PENGUIN BOOKS

THE ALEXANDER TRILOGY

Mary Renault was educated at Clifton High School, Bristol, and St Hugh's College, Oxford. Having completed her nursing training in 1937, she returned to nursing in 1939 until the end of the war. In 1948 she went to live in South Africa. Her other publications include *Purposes of Love, Kind Are Her Answers, The Friendly Young Ladies, Return to Night, North Face, The Charioteer, The Last of the Wine, The King Must Die, The Bull from the Sea, The Lion in the Gateway* (for children), *The Mask of Apollo, The Nature of Alexander* and *The Praise Singer*. The Alexander Trilogy consists of *Fire From Heaven*, which received the Silver Pen Award in 1971, *The Persian Boy* and *Funeral Games*. Many of her books have been published in Penguin. She was made a Fellow of the Royal Society of Literature in 1959. Mary Renault died on 13 December 1983.

MARY RENAULT

THE
ALEXANDER
TRILOGY

PENGUIN BOOKS

Penguin Books Ltd, Harmondsworth, Middlesex, England
Viking Penguin Inc., 40 West 23rd Street, New York, New York 10010, U.S.A.
Penguin Books Australia Ltd, Ringwood, Victoria, Australia
Penguin Books Canada Limited, 2801 John Street, Markham, Ontario, Canada L3R 1B4
Penguin Books (N.Z.) Ltd, 182–190 Wairau Road, Auckland 10, New Zealand

Fire from Heaven first published by Longman Group Ltd 1970
Published in Penguin Books 1970
Copyright © Mary Renault, 1970

The Persian Boy first published by Longman Group Ltd 1972
Published in Penguin Books 1974
Copyright © Mary Renault, 1972

Funeral Games first published by John Murray 1981
Published in Penguin Books 1982
Copyright © Mary Renault, 1981

This collection published as *The Alexander Trilogy* 1984
Reprinted 1986

Copyright © Mary Renault, 1984
All rights reserved

Made and printed in Great Britain by
Richard Clay (The Chaucer Press) Ltd, Bungay, Suffolk
Filmset in 9/11pt Monophoto Photina by
Northumberland Press Ltd, Gateshead

Contents

FIRE FROM HEAVEN

When Perdikkas asked him at what times he
wished divine honours paid to him, he answered that
he wished it done when they themselves were happy.
These were the last words of the King.

Quintus Curtius.

ILLYRIA

T R

Ister

PAIONIA

LYNKESTIS

M A C E D O N

Philippi

L. Lychnidis

Amphipolis

Pella

Aigai

Stagira

Methone

Olynthos

Dion

Mt
Athos

Mt Olympus

EPIROS

MOLOSSIANS

THESSALY

Dodona

Thermopylai

EUBOIA

PHOKIS

Elateia

ACARNANIA

Delphi

Cheironeia

Mt
Parnassos

BOEOTIA

Thebes

Marathon

Corinth

Athe

ATTICA

Olympia

Argos

N

Sparta

0   40   80   120   160
STATUTE MILES

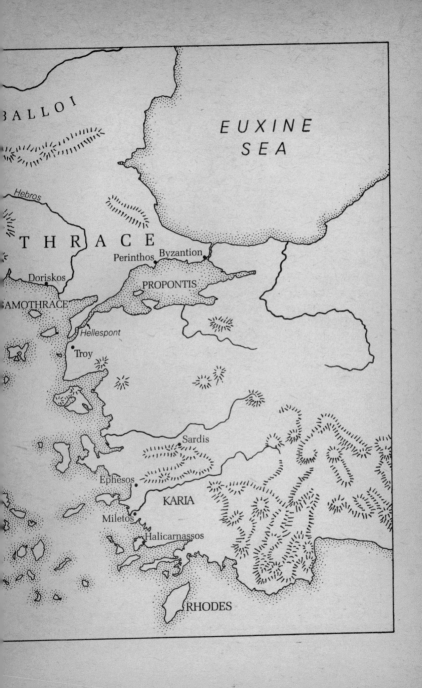

BALLOI

EUXINE
SEA

Hebros

THRACE

Perinthos Byzantion

Doriskos

PROPONTIS

SAMOTHRACE

Hellespont

Troy

Sardis

Ephesos

KARIA

Miletos

Halicarnassos

RHODES

I

The child was wakened by the knotting of the snake's coils about his waist. For a moment he was frightened; it had squeezed his breathing, and given him a bad dream. But as soon as he was awake, he knew what it was, and pushed his two hands inside the coil. It shifted; the strong band under his back bunched tightly, then grew thin. The head slid up his shoulder along his neck, and he felt close to his ear the flickering tongue.

The old-fashioned nursery lamp, painted with boys bowling hoops and watching cock-fights, burned low on its stand. The dusk had died in which he had fallen asleep; only a cold, sharp moonlight struck down through the tall window, patching the yellow marble floor with blue. He pushed down his blanket to see the snake, and make sure it was the right one. His mother had told him that the patterned ones, with backs like woven borderwork, must always be let alone. But all was well; it was the pale brown one with the grey belly, smooth as polished enamel.

When he turned four, nearly a year ago, he had been given a boy's bed five feet long; but the legs were short in case he fell, and the snake had not had far to climb. Everyone else in the room was fast asleep; his sister Kleopatra in her cradle beside the Spartan nurse; nearer, in a better bed of carved pearwood, his own nurse Hellanike. It must be the middle of the night; but he could still hear the men in Hall, singing together. The sound was loud and discordant, slurring the ends of the lines. He had learned already to understand the cause.

The snake was a secret, his alone in the night. Even Lanike, so near by, had not discerned their silent greetings. She was safely snoring. He had been slapped for likening the sound to a mason's saw. Lanike was not a common nurse, but a lady of the royal kindred, who reminded him twice a day that she would not be doing this for anyone less than his father's son.

The snores, the distant singing, were sounds of solitude. The only waking presences were himself and the snake, and the sentry pacing the passage, the click of his armour-buckles just heard as he passed the door.

The child turned on his side, stroking the snake, feeling its polished strength slide through his fingers over his naked skin. It had laid its flat head upon his heart, as if to listen. It had been cold at first, which had helped to wake him. Now it was taking warmth from him, and growing lazy. It was going to sleep, and might stay till morning. What would Lanike say when she found it? He stifled his laughter, lest it should be shaken and go away. He had never known it stray so far from his mother's room.

He listened to hear if she had sent her women out in search of it. Its name was Glaukos. But he could only hear two men shouting at each other in Hall; then the voice of his father, the loudest, shouting them both down.

He pictured her, in the white wool robe with yellow borders she wore after the bath, her hair loose on it, the lamp glowing red through her shielding hand, softly calling 'Glaukos-s!' or perhaps playing snake-music on her tiny bone flute. The women would be looking everywhere, among the stands for the combs and paint-pots, inside the bronze-bound clothes-chests smelling of cassia; he had seen such a search for a lost ear-ring. They would get scared and clumsy, and she would be angry. Hearing the noise from Hall again, he remembered his father did not like Glaukos, and would be glad that he was lost.

It was then he resolved to bring him back to her now, himself.

This must be done, then. The child stood in the blue moonlight on the yellow floor, the snake wound round him, supported in his arms. It must not be disturbed by dressing; but he took his shoulder-cloak from the stool, and wrapped it around both of them, to keep it warm.

He paused for thought. He had two soldiers to pass. Even if both turned out to be friends, at this hour they would stop him. He listened to the one outside. The passage had a bend in it, and a strongroom was round the corner. The sentry looked after both doors.

The footfalls were receding. He got the door unlatched, and looked out to plan his way. A bronze Apollo stood in the angle of the wall, on a plinth of green marble. He was still small enough to squeeze behind it. When the sentry had passed the other way, he ran. The rest was easy, till he got to the small court from which rose the stair to the royal bedchamber.

The steps went up between walls painted with trees and birds. There was a little landing at the top, and the polished door with its great ring handle in its lion's mouth. The marble treads were still scarcely worn. There had been nothing but a small harbour town on the lagoon at Pella, before King Archelaos' day. Now it was a city, with temples and big houses; on a gentle rise, Archelaos had built his famous palace, a wonder to all Greece. It was too famous ever to have been changed; everything was splendid, in a fashion fifty years old. Zeuxis had spent years painting the walls.

At the stair foot stood the second sentry, the royal bodyguard. Tonight it was Agis. He was standing easy, leaning on his spear. The child, peeping from the dark side-passage, drew back, watching and waiting.

Agis was about twenty, a lord's son of the royal demesne. He had on his parade armour, to wait upon the King. His helmet had a crest of red and white horsehair, and its hinged cheek-flaps were embossed with lions. His shield was elegantly painted with a striding boar; it hung upon his shoulder, not to be put down till the King was safe in bed, and then not out of arm-reach. In his right hand was a seven-foot spear.

The child gazed with delight, feeling within his cloak the snake softly stir and twine. He knew the young man well; he would have liked to jump out with a whoop, making him throw up his shield and point his spear; to be tossed up on his shoulder, in reach of the tall crest. But Agis was on duty. It would be he who would scratch upon the door, and hand Glaukos to a waiting-woman; for himself there would be Lanike and bed. He had tried before to get in at night, though never so late as this; they always told him nobody could enter except the King.

The floor of the passage was made of pebble mosaic, checkered black and white. His feet grew sore from standing, and the night chill came on. Agis had been posted to watch the stairs, and only that. It was a different matter from the other guard.

For a moment he considered coming out, having a talk with Agis, and going back. But the slither of the snake against his breast reminded him that he had set out to see his mother. That, therefore, was what he was going to do.

If one kept one's mind upon what one wanted, the chance appeared. Glaukos, too, was magical. He stroked the snake's thinned neck, saying voicelessly, 'Agathodaimon, Sabazeus-Zagreus, send him away, come, come.' He added a spell he had heard his mother use. Though he did not know what it was for, it was worth a trial.

Agis turned from the stairs into the passage opposite. There was a statue a long way along, of a lion sitting up. Agis leaned his shield and spear on it, and went round behind. Though stone sober by local reckoning, he had drunk before going on duty too much to hold till the next watch. All the guards went behind the lion. Before morning, the slaves would wipe it up.

The moment he started walking, before he put down his weapons, the child knew what it meant and started to run. He flew up the cold smooth stairs on silent feet. It always amazed him, when with children of his own age, how easily they could be out-run or caught. It seemed impossible they could really be trying.

Agis behind the lion had not forgotten his duty. When a watch-dog barked, his head went up at once. But the sound came from the other way.

It ceased, he straightened his clothes and picked up his arms. The stairs were empty.

The child, having pushed-to behind him, silently, the heavy door, reached up to fasten the latch. It was well-polished and oiled; he coaxed it home without a sound. This done, he turned into the room.

A single lamp was burning, on a tall standard of bright bronze, twined with a gilded vine and resting on gilded deer's-feet. The room was warm, and breathing all over with secret life. The deep curtains of blue wool with embroidered edges, the people painted on the walls, all stirred with it; the flame of the lamp breathed too. The men's voices, shut off by the heavy door, were no more than murmurs here.

There were close scents of bath-oil, incense and musk, of resined pine-ash from the bronze hearth-basket; of his mother's paints and oils and the phial from Athens; of something acrid she burned for magic; of her body and her hair. In the bed whose legs were inlaid with ivory and tortoiseshell and ended in lion's paws, she lay sleeping, her hair falling across the worked linen pillow. He had never seen her in such a deep sleep before.

It seemed she had never missed Glaukos, to sleep so soundly. He paused, to enjoy his stealthy undisturbed possession. On her tiring-table of olive wood, the pots and bottles were clean and closed. A gilded nymph upheld the moon of her silver mirror. The saffron night-robe was folded on a stool. From the room beyond where her women slept came a faint distant snore. His eyes strayed to the loose stone by the hearth, under which lived forbidden things; he had often wished to try working his own magic. But Glaukos might slip away. She must have him now.

He stepped softly up, the unseen guard and lord of her sleep. Gently the cover of marten-skins, edged with scarlet and fringed with bullion, rose and fell above her. Her brows were drawn clearly above the thin smooth lids which seemed to show through them the smoke-grey eyes beneath. Her lashes were darkened; her mouth was firmly closed, the colour of watered wine. Her nose was white and straight, and whispered faintly as she breathed. She was twenty-one years old.

The cover had fallen back a little from her breast, where, till lately, Kleopatra's head had too often lain. She had gone to the Spartan nurse now, and his kingdom was his own again.

A strand of hair spilled down towards him, dark-red, strong, and shining in the moving lamplight with streaks of fire. He pulled forward some of his own, and set them together; his was like rough-wrought gold, gleaming and heavy; Lanike grumbled on feast-days that it never held a curl. Hers had a springy wave. The Spartan woman said Kleopatra's would be the same, though now it was like feathers. He would hate her, if she grew more like his mother than he was. But perhaps she would die; babies often did.

In the shadows, the hair looked dark and different. He looked round at the great mural on the inner wall: the Sack of Troy, done by Zeuxis for Archelaos. The figures were life sized. The Wooden Horse towered in the background; in front, Greeks plunged swords into Trojans, rushed at them with spears, or carried on their shoulders women with screaming mouths. In the foreground, old Priam and the child Astyanax weltered in their blood. That was the colour. Satisfied of this he turned away. He had been born in this room; the picture held nothing new for him.

Round his waist, under his cloak, Glaukos was wriggling, no doubt glad to be home. The child looked again into his mother's face; then let fall his single garment, lifted delicately the blanket's edge, and still twined with the snake slid in beside her.

Her arms came round him. She purred softly, and sank her nose and mouth into his hair; her breathing deepened. He pushed down his head under her chin; her yielding breasts enclosed him, he could feel his bare skin cling to hers, all the length of his body. The snake, too tightly pressed between them, squirmed strongly and slid aside.

He felt her wake; her grey eyes with their inner smoke-rings were open when he looked up. She kissed and stroked him, and said, 'Who let you in?'

While she still half-slept and he lay wrapped in bliss, he had been ready for this question. Agis had not kept proper lookout. Soldiers were punished for it. Half a year had gone by since he had seen from the window a guard put to death on the drill-field by the other guards. After so long an age, he had forgotten the offence, if he had ever known it; but he remembered the small distant body bound to the post, the men standing round with javelins poised at the shoulder; the shrill taught command followed by a single cry; then, when they had all crowded in to jerk out the bristling shafts, the head lolling, and the great spill of red.

'I told the man you wanted me.' No need for names. For a child fond of talking, he had learned early how to hold his tongue.

Her cheek moved in a smile against his head. He had hardly ever heard her speak to his father, without being aware she was lying about one or another thing. He thought of it as a skill she had, like the snake-music on the bone flute.

'Mother, when will you marry me? When I'm older, when I'm six?'

She kissed the nape of his neck, and ran her finger along his backbone. 'When you are six, ask me again. Four is too young to get handfast.'

'I'm five in Lion Month. I love you.' She kissed him saying nothing. 'Do you love me best?'

'I love you altogether. Perhaps I shall eat you up.'

'But best? Do you love me best?'

'When you are good.'

'*No!*' He rode her waist with his knees, pummelling her shoulders. 'Really best. Better than anyone. Than Kleopatra.' She made a soft sound, less reproof than caress. 'You do! You do! You love me more than the King.'

He seldom said 'Father' if he could help it, and knew it did not displease her. Through her flesh he felt her silent laughter. She said, 'Perhaps.'

Victorious and exulting, he slipped down beside her. 'If you promise you love me best, I'll give you something.'

'Oh, tyrant. What can it be?'

'Look, I've found Glaukos. He came into my bed.'

Folding the blanket back he displayed the snake. It had coiled round his waist again, having found this pleasant.

She looked at the burnished head, which lifted from its resting-place on the child's white breast, and softly hissed at her.

'Why,' she said, 'where did you find this? This is not Glaukos. The same kind, yes. But this one is much bigger.'

They gazed together at the coiled snake; the child's mind filled with pride and mystery. He stroked the reared neck, as he had been taught, and the head sank down again.

The lips of Olympias parted, and the blacks of her eyes grew wide, invading the grey irises; he saw them like soft silk, pleating together. Her arms slackened about him; he was held in the grasp of her eyes.

'He knows you,' she whispered. 'Tonight, when he came, be sure it was not for the first time. He must have come often, while you slept. See how he clings to you. He knows you well. He comes from the god. He is your daimon, Alexander.'

The lamp flickered. The end of a pine-brand slipped into the embers, and threw up blue flame. The snake squeezed him swiftly, as if to share a secret; its scales trickled like water.

'I shall call him Tyche,' he said presently. 'He shall have his milk in my gold cup. Will he talk to me?'

'Who knows? He is your daimon. Listen, I will tell you – '

The muted noises from the Hall broke out loud as its doors were opened. Men shouted to each other good nights, jokes or drunken taunts. The noise flowed in on them through their closed defences. Olympias broke off, gathered him close into her side, and said softly, 'Never mind, he won't come here.' But he felt her taut with listening. There was a sound of heavy feet, a stumble and a curse; then the rap of Agis' spear-butt on the floor, and the slap of his soles as he presented arms.

The feet came scuffing and tramping up the stairs. The door flew open. King Philip crashed it behind him, and without a glance at the bed started taking off his clothes.

Olympias had pulled up the blanket. The child, eyes round with alarm, had for a moment been glad to lie hidden. Then, cowered in the womb of soft wool and scented flesh, he began to feel horror of the danger he could not confront or see. He worked down a fold to make a peephole; it was better to know than to guess.

The King stood naked, one foot up on the cushioned stool of the toilet-table, loosing his sandal strap. His black-bearded face was cocked sideways to see what he was doing; his blind eye was towards the bed.

For a year or more, the child had run in and out of the wrestling-ground, when anyone dependable would take him off the women's hands. Bare bodies or clothed, it was all one, except for being able to see men's war-scars. Yet his father's nakedness, seldom seen, always disgusted him. Now, since one eye had been blinded at the siege of Methone, he had become frightful. At first he had kept it covered with a bandage, from which blood-tinged tears had stained a track down into his beard. Then these had dried, and the bandage had come off. The lid, which the arrow had pierced on its way in, was puckered and streaked with red; the lashes were gummed with yellow matter. They were black, like his good eye and his beard, and the mats of hair on his shins and forearms and chest; a track of black hair led down his belly to the bush, like a second beard, between his loins. His arms and neck and legs were seamed with thick scars, white, red or purple. He belched, filling the air with the smell of stale wine, and showing the gap in his teeth. The child, glued to his peephole, knew suddenly what his father looked like. It was the ogre, one-eyed Polyphemos, who had picked up Odysseus' sailors and crunched them raw.

His mother had risen on one elbow, with the clothes pulled up to her chin. 'No, Philip. Not tonight. It is not the time.'

The King took a stride towards the bed. 'Not the time?' he said loudly. He was still panting from the stairs on a full stomach. 'You said that half a month ago. Do you think I can't count, you Molossian bitch?'

The child felt his mother's hand, which had been curved around his body, clench into a fist. When she spoke again it was in her fighting voice. 'Count, you wineskin? You're not fit to know summer from winter. Go to your minion. Any day of the month is the same to *him*.'

The child's knowledge of such things was still imperfect; yet he had a feeling of what was meant. He disliked his father's new young man, who put on airs; he loathed the secrets he sensed between them. His mother's body had tightened and hardened all over. He held his breath.

'You cat-a-mountain!' said the King. The child saw him rush upon them, like Polyphemos on his prey. He seemed to bristle all over; even the rod that hung in his black bushy crotch had risen by itself and was thrusting forward, a sight of mysterious horror. He pulled back the bedclothes.

The child lay in his mother's arms, his fingers dug into her side. His father started back, cursing and pointing. But it was not at them; the blind eye was still turned that way. The child perceived why his mother had not been surprised to feel his new snake beside her. Glaukos had been there already. He must have been asleep.

'How dare you?' panted Philip hoarsely. He had had a sickening shock. 'How dare you, when I forbade it, bring your filthy vermin in my bed? Sorceress, barbarian witch ...'

His voice stopped. Drawn by the hatred in his wife's two eyes, his one eye had moved that way, and he had seen the child. The two faces confronted one another: the man's empurpled, with the wine, and with anger heightened now by shame; the child's as brilliant as a jewel set in gold, the blue-grey eyes fixed and wide, the skin transparent, the delicate flesh, taught with uncomprehended agony, moulded close to the fine bones.

Muttering something, Philip reached by instinct for his robe to cover his nakedness; but there was no more need. He had been wronged, insulted, exposed, betrayed. If his sword had been at hand, he might well have killed her.

Disturbed by all this, the child's living girdle writhed, and lifted its head. Till now, Philip had not seen it.

'What's that?' His pointing finger shook. 'What's that upon the boy? That thing of yours? Are you teaching *him* now? Are you making *him* into a back-country, snake-dancing, howling mystagogue? I tell you, I'll not endure it, take heed of what I say, before you suffer; for by Zeus I mean it, as you will feel. My son is a Greek, not one of your barbarous cattle-lifting hillmen ...'

'Barbarous!' Her voice rose ringing, then sank to a deadly undertone, like Glaukos' when angered. 'My father, you peasant, sprang from Achilles, and my mother from the royal house of Troy. My forbears were ruling men, when yours were hired farm-hands in Argos. Have you looked in a mirror? One can see the Thracian in you. If my son is Greek, it is from me. In Epiros, our blood runs true.'

Philip gritted his teeth. It squared his chin and broadened his cheek-bones, which were wide already. Even under these mortal insults, he remembered the child was there. 'I scorn to answer you. If you are Greek, then show a Greek woman's manners. Let us see some modesty.' He felt the lack of clothes. Two pairs of grey eyes, smokily rimmed, stared from the bed. 'Greek schooling, reason, civility, I mean the boy to have them as I have had. Make up your mind to that.'

'Oh, *Thebes!*' She threw out the word like a ritual curse. 'Is it Thebes again, now? I know enough of Thebes. In Thebes they made you a Greek, in Thebes you learned civility! In Thebes! Have you heard an Athenian speak of Thebes? The byword of Greece for boorishness. Don't make such a fool of yourself.'

'Athens, that talking-shop. Their great days are done there. They should keep quiet about Thebes for shame.'

'It is you should do that. What were *you* in Thebes?'

'A hostage, a pledge of policy. Did I make my brother's treaty? Do you throw that in my face? I was sixteen. I found more courtesy there than you ever showed me. And they taught me war. What was Macedon, when Perdikkas died? He had fallen to the Illyrians with four thousand men. The valleys lay fallow; our people were afraid to come down out of the hill-forts. All they had were the sheep whose skins they wore, and those they could hardly keep. Soon the Illyrians would have taken everything; Bardelys was making ready. Now you know what we are and where our frontiers stand. Through Thebes, and the men who made me a soldier there, I came to you a king. Your kindred were glad enough of it.'

The child, pressed to her side, felt her breath drawn in and in. Blindly he waited for the unknown storm to break from the lowering sky. His fingers clenched on the blanket. He knew himself forgotten now, and alone.

The storm broke. 'A soldier, was it, they made you there? And what else? What else?' He could feel her ribs convulsed with rage. 'You went south at sixteen, and by then already the country all around was full of your by-blows, don't you think I know who they are? That whore Arsinoe, Lagos' wife, old enough to be your mother ... Then the great Pelopidas taught you all the learning Thebes is famous for. Battle and boys!'

'Be silent!' roared Philip, loud enough for a battlefield. 'Have you no decency before the child? What does he see in this room? What does he hear? I tell you, my son shall be brought up civilized, if I have to ...'

His voice was drowned by her laughter. She drew back her hand from the child, to thrust her body forward. With her arms and open palms propping her weight, her red hair falling forward over her naked breasts and the child's open mouth and eyes, she laughed till the high room echoed. '*Your* son?' she cried. '*Your* son!'

King Philip breathed as if he had just run the long-race. He strode forward and raised his hand.

Starting out of a perfect stillness, in one flash of movement the child threw off the curtain of his mother's hair, and stood upright on the bed. His grey eyes, dilated, looked almost black; his mouth had whitened. He struck at the lifted arm of his father, who from mere astonishment withdrew it. 'Go away!' screamed the child, glittering and fierce as a forest wildcat. 'Go away! She hates you! Go away! She will marry me!'

For three long breaths, Philip stood rooted, mouth and eyes gaping, like a man clubbed on the head. Then diving forward, he seized the child by both shoulders, swung him through the air, let go with one hand while he wrenched the great door open, and tossed him outside. Taken unawares, rigid with shock and fury, he did nothing to help himself. His sliding body reached the head of the stairs and began to tumble down them.

With a great clattering din, young Agis let fall his spear, dragged his arm out of his shield-straps, and taking the stairs in threes and fours leaped forward to catch the child. At the third stair down he reached him, and picked him up. His head seemed not to have been struck, and his eyes were open. Up above, King Philip had paused with the door in his hand. He did not slam it till he had seen that all was well; but of this the child knew nothing.

Caught up along with him, startled and bruised, the snake whipped free of him as he began to fall, poured itself down the stairs, and was gone into the dark.

Agis, after his first start, had seen what it was. The child was enough to think about. He carried him downstairs, and sitting at their foot took him on his knees, looking him over by the light of the torch in its wall-sconce. He felt stiff as a board, and his eyes were turned up to show the whites.

In the name of all gods below, thought the young man, what shall I do? If I leave my post, the Captain will have my blood. If his son dies on my hands, the King will. One night last year, before the new favourite's reign began, Philip had looked his way, and he had pretended to be dense. Now he had seen too much; his fortunes, he thought, would sell dear at a sack of beans. The child was looking blue about the lips. In the far corner was Agis' thick wool night cloak, ready for the cold small hours. He picked it up, wadded a fold between the child and his own hard corselet, and wrapped him round. 'Come,' he said anxiously. 'Come, look, all's well.'

He seemed not to be breathing. What to do? Slap him, like a woman in a laughing-fit? It might kill him instead. His eyes were moving, and focusing. He drew in a crowing breath, and gave a violent scream.

Deeply relieved, Agis loosed the cloak round the struggling limbs. He clucked and muttered as if to a frightened horse, not holding him in too hard but letting him feel firm hands. In the room above, his parents were calling down curses on one another. After a time Agis did not reckon – he had most of the night before him – these sounds died down, and the child began to weep, but not for long. Having come thus far to himself, soon he fell quiet. He lay biting his lower lip, swallowing, and gazing up at Agis, who tried suddenly to remember how old he was.

'That's my young captain,' he said gently, moved by the almost manlike struggle on the childish face. He dried it with the cloak, and kissed it, trying as he did so to picture what this golden boy would look like when he was old enough for love. 'Come, sweetheart, you and I will stand guard together. We'll look after one another, eh?'

He enfolded the child and stroked him. After a time, the quiet, the warmth, the unconscious sensuality of the young man's caresses, a vague awareness of being more admired than pitied, began to heal the enormous wound which had seemed his whole and only self. It began to close, sealing in all within it.

Presently he put out his head from the cloak and looked about. 'Where is my Tyche?'

What did the strange child mean, calling upon his fortune? Seeing Agis' face look blank, he added, 'My snake, my daimon. Where did he go?'

'Ah, your lucky snake.' Agis thought the Queen's pets entirely loathsome. 'He's hiding awhile, he'll soon be back.' He wrapped more cloak round the child; he had begun to shiver. 'Don't take it to heart, your father didn't mean it. It was only the wine in him. Many a clip on the head I've had from mine.'

'When I'm big . . .' He paused to count on his fingers, up to ten. 'When I'm big, I'll kill him.'

Agis sucked in his breath through his lower teeth. 'Ss-ss! Don't say such a thing. It's god-cursed to kill a father, it sets the Furies after a man.' He began to describe them, but broke off as the child's eyes widened; he had had more than enough. 'All these knocks we get when we're young, that's how we learn to bear our wounds, when we go to war. Look. Move over. Look what I got, the first time I fought the Illyrians.'

He pulled back the kilt of scarlet wool from his thigh, and showed the long ridged scar, with a pit where the spear-head had ploughed through almost to the bone. The boy gazed with respect, and felt it with his finger.

'Well,' said Agis, covering it again, 'that hurt, you can guess. And what kept me from yelling out, and being shamed before the Companions? My father's clips on the ear. The fellow who gave me that never lived to boast of it. My first man, he was. When I showed my father his head, he gave me my sword-belt, offered up my boy's girdle-cord, and feasted all our kindred.' He looked along the passage. Would no one ever come by, and take the child to his bed?

'Can you see my Tyche?' he was asking.

'He'll not be far. He's a house-snake. They don't wander. He'll come for his milk, you'll see. It's not every boy can take a house-snake. That's the blood of Herakles in you, I daresay.'

'What was *his* snake called?'

'When he was a new-born babe, two snakes crept into his cradle – '

'Two?' His fine brows drew together, frowning.

'Ah, but these were bad ones. Zeus' wife Hera sent them, to choke him dead. But he grabbed them by their necks, one in each hand ...' Agis paused, silently cursing himself. Either it would give the child nightmares, or, maybe likelier, he would go off and try to throttle a viper. 'No, this only happened, you see, to Herakles because he was the son of a god. He passed as King Amphitryon's son, but Zeus had begot him on Amphitryon's Queen. So Hera was jealous.'

The child listened alertly. 'And he had to work. Why did he work so hard?'

'Eurystheus, the next King, was envious of him, because he was the better man, a hero, and half divine. Eurystheus was only a mortal, you understand, and Herakles had been meant to have the kingdom. But Hera caused Eurystheus to be born first. That's why Herakles had to do his Labours.'

The child nodded, like one to whom all has been made clear. 'He had to do them, to show he was the best.'

Agis missed these words. He had heard at last, along the passage, the captain of the night guard, going his rounds.

'No one's been by, sir,' he explained. 'I can't think what the nurse can have been about. The child was blue with cold, running about the Palace mother naked. He says he's looking for his snake.'

'Lazy bitch of a woman. I'll shake up some slave-girl to go in and rouse her. It's too late to disturb the Queen.'

He strode rattling off. Agis hoisted the child across his shoulder, patting his buttocks. 'Bed for you, Herakles, and not before time.'

The child wrigged down, to clasp both arms round his neck. Agis had sheltered his wounds and not betrayed them. Nothing was too good for such a friend. He shared his secret, since it was all he had to give.

'If my Tyche comes back, tell him where I've gone. He knows my name.'

Ptolemy, known as the son of Lagos, cantered his new chestnut towards the lake of Pella; there was good riding land along the shore. The horse was a gift from Lagos, who had grown fonder of him with the years, though his childhood had been less happy. He was eighteen, a dark big-boned youth whose strong profile would grow craggy in later life. He had speared his boar, and could sit at table with the men; had killed his man in a border skirmish, and changed his boy's waist-cord for a red leather swordbelt with a horn-handled dagger in its slot. It was agreed he brought Lagos credit. In the end they had done pretty well by one another; and the King had done well by both.

Between the pinewoods and the lake, he saw Alexander waving to him, and rode that way. He was fond of the boy, who seemed to belong nowhere: too bright for the seven-year-olds, though not yet seven; too small for the older boys. He came running through the marshland, hard-caked with summer around its scrubby reeds; his huge dog rooted after voles, coming back to push its dirty nose in his ear, which it could do with both forepaws on the ground.

'Hup!' said the youth, and hoisting him in front on the cloth saddle-square. They trotted along in search of a stretch to gallop. 'Is that dog of yours still growing?'

'Yes. He's not big enough for his paws.'

'You were right; he's Molossian both sides sure enough. He's growing his mane.'

'It was just about here, where we are now, the man was going to drown him.'

'When you don't know the sire, they don't always pay for rearing.'

'He said he was rubbish; he had a stone tied round him.'

'Someone got bitten in the end, or so I heard. I shouldn't like a bite from that dog.'

'He was too little to bite. I did it. Look, we can go.'

The dog, glad to stretch its great legs, raced by them along the broad lagoon which linked Pella with the sea. As they galloped full-out along its verge, mallards and gulls, dangle-foot herons and cranes, came beating and honking from the sedges, startled by their thunder. The boy in his clear voice sang loudly the paean of the Companion Cavalry, a fierce crescendo tuned to the rhythm of the charge. His face was flushed, his hair fluttered from the peak upon his brow, his grey eyes looked blue, he shone.

Ptolemy slowed to breathe the horse, and extolled its virtues. Alexander replied in terms as expert as a groom's. Ptolemy, who sometimes felt responsible, said, 'Does your father know you spend so much time with the soldiers?'

'Oh, yes. He said Silanos could teach me throwing at the mark, and Menestas could take me hunting. I only go with my friends.'

Least said, then, soonest mended. Ptolemy had heard before that the King preferred even rough company for the boy, to leaving him all day with his mother. He flicked the horse to a canter, till a stone lodged in its frog and he had to dismount and see to it. The voice of the boy above him said, 'Ptolemy. Is it true you're really my brother?'

'What?' His start freed the horse; it began to trot away. The boy, who had at once got hold of the reins, pulled it firmly up again. But the young man, disconcerted, walked at its head without mounting. Perceiving something amiss, the boy said soberly, 'They were saying it in the Guard Room.'

They paced on in silence. The boy, sensing consternation more than anger, waited gravely.

Ptolemy said at length, 'They may; but they don't say it to me. Nor must you. I'd have to kill a man if he said it.'

'Why?'

'Well, one must, that's all.'

There was no answer. Ptolemy saw with dismay that the boy was bitterly wounded. It was something he had not thought of.

'Come,' he said awkwardly, 'a big growing boy like you, if you don't know why ... Of course I'd gladly be your brother, that's nothing to do with it, that's not it. But my mother's married to Father. It would mean I was a bastard. You know what that is.'

'Yes,' said Alexander, who knew it was a deadly insult.

Sensing confusion if not ignorance, Ptolemy did a brother's duty. His blunt questions got blunt answers; the boy had used his ears among his guardroom friends. It seemed, though, that he thought the birth of off-spring called for some further magic. The young man, having dealt sensibly with the matter, was surprised by the long intent silence at the end.

'What is it? It's the way we are all born, nothing wrong with it, the gods made us so. But women must only do it with their husbands, or the child's a bastard. That's why the man wanted to drown your dog: for fear he'd not run true to strain.'

'Yes,' said the boy, and returned to his thoughts.

Ptolemy felt distressed. In his childhood, when Philip had been only a younger son and a hostage too, he had been made to suffer; later he had ceased to be ashamed. If his mother had been unmarried he could have been acknowledged, and would not have been sorry. It was a matter of the decencies; he felt he had treated the boy meanly, not to have made this clear.

Alexander was looking straight ahead. His dirty childish hands kept a managing grip on the reins, minding their own business, making no demand on his thought. Their capacity, so far beyond their growth, approached the freakish; it gave an uneasy feeling. Through his face's puppy roundness, a gem-clear profile already began to show. Ptolemy thought, 'The image of his mother, nothing of Philip at all.'

A thought struck him like a thunderflash. Ever since he had been eating with the men, he had been hearing tales about Queen Olympias. Strange, turbulent, uncanny, wild as a Thracian maenad, able if she was crossed to put the Eye on you: fittingly the King had met her in a cave by torchlight, at the Mysteries of Samothrace; had been mad for her at first sight, even before he knew what house she came of; and had brought her, with a useful treaty of alliance, in triumph home. In Epiros, it was said, until quite lately women had ruled without men. Sometimes the drums and cymbals sounded all night in her pine-grove, and strange piping came from her room. It was said she coupled with serpents; old women's tales, but what happened in the grove? Did the boy, so long her shadow, know more than he should? Had it only now come home to him?

As if he had turned a stone from a cave-mouth of the Underworld, letting loose a swarm of bat-squeaking shades, there passed through Ptolemy's mind a score of bloody tales going back for centuries, of struggles for the throne of Macedon: tribes fighting for High Kingship, kindred killing kindred to be High King; wars, massacres, poisoning; treacherous spears in the hunting-field, knives in the back, in the dark, in the bed of love. He was not without ambition; but the thought of plunging in that stream made his marrow cold. Dangerous guesswork, and what proof could there ever be? Here was the boy in trouble. Forget the rest.

'Listen,' he said. 'Can you keep a secret?'

Alexander lifted his hand and pronounced with care an oath enforced by deadly curses. 'It's the strongest,' he finished. 'Silanos taught it me.'

'That's too strong. I absolve you of it. You must be careful of oaths like that. Now the truth is, your father did get me on my mother; but he was no more than a boy, fifteen. It was before he went to Thebes.'

'Oh, Thebes.' His voice echoed another.

'He was old for his age that way, well known for it. Well, never mind that, a man can't wait till he's wedded, nor have I done if you want the truth. But my mother was married to Father already, so it dishonours them to talk of it. It's one of the things a man must have blood for. Never mind if you see why or not; that's how it is.'

'I won't talk.' His eyes, already deeper-set than other children's, were fixed upon the distance.

Ptolemy fiddled with the horse's cheekstrap, thinking unhappily, Well, what could I say? Someone else would have told him. The boy still in him rescued the defeated man. He halted the horse.

'Now, if we were sworn blood-brothers, we could tell everyone that.' He added, cunningly, 'But you know what we have to do?'

'Of course I know!' He gathered the reins in his left hand, and held out the right, clenched fist turned upward, a blue vein showing at the wrist. 'Come on; here, do it now.'

Ptolemy drew from his red belt the new sharp dagger, seeing the boy focused by pride and resolution to a single gleam. 'Now wait, Alexander. It's a solemn thing we're doing. Your enemies will be mine and mine yours, until we die. We will never take up arms against each other, even

if our own kin are at war. If I die in a strange land you will give me my
rites, and so I will do for you. It means all that.'

'I promise. You can do it here.'

'We don't need so much blood.' He avoided the offered vein, lightly
nicking the white skin. The boy looked down smiling. Having pricked his
own wrist, Ptolemy pressed the cuts together. 'It's done,' he said. And well
done, he thought; some good daimon prompted me. Now they can't come
to me saying, 'He is only the Queen's bastard and you're the King's, so
claim your rights.'

'Come on, brother,' said the boy. 'Get up, he's got his wind now. We
can really go.'

The royal stables were built in a broad square of stuccoed brick, with
stone pilasters. They were half empty; the King was holding manoeuvres,
as he did whenever a new thought about tactics came to him.

Alexander, on his way to watch, had stopped to see a mare which had
just foaled. As he had hoped, no one was about to say she was dangerous
at such a time. He slipped in with her, coaxed her, and stroked the foal
while her warm nostrils stirred his hair. Presently she nudged him, to say
that was enough, and he let them be.

In the trodden yard, with its smells of horse-piss and straw, leather and
wax and liniment, three strange horses had just come in. They were being
rubbed down by foreign grooms in trousers. Their head-stalls, which a
stable slave was cleaning, were oddly bedizened; glittering with gold
plates, topped with red plumes, and with winged bulls worked on the bit-
pieces. They were fine tall horses, powerfully built, not over-ridden; a spare
string was being led through.

The household officer on duty remarked to the horse-master that the
barbarians would have a good wait ahead of them, before the King came
back.

'Brison's phalanx,' said the boy, 'are all ways still with their sarissas.
It takes a long time to learn.' He was able, so far, to lift up one end of these
giant spears. 'Where are those horses from?'

'All the way from Persia. Envoys from the Great King, to fetch back
Artabazos and Menapis.'

These satraps, after an ill-judged revolt, had fled to Macedon for refuge.
King Philip had found them useful; the boy had found them interesting.
'But they're guest-friends,' he said. 'Father won't let the Great King have
them back to kill them. Tell the men not to wait.'

'No, it's a pardon, I understand. They can go home free. In any case,
envoys are entertained whatever message they carry. It's the proper
thing.'

'Father won't be back before noon. I think later, because of the Foot Companions. They can't do close-and-open order yet. Shall I fetch Menapis and Artabazos?'

'No, no, the envoys must have an audience first. Let these barbarians see we know how to do things. Attos, stable all those horses by themselves, it's always the foreigners bring sickness in.'

The boy had a good look at the horses and their harness, then stood in thought. Presently he washed his feet at the conduit, looked at his chiton, went in and put on a clean one. He had listened often when people questioned the satraps about the splendours of Persepolis: the throne room with its gold vine and tree, the stairway up which a cavalcade could rise, the curious rites of homage. Persians, it was clear, were ceremonious. As far as he was able without help, and at the cost of some pain, he combed his hair.

In the Perseus Room, one of Zeuxis' show-pieces where guests of rank were received, a chamberlain was watching two blue-tattooed Thracian slaves set small tables with cakes and wine. The envoys had been seated in chairs of honour. On the wall above them, Perseus was rescuing Andromeda from the sea-dragon. He was one of the ancestors, and was said to have founded Persia too. It seemed that his breed had changed. He was naked, except for his winged sandals; the envoys wore the full Median dress which the exiles during their stay had laid aside. Every inch of these men but their hands and faces was covered up with clothes; every inch of the clothes with embroidery. Their round black hats were stitched with spangles; even their beards, trimmed into little round curls like snail-shells, seemed embroidered too. Their fringed tunics had sleeves; their legs were cased in trousers, notorious sign of a barbarian.

Three chairs had been placed; only two bearded men were sitting. The youth with them, an aide, stood behind the senior envoy's chair. He had long silky blue-black hair, a skin of ivory, a face both haughty and delicate, and dark brilliant eyes. His elders being in talk, he was the first to see the boy standing in the doorway, and flashed at him a charming smile.

'May you live,' he said walking in. 'I am Alexander son of Philip.'

Both bearded heads came round. After a moment both men rose, and invoked the sun to shine on him. The chamberlain, retaining his self-command, pronounced their names.

'Please sit down. Refresh yourselves, you must be tired after your journey.' He had often heard this stock phrase. He became aware they were waiting for him to sit first, the first time this had happened to him. He clambered into a chair which had been put ready for the King. His sandal-tip did not reach the floor; the chamberlain beckoned a slave to get a foot-stool.

'I have come to entertain you, because my father is out reviewing the army. We expect him back about noon. It depends on the Foot Companions, whether they get close-and-open order right. They may be better today. They have been working very hard at it.'

The envoys, chosen for their fluent Greek, leaned forward. Both were somewhat unsure with the broad patois of Macedon, its Doric vowels and blunt consonants; but the child's voice was very clear. 'Is this your son?' he asked.

The senior envoy answered, demurely, that he was the son of a friend, and presented him. The youth, with a deep bow, declined again to sit, but smiled. For a moment they lit up at one another. The envoys exchanged delighted glances. It was all charming; the pretty grey-eyed prince, the little kingdom, the provincial naïvety. The King drilled the troops himself! It was as if the child had boasted that the King cooked his own dinner.

'You don't eat your cakes. I will have one too.' He took a small bite; he did not want his mouth full. What he knew of etiquette did not stretch to small-talk during meals. He came straight to business.

'Menapis and Artabazos will be glad they're pardoned. They often talk about home. I don't think they'll ever rebel again. You can tell King Ochos.'

The senior envoy had followed most of this in spite of the uncouth tongue. He smiled into his black moustaches, and said he would not fail to do so.

'And what about General Memnon? Is he pardoned too? We thought he might be, after his brother Mentor won the war in Egypt.'

The envoy's eyes blinked a moment. Mentor the Rhodian, he said presently, was a worthy mercenary, and no doubt the Great King was grateful.

'Memnon's married to Artabazos' sister. Do you know how many children they have now? Twenty-one! All alive! They keep having twins. Eleven boys and ten girls. I only have one sister. But I think that is enough.'

Both envoys bowed. They were informed of the King's domestic discords.

'Memnon speaks Macedonian. He told me how he lost his battle.'

'My prince,' smiled the elder envoy, 'you should study war from victors.'

Alexander looked at him thoughtfully. His father always took trouble to find out where losers had gone wrong. Memnon had cheated a friend of his over a horse-deal; he would not have minded telling how he lost his battle; but he smelled patronage. If the youth had asked, it would have been different.

The chamberlain sent off the slaves, lingering himself for the rescue which would surely soon be needed. The boy bit sparingly at his cake, going over in his mind his most important questions; there might not be time for all. 'How many men has the Great King in his army?'

Both envoys heard this aright; both smiled. The truth could do only good; he could be trusted, no doubt, to remember most of it.

'Beyond number,' said the elder. 'Like the sands of the sea, or the stars on a moonless night.' They told him of the Median and the Persian bowmen, the cavalry on the great horses of Nisaia; and the troops of the outer empire, Kissians and Hyrkanians, Assyrians with plaited bronze helmets and iron-spiked maces, Parthians with bow and scimitar; Ethiopians in leopard and lion skins who painted their faces red and white for battle and shot arrows tipped with stone; the Arab camel corps; the Bactrians; and so on as far as India. He listened round-eyed, like any child hearing marvels, till the tale was over.

'And they all have to fight when the Great King sends for them?'

'Every one, upon pain of death.'

'How long does it take them to come?'

There was a sudden pause. It was a century since Xerxes' expedition; they themselves did not know the answer. They said the King ruled over vast dominions and men of many tongues. From India, say, to the coast it might be a year's journey. But there were troops wherever he might need them.

'Do have some more wine. Is there a road all the way to India?'

It took time to dispose of this. In the doorway people were elbowing to listen, the news having spread.

'What's King Ochos like in battle? Is he brave?'

'Like a lion,' said the envoys both together.

'Which wing of the cavalry does he lead?'

The mere awe of him ... The envoys became evasive. The boy took a larger bite of cake. He knew one must not be rude to guests, so he changed the subject. 'If the soldiers come from Arabia and India and Hyrkania, and can't speak Persian, how does he talk to them?'

'Talk to them? The King?' It was touching, the little strategist a child again. 'Why the satraps of their provinces choose officers who speak their tongues.'

Alexander tilted his head a little, and creased his brows. 'Soldiers like to be talked to before a battle. They like you to know their names.'

'I am sure,' said the second envoy charmingly, 'they like *you* to know them.' The Great King, he added, conversed only with his friends.

'My father converses with those at supper.'

The envoys murmured something, not daring to catch each other's eyes. The barbarity of the Macedonian court was famous. The royal symposiums, it was said, were more like the feasts of mountain bandits snowed-up with their spoils, than the banquets of a ruler. A Milesian Greek, who swore to having witnessed it, had told them King Philip thought nothing of stepping down from his couch to lead the line of dancers. Once, during an argument carried on in shouts across the room, he had shied a pomegranate at a general's head. The Greek, with the effrontery of that race of liars, had gone on to claim that the general had replied with a hunk of bread, and was still alive, in fact still a general. But if one believed no more than half, the least said the best.

Alexander for his part had been wrestling with a problem. A tale he disbelieved, and wished to check, had been told by Menapis. An exile might want to make the Great King look foolish. But these people would inform on him, and he would be crucified when he got home. It was wicked to betray a guest-friend.

'A boy here told me,' he therefore said, 'that when people greet the Great King they have to lie flat down on the ground. But I told him he was silly.'

'The exiles could have told you, my prince, the wisdom of that homage. Our master rules not only many peoples, but many kings. Though we call them satraps, some are kings by blood, whose forbears once ruled for themselves, till they were brought into the empire. So he must be raised as far above other kings as they above their subjects. Under-kings must feel no more shame to fall down before him than before the gods. If he seemed less than this, his rule would soon pass away.'

The boy had listened and understood. He answered courteously, 'Well, here we don't fall down before the gods. So you need not do it to my father. He's not used to it; he won't mind.'

The envoys clutched at their gravity. The thought of prostrating themselves before this barbaric chief, whose ancestor had been Xerxes' vassal (and a treacherous one at that) was too grotesque to offend.

The chamberlain, seeing it was high time, came forward, bowed to the child, who he thought deserved it, and invented a summons which could be explained away outside. Sliding down from the throne, Alexander bade good-bye to each, remembering all their names. 'I am sorry I can't come back here. I have to go to the manoeuvres. Some of the Foot Companions are friends of mine. The sarissa is a very good weapon in a solid front, my father says; the thing is to make it mobile. So he'll go on till they get it right. I hope you won't have long to wait. Please ask for anything you want.'

Turning beyond the doorway, he saw the beautiful eyes of the youth still fixed on him, and paused to wave good-bye. The envoys, chattering together in excited Persian, were too busy to see their exchange of smiles.

*

Later that day, he was in the Palace garden teaching his dog to fetch things, among the carved urns from Ephesos whose rare flowers died in the bitter winters of Macedon unless they were brought indoors. From the painted stoa above, his father walked down towards him.

He called the dog to heel. Side by side they waited, prick-eared and wary. His father sat down on a marble bench, and beckoned towards the side of his seeing eye. The blind eye had healed now; only a white patch on the iris showed where the arrow had gone in. It had been a spent one, to which he owed his life.

'Come here, come here,' he said, grinning and showing strong white teeth with a gap in them. 'Come tell me what they said to you. You set them some hard questions, I hear. Tell me the answers. How many troops has Ochos, if he's put to it?'

He spoke in Macedonian. As a rule he spoke Greek to his son, for the good of his education. His tongue freed by this, the boy began to talk; of the Ten Thousand Immortals, of archers and javelineers and axemen; how cavalry chargers would bolt from the smell of camels; and how kings in India rode on black hairless beasts, so huge they could carry towers upon their backs. Here he cocked his eye at his father, not wanting to seem gullible. Philip nodded. 'Yes, elephants. They are vouched for by men I have found honest in other ways. Go on; all this is very useful.'

'They say people who greet the Great King have to lie down on their faces. I told them they need not do it to you. I was afraid someone might laugh at them.'

His father's head went back. He gave a great belly-laugh and slapped his knee.

'They didn't do it?' asked the boy.

'No, but they had your leave. Always make virtue of necessity and see you're thanked for it. Well, they were lucky to get off better from you than Xerxes' envoys did from your namesake, in the hall at Aigai.' He settled himself at ease. The boy stirred restlessly, disturbing the dog, which had its nose on his instep.

'When Xerxes bridged the Hellespont and brought his hosts to eat up Greece, he sent envoys first to all the peoples, demanding earth and water. A handful of earth for the land, a flask of water for the rivers; it was the homage of surrender. Our land stood clear in his way southward; we should be at his back when he went on; he wanted to make sure of us. So he sent us seven envoys. It was when the first Amyntas was King.'

Alexander would have liked to ask if this Amyntas was his great-grandfather or what; but nobody would tell one straight about the ancestors, any later than the heroes and the gods. Perdikkas, his father's elder brother, had been killed in battle, leaving a baby son. But the

Macedonians had wanted someone who could fight off the Illyrians and rule the kingdom; so they had asked his father to be King instead. Further back than this, he was always told he would know when he was older.

'In those days, there was no Palace here at Pella; only the castle up at Aigai. We held on then with our teeth and nails. The western chiefs, the Orestids and Lynkestids, thought themselves kings; Illyrians, Paionians, Thracians crossed the border every month to take slaves and drive off cattle. But all those were children beside the Persians. Amyntas had prepared no defences, as far as I could learn. By the time the envoys came, the Paionians, who might have been sought as allies, had been overrun. So he gave up, and did homage for his own land. You know what a satrap is?'

The dog started erect and looked about it fiercely. The boy patted it down.

'Amyntas' son was called Alexandros. He would be about fourteen or fifteen; he had his own Guard already. Amyntas feasted the envoys in the hall of Aigai, and he was there.'

'Then he had killed his boar?'

'How do I know? It was a state banquet, so he was there.'

The boy knew Aigai almost as well as Pella. All the old shrines of the gods, where the great festivals were held, were up at Aigai; and the royal tombs of the ancestors, the ancient grave-mounds kept clear of trees, with their cavelike doorways, their massive doors of worked bronze and marble. It was said that when a King of Macedon was buried away from Aigai, the line would die. When the summer grew hot at Pella, they would go up there for the cool. The streams never dried there, coming down from their ferny mountain glens, cold from the upper snows; tumbling down all over the bluff, by the houses, through the castle court, till they joined together and plunged sheer down in the great fall which curtained the sacred cave. The castle was old, thick and strong, not like the fine columned Palace; the great hall had a round hearth, and a hole in the roof to let out the smoke. When men shouted there at the feasts, the sound would echo. He pictured Persians with curled beards and spangled hats, picking their way over the rough floor.

'There was drinking. Maybe the envoys were used to weaker wine; maybe they felt free to do as they liked, having got what they came for without trouble. One of them asked where the royal ladies were, saying it was the custom in Persia for them to attend the feasts.'

'Do Persian ladies stay on for the drinking?'

'It was a barefaced lie, not even meant to deceive; pure insolence. Persian ladies are closer kept than ours.'

'Did our men fight?'

'No, Amyntas sent for the women. Those of Paionia were already slaves in Asia, because their men had defied Xerxes. In justice to him, I don't think he could have done better than they. He had no army, as we would understand it. The Companions from his own demesne; and the tribal levies, whom their lords would train if and how they chose, and would not bring at all if they did not choose. He had not taken Mount Pangaios with the gold-mines. I did that. Gold, my boy, gold is the mother of armies. I pay my men round the year, war or no war, and they fight for *me*, under my officers. Down south, they turn them off in the slack times, and the hired men find work where they can. So they fight only for their own strolling generals, who are often good in their way, but still just hirelings themselves. In Macedon, *I* am the general. And that, my son, is why the Great King's envoys don't come asking for earth and water now.'

The boy nodded thoughtfully. The bearded envoys had been civil because they must, though the youth was different. 'And did the ladies really come?'

'They came, affronted as you can guess, not deigning to dress their hair or put on a necklace. They expected to appear a moment, and then retire.'

Alexander pictured his mother getting such a summons. He doubted she would show herself, even to keep the people of the land from slavery. If she did, she would dress her hair and put on every jewel she had.

'When they learned they were to stay,' Philip went on, 'they went over, as decent women would, to the far seats by the wall.'

'Where the pages sit?'

'Yes, there. An old man who had it from his grandfather showed me the place. The boys got up for them. They drew their veils and sat silent. The envoys called out compliments, urging them to unveil; for which, if their own women had done so before strange men, they would have cut off their noses; oh yes, and worse, believe me. In this indignity, young Alexandros saw his mother and sisters and the rest of the royal kin. He was enraged, and reproached his father. But if the Persians saw, they thought nothing of it. Who cares if the whelp barks, when the dog is quiet? One said to the King, "My Macedonian friend, better these ladies had not come at all, than sit there a mere torment to our eyes. Pray observe our custom; our ladies converse with guests. Remember, you gave our King earth and water."

'It was the sight of the naked sword. One may suppose a silence. Then the King went over to his womenfolk, and led them to sit on the ends of the Persians' supper-couches, as the flute-girls and the dancing-girls sit in the southern cities. The young prince saw the men lay hands on them, and his friends hardly held him back. Then suddenly he grew quiet. He beckoned the young men of his guard, and chose seven who were still beardless. These he spoke to in private and sent out. Going up to his father, who no doubt looked sick if any shame was in him, he said, "Sir, you are tired. Don't sit out the drinking, leave the guests to me. They shall lack nothing that befits them, I give my word."

'Well, it was a way for the man to save his face. He warned his son to do nothing rash, and then excused himself. The envoys, of course, supposed that nothing was now forbidden. The prince showed no anger. He came up all smiles, and did a round of the couches. "Dear guests, you honour our mothers and our sisters. But they came in so much haste, eager to do you courtesy, they feel hardly fit to be seen. Let us send them along to the bath, to dress and put on their ornaments. When they return, you will be able to say that here in Macedon, you were treated as you deserve."'

Alexander sat upright with shining eyes. He had guessed the prince's plan.

'The Persians had wine, and the night before them. They did not complain. Presently in came seven veiled ladies in splendid clothes. One walked to each envoy's couch. Even then, though they had forfeited by their insolence the rights of guest-friends, he waited to see if they would behave themselves. When the truth was plain, he gave a signal. The young men in the women's robes whipped out their daggers. The bodies rolled down on the platters and fruit-stands and spilled wine, almost without a cry.'

'Oh good!' said the boy. 'It served them right.'

'They had of course their retinue somewhere in the hall. The doors had been made fast; none could be let out alive to bring word to Sardis. It could never be proved they had not been waylaid by bandits as they went through Thrace. When all was done, the bodies were buried in the forest. As the old man told me, young Alexandros said, "You came for earth and water. Be content with earth."'

The father paused, to enjoy the applause of a glowing silence. The boy, who had been hearing tales of vengeance since he could follow human speech – no old house or peasant tribe in Macedon was without one – thought it as good as the theatre.

'So when King Xerxes came, Alexandros fought him?'

Philip shook his head. 'He was King by then. He knew he could do nothing. He had to lead his men in Xerxes' train with the other satraps. But before the great battle of Plataia, he rode over himself, by night, to tell the Greeks the Persian dispositions. He probably saved the day.'

The boy's face had fallen. He frowned with distaste. Presently he said, 'Well, he was clever. But I'd rather have fought a battle.'

'Would you so?' said Philip grinning. 'So would I. If we live, who knows?' He rose from the bench, brushing-down his well whitened robe with its purple edge. 'In my grandfather's time, the Spartans, to secure their power over the south, made treaty of alliance with the Great King. His price was the Greek cities of Asia, which till then were free. No one has yet lifted that black shame from the face of Hellas. None of them would stand up to Artaxerxes and the Spartans both together. And I tell you this: the cities will not be freed, till the Greeks are ready to follow a single war-leader. Dionysius of Syracuse might have been the man; but he had enough with the Carthaginians, and his son is a fool who has lost every-thing. But the time will come. Well, if we live we shall see.' He nodded, smiling. 'Is that great ugly brute the best you can find for a dog? I will see the huntsman, and find you something with good blood in it.'

Leaping before the dog, whose hackles had risen bristling, the boy cried out 'I love him!' in a voice not of tenderness but challenge to the death.

Cross with disappointment, Philip said, 'Very well, very well. You need not shout at me. The beast is yours, who is going to harm it? I was offering you a gift.'

There was a pause. At length the boy said stiffly, 'Thank you, Father. But I think he'd be jealous, and kill the other one. He's very strong.'

The dog pushed its nose into his armpit. They stood side by side, a solid alliance. Philip shrugged and went indoors.

Alexander and the dog started wrestling on the ground. The dog knocked him about, holding back as it would with a growing pup. Presently, their limbs involved together, they lay drowsing in the sun. He pictured the hall at Aigai, littered with cups and plates and cushions and Persians sprawling in gore, like the Trojans on his mother's wall. At the far end, where the attendants were being killed, the youth who had come with the envoys was fighting on, the last one left, standing his ground against a score. 'Stop!' cried the Prince. 'Don't dare to kill him, he's my friend.' When the dog woke him by scratching itself, they had been riding off on horses with plumed head-stalls, to see Persepolis.

The mild summer day declined to evening. On the salt lake of Pella fell the shadow of its island fort, where the treasury and the dungeons were. Lamps glimmered in windows up and down the town; a household slave came out with a resined torch, to kindle the great cressets upheld by seated lions at the foot of the Palace steps. The lowing of homebound cattle sounded on the plain; in the mountains, which turned towards Pella their shadowed eastern faces, far-distant watch fires sparked the grey.

The boy sat on the Palace roof, looking down at the town, the lagoon, and the little fisher-boats making for their moorings. It was his bedtime, and he was keeping out of his nurse's way till he had seen his mother, who might give him leave to stay up. Men mending the roof had gone home, without removing their ladders. It was a chance not to be wasted.

He sat on the tiles of Pentelic marble, shipped in by King Archelaos; the gutter under his thighs, between his knees an antefix in the shape of a gorgon's head, the paint faded by weather. Grasping the snaky hair, he was outstaring the long drop, defying its earth-daimons. Going back he would have to look down; they must be settled with beforehand.

Soon they gave in, as such creatures did when challenged. He ate the stale bread he had stolen instead of supper. It should have been hot posset, flavoured with honey and wine; the smell had been tempting, but at supper one was caught for bed. Nothing could be had for nothing.

A bleat sounded from below. They had brought the black goat, it must be nearly time. Better now not to ask beforehand. Once he was there, she would not send him away.

He picked his way down the long spaces of the ladder-rungs made for men. The beaten earth-daimons kept their distance; he sang himself a song of victory. From the lower roof to the ground; no one was there but a few tired slaves going off duty. Indoors Hellanike would be searching; he must go around outside. He was getting too much for her; he had heard his mother say so.

The Hall was lit; inside, kitchen-slaves were talking Thracian and shifting tables. Just ahead was a sentry, pacing his round; Menestas with his red bushy beard. The boy smiled and saluted.

'Alexander! Alexander!'

It was Lanike, behind the corner he had only just turned. She had come out after him herself. She would see him in a moment. He started running and thinking together. Here was Menestas. 'Quick!' he whispered. 'Hide me in your shield.' Not waiting to be lifted, he clambered up the man and wrapped arms and legs around him. The wiry beard tickled his head. 'Little monkey!' muttered Menestas, clapping the hollow shield across him just in time, and backing up to the wall. Hellanike passed, calling angrily, but too well-bred to talk to soldiers. 'Where are you off to? I've no business ...' But the boy had hugged his neck, dropped away and gone.

He threaded byways, avoiding the middens, for one could not come dirty to serve a god; and reached safely the garden-close by his mother's postern. Outside on the steps a few women were waiting already with their unlit torches. He kept out of their way beyond the myrtle hedge; he did not mean to be seen till they were in the grove. He knew where to go meantime.

Not far away was the shrine of Herakles, his paternal ancestor. Inside its little portico, the blue wall was dusky in evening shade, but the bronze statue shone out clearly, and its eyes of inlaid agate caught the last of the light. King Philip had dedicated it soon after his accession; he had been twenty-four, and the sculptor, who knew how to treat a patron, had done

Herakles about that age, but beardless in the southern style, with his hair and the lion-skin gilded. The fanged mask of the lion was put on like a hood above his brow, the rest formed a cloak on his shoulders. The head had been copied for Philip's coinage.

No one was watching; Alexander went up to the shrine, and rubbed the right toe of the hero above the edge of the plinth. Just now on the roof he had called upon him in their secret words, and he had come at once to tame the daimons. It was time to thank him. His toe was brighter than the rest of his foot, from many such rubbings.

From beyond the hedge he heard the sistrum tinkle, and the mutter of a finger-drum lightly brushed. A torch threw its glow on the painted doorway, turning dusk to night. He crept up to the hedge. Most of the women had come. They had on bright thin dresses; they were only going to dance before the god. At the Dionysia, when they went up from Aigai into the mountain forests, they would wear the real maenad dress, and carry the reed thyrsos with its pine-cone top and wreath of ivy. Their dappled robes and fawnskins would not be seen again, but be thrown away with their bloody stains. The little pelts they wore now were softly dressed and buckled with wrought gold; their thyrses were delicate sceptres, gilded and trimmed with jewellers' work. The priest of Dionysos had just arrived, and a boy leading the goat. They were only waiting for his mother to come out.

She came, laughing in the doorway with Hyrmina from Epiros; dressed in a saffron robe, and gilt sandals with garnet clasps. The ivy-wreath in her hair was gold, its fine sprays trembled glittering in the torchlight, whenever she moved her head. Her thyrsos was twined with a little enamel snake. One of the women carried the basket with Glaukos in it. He always came to the dance.

The girl with the torch carried it round to all the others; their flames leaped up, making eyes shine, and the red, green, blue, yellow of the dresses deepen like jewels. Standing from the shadows, there hung like a mask the sad, wise, wicked face of the goat, its topaz eyes and its gilded horns. A wreath of young green vine-clusters hung round its neck. With the priest and his serving-boy, it led the way to the grove; the women followed talking quietly. The sistra gave soft jangles as their bearers walked. Frogs croaked in the stream that fed the fountains.

They went up on the open hill above the garden; this was all royal land. The path threaded winding, between myrtles and tamarisk and wild olive bushes. Behind them all, out of sight, led by the torches, the boy stepped lightly.

The tall dark of the pinewood loomed ahead. He left the path, and slipped cautiously along through the bush. It was too soon to be seen.

Lying flat on the springy pine-needles, he looked out from a sheltering hollow at the grove. They had stuck their torches into sconces speared into the ground. The dancing-place had been prepared, the altar garlanded, the rustic trestle set with the wine-cups and the mixing-bowl and the sacred fans. On his plinth, cared-for as always, cleansed from bird-droppings, washed and polished so that his brown-tinted marble limbs had the sheen of youthful flesh, stood Dionysos.

Olympias had had him brought here from Corinth, where he had been carved to her commands. He was nearly life-sized, a youth of about fifteen, fair-haired, with the slim muscles of a dancer. He wore ornate red boots, and a leopard-skin on one shoulder. A long-shafted thyrsos was grasped in his right hand; the left held out a gilt cup in welcome. His smile was not Apollo's, which says, 'Man, know yourself; that is enough for your little life.' This was a beckoning smile; its secret was for sharing.

They stood in a ring with joined hands, and sang an invocation, before the goat was sacrificed. It had rained since the last blood was shed there; he came up without fear, and only when the knife went in gave one wild lonely cry. His blood was caught in a shallow cup and mixed with wine for the god. The boy watched quietly, his chin propped on his hands. He had seen countless sacrifices, in the public sanctuaries and in this grove, where in infancy he had been carried to the dancing, and slept on pinemats to the blood-pulse of the drums.

The music had started. The girls with the finger-drums and sistra, the girl with the double flute, began softly swaying to their own time. Glaukos' head in his opened basket was swaying too. Pace and sound built up; arms linked behind waists, the women beat the ground with their feet, their bodies arching forward and back, their hair falling loose and swinging. They drank neat wine, for the dances of Dionysos; after the sacrifice, they had drunk along with the god.

He could come out soon; he would never be sent back now.

The girl with the cymbals brought them together high over her head in a throbbing clang. He crept forward till he was almost in the torchlight; no one saw him. Turning slowly at first, to leave breath for singing, they were hymning the Triumph of the God.

He could hear most of the words, but he knew the hymn from memory. He had often heard it here. After each verse the cymbals clanged, and they sang each time louder the chorus, 'Euoi, Bakchos! Euoi! Euoi!'

His mother began the hymn, hailing the god as son of Semele, born of fire. Her eyes and cheeks and hair were bright, her gold garland shimmered, her yellow dress threw back the torchlight, as if she herself were alight.

Hyrmina from Epiros, shaking her black hair, sang how the infant god had been hidden in Naxos to save him from jealous Hera, and guarded by singing nymphs. The boy crawled nearer. Above his head was the wine-table; he peered over its edge, the cups and the mixer were old, with pictures painted on them. He reached down a cup to look; there was some wine still in it. He tipped out a drop or two, in libation to the god, for he was well-trained in such matters; then he drank the rest. The strong unwatered taste was sweet enough to please him. The god seemed glad to have been honoured; for the torches were brighter, the music became magical. He knew that soon he would dance.

They sang how Zeus' child was brought to the woodland lair of old Silenos, who taught him wisdom till, outstripping his teacher, he found the power in the purple grape. Then all the satyrs worshipped him, for the joys and furies in his hand. The song had a twirling lilt, the dance spun round like a wheel round a well-greased axle. By himself among the trees, the boy began to step out the time and clap his hands.

The god grew to a youth, fair-faced and graceful as a girl, but burning with the levin-fire that had been his mother's midwife. He went out to mankind, showering all good gifts on those who perceived his godhead, but dreadful to unbelievers as a ravening lion. His fame increased, he grew too bright to be hidden. Jealous Hera could be deceived no longer. By his shining and his power she knew him, and sent him mad.

The music spiralled, quicker and higher, the music skirled like the death-shriek of small prey in a midnight wood, the cymbals dinned. The boy, hungry already and thirsty now from the dance, stretched tiptoe to reach another cup. This time it did not catch his breath. It was like the fire from heaven in the hymn.

The wild god wandered, through Thrace and across Hellespont, over the Phrygian heights and south to Karia. His worshippers who had shared his joy did not forsake him, but stayed to share his madness. It brought them ecstasy, for even his madness was divine. He followed the Asian coast to Egypt, whose wise race welcomed him; he rested there to learn their wisdom and teach them his. Then filled with madness and divinity, he set out over the unmeasured leagues of Asia, travelling east. On he danced, gathering worshippers as fire kindles fire; he crossed the Euphrates on a bridge of ivy, the Tigris on a tiger's back. Still he danced on, over plains and rivers and mountains high as Caucasus, till he came to the land of India at the outer edge of the world. Beyond was nothing but the encircling Stream of Ocean. The curse of Hera was spent. The Indians worshipped him; wild lions and panthers came meekly to draw his chariot. Thus he came back in glory to the Hellene lands; the Great Mother cleansed him of all the blood he had shed when he was mad; and he gave gladness to the hearts of men.

They raised the chorus; the boy's voice shrilled with the flute. He had thrown off his chiton, hot with the dance, the torch-flames and the wine. The gold wheels of the lion-drawn chariot turned beneath him, the paeans sounded, rivers drew back for him, the peoples of India and Asia danced to his song. The maenads were invoking him; he leaped from his chariot to dance among them. They broke their whirling ring, laughing and crying aloud to him, and closed the ring again, so that he could circle his own altar. As they sang, he danced around it, trampling the dew, making his magic, till the grove spun round him and he did not know earth from sky. But there before him was the Great Mother, with a wreath of light in her hair; she caught him in her arms, and kissed him over; and he saw on her golden gown the red prints from his bloodstained feet, where he had trodden in the place of sacrifice. His feet were as red as the boots on the painted statue.

He was wrapped in a cloak, and laid on a deep pine-mat, and kissed again, and told softly that even the gods, when they are young, must sleep. He must stay there and be good, and in a little while they would all go home. It was warm on the pine-smelling needles, in the crimson wool; the heave of sickness had passed and the torches had stopped turning. They burned lower in their sconces, but still friendly and bright. Looking out from the folded cloak, he saw the women go off into the pine-grove, hand in hand or with arms entwined. In other years, he would try to remember if he had heard deeper voices, answering theirs down in the wood; but the memories were deceitful, and each time they were invoked spoke with a different voice. At all events, he was not afraid, nor lonely; there was whispering and laughter not far away. A dancing flame was the last thing he saw before his closing eyes.

2

He was seven years old, the age at which boys left the care of women. It was time to make a Greek of him.

King Philip was at war again on the north-east Chalkidian coast, securing his boundaries, which meant stretching them. His marriage grew no easier; rather than a wife, it seemed to him, he had wedded a great and dangerous noble who could not be reduced by war, and whose spies knew everything. From a girl she had grown into a woman of striking beauty; but, girl or youth, it was the young who roused desire in him. For a while young men had contented him; then, after his father's custom, he had taken a well-born young concubine with the status of a minor wife. Olympias' outraged pride had shaken the Palace like an earthquake. She had been seen at night, near Aigai, going with a torch to the royal tombs; it was ancient witchcraft, to write a curse on lead and leave it for the ghosts to work on. It was said a child had been with her. He had looked at his son when next they met; the smoke-grey eyes had met his, unflinching, haunted, mute. As he went away he felt the eyes in his back.

The war in Chalkidia could not wait; nor should the boy. Though not big for his years, he was forward in everything else. Hellanike had taught him his letters and his scale (his high voice was true and its pitch was perfect); the soldiers of the Guard, and even of the barracks, to whom he escaped every second day, had taught him their peasant dialect, and what else one could only guess. As for what he had learned from his mother, that was best not thought of.

When Kings of Macedon went to war, it was second nature to guard their backs. To the west, the Illyrians had been subdued in the first years of his reign. The east he was about to deal with. There remained the old dangers of tribal kingdoms: conspiracies at home, and feuds. If before he marched he had taken the boy from Olympias, and appointed some man of his own as governor, both these evils were certain.

Philip took some pride in seeing where a pass could be turned without a battle. He slept on the problem, and woke remembering Leonidas.

He was Olympias' uncle; but more Hellenized than Philip himself. As a young man, in love with the idea rather than the ideas of Greece, he had travelled south, making first for Athens. Here he had acquired a pure Attic speech, studied oratory and composition; and sampled the philosophic schools just long enough to decide they could only undermine sound tradition and the findings of common sense. As was natural to a man of his birth, he made friends among the aristocracy, hereditary oligarchs who looked to the good old days, deplored the times, and, like their forbears back to the Great War, admired the customs of Sparta. In due course Leonidas went to see it.

Used by now to the high diversions of Athens, drama festivals, music contests, sacred processions put on like great performances, supper-clubs with their verse-capping and well-read wit, he had found Lakedaimon stiflingly provincial. To a feudal lord of Epiros, with deep roots in his demesne, the racial rule of Spartiate over Helot was foreign and uneasy; the blunt-spoken familiarity of Spartiate with Spartiate, and with himself, struck him as boorish. And here too, as in Athens, the great days were

over. Like an old dog thrashed by a younger one, which will show its teeth
but keep its distance, Sparta had not been the same since the Thebans had
marched up to the walls. Barter had gone out, money had come in and
was prized here as elsewhere; the rich had amassed great lands, the poor
could no longer pay their shot at the citizens' public mess-tables, and sunk
to mere 'by-dwellers' whose gallantry had bled out of them with their
pride. But in one respect he had found them equal to their past. They could
still rear disciplined boys, hardy, uncoddled and respectful, who did what
they were told at once without asking why, stood up when their elders
entered, and never spoke till spoken to. Attic culture and Spartan
manners, he had thought as he sailed homeward; combine them in the
pliant mind of youth and they would give you the perfect man.

He returned to Epiros, the consequence of his rank increased by his
travels. Long after his knowledge was out of date it had been universally
deferred to. King Philip, who had agents in all the Greek cities, knew better
than this; nonetheless, when he talked with Leonidas he became aware
that his own Greek was rather Boeotian. Along with the Attic speech went
the Hellene maxims: 'Nothing in excess'; 'Well begun, half done'; and 'It
is a woman's glory not to be spoken of, either for praise or blame.'

Here was the perfect compromise. Olympias' kin was honoured.
Leonidas, who had a passion for correctness, would allot her the dues of
a high-born lady, himself the dues of a man. She would find him harder
than even Philip to meddle with. Through his southern guest-friends he
could engage all the proper tutors the King had not time to find, and
ensure they were sound in politics and morals. Letters were exchanged.
Philip rode off, his mind at rest, leaving orders that Leonidas be given a
state welcome.

On the day he was expected, Hellanike laid out Alexander's best clothes,
and had her slave fill him a bath. Kleopatra came in while she was
scouring him. She was a podgy child, with Olympias' red hair and the
square build of Philip. She ate too much because she was often unhappy,
knowing their mother loved Alexander more, and differently.

'You're a schoolboy now,' she said. 'You can't come in the women's
rooms.'

When he found her in trouble he would often console her, amuse her
or give her things. When she threatened him with her womanhood, he
hated her. 'I shall come in when I like. Who do you think will stop me?'

'Your teacher will.' She began chanting it, jumping up and down. He
leaped out, soaking the floor, and threw her in with all her clothes on.
Hellanike laid him wet across her knee and beat him with her sandal.
Kleopatra mocked him, was beaten in turn, and thrust out screaming, to
be dried by the maid.

Alexander did not weep. He had understood the whole business of the appointment. No one had needed to tell him that if he did not obey this man, it would lose his mother a battle in her war; nor that the next one would then be fought over himself. He was scarred within by such battles. When another threatened, the scars throbbed like old wounds before the rain.

Hellanike combed his tangled hair, making him clench his teeth. He cried easily at old war-songs where sworn comrades died together, at a falling cadence of the flute. He had cried half a day, when his dog fell sick and died. Already he knew what it was to mourn the fallen; for Agis he had wept his heart out. But to cry for his own wounds would make Herakles forsake him. This had long been a part of their secret compact.

Bathed, combed and dressed, he was summoned to the Perseus Room, where Olympias and the guest sat in chairs of honour. The boy had expected an aged scholar; he saw a spruce upright man in the forties, his dark beard scarcely grizzled, looking about like a general who, though off duty, will remember it all tomorrow. The boy knew a good deal about officers, mostly from below. His friends kept his secrets, and he kept theirs.

Leonidas was genial, kissed him on both cheeks, set firm hands on his shoulders, was sure he would be a credit to his ancestors. Alexander submitted civilly; his sense of the realities made him stand through it all like a soldier on parade. Leonidas had not hoped to see the Spartan training so well begun. The boy, though too beautiful for safety, looked healthy and alert; no doubt he would prove teachable. 'You have reared a fine child, Olympias. These pretty baby-clothes show your care. Now we must find him something for a boy.'

His eyes moved to his mother, who had embroidered herself his tunic of soft combed wool. Sitting straight in her chair, she gave him a little nod, and looked away.

Leonidas moved into his palace quarters. To negotiate for suitable teachers would take time. Those eminent enough would have schools to leave; some must be looked into, for dangerous thoughts. His own work must begin at once; he saw it could not be too soon.

The drilled look had been illusion. The boy had done as he liked; got up at cocklight or had his sleep out; run about with boys or men. Though grossly spoilt, one must own him not a milksop; but his speech was dreadful. Not only was he nearly Greekless; but where had he learned his Macedonian? One might suppose he had been begotten against a barrack wall.

Clearly, school hours were insufficient. His life must be taken in hand from dawn till dusk.

Every morning before sun-up he was at exercise; twice round the running-track, swinging the hand-weights, leaping and hurling. When breakfast came at last, it was never quite enough. If he said he was still hungry, he was told to say it in proper Greek; to be answered, in proper Greek, that spare breakfasts were good for the health.

His clothes had been changed for homespun, harsh to the skin and unadorned. It was good enough for the kings' sons of Sparta. Autumn came on; in colder and colder weather, he was hardened-off by going cloakless. Running about to keep warm made him much hungrier, but he did not get much more food.

Leonidas found himself obeyed; doggedly, without complaint, with steady unconcealed resentment. It was all too clear that he and his regime were simply a detested ordeal, which the boy endured for his mother's sake, sustained by pride.

He was uneasy, but could not breach the wall. He was one of those men in whom the role of father, once achieved, blots out all memories of childhood. His own sons could have told him so, had they ever told him anything. He would do his duty by the boy, and knew of no one who could do it better.

Greek lessons began. It soon appeared that Alexander was in fact quite fluent. He simply disliked it; a disgrace, as his tutor told him, when his father spoke it so well. He repeated it briskly; soon learned to write it; and expected, as soon as he left the schoolroom, to lapse into broad Macedonian and the argot of the phalanx.

When he understood he had to speak Greek all day, he could scarcely credit it. Even slaves could use their home tongue to one another.

He had respites. To Olympias, the tongue of the north was the heroes' unspoilt heritage, Greek a degenerate patois. She spoke it to Greeks as a courtesy to inferiors, and to them alone. Leonidas had social duties, during which his captive could escape. If he could get to the barracks at mess-time, there was always porridge to spare.

Riding he still enjoyed; but he soon lost his favourite escort, a young officer of the Companions, to whom he offered an accustomed kiss as the man lifted him down. Leonidas saw from the stable yard. Ordered out of hearing, and seeing his friend flush scarlet, the boy thought a limit had been passed. He walked back, and stood between.

'I kissed him first. And he had never tried to have me.' He used the barrack term, knowing no other.

After a speechless pause, he was marched away in silence. In the schoolroom, still without a word, Leonidas beat him.

He had given far worse to his own sons. Rank and Olympias had their claims. But it was a boy's beating, not a child's. Leonidas did not own to himself that he had been waiting for the chance, to see how his charge would take it.

He heard no sound but the blows. He had meant at the end to bid the
boy turn and face him; but was forestalled. He had looked only for a
Spartan fortitude, or self-pity. He confronted dry wide eyes, their irises
stretched to a pale rim round the black; hard-shut white lips and dilated
nostrils; a blazing rage, condensed by silence like the core of a furnace. For
a moment, he had a sense of actual menace.

Alone among those at Pella, he had seen Olympias' childhood. But *she*
would have flown in straight away with her nails; her nurse's face had
been scored with them. This containment was another thing. One even
dreaded lest it break.

His first instinct was to take the boy by his scruff, and thrash the
defiance out of him. But though a narrow man he was by his lights a just
one, with an exacting self-esteem. Moreover, he had been brought here
to rear a fighting King of Macedon, not to break in a slave. The boy had
at least controlled himself.

'The silence of a soldier. I approve a man who can bear his wounds. No
further work today.'

He received in exchange the look which accords grudging respect to a
mortal enemy. As the boy went out, Leonidas saw a bloodstain on the back
of his homespun chiton. It would have been nothing in Sparta; yet he
found himself wishing he had not hit quite so hard.

The boy said nothing to his mother; but she found the weals. In the
room where they had shared many secrets, she clasped him weeping, and
presently they wept together. He stopped first; went to the loose stone
under the hearth, pulled out a wax mammet he had seen there, and urged
her to bewitch Leonidas. She took it quickly away, saying he must not
touch, and besides it was not for that. It had a long thorn stuck through
its phallos, but had failed to work on Philip, though often tried. She had
not known the child was watching.

For him, the comfort of tears had been brief and false. He felt betrayed,
when he met Herakles in the garden. He had not cried for the pain, but
for his lost happiness; he could have held back if she had not softened him.
Next time she must not know.

They shared a plot, however. She had never been reconciled to the
Spartan clothes; she had loved to dress him. Reared in a house where
ladies sat in Hall like the queens of Homer, to hear the ancestral heroes
sung by bards, she was contemptuous of Spartans, a race of faceless
obedient infantry, and unwashed women half soldier, half brood-mare.
That her son should be forced into the likeness of this grey and plebeian
race would have enraged her, had she thought it could be done. Resenting
even the attempt, she brought him a new chiton worked in blue and
scarlet, saying, as she tucked it into his clothes chest, that there was no

harm in his looking like a gentleman when his uncle was away. Later she added Corinthian sandals, a chlamys of Milesian wool, and a gold brooch for its shoulder.

Good clothes made him feel himself again. Discreet at first, he grew careless with success. Leonidas, knowing where to lay the blame, said nothing. He merely went to the chest and took the new clothes away, along with an extra blanket he found hidden there.

He had challenged the gods at last, thought Alexander; this must be the end of him. But she only smiled ruefully, and asked how he could have let himself be found out. Leonidas must not be defied; he might be offended and go home. 'And then, my darling, we might find our troubles only starting.'

Toys were toys, power was power. Nothing to be had for nothing. Later she smuggled him other gifts. He was more wary, but Leonidas was more vigilant, and took to searching the chest every so often, as a matter of course.

More manly gifts, he was allowed to keep. A friend had made him a quiver, a perfect miniature with a shoulder-sling. Finding it hang too low on him, he sat in the Palace forecourt to undo the buckle. The tongue was awkward, the leather stiff. He was about to go in and find an awl to prise it, when a bigger child walked up and stood in the light. He was handsome and sturdy with bronze-gold hair and dark grey eyes. Holding out his hand he said, 'I'll try, let me.' He spoke with confidence, in a Greek which had got beyond the schoolroom.

'It's new, that's why it's stiff.' He had had his day's work of Greek, and answered in Macedonian.

The stranger squatted beside him. 'It's like a real one, like a man's. Did your father make it?'

'Of course not. Doreios the Cretan did. He can't make me a Cretan bow, those are horn, only men can pull them. Koragos will make a bow for me.'

'Why do you want to undo it?'

'It's too long.'

'It looks right to me. No, but you're smaller. Here, I'll do it.'

'I've measured it. It wants taking in two holes.'

'You can let it out when you're bigger. It's stiff, but I'll do it. My father's seeing the King.'

'What does he want?'

'I don't know, he said to wait for him.'

'Does he make you speak Greek all day?'

'It's what we all speak at home. My father's a guest-friend of the King. When I'm older, I'll have to go to Court.'

'Don't you want to come?'

'Not much; I like it at home. Look, up on that hill; no, not the first one. the second; all that land's ours. Can't you speak Greek at all?'

'Yes, I can if I want. I stop when I get sick of it.'

'Why, you speak it nearly as well as I do. Why did you talk like that, then? People will think you're a farm boy.'

'My tutor makes me wear these clothes to be like the Spartans. I do have good ones; I wear them at the feasts.'

'They beat all the boys in Sparta.'

'Oh, he drew blood on me once. But I didn't cry.'

'He's no right to beat you, he should only tell your father. How much did he cost?'

'He's my mother's uncle.'

'Mm, I see. My father bought my pedagogue, just for me.'

'Well, it teaches you to bear your wounds when you go to war.'

'War? But you're only six.'

'Of course not, I'm eight next Lion Month. You can see that.'

'So am I. But *you* don't look it, you look six.'

'Oh, let me do that, you're too slow.'

He snatched away the sling-strap. The leather slipped back into the buckle. The stranger grabbed it angrily. 'Silly fool, I'd nearly done it.'

Alexander swore at him in barrack Macedonian. The other boy opened his mouth and eyes, and listened riveted. Alexander, who could keep it up for some time, became aware of respect and did so. With the quiver between them, they crouched in the pose of their forgotten strife.

'*Hephaistion!*' came a roar from the columned stoa. The boys sat like scuffling dogs over whom a bucket has been emptied.

The lord Amyntor, his audience over, had seen with concern that his son had left the porch where he had been told to wait, invaded the Prince's playground and snatched his toy. At that age they were not safe a moment out of one's sight. Amyntor blamed his own vanity; he liked to show the boy off, but to have brought him here was stupid. Angry with himself, he strode over, grabbed him by the back of his clothes, and gave him a clout on the ear.

Alexander jumped to his feet. He had already forgotten why he had been angry. 'Don't hit him. I don't mind him. He came to help me.'

'You are good to say so, Alexander. But he disobeyed.'

For a moment the boys exchanged looks, confusedly sharing their sense of human mutability, as the culprit was dragged away.

It was six years before they met again.

'He lacks application and discipline,' said Timanthes the grammarian. Most of the teachers Leonidas had engaged found the drinking in Hall too much for them, and would escape, with excuses which amused the Macedonians, to bed, or to talk in each other's rooms.

'Maybe,' said the music-master, Epikrates. 'But one values the horse above the bridle.'

'He applies when it suits him,' said Naukles the mathematician. 'At first he could not have enough. He can work out the height of the Palace from its noon shadow, and if you ask him how many men in fifteen phalanxes, he hardly has to pause. But I have never brought him to perceive the beauty of numbers. Have you, Epikrates?'

The musician, a thin dark Ephesian Greek, shook his head smiling. 'With you he makes them serve the use; with me, the feeling. Still, as we know, music is ethical; and I've a king to train, not a concert artist.'

'He will get no further with me,' said the mathematician. 'I would say I don't know why I stay, if I thought I should be believed.'

A roar of bawdy laughter sounded from the hall, where someone with talent was improving a traditional skolion. For the seventh time they bawled the chorus.

'Yes, we are well paid,' said Epikrates. 'But I could earn as much in Ephesos, between teaching and concert work; and earn it as a musician. Here I am a conjuror, I call up dreams. It's not what I came to do. Yet it holds me. Does it never hold you, Timanthes?'

Timanthes sniffed. He thought Epikrates' compositions too modern and emotional. He himself was an Athenian, pre-eminent for the purity of his style; he had in fact been the teacher of Leonidas. He had closed his school to come, finding at his age the work grow burdensome, and glad to provide for his last years. He had read everything worth reading, and when young had once known what the poets meant.

'It appears to me,' he said, 'that here in Macedon they have enough of the passions. One heard a great deal about the culture of Archelaos, in my student days. With the late wars of succession, it seems chaos returned. I will not say the court is without refinements; but on the whole, we are in the wilds. Do you know youths come of age here when they have killed a boar and a man? One might suppose oneself in the age of Troy.'

'That should lighten your task,' said Epikrates, 'when you proceed to Homer.'

'System and application are what we need for that. The boy has a good memory, when he cares to use it. At first he learned his lists quite well. But he cannot keep his mind on system. One explains the construction; one quotes the proper example. But apply it? No. It is "Why did they chain Prometheus to the rock?" or, "Who was Hekabe mourning for?"'

'Did you tell him? Kings should learn to pity Hekabe.'

'Kings should learn self-discipline. This morning he brought the lesson to a stop, because, purely for syntax, I gave him some lines from *Seven against Thebes*. Why, if you please, were there seven generals, which led the cavalry, the phalanx, the light-armed skirmishers? "It is not to the purpose," I said, "not to the purpose; attend to syntax." He had the insolence to answer in Macedonian. I had to put my thong across his palm.'

The singing in Hall was broken by quarrelsome drunken shouts. Crockery crashed. The King's voice roared out; the noise subsided; a different song began.

'Discipline,' said Timanthes meaningly. 'Moderation, restraint, respect for law. If we do not ground him in them, who will? His mother?'

There was a pause while Naukles, whose room it was, nervously opened the door and looked outside. Epikrates said, 'If you want to compete with *her*, Timanthes, you had best sweeten your medicine, as I do mine.'

'He must make the effort to apply. It is the root of all education.'

'I don't know what you are all talking about,' said Derkylos, the gymnastic trainer, suddenly. The others had thought he was asleep. He was reclining on Naukles' bed; he thought effort should alternate with relaxation. He was in his mid thirties, with the oval head and short curls admired by sculptors, and a fine body kept painstakingly in shape; as an example to pupils, he used to say, but, thought the envious schoolmasters, no doubt from vanity. He had a list of crowned victors to his credit, and no pretensions to intellect.

'We were wishing,' said Timanthes with patronage, 'that the boy would make more effort.'

'I heard you.' The athlete raised himself on one elbow, looking aggressively statuesque. 'You have spoken words of ill omen. Spit for luck.'

The grammarian shrugged. Naukles said tartly, 'Will you tell us, Derkylos, *you* don't know why you stay?'

'It seems I'm the one with the best reason. To keep him, if I can, from killing himself too young. He has no safety-stop. Surely you've seen that?'

'I fear,' said Timanthes, 'that the terms of the palaestra are to me arcane.'

'I've seen it,' said Epikrates, 'if you mean what I suppose.'

'I don't know all your life-histories,' said Derkylos. 'But if any of you has seen red in battle, or been frightened out of his skin, you may remember putting out strength you had never known was in you. At exercise, even in a contest, you could not find it. There is a lock on it, put there by nature or the gods' wisdom. It is the reserve against extremity.'

'I remember,' said Naukles presently, 'in the earthquake, when the house fell on our mother, I lifted the beams. Yet later I could not move them.

'Nature wrung it out of you. Few men are born whose own will can do it. This boy will be one.'

Epikrates said, 'Yes, you may well be right.'

'And I reckon it something off a man's life each time. I have to watch him already. He told me once that Achilles chose between glory and length of days.'

'What?' said Timanthes startled. 'But we've scarcely begun Book One.'

Derkylos gazed at him in silence, then said mildly, 'You forget his maternal ancestry.'

Timanthes clicked his tongue, and bade them good night. Naukles fidgeted; he wanted to get to bed. The musician and the athlete strolled off through the park.

'It's useless talking to *him*,' said Derkylos. 'But I doubt the boy gets enough to eat.'

'You must be joking. Here?'

'It's the regime of that stiff-necked old fool Leonidas. I check his height each month; he's not growing fast enough. Of course you can't call him starved; but he burns it all up, he could take as much again. He's very quick-thinking, and his body has to keep pace, he won't take a no from it. Do you know he can hit the mark with a javelin while he's running?'

'You let him handle edged weapons? At his age?'

'I wish grown men were all as neat with them. It keeps him quiet ... What is it drives him like this?'

Epikrates looked round. They were in the open, no one near. 'His mother has made a good many enemies. She's a foreigner from Epiros; she has the name of a witch. Have you never heard whispers about his birth?'

'I remember once – But who'd dare let *him* hear word of it?'

'He seems to me to have a burden of proof upon him. Well, he enjoys his music for itself, he finds release in it. I have studied that side of the art a little.'

'I must speak to Leonidas again about his diet. Last time, I was told that in Sparta it would be one spare meal a day, and find the rest off the land. Don't tell it abroad, but I feed him myself sometimes. I used to do it now and then at Argos, for some good boy from a poor home ... These tales – do you believe them?'

'Not with my reason. He has Philip's capacity, if not his face or his soul. No, no, I don't believe them ... Do you know that old song about Orpheus, how he played his lyre on the mountainside, and found a lion had crouched at his feet to listen? I'm no Orpheus, I know; but sometimes I see the lion's eyes. Where did it go, after the music, what became of it? The story doesn't say.'

*

'Today,' said Timanthes, 'you have made better progress. For the next lesson, you may memorize eight lines. Here they are. Copy them on the wax, on the right side of the diptych. On the left, list the archaic word-forms. See you have them correctly; I shall expect you to repeat those first.' He handed over the tablet, and put away the roll, his stiff blue-veined hands shaking as he worked it into its leather case. 'Yes, that is all. You may go.'

'Please, may I borrow the book?'

Timanthes looked up, amazed and outraged.

'The *book*? Most certainly you may not, it is a valuable recension. What do you want with the book?'

'I want to see what happened. I'll keep it in my casket, and wash my hands each time.'

'We should all like, no doubt, to run before we can walk. Learn your passage, and pay attention to the Ionic forms. Your accent is still too Doric. This, Alexander, is not some supper-time diversion. This is Homer. Master his language, then you may talk of reading him.' He tied the strings of the case.

The lines were those in which vengeful Apollo comes striding down the peaks of Olympos with his arrows rattling at his back. Worked over in the schoolroom, hammered out piecemeal like some store-list being inventoried by kitchen slaves, once the boy was alone they came together: a great landscape of clanging gloom lit by funereal fires. He knew Olympos. He pictured the dead light of an eclipse; the tall striding darkness, and round it a faint rim of fire, such as they said the hidden sun had, able to strike men blind. *He came down like the fall of night.*

He walked in the grove above Pella, hearing the deep shuddering note of the bowstring, the hiss of the shafts, and thinking it into Macedonian. It found its way, next day, into his repetition. Timanthes rebuked at length his idleness, inattention, and lack of interest in his work, and set him at once to copy the passage twenty times, with the mistakes again by themselves.

He dug away at the wax, the vision dispersed and faded. Timanthes, whom something had caused to look up, found the grey eyes considering him with a cold distant gaze.

'Do not daydream, Alexander. What are you thinking of?'

'Nothing.' He bent again over his writing-stick. He had been wondering if there was any way of getting Timanthes killed. He supposed not; it would be unfair to ask his friends, who might be punished, and would feel it a disgrace to kill such an ancient man. It would make trouble, too, for his mother.

He went missing next day.

After huntsmen had been out after him with dogs, he was brought back at evening by a woodcutter on his lean old donkey; bruised black, covered with bloody grazes from a tumble down some rocks, and with a swollen foot which would not bear him. He had been trying, said the man, to get along on hands and knees; at night the forest was full of wolves, no place for the young lord alone.

He opened his mouth long enough to thank this man; to demand that he be fed, because he was hungry, and given a younger ass, which he had promised him on the way. These things attended to he became mute. The doctor could scarcely get from him more than yes or no, and a wince when the foot was moved. The compress and splint were put on; his mother came to his bedside. He turned his face away.

She put aside her anger, which belonged elsewhere; brought him a supper of all the treats Leonidas had banned; propped him against her breast while she fed him with sweet mulled wine. When he had told her all the trouble, as far as himself he understood it, she kissed him, tucked him in, and went off in a towering rage to quarrel with Leonidas.

The tempest shook the Palace, like a clash of gods above the Trojan plain. But many weapons which had served her against Philip were here denied her. Leonidas was very correct, very Athenian. He offered to leave, and tell the boy's father why. When she emerged from his study (she had been too angry to wait and have him sent for) everyone hid who saw her coming; but the truth was, she was in tears.

Old Lysimachos, who had lain in wait for her since, starting out, she had swept by him unseeing, greeted her as she returned, and said with no more fuss than if she had been a farmer's wife in his native Akarnania, 'How is the boy?'

No one paid attention to Lysimachos. He was always about, a Palace guest-friend since early in Philip's reign. He had backed his accession when support was urgent; had proved good company at supper, and been rewarded with the hand of an heiress in royal wardship. On the estate it brought him, he farmed and hunted. But the gods had denied him children; not only by her, but by all women he had ever lain with. This reproach being ready to any man's hand who chose to throw it, he thought hubris would ill become him, and was an unpretentious man. His one distinction was to have the run of the royal library; Philip had added to Archelaos' fine collection, and was careful whom he let loose inside. From the depths of his reading-cell, Lysimachos' voice could be heard murmuring by the hour over the scrolls, tasting words and cadences; but nothing had come of it, no treatise, history or tragedy. His mind, it seemed, was as infertile as his loins.

Olympias, at the sight of his square blunt face, his grey-blond hair and beard and faded blue eyes, felt a homely comfort, and asked him into her private guest-room. Once bidden to sit, he sat while she paced about, and offered harmless murmurs whenever she paused for breath, till she had run herself to a stop. Then he said, 'My dear Madam, now the boy has outgrown his nurse's care, don't you think he may need a pedagogue?'

She wheeled round so sharply that her jewels clattered. 'Never! I will not have it, the King knows that. What do they want to make of him, a clerk, a merchant, a steward? *He* feels what he is. All day these low-bred pedants are working to break his spirit. He has scarcely an hour, from his rising to his lying down, when his soul has space to breathe. Now is he to live like some captive thief, marched about in charge of a slave? Let no one speak of it in my hearing. And if the King sent you word to do it, tell him, Lysimachos, that before my son shall suffer that I will have blood for it, yes, by the Threefold Hekate, I will have blood!'

He waited till he thought that she would hear him, then said, 'I should be sorry too to see it. Rather than that, I myself would be his pedagogue. In fact, Madam, that is what I came to ask for.'

She sat down in her tall chair. He waited patiently, knowing she had paused, not to ask herself why a gentleman should offer for a servant's work, but whether he would do.

Presently he said, 'It has often seemed to me that Achilles has come again in him. If so, he needs a Phoinix ... *You, godlike Achilles, were the son I chose for my own, That some day you would keep the hard times from me.*'

'Did he do so? When Phoinix spoke those words, he had been rooted up in his age from Phthia, and brought to Troy. And what he was asking, Achilles did not grant.'

'If he had, it would have saved him sorrow. Maybe his soul has remembered. As we know, the ashes of Achilles and Patroklos were mingled in one urn. Not even a god could sift the one from the other. Achilles has come back with his fierceness and his pride, and with Patroklos' feeling. Each of them suffered for what he was; this boy will suffer for both.'

'There is more,' she said, 'as men will find.'

'I do not question it. Just now, this is enough. Let me try with him; if he cannot do with me, I will let him be.'

She got up again, and took a turn about the room.

'Yes, try,' she said. 'If you can stand between him and those fools, I shall be your debtor.'

Alexander was feverish at night, and slept most of next day. Lysimachos, looking in next morning, found him sitting up in the window, his good foot dangling outside, and shouting down in his high clear voice; two Companion Cavalry officers had come in from Thrace on the King's business, and he wanted news of the war. This they gave; but refused to take him riding, when they learned they were to catch him as he jumped down from the upper floor. Laughing and waving they clattered off. As the boy turned away with a sigh, Lysimachos reached up and carried him back to bed.

He submitted easily, having known the man all his life. As early as he had been able to run about, he had sat on his knee to hear his stories. Timanthes indeed had said of him to Leonidas that he was, rather than a scholar, a learned schoolboy. The boy at least was glad to see him, and confided to him the whole tale of his day in the woods, not without bragging.

'Did you walk on that foot just now?'

'I can't, I hopped.' He frowned at it with displeasure; it was hurting him. Lysimachos eased the pillow under.

'Look after it. The ankle was Achilles' weakness. His mother held him by it, when she dipped him in the Styx, and forgot to wet it after.'

'Is that in the book, how Achilles died?'

'No. But he knows he will, because he has fulfilled his death-fate.'

'Didn't the diviners warn him?'

'Yes, he was warned that his death would follow Hektor's, but still he killed him. He was avenging Patroklos, his friend, whom Hektor had killed.'

The boy considered this intently. 'He was his best friend of all?'

'Yes, from when they were boys together.'

'Why didn't Achilles save him first, then?'

'He had taken his men out of the battle, because the High King had insulted him. The Greeks were getting the worst of it without him; that was as he'd been promised by the god. But Patroklos, who had a feeling heart, when he saw old comrades falling came to Achilles weeping for pity. "Lend me only your armour," he said, "and let me show myself in the field. They will think you are back; it will be enough to scare them off." So Achilles gave him leave, and he did great deeds, but ...' He was stopped by the boy's shocked stare.

'He couldn't do that! He was a general! And he sent a junior officer, when he wouldn't go! It was his *fault* Patroklos died.'

'Oh, yes, he knew. He had sacrificed him to his pride. That was why he fulfilled his death-fate.'

'How did the King insult him? How did it start?'

Lysimachos settled himself on the stool of dyed sheepskin by the bed.

As the tale unfolded, Alexander found to his surprise that it could all have happened, any day, in Macedon.

The harebrained younger son, stealing the wife of his powerful host;

bringing her and the feud to his father's hold – the old houses of Macedon and Epiros could tell such tales by the score. The High King had called up his levies and his under-chiefs. King Peleus, being over age, had sent his own son, Achilles, born of a goddess queen. When at sixteen he came to the plain of Troy, he was already the best of the warriors.

The war itself was just like some tribal skirmish in the hills: warriors whooping each other on into single combats without asking leave; the infantry, it seemed, scrambling about in rabbles behind the lords. He had heard of a dozen such wars in the lifetime of men who told the story, breaking out from old feuds, or flaring up over blood shed in a drinking-brawl, the moving of a boundary stone, an unpaid bride-price, a cuckold mocked at a feast.

Lysimachos told it as he had pictured it in his youth. He had read the speculations of Anaxagoras, the maxims of Herakleitos, the history of Thukydides, the philosophy of Plato, Euripides' melodramas and Agathon's romantic plays; but Homer returned him to his childhood, when he had sat on his father's knee to hear the bard, and watched his tall brothers walk clanking sword at hip, as men still did in the streets of Pella.

The boy, who had always thought less of Achilles for making all this trouble only about a girl, now learned that she was a prize for valour, which the King had taken away to humble him. Now he well understood Achilles' anger. He pictured Agamemnon as a stocky man, with a strong black beard.

So, then, Achilles was sitting in his war-hut, self-exiled from his glory, playing his lyre to Patroklos, the only one who understood his mind, when the King's envoys came to him. The Greeks were in extremity; the King had had to eat dirt. Achilles should have his girl returned. Also, he could marry Agamemnon's own daughter with a huge dowry of lands and cities. If he liked, he could even have the dowry without her.

As people do at the crux of a tragedy though they know the end, the boy willed that all should be well now: that Achilles should relent, that he and Patroklos should go into battle side by side, happy and glorious. But Achilles turned away his face. They still asked too much, he said. 'For my goddess mother has told me I bear two death-fates within me. If I stay before Troy and fight, I lose my homecoming, but win everlasting fame. Or, if I go home to my dear fatherland, I lose the height of my glory, but have a long life left me, death will not come for me soon.' Now his honour had been blown on, he would choose the second fate, and sail home.

The third envoy had not yet spoken. Now he came forward; old Phoinix, who had known Achilles since he was a child upon his knee. King Peleus had adopted him, after his own father had cursed him out of doors. He had been happy at Peleus' court; but the father's curse had worked, making him forever childless. Achilles was the child he had chosen for his own, so that one day he would keep the hard times from him. Now, if he sailed, he would go along with him; he would never forsake him, even in exchange for being made young again. But he begged Achilles rather to heed his prayers, and lead out the Greeks to battle.

A moral digression followed; the boy, his attention wandering, withdrew into himself. Impatient of delays, he wished to bestow at once on Lysimachos some gift he had always wanted. It seemed to him that he could.

'I'd have said yes, if you had asked me.' Scarcely feeling his sprained foot as he moved, he clasped Lysimachos' neck.

Lysimachos embraced him, openly weeping. The boy was undisturbed at it; Herakles allowed such tears. It was great luck to have had the right gift at hand. It was real too, he had not lied at all to him; he truly loved him, would be like his son and keep the hard times from him. If he had come like Phoinix to Achilles, he would have given him what he asked: have led out the Greeks to fight, taking the first of the death-fates, never to come home to the dear fatherland, never to grow old. It was all quite true, and had given happiness. Why add, then, that though he would give consent, it would not be for Phoinix' sake?

He would do it for the everlasting fame.

The great city of Olynthos, on the north-east coast, had fallen to King Philip. His gold got in first, his soldiers later.

The Olynthians had looked askance at his rising power. For years they had harboured two bastard half-brothers of his who claimed his throne; had played him and Athens off against each other whenever it served their turn, and then allied with Athens.

First he took care that his bought men in the town should grow rich, and show it. Their party grew. Down south in Euboia, he fomented a rising to keep the Athenians minding their own business. Meantime he kept exchanging envoys with Olynthos, haggling at length over peace terms, while he reduced strategic country all around.

This done, he sent them an ultimatum. Either they or he would have to go; he had decided they should. If they surrendered, they could leave with a safe-conduct. No doubt their Athenian allies would look after them.

In spite of Philip's party, the vote went for holding out. They gave him some costly fighting, before his clients contrived to lose a couple of battles, and let him through the gates.

Now, he thought, was the time to warn others against giving so much trouble. Let Olynthos be an example. The rebel half-brothers died by the

Companions' spears. Soon the chain-gangs of slaves were going down through Greece, driven by the dealers, or men whose usefulness had deserved a gift. Cities which had seen, time out of mind, their heavy work done by Thracians or Ethiops or broad-cheeked Scythians, gazed in outrage at Greek men bearing burdens under the lash. Greek girls sold to the brothels in the open market. Demosthenes' voice rallied all decent men to stand against the barbarian.

The boys of Macedon saw the hopeless convoys pass, the children wailing in the dust as they trudged at their mothers' skirts. It brought the millennial message. This is defeat: avoid it.

At the sea-foot of Mount Olympos stood the town of Dion, the holy footstool of Olympian Zeus. Here Philip held his victory feast, in the god's sacred month, with splendours which Archelaos had never equalled. Distinguished guests came north from all over Greece; kitharists and flautists, rhapsodes and actors, competed for gold wreaths, purple gowns, and bags of silver.

Euripides' *Bachkai* was to be staged; Euripides had first put it on in this very theatre. The best scene-painter of Corinth was painting the flats with Theban hills and a royal palace; the tragedians were heard each morning in their lodgings, practising the gamut of all their voices from the boom of gods to maiden trebles. Even the schoolmasters were on holiday. Achilles and his Phoinix (the nickname had stuck at once) had the threshold of Olympos, and the sights of the festival, to themselves. Phoinix had given Achilles his own Iliad, a secret from Timanthes. They gave trouble to no one, absorbed in their private game.

On the god's annual feast day, the King gave a grand banquet. Alexander was to appear, but to leave before the drinking. He wore a new blue chiton stitched with gold; his heavy loose-waving hair was curled. He sat on the end of his father's supper-couch, his own silver bowl and cup beside him. The hall was brilliant with lamps; the lords' sons of the royal bodyguard came and went between the King and his guests of honour, bringing them his gifts.

There were some Athenians, of the party which favoured peace with Macedon. The boy noticed his father taking care with his accent. The Athenians might have helped his enemies; they might have sunk to intrigue with the Persians their forbears had fought at Marathon; but they still had in their gift the prize of Greekness.

The King, shouting down the hall, was asking some guest why he looked so glum. It was Satyros, the great comedian of Athens. Having got the feed he had worked for, he mimed fear amusingly, and said he hardly dared ask for what he wanted. Only name it, cried the King with extended hand. It turned out to be the freedom of two young girls he had seen among the slaves, daughters of an old Olynthian guest-friend; he wanted to save them from their fate and give them marriage-portions. A happiness, cried the King, to grant a request itself so generous. There was a buzz of applause; good feeling warmed the room. The guests who had passed the slave-pens found their food tasted a little better.

The garlands were coming in, and big wine-coolers packed with Olympian snow. Philip turned to his son, stroked back the moist fair hair, already losing its curl, from his warm brow, gave it a bristly kiss while the guests murmured delight, and bade him run off to bed. He slipped down, said good night to the guard at the door, who was a friend of his; and made his way to his mother's room to tell her all about it.

Before his hand was on the door, some warning reached him from within.

The place was in confusion. The women stood huddled like frightened hens. His mother, still dressed in the robe she had worn for the choral odes, was pacing to and fro. The mirror-table was overturned; a maid was on hands and knees, scrambling for jars and pins. As the door opened she dropped a jar and the kohl spilled out. Olympias strode across, and sent her sprawling with a blow on the head.

'Out, all of you!' she shouted. 'Sluts, useless gaping half-wits! Get out, and leave me with my son.'

He came in. The flush of the hot hall and his watered wine drained from his face; his stomach clenched itself on its meal. Silently he walked forward. As the women scurried out, she flung herself on the bed, beating and biting the pillows. He came and knelt beside her, feeling the coldness of his own hands as he stroked her hair. He did not ask the trouble.

Olympias writhed round on the bed, and grasped him by the shoulders, calling all gods to witness her injuries and avenge her. She gripped him to her so that they both shook to and fro; the heavens forbid, she cried, that he should ever learn what she suffered from the vilest of all men; it was unfit for the innocence of his years. She always said this at first. He moved his head so that he could breathe. Not a young man this time, he thought; it must be a girl.

It was a proverb in Macedon, that the King took a wife for every war. It was true these matches, always sealed with rites to please the kindred, were a good way of making reliable allies. The boy only knew the fact. He now remembered a sleekness about his father which he had known before. 'A Thracian!' his mother cried. 'A filthy, blue-painted Thracian!' Somewhere in Dion, then, all this while, the girl had been hidden away. Hetairas went about, everyone saw them.

'I'm sorry, Mother,' he said leadenly. 'Did Father marry her?'

'Don't call that man your father!' She held him at arms' length, staring into his face; her lashes were matted, the lids streaked with black and blue; her dilated eyes showed white all round the iris. One shoulder of her gown had fallen; her thick dark-red hair stood out all round her face and fell tangled on her bared breast. He remembered the Gorgon's head in the Perseus room, and shook off the thought with horror. 'Your father!' she cried to him. 'Zagreus be my witness, you are clean of *that*!' Her fingers dug into his shoulders, so that he clenched his teeth with pain. 'The day will come, yes it will come, when he will learn what part *he* had in you! Oh yes, he will learn a greater was here before him!' Letting go, she flung herself back on her elbows and began to laugh.

She rolled in her red hair, laughing in sobs, catching her breath with shrill crowing gasps, the pitch of her laughter mounting louder and higher. The boy, to whom this was new, knelt by her in stifling terror, pulling at her hands, kissing her sweat-smeared face, calling in her ear to her to stop, to speak to him; he was here with her, he, Alexander; she must not go mad or he would die.

At last she moaned deeply, sat up, gathered him in her arms and stroked her cheek against his head. Weak with relief, he lay against her with closed eyes. 'Poor boy, poor child. It was only the laughing-sickness; that is what he has brought me to. I should be ashamed, before anyone but you; but you know what I have to bear. See darling, I know you, I am not mad. Though he would gladly see it, the man who calls himself your father.'

He opened his eyes and sat up. 'When I'm a man, I'll see right done you.'

'Ah, he does not guess what you are. But I know. I and the god.'

He asked no question. Enough had happened. Later, in the night, when, empty with vomiting, he lay dry-lipped in bed listening to the distant roar of the feast, her words came back to him.

Next day the games began. The two-horse chariots ran their laps, the dismounter leaping off and running with the car and vaulting on again. Phoinix, who had noticed the boy's hollow eyes and guessed the cause, was glad to see him held by it.

He woke just before midnight, thinking of his mother. He got out of bed and dressed. He had dreamed she called to him from the sea, like the goddess mother of Achilles. He would go to her, and ask her what she had meant last night.

Her room was empty. Only an old crone, belonging to the house, crept muttering about, picking things up; they had all forgotten her. She looked at him with a little wet red eye, and said the Queen had gone to the Hekate shrine.

He slipped out into the night, among the drunks and whores and soldiers and pickpurses. He needed to see her, whether she saw him or not. He knew the way to the crossroads.

The city gates stood open for the festival. Far ahead were the black cloaks and the torch. It was a Hekate night, moonless; they did not see him stalking them. She had to fend for herself, because she had not a son of age to help her. It was his business, what she did.

She had made her women wait, and gone on alone. He skirted the oleanders and the tamarisks, to the shrine with its three-faced image. She was there, with something whining and whimpering in her hands. She had set her torch in the sooty socket by the altar-slab. She was all in black, and what she held was a young black dog. She held it up by the nape, and hacked a knife at its throat. It writhed and squealed, the whites of its eyes shone in the torchlight. Now she grasped it by its hindfeet, jerking and choking while the blood ran down; when it only twitched, she laid it down on the altar. Kneeling before the image, she beat her fists on the ground. He heard the furious whisper, soft as a snake's, rise to a howl the dog itself might have made; the unknown words of the incantation, the known words of the curse. Her long hair trailed in the puddled blood; when she got up the ends were sticky, and her hands were clotted with black.

When it was over he tracked her home, keeping himself hidden. She looked familiar again, in her black cloak, walking among her women. He did not want to let her out of his sight.

Next day Epikrates said to Phoinix, 'You must spare him to me today. I want to take him to the music-contest.' He had meant to go with friends, with whom he could discuss technique; but the boy's looks disturbed him. Like everyone else, he had heard the talk.

It was the contest for the kitharists. There was hardly a leading artist from the mainland or Greek Asia or the cities of Sicily and Italy who had not come. The unguessed-at beauty caught the boy up, breaking his mood and throwing him straight into ecstasy. So Hektor, stunned by Ajax's great stone, had looked up at a voice that raised the hair on his head, and found Apollo standing by him.

After this, he took up his life much as before. His mother reminded him often with a sigh or a meaning look; but the shock had passed the worst, his body was strong and his age resilient; he sought healing as nature taught him. On the footslopes of Mount Olympos, he rode with Phoinix through chestnut groves, chanting line for line of Homer, first in Macedonian and then in Greek.

Phoinix would gladly have kept him from the women's rooms. But if once the Queen mistrusted his loyalty, the boy would be lost to him for ever. She must not look for her son in vain. At least he seemed now to come away in better spirits.

He had found her busy with some plan which made her almost cheerful. He had waited in dread, at first, for her to come with her midnight torch, and fetch him to the Hekate shrine. She had never yet bade him call down a curse himself upon his father; the night they went to the tomb, he had only had to hold things and stand by.

Time passed; it was clearly no such thing; at last he even questioned her. She smiled, the subtle shadows curving under her cheekbones. He should know in good time, and it would surprise him. It was a service she had vowed to Dionysos; she promised he should be there. His spirits lightened. It must be the dancing for the god. These last two years she had been saying he was too old for women's mysteries. He was eight now. It had been bitter to think that Kleopatra would soon go with her instead.

Like the King, she gave audience to many foreign guests. Aristodemos the tragedian had come not to perform, but as a diplomat, a role often entrusted to well-known actors; he was arranging ransoms for Athenians taken at Olynthos. A slender elegant man, he managed his voice like a polished flute; one could almost see him caress it. Alexander admired the good sense of his mother's questions about the theatre. Later she received Neoptolemos of Skyros, a protagonist even more distinguished, who was rehearsing for *The Bachkai*, playing the god. This time, the boy was absent.

He would not have known his mother was working magic, if he had not heard her through the door one day. Though the wood was thick, he caught some of the incantation. It was one he did not know, about killing a lion on the mountain; but the meaning was always the same. So he went away without knocking.

It was Phoinix who roused him at dawn to see the play. He was too young for the chairs of honour; he would sit with his father when he came of age. He had asked his mother if he could sit with her, as he had done till only last year; but she said she would not be watching, she had other business then. He must tell her afterwards how he had liked it.

He loved the theatre; waking to a treat which would begin at once; the sweet morning smells, dew-laid dust, grass and herbs bruised by many feet, the smoke of the early workers' torches just quenched at daybreak; people clambering down the tiers, the deep buzz of the soldiers and peasants up at the top, the fuss with cushions and rugs down among the seats of honour, the chatter from the women's block; then suddenly the first notes of the flute, all other sound dying but the morning bird-song.

The play began eerily in the dawn-dusk; the god, masked as a beautiful fair-haired youth, saluting the fire on his mother's tomb, and planning revenge on the Theban King who scorned his rites. His young voice, the boy perceived, was being skilfully done by a man; his maenads had flat breasts, and cool boys' voices; but, this knowledge once stored away, he gave himself to the illusion.

Dark-haired young Pentheus spoke wickedly of the maenads and their rites. The god was bound to kill him. Several friends had described the plot beforehand. Pentheus' death was the most dreadful one could conceive; but Phoinix had promised one did not see it.

While the blind prophet rebuked the King, Phoinix whispered that this old voice from the mask was the same actor's who played the youthful god; such was the tragedian's art. When Pentheus had died offstage, this actor too would change masks, and enact the mad queen Agave.

Imprisoned by the King, the god broke out with fire and earthquake; the effects, set up by Athenian craftsmen, entranced the boy. Pentheus, defying miracles, infatuate for doom, still rejected the divinity. His last chance gone, Dionysos wound him in deadly magic and stole his wits away. He saw two suns in the sky; thought he could move mountains; yet let the mocking god disguise him absurdly as a woman, to spy on the maenad rites. The boy joined in the laughter whose edge was sharpened by the sense of terrors to come.

The King went off to his agony; the chorus sang; then the Messenger brought the news. Pentheus had climbed a tree to spy from; the maenads had seen him, and in their god-crazed strength uprooted it. His mad mother, seeing only a wild beast, had led them to tear him in pieces. It was over, and as Phoinix had said, need not be seen. The mere telling had been enough.

Agave was coming, cried the Messenger, with the trophy of her kill.

They ran in through the parodos in bloody robes. Queen Agave carried the head, spiked on a spear as hunters did it. It was made of the Pentheus mask and wig with stuffing in them, and bits of red rag hanging down. She wore a terrible mad mask, with an agonized brow, deep staring eyes and frenziedly grimacing mouth. From his mouth came a voice. At its first words, he sat as if he too had seen two suns in the sky. He was not far above the stage; his ears and eyes were sharp. The wig of her mask was fair; but in its streaming tresses live hair was spilling through, the dark red showed clearly. The Queen's arms were bare. He knew them; even their bracelets.

The players, enacting shock and horror, drew back to give her the stage. The audience began to buzz; they had heard at once, after the sexless boys, that this was a real woman. Who ... what ...? The boy seemed to himself to have been hours alone with his knowledge, before questions began to get answers and the word ran round. It spread like a brush-fire; good eyes insisting to dim ones, the women's high chatter and outraged sibilance; the deep ebb-shoal murmur from the men above; from the seats of honour, a stunned dead silence.

The boy sat as if his own head had been transfixed. His mother tossed her hair and gestured at the bleeding trophy. She had grown into the dreadful mask, it had become her face. He broke his nails, gripping the edge of his stone seat.

The flautist blew on his double pipes; she sang.

> *'I am exalted*
> *Great upon earth!*
> *Let men praise me –*
> *This hunt was mine!'*

Two rows down, the boy saw his father's back, as he turned towards a guest beside him. His face was out of sight.

The curse in the tomb, the black dog's blood, the thorn-pierced mammet, had all been secret rites. This was the Hekate spell by daylight, a sacrifice for a death. The head on the Queen's spear was her son's.

It was the voices all around that roused him from the nightmare. They waked him into another. They rose like the hum of flies disturbed from carrion, almost drowning the actors' lines.

It was of her they were talking, not of Queen Agave in the play. They were talking of her! The southerners who said Macedon was barbarous; the lords and farmers and peasants. The soldiers were talking.

A sorceress they might call her. The goddesses worked magic. This was another thing; he knew these voices. So the men of the phalanx talked in the guardroom, about a woman half of them had had; or some village wife with a bastard.

Phoinix too was suffering. A steady man rather than a quick one, he had been stunned at first; he had not thought even Olympias capable of such wildness. Without doubt, she had vowed this to Dionysos while giddy with wine and dancing at her rites. He began to put out a hand for comfort; looked again and refrained.

Queen Agave came out of frenzy to knowledge and despair; the relentless god appeared above, to close the play. The chorus sang the tag-lines.

> *'The gods have many faces,*
> *And many fates fulfil,*
> *To work their will.*
> *The end expected comes not;*
> *God brings the unthought to be,*
> *As here we see.'*

It was finished; but no one stirred to go. What would she do? She made a reverence to the cult-statue of Dionysos in the orchestra, before sweeping out with the others; some extra picked up the head; it was clear she would not return. From high up in the faceless crush of men came a long shrill whistle.

The protagonist came back to take absent-minded applause. He had not been at his best, with this freak on his mind; however, it had been made well worth his while.

The boy rose, without looking at Phoinix. Chin up, looking straight ahead, he thrust his way through the lingering chattering crowd. All along their way, talk stopped for them; but not soon enough. Just outside the propylon, he turned round, looked Phoinix in the face, and said, 'She was better than the actors.'

'Yes indeed. The god inspired her. It was her dedication to do him honour. Such offerings are very pleasing to Dionysos.'

They came out into the square of tramped earth outside the theatre. The women, in twittering groups, were drifting homeward, the men standing about. Close by, exempt from convention, stood a cluster of well-dressed hetairas, expensive girls from Ephesos and Corinth, who served the officers at Pella. One said in a sweet carrying voice, 'Poor dear little lad, you can see he feels it.' Without turning, the boy walked on.

They were nearly out of the press; Phoinix was starting to breathe more easily, then found him gone. How not, indeed? But no; there he was not twenty feet off, near a huddle of talking men. Phoinix heard their laughter; he ran, but was still too late.

The man who had spoken the last and unambiguous word, had been aware of nothing amiss. But another, whose back was to the boy, felt a quick low tug at his sword-belt. Looking about at man-height, he was only just in time to knock up the boy's arm. The man who had spoken got the dagger along his side, instead of straight in his belly.

It had been so swift and silent, no bystander had turned. The group stood stock-still; the stabbed man with a snake of blood running down his leg; the dagger's owner, who had grabbed the boy before he saw who it was, gazing blankly at the stained weapon in his hand; Phoinix behind the boy, both hands on his shoulders; the boy staring into the face of the wounded man, and finding it one he knew. The man, clutching the warm ooze from his side, stared back in astonishment and pain; then with a shock of recognition.

Breath was drawn in all round. Before anyone spoke, Phoinix lifted his hand as if he had been at war; his square face grew bull-like, they would hardly have known him. 'It will be better for you all to keep your mouths shut.' He pulled at the boy, breaking off the exchange of looks still unresolved, and led him away.

Knowing nowhere else to hide him, he took him to his own lodging in the one good street of the little town. The small room was frowsty with old wool, old scrolls, old bedding, and the ointment Phoinix rubbed on his stiff knees. On the bed, with its blanket of blue and red squares, the boy fell face down and lay soundless. Phoinix patted his shoulders and his head, and, when he broke into convulsive weeping, gathered him up.

Beyond this instant and its needs, the man saw no call to look. His love, being sexless, seemed to him proved selfless. Certainly he would have given all he had, shed his own blood. Much less was wanted now, only comfort and a healing word.

'A filthy fellow. Small loss if you had killed him. No man of honour could let it pass ... A godless fellow who mocks a dedication ... There, my Achilles, don't weep that the warrior came out in you. He'll mend, it's more than he deserves; and keep quiet if he knows what's good for him. No one shall hear a word from me.'

The boy choked into Phoinix' shoulder. 'He made me my bow.'

'Throw it out, I'll get you a better.'

There was a pause. 'It wasn't said to me. He didn't know I was there.'

'And who wants such a friend?'

'He wasn't ready.'

'Nor were you, to hear him.'

Gently, with a careful courtesy, the boy disengaged himself, and lay down again with his face hidden. Presently he sat up, wiping his hand across his eyes and nose, Phoinix wrung out a towel from the ewer and cleaned his face. He sat staring, saying 'Thank you' now and then.

Phoinix got out his best silver cup from his pillow-box, and the last of his breakfast wine. The boy drank, with a little coaxing; It seemed to run straight through to his skin, flushing his drawn face, his throat and breast. Presently he said, 'He insulted my kin. But he wasn't ready.' He shook out his hair, pulled down his creased chiton, re-tied a loosened sandal string. 'Thank you for having me in your house. Now I am going to ride.'

'Now that's foolish. You've had no breakfast yet.'

'I have had enough, thank you. Good-bye.'

'Wait, then, I'll change and go with you.'

'No, thank you. I want to go alone.'

'No, no; let's be quiet a while, read, or go walking – '

'*Let me go.*'

Phoinix's hand withdrew like a scared child's.

Later, going to see, he found the boy's riding boots gone, his pony, his practice javelins. Phoinix hurried about for word of him. He had been seen above the town, riding towards Mount Olympos.

It still wanted some hours to noon. Phoinix, waiting his return, heard people agree that the Queen had done this outlandish thing as an offering. Epirotes were mystai with their mothers' milk, but it would do her no good with Macedonians. The King had put the best face he could on it for the guests, and been civil to Neoptolemos the tragedian. And where was young Alexander?

Oh, gone riding, answered Phoinix, hiding his mounting fear. What had possessed him, to let the boy walk off like a grown man? He should not have let him for a moment out of his sight. No use to follow; in the huge Olympian massif, two armies could be hidden from one another. There were fathomless crags, whose feet were inaccessible; there were boar, wolves, leopards; even lions lived there still.

The sun westered; the steep eastern faces, under which Dion stood, grew darker; cloud swirled round the hidden summits. Phoinix rode about, quartering the cleared land above the town. At the foot of a sacred oak he stretched up his arms to the ever-sunlit peak, King Zeus' throne bathed in its clear aether. Weeping he prayed and vowed his offerings. When night came, he would be able to hide the truth no longer.

The great shadow of Olympos crept beyond the shoreline, and quenched the sea's evening glow. Dusk filled the oak-grove; further in, the woods were already black. Between the dusk and the night, something moved. He flung himself on his horse, his stiff joints stabbing him, and rode towards it.

The boy came down through the trees, walking at the pony's head. The beast, bone-weary, head down, plodded beside him, pecking a little with one foot. They moved steadily down the glade; when the boy saw Phoinix, he raised his hand in greeting, but did not speak.

His javelins were tied across his saddle-cloth; he did not yet own a holster. The pony like a conspirator leaned its cheek to his. His clothes were torn, his knees grazed and caked with dirt, his arms and legs scribbled with scratches; he seemed, since morning, visibly to have lost weight. His chiton was darkened all down the front with blood. He came calmly forward between the trees, his eyes hollow and dilated; walking lightly, floatingly; inhumanly tranquil and serene.

Phoinix dismounted by him, grasping, scolding, questioning. The boy ran his hand over the pony's nose and said, 'He was going lame.'

'I have been running about here, half out of my mind. What have you done to yourself? Where are you bleeding? Where have you been?'

'I'm not bleeding.' He held out his hands, which he had rinsed in some mountain stream; there was blood around the nails. His eyes dwelt on Phoinix's, revealing only the impenetrable. 'I made an altar and a shrine, and sacrificed to Zeus.' He lifted his head; his white brow under the springing peak of hair looked transparent, almost luminous. His eyes widened and glowed in their deep sockets. 'I sacrificed to the god. And he spoke to me. *He spoke to me.*'

3

King Archelaos' study was more splendid than the Perseus Room, having been nearer his heart. Here he had received the poets and philosophers whom his open-handed hospitality and rich guest-gifts had tempted up to Pella. On the sphinx-headed arms of the chair from Egypt had rested the hands of Agathon and of Euripides.

The Muses, to whom the room was dedicated, sang round Apollo in a vast mural which filled the inner wall. Apollo, as he played his lyre, gazed out inscrutably at the polished shelving with its precious books and scrolls. Tooled bindings, cases gilded and jewelled; finials of ivory, agate and sardonyx; tassels of silk and bullion; from reign to reign, even during the succession wars, these treasures had been dusted and tended by well-trained slaves. It was a generation since anyone else had read in them. They were too valuable; the real books were in the library.

There was an exquisite Athenian bronze of Hermes inventing the Lyre, bought from some bankrupt in the last years of the city's greatness; two standing lamps, in the form of columns twined with laurel-boughs, stood by the huge writing-table inlaid with lapis and chalcedony, and supported on lions' feet. All this was little changed since Archelaos' day. But through the door at the far end, the painted walls of the reading-cell had vanished behind racks and shelves, stuffed with the documents of administration; its couch and table given place to a laden desk, where the Chief Secretary was working through the day's letter-bag.

It was a sharp bright March day with a north-east wind. The fretted shutters had been closed to keep the papers from blowing about; a cold dazzling sun came splintering through, mixed with icy draughts. The Chief Secretary had a heated brick hidden in his cloak to warm his hands on; his clerk blew enviously on his fingers, but silently lest the King should hear. King Philip sat at ease. He had just come back from campaign in Thrace; after winter there, he thought his Palace a Sybaris of comfort.

As his power reached steadily towards the immemorial corn-route of the Hellespont, the gullet of all Greece; as he encircled colonies, wrested from Athens the allegiance of tribal lands, laid siege to her allies' cities, the southerners counted it among their bitterest wrongs that he had broken the old decent rule of abandoning war in winter-time, when even bears holed up.

He sat at the great table, his brown scarred hand, chapped with cold and calloused from reins and spear-shaft, grasping a silver stylos he kept to pick his teeth with. On a cross-legged stool, a clerk with a tablet on his knees waited to take a letter to a client lord in Thessaly.

There he could see his way; it was business of the south had brought him home. At last his foot was in the door. In Delphi, the impious Phokians were turning like mad dogs on one another, worn out with war and guilt. They had had a good run for the money they had melted down, coining the temple treasures for soldiers' pay; now far-shooting Apollo was after them. He knew how to wait; on the day they had dug below the Tripod itself for gold, he had sent the earthquake. Then panic, frantic mutual accusations, exilings, torturings. The losing leader now held with his outcast force the strongpoints of Thermopylai, a desperate man who could soon be treated with. Already he had turned back a garrison relief from Athens, though they were the Phokians' allies; he feared being handed over to the ruling faction. Soon he would be ripe and ready. King Leonidas under his grave-mound, thought Philip, must be tossing in his sleep.

Go tell the Spartans, traveller passing by ... Go tell them all Greece will obey me within ten years, because city cannot keep faith with city, nor man with man. They have forgotten even what you could show them, how to stand and die. Envy and greed have conquered them for me. They will follow me, and be reborn from it; under me they shall win back their pride. They will look to me to lead them; and their sons will look to my son.

The peroration reminded him he had sent for the boy some time ago. No doubt he would come when found; at ten years, one did not expect them to be sitting still. Philip returned his thoughts to his letter.

Before he was through it, he heard his son's voice outside, greeting the bodyguard. How many score – or hundred – men did the boy know by name? This one had only been in the Guard five days.

The tall doors opened. He looked small between them, shining and compact, his feet bare on the cold floor of figured marble, his arms folded inside his cloak, not to warm them, but in the well-drilled posture of modest Spartan boyhood, taught him by Leonidas. In this room served by pale bookish men, father and son had the gloss of wild animals among tame: the swarthy soldier, tanned almost black, his arms striped with pink cockled war-scars, the forehead crossed with the light band left by the helmet-rim, his blind eye with its milky fleck staring out under the half-drooped lid; the boy at the door, his brown silky skin flawed only with the grazes and scratches of a boy's adventures, his heavy tousled hair making Archelaos' gildings look dusty. His homespun clothes, softened and bleached by many washings and beatings on the river-stones, long since subdued to their wearer, now carried his style as if he had chosen them himself in a wilful arrogance. His grey eyes, which the cold slanting sun had lightened, kept to themselves some thought he had brought with him.

'Come in, Alexander.' He was already doing so; Philip had spoken only to be heard, resenting this withdrawal.

Alexander came forward, noting that like a servant he had been given leave to enter. The glow of the wind outside ebbed from his face, the skin seemed to change its texture, becoming more opaque. He had been thinking at the door that Pausanias, the new bodyguard, had the sort of looks his father liked. If anything came of it, for a time there might be no new girl. There was a certain look one came to know, when they met one's eyes, or did not; it had not happened yet.

He came up to the desk and waited, his hands disposed in his cloak. One part of the Spartan deportment, however, Leonidas had never managed to impose; he should have been looking down till his elders spoke to him.

Philip, meeting the steady eyes, felt a stab of familiar pain. Even hate might have been better. He had seen such a look in the eyes of men prepared to die before they would yield the gate or the pass; not a challenge, an inward thing. How have I deserved it? It is that witch, who comes with her poison whenever my back is turned, to steal my son.

Alexander had been meaning to ask his father about the Thracian battle-order; accounts had differed, but he would know ... Not now, however.

Philip sent out the clerk, and motioned the boy to the empty stool. As he sat straight-backed on the scarlet sheepskin, Philip felt him already poised to go.

It pleased Philip's enemies, hate being blinder than love, to think his men in the Greek cities had all alike been bought. But though none lost by serving him, there were many who would have taken nothing from him, had they not first been won by charm. 'Here,' he said, picking up from the desk a glittering tangle of soft leather. 'What do you make of this?'

The boy turned it over; at once his long square-ended fingers began to work, slipping thongs under or over, pulling, straightening. As order came out of chaos his face grew intent, full of grave pleasure. 'It's a sling and a shot-bag. It should go on a belt, through here. Where do they do this work?'

The bag was stitched with gold plaques cut out in the bold, stylized, flowing forms of stags. Philip said, 'It was found on a Thracian chief, but it comes from far north, from the plains of grass. It's Scythian.'

Alexander pored over this trophy from the edge of the Kimmerian wilderness, thinking of the endless steppes beyond the Ister, the fabled burial-grounds of the kings with their rings of dead riders staked around them, horses and men withering in the dry cold air. His longing to know more was too much for him; in the end he asked all his stored-up questions. They talked for some time.

'Well, try the sling; I brought it for you. See what you can bring down. But don't go off too far. The Athenian envoys are on the way.'

The sling lay in the boy's lap, remembered only by his hands. 'About the peace?'

'Yes. They landed at Halos and asked for safe conduct through the lines, without waiting for the herald. They are in a hurry, it seems.'

'The roads are bad.'

'Yes, they'll need to thaw out before I hear them. When I do, you may come and listen. This will be serious business; it is time you saw how things are done.'

'I'll stay near Pella. I'd like to come.'

'At last, we may see action out of talk. They have been buzzing like a kicked bee-skep ever since I took Olynthos. Half last year they were touting the southern cities, trying to work up a league against us. Nothing came of it but dusty feet.'

'Were they *all* afraid?'

'Not all; but all mistrusted each other. Some trusted men who trusted me. I shall redeem their trust.'

The fine inner ends of the boy's gilt-brown eyebrows drew together, almost meeting, outlining the heavy bone-shelf over his deep-set eyes. 'Wouldn't even the Spartans fight?'

'To serve under Athenians? They won't lead, they've had their bellyful; and they'll never follow.' He smiled to himself. 'And they're not the audience for a speechmaker beating his breast in tears, or scolding like a market-woman short-changed of an obol.'

'When Aristodemos came back here about that man Iatrokles' ransom, he told me he thought the Athenians would vote for peace.'

It was long since such remarks had had power to startle Philip. 'Well, to encourage them, I had Iatrokles home before him, ransom free. Let them send me envoys by all means. If they think they can bring Phokis into their treaty, or Thrace either, they are fools; but so much the better, they can be voting on it while I act. Never discourage your enemies from wasting time ... Iatrokles will be an envoy; so will Aristodemos. That should do us no harm.'

'He recited some Homer at supper, when he was here. Achilles and Hektor, before they fight. But he's too old.'

'That comes to us all. Oh, and Philokrates will be there, of course.' He did not waste time in saying that this was his chief Athenian agent; the boy would be sure to know. 'He will be treated like all the others; it would do him no good at home to be singled out. There are ten, in all.'

'*Ten?*' said the boy staring. 'What for? Will they all make speeches?'

'Oh, they need them all to watch each other. Yes, they will all speak, not one will consent to be passed over. Let us hope they agree beforehand to divide their themes. At least there will be one show-piece. Demosthenes is coming.'

The boy seemed to prick his ears, like a dog called for a walk. Philip looked at his kindling face. Was every enemy of his a hero to his son?

Alexander was thinking about the eloquence of Homer's warriors. He pictured Demosthenes tall and dark, like Hektor, with a voice of bronze and flaming eyes.

'Is he brave? Like the men at Marathon?'

Philip, to whom this question came as from another world, paused to bring round his mind to it, and smiled sourly in his black beard.

'See him and guess. But do not ask him to his face.'

A slow flush spread up from the boy's fair-skinned neck into his hair. His lips met hard. He said nothing.

In anger he looked just like his mother. It always got under Philip's skin. 'Can't you tell,' he said impatiently, 'when a man is joking? You're as touchy as a girl.'

How dare he, thought the boy, speak of girls to me? His hands clenched on the sling, so that the gold bit into them.

Now, Philip thought, all the good work was undone. He cursed in his heart his wife, his son, himself. Forcing ease into his voice, he said, 'Well, we shall both see for ourselves, I know him no more than you.' This was less than honest; through his agents' reports, he felt he had lived with the man for years. Feeling wronged, he indulged a little malice. Let the boy keep himself to himself, then, and his expectations too.

A few days later, he sent for him again. For both, the time had been full; for the man with business, for the boy with the perennial search for new tests on which to stretch himself, rock-clefts to leap, half-broken horses to ride, records to beat at throwing and running. He had been taught a new piece, too, on his new kithara.

'They should be here by nightfall,' Philip said. 'They will rest in the morning; after luncheon I shall hear them. There is a public dinner at night; so time should limit their eloquence. Of course, you will wear court dress.'

His mother kept his best clothes. He found her in her room, writing a letter to her brother in Epiros, complaining of her husband. She wrote well, having much business she could not trust to a scribe. When he came she closed the diptych, and took him in her arms.

'I have to dress,' he told her, 'for the Athenian envoys. I'll wear the blue.'

'I know just what suits you, darling.'

'No, but it must be right for Athenians. I'll wear the blue.'

'T-tt! My lord must be obeyed. The blue, then, the lapis brooch ...'

'No, only women wear jewels in Athens, except for rings.'

'But my darling, it is proper you out-dress them. They are nothing, these envoys.'

'No, Mother. They think jewels barbarous. I shan't wear them.'

She had begun lately to hear this new voice sometimes. It pleased her. She had never yet conceived of its being used against her.

'You shall be all man, then, my lord.' Seated as she was, she could lean on him and look up. She stroked his windblown hair. 'Come in good time; you are as wild as a mountain lion, I must see to this myself.'

When evening came, he said to Phoinix, 'I want to stay up, please, to see the Athenians come.'

Phoinix looked out with distaste at the lowering dusk. 'What do you expect to see?' he grumbled. 'A parcel of men with their hats pulled down to their cloaks. With this ground-mist tonight, you'll not know master from servant.'

'Never mind. I want to see.'

The night came on raw and dank. The rushes dripped by the lake, the frogs trilled ceaselessly like a noise in the head. A windless mist hung round the sedge, winding with the lagoon till it met the breeze off the sea. In the streets of Pella, muddy runnels carried ten days' filth and garbage down to the rain-pocked water. Alexander stood at the window of Phoinix's room, where he had gone to rouse him out. He himself was dressed already in his riding-boots and hooded cloak. Phoinix sat at his book with lamp and brazier, as if they had the night before them. 'Look! There are the outriders' torches coming round the bend.'

'Good, now you can keep your eye on them. I shall go out in the weather when it is time, and not a moment sooner.'

'It's hardly raining. What will you do when we go to war?'

'I am saving myself for that, Achilles. Don't forget Phoinix had his bed made up by the fire.'

'I'll set light to that book of yours, if you don't hurry. You've not even got your boots on.' He hung in the window; small with darkness and furred with mist, the torches seemed to creep like glow-worms on a stone. 'Phoinix . . .?'

'Yes, yes. There's time enough.'

'Does he mean to treat for peace? Or just to keep them quiet till he's ready, like the Olynthians?'

Phoinix laid down his book on his knee. 'Achilles, dear child.' He dropped artfully into the magic rhythm. 'Be just to royal Peleus, your honoured father.' Not long ago, he had dreamed he stood on a stage, robed to play Leader of the Chorus in a tragedy, of which only one page had yet been written. The rest was already on the wax, but not fair-copied, and he had begged the poet to change the ending; but when he tried to recall it, he remembered only his tears. 'It was the Olynthians who first broke faith. They treated with the Athenians, and took in his enemies, both against their oath. Everyone knows a treaty is made void by oath-breaking.'

'The cavalry generals gave up their own men in the field.' The boy's voice rose a tone. 'He paid them to do it. *Paid them.*'

'It must have saved a good many lives.'

'They are slaves! I would rather die.'

'If all men would rather, there would be no slaves.'

'I shall never use traitors, never, when I'm King. If they come to me I shall kill them. I don't care whom they offer to sell me, if he's my greatest enemy, I shall still send them their heads. I hate them like the gates of death. This man Philokrates, he's a traitor.'

'He may do good in spite of it. Your father means well by the Athenians.'

'If they do as he tells them.'

'Come, one might suppose he meant to set up a tyranny. When the Spartans conquered them in my father's day, then indeed they had one. You know your history well enough, when you've a mind. As far back as Agamemnon the High King, the Hellenes have had a war-leader; either a city or a man. How was the host called out to Troy? How were the barbarians turned in Xerxes' war? Only now in our day they snap and bicker like pi-dogs, and no one leads.'

'You don't make them sound worth leading. They can't have changed so soon.'

'Two generations running, there has been a great killing of their best. In my opinion, the Athenians and the Spartans have both drawn Apollo's curse, since they hired out troops to the Phokians. They knew well enough what gold was used to pay them. Wherever that gold has gone, it has brought death and ruin, and we have not seen the end of it. Now your father, he took the god's part, and look how he has prospered; it is the talk of Greece. Who is more fit for the leader's sceptre? And one day, it will come to you.'

'I had rather – ' the boy began slowly. 'Oh, look, they're past the Sacred Grove, almost in town. Hurry, get ready.'

As they mounted in the muddy stable-yard, Phoinix said, 'Keep your hood well down. When they see you at the audience, you don't want them to know you were out in the street, staring at them like a peasant. What you expect from this outing is more than I can guess.'

They backed their horses into a little grassy patch before a hero-shrine. Overhanging chestnut buds, half unfurled, looked like worked bronze against the pale watery clouds which filtered the moonlight. The out-riders' torches, burned almost to the sockets, danced to the mules' pacing in the quiet air. They showed the leading envoy escorted by Antipatros; Alexander would have known the general's big bones and square beard, even if he had been muffled like the others; but having just come from Thrace, he thought it a warm night. The other must be Philokrates. The body shapeless in its wraps, the eyes peering between cloak and hat, looked the soul of evil. Riding after, he recognized the grace of Aristo-demos. So much for those. His eye raked through the train of riders, mostly craning under their limp hat-brims to see where their horses' feet were going in the muck. Not far from the tail, a tall well-built man was sitting up like a soldier. He was short-bearded, seemed neither old nor young; the torchlight showed up a bold bony profile. When he had passed, the boy looked after, fitting the face upon his dreams. He had seen great Hektor, who would not be old before Achilles was ready.

Demosthenes son of Demosthenes, of Paionia, woke at first light in the royal guest-house, pushed up his head a little from the clothes, and looked around him. The room was grandiose, with a green marble floor; the pilasters at door and window had gilded capitals; the stool for his clothes was inlaid with ivory; the chamber-pot was Italian ware with garlands in relief. The rain was over, but the gusty air felt freezing. He had three blankets and could have done with as many more. Need for the pot had waked him; but it was at the far side of the room. The floor was rugless. He lingered in discomfort, hunched in his folded arms. Swallowing, he felt a soreness in his throat. His fears, first formed during the ride, were realized; on this day of all days, he was starting a cold in the head.

He thought with longing of his snug house in Athens, where Kyknos, his Persian slave, would have fetched more blankets, brought up the pot and brewed the hot posset of herbs and honey which soothed and toned his throat. Now he lay like the great Euripides who had met his end here, sick among barbaric splendours. Was he to be one more sacrifice to this harsh land, breeder of pirates and tyrants; the crag of that black eagle which hung ravening over Hellas, ready to swoop on any city which flagged, stumbled or bled? Yet with the pinions darkening the sky above them, they would straggle after petty gains or feuds and scorn the shep-herd's warning. Today he would meet the great predator face to face; and his nose was thickening.

On the ship, on the road, he had been over and over his speech. It would come last; for to settle contested precedence on the way, they had agreed it should go by age. Eagerly, while others thrust forward evidence of seniority, he had proclaimed himself the youngest, hardly believing they could be so blind to what they were giving away. Not till the final list had been drawn up, had he seen his handicap.

From the distant pot, his eye moved to the other bed. His room-mate, Aischines, slept soundly on his back; his height had pushed his feet nearly through the bedclothes, his broad chest gave resonance to his snores. When he woke, he would run briskly to the window, do the showy voice-exercises he kept up from his theatre days, and, if one mentioned the cold, say it had been worse in some army bivouac or other. He would speak ninth, Demosthenes tenth. No good, he felt, seemed ever to reach him unalloyed. He had the final word, an asset beyond price in the lawcourts, and no price could buy it. But some of the best arguments had been claimed by earlier speakers; and then he must follow this man's portentous presence, his deep voice and artful sense of timing, his actor's memory which could keep him going a run of the water-clock without a note, and – most enviable gift of the unjust gods – his power to speak extempore at need.

A mere nobody, pinchpenny reared, his schoolmaster father beating enough letters into him to give him a pittance from clerking; his mother a priestess of some immigrant back-street cult, which ought to be put down by law; who was he to swagger in the Assembly, amongst men taught in the schools of rhetoric? No doubt he kept going on bribes; but nowadays one heard forever about his forbears, eupatrids of course – that worn-out tale! – ruined in the Great War, his military record in Euboia, and his tedious mention in dispatches.

A kite screamed in the raw air, a piercing gust blew round the bed. Demosthenes clutched the blankets round his meagre frame, recalling bitterly how last night, when he had complained of the marble floor, Aischines had said off-handedly, 'I should have thought you'd mind it the least, with your northern blood.' It was years since anyone had brought up his grandfather's metic marriage to his Scythian grandmother; only his father's wealth had scraped him citizenship, but he had thought it all forgotten long ago. Staring down his cold nose at the sleeping form, putting off for a moment longer the urgent walk to the pot, he murmured viciously, 'You were an usher, I was a student; you were an acolyte, I was an initiate; you copied the minutes, I moved the motion; you were third actor, I sat in front.' He had never in fact seen Aischines play; but his wishes added, 'You were booed off, I hissed.'

The marble was green ice underfoot, his urine steamed in the air. His bed would be cold already; he could only dress now, keep moving and stir his blood. If Kyknos were only here! But the Council had bidden them hurry; the others had stupidly offered to dispense with attendants; it would have been worth a thousand words to any hostile orator, if he alone had brought one.

A pale sun was rising; the wind grew less; it might be warmer out than in this marble tomb. The paved garden-court was empty, but for one slave-boy loitering. He would take his roll with him, and run over his speech again. Doing it here would wake Aischines, who would express surprise at his still needing a script, and boast of having always been a quick study.

No one stirred in the house but slaves. He glanced at each, in search of Greeks; many Athenians had been caught in the siege of Olynthos, and all the envoys had commissions to arrange ransoms where they could. He had resolved to redeem any he found, if it had to be at his own cost. In the bitter cold, in this haughty and boastful Palace, he warmed his heart at the thought of Athens.

His childhood had been pampered, his boyhood wretched. His rich merchant father had died leaving him to uncaring guardians. He had been a puny lad, exciting no one's desire but readily excited; in the boys' gymnasium this had been starkly exposed, and the dirty nickname had stuck to him for years. In his teens he had known his guardians were robbing his inheritance; he had no one to fight his law-suit but himself, with his nervous stutter. He had trained stubbornly, wearily, in secret, copying actors and rhetors, till he was ready; but when he won, the money was two thirds gone. He had made a living at the one thing he had skill in, building up capital from such pickings as were half-respectable; and at last had begun to taste the great wine of power, when the crowd on the Pnyx was one ear, one voice, and his. All these years, he had armoured his tender bruised pride in the pride of Athens. She should be great again; it should be his victor's trophy, one to last till the end of time.

He hated many men, some with good cause, others from envy; but more than them all he hated the man, still unseen, in the heart of this old hubristic Palace, the Macedonian tyrant who would debase her to a client city. In the hallway, a blue-tattooed Thracian slave was scrubbing. The sense of being an Athenian, inferior to no other breed on earth, sustained him now as always. King Philip should learn what it meant. Yes, he would sew up the man's mouth, as they said in the law-courts. He had assured his colleagues of that.

If the King could be defied, there would have been no embassy. Yet subtly, with reminders of old bonds, one could prick out neatly enough his broken promises, reassurances meant only to gain him time, his playing off of city against city, faction against faction; his comfort to Athens' enemies while he seduced or crushed her friends. The preamble was word-perfect; but he had a telling little anecdote to work in just after, which could do with polishing. He had the other envoys to impress, as well as Philip; in the long run they might matter more. He would publish, in any case.

The paved court was scattered with windblown twigs. Against its low wall stood pots of pruned leafless rose-trees; was it possible they ever flowered? The far skyline was a blue-white mountain range, split with black gorges, skirted with forests as thick as fur. Two young men ran past, cloakless, beyond the wall, calling to each other in their barbaric patois. Flogging his chest with his arms, stamping his feet, swallowing in a vain hope that his sore throat might be better, he allowed the unwilling thought that men reared in Macedon must be hardy. Even the slave-boy, who should no doubt have been sweeping the twigs away, seemed at ease in his one drab garment, sitting on the wall, warm enough to be idle. His master, though, might at least have given him shoes.

To work, to work. He opened his scroll at the second paragraph, and, pacing to keep from freezing, began to speak, trying it this way and that. The linking of cadence with cadence, rise with fall, attack with persuasion, made each finished speech a seamless garment. If some interjection forced reply, he made it as brief as he could, never happy till he was back with the written script. Only when well rehearsed was he at his best.

'Such,' he told the air, 'were the generous services of our city to your father Amyntas. But since I have spoken of things which are naturally outside your remembrance since you were unborn, let me speak of kindnesses you witnessed and received yourself.' He paused; at this point Philip would be curious. 'And kinsmen of yours who are now old will bear out what I say. For after your father Amyntas, and your uncle Alexandros, both were dead, while your brother Perdikkas and yourself were children, Eurydike your mother had been betrayed by those who had claimed to be her friends; and the exiled Pausanias was returning to contest the throne, favoured by opportunity, and not without support.'

Walking and declaiming together made him pause for breath. He became aware that the slave-boy had jumped down from the wall to walk just behind him. In a moment, he was returned to the years of mockery. He turned round sharply, to catch a grin or lewd gesture. But the boy looked back with a grave open face and clear grey eyes. He must be held by the mere novelty of gestures and inflections, like some animal by a shepherd's flute. One was used, at home, to servants coming and going while one rehearsed.

'When, therefore, our general, Iphikrates, came into those parts, Eurydike your mother sent for him, and, as all who were there confirm, she led into his arms your eldest brother Perdikkas; and you who were only a little child she put on his knee. "The father of these orphans," she said, "while he lived, adopted you as his son ..."'

He stopped in his tracks. The boy's stare had pierced his back. To be gaped at like a mountebank by this peasant brat was growing tiresome. He made a shooing gesture, as if sending home a dog.

The boy fell back a few steps, and paused looking up, his head tilted a little. In rather stilted Greek, with a strong Macedonian accent, he said, 'Do please go on. Go on about Iphikrates.'

Demosthenes started. Used to addressing thousands, he found this audience of one, only now disclosed, absurdly disconcerting. Moreover, what did it mean? Though dressed like a slave, this could not be a garden-boy. Who had sent him, and why?

A closer scrutiny showed him clean, even to his hair. One could guess what that meant, when it went with looks like these. This was his master's bed-fellow, without a doubt, employed, young as he was, on the man's secret business. Why had he been listening? Demosthenes had not lived among intrigue for thirty years in vain. His mind explored, in moments, half a dozen possibilities. Was some creature of Philip's trying to brief him in advance? But so young a spy was too unlikely. What else, then? A message? Then for whom?

Somewhere, among the ten of them, must be a man in Philip's pay. On the journey the thought had haunted him. He had begun to doubt Philo-krates. How had he paid for his big new house, and bought his son a racehorse? His manner had changed, as they got near Macedon.

'What is it?' asked the boy.

He became aware that while he had been engrossed within himself, he had been observed. An unreasoning anger rose in him. Slowly and clearly, in the kitchen Greek one used to foreign slaves, he said, 'What you want? You look someone? Which master?'

The boy tilted his head, began to speak, and seemed to change his mind. In Greek which was quite correct, and less accented than before, he said, 'Can you please tell me if Demosthenes has gone out yet?'

Even to himself, he did not admit feeling affronted. His ingrained caution made him say, 'We are all envoys alike. You can tell me what you want with him.'

'Nothing,' said the boy, unmoved it seemed by the voice of inquisition. 'I only want to see him.'

There seemed no more to be gained by hedging. 'I am he. What have you to say to me?'

The boy gave one of those smiles with which civil children meet inept grown-up jokes. 'I know which he is. Who are you really?'

These were deep waters indeed! A secret beyond price might be in reach here. Instinctively he looked about him. The house might be full of eyes; he had no one to help, to hold the boy and stop him from crying out, which would stir up a hornet's nest. Often, in Athens, he had stood beside the rack, when slaves were questioned as law allowed; there must be some-thing for them to fear more than their masters, or they would never witness against them. Now and then they had been as young as this; one could not be soft in a prosecution. However, here he was among barbarians, no legal resource at hand. He must do as best he could.

Just then, from the guest-room window, a deep melodious voice started running up and down the scale. Aischines stood, his bare torso visible to the waist, his broad chest expanded. The boy, who had turned at the sound, cried, 'There he is!'

Demosthenes' first feeling was blind fury. His stored envy, goaded and taunted, almost burst him. But one must be calm, one must think, go step by step. There, then, was the traitor! Aischines! He could have wished for no one better. But he must have evidence, a lead; it was too much to hope for proof.

'That,' he said, 'is Aischines son of Atrometos, an actor by trade till lately. Those are actors' exercises he is doing. Anyone in the guest-house will tell you who he is. Ask, if you wish.'

Slowly the boy gazed from man to man. Slowly a crimson flush spread from his chest, dyeing his clear skin up to his brow. He remained quite silent.

Now, thought Demosthenes, we may learn something to the purpose. One thing was certain – the thought thrust in, even while he pondered his next move – he had never seen a handsomer boy. The blood showed like wine poured into alabaster and held up to the light. Desire became insistent, disturbing calculation. Later, later; everything might hang upon keeping one's head now. When he had found out who owned the boy, he might try to buy him. Kyknos had long since lost his looks, and was merely useful. One would need to take care, use a reliable agent ... This was folly. He should have been pinned down in his first confusion. Demosthenes said sharply, 'And now tell me the truth, no lies. What did you want with Aischines? Come, out with it. I know enough already.'

He had paused too long; the boy had collected himself; he looked quite insolent. 'I don't think you do,' he said.

'Your message for Aischines. Come, no lies. What was it?'

'Why should I tell lies? I'm not afraid of you.'

'We shall see. What did you want with him?'

'Nothing. Nor with you, either.'

'You are an impudent boy. I suppose your master spoils you.' He went on to improve on this, for his own satisfaction.

The boy had followed the intention, it seemed, if not the Greek. 'Goodbye,' he said curtly.

This would never do. 'Wait! Don't run off before I have finished speaking. Whom do you serve?'

Coolly, with a slight smile, the boy looked up. 'Alexander.'

Demosthenes frowned; it seemed to be the name of every third well-born Macedonian. The boy paused thoughtfully, then added, 'And the gods.'

'You are wasting my time,' said Demosthenes, his feelings getting the better of him. 'Don't dare go away. Come here.'

He grasped the boy's wrist as he was turning. He drew back the length of his arm, but did not struggle. He simply stared. His eyes in their deep sockets seemed to grow first wide, then pale as the pupils narrowed. In slow Greek, with fastidious correctness, he said quietly, 'Take your hand off me. Or you are going to die. I am telling you.'

Demosthenes let go. A frightening, vicious boy; clearly, some great lord's minion. No doubt his threats were empty ... but this was Macedon. The boy though released still paused, brooding intently on his face. A cold creeping moved in his bowels. He thought of ambushes, poison, knives in dark bedrooms; his stomach turned, his skin chilled. The boy stood motionless, gazing from under his mane of tousled hair. Then he turned, vaulted the low wall, and was gone.

From the window, Aischines' voice boomed in its lowest register, and soared, for effect, to a pure falsetto. Suspicion, only suspicion! Nothing one could pin to an indictment. The soreness climbed from Demosthenes' throat to his nose; he gave a violent sneeze. Somehow he must get a hot tisane, even if some ignorant fool would make it. How often, in his speeches, he had said of Macedon that it was a land from which it had never yet been possible even to buy a decent slave.

Olympias sat in her gilded chair carved with palmettes and roses. Noon sun streamed from the window, warming the high room, lacing the floor with shadows of budding branches. A small table of cypress-wood was at her elbow; on a stool by her knees sat her son. His teeth were clenched, but low gasps of agony now and then escaped him. She was combing his hair.

'The very last knot, my darling.'

'Can't you cut it off?'

'And have you ragged? Do you want to look like a slave! If I did not watch you, you would be lousy. There; all done. A kiss for being good, and you may eat your dates. Don't touch my dress while your hands are sticky. Doris, the irons.'

'They are too hot still, Madam; hissing-hot.'

'Mother, you must stop curling it. None of the other boys have it done.'

'What is that to you? You lead, you do not follow. Don't you want to look beautiful for me?'

'Here, Madam. I don't think they will scorch now.'

'They had better not! Now don't fidget. I do it better than the barbers. No one will guess it's not natural.'

'But they see me every day! All but the ...'

'Keep still, you will get a burn. What did you say?'

'Nothing. I was thinking about the envoys. I think after all I'll wear my jewels. You were right, one shouldn't dress down to the Athenians.'

'No, indeed. We will look out something presently, and proper clothes.'

'Besides, Father will wear jewels.'

'Oh, yes. Well, you wear them better.'

'I met Aristodemos just now. He said I'd grown so much he'd hardly have known me.'

'A charming man. We must ask him here, by ourselves.'

'He had to go, but he presented another man who used to be an actor. I liked him; he's called Aischines, he made me laugh.'

'We might ask him too. Is he a gentleman?'

'It doesn't matter with actors. He told me about the theatre, how they tour; how they get their own back on a man who's bad to work with.'

'You must be careful with these people. I hope you said nothing indiscreet.'

'Oh, no. I asked about the war party and the peace party in Athens. He was in the war party, I think; but we're not like he thought. We got on well.'

'Don't give any of these men the chance to boast of being singled out.'

'He'll not do that.'

'What do you mean? Was he familiar?'

'No, of course not. We only talked.'

She tilted his head back, to curl the locks above his brow. As her hand passed his mouth he kissed it. There was a scratch upon the door.

'Madam, the King sends to say he has had the envoys summoned. He would like the Prince to enter with him.'

'Say he will be there.' She stroked out the hair lock by lock, and looked him over. His nails were trimmed, he was freshly bathed, his gold-studded sandals stood ready. She found him a chiton of saffron wool, with a border she had worked herself in four or five colours; a red chlamys for his shoulder and a big gold pin. When the chiton was on, she clasped round his waist a belt of golden filigree. She was leisurely; if he were early, it would be with Philip he would wait.

'Isn't it finished?' he asked. 'Father will be waiting.'

'He has only just summoned the envoys.'

'I expect they were all ready.'

'You will find the afternoon quite long enough, with their tedious speeches.'

'Well, one must learn how things are done ... I've seen Demosthenes.'

'That great Demosthenes! Well, what did you think of him?'

'I don't like him.' She looked up from the golden girdle, raising her brows. He turned towards her, with an effort she noticed. 'Father told me, but I didn't listen. He was right, though.'

'Put on your cloak. Or do you want it done for you like a baby?'

Silently he threw it round his shoulder; silently, with untender fingers, she drove the pin through the stuff, which gave too quickly. He made no movement. She said sharply, 'Did I prick you?'

'No.' He knelt to lace his sandals. The cloth fell away from his neck, and she saw blood.

She held a towel to the scratch, kissing his curled head, making peace before he went to meet her enemy. As he went towards the Perseus Room, the smart of the pin was soon forgotten. For the other, it was like a pain he had been born with. He could not remember a time when it had not been.

The envoys stood facing the empty throne, with the great mural behind it of Perseus freeing Andromeda. At their backs were ten ornate hard chairs; it had been made clear, even to the most ardent democrats, that they would sit when, and not before, the King invited them. The leader, Philokrates, looked demurely about him, straight-faced, at pains not to seem at ease. As soon as the order and matter of the speeches had been determined, he had made a brief digest and sent it secretly to the King. Philip was known to speak extempore with force and wit, but would be grateful for the chance to do himself full justice. His gratitude to Philokrates had already been very solid.

Down at the far left (they stood in order of speaking) Demosthenes swallowed painfully, and mopped his nose with the corner of his cloak. Lifting his eyes, they met the painted eyes of a splendid youth, poised wing-footed on blue air. In his right hand he held a sword; in his left, by its hair, the ghastly head of Medusa, aiming its lethal gaze at the sea-dragon in the waves below. Manacled to a leafy rock by her outspread arms, her body shimmering through her thin robe, her fair hair lifted by the breeze which upbore the hero, Andromeda gazed at her saviour with soft wild eyes.

It was a masterpiece; as good as the Zeuxis on the Acropolis, and bigger. Demosthenes felt as bitter as if it had been looted in war. The beautiful tanned youth, superbly naked (some Athenian athlete of the great days must have posed for the first cartoon) looked down with hauteur on the heirs of his city's greatness. Once again, as in old years at the palaestra, Demosthenes felt the pause of dread before he stripped his thin limbs; the admired boys strolling by, elaborately careless of their public; for himself, the giggle and the hateful nickname.

You are dead, Perseus; beautiful, brave, and dead. So you need not look at me. You died of malaria in Sicily, you drowned in Syracuse harbour, or parched in the waterless retreat. At Goat's River the Spartans bound you and cut your throat. The hangman of the Thirty burned you with his irons and choked you. Andromeda must do without you. Let her take help where she can, for the waves are parting to show the dragon's head.

With her feet on a cloud, bright-helmed Athene hovered to inspire the hero. Grey-eyed Lady of Victories! Take and use me; I am yours, for what I am. If I have only words to serve you with, your power can turn them to sword and Gorgon. Let me only guard your citadel till it brings forth heroes again.

Athene returned him a level stare. As was proper, her eyes were grey. He seemed to feel again the dawn chill, and his fasting belly griped with fear.

There was a stir at the inner door. The King came in, with his two generals, Antipatros and Parmenion; a formidable trio of hard-bitten warriors, each of whom by himself would have filled the eye. Along with them, almost lost beside them, walked at the King's elbow a curly-haired, overdressed boy with downcast eyes. They disposed themselves in their chairs of honour; Philip greeted the envoys graciously, and bade them sit.

Philokrates made his speech, full of openings which would be useful to the King, masked by spurious firmness. Demosthenes' suspicions grew. They had all been given the precis; but could these weak links be merely slipshod? If only he could keep his mind on it; if only his eye did not keep straying to the King.

Hateful he had expected Philip to be; but not unnerving. His speech of welcome, though perfectly courteous, had not wasted a word, its brevity subtly hinting that smoke-screens of verbiage would not serve. Whenever a speaker turned to the other envoys for support, Philip would scan the line of faces. His blind eye, which was as mobile as the good one, seemed to Demosthenes the more baleful of the two.

The day wore on; the steep sun-patches under the windows stretched along the floor. Speaker after speaker urged Athens' claims to Olynthos, to Amphipolis, to her old spheres of influence in Thrace and Chersonesos; referred to the Euboian war, to this naval brush or that; dragged up old dealings with Macedon in the long complex wars of her succession; talked of the Hellespont corn route, of the aims of Persia and the intrigues of her coastal satraps. Every so often, Demosthenes would see the bright black eye and its spatchcock yokefellow move his way and linger.

He was being awaited, he the famous tyrannophobe, as the protagonist is awaited through the opening chorus. How often, in the law courts and at Assembly, this knowledge had quickened his blood and wits! Now, it came to him that never before had he so addressed himself to a single man.

He knew every string of his instrument, could measure the lightest turn of each key; he could transpose righteousness into hatred; play on self-interest till it seemed even to itself a self-denying duty; he knew where thrown mud would stick on a clean man, and whitewash on a dirty one; even for a lawyer–politician of his day, when standards of skill were high, he was a first-class professional. And he had known himself to be more; on great days he had tasted the pure ecstasy of the artist when he had kindled them all with his own dream of Athenian greatness. He was reaching the peak of his powers; he would be better yet; but now it was borne in on him that the medium of his art was the crowd alone. When it left for home, it would still be praising his oration; but it would break up into so many thousand men, not one of whom really liked him. There was no one at whose side he had locked shields in battle. And when he wanted love, it cost two drachmas.

They were down to the eighth speaker, Ktesiphon. Soon he himself would be speaking; not to the manifold ear he knew, but to this one black probing eye.

His nose was blocked again; he had to blow it on his cloak, the floor looked too pretentiously ornate. What if it ran while he was speaking? To keep his mind off the King, he looked at red big-boned Antipatros, and Parmenion with his broad shoulders, brown bush of beard, and bowed horseman's knees. This was unwise. They had not Philip's obligations to the speaker, and were frankly appraising the envoys together. The fierce blue eye of Antipatros brought back, the moment it met his, the eye of the phylarch under whom he had done his compulsory army training, as a spindly youth of eighteen.

All this while, the gaudy princeling sat unmoving in his low chair, his eyes bent towards his knees. Any Athenian lad would have been looking about him, impertinent perhaps (alas, manners were declining every-where) but at least alert. A Spartan training. Sparta, symbol of past tyranny and present oligarchy. It was just what one would expect in Philip's son.

Ktesiphon had done. He bowed; Philip spoke a few words of thanks. He had managed to make each speaker feel noticed and remembered. The herald announced Aischines.

He rose to his full height (he had been too tall to do well in women's roles, one cause of his leaving the stage). Would he betray himself? Not a word or tone must be missed. The King must be watched too.

Aischines went into his preamble. Once more, Demosthenes was forced to see how training told. He himself relied much on gesture; he indeed had brought it into public speaking, calling the old sculpted stance a relic of aristocracy; but when warmed up, he tended to do it from the elbow.

Aischines' right hand rested easily just outside his cloak; he wore a manly dignity, not trying to old-soldier the three great generals before him, but hinting the respect of one who knows the face of war. It was a good speech, following the scheme arranged. He would give nothing away, whatever he had been up to. Giving up in disgust, Demosthenes blew his nose again, and turned to a mental run-through of his own oration.

'And your elder kinsmen will bear out what I say. For after your father Amyntas and your uncle Alexandros had both fallen, while your brother Perdikkas and you were children . . .'

His mind hung suspended in the pause between shock and thought. The words were right. But Aischines, not he, had spoken them.

'. . . betrayed by false friends; and Pausanias was coming back from exile to contest the throne . . .'

The voice ran on, unforced, persuasive, expertly timed. Wild thoughts of coincidence rose and died, as word followed word, confirming infamy. 'You yourself were only a small child. She put you on his knee, saying . . .'

The early years of anguished struggle to cure his stammer, project his thin voice and temper its shrillness, made him need his own reassurance. Again and again, in audible undertones, script in hand, he must have rehearsed this passage on the journey, on board ship or at inns. This mountebank pedlar of others' words; of course he could have mastered it.

The anecdote reached its well-turned close. Everyone looked impressed; the King, the generals, the other envoys; all but the boy, who, growing restless at last after the hours of stillness, had begun to scratch his head.

Demosthenes confronted not only the loss of his most telling passage; that was the least of it. It should have led his theme to the central matter. Now, at this last moment, he would have to recast his speech.

He had never been good extempore, even with the audience on his side. The King's eye had swivelled his way again, expectantly.

Frantically he gathered in mind the fragments of his speech, trying edge against edge for joins, bridging, transposing. But having taken no interest in Aischines' speech, he had no idea how much of it was left, how soon his own turn would come. The suspense scattered his thoughts. He could only remember the times when he had put down Aischines' upstart pretensions, reminding him, and people of influence along with him, that he came of broken-down gentlefolk, that as a boy he had ground ink for his father's school and copied civil service lists; that on the stage he had never played leading roles. Who could have reckoned on his bringing to the noble theatre of politics the sleights of his sordid trade?

And he could never be accused of it. To own the truth would make any orator the laughing-stock of Athens. One would never live it down.

Aischines' voice had the swell of peroration. Demosthenes felt cold sweat on his brow. He clung to his opening paragraph; its momentum might lead him on. Perseus hovered scornfully. The King sat stroking his beard. Antipatros was muttering something to Parmenion. The boy was raking his fingers through his hair.

Deftly, in his final paragraph, Aischines slipped the key passage of Demosthenes' prepared finale. He bowed, was thanked. 'Demosthenes,' said the herald, 'son of Demosthenes, of Paionia.'

He rose and began, advancing as to a precipice; all sense of style had deserted him, he was glad to remember the mere words. Almost at the last, his normal quick sense revived; he saw how to bridge the gap. At this moment, a movement drew his eye. For the first time, the boy had lifted his head.

The crimped curls, already loosening before he had begun work on them, had changed to a tousled mane springing strongly from a peak. His grey eyes were wide open. He was very slightly smiling.

'To take a broad view of the question ... a broad view ... to take ...'

His voice strangled in his throat. His mouth closed and opened; nothing came out but breath.

Everyone sat up and stared. Aischines, rising, patted him solicitously on the back. The boy's eyes were levelled in perfect comprehension, missing nothing, awaiting more. His face was filled with a clear, cold brightness.

'To take a broad view ... I ... I ...'

King Philip, astounded and bewildered, had grasped the one fact that he could afford to be magnanimous. 'My dear sir, take your time. Don't be disturbed; it will come back to you in a moment.'

The boy had tilted his head a little to the left; Demosthenes recalled the pose. Again the grey eyes opened, measuring his fear.

'Try to think of it little by little,' said Philip good-humouredly, 'back from the beginning. No need to be put off by a moment's dry-up, like the actors in the theatre. I assure you, we can wait.'

What cat-and-mouse game was this? It was impossible the boy should not have told his father. He remembered the school-room Greek: 'You are going to die. I am telling you.'

There was a buzz from the envoys' chairs; his speech contained matter of importance, not yet covered. The main headings, if he could find only those ... In dull panic, he followed the King's advice, stumbling again through the preamble. The boy's lips moved gently, smilingly, silently. Demosthenes' head felt empty, like a dried gourd. He said, 'I am sorry,' and sat down.

'In that case, gentlemen ...' said Philip. He signed to the herald. 'When you have rested and refreshed yourselves, I will let you have my answer.'

Outside, Antipatros and Parmenion were telling each other how they thought the envoys would shape in cavalry. Philip, as he turned towards his study where he had his written speech (he had kept a few spaces for matters arising) became aware of his son looking up at him. He signed with his head; the boy followed him into the garden, where, in reflective silence, they relieved themselves among the trees.

'You could have gone out,' said Philip. 'I didn't think to tell you.'

'I didn't drink anything first. You told me once.'

'Did I? Well; what did you make of Demosthenes?'

'You were right, Father. He isn't brave.'

Philip let fall his robe and looked round; something in the voice had arrested him. 'What ailed the man? Do *you* know?'

'That man's an actor, who spoke before him. He stole his lines.'

'However do you know that?'

'I heard him practising them in the garden. He spoke to me.'

'*Demosthenes?* What about?'

'He thought I was a slave and asked if I was spying. Then when I spoke in Greek, he said he supposed I was someone's bed-boy.' He used the barrack word which came to him most readily. 'I didn't tell him; I thought I'd wait.'

'*What?*'

'I sat up when he started speaking, and he knew me then.'

The boy saw, with unmixed pleasure, his father's slow laughter inform his gap-toothed grin, his good eye, even his blind one. 'But why didn't you tell me first?'

'He'd have expected that. He doesn't know what to think.'

Philip looked at him glintingly. 'Did the man proposition you?'

'He wouldn't *ask* a slave. He just wondered how much I'd cost.'

'Well; we may suppose that now he knows.'

Father and son exchanged looks, in a moment of perfect harmony; unalienated heirs of bronze-sworded chariot lords from beyond the Ister, who had led their tribes down in past millennia, some driving further to seize the southlands and learn their ways, some taking these mountain kingdoms where they kept old customs on; burying their dead in chamber tombs alongside their forbears whose skulls were cased in boar-tusk helms and whose handbones grasped double axes; handing down, father to son, elaborate niceties of blood-feud and revenge.

Affront had been requited, on a man immune from the sword and in any case beneath its dignity; with finesse, in terms cut to his measure. It had been as neat, in its way, as the vengeance in the hall at Aigai.

The peace-terms were debated at length in Athens. Antipatros and Parmenion, who went to represent Philip, watched fascinated the strange ways of the south. In Macedon, the only thing ever voted on was the putting of a man to death; all other public matters were for the King.

By the time the terms had been accepted (Aischines urging it strongly), and the envoys had journeyed back to ratify, King Philip had had time to reduce the Thracian stronghold of Kersobleptes, and take his surrender on terms, bringing back his son to Pella, as a hostage for his loyalty.

Meantime, in the hill-forts above Thermopylai, the exiled temple-robber, Phalaikos the Phokian, was running out of gold, food and hope. Philip was now treating with him in secret. News that Macedon held the Hot Gates would strike Athenians like an earthquake; they could bear the Phokians' sins (and had indeed an alliance with them) far more lightly than this. It must be hidden till the peace had been ratified by sacred and binding oaths.

Philip was charming to the second embassy. Aischines was most valuable, a man not bought but changed in heart. He accepted gladly the King's assurance that he meant no harm to Athens, which was sincere; and, which he saw as not false, that he would deal mildly with the Phokians. Athens needed Phokis; not only to hold Thermopylai, but to contain the ancient enemy, Thebes.

The envoys were entertained and given conspicuous guest-gifts, which they all took except Demosthenes. He had spoken first this time, but his colleagues had all agreed that he lacked his usual fire. They had in fact been quarrelling and intriguing all the way from Athens. Demosthenes' suspicions of Philokrates had reached certainty; he was eager to convince the others, but also to convict Aischines; this charge, being doubted, discredited the other. Brooding on these injuries, he had gone in to dinner, where the guests had been entertained by young Alexander and another boy singing part-songs to the lyre. Across the instrument, two cool grey eyes had lingered on Demosthenes; turning quickly, he had seen Aischines smile.

The oaths were ratified; the envoys went home. Philip escorted them south as far as Thessaly, without revealing that it was on his way. As soon as they had gone, he marched over to Thermopylai, and received the hill-forts from Phalaikos in return for a safe-conduct. The exiles went gratefully, wandering off to hire out their swords in the endless local wars of Greece, dying here and there as Apollo picked them off.

Athens was in panic. They waited for Philip to sweep down on them like Xerxes. The walls were manned, refugees from Attica crowded in. But Philip only sent word that he wished to set in order the affairs of Delphi, so long a scandal, and invited the Athenians to send an allied force.

Demosthenes made a fiery speech against the treachery of tyrants. Philip, he said, wanted the flower of their youth delivered him to use as hostages. No force was sent. Philip was sincerely puzzled; affronted, wounded in his soul. He had shown mercy when none was looked for, and had not even had thanks for it. Leaving Athens to herself, he pressed on with the Phokian war. He had the blessing of the Sacred League, the states who with the Phokians had been guardians of the shrine.

Affairs in Thrace being settled, he could attack with all his force. Fort after Phokian fort surrendered or fell; soon all was over, and the Sacred League met to decide the Phokians' fate. They had become a detested people, whose god-cursed plunder had ruined all in its path. Most of the deputies wanted them tortured to death, or hurled from the summits of the Phaidriades, or at least sold off as slaves. Philip had long been sickened by the savageries of the war; he foresaw endless further wars for possession of the empty lands. He argued for mercy. In the end, it was decided to re-settle the Phokians in their own country, but in small villages they could not fortify. They were forbidden to rebuild their walls, and had to pay yearly reparations to Apollo's temple. Demosthenes made a fiery speech, denouncing these atrocities.

The Sacred League passed a vote of thanks to Philip, for cleansing from impiety the holiest shrine in Greece; and conferred on Macedon the two seats in the Council, from which Phokis had been deposed. He had re-turned to Pella when they sent two heralds after him, inviting him to preside at the next Pythian Games.

After the audience, he stood alone at his study window, tasting his happiness. It was not only a great beginning, but a longed-for end. He was received, now, as a Hellene.

He had been the lover of Hellas since he was a man. Her hatred had burned him like a whip. She had forgotten herself, fallen below her past; but she only needed leading, and in his soul he felt his destiny.

His love had been born in bitterness, when he had been led by strangers from the mountains and forests of Macedon to the dreary lowlands of Thebes, a living symbol of defeat. Though his jailer-hosts were civil, many Thebans were not; he had been torn from friends and kin; from willing girls, and the married mistress who had been his first instructor. In Thebes, free women were barred to him; his comings and goings watched; if he went to a brothel, he had not the price of a whore who did not disgust him.

In the palaestra he had found his only comfort. Here no one could look down on him; he had proved himself an athlete of skill and stubborn fortitude. The palaestra had accepted him, and let him know that its loves were not denied him. Begun at first in mere loneliness and need, they had proved consoling; by degrees, in a city where they had tradition and high prestige, they had grown as natural as any other.

With new friendships had come visits to the philosophers and teachers of rhetoric; and, presently, the chance to learn from experts the art of war. He had longed for home and had returned with gladness; but by then he had been received into the mystery of Hellas, forever her initiate.

Athens was her altar, almost her self. All he asked of Athens was to restore her glories; her present leaders seemed to him like the Phokians at Delphi, unworthy men who had seized a holy shrine. Deep in his mind moved a knowledge that for Athenians freedom and glory went together; but he was like a man in love, who thinks the strongest trait of the loved one's nature will be easily changed, as soon as they are married.

All his policies, devious and opportunist as they had often been, had looked forward to the opening of her door to him. Rather than lose her, in the last resort he would break it down; but he longed for her to open it. Now he held in his hand the elegant scroll from Delphi; the key, if not to her inner room, at least to her gate.

In the end, she must receive him. When he had freed her kindred cities of Ionia from their generations of servitude, he would be taken to her heart. The thought grew in his mind. Lately, he had had like an omen a long letter from Isokrates, a philosopher so old that he had been a friend of Sokrates while Plato was still a schoolboy, and had been born before Athens declared war on Sparta, to begin that long mortal bloodletting of Greece. Now in his tenth decade still alert to a changing world, he urged Philip to unite the Greeks and lead them. Dreaming at the window, he saw a Hellas made young again, not by the shrill orator who called him tyrant, but by a truer Heraklid than those effete and bickering Kings of Sparta. He saw his statue set up on the Akropolis; the Great King set down to the proper place of all barbarians, to furnish slaves and tributes; with Philip's Athens once more the School of Hellas.

Young voices broke his thoughts. On the terrace just below, his son was playing knucklebones with the young hostage son of Teres, King of the Agrianoi.

Philip looked down with irritation. What could the boy want with that little savage? He had even brought him to the gymnasium, so had said one of the Companion lords, whose son went there too, and who did not like it.

The child had been treated quite humanely, well clad and fed, never made to work or do anything disgraceful to his rank. Of course none of the noble houses had been prepared to take him in, as they would have done a civilized boy from a Greek city of coastal Thrace; he had had to be found quarters in the Palace, and, since the Agrianoi were a warlike race whose submission might not be lasting, a guard put over him in case he ran away. Why Alexander, with every boy of decent birth in Pella to choose from, should have sought out this one, was past comprehension. No doubt he would soon forget the whim; it was not worth interfering.

The two princes squatted on the flagstones, playing their game in mixed Macedonian and Thracian helped out with mime; more Thracian, because Alexander had learned faster. The guard sat, bored, on the rump of a marble lion.

Lambaros was a Red Thracian of a conquering northern strain which, a thousand years before, had come south to hew out mountain chiefdoms among the dark Pelasgians. He was about a year older than Alexander and looked more, being big-boned. He had a shock of fiery hair; on his upper arm was tattooed an archaic, small-headed horse, the sign of his royal blood – like every high-born Thracian, he claimed direct descent from the demigod, Rhesos the Rider. On his leg was a stag, the mark of his tribe. When he came of age and his further growth would not spoil them, he would be covered with the elaborate design of whorls and symbols to which his rank entitled him. Round his neck on a greasy thong was a gryphon amulet in yellow Scythian gold.

He held the leather dice-bag, muttering an incantation over it. The guard, who would have liked to go where he had friends, gave an impatient cough. Lambaros threw a wild look over his shoulder.

'Take no notice,' said Alexander. 'He's a guard, that's all. He can't tell you what to do.' He thought it a great dishonour to the house, that a royal hostage should be worse treated in Pella than in Thebes. It had been in his mind, even before the day he had come upon Lambaros crying his heart out with his head against a tree, watched by his indifferent warder. At the sound of a new voice he had turned like a beast at bay, but had understood an outstretched hand. Had his tears been mocked, he would have fought even if they killed him for it. This knowledge had passed between them without words.

There had been red lice in his red hair, and Hellanike had grumbled even at asking her maid to see to it. When Alexander had sent for sweets to offer him, they had been brought by a Thracian slave. 'He's only on sentry-go. You're my guest. Your throw.'

Lambaros repeated his prayer to the Thracian sky-god, called fives, and threw a two and three.

'You ask him for such little things; I expect he was offended. Gods like to be asked for something great.'

Lambaros, who now prayed less often to go home, said, 'Your god won for you.'

'No, I just try to feel lucky. I save prayer up.'

'What for?'

'Lambaros; listen. When we're men, when we're kings – you understand what I'm saying?'

'When our fathers die.'

'When I go to war, will you be my ally?'

'Yes. What is an ally?'

'You bring your men to fight my enemies, and I'll fight yours.'

From the window above, King Philip saw the Thracian grasp his son's hands, and, kneeling, arrange them in a formal clasp about his own. He lifted his face, speaking long and eloquently; Alexander knelt facing him, holding his folded hands, patient, his whole frame attentive. Presently Lambaros leaped to his feet, and gave a high howl like a forsaken dog's, his treble attempting the Thracian war-yell. Philip, making nothing of the scene, found it distasteful; he was glad to see the guard stop idling and walk over.

It brought back to Lambaros the truth of his condition. His paean stopped; he looked down, sullen with misery.

'What do you want? Nothing is wrong, he is teaching me his customs.' The guard, come to separate brawling children, was startled into apology. 'Go back. I shall call you if I need you. That's a fine oath, Lambaros. Say the end again.'

'I will keep faith,' said Lambaros slowly and gravely, 'unless the sky fall and crush me, or the earth open and swallow me, or the sea rise and overwhelm me. My father kisses his chiefs when he swears them in.'

Philip watched, incredulous, his son take in his hands the red head of the young barbarian, and plant the ritual kiss on his brow. This had gone far enough. It was un-Hellenic. Philip remembered he had not yet given the boy the news about the Pythian Games, to which he intended taking him. That would give him better things to think about.

There was a drift of dust on the flags. Alexander was scribbling in it, with a whittled twig. 'Show me how your people form up for battle.'

From the library window on a floor above, Phoinix saw with a smile the gold and the rufous head bent together over some solemn game. There was always relief in seeing his charge a child awhile, the bow unbent. The presence of the guard had lightened his duties. He returned to his unrolled book.

'We'll win a thousand heads,' Lambaros was saying. 'Chop-chop-chop!'

'Yes, but where do the slingers stand?'

The guard, who had had a message, came up again. 'Alexander, you must leave this young lad to me. The King your father wants you.'

Alexander's grey eyes lifted for a moment. In spite of himself, he shifted his feet.

'Very well. Don't stop him from doing everything he wants. You're a

soldier, not a pedagogue. And don't call him this young lad. If I can give
him his rank, then so can you.'

He walked up between the marble lions, followed by Lambaros' eyes,
to hear the great news from Delphi.

4

'It is a pity,' said Epikrates, 'that you cannot give more time to it.'

'Days should be longer. Why must one sleep? One should be able to do
without.'

'You would not find it improved your execution.'

Alexander stroked the polished box of the kithara with its inlaid scrollwork and ivory keys. The twelve strings sighed softly. He slipped off the
sling which let it be played standing (sitting muted its tone) and sat down
by it on the table, plucking a string here and there to test the pitch.

'You are right,' said Epikrates. 'Why must one die? One should be able
to do without.'

'Yes, having to sleep reminds one.'

'Well, come! At twelve years, you are still pretty rich in time. I should
like to see you entered for a contest; it would give you an aim to work for.
I was thinking of the Pythian Games. In two years, you might be ready.'

'What's the age limit for the youths?'

'Eighteen. Would your father consent?'

'Not if music was all I entered for. Nor would I, Epikrates. Why do you
want me to do it?'

'It would give you discipline.'

'I thought as much. But then I shouldn't enjoy it.'

Epikrates gave his accustomed sigh.

'Don't be angry. I get discipline from Leonidas.'

'I know, I know. At your age, my touch was not so good. You started
younger, and I may say without hubris that you have been better taught.
But you will never make a musician, Alexander, if you neglect the philosophy of the art.'

'One needs mathematics in the soul. I shall never have it, you know
that. In any case, I could never be a musician. I have to be other
things.'

'Why not enter the Games,' said Epikrates temptingly, 'and take in the music contest too?'

'No. When I went to watch, I thought nothing would be so wonderful. But we stayed on after, and I met the athletes; and I saw how it really is. I can beat the boys here, because we're all training to be men. But these boys are just boy athletes. Often they're finished before they're men; and if not, even for the men, the Games is all their life. Like being a woman is for women.'

Epikrates nodded. 'It came about almost within my lifetime. People who have earned no pride in themselves, are content to be proud of their cities through other men. The end will be that the city has nothing left for pride, except the dead, who were proud less easily ... Well, with music every man's good is ours. Come, let me hear it again; this time, with a little more of what the composer wrote.'

Alexander slung and strapped on the big instrument sideways to his breast, the bass strings nearest; he tested them softly with his left-hand fingers, the trebles with the plectrum in his other hand. His head inclined a little, his eyes rather than his ears seemed to be listening. Epikrates watched him with exasperation mingled with love, asking himself as usual whether, if he had refused to understand the boy, he could have taught him better. No; more likely he would simply have given it up. Before he was ten, he had already known enough to strum a lyre at supper like a gentleman. No one would have insisted on his learning more.

He struck three sonorous chords, played a long rippling cadenza, and began to sing.

At an age when the voices of Macedonian boys were starting to roughen, he kept a pure alto which had simply gained more power. As it went soaring up with the high grace-notes flicked by the plectrum, Epikrates wondered that this never seemed to trouble him. Nor did he hesitate to look bored when other lads were exchanging the obsessive smut of their years. A boy never seen afraid can dictate his terms.

> 'God brings all things to pass as he would have them be;
> God overtakes the flying eagle, the dolphin in the sea.
> He masters mortal men, though their pride be bold;
> But to some he gives glory that will never grow old.'

His voice floated and ceased; the strings echoed and re-echoed it, like wild voices in a glen.

Epikrates, sighing, thought, 'He's off.'

As the dramatic, headlong, passionate impromptu swept from climax to climax, Epikrates gazed at leisure; he would not be noticed. He felt bewildered by the misuse to which, with open eyes, he was dedicating his aesthetic life. He was not even in love, his tastes were otherwise. Why did he stay? This performance, at the Odeon of Athens or of Ephesos, would have enraptured the upper tiers and had them booing the judges. Yet nothing here was for show; it was redeemed not indeed by ignorance, Epikrates had seen to that; but by a perfect innocence.

And this, he thought, is why I stay. I feel here a necessity, whose depth and force I cannot measure; and to deny it makes me afraid.

There was a tradesman's son in Pella, whom he had overheard playing once, a real musician; he had offered to teach him for nothing, to redeem his peace of mind. The lad would make a professional, worked hard, was grateful; yet those fruitful lessons engaged Epikrates' mind less than these, when all that was sacred to the god he served was flung like wasteful incense on an unknown altar.

'Garland the prow with flowers, my song is for the brave . . .'

The music climbed to a rapt crescendo. The boy's lips were parted in the fierce and solitary smile of an act of love performed in darkness; the instrument could not sustain his onslaught, and was going out of tune; he must have heard it, but went on as if his will could compel the strings. He is using it, thought Epikrates, as one day he will use himself.

I must go, it is more than time; I have given him all he will ever take from me. All this he could do alone. In Ephesos, all round the year one can hear good music, and once in a while the best. And I should like to work in Corinth. I could take young Peithon; he ought to be hearing the masters. This one here, I am not teaching him, he is corrupting me. He comes to me for a listener who knows the language, and I listen, though he murders my native tongue. He must play to what gods will hear him, and let me go.

'You have learned your begetting; live as what you are!'

He swept the plectrum across the strings. One snapped, and whipped around the others; there was discord, and silence. He stared at it unbelievingly.

'Well?' said Epikrates. 'What did you expect? Did you think it was immortal?'

'I though it would last till I'd finished.'

'You would not treat a horse so. Come, give it me.'

He took a new string from his box, and began to put the instrument in order. The boy walked restlessly to the window; what had been about to be revealed would not return. Epikrates worked on the tuning, taking his time. I wish I could make him show what he really does know, before I leave.

'You have never yet played to your father and his guests, except on the lyre.'

'The lyre is what people want at supper.'

'It is what they get for want of better. Do me a kindness. Work on one piece for me and play it properly. I am sure he would like to see how you have got on.'

'I don't think he knows I have a kithara. I bought it myself, you know.'

'So much the better, you will show him something new.' Like everyone else at Pella, Epikrates knew there was trouble in the women's quarters. The boy was on edge with it, and had been for some time. It was not only his practice he had missed, but a lesson too. As soon as he had walked in, Epikrates had seen how it would be.

Why, in the name of all gods of reason, could the King not be content with paid hetairas? He could afford the best. He had his young men as well; was it too much to ask? Why must he always do his rutting so ceremoniously? He must have gone through at least three such weddings before this last one. It might be an old royal custom in this backward land, but if he wanted to be thought a Hellene, he should remember 'Nothing too much'. One could not make over barbarians in a generation; it came out in the boy as well; and yet . . .

He was still gazing from the window as if he had forgotten where he was. His mother must have been at him. One could have pitied the woman, if she had not begged for half her troubles, and her son's as well. He must be hers, hers only, and only the gods could say what else, for the King was civilized when set beside his Queen. Could she not see she might cry stinking fish once too often? From any one of these other brides might come a boy glad enough to be his father's son. Why could she not show some policy? Why could she never spare the boy?

There was no hope, thought Epikrates, of his learning anything today. As well put away the kithara . . . Well, but if I myself have learned, what have I learned for? Epikrates put on the instrument, stood up and began to play.

After a while Alexander turned back from the window, and came to sit on the table, fidgeting at first, then quiet, then still, his head tilted a little, his eyes finding a distance for themselves. Presently tears filled their lashes. Epikrates saw it with relief; it had always happened when music moved him, and embarrassed neither of them. When it was over, he wiped his eyes on his palms and smiled. 'If you want me to, I'll learn a piece to play in Hall.'

Epikrates said to himself as he went away, I shall have to go soon; the turbulence here is too much for any man who wants harmony and balance in his soul.

A few lessons later, Alexander said, 'There will be guests at supper; if I'm asked to play, shall I try it?'

'Certainly. Play it just as you did this morning. Will there be a place for me?'

'Oh yes; it will be all men we know, no foreigners. I'll tell the steward.'

Supper was late; it had to wait for the King. He greeted his guests with civility, but was rather short with the servants. Though his cheeks were flushed and his eyes injected, he was clearly sober, and anxious to forget whatever had put him out. Slaves passed along the news that he had just come from the Queen.

The guests were old campaigning friends from the Companion Cavalry. Philip looked down the couches with relief; no state envoys to put on a show for, or to complain if they got along early to the wine. Good full-bodied Akanthian, and no water with it; he needed it, after what he had had to endure.

Alexander sat on the end of Phoinix's supper-couch and shared his table. He never sat with his father unless invited. Phoinix, who had no ear to speak of but knew all the literary references to music, was pleased to hear of the boy's new piece and cited Achilles' lyre. 'And I shall not be like Patroklos, who Homer says was sitting waiting for his friend to leave off.'

'Oh, unfair. It only means Patroklos wanted to talk.'

'Now, now, boy, what are you up to? That's my cup you're drinking from, not yours.'

'Well, I pledge you in it. Try mine. If they rinsed wine round it before they put in the water, that was all.'

'It's the proper mixture for boys, one in four. You can pour some in my cup, we can't all take it neat as your father can, but it looks bad to call for the water-pitcher.'

'I'll drink some to make room, before I pour.'

'No, no, boy, stop, that's enough. You'll be too drunk to play.'

'Of course not, I only had a mouthful.' And indeed he showed no sign beyond a little heightened colour. He came of well-seasoned stock.

The noise was rising as the cups were topped up. Philip, shouting above it, invited anyone to give them a tune or a song.

'Here's your son, sir,' called Phoinix, 'who has learned a new tune for this very feast.'

Two or three cups of strong neat wine had made Philip feel much better. It was a known cure for snakebite, he thought with a grim smile. 'Come up, then, boy. Bring your lyre and sit up here.'

Alexander signed to the servant with whom he had left the kithara. He put it on with care, and went over to stand by his father's couch.

'What's this?' said the King. 'You can't play that thing, can you?' He had never seen it used by a man not paid to do it; it struck him as unsuitable.

The boy smiled, saying, 'You must tell me that when I've finished, Father.' He tested the strings and began.

Epikrates, listening down the hall, looked at the boy with deep affection. At this moment he could have posed for a young Apollo. Who knows, this may be the true beginning; he may come to a pure knowledge of the god.

All the Macedonian lords, who had been awaiting the cue to shout a chorus, listened amazed. They had never heard of a gentleman playing like this, or wanting to. What had those schoolmasters been up to with the boy? He had the name of being plucky and game for anything. Were they making a southerner of him? It would be philosophy next.

King Philip had attended many music-contests. Though without sustained interest in the art, he could recognize technique. He was aware of it here, together with its lack of fitness. The company, he could see, did not know what to make of it. Why had the teacher not reported this morbid fervour? The truth was plain. *She* had been bringing him again to those rites of hers, steeping him in their frenzies, making a barbarian of him. Look at him now, thought Philip; look at him now.

Out of civility to foreign guests, who always expected it, he had got into the way of bringing the boy to supper in the Hellene fashion; his friends' sons would not appear till they came of age. Why had he broken this good custom? If the boy had a girl's voice still, must he tell the world? That Epirote bitch, that malignant sorceress; he would long since have put her away, had her powerful kin not been like a spear poised at his back when he went to war. Let her not be too sure of herself. He would do it yet.

Phoinix had had no notion the boy could play like this. He was as good as that fellow from Samos a few months back. But he was letting himself get carried away, as he did sometimes with Homer. Before his father, he had always held himself in. He should never have had that wine.

He had reached the cadenzas which led to the finale. The stream of sound cascaded through its gorges, the bright spray glittered above.

Philip gazed, almost unhearing, taken up with what he saw: the brilliant glow of the face, the deep-set eyes unfocused and glittering with unshed tears, the remotely smiling mouth. To him, it mirrored the face he had left upstairs, its cheekbones flushed red, its defiant laughter, its eyes weeping with rage.

Alexander struck the last chord and drew a long deep breath. He had not made one mistake.

The guests broke into uneasy applause. Epikrates joined in eagerly. Phoinix shouted rather too loudly, 'Good! Very good!'

Philip banged down his wine-cup on the table. His forehead had flushed dark crimson; the lid of his blind eye had dropped a little, showing the white spot; his good eye started in its socket.

'Good?' he said. 'Do you call that music for a man?'

The boy turned slowly, as if waking from sleep. He blinked his eyes clear, and fastened them on his father.

'Never,' said Philip, 'let me see you make such a show of yourself again. Leave it to Corinthian whores and Persian eunuchs; you sing well enough for either. You should be ashamed.'

With the kithara still strapped on to him, the boy stood stock-still for a few moments, his face blank, and, as the blood receded, growing sallow. Looking at no one, he walked out between the couches and left the hall.

Epikrates followed. But he had wasted a few moments thinking what to say, and did not find him.

A few days later, Gyras, a tribal Macedonian from the inland hills, set out along ancient tracks, returning home on leave. He had told his commander formally, that his father was dying and had begged for a last sight of him. The officer, who had expected it since the day before, told him not to waste time at home when he had done his business, if he wanted to draw his pay. Tribal wars were winked at, unless they showed signs of spreading; they were immemorial; to put down blood-feud would have taken the army all its time, even had it not been itself steeped in tribal loyalties. Gyras' uncle had been killed, the wife raped and left for dead; if Gyras was refused leave he would desert. Some such thing happened once a month or so.

It was his second day out. He was a light cavalryman with his own horse, small and scrubby but tough, qualities Gyras shared; a gingery brown man, with a broken nose set slightly skew and a short bristly beard, dressed mainly in leather, and armed to the teeth, this being required for the journey as well as for his errand. He had been favouring his horse over grass wherever he could find it, to keep its unshod hooves sound for the work ahead. At about noon, he was crossing a rolling heathland between the mountain ribs of Macedon. In the wooded dips, birches and larches swayed in a gentle breeze; it was late summer, but up here the air was fresh. Gyras, who did not want to be killed, but preferred it to the life of disgrace which followed a failure to take vengeance, looked about him at the world he might shortly have to leave. Meantime, however, there was an oak-grove ahead; in its hushed and grateful shade a stream burbled over pebbles and black oak-leaves. He watered and tethered his horse; dipping the bronze cup he carried on his belt, he approved the water's sweetness. From his saddle-bag he took goat cheese and black bread, and sat on a rock to eat.

Hoof-beats cantered on the track behind him. At a walk, some stranger entered the wood. Gyras reached for his javelins, already laid at hand.

'Good day to you, Gyras.'

Till the lastest moment he had not believed his eyes. They were a good fifty miles out from Pella.

'Alexander!' His bread had stuck in his throat; he dislodged and bolted it, while the boy dismounted and led his horse to the stream. 'How did you get here? Is no one with you?'

'You are, now.' He invoked the god of the stream in proper form, restrained his mount from drinking too much, and tethered it to an oak-sapling. 'We can eat together.' He unpacked food and came over. He wore a man's long hunting-knife on a shoulder sling; his clothes were tumbled and dirty, his hair had pine-needles in it. Clearly he had slept out. His horse carried, among other things, two javelins and a bow. 'Here, take an apple. I thought I should catch up with you about mealtime.'

Dazedly Gyras complied. The boy drank from cupped hands and splashed his face. Concerned with his own affairs, for him momentous, Gyras had heard nothing of King Philip's supper-party. The thought of this charge on his hands appalled him. By the time he had returned him and set out again, anything might have happened at home. 'How did you come so far alone? Are you lost? Were you out hunting?'

'I am hunting what you are hunting,' said Alexander, biting into his apple. 'That is why I am coming with you.'

'But ... but ... what notion ... You don't know what I'm about.'

'Of course I do. Everyone in your squadron knows it. I need a war, and yours will do very well. It is quite time, you know, that I got my swordbelt. I have come out to take my man.'

Gyras gazed transfixed. The boy must have tracked him all this way, keeping out of sight. He was equipped with care and forethought. Also, something had changed his face. His cheeks had sunk and flattened below the cheekbones; his eyes looked deeper under the shelf of his brows, his high-bridged nose stood out more. There was a line across his forehead. It was scarcely a boy's face at all. Nonetheless he was twelve years old, and Gyras would have to answer for him.

'It's not right,' he said desperately, 'what you've done. You know it's not right. I was needed at home, you know that. Now I'll have to leave them in their trouble, and take you back.'

'You can't, you've eaten with me, we're guest-friends.' He was reprov-ing, not alarmed. 'It's wicked to betray a guest-friend.'

'You should have told me the right of it first, then. I can't help it now. Come back you must and will. You're no more than a child. If harm came to you, the King would have me crucified.'

The boy got up without haste, and strolled to his horse. Gyras started up, saw he was not untying it, and sat down again.

'He won't kill you if I come back. If I die, you'll have plenty of time to run away. I don't suppose he'd kill you anyway. Think about me, instead. If you do anything to get me sent home before I'm ready, if you try to ride back or send a message, then I shall kill you. And that you can be sure of.'

He had turned from the horse with lifted arm. Gyras looked along a javelin, balanced and poised. The narrow leaflike blade shone blue with honing, the point looked like a needle.

'Keep still, Gyras. Sit just as you are, don't move. I'm quick, you know, everyone knows it. I can throw before you can do anything. I don't want you for my first man. It wouldn't be enough, I should still have to take another in battle. But you will be, if you try to stop me now.'

Gyras looked at his eyes. He had faced such eyes through helmet-slits. He said, 'Now, come, now, you don't mean that.'

'No one will even know I did it. I shall just leave your body in that thicket, for the wolves and kites. You'll never be buried, or given your rites to set you free.' His voice grew rhythmic. 'And the shades of the dead will not let you cross the river to join their company, but you will wander alone for ever before the wide gates of Hades' house. No, don't move.'

Gyras sat immobile. It gave him time to think. Though ignorant of the supper-party, he knew about the King's new wedding, and those before. There was already a boy from one of them. Folk said it had started bright enough, but had turned out an idiot, no doubt poisoned by the Queen. Maybe she had only bribed the nurse to drop it on its head. Maybe it was just a natural. But there might be others. If young Alexander wanted to make himself a man ahead of time, one could see why.

'Well?' said the boy. 'Will you pledge yourself? I can't stand like this all day.'

'What I've ever done to deserve this of the gods, they only know. What do you want me to swear to?'

'Not to get word to Pella of me. To tell no one my name without my leave. Not to keep me from going into battle, or get anyone else to do it. You must swear all that, and call down a death-curse on yourself if you break your oath.'

Gyras felt himself flinch. He wanted no such compacts with a witch's son. The boy lowered his weapon but kept the thong in his fingers, twisted for a throw. 'You'll have to do it. I don't want you creeping up to bind me when I'm asleep. I could sit up to watch, but it would be stupid before a battle. So if you want to come out of this wood alive, you'll have to swear.'

'And what's to become of me after?'

'If I live I'll see you right. You must chance my dying, that's war.' He reached into his leather saddle-bag, looking over his shoulder at the still unsworn Gyras, and took out a piece of meat. It smelled high, not having been fresh when it left Pella. 'This is from a haunch of sacrifice,' he said, slapping it down upon a boulder. 'I knew we should have to do this. Come here. Lay your hand on it. Have you respect for oaths before the gods?'

'Yes.' His hand was so chilly that the dead goat-flesh felt quite warm.

'Then say this after me.'

The oath was elaborate and exact, the death-fate invoked was ghastly. The boy was well-versed in such things, and had on his own account a ready awareness of loopholes. Gyras finished binding himself as he was told, and went to swill his bloody hand in the running stream. The boy sniffed at the meat. 'I don't think this is fit to eat, even if we were to waste time making fire.' He tossed it away, holstered his javelin, and came back to Gyras' side. 'Well, that's done, now we can go on like friends. Let's finish eating, while you tell me about the war.'

Passing his hand across his brow, Gyras began to recite his kinsmen's injuries. 'No, I know about that. How many are you, how many are they? What kind of country is it? Have you horses?'

Their track threaded green hills, steadily rising. Grass gave way to bracken and thyme, the track wound past pine-woods and thickets of arbutus. The ranges heaved up all round them; they met mountain air, with its lifegiving holy pureness. They entered the open secrecy of the heights.

Gyras traced back the feud three generations. The boy, his first questions once answered, proved a good listener. Of his own affairs, he said only, 'When I've taken my man, you must be my witness at Pella. The King didn't take his man till he was fifteen. Parmenion told me so.'

Gyras planned to spend the last night of the journey with distant kinsmen, half a day's ride from home. He pointed out their village, clinging to the edge of a gorge, with rocky slopes above it. There was a mule-track along the precipice; Gyras was for taking a good road round the slope, one of King Archelaos'; but the boy, having learned that the pass was just usable, insisted on going that way to see what it was like. Between the steep bends and giddy drops, he said, 'If these are your clansmen, it's no use our saying I'm your kin. Say I'm your commander's son, come to learn about war. They can never claim you lied to them.'

Gyras readily agreed; even this would hint that the boy must be kept an eye on. He could do no more, on account of the death-fate. He was a believing man.

On a flattish shelf a few furlongs round about, between a broken hillside and the gorge, was the hamlet of Skopas, built of the brown stone which lay loose all round it, looking like an outcrop itself. On its open side was a stockade of boulders filled in with thorn-brush. Within, the coarse grass was full of cow-pats from the cattle that spent the night there. One or two small hairy horses were at graze; the rest would be out with the herders and hunters. Goats and some ragged sheep moved on the hill; a goat-boy's piping sounded from above, like the call of some wild bird.

Above the pass, on a gnarled dead tree, were spiked a yellow skull, and a few bones left of a hand. When the boy asked about it, Gyras said, 'That was a long time back, when I was a child. That was the man killed his own father.'

Their coming was the news of half a year. A horn was blown to tell the herdsmen; the oldest Skopian was carried in from the lair of still older rags and skins where he lived, waiting to die. In the headman's house they were offered sweet small figs, and some turbid wine in the best, least-chipped cups; people waited with ritual courtesy till they had done, before the questions began, about themselves, and the distant world. Gyras said the Great King had Egypt under his heel again; King Philip had been called in to set things to rights down in Thessaly, and was Archon there now, as good as King; it had put the southerners in a taking. And was it true, asked the headman's brother, that he had taken a new wife, and put the Epirote Queen away?

Aware of a stillness more piercing than all the voices, Gyras said that this was a pack of lies. The King as he got new lands in order might honour this lord or that by taking a daughter into his house; to Gyras' mind, they were by way of a kind of hostage. As for Queen Olympias, she stood in high respect as the mother of the King's heir, a credit to both his parents. Having got off this speech, sweated over in silence some hours before, Gyras cut off comment by asking in his turn for news.

News of the feud was bad. Four enemy Kimolians had met in a glen two of Gyras' clansmen, out after deer. One had lived just long enough to creep home and tell them where to find his brother's corpse before the jackals had it. The Kimolians were puffed with pride; the old man had no hold upon his sons; soon no one would be safe from them. Many deeds were milled over, many words quoted which had struck someone as telling, while the livestock was driven in, and the women cooked the goat which had been slaughtered to feast the guests. With the fall of dark, everyone went to bed.

Alexander shared with the headman's son, who had a proper blanket. It was verminous; so was the child, but being in awe of his guest he let him sleep in what peace the fleas allowed.

He dreamed that Herakles came up to the bed and shook him. He looked as he did in the garden shrine at Pella, beardless and young, hooded in the fanged mask of the lion, its mane hanging down behind. 'Get up, lazy boy,' he said, 'or I shall start without you. I have been calling you this long time.'

All the people in the room were sleeping; he took his cloak and stepped softly out. A late bright moon lit the wide uplands. No one kept watch but the dogs. One huge wolflike beast ran up to him; he stood still to be smelled, and it let him be. It was movement outside the fence that would have had them baying.

All was quiet, why had Herakles called him? His eye fell on a tall crag, with an easy way up well worn by feet, the village lookout. If a guard was there . . . But no guard was. He scrambled up. He could trace the good road of Archelaos, winding on down the hill; and on it a creeping shadow.

Twenty-odd horsemen, riding light, without burdens. Even in the far-sounding hills, they were too far off to hear; but something twinkled under the moon.

The boy's eyes widened. He raised both hands to the sky, his shining face uplifted. He had committed himself to Herakles, and the god had answered. Not leaving him to find the battle, he had sent the battle to him.

In the light of the gibbous moon, he stood printing on his mind the shape of the place, the vantage points and the hazards. There was nowhere down there to ambush them. Archelaos, a good road-builder, had no doubt planned against ambushes. They would have to be ambushed here; for the Skopians were out-numbered. They must be roused at once, before the enemy got near enough to hear the stir. If he ran about shaking them up, they would forget him in the scramble; they must be made to listen. Outside the headman's hut hung the horn which had called the villagers. He tested it softly, and blew.

Doors opened, men ran out with clouts clutched round them, women squealed to each other, sheep and goats bleated. The boy, standing up on a high boulder against the glimmering sky, called, 'War! It is war!'

The gabble hushed. His clear voice cut in. Ever since he left Pella, he had been thinking in Macedonian.

'I am Alexander, King Philip's son. Gyras knows who I am. I have come to fight in your war for you, because the god has warned me. The Kimolians are there on the valley road, twenty-three riders. Listen to me, and before sun-up we'll make an end of them.' He called up, by name, the headman and his sons.

They came forward in stunned silence, their eyes starting in the gloom. This was the witch's child, the son of the Epirote.

He sat on the boulder, not wishing to part with the height it lent him, and spoke earnestly, aware all the while of Herakles at his shoulder.

When he had done, the headman sent the women indoors, and told the men to do as the boy had said. They argued at first; it went against the grain to strike no blow at the accursed Kimolians till they were in the stockade among the cattle they had come to steal. But Gyras came out too for it. So in the loom of the false dawn the Skopians armed themselves and caught their ponies, and clustered the far side of the houses. It was clear the Kimolians reckoned on attacking when the men had gone out about their work. The bar of thorn-brush which closed the gateway had been thinned enough to let them in, but not to make them think. The shepherd boys and goat-herds were sent up on the hill, to make it look like a common morning.

The peaks stood dark against the sky, in whose deeps the stars were paling. The boy, holding his bridle and his javelins, watched for the first rose of dawn; he might be seeing it once for all. This he had known; for the first time, now, he felt it. All his life he had been hearing news of violent death; now his body told back the tale to him; the grinding of the iron into one's vitals, the mortal pain, the dark shades waiting as one was torn forth to leave the light, for ever, for ever. His guardian had left his side. In his silent heart he turned to Herakles, saying, 'Why have you forsaken me?'

Dawn touched the highest peak in a glow like flame. He had been perfectly alone; so the voice of Herakles, still as it was, reached him unhindered. It said, 'I left you to make you understand my mystery. Do not believe that others will die, not you; it is not for that I am your friend. By laying myself on the pyre I became divine. I have wrestled with Thanatos knee to knee, and I know how death is vanquished. Man's immortality is not to live for ever; for that wish is born of fear. Each moment free from fear makes a man immortal.'

The rose-red on the hill-tops changed to gold. He stood between death and life as between night and morning, and thought with a soaring rapture, 'I am not afraid.' It was better than music or his mother's love; it was the life of the gods. No grief could touch him, no hatred harm him. Things looked bright and clear, as to the stooping eagle. He felt sharp as an arrow, and full of light.

The Kimolians' horses sounded on the hard earth of the road.

They paused outside the stockade. A goat-herd piped on the hill. In the houses children talked, innocent of guile; a guileful woman was singing. They kicked the thorn-brush aside, and rode in laughing. The cattle they had come for were still within the pound. They would have the women first.

Suddenly came a yell so loud and high that they thought some wild girl had seen them. Then came the shouts of men.

Horse and foot, the Skopians burst out on them. Some were already making for the houses; these were dealt with quickly. Soon numbers were almost even.

For a while there was only chaos, as men dived and stumbled about among the bawling cattle. Then one of the raiders made a bolt for the gate, and was off. Cheers of triumph rose from the Skopians. The boy perceived that this was the beginning of flight; and that the Skopians were going to allow it, content that the day was theirs, not looking to another day when the enemy would come back, sore from defeat and bent on vengeance. Did they take this for victory? With a shout he rode towards the gate, calling fiercely 'Head them off!'; and, drawn by his certainty, the Skopians followed. The gate was blocked. Cattle still milled about; but men were facing men; there had formed, in miniature, opposing battle-lines.

'Now!' thought the boy. He looked at the man across from him.

He had on a war-cap of greasy black old leather, stitched with crudely-forged plates of iron, and a corselet of goat's hide with the hair on, worn bald here and there. His red beard was young, his face freckled and peeled with sunburn. He was frowning deeply, not in anger but like a man charged with some work he is not skilled in, who has time for no one's concerns except his own. Nonetheless, thought the boy, that is an old war-cap, often used; and he's a grown man, quite tall. One must take the first comer, that is the proper thing.

He had his two javelins, the first to throw, the second to fight with. Spears were flying, and one Skopian had jumped on a house-roof with a bow. A horse neighed and reared, a shaft sticking in its neck; the rider fell, and scrambled off hopping on one leg; the horse bolted round the houses. Much time seemed to pass in these beginnings. Most of the spears had missed, through impatience, distance or lack of skill. The red-haired man's eyes shifted, waiting for the melee to throw up the opponent he must fight. Before long, someone else would have him.

The boy poised his throwing spear as he kicked his pony forward. An easy mark; there was a black patch on the goat-skin over the heart. No; this was his first man, it must be hand to hand. Alongside was a dark, stocky, swarthy man with a black beard; the boy jerked back his arm, and threw almost without looking; his fingers reaching for the second shaft the moment the first was gone, his eyes seeking the red-haired man's. The man had seen him, their eyes met. The boy shouted a wordless battle-yell, and urged on his horse with his spear-butt. It leaped forward jerkily over the broken ground.

The man levelled his spear, a longer one, peering about. His eyes passed over the boy, shifting and seeking. He was waiting for someone; for a grown man, whom he must heed.

The boy threw up his head, and shouted at his lungs' full pitch. The man must be roused, made to believe in him, or it would not be a proper killing; it would be like taking him in the back, or half asleep. It must be perfect, there must be nothing that could ever be said against it. He yelled again.

The raiders were a big-made tribe. To the red-haired man, it seemed a child who came riding. He gazed in unease, disliking the need to keep an eye on him, fearing that while he beat him off some man would rush in and take him off guard. His eyesight was only middling; though the boy had seen him clearly, he took some moments to make out the approaching face. It was not a child's. It raised the hair on his neck.

The boy set his face into a warrior's, that he might be believed in and challenge death. In a perfect singleness, free from hatred, anger, or doubt, pure in dedication, exultant in victory over fear, he swooped towards the red-haired man. With this face of inhuman radiance; with this being, whatever it was, eerie, numinous, uttering its high hawklike cries, the man wanted no more to do. He swerved his horse; a burly Skopian was nearing, perhaps to single him out; someone else should deal with the matter. His eye had strayed too long. With a shrill 'Ahii-i!' the shining man-child was on him. He thrust with his spear; the creature swung past it; he saw deep sky-filled eyes, a mouth of ecstasy. A blow struck his breast, which at once was more than a blow, was ruin and darkness. As sight faded from his eyes, it seemed to him that the smiling lips had parted to drink his life.

The Skopians cheered the boy, clearly a luckbringer; it had been the quickest kill of the fight. The raiders were shaken; this was the favourite son of their headman, who was old and would get no more. They struggled in bad order to the gate-gap, forcing their horses through the cattle and the men; not all the Skopians were resolute. Horses squealed, cows bawled and trampled the fallen; there was a stink of fresh-dropped dung, crushed herbage, sweat and blood.

As the flight cohered, it was seen to head for the road. The boy, steering his horse through goats, remembered the lie of the land, seen from the lookout. He burst out of the press, with an ear-piercing yell of 'Stop them! The pass! Head them for the pass!' He never looked back; had the spell-bound Skopians not streamed after him, he would have confronted the Kimolians all alone.

They were in time; the raiders were contained, all ways but the one. In full panic now, unfit for a wise choice of evils, scared of the precipices, but ignorant of the goat-ways on the rocky hill, they crowded on to the narrow track above the gorge.

At the back of the rout, a single man wheeled round to face the pursuers. Straw-haired, darkly tanned, hawk-nosed, he had been first in attack and last to fly; last, too, to give up struggling to reach the road. Knowing the choice of evils had been wrong, he waited where the mouth of the pass grew narrow. He had planned and led the raid; his youngest brother had fallen, at the hand of a boy who should still have been herding goats; he would have to face their father with it. Better redeem shame in death; the odds were on death in any case; a few might escape, if he could hold the pass awhile. He drew the old iron sword which had been his grandfather's, and, dismounting, straddled the rough way.

The boy, riding up from his place in the drag-net, saw him hold his own against three, take a head-blow, give at the knees. The chase broke over him. Ahead, the raiders were strung along the ledge. Yelling with joy, the Skopians hurled rocks at them, the archer loosed his bow. Horses fell screaming down the cliff, men followed the horses. They had lost half their strength, before the remnant turned out of range.

It was over. The boy reined in his pony. Its neck had been cut, it began to feel the pain and be plagued by flies. He caressed and reassured it. He had only come to take his man, and he had won a battle. This the god had given him from the sky.

The Skopians crowded round him, those who had not climbed down to strip the bodies in the gorge. Their heavy hands were on his back and shoulders, the air round him steamed with their strong breath. He was their captain, their fighting quail, their little lion, their luck-piece. Gyras walked by him with the air of a man whose status is changed for ever.

Someone shouted, 'This whore's son is moving still.' The boy, not to miss anything, shoved in. The straw-haired man lay where he had been beaten down, bleeding from his torn scalp, trying to struggle up on one arm. A Skopian grasped him by the hair, so that he cried out with pain, and pulled back his head to cut his throat. The others gave scarcely a second glance to this natural action.

'No!' said the boy. They all turned, surprised and puzzled. He ran up and knelt by the man, pushing aside the knife. 'He was brave. He did it for the others. He was like Ajax at the ships.'

The Skopians broke into lively argument. What did he mean? Something about some sacred hero, about an omen, that it would be bad luck to kill the man? No, said another, it was just some fancy of the boy's, but war was war. Laughing, pushing aside the first comer, he came knife in hand to the man upon the ground.

'If you kill him,' said the boy, 'I will make you sorry. I swear it by my father's head.'

The knife-bearer looked round with a start. A moment ago, the lad had been all sunshine. Gyras muttered, 'You had better do as he says.'

He stood up, saying, 'You must let this man go. I claim him as my battle-prize. He is to have his horse; I'll give you the horse of the man I killed, to make good.' They listened open-mouthed; but, he thought looking round, they were reckoning he would soon forget and they could finish the man off later. 'Get him mounted now, at once, and put him on the road. Gyras, help them.'

The Skopians escaped into laughter. They bundled the man along to his horse, amusing themselves till the sharp young voice behind them called, 'Stop doing that.' They slashed the horse's rump and it went walloping off along the road, its limp rider clinging to its mane. The boy turned back, the frown-line smoothed from his brow. 'Now,' he said. 'I must find my man.'

No living wounded were left upon the field. The Skopians had been carried home by their women, the raiders butchered, mostly by the women too. Now they had come to their dead, flinging themselves across the bodies, beating their breasts, clawing at their faces, wrenching their loosened hair. Their keening hung in the air like the voices of wild things native to the place, young wolves or crying birds or goats at yeaning-time. White clouds sailed the sky, calmly, sending dark wings over the mountains, touching far forest-tops with black.

The boy thought, This is a battlefield. This is what it is like. The enemy dead lay littered and bundled about, forsaken, ungainly, sprawling. The women, clustered like crows, hid the fallen victors. Already, balanced swaying on high air, by one and one vultures appeared.

The red-haired man lay on his back, one knee bent up, his young beard cocked at the sky. The iron-patched war cap, two generations older than he, had been taken already; it would serve many other men. He was not bleeding much. There had been a moment, while he was falling, when the javelin had stuck in him, and the boy had thought he would have to let go or be dragged off too. But he had tugged once more and it had pulled free, just in time.

He looked at the white face, already growing livid, the gaping mouth, and thought again, This is a battlefield, a soldier must learn to know it. He had taken this man, and must show a trophy. There was no dagger, not even a belt; the goatskin corselet had gone. The women had been quickly over the field. The boy was angry in himself, but knew that complaint would bring no redress and would lose him face. He must have a trophy. Nothing was left, now, except . . .

'Here, little warrior.' A Skopian youth with black tangled hair stood over him, showing broken teeth in a friendly smile. In his hand was a cleaver with half-dry blood all over it. 'Let me take off the head for you. I know the knack.'

Between the grinning and the gaping face, the boy paused silent. The cleaver, light in the youth's big hand, looked heavy for his own. Gyras said quickly, 'They only do that in the back-country now, Alexander.'

'I had better have it,' he said. 'There's nothing else.' The youth came forward eagerly. Gyras might be citified, but for the King's son old customs were good enough; that was the way of quality. He tried the edge on his thumb. But the boy had found himself too glad to have this work done for him. 'No. I must cut it off myself.' While the Skopians laughed and swore admiringly, the cleaver, warm, sticky, slimy, raw-smelling, was put in his hand. He knelt by the corpse, forcing himself to keep his eyes open, doggedly chopping at the neckbone, spattering himself with bloody shreds, till the head rolled free. Grasping a handful of dead hair – for there must be nothing he could know after in his most secret soul that he had feared to do – he stood upright. 'Fetch me my game-bag, Gyras.'

Gyras unstrapped it from the saddle-cloth. The boy dropped the head in, and rubbed his palms on the bag. There was still blood between his fingers, sticking them together. The stream was a hundred feet down, he would wash them going home. He turned to bid his hosts farewell.

'Wait!' shouted someone. Two or three men, carrying something, were running and waving. 'Don't let the little lord go. Here, we have this other trophy for him. Two, yes, look, he killed two.'

The boy frowned. He wanted to go home now. He had only fought one combat. What did they mean?

The foremost man ran up panting. 'It's true. This one here' – he pointed to the raw-necked trunk – 'that was his second man. He took the first with a javelin-throw, before ever we closed with them. I saw it myself; he pitched straight down stuck like a pig. He was creeping about awhile, but he was finished before the women got to him. Here you are, little lord. Something to show your father.'

The second man displayed the head, holding it up by its black hair. The strong bushy beard hid the shorn neck. It was the head of the man he had thrown his first javelin at, before he fought hand to hand. There had been an eye-blink moment, when he had seen this was the man to have it. He had forgotten, his mind had shut on it as if it had never been. Held by the forelock, it had an arrogant upward tilt; rigor had set a gap-toothed grin on it; the skin was swarthy, one of the eyes was half closed, showing only the white.

The boy looked at the face confronting his. A coldness spread in his belly; he felt a great heave of nausea, a clammy sweat in his palms. He swallowed, and fought to keep from vomiting.

'I didn't kill him,' he said. 'I never killed that man.'

They began all three at once to reassure him, describing the body, swearing it had no other wound, offering to take him there, thrusting the head towards him. Two men at his first blooding! He could tell his grandsons. They appealed to Gyras; the little lord was overdone, and no wonder; if he left his prize behind, when he was himself again he would be sorry; Gyras must keep it for him.

'No!' The boy's voice had risen. 'I don't want it. I didn't see him die. You can't bring him to me if the women killed him. You can't tell what happened. Take it away.'

They clicked their tongues, sorry to obey him to his later loss. Gyras took aside the headman, and whispered in his ear. His face changed; he took the boy kindly round the shoulders, and said he must be warmed with a drop of wine before the long ride home. The boy walked with him quietly, his face with its clear pallor remote and gentle, a faint blueness under his eyes. Presently with the wine the colour came back into his skin; he began to smile, and before long joined in the laughter.

Outside there was a buzz of praise. What a fine boy! Such pluck, such a head on his shoulders; and now such proper feeling. Not much of a likeness, yet it had moved his heart. What father would not be proud of such a son?

'*Look well at the horn of the hoof. A thick horn makes for much sounder feet than a thin one. Take care, too, to see the hoofs are high front and back, not flattened; a high hoof keeps the frog clear of the ground.*'

'Is there any of that book,' asked Philotas, Parmenion's son, 'that you don't know by heart?'

'One can't know too much of Xenophon,' Alexander said, 'when it comes to horses. I want to read his books about Persia, too. Are you buying anything today?'

'Not this year. My brother's buying one.'

'Xenophon says a good hoof ought to make a ringing noise like a cymbal. That one there looks splay to me. My father wants a new battle-charger. He had one killed under him, fighting the Illyrians last year.' He looked at the dais beside them, run up as usual for the spring horse-fair; the King had not yet arrived.

It was a sharp brilliant day; the lake and the lagoon were ruffled and darkly gleaming; the white clouds that skimmed across to the distant mountains had edges honed blue, like swords. The bruised turf of the meadow was green from the winter rains. All morning the soldiers had been buying; officers for themselves, tribal chiefs for the vassals who made up their squadrons (in Macedon, the feudal and the regimental always overlapped), tough stocky thick-maned beasts, lively and sleek from the winter grazing. By noon, this common business was done; now the bloodstock was coming out, racers and parade show-horses and chargers, curried and dressed up to the eyes.

The horse-fair at Pella was a rite not less honoured than the sacred feasts. Dealers came from the horse-lands of Thessaly, from Thrace, from Epiros, even across Hellespont; these would always claim their stock was crossed with the fabled Nisaian strain of the Persian kings.

Important buyers were only now arriving. Alexander had been there most of the day. Following him about, not yet at ease with him or with one another, were half a dozen boys whom Philip had lately collected from fathers he wished to honour.

It was long since a Prince's Guard had been formed in Macedon for an heir just come of age. The King himself had never been heir-apparent. In the wars of succession before that, no heir for generations had had time to come of age before he was murdered or dispossessed. Records revealed that the last Prince of Macedon to have his Companions chosen for him in proper form had been Perdikkas the First, some fifty years before. One ancient man survived of them; he had tales as long as Nestor's about border wars and cattle raids, and could name the grandchildren of Perdikkas' bastards; but he had forgotten everything about procedure.

The Companions should have been youths of about the Prince's age, who had also passed the test of manhood. No such boy was now to be found in the royal lands. Fathers put forward eagerly the claims of sons sixteen or seventeen years old, who already looked and talked like men. They argued that most of Alexander's current friends were even older. It was natural, they added tactfully, with so brave and forward a boy.

Philip endured the compliments with a good grace, while he lived with the remembered eyes which had met his when the head, already stinking from its journey, was laid before him. During the days of waiting and seeking news, it had been clear to him that if the boy never came back, he would have to have Olympias killed before she could kill him. All this was tough meat to feast on. Epikrates, too, had left, telling him the Prince had decided to give up music, and not meeting his eyes. Philip bestowed lavish guest-gifts, but could see an unpleasant tale going round the odeons of Hellas; these men went everywhere.

In the upshot, no real attempt had been made to muster a formal Prince's Guard. Alexander took no interest in this dead institution; he had picked up for himself the group of youths and grown men who were already known everywhere as Alexander's Friends. They themselves were apt to forget that he was only thirteen last summer.

The morning, however, of the Horse Fair, he had been spending with the boys attached to him by the King. He had been pleased to have their company; if he treated them all as his juniors, it was not to assert himself or put them down, but because he never felt it otherwise. He had talked horses untiringly and they had done their best to keep up. His sword-belt, his fame, and the fact that with all this he was the smallest of them,

bewildered them and made them awkward. They were relieved that now,
for the showing of the blood-stock, his friends were gathering, Ptolemy
and Harpalos and Philotas and the rest. Left on one side, they clumped
together and, with their pack-leader gone, started edging for precedence
like a chance-met group of dogs.

'My father couldn't come in today. It's not worth it; he imports his
horses straight from Thessaly. All the breeders know him.'

'I shall need a bigger horse soon; but my father's leaving it till next year,
when I've grown taller.'

'Alexander's a hand shorter than you, and *he* rides men's horses.'

'Oh, well, I expect they trained them specially.'

The tallest of the boys said, 'He took his boar. I suppose you think they
trained a boar for him.'

'That was set up, it always it,' said the boy with the richest father, who
could count on having it set up for him.

'It was not set up!' said the tall boy angrily. The others exchanged looks;
he reddened. His voice, which was breaking, gave a sudden startling
growl. 'My father heard about it. Ptolemy tried to set it up without his
knowing, because he was set on doing it, and Ptolemy didn't want him
killed. They cleared the wood except for a small one. Then when they
brought him there in the morning, overnight a big one had got in. Ptolemy
went as white as a fleece, they said, and tried to make him go home. But
he saw through it then; he said this was the boar the god had sent him,
and the god knew best. They couldn't budge him. They were in a sweat
with fright, they knew he was too light to hold it, and the net wouldn't
hold it long. But he went straight for the big vein in the neck; no one had
to help him. Everyone knows that's so.'

'No one would dare spoil the story, you mean. Just look at him now.
My father would belt me if I stood in the horse-field letting men make up
to me. Which of them does he go with?'

One of the others put in, 'No one, my brother says.'

'Oh? Did he try?'

'His friend did. Alexander seemed to like him, he even kissed him once.
But then when he wanted the rest, he seemed surprised and quite put out.
He's young for his age, my brother says.'

'And how old was your brother when he took his man?' asked the tallest
boy. 'And his boar?'

'That's different. My brother says he'll come to it all of a sudden, and
be mad for girls. His father did.'

'Oh, but the King likes – '

'Be quiet, you fool!' They all looked over their shoulders; but the men
were watching two race-horses whose dealer had set them to run round

the field. The boys ceased squabbling, till the Royal Bodyguard began to form up around the dais, in readiness for the King.

'Look,' whispered someone, pointing to the officer in command. 'That's Pausanias.' There were knowing looks, and inquiring ones. 'He was the King's favourite before the one who died. He was the rival.'

'What happened?'

'Shsh. Everyone knows. The King threw him over and he was madly angry. He stood up at a drinking-party and called the new boy a shameless whore who'd go with anyone for pay. People pulled them apart; but either the boy really cared for the King, or it was the slight to his honour; it gnawed at him, and in the end he asked a friend, I think it was Attalos, to give the King a message when he was dead. The next time they fought the Illyrians, he rushed straight in front of the King among the enemy, and got hacked to death.'

'What did the King do?'

'Buried him.'

'No, to Pausanias?'

There were confused whispers. No one really knows if ...' 'Of course he did!' 'You could be killed for saying that.' 'Well, he can't have been sorry.' 'No, it was Attalos and the boy's friends, my brother says so.'

'What did they *do*?'

Attalos got Pausanias dead drunk one night. Then they carried him out to the grooms and said they could enjoy themselves, he'd go with anyone without even being paid. I suppose they beat him up as well. He woke in the stable yard next morning.'

Someone whistled softly. They stared at the officer of the guard. He looked old for his years, and not strikingly handsome. He had grown a beard.

'He wanted Attalos put to death. Of course the King couldn't do it, even if he'd wanted; imagine putting *that* to the Assembly! But he had to do something, Pausanias being an Orestid. He gave him some land, and made him Second Officer of the Royal Guard.'

The tallest boy, who had heard the whole tale in silence, said, 'Does Alexander get to know of things like this?'

'His mother tells him everything, to turn him against the King.'

'Well, but the King insulted him in Hall. That's why he went out to take his man.'

Is that what he told you?'

No, of course he wouldn't speak of it. My father was there; he often has supper with the King. Our land's quite near.'

'So you've met Alexander before, then?'

Only once when we were children. He didn't know me again, I've grown too much.'

'Wait till he hears you're the same age, he won't like that.'

'Who said I was?'

'You told me you were born in the same month.'

'I never said the same year.'

'You did, the first day you came.'

'Are you calling me a liar? Well, come on, are you?'

'Hephaistion, you fool, you can't fight here.'

'Don't call me a liar, then.'

'You do look fourteen,' said a peacemaker. 'In the gymnasium, I thought you were more.'

'You know who Hephaistion has a look of? Alexander. Not really *like*, but, say, like his big brother.'

'You hear that, Hephaistion? How well does your mother know the King?'

He had counted too much on the protection of place and time. Next moment, with a split lip, he was on the ground. In the stir of the King's approach, few people saw it. Alexander all this while had kept the tail of his eye on them, because he thought of himself as their commanding officer. But he decided not to notice it. They were not precisely on duty, and the boy who had been knocked down was the one he liked the least.

Philip rode up to the stand, escorted by the First Officer of the Guard, the Somatophylax. Pausanias saluted and stepped aside. The boys stood respectfully, one sucking his lip, the other his knuckles.

The Horse Fair was always easy-going, an outing where men were men. Philip in riding-clothes lifted his switch to the lords and squires and officers and horse-dealers; mounted the stand, shouted to this friend or that to join him. His eye fell on his son; he made a movement, then saw the little court around him and turned away. Alexander picked up his talk with Harpalos, a dark lively goodlooking youth with much offhand charm, whom fate had cursed with a clubfoot. Alexander had always admired the way he bore it.

A racehorse came pounding by, ridden by a little Nubian boy in a striped tunic. Word had gone round that this year the King was only in the market for a battle-charger; but he had paid the sum, already a legend, of thirteen talents for the racer that had won for him at Olympia; and the dealer had thought it worth a try. Philip smiled and shook his head; the Nubian boy, who had hoped to be bought with the horse, to wear gold earrings and eat meat on feast-days, cantered back, his face a landscape of grief.

The chargers were led up, in precedence fiercely fought over by the dealers all the forenoon, and settled in the end by substantial bribes. The King came down to peer into mouths and at upturned hooves, to feel shanks and listen to chests. The horses were led away, or kept by in case nothing better turned up. There was a lag. Philip looked impatiently about. The big Thessalian dealer, Philonikos, who had been fuming for some time, said to his runner, 'Tell them I'll have their guts for picket-ropes, if they don't bring the beast *now*.'

'Kittos says, sir, they can *bring* him, but . . .'

'I had to break the brute myself, must I show him too? Tell Kittos from me, if I miss this sale, they won't have hide enough left between them for a pair of sandal soles.' With a sincere, respectful smile, he approached the King. 'Sir, he's on his way. You'll see he's all I wrote you from Larissa, and more. Forgive the delay; they've just now told me, some fool let him slip his tether. In prime fettle as he is, he was hard to catch. Ah! Here he comes now.'

They led up, at a careful walk, a black with a white blaze. The other horses had been ridden, to show their paces. Though he was certainly in a sweat, he did not breathe like a horse that had been running. When they pulled him up before the King and his horse-trainer, his nostrils flared and his black eye rolled sidelong; he tried to rear his head, but the groom dragged it down. His bridle was costly, red leather trimmed with silver; but he had no saddle-cloth. The dealer's lips moved viciously in his beard.

A hushed voice beside the dais said, 'Look, Ptolemy. Look at *that*.'

'There, sir!' said Philonikos, forcing rapture into his voice. 'There's Thunder. If there ever stepped a mount fit for a King . . .'

He was indeed, at all points, the ideal horse of Xenophon. Starting, as he advises, with the feet, one saw that the horns of the hooves were deep before and behind; when he stamped, as he was doing now (just missing the groom's foot) they made a ringing sound like a cymbal. His leg-bones were strong but flexible; his chest was broad, his neck arched, as the writer puts it, like a gamecock's; the mane was long, strong, silky and badly combed. His back was firm and wide, the spine well padded, his loins were short and broad. His black coat shone; on one flank was branded the horned triangle, the Oxhead, which was the mark of his famous breed. Strikingly, his forehead had a white blaze which almost copied its shape.

'That,' said Alexander with awe, 'is a perfect horse. Perfect everywhere.'

'He's vicious,' Ptolemy said.

Over at the horse-lines, the chief groom Kittos said to a fellow-slave who had watched their struggles, 'Days like this, I wish they'd cut my throat along with my father's, when they took our town. My back's not healed from last time, and he'll be at me again before sundown.'

'That horse is a murderer. What does he want, does he want to kill the King?'

'There was nothing wrong with that horse, I tell you nothing, nothing beyond high spirits, till he lost his temper when it took against him. He's like a wild beast in his drink; mostly it's us men he takes it out of, we come cheaper than horses. Now it's anyone's fault but his; he'd kill me if I told him its temper's spoiled for good. He only bought it from Kroisos a month ago, just for this deal. Two talents he paid.' His hearer whistled. 'He reckoned to get three, and he well might if he'd not set out to break its heart. It's held out well, I'll say that for it. He broke mine long ago.'

Philip, seeing the horse was restive, walked round it a few paces away. 'Yes, I like his looks. Well, let's see him move.'

Philonikos took a few steps towards the horse. It gave a squeal like a battle-trumpet, forced up its head against the hanging weight of the groom, and pawed the air. The dealer swore and kept his distance; the groom got the horse in hand. As if dye were running from the red bridle, a few drops of blood fell from its mouth.

Alexander said, 'Look at that bit they've put on him. Look at those barbs.'

'It seems even that can't hold him,' said big Philotas easily. 'Beauty's not everything.'

'And still he got his head up.' Alexander had moved forward. The men strolled after, looking out over him; he barely reached Philotas' shoulder.

'You can see his spirit, sir,' Philonikos told the King eagerly. 'A horse like this, one could train to rear up and strike the enemy.'

'The quickest way to have your mount killed under you,' said Philip brusquely, 'making it show its belly.' He beckoned the leathery bow-legged man attending him. 'Will you try him, Jason?'

The royal trainer walked round to the front of the horse, making cheerful soothing sounds. It backed, stamped and rolled its eyes. He clicked his tongue, saying firmly. 'Thunder, boy, hey, Thunder.' At the sound of its name it seemed to quiver all over with suspicion and rage. Jason returned to noises. 'Keep his head till I'm up,' he told the groom, 'that looks like one man's work.' He approached the horse's side, ready to reach for the roots of the mane; the only means, unless a man had a spear to vault on, of getting up. The saddle-cloth, had it been on, would have offered comfort and show, but no kind of foothold. A hoist was for the elderly, and Persians, who were notoriously soft.

At the last moment his shadow passed before the horse's eyes. It gave a violent start, swerved, and lashed out missing Jason by inches. He stepped back and squinted at it sideways, screwing up one eye and the side of his mouth. The King met his look and raised his eyebrows.

Alexander, who had been holding his breath, looked round at Ptolemy and said in a voice of anguish, 'He won't buy him.'

'Who would?' said Ptolemy, surprised. 'Can't think why he was shown. Xenophon wouldn't have bought him. You were quoting him only just now, how the nervous horse won't let you harm the enemy, but he'll do plenty of harm to you.'

'Nervous? He? He's the bravest horse I ever saw. He's a fighter. Look where he's been beaten, under the belly too, you can see the weals. If Father doesn't buy him, that man will flay him alive. I can see it in his face.'

Jason tried again. Before he got anywhere near the horse it started kicking. He looked at the King, who shrugged his shoulders.

'It was his shadow,' said Alexander urgently to Ptolemy. 'He's shy of his own, even. Jason should have seen.'

'He's seen enough; he's got the King's life to think of. Would you ride a horse like that to war?'

'Yes, I would. To war most of all.'

Philotas raised his brows, but failed to catch Ptolemy's eye.

'Well, Philonikos,' said Philip, 'if that's the pick of your stable, let's waste no more time. I've work to do.'

'Sir, give us a moment. He's frisky for want of exercise; too full of corn. With his strength, he – '

'I can buy something better for three talents than a broken neck.'

'My lord, for you only, I'll make a special price.'

'I'm busy,' Philip said.

Philonikos set his thick mouth in a wide straight line. The groom, hanging for dear life on the spiked bit, began to turn the horse for the horse-lines. Alexander called out in his high carrying voice, 'What a waste! The best horse in the show!'

Anger and urgency gave it a note of arrogance that made heads turn. Philip looked round startled. Never, at the worst of things, had the boy been rude to him in public. It had best be ignored till later. The groom and the horse were moving off.

'The best horse ever shown here, and all he needs is handling.' Alexander had come out into the field. All his friends, even Ptolemy, left a discreet space round him; he was going too far. The whole crowd was staring. 'A horse in ten thousand, just thrown away.'

Philip, looking again, decided the boy had not meant to be so insolent. He was a colt too full of corn, ever since his two precocious exploits. They had gone to his head. No lesson so good, thought Philip, as the one a man teaches to himself. 'Jason here,' he said, 'has been training horses for twenty years. And you, Philonikos; how long?'

The dealer's eyes shifted from father to son; he was on a tight-rope. 'Ah, well, sir, I was reared to it from a boy.'

'You hear that, Alexander? But you think you can do better?'

Alexander glanced, not at his father but at Philonikos. With an un-pleasant sense of shock, the dealer looked away.

'Yes. With this horse, I could.'

'Very well,' said Philip. 'If you can, he's yours.'

The boy looked at the horse, with parted lips and devouring eyes. The groom had paused with it. It snorted over its shoulder.

'And if you can't?' said the King briskly. 'What are you staking?'

Alexander took a deep breath, his eyes not leaving the horse. 'If I can't ride him, I'll pay for him myself.'

Philip raised his dark heavy brows. 'At three talents?' The boy had only just been put up to a youth's allowance; it would take most of this year's, and the next as well.

'Yes,' Alexander said.

'I hope you mean it. I do.'

'So do I.' Roused from his single concern with the horse, he saw that everyone was staring: the officers, the chiefs, the grooms and dealers. Ptolemy and Harpalos and Philotas; the boys he had spent the morning with. The tall one, Hephaistion, who moved so well that he always caught the eye, had stepped out before the others. For a moment their looks met.

Alexander smiled at Philip. 'It's a bet, then, Father. He's mine; and the loser pays.' There was a buzz of laughter and applause in the royal circle, born of relief that it had turned good-humoured. Only Philip, who had caught it full in the eyes, had known it for a battle-smile, save for one watcher of no importance who had known it too.

Philonikas, scarcely able to credit this happy turn of fate, hastened to overtake the boy, who was making straight for the horse. Since he could not win, it was important he should not break his neck. It would be too much to hope that the King would settle up for him.

'My lord, you will find that – '

Alexander looked round and said, 'Go away.'

'But, my lord, when you come to – '

'Go away. Over there, down wind, where he can't see you or smell you. You've done enough.'

Philonikas looked into the paled and widened eyes. He went, in silence, exactly where he was told.

Alexander remembered, then, that he had not asked when the horse was first called Thunder, or if it had had another name. It had said plainly enough that Thunder was the word for tyranny and pain. It must have a new name, then. He walked round, keeping his shadow behind, looking at the horned blaze under the blowing forelock.

'Oxhead,' he said, falling into Macedonian, the speech of truth and love. 'Boukephalas, Boukephalas.'

The horse's ears went up. At the sound of this voice, the hated presence had lost power and been driven away. What now? It had lost all trust in men. It snorted, and pawed the ground in warning.

Ptolemy said, 'The King may be sorry he set him on to this.'

'He was born lucky,' said Philotas. 'Do you want to bet?'

Alexander said to the groom, 'I'll take him. You needn't wait.'

'Oh, no, sir! When you're mounted, my lord. My lord, they'll hold me accountable.'

'No, he's mine now. Just give me his head without jerking that bit ... I said, Give it me. *Now.*'

He took the reins, easing them at first only a little. The horse snorted, then turned and snuffed at him. The off forefoot raked restlessly. He took the reins in one hand, to run the other along the moist neck; then shifted his grip to the head-stall, so that the barbed bit no longer pressed at all. The horse only pulled forward a little. He said to the groom, 'Go that way. Don't cross the light.'

He pushed round the horse's head to face the bright spring sun. Their shadows fell out of sight behind them. The smell of its sweat and breath and leather bathed him in its steam.

'Boukephalas,' he said softly.

It strained forward, trying to drag him with it; he took in the rein a little. A horse-fly was on its muzzle; he ran his hand down, till his fingers felt the soft lip. Almost pleadingly now, the horse urged them both onward, as if saying, 'Come quickly away from here.'

'Yes, yes,' he said, stroking its neck. 'All in good time, when I say, we'll go. You and I don't run away.'

He had better take off his cloak; while he spared a hand for the pin, he talked on to keep the horse in mind of him. 'Remember who we are. Alexander and Boukephalas.'

The cloak fell behind him; he slid his arm over the horse's back. It must be near fourteen hands, a tall horse for Greece; he was used to thirteen. This one was as tall as Philotas' horse about which he talked so much. The black eye rolled round at him. 'Easy, easy, now. I'll tell you when.'

With the reins looped in his left hand he grasped the arch of the mane; with his right, its base between the shoulders. He could feel the horse gather itself together. He ran a few steps with it to gain momentum, then leaped, threw his right leg over; he was up.

The horse felt the light weight on its back, compact of certainty; the mercy of invincible hands, the forbearance of immovable will; a nature it knew and shared, transfigured to divinity. Men had not mastered it; but it would go with the god.

The crowd was silent at first. They were men who knew horses, and had more sense than to startle this one. In a breathing hush they waited for it to get its head, taking for granted the boy would be run away with, eager to applaud if he could only stick on and ride it to a standstill. But he had it in hand; it was waiting his sign to go. There was a hum of wonder; then, when they saw him lean forward and kick his heel with a shout, when boy and horse went racing down towards the water-meadows, the roar began. They vanished into the distance; only the rising clouds of wildfowl showed where they had gone.

They came back at last with the sun behind them, their shadow thrown clear before. Like the feet of a carved pharaoh treading his beaten enemies, the drumming hooves trampled the shadow triumphantly into the ground.

At the horse-field they slowed to a walk. The horse blew and shook its bridle. Alexander sat easy, in the pose which Xenophon commends: the legs straight down, gripping with the thigh, relaxed below the knee. He rode towards the stand; but a man stood waiting down in front of it. It was his father.

He swung off cavalry style, across the neck with his back to the horse; considered the best way in war, if the horse allowed it. The horse was remembering things learned before the tyranny. Philip put out both arms; Alexander came down into them. 'Look out we don't jerk his mouth, Father,' he said. 'It's sore.'

Philip pounded him on the back. He was weeping. Even his blind eye wept real tears. 'My son!' he said choking. There was wet in his harsh beard. 'Well done, my son, my son.'

Alexander returned his kiss. It seemed to him that this was a moment nothing could undo. 'Thank you, Father. Thank you for my horse. I shall call him Oxhead.'

The horse gave a sudden start. Philonikos was coming up, beaming and full of compliments. Alexander looked round, and motioned with his head. Philonikos withdrew. The buyer was never wrong.

A surging crowd had gathered. 'Will you tell them to keep off, Father? He won't stand people yet. I'll have to rub him down myself, or he'll catch a chill.'

He saw to the horse, keeping the best of the grooms beside him for it to know him another time. The crowd was still in the horse-field. All was quiet in the stable-yard when he came out, flushed from the ride and the work, tousled, smelling of horse. Only one loiterer was about; the tall boy Hephaistion, whose eyes had wished him victory. He smiled an acknowledgement. The boy smiled back, hesitated, and came nearer. There was a pause.

'Would you like to see him?'

'Yes, Alexander ... It was just as if he knew you. I felt it, like an omen. What is he called?'

'I'm calling him Oxhead.' They were speaking Greek.

'That's better than Thunder. He hated that.'

'You live near here, don't you?'

'Yes. I can show you. You can see from over here. Not that first hill there, the second, the one behind it – '

'You've been here before. I remember you. You helped me fix a sling once, no, it was a quiver. And your father hauled you off.'

'I didn't know who you were.'

'You showed me the hills before; I remembered then. And you were born in Lion Month, the same year as me.'

'Yes.'

'You're half a head taller. But your father's tall, isn't he?'

'Yes he is, and my uncles too.'

'Xenophon says you can tell a tall horse when it's foaled, by the length of leg. When we're men you'll still be taller.'

Hephaistion looked into the confident and candid eyes. He recalled his father saying that the King's young son might have more chance to make his growth, if that stone-faced tutor would not overwork and underfeed him. He should have been protected, some friend should have been there.

'You'll still be the one who can ride Boukephalas.'

'Come and look at him. Not too near just yet; I shall have to be here at first every time they groom him, I can see that.'

He found he had fallen into Macedonian. They looked at each other and smiled.

They had been talking some time, before he remembered he had meant to go straight up from the stable, just as he was, and bring the news to his mother. For the first time in his life, he had forgotten all about her.

A few days after, he made a sacrifice to Herakles.

The hero had been generous. He deserved something richer than a goat or a ram.

Olympias agreed. If her son thought nothing too good for Herakles, she thought nothing too good for her son. She had been writing letters to all her friends, and her kindred in Epiros, relating that Philip had tried again and again to mount the horse, and had been thrown with indignity before all the people; how it was as savage as a lion, but her son had tamed it. She opened her new bale of stuffs from Athens, inviting him to choose stuff for a new festal chiton. He chose plain, fine white wool, and, when she said it was too mean for so great a day, answered that it was proper for a man.

He brought his offering in a gold cup to the hero-shrine in the garden. His father and mother were present; it was a court occasion.

Having made the proper invocation to the hero, with his praises and his epithets, he thanked him for his gifts to mankind, and finished, 'As you have been to me, so remain; be favourable to me in what I shall henceforth undertake, according to my prayers.'

He tilted the cup. A translucent stream of incense, like grains of amber, shone in the sunlight, and fell on the glowing wood. A cloud of sweet blue smoke rose to heaven.

All the company, but one, pronounced Amen. Leonidas, who had come to watch because he thought it his duty, compressed his lips. He was leaving soon; another was taking up his charge. Though the boy had not yet been told, his good spirits were offensive. The Arabian gum was still showering from the chalice; the cost might run into scores of drachmas. This after his constant training in austerity, his warnings against excess!

Among the cheerful pieties, his voice said tartly, 'Be less wasteful of such precious things, Alexander, till you are master of the lands they grow in.'

Alexander turned from the altar, with the emptied cup in his hand. He looked at Leonidas with an alert kind of surprise, followed by grave attention. At length he said, 'Yes. I will remember.'

As he came down the steps from the shrine, his eyes met the waiting eyes of Hephaistion, who understood the nature of omens. There was no need for them to speak of it after.

5

'I know now who it will be. Father's had a letter, he sent for me this morning. I hope this man will be bearable. If not, we must make a plan.'

'You can count on me,' said Hephaistion, 'even if you want to drown him. You've put up with more than enough. Is he a real philosopher?'

They were sitting in the trough between two of the Palace gables; a private spot, since only Alexander had climbed there till he showed Hephaistion the route.

'Oh, yes, from the Academy. He was taught by Plato. You'll come to the lessons? Father says you can.'

'I'd only hold you back.'

'Sophists teach by disputation, he wants my friends. We can think later who else to have. It won't just be logic-chopping, he'll have to teach things

I can use, Father told him that. He wrote back that a man's education should be suited to his station and his duties. That doesn't tell us much.'

'At least this one can't beat you. He's an Athenian?'

'No, a Stagirite. He's the son of Nikomachos, who was my grandfather Amyntas' doctor. My father's too I suppose, when he was a child. You know how Amyntas lived, like a wolf in hunting-country, throwing out his enemies or trying to get back himself. Nikomachos must have been loyal, I don't know how good a doctor he was. Amyntas died in bed; that's very rare in our family.'

'So this son – what's he called – ?'

'Aristotle.'

'He knows the country, that's something. Is he very old?'

'About forty. Not old for a philosopher. They live for ever. Isokrates, who wants Father to lead the Greeks, is ninety-odd, and *he* applied for the job! Plato lived to over eighty. Father says Aristotle had hoped to be head of the School, but Plato had chosen a nephew of his. That's why Aristotle left Athens.'

'So then he asked to come here?'

'No, he left when we were nine. I know the year, because of the Chalkidian war. And he couldn't go home to Stagira, Father had just burned it and enslaved the people. What is it pulling my hair?'

'It's a stick from the tree we came up.' Hephaistion, who was not very neat-handed, unwound with anxious care the walnut-twig from its shining tangle, which smelt of some expensive wash used on it by Olympias, and of summer grass. This done, he slid his arm down to Alexander's waist. He had done it the first time almost by accident; though not rebuffed, he had waited two days before daring to try again. Now he watched his chance whenever they were alone; it had become a thing he thought about. He could not tell what Alexander thought, if he thought at all. He accepted it contentedly, and talked, with ever more ease and freedom, about other things.

'The Stagirites,' he said, 'were confederates of Olynthos; he made examples of those who wouldn't treat with him. Did your father tell you about the war?'

'What? . . . Oh yes. Yes, he did.'

'Listen, this is important. Aristotle went off to Assos, as Hermeias' guest-friend; they'd met at the Academy. He's tyrannos there. You know where Assos is; it's opposite Mytilene, it controls the straits. So, as soon as I thought, I saw why Father chose this man. This is only between us two.'

He looked deeply into Hephaistion's eyes, as always before a confidence. As always, Hephaistion felt as if his midriff were melting. As always, it was some moments before he could follow what he was being told.

'... who were in other cities and escaped the siege, have been begging Father to have Stagira restored and the citizens enfranchised. That's what this Aristotle wants. What Father wants is an alliance with Hermeias. It's a piece of horse-trading. Leonidas came for politics, too. Old Phoinix is the only one who came for *me*.'

Hephaistion tightened his arm. His feelings were confused; he wanted to grasp till Alexander's very bones were somehow engulfed within himself, but knew this to be wicked and mad; he would kill anyone who harmed a hair of his head.

'They don't know I've seen this. I just say "Yes, Father," I've not even told my mother. I want to make my own mind up when I've seen the man, and do what I think good without anyone knowing why. This is only between us two. My mother is entirely against philosophy.'

Hephaistion was thinking how fragile his rib-cage seemed, how terrible were the warring desires to cherish and to crush it. He continued silent.

'She says it makes men reason away the gods. She ought to know I would never deny the gods, whatever anyone told me. I know the gods exist, as surely as I know that you do ... I can't breathe.'

Hephaistion, who could have said the same, let go quickly. Presently he managed to reply, 'Perhaps the Queen will dismiss him.'

'Oh, no, I don't want that. That would only make trouble. I've been thinking, too, he may be the kind of man who'll answer questions. Ever since I knew a philosopher was coming, I've been writing them down, things nobody here can tell me. Thirty-five already, I counted yesterday.'

He had not withdrawn, but, backed to the sloping gable-roof, sat propped lightly against Hephaistion, trustful and warm. This, thought Hephaistion, was the true perfection of happiness; it ought to be; it must be. He said restlessly, 'I should like to kill Leonidas, do you know that?'

'Oh, I thought that once. But now, I think he was sent by Herakles. A man doing one good against his will, that shows the hand of a god. He wanted to keep me down, but he taught me to put up with hardship. I never need a fur cloak, I never eat after I'm full, or lie in bed in the morning. It would have come harder to start learning now, as I'd have had to do, without him. You can't ask your men to put up with things you can't bear yourself. And they'll all want to see if I'm softer than my father.'

His ribs and their muscle-layer had knit together; his side felt like armour. 'I wear better clothes, that's all. I like to do that.'

'You'll never wear this chiton again, I'm telling you. Look what you did in the tree, I can get my whole hand inside it ... Alexander. You won't ever go to war without me?'

Alexander sat up staring; Hephaistion was jolted into taking his hand away. 'Without *you*? What do you mean, how could you even think of it? You're my dearest friend.'

Hephaistion had known for many ages that if a god should offer him one gift in all his lifetime, he would choose this. Joy hit him like a lightning-bolt. 'Do you mean it?' he said. 'Do you really mean it?'

'Mean it?' said Alexander, in a voice of astonished outrage. 'Did you doubt I meant it? Do you think I tell everyone the things I've told to you? Mean it – what a thing to say!'

Only a month ago, Hephaistion thought, I should have been too scared to answer. 'Don't fight me. One always doubts great good fortune.'

Alexander's eyes relented. Raising his right hand, he said, 'I swear by Herakles.' He leaned and gave Hephaistion a practised kiss; that of a child who is affectionate by nature, and fond of grownup attention. Hephaistion had hardly time to feel the shock of delight before the light touch had gone. By the time he had nerved himself to return the kiss, Alexander's attention had been withdrawn. He seemed to be gazing at heaven.

'Look,' he said pointing. 'You see that Victory statue, on the top gable of all? I know how to get up there.'

From the terrace, the Victory looked as small as a child's clay doll. When the dizzy climb had brought them to its base, it turned out to be five feet tall. Its hand held a gilded laurel wreath, extended over the void.

Hephaistion, who had questioned nothing all the way because he had not dared think, clasped in his left arm, at Alexander's bidding, the bronze waist of the goddess. 'Now hold my wrist,' Alexander said.

Thus counterpoised, he leaned out, off balance, into empty space, and broke two leaves from the wreath. One came easily; the second he had to worry at. Hephaistion felt clammy sweat in his palms; the dread that it would make his grip slide off turned his belly to ice, and crept in his hair. Through this terror he was aware of the wrist he held. It had looked delicate, against his own big frame; it was hard, sinewy, the fist clenched on itself in a remote and solitary act of will. After a short eternity, Alexander was ready to be pulled back. He climbed down with the leaves in his teeth; when they were back on the roof, he gave one to Hephaistion, saying, 'Now do you know we shall go to war together?'

The leaf sat in Hephaistion's hand, about the size of a real one. Like a real one it was trembling; quickly he shut his fingers on it. He felt now the full horror of the climb, the tiny mosaic of great flagstones far below, his loneliness at the climax. He had gone up in a fierce resolve to face, if it killed him, whatever ordeal Alexander should set to test him. Only now, with the gilt-bronze edges biting his palm, he saw that the test had not been for him. He was the witness. He had been taken up there to hold in his hand the life of Alexander, who had been asked if he meant what he had said. It was his pledge of friendship.

As they climbed down through the tall walnut-tree, Hephaistion called to mind the tale of Semele, beloved of Zeus. He had come in a human shape, but that was not enough for her; she had demanded the embrace of his divine epiphany. It had been too much, she had burned to ashes. He would need to prepare himself for the touch of fire.

It was some weeks before the philosopher arrived; but his presence came before him.

Hephaistion had underrated him. He not only knew the country, but the court, and his knowledge was up-to-date; he had family guest-ties at Pella, and many travelled friends. The King, well aware of this, had written offering to provide, if it seemed of use, a precinct where the Prince and his friends could study undisturbed.

The philosopher read, approvingly, between the lines. The boy was to be taken from his mother's claws; in return, the father too would let well alone. It was more than he had dared hope; he wrote back promptly, suggesting the Prince and his fellow-students be lodged at some distance from the court's distractions, and adding, as an afterthought, a recommendation of pure upland air. There were no sizeable hills within miles of Pella.

On the footslopes of Mount Bermion, west of the Pella plain, was a good house which had gone downhill in the wars. Philip bought it, and put it in order. It was more than twenty miles out; it would do very well. He added a wing and a gymnasium; and, since the philosopher had asked for somewhere to walk about, had a garden cleared; nothing formal, a pretty editing of nature, what the Persians called a 'paradise'. It was said that the legendary pleasance of King Midas had been thereabouts. Everything flourished there.

These orders given, he sent for his son; his wife would hear of them from her spies within the hour, and somehow twist their meaning to the boy.

In the talk which followed, much more was exchanged than was said in words. This was the self-evident training of a royal heir. Alexander saw his father took it as a matter of course. Had all the rebuffs, ambiguous double-edged words, been more than sparring in the endless war with his mother? Had all the words really been said? Once he had believed she would never lie to him; but he had known for some time that this was vanity.

'In the next few days,' said Philip, 'I'd like to know which friends of your own you want to spend your time with. Think it over.'

'Thank you, Father.' He remembered the hours of tortuous stifling talk in the women's rooms, the reading of gossip and rumour, the counter-intrigues, the broodings and guessings over a word or look; cries, tears, declarations before the gods of outrage; smells of incense and magic herbs and burning meat; the whispered confidences that kept him awake at night, so that next day he was slower in the race or missed his aim.

'Those you go about with now,' his father was saying, 'if their fathers agree, will all be quite acceptable. Ptolemy, I suppose?'

'Yes, Ptolemy of course. And Hephaistion. I asked you about him before.'

'I remember. Hephaistion by all means.' He was at pains to sound easy; he had no wish to disturb a state of things which had taken a load off his mind. The erotic patterns of Thebes were engraved on it; a youth and a man, to whom the youth looked for example. Things being as it began to seem they were, there was no one he wished to see in this place of power. Even Ptolemy, brotherly and a man for women, had been throwing too long a shadow. What with the boy's startling beauty, and his taste for grownup friends, he had been an anxiety for some time. It was of a piece with his oddness, suddenly to throw himself into the arms of a boy his own age almost to a day. They had been inseparable now for weeks; Alexander, it was true, was giving nothing away, but the other could be read like an open book. However; here there was no doubt at all who looked for example to whom. An affair, then, not to be interfered with.

There was trouble enough outside the kingdom. The Illyrians had had to be thrown back last year on the west border; it had cost him, as well as much grief, trouble and scandal, a sword-slash on the knee from which he was still limping.

In Thessaly, all was well; he had put down a dozen local tyrannies, made peace in a score of blood-feuds, and everyone, except a tyrant or two, was grateful. But he had failed with Athens. Even after the Pythian Games when, because he was presiding, they had refused to send competitors, he had still not given them up. His agents all said that the people could be reasoned with, if the orators would let them be. Their first concern was that the public dole should not be cut; no policy was ever passed if it threatened that, not even for home defence. Philokrates had been indicted for treason, and got away just ahead of a death-sentence, to enjoy a generous pension; Philip rested his best hopes now on men never for sale, who yet favoured the alliance because they thought it best. They had seen for themselves that, his first aim being the conquest of Asian Greece, the last thing he wanted was a costly war with Athens in which, win or lose, he must stand as Hellas' enemy, for no better reward than to secure his back.

He had sent therefore this spring another embassy, offering to revise the peace treaty, if reasonable amendments were put up. An Athenian envoy had been sent back, an old friend of Demosthenes, a certain Helgesippos known to his fellow-citizens as Tufty, from his effeminate topknot of long curls tied in a ribbon. At Pella it became clear why he had been chosen; to unacceptable terms he added, on his own account, uncompromising rudeness. No risk had been taken of Philip winning him over; he was the man who had arranged Athens' alliance with the Phokians, his mere presence was an affront. He came and went; and Philip, who had not yet enforced the Phokians' yearly fine to the plundered temple, gave them notice to start paying up.

Now there was a war of succession boiling up in Epiros, where the King had lately died. He had been scarcely more than one chieftain among many; soon there would be chaos, unless a hegemon could be set up. Philip meant to do so, for the good of Macedon. For once he had his wife's blessing on his work, since he had chosen her brother Alexandros. He would see where his interest lay and be a curb on her intrigues; he was eager for support and should be a useful ally, Philip thought. It was a pity that, the affair being so urgent, he could not stay to welcome the philosopher. Before he limped out to his war-horse, he sent for his son and told him this. He said no more; he had been using his eyes, and had been many years a diplomat.

'He will be here,' said Olympias ten days later, 'about noon tomorrow. So remember to be at home.'

Alexander was standing by the little loom on which his sister was learning fancy border-work. She had newly mastered the egg-and-dart pattern and was anxious to be admired for it; they were friends just now and he was generous with applause. But now he looked round, like a horse when it pricks its ear.

'I shall receive him,' said Olympias, 'in the Perseus room.'

'I shall receive him, Mother.'

'Of course you must be there, I said so.'

Alexander walked away from the loom. Kleopatra, forgotten, stood with the shuttle in her hand, and looked from face to face with a familiar dread.

Her brother patted his sword-belt of polished chestnut leather. 'No, Mother, it's for me to do it, now that Father's away. I shall make his apologies, and present Leonidas and Phoinix. Then I shall bring Aristotle up here, and present him to you.'

Olympias stood up from her chair. He had grown faster lately; she was not so much the taller as she had thought. 'Are you saying to me, Alexander,' she said in a swelling voice, 'that you do not want me there?'

There was a short, unbelievable silence.

'It's for little boys, to be presented by their mothers. It's no way to come to a sophist, when one is grown-up. I'm nearly fourteen, now, I shall start with this man in the way I mean to go on.'

Her chin rose, her back stiffened. 'Did your father tell you this?'

The moment found him unprepared, but he knew it for what it was. 'No,' he said. 'I didn't need Father to tell me I'm a man. It was I who told him.'

There was a flush on her cheekbones; her red hair seemed to rise by itself from its central peak. Her grey eyes had widened. He gazed transfixed, thinking no other eyes in the world could look so dangerous. No one had yet told him otherwise.

'So, you are a man! And I, your mother, who bore you, nursed you, suckled you, who fought for your rights when the King would have thrown you off like a stray dog to set up his bastard – ' She had fixed him with the stare of a woman who drives home a spell. He did not question her; that she willed his hurt was truth sufficient. Word followed word like a flight of burning arrows. 'I who have lived for you each day of my life since you were conceived, oh, long before you saw the light of the sun; who have gone through fire and darkness for you and into the houses of the dead – ! Now you plot with him to beat me down like a peasant wife. Now I can believe that you are his son!'

He stood silent. Kleopatra dropped her shuttle and cried urgently, 'Father's a wicked man. I don't love him, I love Mother best.' Neither of them looked at her. She started to cry, but no one heard.

'The time will come when you look back upon this day.' Indeed, he thought, it would not soon be forgotten. 'Well? Have you no answer for me?'

'I am sorry, Mother.' His voice had been breaking for some time; it betrayed him, cracking upward. 'I have done my tests of manhood. Now I must live like a man.'

For the first time, she laughed at him as he had heard her laugh at his father. 'Your tests of manhood! You silly child. Come and tell me that when you have lain with a woman.'

A shocked pause fell between them. Kleopatra, unheeded, ran outside. Olympias flung herself back into her chair, and burst into a storm of tears.

He went up presently, as so often before, and stroked her hair. She wept on his breast, murmuring of the cruelties she suffered, crying that she would no longer wish to see the light of day if he turned against her. He said that he loved her, that she knew it well enough. Much time passed in such words. In the end, he hardly knew how, it was decided he should receive the sophist himself, with Leonidas and Phoinix; and a little after, he went away. He felt neither defeated nor victorious, merely drained.

At the stair-foot Hephaistion was waiting. He happened to be there, as he happened to have a ball handy if Alexander wanted a game, or water if he was thirsty; not by calculation, but in a constant awareness by which no smallest trifle was missed. Now, when he came down the stairs with a shut mouth and blue lines under his eyes, Hephaistion received some mute signal he understood, and fell into step beside him. They went up along the path which wandered into the wood; in an open glade was an old fallen oak-bole with orange fungus and a lace of ivy. Hephaistion sat down with his back to it. Alexander, in a silence unbroken since setting out, came and settled into his arm. After a while he sighed; no other word was spoken for some time.

'They claim to love you,' he said at length. 'And they eat you raw.'

Words made Hephaistion anxious; it had been simpler and safer to do without. 'It's that children belong to them, but men have to go away. That's what my mother says. She says she wants me to be a man, and yet she doesn't.'

'Mine does. Whatever she likes to say.' He edged himself closer; like an animal, Hephaistion thought, which is reassured by handling. It was nothing more for him. No matter, whatever he needed he must have. The place was solitary, but he spoke softly as if the birds were spies. 'She needs a man to stand up for her. You know why.'

'Yes.'

'She's always known I shall do that. But I saw today, she thinks when my time comes I shall let her reign for me. We didn't speak of it. But she knows that I told her no.'

Hephaistion's back prickled with danger, but his heart was full of pride. He had never hoped to be called in alliance against this mighty rival. He expressed his allegiance, but without risking words.

'She cried. I made her cry.'

He was still looking quite pale. Words must be found. 'She cried too when you were born. But it had to be. So has this.'

There was a long pause; then, 'You know that other thing I told you?'

Hephaistion assented. They had not spoken of it since.

'She promised to tell me everything one day. Sometimes she says one thing, sometimes another ... I dreamed I caught a sacred snake and I was trying to make it speak to me, but it kept escaping and turning away.'

Hephaistion said, 'Perhaps it wanted you to follow it.'

'No, it had a secret, but it wouldn't speak ... She hates my father. I think I'm the only one she ever truly loved. She wants me all hers, none of me his. Sometimes I've wondered ... is that *all*?'

In the sun-steeped wood, Hephaistion felt a fine tremor running through him. Anything he needed, he must have. 'The gods will reveal it. They revealed it to all the heroes. But your mother ... in any case ... *she* would be mortal.'

'Yes, that's true.' He paused, turning it over. 'Once when I was by myself on Mount Olympos, I had a sign. I vowed to keep it for ever between me and the god.' He made a little movement, asking to be released, and stretched his whole frame in a long shuddering sigh. 'Sometimes I forget all this for months on end. Sometimes I think of it day and night. Sometimes I think, unless I find out the truth of it, I shall go mad.'

'That's stupid. You've got me now. Do you think I'd let you go mad?'

'I can talk to you. As long as you're there ...'

'I promise you before God, I'll be there as long as I'm alive.'

They looked up together into the tall clouds, whose scarcely visible drift was like stillness in the sky of the long summer day.

Aristotle, son of Nikomachos the physician of the line of the Asklepiads, gazed round him as the ship rowed into harbour, trying to recall the scenes of boyhood. It was a long time; everything looked strange. He had had a quick smooth voyage from Mytilene, sole passenger in a fast war-galley sent to fetch him. It was no surprise, therefore, to see a mounted escort waiting on the wharf.

He hoped to find its leader helpful. He was well-informed already, but no knowledge was ever trivial; truth was the sum of all its parts.

A gull swooped over the ship. With the reflex of many years' self-training, he noted its species, the angle of its flight, its wing-spread, its droppings, the food it dived for. The lines of the vessel's bow-wave had changed with its lessening speed; a mathematical ratio formed in his mind, he stored it where he would find it again when he had time. He never needed to carry tablets and stylos with him.

Through the cluster of small craft, he could not see the escort clearly. The King would have sent someone responsible. He prepared his questions; those of a man formed by his era, when philosophy and politics were totally engaged, when no man of intellect could conceive for his thought a higher value than that of being physician to Hellas' sickness. Barbarians, by definition, were hopeless cases; as well try to make a hunchback straight. Hellas must be healed to guide the world.

Two generations had seen each decent form of government decay into its own perversion: aristocracy into oligarchy, democracy to demagogy, kinship to tyranny. With mathematical progression, according to the number who shared the evil, the dead-weight against reform increased. To change a tyranny had lately been proved impossible. To change an oligarchy called for power and ruthlessness, destructive to the soul. To change a demagogy, one must become a demagogue and destroy one's mind as well. But to reform a monarchy, one need only mould one man. The chance to be a king-shaper, the prize every philosopher prayed for, had fallen to him.

Plato had risked death for it in Syracuse, once with the tyrant father, again with the trivial son. He had thrown away half his last harvest-time, sooner than refuse the challenge he himself had first defined. It was the aristocrat and soldier in him; or maybe the dreamer. Far better have collected reliable data first, and saved the journey ... Yet even this crisp thought evoked that formidable brooding presence; the old unease, the sense of something eluding the tools of measurement, defeating category and system, came hauntingly back with the summer scents of the Academy garden.

Well, in Syracuse he had failed. Maybe for want of good stuff to work on; but his failure had resounded through all Greece. And before the end, his mind must have been failing too, to bequeath the School to Speusippos, that barren metaphysician. At all events, Speusippos had been eager to give up even that, and come to Pella. The King cooperative, the boy intelligent and strong-willed, without known vices, the heir to yearly-increasing power; no wonder that Speusippos had been tempted, after the squalors and miseries of Syracuse. But Speusippos had been turned down. Demosthenes and his faction had achieved this if nothing else, that no one from Athens had stood a moment's chance.

For himself, when friends had praised his courage in braving the backward and violent northland, he had brushed it aside with his astringent smile. His roots were here; in the air of these mountains he had known childhood happiness, tasting their beauty while his elders' minds were clenched in the cares of war. As for violence, he was no innocent, having lived in the shadow of Persian power. If there he had succeeded in making of a man with so dark a past a friend and a philosopher, he need hardly fear failure with an unformed boy.

As the galley threaded the shipping, backing oars to let through a troop-trireme, he thought with affection of the hillside palace at Assos, looking out to the wooded mountains of Lesbos and the straight he had crossed so often; the terrace with its burning cresset on summer nights; debate or thoughtful silence, or a book read together. Hermeias read well, his high voice was musical and expressive, never shrill. Its epicene pitch did not reflect his mind; as a boy he had been gelded to prolong the beauty his master prized; he had been through the depths, before he made himself ruler, but like a smothered sapling he had grown through to the light. He had been persuaded to visit the Academy, and from there he had never fallen back.

He had adopted a niece, being condemned to childlessness. For their friendship's sake, Aristotle had married her; the fact that she adored him had come as a surprise. He was glad to have shown gratitude, for she was lately dead; a thin dark studious girl, who had held his hand, gazed at him dimly with near-sighted eyes already beginning to wander, and begged that her ashes and his might share one urn. He had vowed it to her, and added of his own accord that he would never take another wife. He had brought the urn with him, in case he should die in Macedon.

There would of course be women. He took some pride, not improper, he thought, to a philosopher, in his own healthy normality. Plato, in his opinion, had committed too much to love.

The galley was docking, turning in with the suddenness of such manoeuvres in crowded harbours. Ropes were flung and hitched, the gangplank clattered. The escort stood dismounted, five or six men. He turned to his two servants to make sure of all his baggage. Some stir among the seamen made him look up. At the top of the gangplank stood a boy gazing about. His hands were poised on the man's sword-belt round his waist, his bright heavy hair was ruffled in the offshore breeze. He looked as alert as a young hunting-dog. As their eyes met he jumped down, not waiting for the sailor who ran to help, landing so lightly that it did not check his pace.

'Are you Aristotle the philosopher? May you live happy. I am Alexander son of Philip. Be welcome to Macedon.'

They exchanged the formal courtesies, taking stock of one another.

Alexander had planned his expedition at short notice, adjusting his strategy to events.

Instinct had made him watchful. His mother was taking it too well. He had known her agree with his father on this or that, only to cover her next move. Going to her room in her absence, he had seen a state gown laid out. A new battle would be bloodier than the last, and still indecisive. He had bethought him of the admirable Xenophon, who, when cornered in Persia, had decided to steal a march.

It must be done correctly, not turned into an escapade. He had gone to Antipatros, his father's Regent in Macedon, and asked him to come too. He was a King's man of unshaken loyalty; he read the lie of the land with satisfaction, which he was not fool enough to show. He was here now on the quay; the reception was an official one; and here was the philosopher.

He was a lean smallish man, not ill-proportioned, who yet gave at first sight the effect of being all head. His whole person was commanded by his wide bulging brow, a vessel stretched by its contents. Small piercing eyes were busy recording, without prejudgement or error, just what they saw. The mouth was closed in a line precise as a definition. He had a short neat beard; his thinning hair looked as if its roots had been forced apart by the growth of the massive brain.

A second glance revealed him to be dressed with some care and with the elegance of Ionia, wearing one or two good rings. Athenians thought him rather foppish; in Macedon, he looked tasteful and free from harsh austerity. Alexander offered him a hand to mount the gangplank, and tried the effect of a smile. When the man returned it, it could be seen that smiling was what he would do best; he would not often be caught with his head back laughing. But he did look like a man who would answer questions.

Beauty, thought the philosopher; the gift of god. And it moved with mind; in that house there was someone living. This enterprise was no such forlorn hope as poor Plato's trips to Syracuse. He must take care that Speusippos had the news.

Presentations went forward, the Prince performing them with address. A groom led up a mount for the philosopher, offering a leg-up, Persian style. This seen to, the boy turned round; a taller boy moved forward, his hand on the head-stall of a magnificent black charger with a white blaze. All through the formalities, Aristotle had been aware of the creature fretting; he was surprised therefore to see the youth release it. It trotted straight to the Prince, and muzzled the air behind his ear. He stroked it, murmuring something. With neatness and dignity, the horse sank its crupper on its haunches, waited while he mounted, and at his finger-touch straightened up. There was a moment in which the boy and the beast seemed like initiates who have exchanged in secret a word of power.

The philosopher swept aside this fantasy. Nature had no mysteries, only facts not yet correctly observed and analysed. Proceed from this sound first principle, and one would never miss one's way.

The spring of Mieza was sacred to the Nymphs. Its waters had been led into an old stone fountain-house, where they tinkled hollowly; but the ferny pool below had been carved by the falling stream itself, swirling between the rocks. Its brown surface caught the sun; it was a pleasant place to bathe in.

Runnels and conduits threaded about the gardens, glittering streamlets sprang out in jets, or tumbled in little falls. Bay and myrtle and rowan grew there; in rough grass beyond the tended orchard, old gnarled apple-trees and crabs still bloomed in spring. Fine green turf had been laid where the scrub had been cleared away; from the pink-washed house, paths and rough steps meandered, circling some rock with its small wiry mountain flowers, or crossing a wooden bridge, or widening round a stone seat with a view. In summer, the woods beyond were a tangle of huge wild roses, the gift of the Nymphs to Midas; the night dews were full of their briery scent.

The boys would ride out at cocklight, to go hunting before the day's school began. They would set up their nets in the coverts, and get their buck or their hare. Under the trees the smells were dank and mossy; on the open slopes, spicy with crushed herbs. At sun-up there would be smells of wood-smoke and roasting meat, horse-sweat on leather, dog-smells as the hounds came coaxing up for scraps. But if the quarry was rare or strange, they would go fasting home and save it for dissection. Aristotle had learned this skill from his father; it was the Asklepiad heritage. Even insects, they found, he did not disdain. Most of what they brought in he knew already; but now and then he would say sharply, 'What's this, what's this?' then get out his notes with their fine pen-drawings, and be in good humour for the day.

Alexander and Hephaistion were the youngest boys. The philosopher had made it clear that he wanted no children under his feet, however great their fathers. Many youths and older boys who had been friends of the Prince's childhood were now grown men. None of those chosen refused the invitation to join the School. It established them as Companions of the Prince, a privilege which might lead anywhere.

Antipatros, after waiting some time in vain, put forward to the King the claims of his son Kassandros. Alexander, to whom Philip had given this news before he left, had not taken it well. 'I don't like him, Father. And he doesn't like me, so why does he want to come?'

'Why do you suppose? Philotas is going.'

'Philotas is one of my friends.'

'Yes, I said your friends should go, and as you know I have not refused one of them. But I did not promise to let in no one else. How can I admit Parmenion's son, and reject Antipatros'? If you're on bad terms, now's the time to mend it. It will be of use to me. And it is an art that kings must learn.'

Kassandros was a youth with bright-red hair, and a bluish-white skin patched with dark freckles; thickly built, and fond of exacting servility from anyone he could frighten. He thought Alexander an insufferable young show-off, spoiling for a good set-down, but protected by his rank and the ring of toadies it brought him.

Kassandros had not wanted to go to Mieza. Not long before, he had been beaten up by Philotas, to whom he had said something ill-advised, unaware that Philotas' chief concern just then was to get accepted in Alexander's set. No exploit of Philotas' was likely to lose in the telling. Kassandros found himself cut by Ptolemy and Harpalos; Hephaistion looked at him like a leashed dog at a cat; Alexander ignored him, but was charming in his presence to anyone he was known to dislike. Had they ever been friends it could have been righted; Alexander was fond of reconciliations, and, to refuse one, had to be very angry indeed. As it was, casual dislike had become hostility. Kassandros would see them all rot, before he came fawning to that vain little whelp, who, in the proper course of nature, ought to be learning a wholesome respect for him.

He had pleaded in vain to his father that he could not learn philosophy; that it was known to turn men's brains; that he wanted only to be a soldier. He dared not confess that he was disliked by Alexander and his friends; he would have had a belting for letting it happen. Antipatros valued his own career and was ambitious for his son's. As it was, he fixed Kassandros with a fierce blue eye, whose bristling brows had once been as red as his, and said, 'Behave yourself there. And be careful with Alexander.'

Kassandros said dismissively, 'He's only a little boy.'

'Don't make yourself out a bigger fool than you were born. Four or five years between you, it's nothing once you're men. Now pay heed to what I tell you. That boy has his father's wits about him; and if he doesn't turn out as bad to cross as his mother, then I'm an Ethiop. Don't cross him. The sophist is paid to do it. You I'm sending to improve yourself, not to make enemies. If you stir up brawls there, I'll tan your hide.'

So Kassandros went to Mieza, where he was homesick, bored, lonely and resentful. Alexander was civil to him, because his father had said it was the art of kings, and because he had more serious things to think about.

The philosopher had turned out not only willing, but eager to answer questions. Unlike Timanthes, he would do this first, and only afterwards explain the value of system. The exposition, however, when it came was always rigorous. He was a man who hated loose ends and cloudy edges.

Mieza faced east; the tall rooms with their faded frescoes were sun-drenched all morning, and cool from noontime on. They worked indoors when they needed to write or draw or study specimens; when they discoursed or were lectured to, they walked the gardens. They talked of ethics and politics, the nature of pleasure and of justice; of the soul, virtue, friendship and love. They considered the causes of things. Everything must be traced to its cause; and there could be no science without demonstration.

Soon a whole room was full of specimens: pressed flowers and plants, seedlings in pots; birds' eggs with their embryos preserved in clear honey; decoctions of medicinal herbs. Aristotle's trained slave worked there all day. At night they observed the heavens; the stars were stuff more divine than any other thing man's eye could reach, a fifth element not to be found on earth. They noted winds and mists and the aspect of the clouds, and learned to prognosticate storms. They reflected light from polished bronze, and measured the angles of refraction.

For Hephaistion, it was a new life. Alexander was his own in the sight of everyone. His place was recognized even by the philosopher.

The school discussed friendship often. It is, they learned, one of the things man can least afford to lack; necessary to the good life, and beautiful in itself. Between friends is no need of justice, for neither wrong nor inequality can exist. He described the degrees of friendship, up from the self-seeking to the pure, when good is willed to the friend for the friend's own sake. Friendship is perfect when virtuous men love the good in one another; for virtue gives more delight than beauty, and is untouched by time.

He went on to value friendship far above the shifting sands of Eros. One or two of the young men argued this. Hephaistion, who was not very quick at shaping his thoughts into words, usually found that someone else got in before him. He preferred this to making a fool of himself. Kassandros, for one thing, would count it as a score against Alexander.

Hephaistion was quickly growing possessive. Everything led him that way: his nature, the integrity of his love and his own sense of it; the tenet of the philosopher that for each man there was only one perfect friend; the certainty of his unspoiled instincts that Alexander's loyalty matched his own; and their acknowledged status. Aristotle was a man to proceed from facts. He had seen at once the attachment already fixed for good or ill; one of real affection, not of incontinence or flattery. It should not be opposed, but moulded in its innocence. (Had some wise man only done as much for the father . . .!) When therefore he spoke of friendship, he let his eyes fall kindly on the two handsome boys unfailingly side by side. In the stolen intimacies of Pella, Hephaistion had only had eyes for Alexander; now he saw refracted, as clearly as in the optics class, the fact that they made a very goodlooking pair.

There was nothing to do with Alexander of which he was not proud; this included his rank, for he could not be imagined without it. Had he lost it, Hephaistion would have followed him to exile, prison or death; this knowledge gave self-respect to his pride. He was never jealous over Alexander, since he never doubted him; but he was jealous of his own standing, and liked to have it recognized.

Kassandros at least was well aware of it. Hephaistion, who had eyes for him in the back of his head, knew that though Kassandros wanted neither of them, he hated in both their closeness, their trust, their beauty. He hated Alexander because with Antipatros' soldiers he came before Antipatros' son; because he had won his belt at twelve, because Oxhead sat down for him. Hephaistion he hated for not being after Alexander in hope of gain.

All this Hephaistion knew, and mirrored back his deadly knowledge to Kassandros, whose self-esteem craved assurance that he hated Alexander for his faults alone.

Most hateful of all was his going to Aristotle for private lessons in statecraft. Indeed, Hephaistion offered Kassandros' envy to cheer Alexander up, when he complained that he found the lessons boring.

'I thought they'd be the best. He knows Ionia and Athens and Chalkidike, and even Persia a little. I want to know what men are like there, their customs, how they behave. What *he* wants, is to fit me out with answers beforehand to everything. What would I do if this happened, or that? I'd see when it happened, I said; happenings are made by men, one would need to know them. He thought I was being obstinate.'

'The King might let you drop it?'

'No. I've a right to it. Besides, disagreeing makes one think. I know what's wrong. He thinks it's an inexact science, but still a kind of science. Put a ram to a ewe and you get a lamb each time, even if not identical; heat snow and it melts. That's science. Your demonstrations should be repeatable. Well, say in war, now; even if one could repeat all other conditions, which is impossible, one could still not repeat surprise. Nor the weather. Nor the mood the men are in. Armies and cities, they're all made up of men. Being a king . . . being a king is like music.'

He paused, and frowned. Hephaistion said, 'Has he been asking you again to play?'

'"With mere listening, half the ethical effect is lost."'

'When he's not as wise as a god, he's as silly as some old henwife.'

'I told him I'd learned the ethical effect by an experiment, but it was not repeatable. I suppose he took the hint.'

The matter was indeed never raised again. Ptolemy, who did not deal in hints, had taken the philosopher aside and explained the facts.

The young man had borne without rancour the rise of Hephaistion's star. Had the new friend been adult, a clash would have been certain; but Ptolemy's fraternal role remained untrespassed on. Though still unmarried, he was several times a father, with a sense of duty to his scattered offspring; into this feeling, his friendship for Alexander began to merge. The world of passionate adolescent friendship was unknown country to him; he had been entranced by girls since puberty. He had lost nothing to Hephaistion; except that he no longer came first of all. This being not the least of human losses, he was inclined not to take Hephaistion more seriously than he had to. No doubt they would soon grow out of it. But meantime, Alexander should get the boy to be less quarrelsome. One could see the two of them never fell out, one soul in two bodies as the sophist put it; but Hephaistion on his own could be pugnaciously assertive.

There was just then some excuse for this. Mieza, sanctuary of the Nymphs, was a shelter too from the court with its turmoil of news, events, intrigues. They lived with ideas, and with one another. Their minds were ripening, a growth they were daily urged to hasten; less was said about the fact that their bodies were ripening too. At Pella, Hephaistion had lived in a cloud of vague, inchoate longings. They had become desires, and no longer vague.

True friends share everything; but Hephaistion's life was filling with concealments. It was Alexander's nature to love the proofs of love, even when he was sure of it; in this spirit he welcomed and returned his friend's caresses. Hephaistion had never dared do anything which would tell him more.

When one so quick-minded was so slow to understand, he must lack the will. When he delighted in giving, what he did not offer he might not possess. If then the knowledge were forced home to him, one would have made him fail. His heart might forgive it; his soul would never forget.

And yet, thought Hephaistion, sometimes one could swear ... But it was no time to trouble him, he had trouble enough.

Every day they had formal logic. The King had forbidden, and the philosopher did not want, the quibbling logomachy of eristics, that science which Sokrates had defined as making the worse cause look the better. But the mind must be trained to detect a fallacy, a begged question, false analogy or undistributed middle; all science hung on knowing when two propositions excluded one another. Alexander had picked up logic quickly. Hephaistion kept his misgivings to himself. He alone knew the secret of impossible alternatives, avoided by half-believing two things at once. At night, for they shared a room, he would look across to his bed and see him open-eyed in the moonlight, confronted by the syllogism of his own being.

For Alexander, their sanctuary was not inviolate. Half a dozen times a month would come his mother's courier, with a gift of sweet figs, a riding-hat or a pair of worked sandals (the last pair too small, for his growth was quickening); and a thick letter, thread-bound and sealed.

Hephaistion knew what the letters contained. He read them. Alexander said that true friends share everything. He did not try to hide that he needed to share his trouble. Sitting on the edge of his bed, or in one of the garden arbours, with an arm around him to read over his shoulder, Hephaistion would be scared by his own anger, and shut his teeth on his tongue.

The letters were full of secrets, detraction and intrigue. If Alexander wanted news of his father's wars, he had to question the courier. Anti-patros had been left again as Regent, while Philip campaigned in the Chersonese; Olympias thought she herself should have been governing, with the general as garrison commander. He could do nothing right for her; he was Philip's creature; he was plotting against her, and against Alexander's succession. She always ordered the courier to await his answer; and he would do no more work that day. If he seemed lukewarm against Antipatros, a letter full of reproaches would come back; had he supported her accusations, he knew her not above showing Antipatros his letter, to score in their next quarrel. In time came the inevitable day when news reached her that the King had a new girl.

This letter was terrible. Hephaistion was amazed, even dismayed, that Alexander should let him read it. Half-way through he drew back; but Alexander reached for him and said, 'Go on.' He was like someone with a recurring illness, who feels the familiar grip of the pain. At the end he said, 'I must go to her.'

He had grown chilly to the touch. Hephaistion said, 'But what can you do?'

'Only be there. I'll come back tomorrow, or the day after.'

'I'll go with you.'

'No, you'd be angry, we might quarrel. It's enough without that.'

The philosopher, when told that the Queen was sick and her son must visit her, was nearly as angry as Hephaistion, but did not say so. The boy did not look like a truant going off to a party; nor did he come back looking as if he had had one. That night he woke Hephaistion by shouting 'No!' in his sleep. Hephaistion went over and got in with him; Alexander grasped his throat with savage strength, then opened his eyes, embraced him with a sigh of relief that was like a groan, and fell asleep again. Hephaistion lay awake beside him, and just before daybreak returned to his own cold bed. In the morning, Alexander remembered nothing of it.

Aristotle too, in his way, attempted consolation, making next day a special effort to draw back his charge into the pure air of philosophy. Grouped round a stone bench with a view of clouds and distances, they discussed the nature of the outstanding man. Is self-regard a flaw in him? Certainly yes, in respect of common greeds and pleasures. But then, what self should be regarded? Not the body nor its passions, but the intellectual soul, whose office it is to rule the rest like a king. To love *that* self, to be covetous of honour for it, to indulge its appetite for virtue and noble deeds; to prefer an hour of glory closed by death, to a slothful life; to reach for the lion's share of moral dignity: there lies the fulfilling self-regard. The old saws are wrong, said the philosopher, which tell man to be forever humble before his own mortality. Rather he should strain his being to put on immortality, never to fall below the highest thing he knows.

On a grey boulder before a laurel-bush, his eyes upon the skyline, Alexander sat with his hands clasping his knees. Hephaistion watched him, to see if his soul was being calmed. But he seemed more like one of those young eagles which, they had read, were trained by their parents to stare into the noonday sun. If they blinked, the books said, they were thrown out of the nest.

Afterwards Hephaistion took him away to read Homer, having more faith in this remedy.

They now had a new book for it. Phoinix's gift had been copied some generations back, by an untalented scribe from a corrupt text. Asked about one unclear passage, Aristotle had compressed his lips over the whole, had sent to Athens for a good recension, and gone over it himself for errors. Not only did it contain some lines the old book had dropped out, but it now scanned everywhere and made sense. Here and there it had also been edited for moral tone; a footnote explained that when Achilles called 'Lively!' for the wine, he wanted it soon, not strong. The pupil was keen and grateful; but to the teacher, this time, the causes of things were not revealed. He had been concerned to make an archaic poem edifying; Alexander, that a sacred scripture should be infallible.

The philosopher felt less easy when, at one of the feasts, they rode into town and went to the theatre. To his regret it was Aischylos' *Myrmidons*, which showed Achilles and his Patroklos as more (or in his own view less) than perfect friends. In the midst of his critical concerns, when the news of Patroklos' death had reached Achilles, he became aware that Alexander was sitting trance-bound, tears streaming from his wide-open eyes, and that Hephaistion was holding his hand. A reproving stare made Hephaistion let go, red to the ears; Alexander was unreachable. At the end they vanished; he ran them down backstage, with the actor who had played Achilles. He was unable to stop the Prince from actually embracing this person, and giving him a costly arm-ring he had on, which the Queen was sure to inquire for. It was most unsuitable. All next day's work was devoted to mathematics, as a healthy antidote.

No one had informed him that his school, when not required to discuss law, rhetoric, science or the good life, was busy debating whether those two did anything, or not. Hephaistion knew it well, having lately thrashed someone for asking him outright, because there was a bet on it. Was it possible for Alexander not to know? If he did, why did he never speak of it? Was it loyalty to their friendship, lest anyone should think it incomplete? Did he, even, think they were lovers already, as he understood it himself? Sometimes in the night Hephaistion wondered if he was a fool and coward, not to try his luck. But the oracle of instinct signed against it. They were being daily told that all things were open to reason; he knew better. Whatever it was that he was waiting for – a birth, a healing, the intervention of a god – he would have to wait, if he waited for ever. Only with what he had, he was rich beyond his dreams; if, reaching for more, he lost it, he would as soon be dead.

In the month of the Lion, when the first of the grapes were harvested, they had their birthdays and turned fifteen. In the week of the first frosts the courier brought a letter, not from the Queen but from the King. He greeted his son; expected he would like a change from sitting down with the philosophers; and invited him to visit his headquarters. It was none too soon, since he was forward in such matters, for him to see the face of war.

Their road led by the shore, skirting the mountains when marsh or river-mouth drove it inland. The armies of Xerxes had first levelled it, moving westward; the armies of Philip had repaired it, moving east.

Ptolemy came, because Alexander thought it due to him; Philotas, because his father was with the King; Kassandros because if the son of Parmenion came, Antipatros' could not be left behind; and Hephaistion as a matter of course.

The escort was commanded by Kleitos, Hellanike's younger brother. The King had detailed him for it, because Alexander had known him so long. This was indeed one of the first beings he could remember, as a dark thickset young man who would walk into the nursery and talk to Lanike across him, or come roaring across the floor playing bears. He was now Black Kleitos, a bearded captain of the Companion Cavalry; highly reliable, and with an archaic forthrightness. Macedon had many such survivals from a Homeric past, when the High King had to take, if his chieftains chose to give it, a wholesome piece of their minds. Now, escorting the King's son, he was hardly aware of harking back to the rough teasing of the nursery; Alexander scarcely knew what it was he half-remembered; but there was an edge to their sparring, and though he laughed, he took care to give as good as he got.

They forded streams which, it was said, had been drunk dry by the Persian hordes; crossed the Strymon by King Philip's bridge, and climbed Pangaion's shoulder to the terraced city of Amphipolis. There at the Nine Ways, Xerxes had buried nine boys and nine girls alive, to please his gods. Now between mountain and river stood a great fortress shining with new squared ashlar; gold-smelters' furnaces smoked within its walls; it was a strongpoint Philip did not mean to lose, the first of his conquests beyond the river which had once been Macedon's furthest boundary. Above them towered Pangaion, dark with forests and scarred with the workings of the mines, its white marble outcrops gleaming in the sun; the rich womb of the royal armies. Wherever they went, Kleitos pointed out to them the spoor of the King's wars; weed-covered siege works, ramps where his towers and his catapults had been reared against city walls still laid in ruins. There was always a fort of his along the way, to take them in for the night.

'What's to become of us, boys,' said Alexander laughing, 'if he leaves us nothing to do?'

When the coastal plain was firm, the boys would wheel off at a gallop, and charge back with streaming hair, splashing along the sea-shore, shouting to each other above the crying of the gulls. Once, when they were singing, some passing peasants took them for a wedding-party, bringing the bridegroom to the house of the bride.

Oxhead was in high spirits. Hephaistion had a fine new horse, red with a blonde mane and tail. They were always giving each other things, on impulse, or at the feasts, but they had been boys' small keepsakes; this was the first costly and conspicuous gift he had had from Alexander. The gods had only made one Oxhead; but Hephaistion's mount must excel all others. It handled well. Kassandros admired it pointedly. After all, then, Hephaistion was making a good thing out of his sycophancy. Hephaistion felt the meaning, and would have given much for the chance of vengeance; but nothing had been said in words. Before Kleitos and the escort, it was unthinkable to make a scene.

The road ran inland to skirt a brackish swamp. Perched on a spur of hill to command the passage, towering proudly above the plain, was the citadel rock of Philippi. Philip had taken it, and sealed it with his name, in a famous year.

'My first campaign,' Kleitos said. 'I was there when the courier brought the news. Your father, Philotas, had pushed back the Illyrians and run them half-way to the western sea; the King's horse had won at Olympia; and you, Alexander, had come into the world – with a great yell as we were told. We were issued a double wine-ration. Why he didn't make it a treble one, I don't know.'

'I do. He knew how much you could hold.' Alexander trotted ahead, and murmured to Hephaistion, 'Since I was three I've been hearing that story.'

Philotas said, 'All this used to be Thracian tribal land.'

'Yes, Alexander,' said Kassandros. 'You'll need watch your blue-painted friend, young Lambaros. The Agrianoi' – he waved his hand northwards – 'must be hoping to make something of this war.'

'Oh?' Alexander raised his brows. 'They've kept their pledges. Not like King Kersobleptes, who made war as soon as we'd given his hostage back.' It was known that Philip had had enough of this chief's false promises and brigand raids; the aim of the war was to make his lands a province of Macedon.

'These barbarians are all alike,' Kassandros said.

'I heard from Lambaros last year. He got a merchant to write for him. He wants me to visit their city as his guest.'

'I don't doubt it. Your head would look well on a pole at the village gate.'

'As you just now said, Kassandros, he's my friend. Will you remember that?'

'And shut your mouth,' said Hephaistion audibly.

They were to sleep at Philippi. The tall acropolis flamed like a cresset in the red light of the westering sun. Alexander gazed long in silence.

The King, when at last they reached him, was camped before the fort of Doriskos, on the near side of the Hebros valley. Beyond the river was the Thracian city of Kypsela. Before investing that, he must take the fort.

It had been built by Xerxes, to guard his rear after he had crossed the Hellespont. On the flat sea-meadow below it, he had rough-reckoned the number of his host, too vast for counting, by marching troop after troop into a square drawn around the first ten thousand men. The fort was solid; he had had no lack of slaves. But it had grown ramshackle in its century and a half of Thracians; cracks were filled in with rubble, the battlements patched with thorn like a goat-pen in the mountains. It had withstood Thracian tribal wars; till now, no more had been asked of it.

Dusk was falling as they came near. From within the walls rose the smell of cook-fires and the distant bleat of goats. Just out of arrow-shot was the camp of the Macedonians, a workmanlike shanty town of hide tents, lean-to's roughly thatched with reeds from the Hebros river, and propped upturned carts. Drawn geometric and black against the sunset sky stood a sixty-foot wooden siege-tower; its guards, shielded by thick ox-hide housing against missiles from the ramparts, were cooking supper within its base. In the cavalry lines, the horses whinnied at their pickets. The platforms had been set up for the catapults; the great engines seemed to crouch like dragons about to spring, their timber necks extended, their massive bolt-firing bows outspread from their sides like wings. The out-lying scrub stank of ordure; the nearer air smelled of woodsmoke, grilling fish, and the unwashed bodies of many men and women. The camp-followers were busy with supper; here and there one of their incidental children chirped or wailed. Someone was playing a lyre in need of tuning.

A little hamlet of huts, its people fled to the fort or mountains, had been cleaned out for the officers. The headman's place, two stone rooms and a lean-to, housed the King. They saw his lamp at some distance.

Alexander moved into the lead, lest Kleitos take it on himself to deliver him like a child. His eyes and nose and ears took in the presence of war, the difference from barracks or home camp. When they reached the house, Philip's square shape darkened the doorway. Father and son embraced, and viewed each other in the light of the watch-fire. 'You're taller,' said the King.

Alexander nodded. 'My mother,' he said for the escort's ears, 'sends you greeting and hopes you are in good health.' There was a loaded pause; he went on quickly, 'I've brought you a sack of apples from Mieza. They're good this year.'

Philip's face warmed; Mieza apples were famous. He clapped his son on the shoulder, greeted his companions, directed Philotas to his father's lodging, and said, 'Well, come in, come in and eat.

Joined presently by Parmenion, they ate at a trestle, waited on by the royal squires, youths in their mid teens whose fathers' rank entitled them to learn manners and warfare by acting as body-servants to the King. The sweet golden apples were brought in a silver dish. Two lamps stood on bronze standards. The King's weapons and armour leaned in a corner. An ancient smell of humanity sweated out from the walls.

'Only a day later,' said Philip, 'and we might have lodged you inside.' He gestured with his apple-core at the fort.

Alexander leaned forward across the table. The long ride had sun-burned him; the clear colour glowed in his cheeks, his hair and eyes caught the lamplight brilliantly; he was like kindling caught with the spark.

'When do we attack?'

Philip grinned across at Parmenion. 'What can one do with such a boy?'

They were to go in just before dawn.

After supper, the officers came in for briefing. They were to approach the fort in darkness; then flame-arrows were to be shot at the brushwood in the walls, the catapults and siege-tower would open covering fire to clear the ramparts while scaling-ladders were set up. Meantime the ram, slung in its mighty cradle, would be swung against the gates, the siege-tower would thrust out its drawbridge; the assault would begin.

It was an old story to the officers, only small details imposed by the site were new. 'Good,' Philip said. 'Time for a little sleep, then.'

The squires had brought in a second bed to the room behind. Alexander's eyes had followed it for a moment. Just before bedtime, when he had honed his weapons, he went out to find Hephaistion, to tell him he had arranged they should be posted together for the assault, and to explain that he himself had to share his father's lodging. For some reason he had not thought to expect it.

When he got back, his father had just stripped, and was handing a squire his chiton. Alexander checked a moment in the doorway, then entered, saying something to seem at ease. He could not, indeed, account

for the deep distaste and shame the sight of his father gave him. As far
as he could remember, he had never seen him naked before.

By sun-up the fort had fallen. A pure, clear golden light came lifting from
behind the hills that hid the Hellespont. A fresh breeze blew from the sea.
Over the fort hung the acrid smells of smoke and smoulder, the stink of
blood and entrails and grimy sweat.

The ladders, solid structures of undressed pine which would take two
men abreast, still leaned against the firestained walls, with here and there
a broken rung where the rush had overloaded one. Before the burst
splintered gates hung the ram in its hide-roofed cradle; the gangway from
the siege-tower lolled on the ramparts like a great tongue.

Inside, the Thracian men who survived were being fettered for their
march to the slave-market at Amphipolis; the clink sounded musical, at
a little distance. An example, Philip thought, might encourage the
Kypselans to surrender when their turn came. All round the huts and
hovels that clung like swallows' mud nests to the inside of the walls, the
soldiers were on the hunt for women.

The King stood, with Parmenion and a couple of runners by whom he
was sending orders, up on the ramparts; solid, workmanlike, relaxed, like
an able farmer who has ploughed a big field and got it sown before the
rain. Once or twice, when a shriek rose shrilling to hurt the ears, Alexander
looked towards him; but he went on talking to Parmenion, undisturbed.
The men had fought well, and deserved what meagre spoils the place could
offer. Doriskos should have surrendered; then no one would have been
hurt.

Alexander and Hephaistion were by themselves in the gatehouse, talking about the battle. It was a small stone room, containing besides themselves a dead Thracian, a slab carved with the name and styles of Xerxes,
King of Kings; some rough wooden stools; half a loaf of black bread; and,
by itself, a man's forefinger with a black broken nail. Hephaistion had
kicked it aside; it was a trifle to what they had seen already.

He had won his sword-belt. One man he had killed for certain, dead on
the spot; Alexander thought it might well be three.

Alexander had taken no trophies, nor counted his men. As soon as they
were on the walls, the officer who led their party had been hurled down.
Alexander, giving no one else time to think, had shouted that they must
take the gatehouse, whence missiles were being showered on the ram
below. The appointed second-in-command, an untried man, had wavered,
and in that moment had lost his men to Alexander's certainty; they were
already running after him, clambering, scrambling, stabbing and thrusting along Xerxes' old ragged masonry, with its wild blue-stained defenders

and clefts of crackling fire. The entry to the gatehouse was narrow; there had been a minute, after Alexander had hurled himself inside, when the following press had jammed in it, and he had been fighting alone.

He stood now with the blood and dust of combat on him, looking down on the other face of war. But, Hephaistion thought, he was not really seeing it. He talked quite clearly, remembered every detail where for Hephaistion things were already flowing together like a dream. For him it was fading; Alexander was living in it still. Its aura hung about him; he was in a mode of being he did not want to leave, as men linger on in a place where they saw a vision.

He had a sword-cut across his forearm. Hephaistion had stopped the bleeding with a strip of his kilt. He looked out at the pale clean sea, saying, 'Let's go down and bathe, to wash off the muck.'

'Yes,' said Alexander. 'I ought to see Peithon first. He put out his shield to cover me when two of them were at me, and that man with the forked beard caught him under it. But for you he'd have been killed outright.' He took off his helmet (they were both armed, at short notice, from the common stock of the Pella armoury) and ran his hand through his damp hair.

'You ought to have waited, before you dashed in alone, to see if we'd come up with you. You know you run faster than anyone else. I could have killed you for it, when we were milling in the doorway.'

'They were going to drop that rock there, look at the size of it. I knew you weren't far off.'

Hephaistion was feeling the reaction, not only to his fears for Alexander, but to all he had seen and done. 'Rock or no rock, you'd have gone in. It was written all over you. It's only luck you're alive.'

'It was the help of Herakles,' said Alexander calmly. 'And hitting them quickly, before they could hit me.'

He had found this easier than he had foreseen. The best he had hoped from his constant weapon-practice had been some lessening of disadvantage, against seasoned men. Hephaistion, reading his thought, said, 'These Thracians are peasants. They fight two or three times a year, in a cattle-raid or a brawl. Most of them are stupid, none of them are trained. Real soldiers, like your father's men, would have cut you down before you were well inside.'

'Wait till they do it,' said Alexander sharply, 'and tell me about it then.'

'You went in without me. You didn't even look.'

Suddenly transformed, Alexander gave him a loving smile.

'What's the matter with you? Patroklos reproached Achilles for *not* fighting.'

'He was listened to,' said Hephaistion in a different voice.

From below in the fort, the wail of a woman keening rhythmically over some dead man broke off in a shriek of terror.

'He should call the men in,' Alexander said. 'It's enough. I know there was nothing else worth taking, but – '

They looked along the wall; but Philip had gone off on some other business.

'Alexander. Listen. It's no use to be angry. When you're a general, you'll not be able to expose yourself like that. The King's a brave man, but he doesn't do it. If you'd been killed, it would have been like a battle won for Kersobleptes. And later, when you're King . . .'

Alexander turned round, and riveted on him that gaze of peculiar intensity with which he told a secret. Dropping his voice, a needless caution in so much noise, he said, 'I can never not do it. I know it, I've felt it, it's the truth of the god. It's then that I – '

A sound of panting breath, catching in shrill sobs, broke in on them. A young Thracian woman rushed in from the ramparts and, without looking right or left, dashed towards the wide parapet above the gate. It was some thirty feet from the ground. As she got her knee on the sill, Alexander jumped after and grasped her arm. She screamed, and clawed at him with her free hand, till Hephaistion caught it back. She stared into Alexander's face with the fixity of a cornered animal, writhed suddenly free, crouched down and clutched his knees.

'Get up, we won't harm you.' Alexander's Thracian had been improved by his talks with Lambaros. 'Don't fear, get up. Let go.'

The woman gripped harder, pouring out a stream of half-smothered words as she pressed her face with its running eyes and nose against his bare leg.

'Get up,' he said again. 'We won't . . .' He had never learned the essential word. Hephaistion supplied a gesture of universal meaning, followed by a strongly negative sign.

The woman let go and sat back on her heels, rocking and wailing. She had red matted hair, and a dress of some coarse raw wool, torn at the shoulder. The front was splashed with blood; there were damp patches of leaked milk over the heavy breasts. She wrenched at her hair, and began to wail again. Suddenly she started, leaped to her feet, and flattened herself against the wall behind them. Footsteps approached; a thick breathless voice called, 'I saw you, you bitch. Come here. I saw you.' Kassandros entered. His face was crimson, his freckled brow beaded with sweat. He charged blindly in, and stopped dead.

The girl, shouting out curses, entreaties, and the incomprehensible tale of her wrongs, ran up behind Alexander and grabbed his waist, holding him like a shield. Her hot breath was in his ear; her wet softness seemed to seep even through his corselet; he was half stifled with the rank female smell of dirty flesh and hair, blood, milk and sex. Pushing her arms away, he gazed at Kassandros with mystified repugnance.

'She's mine,' panted Kassandros, with an urgency hardly capable of words. 'You don't want her. She's mine.'

Alexander said, 'No. She's a suppliant, I've pledged her.'

'She's *mine*.' He spoke as if the word must produce effect, staring across at the woman. Alexander looked him over, pausing at the linen kilt below his corselet. In a withdrawn distaste he said, 'No.'

'I caught her once,' Kassandros insisted. 'But she got away.' His face was ploughed down one side with scratches.

'So you lost her. I found her. Go away yourself.'

Kassandros had not quite forgotten his father's warnings. He kept his voice down. 'You can't interfere here. You're a boy. You know nothing about it.'

'Don't dare call him a boy!' said Hephaistion furiously. 'He fought better than you did. Ask the men.'

Kassandros, who had blundered and hacked his way through the complex obstacles of battle, confused, harassed, and intermittently scared, recalled with hatred the enraptured presence cleaving the chaos, as lucid as a point of flame. The woman, supposing all this to be concerned with her, began to pour out another flood of Thracian. Above it Kassandros shouted, 'He was looked after! Whatever fool thing he did, they were bound to follow him! He's the King's son. Or so they say.'

Stupid with anger, and looking at Hephaistion, he was an instant too late for Alexander, whose standing leap at his throat took him off balance and hurled him to the rugged floor. He threshed and flailed; Alexander, intent on choking him, took kicks and blows with indifference. Hephaistion hovered, not daring to help without leave. Something rushed past him from behind. It was the woman, whom they had all forgotten. She had snatched up a three-legged stool; missing Alexander by an inch, she brought it down in a side-sweep on Kassandros' head. Alexander rolled out of the way; with a frenzied rage she began to beat Kassandros over the body, slamming him back whenever he tried to rise; taking both hands to it, as if she were threshing corn.

Hephaistion, who was becoming over-wrought, burst out laughing. Alexander, regaining his feet, stood looking down, stone cold. It was Hephaistion who said, 'We must stop her. She'll finish him off.'

Without moving, Alexander answered, 'Someone killed her child. That's its blood on her.'

Kassandros had begun to roar with pain. 'If he dies,' said Hephaistion, 'she'll be stoned. The King couldn't refuse. You pledged her.'

'Stop!' said Alexander in Thracian. Between them they got the stool away. She burst into wild weeping, while Kassandros rolled about on the cobbled floor.

'He's alive,' said Alexander, turning away. 'Let's find someone reliable, and get her out of the fort.'

A little later, rumours reached King Philip that his son had thrashed Antipatros' son in a fight over a woman. He said off-handedly, 'Boys will be men, it seems.' The note of pride was too clear for anyone to risk taking it further.

Hephaistion, walking back with Alexander, said grinning, 'He can hardly complain to Antipatros that you stood by and let a woman beat him.'

'He can complain where he likes,' said Alexander. 'If he likes.' They had turned into the gate. A sound of groaning came from a house within the wall. Here on makeshift bedding the wounded lay; the doctor and his two servants were going to and fro. Hephaistion said, 'Let him see properly to your arm.' It had started to bleed again, after the brawl in the gatehouse.

'There's Peithon,' Alexander said, peering into the gloom with its buzzing flies. 'I must thank him first.'

He picked his way between mats and blankets, by the light from holes in the roof. Peithon, a youngish man who in battle had looked stern and Homeric, lay with his bandage seeping, limp with loss of blood. His pale face was pinched, his eyes shifted anxiously. Alexander knelt by him and clasped his hand; presently, as his exploits were recalled to him, his colour livened a little, he bragged, and essayed a joke.

When Alexander got up, his eyes had grown used to the shadows. He saw they were all looking at him, jealous, despondent, hopeful; feeling their pain, and wanting their contribution recognized. In the end, before he left, he had spoken to every one of them.

It was the hardest winter old men remembered. Wolves came down to the villages and took the watch-dogs. Cattle and herdboys died of cold on the low slopes of the winter grazing. The limbs of fir-trees cracked under their weight of snow; the mountains were blanketed so thick that only great cliffs and clefts in them still showed dark. Alexander did not refuse the fur cloak his mother sent him. Taking a fox among the stark black tangle of the rose-thorns near Mieza, they found that its pelt was white. Aristotle was very pleased with it.

The house was pungent and smoky with its braziers; nights were so bitter that the young men doubled up together, only for warmth. Alexander was anxious to keep well hardened (the King was still in Thrace, where winter blew down straight from the Scythian steppes). He thought he should get through the cold spell without such coddling; but gave way to Hephaistion's view that people might suppose they had quarrelled.

Ships were lost at sea, or land-bound. Even from as near as Pella, the roads were sometimes snowed up. When the mule-train got through, it was like a feast-day.

'Roast duck for supper,' said Philotas.

Alexander smelled the air and nodded. 'Something's wrong with Aristotle.'

'Has he gone to bed?'

'No, it's bad news. I saw him in the specimen-room.' Alexander went there often; he was now apt to set up his own experiments. 'My mother sent me some mitts; I don't need two pairs, and no one sends him presents. He was there with a letter. He looked dreadful; like a tragic mask.'

'I daresay some other sophist has contradicted him.'

Alexander held his peace, and went off to tell Hephaistion.

'I asked him what the trouble was, if I could help. He said no, he'd tell us about it when he was more composed; and that womanishness would be unworthy of a noble friend. So I went off, to let him weep.'

At Mieza, the winter sun went down quickly behind the mountain, while the eastward heights of Chalkidike still caught its light. Around the house, the dusk was whitened by the snow. It was not yet time to eat; in the big living-room with its peeling frescoes of blue and rose, the young men hung round the fire-basket on the hearth, talking about horses, women or themselves. Alexander and Hephaistion, sharing the wolfskin cloak sent by Olympias, sat near the window because the lamps were not yet lit. They were reading Xenophon's *The Upbringing of Kyros*, which, next to Homer, was just then Alexander's favourite book.

'*And she could not hide her tears,*' read Hephaistion, '*falling down her robe to her feet. Then the eldest man of us said, "Don't be afraid, Lady. We know your husband was noble. But we are choosing you out for one who is not below him in beauty, or mind, or power. We believe that if any man is admirable, it is Kyros; and to him you will belong." When the lady heard this, she rent her peplos from top to bottom crying aloud, while her servants wept with her; and we then had a sight of her face, her neck and arms. And let me tell you, Kyros, it seemed to me and all of us that there was never so beautiful a woman of mortal birth in Asia. But you must be sure to see her for yourself.*

'"*No, by God," said Kyros. "Especially if she is as lovely as you say."*'

'They keep asking me,' said Hephaistion looking up, 'why Kassandros doesn't come back.'

'I told Aristotle he fell in love with war and forsook philosophy. I don't know what he told his father. He couldn't have come back with us; she broke two of his ribs.' He pulled another roll out of the cloak. 'This part

I like. *"Bear in mind that the same toils do not bear equally on the general and the common soldier, though their bodies are of the same kind; but the honour of the general's rank, and his knowing that nothing he does will go unnoticed, make his hardships lighter to endure."* How true that is. One can't bear it in mind enough.'

'Can the real Kyros have been quite so much like Xenophon?'

'The Persian exiles used to say he was a great warrior and a noble king.'

Hephaistion peered into a roll. *'He trained his companions not to spit or blow their noses in public, not to turn round and stare ...'*

'Well, the Persians were rough hill-people in his day. They must have seemed to the Medes like, say, Kleitos would to an Athenian ... I like it that when his cooks served him something good, he sent pieces round to his friends.'

'I wish it were supper-time. I'm clemmed.'

Alexander edged more of the cloak around him, remembering that at night he was always drawing close because of the cold. 'I hope Aristotle will come down. It must be icy upstairs. He ought to have some food.'

A slave came in with a hand-lamp and tinder-stick, and kindled the tall standing lamps, then reached his flame to the hanging lamp-cluster. The raw young Thracian he was training closed up the shutters, and gingerly pulled the thick wool curtains across.

'A ruler,' read Alexander, *'should not only be truly a better man than those he rules. He should cast a kind of spell on them ...'*

There were footsteps on the stairs, which paused till the slaves had gone. Into the evening snugness, Aristotle came down like a walking corpse. His eyes were sunken; the closed mouth seemed to show beneath it the rigid grin of the skull.

Alexander threw off the cloak, scattering the scrolls, and crossed the room to him. 'Come to the fire. Bring a chair, someone. Come and get warm. Please tell us the trouble. Who is dead?'

'My guest-friend, Hermeias of Atarneus.' Given a question of fact to answer, he could bring out the words. Alexander shouted in the doorway for some wine to be mulled. They all crowded round the man, grown suddenly old, who sat staring into the fire. For a moment he stretched his hands to warm them; then, as if even this stirred some thought of horror, drew them back into his lap.

'It was Mentor the Rhodian, King Ochos' general,' he began, and paused again. Alexander said to the others, 'That's Memnon's brother, who reconquered Egypt.'

'He has served his master well.' The voice too had thinned and aged. 'Barbarians are born so; they did not make their own base condition. But a Hellene who sinks to serve them ... Herakleitos says, *The best corrupted is the worst*. He has betrayed nature itself. So he sinks even below his masters.'

His face looked yellow; those nearer saw his tremor. To give him time, Alexander said, 'We never liked Memnon, did we, Ptolemy?'

'Hermeias brought justice and a better life to the lands he ruled. King Ochos coveted his lands, and hated his example. Some enemy, I suspect Mentor himself, carried to the King tales he gladly believed. Then Mentor, pretending a friend's concern, warned Hermeias of danger, and invited him to come and take counsel on it. He went, believing; in his own walled city he could have held out a long time, and was in reach of help from ... a powerful ally, with whom he had agreements.'

Hephaistion looked at Alexander; but he was fixed in entire attention.

'As a guest-friend he came to Mentor; who sent him in fetters, to the Great King.'

The young men made sounds of outrage, but briefly, being eager to learn what next.

'Mentor took his seal and fixed it to forged orders, which opened all the strongpoints of Atarneus to Mentor's men. King Ochos now owns them, and all the Greeks within them. As for Hermeias ...'

A brand fell out of the hearth; Harpalos picked up the fire-iron and shoved it back. Aristotle wetted his lips with his tongue. His folded hands did not move, but their knuckles whitened.

'From the first his death had been determined; but that was not enough for them. King Ochos wished first to know what secret treaties he might have made with other rulers. So he sent for the men whose skill it is to do such things, and told them to make him speak. It is said they worked on him a day and a night.'

He went on to tell them what had been done; forcing his voice, when he could, into the tone of his lectures on anatomy. The young men listened wordless; their breath hissed as they sucked it in through their shut teeth.

'My pupil Kallimachos, whom you know, sent me the news from Athens. He says that when Demosthenes announced to the Assembly that Hermeias had been taken, he numbered it among the gifts of fortune, saying, "The Great King will now hear of King Philip's plots, not as a complaint from us, but from the lips of the man who worked them." *He* knows, none better, how such things are done in Persia. But he rejoiced too soon. Hermeias told them nothing. At the end, when after all they could do he was still alive, they hung him on a cross. He said to those in hearing, "Tell my friends I have done nothing weak, nor unworthy of philosophy."'

There was a deep-voiced murmuring. Alexander stood rooted and still. Presently, when no one else spoke, he said, 'I am sorry. Indeed I am truly sorry.' He came forward, put his arm around Aristotle's shoulders and kissed his cheek. He stared on into the fire.

A servant brought the warmed wine; he sipped it, shook his head, and put it aside. Suddenly he sat up, and turned towards them. In the upward glow of the fire, the lines of his face looked as if carved in clay, ready for casting in the bronze.

'Some of you will command in war. Some of you will have the ruling of lands you conquer. Always remember this: as the body is worth nothing without the mind to rule it, as its function is to labour that the mind may live, such is the barbarian in the natural order God ordained. Such peoples may be bettered, as horses are, by being tamed and put to use; like plants or animals, they can serve purposes beyond what their own natures can conceive. That is their value. They are the stuff of slaves. Nothing exists without its function; that is theirs. Remember it.'

He stood up from the chair, giving as he turned a haunted look at the fire-basket, whose bands were reddening. Alexander said, 'If I ever take the men who did this to your friend, the Persians or the Greek, I swear I will avenge him.'

Without looking back, Aristotle walked to the dark staircase and went up it out of their sight.

The steward came in, to announce that supper was ready.

Talking loudly of the news, the young men made for the dining-room; there was not much formality at Mieza. Alexander and Hephaistion lingered, exchanging looks. 'So,' said Hephaistion, 'he did arrange the treaty.'

'My father and he caused this between them. What must he feel?'

'At least he knows his friend died faithful to philosophy.'

'Let's hope he believes it. A man dies faithful to his pride.'

'I expect,' said Hephaistion, 'the Great King would have killed Hermeias in any case, to get his cities.'

'Or he did it because he doubted him. Why was he tortured? They guessed there was something he knew.' The firelight burnished his hair and the clear whites of his eyes. He said, 'If ever I get my hands on Mentor, I shall have him crucified.'

With a complex inward shudder, Hephaistion pictured the beautiful vivid face watching unmoved. 'You'd better go in to supper. They can't start without you.'

The cook, who knew how young men eat in cold weather, had allowed a whole duck to each. First helpings, with the breast, were being carved and handed; a warm aromatic smell enriched the air.

Alexander picked up the plate they had put before him, and swung down his feet from the dining-couch he was sharing with Hephaistion.

'Everyone eat, don't wait. I'm only going to see Aristotle.' To Hephaistion he said, 'He must eat before night. He'll fall sick if he lies fasting in the cold, in all that grief. Just tell them to get me something, anything will do.'

The plates were being wiped with bread when he came back. 'He took a little. I thought he would, once he got the smell of it. I daresay he'll have more, now ... There's too much here, you've been giving me yours.' Presently he added, 'Poor man, he was half out of his mind. I could tell, when he made us that speech about the nature of barbarians. Imagine calling a great man like Kyros the stuff of slaves, only because he was born a Persian.'

The pale sun rose earlier and gained strength; steep mountain faces let slip their snow-loads, roaring, to flatten great pines like grass. Torrents foamed down their gorges, grinding boulders with thunderous sound. Shepherds waded thigh-deep through wet snow to rescue the early lambs. Alexander put his fur cloak away, in case he should come to depend on it. The young men who had been doubling-up went back to sleep alone; so he put away Hephaistion too, though not without some regret. Secretly Hephaistion exchanged their pillows, to take with him the scent of Alexander's hair.

King Philip came back from Thrace, where he had deposed King Kersobleptes, left garrisons in his strong points, and planted the Hebros valley with Macedonian colonists. Those who applied for lands in these uncouth wilds were mostly men unwanted, or wanted too much, else-where; the wits of the army said he should have called his new city not Philipopolis, but Knavestown. However, the foundation would serve its purpose. Pleased with his winter's work, he returned to Aigai to celebrate the Dionysia.

Mieza was abandoned to its slaves. The young men and their teacher packed up their things, and rode along the track which skirted the ridge to Aigai. Here and there they had to descend to the plain, to ford swollen streams. A long while before they sighted Aigai, on the forest trail they felt the earth below them shudder from the pounding of the falls.

The old rugged castle was full of lights and bright stuffs and beeswax polish. The theatre was being readied for the plays. The half-moon shelf Aigai stood on was like a great stage itself, looked down on by wild hills whose audience one could only guess at, when in the windy spring nights they cried to each other over the sounds of water, in defiance, terror, loneliness or love.

The King and Queen were installed already. Reading as he crossed the threshold those signs in which the years had made him expert, Alexander judged that, publicly at least, they were on speaking terms. But they were unlikely to be found together. This had been his first long absence; which should be greeted first?

It ought to be the King. Custom decreed it; to omit it would be an open slight. Unprovoked too; in Thrace, Philip had gone to trouble to keep things decent before him. No girl about the place; never a glance too many at the handsomest of the body-squires, who thought himself a cut above the rest. His father had commended him handsomely after the battle, and promised him his own company when next he went into action. It would be boorish now to insult him. Indeed, Alexander found that he wished to see him; he would have much to tell.

The King's business room was in the ancient tower which had been the first core of the castle, filling its upper floor. A ponderous wooden ladder, mended through the centuries, still had beside it the heavy ring to which earlier kings, whose bed-chamber it had been, had chained a watch-dog of the great Molossian breed that could rear up taller than a man. King Archelaos had hung a smoke-hood over the hearth; but he had made few changes at Aigai, the palace at Pella had been his love. Philip's clerks had the anteroom below the ladder. Alexander had one of them announce him, before he went up.

His father got up from his writing-table, to thump him on the shoulders. Their greetings had never been so easy. Alexander's questions burst from him. How had Kypsela fallen? He had been sent back to school while the army still sat before it. 'Did you go in from the river side, or breach that blind bit next the rocks?'

Philip had been saving him a reprimand for visiting, without leave, the wild eyrie of young Lambaros on his journey home, but this was now forgotten. 'I tried a sap on the river side, but the soil was sandy. So I built a siege-tower for them to think about, while I sapped the north-east wall.'

'Where did you put the tower?'

'On that rise where – ' Philip looked for his tablet, found it filled with notes, and made gestures in the air to sketch the site.

'Here.' Alexander ran to the log-basket by the hearth, and came back with both hands full of kindling. 'Look, this is the river.' He laid down a stick of pine. 'Here's the north watchtower.' He stood a log on its end. Philip reached for another, and made a wall next the tower. They began eagerly to push bits of wood about.

'No, that's too far out, the gate was here.'

'Look, but Father, your siege-tower ... Oh, there, I see. And the sap was here?'

'Now the ladders, give me those sticks. Now here was Kleitos' company. Parmenion – '

'Wait, we left out the catapults.' Alexander dived into the basket for fir-cones. Philip set them up.

'So Kleitos was partly covered, while I – '

Silence fell like a sword-stroke. Alexander, whose back was to the door, needed only to read his father's face. It had been easier to leap into the gatehouse at Doriskos than now it was to turn; so he turned at once.

His mother was dressed in a robe of purple bordered with white and gold. Her hair was bound with a gold fillet, and draped with a veil of byssos silk from Kos, through which its red showed like fire through wood-smoke. She did not glance at Philip. Her burning eyes sought not the enemy, but the traitor.

'When you have done your game, Alexander, I shall be in my room. Do not hurry. I have waited half a year; what are a few hours more?'

She turned rigidly and was gone. Alexander stood unmoving. Philip read into this what he wished to see. He raised his brows with a smile, and turned again to the battle-plan.

'Excuse me, Father. I had better go along.'

Philip was a diplomat; but the rancour of years, the present exaspera-tion, robbed him of his instinct for the moment when generosity would pay. 'You can stay, I suppose, till I have finished speaking.'

Alexander's face changed to that of a soldier awaiting orders. 'Yes, Father?'

With a folly he would never have shown in parley with his enemies, Philip pointed to a chair and said, 'Sit down.' Challenge had been offered, beyond recall.

'I am sorry. I must see Mother now. Good-bye, Father.' He turned towards the door.

'Come back,' barked Philip. Alexander looked round from where he was. 'Do you mean to leave all this filth on my table? You put it there; clear it up.'

Alexander walked back to the table. Crisply, precisely, he put the wood in a pile, strode with it to the fire-basket, and flung it in. He had knocked a letter off the table. Ignoring it, he gave one deadly look at Philip and left the room.

The women's quarters had been the same since the first days of the castle. From here they had been summoned, in Amyntas' day, to greet the Persian envoys. He went up the narrow stairs to the little anteroom. A girl he had not seen before was coming out, looking over her shoulder. She had fine feathery dark hair, green eyes, a clear pale skin, and a deep bosom over which her thin red dress was tightly bound; her lower lip was caught in a little, in a natural line. At the sound of his step she started. Her long lashes swept up; her face, as frank-looking as a child's, showed admiration, realization, fright. He said, 'Is my mother there?' and knew there had been no need to ask the question, he had done it from choice. 'Yes, my lord,' she said, dipping nervously. He wondered why she looked scared, though a mirror might have told him; felt sorry for her and smiled. Her face changed as if a pale sun had touched it. 'Shall I tell her, Alexander, that you are here?' 'No, she expects me, you need not stay.' She paused a moment, looking at him earnestly, as if not satisfied that she had done enough for him. She was a little older than he, perhaps a year. Then she went on down the stairs.

He paused a moment outside the door, staring after. She had looked fragile and smooth to touch, like a swallow's egg; her mouth had been unpainted, pink and delicate. She had been a sweet taste after a bitter one. From outside the window came drifting the sound of a men's chorus, practising for the Dionysia.

'You have remembered, then, to come,' said his mother as soon as they were alone. 'How soon you have learned to make your life without me?'

She stood by the window in the thick stone wall; a slanting light touched the curve of her cheek and shone in her thin veil. She had dressed for him, painted; intricately done her hair. He saw it; as she saw that he had grown again, that the bones of his face had hardened, his voice lost the last flaws of boyhood. He had come back a man, and faithless like a man. He knew that he had longed for her; that true friends share everything, except the past before they met. If only she would weep, even that, and let him comfort her; but she would not humble herself before a man. If only he would run to her side and cling to her; but his manhood was hard-won, no mortal should make him a child again. So, blinded by their sense of their own uniqueness, they fought out their lovers' quarrel, while the roar of the Aigai falls pounded in their ears like blood.

'How shall I be anything, without learning war? Where else can I learn it? He is my general; why affront him without a cause?'

'Oh, you have no cause now. Once you had mine.'

'What? What has he done?' He had been gone so long, Aigai itself had looked changed, like the promise of some new life. 'What is it, tell me.'

'Never mind, why should you be troubled? Go and enjoy yourself with your friends. Hephaistion will be waiting.'

She must have been questioning someone, he had always been careful. 'I can see them any time. All I wanted was to do the proper thing. For your sake too, you know that. One would think you hated me.'

'I only counted on your love. Now I know better.'

'Tell me what he's done.'

'Never mind. It is nothing, except to me.'

Mother.'

She saw the crease drawn across his forehead, deeper now; two little new lines came down between his brows. She could no longer look down at him; his eyes, drawn at the inner corners, met hers level. She came forward and laid her cheek to him. 'Never be so cruel to me again.'

Once through this rising river, and she would forgive him everything, all would be rendered back. But no. He would not give her this. Before she could see his tears, he broke from her and ran down the narrow stair.

At the turn, his eyes blurred, he collided with someone head-on. It was the dark-haired girl. 'Oh,' she cried, fluttering and soft like a pigeon, 'I am sorry, I am sorry, my lord.'

He took her slender arms in his hands. 'My fault. I hope I did not hurt you?'

'No, no indeed.' They paused a moment, before she swept down her thick lashes and went on up the stairs. He touched his eyes, in case there had been anything to notice; but they were scarcely wet.

Hephaistion, who had been looking for him everywhere, found him an hour later in a little old room which looked towards the falls. Their sound was deafening here when the water was in spate; the very floor seemed to shudder with the grinding of the rocks below. The room was lined with chests and shelves of old musty records and title deeds, treaties, and long family trees going back to heroes and gods. There were a few books too, left there by Archelaos or by the accidents of time.

Alexander sat curled in the small deep window-hole, like an animal in a cave. A handful of scrolls was strewed around him.

'What are you doing here?' Hephaistion asked.

'Reading.'

'I'm not blind. What's the matter?' Hephaistion came up nearer, to see his face. It had the fierce secretiveness of a wounded dog which will bite the hand that strokes it. 'Someone said you went up here. I've never seen this room before.'

'It's the archives room.'

'What are you reading?'

'Xenophon on hunting. He says the tusk of the boar is so hot that it singes dogs' fur.'

'I never knew that.'

'It's not true. I put a hair on one to see.' He picked up the scroll.

'It will soon be dark in here.'

'Then I'll come down.'

'Don't you want me to stay?'

'I just want to read.'

Hephaistion had come to tell him that their sleeping-quarters had been set out in the archaic manner, the Prince in a small inner room, the

Companions in a dormitory outside it, devoted to that purpose immemori-
ally. Now, without asking, Hephaistion could see that the Queen would
take notice if this arrangement were changed. The groan of the waterfall,
the lengthening shadows, spoke of grief.

Aigai was in its yearly bustle for the Dionysia, enhanced by the presence
of the King, so often absent at war. The women ran from house to house,
the men met to practise their phallic dances. Mule-trains of wine came in
from the vineyards and up from the castle store-rooms. The Queen's rooms
were a buzzing secret hive. Alexander was barred from them, not in
disgrace but because he was a man. Kleopatra was inside, though she was
not yet a woman. She must know nearly all the secrets now. But she was
too young yet to go with them up the mountain.

On the day before the feast, he woke early and saw dawn glimmer in
the window. The first birds were chirping; the water sounded more
distantly here. He could hear a woodman's axe, and cattle lowing for the
milkers. He rose and dressed, thought of waking Hephaistion, then looked
at the little postern-stair which would let him out alone. It was built within
the wall, so that the Prince could have women brought in discreetly. It
could have told some tales, he thought as he stepped quietly down and,
at the bottom, turned the key in its massive lock.

There was no garden at Aigai, only an old orchard enclosed in the outer
wall. On the black bare trees, one or two buds were splitting at the thrust
of unfolding flowers. Dew was heavy in the long grass; it hung in the
spiders' webs like crystal beads. The peaks, still snowbound, were flushed
with pink. The cold air was quickened with spring and violets.

He traced them by their scent to the bank where they grew deep in rank
grass. When he was a child, he had gathered them for his mother. He
would pick some now, and bring them while the women were doing her
hair. It was as well he had come alone; even with Hephaistion, he could
not very well have done it.

His hands were full of the cold wet flowers, when he saw something
gliding through the orchard. It was a girl, with a thick brown wrap over
a pale filmy gown. He knew her at once, and went towards her. She was
like the plum-buds, the light enfolded in the dark. When he came out from
the trees, she gave a great start, and went as white as her linen. What a
shy girl she was. 'What is it? I shan't eat you. I only came to say good day.'
'Good morning, my lord.' 'What's your name?' 'Gorgo, my lord.'

She still looked quite blanched with fright; she must be extremely
modest. What should one say to girls? He knew only what his friends, and
the soldiers, claimed that they had said. 'Come, smile for me, Gorgo, and
you shall have some flowers.' She gave him with dropped lashes a little
smile, fragile, mysterious, like a hamadryad slipping out briefly from her

tree. He almost found himself dividing the flowers in two, to keep some for his mother; what a fool he would have looked. 'Here,' he said, and, as she took them, bent and kissed her cheek. She leant it a moment to his lips, then drew back, not looking at him, softly shaking her head. Opening her thick cloak she tucked the violets between her breasts, and slipped away through the trees.

He stood looking after her, seeing again the cold crisp stems of the violets going down into the warm silky crease. Tomorrow was the Dionysia. *And holy Earth made fresh young grass grow under them, dewy clover and crocuses and hyacinths, a thick soft bed between them and the hard ground.*

He said nothing of it to Hephaistion.

When he went to greet his mother, he saw that something had happened. She was raging like a banked-down fire; but from her looks he was not the offender. She was asking herself whether or not to tell him of it. He kissed, but did not question her. Yesterday had been enough.

All day his friends were telling each other about the girls they meant to have next day, if they could catch them on the mountain. He threw back the old jokes, but kept his own counsel. The women would be setting out from the sanctuary, long before the dawn.

'What shall we do tomorrow?' Hephaistion asked him. 'I mean, after the sacrifice?'

'I don't know. It's unlucky to make plans for the Dionysia.'

Hephaistion gave him a secret, startled glance. No, it was not possible; he had been moody since he got here, and cause enough. Till he got over it, one must let him be.

Supper was early; everyone would be up next day before cock-light; and on the eve of Dionysos no one, even in Macedon, sat late over the wine. The spring twilight fell early, when the sun sank under the western ridges; there were corners in the castle where lamps were kindled half way through the afternoon. The meal in Hall had a transit air; Philip made use of its sobriety to seat Aristotle by him, a compliment less convenient on other nights, for the man was a poor drinker. After supper, most people went straight to bed.

Alexander was never fond of sleeping early. He decided to look up Phoinix, who often read late; he was lodged in the western tower.

The place was a warren; but he knew the short cuts from childhood. Beyond an anteroom, where spare furniture for guests was kept, was the well of a little stair which took one straight there. The lobby was unlit, but a wall-cresset from beyond shone through. He was almost inside, when he heard a sound, and saw a movement.

Silent and motionless, he stood in shadow. In the patch of light, the girl Gorgo faced towards him, wriggling and squirming in the arms of a man who stood behind her, one dark square hairy hand squeezing her groin and the other her breast. Breathless soft giggles stirred her throat. The dress slid off her shoulder under the working hand; a couple of dead violets fell out on the flagstones. The man's face, muzzling for her ear, appeared from behind her head. It was his father's.

Stealthily as in war, his footfalls covered by her squeaking, he drew back, and went through the nearest door into the cold, water-loud night.

Upstairs, in the lodging of the Prince's Guard, Hephaistion lay awake, waiting for Alexander to come to bed so that he could go in and say good night. Other nights here, they had all gone up together; but tonight, no one had seen him since supper. To go searching about for him might make people laugh; Hephaistion lay in the darkness, staring at the line of light under the thick old door of the inner room, watching for the shadows of feet to cross it. No shadow stirred. He drifted into sleep, but dreamed he was watching still.

In the dark small hours, Alexander went up by the postern to change his clothes. The lamp, nearly burned out, flickered dimly. Stripping in the bitter cold, his fingers almost too numb to fasten things, he got into the dressed leather tunic, boots and leggings he used for hunting. He would get warm when he began to climb.

He leaned from the window. Already here and there, wavering among trees, twinkling like stars in the down-draughts from the snows, the first torches shone.

It was long since he had followed them to the grove. Never, at any time of his life, had he followed them to the rites upon the mountain. He could have given no reason now, except that it was the only thing. He was returning, though it was unlawful. There was nowhere else to go.

He had always been a quick, light-footed hunter, impatient of others' noise. Few men were astir so early; they were easily heard, laughing and talking with time in hand to find in the footslopes the willing tipsy stragglers who would be their prey. He slipped past unseen; soon he had left them all below him, going up through the beech-woods along the immemorial track. Long ago, the day after an earlier Dionysia, he had traced this path in secret, all the way to the trodden dancing-place, by footprints, threads caught on thorns, fallen sprays of vine and ivy, torn fur and blood.

She should never know; even in after years, he would never tell her. For ever possessed in secrecy, this would belong only to him. He would be with her invisibly, as the gods visit mortals. He would know of her what no man had known.

The mountain-side grew steep, the path doubled to and fro; he threaded its windings quietly, lit by the sinking moon and the first glimmer of dawn.

Down in Aigai, the cocks were crowing; the sound, thinned by distance, was magical and menacing, a ghostly challenge. On the zig-zag path above him, the line of torches twined like a fiery snake.

Dawn rose up out of Asia and touched the snow-peaks. Far ahead in the forest he heard the death squeal of some young animal, then the bacchic cry.

A steep bluff was split by a timbered gorge; its waters spread from their narrow cleft in a chuckling bed. The path turned left; but he remembered the terrain, and paused to think. This gorge went right up till it flanked the dancing-place. It would be a hard climb through virgin woods to the other edge, but it would make a perfect hide, out of reach yet near; the cleft was narrow there. He could hardly reach it before the sacrifice; but he would see her dance.

He forded the fast ice-cold water, clinging to the rocks. The pine-woods above were thick, untouched by man, dead timber lying where time had felled it; his feet sank in the black sheddings of a thousand years. At last he glimpsed the torches flitting, small as glow-worms; then, as he drew nearer, the bright clear flame from the altar fire. The singing too was like flames, shrilling and sinking and rising in some new place as one voice kindled another.

The first shafts of sunlight shone ahead, at the open edge of the gorge. Here grew a fringe of small sun-fed greenery, myrtle and arbutus and broom. On hands and knees, stealthily as if stalking leopard, he crept behind their screen.

On the far side it was clear and open. There was the dancing-place, the secret meadow screened from below, exposed only to the peaks and the gods. Between its rowan-trees it was scattered with small yellow flowers. Its altar smoked from the flesh of the victim and blazed with resin; they had thrown the butts of their torches on it. Below him the gorge plunged a hundred feet, but across it was only a javelin-cast. He could see their dew-dabbled, bloodstained robes and their pine-topped thyrses. Even from so far, their faces looked emptied for the god.

His mother stood by the altar, the ivy-twined wand in her hand. Her voice led the hymn; her unbound hair flowed over her robe and fawnskin and her white shoulders, from under her ivy crown. He had seen her, then. He had done what men must not do, only the gods.

She held one of the round wine-flasks proper to the festival. Her face was not wild or blank, like some of the others', but bright, clear and smiling. Hyrmina from Epiros, who knew most of her secrets, ran up to her in the dance; she held the flask to her mouth and spoke in her ear.

They were dancing round the altar, running out and back from it, then in on it with loud cries. After a while, his mother threw away her thyrsos, and sang out a magic word in old Thracian, as they called the unknown tongue which was the language of the rites. They all threw their wands away, left the altar and joined hands in a ring. His mother beckoned to a girl along the line, to come out in the middle. The girl came slowly, urged on by the others' hands. He stared. Surely, he knew her.

Suddenly, she ducked under their joined arms, and started running towards the gorge, taken no doubt by the maenad frenzy. As she came nearer, he saw it was certainly the girl Gorgo. The divine frenzy, like terror, had made her eyes start and stretched her mouth. The dance stopped, while some of the women ran after her. Such things, no doubt, were common at the rites.

She ran furiously, keeping well ahead, till her foot tripped on something. She was up again in a moment, but they caught her. In her bacchic madness, she began to scream. The women ran her back towards the others; on her feet at first, till her knees gave way and they pulled her along the ground. His mother waited, smiling. The girl lay at her feet, neither weeping nor praying, only shrieking on and on, a thin shrill note like a hare in a fox's jaws.

It was past noon. Hephaistion walked about the footslopes, calling as it seemed to him he had been doing for many hours, though it was not so long; earlier he had been ashamed to search, not knowing what he might find. Only since the sun was high had misery changed to fear.

'Alexander!' he called. A cliff-slab at the head of the glade flung '... ander!' back and forth. A stream ran out from a gorge, spreading through scattered rocks. On one of them Alexander sat, looking straight before him.

Hephaistion ran to him. He did not rise, scarcely looked round. It's true, thought Hephaistion, it's done. A woman, he is changed already. Now it will never be.

Alexander looked at him strainingly, with sunken eyes, as if feeling it urgent to remember who he was.

'Alexander. What is it? What happened, tell me. Did you fall, have you hurt your head? Alexander!'

'What are you doing,' said Alexander in a flat clear voice, 'running about on the mountain? Are you looking for a girl?'

'No. I was looking for you.'

'Try the gorge up there, you'll find one. But she's dead.'

Hephaistion, sitting down on the rock beside him, almost said, 'Did you kill her?' for nothing seemed impossible to this face. But he dared not speak.

Alexander rubbed the back of a dirt-crusted hand across his brow, and blinked. 'I didn't do it. No.' He gave the dry rictus of a smile. 'She was a pretty girl, my father thought so, my mother too. It was the frenzy of the god. They had a wild-cat's kittens, and a fawn, and something else one couldn't tell. Wait if you like, she'll come down with the stream.'

Speaking quietly, watching him, Hephaistion said, 'I'm sorry you saw that.'

'I shall go back and read my book. Xenophon says, if you lay the tusk of a boar on them, you can see it shrivel. It's the heat of their flesh. Xenophon says it scorches violets.'

'Alexander. Drink some of this. You've been up since yesterday. I brought you some wine along ... Alexander, look, I brought some wine. Are you sure you're not hurt?'

'Oh no, I didn't let them catch me, I saw the play.'

'Look. Look here. Look at me. Now drink this, do as I tell you. Drink it.' After the first swallow, he took the flask from Hephaistion's hand, and emptied it thirstily.

'That's better.' Instinct told Hephaistion to be common and plain. 'I've some food too. You shouldn't follow the maenads, everyone knows it's unlucky. No wonder you feel bad. You've a great thorn in your leg here, hold still while I get it out.' He grumbled on, like a nurse sponging a child's bruises. Alexander sat docile under his hands.

'I've seen worse,' said Alexander suddenly, 'on a battlefield.'

'Yes. We have to get used to blood.'

'That man on the wall at Doriskos, his entrails fell out and he tried to put them back.'

'Did he? I must have looked away.'

'One must be able to look at anything. I was twelve when I took my man. I cut off the head myself. They'd have done it for me, but I made them give me the axe.'

'Yes, I know.'

'She came down from Olympos to the plain of Troy, walking softly, that's what the book says, walking softly with little steps like a quivering dove. Then she put on the helm of death.'

'Of course you can look at anything, everyone knows you can. You've been up all night ... Alexander, are you listening? Can you hear what I say?'

'Be quiet. They're singing.'

He sat with hands on knees, his eyes upturned towards the mountain. Hephaistion could see white below the iris. He must be found, wherever he was. He ought not to be alone.

Quietly, insistently, without touching him, Hephaistion said, 'You're with me now. I promised you I'd be here. Listen, Alexander. Think of

Achilles, how his mother dipped him in the Styx. Think how black and terrible, like dying, like being turned to stone. But then he was invulnerable. Look, it's finished, it's over now. Now you're with me.'

He put out his hand. Alexander's came out and touched it, deathly cold; then closed on it crushingly, so that he caught his breath with mingled relief and pain. 'You're with me,' Hephaistion said. 'I love you. You mean more to me than anything. I'd die for you any time. I love you.'

For some time they sat like this, with their clasped hands resting on Alexander's knee. After a while the vice of his grip relaxed a little; his face lost its mask-like stiffness, and looked only rather ill. He gazed vaguely at their joined hands.

'That wine was good. I'm not so very tired. One should learn to do without sleep, it's useful in war.'

'Next time, we'll stay up together.'

'One should learn to do without anything one can. But I should find it very hard to do without you.'

'I'll be there.' The warm spring sun, slanting now towards afternoon, slid into the glade. A thrush was singing. Hephaistion's omens spoke to him, telling him there had been a change: a death, a birth, the intervention of a god. What had been born was bloodstained from a hard passage, still frail, not to be handled. But it lived, it would grow.

They must be getting back to Aigai, but there was no hurry yet, they were well enough as they were; let him have some quiet. Alexander rested from his thoughts in a waking sleep. Hephaistion watched him, with the steadfast eyes and tender patience of the leopard crouched by the pool, its hunger comforted by the sound of light distant footfalls, straying down the forest track.

6

The plum-blossom had fallen, and lay beaten with spring rain; the time of violets was done, and the vines were budding.

The philosopher had found some of his students a little scatterbrained after the Dionysia, a thing not unknown even in Athens; but the Prince was studious and quiet, doing well at ethics and logic. He remained sometimes unaccountable; when found sacrificing a black goat to Dionysos, he evaded questions; it was to be feared philosophy had not yet rid him of superstition; yet this reticence showed, perhaps, a proper self-questioning.

Alexander and Hephaistion stood leaning on one of the small rustic bridges which spanned the stream of the Nymphs.

'Now,' Alexander said, 'I think I've made my peace with the god That's why I've been able to tell you everything.'

'Isn't it better?'

'Yes, but I had to master it first in my own mind. It was the anger of Dionysos pursuing me, till I made my peace with him. When I think about it logically, I see it would be unjust to be shocked at what my mother did, only because she's a woman, when my father has killed men by thousands. You and I have killed men who never injured us except for the chance of war. Women can't issue challenges to their enemies, as we can; they can only be avenged like women. Rather than blame them, we ought to be thankful to the gods for making us men.'

'Yes,' said Hephaistion. 'Yes, we should.'

'So then I saw it was the anger of Dionysos, because I profaned his mystery. I've been under his protection, you know, ever since I was a child; but lately I've sacrificed more to Herakles than to him. When I presumed, he showed his anger. He didn't kill me, like Pentheus in the play, because I was under his protection; but he punished me. It would have been worse, but for you. You were like Pylades, who stayed with Orestes even when the Furies came for him.'

'Of course I stayed with you.'

'I'll tell you something else. This girl, I'd thought, perhaps, at the Dionysia . . . But some god protected me.'

'He could protect you because you'd a hold over yourself.'

'Yes. All this happened because my father couldn't be continent, even for decency in his own house. He's always been the same. It's known everywhere. People who should be respecting him, because he can beat them in battle, mock him behind his back. I couldn't bear my life, to know they talked like that of me. To know one's not master of oneself.'

'People will never talk like that about you.'

'I'll never love anyone I'm ashamed of, that I know.' He pointed to the clear brown water. 'Look at all those fish.' They leaned together over the wooden rail, their heads touching; the shoal shot like a flight of arrows into the shadow of the bank. Presently straightening up Alexander said, 'Kyros the Great was never enslaved by women.'

'No,' said Hephaistion. 'Not by the most beautiful woman of mortal birth in Asia. It's in the book.'

Alexander had letters from both his parents. Neither had been much disturbed by his unwonted quiet after the Dionysia, though each, at parting, had been aware of a certain scrutiny, as if from a window in a doorless wall. But the Dionysia left many young lads changed; there would be more cause for concern if it passed them by.

His father wrote that the Athenians were pouring colonists into the Greek coastal lands of Thrace, such as the Chersonesos; but, faced with a cut in the public dole, had refused to maintain the supporting fleet, which kept going perforce on piracy and inshore raids, like the rievers of Homer's day. Macedonian ships and steadings had been looted; they had even seized a Macedonian envoy sent to ransom prisoners, tortured him, and extracted nine talents' ransom for his life.

Olympias, for once almost at one with Philip, had a similar tale to tell. A Euboian dealer, Anaxinos, who imported southern goods for her, had been seized in Athens on the orders of Demosthenes, because the house of his host had been visited by Aischines. He was tortured till he confessed to being a spy of Philip, on which he was put to death.

'I wonder how long,' Philotas said, 'before it comes to war.'

'We are at war,' said Alexander. 'It's only a matter of where we shall fight the battle. It would be impious to lay Athens waste; like sacking a temple. But sooner or later, we shall have to deal with the Athenians.'

'Will you?' asked crippled Harpalos, who saw in the fighters round him a friendly but alien race. 'The louder they bark, the more you can see their rotten teeth.'

'Not so rotten that we can do with them in our backsides when we cross to Asia.'

The war for the Greek cities of Asia was no longer a vision; its essential strategy had begun. Each year saw the causeway of conquered lands pushed nearer to the Hellespont. The strongpoints of the narrow seas, Perinthos and Byzantion, were the last great obstacles. If they could be taken, Philip would need only to secure his rear.

This fact being plain, the Athenian orators were touring Greece again in search of allies whom Philip had not yet persuaded, scared or bought. The fleet off Thrace was sent a little money; an island base was garrisoned in Thasos, close at hand. In the garden of Mieza, the young men debated together how soon they would get another taste of fighting, or, under the eye of the philosopher, discussed the nature and attributes of the soul.

Hephaistion, who had never imported anything in his life before, had gone through the complex business of ordering from Athens a copy of *The Myrmidons*, which he gave to Alexander. Under a flower-bowed lilac beside the pool of the Nymphs, they discussed the nature and attributes of love.

It was the time when the wild beasts mated in the woods. Aristotle was preparing a thesis on their coupling and the generation of their young.

His pupils, instead of hunting, hid in the coverts and made notes. Harpalos and a friend of his amused themselves by inventing far-fetched procedures, carefully doctored with enough science to secure belief. The philosopher, who thought himself too useful to mankind to risk a chill crouching for hours on wet ground, thanked them warmly and wrote all of it down.

One beautiful day, Hephaistion told Alexander he had found a vixen's earth, and thought she was mating. An old tree near by had been uprooted in the storms, leaving a deep hollow; one could watch from there. In the late sunlight, they went into the forest, not crossing the paths of their friends. Neither remarked on this, or offered the other any reason.

The dead roots of the fallen tree sheltered the hollow; its bottom was soft with last year's deep-drifted leaves. After some time the vixen, heavy with young, came slipping through the shadows with a partridge-chick in her mouth. Hephaistion half-raised his head; Alexander, who had closed his eyes, heard the rustle of her passage but did not open them. She took fright at their breathing, and ran like a red streak into her lair.

Soon after, Aristotle expressed the wish to dissect a pregnant fox-bitch; but they spared the guardian of their mystery. She grew used to them, after a while, would bring out her cubs without fear, feed them and let them play.

Hephaistion liked the cubs, because they made Alexander smile. After love he would grow silent, drifting into some private darkness; if recalled he was not impatient, but too gentle, as if with something to hide.

Both agreed that all this had been ordained by their destinies before their birth. Hephaistion still felt an incredulous sense of miracle; his days and nights were lived in a glittering cloud. It was only at these times that a shadow pierced it; he would point to the fox-cubs playing, the deep brooding eyes would move and lighten, and all was well again. The pools and streams were fringed with forget-me-not and iris; in sunny copses the famous dog-roses of Mieza, blessed by the Nymphs, opened their great bland faces and spread their scent.

The young men read the signs with which their youth made them familiar, and paid up their bets. The philosopher, less expert and not so good a loser, while they all walked or sat in the rose-starred gardens looked doubtfully at the two handsome boys unfailingly side by side. He risked no questions; there was no place in his thesis for the answers.

The olives were powdered with fine pale-green flowers, whose faint sweet waxy scent blew everywhere. The apple-trees let fall their false fruit; small and green the true apples began to set. The vixen led her cubs into the forest; it was time they learned the craft by which they would live.

Hephaistion, too, became a patient and skilful hunter. Till his prey first came to his lure, he had not doubted that the passionate affection bestowed on him so freely held the germ of passion itself. He found matters less simple.

Once more he told himself that when the gods are bountiful, man must not cry for more. He thought how, like the heir of great wealth who is happy at first only to know his fortune, he had gazed at the face before him; the wind-tossed hair springing loosely from its peak, the forehead already traced with faint creases by the eyes' intensity; the eyes in their beautiful hollows, the firm yet feeling mouth, the aspiring arch of the golden eyebrows. It had seemed he could sit for ever, content simply with this. So it had seemed at first.

'Oxhead wants exercise, let's go riding.'

'Has he thrown the groom again?'

'No, that was just to teach him. I'd warned him, too.' The horse had consented, by degrees, to be mounted for the routine of the stables. But once his headstall was on with its buckles and plaques of silver, his collar worked with filigree, and his fringed saddle-cloth, then he knew himself the seat of godhead, and avenged impiety. The groom was still laid up.

They rode through red new-leaved beechwoods to the grassy uplands, at an easy pace set by Hephaistion, who knew Alexander would not let Oxhead stand in a sweat. At a coppice edge they dismounted, and stood looking out to the Chalkidian mountains beyond the plain and the sea.

'I found a book at Pella,' Alexander said, 'last time we were there. It's one by Plato, that Aristotle never showed us. I think he must have been envious.'

'What book?' Hephaistion smiling tested the hitch of his horse's bridle.

'I learned some, listen. *Love makes one ashamed of disgrace, and hungry for what is glorious; without which neither a people nor a man can do anything great or fine. If a lover were to be found doing something unworthy of himself, or basely failing to resent dishonour, he would rather be exposed before family or friends or anyone, than before the one he loves.* And somewhere it says, *Suppose a state or an army could be made up only of lovers and beloved. How could any company hope for greater things than these, despising infamy and rivalling each other in honour? Even a few of them, fighting side by side, might well conquer the world.*'

'That's beautiful.'

'He was a soldier when he was young, like Sokrates. I expect Aristotle was envious. The Athenians never founded a lovers' regiment, they left it to the Thebans. No one's yet beaten the Sacred Band, did you know that?'

'Let's go in the wood.'

'That's not the end, Sokrates ends it. He says the best, the greatest love can only be made by the soul.'

'Well,' said Hephaistion quickly, 'but everyone knows he was the ugliest man in Athens.'

'The beautiful Alkibiades threw himself at his head. But he said that to make love with the soul was the greatest victory, like the triple crown at the games.'

Hephaistion stared out in pain to the mountains of Chalkidike. 'It would be the greatest victory,' he said slowly, 'to the one who minded most.'

Knowing that in the service of a ruthless god he had baited his trap with knowledge gained in love, he turned to Alexander. He stood staring out at the clouds, in solitude, conferring with his daimon.

Guilt-troubled, Hephaistion reached out and grasped his arm. 'If you mean that, if it's what you really want ...'

He raised his brows, smiled, and tossed back his hair. 'I'll tell you something.'

'Yes?'

'If you can catch me.'

He was always the quickest off the mark. While his voice still hung in the air he was gone. Hephaistion threaded light birches and shadowy larches to a rocky scarp. At its foot Alexander lay motionless with closed eyes. Distraught and breathless Hephaistion clambered down, knelt by him, felt him for injuries. Nothing whatever was wrong. He eyed Hephaistion smiling. 'Hush! You'll scare the foxes.'

'I could kill you,' said Hephaistion with rapture.

The sunlight, sifting through the larch-boughs, had moved westward a little, striking glints like topaz from the wall of their rocky lair. Alexander lay watching the weaving tassels with his arm behind his head.

'What are you thinking of?' Hephaistion asked him.

'Of death.'

'It does leave people sad sometimes. It's the vital spirits that have gone out of one. I'd not have it undone; would you?'

'No; true friends should be everything to one another.'

'It *is* what you really want?'

'You should know that.'

'I can't bear you to be sad.'

'It soon goes by. It's the envy of some god perhaps.' He reached up to Hephaistion's head, bent anxiously above him, and settled it on his shoulder. 'One or two of them were shamed by unworthy choices. Don't name them, they might be angry; still, we know. Even the gods can be envious.'

Hephaistion, his mind freed from the clouds of longing, saw in a divining moment the succession of King Philip's young men: their coarse good looks, their raw sexuality like a smell of sweat, their jealousies, their intrigues, their insolence. Out of all the world, he had been chosen to be everything which those were not; between his hands had been laid, in trust, Alexander's pride. As long as he should live, nothing greater could ever happen to him than this; to have more, one would need to be made immortal. Tears burst from his eyes, and trickled down on the throat of Alexander, who, believing he too felt the after sadness, smilingly stroked his hair.

In the next year's spring, Demosthenes sailed north to Perinthos and Byzantion, the fortified cities on the narrow seas. Philip had negotiated a peace treaty with each: if let alone, they would not impede his march. Demosthenes persuaded both cities to denounce the treaties. The Athenian forces based on Thasos were conducting an undeclared war with Macedon.

On the drillfield of the Pella plain, a sea-flat left bare in old men's living memory, the phalanxes wheeled and counter-marched with their long sarissas, graded so that the points of three ranks, in open order, should strike the enemy front in a single line. The cavalry did their combat exercises, gripping with the thighs, the knees, and by the mane, to help them keep their seats through the shock of impact.

At Mieza, Alexander and Hephaistion were packing their kit to start at dawn next day, and searching each other's hair.

'None this time,' said Hephaistion laying down the comb. 'It's in winter, with people huddling together, that one picks them up.'

Alexander, sitting at his knees, shoved off a dog of his that was trying to lick his face, and changed places. 'Fleas one can drown,' he said as he worked, 'but lice are like Illyrians creeping about in the woods. We'll have plenty on campaign, one can at least start clean. I don't think you've ... no, wait ... Well, that's all.' He got up to reach a stoppered flask from a shelf. 'We'll use this again, it's far the best. I must tell Aristotle.'

'It stinks.'

'No, I put in some aromatics. Smell.' During this last year, he had been taken up with the healing art. Among much theory, little of which he thought could issue well in action, this was a useful thing, which warrior princes had not disdained on the field of Troy; the painters showed Achilles binding Patroklos' wounds. His keenness had somewhat disconcerted Aristotle, whose own interest now was academic; but the science had been his paternal heritage, and he found after all a pleasure in teaching it. Alexander now kept a notebook of salves and draughts, with hints on the treatment of fevers, wounds and broken limbs.

'It does smell better,' Hephaistion conceded. 'And it seems to keep them off.'

'My mother had a charm against them. But she always ended in picking them out by hand.'

The dog sat grieving by the baggage, whose smell it recognized. Alexander had been in action not many months before, commanding his own company as the King had promised. All of today the house had sounded with shrill susurrations, like crickets' chirping; the scrape of whetstones on javelins, daggers and swords, as the young men made ready.

Hephaistion thought of the coming war without fear, erasing from his mind, or smothering in its depths, even the fear that Alexander would be killed. Only so was life possible at his side. Hephaistion would avoid dying if he could, because he was needed. One must study how to make the enemy die instead, and beyond that trust in the gods.

'One thing I'm scared of,' said Alexander, working his sword about in its sheath till the blade glided like silk through the well-waxed leather. 'That the south will come in before I'm ready.' He reached for the brush of chewed stick with which he cleaned the goldwork.

'Give me that, I'll do it along with mine.' Hephaistion bent over the elaborate finial of the sheath, and the latticed strapwork. Alexander always rid himself of his javelins quickly, the sword was already his weapon, face to face, hand to hand. Hephaistion muttered a luck-charm over it as he worked.

'Before we march into Greece, I hope to be a general.'

Hephaistion looked up from rubbing the hilt of polished shark-skin. 'Don't set your heart on it; time's looking short.'

'They'd follow me already, in the field, if it came to a push in action. That I know. They'd not think it proper to appoint me yet, though. A year, two years ... But they'd follow me, now.'

Hephaistion gave it thought; he never told Alexander what he wished to hear, if it could cause him trouble later. 'Yes, they would. I saw that last time. Once they thought you were just a luck-bringer. But now they can tell you know what you're about.'

'They've known me a long time.' Alexander took down his helmet from the wall-peg, and shook out its white horsehair crest.

'To hear some of them talk, one would think they'd reared you.' Hephaistion dug too hard with the brush, broke it, and had to chew a new end.

'Some of them have.' Alexander, having combed the crest, went over to the wall-mirror. 'I think it will do. It's good metal, it fits, and the men can see me.' Pella had no lack of first-class armourers. They came north from Corinth, knowing where good custom was. 'When I'm a general, I can have one to show up.'

Hephaistion, looking over his shoulder at his mirrored face, said, 'I'll bet on that. You're like a gamecock for finery.'

Alexander hung back the helmet. 'You're angry, why?'

'Get made a general, then you'll have a tent of your own. We'll never be out of a crowd from tomorrow till we get back.'

'Oh ... Yes, I know. But that's war.'

'One has to get used to it. Like the fleas.'

Alexander came swiftly over, struck with remorse at having forgotten. 'In our souls,' he said, 'we'll be more than ever united, winning eternal fame. *Son of Menoitios, great one, you who delight my heart.*' He smiled deeply into Hephaistion's eyes, which faithfully smiled back. 'Love is the true food of the soul. But the soul eats to live, like the body; it mustn't live to eat.'

'No,' said Hephaistion. What he lived for was his own business, part of which was that Alexander should not be burdened with it.

'The soul must live to *do*.'

Hephaistion put aside the sword, took up the dagger with its dolphin hilts and agate pommel, and agreed that this was so.

Pella rang and rattled with sounds of war. The breeze brought Oxhead the noise and smell of war-chargers; he flared his nostrils and whinnied.

King Philip was on the parade-ground. He had had scaling-ladders rigged up against tall scaffolding, and was making the men climb up in proper order, without crowding, jostling, pinking each other with their weapons, or undue delay. He sent his son a message that he would see him after manoeuvres. The Queen would see him at once.

When she embraced him, she found he was the taller. He stood five feet seven; before his bones set, he might make another inch or so, not more. But he could break a cornel spear-shaft between his hands, walk thirty miles in a day over rough country without food (for a test, he had done it once without drink either). By gradual unnoticed stages, he had ceased to grieve that he was not tall. The tall men of the phalanx, who could wield a twenty-foot sarissa, liked him very well as he was.

His mother, though there was only an inch between them, laid her head on his shoulder, making herself soft and tender like a roosting dove. 'You are a man, really a man now.' She told him all his father's wickedness; there was nothing new. He stroked her hair and echoed her indignation, his mind upon the war. She asked him what kind of youth was this Hephaistion; was he ambitious, what did he ask for, had he exacted any promises? Yes. That they should be together in battle. Ah! Was that to be trusted? He laughed, patted her cheek, and saw the real question in her eyes, which sought, like wrestlers, for a moment's failure of nerve which would let her ask it. He faced her out, and she did not ask. It made him fond of her and forgiving; he leaned to her hair to smell its scent.

Philip was in the painted study at a littered desk. He had come straight from the drill-field, the room smelled acridly of his horse's sweat and his own. At the kiss of greeting, he noticed that his son, after a ride of less than forty miles, had already bathed to wash off the dust. But the real shock was to perceive on his jaw a fine golden stubble. With astonishment and dismay, Philip perceived that the boy was not, after all, behindhand with his beard. He had been shaving.

A Macedonian, a king's son, what could have possessed him to make him ape the effete ways of the south? Smooth as a girl. For whom was he doing this? Philip was well-informed about Mieza; Parmenion had arranged this secretly with Philotas, who made regular reports. It was one thing to take up with Amyntor's son, a harmless and comely youth whom Philip, indeed, could himself have fancied; it was another to go about looking like someone's minion. He cast his mind back to the troop of young men he had seen arriving; it now occurred to him that there had been older chins there, beardless too. It must be a fashion among them. A vague feeling of subversion stirred under his skin; but he pushed it out of the way. In spite of the boy's oddities, he was trusted by the men; and, since business stood where it did, this was no time to cross him.

Philip waved his son to the seat beside him. 'Well,' he said, 'as you see, we're well forward here.' He described his preparations; Alexander listened, elbows on knees, hands clasped before him; one could see his mind running a step ahead. 'Perinthos will be tough to crack, but we shall have Byzantion on our hands as well; openly or not they'll support Perinthos. So will the Great King. I doubt he's in a state to make war, from what I hear; but he'll send supplies. He has a treaty for that with Athens.'

For a moment, their faces shared a single thought. It was as if they spoke of some great lady, the strict mentor of their childhood, now found to be plying the streets in a seaport town. Alexander glanced at the beautiful old bronze by Polykleitos, of Hermes inventing the lyre. He had known it all his life; the too-slender youth with his fine bones and runner's muscles had always seemed, under the divine calm imposed by the sculptor, to conceal a deep inward sadness, as if he knew it would come to this.

'Well, then, Father; when do we march?'

'Parmenion and I, seven days from now. Not you, my son. You will be at Pella.'

Alexander sat bolt upright staring; he seemed to stiffen all over. 'At Pella? What do you mean?'

Philip grinned. 'You look for all the world like that horse of yours, shying at his shadow. Don't be so quick off the mark. You won't be sitting idle.'

From his scarred and knotted hand he drew a massive ring of antique goldwork. Its signet of sardonyx was carved with a Zeus enthroned, eagle on fist; it was the royal seal of Macedon.

'You will look after this.' He flipped it up and caught it. 'Do you think you can?'

The fierceness left Alexander's face; for a moment it looked almost stupid. In the King's absence, the Seal was held by his Regent.

'You've had a good grounding in war,' his father said. 'When you're old enough to be up-graded without a fuss, you can have a cavalry brigade. Let's say two years. Meantime, you must learn administration. It's worse than useless to push out frontiers, if the realm's in chaos behind you. Remember, I had to deal with that before I could move anywhere, even against the Illyrians who were inside our borders. Don't think it can't come back again. Moreover, you'll have to protect my lines of communication. This is serious work I'm giving you.'

Watching the eyes before him, he saw a look in them he had not met since the day of the horse-fair, at the end of the ride. 'Yes, Father. I know it. Thank you; I'll see that you don't repent of it.'

'Antipatros will stay too; if you've sense you'll consult him. But that's your own choice; the Seal's the Seal.'

Each day till the army marched, Philip held councils: with the officers of the home garrisons, the tax-collectors, the officers of justice, the men whom the tribal chiefs, enrolled with the Companions, had left to rule their tribes; the chiefs and princes who for reasons historic, traditional or legal remained at home. Amyntas was one, the son of Perdikkas, Philip's elder brother. When his father fell he had been a child. Philip had been elected Regent; before Amyntas came of age, the Macedonians had decided they liked Philip's work and wanted to keep him on. With the royal kin, the throne was elective by ancient right. He had dealt graciously with Amyntas, giving him the status of a royal nephew, and one of his own half-legal daughters for a wife. He had been conditioned to his lot from infancy; he came now to the councils, a thick-set, dark-bearded young man of five and twenty, whom any stranger might have picked out of a crowd as Philip's son. Alexander, sitting on his father's right at the conference, would steal a look sometimes, wondering if such inertia could be real.

When the army marched, Alexander escorted his father to the coast road, embraced him, and turned for Pella. Oxhead, as the cavalry went off without him, blew restively down his nose. Philip was pleased he had told the boy he would be in charge of the communication lines. A happy thought; it had delighted him; and in fact the route was very well secured.

The first act of Alexander's regency was a private one; he bought a thin slip of gold, which he wound round the hoop of the royal signet to make it fit his finger. He knew that symbols are magical, in perfection and in defect.

Antipatros proved most helpful. He was a man for acting on facts, not wishes. He knew his son had fallen foul of Alexander, disbelieved Kassandros' version of it, and had been keeping him well out of the Prince's way; for here, if Antipatros had ever seen one, was a boy needing only a clumsy push at a crucial moment to discover in himself a very dangerous man. He must be served and served well, or else destroyed. In Antipatros' youth, before Philip secured the kingdom, a man might find himself any day standing siege in his own home against a vengeful neighbour prince, a horde of Illyrian raiders, or a brigand band. His choice had long since been made.

Philip had sacrificed his useful Chief Secretary, to take care of the young Regent. Alexander thanked him politely for the digests he had prepared, then asked for the original correspondence; he wished, he explained, to get the feel of the men who wrote. When he met anything unfamiliar, he asked questions. After everything was clear in his mind, he consulted with Antipatros.

They had no differences, till one day when a certain soldier was accused of rape, but swore to the woman's willingness. Antipatros was inclined to accept his well-argued case; but since a blood-feud threatened, he felt obliged to consult the Regent. With some diffidence he laid the unsavoury tale before the fresh-faced youth in Archelaos' study, who answered without a pause that Sotion, as all his phalanx knew, when sober could talk his way out of a wolf-trap, but in drink he'd not know a farrow sow from his sister, and either would do as well.

A few days after the King marched east, the whole garrison force around Pella was called out on manoeuvre. Alexander had had some thoughts about the use of light cavalry against flanking infantry. Besides, he said, they must not be allowed to gather moss.

Relieved or frustrated at being left behind, in either case the men were inclined to take things easy. Before the trim well-burnished youth on his sleek black horse had ridden half down the line, they were dressing ranks with nervous care and trying, with scant success, to conceal defects. One or two were sent in disgrace straight back to barracks. The rest spent a strenuous morning. Afterwards, the veterans who beforehand had grumbled loudest, jeered at raw men's complaints; the youngster might have sweated them, but he knew how many beans make five.

'They shaped quite well,' said Alexander to Hephaistion. 'The chief thing is, they know now who's in command.'

It was not, however, the troops who first tested this.

'My darling,' said Olympias, 'there is a little thing you must do for me

before your father comes back; you know how he crosses me in everything. Deinias has done me so many kindnesses, looked after my friends,
kept me warned of enemies. Your father has held back his son's promotion,
just out of spite. Deinias would like him to have a squadron. He is a most
useful man.'

Alexander, half whose mind had been on mountain manoeuvres, said,
'Is he? Where is he serving?'

'Serving? It is Deinias, of course, I meant is useful.'

'Oh. What's the son's name, who's his squadron commander?'

Olympias looked reproach, but referred to her notes and told him.

'Oh, Heirax. He wants *Heirax* to have a squadron?'

'It's a slight to a distinguished man like Deinias; he feels it is.'

'He feels this is the time to say so. I expect Heirax asked him.'

'Why not, when your father has taken against him for my sake?'

'No, Mother. For mine.'

She swept round to face him. Her eyes seemed to explore some dangerous stranger.

'I've been in action,' he said, 'with Heirax, and I told Father what I saw
of him. That's the reason he's here instead of in Thrace. He's obstinate,
he resents men who are quicker-thinking than he is; and then when things
go wrong he tries to shift the blame. Father transferred him to garrison
duty, rather than demote him. I'd have demoted him, myself.'

'Oh! Since when is it Father this and Father that! Am I no one to you
now, because he gives you the Seal to wear! Do you take his part against
me?'

'I take the men's part. They may have to be killed by the enemy; that's
no reason to have them killed by a fool like Heirax. If I gave him a
squadron, they'd never trust me again.'

She struck back at the man in him, with love and hatred. Once long ago,
in the torchlit cave of Samothrace, when she was fifteen, she had met the
eyes of a man before she knew what men were. 'You are growing absurd.
What do you think it means, that thing stuck on your finger? You are only
Antipatros' pupil; it was to watch him govern that Philip left you here.
What do you know of men?'

She was ready for the battle, the tears and the bloodstained peace. For
a moment he said nothing. Suddenly he grinned at her. 'Very well, then,
Mother. Little boys should leave affairs to the men, and not interfere.'

While she still stared, he took three quick strides across and put his arm
round her waist. 'Dearest Mother! You know I love you. Now leave all
these things and let me deal with them. I can see to them. You're not to
be troubled with them any more.'

For a moment she stood rigid. Presently she told him he was a wicked

cruel boy, and she could not think what she would say to Deinias. But she
had softened in his arm; and he knew she had been glad to feel its strength.

He gave up his hunting-trips to stay near Pella. In his absence, Antipatros would feel justified in taking decisions without him. Feeling short
of exercise, and rambling through the stables, he found a chariot fitted up
for the dismounters' race. Years ago he had meant to learn the trick, but
then had come Mieza. The chariot was a synoris, a two-horse racer of
walnut and pearwood; the bronze hand-grip for the dismounter was about
the right height; it was not a race for big men. He had two Venetian ponies
yoked to it, called for the royal charioteer, and began to practise jumping
down in mid-course, running with the car and leaping up again. Besides
being good exercise, it was Homeric; the dismounter was the last heir of
the chariot-borne hero, who drove to the fray in order to fight on foot. His
spare hours were given to acquiring this archaic skill; he became very fast
at it. Old chariot-sheds were rummaged, so that friends could give him a
race; this he enjoyed, but never arranged a formal one. He had disliked
set contests, from as soon as he had been old enough to perceive that there
were people who would let him win.

Dispatches came from Propontis, where Philip, as he had foretold, was
finding Perinthos hard to crack. It stood on a headland impregnable from
the sea, and strongly walled inland. The Perinthians, prospering and
increasing on their steep rocks, had for years been building upward; four-
and five-storey houses, rising in tiers like theatre benches, overlooked the
ramparts, and now harboured slingers and javelineers to repel assaults.
Philip, to give his men covering fire, had built hundred-foot siege towers,
and mounted a platform of catapults; his sappers had brought down part
of the wall, only to find an inner one, made from the first row of houses
packed solid with rock, rubble and earth. As he had expected, too, the
Byzantines were supplying the enemy; their fast triremes, with pilots
expert in local waters (Macedon had never been a strong naval power),
brought in crack troops, and kept open the way for the Great King's store-
ships. He was fulfilling his pact with Athens.

King Philip, who dictated these reports, was a crisp and clear expositor.
After reading one, Alexander would pace about, aware of the great
campaign he was missing. Even the Seal was scant amends.

He was on the race-track one morning, when he saw Harpalos waving.
A Palace messenger had passed the word to someone who could stop him
without disrespect; it must be urgent. He jumped down from the car, ran
with it a few steps to keep his balance, and came over, plastered with track-
dust which coated his legs to the knee as thick as buskins. Through the
mask of sweat-striped dirt shone his eyes, looking by contrast turquoise-
blue. His friends stood well away, not from good manners but to keep him

off their clothes. Harpalos murmured behind him, 'It's an odd thing; have you noticed he never stinks, when anyone else would be rank as a dog-fox?' 'Ask Aristotle,' said someone. 'No, I think he must burn it up.'

The messenger reported that a courier was in from the north-east border, awaiting the Prince's leisure.

He sent a servant running to fetch him a fresh chiton; stripped and scraped-down under the horse-yard fountain; and appeared in the audience-room just before Antipatros, the scroll still correctly sealed, had finished questioning the courier, who had more to tell. He had barely got back with his life from the highlands up the Strymon river, where Macedon knit with Thrace in a mesh of disputed gorges, mountains, forests and grazing-grounds.

Antipatros blinked with surprise at Alexander's uncanny promptness; the messenger blinked with exhaustion, his eyes gummed by lack of sleep. Having asked his name, Alexander said, 'You look dead tired; sit down.' Clapping his hands he ordered wine for the man; while it came, he read the dispatch to Antipatros. When the man had drunk, he asked him what he knew.

The Maidoi were hillmen of a strain so ancient that Achaians, Dorians, Macedonians and Celts had all, in their southward drift, passed by the tribe's savage homeland in hope of better things. They had survived in the mountains and the Thracian weather, tough as wild goats, keeping up customs older than the age of bronze, and, when in spite of human sacrifice their food-gods were still unkind, raiding the settled lands. Philip had conquered them long ago, and taken their oaths of fealty; but with time he had grown dim to them and faded into legend. Their numbers had increased; boys come to manhood needed to blood their spears; they had broken south like a flash-flood in a river bed. Farms had been stripped and burned; Macedonian settlers and loyal Thracians had been cut up alive, their heads taken for trophies, their women carried away.

Antipatros, for whom this was a second hearing, watched the youth in the chair of state, waiting kindly to meet his need with reassurance. He remained, however, with his eyes fixed on the messenger, sitting forward eagerly.

'Rest awhile,' he said presently. 'I want a few things in writing.' When the scribe appeared, he dictated, checking them with the messenger, the Maidoi's movements and the main features of the country; adding, himself, a sketch-map worked up in the wax. Having checked this too, he ordered that the man be bathed, fed and put to bed, and sent out the clerk.

'I thought,' he said scanning the tablets, 'we should get all this from him now. A night's sleep should set him up, but one never knows, he might die. I want him well rested till I start out, so that I can take him as a guide.'

Antipatros' brows with their foxy grizzle met over his fierce nose. He had felt this coming, but decided not to believe in it.

'Alexander, you know how gladly I would have you with me. But you know too it is impossible we should both be out of Macedon, with the King at war.'

Alexander sat back in his chair. His hair, streaked with dust and damp from his makeshift bath, hung limply on his brow; his nails and his toes were grimy. His eyes were cool, and made no pretence at naïvety. 'But of course, Antipatros. I should never think of such a thing. I shall leave you the Seal, while I am gone.'

Antipatros opened his mouth, breathed deep and paused. Alexander cut in ahead, with inflexible courtesy. 'I haven't it on me, I've been at exercise. You shall have it when I leave Pella.'

'Alexander! Only consider ...'

Alexander, who had been watching him like a duellist, made a small gesture to say he had not done speaking. After a crucial instant, Antipatros' voice trailed off. With stately formality, Alexander said, 'Both my father and I know our great good fortune, in having such a man to entrust the realm to.' He stood up, feet apart, hands on his belt, and tossed back his tousled hair. 'I'm going, Antipatros. Settle your mind to it, because we're short of time. I shall start at dawn tomorrow.'

Antipatros, who perforce had risen too, tried to use his height but found it ineffectual. 'If you will, you will. But just think first. You're a good field officer, that's common knowledge. The men like you, agreed. But you've never mounted a campaign, or kept it in supplies, or planned its strategy. Do you know what that country's like?'

'By this time they'll be down in the Strymon valley; that's what they came for. We'll discuss supplies at the war-council. I'm calling one in an hour.'

'Do you realize, Alexander, that if you lose, half Thrace will blaze up like a fire of myrtle-brush? Your father's lines will be cut; and once the news is out, I'll be holding the north-west against the Illyrians.'

'What troops would you need for that?'

'If you lose, there wouldn't be enough in Macedon.'

Alexander tilted his head a little to the left; his gaze, floating beyond Antipatros' head, went slightly out of focus. 'Also, if I lose, the men won't trust me again and I shall never be a general. Also, my father may well say I'm no son of his, and I shall never be a king. Well, I shall have to win, it seems.'

Antipatros thought, Kassandros should never have crossed him ... The eggshell was cracking indeed. One must already be very careful. 'What about me? What will he say to me for letting you go?'

'If I lose, you mean? That I should have taken your advice. Write it down, and I'll sign to say you gave it to me; win or lose, it goes to my father. How's that for a fair bet?'

Antipatros looked sharply from under his shaggy brows. 'Ah. But you'd hold it against me after.'

'Oh yes,' said Alexander blandly. 'Of course I should; what do you suppose? You make your bet, Antipatros. You can't expect to hedge it. I can't hedge mine.'

'I think the stakes as they stand are high enough.' Antipatros smiled, remembering that already one must be careful. 'Let me know what you want, then. I've bet on worse horses in my time.'

Alexander was on his feet all day, except during the war-council. He could have sat while he was sending out orders, but he could think more quickly pacing to and fro; perhaps it came from the walking discussions at Mieza. He had meant to see his mother earlier, but there had been no time. He went when he had settled everything, but did not stay very long; she was inclined to make a fuss, though surely this was what she had been wanting. She would see that later. Meantime he had Phoinix to say good-bye to; and it was important to get some sleep.

It was a quiet morning in the camp before Perinthos; there had been an engagement on the wall the night before, and the men were being rested. The noises were those of lull: mules whinnied, men serviced the engines with shouts and clanks, a man with a head-wound shouted insanely from the hospital shed; a captain of artillery, detailed to see the besieged did not take a holiday, shouted to his crew to lift her up a chock, and grease the bolt-track; there was a clang from the pile of massive bolt-heads, each stamped with the laconic message, FROM PHILIP.

Philip had had a large timbered hut put up for him; when not on the move, there was no sense in using the royal tent, to sweat under stinking leather. He had made himself snug like an old campaigner; local straw matting covered the floor, his baggage-train had carried chairs, lamp-stands, a bath, and a bed broad enough for company. At a pinewood table, made by the camp carpenters, he sat with Parmenion, reading a dispatch.

'Having summoned also the troops from Pydna and Amphipolis, I marched north to Therma. I had planned to go by the Great East Road to Amphipolis, to learn the enemy's movements, and to make whatever dispositions seemed best, before going north up river.

'But at Therma, a rider met me, from the country of the Agrianoi. He had been sent by Lambaros, my guest-friend, in fulfilment of a vow.

'Guest-friend?' said Philip. 'Guest-friend? What does he mean? The boy was a hostage. You remember, Parmenion. I'd have bet a talent the Agrianoi would have joined the Maidoi.'

'What was it you told me,' said Parmenion, 'about the Prince slipping off for a jaunt among the tribesmen, after you'd sent him back to school? I well remember you swearing when you heard.'

'That's so, that's so. It slipped my memory. A crazy escapade, he was lucky not to have had his throat cut. I don't take hostages from tribes I think are safe. Guest-friend! Well, let's see.

'*Having heard you were in the east, he sent me word that the Maidoi were in the upper Strymon valley, laying everything waste. They had invited his people to join them in the war; but King Teres respected the oaths exchanged when you returned his son to him.*'

'Wouldn't burn his fingers. But it was the boy who sent the message. How old will he be now? About seventeen.

'*He advised me to march quickly up river to Rushing Gate, as they call the steep throat of the gorge, and reinforce the old fort there, before they came down into the plain. I therefore decided not to lose time myself by going to Amphipolis, but to send Koinos with my orders to bring on the troops from there; I would lead the men I had straight up over the Krousia range by the trackways, and ford the Strymon at Siris, where Koinos would meet me with men, fresh horses and supplies, we ourselves travelling light. When I told the men what kind of dangers threatened our colonists in the plain, they made good going; the tracks being difficult, I went on foot with them, encouraging them to hurry.*'

Philip looked up. 'Some secretary polished this. But touches of nature show.

'*We crossed over Krousia and forded Strymon by noon on the third day.*'

'What?' said Parmenion staring. 'Over Krousia? It's sixty miles.'

'He moved light, and encouraged them to hurry.

'*Koinos met me promptly with all orders carried out. This officer acted with speed and address, and I commend him highly. Also he talked sense to Stasandros commanding at Amphipolis, who thought I should have wasted three days marching out that way and asking him what to do.*'

'Added,' said Philip with a grin, 'in his own hand.

'*Through Koinos' good management of his mission, I got the forces I had asked for, one thousand men . . .*'

Parmenion's jaw dropped. He did not attempt comment.

'*Which, though it left Amphipolis undermanned, still seemed to me most prudent, since for every day the Maidoi went undefeated, the chance grew greater of their being joined by other tribes. I had lookouts and beacons between me and the coast, to warn me if the Athenians should attack by sea.*'

'Ah,' mused Parmenion. 'Still, I wonder he got a steady man like Koinos to take it on.'

'*But before we reached the Strymon, the Maidoi had already overrun the fort at Rushing Gate, had reached the plain and begun to ravage the farms. Some had crossed the Strymon westward to the silver mine, killed the guards and slaves, and carried home the bar silver through the river pass. This decided me that it would not be enough to beat them off the farmlands; their own settlement ought to be reduced by war.*'

'Did he know,' asked Parmenion incredulously, 'where it is?'

'*When I had looked over the troops, I sacrificed to the appropriate gods, and to Herakles, and was given good auguries by the diviners. Also, one of the loyal Paionians told me that while hunting early, he had seen a wolf as it fed upon a carcase, taken by a young lion. The soldiers were pleased with the omen, and I rewarded the man with gold.*'

'He deserved it,' said Philip. 'The shrewdest of the diviners.

'*Before starting my advance, I sent five hundred chosen hillmen to go under cover of the woods and surprise the fort at the Gate. Lambaros my guest-friend had advised me that it would be held by the worst of the enemy, since none of their foremost warriors would forego his share of the loot to secure their rear. My men found this to be true. They found also the bodies of our garrison, and saw that our wounded had been maltreated. As I had ordered should this be so, they threw the Maidoi down the cliffs into the rapids. They then manned the fort and both flanks of the gorge. Kephalon led; an energetic officer.*

'*In the valley, some of our colonists had sent off their families to safety, and stayed themselves to fight off the enemy. I commended them for their courage, issued them with arms, and promised them a year's tax remission.*'

'Young men never know where money comes from,' said the King. 'You can be sure he never thought to ask what their tax was worth.

'*I now led all my forces north up the valley, with my right flank advanced to deny the high ground to the enemy. Where we came on dispersed bands looting, these we destroyed; the rest we worked north-east, worrying them like herd-dogs getting the flock together, lest they should scatter off into the hills without giving us battle. Thracians trust everything to their first headlong rush, and do not like to stand.*

'*They collected where I had hoped, in a tongue of land where the river makes an elbow with the lake. They reckoned, as I thought they would, on the river securing their backs; I reckoned to push them into it. There was a ford at their rear, known for being deep and treacherous. By the time they had wet their bowstrings and lost their heavy arms, they should be ready to make for home through the pass, not knowing that my men held it.*

'*This, then was the order of battle . . .*'

A workmanlike summary followed. Philip muttered through it, forgetting to recite aloud to Parmenion, who craned forward to hear. Lured out, rolled up, and thrown into confusion, the Maidoi had duly struggled off through the river, into the iron trap of the gorge. Alexander had returned to Amphipolis most of its borrowed garrison, in charge of his many prisoners.

'*Next day I pressed on up river beyond the pass; a number of the Maidoi had crossed the mountains by other ways, and I did not want to give them leisure to re-form. So I came to the country of the Agrianoi. Here Lambaros, my guest-friend, met me with a troop of horse, his friends and kinsmen. He had asked leave of his father to ride to war with us, in fulfilment of a vow. They showed us the easiest passes; later they did very well in battle.*

'Teres saw which way the cat was jumping,' said Philip. 'Yet the boy didn't wait. Why? A child when he was at Pella, I can't even remember what he looked like.'

He muttered his way through the breakneck mountain campaign that followed. Guided by his allies to the enemy's craggy nest, Alexander had attacked its main approach, while his mountaineers crept up the sheer side left unguarded.

'*The men of the valley, wanting to revenge their wrongs, were about to kill everyone they found; but I ordered them to spare the women and the children, who had injured no one. These I sent to Amphipolis; do with them as you think best.*'

'Sensible lad,' said Parmenion. 'Those strong hill-women always fetch good prices; work better than the men.'

Philip skimmed on, through rounding-up operations and commendations (*Hephaistion son of Amyntor, of Pella, fought with great distinction*), his voice fading to the murmur of routine business. Suddenly, making Parmenion jump, he shouted, '*What?*'

'Well, what, then?' asked Parmenion presently.

Philip, looking up from the roll, said in a measured voice, 'He has stayed on there to found a city.'

'It must be the clerk's writing.'

'The clerk writes like a book. The Maidoi had some good grazing-lands, and the footslopes will grow vines. So he is refounding their city, in counsel with Lambaros, his guest-friend. I reckon they can notch up thirty-three years between them.'

'If as much,' Parmenion grunted.

'He has considered suitable colonists. Agrianoi of course; loyal Paionians; some landless Macedonians he knows of, and ... Yes, wait. An afterthought, this. Have I any good men I would like to reward with a gift of land? He thinks he could take twenty.'

Parmenion, deciding that only a fool would open his mouth, cleared the back of his throat to fill the pause.

'Of course he has named the city. Alexandropolis.'

He stared down at the parchment. Parmenion looked at the shrewd, scarred, ageing face, the grizzled black brows and beard; the old bull snuffing the new spring air, tilting his battle-frayed old horns. I'm getting on too, Parmenion thought. They had shared the Thracian winters, stood together through the Illyrian battle-rush; they had shared muddy water in drought, wine after the battle; they had shared a woman, when they were young; she had never known for sure which had fathered her child; they had shared the joke. Parmenion cleared the back of his throat again.

'The boy's for ever saying,' he brought out brusquely, 'that you'll leave him nothing to do, to make his name on. He's taking what chance he can.'

Philip brought down his fist on the table. 'I'm proud of him,' he said decisively. 'Proud of him.' He pulled a blank tablet towards him, and with deep quick strokes sketched the battle. 'That's a pretty plan, nice dispositions. But let them get out of touch; let a gap open, now say, *here*, and where would he have been then, eh? Or if the cavalry pressed on out of hand? But no, he kept his hand on everything, there in the front line. And when they broke the wrong way, he changed his movement like *that*.'

He snapped his fingers. 'We shall see things, Parmenion, with this boy of mine. I'll find him those twenty settlers for his Alexandropolis, by God I will.'

'I'll ask about, then. Why don't we drink to it?'

'Why not?' He called for wine, and began rolling up the letter. 'What's this, wait, what's this? I never finished it.'

'Since I have been in the north, I hear everywhere of the Triballoi who live on the heights of Haimon, how they are unruly and warlike and a threat to the settled lands. It seems to me that while I am at Alexandropolis, I could carry the war up there, and bring them into order. I would like to ask your leave before drawing the troops I would need from Macedon. I propose . . .'

The wine came and was poured. Parmenion took a great gulp, forgetting to wait for the King, who forgot to notice it. 'The Triballoi! What does the boy want, does he want to push on up to the Ister?'

Philip, skipping the requisitions, read, *'These barbarians might annoy us, if they come on our rear when we cross to Asia; and if they were subdued, we could push our frontiers as far north as the Ister, which is a natural defence wall; being, as men say, the greatest river on earth after the Nile and the Encircling Ocean.'*

The two weathered men searched one another's faces, as if consulting omens. Philip broke the pause, throwing back his head in a great laugh full of broken teeth, and slapping his knee. Parmenion joined in with the loudness of relief.

'Simmias!' called the King at length. 'Look after the Prince's courier. A fresh horse tomorrow.' He threw back his wine. 'I must get off his recall at once, before he starts to mobilize; I don't want to disappoint the lad. Ah, I know. I'll propose he consults with Aristotle over the constitution of his city. What a boy, eh? What a boy!'

'What a boy!' echoed Parmenion. He gazed into his cup, seeing his own image in the dark face of the wine.

The long train of men marched south, by phalanxes and squadrons, along the Strymon plain. Alexander led, at the head of his personal squadron. Hephaistion rode beside him.

The air was loud with sound; thin harsh crying and keening, deep creaks as of strained wood. It was the call of kites, hovering and stooping and fighting for choice shreds, mixed with the croak of ravens.

The settlers had buried their dead, the soldiers burned theirs on ceremonial pyres. At the rear of the column, behind the straw-bedded hospital wagons, a cart trundled along with straw-packed urns of local pottery, each painted with a name.

Losses had been light, for victory had come quickly. The soldiers talked of it as they marched, gazing at the enemy's scattered thousands, lying where they had fallen to receive the rites of nature. By night the wolves and jackals had gorged on them; with daylight the village pi-dogs, and the birds which clustered in a moving pall. When the column passed near, they rose in a screaming cloud and hovered angrily over their meal; only then could one see the raw bones, and the rags torn by wolves in haste to reach the entrails. The stench, like the noise, shifted with the breeze.

In a few days they would be picked clean. Whoever owned the land, the worst of the work done for him, would burn the bones in a heap, or shovel them into a pit.

Over a dead horse danced vultures, bouncing up and down with half-opened wings, scrawking at one another. Oxhead gave a smothered squeal, and shied away. Alexander signed to the column to proceed, dismounted, and led the horse gently towards the mound of reeking flesh; stroking his muzzle, going ahead to scare off the vultures, and, when they scolded and flapped, returning with soothing words. Oxhead stamped and blew, disgusted but reassured. When they had stood there a few moments, Alexander mounted and cantered back to his place. 'Xenophon says,' he told Hephaistion, 'one should always do that with whatever scares a horse.'

'I didn't know there were so many kites in Thrace. What do they live on when there's no war?' Hephaistion, who felt sick, was talking to keep his mind off it.

'There's never no war in Thrace. But we'll ask Aristotle.'

'Are you still sorry,' said Hephaistion dropping his voice, 'that we didn't fight the Triballoi?'

'Why, of course,' said Alexander, surprised. 'We were half-way there. They'll have to be dealt with in the end; and we'd have seen the Ister.'

A small cavalry detail on the flank cantered ahead at his signal; there were some bodies blocking the road. They were raked into a hunting-net, and dragged out of the way.

'Ride on ahead,' Alexander ordered, 'and see it's clear ... Yes, I'm sorry still, of course; but I'm not angry. It's true, as he says, his forces are stretched just now. He sent me a very handsome letter; I read it too quickly, when I saw it was a recall.'

'Alexander,' said Hephaistion, 'I think that man there's alive.'

A council of vultures was considering something out of sight; bouncing forward, then recoiling as if offended or shocked. There came into view a feebly flailing arm.

'So long?' said Alexander wondering.

'It rained,' Hephaistion said.

Alexander turned and beckoned the first rider whose eye he met. The man cantered up smartly, and gazed at the wonderful boy with fervent affection.

'Polemon. If that man's not past help, have him picked up. They fought well, hereabouts. Or else finish him quickly.'

'Yes, Alexander,' said the man adoringly. Alexander gave him a slight approving smile; he went radiant off on his mission. Presently he re-mounted; the vultures, with satisfied croaks, closed in together.

Far on ahead of them shone the blue sea; soon, thought Hephaistion with relief, they would be past the battlefield. Alexander's eyes wandered over the bird-haunted plain, and beyond it skywards. He said:

> *Many brave men's souls it flung down to the house of Hades,*
> *While their flesh made a feast for dogs, and all the birds of the air.*
> *And the will of Zeus was fulfilled.'*

The rhythm of the hexameters matched itself smoothly to Oxhead's pacing. Hephaistion gazed at him silent. He rode on, at peace, with his unseen companion.

The Seal of Macedon stayed some time with Antipatros. Alexander had been met by a second courier, bidding him come to his father's siege-lines to be commended. He turned east to Propontis, taking his companions with him.

In the King's lodging before Perinthos, a well-lived-in home by now, father and son would sit at the pinewood trestle, over a tray of sea-sand

and stones; heaping up mountains, digging out defiles with their fingers, drawing with writing-sticks the disposition of cavalry, skirmishers, phalanxes and archers. Here no one disturbed their game, except sometimes the enemy. Philip's handsome young squires were decorous; bearded Pausanias with his ruined beauty, now promoted to Somatophylax, Commander of the Guard, watched impassively, never interrupting except for an alarm. Then they would buckle on their armour, Philip with veteran curses, Alexander eagerly. The troops whose section he joined would raise a cheer. Since his campaign he had a nickname: Basiliskos, the Little King.

His legend had run before him. Leading a scouting party against the Maidoi, he had walked round a crag straight into two of them, and dispatched them both while the men behind him were still catching their breath; neither had had time to shout a warning. He had kept a twelve-year-old Thracian girl in his tent all night, because she had run to him when the men were after her; had never laid a finger on her, and had given her a marriage dower. He had run between four big Macedonians brawling with their swords already out, and shoved them apart with his bare hands. In a mountain storm which had rained thunderbolts, so that it seemed the gods had resolved to destroy them all, he had read luck into it, kept them moving, made them laugh. Someone had had his wound staunched with the Basiliskos' own cloak, and been told his blood was a dye more honourable than purple; someone had died in his arms. Someone else, who had thought him raw enough to try old soldiers' tricks on, was sorry and sore. You would need to watch out, if he took against you. But put a fair case to him straight, he would see you right.

So, when in the light of the falling fires they saw him running towards the ladders, burnished like a dragonfly, greeting them as if they had all been bidden to a feast, they would call to him, and race for places near him. It was well to keep your eye on him; he would think quicker than you.

For all this, the siege went badly. Making an example of Olynthos had cut two ways; the Perinthians had decided that at the pinch they would rather die. And the pinch was still far off. The defenders, well supplied by sea, met assaults in strength and often went over to attack. They were setting their own example. From the Chersonesos, just south of the Great East Road, word came that the subject cities were taking heart. The Athenians had long urged revolt on them; but they would not take in Athenian troops, who were seldom paid and forced to live off the country. Now the cities had been emboldened. Macedonian outposts had been seized, and strongpoints threatened. War had begun.

'I swept one side of the road for you, Father,' Alexander said as soon as the news arrived. 'Now let me sweep the other.'

'So I will, as soon as the new troops come. I'll use them here; you'll need men who know the country.'

He was planning a surprise assault upon Byzantion, to stop their aid to Perinthos; as well deal with them now as later. He was committed, more deeply than he liked, to this costly war, and had needed to hire more mercenaries. They were coming up from Argos and Arkadia, states friendly to his power because for generations they had lived under the threat of Sparta; they did not share the anger and dread of Athens. But they cost money; which had been swallowed by the siege like water poured in sand.

At length they came, square stocky men of Philip's own build; his Argive descent still showed in him, bridging the generations. He reviewed them and conferred with their officers, from whom for better or worse hired troops would never be divided; it made a weak link in the chain of command. However, they were trained men who would earn their pay. Alexander and his troops marched west; already the men who had served with him in Thrace were patronizing the others.

His campaign was rapid. Revolt was still in the bud; several towns took fright, exiled their rash insurgents and pledged their loyalty. Those already committed, however, rejoiced to hear that Philip, the gods having sent him mad, had trusted his forces to a boy of sixteen years. They sent defiances, Alexander rode to their citadels, sat down before them one by one, looked for the flaws in their defences, or, if there were none, created them with saps or ramps or breaches. He had learned his lessons at Perinthos, and improved on some of them. Resistance soon died out; the remaining towns opened their gates on his terms.

Riding out from Akanthos he viewed Xerxes' Ditch, the ship canal through the isthmus neck of Athos, cut for the Persian fleet to bypass its mountain storms. Its great snowy peak reared up from its shaggy buttresses. The army turned north, along the curve of a pleasant bay. Perched on the foot-slopes below the wooded hills stood a long-ruined town. Brambles grew on its fallen walls; the terracing of its vineyards was collapsing from the winter rains; its weed-grown olive groves were forsaken, but for a herd of goats nibbling the bark, and some naked little boys tearing off low branches. Alexander asked, 'What place was this?'

A trooper rode to ask, and, when all the boys fled yelling at the sight of him, grabbed up the slowest, who struggled like a netted lynx. Dragged before the general, and finding him no older than his own brother, he was struck dumb. When the portent let him know that all they wanted of him was the name of the spot they stood on, he answered, 'Stagira.'

The column rode on. Alexander said to Hephaistion, 'I must speak to Father. It's time for the old man to have his fee.'

Hephaistion nodded. He had seen that schooldays were over.

When the treaties had been signed, the hostages delivered, the strong-points manned, Alexander went back to Philip, still sitting before Perinthos.

The King had waited for him, before moving against Byzantion; he had needed to know that all was well. He was marching himself, leaving Parmenion here; for Byzantion would be tougher than Perinthos, three sides protected by Propontis and Golden Horn, the land side by massive walls. He set his hopes upon surprise.

They milled over the campaign together, over the pinewood trestle. Often Philip would forget it was not a grown man he was talking to, till some careless bluntness would set up the boy's back. It was rarer now; rough, wary, touchy, their contact was warmed by a secret, mutual pride in one another's acceptance.

'How are the Argives shaping?' asked Alexander not long after, over a midday meal.

'I shall leave them here. Parmenion must cope with them. They came here I suppose to swagger about before half-trained citizen levies, as they can in the southern cities. Our men think them raw hands, and let them know it. But what are they, soldiers or bridesmaids? Fair pay, good rations, good quarters; yet nothing's right for them. They sulk at drill; they don't like the sarissa; all they mean is they're clumsy still and our own men laugh. Well, they can stay here and use the short spear, for this work it's well enough. When I've marched with my people, and they're cocks of the walk, they'll pick up, their officers tell me.'

Alexander, scooping up fish sauce with his bread, said, 'Listen.' His first question had been prompted by half-heard sounds of discord. They were getting louder.

'Hades take them,' said the King. 'What now?'

Shouted insults, in Greek and Macedonian, could now be heard.

'Anything looses it off, when they're at odds like this.' Philip pushed back his chair, wiping-off his fingers on his bare thigh. 'A cockfight, a squabble over a boy ... Parmenion's on reconnaissance.' The noise was growing; each side was being reinforced. 'Nothing for it, I shall have to sort them myself.' He walked with his stolid limp towards the doorway.

'Father. They sound ugly. Why not get armed?'

'What? No, that would make too much of it. They'll give over when they see me. They won't heed one another's officers, there's the mischief.'

'I'll come too. If the officers can't quieten them ...'

'No, no; I don't need you. Finish your food. Simmias, keep mine hot.'

He went out as he was, unarmed but for the sword he always wore. Alexander got up and looked after him from the door.

Between the town, and the straggling village of the siege-lines, was a wide space through which slit trenches ran out to the siege-towers, and fortified guard-posts stood. Here between men on duty or changing guard the brawl must have begun, visible all along the lines, so that the factions had gathered quickly. There were already some hundreds; Greeks, who had been nearer, outnumbered Macedonians. Racial taunts were flying. Above the din, voices that sounded like officers' were exchanging recriminations, and threatening each other with the King. Philip stumped forward a few paces, looked again; then shouted to a trooper who had been riding towards the crowd. The man dismounted and gave him a leg up. Provided now with a living rostrum, he cantered purposefully forward, and shouted for silence.

He chose seldom to be formidable. Silence fell; the crowd divided to let him in. As it closed again, Alexander saw that the horse was restive.

The squires who had waited at table were talking in excited undertones. Alexander gave them a look; they should have been waiting for orders. The next hut was the lodging of all the body-squires; the doorway was full of heads. He called out, 'Get armed. Be quick.'

Philip was wrestling with the horse. His voice, which had carried power, now sounded angry. The horse reared; there was a roar of abuse and cursing; it must have struck a man with its forefeet. Suddenly it gave a great scream, stood almost upright, and sank down, the King still doggedly clinging. Horse and man vanished into a threshing, shouting vortex.

Alexander ran to the armour-pegs on the wall, snatched his shield and helmet – the corselet would take too long – and called to the squires, 'They've killed his horse under him. Come.' Soon outdistancing all the others, he ran without looking back. The Macedonians were pouring out of barracks. It was the next moments that counted.

At first he simply shoved at the mob, and it let him through. These were sightseers, or mere accretions, easily shifted by anyone who knew his own mind. 'Let me pass. Let me through to the King.' He could hear the squeals of the dying horse, weakening to groans; no sound from his father. 'Back, get back, let me pass. Make way, I want the King.'

'He wants his dad.' The first defiance; a square-shouldered, square-bearded Argive stood grinning in his way. 'Look, here's the cockalorum.' The last word choked off. His eyes and mouth gaped, a retch came up from his throat. Alexander with an expert jerk freed his sword.

A gap appeared; he could see the still twitching horse, on its side, his father lying with one leg under it, unmoving; over him stood an Argive with a lifted spear, irresolute, waiting for encouragement. Alexander ran him through.

The crowd heaved and swayed, as the Macedonians flung themselves at its edges. Alexander bestrode his father's body, one leg braced against the horse which had stiffened in death; he yelled, 'The King!' to guide the rescuers. All round him, uncertain men were urging each other to strike. For anyone behind him, he was a gift.

'This is the King. I will kill the first man who touches him.' Some were scared; he fixed his eyes on the man they had been looking at for guidance. He stuck out his jaw and mumbled, but his eyes were flickering. 'Get back all of you. Are you mad? Do you think if you kill him or me, you can get out of Thrace alive?' Someone said they had got out of worse places; but no one moved. 'Our men are either side of you, and the enemy has the harbour. Are you tired of life?'

Some warning, a gift of Herakles, made him whip round. He hardly saw the face of the man whose spear was lifted, only the exposed throat. His stab severed the windpipe; the man reeled back, bloody fingers clawing at the hissing wound. He swung round to confront the others; in this instant the scene had changed, he saw instead the backs of the royal squires, shields locked, heaving off the Argives. Hephaistion came breasting through like a swimmer through surf, and stood to shield his back. It was over, in about as long as it would have taken him to finish his half-eaten fish.

He looked round. He had not a scratch, he had been a stroke ahead each time. Hephaistion spoke to him and he answered smiling. He was shining and calm at the centre of his mystery, the godlike freedom of killing fear. Fear lay dead at his feet.

Loud voices, expert in command, cleft the confusion; the Argive general, and Parmenion's deputy, roared at their troops in familiar tones. Hangers-on turned swiftly to spectators; the centre fell apart revealing a scatter of dead and wounded; all the men near the fallen King were arrested and led away. The horse was dragged aside. The riot was over. When shouts began again, they came from those on the outskirts who could not see, spreading rumours or asking news.

'Alexander! Where's our boy? Have those whores' sons killed him?' Then, running the other way in a deep bass counterpoint, 'The King, they killed the King! The King is dead!' and higher, as if in answer, 'Alexander!'

He stood, a point of stillness in all the clamour, looking beyond it into the blue dazzling sky.

There were other voices, down by his knees. 'Sir, sir, how are you?' they were saying. 'Sir?' He blinked a moment, as if awaking from sleep; then knelt down with the others and touched the body, saying, 'Father? Father?'

He could feel at once that the King was breathing.

There was blood in his hair. His sword was half-out; he must have felt for it as he was struck, perhaps with a pommel by someone whose nerve had failed him to use the edge. His eyes were closed, and he came limply with their lifting hands. Alexander, remembering a lesson of Aristotle's, pulled back the lid of his good eye. It closed again with a twitch.

'A shield,' Alexander said. 'Roll him gently. I'll take his head.'

The Argives had been marched off; the Macedonians crowded round, asking if the King was alive or dead. 'He is stunned,' said Alexander. 'He will be better presently. He has no other wound. Moschion! The herald is to give that out. Sippas! Order the catapults to fire a volley. Look at the enemy gaping on the wall; I want the fun knocked out of them. Leonnatus, I'll be with my father till he's himself again. Bring anything to me.'

They laid the King on his bed. Alexander drew a blood-stained hand from holding his head, to settle it on the pillow. Philip groaned, and opened his eyes.

The senior officers, who had felt entitled to crowd in, assured him all was well, all the men in hand. Alexander standing by the bed-head said to one of the squires, 'Bring me water, and a sponge.'

'It was your son, King,' said someone, 'your son saved you.' Philip turned his head and said weakly, 'So? Good boy.'

'Father, did you see which of them struck you?'

'No,' said Philip, his voice strengthening. 'He took me from behind.'

'Well, I hope I killed him. I killed one there.' His grey eyes dwelt deeply on his father's face.

Philip blinked dimly, and sighed. 'Good boy. I remember nothing; nothing till I woke up here.'

The squire came up with the water-bowl and held it out. Alexander took the sponge, and washed his hand clean of blood, going over it carefully, two or three times. He turned away; the squire paused with the bowl, at a loss, then went round to sponge the King's hair and brow. He had supposed that this was what the Prince had meant it for.

By evening, though sick and giddy if he moved, Philip could give orders. The Argives were marched off on exchange to Kypsela. Alexander was cheered wherever he was seen; men touched him for luck, or for his virtue to rub off on them, or merely for the sake of touching him. The besieged, encouraged by these disorders, came out on the wall at dusk and attacked a siege tower. Alexander led out a party and beat them off. The doctor announced that the King was mending. One of the squires sat up with him. It was midnight before Alexander got to bed. Though he ate with his father, he had his own lodging. He was a general now.

There was a scratch on the door, in a familiar rhythm. He folded back the blanket, and moved over. Hephaistion had known, when this tryst was made, that what Alexander wanted was to talk. He could always tell.

They milled over the fight, talking softly into the pillow. Presently they fell quiet; in the pause they could hear the sounds of the camp, and, from the distant ramparts of Perinthos, the night watch passing the bell along from man to man, the proof of wakefulness. 'What is it?' Hephaistion whispered.

In the dim glimmer of the window, he saw the shine of Alexander's eyes coming close to his. 'He says he remembers nothing. He'd already come to himself when we picked him up.'

Hephaistion, who had once been hit by a stone from a Thracian wall, said, 'He'll have forgotten.'

'No. He was shamming dead.'

'Was he? Well, who can blame him? One can't even sit up, everything spins round. He hoped they'd be scared at what they'd done, and go away.'

'I opened his eye, and I know he saw me. But he gave me no sign, though he knew it was over then.'

'Very likely he just went off again.'

'I watched him, he was awake. But he won't say he remembers.'

'Well, he's the King.' Hephaistion had a secret kindness for Philip, who had always treated him with courtesy, even with tact; with whom, too, he shared an enemy. 'People might misunderstand, you know how tales get twisted.'

'To me he could have said it.' Alexander's eyes, glittering in the near-darkness, fastened upon his. 'He won't own that he was lying there, knowing he owed his life to me. He didn't want to admit it, he doesn't want to remember.'

Who knows? thought Hephaistion. Or ever will? But *he* knows, and nothing will ever shift it. His bare shoulder, crossed by Hephaistion's arm, had a faint sheen like darkened bronze. 'Supposing he had his pride? You ought to know what that is.'

'Yes, I do. But in his place I'd still have spoken.'

'What need?' He slid his hand up the bronze shoulder into the tousled hair; Alexander pushed against it, like a powerful animal consenting to be stroked. Hephaistion remembered his childishness in the beginning; sometimes it seemed like yesterday, sometimes half a lifetime. 'Everyone knows. He does; so do you. Nothing can take it away.'

He felt Alexander draw a long deep breath. 'No; nothing. You're right, you always understand. He gave me life, or he claims so. Whether or not, now I've given it him.'

'Yes, now you're quits.'

Alexander gazed into the black peak of the rafters. 'No one can equal the gifts of the gods, one can only try to know them. But it's good to be clear of debt to men.'

Tomorrow he would sacrifice to Herakles. Meantime, he felt a deep wish at once to make someone happy. Luckily he had not far to seek.

'I warned him,' said Alexander, 'not to put off dealing with the Triballoi.' He sat with Antipatros at the great desk of Archelaos' study, over a dispatch full of bad news.

'Is his wound thought dangerous?' Antipatros asked.

'He couldn't sign this; just his seal, and Parmenion's witness. I doubt he even finished dictating it. The last part reads more like Parmenion.'

'He has good-healing flesh, your father. It's in the family.'

'What were his diviners doing? Nothing's gone right with him since I left. Perhaps we should consult Delphi or Dodona, in case some god needs appeasing.'

'It would spread through Greece like wildfire that his luck was out. He'd not thank us for that.'

'That's true, no, better not. But look at Byzantion. He did everything right; got there fast, while their best forces were at Perinthos; chose a cloudy night; got up to the very walls. But of a sudden the clouds part, out comes the moon; and all the town dogs start barking. Barking at the crossroads ... they light the torches ...'

'Crossroads?' asked Antipatros into the pause.

'Or,' said Alexander briskly, 'maybe he misread the weather, it's changeable on Propontis. But once he'd decided to lift both sieges, why not have rested his men, and let me take on the Scythians?'

'They were there on his flank, and had just denounced their treaty; but for them he might have hung on at Byzantion. Your father's always known when to write off his losses. But his troops had their tails down; they needed a solid victory, and loot; both of which he got.'

Alexander nodded. He could get along well with Antipatros, a Macedonian of ancient stock, bone-loyal to the King beside whom he had fought in youth, but to the King before the man. It was Parmenion who loved the man before the King. 'He did indeed. So there he was, lumbered-up with a thousand head of cattle, a slave-train, wagons of loot, on the north border where they can smell plunder further than buzzards. Tails up or not, his men were tired ... If only he'd let me go on north from Alexandropolis; he'd have had no raid from the Triballoi then.' The name was established now; the colonists had settled. 'The Agrianoi would have come in with me, they'd already agreed ... Well, done's done. It's lucky his doctor wasn't killed.'

'I should like to wish him well when the courier leaves.'

'Of course. Let's not trouble him with business.' (If orders came back would they be Philip's or Parmenion's?) 'We shall have to shift for ourselves awhile.' He smiled at Antipatros, whom he liked none the worse for being charmable, and amusingly unaware of it. 'War we can deal with well enough. But the business of the south – that's another thing. It means a great deal to him; he sees it differently; he knows more about it. I should be sorry to act without him there.'

'Well, they seem to be working for him there better than we could.'

'At Delphi? I was there when I was twelve, for the Games, and never since. Now, once again, to be sure I understand it: this new offering-house the Athenians put up; they put in their dedications before it had been consecrated?'

'Yes, a technical impiety. That was the formal charge.'

'But the real quarrel was the inscription: SHIELDS TAKEN FROM PERSIANS AND THEBANS FIGHTING AGAINST GREECE ... Why *did* the Thebans Medize, instead of allying with the Athenians?'

'Because they hated them.'

'Even then? Well, this inscription enraged the Thebans. So when the Sacred League of Delphi met, being I suppose ashamed to come forward themselves, they got some client state to accuse the Athenians of impiety.'

'The Amphissians. They live below Delphi, up river.'

'And if this indictment had succeeded, the League would have had to make war on Athens. The Athenians had sent three delegates; two went down with fever, and the third of them was Aischines.'

'You may remember the man; he was one of the peace-envoys, seven years ago.'

'Oh, I know Aischines, he's an old friend of mine. Did you know he was an actor once? He must have been good at gagging; because when the Council was about to pass the motion, he suddenly recalled that the Amphissians had been raising crops on some river land which had once been forfeited to Apollo. So he went rushing in, somehow got a hearing, and counter-accused the Amphissians. Is that right? Then, after his great oration, the Delphians forgot Athens, and rushed down pell-mell to wreck the Amphissians' farms. The Amphissians fought; and some of the Councillors had their sacred persons knocked about. This was last autumn after the harvest.'

It was now winter. The study was as draughty and cold as ever. The King's son, thought Antipatros, seemed to notice it even less than the King.

'Now the League is meeting at Thermopylai to pass judgement on the Amphissians. It's clear my father won't be fit to go. I am sure what he would like would be for you to represent him. Will you?'

'By all means, yes,' said Antipatros, relieved. The boy knew his own limits, eager as he was to stretch them. 'I shall try to influence whom I can, and, where I can, postpone decisions for the King.'

'Let's hope they've found him a warm house; Thrace in winter is no place for healing wounds. Before long, we shall have to consult him about this. What do you expect will happen?'

'In Athens, nothing. Even if the League condemns Amphissa, Demosthenes will keep the Athenians out. The counter-charge was a personal triumph for Aischines, whom he hates like poison, and indicted on a capital charge of treason after their embassy here, as I daresay you know.'

'No one better. Part of the charge was that he was too friendly with me.'

'These demagogues! Why, you were only ten years old. Well, the charge failed, and now Aischines comes back from Delphi a public hero. Demosthenes must be chewing wormwood. Also, a larger issue, the Amphissians support the Thebans, whom he won't wish to antagonize.'

'But the Athenians hate the Thebans.'

'He would like them to hate us more. A war-pact with Thebes is what any man of sense would work for, in his place. With the Thebans he may succeed; the Great King has sent him a fortune to buy support against us. It's the Athenians will give him trouble; that feud's too old.'

Alexander sat in thought. Presently he said, 'It's four generations now since they threw back the Persians; and we Medized, as the Thebans did. If the Great King crossed now from Asia, they'd be intriguing and impeaching one another, while we turned him back in Thrace.'

'Men change in less time than that. *We* have come up in one generation, thanks to your father.'

'And he's still only forty-three. Well, I shall go out and take some exercise, in case he should leave me anything to do.'

On his way to change, he met his mother, who asked the news. He went with her to her room, and told her as much as he thought good. The room was warm, soft and full of colour; bright firelight danced on the pictured flames of Troy. His eyes turned to the hearth; he stared unnoticed at the loose stone he had explored in childhood. She found him withdrawn, and accused him of weak compliance with Antipatros, who would stop at nothing to do her harm. This happened often, and he passed it off with the usual answers.

Leaving, he met Kleopatra on the stairs. Now at fourteen she was more like Philip than ever, square-faced, with strong curly hair; but her eyes were not his, they were sad as an unloved dog's. His half-wives had borne him prettier girls; she was plain at the age when, for him, it mattered most; and for her mother she wore the mask of the enemy. Alexander said, 'Come with me, I want to speak to you.'

In the nursery they had been struggling rivals. Now he was above the battle. She longed for, yet feared, his notice, feeling unequal to anything it could mean. It was unheard-of for him to confer with her. 'Come in the garden,' he said, and, when she shivered and crossed her arms, gave her his cloak. They stood in a leafless rose-plot by the Queen's postern, close against the wall. Old snow lay in the hollows and between the clods. He had spoken to her quietly, he had not wished to frighten her, she saw that in herself she was unimportant; but she was afraid.

'Listen,' he said. 'You know what happened to Father at Byzantion?' She nodded. 'It was the dogs betrayed him. The dogs, and the sickle moon.'

He saw the dread in her sad eyes, but read no guilt in it. Neither of Olympias' children looked for innocence in the other. 'You understand me. You know the rites I mean. Did you . . . see anything done?'

She shook her head dumbly; if she told, it would come out in one of their dreadful love-quarrels. His eyes searched her like the winter wind; but her fear hid everything. Suddenly he became gentle and grave, and took her hand through the folds of cloak. 'I won't tell that you told me. By Herakles. I could never break that oath.' He looked round at the garden shrine. 'Tell me, you must. I must know.'

Her hidden hand shifted in his. 'Only the same as other times, when nothing came of it. If there was more, I didn't see it. Truly, Alexander, that's all I know.'

'Yes, yes, I believe you,' he said impatiently; then grasped at her hand again. 'Don't let her do it. She hasn't the right, now. I saved him at Perinthos. He'd be dead now, but for me.'

'Why did you?' Much could be left unsaid between them. Her eyes dwelt on the face that was not Philip's, the rough-cut, shining hair.

'It would have been disgraceful not to.' He paused, seeking, she thought, some words that would serve for her. 'Don't cry,' he said, and passed a finger-tip gently under her eyes. 'That's all I wanted to know. You couldn't help it.'

He began to lead her in; but paused at the doorway, and looked about them. 'If she wants to send him a doctor, medicines, sweets, anything, you must let me know. I charge you with it. If you don't, it will rest on you.'

He saw her face pale with shock. Her surprise, not her distress, arrested him. 'Oh, Alexander! No! Those things you spoke of, they've never worked, she must know it. But they're terrible, and when – when she can't contain her soul, they purge it. That's all they are.'

He looked at her almost with tenderness, and slowly shook his head. 'She meant them.' He gave her one of his secret looks. 'I remember,' he said softly.

He saw her sad dog's eyes, flinching from this new burden. 'But that's long ago. I expect it's as you say. You're a good girl.' He kissed her cheek, and squeezed her shoulders as he took back his cloak. From the doorway she watched him go shining off through the dead garden.

Winter dragged on. In Thrace the King mended slowly, and could sign letters with the shake of an old man. He had understood the news from Delphi, and directed that Antipatros should support, discreetly, the Amphissian war. The Thebans, though pledged to Macedon, had been doubtful allies, intriguing with the Persians; they were expendable at need. He foresaw the League states voting for the war, each hoping that its burden would be borne by others; Macedon should stand by, without officiousness, in friendly willingness to assume the tiresome duty. It would put the key to the south into his hand.

Soon after midwinter, the Council voted for war. Each state offered only a token force; none would yield leadership to a rival city. Kottyphos, a Thessalian, being President of the Council, had flung in his lap command of this awkward army. Thessalians, whom Philip had rescued from tribal anarchy, remained mostly grateful. There was small doubt where Kottyphos would turn in his hour of need.

'It has begun,' said Alexander to his friends, as they sluiced-down under the fountain by the stadium. 'If one only knew how long.'

Ptolemy, pushing his head out of his towel, remarked, 'Women say a watched pot never boils.' Alexander, dedicated to constant readiness, had been working them hard; Ptolemy had a new mistress, of whom he would have liked to be seeing more.

'They say too,' Hephaistion countered, 'that when you take your eye off it, it boils over.' Ptolemy looked at him with irritation; it was well for him, *he* was getting enough of what he wanted.

He was getting, at least, what he would not have changed for any other human lot; and the world could know it. The rest was his secret; he came to what terms he could with it. Pride, chastity, restraint, devotion to higher things; with such words he made tolerable to himself his meetings with a soul-rooted reluctance, too deep to suffer questioning. Perhaps Olympias' witchcraft had scarred her child; perhaps his father's example. Or, thought Hephaistion, perhaps it was that in this one thing he did not want the mastery, and all the rest of his nature was at war with it; he had entrusted his very life much sooner and more willingly. Once in the dark he had murmured in Macedonian, 'You are the first and the last,' and his voice might have been charged with ecstasy or intolerable grief. Most of the time, however, he was candid, close, without evasions; he simply did not think it very important. One might have supposed that the true act of love was to lie together and talk.

He talked of man and fate; of words heard in dreams from speaking serpents; of the management of cavalry against infantry and archers; he quoted Homer on heroes, Aristotle on the Universal Mind, and Solon on love; he talked of Persian tactics and the Thracian battle-mind; about his dog that had died, about the beauty of friendship. He plotted the march of Xenophon's Ten Thousand, stage by stage from Babylon to the sea. He retailed the backstairs gossip of the Palace, the staff room and the phalanx, and confided the most secret policies of both his parents. He considered the nature of the soul in life and death, and that of the gods; he talked of Herakles and Dionysos, and how Longing can achieve all things.

Listening in bed, in the lee of mountain crags, in a wood at daybreak; with an arm clasping his waist or a head thrown back on his shoulder, trying to silence his noisy heart, Hephaistion understood he was being told everything. With pride and awe, with tenderness, torment and guilt, he lost the thread, and fought with himself, and caught the drift again to find something gone past recall. Bewildering treasures were being poured into his hands and slipping through his fingers, while his mind wandered to the blinding trifle of his own desire. At any moment he would be asked what he thought; he was valued as more than a listener. Knowing this he would attend again, and be caught up even against his will; Alexander could transmit imagination as some other could transmit lust. Sometimes, when he was lit up and full of gratitude for being understood, Longing, who has the power to achieve all things, would prompt the right word or touch; he would fetch a profound sigh, dragged up it seemed from the depth of his being, and murmur something in the Macedonian of his childhood; and all would be well, or as well as it could ever be.

He loved giving, to gods or men; he loved achievement here as elsewhere; he loved Hephaistion, whom he forgave for having confronted him, irrevocably now, with his human needs. The profound melancholy after, he bore uncomplaining like a wound. Nothing could be had for nothing. But if later he threw a javelin wide, or won a race by two lengths instead of three, Hephaistion always suspected him, without a word or a look to show it, of thinking that virtue had gone out of him.

In his waking dreams, from which hard clear thought emerged like iron from fire, he would lie back in the grass with his arm behind his head, or sit with his hands loose on the boar-spear across his knees, or pace a room, or stare from a window, his head tilted up and a little leftward, his eyes seeing what his mind conceived. His forgotten face told truths no sculptor would ever catch; behind dropped curtains the secret lamp flared high, one saw the glow, or a dazzling glint through a chink. At times like these, when, Hephaistion thought, even a god could scarcely have kept his hands off him, then above all he must be let alone. But this, after all, one had known from the very beginning.

Once having understood it, Hephaistion could himself achieve, in some degree, Alexander's power to drive the force of sexual energy into some other aim. His own ambitions were more limited; he had already attained the chief of them. He was entirely trusted, constantly and deeply loved.

True friends share everything. One thing, however, he thought well to keep to himself: that Olympias hated him, and her hatred was returned.

Alexander did not speak of it; she must have known that here she would meet with rock. Hephaistion, when she passed him without a greeting, put it down to simple jealousy. It is hard for a generous lover to pity a devouring one; he could not feel much for her, even while he believed that this was all.

It took him time to credit what he saw in front of him, that she was throwing women in Alexander's way. Surely she would hate their rivalry even more? Yet waiting-maids, visiting singers and dancers, young wives not strictly kept, girls who dared not for their lives have risked her anger, now hung about and made eyes. Hephaistion waited for Alexander to talk about it first.

One evening just after lamp-lighting, in the Great Court, Hephaistion saw him waylaid by a young notorious beauty. He flashed his eyes at her languid ones, said something crisp, and walked on with a cool smile, which disappeared at sight of Hephaistion. They fell into step; Hephaistion seeing him on edge said lightly, 'No luck for Doris.' Alexander looked ahead frowning. The newly-lit cressets flung deep shadows and shifting gleams into the painted stoa.

Alexander said abruptly, 'She wants me to marry young.'

'*Marry?*' said Hephaistion staring. 'How could you marry Doris?'

'Don't be a fool,' said Alexander irritably. 'She's married, she's a whore, she had her last child by Harpalos.' They walked on in silence. He paused beside a column. 'Mother wants to see me going with women, to know I'm ready.'

'But no one marries at our age. Only girls.'

'She has her mind on it, and she wishes I had mine.'

'But why?'

Alexander glanced at him, not in wonder at his slowness but envy of his innocence. 'She wants to bring up my heir. I might fall in battle without one.'

Hephaistion understood. He was impeding more than love, more than possession. He was impeding power. The cressets flickered, the night breeze blew coldly down his neck. Presently he said, 'And will you do it?'

'Marry? No, I shall suit myself, when I choose, when I've time to think of it.'

'You'd have to maintain a household, it's a great deal of business.' He glanced at Alexander's creased brows and added, 'Girls, you can take or leave whenever you like.'

'That's what I think.' He looked at Hephaistion with a gratitude not quite aware of itself. Drawing him by the arm into the thick column's shadow, he said softly, 'Don't be troubled about it. She would never dare do anything to take you from me. She knows me better than that.'

Hephaistion nodded, not liking to admit that he understood what was meant. It was true that he had begun lately to notice how his wine was poured.

A little while later, Ptolemy said in private to Alexander, 'I've been asked to give a party for you and invite some girls.'

Their eyes met. Alexander said, 'I might be busy.'

'I'd be grateful if you'd come. I'll see you're not plagued, they can sing and amuse us. Will you? I don't want to be in trouble.'

It was not a custom of the north to bring in hetairas at dinner; a man's women were his own concern; Dionysos, not Aphrodite, closed the feast. But lately, among up-to-date young men at private parties, Greek ways were admired. Four guests came to the supper; the girls sat on the ends of their couches, talked prettily, sang to the lyre, filled up their wine-cups and patted their wreaths in place; they might almost have been in Corinth. To Alexander his host had allotted the eldest, Kallixeina, an expert and cultured courtesan of some fame. While a girl acrobat was throwing somersaults naked, and on the other couches understandings were being reached with covert tickles and pinches, she talked in her mellow voice about the beauties of Miletos, where she had lately been, and the oppression of the Persians there; Ptolemy had briefed her well. Once, leaning gracefully, she let her dress dip to show him her much-praised breasts; but as he had been promised, her tact was faultless. He enjoyed her company, and at parting kissed the sweetly-curving lips from which she took her trade name.

'I don't know,' he confided to Hephaistion in bed, 'why my mother should want to see me enslaved by women. You'd think with my father she'd have seen enough.'

'All mothers are mad for grandchildren,' said Hephaistion tolerantly. The party had left Alexander vaguely restless, and receptive to love.

'Think of the great men it has ruined. Look at Persia.' His sombre mood being on him, he retailed from Herodotos a hideous tale of jealousy and vengeance. Hephaistion expressed a proper horror. His sleep was sweet.

'The Queen was pleased,' said Ptolemy next day, 'to hear you enjoyed the party.' He never said more than enough, a trait Alexander valued. He sent Kallixeina a necklace of gold flowers.

Winter began to break. Two couriers from Thrace, the first having been delayed by swollen streams, arrived together. The first dispatch said that the King could walk a little. He had had news from the south by sea. The League army, after troubles and delays, had won a partial victory; the Amphissians had accepted peace-terms, to dismiss their leaders and put in their exiled opposition. This was always a hated condition, since exiles returned bent on settling their old scores. The Amphissians had not fulfilled their agreement yet.

From the second courier's letter, it was clear that Philip was now dealing direct with his southern agents, who had reported the Amphissians still harboured their former government, and ignored remonstrances; the opposition dared not return. Kottyphos, the League general, had written to the King in confidence: if the League were forced into action, would Philip be prepared to undertake the war?

With this came a second letter, bound up and double-sealed, addressed to Alexander as Regent. It commended his good government; and informed him that though Philip hoped soon to be fit for the journey home, affairs could not wait so long. He wanted the whole army mobilized for action; but no one must suspect that his plans led southward; Antipatros alone could share the knowledge. Some other pretext must be sought. There had been tribal musterings in Illyria; it should be given out that the western border was threatened, and the troops were standing by for that. Terse notes on training and staffing were closed with fatherly blessings.

Like a caged bird set free, Alexander flew into action. As he ranged about in search of good country for manoeuvres, he could be heard singing to the beat of Oxhead's hooves. If some girl he had loved for years, Antipatros thought, had suddenly been promised him, he could not have glowed more brilliantly.

War-councils were called; the professional soldiers conferred with the tribal lords who commanded their own levies. Olympias asked Alexander what kept him so often away, and why he looked so full of business. He answered that he hoped soon to see action against the Illyrians on the border.

'I have been waiting to speak to you, Alexander. I hear that after Kallixeina the Thessalian entertained you all one evening, you made her a present and never sent again for her. These women are artists, Alexander; a hetaira of that standing has her pride. What will she think of you?'

He turned round, for a moment quite bewildered. He had forgotten the existence of such a person. 'Do you think,' he said staring, 'that I've time now to be playing about with girls?'

She tapped with her fingers on her gilded chair-arm. 'You will be eighteen this summer. People may be saying you do not care for them.'

He stared at the Sack of Troy, the flames and blood and the shrieking women flung back across warriors' shoulders, waving their arms. After a moment he said, 'I shall find them something else to talk about.'

'You have always time for Hephaistion,' she said.

'He thinks of my work, and helps.'

'What work? You tell me nothing. Philip sent you a secret letter; you did not even tell me. What did he say?'

With cool precision, without a pause, he gave her the tale about the Illyrian war. She saw, and was shaken by, the cold resentment in his eyes.

'You are lying to me,' she said.

'If you think so, why ask?'

'I am sure you told Hephaistion everything.'

Lest Hephaistion should suffer for the truth, he answered, 'No.'

'People talk. Hear it now from me, if you do not know. Why do you shave, like a Greek?'

'Am I not Greek, then? This is news, you should have told me sooner.'

Like two wrestlers who in their grapple reel towards a cliff, and let go in a common fear, they paused and swerved.

'Your friends are known by it, the women point at them. Hephaistion, Ptolemy, Harpalos . . .'

He laughed. 'Ask Harpalos why they point.'

She was angered by his endurance, when instinct told her she was drawing blood. 'Soon your father will be making you a marriage. It is time you showed him it is a husband he has to offer, and not a wife.'

After a moment's stillness he walked forward, very slowly, and lightly as a golden cat, till he stood straight before her looking down. She opened her mouth, then closed it; little by little she shrank back into her thronelike chair, till its high back held her and she could retreat no further. Judging this with his eyes, he then said softly, 'You will never say that to me again.'

She was still there, and had not moved, when she heard Oxhead's gallop thudding away.

For two days he did not come near her; her orders to deny him her door were wasted. Then came a feast; each found a gift from the other. The breach was healed; except that neither spoke of it, or asked forgiveness.

He forgot it, when the news came in from Illyria. Word having spread that King Philip was arming against them, the tribes, which had been settling, were in ferment from the border to the western sea.

'I expected no less,' said Antipatros in private to Alexander. 'The price of a good lie is that it gets believed.'

'One thing's certain, we can't afford to undeceive them. So they'll be over the border any day. Let me think about this; tomorrow I'll tell you what troops I need to take.'

Antipatros saved his breath; he was learning when to do so.

Alexander knew what forces he wanted; what most concerned him was how to avoid, without suspicion, committing too many troops to the work they were supposed to be standing-by for. Soon fact supplied a pretext. Since the Phokian war, the Thermopylai fort had been held by a Macedonian garrison. It had just been 'relieved', in strength and without agreement, by a force of Thebans. Thebes, they explained, had to protect herself from the Delphi League, which, by attacking her allies the Amphissians, was clearly threatening her. This seizure was as near a hostile act as a formal ally could compass. It would be natural, now, to leave a good holding force at home.

The Illyrians were lighting war-fires. Alexander got out his father's old maps and records; questioned veterans about the terrain, which was mountainous and cleft with gorges, and tested his men in marches across country. From one such day he got back at fall of dusk, bathed, greeted friends, had dinner, and, ready for sleep, went straight up to his room. He threw off his clothes at once; with the cold draught from the window came a warm drift of scent. The tall standing lamp shone in his eyes. He stepped past it. On the bed a young girl was sitting.

He stared at her in silence; she gasped and looked down, as if the last thing she had looked for here was an unclothed man. Then slowly she got to her feet, unclasped her hands to let them fall at her sides, and raised her head.

'I am here,' she said like a child repeating lessons, 'because I have fallen in love with you. Please don't send me away.'

He walked steadily across to her. The first shock had passed; one must not be seen to hesitate. This one was not like the painted jewelled hetairas with their easy charm, the patina of much handling. She was about fifteen, a fair-skinned girl, with fine flaxen hair falling unbound over her shoulders. Her face was heart-shaped, her eyes were dark blue, her small breasts firm and pointed; the dress of snow-white byssos showed the pink nipples through. Her mouth was unpainted, fresh as flowers. Before he reached her, he felt her steeped in fear.

'How did you get in?' he asked. 'There's a guard outside.'

She clasped her hands again. 'I – I have been trying a long time to come to you. I took the first chance I saw.' Her fear shivered like a curtain round her, it almost stirred the air.

He had expected no answer to the purpose. He touched her hair, which felt like thin silk clothing her; she was shaking like the bass-string of a kithara lately struck. Not passion, fear. He took her shoulders between his hands and felt her a little calmed, like a scared dog. It was because of him, not of him, she was afraid.

They were young; their innocence and their knowledge spoke together, without their will. He stood holding her between his hands, no longer heeding her, listening. He heard nothing; yet the whole room seemed to breathe.

He kissed her lips, she was just the right height for him. Then he said crisply, 'The guard must have gone to sleep. If he let you in, let's make sure there is no one else here.'

She grasped him with a clutch of terror. He kissed her again, and gave her a secret smile. Then he went to the far end of the room, shaking the window-curtains loudly on their rings, one after another, looking into the great chest and slamming its lid. He left to the last the curtain before the postern door. When at length he pulled it aside, no one was there. He shot the bronze bolt home.

Going back to the girl, he led her towards the bed. He was angry, but not with her; and he had been offered a challenge.

Her white gauze dress was pinned on the shoulders with golden bees. He loosened them, and the girdle; it all fell on the floor. She was milky as if her flesh never saw the sun, all but the rosy nipples, and the golden fuzz which painters never put in. Poor soft pale thing, for which the heroes had fought ten years at Troy.

He lay down beside her. She was young and scared, she would thank him for time and gentleness, there was no hurry. One of her hands, ice-cold with fright, started travelling down his body; hesitant and inexpert, remembering instruction. It was not enough that she had been sent to learn if he was a man, this child had been told to help him. He found himself handling her with the most delicate care, like a day-old pup, to protect her from his anger.

He glanced at the lamp; but it would be a kind of flight to quench it, shameful to fumble in the dark. His arm lay across her breast, firm, brown, scratched from the mountain brambles; how weak she looked, even a real kiss would bruise her. She had hidden her face against his shoulder. A conscript without doubt, not a volunteer. She was thinking what would become of her if she failed.

And at the best, he thought; at the best? The loom, the bed, the cradle; children, the decking of bride-beds, clacking talk at the hearth and the village well; bitter old age, and death. Never the beautiful ardours, the wedded bond of honour, the fire from heaven blazing on the altar where fear was killed. He turned up her face in his hand. For this lost life, the creature that looked at him with these flax-blue eyes, helpless and waiting, had been created a human soul. Why had it been ordered so? Compassion shocked him, and pierced him with darts of fire.

He thought of the fallen towns, the rafters burning, the women running from the smoke as rats and hares run out when the last stand of wheat falls to the sickle and the boys wait stick in hand. He remembered the bodies, left behind by men for whom the victor's right of mating, with which wild beasts were content, was not enough. They had something to revenge, some unsated hatred, of themselves perhaps, or of one they could not name. His hand traced softly on her smooth body the wounds he had seen; there was no harm, she did not understand it. He kissed her so that she would be reassured. She was trembling less, knowing now that her mission would not fail. He took her carefully, with the greatest gentleness, thinking of blood.

Later she sat up softly, thinking him asleep, and began to slip out of bed. He had only been thinking. 'Don't go,' he said. 'Stay with me till morning.' He would have been glad to lie alone, not crowded by this alien soft flesh; but why should she face her questioning at such an hour? She had not cried, but only flinched a little, though she had been a virgin. Of course, how not? She was to furnish proof. He was angry on her behalf, no god having disclosed to him that she would outlive him by fifty years, boasting to the last of them that she had had the maidenhood of Alexander. The night grew cool, he pulled up the blanket over her shoulders. If anyone was sitting up for her, so much the better. Let them wait.

He got up and snuffed the lamp, and lay looking into the darkness, feeling the lethargy of soul which was the price of going hostage to mortality. To die, even a little, one should do it for something great. However, this might pass for a kind of victory.

He woke to birdsong and first light; he had overslept, some men he had meant to look at would be at drill already. The girl was fast sleeping still, her mouth a little open; it made her look foolish more than sad. He had never asked her her name. He shook her gently; her mouth closed, her deep-blue eyes opened; she looked tumbled, sleek and warm. 'We had better get up, I have work to do.' Out of courtesy he added, 'I wish we could stay longer.'

She rubbed her eyes, then smiled at him. His heart lifted; the ordeal was over, and well achieved. There on the sheet was the little red stain the old wives showed the guests on the wedding morrow. It would be practical, but unkind, to suggest she should take it with her. He had a better thought.

He belted on his chiton, went to his casket where his dress jewels were kept, and took out a pouch of soft kidskin, old and worn, with gold embroidery. It was not long ago that, with much solemnity, it had been given him. He slipped it out, a big brooch of two gold swans, their necks entwined in the courtship dance. The work was ancient, the swans wore crowns. 'It has come down from queen to queen for two hundred years. Look after it, Alexander; it is an heirloom for your bride.'

He tossed the stitched pouch away, his mouth hardening; but he walked over with a smile. The girl had just fastened her shoulder-pins and was tying her girdle. 'Here's something for remembrance.' She took it wide-eyed, staring and feeling its weight. 'Tell the Queen that you pleased me very much, but in future I choose for myself. Then show her this; and remember to say I told you to.'

In fresh blowy spring weather they marched west from the coast and up to Aigai. Here on Zeus' ancient altar Alexander offered an unblemished pure-white bull. The seers, poring over the steaming vitals, announced the good portents of the liver.

They passed Lake Kastoria flooded from the snow-streams, half-drowned willows shaking green locks over its wind-ruffled blue water; then wound up through winter-brown scrub, into the rocky heights of the Hills of Lynxes, the Lynkestid lands.

Here he thought well to put on his helmet, and the leather guard for his bridle-arm which he had had made to Xenophon's design. Since old Airopos had died, and young Alexandros had been chief, he had given no trouble, and had aided Philip in the last Illyrian war; nonetheless this was perfect ambush country, and Lynkestids were Lynkestids, time out of mind.

However, they had done their vassal duty; here were all three brothers on strong hairy mountain ponies, armed for campaign with their high-landers behind them; tall brown bearded men, no longer the lads he had met at festivals. They exchanged greetings of scrupulous courtesy, the common heirs of an ancient patched-up feud. For generations their houses had been linked by kinship, war, rivalry and marriage. The Lynkestids had once been kings here; they had contended for the High Kingship more than once through the generations. But they had not been strong enough to hold back the Illyrians. Philip had; and that had settled the matter.

Alexander accepted their formal host-gifts of food and wine, and called them to conference with his chief officers, on a rocky outcrop patched with lichen and flowering moss.

Dressed, themselves, with the rough usefulness of the border, leather tunics stitched with plates of iron, cap-shaped Thracian helmets, they could not take their eyes off the smooth-shaved youth who had chosen, while he outdid men, to keep the face of a boy, and whose panoply glittered with all the refinements of the south. His corselet was shaped to measure over every muscle; elegantly inlaid, but finished so smoothly that no ornament would hold a point. His helmet had a tall white crest, not to give him height but to be seen by his men in battle; they must be ready for change of plan whenever the action called for it. He explained this to the Lynkestids, since they were new to his wars. They had not believed in him before he came; when they saw him, they believed still less; but when they watched the war-scarred faces of warriors forty years old, intent on his every word, they believed at last.

They pressed on, to command the heights above the passes before the enemy; and came to Herakleia, whose fertile valley had been fought for in many wars. The Lynkestids were as familiar here as the storks on the house-roofs; they heartened their people with gnarled country jokes, and saluted shrines of immemorial gods elsewhere unknown. At Alexander the folk gazed as at a fable, and placed his acquisition to the credit of their lords.

The army rode up between vine-terraces, stone-edged in good red earth, to the next range; down past Lake Prespa cupped in its rocky hills, and on till Lychnidis smiled blue below them, sky-clear, fringed with its poplars and white acacias and groves of ash, shapely with bays and rocky head-lands. From the near side, war-smoke was rising. Illyria had crossed over into Macedon.

At a small hill-fort on the pass, Lynkestid clansmen greeted their chief with loyal cries. To their own kinsmen in the force, they said out of his hearing, 'A man only lives once; we'd not have waited so long with that horde so near, only that we heard the witch's son was coming. Is it true that a snake-daimon got him on the Queen? That he's weapon-proof? Is it true he was born in a caul?' Peasants to whom a visit to the nearest market ten miles off was a thing for the greater festivals, they had never seen a shaved man and asked the easterners if he was a eunuch. Those who had managed to press near reported it false that he was weapon-proof; young as he was, he was already battle-scarred; but they could attest that he was magical, having seen his eyes. Also he had forbidden the soldiers, on the way, to kill a great viper which had slid along the pass in front of them, calling it a messenger of good fortune. They eyed him warily, but with hope.

The battle was fought by the lake, among the ash-groves and orchards and glittering poplar-trees, on slopes starred with yellow mallows or blue with irises, which the soldiers crushed under trampling feet or stained with blood. The lapis-blue waters were churned and fouled; the storks and the herons fled the reeds; the eaters of carrion watched each his neighbour drop from the sky, and swooped to the glut of corpses heaped on the grassy shores, or floating under the small-flowered rocks.

The Lynkestids obeyed orders, and fought to the honour of their house. They recognized, though they could not have planned, the neat tactics which had trapped the Illyrian raiders between the steeps and the shore. They joined in the pursuit, on into the snow-topped western mountains and down the gorges, where Illyrians who made a stand were dislodged from their fastnesses to die or yield.

The Lynkestids were surprised to see him taking prisoners, after his fierceness in the battle. They had been thinking that those who nicknamed him Basiliskos must have had in mind the crowned dragon whose stare is death. But now, when they themselves would not have spared one of the ancient foes, he was taking oaths of peace as though they were not barbarians.

The Illyrians were tall lean mountaineers, leathery, brown-haired, not unlike the Lynkestids whose forbears had often married with them. Kossos, the chief who had led the raid, had been trapped in a river-gorge and taken alive. They brought him bound before Alexander by the rushing stream which foamed brown between the borders. He was a younger son of the great Bardelys, King Philip's old enemy, the terror of the border till he fell spear in hand at ninety years old. Now, the greybeard of fifty, hard and straight as a spear, stared impassively, hiding his wonder, at the boy with a man's eyes, sitting on a horse which by itself would have been worth a border raid.

'You have wasted our lands,' said Alexander, 'driven off the cattle, looted our towns and forced our women. What do you think you deserve?'

Kossos knew little Macedonian, but enough for this. He wanted no interpreter coming between them. He looked long into the young man's face and answered, 'What is due to me, we might not agree on. Do with me, son of Philip, what you think is due to yourself.'

Alexander nodded. 'Unbind him, and give him back his sword.'

He had lost in the battle two of his twelve sons; five more had been taken captive. Alexander freed three of them without ransom, and took two as hostages.

He had come to settle the border, not to breed new feuds. Though he had gone deep into Illyria, he did not try to push the frontier beyond Lake Lychnidis, where Philip had won it long ago and where the earth-shaping gods had drawn it. One thing at a time.

This was his first real war in sole command. He had gone into unknown country, and dealt with what he found; everyone thought it a great victory. With him rested the secret that it was the mask for a greater war. Alone with Hephaistion, he said, 'It would have been base to take revenge on Kossos.'

By the clear lake of Lychnidis, the mud of combat settled, pike and eels picked clean the drifting dead. The crushed lilies slept to sprout green another year; the white acacia-flowers fell like snow in the next fresh wind, and hid the blood. Widows mourned, maimed men fumbled at former skills, orphans knew hunger who had never lacked before. The people bowed to fate, as to a murrain on the cattle, or untimely hail stripping the olive-trees. They went, even the widows and orphans, to make thank-offerings at the shrines; the Illyrians, notorious pirates and slavers, might have won. Their gods, regarding their offerings kindly, kept from them the knowledge that they had been a means and not an end. In grief more than in joy, man longs to know that the universe turns around him.

A few weeks later, King Philip came back from Thrace. With the ships of Athens ranging the coasts, the comfort of a sea-trip had been denied him; he had come most of the way by litter, but, for the last lap to Pella, mounted a horse to show that he could do it. He had to be helped down; Alexander, seeing he still walked with pain, came up to offer his shoulder. They went in together to a muted hum of comment; a sick bent man who had put on ten years and lost a stone; and a glowing youth who wore victory like the spring velvet on young stags' horns.

Olympias at her window exulted in the sight. She was less pleased when as soon as the King was rested, Alexander went to his room and stayed two hours.

Some days later the King managed to hobble down for supper in Hall. Alexander, helping him up on his couch, noticed that the smell of pus still clung to him. Himself fastidiously clean, he reminded himself it was the smell of an honourable wound, and, seeing everyone's eyes on the ungainly scramble, said, 'Never mind, Father, every step you take is the witness of your valour.' The company was much pleased. It was five years now since the evening of the kithara, and few of them remembered it.

With home comfort and good doctoring, Philip mended quickly. But his limp was much worse; the same leg had been pierced again, this time in the hamstring. In Thrace the wound had putrefied; he had lain days near to death in fever; when the rotten flesh sloughed off, Parmenion said, there had been a hole you could get your fist into. It would be long before he could mount a horse without a leg-up, if he ever did; but once up, he sat handsomely with the straight-leg grip of the riding schools. In a few weeks he took over the army's training; praised the good discipline he found, and kept to himself the thought that there had been a spate of innovations. Some of them were even worth following up.

In Athens, the marble tablet which witnessed the peace with Macedon had been torn down, in formal declaration of war. Demosthenes had convinced nearly all the citizens that Philip was a power-drunk barbarian, who looked to them as a source of plunder and slaves. That they had lain an easy prey five years before, and he had not harmed them, was credited to anything but himself. He had offered, later, to treat Athenian troops as allies in the Phokian war; but Demosthenes had kept them at home by declaring they would be held as hostages; so many men going to see for themselves could only come back and confuse the issue. Phokion, the general who had done best in action against Macedon, declared Philip's offer to be sincere, and narrowly escaped a treason charge; he was only saved by a known probity which rivalled that of Aristeides the Just.

Demosthenes found it a constant nuisance. He had no doubt that he was laying out in the City's interests the gold that the Persians sent him; but a great deal passed through his hands, he was accountable to no one, and the agent's cut was naturally allowed for. It freed him from daily cares, and his time for public service; what object could be worthier? But he had to take care with Phokion.

In the Great War with Sparta, the Athenians had fought for glory and for empire; they had ended beaten to the dust and stripped of everything. They had fought for freedom and democracy, and had finished under the most brutal tyranny of their recorded years. Old men still lived who had starved through the winter siege; the middle-aged had heard of it at first hand, mostly from people it had ruined. They had lost faith in war. If they turned to it again, it could only be in one cause, for mere survival. Step by step they had been brought to think that Philip meant to destroy them. Had he not destroyed Olynthos? So at last they gave up the public dole, to spend it on the fleet; the tax on the rich was raised above the old flat rate, in proportion to what they owned.

It was the Athenian navy which made her safer than Thebes. Few understood that its high command was not just then very talented; Demosthenes took for granted that mere numbers must be decisive. Sea-power had saved Perinthos and Byzantion and the corn-route of the Hellespont. If Philip forced his way south it must be by land. Demosthenes was now the most powerful man in Athens, her symbol of salvation. Alliance with Thebes was in his grasp; he had replaced the ancient enmity by a greater.

Thebes paused in doubt. Philip had confirmed her rule over the Boeotian countryside around her, an age-long issue; where Athens, declaring it anti-democratic, had sought to weaken her by giving the Boeotians self-rule. But Thebes controlled the land-route into Attica; this was her value to Philip; all her bargaining power with him would vanish, if he and Athens made a separate peace.

So they debated, willing things to be as they had always been, unwilling to know that events are made by men, and that men had changed.

In Macedon, Philip grew brown and weathered, he could endure first half a day on horseback, and then a day; on the great horse-field by Pella lake, the cavalry wheeled and charged in complex manoeuvres. There were now two royal squadrons, Philip's and Alexander's. Father and son were seen riding together deep in counsel, the gold head bent towards the grizzled one. Queen Olympias' maids looked pale and fretted; one had been beaten, and was two days laid up.

In midsummer, when the grain was tall and green, the Council of Delphi met again. Kottyphos reported the Amphissians still defaulting, the proscribed leaders unexpelled; it was beyond his makeshift army to force them to their knees. He proposed in Council that King Philip of Macedon, who had championed the god against the impious Phokians, be asked to undertake the holy war.

Antipatros, who was there as envoy, rose to say he was empowered to give the King's consent. What was more, Philip, as a pious offering, would campaign at his own expense. Votes of thanks and an elaborate commission were drafted, and inscribed by the local writing-master; he finished his task about the time when Antipatros' courier, for whom fresh horses had stood by all the way, arrived at Pella.

Alexander was in the ball-court, playing odd-man out with his friends. It was his turn to stand in the centre of the ring, and try to stop the ball on its way. He had just got it with a four-foot jump, when Harpalos, condemned as usual to watch others limbering up, caught a flying rumour from outside, and called that the courier was here from Delphi. Alexander, in his eagerness to see the letter opened, brought it in to the King while he was in his bath.

He stood in a broad basin of ornate bronze, steaming his wounded leg while one of the squires rubbed in a strong-smelling liniment. His flesh was still sunken, his scars were ploughed and knotted all over him; one collarbone, broken long ago when his horse was killed in battle, had knit with a thick callus. He was like some old tree on which the cattle year after year have rubbed their horns. With unthinking instinct, Alexander saw what kind of weapon had made each wound. *What scars shall I carry, when I am as old as he?*

'Open it for me,' said Philip. 'My hands are wet.' He drooped his eyelid as a sign to hide bad news. But there was no need.

When Alexander ran back to the ball-court, the clean-shaved young men were splashing in the fountain, throwing jars of water at each other to sluice off the dust and cool down. Seeing his face, they paused, arrested in action like a sculpture-group by Skopas.

'It has come!' he said. 'We are going south.'

7

At the foot of the painted stairway, the bodyguard leaned on his spear. It was Keteus, a stocky iron-bearded veteran rising sixty. It had not been thought seemly for youths to guard the Queen, since the King had ceased to visit her.

The young man in the black cloak paused in the shadowed passage with its checkered floor-mosaic. He had never been so late to his mother's room.

At his footfall, the guard threw up his shield and pointed his spear, bidding him declare himself. He showed his face, and went up the stairs. When he scratched on the door there was no answer. He drew his dagger, and rapped sharply with the hilt.

A sleepy bustle sounded within, followed by a breathing silence.

'It is Alexander,' he said. 'Open the door.'

A blinking rumpled woman, a robe dragged round her, put out her head; behind her the voices rustled like mice. They must have thought, before, that it was the King.

'Madam is sleeping. It is late, Alexander, long past midnight.'

His mother's voice from beyond said, 'Let him in.'

She stood by the bed, tying the girdle of her night-robe, made of wool the colour of curded cream edged with dark fur. He could just see her by the flickering night-light; a maid, clumsy from sleep, was trying to kindle from it the wicks of the standing lamp-cluster. The hearth was swept clean, it was summer now.

The first wick of the three burned up. She said, 'That is enough.'

Her red hair mixed on her shoulders with the dark sleekness of the fur. The slanting lamplight etched the frown-creases between her brows, the lines that framed the corners of her mouth. When she faced the light full, one saw only the fine structure, the clear skin and the firm closed lips. She was thirty-four years old.

The one lamp left the room's edges dark. He said, 'Is Kleopatra here?'

'At this hour? She is in her room. Do you want her?'

'No.'

She said to the women, 'Go back to bed.'

When the door closed, she threw the embroidered coverlet over the tumbled bed, and motioned him to sit by her; but he did not move.

'What is it?' she said softly. 'We have said good-bye. You should be sleeping, if you march at dawn. What is it? You look strange. Have you had a dream?'

'I have been waiting. This is not a little war, it is the beginning of everything. I thought you would send for me. You must know what brings me here.'

She stroked back the hair across her brow, her hand masking her eyes. 'Do you want me to make a divination for you?'

'I need no divination, Mother. Only the truth.' She had let fall her hand too quickly, his eyes had seized on hers. 'What am I?' he said. 'Tell me who I am.'

She stared. He saw she had expected some other question.

'Never mind,' he said, 'whatever you have been doing. I know nothing about it. Tell me what I ask.'

She saw that in the few hours since they had last met, he had grown haggard. She had nearly said to him, 'Is that all?'

It was long past, overlaid with living; the dark shudder, the fiery consuming dream, the shock of waking, the words of the old wise-woman brought by night to this room in secret from her cave. How had it been? She no longer knew. She had brought forth the child of the dragon, and he asked, 'Who am I?'. It is I who need to ask that of him.

He was pacing, quick and light as a caged wolf, about the room. Coming to a sudden stop before her, he said, 'I am Philip's son. Isn't it so?'

Only yesterday she had seen them together going to the drill-field; Philip had spoken grinning, Alexander thrown back his head and laughed. She grew quiet, and with a long look under her eyelids said, 'Do not pretend you can believe that.'

'Well, then? I have come to hear.'

'These things cannot be scrambled at, on a whim at midnight. It is a solemn matter. There are powers one must propitiate . . .'

His searching, shadowed eyes seemed to pass clean through her, going too deep. 'What sign,' he said softly, 'did my daimon give you?'

She took both his hands, pulled him near and whispered. When she had done, she drew back to look. He was wholly within, scarcely aware of her, wrestling it out. His eyes did not tell the outcome. 'And that is everything?'

'What more? Even now are you not satisfied?'

He looked into the dark beyond the lamp. 'All things are known to the gods. The thing is how to question them.' He lifted her to her feet, and for a few moments held her at arms' length, the corners of his brows pulled together. At last her eyes fell before his.

His fingers tightened; then he embraced her, quickly and closely, and let her go. When he had left, the dark crept up all around her. She kindled the other two lamps, and slept at last with all three burning.

Alexander paused at the door of Hephaistion's room, opened it quietly and went in. He was fast asleep, one arm thrown out, in a square of moonlight. Alexander stretched out a hand, and then withdrew it. He had meant, if his mind had been satisfied, to wake him and tell him everything. But all was still dark and doubtful, she too was mortal, one must await the certain word. Why break his good sleep with that? It would be a long ride tomorrow. The moon shone straight down on his closed eyes. Softly Alexander drew the curtain half across, lest the powers of night should harm him.

In Thessaly they picked up the allied cavalry; they came streaming down over the hills, without formation, yelling and tossing their lances, showing off their horsemanship. It was a land where men rode as soon as they could walk. Alexander raised his brows; but Philip said they would do what they were told in battle, and do it well. This show was a tradition.

The army bore south-west, towards Delphi and Amphissa. Some levies from the Sacred League joined them along the way; their generals were made welcome, and swiftly briefed. Used to the confederate forces of small rival states, the edging for precedence, the long wrangles with whichever general had been given chief command, they were drawn amazed into a moving army of thirty thousand foot and two thousand horse, each man of which knew where he had to be, and went there.

There were no forces from Athens. The Athenians had a seat on the League Council; but when it commissioned Philip, no Athenian had been present to dissent. Demosthenes had persuaded them to boycott it. A vote against Amphissa would have antagonized Thebes. He had seen no further.

The army reached Thermopylai, the hot gates between the mountains and the sea. Alexander, who had not passed this way since he was twelve, went with Hephaistion to bathe in the warm springs for which the pass was named. On the grave-mound of Leonidas, with its marble lion, he laid a garland. 'I don't think,' he remarked after, 'that he was really much of a general. If he'd made sure the Phokian troops understood their orders, the Persians could never have turned the pass. These southern states never work together. But one must honour a man as brave as that.'

The Thebans still had the fort above. Philip, playing their own game, sent up an envoy, politely asking them to leave so that he could relieve them. They looked down at the long snake of men filling the shore-road and thickening into distance; stolidly they picked up their gear, and left for Thebes.

Now the army was on the great south-east road; they saw on their right the stark mountains of Hellas' spine, barer and bleaker, more despoiled by man's axes and man's herds, than the wooded heights of Macedon. In the valleys between these tall deserts, flesh between bones, lay the earth and water that fed mankind.

'Now I see it again,' said Alexander to Hephaistion as they rode, 'I can understand just why the southerners are as they are. They're land-starved; each man covets his neighbour's, and knows the neighbour covets his. And each state has its fringe of mountains. Have you seen two dogs by the fence where one of them lives, running up and down barking?'

'But,' said Hephaistion, 'when dogs come to a gap, they don't rush through and fight, they just look surprised and walk off. Sometimes dogs have more sense than men.'

The road towards Amphissa turned due south; an advance party under Parmenion had gone ahead, to take the strong-point of Kytinion and secure this road, as earnest of Philip's purpose to pursue the holy war. But the main force marched on by the highway, still going south-east, towards Thebes and Athens.

'Look,' said Alexander, pointing ahead, 'there's Elatia. Look, the masons and engineers are there already. It shouldn't take long to raise the walls, they say all the stone's still there.'

Elatia had been a fort of the god-robbing Phokians, pulled down at the end of the previous holy war. It commanded the road. It was two days' fast march from Thebes, and three from Athens.

A thousand slaves, under skilled masons, soon put back the well-squared ashlar. The army occupied the fort and the heights around it. Philip set his headquarters up, and sent an envoy to Thebes.

For years, his message said, the Athenians had made war on him, first covertly, then openly; he could no longer hold his hand. To Thebes they had been hostile even longer; yet now they were trying to draw Thebes, too, into war against them. He must ask the Thebans therefore to declare themselves. Would they stand by their allegiance, and give his army passage south?

The royal tent had been put up within the walls; the shepherds who had made hovels in the ruins had fled when the army came. Philip had had a supper-couch carted along, to rest his game leg after the day's work. Alexander sat on a chair beside him. The squires had set out wine, and withdrawn.

'This should settle it,' said Philip, 'once for all. Time comes when one must put down the stake and throw. I think it's long odds against war. If the Thebans are sane, they'll declare for us; the Athenians will wake up and see where their demagogues have brought them; Phokion's party will come in; and we can cross to Asia without a drop of blood shed in Greece.'

Alexander turned his winecup in his hands, and bent to smell the local vintage. They made better wine in Thrace, but Thrace had been given it by Dionysos. 'Well, yes ... but look what happened while you were laid up and I was raising the army. We gave out we were arming against the

Illyrians; and everyone believed it, the Illyrians most of all. Now, what about the Athenians? They've been told for years by Demosthenes to expect us; here we are. And what becomes of *him*, if Phokion's party gets the vote?'

'He can do nothing, if Thebes has declared for us.'

'They've ten thousand trained mercenaries in Athens.'

'Ah, yes. But it's the Thebans who will decide. You know their constitution. A moderate oligarchy they call it, but the franchise test is low; it takes in any man who can afford a hoplite panoply. There you have it. In Thebes, it's the electorate that will fight in any war it votes for.'

He began to talk about his hostage years there, almost with nostalgia. Time had misted the hardships; it had the taste of vanished youth. He had been smuggled once by friends into action under Epaminondas. He had known Pelopidas. Alexander as he listened thought of the Sacred Band, which Pelopidas had gathered into one corps, rather than founded; for their heroic vows were ancient, going back to Herakles and Iolaos, at whose altar they were sworn. Men of the Band, having each in his charge a twofold honour, did not retreat; they advanced, or stood, or died. There was much Alexander would have liked to know of them, and tell Hephaistion, had there been anyone else to ask.

'I wonder,' he remarked instead, 'what is going on now in Athens.'

Athens had had the news at sunset, on the day Elatia was occupied. The City Councillors were at their civic meal in the Council Hall, with some old Olympic victors, retired generals and other worthies honoured with this privilege. The Agora was clamorous; the courier from Thebes came only on the heels of rumour. All night the streets were like market-time, with kindred running to kindred, merchants to the Piraeus; strangers talking passionately to strangers, women running with half-veiled faces to the women's rooms of houses where they had friends. At daybreak the City Trumpeter called Assembly; in the Agora the hurdles of the stock-pens and the market stalls were set alight to beacon the outer suburbs. The men poured across to Pnyx Hill with its stone rostrum. They were told the news; that Philip was expected to march south at once, and that Thebes would make no resistance. Old men recalled a black day of their childhood, the beginning of shame, starvation, tyranny, when the first stragglers had come in from Goat River on the Hellespont, where the fleet had been annihilated; the Great War lost and the death-throes still to come. The crisp cool air of an autumn morning struck to the bone like a winter frost. The presiding Councillor called aloud. 'Does anyone wish to speak?'

A long silence followed. All eyes turned one way. Nobody had the folly to come between the people and their choice. When they saw him mount the bema, no one cheered; the chill was too deep for that; there was only a deep murmur, like the sound of prayer.

All night the lamp had burned in Demosthenes' study; men walking the streets, too troubled to go to bed, had been comforted by its light. In the dark before the dawn, the draft of his speech was ready. The city of Theseus, Solon, Perikles, at her crux of fate had turned to him. She had found him ready.

Firstly, he said, they could dismiss their fear that Philip was sure of Thebes. If he were, he would not be sitting in Elatia; he would be here now before their walls, he who had always aimed at their destruction. He was making a show of force, to hearten his bought friends in Thebes and daunt the patriots. Now at last they must resolve to forget the ancient feud, and send envoys to offer generous terms of alliance, before Philip's men had done their evil work there. He himself, if summoned, would not refuse the call. Meantime, let the men of fighting age put on their arms, and march up the Theban road as far as Eleusis, in token of readiness to take the field.

As he ended, the sun rose, and they saw across the dip the Acropolis bathed in splendour; the mellow old marble, the white new shrines, the colour and the gold. A great cheer ran over the hill. Those who had been too far to hear all joined in it, sure that salvation had been proclaimed.

Demosthenes went back home, and drafted a diplomatic note to Thebes, heaping scorn on Philip. '... acting as might be looked for in one of his race and nature; insolently using his present fortune, forgetful of his unforeseen rise to power from small mean origins ...' Thoughtfully he chewed his pen; the stylos moved on over the wax.

Outside his window, young men still new to war, on the way to report to their tribal officers, were shouting to each other; the jokes of the young, whose meaning he no longer knew. A woman was crying somewhere. Surely, it was in the house. It must be his daughter. If she had anyone to weep over, it was the first he knew of it. Angrily he closed the door; the noise was ill-omened, and disturbed his thoughts.

When the Assembly met at Thebes, no man who could stand on his feet was absent. The Macedonians, being formal allies, had first hearing.

They recalled Philip's good offices to Thebes; his help in the Phokian War, his support for her hegemony over Boeotia; rehearsed her ancient injuries from the Athenians, their efforts to weaken her, their alliance with the impious Phokians, paying their troops with Apollo's gold. (With this too, no doubt, they had gilded the Theban shields they had set up, in blasphemous affront to Thebes and to the god.) Philip did not ask that Thebes should take up arms against Athens; Thebans might do so if they chose, and share the fruits of victory; but he would still count them as friends, if they gave him only right of passage.

The Assembly turned it over. They had been angered by Philip's surprise of Elatia; if he was an ally, he was a high-handed one, it was late to consult them now. For the rest, it was true enough. The great issues of power remained unspoken. Once Athens had fallen, what would they be worth to him? And yet, he had power in Thessaly and had done no harm there. They had fought the long Phokian war; Thebes was full of dead men's sons with a family on their shoulders, the widowed mother and the younger ones. Was it not enough?

Antipatros ceased, and sat down. A not unfriendly murmur, almost applause, was heard. The marshal called the Athenian envoys. Demosthenes climbed the rostrum, in a hush of expectation, mostly hostile. Not Macedon, but Athens, had been the threat here for generations. There was no house without a blood-debt from the endless border wars.

He could strike one answering nerve; the common hate for Sparta. He recalled how after the Great War, when Sparta had imposed on Athens the Thirty Tyrants (traitors like those who wanted peace with Philip now), Thebes had given harbour to the Liberators. Beside Philip, the Thirty were merely schoolboy bullies; let the past be forgotten, only that noble act remembered. With skilled timing, he brought out the Athenian offers. Theban rights over Boeotia should be undisputed; if the Boeotians should rebel, Athens would even send troops to put them down. Plateia too, that old bone of contention. He did not remind his hearers that Plateia, in return for Athens' protection against Thebes, had joined in the stand at Marathon, and been granted Athenian citizenship for ever. It was no time for hair-splitting; Plateia should be conceded. Also, if there was war with Philip, Thebes should command all land-forces, while Athens would meet two-thirds of the expense.

The burst of applause was missing. Thebans in doubt were looking at other Thebans they knew and trusted, not at him. They were slipping his grip.

Striding forward, lifting his arm, he invoked the heroic dead, Epaminondas and Pelopidas; the glorious fields of Leuktra and Mantinea; the record of the Sacred Band. His ringing voice dropped to a note of silken irony. If these things were no longer of account to them, he had only one request to make on behalf of Athens; right of passage, to oppose the tyrant alone.

He had caught them now. That nip of the old rivalry had done it.

They were shamed, he could hear it in the deep muted sound. Here and there two voices called together for the voting to begin; the men of the Sacred Band were considering their honour. The pebbles rattled into the urns; tally-clerks under close scrutiny flicked their abacuses; a long tedious business, after the efficient slot-counters at home. The Thebans had voted to tear up the treaty with Macedon, and ally with Athens.

He walked back to his lodging, hardly feeling his feet touch ground. Like Zeus with his scales, he had held and tilted the destiny of Greece. If ordeal lay ahead, what new life came forth without birth-pangs? They would say of him now, for ever, that the hour had found the man.

They brought Philip the news next day, as he ate his noon meal with Alexander. The King sent his squires out, before even opening the dispatch; like most men of the time, he had not mastered the knack of reading with the eye alone, he needed to hear himself. Alexander, taut with suspense, wondered why his father could not have trained himself, as he had done, to read in silence; it was only a matter of practice; though his lips still moved with the words, Hephaistion had assured him that no sound at all came out.

Philip read levelly, without anger; the lines of his face only deepened into seams. He laid down the scroll by his dish, and said, 'Well, if they will have it, they will have it.'

'I'm sorry, Father; I suppose it had to be.' Could he not see that however the Thebans had voted, Athens would still have hated him? That there was no way he could have entered her gates, but as a victor? How had he nursed so long this insubstantial dream? Better leave him in peace, and think about realities. It would be the second war-plan, now.

Athens and Thebes made ready at fever-heat to meet Philip's southward march. Instead he went west, into the mountain ribs and gorges that fringed the Parnassos massif. He had been commissioned to drive the Amphissians from the sacred plain; this he would do. As for Thebes, let it be said he had only tested a doubtful ally's loyalty, and knew the answer.

The young men of Athens, roused for war, prepared to go north to Thebes. The omens were taken; the first smouldered, the diviners misliked the entrails. Demosthenes, finding the dead hand of superstition raised against him, declared these portents were meant to reveal the traitors in their midst, paid by Philip to stop the war. When Phokion, back from a mission too late to change events, urged that the city should get an oracle from Delphi, Demosthenes laughed, and said that all the world knew Philip had bought the Pythia.

The Thebans received the Athenians as the Lynkestids had welcomed Alexander, with careful courtesy. The Theban general disposed his joint force to guard the southern passes, and to block Philip from Amphissa. All over the wild stony uplands of Parnassos, and in the gorges of Phokis, the armies scouted and manoeuvred. Trees turned brown, then bare; on the tops the first snows fell. Philip took his time. He was busy rebuilding the forts of the impious Phokians, who gratefully leased them to his men, in exchange for a cut in their fines to the plundered god.

He would not be tempted into a major battle. There was a skirmish in a river-gorge, another in an upland pass, both broken off when he saw his troops being drawn into awkward country. Athens hailed them as victories, and thanksgiving feasts were held.

One winter night, Philip's tent was pitched out of the wind against a cliff-face, above a river in snow-spate churning its stony gorge. On the slopes between, a pine-wood had been felled for cook-fires. Dusk was falling; eddies of pure mountain air pierced through the heavy mingled smells of wood-smoke, porridge, bean broth, horses, crudely-cured tent hides, and many thousand unwashed men. On leather camp-chairs, Philip and Alexander sat warming their wet boots at the glowing crumble of their fire. The steamy reek of his father's feet blended for Alexander with the other homely and familiar scents of war. He himself was no more than fairly dirty; when streams were hard to come at, he would rub himself down with snow. His attention to these things had created a legend, of which he was still unaware, that he was endowed with a natural fragrance. Most of the men had not bathed for months. Their wives would scrub them, when they returned to the marriage bed.

'Well,' said Philip, 'didn't I tell you Demosthenes' patience would wear out before mine? I heard just now. He's sent them.'

'What? How many?'

'The whole ten thousand.'

'Is the man mad?'

'No, he's a party politician. The voters didn't like to see paid troops drawing pay and rations in Attica, while citizens went to war. They've been on my mind; trained men, and too mobile where they were, too mobile by far. At the clinch, ten thousand extra men is a good many. Now we can deal with them first; they're being sent direct to Amphissa.'

'So we wait till they're there. Then what?'

Philip's yellow teeth grinned in the firelight. 'You know how I slipped away at Byzantion? We'll try that again. We'll have bad news, very bad news from Thrace. Revolt, Amphipolis threatened, every man needed to hold the frontier. I shall reply, in good clear writing, that we are marching north with all our forces. My courier will be captured, or maybe sell the letter. The enemy's scouts will see us starting northward. At Kytinion we'll go to ground, lie low, and wait.'

'Then over the Grabian Pass, and attack at dawn?'

'A stolen march, as your friend Xenophon says.'

They stole it, before spring thaw had drowned the river-crossings. The mercenaries of Athens did their duty, as long as there was hope in it; after that, being professionals, they either got away to the coast, or asked for terms. Most of these last ended by enlisting with Philip, had their wounds dressed, and sat down to a good hot meal.

The Amphissians surrendered without condition. Their government was exiled as the Sacred League had decreed. The holy plain was stripped of their impious husbandry, and left fallow for the god.

In the first warmth of spring, at the theatre of Delphi, the steep pale eagle-cliffs of the Phaidriades behind them, the great temple of Apollo before, and the vast gulf beyond, King Philip was crowned by the League with a golden laurel crown. He and his son were eulogized in long speeches and choric odes; a sculptor sketched them, for statues to adorn the temple.

Afterwards, Alexander walked with his friends on the jostling terrace. It hummed and stank with the throng from all over Greece, and as far as Sicily, Italy and Egypt. Rich votaries marched with their offerings displayed on the heads of slaves, goats bleated, doves moaned in wicker cages; faces eager, devout, relieved, drawn with anxiety, came and went. It was one of the days for the oracle.

Under the noise, Hephaistion said in Alexander's ear, 'Why don't you, while you're here?'

'Not now.'

'It would set your mind at rest.'

'No, the time's not right. One should take the seer by surprise, I think, in a place like this.'

A sumptuous performance was put on in the theatre; the protagonist was Thettalos, renowned for his heroic roles. He was a handsome ardent young man, whose Thessalian blood was mixed with some Celtic strain; his training in Athens had contained his fire in good technique, and his natural rashness in good manners. He had often played in Pella, and was a favourite with Alexander, for whom he conjured some special vision of the hero's soul. Now in Sophokles' *Ajax*, doubling Ajax and Teukros, he made it unthinkable the one should outlive his honour, the other fail in loyalty to the dead. Alexander went round afterwards with Hephaistion to the skene-room. Thettalos had pulled off the mask of Teukros, and was towelling the sweat from his strongly-carved face and short curly chestnut hair. At the sound of Alexander's voice he emerged and glowed at him with large hazel eyes, saying, 'I am glad if you were pleased. I was playing it all to you.'

They talked awhile about his recent travels. At the end he said, 'I get about a good deal. If ever you have any business, never mind what, and need someone you can trust, you know it would be a privilege.'

He was understood. Actors, the servants of Dionysos, were protected persons; often used as envoys, as secret agents even oftener. Alexander said, 'Thank you, Thettalos. There is no one I would sooner ask.'

When they were walking away towards the Stadium, Hephaistion said, 'You know that man's still in love with you?'

'Well, one can at least be civil. He's sensible, he doesn't misunderstand. Some day I might need to trust him, one never knows.'

With good spring weather, Philip moved down to the Gulf of Corinth, and took Naupaktis, which commanded its outer strait. In summer, he moved about in the country behind Parnassos, strengthening strong-points, keeping alliances warm, making roads, feeding-up his cavalry mounts. Now and again he would make feints to the east, where Athenians and Thebans tensely manned the passes. Then he would march away, leaving them flat and stale, and would hold manoeuvres or games, to make sure his own men were neither.

Even now, he sent once more envoys to Thebes and Athens, offering to discuss terms for a peace. Demosthenes proclaimed that Philip, twice repulsed by their arms, must be growing desperate; these offers proved it. One good push would finish him in the south.

In late summer, when the barley between the trees in the olive-orchards of Attica and Boeotia was yellowing in the ear, he went back to his base at Elatia, but left his strongpoints manned. The forward outposts of Thebes and Athens were at a pass about ten miles south. Till his offers were thrown back, he had done no more than tease them. Now he displayed his strength; they were outflanked, and could be cut off when he chose. Next day his scouts found them gone; he took and manned the pass.

The men of the cavalry looked happy, polished their gear and made much of their horses. Now, the coming battle would be in the plains.

The barley whitened, the olives ripened. By the calendar of Macedon, it was the month of the Lion. King Philip gave a birthday feast in the fort for Alexander. He was eighteen.

Elatia had been made snug; woven hangings on the wall of the royal quarters, tiles on the floor. While the guests were singing, Philip said to his son, 'You've not named your gift yet. What would you like?'

Alexander smiled. 'You know that, Father.'

'You've earned it; it's yours. It won't be long now. I shall take the right wing, that goes back time out of mind. You will command the cavalry.'

Slowly Alexander set down on the table his golden cup. His eyes, shimmering and wide with wine and visions, met Philip's lop-sided black glint. 'If you ever regret it, Father, I shan't be there to know.'

The appointment was cheered, and toasted. Once more the birth-omens were remembered: the Olympic racing win, the Illyrian victory.

'And the third,' said Ptolemy. 'It's the one I remember best, I was at the age for marvels. It was the day the great temple of Artemis was burned at Ephesos. A fire in Asia.'

Someone said, 'I never heard how it came to happen, without a war. Was it a thunderbolt, or did some priest upset a lamp?'

'No, a man did it on purpose. I heard his name once. Heiro – Hero –
a longer name than that. Nearchos, can you remember?'

No one could. Nearchos said, 'Did they find out why he did it?'

'Oh, yes. He told them all willingly, before they killed him. He did it so
that his name should be remembered for ever.'

Dawn glimmered over the low hills of Boeotia, heather and scrub
burned brown with summer, scattered with grey boulders and gravelly
stones. Dark and rusty like the heath, weathered like the stones, spiny like
the thorn-trees, the men poured over the hills towards the plain. They
trickled down the slopes and silted in the river-valley; the silt thickened,
but steadily flowed on.

Along the smoothest inclines the cavalry came ambling, careful of
unshod hooves. The horses made only a muffled thudding as they picked
their way among the heather, their bare backs gripped by the men's bare
thighs. It was the harness of the men that clicked and rattled.

The sky lightened, though the sun still stood behind the great eastward
bulk of Parnassos. The valley, scoured out by primeval floods and filled in
with their topsoil, began to flatten and widen. Along it burbled through
stones the Kephissos river in its summer bed. East of it, low on the terraced
slopes, its pink-washed houses still mauve with shadow, stood the village
of Chaironeia.

The flood of men slowed its onward course, paused, and spread sideways
across the plain. Ahead of it was stretched a dam. Its thick line bristled,
and glinted in the first slanting sunbeams; a dam of men.

Between lay a clear space of innocent fields, fed by the river. Mown
barley-stubble round the olive trees was pretty with poppies and vetch.
There was a noise of crowing cocks, a bleating and lowing of farm-stock,
sharp cries of boys and women driving the herds away uphill. The flood
and the dam both waited.

In the broad throat of the pass, the northern army made camp
along the river. The cavalry went downstream, to water their horses
without fouling it for the rest. The men untied their cups from their
belts and unpacked their food for their noon meal; flat griddle-cakes,
an apple or an onion, a crumble of dirty grey salt from the heel of the
bag.

The officers looked about for unsound spear-shafts or javelin thongs,
and took the feel of morale. They found a healthy tension, like a drawn
bow's; the men had caught the sense of something momentous. They were
thirty-odd thousand foot, two thousand horse; the host ahead was as
many; this would be the greatest battle of all their lives till now. They were
aware too of the men they knew, the captain who was the squire at home,

the village neighbour, the fellow-tribesmen and kin, who would report their honour or their shame.

Towards afternoon the long baggage-train laboured down with the tents and bedding. They could sleep well, all but the outposts; the King held all the flanking passes, their position could not be turned. The army ahead could only sit and wait his pleasure.

Alexander rode up to the ox-cart with the royal tents, and said, 'Put mine there.' A young oak gave shade by the river; under the bank was a clear gravelly pool. Good, said his servants, it would save carrying water. He liked his bath, not only after a battle but, if he could manage it, even before. Some grumbler had said he would be vain even of his corpse.

The King sat in his tent, giving audience to Boeotians, eager to tell him all they knew of the enemy's plans. The Thebans had oppressed them; the Athenians, their sworn allies, had just sold them publicly to the Thebans; they had nothing much to lose by a leap in the dark. He received them with charm, listened to all their involved and ancient grievances, promised redress, and made notes in his own hand of all they had to tell. Before dusk, he rode up the hill to look for himself, with Alexander, Parmenion, and the next in command, a Macedonian lord called Attalos. The royal body-guard under Pausanias rode behind.

Below them spread the plain which some old poet had called 'the dancing-floor of war', so often had armies met there. The confederate troops spread across from the river to the southern foothills, a front of about three miles. The smoke of their evening fires was rising, with here and there a spurt of flame. Not yet in line of battle, they were clumped, like birds of different species, each city and state apart. Their left wing, which would face the Macedonian right, was based firmly on rising ground. Philip narrowed his good eye at it.

'The Athenians. Well, I must have them out of there. Old Phokion, their only general who's good for anything, has been given the navy; he was too canny to please Demosthenes. Our luck; they've sent Chares, who fights by the book . . . Hm, yes; I must put on a good-looking assault before I start falling back. They'll swallow it, from the old general who writes off his losses.' He leaned over with a grin to clap Alexander's shoulder. 'It wouldn't do for the Little King.'

Alexander's brow creased, then cleared. He returned the grin, and went back to considering the long bar of men below, as an engineer who must divert a river considers obstructing rock. Tall lank-cheeked Attalos, with his forked yellow beard and pale blue eyes, had edged his horse up nearer, but now moved quietly back.

'So, then,' said Alexander, 'in the centre we've the odds and ends; Corinthians, Achaians, and so on. And on the right . . .'

'The high command. For you, my son, the Thebans. You see, I've not stinted your dish.'

The river gleamed in the light of the paling sky, between tapering poplars and shady planes. Beside it, in orderly patterns, the Theban watch-fires budded into flame. Alexander gazed in deep concentration; for a moment he pictured in this distant firelight the human faces; then they dwindled into the spread of the great design. *And all the gates were opened, and the warriors came pouring out. Foot and horse, and the din of onset resounded.*

'Wake up, lad,' said Philip. 'We've seen all we need; I want my supper.'

Parmenion always ate with them; so tonight did Attalos, newly come in from Phokis. Alexander saw with discomfort that Pausanias was on guard. Those two together in one room always put his teeth on edge. He greeted Pausanias with special warmth.

It was Attalos, friend and kin of the dead rival, who had planned the obscene revenge. It was a mystery to Alexander why Pausanias, a man with no lack of courage, should have come to the King demanding vengeance, rather than take it with his own hand. Could it be that he had wanted a sign of Philip's loyalty? Long ago, before the change, he had had a kind of archaic beauty, which could have housed such an arrogant Homeric love. But Attalos was chief of a powerful clan, a good friend of the King, and useful; the dead boy's loss had been bitter, too. Pausanias had been talked out of it, and his honour patched up with rank. Six years had gone by, he had been laughing oftener, talking more, becoming an easier presence, till Attalos was made a general. Now once more he never met one's eyes, and ten words were a long speech for him. Father shouldn't have done it. It looks like a reward. People say already . . .

His father was talking of the coming battle. He brushed clear his mind; but an aftertaste lingered, as of tainted food.

Alexander had his bath in the gravelly pool, and lay on his bed, going over in his mind the battle-plan, point by point. There was nothing he had forgotten. He got up, dressed, and walked along quietly between the watch-fires, till he reached the tent Hephaistion shared with two or three other men. Before he had touched the flap, Hephaistion had risen soundlessly, thrown on his cloak and come out. They stood for a while talking, then went back to their beds. Alexander slept well till the morning watch.

The din of onset resounded.

Over the barley stubble and round the olive-trees, crashing through vineyards half-picked when the labourers fled, knocking down the props and treading the grapes into bloody wine, the press of men swayed and mixed and seethed, their mass swelling and bursting like bubbles, rising and settling like yeast. The noise was deafening. Men yelled to one another, or to the enemy, or to themselves; or screamed in some piercing agony beyond what they had known that flesh could feel. Shields clashed, horses squealed, each corps of the confederate army shouted its own battle-paean at full stretch of its lungs. Officers roared orders, trumpets blew. Over everything hung a great cloud of rusty, choking dust.

On the left, where the Athenians held the foothills which formed the confederates' anchor, the Macedonians shoved their long sarissas doggedly from below, the points of three graded ranks forming one row of weapons, bristling like a porcupine. The Athenians took them on their shields when they could; the bravest pressed between them, stabbing with the short spear or hacking with the sword, sometimes overwhelmed, sometimes denting the line. Along the far flank Philip sat his strong cobby war-horse, his couriers by him, waiting; for what, his men all knew. They heaved and strained in the line, as if their failure to break it was killing them with shame. Though huge noise was everywhere, among them it was somewhat less; they had been told to listen for the word.

In the centre, the long front leaned to and fro. The confederate troops, strangers to their neighbours, sometimes rivals, shared the common knowledge that where the line broke disgrace and death would enter. Wounded men fought on till with luck the shields closed before them; or fell, and were trampled on by men who could not drop their guard or pause. The hot press churned in the hot dust, sweating, grunting, cursing, hacking, thrusting, panting, moaning. Where rock broke the ground, the melee heaved round it like sea-foam, and splashed it with crimson spray.

At its north end, where the river guarded its flank, there stretched as evenly as a string of beads the unflawed shield-line of the Sacred Band of Thebes. Now in action the couples were forged into a single bar, each man's shield overlapping the left-hand man. The elder of each pair, the erastes, kept the right, the spear side; the younger, the eromenos, the side of the shield. The right was the side of honour, for a corps or a man; though the youth might grow up the stronger, he would never ask his friend to cede it. All this was governed by ancient laws. Newly-sworn lovers were here, intent upon their proving; and couples who had been in the corps ten years, solid bearded fathers of families, love rendered-down to comradeship; the Band was too famous to be renounced at a dream's passing. Its lifelong vows were battle-vows. Even through the dust, it glittered. Its bronze hatlike Boeotian helmets and its round shields edged with cable-work had been burnished to shine like gold. Its weapons were six-foot spears with iron blades, and short stabbing swords, still sheathed, the spear-hedge being unbroken.

Parmenion, whose phalanx faced them, had all he could do to hold them. Now and then they gave a great heave forward, and could have gone further yet, but for fear of breaking contact with the Achaians next to them in the line. They were polished and smooth like some old well-made weapon a man knows the feel of in the dark. Hurry up, Philip; these fellows have been to school. I hope you know what you've given your boy to bite on. I hope he has the teeth for it.

Behind the labouring phalanx, just out of bowshot, the cavalry waited. They were massed in a thick column like a catapult-bolt, with a tapering head, whose point was a single horseman.

The horses fidgeted at the noise, at the drifts of blood-smell on the wind, and the tension in the riders' bodies; they blew from the tickle of the dust. The men talked to neighbours or called to friends, rebuked or fondled the horses, straining to see through the ten-foot dust cloud how the battle went. They were to charge a line of hoplites, the horseman's nightmare. Cavalry against cavalry, the other man could fall off as easily as you, pushed with the spear, or over-reaching himself; he could be out-manoeuvred, slashed with the sabre. But to run at firm up-pointed spears went against a horse's nature. They fingered the hard-cured bullhide pectorals on their chargers' breasts. The Companions found their own equipment; but they were glad they had listened to the Boy.

The foremost rider flicked off a fly from his horse's eyelid, feeling with his thighs its strength, its knowledge of the coming fury, its implicit trust, its complicit horse-sense. Yes, yes; we'll be going when I say go. Remember who we are.

Hephaistion in the next short rank felt at his sword-belt; should it be one hole tighter? No, nothing makes him so angry as a man fixing his turnout in the line. I must catch him up before he gets there. His colour's high. It often is before an action. If it was fever he'd never say. Two days with it before the fort fell, and not a word, I could have carried extra water. A fine night I had of it.

A courier rode through the dusty trampled stubble, and hailed Alexander in the King's name. The message was word-of-mouth: 'They are taking the bait. Be ready.'

Up on the hill, above the pink-washed village of Chaironeia, in the tenth row back of the Athenian force, Demosthenes stood with his tribal regiment. The young men held the front; next behind were the strongest of the middle-aged. The whole depth of the line shifted and strained, as a man's whole body does when his right arm alone makes some great effort. The day grew hot. It seemed they had been standing and swaying and staring down for hours; suspense ached in him like a tooth. Ahead men were falling, getting spears in their guts and chests; the shock of the blows seemed to travel all through the thick ranks, back to where he stood. How many fallen already; how many ranks still left between that and him? I should not be here, I am wronging the City by risking myself in war. The milling press made a long shove forward; it was the second in a short time; without doubt now, the enemy was giving ground. There were still nine ranks between him and the long sarissas; and their line was wavering. It is not unknown to you, men of Athens, that I carried shield and spear on the field of Chaironeia, counting as nought my life and my own concerns, though some might have called them weighty, and indeed you might have reproached me with hazarding your welfare in risking mine ... A choking cry of pain came from the front rank, which had been the second. Men of Athens ...

The roar of battle changed. An exultant shout ran like fire through the packed mass. It began to move, no longer in laboured heaves but like a gathering landslide. The enemy was retreating! The glories of Marathon, of Salamis, of Plataia, flashed before his eyes. Men in front were yelling, 'On to Macedon!' He started running with the rest, calling in his high sharp voice, 'Catch Philip! Take him alive!' He should be led in chains through the Agora; after that they would make him talk, name every traitor. There would be a new statue on the Acropolis, next to Harmodios and Aristogeiton: DEMOSTHENES THE LIBERATOR. He shouted to those ahead who could run faster, 'On to Macedon! Take him alive!' In this haste to be there and see it, he almost stumbled over the bodies of the young men who had fallen in the front line.

Theagenes the Theban, commander-in-chief of the confederate army, urged his horse behind the battle-lines towards the centre. The long front fermented with shouted rumour, too garbled to be of use. Here at last came one of his own scouts. The Macedonians were indeed, he reported, in retreat.

How? asked Theagenes. In disorder? In fair order, but getting away pretty fast. They had already fallen right back from the heights, with the Athenians after them. After them? What! Had they left their station, then, without orders? Well, orders or not, they were already in the plain; it was the King himself they were chasing.

Theagenes, cursing, beat his fist on his thigh. Philip! The fools, the misbegotten, fribbling, vainglorious Athenian fools. What had become of the line up there? There must be a gap as long as a hippodrome. He sent off the scout with orders that it must at all costs be filled, and the left flank covered. No sign anywhere else of the enemy falling back; they were laying on harder than ever.

The leader of the Corinthians received the order. How better guard the flank, than get up on the good rising ground where the Athenians had been? The Achaians, left feeling naked, spread out towards the Corin-

thians. Theagenes stretched out his own troops in turn. Let these
Athenian speechmakers see what real soldiers look like. In their place of
honour on the right wing, the Sacred Band changed order; briefly, as they
moved, they showed in twos.

Theagenes surveyed the long threshing chain of men, now loose at one
end, and weaker overall. Before him, the enemy rear was obscured by a
tree-tall thicket of sarissas; ranks not engaged held them high, for the
safety of those in front. With them and the dust-cloud, one could see
nothing. A thought hit him, like a jolt in the midriff. No word of young
Alexander. Where is he? On garrison duty in Phokis? Toiling unnoticed
in the line? Yes, when iron floats. Then where is he?

There was a lull in the fight before him; almost a stillness, after the noise
before; the heavy pause of earthquake weather. Then the deep bristling
phalanx swung sideways, ponderously but smoothly, like an enormous
door.

It stood open. The Thebans did not go out of it; they waited for what
was coming in. The Sacred Band, turning face to face before they locked
the shield-line and settled their spears, showed up in twos, once and for
all.

In the stubble-field among the trampled poppies, Alexander lifted his
sword-arm, and yelled the note of the paean.

Strong and sustained, the voice trained by Epikrates rang down the
great square of horsemen. They took up the paean; it lost in its passage
the sound of words, dinning like the fierce outcry from a cloud of swooping
hawks. It goaded the horses more than spurs. Before ever they came in
sight, the Thebans had felt their thunder through the ground.

Watching his men like a shepherd on a mountain trail, Philip waited
for news.

The Macedonians were plodding back, sullenly, carefully, fighting for
every few yards of ground. Philip rode about, directing their retreat just
where it should go. Who could believe it, he thought. When Iphikrates was
alive, or Chabrias ... But their orators appoint their generals now. So soon,
so soon. A generation ... He shielded his eyes to scan the line. The charge
had begun, he knew no more.

Well, he's alive; if he fell, the news would fly quicker than a bird. Curse
this leg, I'd like to take a walk among the men, they're used to it. A
spearman all my life. I never thought I'd breed a cavalry general. Ah well,
the hammer still needs the anvil. When he can bring off a planned fighting
withdrawal like this ... He understood his briefing. Everything pat. But
only half there, he had that look of his mother.

Thought changed to tangled images like a knot of snakes. He saw the

proud head lying in blood; the mourning, the tomb at Aigai, the choice
of a new heir; idiot Arridaios' jerking face, I was drunk when I got him;
Ptolemy, too late now to acknowledge him, I was a boy, what could I do?
... What's four-and-forty, I've good seed in me yet. A sturdy square dark-
haired boy ran up to him, calling, 'Father!' ...

Shouts sounded, nearing, directing a rider to the King.

'He's through, sir. He's broken the line. The Thebans are standing, but
they're cut off beside the river, the right wing's rolled up. I didn't speak
with him, he said ride straight to you when I saw it, you were waiting for
the word. But I saw him there in the van, I saw his white crest.'

'The gods be thanked. A bringer of such news deserves something. See
me after.' He summoned the trumpeter. For a moment, like a good farmer
at harvest-time, he viewed the field which through his careful husbandry
stood for the reaping just as it ought. His cavalry reserve had appeared
upon the heights, before the Corinthians could command them. His withdrawing infantry had spread into the shape of a sickle blade. Enclosed in
its curve were the jubilant Athenians.

He gave the order to attack.

The knot of young men was still resisting. They had found a stone sheep-
pen, nearly breast high, but the sarissas came thrusting over. In the filth
on the ground a lad of eighteen was kneeling, clutching at his eye which
was falling down his cheek.

'We should get away,' said the older man in the middle, urgently. 'We
shall be cut off. Look, you can see, look round.'

'We're staying here,' said the young man who had assumed command.
'You go if you want, we'll never notice the difference.'

'Why throw away our lives? Our lives belong to the City. We should go
back and dedicate our lives to restoring Athens.'

'Barbarians! Barbarians!' yelled the young man to the troops outside.
They replied with some uncouth battle-cry. When he had time to spare,
he said to the older man, 'Restore Athens? Let us rather perish with her.
Philip will blot her from the earth. Demosthenes has always said so.'

'Nothing is certain, terms can be made ... Look, they have almost closed
us round, are you mad, wasting all our lives?'

'Not even slavery, but annihilation. That's what Demosthenes said. I
was there, I heard him.'

A sarissa, poking forward out of the thick of the attackers, caught him
under the chin and went tearing up through his mouth into his brain-
base.

'This is madness, madness,' said the middle-aged man. 'I'll have no more
part in it.' Dropping shield and spear, he scrambled over the far wall. Only

one man, inactive with a broken arm, was looking when he shed his helmet too.

The rest fought on, till a Macedonian officer came up, calling that if they surrendered the King would spare their lives. At this they laid down their arms. While they were being marched off, between the dying and dead strewed everywhere, to join the herd of captives, one of them said to the rest, 'Who was the little fellow who ran away, the one poor Eubios was quoting Demosthenes to?'

The man with the broken arm, who had been a good while silent, answered, 'That was Demosthenes.'

The prisoners were under guard, the wounded were being carted off on shields, beginning with the victors. This would take many hours, many would be there at nightfall. The defeated lay at the mercy, for good or ill, of those who found them; many, unfound, would be with the dead tomorrow. Among the dead too there was precedence. The conquered would lie till their cities sued for them; their bodies, asked and granted, were formal acknowledgement that the victors possessed the field.

Philip with his staff rode down the long wreck-strewn shore of battle from south to north. The moans of the dying sounded in fitful gusts, like wind in the high woods of Macedon. Father and son said little; sometimes a landmark of the fight would prompt a question; Philip was trying to make real to himself the event with all its meaning. Alexander had been with Herakles; it took time to come down from that possession. He did his best to attend to his father, who had embraced him when they met, and said everything that was proper.

At length they reached the river. Here by its shore, there was no straggle among the dead of men caught flying. They lay compactly, facing all ways outward, except where the river for a time had guarded their backs. Philip looked at the cable-trimmed shields. He said to Alexander, 'You went in here?'

'Yes. Between them and the Achaians. The Achaians stood well; but these died harder.'

'Pausanias,' called Philip. 'Have them counted.'

Alexander said, 'You will find there is no need.'

The count took time. Many were buried under Macedonians they had killed, and had to be disentangled. There were three hundred. All the Band was there.

'I called on them to yield,' Alexander said. 'They called back that they didn't know the word; they supposed it was Macedonian.'

Philip nodded, and sank back into his thoughts. One of the bodyguard who had done the counting, a man fond of his own wit, turned one of the bodies over on another and made an obscene joke.

'Let them alone,' said Philip loudly. The uncertain titters died. 'Perish the man who said they did or bore anything base.'

He wheeled round his horse, followed by Alexander. Unseen by either, Pausanias turned and spat on the nearest body.

'Well,' Philip said, 'the day's work done. I think we have earned a drink.'

It was a fine night. The flaps of the royal tent were opened; tables and benches overflowed outside. All the chief officers were there, old guest-friends, tribal chiefs, and various allied envoys who had been following the campaign.

The wine was tempered at first, because people were dry; when thirst was slaked, it went round neat. Everyone who felt happy, or thought it useful, started a new round of toasts, and pledged the King.

To the rhythm of old Macedonian drinking-songs, the guests began clapping, slapping their thighs, or banging the tables. Their heads were crowned with wreaths from the broken vineyards. After the third chorus, Philip rose to his feet, and proclaimed a komos.

An unsteady line was formed. Anyone in reach of a torch snatched it up and waved it. Those who were giddy grasped the next man's shoulder. Swaying and limping, Philip lurched along at the head of the line, arm in arm with Parmenion. His face glistened red in the shaking torchlight, the lid of his dead eye drooped, he bawled out the song like battle-orders. The truth of the wine had lit for him the vastness of his deed; the long plans ended, the vista of power ahead, the downfall of his enemy. Freed from careful southern graces as from a hampering cloak, one in soul with his highland forbears and nomad ancestors, he was a chieftain of Macedon, feasting his clansmen after the greatest of all border raids.

The lilt of the song inspired him. 'Hark!' he roared. 'Listen to this:

> *Demosthenes decrees!*
> *Demosthenes decrees!*
> *Demosthenes of Paionia,*
> *Son of Demosthenes.*
> *Euoi Bakchos! Euoi Bakchos!*
> *Demosthenes decrees!'*

It spread down the line like fire in tinder. It was easy to learn, and even easier to sing. Stamping and shouting, the komos wavered out through the moonlit night over the olive fields by the river. A little way down-stream, where they would not foul the water for the victors, were the prisoners' pens. Roused by the noise from exhausted sleep or lonely brooding, the drawn grimy men got to their feet and stared silently, or looked at one another. The torches shone on still rows of eyes.

Near the tail of the komos, among the young, Hephaistion slipped from his neighbours' convivial arms, and walked along through the olives' shadows, looking out and waiting. He kept along by the komos till he saw Alexander leave it; he too looked about, knowing Hephaistion would be there.

They stood together under an old tree with a gnarled intricate stem, thick as a horse's body. Hephaistion touched it. 'Someone told me they live a thousand years.'

'This one,' Alexander said, 'will have something to remember.' He felt at his brow, dragged off the vine-wreath and stamped it under his heel. He was cold sober. Hephaistion had been drunk when the komos started, but that had soon cleared his head.

They walked on together. The lights and noise still meandered before the prisoners' pens. Alexander walked steadily down river. They picked their way over broken spears and sarissas and javelins, round dead horses and dead men. At length Alexander stopped by the river bank, where Hephaistion had known he would.

No one had stripped the bodies yet. The bright shields, the victor's trophies, glimmered softly under the moon. The smell of blood was stronger here; bleeding men had fought on longer. The river chuckled gently among the stones.

One body lay by itself, face down, feet towards the river; a young man, with dark crisply-curling hair. His dead hand still grasped his helmet, which stood by him upside down, with water in it. It was unspilled, because he had been crawling when death overtook him. A blood-spoor, along which he had been returning, led from him to the heap of dead. Alexander picked up the helmet, carrying the water carefully, and followed the trail to its end. This man too was young; he had bled a wide pool, the great vein of his thigh being severed. His open mouth showed the dry tongue. Alexander bent, with the water ready, and touched him, then laid the helmet aside.

'The other had stiffened, but this one is hardly cold. He had a long wait.'

'He would know why,' Hephaistion said.

A little way on, two bodies lay across each other, both facing upward to where the enemy had been. The elder was a strong-looking man with a fair clipped beard; the younger, on whom he had fallen back in death, was bare-headed. On one side he was bare-skulled; a downward slash of a cavalry sabre had flayed off the face to show a bony grin. From the other side, one could see that beauty had been there.

Alexander knelt, and as one might straighten a garment, replaced the flap of flesh. It adhered, sticky with blood. He looked round at Hephaistion and said, 'I did this. I remember it. He was trying to spear Oxhead through the neck. I did it.'

'He shouldn't have lost his helmet. I suppose the chin-strap was weak.'

'I don't remember the other.'

He had been speared through the body, and the spear wrenched back in the urgency of battle, leaving a great torn hole. His face was set in a grimace of agony; he had died wide awake.

'I remember him,' said Hephaistion. 'He came at you after you struck the first one down. You had your hands full already. So I took him on.'

There was a silence. Small frogs chirrupped in the river shallows. A night bird sang liquidly. Behind them sounded the blurred chant of the komos.

'It's war,' said Hephaistion. 'They know they'd have done the same to us.'

'Oh yes. Yes, it is with the gods.'

He knelt down by the two bodies, and tried to compose the limbs; but they were set hard as wood, the eyes, when he had closed the lids, opened again to stare. Finally he dragged the man's corpse over, till it lay by the youth's with one stiff arm across it. Taking off his shoulder-cloak he spread it so that both faces were covered.

'Alexander. I think you should go back to the komos. The King will be missing you.'

'Kleitos can sing much louder.' He looked round at the still shapes, the dried blood blackened by moonlight, the palely shining bronze. 'It is better here among friends.'

'It's only right you should be seen. It's a victory komos. You were first through the line. He waited for that.'

'Everyone knows what I did. There's only one honour I want tonight; to have it said I wasn't *there*.' He pointed at the wobbling torchlight.

'Come, then,' said Hephaistion. They went down to the water and washed the blood from their hands. Hephaistion loosened his shoulder-cloak and wrapped it around both of them. They walked on by the river into the hanging shadow of the willows fed by the stream.

Philip finished the evening sober. As he danced before the captives, a certain Demades, an Athenian eupatrid, had said to him with quiet dignity, 'When fortune has cast you for Agamemnon, King, aren't you ashamed to play Thersites?'

Philip was not too drunk to feel, through this harshness, a rebuke from Greek to Greek. He stopped the komos, had Demades bathed and freshly clothed, gave him supper in his tent, and, the next day, sent him back to

Athens as an envoy. Even in drink, Philip's eye had been good; the man was one of Phokion's party, who had worked for peace but obeyed the call to war. By him, the King's terms were conveyed to Athens. They were proclaimed to an Assembly stunned silent with incredulous relief.

Athens was to acknowledge the hegemony of Macedon; so far the condition was Sparta's of sixty years before. But the Spartans had cut the throats of all their captives at Goat's River, three thousand men; they had pulled down the long Walls to the sound of flutes, and set up a tyranny. Philip would release his prisoners without ransom; he would not march into Attica; he left their form of government to their own choice.

They accepted; and were granted in due form the bones of their dead. They had been burned on a common pyre, since they could not last out the days of peace-making. The pyre was broad; one party of troops stoked it all day with timber, another fed it with corpses; it smoked up from sunrise to sunset, and both details finished worn out. There were more than a thousand men to burn. The ashes and calcined bones were boxed in oaken chests, awaiting a state cortège.

Thebes, stripped and helpless, had surrendered without condition. Athens had been an open enemy; but Thebes, a faithless ally. Philip garrisoned her citadel, killed or dispossessed her leading anti-Macedonians, and freed the Boeotians from her rule. There being no parleys, her dead were quickly gathered. The Band were given the heroes' right of a common tomb, and remained together; above them the Lion of Chaironeia sat down to its long watch.

When his envoys returned from Athens, Philip let the Athenian prisoners know they were free to go, and went off to his mid-day meal. He was eating in his tent when a senior officer asked leave to enter. He was in charge of dispatching the convoy. 'Yes?' said Philip. 'What's wrong?'

'Sir, they're asking for their baggage.'

Philip put down his soup-soaked bannock. 'Asking for *what?*'

'Their stuff from their camp, bedding-rolls and so on.'

Macedonian mouths and eyes fell open. Philip gave a bark of laughter. He grasped his chair-arms, and jutted his black beard. 'Do they think,' he roared, 'that we beat them at a game of knucklebones? Tell them to get out.'

As the grumbling exodus was heard, Alexander said, 'Why not have marched on? We need not have damaged the city; they'd have left it when you came in sight.'

Philip shook his head. 'One can't be sure. And the Acropolis has never fallen, so long as it was manned.'

'Never?' said Alexander. A dreaming aspiration shone in his eyes.

'And when it did fall, it was to Xerxes. No, no.'

'No. That's true.' Neither had spoken of the komos, or of Alexander's leaving it; each had welcomed the other's forbearance. 'But I wonder you didn't at least make them hand over Demosthenes.'

Philip swept his bread around his soup-bowl. 'Instead of the man, there would be his hero-statue. The man will be truer to life ... Well, you can see Athens for yourself very shortly. I am sending you as my envoy, to return their dead.'

Alexander looked round slowly; he had supposed for a moment he was the object of some obscure joke. He had never thought it possible that, having spared Athens both invasion and occupation, his father would not himself ride in as a magnanimous victor, to receive her thanks. Was it shame for the komos? Policy? Could it be even hope?

'To send you,' said Philip, 'is a civility. For me to go would be thought hubristic. They have the status of allies now. A more fitting time may come.'

Yes, it was still the dream. He wanted the gates opened from within. When he had won the war in Asia and freed the cities, it was in Athens, not as conqueror but honoured guest, that he would hold the feast of victory. And he had never even seen it.

'Very well, Father, I'll go.' A moment later, he remembered to express thanks.

He rode between the towers of the Dipylon Gate, and into the Kerameikos. On either side were the tombs of the great and noble; old painted grave-steles faded with weather, new ones whose withered grave-wreaths were tasselled with the mourners' hair. Marble knights rode heroically nude, ladies at tiring-tables remembered beauty; a soldier gazed out at the sea that kept his bones. They were quiet people. Among them, the noisy crowds of the living milled to stare.

A pavilion had been built, to house the ossuaries till the tomb was ready; they were lifted in from the train of biers. As he rode on between obsequious faces, a shrill keening swelled up behind him; the women had surged upon the catafalque, to wail the fallen. Oxhead started under him; from behind a grave, someone had hurled a clod. Horse and rider had known worse, and neither deigned to look round. If you were at the fight, my friend, this does not become you; still less if you were not. But if you are a woman, I understand it.

Ahead towered the steep north-west cliffs of the Acropolis. He ran his eye over them, wondering about the other sides. Someone was inviting him to a civic function; he bowed acceptance. By the road, a marble hoplite in antique armour leaned on his spear; Hermes, guide of the dead, bent to offer a child his hand; a wife and husband bade farewell; two friends clasped hands on an altar, a cup beside them. Everywhere Love faced Necessity in silence. No rhetoric here. Whoever had come after, these people had built this city.

He was led through the Agora to hear speeches in the Council Hall. Sometimes far back in the crowd he heard a shouted curse; but the war party, its prophecies made void, mostly kept away. Demosthenes might have vanished into air. Old Macedonian guest-friends and supporters were thrust forward; he did his best with these awkward meetings. Here came Aischines, carrying it off well, but defensive under it. Philip had showed more mercy than even the peace party had dared predict; they were smeared with the odium of men who have been too right. The bereaved, the ruined, watched them Argus-eyed for a gleam of triumph and were sure to find it. Philip's hirelings came too, some cautious, some fawning; these found Philip's son civil, but opaque.

He ate at the house of Demades, with a few guests of honour; the occasion was not one for feasting. But it was very Attic: well-worn spare elegance, couches and tables whose ornament was perfect shaping and silky wood; wine-cups of old silver thin with polishing; quiet expert service, talk in which no one interrupted or raised his voice. In Macedon, Alexander's mere lack of greed put his table manners above the common run; but here he took care to observe the others first.

Next day on the Acropolis he made dedications to the City's gods, in earnest of the peace. Here were the fabled glories, towering Athene of the Vanguard whose spear-tip guided ships – where were you, Lady, did your father forbid you the battle, as he did at Troy? This time were you obedient? Here in her temple stood Pheidias' ivory Maiden in her robe of folded gold; here were the trophies and dedications of a hundred years. (Three generations; only three!)

He had been reared in the Palace of Archelaos; fine building was nothing new to him; he talked of history, and was shown Athene's olive, which sprouted green overnight when the Persians had burned it. They had carried off, too, the old statues of the Liberators, Harmodios and Aristogeiton, to adorn Persepolis. 'If we can get them back,' he said, 'we will let you have them. Those were brave men and faithful friends.' No one answered; Macedonian boastfulness was a byword. From the parapet he looked for the place where the Persians had climbed up, and found it without help; it had seemed impolite to ask.

The Peace party had got a motion passed that, to recognize Philip's clemency, his statue and his son's should be set up in the Parthenon. As he sat for the sculptor's sketch, he thought of his father's image standing there, and wondered how soon the man would follow it.

Was there anything else, they asked, any sight he would like to visit before he left? 'Yes; the Academy. Aristotle my tutor studied there. He lives now in Stagira; my father rebuilt the town and brought the people back. But I should like to see where Plato taught.'

Along the road there, all the great soldiers of Athens' past were buried. He saw the battle-trophies, and his questions delayed the ride. Here, too, men who had died together in famous actions lay in fraternal tombs. A new site was being cleared; he did not ask for whom.

The road petered out into a grove of ancient olives, whose long grass and field-flowers were dried with autumn. Near the altar of Eros was another, inscribed EROS AVENGED. He asked the story. An immigrant, they said, had loved a beautiful Athenian youth, and vowed there was nothing he would not do for him. He had said, 'Then go jump off the Rock.' When he found he had been obeyed, he made the same leap himself. 'He did right,' said Alexander. 'What does it matter where a man comes from? It's what he is in himself.' They changed the subject, exchanging looks; it was natural the son of the Macedonian upstart should have such thoughts.

Speusippos, who had inherited the school from Plato, had died the year before. In the cool, plain white house that had been Plato's, the new head, Xenokrates, received him, a tall big-boned man whose gravity, it was said, cleared a path before him even through the Agora at market-time. Alexander, entertained with the courtesy of eminent teacher to promising student, felt the man to be solid and took to him on sight. They talked a little about Aristotle's methods. 'A man must follow his truth,' Xenokrates said, 'wherever it leads him. It will lead Aristotle, I think, away from Plato, who was a man for making How serve Why. Me it keeps at Plato's feet.'

'Have you a likeness of him?'

Xenokrates led him out past a dolphin fountain to Plato's myrtle-shaded tomb; the statue stood near it. He sat scroll in hand, his classic oval head stooped forward from heavy shoulders. To the end of his days he had kept the athlete's short-cut hair of his youth. His beard was cleanly trimmed; his brow was furrowed across and down; from under its weight looked the haunted unwavering eyes of a survivor who has fled from nothing. 'Yet still he believed in good. I have some books of his.'

'As to the good,' said Xenokrates, 'he himself was his own evidence. Without that, a man will find no other. I knew him well. I am glad you read him. But his books, he always said, contained the teaching of his master, Sokrates; there would never be a book of Plato, for what he had to teach could only be learned as fire is kindled, by the touch of the flame itself.'

Alexander gazed eagerly at the brooding face, as if at a fort on some impregnable rock. But the crag was gone, overthrown by the floods of time, never to be assailed again. 'He had a secret doctrine?'

'An open secret. You, who are a soldier, can only teach your wisdom to men whose bodies have been prepared for hardship, and their minds to resist fear; isn't that so? Then the spark can kindle the spark. So with him.'

With regret and surmise, Xenokrates gazed at the youth who looked, with surmise and regret, at the marble face. He rode back past the dead heroes to the City.

He was about to change for supper when a man was announced and left alone with him; a well-dressed, well-spoken person, who claimed to have met him at the Council Hall. Everyone, he learned, had praised the modesty and restraint he had shown, so proper to his mission. Many regretted he should have denied himself, from respect for public mourning, the pleasures of a city so well able to provide them. It would be disgraceful were he not offered the chance to taste them in harmless privacy. 'Now I have a boy ...' He described the graces of a Ganymede.

Alexander heard him out without interruption. 'What do you mean,' he then said, 'that you have a boy? Is he your son?'

'Sir! Ah, you will have your joke.'

'Your own friend, perhaps?'

'Nothing of the kind, I assure you, entirely at your disposal. Only see him for yourself. I paid two hundred staters for him.'

Alexander stood up. 'I don't know,' he said, 'what I have done to deserve you, or your merchandise either. Get out of my sight.'

He did so, returning with consternation to the peace party, which had wished the young man to take away grateful memories. A curse on false reports! Too late now to offer a woman.

He rode north next day.

Soon after, the dead of Chaironeia were brought to their common tomb in the Street of Heroes. The people debated who should speak their funeral praises. Aischines was proposed, and Demades. But the one had been too right, the other too successful; to the sore hearts in Assembly, they looked sleek and smug. All eyes returned to the ravaged face of Demosthenes. Perfect defeat, enormous shame had burned out, for the time, all spite from him; the new lines on his tight-drawn skin were of a pain greater than hate. Here was one they could all trust not to rejoice when they were mourning. They chose him to speak the epitaph.

All the Greek states but Sparta sent envoys to the Council at Corinth. They acknowledged Philip supreme war-leader of Hellas against the Persians, for defence. At this first meeting he asked no more. All the rest would follow.

He marched to the frontier of sullen Sparta, then changed his mind. Let the old dog keep its kennel. It would not come out; but if cornered, it would die hard. He had no wish to be the Xerxes of a new Thermopylai.

Corinth, city of Aphrodite, proved readier to please than Athens.

The King and Prince were splendidly entertained. Alexander found time to climb the long path to Acrocorinth, and survey the great walls which, from below, looked narrow as ribbons round the mount's towering brow. With Hephaistion he gazed, the day being clear, south to Athens and northward to Olympos; appraised the walls; saw where one could build better ones and scale those that were there; and was reminded to admire the monuments. At the very top was the small graceful white temple of Aphrodite. Some of the goddess's famous girls, the guide advised them, would certainly at this time have come up from the city precinct to serve her there. He paused expectantly, but in vain.

Demaratos, a Corinthian aristocrat of the ancient Dorian stock, was an old guest-friend of Philip, and played host to him during the Council. At his great house on the footslopes of Acrocorinth, he gave one night a small intimate party, promising the King a guest who would interest him.

It was Dionysios the Younger, son of Dionysios the Greater, late of Syracuse. Since Timoleon had expelled him from his tyranny, he had earned his bread here by running a school for boys. He was a short-sighted, gangling, mouse-coloured man of about Philip's age; his new calling, and lack of means, had ended his once notorious dissipations, but he had an old drunkard's broken-veined nose. A combed, scholarly beard masked his weak chin. Philip, who had surpassed the achievements of even his formidable father the elder tyrant, treated him with charming tact, and when the wine had been round was rewarded by his confidences.

'I had no experience, when I inherited from my father, none at all. My father was a very suspicious man. You will have heard the stories; they are mostly true. All the gods could have witnessed, I never had a thought of doing him any wrong; but to the day of his death, I was searched to the skin before I was admitted to his presence. I never saw state papers, never attended a war-conference. Now if he had left me, as you did your son, to govern at home while you were on campaign, history might have a different tale to tell.'

Philip nodded gravely, and said he could well believe it.

'I would have been content if he had only left me to enjoy a young man's pleasures in peace. He was a hard man; very able, but hard.'

'Well, many causes go to these reversals.'

'Yes. When my father took power, the people had had a bellyful of democracy; and when it passed to me, they'd had a bellyful of despotism.'

Philip had perceived he was not always as foolish as he seemed. 'But was Plato no help to you? They say you had two visits from the philosopher.'

There was a working in the ineffectual face. 'Don't you think I learned some philosophy from Plato, when you see me bear so great a change of fortune?'

The watery eyes had taken on almost dignity. Philip looked at the well-darned splendour of his one good gown, laid a kindly hand on his, and beckoned up the wine-pourer.

On a gilded bed, whose headpiece was carved with swans, Ptolemy lay with Thais the Athenian, his newest girl.

She had come young to Corinth, and had her own house already. There were wall-paintings of twining lovers; the bed-table held two exquisitely shallow cups, a wine-jar, and a round flask of scented oil. A triple lamp, upheld by gilt nymphs, glowed on their pleasures; she was nineteen, and had no need of mystery. Her black hair was feather-soft, her eyes were dark blue; her rose-red mouth was unpainted, though she had tinted like pink shells her nails and nipples and nostrils. Her creamy skin had been polished and plucked as smooth as alabaster. Ptolemy was enchanted with her. Languidly, for the hour was late, he stroked her over, hardly caring whether reminiscence renewed desire.

'We must live together. This is no life for you. I shan't marry for many years. Don't fear that I won't take care of you.'

'But, darling man, I have all my friends here. Our concerts, play-readings ... I should be quite lost in Macedon.' Everyone said he was Philip's son. One must never sound too eager.

'Ah, but soon it will be Asia. You shall sit by a blue-tiled fountain, with roses round you; I shall come back from battle and fill your lap with gold.' She laughed, and nibbled his ear.

He was a man, she thought, whom one could really put up with every night. When one considered some of the others ... 'Let me think a little longer. Come to supper tomorrow; no, it's today. I'll tell Philetas I'm sick.'

'Little finch. What shall I bring you?'

'Only yourself.' She had seldom known this to fail. 'Macedonians are really men.'

'Ah, well, you would move a statue.'

'I'm glad you've begun to take your beards off. One can see the handsome faces now.' She ran her finger along his chin.

'Alexander set the fashion. He says a beard gives the enemy a handhold.'

'Oh, is that why? ... That beautiful boy. They are all in love with him.'

'All the girls but you?'

She laughed. 'Don't be jealous. I meant all the soldiers. He's one of us, you know, at heart.'

'No. No, there you're wrong. He's as chaste as Artemis; or nearly.'

'Yes, that one can see; it's not what I meant.' Her feathery brows moved in meditation. She liked her bedfellow, and for the first time bestowed on him her real thoughts. 'He is like the great, the famous ones; like Lais or Rhodope or Theodotis they tell tales of in those old days. They don't live for love, you know; but they live upon it. I can tell you, I have seen, they are the very blood of his body, all those men who he knows would run after him through fire. If ever the day comes when they will follow him no longer, it will be the same with him as with some great hetaira when the lovers leave her door and she puts away her mirror. He will begin to die.'

A sigh replied to her. Softly she fished up the coverlet and drew it over both of them. He was fast asleep, and it would soon be morning. Let him stay. She might as well start getting used to him.

From Corinth, Philip went homeward to prepare for the war in Asia. When he was ready, he would seek the Council's sanction to begin.

Most of the troops had gone on ahead under Attalos, and dispersed to their homes on leave; Attalos also. He owned an old grey ancestral fort on the footslopes of Mount Pydna; Philip received a message from him, begging the King to honour his rough house by breaking the journey there. The King, who had found him both keen and capable, sent an acceptance back.

As they turned off the high road into the hills, and the sea-horizon widened, Alexander grew taciturn and withdrawn. Presently he rode off from Hephaistion's side, overtook Ptolemy, and beckoned him away from the cavalcade among the heath and scrub of the hillside. Ptolemy followed, puzzled; his mind had been on his own concerns. Would she keep her word? She had made him wait for her answer to the very last.

'What can Father be thinking of,' said Alexander, 'not to send Pausanias on to Pella? How *can* he bring him here?'

'Pausanias?' said Ptolemy vaguely. His face changed. 'Well, it's his right to guard the King's person.'

'It's his right to be spared this, if he has a right to anything. Don't you know, it was at Attalos' house it happened?'

'He has a house at Pella.'

'It was here. I've known that since I was twelve. I was in the stables at home, in one of the stalls, they didn't see me; Attalos' grooms were telling ours. Mother told me too, years later; I didn't tell her it was stale fish. It happened here.'

'It's a good while back, now. Six years.'

'Do you think one could forget in sixty?'

'He's at least on duty, he needn't feel himself a guest.'

'He should have been released from duty. Father should have helped him out.'

'Yes,' said Ptolemy slowly. 'Yes, a pity ... You know, I'd not recalled the matter till you spoke of it, and I've had less business to think of than the King.'

Oxhead, feeling some shock through his rider, snorted and shook his glittering head. '*That* I'd not thought of! Even in our family, there's a limit on what one can remind one's father of. Parmenion should do it, they were young men together. But maybe he's forgotten, too.'

'It's only for this one night ... I've been thinking, if all goes well she may have sold her house by now. You must see her. Wait till you hear her sing.'

Alexander rejoined Hephaistion. They rode on in silence till the rock-hewn walls of the fort, a grim relic of the lawless years, came in sight round a bluff. A group of horsemen appeared from the gate, to meet them.

Alexander said, 'If Pausanias is sullen, don't fall out with him.'

'No. I know.'

'Even kings have no right to wrong men and then forget it.'

'I don't fancy,' said Hephaistion, who had been giving it thought, 'that he does forget. You need to bear in mind how many blood-feuds the King has settled, in his reign. Think of Thessaly; the Lynkestids. My father says, when Perdikkas died there wasn't a house or tribe in Macedon without one at least. You know Leonnatos and I should be at feud, his great-grandfather killed mine, I must have told you that. The King often asks our fathers to supper the same night, to prove all's well; they don't mind it now.'

'But that was old family business, not their own.'

'It's the King's way, Pausanias must know it. That removes the affront.'

And when they reached the fort, he did indeed go about his duties as usual. It was his office to keep the door while the King was feasting, not to sit down with the host. His meal would be served him later.

The King's train was hospitably looked after; he himself with his son and a few chief friends were led to the inner rooms. The fort was ruder, and little later, than the castle at Aigai, which was as old as Macedon itself. The Attalids were an ancient clan. Within, the rooms had been well decked out with Persian hangings and inlaid chairs. In supreme compliment to the honoured guests, the ladies came in, to be presented and offer sweets.

Alexander, whose eye had been drawn off by a Persian archer on the tapestry, heard his father say, 'I never knew, Attalos, that you'd another daughter.'

'Nor had I, King, till lately. The gods, who took away my brother, gave her to us. This is Eurydike, poor Bion's child.'

'Poor indeed,' said Philip, 'to watch over such a child and die before her wedding.'

Attalos said easily, 'We don't yet think of that; we're too pleased with our new daughter to let her go.'

At the first sound of his father's voice, Alexander had turned like a house-dog at a stealthy footfall. The girl stood before Philip, with a polished silver sweet-bowl in her right hand. He had taken her left in his, as a kinsman might have done, and now released it, perhaps because he had seen her blush. She had a family look of Attalos, but with his defects all turned to graces: for gaunt cheeks, delicate hollows under fine bones; for straw hair, gold; he was lanky, she was willowy. Philip spoke some praise of her dead father; she made a little reverence, met his eyes and dropped hers; then went on with her sweet-bowl to Alexander. Her sweet bland smile fixed for a moment; she had looked before he was ready.

Next day, their departure was delayed till noon, Attalos having revealed that it was a feast-day for some local river-nymphs, and the women would be singing. They came with their garlands; the girl's voice was light, childish, but true. The clear water of the nymphs' spring was tasted and praised.

When they set out, the heat of the day was well advanced. A few miles on, Pausanias left the column. Another officer, seeing him go down towards a stream, called after him to wait a mile or two more for better water; here it got staled by cattle. He pretended not to hear, filled his cupped hands and drained them thirstily. He had neither eaten nor drunk, all the while he was at the house of Attalos.

Alexander stood with Olympias under Zeuxis' painting of the sack of Troy. Above her, Queen Hekabe rent her garments; behind his head spread like a crimson nimbus the blood of Priam and Astyanax. Winter firelight leaped in the painted flames, and drew hollows in the living faces.

Olympias' eyes were ringed with black, and her face was lined like a woman's ten years older. Alexander's mouth looked dry and set; he too had been sleepless, but showed it less.

'Mother. Why send for me again? All's said and you know it. What was true yesterday is true today. I shall have to go.'

'Expediency! Expediency! He has made a Greek of you. If he kills us for defying him, good, let him kill us. Let us die with our pride.'

'You know he'd not kill us. We should be where our enemies want, that's all. If I go to this wedding, if I give it countenance, everyone can see I rate it with all the rest, the Thracians and Illyrian girls and the other nobodies. Father knows that; can't you see that's why he asked me? He did it to save our faces.'

'What? When you drink to my disgrace?'

'Would I do so? Accept, since it's true, that he won't forego this girl. Very well: she's a Macedonian, the family's as old as ours; of course they stand out for marriage. That's why they threw her in his way, I knew it the first moment. Attalos has won this action. If we play into his hands, he'll win the war.'

'They will only think you are taking your father's part against me, to keep his favour.'

'They know me better ' This thought had tormented him half the night. 'Feasting with his whore's kindred.'

'A virgin of fifteen. She's only the bait, like the kid in a wolf-trap. Oh, she'll do her part, she's one of them; but in a year or two he'll have seen a younger one. It's Attalos who will use the time. Keep your mind on nim.'

'That we should come to this!' Though she spoke with bitter reproach, he took it as assent, having had enough.

In his room he found Hephaistion waiting. Here, too, most things had been said. For some time they sat side by side on the bed in silence. At length Hephaistion said, 'You will know your friends.'

'I know them now.'

The King's own friends should advise him. Can't Parmenion do it?'

'He tried, Philotas tells me ... I know what Parmenion thinks. What I can't tell Mother is that I understand it.'

Hephaistion, after a long wait, said, 'Yes?'

'Since Father was sixteen, he's been in love with one who'll never have him. He's sent her flowers, she's thrown them out on the midden; he's sung at her window, she's emptied the chamberpot on his head; he's offered for her hand, she's flaunted with his rivals. At last he couldn't stand more, and struck her; but he couldn't bear to see her lie at his feet, so he picked her up again. Then, though he'd mastered her, he was ashamed to go to her door; he sent me instead. Well, I went; and when all's done she's an old painted whore. And I pity him. I never thought I'd see the day, but it's true, I pity him. He deserves better. This girl here, I wish she were a dancer or a flute player, or a boy for that matter; then we'd be out of trouble. But since she's what he wants ...'

'And *that's* why you're going?'

'Oh, I can find better reasons. But that's why.'

*

The wedding feast was held at Attalos' town house not far from Pella. He had just refurbished it, and not by halves; the columns were twined with gilded garlands, and statues of inlaid bronze had been shipped in from Samos. Nothing had been left out which could show that this marriage of the King's was unlike all others, except the first. As Alexander entered with his friends, and they looked about them, all their eyes exchanged one thought. This was the mansion for a King's father-in-law, not the uncle of a concubine.

The bride sat throned among the splendours of her dowry and the groom's gifts; Macedon kept up older customs than the south. Gold and silver cups, rolls of fine weaving, trinkets and necklaces spread out on linen coverlets, inlaid tables on which stood caskets of spices and phials of scent, filled the bridal dais. Robed in saffron and crowned with white roses, she sat looking down at her folded hands. The guests called ritual blessings on her; her aunt beside her spoke thanks on her behalf.

In due time the women bore her off to the house prepared for her. The procession in the wedding car had been left out, as inappropriate. Alexander, viewing the kindred, felt sure that they had hankered for it. He had thought his anger was spent, till he saw their faces watching him.

The meat from the marriage sacrifice, richly dressed, was eaten, and the kickshaws after. Though the chimney had a hood, the hot room grew smoky. He noticed he was being left alone a good deal with his own friends. He was glad to have Hephaistion next to him; but it should have been a kinsman of the bride's. Even the younger Attalids were clustered about the King.

Alexander murmured to Hephaistion, 'Hurry up, Dionysos, we need you badly.'

In fact, however, when the wine came in he drank lightly, as usual, being as moderate in this as in eating. Macedon was a land of good springs with safe pure water. One need never come to table thirsty, as men did in the hot lands of Asia with their deadly streams.

But, with no hosts in hearing, he and Hephaistion allowed themselves the kind of joke guests save for the journey home. The young men of his following, jealous that he had been slighted, read their smiles, and followed their lead with less discretion. The banquet-hall became tinged with a scent of faction.

Alexander, growing uneasy at it, murmured to Hephaistion, 'We had better make ourselves pleasant,' and turned towards the company. When the bridegroom left the feast, they could slip away. He looked at his father; and saw he was already drunk.

His face was glazed and shining, he was bawling out old army songs with Attalos and Parmenion. Grease from the roast was streaked in his beard. He flung back to the company the immemorial jokes of defloration and prowess, showered on the bridegroom as ritually as the earlier raisins and grain. He had won his girl, he was among old friends, goodfellowship prevailed, wine made his glad heart gladder. Alexander, scrupulously bathed, almost empty, and nearly sober, though not so sober as if he had eaten more, looked on in a silence which began to be felt around him.

Hephaistion, controlling his own anger, talked to neighbours to draw off notice. No decent master, he thought, would have inflicted this ordeal on a slave. He was angry, too, with himself. How had he not foreseen all this, why had he said nothing to keep Alexander away? He had held his peace, because he had a kindness for Philip, because it had seemed politic, and – he faced it now – in order to spite Olympias. Alexander had made this sacrifice, in one of those flashes of reckless magnanimity for which Hephaistion loved him. He should have been protected; some friend should have stepped in. He had been betrayed.

Through the rising noise he was saying something. '. . . she's one of the clan, but she's had no choice, she's barely out of the nursery . . .'

Hephaistion looked round startled. With all he had on his mind, this was one thing he had never thought of, that Alexander could be angry for the girl.

'It's mostly like this at weddings, you know that; it's custom.'

'She was scared when first she met him. She kept a good face, but I could see.'

'Well, he'll not be rough with her. It's not like him. He's used to women.'

'Imagine it,' murmured Alexander into his wine-cup. He emptied it quickly and held it out. The boy came with the snow-cooled rhyton; soon after, attentive to his duties, he returned to fill it again.

'Save this one for the toasts,' said Hephaistion watchfully.

Parmenion rose on the King's behalf to praise the bride, properly the office of the groom's nearest kinsman. Alexander's ironic smile was noticed by his friends, and returned too openly.

Parmenion had spoken at many weddings, some of them the King's. He was correct, simple, careful and brief. Attalos, a huge ornate gold goblet in his hand, swung down from his supper-couch to make the speech of bestowal. It was clear at once that he was as drunk as Philip, and not carrying it so well.

His praise of the King was rambling and wordy, clumsiness defeating fulsomeness; the climaxes were maudlin and badly timed; the applause, which was rapturous, was a tribute to the King. It grew less carefree as the speech warmed up. Parmenion had wished luck to a man and woman. Attalos was wishing it, in all but the naked words, to a King and Queen.

His supporters cheered, and knocked cups on tables. Alexander's friends talked in under-voices meant to be heard. The uncommitted, taken by surprise, dismayed, were revealed by silence.

Philip, not too drunk to know what it meant, fixed his bloodshot black eye on Attalos, wrestling with his own fuddled slowness, thinking how to stop the man. This was Macedon; he had quieted plenty of after-dinner brawls; but he had never had to deal before with a new father-in-law, self-styled or not. The others had known their places and been grateful. His eye slewed round to his son.

'Don't notice it,' Hephaistion was whispering. 'The man's soused, they all know it, they'll all have forgotten by morning.' Early on in the speech he had made his way from his own supper-couch to stand by Alexander's, who, his eyes fixed on Attalos, felt hard and taut to the touch, like a catapult wound up.

Philip, looking that way, saw under the flushed brow and the gold hair smoothed for the feast, the wide staring grey eyes pass from Attalos' face to his. Olympias' rage; no, but that boiled quickly, this was held in. Nonsense, I'm drunk, he's drunk, we're all drunk, and why not? Why can't the boy take it easy like anyone else at a feast? Let him swallow it, and behave.

Attalos was running on about the good old native blood of Macedon. He had conned his speech well; but lured on by smiling Dionysos, he knew he could now do better. In the person of this fair maiden, the dear homeland took back her King to her breast, with the blessing of the ancestral gods. 'Let us pray to them,' he cried in sudden inspiration, 'for a lawful, true-born heir.'

There was an outbreak of muddled noise; applause, protest, dismay, clumsy efforts to smother danger in jollity. The voices changed, and checked. Attalos, instead of drinking the toast, had clapped his other hand to his head; blood showed between his fingers. Something bright, a silver drinking-cup, was clattering along the mosaic floor. Alexander leaned on his supper-couch, propped upon one hand. He had thrown without getting up. Uproar began, echoing in the high hall. His voice, which had carried through the din of Chaironeia, called out, 'You blackguard, are you calling me a bastard?' The young men, his friends, yelled out indignant applause. Attalos, perceiving what had hit him, made a choking sound, and hurled his heavy goblet at Alexander, who measured its course and did not trouble to move; it fell short half-way. Friends and kinsmen shouted; it began to sound like a battlefield. Philip, furious and knowing now where to vent his anger, roared over the clamour, 'How dare you, boy? How dare you? Behave yourself or go home.'

Alexander hardly raised his voice. Like his cup, it struck where it was aimed.

'You filthy old goat. Will you never have any shame? All Hellas can wind your stink; what will you do in Asia? No wonder the Athenians laugh.'

For a moment, the only answer was a sound of breathing like a labouring horse's. The red of the King's face deepened to purple. His hand fumbled about the couch. He alone here, in the ceremonial dress of the bridegroom, had a sword.

'Son of a whore!' He swung off the couch, upsetting his taper-legged supper table. There was a crash of cups and dessert-plates. He grasped his sword-hilt.

'Alexander, Alexander,' muttered Hephaistion desperately. 'Come away, quick, come.' As if he had not existed, Alexander slid neatly down on the far side of the couch, grasped the wood in both hands, and waited with a cold eager smile.

Panting and limping, drawn sword in hand, Philip stumbled through the mess upon the floor towards his enemy. His foot slipped on a fruit-paring; he came down hard on the lame leg, skidded, and crashed head-long among sweets and sherds.

Hephaistion took a step forward; for a moment, it had been instinct to help him up.

Alexander came round the supper-couch. Hands on belt, head tilted, he looked down at the red stertorous cursing man sprawling in spilled wine and reaching about for his sword. 'Look, men. Look who is getting ready to cross from Europe into Asia. And he falls flat crossing from couch to couch.'

Philip pushed himself up with both hands on to his good knee. He had cut his palm on a broken plate. Attalos and his kinsmen ran, stumbling over each other, to his aid. During the scramble, Alexander signed to his friends. They all followed him out, silently and promptly, as if in some night-action at war.

From his post at the doorway, which through all this he had made no move to leave, Pausanias gazed after Alexander. So might a traveller in a thirsty desert look after the man who gave him a cool delicious drink. No one noticed. Alexander, gathering up supporters, had never given him a thought. From the beginning, he had never been an easy man to talk to.

Oxhead neighed in the courtyard; he had heard his master's war-voice. The young men tossed their festal wreaths upon the midden furred with frost, mounted without waiting for service, and galloped off on the rutted track with its thin-iced puddles towards Pella. In the Palace courtyard, in the glow of the night-flares, Alexander looked them over, reading all their faces.

'I am taking my mother to her brother's house in Epiros. Who will come with me?'

'I for one,' said Ptolemy. 'And *that* for their true-born heirs.'

Harpalos, Nearchos and the others crowded up; from love, from loyalty, from ingrained faith in Alexander's fortune, from fear that the King and Attalos had marked them down; or from shame at being seen by others to hold back.

'No, not you, Philotas; you stay.'

'I'll come,' said Philotas quickly, looking round. 'My father will forgive me, and if not what of it?'

'No, he's a better one than mine, you shan't offend him for me. Listen, the rest of you.' His voice took the habit-formed note of brisk command. 'We must get away now, before I'm locked up and my mother poisoned. Travel light, bring spare horses; all your weapons, and what money you can lay your hands on; one day's food; any good servants fit to bear arms, I'll mount and arm them. All of you meet me here when the horn sounds for the next guard-change.'

They dispersed, all but Hephaistion, who looked at him as someone in a sea without horizon looks at the steersman.

'He'll be sorry for this,' Alexander said. 'He counted on Alexandros of Epiros. He put him on the throne, he's been to a deal of trouble for that alliance. Now he can go whistle for it, till Mother has her rights.'

'And you?' said Hephaistion blankly. 'Where are we going?'

'To Illyria. I can do more there. I understand the Illyrians. You remember Kossos? Father's nothing to him, he rebelled once and he would again. It's me he knows.'

'You mean . . .?' said Hephaistion, wishing there were need to ask.

'They're good fighters. They might do better, if they had a general.'

Done is done, thought Hephaistion; and what did I do to save him? 'Very well, if you think that best.'

'The others need not come on beyond Epiros, unless they choose. Today's work today. We'll see how the Supreme Commander of all the Greeks likes to start for Asia with Epiros doubtful and Illyria arming for war.'

'I'll pack for you. I know what to put in.'

'It's lucky Mother can ride, we've no time for litters.'

He found her with her lamp still burning, sitting in her high chair staring before her. She looked at him with reproach, knowing only that he came from the house of Attalos. The room smelled of bruised herbs and burned blood.

'You were right,' he said, 'and more than right. Get your jewels together; I have come to take you home.'

His campaign bag, when he found it in his room, held as Hephaistion had promised all he would need. At the top sat the leather scroll-case of the Iliad.

The high road to the west led by way of Aigai. To avoid it, Alexander led them through the passes he had learned when he was training his men in hill-warfare. The oaks and chestnuts on the foothills were black and bare; the tracks above the gorges were wet and slippery with fallen leaves.

In this back country, people seldom saw a stranger. They said they were pilgrims, going to Dodona to consult the oracle. No one who had glimpsed him on manoeuvre knew him now, in an old travelling hat and sheepskin cloak, unshaven, looking older. Coming down to Kastoria lake with its willows and marshes and beaver dams, they spruced themselves up, knowing they would be recognized; but their story was the same and was not questioned. That the Queen was at odds with the King was ancient history; if she wanted advice from Zeus and Mother Dione, it was her own affair. They had outstripped rumour. Whether pursuit were following; whether they were being left to stray like unwanted dogs; whether Philip was sitting back in his old way to let time work for him, they could not tell.

Olympias had made no such journey since girlhood. But she had spent that in Epiros, where all journeys were overland because of the pirates from Korkyra with whom its coastline swarmed. The first day out, she was white with fatigue and shivering in the evening chill; they camped in a shepherd's bothie left empty when the flocks went down to the winter grazing-lands, not daring to trust a village so near home; but next day she woke fresh, and soon kept up with them like a man, eyes and cheeks glowing. Till they sighted a village she would ride astride.

Hephaistion rode behind among the others, watching the slight, cloaked figures, their heads together, conferring, planning, confiding. His enemy possessed the field. Ptolemy patronized him, meaning no harm, scarcely aware of it, bearing well the prestige of sacrifice. He had left Thais at Pella, after only a few months' bliss. Hephaistion, on the other hand, had done the only thing that was in him; like Oxhead, he was seen as a limb of Alexander. No one noticed him. It seemed to him they would journey on forever, just like this.

They struck south-east, towards the great watershed ranges between Macedon and Epiros, struggling through swollen streams; making for the hard short way, between the heights of Grammos and Pindos. Before they had climbed to the ridge where the red earth of Macedon peters out, it had begun to snow. The tracks were treacherous, the horses laboured; they debated whether to turn back to Kastoria, rather than be benighted in the open. A rider threaded down to them between the beeches, and bade them honour the house of his absent master, who, though detained by duty, had sent word that they be entertained.

'This is Orestid country,' said Alexander. 'Who is your master, then?'

'Don't be foolish, my dear,' Olympias murmured. She turned to the messenger. 'We shall gladly be Pausanias' guests. We know he is our friend.'

In the massive old fort which stuck out on a spur from the woods behind it, they were given hot baths, good food and wine, warm beds. Pausanias it seemed kept a wife here, though all other court officers brought their wives to Pella. She was a tall strapping mountain girl, born to simplicity but burdened with half-knowledge. Her husband, in some distant place before they met, had once been wronged, in a way never made clear to her; his day was yet to come; these were his friends against his enemies, and must be made welcome. But against whom would Olympias be a friend? Why was the Prince here, when he was a general of the Companions? She lapped them in comfort; but alone at bedtime, in the great room Pausanias visited for two or three weeks a year, she heard an owl hoot and a wolf howl, and round her lamp the shadows thickened. Her father had been killed in the north by Bardelys, her grandfather in the west by Perdikkas. When the guests had gone next day, in charge of a good guide as Pausanias had directed, she went down into the rock-cut cellars, counting over the arrow-heads and the stores.

They climbed through a chestnut forest, where even the local bread was of chestnut flour; then up through firs to the head of the pass. The sun gleamed on the fallen snow, and filled the huge horizons; here was the frontier set by earth-shaping gods. Olympias looked back eastward; her lips moved in ancient words she had learned of a witch from Egypt; she whispered them to a stone of the proper shape she had brought along, and cast the stone behind her.

In Epiros the snows were melting; they had to wait three days in a peasant village to cross a flooded river, their horses stabled in a cave. But at last they reached the Molossian lands.

The rolling plateau was famous for hard winters; but their snow-waters made rich pasture. Huge long-horned cattle grazed; the choicest sheep wore leather jackets, to shield their fine wool from thorns; their guard-dogs were as big as they. The towering oaks prized by shipwrights and builders, the sacred wealth of the land, stood bare, weathering themselves for coming centuries. Villages were well-built, with crowds of healthy children.

Olympias had dressed her hair, and put on a gold chain. 'Achilles' forebears came from here. His son Neoptolemoas lived here with Andromache, when he came from Troy. It is through me that their blood comes down to you. We were the first of all the Hellenes. They all took the name from us.'

Alexander nodded; he had been hearing this all his life. This was a rich land; it had had no High King till lately; and the King, for all he was Olympias' brother, owed it all to Philip. He rode in thought.

While their courier rode on to announce them, the young men shaved and combed by a rocky pool. It was icy, but Alexander bathed. They all unpacked their best clothes and put them on.

Soon, showing dark and glittering against the half-melted snow, they descried a train of horsemen. King Alexandros was giving them a kinsman's welcome.

He was a tall auburn man, not much over thirty; his strong beard hid the family mouth, but one could see the family nose; his eyes were deep-set, restless, alert. He kissed his sister in greeting and said proper things. He had long been prepared for this unwelcome moment, and brought as good a grace to it as he could. To her marriage he owed his kingdom; but since then, he could not think of much she had left undone to pull him down. From her raging letter, he could not make out if Philip had yet divorced her; in any case he must take her in, and maintain her injured innocence, to keep the family honour out of the dirt. By herself she was trouble enough. He had hoped against certainty that she would not bring along that firebrand son, reputed to have killed his man at twelve and never sat down a day in quiet since.

With distrust, quickly concealed by civil gestures, the King glanced at the troop of young men with firm-boned Macedonian faces, barbered like southern Greeks. They looked tough, watchful, close-knit; what trouble did they mean to brew here? The kingdom was settled, the tribal lords called him hegemon, followed him to war and paid their taxes; the Illyrians kept their own side of the border; he had dislodged, only this year, two pirate holds, the local peasants had thanked him with hymns. Who would follow him to war against the might of Macedon, who would bless him after? No one. Philip, if he marched, would march right up to Dodona and make a new High King. Moreover, Alexandros had always liked the man. As he rode between his sister and his nephew and felt the crackling air, he hoped his wife at home would be fit to receive the guests; he had left her in tears, she was pregnant, too.

Coming down to Dodona, a twisting pass strung them out, the King ahead. Alexander, riding close to Olympias, murmured, 'Don't tell him what I mean to do. About yourself, what you like. About me, know nothing.'

Startled and angry, she said, 'What has he done that you doubt him?'

'Nothing. I have to think, I need time.'

Dodona sat in a high valley, under a long snow-swept range. A fierce wind crusted them with fine hail like meal. The walled town clasped the hillside; below, the sacred precinct was guarded only by a low fence, and its gods. In the midst of it, dwarfing altars and shrines like toys, a vast oak lifted its bare black labyrinth above the snow. The wind carried up to them a deep booming resonance, rising and falling with the blasts.

The town gates swung open. As they formed up for their entry, Alexander said, 'Uncle, I should like to visit the oracle before I go. Will you ask when the next auspicious day is?'

'By all means, yes.' He spoke with new warmth, adding the proper well-omened formula, 'God and good luck.' The auspicious day could not come too soon. He had been little more than a boy when Olympias married; she had always bullied him, though he was the elder. Now she must learn he was master of his house. This war-weathered, war-scarred youth, with his mad brooding eyes and his troop of well-groomed outlaws, would not help. Let him go his own way to Hades, and leave sensible men in peace.

The townsmen greeted their King with unforced loyalty. He had led them well against their many enemies, and was less greedy than the warring chiefs had been. A crowd gathered; for the first time since leaving Pella, Oxhead heard the familiar cheers, the shouts of 'Alexandros!' His head went up, he fell into his proud parade-gait. Alexander sat straight-backed, looking ahead; Hephaistion glancing sidelong saw him pale as if half his blood had been drained away. He kept his countenance, and answered his kinsman calmly; but when they reached the royal house, he was still white about the mouth. The Queen forgot her own sickness, and called to her servants to hurry the mulled wine; only yesterday, a drover had been found frozen on the pass above.

The snow had ceased, but still lay on the ground, frosted over, and brittle to the foot. A pale hard sun glittered on the drifts and the tufted shrubs; a thin icy wind came searching down from the mountains. In the white landscape, like an old cloth, was a cleared space of winter-browned grass and black dank oak-mast. The sanctuary slaves had shovelled the snow away against the oaken palings; it lay in soiled heaps, speckled with leaves and acorn-husks.

A young man in a sheepskin cloak walked up to the doorless gateway of massive, time-blackened beams.

From the lintel, dangling on ropes of hide, hung a deep bronze bowl. He picked up a staff propped by the post, and struck smartly. Long shudders of sound, like rings in water, throbbed on and on; a deep answering hum came from somewhere beyond. The great tree brooded, its crotches and knots and old birds' nests full of snow. Ancient rude altars, the dedications of centuries, stood in the open round it.

It was the oldest oracle in Greece. Its power came from Egyptian Ammon, the father of all oracles, older than time. Dodona had spoken before Apollo came to Delphi.

The wind, which had been quietly keening in the high branches, swept down in a violent gust. A wild clangour broke out ahead; on a marble column stood a bronze boy holding a scourge, with lashes of bronze chain which, whirled by the wind, struck a bronze cauldron with their weighted ends. It was an acoustic vessel like those sometimes used in the theatres. The din was thunderous. All round the sacred tree, standing on tripods, were hollow bronzes; the sound dwindled along them, like thunder rumbling away after a great clap. Before it had died, another gust lifted the scourge. From a little stone house beyond the tree, peering grey heads poked out.

Alexander's mouth smiled as it did when he charged in battle. He strode on towards the thrumming precinct. A third gust blew; a third time the cycle of noise revolved and faded. The former murmurous quiet returned.

From the thatched stone hut, muttering together, mothy fur cloaks clutched round them, came three old women. They were the Doves, the servants of the oracle. As they shuffled forward over the wet black oak-mast, it could be seen that their ankles were wrapped in woollen rags, but their feet were bare, cracked, and ingrained with grime. They drew power from the touch of earth and must never lose it; it was the law of the sanctuary.

One was a strong old woman, big-boned, who looked to have done a man's farm-work most of her life. The second was short, round and severe, with a pointed nose and out-thrust lower lip. The third was a tiny bent crone, dry and brown as an old acorn-husk. She was reputed to have been born in the year Perikles died.

Shrugged in their furs, they looked about, their eyes returning, it seemed, in surprise to this single pilgrim. The tall one whispered to the round one. The old one trotted forward on shrivelled bird-feet, and fingered him like a curious child. Her eyes had a blue-white film, she was almost blind.

The round one said, in a sharp voice edged with wariness, 'How do you wish to question Zeus and Dione? Do you want the name of the god you should offer to, to win your wish?'

Alexander said, 'I shall tell my question to the god alone. Give me the things to write with.'

The tall one bent towards him with awkward kindness; she moved like a farm animal, and smelled like one. 'Yes, yes, only the god will see. But the lots are in two jars; one for the gods to be propitiated; the other for Yes or No. Which shall we set out?'

'Yes or no.'

The old one still clutched a fold of his cloak in her tiny fist, with the assurance of a child whose beauty makes it welcome. Suddenly she piped up, from down near his waist, 'Take care with your wish. Take care.'

He bent down over her, and asked softly, 'Why, Mother?'

'Why? Because the god will grant it.'

He put his hand on her head, a little shell of bone in a woollen clout, and, caressing it, looked over her at the black depths of the oak. The other two looked at one another. Neither spoke.

He said, 'I am ready.'

They went off into a low-roofed sanctuary house beside their dwelling, the old one trotting behind squeaking muddled orders, like any great-grandmother who has got into a kitchen to annoy the women at work. They could all be heard bustling and grumbling, as at some inn caught unready by a guest who cannot be turned away.

The huge ancient branches stretched above him, splintering the pale sun. The central trunk was folded and ribbed with age; into its fissures small votives had been thrust by worshippers, in times so remote that the bark had almost engulfed them. A part was crumbled with rot, and worm-holed. Summer would reveal what bare winter hid, that some of the main limbs were dead. Its first root had thrust from the acorn while Homer was still alive; it was near its time.

From around its massive centre, where the boughs forked, came a sleepy cooing and moaning; in hollows, and little cotes nailed here and there, the sacred doves were huddled, couple by couple, fluffed-up and pressed together against the cold. As he came near, one gave from its hidden darkness a loud 'Roo-co-coo!'

The women came out, the tall one with a low wooden table, the round one with an ancient jar, painted black on red. They set the jar on the table under the tree. The old one put into his hands a strip of soft lead, and a bronze stylos.

He laid the strip on an old stone altar, and wrote firmly: the deep letters shone silvery in the dull lead. GOD AND GOOD LUCK. ALEXANDER ASKS ZEUS OF THE SANCTUARY, AND DIONE, WILL THE THING I HAVE IN MY MIND COME TO PASS? Having folded the strip in three, so that the words were hidden, he dropped it in the jar. He had learned what to do, before he came.

The tall woman stood by the table, and lifted her arms. There was a priestess painted on the jar, standing just so. The invocation was in the jargon of some foreign tongue, corrupted long since by time and ignorance; the vowels were drawn out, to mimic a dove. Presently one replied; there was a low murmuring, all round the heart of the tree.

Alexander stood watching, his mind upon his wish. The tall priestess put her hand in the jar, and was beginning to grope about, when the old one came up and twitched her cloak, scolding as shrilly as a monkey. 'It was promised me,' she chattered. 'Promised me.' The other stood back, her eyes startled, stealing a glance at him; the round one clucked, but did nothing. The old woman pushed back her robe from her stick-thin arm, like a housewife pot-scouring, and thrust it inside. There was a rattling of the small oak tablets on which the lots were carved.

Through these delays, Alexander stood waiting, his eyes fixed on the jar. The black-painted priestess stood in her stiff archaic posture, showing her lifted palms. At her feet, twined round the leg of her painted table was a painted snake.

It was drawn with skill and vigour, its head thrust upward. The table-leg was short, like a low bed's, it would climb up easily. It was a house-snake, which knew a secret. While the old woman muttered and scratched about, he frowned at it, trying to trace back, into the darkness from which it had crept forth, a sense of some ancient anger, some enormous wound, some mortal insult unavenged. Images formed. He faced again a giant enemy. The steam of his breath dispersed in the cold air; through a long pause no new breath followed, then a sound escaped him, bitten off into silence. His fingers and teeth had clenched themselves. His memories opened and bled.

The old woman straightened up. In her grimy claw she held the folded lead, and two wooden lots. The others hurried to her; the law was to bring out one lot, that lying nearest to the lead; they hissed at her, like nurses at a child who does an unseemly thing in ignorance. She lifted her head – her backbone was past straightening – and in a younger, commanding voice said, 'Stand back! I know what I have to do.' For a moment it could be seen that she had once been beautiful.

Leaving the lead on the table, she came towards him, both hands held out, a lot in each. Opening the right, she said, 'For the wish in your mind.' She opened the left, saying, 'And for the wish in your heart.'

Each of the little black wood-blocks was carved with 'Yes'.

8

King Philip's newest wife had had her firstborn. It was a girl.

The downcast midwife brought it from the lying-in room. He took in his hands, with ritual signs of approval, the little red crumpled thing, brought naked to prove it free from blemish. Attalos, who had been haunting the house since the birth-waters broke, craned over, his face red and crumpled too; he must have hoped against hope till he saw the sex for himself. His pale blue eyes followed it with hatred as it was carried back; he would as soon have thrown it in the lake like an unwanted bitch-pup, Philip thought. Often it made him feel foolish that he seemed to sire five girls for every boy; but this time he had heard the news with deep relief.

Eurydike was all he liked in a girl, sensual without looseness, eager to please without fuss, never making scenes. Gladly, any day, he would have put her in Olympias' place. He had half-thought, even, of having the witch put out of the way for good; it would solve all problems, she had blood-guilt enough on her hands to make it a rough justice, and there were people to be hired as skilled in such matters as she. But however well it was managed, the boy would know. Nothing would hide it from him; he would pluck the truth from air. And then?

And now? Well, this girl-child gave breathing-space. Attalos had told him a dozen times that their family ran to boys. Now let him keep quiet awhile. Philip put off decision, as he had been doing these ten months.

His plans for the war in Asia went forward smoothly. Weapons were made and stored, levies came in, horses were broke for cavalry; gold and silver flowed out like water, to contractors, to paymasters, to agents and client rulers. The troops drilled and manoeuvred, ready and disciplined, swapping legends about the fabled wealth of Asia and the vast ransoms of captive satraps. But a gloss had gone, a resonance, a crackle and spark, a smile on the face of danger.

There were also rubs more palpable. A savage brawl, which would beget half a dozen blood-feuds, had broken out in a Pella wine-shop, between cavalry of Attalos' tribal levy, and those of a corps lately re-named Nikanor's Horse, though no one who valued his life would call it this in hearing of its men. Philip sent for the chief offenders; they glared at each other and were evasive till the youngest, heir of an ancient house that had helped a dozen kings in or out and well remembered it, lifted his shaven chin and said defiantly, 'Well, sir, they were slandering your son.'

Philip told them to look after their own households, and leave his to him. Attalos' men, who had hoped to hear him say, 'I have no son yet,' went grieved away. Soon after, he sent out yet another spy, to learn what was going on in Illyria.

To Epiros he sent none; he knew where he was, there. He had had a letter he perfectly understood; the protest of a man of honour, carried just as far as honour required. One could almost see the drawn line. He replied with equal nicety. The Queen had left him from self-will and sullen temper, having suffered no legal injuries. (He was on good ground here; not every Epirote royal house had been monogamous.) She had turned his son against him; the young man's present exile was her fault alone. The letter contained no mortal insults. It would be understood in its turn. But what was happening in Illyria?

Some few of the young men had ridden home from Epiros, bringing a letter.

Alexander to Philip King of the Macedonians, greeting. I send back to you and to their fathers these men, my friends. They are guilty of no wrong. In kindness they escorted the Queen and me into Epiros; this done, we required no more of them. When the Queen, my mother, is restored to her rights and dignity, we will return. Till then I shall do as I think good, asking no man's leave.

Greet for me the soldiers I led at Chaironeia, and those who served under me in Thrace. And do not forget the man who was saved by my shield, when the Argives mutinied before Perinthos. You know his name. Farewell.

In his private reading-cell, Philip crumpled the letter and threw it down; then, bending stiffly with his lame leg, picked it up, flattened out the creases, and locked it away.

One after another, the spies from the west brought in uneasy news, never facts one could grip on. The names of the small close band were always there. Ptolemy: ah, if I could have bride-bedded his mother it would have been a different tale. Nearchos: a good sea-officer, due for promotion if he'd had sense. Harpalos: I never trusted that limping fox, but the boy would have him. Erigyios . . . Laomedon . . . Hephaistion, well, as soon part a man from his shadow. Philip brooded a moment, in the sad resenting envy of the man who believes himself always to have sought the perfect love, not owning that he has grudged the price.

The names never varied; the news always did. They were at Kossos' fort; at the castle of Kleitos, who was as near a High King as Illyria would stomach; they were on the Lynkestid border. They were on the coast, said to be asking after ships for Korkyra, for Italy, for Sicily, even for Egypt. They had been sighted in the ranges beside Epiros. They were rumoured to be buying arms, to be hiring spearmen, to be training an army in some forest lair. Whenever Philip needed to dispose his troops for the war in Asia, one of these alarms would come in, and he must spare a regiment for the border. Without doubt, the boy was in touch with friends in

Macedon. On paper, the King's war plans remained unaltered; but his generals could feel him hanging fire, awaiting the next report.

In a castle perched on a craggy headland by a wooded Illyrian bay, Alexander stared up at the night-shrouded, smoke-black rafters. He had spent the day hunting, like the day before. His bed was of rushes, full of fleas, in the guest-corner of the hall; here, among dogs crunching the bones from old suppers, the bachelors of the household slept. His head ached. A draught of clean air blew from the doorway; the moonlit sky looked bright there. He got up and threw his blanket round him. It was soiled and torn; his good one had been stolen some months before, about the time of his birthday. In a nomad camp near the border, he had turned nineteen.

He steered past sleeping bodies, stumbling on one, which grunted curses. Outside on the bare crag ran a narrow rampart. The cliff plunged straight to the sea; far down, moon-gleaming foam crawled round the boulders. He knew the footsteps behind and did not turn. Hephaistion leaned on the wall beside him.

'What is it? Couldn't you sleep?'

'I woke,' Alexander said.

'Have you got the gripes again?'

'It stinks in there.'

'Why do you drink that dog-piss? I'd sooner go to bed sober.'

Alexander gave him a look like a silent growl. His arm propped on the wall was scored by the claws of a dying leopard. All day he had been in movement; now he was still, looking down the giddy drop to the sea.

At last he said, 'We can't keep it up much longer.'

Hephaistion frowned at the night. He was glad, however, to be told; it was being asked he had most dreaded. 'No,' he said. 'I doubt we can.'

Alexander picked some stone chips from the wall-top, and pitched them down at the shimmering sea. No ripple showed, no sound returned from the depth, even when they struck rock. Hephaistion did nothing. He offered his presence, as his omens had directed him.

'Even a fox,' said Alexander presently, 'runs through all its tricks in time. And the second time round, the nets are waiting.'

'You've often had luck from the gods.'

'Time's running out,' Alexander said. 'It's a feel one gets in war. You remember Polydoros with his dozen men, trying to hold that fort in the Chersonese. All those helmets propped on the walls; moved, too, now and again. I was fooled into sending for reinforcements, two days, remember? Then a catapult knocked off a helmet and showed the stake. It was bound to happen; his time ran out. Mine will run out when some Illyrian chief crosses the border on his own account, for cattle, or a feud, and Philip hears I wasn't leading. I'll never fool him after that, he knows me too well.'

'You could still lead a raid, it's not too late to change your mind. If you pushed a little way in, and withdrew from strength ... With all he has to do, it's not likely he'll come in person.'

'How can I know that? No, I had a warning ... a kind of warning ... at Dodona.'

Hephaistion stored away this news in silence. It was the most Alexander had ever told him of it.

'Alexander. Your father wants you back. I know it. You should believe me. I've known it all along.'

'Good. Then he can do right by my mother.'

'No, not only for the war in Asia. You don't want to hear this, but he loves you. You may not like the way it takes him. The gods have many faces, Euripides says.'

Alexander laid his hands on the broken stone, and turned on his friend his entire attention. 'Euripides wrote for actors. Masks, you can say; yes, masks. Some pretty, some not. But one face. Only one.'

A meteor flared down with a yellow-green glowing head and fading red trail, and plunged into the distant sea. Hephaistion put happiness briskly by, like a cup drunk down in haste. 'It's an omen for you. You must decide tonight. You know; you came out to do it.'

'I woke up, and the place stank like a midden.' A tuft of pale wallflower had rooted itself among the stones; he fingered it unseeingly. Like a great weight thrown suddenly on his shoulder, Hephaistion felt an awareness of being leaned upon, of being needed for more than love. It brought no joy; it was like glimpsing the first mark of a deadly sickness. Rust; he can bear anything but rust.

'Tonight,' he said quietly. 'Nothing to wait for, you know it all.'

Without movement, Alexander seemed to gather himself together, to grow more compact. 'Yes. First, I'm spending time, not using it. This I've never felt before. Second, there are two or three men, and I think King Kleitos is one of them, who once they're sure they can't use me against my father, will want to send him my head. And, third ... he's mortal, no man knows his hour. If he died, and I away over the border ...'

'That, too,' said Hephaistion calmly. 'Well, then, as you say. You want to go home, he wants you back. You've exchanged mortal insults, no one will speak first. So you must find a proper go-between. Who is it going to be?'

Firmly now, as if it had been some time settled, Alexander said, 'Demaratos of Corinth. He likes us both, he'll enjoy the importance, he'll do it well. Whom shall we send him?'

It was Harpalos, with his sad graceful limp, his dark vivid face, his quick smile and flattering grave attentiveness, who rode south. They convoyed him to the Epirote border, for fear of robbers; but he carried no letter with him. It was the essence of his mission, that no record of it should exist. He took only his mule, a change of clothing, and his golden charm.

Philip learned with pleasure that his old guest-friend Demaratos had business in the north, and would like to visit him. He was at pains to choose the supper, and hire a good sword-dancer to enliven it. Food and dancer were cleared away; they settled down to their wine. Corinth being the listening-post for all southern Greece, Philip asked at once for news. He had heard of some rub between Thebes and Sparta; what did Demaratos think?

Demaratos, a privileged guest and proud of it, fed with the expected cue, shook his distinguished iron-grey head. 'Ah, King! That I should hear you ask if the Greeks are living in harmony! With your own house in the midst of war.'

Philip's dark eye, not yet much engorged with wine, slewed sharply round. His trained diplomatist's ear had picked up a certain note, a shade of preparation. He gave no sign of this. 'That boy. He flares up at a spark, like pitch. A silly speech from a man in liquor, only worth a laugh next day if he'd kept the sense he was born with. But he runs off in a blaze to his mother; and you know *her*.'

Demaratos made sounds of fellow-feeling. A thousand pities, he said, that with the mother of such a jealous temper, the young man should feel his future threatened by her disgrace. He quoted faultlessly (having had them ready) some apt elegiacs of Simonides.

'Cutting off his own nose,' said Philip, 'to spite his face. A boy with his gifts, the waste of it. We'd get along well enough, but for that witch. He should know better. Well, by now he'll have paid for it. He'll have had a bellyful of Illyrian hill-forts. But if he thinks I'll . . .'

It was not till next morning that the talking began in earnest.

Demaratos was in Epiros, the King's most honoured guest. He would be escorting back to Pella the King's sister and her pardoned son. Being rich already, he must chiefly be paid in kudos. King Alexandros toasted him in an heirloom gold cup, and begged him to accept it as a small memento. Olympias put out for him all her social graces; if her enemies called her vixenish, let him judge for himself. Alexander, wearing the one good chiton he had left, was most attentive; till one evening when a tired stiff old man came plodding down to Dodona on a weary mule. It was

Phoinix. He had met hard weather on the pass, and almost fell from the saddle into his foster-son's lifted arms.

Alexander demanded a hot bath, sweet oils, and a skilled bathman; no one in Dodona, it turned out, had ever heard of such a calling. He went in to rub Phoinix down himself.

The royal bath was an antique affair of painted clay, much mended and prone to leak; there was no couch, he had had to send for one. He worked on the knotted-up thigh muscles, following their path as Aristotle had shown him, kneading and tapping as, at home, he had taught his slave to do. In Illyria, he had been doctor to all the others. Even when, knowledge or memory failing, he had relied upon omens seen in dreams, they had preferred him to the local witch-wife.

'Ugh, aah, that's better, that's where it always catches me. Have you studied with Cheiron, like Achilles?'

'No teacher like necessity. Now turn over.'

'Those scars on your arm are new.'

'My leopard. I had to give the skin to my host.'

'Did the blankets reach you safely?'

'Did you send blankets too? They're all thieves in Illyria. I got the books; they can't read, and by luck they weren't short of tinder. The books were the best. They stole Oxhead, once.'

'What did you do?'

'Went after the man and killed him. He'd not gone far, Oxhead wouldn't let him mount.' He kneaded Phoinix' hamstring.

'You had us all on edge half a year and more. Here and there like a fox.' Alexander laughed shortly, not pausing in his work. 'But time went by, and you're not one for putting off. Your father set it down to your natural feeling. As I told him he should.' Phoinix screwed round his head to look.

Alexander straightened up, wiping-off his oily hands on a towel. 'Yes,' he said slowly. 'A natural feeling, yes, you may call it that.'

Phoinix withdrew his steps from the deep water, as he had learned when to do. 'And did you see battle, Achilles, in the west?'

'Once, a tribal war. One has to support one's host. We won.' He pushed back his steam-moistened hair. His nose and mouth looked pinched. He threw the towel hard into a corner.

Phoinix thought, He has learned to boast of what he suffered under Leonidas; it taught him endurance; I have heard him at Pella and smiled. But these months he will never boast of; and the man who smiles should take care.

As if he had spoken aloud, Alexander said, in sudden anger, 'Why did my father demand I should ask his pardon?'

'Well, come, he's a bargaining man. Every bargain starts with asking too much. In the end he didn't press it.' Phoinix swung down his stocky wrinkled legs from the couch. By it was a little deep window, with a marten's nest in an upper corner; on the sill, speckled with droppings, lay an ivory comb with chipped teeth, in which clung some reddish hairs from King Alexandros' beard. Combing himself, his face shielded, Phoinix looked his nurseling over.

He has conceived that he could fail. Yes, even he. He has seen there are rivers over which, once the spate has risen, there is no way back. Some dark night in that land of robbers, he has seen himself, who knows what? A strategos of mercenaries, hired out to some satrap at war with the Great King, or to some third-rate Sicilian tyrant; maybe a wandering comet, such as Alkibiades once was, a nine days' wonder every few years, then burnt out in darkness. For a moment he has seen it. He likes to show his war-scars; this scar he will cover like a slave-brand, he hides it even from me.

'Come! The bargain's struck; wipe old scores away and start with the tablet clean. Remember what Agamemnon said to Achilles, when they were reconciled:

> But what could I do? All things come to pass from God.
> Blindness of heart is old-born of Zeus, Ate the deadly,
> Who fools us all

Your father has felt it. I have seen it in his face.'

Alexander said, 'I can lend you a cleaner comb that that.' He put it back under the bird's-nest, and brushed his fingers. 'Well, we know what Achilles said;

> This has been all to the good for Hector, and for the Trojans;
> The Greeks, though, I think will long remember our falling out.
> Even so, we will put it all by, finished and done with,
> Though it hurts us, beating down the inward passion because we must.'

He picked up the fresh chiton creased from Phoinix' saddlebag, dropped it neatly over his head like a well-trained page, and handed him his sword-belt.

'Ah, child, you've always been a good boy to me.' Phoinix fiddled with the buckle, head down. He had meant these words to open an exhortation; but, the rest failing him, he left them to stand as they were.

Nikanor's Horse was again Alexander's squadron.

The haggling had lasted some time; many couriers between Demaratos and the King had crossed the rough tracks into Epiros. It was the centre of the bargain, achieved with much manoeuvring, that neither party should claim an outright victory. When father met son at length, both felt that enough had been said already; they excused themselves from going over it again in words. Each eyed the other with curiosity, resentment, suspicion, regret, and a half-hope which each hid too well.

Under Demaratos' complacent eyes, they exchanged a symbolic kiss of reconcilement. Alexander led up his mother; Philip kissed her too, noting to himself the lines of pride and rancour etched deeper in, and recalling with wonder, for a moment, his youthful passion. Then they all went off to take up their lives as they found them now.

Most men about the court had been able, so far, to avoid taking sides. Only small groups of partisans, Attalids, agents of Olympias, friends and comrades of Alexander, had bickered and intrigued. But the exiles' living presence was like verjuice stirred into milk. Separation began.

The young knew that he was young and had excelled his elders; that when old envious men had tried to put him down, he had stood up to it and won. He was all their own smouldering rebellions, expressed in flame; their hero-victim. Because it was his, they made even Olympias' cause their own. To see one's mother shamed, and one's father, an old man past forty, make a public show of himself with a girl of fifteen; why should one swallow that? When they saw him, therefore, they greeted him with defiant fervour. He never failed to acknowledge it.

His face was thinner. It had been weathered for years, but the closed drawn look was new. Their salutations changed it; his warm confiding smile made them feel rewarded.

Hephaistion, Ptolemy, Harpalos and the rest, the companions of his exile, were treated with awed respect, their stories becoming legend. They did not fail their friend. All the tales were of success; the leopard, the lightning marches to the border, a glorious victory in the tribal war. Their pride was invested in him, besides their love; they would have changed, if they could, his very memories. His thanks, though unspoken, were enough; they felt themselves beloved. Soon they seemed acknowledged leaders, to the young men and to themselves as well; they began to show it, sometimes with discretion, sometimes not.

His party gathered; made up of men who liked him, or had fought beside him; who, perhaps, wounded and half-frozen in Thrace had been given his own place by the fire and a drink from his own wine-cup; or whose courage had been damping-out when he came along and kindled it; or who had told him tales in the guard-room when he was a child: supported by men who looked back to the lawless years, and wanted a strong heir; by men, also, who hated his enemies. The Attalids were daily growing in power and pride. Parmenion, some time widowed, had lately married Attalos' daughter, and the King had stood as groom's man.

The first time Alexander met Pausanias out of others' hearing, he thanked him for his house's hospitality. The bearded lips moved stiffly, as if they would have returned his smile had they not lost the knack. 'It was nothing, Alexander. We were honoured ... I would do more than that.' For a moment their eyes met, Pausanias' exploring, Alexander's questioning; but he had never been an easy man to understand.

Eurydike had a fine new house on the slope, a short walk from the Palace. A pine-wood had been felled to clear the site, and a statue of Dionysos, which had stood in the grove, returned to Queen Olympias, who had set it up. It had not been a shrine of ancient sanctity, only a fancy of hers, to which rumour attached some scandal.

Hephaistion, who had arrived too late to know much about such things, knew like anyone else that a son's legitimacy hangs on his mother's honour. Of course he must defend her, he had no choice; but why with such passion, such bitterness to his father, such blindness to his own good? True friends share everything, except the past before they met.

That she had her faction, everyone knew too well; her rooms were like the meeting-house of some exiled opposition in the southern states. Hephaistion felt his teeth on edge, whenever Alexander went there. Did even he know all she was up to? Whatever it was, if trouble broke the King would believe he knew.

Hephaistion too was young; he had shared the shock when time-servers, once assiduous, now kept their distance. Alexander's very victories were their warning. In Macedon with its history, he was marked dangerous as brightly as the panther. He had always despised servility; but rooted in him was the need to be beloved. Now he was learning which men had known and used it. Watching the lesson, with grim quiet irony, was the King.

'You should try to mend matters,' Hephaistion would say. 'He must want to, or why recall you? It's always for the younger to come forward first, no disgrace in that.'

'I don't like the way he looks at me.'

'He may think the same, you're both on edge. But how can you doubt you're his heir? Who else is there? Arridaios?'

The idiot had been in Pella lately, for one of the great festivals. His mother's kin always brought him, spruced and combed, to pay his respects to his father, who had acknowledged him with pride when, a fine healthy-looking infant, he had been brought out of the birth-room. Now at seventeen, he was taller than Alexander, and favoured Philip's looks except when his mouth fell open. He was no longer taken to the theatre, where he would laugh loudly at the tragic climaxes, nor to solemn rites, in case one of his fits should take him, when he would flap on the ground like a landed fish, wetting and dirtying himself. It was the fits had done some violence to his mind, the doctors said; he had been a likely child before them. He enjoyed the side-shows of the feast, led about by an old family slave like a little boy with his pedagogue. This year his black beard had grown; but he would not be parted from his doll.

'What a rival!' Hephaistion said. 'Why can't you be easy?'

After giving this good advice, he would go out, run into some man of the Attalid faction, or even one of Olympias' many enemies; would resent what they said, and hit them in the teeth. All Alexander's friends were doing their share of this; Hephaistion, being quick-tempered, did rather more. True friends share everything, especially their quarrels. Later he might reproach himself; but all of them knew they would get no reproach from Alexander for these proofs of love. It was not that he set them on to make trouble; only that there grew up around him that kind of defiant loyalty from which sparks are struck, as if from flint.

He hunted untiringly, best pleased when the quarry was dangerous, or gave him a long hard chase. He read little, but to the purpose; his restlessness needed action, he was only content when readying his men for the coming war. He seemed everywhere, demanding from the engineers catapults which could be taken apart and carted, not left behind to rot after every siege; in the horse lines, looking at feet, inspecting the stable floors and discussing fodder. He talked much with travelling men, traders and envoys, actors, paid-up mercenaries, who knew Greek Asia and even the lands beyond. All they told him, he checked stage by stage against Xenophon's *Inland March*.

Hephaistion, whom he shared his studies with, saw all his hopes staked on the war. He was scarred by the months of impotence as if by a fetter; he needed the medicine of command, victory to confound his enemies and heal his pride. He still took for granted he would be sent ahead, alone or with Parmenion, to make good an Asian bridgehead for the main force. Hephaistion, concealing his own uneasiness, asked if he had talked of it with the King. 'No. Let him come to me.'

The King, though busy himself, was watchful. He saw tactical changes which should have had his sanction, and waited to be asked, in vain. He saw the young man's altered face, and his friends as thick as thieves. It had never been easy to read his mind, but once he would have come with all this as soldier to soldier; he could not have kept it in. As a man, Philip was hurt and angry; as a ruler, he was distrustful.

He had just had good news; he had brought off an alliance of priceless strategic value. In his heart, he was longing to boast of it to his son. But, if the boy was too stiff-necked to consult his father and King, he could not expect to be consulted. Let him learn for himself, or from his mother's spies.

It was from Olympias, therefore, that he heard of Arridaios' coming marriage.

The satrapy of Karia, on the southern curve of the Asian coast, was ruled under the Great King by its native dynasts. The great Mausolos, before he was laid in his grandiose Mausoleum, had built himself a little empire, seawards to Rhodes, Kos and Chios, south down the coast to Lykia. The succession, though in dispute, had passed firmly to Pixodoros, his younger brother. He paid tribute and did formal homage; the Great King took care to ask no more. After Syracuse sank back to anarchy, and before the rise of Macedon, Karia had been the greatest power on the Middle Sea. Philip had long been watching her, sending secret envoys, playing her on a silken line. Now he was hauling in. He had betrothed Arridaios to Pixodoros' daughter.

Olympias learned of it one morning at the theatre, during a tragedy put on to honour the Karian envoys.

Alexander, when she sent for him, was not found at once. He had gone back-stage with Hephaistion, to congratulate Thettalos. The play had been *The Madness of Herakles*. Hephaistion wondered, after, how he could have missed the omen.

Thettalos was now about forty, at the height of his powers and fame. So versatile that he could give a performance in any mask from Antigone to Nestor, he still triumphed in hero roles. This one had been demanding. His mask only just off, he was careless of his face, which for a moment revealed concern at what he saw; after absence, changes show. He had heard things, too, and took trouble to make it clear that his own loyalty was unshaken.

From the theatre, Hephaistion went off to spend an hour with his parents, who had come into town for the feast. When he returned, it was to the centre of a hurricane.

Alexander's room was milling with his friends, all talking at once, indignant, guessing, plotting. Seeing Hephaistion at the door, Alexander broke through the crowd to him, grasped him by the arm and shouted the news in his ear. Dazed by his rage, Hephaistion made sounds of sympathy; certainly he should have heard of it from the King, certainly he had been slighted. The truth came piecemeal through the din: he believed this to prove Arridaios had been adopted as heir of Macedon. Olympias was sure of it.

I must get him alone, Hephaistion thought; but he dared not try. Alexander was flushed as if with fever; the young men, recalling his victories, cursing the King's ingratitude, offering wild advice, had felt his need of them and did not mean to leave him. He wanted from Hephaistion what he wanted from all the rest, only more urgently. It would be madness to cross him now.

Illyria, Hephaistion thought. It's like a sickness he can't shake off. Later I'll talk to him. 'Who'd be a woman?' he said. 'Does she know she's promised to a wittol?'

'What do you think?' said Alexander, his nostrils flaring. 'Or her father either.' His brows drew together in thought; he began to pace about. Hephaistion recognized the prelude to coming action.

Ignoring the danger signs, falling into step beside him, Hephaistion said, 'Alexander, this can't be true unless the King's gone mad. Why, he was elected King himself because the Macedonians wouldn't accept a child. How could he suppose they'd accept a halfwit?'

'I know what he's doing.' A dry heat seemed to radiate from him. 'Arridaios is a stopgap till Eurydike has a boy. This is Attalos' work.'

'But . . . but think! This boy's not even born. Then he has to grow up. Say eighteen years. And the King's a soldier.'

'She's pregnant again, didn't you know?' If one touched his hair, Hephaistion thought, one would hear it crackle.

'He can't think he's immortal. He's going to war. What does he think would happen if he died in the next five years? Who is there but you?'

'Unless he has me killed.' He threw it off like a commonplace.

'*What?* How can you believe it? His own son.'

'They say I'm not. Well, then, I must look out for myself.'

'Whoever says so? Do you mean that sottish wedding speech? I think all the man really meant by a true-born heir, was Macedonian blood both sides.'

'Oh, no. That's not what they're saying now.'

'Listen. Come out awhile. We'll go hunting. Then we'll talk later.'

Looking quickly round to be sure no one else could hear, Alexander said in a desperate undertone, 'Be quiet, be quiet.' Hephaistion went back to the others; Alexander paced, like a caged wolf, to and fro.

Suddenly he faced round to them, and said, 'I shall deal with this.'

Hephaistion, who had never before heard this voice of decision with less than perfect trust, felt an instant presage of disaster.

'We'll see who wins,' Alexander said, 'at this marriage-broking.' Prompt as a chorus, the others begged to hear. 'I shall send to Karia, and tell Pixodoros what kind of bargain he's made.'

There was applause. Hephaistion thought, Everyone's gone insane. Over the noise, Nearchos the naval officer called out, 'You can't do that, Alexander. You might lose us the war in Asia.'

'You might let me finish,' Alexander shouted back. 'I shall offer for the girl myself.'

Almost in silence, they took it in. Then Ptolemy said, 'Do it, Alexander. I'll stand by you, here's my hand on it.'

Hephaistion stared, appalled. He had counted upon Ptolemy, the big brother, the steady one. He had lately fetched his Thais back from Corinth, where she had spent his time of exile. But now it was clear he was as angry as Alexander. He was, after all, though unacknowledged, the eldest of Philip's sons. Personable and capable, ambitious and turned thirty, he thought he could have managed in Karia very well. It was one thing to uphold a loved and legitimate brother; something else to stand aside for slobbering Arridaios. 'What do you say, everyone? Do we all stand by Alexander?'

There were sounds of confused assent. Alexander's certainties were always catching. They exclaimed that this marriage would secure his place, that it would force the King to take care with him. Even the faint-hearted, seeing him count heads, joined in; this was no Illyrian exile, there was nothing they need do, all the risks would be taken, they thought, by him.

This is treason, Hephaistion thought. Arrogant with desperation, he took Alexander by the shoulders, with the firmness of one who claims his rights. At once Alexander turned aside with him.

'Sleep on it. Think tomorrow.'

'Never put off.'

'Listen. What if your father and Pixodoros are swapping stinking fish? What if she's a slut or a hag? Just fit for Arridaios? You'd be a laughing-stock.'

With an effort he could see, Alexander turned on him dilated glittering eyes, and said with controlled forbearance, 'What is it? This will make no difference to us, you know that.'

'Of course I know that!' said Hephaistion angrily. 'You're not talking to Arridaios, what sort of fool do you ...' No, no; one of us must keep his head. Suddenly, for no reason that was clear to him, Hephaistion thought, he's proving he can take a woman from his father. She's for Arridaios, that keeps it decent, he need not know. And who dares tell him? No one, not even I.

Alexander, his head tilted defiantly, had started to assess the strength of the Karian navy. Through all this, Hephaistion sensed appeal. He wanted not advice, but the proofs of love. Anything he needed, he must have.

'You know I'm with you, whatever comes of it. Whatever you do.'

Alexander pressed his arm, gave him a quick secret smile, and turned back to the rest.

'Whom will you send to Karia?' asked Harpalos. 'I'll go, if you want.'

Alexander strode over and clasped his hands. 'No; no Macedonian; my father could make you pay. It was noble to offer, Harpalos, I'll never forget it.' He kissed Harpalos' cheek; he was getting very emotional. Two or three others crowded up, offering to go. This is like the theatre, Hephaistion thought.

It was then that he guessed whom Alexander would send.

Thettalos came after dark, and was let in through Olympias' private postern. She had wished to be present at the conference, but Alexander saw him alone. He went away with a gold ring on, and his head held high. Olympias, too, thanked him with the charm she could still sometimes command, and gave him a talent of silver. He replied with grace; he had had practice in making speeches when his mind was on other things.

Some seven days later, Alexander met Arridaios in the Palace court-yard. He came oftener now; the doctors advised he should mix more in company, to stir his wits. He trotted eagerly forward to meet Alexander, the old servant, now half a head shorter, bustling anxiously behind. Alexander, who bore him no more malice than his enemy's horse or dog, returned his greeting. 'How's Phryne?' he asked. The doll was missing. 'Have they taken her away?'

Arridaios grinned. There was a wet trickle in his soft black beard. 'Old Phryne's in the box. I don't need *her*. They're bringing me a real girl, from Karia.' He added, like a dull child echoing adults, an obscene boast.

Alexander looked at him with pity. 'Take care of Phryne. She's a good friend. You might want her after all.'

'Not when I've a wife.' He nodded down at Alexander, and added with friendly confidence, 'When you're dead I shall be King.' His keeper tugged quickly at his belt; he went on towards the stoa, singing to himself a tuneless song.

Philotas was growing concerned. He had seen looks exchanged whose meaning he would have given much to know. Again he had been left outside a secret. Half a month he had scented it, but they were all holding their tongues. Who they were, at least, he knew; they were too pleased with themselves, or too scared, to hide it.

It was an uneasy time for Philotas. Though he had lived for years on the fringe of Alexander's set, he had always failed to reach the inmost ring. He had a good war record; impressive looks, but for rather prominent blue eyes; he was good company at supper, and in the van of fashion; his reports to the King had always been discreet, and he was certain were undetected. Why then was he not trusted? His instincts blamed Hephaistion for it.

Parmenion was badgering him for news. If he missed this, whatever it was, it would set him back, both with his father and the King. It might even have been better to have shared the exile, he could have been useful there, and now he would have been told everything. But it had been too sudden, the choice at the wedding brawl; though brave in the field, he was comfort-loving off it, and in doubtful issues he liked hot chestnuts pulled out of the fire by others.

He wanted no one reporting to Alexander, or to Hephaistion which was the same, that he had been asking dangerous questions. It therefore took him some time, picking up trifles here and there, and seeking the missing pieces where he would least be noticed, before he learned the truth.

It had been agreed that Thettalos was too conspicuous to report, himself, upon his mission. He sent a confidential messenger from Corinth, announcing his success.

Pixodoros had known something, though not enough, about Arridaios; Philip was too old a hand to think a lasting treaty could be won by downright fraud. When, therefore, the satrap learned that at no more cost he could exchange the ass for the racehorse, he was enchanted. In the audience room at Halikarnassos, with its columns of serpentine, Persian wall-tiles and Greek chairs, the daughter was modestly paraded; no one had been at the trouble of telling Arridaios that she was eight years old. Thettalos expressed a proxy's rapture. The marriage, of course, would have to be by proxy too; but once performed, the bridegroom's kin would have to accept it. It only remained to choose someone of proper standing, and send him off.

For the better part of a day, in Alexander's presence and out of it, nothing else was talked of among his friends. When others were about, they endeavoured to speak darkly. But that day gave Philotas the last link in his chain.

There was nothing King Philip did better than to act when he was ready, and keep quiet meantime. He wanted no clamour and no rallying-cries; enough harm had been done already. Seldom in his life had he been so angry; this time he was angry cold sober.

The day passed without event. Night came; Alexander went to his room. When he was certainly alone, which meant when Hephaistion left, a guard was put on it. The window was twenty feet up, but there was a guard under that as well.

He knew nothing of it till morning. The men had been chosen with care; they answered no questions. He waited, fasting, till noon.

There was a dagger under his pillow. In the royal house of Macedon, this was as natural as wearing clothes. He slung it on inside his chiton. If food had been brought him, he would have left it; poison was not a fighting death. He waited for the footsteps.

When at last they came, he heard the guard presenting arms. It was not, then, the executioner. He felt no relief; he knew the tread.

Philip came in, with Philotas following.

'I need a witness,' said the King. 'This man will do.'

Out of his sight, behind his shoulder, Philotas gave Alexander a look of shocked concern, mixed with dazed bewilderment. His hand sketched a little gesture, offering in the unknown trouble his helpless loyalty.

Alexander half-perceived it; but the King's presence filled the room. His big mouth was set in his broad face; his thick brows, which had always an outward tilt, flared up from his frown like a hawk's spread wings. Force came from him like heat. Alexander planted his feet and waited; he felt the dagger with the nerves under his skin.

'I knew,' said his father, 'that you were as headstrong as a wild pig, and as vain as a Corinth whore. Treacherous I knew you could be, as long as you listened to your mother. But one thing I didn't reckon on, that you were a fool.'

At 'treacherous' Alexander had caught his breath; he began to speak.

'*Be quiet!*' said the King. 'How dare you open your mouth? How dared you meddle in my business with your insolence and your ignorant childish spite, you blundering, brainsick fool?'

'It was to hear this,' said Alexander into the pause, 'that you brought Philotas?' A jar had gone through him, like a wound one does not yet feel.

'No,' said the King menacingly. 'You can wait for that. You have lost me Karia. Can't you see it, you fool? Before God, since you think so much of yourself, you might have thought better this time. Do you want to be a Persian vassal? Do you want to pick up a horde of barbarian marriage-kin, who'll hang about you when war begins, selling the enemy our plans and bargaining for your head? Well, if so your luck's out, for I'll see you to Hades first, you'd be less hindrance there. And after this, do you think Pixodoros will accept Arridaios? Not unless he's a greater fool than you, and small chance of that. I thought I could spare Arridaios better. Well, I was a fool, I deserve to beget fools.' He drew a heavy breath. 'I have no luck with my sons.'

Alexander stood quiet. Even the dagger on his ribs hardly moved against them. Presently he said, 'If I am your son, then you have wronged my mother.' He spoke without much expression; he was taken up with inward things.

Philip's lower lip thrust out. 'Don't tempt me,' he said. 'I brought her back for your sake. She's your mother; I'm trying to remember it. Don't tempt me before a witness.'

In the background, Philotas shifted his tall bulk, and gave a quiet, sympathetic cough.

'And now,' said Philip, 'attend to me; I am coming to business. First: I am sending an envoy to Karia. He can carry a formal letter from me, refusing my consent to your betrothal, and one from you withdrawing. Or, if you won't write, he can carry one from me telling Pixodoros he is welcome to you, but he'll be getting no son of mine. If that's your choice, tell me now. No? Very well. Then, second: I don't ask you to control your mother, you couldn't do it. I don't ask you to bring her intrigues to me, I've never asked it, I don't ask now. But while you are here in Macedon as my heir, which is while I choose and no longer, you will keep your hands out of her plots. If you meddle in them again, you can go back where you have been, and stay there. To help keep you out of mischief, the young fools you've embroiled so far can go looking for trouble outside the kingdom. Today they are settling their affairs. When they are gone, you may leave this room.'

Alexander heard in silence. He had long prepared his mind for torture, lest he should somehow be taken alive in war. But it was his body he had thought of.

'Well?' said the King. 'Don't you want to know who they are?'

He answered, 'You may suppose so.'

'Ptolemy: I have no luck with my sons. Harpalos: a sleek greedy fox, I could have bought him if he were worth it. Nearchos: his Cretan kin may have joy of him. Erigyios and Laomedon ...' The names came slowly. He was watching the face before him whiten. It was time the boy learned once for all who was the master. Let him wait.

Gladly as Philotas would have removed Hephaistion, he had not named him; neither justice nor kindness, but an ineradicable fear, had held his hand. The King for his part had never thought Hephaistion dangerous in himself. Though it was certain that, at the pinch, there was nothing he would not do for Alexander, he was worth taking a risk on. This was the one pardon which would disoblige Olympias. It had another use, besides.

'Concerning Hephaistion son of Amyntor,' he said, taking his time, 'I have considered that matter by itself.' He paused again, while something within him, between contempt and deep secret envy, thought, The man does not live I could feel that for, or the woman either. 'You will not pretend, I take it, that he was not told your plans, or that he refused assent to them.'

In the distant voice of great pain, Alexander said, 'He disagreed, but I overbore him.'

'So? Well, be that as it may, I take into account that placed as he is, he could not escape blame either by keeping your counsel or revealing it.' His voice was dry, putting Hephaistion where he belonged. 'Therefore, at present I have exempted him from exile. If he gives you more good advice, you will do well to take it, both for your own sake and for his. For I am saying this before a witness, in case you should dispute it later: if you are found again in treasonable conspiracy, I shall consider him a party to it, both by knowledge and consent. I shall accuse him before the Assembly of the Macedonians, and ask them for his death.'

Alexander answered, 'I have heard you. You need not have brought a witness.'

'Very well. Tomorrow, if your friends have taken themselves off, I will dismiss the guard. Today you can give thought to your life. It is more than time.'

He turned. The guard outside presented arms. Philotas, leaving after him, had meant to look back at Alexander with discreet support and a meaning indignation. But at the last, he went out with averted face.

Days passed; Alexander, now he was about again, found his following well sifted. It can cost too much to be in fashion, even for the young. The chaff was all winnowed out now. The solid grain remained. He took note of these faithful ones; they were never forgotten.

A few days later, he was sent for to the small audience room. The message only said that the King required his presence.

Philip was in his chair of state, with an officer of justice, some clerks, and a number of litigants waiting audience. Without speaking, he motioned his son to a seat below the dais, and went on dictating a letter.

Alexander stood a moment, then sat down. Philip said to the guard at the door, 'They can bring him in.'

A four-man guard brought in Thettalos. His hands and his legs were fettered. He walked forward with the heavy shuffling gait imposed by the leg-irons. His wrists had raw bloody sores, from the rubbing of the bracelets.

He was unshaven and unkempt, but he kept his head well up. His bow to the King was not more, nor less respectful than if he had been a guest. He made another to Alexander; his eyes held no reproach.

'So you are here,' said the King grimly. 'If you were an honest man, you would have come to give account of your embassy. And if you were a wise one, you would have run further than to Corinth.'

Thettalos inclined his head. 'So it seems, King. But I like to fulfil my contracts.'

'It is a pity, then, that your sponsors will be disappointed. You will give your last show in Pella. And you will give it alone.'

Alexander stood up. Everyone looked at him; they could see now why he was there.

'Yes,' said the King. 'Let Thettalos see you. He owes his death to you.'

Alexander said in a high taut voice, 'He is an artist of Dionysos, his person is sacred.'

'He should have kept to his art.' Philip nodded to the officer of justice, who began to write something.

'He's a Thessalian,' Alexander said.

'He is a citizen of Athens these twenty years. After the peace was signed he has acted as my enemy. He has no rights, and he knows it.'

Thettalos looked, with an almost imperceptible shake of the head, at Alexander; but his eyes were fixed on the King.

'If he has his deserts,' Philip said, 'he will hang tomorrow. If he wants clemency, he must ask me for it. *And so must you.*'

Alexander stood rigid, holding an indrawn breath. Everyone's eyes were on him. He took a step towards the throne.

With a clank, Thettalos advanced one weighted foot. It brought him into the pose of heroic fortitude beloved of audiences. Every eye was drawn his way.

'Let me answer for it all. One should not exceed one's instructions. I was officious in Karia. Rather than your son, I will ask Sophokles to be my pleader.' He brought both hands forward in a classic movement which also, to the best advantage, displayed his sores. There was a faint shocked murmur. He had been oftener crowned than any Olympic victor, and Greeks who had scarcely seen a theatre knew his name. In his resonant voice which could have reached an audience of twenty thousand, now pitched perfectly to the room, he delivered his supplication.

The lines were fairly appropriate; not that it mattered. It was an exhibition piece. Its real meaning was, 'Oh, yes, I know who you are. And you know who I am. Isn't it time to end the comedy?'

Philip narrowed a hard black eye. The message was understood. He was quite startled to see his son, blazing with controlled emotion, come out and stand by the actor's side.

'Certainly, sir, I will ask clemency for Thettalos. It would be far more shameful not to. He has risked his life for me; I shall not grudge him a little of my pride. Please pardon him; all the fault was mine. And you, Thettalos, please forgive me.'

Thettalos with his fettered hands made a gesture more exquisite than words. Applause, though unheard, hung in the air.

Philip nodded at Thettalos, like a man who has fulfilled his purpose. 'Very well. I hope this has taught you not to hide behind the god when you are making mischief. This time you are pardoned; don't presume on it. Take him away, and strike off his chains. I will hear the other business presently.' He went out. He needed time to recover his temper, lest he make mistakes. Between them, they had nearly managed to make a fool of him.

Yet they had had no time to concert it. A couple of tragedians, cueing one another to steal his scene.

Thettalos sat that evening at the lodging of his old friend Nikeratos, who had followed him up to Pella in case he needed ransoming, and was rubbing salve on his sores.

'My dear, I bled for the boy. One forgets how little he travels. I tried to signal him, but he swallowed every word. He saw the rope round my neck.'

'So did I. Will you never learn sense?'

'Come come, what do you think Philip is, some Illyrian pirate? You should have seen him being Greek at Delphi. He knew already he'd gone too far, before I told him so. A disgusting journey. Let us go home by sea.'

'You know the Corinthians are fining you half a talent? Aristodemos got your roles. No one will pay you for acting King Philip off his own stage.'

'Oh, not I alone. I never reckoned on the boy being such a natural. What a sense of theatre! Wait till he finds himself; I tell you, we shall see something. But it was a monstrous thing to do to him. I bled for him, truly bled.'

Hephaistion was whispering in the midnight room, 'Yes, I know. I know. But you must get some sleep now. I'll stay with you. Try to sleep.'

In a colourless white-hot voice Alexander repeated, 'He put his foot on my neck.'

'He's getting no praise for it. It's a scandal, his chaining Thettalos; everyone says so. They all say you came off best.'

'He put his foot on my neck, to show me he could do it. Before Thettalos; before them all.'

'They'll forget. So must you. All fathers are unfair sooner or later. I remember once – '

'*He's not my father.*'

Hephaistion's comforting hands froze in a moment's stillness. 'Oh, not in the eyes of the gods; they choose whom – '

'Never use that word again.'

'The god will reveal it. You must wait the god's sign, you know that ... Wait till the war begins. Wait till you win your next battle. He'll be bragging of you then.'

Alexander was lying flat on his back, staring upward. Suddenly he grasped Hephaistion in an embrace so fierce that it knocked the breath out of him, and said, 'Without you I should go mad.'

'I too without you,' said Hephaistion with loving ardour. Change the meaning, he thought, and you avert the omen.

Alexander said nothing. His strong fingers gripped into Hephaistion's ribs and shoulder; the bruises would be there a week. Hephaistion thought, I am in the King's gift too, a favour he can take away. Presently, having no more words, he offered instead the sadness of Eros, for this at least brought sleep.

The young slave-girl glided out from the shadow of the column; a black Nubian girl in a scarlet dress. She had been given as a child to Kleopatra in her childhood, to grow up with her, as a puppy might have been given. Her dark eyes with their smoky whites, like the agate eyes of statues, looked left and right before she spoke.

'Alexander, my lady says, please see her in the Queen's garden. By the old fountain. She wants to speak with you.'

He looked at her with a sharp alertness, then seemed to draw into himself. 'I can't come now. I am busy.'

'Please see my lady now. Please come. She is crying.' He saw that on her own dark polished face drops were lying like rain on bronze.

'Tell her yes, I'll come.'

It was early spring. The old tangled roses were beaded with hard red buds; in the slant evening light they glowed like rubies. An almond-tree growing between ancient tilted flag-stones looked weightless in its cloud of pink. The shadowed water gushed out from the columned fountain-house into a basin of worn porphyry with ferns growing in its cracks. Seated on its edge, Kleopatra looked up at his footstep. She had dried her tears. 'Oh, I am glad Melissa found you.'

He rested a knee on the coping and made a quick movement with his hand. 'Wait. Before you say anything, wait.'

She looked at him blankly. He said, 'There was something I asked you once to warn me of. Is it anything like that?'

'Warn you?' She had been full of other things. 'Oh, but not – '

'Wait. I am not to interfere with any of her business. In any plot. That was the condition.'

'Plot? No, no, please don't go away.'

'I am telling you, I release you from the promise. I don't wish to know.'

'No, truly. Please stay, Alexander, when you were in Molossia ... with King Alexandros ... What was he like?'

'Our uncle? But he was here a few years ago, you must remember him. A big man, red-bearded, young for his age – '

'Yes, I know; but what kind of man?'

'Oh, ambitious, brave in war I'd say, but I'd doubt his judgement. He governs well, though, watches things for himself.'

'What did his wife die of? Was he kind to her?'

'How should I know? She died in childbed.' He paused and stared, then in a changed voice said, 'Why do you ask?'

'I have to marry him.'

He stood back. The water from the hidden spring murmured in its columned cave. His first words were, 'When did you hear this? I should have been told. The King tells me nothing. Nothing.'

She looked at him silently, then said, 'He sent for me just now,' and turned away.

He crossed over and drew her against his shoulder. He had scarcely embraced her since their childhood, and now it was in Melissa's arms that she had wept. 'I am sorry. You need not be frightened. He's not a bad man, he has no name for being cruel. The people like him. And you'll not be too far away.'

She thought, *You* took for granted you'd choose the best; when you chose, you had only to lift your finger. When they find you a wife, you can go to her if you choose, or stay away with your lover. But I must be grateful that this old man, my mother's brother, has no name for being cruel. All she said was, 'The gods are unjust to women.'

'Yes, I have often thought so. But the gods are just; so it must be the fault of men.' Their eyes met questioningly, but their thoughts had no point of meeting. 'Philip wants to be sure of Epiros, before he crosses to Asia. What does Mother think of it?'

She grasped a fold of his chiton, the gesture of a suppliant. 'Alexander. This is what I wanted to ask you. Will you tell her for me?'

'*Tell* her? But of course she must have heard before you.'

'No, Father says not. He said I could tell her.'

'What is it?' He grasped her wrist. 'You are keeping something back.'

'No. Only that – I could tell he knows she will be angry.'

'So I should think. What an insult! Why go out of his way to slight her, when the thing in itself . . . I should have thought . . .'

Suddenly he released her. His face altered. He began to walk about the pavement, his feet, with a cat's instinct, avoiding the broken edges. She had known he would uncover the secret dread; better he than their mother, she had thought; but now she could scarcely bear the waiting. He turned. She saw a greyness under his skin; his eyes appalled her. He remembered her presence, said abruptly, 'I'll go to her,' and began to walk away.

'Alexander!' At her cry he paused impatiently. 'What does it mean? Tell me what it means?'

'Can't you see for yourself? Philip made Alexandros King of Molossia and hegemon of Epiros. Why isn't that enough? They're brothers-in-law; isn't *that* enough? Why not? Why make him a son-in-law besides? Can't you see? Not besides – instead.'

She said slowly, 'What?' and then, 'Ah, no, God forbid it!'

'What else? What does he mean to do, that would make an enemy of Alexandros unless he's sweetened with a new marriage-tie? What else, but throw him back his sister? For Eurydike to be Queen.'

Suddenly she began to wail, tearing her hair and dress, clawing and beating her bared breasts. He pulled back her hands, straightened her clothes and gripped her hard by the arms. 'Quiet! Don't tell the world our business. We must think.'

She looked up with terror-stretched eyes. 'What will she do? She will kill me.' The words passed without shock, between the children of Olympias; but he took her in his arms and patted her, as he might have soothed a hurt dog. 'No, don't be foolish, you know she won't harm her own. If she killed anyone . . .' He broke off with a violent movement, which in the moment of making it he changed to a clumsy caress. 'Be brave. Sacrifice to the gods. The gods will do something.'

'I thought,' she said sobbing, 'if he's not a bad man . . . I can take Melissa . . . at least I would get away. But with *her* there in the house, and after this . . .! I wish I were dead. I wish I were dead.'

Her dishevelled hair fell against his mouth, he could taste it damp and salt. Looking past her, he saw behind a laurel-bush a glimpse of scarlet, and freed an arm to beckon. The girl Melissa came out flinching. But, he thought, she could have overheard nothing she would not soon have been told. He said to Kleopatra, 'Yes, I'll see Mother. I'll go now.'

He put his sister into the dark outstretched hands with their pink palms. Looking back on his way to the furnace he was bound for, he saw the slave-girl seated on the rim of the porphyry fountain, bending over the head of the princess crouched by her lap.

News of the betrothal spread quickly. Hephaistion considered what Alexander would think of it, and guessed right. He did not appear at supper; he was said to be with the Queen. Hephaistion, waiting in his room, had fallen asleep on the bed before the sound of the latch aroused him.

Alexander came him. His eyes looked hollow, but full of a feverish exaltation. He walked over, put out his hand and touched Hephaistion, as a man might touch a sacred object for luck or a good omen, while deeply concerned with something else. Hephaistion looked, and was silent.

'She has told me,' said Alexander.

Hephaistion did not ask, 'What is it now?' He knew.

'She has told me at last.' He looked deeply at, and through Hephaistion, including him in his solitude. 'She made the conjuration, and asked the god's leave to tell me. He had always signed against it. That I never knew before.'

Hephaistion sitting on the edge of the bed, unmoving, watched Alexander with all his being. He had perceived that his being was all he had to give. Men must not be spoken to on their way up from the shades, or they might sink back again for ever. This was well known.

With the verge of consciousness, Alexander was aware of the quiet body, the face made beautiful by its intentness, the still dark-grey eyes, their whites lit by the lamp. He gave a deep sigh, and rubbed his hand across his brow.

'I was present,' he said, 'at the conjuration. For a long time the god did not speak, either yes or no. Then he spoke, in the form of the fire and in the – '

Suddenly he seemed aware of Hephaistion as a presence separate from his own. He sat down by him, and laid a hand on his knee. 'He gave me leave to hear, if I vowed not to disclose it. It is the same with all the Mysteries. Anything of mine I would share with you, but this belongs to the god.'

No, to the witch, thought Hephaistion; that condition was made for me. But he took Alexander's hand in both of his, and pressed it reassuringly. It felt dry and warm; it rested between his in trust, but sought no consolation.

'You must obey the god, then,' said Hephaistion; and thought, not for the first time, nor for the last, Who knows? Aristotle himself never denied that such things have been; he would not be so impious. If it was ever possible, it must be so still. But it is a great burden for the mortal part to carry. He clasped more tightly the hand he held. 'Only tell me this, whether you are satisfied.'

'Yes.' He nodded at the shadows beyond the lamp. 'Yes, I am satisfied.'

Suddenly his face was drained and drawn; his cheeks seemed to sink in as one looked, and his hand grew chilly. He began to shiver. Hephaistion had seen the same thing after battle, when men's wounds got cold. This needs the same remedy, he thought. 'Have you any wine in here?'

Alexander shook his head. He withdrew his hand to hide its tremor, and began to walk about.

Hephaistion said, 'We both need a drink. I do. I left supper early. Come and drink with Polemon. His wife's had a boy at last. He was looking for you in Hall. He's always been loyal.'

This was true. That night, being happy, he grieved to see the Prince look so worn down by his troubles, and kept his cup well filled. He did grow gay, even noisy; it was a party of friends; most had fought in the charge at Chaironeia. In the end, Hephaistion just got him up to bed on his feet, and he slept on till mid-morning. About noon, Hephaistion went to see how he was getting on. He was reading at his table, with a pitcher of cold water by him.

'What book is it?' asked Hephaistion leaning over his shoulder; he had been reading so quietly one could hardly make out the words.

He put the book quickly aside. 'Herodotos. *Customs of the Persians.* One should understand the kind of man one is going to fight.'

The ends of the scroll, curling up together, had met at the place where he had read. A little while after, when he was out of the room, Hephaistion rolled it open.

. . . the transgressor's services shall always be set against his misdeeds; only if the second are found the greater, shall the wronged party go on to punishment.

The Persians hold that no one ever yet killed his own father or mother. They are sure that if every such case were fully searched, it would be found out that the child was either a changeling, or born of adultery; for it is inconceivable, they say, that the true father should die by the hands of his child.

Hephaistion let the scroll spring back over the writing. For some time he stood looking out of the window, with his temple pressed against its frame, till Alexander, returning, smiled at the print of the carved laurel-leaves stamped into his flesh.

The troops drilled for the war. Hephaistion, long eager for it to begin, now almost craved for it. Philip's threats had angered more than frightened him; like any hostage, he was worth more alive than dead, and the Great King's soldiers would kill him much more readily; yet here it was as if they were all being driven down the funnel of a narrowing gorge, a torrent rushing below them; war beckoned like open country, freedom, escape.

After half a month, an envoy came from Pixodoros of Karia. His daughter, he disclosed, had most unhappily fallen into a wasting sickness. It was no small part of his grief that, besides her expected loss, he must renounce the distinguished honour of a union with the royal house of Macedon. A spy, who arrived by the same ship, reported that Pixodoros had sent the new Great King, Darius, pledges of firm allegiance, and betrothed the girl to one of his most loyal satraps.

Next morning, sitting at the desk of Archelaos, with Alexander standing straight-backed before it, Philip gave this news without any comment, and looked up, waiting.

'Yes,' said Alexander evenly. 'It has turned out badly. But remember, sir, Pixodoros was content with me. It was not my choice to withdraw.'

Philip frowned; yet he had felt something like relief. The boy had been too quiet just lately. This impudence was more like him, except for its restraint. One had always learned from his anger. 'Are you trying to excuse yourself, even now?'

'No, sir. I just say what we both know is true.'

He had still not raised his voice. Philip, his first fury spent and the bad news long expected, did not shout back. In Macedon, insult was a killing matter, but plain speaking the subject's right. He had taken it from simple men, even from women. Once, when after a long day in the judgement-seat he had told some old crone he had no time left to hear her case, she had called out, 'Then leave off being King!' and he had stayed to hear it. Now too he listened; it was his business; he was the King. It should have been more; but he put his grief behind him, almost before he knew it for what it was.

'I forbade the match for good reasons which you know.' He had kept the best to himself; Arridaios would have been his tool, Alexander could have been dangerous. Karia was powerful. 'Blame your mother,' he said. 'She led you into this folly.'

'Can she be blamed?' Alexander still spoke with calm; there was a kind of searching in his eyes. 'You have acknowledged children by other women. And Eurydike is in her eighth month now. Isn't that so?'

'That is so.' The grey eyes were fastened on his face. Appeal in them might have softened him. He had been at trouble enough to train this man for kingship; if he himself fell in the coming war, what other heir could there be? Again he studied the face before him, so unconceding, and so unlike his own. Attalos, a Macedonian of a stock already old when the royal line was still in Argos, had told him country tales about the Bacchic revels, customs brought in from Thrace, which the women kept secret. In the orgy, they themselves did not remember what they had done; what came of it they blamed on the god, in a human form or a snake's; but somewhere a mortal man was laughing. That is a foreign face, thought Philip; then remembered it, flushed and brilliant, coming down from the black horse into his arms. Divided in himself and angry at it, he thought, He is here to be reprimanded; how dare he try to corner me? Let him take what he is given and be thankful, when I choose to give. What more does he deserve?

'Well, then,' he said, 'if I have given you competitors for the kingdom, so much the better for you. Show your quality, earn your inheritance yourself.'

Alexander gazed at him with a piercing, an almost painful concentration. 'Yes,' he said. 'Then that is what I must do.'

'Very well,' Philip reached for his papers, dismissively.

'Sir. Whom are you sending to Asia, in command of the advance force?'

Philip looked up. 'Parmenion and Attalos,' he said curtly. 'If I don't send you where I cannot keep an eye on you, you have yourself to thank. And your mother. That is all. You have leave to go.'

In their fort on the Lynx Hills the three Lynkestids, the sons of Airopos, stood on their brown stone ramparts. It was an open place, safe from eavesdroppers. They had left their guest downstairs, having heard what he had to say, but given no answer yet. Around them stretched a great sky of white towering clouds, fringed with mountains. It was late spring; on the bare peaks above the forests, only the deepest gullies showed veins of snow.

'Say what you like, both of you,' said the eldest, Alexandros, 'but I don't trust it. What if this comes from the old fox himself, to test us? Or to trap us, have you thought of that?'

'Why should he?' asked the second brother, Heromenes. 'And why now?'

'Where are your wits? He is taking his army into Asia, and you ask why now.'

'Well,' said the youngest, Arrabaios, 'that's enough for him surely, without stirring up the west? No, if it had been that, it would have come two years ago, when he was planning to march south.'

'As *he* says' – Heromenes jerked his head towards the stairway – 'now's the time. Once Philip's set out, he will have his hostage for us.' He looked at Alexandros, whose feudal duty it was to lead their tribal levies in the King's war.

He stared back resentfully; already before this, he had been thinking that once his back was turned, the others would ride out on some mad foray that would cost him his head. 'I tell you I don't trust it. We don't know this man.'

'Still,' argued Heromenes, 'we do know those who've vouched for him.'

'Maybe. But those he claims to speak for – *they've* put their name to nothing.'

'The Athenian has,' said Arrabaios. 'If you two have forgotten how to read your Greek, you can take my word for it.'

'*His* name!' said Alexandros, snorting like a horse. 'What was it worth to the Thebans? He puts me in mind of my wife's little dog, who starts the big ones fighting, and does nothing himself but yap.'

Heromenes, who had extravagant tastes as such things went on the border, said, 'He's sent a sweetener.'

'Birdlime. We must send it back. You should learn to judge a horse, then you'd not owe the copers. Don't you value our heads at more than a bag of Persian darics? The real price, the worth of the risk, that's not his to give.'

'That we could take for ourselves, said Heromenes resentfully, 'with Philip out of the way. What ails you, man; are you head of the clan, or our big sister? We're offered our father's kingdom back, and all you can do is cluck like some wet-nurse when the child starts walking.'

'She keeps it from breaking its head. Who says we could do it? An Athenian who ran like a goat at the smell of blood. Darius; a usurper barely settled on his throne, who has enough on his hands without a war. Do you think they care for us? And more, do you think *they* know whom we'd have to deal with, in Philip's room? Of course not; they think he's a spoiled little prince given credit for other men's victories. The Athenian's forever saying it in speeches. But we know. *We've* seen the lad at work. Sixteen he was then, with a head on him like thirty; and that's three years gone. It's not a month since I was at Pella; and I tell you, disgrace or not, put him in the field and the men will follow him anywhere. That you can take from me. Can we fight the royal army? You know the answer. So, is he in the business, as this man says, or not? That's the only question. These Athenians, they'd sell their mothers to the stews if the price was right. Everything hangs on the lad, and we've no proof.'

Heromenes tweaked a bit of broom from its roots between the stones, and switched it moodily. Alexandros frowned at the eastern hills.

'Two things I don't like,' he went on. 'First, he has bosom friends in exile, some no further than Epiros. We could have met in the mountains and no one the wiser; we'd all know then where we were. Why send this go-between, a man I've never seen about him, why trust the man with his head? And the other thing I mislike is that he promises too much. You've met him. Think.'

'We should think first,' said Arrabaios, 'whether he's one who could do it. Not all men could. I think he could. And he's at a pass when he might.'

'And if he's a bastard as they say,' urged Heromenes, 'then it's a dangerous business, but not blood-cursed. I think he could and would.'

'I still say it doesn't smell of him,' said Alexandros. Absently he scratched a louse out of his head, and rubbed it between thumb and finger. 'Now, if it were his dam . . .'

'Dam or whelp, you can be sure they're in it together,' Heromenes said.

'We don't know that. What we do know is, the new wife's with child again. And they say Philip's giving his daughter as a sop to the Epirote King, so that he'll stomach the witch being packed off. So, think which of them can't afford to wait. Alexander can. Philip's seed tends to girls, as everyone knows. Even if Eurydike throws a boy, let the King say what he likes while he lives, but if he dies, the Macedonians won't accept an heir under fighting age; *he* should know that. But Olympias, now, that's another matter. *She* can't wait. Scratch into this deep enough, and I'll stake my best horse you'll find her hand in it.'

'If I thought it came from *her*,' said Arrabaios, 'then I'd think twice.'

'This lad's only nineteen,' said Heromenes. 'If Philip dies now, with no other son besides the lackwit, then *you*' – he stabbed his finger at Alexandros – 'are next in line. Couldn't you see that's what the fellow down there was trying to tell you?'

'O Herakles!' said Alexandros, snorting again. 'Who are you to talk of lackwits? Nineteen, and you saw him at sixteen. Since then, he has led the left at Chaironeia. Go to Assembly, will you, and tell them he's a child too young for war, they must vote for a grown man. Do you think I would live to get there and count my votes? You had better stop dreaming, and look at the man you have to deal with.'

'I am looking,' said Arrabaios. 'That's why I said he has it in him to do this business. Bastard or not.'

'You say he can afford to wait.' Heromenes' blue eyes in his wine-reddened face stared with contempt at Alexandros, whose place he envied. 'Some men can't wait for power.'

'I only say, ask yourself who gains most. Olympias gains everything, because this match will lose her everything, if the King outlives it. Demosthenes gains the blood of the man he hates worse than death, if he hates anything worse; the Athenians gain a civil war in Macedon, if we play our part, with the kingship in doubt, or passed to a boy they make light of, the more since he's in disfavour. Darius, whose gold you want to keep even if it hangs you, gains even more, since Philip's arming for war against him now. Out of them all, not one would care a dog's turd, once the thing's done, if we're all three crucified in a row. Yet you put your bet on Alexander. No wonder you can't win at a cockfight.'

They milled it over a little longer. In the end, they agreed to refuse the go-between and return the gold. But Heromenes had debts, and a younger son's portion; he agreed unwillingly; and it was he who set the guest on his way to the eastern pass.

The scent of raw warm blood mixed with the cool scents of a dewy morning, of pine-resin and wild thyme and some little upland lily. Tall dogs as heavy as men gnawed contentedly at deer-bones; now and then strong teeth would split one with a crack, to reach the marrow. The dead stag's sad empty face lolled on the grass. Over an aromatic fire, two of the hunters were grilling steaks for breakfast; the rest had gone looking for a stream. Two servants rubbed-down the horses.

On a rock-ledge cropping out from small-flowered turf, Hephaistion sprawled beside Alexander in the early sun, seen on the skyline by the rest, but far out of hearing. So, in Homer, Achilles and Patroklos had drawn apart from their dear comrades to share their thoughts. But it had been Patroklos' ghost who recalled it, when they shared their grief; so Alexander thought the lines bad luck, and never quoted them. He had been talking of other things.

'It was like a dark labyrinth,' he said, 'with a monster waiting. Now it is daylight.'

'You should have talked before.' Hephaistion drew his reddened hand over a patch of wet moss, to wash off the blood.

'It would only have burdened you. As it was, you knew, and it did.'

'Yes. So why not have talked it out?'

'It would have been cowardice, then. A man must deal with his own daimon. When I look back on my life, I remember it always there, waiting at every crossroads, where I knew that I would meet it. From the time when I was a child. Even the wish, never acted, the wish alone, was a terrible thing to carry. Sometimes I would dream of the Eumenides, as they are in Aischylos; they would touch my neck with their long cold black claws, saying, "One day you will be ours for ever." For it drew me on, by the very horror of it; some men say that standing on a cliff, they feel the void is drawing them. It seemed my destiny.'

'I have known this a long time. I am your destiny too; did you forget?'

'Oh, we have spoken of it often, without words, and that was better. Things are fixed by words, as fire fixes clay. So I went on; sometimes I thought I could be free of it, then I would doubt again. All that is over, now it's been revealed to me what my true birth is. Once I knew he was no kin to me. I began to think what should be done. And from that moment, my thought was clear. Why do it? To what end? Why now? From what necessity?'

'I tried to say all this.'

'I know; but my ear was closed. It was more than the man himself oppressing me. It was the god's "You may not" stifling my soul's "I must". And the thought of his blood in me, like a sickness. Now I'm free of it, I hate him less. Well, the god delivered me. If I meant to do it, no time could be worse than now, at this ebb-tide of my fortune, with the tide ready to turn. He won't leave me regent here, when he goes to Asia; I'm in disgrace, and besides I doubt he'd dare. He's bound to take me to the war. Once I'm in the field, I hope I can show him something, and the Macedonians too. They were glad enough of me at Chaironeia. If he lives, he'll change to me when I've won some battles for him. And if he falls, I'm the man who will be there, with the army round me. That above all.'

His eye was caught by a small blue flower in a rock-crevice. Delicately he raised his head, named it, and added the use of its decoction for coughs.

'Of course,' he said, 'I shall kill Attalos as soon as I can do it. It will be best in Asia.'

Hephaistion nodded; he himself, at nineteen, had long lost count of men he had already killed. 'Yes, he's your mortal enemy; you'll have to get rid of *him*. The girl's nothing then, the King will find another as soon as he's on campaign.'

'I told Mother that, but ... Well, she must think as she chooses, I mean to act in my own time. She's a wronged woman, it's natural she should want revenge; though of course that's what has set the King on getting her out of the kingdom before he leaves, and it's done *me* harm enough ... She'll intrigue to the last, she can't help it, it's become her life. There's some business now, she keeps hinting she wants to drag me into; but I forbade her even to tell me.' Arrested by this new tone, Hephaistion stole a sidelong glance. 'I have to think and plan. I can't be thrown out from day to day by these fits and starts. She must understand it.'

'It eases her mind, I suppose,' said Hephaistion, whose own was eased. (So she made her conjuration, and the wrong spirit answered; I should like to know her thoughts.) 'Well, the wedding can't but be a day of honour for her; her daughter and her brother. Whatever the King may feel, or mean to do, he'll have to give her her dignities then, for the bridegroom's sake. So he must give you yours.'

'Oh, yes. But it's to be his own day mainly. Memory and history both surpassed. Aigai's teeming already with craftsmen; and the invitations have gone out so far afield, I only wonder he hasn't sent to the Hyperboreans. Never mind, it's something to be lived through, before we cross to Asia. Then it will seem like *that*.' He pointed to the plain below, and the flocks tiny with distance.

'Yes, it will be nothing then. You've already founded a city; but there you'll find yourself a kingdom. I know as if a god had told me.'

Alexander smiled at him; sat up, and with hands clasped round knees looked towards the next range of mountains. Wherever he was, he could never keep his eyes long from the skyline. 'Do you remember, in Herodotos, where the Ionians sent Aristagoras to the Spartans, begging them to come and free the Greek cities of Asia? They cried off, when they heard Susa was three months' march from the sea. Farm dogs, not hunting-dogs ... That's enough, now. Down.' A year-old deerhound, which had just tracked him there by scent after getting loose from the huntsman, ceased its caresses and lay obediently, pressing its nose against him. He had had it in Illyria as a pup, and had spent his spare hours in training it; its name was Peritas.

'Aristogoras,' he said, 'brought them a map on bronze, of the whole world with the encircling ocean, and showed them the Persian empire.

Truly the task is not hard; for the barbarians are people unfit for war, while you are the best and bravest men on earth. (Perhaps it was true in those days.) *This is how they fight: They use bows and arrows and a short spear, they take the field in trousers, and cover their heads with turbans* (not if they can afford a helmet); *that shows how easy they are to conquer. I tell you, too, that the people of those regions have more wealth than all the rest of the world together.* (Now that is true.) *Gold, silver and bronze; embroidered garments; asses, mules and slaves; you can own it all, if you choose.* He goes over the nations with his map, till he gets to Kissia by the River Choaspes. *And on its banks the city of Susa, where the Great King holds court, and where the treasuries are, in which his wealth is stored. Once you are lords of this city, you may challenge Zeus himself to surpass your riches.* He reminded the Spartans how they were always at war around their borders, over bits of poor land, against men who owned nothing worth a battle. Do you need to do that, he said to them, when you might be lords of Asia? They kept him waiting three days, then said it was too far from the sea.'

A horn blew from the cook-fire, to say breakfast was ready. Alexander gazed at the mountains. However hungry he was, he never hurried to food.

'Only Susa. They didn't let him even begin to talk about Persepolis.'

Anywhere along Armourers' Street at Piraeus, the port of Athens, it was hard to make oneself heard above a shout. The shops were open in front, to let out the heat of the forges and show the work. These were not the cheap off-the-peg factories with their hordes of slaves; here the best craftsmen made to measure, from clay moulds of the naked client. Half a morning might go to a fitting, and to choosing from pattern-books the inlaid design. Only a few of the shops made armour meant for war; the most fashionable catered for knights who wanted to be noticed in the Panathenaic procession. They would bring all their friends along, if they could stand the noise; comings and goings were little noticed. In the rooms above the shops, the din was hardly muted; but men could just hear each other speak, if they kept close together; and it was well known that armourers grew hard of hearing, which lessened the fear of eavesdroppers.

In one of these rooms, a conference was going on. It was a meeting of agents. None of the principals could have been seen with any of the others, even had it been possible for all of them to attend. Three men of the four were leaning over an olive-wood table on their folded arms. The feet of their wine-cups rattled to the pounding of the hammers that shook the floor; the wine shivered, sometimes a drop leaped out.

The three who were talking had reached the last stages of a long wrangle about money. One was from Chios; his olive pallor and blue-black beard derived from the long Median occupation. One was an Illyrian, from close to the Lynkestid border. The third, the host, was an Athenian; he wore his hair tied over his brow in a topknot, and his face was discreetly painted.

The fourth man sat back in his chair, his hands on the pinewood arms, waiting for them to have done; his face seeming to say that to tolerate such things was part of his commission. His fair hair and beard had a tinge of red; he was from north Euboia, which had long had commerce with Macedon.

On the table was a wax diptych tablet, and a stylos, the sharp end to write, the flat end to erase what had been written, in the presence of all four parties, before they left the room. The Athenian tapped it impatiently on the table, then on his teeth.

The Chian said, 'It is not as if these gifts were to be the end of Darius' friendship. As I say, Heromenes can always count on a place at court.'

'He is seeking,' said the Illyrian, 'to rise in Macedon, not to prepare for exile. I thought that was understood.'

'Certainly. A generous earnest has been agreed on.' The Chian looked at the Athenian, who nodded, drooping his lids. 'The bulk sum to follow a revolt in Lynkestis as arranged. I am not satisfied that his brother, the chief, has agreed to this. I must stand out for payment by result.'

'Reasonable,' said the Athenian, taking the stylos from his mouth. He had a slight lisp. 'Now do let us take all that as settled, and come back to the man who matters most. My principal wants an undertaking that he will act on the day agreed – no other.'

This brought the Euboian leaning across the table, like the rest. 'You said that before, and I answered that there's no sense in it. He is always about Philip's person. He has entry to the bedchamber. He might have far better chances, both to do it and to get away. This is asking too much of him.'

'My instructions are,' said the Athenian, tapping the stylos on the table, 'that it shall be that day, or we will not offer him asylum.'

The Euboian thumped the already rattling table, making the Athenian shut his eyes protestingly. 'Why, tell me? Why?'

'Yes, why?' said the Illyrian. 'Heromenes doesn't ask for it. The news could reach him anytime.'

The man from Chios raised his dark brows. 'Any day will do for *my* master. If Philip does not cross to Asia, it is enough. Why this insistence on the day?'

The Athenian lifted the stylos by both ends, rested his chin on it, and smiled confidingly.

'First, because on that day every possible claimant to the throne, and

every faction, will be there at Aigai for the rites. Not one can escape
suspicion; they will accuse each other, and very likely fight for the succession; this will be of use to us. Secondly, ... I think my principal deserves
some small indulgence. It will crown his life-work, as anyone aware of his
life can see. He finds it fitting that the tyrant of Hellas be brought down,
not some dark night as he stumbles drunk to bed, but at the climax of his
hubris; in this I agree, let me say.' He turned to the Euboian. 'And, your
man's wrongs being what they are, I should suppose it would please him
too.'

'Yes,' said the Euboian slowly. 'No doubt. But it may not be possible.'

'It will be possible. The order of the ceremonies has just come into our
hands.' He detailed them, till he reached a certain event, when he looked
up meaningly.

'Your ears are good,' said the Euboian, raising his brows.

'This time you may rely on them.'

'I daresay. But our man would be lucky to come off well out of that. As
I say, he could get better chances.'

'None so distinguished. Fame sweetens vengeance ... Well, well, since
we are speaking of fame, I will let you into a little secret. My principal
wants to be first with the news in Athens, even before the news arrives.
Between ourselves, he plans to have had a vision. Later, when Macedon
has sunk back to its tribal barbarism – ' He caught the Euboian's angry
eye, and said hastily, 'That is, has passed to a King who is prepared to stay
at home – then he can proclaim to a grateful Greece his share in the
liberation. Meantime, when one remembers his long battle against
tyranny, can one grudge him this small reward?'

'What risk is *he* taking?' shouted the Illyrian suddenly. Though the
hammers below were noisy, it startled the others into angry gestures,
which he ignored. 'Here's a man risking death to avenge his honour. And
only Demosthenes must choose the time, so that he can prophesy in the
Agora.'

The three diplomats exchanged looks of scandal and disgust. Who but
a backwoodsman of Lynkestis would have sent this rude clansman to
such a conference? There was no knowing what he might say next, so they
broke up the meeting. All that mattered had been determined.

Each left the building separately, with a little time between. The last left
were the Chian and the Euboian. The Chian said, 'Can you be sure your
man will do his part?'

'Oh yes,' said the Euboian. 'We know how to manage that.'

'You were there? You yourself heard it?'

The spring night blew chilly in the hills of Macedon. The torches smoked with the window-draught, the embers of the sacred hearth faded and flickered on their old blackened stone drum. It was late. As the shadows deepened above, the stone walls seemed to lean inward, craning to hear.

The guests had departed, all but one; the slaves had been sent to bed. The host and his son had drawn three couches close round one wine-table; the others, shoved aside in haste, gave the room a disordered look.

'Do you tell me,' said Pausanias again, 'that you were there?' His head and shoulders were thrust forward; he had to grasp the edge of the couch to keep his balance. His eyes were bloodshot with wine; but what he had just heard had sobered him. His host's son met his gaze; a youngish man with expressive blue eyes, and a mean mouth under his short black beard.

'The wine tripped my tongue,' he answered. 'I'll say no more.'

'I ask pardon for him,' said his father, Deinias. 'What possessed you, Heirax? I tried to catch your eye.'

Pausanias turned like a speared boy. '*You* knew of it too?'

'I was not present,' said the host, 'but people talk. I am sorry it should be here in my house that it reached your ears. Even between themselves in secret, you would think both the King and Attalos would be ashamed to boast of such a thing; much more in company. But you know, none better, what they're like when they've had a skinful.'

Pausanias' nails dug at the wood, so that the blood receded. 'He took his oath before me, eight years ago, never to let it be spoken of in his presence. It was that persuaded me to forego vengeance. He knew it, I told him so.'

'Then he was not forsworn,' said Heirax with a sour smile. 'He didn't let it be said, he said it. He thanked Attalos for the good service. When Attalos would have answered, he clapped a hand across his mouth, and they both laughed at that. Now I understand it.'

'He swore to me by the stream of Acheron,' said Pausanias, almost whispering, 'that he had no foreknowledge of it.'

Deinias shook his head. 'Heirax, I take back my rebuke. When so many know, it is better Pausanias hears of it first from friends.'

'He said to me' – Pausanias' voice was thickening – '"In a few years, when you are seen to be held in honour, they will doubt the tale; then they will forget it."'

'So much for oaths,' said Deinias, 'when men feel themselves secure.'

'Attalos is secure,' said Heirax easily. 'Safe with his troops in Asia.'

Pausanias stared past them into the dulling red core upon the hearth. Speaking, it seemed, to that, he said, 'Does he think it is too late?'

'If you like,' said Kleopatra to her brother, 'you may see my dress.'

He followed to her room, where it hung on a T-shaped stand, fine saffron-dyed linen embroidered with jewelled flowers. She was to blame for nothing; soon they would seldom meet again; he gave her waist a pat. In spite of all, the coming pomps began to charm her; shoots of pleasure broke through, like green on a burnt hillside; she began to feel she would be a queen.

'Look, Alexander.' She lifted from its cushion the bridal wreath, wheat-ears and olive sprays worked from fine gold, and walked towards the mirror.

'No! Don't try it on. That's very unlucky. But you will look beautiful.' She had shed most of her puppy-fat, and showed promise of some distinction.

'I hope we shall soon go up to Aigai. I want to see the decorations; when the crowds arrive, one can't go about. Have you heard, Alexander, about the great procession to the theatre, to dedicate the Games? They're to be offered to all the twelve Olympians, and the images are to be carried – '

'Not twelve,' said Alexander drily. 'Thirteen. Twelve Olympians, and divine Philip. But he's modest, his image is going last ... Listen; what's that noise?'

They ran to the window. A party had dismounted from its mules, and was grouping formally, to approach the Palace. The men were crowned with bay, and the leader carried a branch of it.

Sliding down from the sill, Alexander said eagerly, 'I must go. Those are the heralds from Delphi, with the oracle about the war.' He kissed her briskly, and turned to the doorway. In it, just entering, was his mother.

Kleopatra saw her glance pass by, and the old bitterness stirred once more. Alexander, who received the glance, knew it of old. It called him to a secret.

'I can't stay now, Mother. The heralds are here from Delphi.' Seeing her mouth open, he added quickly, 'I've a right to be there. We don't want that forgotten.'

'Yes, you had better go.' She held out her hands to him, and, as he kissed her, began to whisper. He drew back saying, 'Not now, I shall be late,' and loosened her hands. She said after him, 'But we must talk today.'

He went without sign of hearing it. She felt Kleopatra's watching eyes, and answered them with some small business of the wedding; there had been many such moments, over many years. Kleopatra thought of them, but held her peace. Long before Alexander could be a king, she thought, if he ever was one, she would be a queen.

In the Perseus Room, the chief diviners, the priests of Apollo and of Zeus, Antipatros, and everyone whom rank or office entitled to be there, had assembled to hear the oracle delivered. The heralds from Delphi stood before the dais. Alexander, who had run the first part of the way, made a slow entrance and stood at the right of the throne, arriving just before the King. Nowadays he had to manage such things for himself.

There was a pause of whispering expectation. This was a royal embassy. Not for the swarming petitioners about marriages and land-purchases and sea journeys and offspring, who could be dealt with by drawing lots, but for this single question, the grey-haired Pythia had gone into the smoky cave below the temple, mounted the tripod beside the Navel Stone swathed in its magic nets, chewed her bitter laurel, breathed the vapour from the rock-cleft, and uttered her god-crazed mutterings before the shrewd-eyed priest who would interpret them in verse. Old fateful legends drifted like mist from mind to mind. Those of more stolid temper awaited some stock response, advice to sacrifice to the proper gods, or to dedicate a shrine.

The King limped in, was saluted, and sat down, his stiff leg pushed forward. Now he could exercise less, he had begun to put on weight; there was new solid flesh on his square frame, and Alexander, standing behind, saw that his neck had thickened.

There were the ritual exchanges. The chief herald unrolled his scroll.

'Pythian Apollo, to Philip son of Amyntas, King of the Macedonians, answers thus: *Wreathed is the bull for the altar, the end fulfilled. And the slayer too is ready.*'

The company pronounced the well-omened phrases prescribed for such occasions. Philip nodded to Antipatros, who nodded back with relief. Parmenion and Attalos were having trouble on the coast of Asia, but now the main force would set out with good augury. There was a satisfied hum. A favourable answer had been expected; the god had much to thank King Philip for. But it was only to greatly honoured ones, the courtiers murmured, that Two-Tongued Apollo spoke with so clear a voice.

'I have put myself in his way,' Pausanias said. 'But I have had no sign from him. Courteous, yes; but then he always was. From a child he knew the story. I used to see it in his eyes. But he gives no sign. Why not, if all this is true?'

Deinias shrugged and smiled. He had feared this moment. Had Pausanias been prepared to throw his life away, he could have done it eight years before. A man in love with vengeance wanted to outlive his enemy, and taste the sweet on his tongue. This Deinias had known, and it was prepared for.

'Surely that does not surprise you? Such things have a way of being seen, and remembered later. You may rest assured that you will be watched over like a friend; subject of course to a good appearance. Look.

I have brought you something which will set your mind at rest.' He opened
his hand.

Pausanias, peering, said, 'One ring is much like another.'

'Look well at this one. Tonight, at supper, you will be able to look again.'

'Yes,' Pausanias said. 'With that I would be satisfied.'

'Why,' Hephaistion exclaimed, 'you're wearing your lion ring. Where
was it? We looked everywhere.'

'Simon found it in my clothes-chest. I must have run my hand through
the clothes, and dragged it off.'

'I looked there myself.'

'I suppose it lodged in a fold.'

'You don't think he stole it, and then took fright?'

'Simon? He'd have more sense, everyone knows it's mine. It's a lucky
day, it seems.'

He meant that Eurydike had just been delivered of her child; it was
another girl.

'May God fulfil the good omen,' Hephaistion said.

They went down to supper. Alexander paused to greet Pausanias by the
entry. From so grim-faced a man, it was always a small triumph to win
a smile.

It was the dark before dawn. The old theatre at Aigai glowed with
cressets and flambeaux. Small torches flitted like fireflies, as stewards
guided guests to their places on the cushioned benches. The light breeze
from the mountain forests picked up the smells of burning pine-resin and
packed humanity.

Down in the round orchestra were set in a circle the twelve altars of the
Olympians. Fires glowed on them, sweetened with incense, lighting up the
robes of their heirophants, and the strong bodies of the sacrificers with
their shining cleavers. From the fields beyond came the lowing and
bleating of the victims, restless at the stir and torchlight, wreathed already
in their garlands. Above the rest rose the bellow of King Zeus' white bull
with his gilded horns.

On the stage, its ornate setting still dim with dusk, the King's throne
was set, flanked with state chairs for his new son-in-law, and his son.

In the upper tiers were the athletes, the charioteers, the singers and
musicians who would compete in the Games when the coming rite had
hallowed them. With these, and the multitude of the King's invited guests,
the small theatre was packed full. The soldiers and peasants, the tribesmen
ridden in from the hills to see the show, trampled and stirred on the dusky
hillside around the scooped shell of the theatre, or thronged the proces-

sional way. Voices rose and fell and shifted, like waves on a shingle beach. The pine-trees, standing black in the eastward glimmer, creaked under their load of boys.

The old rough road to the theatre had been levelled and widened for the great procession. Laid by the mountain dews, the dust smelled sweet in the sharp daybreak air. Soldiers detailed to clear the route came with torches; the jostling was good-humoured, shover and shoved being often fellow-tribesmen. The torches were extinguished in the lift of a cloudless clear summer dawn.

As pink touched the peaks beyond the Aigai ledge, the splendours of the parade way glimmered into view; the tall scarlet masts with their gilt finials of lion or eagle, the long streaming banners; the festoons of flowers and ribboned ivy; the triumphal arch carved and painted with the Exploits of Herakles, and topped with a Victory holding out her gilded bays. On either side of her stood two live golden-haired boys robed as Muses, with trumpets in their hands.

In the castle forecourt on the ancient stone acropolis, Philip stood in a purple cloak clasped with gold, crowned with a golden laurel-wreath. His head was turned into the light early breeze. Bird-song, the tweeting and twanging of instruments tuning-up, voices of spectators and of marshals giving orders, came to him backed by the bass roar of the Aigai falls. His gaze traversed the plain that stretched east to Pella and the dawn-mirroring sea. His pasture lay lush and green before him; his rivals' horns were broken. His wide nostrils snuffed the rich friendly air.

Behind him, in a scarlet tunic and jewelled sword-belt, Alexander stood beside the bridegroom. His bright hair, freshly washed and combed, was crowned with a garland of summer flowers. Half the states of Greece had sent the King wrought-gold wreaths as gifts of honour; but none had been passed to him.

Round the forecourt were ranged the men of the royal bodyguard, ready to form the escort. Pausanias, their commander, was pacing about before the lines. Those in his path would dress ranks anxiously, or fidget with their equipment; then stand easier, aware that he had not looked at them.

On the north rampart, among her women, was the bride, just risen from her marriage bed. She had had no pleasure in it; but she had been ready for worse. He had been decent, not very drunk, much aware of her youth and maidenhood, and not really old. She no longer feared him. Craning over the rough stone parapet, she saw the long snake of the procession forming along the walls. Beside her, her mother stared down into the courtyard; her lips were moving, a faint murmur of breath came out. Kleopatra did not try to hear the words. She felt the sorcery, like heat from a covered fire. But it was time to set out for the theatre, their litters were ready. Soon she would be on her wedding journey; such things would no longer matter. Even if Olympias came to Epiros, Alexandros would know how to deal with it. It was something after all, to have a husband.

The Muses' trumpets blew. Under the Victory arch, to shouts of wonder, the Twelve Gods passed in progress to their altars. Each float was drawn by matched horses, caparisoned in red and gold. The wooden images were carved god-size, seven feet tall, and had been tinted by the Athenian master who coloured for Apelles.

King Zeus enthroned, with staff and eagle, had been copied in little from the giant Zeus at Olympia, his throne gilded, his robe stiff with gems and bullion. Apollo was robed as a musician, with a gold lyre. Poseidon rode in a sea-horse chariot. Demeter sat crowned with gold corn, between mystai holding torches. Queen Hera had her peacocks; wits remarked that King Zeus' consort came rather far down the line. Virgin Artemis, bow at shoulder, held a kneeling stag by the horns. Dionysos rode nude on a spotted panther. Athene had her shield and helmet, but not her Attic owl. Hephaistos wielded his hammer; Ares, his foot on a prone foe, glared under his crested helmet; Hermes laced a winged sandal. Clad in a narrow drift of veil, a little Eros beside her, Aphrodite sat in a flowered chair. It was observed, in undertones, that she had a look of Eurydike. She was still in the lying-in room, she would not appear today.

The last float of the twelve received its fanfare. The thirteenth float came on.

King Philip's image had an eagle-headed throne with couchant leopards for arms. His feet rested on a winged bull with a Persian tiara and the face of a man. The artist had trimmed down his figure, left out his scars, and put back his age ten years. Allowing for this, he was very lifelike; one almost expected movement from the black painted eyes.

There were cheers; but like a cold current in warm seas, there could be felt a flaw of silence. One old countryman murmured to another, 'He ought to have been made smaller.' They looked askance at the line of jolting gods ahead, and made ancient averting signs.

The chiefs of Macedon followed, Alexandros of Lynkestis and the rest. It was seen that even those from the back hills wore good loom-woven wool with border-work, and a gold brooch. Old folk recalled days of sheepskin cloaks, when bronze pins were riches; their tongues clucked between doubt and wonder.

To the beat of deep-toned pipes playing a Dorian march, came the van of the Royal Guard, Pausanias leading. The men swaggered in their parade armour, smiling at friends in the crowd; a feast-day did not demand the sternness of manoeuvres. But Pausanias looked straight on, at the tall doorway of the theatre.

There was a blare of archaic horns, and cries of 'May the King live!'

Philip paced on a white horse, in his purple cloak and gold olive crown. Half a length behind, at either side, rode his son-in-law and his son.

The peasants made good-luck phallic signs at the bridegroom, and wished him offspring. But by the arch, a troop of young men, who had been waiting with filled lungs, yelled together, 'Alexander!'

He turned his head smiling, and looked at them with love. Long after, when they were generals and satraps, they would boast of it to silence envy.

The rear of the bodyguard came after; then, finishing the procession, the victims for the sacrifice, one for each god, led by the bull with a garland around his dewlaps, and gold foil on his horns.

The sun floated up from its nets of light; everything glittered; the sea, the dewy grass, crystal cobwebs on yellow broom; the jewels, the gilding, the cool gleam of the burnished bronze.

The gods had entered the theatre. Through the tall gateway of the parodos, the cars drove round the orchestra one by one; the guests applauded; the resplendent images were lifted off, and put on bases near their altars. The thirteenth deity, who claimed no shrine but owned the precinct, was set down in the middle.

Outside in the road, the King made a sign. Pausanias barked an order. The van of the Royal Guard wheeled smartly left and right, and fell back on the rearguard, behind the King.

The theatre was some hundred yards away. The chiefs, looking back, saw the Guard retire. The King, it seemed, had entrusted himself to them for this last lap of his progress. Pleased by the compliment, they opened their ranks for him.

Noticed only by his own men, who thought it none of their business, Pausanias strode on towards the parodos.

Philip saw the chiefs waiting. He walked his horse up to them, from the standing ranks of the Guard, and leaned down smiling. 'Go on in, my friends. I shall come after.'

They began moving; but one elderly laird stood planted by his bridle, and said with Macedonian forthrightness, 'No guard, King? In all this crowd?'

Philip leaned down and clapped his shoulder. He had been hoping someone would say it. 'My people are guard enough. Let all these foreigners see it. Thanks for your kindness, Areus; but go on in.'

As the chiefs went forward, he slowed his horse, falling back between the bridegroom and Alexander. From the crowd each side came a buzz of friendly voices. Ahead was the theatre, packed with friends. His broad mouth smiled; he had looked forward to this moment of public proof. An

elected King, whom these southerners had dared call tyrant; let them see
for themselves if he needed the tyrant's square of spearmen. Let them tell
Demosthenes, he thought.

He reined up and beckoned. Two servants came up to the younger men,
and stood ready to hold their horses. 'You now, my sons.'

Alexander, who had been watching the chiefs go in, looked sharply
round. 'Are we not to go with you?'

'No,' Philip said crisply. 'Weren't you told? I go in alone.'

The bridegroom looked away, to hide his embarrassment. Were they
going to bicker over precedence now, before everyone? The last of the
chiefs was going through out of sight. He could not walk over by himself.

Sitting upright on Oxhead's scarlet saddle-cloth, Alexander looked
along the stretch of empty road, empty in sunlight; wide, trampled, wheel-
rutted, hoof-marked; ringing with emptiness. At its end, in the triangle of
deep shadow thrown by the parados, was a gleam of armour, a line of red
cloak. If Pausanias was there, he must have his orders?

Oxhead pricked up his ears. His eye, bright as onyx, looked sideways;
Alexander touched his neck with a finger; he stood like bronze. The
bridegroom fidgeted. Why would the youth not move? There were times
when one could understand the rumours. It was something about the
eyes. There had been a day at Dodona; a bitter wind, a fall of snow lying,
he wore a sheepskin cloak ...

'Get down then,' said Philip impatiently. 'Your brother-in-law is
waiting.'

Alexander glanced again at the dark gateway. He pressed with his knee,
bringing Oxhead nearer, and looked with deep concentration into Philip's
face.

'It is too far,' he said quietly. 'It's better if I go with you.'

Philip raised his brows under his gold garland. It was clear enough now
what the lad was after. Well, he had not earned it yet; let him not push
for it. 'That is my business. I will be judge of what is best.'

The deep-shadowed eyes reached for his. He felt invaded. From any
subject, it was an affront to stare at the King.

'It is too far,' said the high clear voice, inexpressive, steady. 'Let me go
in with you, and I will pledge my life for yours ... I swear it to you by
Herakles.'

Faint, curious murmurs began to be heard among the bystanders,
aware of something unplanned. Philip, though growing angry, was careful of his face. Keeping down his voice, he said sharply, 'That is enough.
We are not going to the theatre to act in tragedy. When I need you I will
tell you so. Obey my orders.'

Alexander's eyes ceased their quest. His presence left them; they were as empty as clear grey glass. 'Very well, sir,' he said. He dismounted; Alexandros followed with relief.

Pausanias in the tall gateway saluted as they came. Alexander returned it in passing, while he spoke to Alexandros. They ascended the short ramp to the stage, acknowledged the acclamations, and took their seats.

Outside, Philip touched his rein. With a stately gait, his well-trained charger went forward, undisturbed by noise. The people knew what the King was doing, admired it, and took care he heard. His anger passed; he had something better to think of. If the boy had chosen some more fitting time . . .

He rode on, acknowledging the cheers. He would sooner have walked, but his limp robbed it of dignity. Already, through the twenty-foot-high parodos, he could glimpse the orchestra with its ring of gods. The music had struck up for him.

From the stone gateway a soldier stepped forward, to help him down and take his horse. It was Pausanias. In honour of the day, he must have posted himself to this page's service. How long ago . . . It was a signal of reconcilement. At last he was ready to forget. A charming gesture. In the old days, he had had a gift for such acts of grace.

Philip slid stiffly down, smiled, and began to speak. Pausanias' left hand took his arm in a tightening grip. Their looks met. Pausanias brought out his right hand from his cloak, so swiftly that Philip never saw the dagger, except in Pausanias' eyes.

The guard up the road saw the King fall, and Pausanias stoop over him. His lame foot must have stumbled, the men thought, and Pausanias been clumsy. Suddenly Pausanias straightened up, and began to run.

He had been eight years in the Guard, and for five of them commanded it. A farmer among the crowd was the first to call out, 'He's killed the King!' As if given leave to credit their senses, with confused shouts the soldiers rushed towards the theatre.

An officer reached the body, stared at it, pointed wildly, and yelled, 'After him!' A stream of men poured round the corner, behind the back-stage buildings. The King's well-trained charger stood stolidly by the parodos. No one had thought fast enough to dare the outrage of mounting it.

A piece of land behind the theatre, sacred to Dionysos its guardian god, had been farmed by the priests with vines. The thick black old stocks were dappled with young shoots and bright green leaves. On the earth glinted Pausanias' helmet, flung away as he ran; his red cloak draped a vine-prop. He raced over the rough clods towards the old stone wall and its open gateway. Beyond it, a mounted man with a spare horse was waiting.

Pausanias was in hard training, and not yet thirty. But in the hunt were youths not yet twenty, who had learned mountain warfare with Alexander; they had trained still harder. Three or four drew out in front. The gap began to narrow.

It was narrowing too slowly, however. The gate was not far ahead. The man with the horses had turned their heads, ready, towards the open road.

Suddenly, as if an invisible spear had struck him, Pausanias hurtled forward. An arched knotted root had caught his toe. He fell flat; then rose on hands and knees, tugging free his booted foot. But the young men were on him.

He twisted over, looking from one to another, searching. No luck. But he had faced this chance from the first. He had cleansed his honour. He dragged at his sword; someone set a foot on his arm, another trod on his corselet. He had had no time to feel the pride of it, he thought as all the iron hacked down. No time.

The man with the horses, after one glance, had unhitched the spare one, lashed his own mount, and raced away. But the stunned pause was over. Hooves drummed on the road beyond the vines. The riders spurred after him through the gates, knowing the value of the prize.

In the vineyard, the press had caught up with the leading hunters. An officer looked down at the body bleeding, like some ancient sacrifice, into the roots of the vine-stock. 'You've finished him. You young fools. Now he can't be questioned.'

'I never thought of it,' said Leonnatos, the drunkenness of the blood-chase leaving him. 'I was afraid he'd still get away.'

'I only thought,' said Perdikkas, 'of what he'd done.' He wiped his sword on the dead man's kilt.

As they walked away, Aratos said to the others, 'Well, it's best. You know the story. If he'd talked, it could only disgrace the King.'

'What King?' asked Leonnatos. 'The King is dead.'

Hephaistion's seat was half-way up the theatre, near the centre steps.

The friends who had waited to cheer Alexander had run round, and scrambled in by an upper gate. These were peasants' seats as a rule; but Companions of the Prince were small fry in today's assembly. He had missed the grand entrance of the gods. His father was seated lower down; his mother would be among the women, in the far end block. The two Queens were already there, in the front row. He could see Kleopatra looking about at the sights, like the other girls; Olympias, it seemed, thought that beneath her. She was staring out fixedly, straight before her, towards the parodos on the other side.

It was out of Hephaistion's sight-line; but he was well-placed for the stage with its three thrones. It was magnificent; the back and wings had columns with carved capitals, supporting embroidered curtains. The music came from behind them, crowded out from the orchestra by so many gods.

He waited for Alexander, to give him another cheer; if they started it well, everyone would take it up. He would be better for that.

Here he came now, with the Epirote King. The cheer spread well through the theatre. Never mind the names being the same; he would know from the sound.

He knew, and smiled. Yes, it had done him good. This was a small theatre; Hephaistion had seen, when he came in, that he was not himself. In one of his dreams, a bad one, and glad to wake. What can one expect today? I'll see him after, if I can get near him before the Games. Everything will be simpler, when we cross to Asia.

Down in the orchestra, King Philip's effigy sat in its gilded throne, on a base swagged with laurel. The throne waiting on the stage was just the same. Cheers sounded from the road; the hidden music grew louder.

It reached a climactic flourish. There was a hiatus, the sense of a dropped cue. Suddenly, from the women's block where the tiers curved to face the parodos, came a shrill scream.

Alexander's head went round. His face, from which the strangeness had been passing, altered. He jumped from his throne and went swiftly downstage where he could see out past the wings. He was running down the ramps and through the orchestra, between priests, altars and gods, before the shouting began outside. His garland fell from his flying hair.

While the audience stirred and chattered, Hephaistion leaped down the steps to the half-way gallery, and began to race along it. The friends followed promptly; they had been trained not to waste time. Around the gallery, the young men with their speed and purpose were a spectacle in themselves, suspending panic till they had passed by. They reached the end steps that led down towards the parodos. These were choked already, with bewildered foreign guests from the lower tiers. Hephaistion shoved through with the ruthlessness of battle, elbowing, shouldering, butting. A fat man fell, tripping others; the stairs were jammed; the tiers were a confusion of people scrambling up or down. In the still centre of chaos, forsaken by their heirophants, the wooden gods in their circle turned all their eyes on the wooden King.

Unmoving as they, straight-backed on her carved chair of honour, ignoring her daughter clutching her arm and crying out to her, Queen Olympias sat staring out towards the parodos.

Hephaistion felt a red rage for anyone in his way. Not caring how he did it, his companions all left behind, he fought through to his goal.

Philip lay on his back, the hilt of the dagger standing out between his ribs. It was Celtic work, with an elaborate plaited pattern of inlaid silver. His white chiton was almost unstained; the blade sealed the wound. Alexander was bent above him, feeling for his heart. The King's blind eye was half-closed, the other turned up at the living eyes above him. His face was set in a stare of shock, and an astonished bitterness.

Alexander touched the lid of the open eye. It gave limply with his fingers, 'Father,' he said. 'Father, Father.'

He put his hand to the clammy brow. The gold crown slipped off, and fell with a brittle clink on the pavement. For a moment his face fixed, as if carved in marble.

The body stirred. The mouth parted, as if to speak. Alexander started forward; he raised the head between his hands, and leaned towards it. But only air came from the corpse, loosened by some spasm of lung or belly; a belch, with a little froth of blood.

Alexander drew back. Suddenly his face and his body changed. He said, as sharply as a battle-order, 'The King is dead.' He got to his feet and looked about him.

Someone called out, 'They caught him, Alexander, they cut him down.' The broad entry of the parodos was seen to be full of chiefs, unarmed for the feast, confusedly trying to form a protective wall.

'Alexander, we are here.' It was Alexandros of Lynkestis, pushing himself into prominence. He had found himself a panoply already. It fitted; it was his own. Alexander's head seemed to point, in silence, as sharply as a hunting dog's. 'Let us escort you to the citadel, Alexander; who can tell where the traitors are?'

Yes, who? thought Hephaistion; that man knows something. What was his armour ready for? Alexander was looking about the crowd; for the other brothers, Hephaistion thought. He was used to reading Alexander's thoughts in the back of his head.

'What is this?'

The press parted. Antipatros, having forced his way through a turmoil of scared guests, had reached Macedonians who at once made way for him. He had long been appointed sole Regent of Macedon, with effect from the royal army's leaving. Tall, garlanded, robed with restrained splendour, clad in authority, he looked about him. 'Where is the King?'

Alexander answered, 'Here.'

He held Antipatros' eyes a moment, then stepped back to show the body.

Antipatros bent, and rose. 'He is dead,' he said unbelievingly. 'Dead.' He passed his hand over his brow. It touched his festal wreath; with a gesture of dazed convention, he dropped it on the ground. 'Who – '

'Pausanias killed him.'

'Pausanias? After so long?' He stopped abruptly, discomposed by what he had said.

'Was he taken alive?' said Alexandros of Lynkestis, just too quickly.

Alexander delayed the answer, to watch his face. Then, 'I want the gates of the city closed, and the walls manned. No one to leave till I give the order.' He scanned the crowd. 'Alketas, your division. Post them now.'

The egg is hatched, thought Antipatros, and I was right. 'Alexander, you must be in danger here. Will you come up to the castle?'

'In good time. What are those men about?'

Outside, the second-in-command of the Royal Guard was trying to get them in hand, with the help of what junior officers he could find. But the soldiers had lost their heads entirely, and were listening to some of their number who cried out that they would all be accused of conspiracy in the murder. They turned with curses on the young men who had killed Pausanias; it would look as if they had needed to stop his mouth. The officers were trying vainly to shout them down.

Alexander stepped from the sharp blue shadow of the parodos into the cool brilliant early light. The sun had scarcely climbed since he had walked into the theatre. He vaulted up on the low wall by the gateway. The noise changed, and died down.

'Alexander!' said Antipatros sharply. 'Take care! Don't expose yourself.'

'Guard – by the right – form phalanx!'

The scuffling mass took shape, like a scared horse calmed by its rider.

'I honour your grief. But don't grieve like women. You did your duty; I know what your orders were. I myself heard them. Meleagros, an escort for the King's body. Bring him to the castle. The small audience room.' Seeing the man look about for some makeshift litter, he said, 'There is a bier behind the stage, with the things for tragedy.'

He stooped over the body, pulled out a fold from the purple cloak crumpled under it, and covered the face with its bitter eye. The men of the escort closed round their charge, hiding it from sight.

Stepping out before the silent ranks of the Guard, he said, 'Fall out, the men who struck down the murderer.'

Between pride and dread, they stood forth uncertainly.

'We owe you a debt. Don't fear it will be forgotten. Perdikkas.' His face smoothed with relief, the young man came forward. 'I left Oxhead in the road outside. Will you see him safe for me? Take a guard of four.'

'Yes, Alexander.' He went off in a blaze of gratitude.

There was a felt silence; Antipatros was looking oddly under his brows.

'Alexander. The Queen your mother is in the theatre. Had *she* not better have a guard?'

Alexander walked past him, and looked in through the parodos. He stood there in perfect stillness. There was a stir about the entry; the soldiers had found the tragic bier, ornately painted and draped with black. They set it down by Philip's body and heaved him on to it. The cloak fell from the face; the officer pulled down the eyelids and pressed them till they closed.

Alexander, motionless, stared on into the theatre. The crowd had gone, thinking it no place to loiter in. The gods remained. In some surge of tumult, Aphrodite had been toppled from her base, and lay awkward and stiff beside it. Flung clear in her fall, young Eros leaned on her fallen throne. King Philip's image sat stockily in its place, its painted eyes fixed on the empty tiers.

Alexander turned away. His colour had changed, but his voice was even. 'Yes; I see she is still there.'

'She must be in distress,' said Antipatros. He spoke without expression.

Alexander gazed at him thoughtfully. Presently, as if something had just chanced to catch his eye, he looked aside.

'You are right, Antipatros. She should be in the safest hands. So I shall be grateful if you, yourself, will escort her up to the citadel. Take what men you think sufficient.'

Antipatros' mouth opened. Alexander waited, his head tilted slightly, his eyes unwavering. Antipatros said, 'If you wish, Alexander,' and went upon his errand.

There was a moment's lull. From his place in the crowd, Hephaistion came out a little, signalling no message, only offering his presence, as his omens prompted him. No message was returned; yet between one step and the next, he saw God thanked for him. His own destiny, too, was opening out before him, in unmeasured vistas of sun and smoke. He would not look back wherever it should take him; his heart accepted it with all its freight, the bright and the dark.

The officer of the bearer party gave an order. King Philip on his gilded bier jogged round the corner. From the sacred vineyard, borne on a hurdle and covered with his torn cloak, his blood dripping through the plaited withies, some troopers brought Pausanias. He too would have to be shown before the people. Alexander said, 'Prepare a cross.'

The noises had died to a restless hum, mingled with the roar of the Aigai falls. Lifting above it his strong unearthly cry, a golden eagle swooped over. In its talons was a lashing snake, snatched from the rocks. Each head lunged for the other, seeking in vain the mortal stroke. Alexander, his ear caught by the sound, gazed up intently, to see the outcome of the fight. But, still in combat, the two antagonists spired up into the cloudless sky, above the peaks of the mountains; became a speck in the dazzle, and were lost to sight.

'All is done here,' he said, and gave orders to march up to the citadel.

As they reached the ramparts which overlooked the Pella plain, the new summer sun stretched out its glittering pathway across the eastern sea.

Author's Note

All records of Alexander by his own contemporaries have perished. We depend on histories compiled three or four centuries later from this lost material, which sometimes gives references, sometimes not. Arrian's main source was the Ptolemy of this story, but Arrian's work opens only at Alexander's accession. Curtius' early chapters have disappeared; Diodoros, who covers the right time and tells us much of Philip, says little of Alexander before his reign begins. For these first two decades, nearly two thirds of his life, the only extant source is Plutarch, with a few retrospective allusions in the other histories. Plutarch does not cite Ptolemy for this section of the Life; he would have been a first-hand witness, so he probably did not cover it.

Plutarch's account has here been set against its historical background. I have used, with due scepticism, the speeches of Demosthenes and Aischines. Some anecdotes of Philip and Alexander have been taken from Plutarch's *Sayings of Kings and Commanders;* a few from Athenaeus.

I have inferred the age at which Alexander entertained the Persian envoys from their recorded surprise that his questions were not childish. On the character of Leonidas, and his searching the boy's boxes for his mother's home comforts, Plutarch quotes Alexander himself verbatim. Of the other teachers, who are described as numerous, only Lysimachos ('Phoinix') is mentioned by name. Plutarch seems not to think much of him. Alexander's estimate appeared later. During the great siege of Tyre, he went for a long hill-walk; Lysimachos, boasting that he was as good as Achilles' Phoinix and no older, insisted on going too. 'When Lysimachos grew faint and weary, though evening was coming on and the enemy were near at hand, Alexander refused to leave him; and encouraging and helping him along with a few companions, unexpectedly found himself cut off from the main body and obliged to spend the night in a wild spot in darkness and extreme cold.' Singlehanded, he raided an enemy watch-fire to snatch a burning brand; the enemy, thinking his troops were at hand, retreated; and Lysimachos had a fire to sleep by. Leonidas, left behind in Macedon, got only a load of expensive incense, with an ironic gift-tag saying that from now on he need not be stingy towards the gods.

Philip's telling Alexander he should be ashamed to sing so well – presumably in public, since it was recorded – is from Plutarch, who says the boy never played again. The tribal skirmish after is invented; we do not know where or when Alexander first tasted war. It can only be back-dated from his regency. At sixteen, he was trusted by the first general in Greece with a command of vital strategic importance, in the full expectation that experienced troops would follow him. By then they must have known him well.

The encounter with Demosthenes at Pella is all invention. It is true, however, that the orator, who as last speaker had had some hours in which to compose himself, broke down after a few stumbling sentences, and though encouraged by Philip was unable to go on. With eight witnesses to his story, Aischines can here be trusted; whether he was to blame – they were already old enemies – cannot be known. Demosthenes never liked to speak extempore, but no reason appears for his needing to. He came back with a virulent dislike of Alexander, remarkable towards so young a boy, and seems to have sneered at Aischines for sycophancy to him.

The taming of Boukephalas is given by Plutarch in such detail that one is tempted to guess the source may have been a favourite after-dinner story of Alexander's. My only addition is to suppose the horse had lately been ill-treated. By Arrian's dating it was already twelve years old; it is not conceivable that a mount with a long record of vice would be offered to the King. Greek war-horses were elaborately trained, and this must have been done already. But I cannot credit the astronomical asking price of thirteen talents. Chargers were too expendable (though Alexander cherished Boukephalas to an age of thirty). Philip may well have paid this huge sum for his victorious Olympic racer, and the stories become con-flated.

Aristotle's years of fame in Athens began only after Philip's death; those of his works which have been preserved are of later date. We do not know what, exactly, he taught Alexander, but Plutarch speaks of his lifelong interest in natural science (while in Asia he kept Aristotle supplied with specimens) and in medicine. I have assumed Aristotle's views on ethics to be already formed. Among lost works of his was a book of letters to Hephaistion, whose special status he must, it seems, have recognized.

Alexander's rescue of his father from the mutineers is from Curtius, who says Alexander complained bitterly that Philip never admitted to the debt, though he had had to take refuge in shamming dead.

Diodoros, and other writers, describe Philip's victory komos after the battle of Chaironeia; but none of the accounts mentions Alexander's presence.

The sexual mores of Alexander have been much discussed, his detractors tending to claim he was homosexual, his admirers to rebut it with indignation. Neither side has much considered how far Alexander himself would have thought it a dishonour. In a society which accepted bisexuality as a norm, his three state marriages qualified him for normality. His general restraint was much noticed; but, for contemporaries, his most striking peculiarity was his refusal to exploit defenceless victims like captive women and slave-boys, a practice then universal.

His emotional commitment to Hephaistion is among the most certain facts of his life. He displayed an open pride in it. At Troy, in the presence of his army, they honoured together the tombs of Achilles and Patroklos. Though Homer does not say the heroes were more than friends, it was widely believed in Alexander's day; had he thought the imputation disgraceful, he would not so have courted it. After his victory at Issus, when the captive women of Darius' family were bewailing their lord for dead, Alexander went to their tent to reassure them, taking Hephaistion along. According to Curtius, they walked in together, dressed much alike; Hephaistion was taller and by Persian standards more impressive; the Queen Mother prostrated herself before him. Warned of her error by the frantic signals of her attendants, she turned in distressed confusion to the real King, who said to her, 'You weren't far out, Mother; he is Alexander, too.'

It is clear they behaved with seemliness in public (though high-ranking officials resented Hephaistion's being seen to read, without rebuke, Olympias' letters over Alexander's shoulder). No physical relationship is proved, and those whom the thought disturbs are free to reject it. It is a recorded saying of Alexander's that sleep and sex put him in mind of his mortality.

Alexander survived his friend by about three months, for two of which he was travelling with the body from Ecbatana to Babylon, the intended capital of his empire. The wild extravagance of the funeral rites, the vast grandiose pyre, the request to Zeus Ammon's oracle to grant the dead man the divine status already accorded to Alexander himself (Ammon allowed Hephaistion only to be a hero), suggest that at this time Alexander was barely in command of his reason. Not long after, he contracted fever, but sat up all night at a party. Though he pushed on with his campaign plans as long as he could stand, indeed much longer, he is not recorded to have had a doctor. (He had hanged Hephaistion's, for neglect.) His stubborn mistreatment of his own condition seems self-destructive, whether consciously or not.

His experience at the Aigai Dionysia is invented, but expresses, I think, a psychological truth. Olympias committed many murders; her eventual execution was entrusted by Kassandros to the relatives of her victims. She killed Eurydike and her infant the moment Alexander's back was turned after Philip's death. Her complicity in the latter has been much suspected, but never proved. The prophetic 'vision' of Demosthenes is historical.

The general reader who wants to follow Alexander's career as King will find it in Plutarch's *Lives* (Volume II in the Everyman Edition), or in Arrian's *History* (Penguin Classics). Both are available in English interleaved with Greek, in the Loeb Classical Library.

Proper Names

Alexander's real name was, of course, Alexandros; it was so common in North Greece that three other bearers of it appear within this tale alone. Because of this, and because of two-thousand-year-long associations, I have given him the traditional Latinized form.

I have kept traditional forms, too, for some other very familiar names: Philip for Philippos, Ptolemy for Ptolemaios, Aristotle for Aristoteles; and for a number of place names. The word Bucephalus, however, comes trailing such clouds of nineteenth-century cliché that I have preferred to translate it: Boukephalas would be the Doric-Macedonian form. In the story of Alexander, no system of nomenclature is likely to please everyone; so, with apology, I have pleased myself.

I have used the name of Eurydike for Philip's bride, though it was a royal honorific bestowed by him, rather than her given name of Kleopatra, to avoid confusion with Alexander's sister.

THE
PERSIAN
BOY

If anyone has the right to be measured by the standards of his own time, it is Alexander.

Hermann Bengtson: *The Greeks and the Persians*

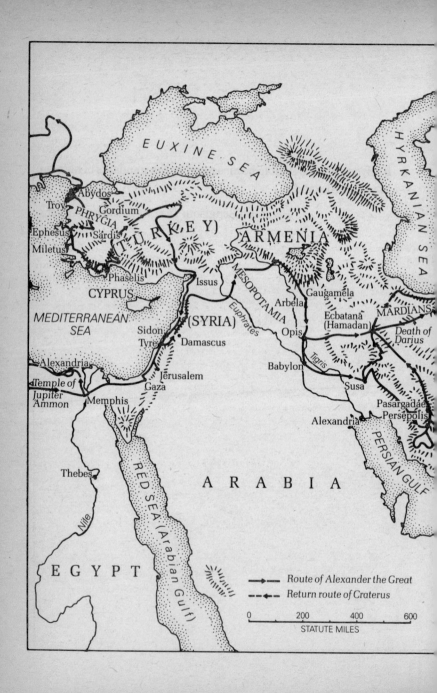

EUXINE SEA

HYRKANIAN SEA

Abydos
Troy
PHRYGIA
Gordium
Ephesus
Sardis
Miletus
(TURKEY)
ARMENIA

Phaselis
CYPRUS
Issus
MESOPOTAMIA
Gaugamela
Arbela
MARDIANS

MEDITERRANEAN SEA
(SYRIA)
Euphrates
Opis
Ecbatana (Hamadan)
Death of Darius

Sidon
Tyre
Damascus

Alexandria
Babylon
Tigris

Temple of Jupiter Ammon
Jerusalem
Gaza
Memphis
Susa

Thebes
RED SEA (Arabian Gulf)
Alexandria
Pasargadae
Persepolis

ARABIA
PERSIAN GULF

Nile

EGYPT

→→→ Route of Alexander the Great
--◄-- Return route of Craterus

0   200   400   600
STATUTE MILES

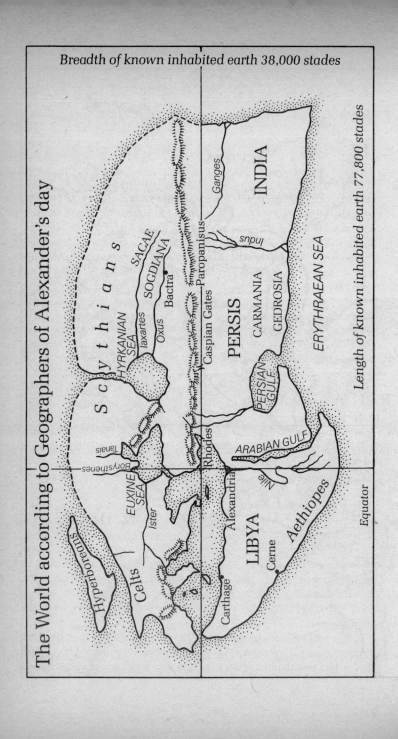

The World according to Geographers of Alexander's day

Breadth of known inhabited earth 38,000 stades

Length of known inhabited earth 77,800 stades

Equator

INDIA

Ganges

Indus

PERSIS

CARMANIA

GEDROSIA

ERYTHRAEAN SEA

Paropanisus

Caspian Gates

PERSIAN GULF

ARABIAN GULF

Bactra

SOGDIANA

SACAE

Iaxartes

Oxus

HYRKANIAN SEA

S c y t h i a n s

Tanais

Borysthenes

Rhodes

Nile

Alexandria

EUXINE SEA

Ister

LIBYA

Cerne

Aethiopes

Carthage

Celts

Hyperboreans

I

Lest anyone should suppose I am a son of nobody, sold off by some peasant father in a drought year, I may say our line is an old one, though it ends with me. My father was Artembares, son of Araxis, of the Pasargadai, Kyros' old royal tribe. Three of our family fought for him, when he set the Persians over the Medes. We held our land eight generations, in the hills west above Susa. I was ten years old, and learning a warrior's skills, when I was taken away.

Our hill-fort was as old as our family, weathered-in with the rocks, its watch-tower built up against a crag. From there my father used to show me the river winding through the green plain to Susa, city of lilies. He pointed out the Palace, shining on its broad terrace, and promised I should be presented, when I was sixteen.

That was in King Ochos' day. We survived his reign, though he was a great killer. It was through keeping faith with his young son Arses, against Bagoas the Vizier, that my father died.

At my age, I might have overheard less of the business, if the Vizier had not borne my name. It is common enough in Persia; but being the only son and much beloved, I found it so strange to hear it pronounced with loathing, that each time my ears pricked up.

Court and country lords whom, as a rule, we hardly saw twice a year, were riding up the mountain track every few days. Our fort was well out of the way, a good place to meet. I enjoyed seeing these fine men on their tall horses, and felt an expectation of events, but not of danger, since none of them owned to fear. More than once they sacrificed at the fire-altar; the Magus would come, a strong old man who could scramble the rocks like a goatherd, killing snakes and scorpions. I loved the bright flames, and their light on the polished sword-hilts, gold buttons and jewelled hats. So it would all go on, I thought, till I could join them as a man.

After the prayer they would take the sacred drink together, and talk about honour.

In honour I had been instructed. Since I was five and had been brought out from among the women, I had been reared to ride and shoot and abhor the Lie. Fire was the soul of the Wise God. The dark Lie was faithlessness.

King Ochos was lately dead. If his sickness had killed him, few would have cried; but it was said that had been nothing much, it was his medicine he had died of. Bagoas had been highest in the kingdom, next the King, for many years; but young Arses had lately come of age and married. Ochos, with a grown heir and grandsons, had begun to trim Bagoas down. He died soon after this was seen.

'So now,' said one of my father's guests, 'the throne comes down by treachery, even though to the lawful heir. Myself, I acquit Arses; I never heard anything against the boy's honour. But his youth will double Bagoas' power; from now on, he might as well be King. No eunuch before has climbed so high.'

'Not often,' my father said. 'But sometimes this lust for power will rule them. It is because they will see no sons.' Finding me near him, he took me in his arm. Someone uttered a blessing.

The guest of highest rank, whose land was near Persepolis but who had followed the court to Susa, said, 'We are all agreed that Bagoas shall never rule. But let us see how Arses deals with him. Young though he is, I think the Vizier has reckoned without his host.'

I don't know what Arses would have done, if his brothers had not been poisoned. It was then he set out to count his friends.

The three princes had been much of an age. All three had been very close. Kings mostly change to their kin; Arses did not. The Vizier distrusted their private councils. Both the younger, without much time wasted between, got cramps in their bellies and died.

Soon after, a messenger came to our house; his letter bore the royal seal. I was the first person my father met, when the man had gone.

'My son,' he said, 'I shall soon have to go away; the King has called for me. A time may come – remember it – when one must stand for the Light against the Lie.' He set his hand on my shoulder. 'It's hard for you to be sharing your name just now with an evil man; you will not for long, God willing. And that monster can't hand it on. It is you who will carry it down in honour; you, and the sons of your sons.' He lifted me up and kissed me.

He had the fort strengthened. It had a sheer cliff one side, and a gatehouse over the mountain track; but he had the walls raised a course or two, with better slits for the archers.

On the day before he was due to leave, a party of warriors rode up. Their letter carried the royal seal. We were not to know it came from a dead man's hand. Arses had gone his brothers' way; his infant sons were smothered; the male line of Ochos was wiped out. My father looked at the seal, and ordered the gates to be opened. The men rode in.

Having watched all this, I went back to some boy's business in the orchard below the tower. There was some shouting; I came to see. Five or six men dragged through the door a man with a dreadful face. Its centre was red and empty; blood streamed from it into his mouth and beard. He had been stripped of his coat; both shoulders dripped blood, for his ears had gone. I knew him by his boots; they were my father's.

Even now, sometimes I think how I let him go to his death without a word, struck dumb with horror. I suppose he understood; when he spoke it was to the purpose. As they led him on, he cried at me in a loud harsh voice, horribly changed by the wound where his nose had been, 'Orxines betrayed us! Orxines, remember the name! Orxines!'

With the mouth open and shouting, the face looked more frightful than before. I did not know I heard the words it uttered. I stood like a post, while they pushed him to his knees, and pulled his head forward by the hair. It took them five or six sword-strokes, to cleave through his neck.

While they were about this, they forgot to watch my mother. She must have run straight up the tower; the moment he was dead she leaped from it, so they lost their sport with her. She screamed as she fell; but that, I think, was because she saw too late I was there below her. She struck the ground about a spear-length away, and her skull burst open.

I hope my father's spirit saw her quick death. They could just as well have taken his ears and nose when his head was off. The Vizier, when they brought it him, would never have known the difference.

My sisters were twelve years old and thirteen. There was another of about nine, by a second wife of my father's who had died of fever. I heard all three of them shrieking. I don't know if they were left for dead when the men had done, or taken away alive.

At last, the captain of the troop set me on his horse and rode with me down the hill. Slung to his saddle-cloth was the bloody bag with my father's head. I wondered, with what power of thought was left me, why he had had mercy on me alone. I learned the answer that same night.

He did not keep me long, being in need of money. In the dealer's courtyard at Susa, city of lilies, I stood stripped naked, while they drank date wine out of little cups, and haggled over my price. Greek boys are reared without shame and used to nakedness; we have more modesty. In my ignorance, I thought one could fall no lower.

Only a month before, my mother had scolded me for looking in her mirror, saying I was too young to be vain. I had no more than glimpsed my face in it. My new owner had more to tell. 'A real thoroughbred, the antique Persian strain, the grace of a roebuck. See those delicate bones, the profile – turn round, boy – the hair shining like bronze, straight and fine as silk from China – come here, boy, let him feel it. Brows drawn with the fine brush. Those great eyes, smudged in with bistre – aha, pools to drown love in! Those slender hands you won't sell cheap to sweep floors.

Don't tell me you've been offered such goods in five years, or ten.'

At his every pause, the dealer told him he did not buy at a loss. At last he reached his final offer; the captain said it was robbing an honest man; but the dealer said there was the risk to reckon for. 'We lose one in five when we geld them.'

Geld them, I thought, while the hand of fear closed the gate of understanding. But I had seen it done to an ox at home. I neither spoke nor moved. I begged for nothing. I had learned better than to hope there was pity in the world.

The dealer's house was strong as a prison, with courtyard walls fifteen feet high. On one side was a shed, where they did the gelding. They had purged and starved me first, which is thought to make it safer; I was led in cold and empty, to see the table with the knives, and the frame with splayed-out legs to which they bind you, with old black blood on it and dirty straps. Then at last I threw myself at the dealer's feet and clasped them crying. But they made no more of it than farmhands of the bawling bull-calf. They did not speak to me, just strapped me down, talking across me of some gossip in the market, till they began and I knew nothing, only the pain and my own screams.

They say women forget the pain of childbirth. Well, they are in nature's hand. No hand took mine. I was a body of pain in an earth and sky of darkness. It will take death to make me forget.

There was an old slave-woman who dressed my wounds. She was skilful and clean, for boys were merchandise, and, as she told me once, they thrashed her if they lost one. My cuts hardly festered; she used to tell me they'd made neat work of me, and later, she said giggling, I would be the gainer. I had no use for her words, and only knew she laughed when I was in pain.

When I was healed, I was sold at auction. Once more I stood stripped, this time before staring crowds. From the block I could see the bright glazes of the Palace, where my father had promised to present me to the King.

I was bought by a gem-stone dealer; though it was his wife who chose me, pointing a red-tipped finger from her curtained litter. The auctioneer had delayed and pleaded; the price had disappointed him. From pain and grief I had lost flesh, and no doubt most of my looks. They had stuffed me with food, but I had brought up most of it as if my body disdained to live; so they got me off their hands. The jeweller's wife wanted a pretty page, to set her above the concubines, and I was pretty enough for that. She had a monkey too, with green fur.

I grew fond of the monkey; it was my work to feed it. When I came it would fly through the air to me, and clasp my neck with its little hard black hands. But one day she wearied of it, and had it sold.

I was still young, living from day to day. But when she sold the monkey, I looked ahead. I would never be free; I would be bought and sold like the monkey; and I would never be a man. In the night I lay and thought of it; and in the morning, it seemed that without manhood I had grown old. She said I looked peaked, and gave me a dose that griped my belly. But she was not cruel, and never beat me unless I broke something she valued.

While I lay at the dealer's, the new King had been proclaimed. Ochos' line being extinguished, he was royal only by side descent; but the people seemed to think well of him. Datis, my master, brought no news to the harem, thinking the only concern of women was to please men, and of eunuchs to oversee them. But the Chief Eunuch would bring us all the gleanings of the bazaar, taking delight in this importance; and why not? It was all he had.

Darius the new King, he said, had both beauty and valour. When Ochos had been at war with the Kardousians, and their giant champion had challenged the King's warriors, only Darius had come forward. He stood six feet and a half himself, and had transfixed the man with a single javelin, living ever since in the renown. There had been consultations, and the Magi had scanned the skies; but no one in council had dared cross Bagoas' choice, he was too much dreaded. However, it seemed that so far the new King had murdered no one; his manners were reported gracious and mild.

As I heard this, waving my mistress's peacock fan, I recalled my father's birthday feast, the last of his life; the guests threading up the mountain and coming in through the gatehouse, the grooms taking their horses; my father, with me beside him, welcoming them at the door. One man had towered over the others, and looked so much a warrior that even to me he did not seem old. He was handsome, with all his teeth still perfect, and had tossed me up like a baby, making me laugh. Had he not been called Darius? But one King or another, I thought as I waved the fan, what is that to me?

Soon all this was stale news, and they were talking about the west. There were barbarians there whom I had heard my father speak of, red-haired savages who painted themselves blue; they lived north of the Greeks, a tribe called Macedonians. First they had come raiding; then they had had the impudence to declare war, and the coastal satraps were arming. But the news now was that not long after King Arses' death, their own King had been killed, at some public spectacle where, in their barbarous way, he had walked about unguarded. His heir was only a young lad, so there was no more need to be concerned about them.

My life went by in the small duties of the harem, making beds, carrying trays, mixing sorbets of mountain snow and citron, painting my mistress's finger-ends, and being petted by the girls; Datis had only one wife, but three young concubines, who were kind to me, knowing the master had no taste for boys. But if ever I waited on them, my mistress would clip my ear.

Soon I was let out on little errands, to buy henna and kohl and herbs for the clothes-chests, and such things beneath the Chief Eunuch's dignity; and would see other eunuchs shopping too. Some were like him, soft and fat with breasts like women's, and after seeing one, though I was growing quickly, I would eat less. Others were shrivelled and shrill like careworn crones. But a few stood tall and straight, with some look of pride in themselves; I used to wonder what their secret was.

It was summer; the orange-trees in the women's court scented the air, mixed with perfumed sweat from the girls, as they sat dabbling their fingers at the rim of the fish-pool. My mistress had bought me a little harp, to hold on the knee, and bade one of the girls teach me to tune it. I was singing, when the Chief Eunuch rushed in, wheezing with haste and quivering all over. He was bursting with news, but paused to mop his brow and complain about the heat, making them wait. One could see it was a great day.

'Madam,' he said, 'Bagoas the Vizier is dead!'

The courtyard twittered like a roost of starlings. My mistress waved her plump hand for quiet. 'But how? Don't you know anything more?'

'Indeed, Madam.' He mopped his brow again, till she invited him to sit. He looked round from his cushion like a market story-teller. 'It is common talk at the Palace, having been witnessed by many, as you shall hear. You are aware, Madam, I know where to ask; if it can be known, it comes to me. It appears that yesterday the King received Bagoas in audience. With men of such rank, of course, only the choicest wine is offered. It was brought in, poured already into cups of inlaid gold. The King took the royal one, Bagoas the other, and the Vizier waited for the King to drink. For some time he held his wine-cup, speaking of some slight matter and watching Bagoas' face; then he made to drink; then he lowered the cup again, watching still. He then said thus: "Bagoas, you have been the faithful servant of three kings. Such a man should be marked with honour. Here is my own cup for you to pledge me in; I will drink from yours." The chamberlain brought it to Bagoas, and brought the other to the King.

'I was told, by one who did me the honour to confide in me, that the face of the Vizier changed to the colour of pale river-mud. The King drank; and there was a stillness. "Bagoas," he said, "I have drunk; I am waiting for you to pledge me." At this, Bagoas laid hand on heart, fetched his breath short, and prayed the King to pardon him; he had been taken faint, and begged leave to withdraw. But the King said, "Sit, Vizier; the wine is your best medicine". He sat, for it seemed his knees failed beneath him; and the cup shook in his hand, so that the wine began to spill. Then the King leaned forward in his chair, raising his voice for all to hear. "Drink your wine, Bagoas. For I tell you this and I do not lie: whatever is in that cup, it will be better for you to drink it."

'At this he drank; and when he would have risen, the Royal Guard stood round him with pointed spears. The King waited till the poison had taken hold, before retiring and leaving them to watch him die. I am told he was an hour about it.'

There was a great deal of exclaiming, like coins in the storyteller's hat. The mistress asked who it was that warned the King. The Chief Eunuch looked sly, and dropped his voice. 'The Royal Cupbearer has been given a robe of honour. Madam, who knows? Some say the King himself cast his eye on the fate of Ochos; that when the cups were changed, the Vizier read his face, but could do nothing. Let the hand of discretion cover the wise mouth.'

So, then, divine Mithra, Avenger of Honour, had kept his day. The traitor had died by treachery, just as he ought. But the time of gods is not like the time of men. My namesake had died, as my father promised me; but he had died too late for me, and for all the sons of my sons.

2

Two years I served the harem, suffering nothing worse than a tedium I wondered, sometimes, I did not die of. I grew taller, and twice had to have new clothes. Yet my growth had slowed. They had said at home I would be as tall as my father; but the gelding must have given some shock that changed me. I am a little better than small, and all my life have kept the shape of a boy.

None the less, I used to hear in the bazaar praise of my beauty. Sometimes a man would speak to me, but I turned away; he would not speak, I thought, if he knew I was a slave. Such was still my simplicity. I was only glad to escape the women's chatter, see the life of the bazaar, and take the air.

Presently my master also gave me errands, taking notes to the jewellers of his new stock, and so on. I used to dread being sent to the royal workshops, though Datis seemed to think he was giving me a treat. The workmen were all slaves, chiefly Greeks, who were prized for skill. Of course they were all branded in the face; but as punishment, or to stop their getting away, most of them had had a foot off, or sometimes both. Some needed both hands and feet, if they used a burin-wheel for carving gems; and these, lest they should slip off untraced, had had their noses taken. I would look anywhere but at them; till I saw the jeweller watching me, supposing me in search of something to steal.

I had been taught at home that, after cowardice and the Lie, the worst disgrace for a gentleman was to trade. Selling was not to be thought of; one lost face even by buying, one should live off one's own land. Even my mother's mirror, which had a winged boy engraved on it and had come all the way from Ionia, had been in her dowry. No matter how often I fetched merchandise, I never ceased to feel the shame. It is a true saying, that men don't know till too late when they have been well off.

It was a bad year for the jewellers. The King had gone to war, leaving the Upper City dead as a tomb. The young King of Macedon had crossed to Asia, and was taking all the Greek cities there from Persian rule. He was not much more than twenty; it had seemed just a matter for the coastal satraps. But he had beaten their forces and crossed the Granikos, and was now thought as bad to reckon with as his father.

It was said he had no wife; that he took no Household with him; only his men, like a mere robber or bandit. But thus he got about very fast, even through mountain land unknown to him. From pride he wore glittering arms, to be singled out in battle. Many tales were told of him, which I leave out, since those that were true are known by all the world, while of the false we have enough. At all events, he had already done all his father had intended, and still did not seem content.

The King, therefore, had mustered a royal army, and gone himself to meet him. Since the King of Kings did not travel naked to war like a young western raider, he had taken the Court and Household, with its stewards and chamberlains and eunuchs; also the harem, with the Queen Mother, the Queen, the Princesses and the little Prince, and their own attendants, their eunuchs and hairdressers and women of the wardrobe and all the rest. The Queen, who was said to be of surpassing beauty, had always brought the jewellers good trade.

The King's attendant lords had also taken their women, their wives and often their concubines, lest the war should last some time. So, in Susa, only such people were buying jewellery as are content with chippings stuck in paste.

The mistress had no new dress that spring, and was sharp with us all for days; the prettiest of the concubines had a new veil, which for a week made life unbearable. The Chief Eunuch had less shopping-money; the mistress was skimped with sweets, the slaves with food. My only comfort was to feel my slim waist, and look at the Chief Eunuch.

If no thicker, I was growing taller. Though I had again outgrown my clothes, I expected to go on wearing them. But to my surprise, I got a new suit from the master; tunic, trousers and sash, and an outer coat with wide sleeves. The sash even had gold thread in it. They were so pretty that I stooped over the pool to see myself, and was not displeased.

The same day, soon after noon, the master summoned me to his business room. I remember finding it strange that he did not look at me. He wrote a few words and sealed the paper, saying, 'Take this to Obares the master jeweller. Go straight there, don't loiter in the bazaar.' He looked at his fingernails, then back at me. 'He is my best customer; so take good care to be civil.'

These words surprised me. 'Sir,' I said, 'I have never been uncivil to a customer. Does anyone say I have?'

'Oh, tut, no,' he said, fidgeting with a tray of loose turquoises. 'I am only telling you to be civil to Obares.'

Even then, I walked to the house thinking no more than that he had some worry about the man's goodwill. The captain who took me from my home, and what he did to me, was smothered up with other things in my mind; when I woke crying in the night, it was mostly from a dream of my father's noseless face, shouting aloud. Without thought of harm I went to the shop of Obares, a stocky Babylonian with a black bush of beard. He glanced at the note, and led me straight through to the inner room, as if I were expecting it.

I hardly remembered the rest, except his stink, which I can recall today; and that, after, he gave me a bit of silver for myself. I gave it to a leper in the market-place, who took it on a palm without thumb or fingers, and wished me the blessing of long life.

I thought of the monkey with green fur, carried away by a man with a cruel face, who'd said he was going to train it. It came to me that perhaps I had been sent on approval to a buyer. I went to the gutter and vomited my heart out. No one took notice. Damp with cold sweat, I returned to my master's house.

Whether or not Obares would have been a buyer, my master was not a seller. It suited him far better to be doing Obares favours, I was lent to him twice a week.

I doubt my master ever called himself what he was. He just obliged a good customer. Then a friend of Obares heard, and must be obliged for his sake. Not being in the trade, he paid in coin; and he passed the good word on. Before long, I was sent out most afternoons.

At twelve years old, it takes too perfect a despair to die alone. I thought of it often; I had dreamed of my father without his nose, and instead of the traitor's name he shouted mine. But Susa has not walls high enough to leap from; there was nothing else with which I could make sure. As for running away, I had for example the leg-stumps of the royal jeweller's slaves.

I went, therefore, to my clients as I was told. Some were better than Obares, some much worse. I can yet feel the cold sinking of my heart, as I walked to some house unknown before; and how, when one required of me something not fit to be described, I remembered my father, no longer a noseless mask, but standing on the night of his birthday feast while by torchlight our warriors did the sword-dance. To honour his spirit, I struck the man and called him what he deserved.

My master did not beat me with the leaded whip he used upon the Nubian porter, for fear of spoiling me; but the cane cut hard. While it still stung, I was sent back to beg pardon and make amends.

This life I led for rather more than a year, seeing no escape till I should be too old. My mistress did not know of it, and I conspired to deceive her; I had always some tale for her of my day's business. She had more decency than her husband, and would have been outraged, but she had no power to save me. If she knew the truth, the house would be in an uproar, till for the sake of peace he would sell me for the best price I'd fetch. When I thought of the bidders, I kept the hand of discretion before my mouth.

Whenever I passed through the bazaar, I imagined people saying, 'There goes Datis' whore.' Yet I had to bring back some news, to satisfy my mistress. The rumours were running, ahead of truth, that the King had fought a great battle with Alexander, at Issos by the sea, and lost, escaping with his bare life on horseback, leaving his chariot and his arms. Well, he got away, I thought; there are some of us would think that luck enough.

As proper news came in by the royal road, we learned that the Harem had been taken, with the Queen Mother, the Queen, her daughters and her son. I pitied them; I had good cause to know their fate. The girls' screams rang in my ears; I pictured the young boy flung upon the spears, as I would have been but for one man's greed. However, never having seen these ladies and being bound for the house of someone I knew too well, I kept some pity for myself.

Later it was put about, by someone who swore it came straight from Kilikia, that Alexander had set up the royal women in their own pavilion, untouched by man, with their Household to serve them, and that even the boy was still alive. This tale was laughed at, for everyone knew that no one behaves like that in war, let alone western barbarians.

The King had fallen back on Babylon, and wintered there. But it grows hot in spring; without much state he returned to Susa, to rest from his labours, while his satraps mustered another army. I was kept at work, and could not see the royal cavalcade, which, like the boy I still partly was, I had set some store by. It seemed that Alexander had not marched inland where he had been expected, but had had the folly to sit down before Tyre, an island stronghold which would not fall in ten years. While he kept up this pastime, the King could take his ease.

Now that the Court was back, even though without the Queen, I hoped the jewel-trade would prosper; then perhaps I might be let off *my* trade, to stay and serve the harem. Once I had thought it tedious; it beckoned now like a palm-grove in the desert.

You might suppose by now I would be reconciled. But ten years are ten years, though one has left them behind for three. Far off on the mountain, I could still discern the ruins of my home.

There were clients from whom, if I had flattered them, I could have had good money I need not have shown my master. I could sooner have made a meal off camel-dung; yet some were drawn by my sullenness, and would court me to win a smile. Others would hurt me in various ways, but I divined they would do so in any case, and servility would encourage them. The worst, who left me covered in weals, my master denied me to, not from pity but because he damaged the goods. With others I learned resources. I did not refuse a small piece of silver, but used it to buy kif. Taking it seldom, I could smoke myself silly beforehand. That is why to this day the mere smell of it makes me sick.

Some, in their way, were kind. With these, it seemed that honour demanded a return. I would try to please them, since I had nothing else to give; and they were glad to teach me how to do it better. Thus I learned the beginnings of art.

There was a carpet-seller who, when he had done, would treat me like a guest, seat me by him on the divan, give me wine and talk to me. The wine I was glad of, since he sometimes put me in pain; not through his fault, for he was gentle and liked to please. I kept it to myself, from pride, or what modesty was left me.

One day he had a carpet of ten years' work hung on the wall, to take pleasure in, he said, before it went to the buyer; a friend of the King's, content with only the finest. 'I expect,' he said, 'he may have known your father.'

I could feel my face drain of blood and my hands grow cold. All this while I had supposed my birth a secret, my father's name sheltered from my disgrace. Now I knew my master had had it from the dealer, and boasted of it. Why not? The Vizier, from whose vengeance I had been stolen, was disgraced and dead; it was no crime to have cheated him. I thought of our name in the mouths of all those who had had their hands on me.

A month's custom dulled me a little to it, but not much. There were some I would gladly have killed for knowing what they knew. When the carpet-seller sent for me again, I was thankful it was no one worse.

I was brought into the fountain-court, where he sometimes sat on cushions under a blue awning, till we went indoors. But, this time, he was not alone; another man sat with him. I stood stock-still in the open doorway, my thought, I suppose, clear on my face.

'Come in, Bagoas,' he said. 'Don't look so startled, my dear boy. Today my friend and I ask nothing but the refreshment of beholding you, and the pleasure of hearing you sing. You have your harp, I am glad to see.'

'Yes,' I answered. 'The master said you wished it.' I had wondered if he had been charged extra.

'Come, then. We are both fretted with the day's business; you shall soothe our souls for us.'

I sang to them, thinking all the while, They will be up to something later. The guest had not a merchant's look; he was almost like my father's friends, but smoother. Some patron of the host's, I thought; presently I shall be served to him on a platter, dressed with green leaves.

I was mistaken. I was asked for another song; then they chatted with me of nothings; then I was given a little present, and dismissed. No such thing had ever happened to me before. As the courtyard door closed behind me, I heard their low voices, and knew they spoke of me. Well, I thought, it had been an easy stint of work. I should hear from the other man later.

So I did. Next day he bought me.

I saw him come to the house. Wine was sent for; the Nubian who had served it, said some hard bargaining was going on. He did not know what about; he had only simple Persian; but already I wondered. When afterwards the master sent for me, I knew before he spoke.

"Well, Bagoas.' He was smiling from ear to ear. 'You are a very fortunate boy; you are going to very good service.' And for a very good price, I thought. 'You will be sent for tomorrow morning.'

He waved me off. I said, 'What kind of service, sir?'

'That is your new master's business. Take care to show him respect. You have had good training here.'

My mouth opened. But I said nothing after all. I just looked him in the face; his colour changed, and his pig-eyes shifted. Then he told me to go; but it had done me good.

So, like the monkey, I was set for an unknown bourne. My mistress drenched me with tears; it was like being enfolded in wet cushions. Of course he had sold me without her leave. 'You have been such a sweet good boy, so gentle. I know you still grieve for your parents, even now; I have seen it in your face. I do pray you have a kind master; you are still a child as the world goes, so quietly you have lived here.'

We cried again, and all the girls embraced me in turn. Their scented freshness was pleasant, compared with certain memories. I was thirteen years old, and felt I could have no more to learn when I was fifty.

I was duly fetched next day, by a very grand eunuch, some forty years old, who had been handsome and still watched his figure. He was so civil, I ventured to ask the new master's name. He smiled discreetly. 'We must first see you made fit for his household. But do not be anxious, boy; all that will be attended to.'

I felt he was keeping something back, though not from malice. As we walked beyond the bazaar to the quiet streets where the big houses were, I hoped the new master's tastes were not too odd.

The house was like all such, shut off from the street by a high wall, with a great bronze-studded gate. The outer court had tall trees, whose tops, even, had hardly shown from the street. It was all old and dignified. The eunuch took me to a little room in the servants' wing, with only one bed. For three years I had fallen asleep to the Chief Eunuch's whistling snores. On the bed were new clothes laid out. They were plainer than mine; only when they were on I saw their quality. The eunuch took my own clothes between finger and thumb, and sniffed. 'Gaudy and shoddy. We can make no use of them here. However, no doubt some child of want will be glad of them.'

I supposed I should now be brought before my master; but it seemed I was not accounted fit to see his face before my training, which began that day.

It was a huge old house, very cool, with a set of rambling rooms upon a court, long out of use it seemed, some with just an antique chest or an old divan with burst cushions. Through these we came to another, with good furniture set out I supposed rather for store than use. At one end was a table with a fine carved chair; there was a sideboard, with good vessels of enamelled copper; yet at the other end stood a stately bed beneath an embroidered canopy. Strangely, this was made up, and had its clothes-stool and its night-table. All was polished and clean, yet had no look of habitation. Creepers festooned the fretted windows; the light came in as green as water in a fishpool.

However, it soon appeared there was method in all this. This was my training-ground.

The eunuch sat in the carved chair enacting the master, instructing me in serving this dish or that, or pouring wine, setting down the cup or putting it in the master's hand. His manners were haughty enough for any lord's, but he never struck or cursed me, and I felt no ill-will to him; I saw the awe he inspired in me was part of my training too. For I perceived that indeed I had changed my state, and was growing scared.

My noon meal was brought here; I did not eat with the servants. I had seen no one but the eunuch, since I entered this house. It began to seem uncanny; I dreaded being told I must sleep here too in the great bed; I was sure there would be ghosts at night. But after my supper I slept in my little cell. Even the privy I went to had no one ever about, but was overgrown and full of spiders, as if not used any more.

Next morning, the eunuch took me through all yesterday's lessons. As far as a man of his dignity could show it, he seemed a little keyed-up, I thought, Of course, he expects the master; and growing anxious, at once let fall a plate.

Suddenly the door swung open, and, as if it had revealed a flower-garden in full bloom, a young man came in. He strode forward, gay, handsome, assured, richly dressed and adorned with gold, smelling of costly essences. It took me some moments to reflect that, though more than twenty, he had no beard. He had seemed no more like a eunuch than a shaven Greek.

'Greeting, Gazelle-eyes,' he said, smiling and showing teeth like fresh-peeled almonds. 'Well, indeed, they said no more than the truth for once.' He turned to my mentor. 'And how is he getting on?'

'Not badly, Oromedon, for one who has had no grounding. We shall make something of him in time.' He spoke, not without respect, but not as one speaks to the master.

'Let us see.' He beckoned to an Egyptian slave behind him to put some burden down, and withdraw. I was taken through all my table-work. As I made to pour wine, he said, 'Your elbow is rather tight. Curve it like this.' He flexed my arm in his hands. 'You see? That makes a much prettier line.'

I continued to the sweets, and stood awaiting censure. 'Good. But now let us try with a proper service.' From the slave's parcel, he unwrapped a treasure that made me stretch my eyes; cups, ewers and dishes of pure chased silver, inlaid with gold flowers. 'Come,' he said, pushing aside the copper. 'There is a certain touch in the handling of precious things, which is only learned by touching them.' He gave me a secret smile from his long dark eyes. When I took the things up, he said, 'Ah! He has it. You see? He is not afraid of them, he feels how they should be cherished. I think we shall do well.' He looked about. 'But where are the cushions? And the low wine-table? He must learn how to serve the inner room.' The other glanced up at him. 'Oh, yes,' he said, laughing softly, his gold earrings twinkling, 'we can be sure of that. Just send the things, and I will show him all that myself. I shan't need to keep you.'

When the cushions came, he sat, and showed me how to hold the tray to him kneeling. He was so friendly, even when correcting me, that I mastered this new work without nervousness. He got up, saying, 'Excellent. Quick, deft and quiet. And now to the rites of the bedchamber.'

I said, 'I'm afraid, sir, I've learned none of that yet, either.'

'You need not keep calling me sir. That was just to keep up your sense of ceremony. No, this is my part of your instruction. There is a great deal of ritual at bedtime, but we need do no more than run over it; most will be done by people of higher rank. However, it is important never to be at a loss. We will first prepare the bed, which should have been done already.' We opened and turned it back; it had sheets of thread-drawn Egyptian linen. 'No perfume? I don't know who got this room ready. Like an inn for camel-drivers. However, let us suppose the perfume scattered.'

He stood by the bed and removed his fluted hat. 'That would be done by someone of very high rank indeed. Now there's a knack in taking off the sash; he will of course not turn around for you. Just slip your hands round and cross them; yes, that's right. And now the robe. Begin unbuttoning at the top. Now lift it off from behind, and slip it down; he will just move his arms from his sides enough for that.' I removed the robe, baring his slender olive-coloured shoulders, on which his black curls fell down, just touched with henna. He sat down on the bed. 'For the slippers, go on both knees, sit back a little, and take each foot on your lap in turn, always beginning with the right. No, don't get up yet. He has loosened the waist of his trousers; you now draw them off, still kneeling, with your eyes cast down all the time.' He lifted his weight a little, so that I could do this. It left him in his linen under-drawers. He was extremely graceful, with a flawless skin; the Median, not the Persian beauty.

'You have not folded them. The chamber-groom will take them away; but there must never be a moment when they lie about untidy. So, then, if this room were set out properly, you would put on the night-robe (my fault, however did I forget it?) under which he would slip off his drawers, in accordance with propriety.' He covered himself modestly with the sheet, and tossed them on to the stool.

'And now, if nothing has been said beforehand, watch carefully for the sign that you are to remain when the rest retire. It will be nothing much; just a glance – like this – or a small movement of the hand. Don't stand about, but occupy yourself with something; I will show you, when all the right things are here. Then, when you are alone, he will motion you, like this, to undress. Go now to the foot of the bed, take off quickly and neatly, and lay them down there out of sight; he does not expect to see a pile of your clothes. That's right, take off everything. You may now allow yourself to walk up with a smile, but don't make it too familiar. That's perfect, perfect; try to keep that touch of shyness. And now—' He opened the bed, with a smile so gracious and commanding that I had got there before I knew it.

I started away, reproach and anger in my heart. I had liked and trusted him; he had tricked and mocked me. He was no better than the rest.

He reached out and caught my arm; his grasp was firm, but without anger or greed. 'Gently, Gazelle-eyes. Hush now, and listen to me.' I had not said a word; but I sat still and ceased to struggle. 'I have never, all this time, told you a word of a lie. I am just a teacher; all this is part of what I am here to do. If I like my work, so much the better for both of us. What you wish to forget, I know; soon you can do so forever. There is a pride in you, wounded but still unyielding; it is perhaps what shaped your prettiness into beauty. With such a nature, living as you have lived between your sordid master and his vulgar friends, you must have been holding back all the while. And very right. But those days are gone. There is a new existence before you. Now you must learn to give a little. I am here for that, to teach you the art of pleasure.' He reached out his other hand, and gently pulled me down. 'Come. I promise you, you will like it much more with me.'

I did not resist persuasion. He might indeed possess some magic, by whose power all would be well. So at first it still appeared, for he was as skilled as he was charming, like a creature from another world than that I had been frequenting; it seemed one could linger forever in the outer courts of delight. I took all that was offered, neglecting my old defences; and the pain, when it swooped on me with all its claws, was worse than ever before. For the first time I could not keep silent.

'I am sorry,' I said as soon as I could. 'I hope I did not spoil it for you. I couldn't help it.'

'But what is it?' He bent over me as if it really concerned him. 'I cannot have hurt you, surely?'

'No, of course.' I turned my eyes to the sheet to blot my tears. 'It always happens like that, if it does at all. As if they brought back the knives.'

'But you should have told me this.' He still spoke as if he cared, which to me was wonderful.

'I thought it must be the same with us all – with all people like me.'

'No, indeed. How long ago were you cut?'

'Three years,' I said, 'and a little more.'

'I don't understand it. Let me look again. But this is beautiful work; I never saw cleaner scars. It would surprise me, cutting a boy with your looks, if they took more than just enough to keep you beardless. Of course it can go wrong. The cuts can fester so deep that all the roots of feeling are eaten away. Or they can butcher you so that nothing is left for feeling, as they do with the Nubians, I suppose from fear of their strength. But with you, short of giving her fill to a woman – and few of us can do that, though one hears of it now and then – I can't see why you shouldn't enjoy it with the best. Do you tell me you have suffered this since you began?'

'What?' I cried. 'Do you think I let myself be moved by those sons of pigs?' Here was one to whom I could speak at last. 'There were one or two ... But I used to think myself away from it, when I could.'

'I see. Now I begin to guess the trouble.' He lay in thought, as grave as a physician, then said, 'Unless it is women. You don't think of women, do you?'

I remember the three girls hugging me by the pool, and their round soft breasts; then my mother's brains spilled on the orchard pebbles, and my sisters screaming. I answered, 'No'.

'Never think of them.' He looked at me earnestly, his lightness gone. 'Don't imagine, if your beauty keeps its promise, that they won't be after you, sighing and whispering, and vowing to be content with anything you have. So they may believe; but they never will. No; in their discontent they will turn spiteful, and betray you. The surest way to end on a spike in the sun.'

His face had turned sombre. I saw there some dreadful recollection, and, to reassure him, told him again I never thought of them.

He caressed me consolingly, though the pain had left me. 'No, I don't know why I considered women. It is clear enough what it is. You have fine senses; for pleasure certainly, for pain therefore as much. Though gelding is bad enough for anyone, there are degrees of feeling. It has haunted you ever since, as if it could happen again. That's not so rare; you'd have got over it long ago, with me. But you have been going with men you despised. Outwardly you had to obey; within, your pride has conceded nothing. You have preferred pain to a pleasure by which you felt degraded. It comes of anger, and the soul's resistance.'

'I didn't resist you,' I said.

'I know. But it has bitten deep; it won't be cured in a day. Later we'll try again, it's too soon now. With any luck in your life, you will outgrow it. And I can tell you one thing more; where you're going now, I don't think it will much trouble you. I have been told to say no more, which is taking discretion to absurdity; but no matter, to hear is to obey.'

'I wish,' I said, 'I might belong to you.'

'I too, Gazelle-eyes. But you are for my betters. So don't fall in love with me; we shall be parting all too soon. Put your clothes on; the getting-up ceremonial will do tomorrow. The lesson has been long enough for today.'

My training took some time longer. He came earlier, dispensed with the haughty eunuch, and taught me himself the service of the table, the fountain court, the inner chamber, the bath; he even brought a fine horse, and in the weed-grown courtyard showed me how to mount and ride with grace; all I'd learned at home was how to stick on my mountain pony. Then we went back to the room with its green glimmering windows and great bed.

He still hoped to exorcise my demon, giving much patience to it; but the pain always returned, its strength increased by the pleasure it had fed on. 'No more,' he said. 'It will be too much for you, and not enough for me. I am here to teach, and am in danger of forgetting it. We must accept this is your lot just now.'

I said in grief, 'I'd be better off like those others, feeling nothing.'

'Oh, no. Never suppose so. They put it all into eating; you can see what becomes of *them*. I'd have liked to cure you; just for your sake and mine; but as to your calling, that's to please, not be pleased. And it seems to me that in spite of this trouble – or maybe because of it, who can tell what makes the artist? – you have a gift. Your responses are very delicate; it is this which made your late employment so disgusting to you. You were a musician forced to hear howling street-singers. All you need is to know your instrument. That I shall teach you, though I think you will excel me. This time, you need not fear being sent where your art will shame you; I can promise that.'

'Can't you tell me yet who it is?'

'Haven't you guessed even yet? But no, how should you? One thing, though, I can say, and don't forget it. He loves perfection; in jewels and vessels, in hangings, carpets and swords; in horses, women and boys. No, don't look so scared; nothing dreadful will be done to you for falling short; but he might lose interest, which would be a pity. I wish to present you flawless; he will expect no less of me. But I doubt if your secret will come to light there. Let us think no more of it, and apply ourselves to useful knowledge.'

Till now, as I found, he had been like the musician who takes up an unknown harp or lyre, testing its resonance. Now lessons began in earnest.

Already I hear the voice of one who has known no more of slavery than to clap his hands and give orders, crying out, 'The shameless dog, to boast of how he was debauched in youth by one corrupted before him.' To such I reply that I had been debauched for a year already, rolled in mire without help or hope; and now to be tended like something exquisite seemed not corruption but the glimpse of some blissful heaven. So too, after being the sport of rutting swine, seemed the subtle music of the senses. It came to me easily, as if by nature or remembrance. At home, I had sometimes had sensual dreams; if let alone, no doubt I should have been precocious. All this had been altered in me, yet not killed.

Like a poet who can sing of battles though not a warrior, I could conjure the images of desire, without suffering the sharpness of its wounds which I knew too well. I could make the music, its pauses and its cadenzas; Oromedon said I was like one who can play for the dancers, yet not dance. It was his own nature to take delight in the measure he gave it; yet I triumphed with him. Then he said, 'I don't think, Gazelle-eyes, you have very much more to learn.'

His words dismayed me like news unknown before. I clung to him, saying, 'Do you love me? You don't only want to teach me? Will you be sorry when I am gone?'

'Have you learned to break hearts already?' he said. 'I never taught you that.'

'But you do love me?' I had asked it of no one since my mother died.

'Never say that to *him*. It would be considered far too oncoming.'

I looked into his face; relenting, he hugged me like a child, which did not seem strange to me. 'Truly I love you, and when you go I shall be desolate.' He spoke like one who reassures a child against ghosts and darkness. 'But then comes tomorrow. I would be cruel to make you pledges; I may never see you again. If I do, maybe I cannot speak to you, and then you would think me false. I promised not to lie to you. When we serve the great, they are our destiny. Count upon nothing, but make your own nest against the storm . . . Do you see this?'

His brow had a scar, growing old and pale. I had thought it gave him distinction. Among my father's friends, anyone without a scar or two seemed scarcely a man. 'How did you get it?' I asked.

'I was thrown at the hunt, doing something that needed doing. It was that same horse you rode; it's still mine, you see; I have not been treated shabbily. But he can't bear flawed things. So try not to get yourself knocked about.'

'I would love you,' I said, 'if you were covered with scars all over. Did he send you away?'

'Oh, no, I am very well provided for. Nothing is done unhandsomely. But I belong no more with the perfect vase and the polished gem. Don't build upon the wind, Gazelle-eyes. That is the last of my lessons. May you not be too young to bear it, for you are not too young to need it. We had better get up. I shall see you again tomorrow.'

'Do you mean,' I said, 'that tomorrow will be the last?'

'Perhaps. There is one more lesson after all. I have never told you the proper motions of the Prostration.'

'Prostration?' I said puzzled. 'But they do that for the King.'

'Just so,' he said. 'Well, that took you long enough.'

I stared at him in a kind of stupor. Then I cried aloud, 'I can't do it! I can't, I can't.'

'Whatever is this, after all my trouble? Don't stare with those great eyes as if I'd brought you a death-warrant, instead of your fortune.'

'You never told me!' I grasped him in terror till my nails dug in. He loosened them gently.

'I dropped you hints enough; it was clear you'd do. But you see, till you are accepted in the Household, you are on probation. It is assumed you might fail, and be turned away. Then, if you had known whose service you were training for, it was thought you might know too much.'

I threw myself on my face, convulsed with weeping. 'Come,' he said, and wiped my eyes on the sheet. 'You have nothing, truly, to fear. He's had some hard times, and is in need of consolation. I am telling you, you will do very well indeed; and I ought to know.'

3

I was some days in the Palace, before being presented. I thought I should never learn my way about this high maze of splendours; everywhere tall columns of marble or porphyry or malachite, with gilded capitals and twisted shafts; on every wall reliefs, coloured and glazed brighter than life, of marching warriors, or tribute-bearers from the further empire, leading bulls or dromedaries, bearing bales or jars. When one lost one's direction, one seemed alone in a solemn crowd, with nobody to ask.

In the eunuch's courtyard I was received without much warmth, as being destined for privilege; but for the same reason, none treated me ill, lest I should take my grudges with me.

It was on the fourth day that I saw Darius.

He had been taking wine and hearing music. The room gave on to a small fountain court, sweet with the scent of lilies; in the flowering trees hung gold cages of bright birds. By the fountain the musicians were putting up their instruments; but the water and the birds made a soft murmuring concert. The court had high walls, and was part of the room's seclusion.

He was on his cushions, looking into the courtyard; by him on the low table were the wine-jug and empty cup. I knew him at once for the man at my father's birthday feast. But he had been dressed then for a long ride up rough roads. Now he was robed in purple worked with white, and wore the Mitra; the light kind he used when at ease. His beard was combed like silk, and he smelled of Arabian spices.

I walked with downcast eyes behind the chamberlain. One must not look up at the King; so I could not tell if he remembered me, or whether I found favour. When my name was pronounced, I prostrated myself as I had been taught, and kissed the floor before him. His slipper was of soft dyed kid, crimson, embroidered with sequins and gold wire.

The eunuch took the wine-tray and placed it in my hands. As I backed out of the Presence, I thought I heard a faint stir among the cushions.

That night I was admitted to the Bedchamber, to assist at the disrobing. Nothing happened, except that I was given things to hold till the appointed person took them away. I tried to show grace and be a credit to my teacher. It seemed he had given me advanced instruction; in reality, some allowance was made for a beginner. For the next night, while we waited for the King to enter, an old eunuch, whose every wrinkle spoke of vast experience, whispered in my ear, 'If his Majesty should beckon you, do not leave with the others, but wait and see if he has any more commands for you.'

I remembered my training; watched under my eyelids for the beckoning; did not stand about, but occupied myself in a seemly way; and recognized, when we were alone, the signal to undress. I laid my clothes out of sight; I only failed in walking up with a smile. I was so scared, I knew it would look like a sheepish grin; so I approached grave and trustful, hoping for the best, as the bed was folded back for me.

At first he kissed and dandled me like a doll. Later I divined what was required of me, for I had been well prepared; and it seemed I was acceptable. Certainly, as Oromedon had said, I was never betrayed into pain by pleasure. In all the time I was with him, he gave no sign of knowing a eunuch can feel anything. One does not tell such things to the King of Kings, if he does not ask.

I was to be enjoyed, like the flame and crimson birds, the fountain and the lutes; and this I soon learned to manage, without jarring his dignity. I was never insulted, never humiliated, never handled roughly. I was dismissed with a civil word, if he was still awake; and often next morning a gift would come. But I too had learned to understand pleasure. He was getting on for fifty, and in spite of the baths and the sprinkled perfume, already he began to smell rather old. For some time, in the royal bed, my one wish was to change this great tall bearded man for the supple body of Oromedon. But it is not for the perfect vase or the polished gem to choose its owners.

If I grew discontented, I had only to remember my former lot. The King was a man jaded with too much pleasure, but unwilling to put it by. I achieved for him what he needed; he was content and gracious. When I thought of those others, the greedy rough hands and stinking breath and nasty wishes, I was shocked that I had felt a moment's repining, and I showed my master the gratitude I felt.

Soon I waited on most of his leisure. He gave me a beautiful little horse, to ride in the royal park with him. No wonder Paradise was named after such a place. For generations, the kings had had rare trees and flowering shrubs brought from all over Asia; full-grown trees sometimes, with their roots and soil, needing a train of ox-carts, and an army of gardeners to tend them on the way. The game, too, was choice; at the hunt, they would drive it towards the King to shoot at, and when he killed we would all applaud.

One day he remembered that I sang, and asked to hear me. My voice was never wonderful, like some eunuchs', which far surpass women's both in strength and sweetness; it was pretty and clear, when I was a boy. I fetched in the little harp my old mistress had bought in the bazaar. He was as shocked as if I had brought in some piece of offal. 'Whatever is that thing? Why did you not ask someone for a proper instrument?' He saw my dismay and said kindly, 'No, I understand your modesty prevented you. But take it away. When you have something fit to play on, then you shall sing.'

I was given a harp of tortoiseshell and boxwood, with ivory keys, and had lessons with the Chief Musician. But one day, before I had learned his difficult pieces, I sat on the fountain-rim in the sunset light, and remembered it slanting far across the plain from our walls at home. When he asked me for a song, I gave one that my father's warriors used to sing at night by the watch-fire.

When I had done, he beckoned me over; I saw he had tears in his eyes. 'That song,' he said, 'sets your poor father before me. What happy days gone by, when we were young together. He was a faithful friend to Arses, whose spirit may the Wise God receive; had he lived, he would have been welcomed here as a friend of mine. Be sure, my boy, I shall never forget you are his son.'

He laid on my head his jewelled hand. Two of his friends were there, and the Chief Steward; from this moment, as he had meant, my standing at the court was changed. I was no longer a bought pleasure-boy, but a favourite of gentle birth, and they were all to know it. I was to know, too, that if my looks were damaged or went off, he would still look after me.

I was given a charming room in the Upper Household, with a window on the park, and my own slave; an Egyptian, who tended me like a prince. I was fourteen, my looks were changing from boy to youth. I heard the King tell friends that he had foreseen my promise, and I had fulfilled it; he did not believe that for beauty all Asia contained my equal. They would of course agree that I surpassed comparison. Certainly I learned to carry myself as if it were true.

His bed was canopied with a lattice, bearing a pure gold vine. Jewelled grape-clusters hung from it, and a great fretted lamp. Sometimes at night, when it threw on us its leaflike shadows, he would stand me by the bed and turn me here and there to take the light. I thought this possession of the eyes would have contented him, but for his respect for his manhood.

However, on other nights he wanted entertainment. The world seems full of people who desire the same thing each time, not enduring the least change in it; this is tedious, but does not tax invention. The King liked variety and surprise; himself he was not inventive. I had run through all that Oromedon had taught me, and began wondering when the day would come for me, too, to start training my successor. There had been a boy before me, I had found out, who had been packed off after a week, because the King found him insipid.

In search of ideas, I visited the most famous whore in Susa, a Babylonian, who claimed to have trained at some temple of love in India. To prove it, she had a bronze in her room (bought I daresay, if truth were told, from a passing caravan) of two demons, with six or eight arms apiece, having intercourse while dancing. I doubted this would delight the King, but kept my hopes. Such women will always oblige a eunuch now and then; they get more men than enough; but her crude squirmings so disgusted me that without regard for good manners, I got up and dressed. As I put down my gold piece, I said I would pay for her time, since I had wasted it, but I could not stay to instruct her. She was so angry, I was halfway downstairs before she found her voice. So I was thrown on my own resource, since it seemed there was no one better.

It was then that I learned to dance.

As a child I had liked it, following the men, or prancing and spinning to some tune out of my head. I knew, if I were taught, I still had it in me. The King was glad for me to learn accomplishments (I did not mention the Babylonian) and hired me the best master in the city. It was not like my infant games; one had to train as hard as a soldier; but this I welcomed. It is idling makes eunuchs flabby; standing about, gossiping, waiting for something to do. It was good to get in a sweat and stir my blood.

So, when my tutor said I was ready, I danced in the fountain court for the King and his friends; an Indian dance with a turban and spangled loin-cloth; a Greek dance (so I believed) in a scarlet chiton; a Kaukasian dance with a little gilded scimitar. Even the lord Oxanthres, the King's brother who had always looked down his nose at me because he liked only women, called out 'Bravo!' and tossed me a piece of gold.

By day I danced in my finery; at night too I danced, wearing only the shadows of the fretted lamp that hung from the golden vine. I soon learned to slow down the pace towards the end; he never gave me time to get my breath.

I often wondered if he would have set such store by me if the Queen had not been captive. She was his half-sister, by a much younger wife of their father, and was of an age to have been his daughter. They said she was the loveliest woman in all Asia; of course he would be content with nothing less. Now he had lost her to a barbarian younger than she, and, from his deeds, it would seem hot-blooded. Of course he never spoke of such things to me. Indeed, once in bed he hardly spoke at all.

About this time, I caught a summer fever. Neshi, my slave from Egypt, nursed me with much kindness. The King sent me his own physician; but he never came himself.

I remember Oromedon's scar. Since my mirror gave me bad news, it was better so. Yet, being young, I must have had something left in me that still looked for – I don't know what. I cried once in the night, when I was weak and silly; Neshi got up from his pallet to sponge my face. Soon after, the King sent me some gold darics, but still did not come. I gave the gold to Neshi.

It was when I was about again, and had been playing my harp in the fountain court with the King alone, that the Grand Vizier himself came in, panting with news. The Queen's Eunuch had escaped from Alexander's camp, and begged audience.

Had others been there, they would have been dismissed and I could have followed. But I was like the birds and the fountain, part of the appointments. Besides, when the man came in, for secrecy they spoke Greek.

No one had ever asked if I understood it. As it happened, there were several Greek jewellers in Susa, whom my old master traded with, in gems, or in me. So I had come to the Palace with a smattering, and had often passed idle time by listening to the Greek interpreter. He did all kinds of business in public, between court officials and suitors to the King; fugitive tyrants from Greek cities freed by Alexander, or envoys from states like Athens, which he had spared, as it seemed, to intrigue against him; generals of Greek mercenaries, shipmasters and spies. With all the Persian repeated in Greek, it was easy to learn by ear.

Impatient even through the Prostration, the King asked if his family were alive. The eunuch said yes, and in good health; moreover, they were given their royal rank, and fitting quarters. This, he said (he was an oldish man and looked the worse for his long journey) was how he had escaped so easily; the guard on the royal women was posted more to keep intruders out, than anyone in.

On the ends of his chair-arms I could see the King's hands working. No wonder. What he had to ask, should not be asked of a servant.

'Never, my lord!' The eunuch's gesture called God to witness. 'My lord, he has not come even into her presence since the day after the battle, when he came to promise his safeguard. We were there all the time; he, also, brought a friend with him. I have heard that his companions, in their wine, recalled the fame of her beauty, and urged him to change his mind; and he too had been drinking, as all Macedonians do, yet he was angry, and forbade them to name her in his presence again. One who was there assured me of it.'

The King was some time silent. Having given a long sigh, he said in Persian, 'What a strange man.' I thought he would go on to ask what he looked like, which I myself wished to know; but of course, he had seen him in the battle.

'And my mother?' He fell now into Persian. 'She is too old for these hardships. Is she well cared for?'

'Great King, My Lady's health is excellent. Alexander always inquires for it. When I left, he was visiting her nearly every day.'

'Visits my mother?' His face had changed suddenly. I thought that he looked pale. I could not think why; the Queen Mother was over seventy.

'Indeed, my lord. He gave her offence at first; but now, when he asks her to admit him, she always gives him leave.'

'What insult did he offer her?' asked the King. He sounded eager.

'He gave her a parcel of wool for weaving.'

'What? Like a slave?'

'So My Lady thought. But when she showed her affront, he begged her pardon. He said his mother and sister did such work, and he thought it would give her pastime. When My Lady perceived his ignorance, she accepted his apology. Sometimes they will be talking, through the interpreter, an hour together.'

The King sat staring before him. Presently he gave the eunuch leave to go, and, remembering my presence, signed to me to play. I played softly, seeing him troubled. It was to be many years before I understood the cause.

I gave the news to my friends at court; for I had friends by now, some in high places, some not, who were glad to hear things first. I took no presents for this; it would have been like selling my friendship. Of course I took bribes, to further suits with the King. To refuse would have been to proclaim enmity, and someone would have poisoned me. Needless to say, I did not bore the King with their tedious suits; it was not for such things he kept me. I would say sometimes, 'So-and-so gave me this to get your favour'; it amused him, because the others did not tell. Now and then he would ask, 'What did he want?' and say, 'Well, we must keep you in credit. I daresay it can be arranged.'

The strange conduct of the Macedonian King was much debated. Some said he liked to show himself a man of iron, above pleasure; some that he was impotent; some that he was keeping the Royal Family unharmed, to get good terms of surrender. Others, again, said he liked only boys.

The Queen's Eunuch said that, indeed, he was waited on by a band of highborn youths; but this was the custom of all their kings. In his own belief, it was in the young man's nature to be generous with suppliants. He quickly added that for beauty and presence he could not compare with our own King; he would scarcely stand higher than Darius' shoulder. 'Indeed, when he visited the ladies to give his safeguard, the Queen Mother bowed to his friend instead. If you will believe it, they walked in together, side by side, and hardly distinguished in dress from one another. The friend was taller, and handsome for a Macedonian. I was distraught, having seen the King in the royal tent already. The friend drew back, and she saw my warning signs. She was of course distressed, and began her prostration again before the King. But he raised her in his hands, and was not even angry with this man; he said, as the interpreter assures me, "Never mind, Mother, you weren't far out; he is Alexander too."'

Well, they are barbarians, I thought. Yet something sighed in my heart.

The eunuch said, 'I never saw a king keep so little state; he lives worse than any general would with us. When he entered Darius' tent, he stared like a peasant at its appointments. He knew what the bath was, and used it, the first thing he did; but for the rest, one had hard work not to smile. In Darius' chair his feet would not touch the ground, so he put them on the wine-table, taking it for a footstool. However, he soon moved in like a poor man with a legacy. He looks like a boy, till you see his eyes.'

I asked what he had done with the royal concubines; had he preferred them to the Queen? The eunuch said they had all been presented to his friends; he had not kept one. 'It's boys then,' I said laughing. 'So now we know.'

The girls from the harem, whom the King had taken along, were of course the choicest, and a great loss to him. However, he still had plenty; some only of his nights were spent with me. Though it is true that, by old custom, there were as many women as days in the year, some were of course past youth; and it is an absurdity such as only Greeks could invent, that they were paraded nightly round his bed to choose from. Now and then he would visit the harem, look over the girls, and learn from the Chief Eunuch there the names of five or six he found most pleasing. Then at night he would send for one; or sometimes for all the group to play and sing to him, later beckoning one to stay. He liked to conduct such matters gracefully.

When he went there he often took me with him. Of course I should never have been brought in the Queen's presence; but I ranked rather higher than the concubines. He liked to have his beautiful possessions admired, if only by one another. Some of the girls were exquisite, with a fragile bloom like that of the palest flowers. Even I could dream of desiring them. Perhaps Oromedon had saved me from great danger; for already one or two had slid their eyes at me.

I met him once, crossing a courtyard in the sun, gaily dressed as ever; it was strange to know my own clothes were richer now. At first sight, I would have run straight up to embrace him; but he smiled softly and shook his head, and I now knew enough of courts to understand. It would never do, to have it seen that from the dish prepared for his master, he had kept a portion back. So I returned his smile in secret, and passed him by.

Sometimes, when the King had a girl at night, I would lie in my pretty room, smelling the scented breezes from the park, looking at moonlight striking my silver mirror, and thinking, How pleasant and cool this is, to lie here alone. If I loved him, I should be grieving. It made me sad and ashamed. He had done me many kindnesses, raised me to honour, given me my horse and the gifts my room was full of. He had not asked love of me, not even to pretend it. Why should I think of such a thing?

The truth was, for ten years I had been beloved by parents who loved each other. I had learned to think well of love; having had none since. I had not learned to think worse. Now I was at the age when boys fumble about and make their first mistakes, laughed at by unkind girls before their elders, or tumbling some sweaty peasant and thinking, So this is all? To me none of this could happen; love was the image of lost happiness, and the stuff of fantasy.

My art had no more to do with love than a doctor's skill. I was good to look at, like the golden vine though less enduring; I knew how to wake appetite grown sluggish with satiety. My love was unspent, my dreams of it were more innocent than a home-bred boy's. I would whisper to some shadow made of moonlight, 'Am I beautiful? It is for you alone. Say that you love me, for without you I cannot live.' It is true, at least, that youth cannot live without hope.

Summer grew hot in Susa; this time of year, the King should have been in the hills, at the summer palace of Ekbatana. But Alexander still sat before Tyre, stubbornly running out a mole to it; this was all I knew then of that great piece of siegecraft. Any time, they said, he might weary of the task, and turn inland; then Ekbatana would have been too far away. Indeed, it came to my ears that the captains thought the King should have stayed in Babylon. One said, 'The Macedonian you would find nearer the action.' Another answered, 'Well, it's only a week from Susa down to Babylon; the generals there are doing well enough on their own. Or better.' I slipped off unseen. It was no part of my duty to inform on men who meant no harm and were only speaking too freely, as my father had once done. To do the King justice, he never asked it of me. He did not mix business with pleasure.

Then Tyre fell.

Alexander had broken the wall and stormed the breach. There had been a great killing; the Tyrians had murdered Alexander's envoys before the siege, and then had flayed his men by pouring red-hot sand on them. The Tyrians who survived the sack had been enslaved, except those in Melkaart's sanctuary. It seemed Alexander revered this god, though he called him Herakles. What all this meant was that Persian ships had no port of call in the Middle Sea north of Egypt, save Gaza, which could not hold out long.

Little as I knew of the western empire, the King's countenance told me how great the disaster was. Alexander's way was now clear to Egypt where our rule was hated ever since Ochos put back our yoke on them. He had defiled their temples and killed their holy bull-god; now, if our satraps there were to shut gates against Alexander, the Egyptians would spear them in the back.

Soon we all knew that the King had sent an embassy, led by his brother Oxathres, suing for peace.

The terms were not divulged. I had never been fool enough to coax the King for secrets. I'd been offered huge bribes to do it; but one learns as one goes along, and I found it policy to take small ones, saying he kept his counsel well, and though I would do my best for them, it would be cheating them to accept more. Thus they bore no grudges, and I could not come under the King's suspicion, for I never asked him anything.

Even though the embassy used the royal post-stages for fresh horses, lords do not ride like King's Messengers racing the wind. While we waited, life at the Palace was at pause, like dead air before a storm. My nights were spent alone. In those weeks, the King took a great turn for women. I think it gave him assurance he was a man.

When the embassy did return, its news was stale. Oxathres had thought Alexander's answer should go quickly, and sent a copy by King's Messenger. Galloping the Royal Road with fresh horses and fresh men, it arrived half a month ahead.

No need to ask questions. You could feel the thud of it all through the Palace and on into the city. All the world can quote it now, even from memory, as I do.

You may keep your ten thousand talents; I am not in want of money, I have taken enough. Why only the half of your kingdom to the Euphrates? You offer me the part in exchange for the whole. Your daughter whom you speak of, I shall marry if I choose, whether given by you or not. Your family is safe; no ransom is required of you; come here yourself and make your suit to me, you shall have them free. If you desire our friendship, you have only to ask.

There was a time, I forget how long, perhaps a day, of still, stunned whisperings. Then suddenly all was trumpeting and shouting. Heralds proclaimed the King was marching west to Babylon, to ready his troops for war.

4

We started in a week. It was without precedent for the Household to move so fast. The Palace was in an uproar. All the chamberlains were clucking about like hens. The Chief Eunuch of the Harem was trying to make the King decide which girls to take; the Warden of the Silverware appealed to me to choose out his favourite pieces. He himself had no time for me; the men he now called to conference wanted no dancing with it, and at night, he was so tired that he even slept alone.

One day I took my horse along the river-bank where the lilies grow in spring. I could see clear to the hills. Our fort was going back to its native stones. I half thought of riding up to say farewell; but I remembered looking back there, from the captain's horse, the saddle-bag with my father's head bouncing and dripping. The flames of the burning rafters had risen thirty feet high. I went back, and saw to my packing.

The eunuchs of the Household would travel like the women, in covered carts with cushions; but no one expected this of me. I saw my horse groomed, and had a try at an ass for Neshi; but he had to walk with the other followers.

I took my good clothes, and a change of clothes for the road, and some dancing-costumes. My money and my jewels were in my belt-wallet; there too, in case of mischance, I put my hand-mirror and combs, and my eye-paint with its brushes. I never used carmine. No one should, who has the true Persian looks. It is vulgar to colour ivory.

I bought also a little dagger. I had never used weapons; but at least, for the dance, one is taught to hold them properly.

The older eunuchs were much distressed at it, and begged me to leave it behind. They meant that unarmed eunuchs taken in war count as women, but with weapons not. I replied that any time I liked I could throw it away.

The truth was, I had dreamed again of my father, the old frightful dream. Though I woke in a sweat, I knew he had the right to come to me, his only son, demanding vengeance. In the dream, I heard the name of the traitor who had betrayed him, as he cried it on his way to death. In the morning, as always, I forgot it. There seemed small chance I would ever give him his rights; but at least for his sake I would go armed. There are eunuchs who become women, and those who do not; we are something by ourselves, and must make of it what we can.

It is the custom for the King to start a march at sunrise; I don't know if it's to give him the blessing of the sacred fire, or to let him have his sleep out. The carts and carriages were drawn up overnight. Most of us were astir soon after midnight getting ready for the road.

At daybreak, I could scarcely believe the real army was at Babylon, and that this horde, stretching a mile both ways, was no more than the Household.

The King's Guard, the Ten Thousand Immortals, who never left his person, took up a good deal of road. Then there were the Royal Kin. It is a title of honour, not of blood; there were fifteen thousand, though ten thousand had gone on to Babylon. They looked very fine; all their shields were worked with gold, and as they formed up by torchlight, the jewels in their helmets flashed.

Presently came the Magi with their silver carrying-altar ready to kindle the holy fire and lead the march.

As I rode to and fro gaping at each new splendour, I wondered if I was working my horse too hard, with the march before him. Then I remembered that however many the horses and chariots were, the column would go at walking-pace, for the foot-men, and the Magi with their silver altar. I thought of the rashly-spoken captain, who had said it was only a week from Susa down to Babylon. He was of course in cavalry. At this rate, we would take a month.

The transport alone seemed to stretch for miles. There were a dozen wagons for the King alone, for his tent, his furniture, his robes and tableware, his travelling bathroom and its appointments. There were the wagons for the Household eunuchs, and for their belongings; then the wagons for all the women. The King had taken all the younger concubines in the end, more than a hundred; they and their gear and their eunuchs were only the beginning. The lords at court, who'd not yet gone ahead to Babylon, had their wives and children with them, their harems, and all *their* luggage, as well. Then there were the store-wagons; such a host could not live off the country. The torches now stretched further than I could see. And behind the wagons and baggage-train there were still the foot-followers: the army of slaves to set up camp and strike it, the cooks and smiths and grooms and harness-menders, and a great troop of personal servants, such as mine.

I rode back from the road to the Palace square, as the torches paled. Now they were bringing out the Chariot of the Sun. It was sheathed all over with gold; a sunburst emblem stood in it on a silver pole; the symbol of the god, its only rider. Not even the body of its charioteer would sully it; its matched pair of great white horses was led on foot.

Last came the King's battle-chariot, nearly as splendid as the god's. (I wondered it if was as good as the one he had left for Alexander.) The charioteer was putting in the King's weapons, javelins and bow and arrows in their holsters. In front of it stood his litter for the journey, with gold shafts, and a sun-canopy fringed with bullion.

As the east began to glow, appeared the Sons of the Kindred, elegant youths a little older than I, who would march before and behind the King, dressed from head to foot in purple.

All this order of the march was fixed by ancient hierarchy. It was time to find my place alongside the eunuchs' wagons; clearly there was none for me near the King.

Suddenly, above the Sun Chariot shone a brilliant point of light. The centre of its sunburst was a globe of crystal. It had caught the first shaft of sunrise. There was a bray of horns and blare of trumpets. In the distance a figure in white and purple, tall even from so far, stepped into the royal litter.

Slowly, without at first any forward movement, the vast train stirred into fidgeting and shuffling. Then, sluggish as a winter snake, it began to crawl. We must have been moving nearly an hour, before one felt to be really marching.

We travelled the Royal Road, through the land of rivers, low and green, with thick crops in rich black earth. Shallow lakes mirrored the sky, spiky with sedge. Sometimes great rough-rock causeways spanned the swamps. Now they were mostly caked and dry, but we never made camp there; they had a name for fever.

I attended the King each evening when his tent was pitched. There was room for most of his usual people. He seemed to like the sight of familiar faces. Often he kept me at night. He was harder to stir up than I had ever known him, and I wished he would settle for sleep instead. But I think the truth was that, if alone, he would lie awake.

Every few days, galloping to meet us, the last man and horse of the long relay as fresh and swift as a stag, a King's Messenger brought despatches from the west.

Alexander had taken Gaza. It seemed he had nearly been put out of the way for good. He had been struck on the shoulder by a catapult-bolt, and felled clean backwards; it had pierced his armour, but he had got up and gone on fighting. Then he had fallen again, and been carried off like the dead. Our people had waited a while to see, he being known by now for a man who was hard to kill; and sure enough, though he had bled himself white, he was still alive. He would be laid up some time; but his advance guard was already on the march to Egypt.

When this was known, I thought to myself, Perhaps he's shamming, so that we take our time; then he could strike east like lightning and take us by surprise. Now if I were the King, I thought, I would be out of my litter into my chariot, and dash on ahead with all the cavalry to Babylon, just in case.

I longed for the trumpet calling us to ride. Each evening, reckoning that Neshi would have had enough with his footmarch, I curried my horse myself. I had called him Tiger. I had only seen the skin of one, but it was a good fierce name.

But when I went to the King at evening, he was playing draughts with one of the lords, in such abstraction that the man had hard work to lose. When the game was over, the King asked me to sing. I remembered the battle-song of my father's men which he had liked before; I hoped it would cheer his soul. After two verses, however, he called for something else.

I thought of his old combat with the Kardousian champion, which had won him his renown; I tried to picture him striding forward in arms, hurling his javelin, stripping the enemy of his weapons, returning to the warriors' cheers. He had been younger then; he had had no palaces, and fewer girls. And then again, a battle is different from such a combat, especially if one is in command; still more, if one is meeting the man from whom one fled last time.

My song drew to its end. I said to myself, Who am I to judge? What action shall I ever see? He has been a good master; that should be enough for me, who will never be a man.

Each morning, the Standard of the Sun was set up by the King's pavilion. Each morning, when the first sunbeam struck the crystal, the horns sounded, the King was escorted to his litter, the chariot was walked behind it. So we followed the Royal Road through the river country, and the night followed each day.

When I grew weary of the eunuchs' talk in the wagons, I would sometimes fall back to the harem train, to have a word with the girls. Each load, of course, was in charge of at least one reverend eunuch; if invited, I was safe enough to hitch my horse to the tailboard and clamber in. I found it instructive. This horde of women was nothing like my old master's little harem. The King was achieved once in a summer, or a year, or never; or he might send for a girl most nights in a month, then never notice her again. On the whole, it was each other they had to live with; they were full of factions, alliances and bitter feuds, few of which came of rivalry for the King, but simply of seeing each other day after day, with nothing to do but talk. It was amusing to visit such a world as this; I hoped never to be employed within it.

It was amazing how fast news flew along the column. People talked from tedium, to enliven the miles. Alexander was already getting about again, and was sending spies to learn where Darius was. From what I had heard by now, I could guess what was baffling the Macedonian. He would have thought of everything, except that his enemy could still be upon the road.

However, he must soon have found out; the next thing we heard, he was making south for Egypt. So there was no hurry after all.

We marched on, fifteen miles a day, till we came to the maze of canals and streams which lead the Euphrates into the Babylonian cornfields. The bridges are built high for the floods of winter. Sometimes the rice-fields spread their tasselled lakes, off which the morning sun would glance to blind us. Then one noon, when the glare had shifted, we saw ahead the great black walls of Babylon, stretched on the low horizon against the heavy sky.

Not that its walls were near; it was their height that let us see them. When at last we passed between the wheatfields, yellowing for the second harvest, which fringed the moat, and stood below, it was like being under mountain cliffs. One could see the bricks and bitumen; yet it seemed impossible this could be the work of human hands. Seventy-five feet stand the walls of Babylon; more than thirty thick; and each side of the square they form measures fifteen miles. We saw no sign of the royal army; there was room for it all to encamp within, some twenty thousand foot and fifty thousand horse.

The walls have a hundred gates of solid bronze. We went in by the Royal Way, lined with banners and standards, with magi holding fire-altars, with trumpeters and praise-singers, with satraps and commanders.

Further on was the army; the walls of Babylon enclose a whole country-side. All its parks can grow grain in case of siege; it is watered from the Euphrates. An impregnable city.

The King entered in his chariot. He made a fine figure, over-topping by half a head his charioteer, shining in white and purple. The Babylonians roared their acclamation, as he drove off with a train of lords and satraps to show himself to the army.

We of the Household were led through back ways along the straight high streets, to enter the Palace through doorways suited to our station, and make ready for the Master.

Knowledge can alter memory. I see in my mind those glories; the fine-clay brick, polished, sculpted, enamelled, glazed or gilded; the furniture of Nubian ebony inlaid with ivory; hangings of scarlet and purple, woven with gold and stitched with Indian pearls. I remember the cool, after the baking heat outside. And it seems that the coolness fell on me like the shadow of blinding grief; that the very walls oppressed me like a tomb. Yet I suppose I went in like any lad after a journey, wide-eyed for all the sights.

When they had laid out the King's own vessels for his food and wine, they made the bed, which was plated all over with gold, a winged deity at each bedpost. Then, for he would surely come back tired and dusty from his ride, they prepared the bath.

Because it is hot in Babylon, the bath is a pleasure-house, where one could spend all day; floored with marble from the west, with glazed walls, white flowers on blue. The bath is a spacious pool, whose lapis-blue tiles have gold fish impressed in them. There are pots with sweet shrubs and trees, changed at each season, jasmine and citron; the fretted screens give on to a bathing-place, let in from the Euphrates.

Everything had been prepared, everything shone; the water was clear as crystal, tepid, just right, the tank warmed with filtered sun. There was a couch with cushions of fine linen, to rest on after the bath.

Not a tile, not a golden fish, not a thread of linen there will ever leave my memory while I live. When I saw it that first time, I just thought it very pretty.

Soon we had settled in, the days turning as smoothly as the water-wheels below the Hanging Gardens; though our lot was lighter than the oxen's there. That beautiful man-made hill with its shady trees and the cool groves within its terraces, needs a deal of watering, and it's a high haul to the top. Often amid its bird-song you can hear, if you listen, the cracking of whips below.

Fresh troops were still coming in from the distant satrapies, after months upon the march. All the city turned out to see the Baktrians. It was cooling down for autumn, but still they sweated, having put on their best for show;

felt coats, quilted trousers, and fur-lined hats, all fine and warm for the
Baktrian winters. You could tell their land was rich, by the lords' adornments, and the sturdy build of the men after so long a march. Each lord
brought from his own stronghold his own warriors, as my father would
have done if he'd been alive. But the Baktrian lords numbered hundreds.
Their baggage was borne by a long train of their two-humped camels,
long-bodied and thick-legged, shaggy, built for endurance.

At the head rode their satrap, Bessos, Darius' cousin. The King greeted
him standing, in the Hall of Audience, and offered his cheek to kiss. He
was the taller, but not much. Bessos was thickset like his camels, war-
scarred, burnt almost black with sun and wind. They had not met since
the defeat at Issos. Now I saw in Bessos' eyes, pale under black brows, a
show of respect over a shadow of scorn; and in the King's, a shadow of
mistrust. Baktria was the most powerful satrapy in the empire.

Meantime, news came that Egypt had opened its arms to Alexander,
hailed him as liberator, and proclaimed him Pharaoh.

I knew little of Egypt then. I know it now; I live there. I have seen him
carved on a temple wall, worshipping Ammon, made to look just like all
the other Pharaohs, even to the little blue strip of ceremonial beard.
Perhaps when they put on him the double crown, and set in his hands
the crook and flail, he even wore it. He was courteous in such things. But
it makes me smile.

He had been to Ammon's oracle, at green Siwah in the desert, where
it seems he was told the god was there before the King his father, when
he was conceived. So rumour ran; he went in alone, and said only, after,
that he was satisfied.

I asked Neshi about this oracle, while he dressed me and combed my
hair. He had been at a school for scribes, till Ochos conquered Egypt, when
they had all been taken from their temple and sold. Even now, he still
shaved his head.

He said the oracle was very old and revered. Long ago (and from an
Egyptian that means at least a thousand years), the god used to speak in
Thebes as he does at Siwah. In the days of the terrible Hatshepsut, the only
woman Pharaoh, her stepson Tuthmosis was a young boy serving the
shrine. The symbol of the god was carried by, as at Siwah now, in a boat
enriched with gold and jewels and tinkling vessels. The bearers say that
the carrying-poles press on their shoulders, when the god wants to speak;
they feel the weight of him telling them where to go. He guided them to
this young prince, who then was a nobody in the crowd, and made the
boat bow before him; and they set him in the royal seat, knowing his
destiny. Neshi had some very good tales like this.

I myself, when I made my pilgrimage (and a hard journey it is, though

I have known a worse one), asked a question of the oracle. I was told it was enough for me to offer the proper sacrifice, and not be curious about one who had been received among the gods. Still, I could not be content never to have seen it.

Meantime at Babylon I had time on my hands, the King being always busy, and went about seeing the sights. I climbed the stair round Bel's temple-tower, though the top was ruinous where his concubine used to lie on his golden bed. I was much beset by bawds, my youth still being enough to explain my beardlessness. And I saw the temple of Mylitta with its famous courtyard.

Every girl in Babylon, once in her life, must offer herself to the goddess. The courtyard is one huge bazaar of women, sitting in rows marked off with scarlet cords. None may refuse the first man to toss in her lap a piece of silver. There were some as fine as princesses, on silk cushions, with slaves to fan them, next to hard-handed peasant girls from the fields. Along the rows strolled the men, as if at a horse-fair; I half expected they'd start to look at their teeth. The pretty ladies don't have to wait long; but if a river bargee gets there before a lord, they must take him. Not a few stretched out their hands to me, hoping to pay their due with someone not too ill-favoured. There was a grove near by, where the rite was done.

Seeing some men standing laughing, I went to look. They were mocking the ugly girls, who sat day after day unchosen. That I might share the joke, they pointed out one to me who had been sitting there three years.

She had grown there from girl to woman. One shoulder was hunched; she had a great nose, and a birthmark on her cheek. The girls round her, plain as they were, seemed to look at her and take comfort. She just sat with folded hands, enduring the laughter, as an ox the whip and goad. Suddenly I was filled with anger at man's cruelty. I thought how the soldiers had cut off my father's nose alive instead of dead; how the men who gelded me had talked lightly across my pain. I took out a silver siglos from my pouch, and tossed it in her lap, saying the ritual words, 'May Mylitta prosper you.'

At first she seemed scarcely to take it in. Then the loafers gave a great bawdy cheer. She grasped the coin and looked up bewildered. I smiled and offered her my hand.

She got to her feet. Nothing could have made her anything but hideous; yet even a clamp lamp is beautiful, when its light shines at dusk. I led her from her tormentors, saying, 'Let them find some other pastime.' She trotted along beside me, shorter by a head, though I was not yet full-grown. Low stature is despised in Babylon as in Persia. Everyone was staring, but I knew I must walk with her as far as the grove.

Inside, it was a disgusting spectacle. No Persian could well conceive it.

The trees and bushes were not nearly enough for decency. In my worst days at Susa, I met no one so lost to shame as to do such things except in the inner room.

When we were just within the gate, I said to her, 'You may be sure I won't put you to such disgrace as that. Farewell; live happy.' She looked at me smiling, still too dazed to take in my words; then pointed into the grove, saying, 'There is a good place.'

That she could really expect such a thing, had never entered my head. I could scarcely credit it. Though I had meant to keep my secret, I said unwillingly, 'I can't go in the grove with you. I am one of the King's eunuchs. I was angry with them for mocking you, I wanted to set you free.'

For a moment she stared at me, her mouth falling open. Then suddenly she screamed out, 'Oh! Oh!' and struck me two great slaps in the face, one with each hand. I stood with singing ears, while she ran off down the street, crying out, 'Oh! Oh! Oh!' and beating her breast.

I was astonished, and wounded by her ingratitude. It was no more my fault I was cut, than hers that she was ugly. But as, brooding on it, I walked home, it came to me that ever since I was born, somewhere I had been wanted, whether for good or ill. I tried to think how it would be, to have lived twenty years and never once have known it. It killed my anger; but I went home sad.

Babylon grew mild with winter. I turned fifteen, though no one knew but I. Our family, like all Persians, had always made much of birthdays. Even in five years, I had never quite grown used to waking on the day, knowing it would be just like any other. The King had never asked me when it was. It seemed childish to mind; he had been generous on many other days.

News came in piecemeal from Egypt. Alexander had been restoring the ancient laws; he had held a great feast, with contests for athletes and musicians. At Nile mouth he had laid out the plan for a city, marking the lines with meal, which flocks of birds had swooped down to feed on; this omen was held to mean that the city would come to nothing.

I wonder how it looked when the birds came down. Flat green land, with papyrus growing; a few palms; some donkeys grazing; a cluster of fisher-huts. It is Alexandria now, a palace among cities. Though he never saw it, he has returned to it for ever; and instead of birds it has taken in men from all quarters under heaven, as it has taken me.

Next after the Baktrians, the Scythians came to Babylon, those who were Bessos' vassals; wild shaggy fair-haired savages, their faces tattooed blue. They wore pointed lynx-skin bonnets, loose blouses, and trousers tied at the ankle; ox-carts bore their black tents and their women. They are great bowmen. But they stink to heaven; if they are washed in their lives, it is by the midwife in mares' milk. They were hurried away into camp. No people could afford to be as shameless as the Babylonians, if they did not bathe every day.

News came that Alexander had left Egypt. He was marching north.

The King called a council in the great audience-room. I hung about outside, to watch the great men leaving. A boy's curiosity took me there; but I learned something of use, which has stayed with me ever since. Only keep quiet at such a time and look like nothing, and you will see men reveal themselves. In the Presence, they have had to show respect and keep half their thoughts unspoken; outside, each will turn to whoever he felt to share his mind; and intrigue begins.

Thus I saw Bessos single out Nabarzanes, who had been in Babylon long before the King, for he was Commander in Chief of the cavalry. He had fought at Issos. His men thought well of him.

It was in the pleasure-houses, where I went to watch the dancing, that I heard them talk. They did not know who I was, as people did at Susa. Certainly, I was never tempted to carry their words to the King. They said that at Issos Nabarzanes had fought a great battle, though the King's choice of ground had been a blunder. The cavalry had charged when the rest were faltering, taken on the Macedonian horse, and hoped to turn the tide; then the King had fled, among the first to leave the battle. With that came rout. No one can fly and fight; but the pursuer can still strike. There had been a great slaughter; they blamed the King.

I had been long with soft-spoken men; I had not thought such words possible. They hurt me; one lives in one's master's name, and shares disgrace. The captain I'd overheard at Susa must have been one of Nabarzanes'.

He was tall and lean, Nabarzanes, with the pure-bred Persian face, clear-carved and proud. Yet he was easy-mannered, and could laugh, though not over often. At court he often greeted me very pleasantly, but it never went beyond that. I could not tell if he had a liking for boys, or not.

He and Bessos looked odd together, Nabarzanes sword-slim, in the plain good clothes of Persia; huge Bessos with his black bush of beard and chest as deep as a bear's, dressed in embroidered leather with chains of barbaric gold. But they were soldiers who had met upon campaign. They walked off quickly out of the press, as if impatient to talk in private.

Most people talked in public; and soon all Babylon knew what had passed in council. The King had proposed that the whole Persian army should retire to Baktria. There he could raise more troops from India and Kaukasos, fortify the eastern empire, or some such thing.

It was Nabarzanes who had stood forward, and quoted the words of

Alexander's first defiance, when he had still been taken for a vaunting boy. 'Come out and fight me. If you will not, I shall follow you wherever you may be.'

So the army stayed in Babylon.

To fall back on Baktria! To surrender, without another blow, with all its people, Persis itself, the ancient land of Kyros, the heart and cradle of our race, even that with the rest. I, who had nothing left there but a memory and a roofless ruin, had been shocked to my soul; what Nabarzanes felt, his face had told me. That night, the King kept me with him. I tried to keep my mind on the kindness he had shown me, and forget the rest.

Soon after, I awaited him one morning in his inner room, when a white-haired, straight old man was shown into the ante-room. He was the satrap Artabazos, who had rebelled against Ochos, and lived an exile in Macedon in King Philip's day. I went in and asked if I could bring him anything while he waited. As I'd hoped, he began to talk to me; and I asked if he had ever seen Alexander.

'Seen him? I have sat him on my knee. A beautiful child. Yes, even in Persia one would call him beautiful.' He sank into himself. He was very old. He could have left it to his many sons, to follow the King to war. I thought he was getting absent, as old men will; when suddenly he opened a bright fierce eye under his thick white brows. 'And afraid of nothing. Nothing at all.'

In spring, Alexander returned to Tyre. He sacrificed, and held some more games and contests. It seemed he was asking the gods' goodwill for a new campaign. When spring turned to summer, the spies reported him on the march for Babylon.

5

It is three hundred miles north up the Tigris valley, from Babylon to Arbela.

Alexander had turned north-east from Tyre, to skirt the Arabian deserts. From the north he would come down. The King marched north with the royal army; and the Household went with the King.

I had pictured an endless column of men, miles long. But the army was spread all over the plain, between the river and the hills. It was as if the land grew men instead of corn. They were wherever one looked, horse, foot and camels. The transport wound along in little trains, where the going was best. Apart, given as wide a berth as lepers, were the scythed chariots, with long curved blades standing out from their wheels and cars. One soldier, who was dim of sight and got in their way, had had a leg taken off, and died of it.

The Household had a fair passage; outriders went ahead to find us the smoothest ground.

Alexander had crossed the Euphrates. He had sent engineers ahead to bridge it; the King had sent Mazaios, the Satrap of Babylon, with his men to stop them. But they pushed it out from their own side by sinking piles; when Alexander came up with all his forces, Mazaios' horse retired. The bridge was finished next day.

Soon we heard he was across the Tigris. He couldn't bridge that; not for nothing is it called The Arrow. He had simply breasted through it, going first himself to feel the way. They had lost some baggage, but no men.

Then we lost him awhile. He had turned from the river plain, to take his men round by the hills, where it was cooler and would keep them fresh.

When his route was known, the King rode out to choose the field of battle.

He had lost at Issos, his generals had told him, because he had been cramped for room and could not use his numbers. There was a fine broad plain, about sixty miles north of Arbela. I never saw it myself; the Household was to be left in town with the gold and stores, when the King took the field.

Arbela is a grey and ancient city, standing on its hill. It is so old, it goes back to the Assyrians. This I believe, for they still worship Ishtar without a consort. She stares at you in the temple, horribly old, with huge eyes, grasping her arrows.

We were all in turmoil, finding quarters for the women; being shoved aside by soldiers who wanted strong houses for the treasure and billets for the garrison; preparing a house for the King while he should need it (the governor had to turn out for that). There was hardly time to think we were on the eve of battle.

Just as we were settling down, there was crying and wailing in the street, and a rush of women to the temple. I felt a strangeness, even before I saw the omen. The moon had been eaten by darkness. I saw her last curve vanish, sombre and red.

I grew cold. The people were wailing. Then I heard the brisk soldier's voice of Nabarzanes, telling his men that the moon is a wanderer, so was the Macedonian, and the omen was for him. All those around were heartened. But from the old grey temple where the women had served Ishtar a thousand years, I could still hear wailing, like a high wind in trees.

The King had sent a great troop of slaves to the battlefield, to level out broken ground for the chariots and the horse. His spies had told him the Macedonian horse were much fewer, and they had no chariots at all, let alone scythed ones.

The next news came not from spies but by envoy. He was Tyriotes, one of the eunuchs attendant on the Queen. Alexander had sent him, to bring word that she was dead.

We wailed as was proper, then the King sent us out. We could hear him shouting aloud, and Tyriotes crying out in fear. At length he came outside, shaking all over, dishevelled from tearing his hair and clothes.

He had been captured before my time in the Household, but the older ones knew him well. They gave him cushions, and wine which he badly needed. We listened in case the King should summon us, but heard no sound. He put his hand to his throat; it looked bruised and red.

Boubakes the Egyptian, the Chief Eunuch of the Household, said, 'It is never good to bring bad news to the great.'

Tyriotes rubbed his throat. 'Why are you not wailing? Mourn, mourn, for the love of God.'

For some time we made the sounds of grief. The King did not call us. We took Tyriotes to a quiet corner. A house is safer for talking than a tent.

'Tell me,' he asked, 'has the King been distempered lately?'

We said, only a little out of spirits.

'He shouted at me that Alexander had killed the Queen trying to rape her. I embraced his feet, I repeated that she had died of sickness in the arms of the Queen Mother. I vowed Alexander had not set eyes on her, from that first day till she was on her bier. When she died, he held up his march for a day and mourned her fasting; that was my message, that she had had all her proper rites. What have the spies been doing? Is the King not informed of anything? Surely he knows Alexander does not care for women?'

We said that he had certainly heard as much.

'He should be thankful Alexander did not give the ladies to his generals, as most victors would. He has burdened himself with a royal harem, from which he is getting nothing. The Queen Mother . . . I don't know what ailed the King; he should be glad she is well cared for, at her age, by so young a man. It was only when I spoke of it, that he broke out. He said all this grief for the Queen was what a man shows his bedfellow. He took me by the throat. You know what huge hands he has; I am still hoarse from it, you can hear. He threatened me with torture unless I told the truth. To quiet him, I said I would submit to it if he wished.' His teeth were chattering; I held the wine-cup for him, lest he spill it. 'At last he believed me; God knows every word was true. But from the first, it seemed to me, he was not himself.'

Still silence from the King. Well, I thought, the bad omen of the moon has been fulfilled. It would calm the people.

The prince Oxathres had been sent for; now he came, and they lamented together. The Queen had been his full sister by the same mother; he was some twenty years younger than the King. After this, the King's grief having been released by weeping, we put him to bed; also Tyriotes, who looked ready to faint. His throat had turned black next day; he had to use a scarf to cover it, when the King summoned him again.

He went in terror, but was not kept for long. All the King asked him was, 'Did my mother send any word to me?' He answered, 'No, my lord; but she was much disordered with grief.' The King then gave him leave to go.

Word came that the battle-ground was ready, as smooth to drive or ride on as a street. On one flank were the hills, on the other was the river. So the King put off his mourning, as not being proper for leading troops in war. All Persian kings lead the centre as all kings of Macedon lead the right. His chariot was brought up, equipped with all his weapons; he was dressed in his coat of mail.

Two or three eunuchs of the Bedchamber, who always saw to his clothes and toilet, went to attend him in camp. To the last I wondered if he would take me. It scared, yet drew me. I thought I could fight, if put to it, and it would be my father's wish. I hung about, but the King said nothing. With the rest I stood to see him mount his chariot, and withdrew from his escort's dust.

Now we were just the Household, women, eunuchs and slaves. The battle-ground was too far even to ride in sight of. We could only wait.

I went up to the walls, and looked to the north, and thought, I am fifteen years old. I would have my manhood, if it had not been taken away. If my father had lived, he would have brought me with him; he never held me back from anything I dared to do, not even for my mother. I would be with him now among our warriors, laughing together and making ready to die. That I was born to; this I am. I must make the best I can of it.

It came into my head to go round the yards where the women's wagons were, to make sure the horses were stabled near, the harness mended, the drivers ready and sober. I told them the King had ordered it, and they believed me.

While about this meddling, I ran, to my surprise, into Boubakes of Egypt,

the Chief Eunuch; a tall and stately person, who had always been civil to
me, but distant; I don't think he approved that the King should keep a boy.
However, he asked me without reproof what I was doing. His own
presence was more remarkable.

'I was thinking, sir,' I said, 'that the wagons should be ready. Supposing,' I said, looking him in the eye, 'the King should pursue the enemy.
He would want the Household with him.'

'My own thought also.' He gave me a grave approving nod. It was no
lie that our thoughts had been just the same. 'The King has a far greater
host than he had at Issos. Half as many again.'

'Truly. And the scythed chariots, too.' We looked at each other, and
then away.

I hired Tiger, my horse, a private stable, with good strong doors, and
took care to keep him exercised.

The King's Messengers had been set up with their relay-posts, to take
despatches between the King and Arbela. Most days one came in. In a day
or two, we heard the Macedonians had appeared on the hills above the
plain of Gaugamela, where the King was awaiting them. Later again, that
Alexander had been sighted, shown up by his flashing armour, riding with
his scouts to survey the field.

That night there was a great play of summer lightning, which brought
no rain. It was as if the north skies were burning. For hours it flickered
and danced, without sound of thunder. The air was heavy and still.

Next day I waked in the dawn-dark. All Arbela was astir, the garrison
were busy about the horse-lines. At sun-up, the walls were full of people
gazing north, though there was nothing to see.

I met Boubakes again, visiting the women's quarters, and guessed he
was telling their eunuchs to look alive. Harem duties make such people
fat and lazy. Still, these were faithful to their trust, as we were soon to
learn.

Taking Tiger for his canter, I felt him on edge; he'd caught it from the
other horses, who'd caught it from the men. Coming back I said to Neshi,
'Keep a watch on the stable. See no one breaks in.' He asked no questions,
but was as twitchy as the horses. In war many chances can happen to
a slave, both good and bad.

At noon came a King's Messenger. The battle had begun soon after sun-
up. Our army had stood-by all night, the King thinking that Alexander,
being outnumbered, might try for a surprise; but he had waited till the sky
was bright, before engaging. The Messenger was the sixth of the relay; he
knew no more.

Night came. The soldiers lit watch-fires along the walls.

Towards midnight, I stood up there near the north gatehouse. It had

been hot all day, but the night wind blew cool, and I went back to get my
coat. As I returned, suddenly Northgate Street was filled with clamour;
men heaving and crushing back from the road, the halting drum-beat of
half-foundered horses, the crack of whips. The riders drove on like
drunken men who have forgotten where they are going. These were not
Messengers; they were soldiers.

As they began to come to themselves and slow down a little, people
came with torches. I saw the men white with caked dust, streaked with
dark blood; the horses' nostrils flaring scarlet as they fought for breath,
their mouths all bloody foam. The men's first word was, 'Water!' Some
soldiers dipped their helmets in a near-by fountain and brought them
dripping. As if the mere sight had given him strength, one of the riders
croaked, 'All's lost . . . The King is coming.'

I shoved forward and shouted, 'When?' One who had had a gulp to
drink said, 'Now'. Their horses, maddened by the smell of water, were
dragging them on, trying to get to the fountain.

The crowd engulfed me. Wailing began, and rose to the night sky. It
crawled and surged in my blood like fever. I raised a voice which I hardly
knew for mine, a shrill crying like a girl's; it flowed from me, without my
will, without shame. I was a part of lamentation, as a raindrop is part of
rain. Yet as I cried, I was fighting to get out through the press. I freed
myself, and made for the King's house.

Boubakes had only just come out upon the threshold, and was calling
a slave to go and learn the news. My wailing ceased. I told him.

Our eyes spoke without more words. Mine, I suppose, said, 'Again the
first to run. But who am I to say so? I shed no blood for him, and he has
given me all I have.' And his answered, 'Yes, keep your thoughts to
yourself. He is our master. That is the beginning and the end.' Then he
cried out, 'Alas! Alas!' and beat his breast in duty. But next moment he
was calling all the servants to make ready for the King.

I said, 'Shall I see the women put in the wagons?' The wailing was
washing all over the city, like a river risen in flood.

'Ride round to tell the wardens, but do not stay. Our duty is with the
King.' He might not approve of his master keeping a boy; but he
would look after all his property and have it ready. 'Have you your
horse?'

'I hope so, if I can get to him fast enough.'

Neshi was watching the stable door, without making a show of it. He
had always had good sense.

I said, 'The King's coming. I shall have to go with him. It looks like a
hard journey, and worse for foot-followers. I don't know where he means
to go. The Macedonians will soon be here. The gates will all be open; they

might kill you, or you might get away, even to Egypt. Will you run with us, or take your freedom? Make your own choice.'

He said he would take his freedom, and if they killed him he would still die blessing my name. He prostrated himself though he was nearly trampled doing it, before he ran off.

(He did get back to Egypt. I found him quite lately, the letter-writer in a good village not far from Memphis. He almost knew me; I have good bones, and have looked after my figure. But he could not place me, and I kept quiet. I said to myself it would not be proper, now where he was respected, to remind him of his slavery. But the truth is too, that though the wise man knows all beauty is born to perish, one does not care to be reminded of that either. So I thanked him for pointing me out my road, and went my way.)

As I took Tiger out from his stall, a man ran up, and offered to buy him for twice what he was worth. I had been just in time; soon horses would be fought over. I was glad my dagger was in my sash.

At all the harem houses, there was a great packing and harnessing-up; you could hear from outside a chittering like a bird-seller's shop, and smell great drifts of scent from the stirred-up clothes. Each eunuch asked me where the King was going. I wished I knew, to set them on their way before their mules were stolen. I knew that some would be caught by the Macedonians, and hated leaving them to their fate; I was less needed where I was going, and my heart was not in it. But Boubakes had been right. Faithfulness in disaster, as my father would have told me, is the only guide.

As I turned back into Northgate Street, my errand done, there was a pause in the wailing, like a storm-wind dropping to silence, and a sound of dead-beat horses. Through the stillness drove the King.

He was still in his chariot, with his armour on. A handful of cavalry came behind him. His face was empty, like a blind man's whose eyes can open.

There was dust on him, but no wound. I saw his escort, with faces slashed, or a limp arm, or a leg half-blackened with clotted blood, gasping with thirst from their bleeding. These men had covered his flight.

On my fresh horse, in my clean clothes, with my whole skin, I had not the face to join this company. I made for the house by side-streets. This was the man who came forward to fight the Kadousian giant, when no other would. How long ago? Ten years – fifteen?

I thought of what he had come from now; the din, the dust-cloud; hurling of man on man and mass on mass; the heaving tide of battle; the sense of some plan reaching out for him, which was the mask for another plan; then the mask whipped off, the trap sprung; finding himself no more than a King of chaos. And then, the presence nearing him that he had seen and fled at Issos, that had haunted him all the way. Should I judge? I thought. On my own face there is not even dust.

It was the last time I could say so for many days. Within an hour, we were off towards the Armenian passes, making for Media.

6

From the hills we climbed to the mountains. We were on the road to Ekbatana. There was no pursuit.

By troops and single stragglers, the remnant of the army caught us up. Soon, if you had not seen what had taken the field, you could have called us a great force. Bessos' Baktrians were all there, but for the dead. Being headed for their homeland, of course they had kept together. They were still nearly thirty thousand. The Immortals, and Royal Kin, and all the remnant of the Medes and Persians, both horse and foot, were now led by Nabarzanes.

We had, also, all the Greek mercenaries, about two thousand. It amazed me that, fighting only for hire, not one of them had deserted.

The most grievous loss was Mazaios, Satrap of Babylon, and all his men. They had held their line, long after the centre had broken with the flight of the King, whose life they may well have saved; Alexander, hot in chase of him, had had to turn back and deal with them. Not one of these brave warriors was with us now; they must all have perished.

Only about a third of the women's wagons had escaped from Arbela; two of the King's; the rest, the harems of lords who had stayed themselves to rescue them. But not one of the eunuchs had run off without his charges. What their fate was, I have never heard.

All the treasure was lost. But there were vaults of it at Ekbatana; the stewards had wisely loaded up with stores for the march, which we would need much more. Boubakes, I found, had had the King's baggage-wagon all packed since morning. In his wisdom he had loaded a second tent, with a few small comforts for the royal eunuchs.

Even so, it was a hard rough journey. It was early autumn by now; still hot in the plains, but cool in the hills, and already cold in the mountains.

Boubakes and I had horses; three eunuchs rode in the baggage-wagon. No more of us were left, except those of the women.

Each pass wound up higher and steeper; we looked down great clefts into stony gorges; wild goats gazed at us from the crags, and were shot for food by the Baktrian archers. At night, short of blankets in our little tent, the five of us huddled like birds for warmth. Boubakes, who had taken me into his grace and behaved to me as a father, shared blankets with me so that we had them double. He favoured some scent with musk, but I was grateful. We were lucky to have a tent at all; nearly all the soldiers, their baggage lost, were sleeping under the sky.

From them, I pieced together the battle as best I could. Later on, I was to hear it gone over by men who knew; tactic by tactic, order by order, blow by blow. I have it by heart; I can't bring myself to go over it all again. To cut it short; our men all started tired, having stood-to all night because the King expected surprise. Alexander, hoping for that very thing, gave his own men a good night's rest, and, when he'd finished his battle-plan, turned in himself. He slept like a log; at sunrise they had to shake him. He told them it was because his mind had been at ease.

Darius leading the centre, Alexander the right, he was expected to sweep centrewards at the onset. Instead, he wheeled round to outflank our left. The King sent troops to prevent this; Alexander lured more and more of them to the left, thinning out our centre. Then he formed up the royal squadron, set himself at its head, gave the note for a deafening war-yell, and came thundering straight for the King.

Darius had fled early, but not, after all, the first. His charioteer had been shot with a flying javelin; when he fell, he had been taken for the King. The first flight began from this.

Perhaps he would have stood in a single fight, as long ago in Kadousia. If he had only seized the chariot-reins, and given his war-cry, and dashed in among the enemy! It would have been quick, his name would have lived in honour. How often, before the end, he must have wished it too. But, caught in the panic like a leaf in storm, seeing Alexander on his black horse loom up through the dust towards him, he wheeled the chariot and joined the rout. From that, the plain of Gaugamela became a slaughterhouse.

One thing I learned from the soldiers. Darius had detailed a troop to sortie behind the Macedonian lines, and rescue his captive family. They had reached the base-camp, shielded by the confusion; freed some captive Persians, and, getting to the ladies, called on them to fly. All had started up, except Sisygambis the Queen Mother. She neither rose, nor spoke, nor made any sign to the rescuers. They rescued no one; the Macedonians drove them off; but the last they saw of her, she was sitting upright in her chair, her hands laid in her lap, looking before her.

I asked one captain why we were going to Ekbatana, instead of holding out in Babylon. 'That whore of cities?' he said. 'She'll open her legs to Alexander the moment he comes in sight. And hand the King over, if she had him there.' Another said sourly, 'When wolves are after your chariot, you either stay and fight them, or throw them something out, to keep them busy. The King's thrown Babylon. And with Babylon goes Susa.'

I fell back to ride beside Boubakes, who did not think it proper I should talk too long with the men. As if he had read my thoughts, he said, 'Did you say, once, you had never seen Persepolis?'

'The King never went there since I joined the Household. Is it better than Susa?'

He sighed and said, 'There is no king's house more beautiful ... Once Susa is gone, I doubt they can hold Persepolis.'

We went on through the passes. The road was clear behind us. Alexander had chosen Babylon and Susa. When the column's pace grew tedious, I practised archery. Some time before, I had picked up the bow of a dead Scythian, who had fled to the hills and then died of his wounds. Horsemen's bows are light, and I could pull it easily. The first game I got was a sitting hare; but the King was pleased to have it for supper, as a change from goat.

He was quiet of an evening, and for some nights slept alone, till the air grew sharp, when he had a girl from the harem. He never sent for me. Perhaps he remembered the song of my father's warriors, that I used to sing him. I do not know.

The high peaks were touched with white, when from the head of the last pass we saw Ekbatana.

It is, if you like, a palace and walled city. But it seemed more like some splendid sculpture wrought from the mountain-side. The westering sun warmed the rich faded colours that crested its sevenfold walls, rising in tiers with the slope; the white, the black, the scarlet and blue and orange. The inmost two, which enclose the palace and treasuries, had a fiery gleam. The outer was sheathed with silver, the innermost with gold.

To me, bred in the hills, it was lovelier than Susa a thousand times. I almost shed tears beholding it. I saw that Boubakes too seemed near to weeping. But what grieved him, he said, was that the King should be driven to his summer palace with winter coming on, and no other left for him.

We entered the city gate, and went up through the sevenfold walls to the palace above the golden battlements. It was all airy balconies, looking to the mountains. The soldiers, overflowing the town, built themselves huts of timber roofed with brush. Winter came on.

The snow that had tipped the mountains crept lower and filled their clefts. My room (there were rooms to spare, for so small a Household) was high in one of the towers. Each day I could see the white descending; till one morning, as in my childhood, I opened my eyes to the snow-light. Snow lay on the city, on the thatched huts of the soldiers, on the sevenfold walls. A raven lighted on the nearest, loosing a little slide, and there showed under his claw a patch of gold. I could have gazed for ever, except that I was freezing. I had to break the ice in my water-ewer; and winter was only starting.

I had no warm clothes, and told Boubakes I must go to the bazaar. 'Don't do that, my boy,' he said. 'I have been going through the Wardrobe. There are things that have been lying there since King Ochos' day. I have just the thing for you. No one will miss it.'

It was a splendid coat, of lynx-skin lined with scarlet; it must have belonged to one of the princes. This was good of Boubakes. He may have noticed the King had not lately sent for me, and wanted to make me pretty.

The mountain air was like health after long sickness. I daresay it did more for my looks than the coat; at all events, the King sent for me before long. But he had changed since the battle. He was restless and hard to please; and I felt, as I never had before, that without warning he might turn against me. It put me on edge; I wanted only to get it over.

However, I could understand, and did not hold it against him. He had just had news of how Babylon the Whore had opened her bed to Alexander.

Even against him, I should think those great walls could have held out a year. But the Royal Gate was opened. The Royal Way was strewn with flowers, and lined each side with altars and tripods burning precious incense. A procession met him bringing kingly gifts; pure-bred Nisaian horses, flower-wreathed oxen, gilded cars with leopards and lions in cages. The Magi and Chaldeans chanted praises, to the sound of harps and lutes. The cavalry of the garrison paraded without their weapons. Compared with this, the welcome to Darius had been like that for some third-rate governor.

Even this was not the worst. The envoy who met Alexander on his march, and put the keys of the citadel in his hands, had been the Satrap, Mazaios, whom we had mourned for dead.

He had done his duty in the battle. No doubt in the dust and din he had not known at first that the King had fled. He had hoped for support, for victory. When he knew, he made his choice. He had led back his men at speed, lest he should be too late for Alexander. He had been in time; Alexander had re-appointed him. He was still Satrap of Babylon.

For all Mazaios' homage, Alexander had marched warily on the city, in battle order, leading the van himself. However, it was not too good to be true. He had Darius' gilded chariot brought, and entered in proper style.

I tried to picture this wild and strange young barbarian in the palace I knew so well. For some reason, perhaps because the first thing he did in Darius' captured tent was to take a bath (by all accounts, he seemed as clean as a Persian), I saw him in the bath-house, with its lapis tiles and gold fish, splashing in the sun-warmed water. It was an envious thought, at Ekbatana.

The servants fared well; their quarters had been unchanged for centuries, since the Median kings had lived there all through the year. It was only the royal rooms which, when the empire grew, had been made open and airy, to catch the mountain breezes in summer heats. Snow blew in at the windows.

We got shutters made, with fifty carpenters at it, and filled the place with braziers. But nothing could really warm it. I could see how it irked the King, to think of Alexander basking in Babylon's mild air.

The Baktrians, who have hard winters at home, would have been well clad, had they not stripped-down in the heat of Gaugamela and then lost their baggage. The Persians and the Greeks were no better off. The men from mountain satrapies went hunting their own furs; others bought in the bazaar, or rode into the country and robbed the peasants.

Prince Oxathres, and the lords and satraps, had quarters in the palace. Bessos laughed at the cold through his black beard; but Nabárzanes noted we had tried to give him some comfort, and thanked us civilly. He was one of the antique school.

The soldiers had been paid from the palace treasury. They brought the town trade; but being short of whores, caused much contention over honest women. When I went out riding, I soon learned to skirt the barracks of the Greeks. Their repute for liking boys is not unearned. Though they must have known I served the King, they would whistle and call, without any sense of propriety. However, it was their custom; and I respected their fidelity in disaster.

The last leaves fell from the lean and spiky trees, stripped by the wind even of snow. Drifts closed the roads. Each day passed like yesterday. I shot at a mark for pastime, and practised my dancing, though it was hard to warm-up and save myself from sprains.

The King's days passed heavily. Oxathres his brother was hardly thirty, unlike him in looks and mind, and would be gone for days on hunting-trips with other young lords. The King would entertain the satraps and nobility by turns to supper; but he would sink into his thoughts, and forget to invite their conversation. He got me to dance, I think, chiefly to relieve him of the need to talk. But the guests, who had few diversions, were gracious and made me gifts.

I thought it would not have been out of place to invite Patron, the Greek commander. But it never entered his head, to have such people indoors.

At last it thawed, and a messenger got through the half-flooded roads; a horse-coper from Susa, who came for the reward. We depended on such people now; they were always well paid, however bad their news was.

Alexander was in Susa. The city, though without the fulsomeness of Babylon, had opened its gates at once. He had taken entire the treasure, hoarded reign after reign; a sum so vast that, when I heard it, I could not believe there were such riches in all the world. Truly, enough to keep the wolf from the chariot.

As winter hardened, closing the roads again, shutting us up together week after week with only the muddy town or the barren hillsides, men grew prickly or dull or sour. The soldiers fell into tribal factions, reviving old feuds from home. Townsmen came up to complain that their wives, or daughters, or sons had been debauched. The King would not be troubled with such trifles; soon all petitioners sought Bessos or Nabarzanes. Yet idleness made him moodier; it fell on one man or another mostly by chance, but everyone was on edge from it. All that befell later, as I believe, was hatched in those long white empty days.

One night he sent for me, the first time in a long while. I saw Boubakes, as he withdrew from the Bedchamber, signal discreet congratulation. But from the first I was ill at ease with myself, uncertain of the King. I remembered the boy before me, packed off for being insipid. So I tried something which had amused him once at Susa. Suddenly he pushed me off, fetched me a great slap on the face, said I was insolent, and ordered me out of his sight.

My hands were shaking so, I could hardly get my clothes on. I stumbled down cold corridors, half-blinded with tears of pain, anger and shock. Putting my sleeve to my eyes to wipe them, I ran clean into someone.

The feel of his clothes told me he was a lord. I stammered an apology. He put both hands on my shoulders, and looked at me by the light of the wall-sconce. It was Nabarzanes. I swallowed my weeping in shame. He had a biting turn of mockery when he chose.

'Why, Bagoas,' he said with the greatest gentleness, 'what is it? Has someone been ill-using you? That lovely face of yours will be bruised tomorrow.'

He spoke as if to a woman. It was natural; yet, fresh from humiliation, I found it too much to bear. Without even dropping my voice, I said, 'He struck me, for nothing. And if he is a man, then I reckon so am I.'

He looked down at me in silence. It sobered me; I had put my life in his hands. Then he said gravely, 'I have nothing to say to that.' While I still stood rooted, feeling my words' enormity, he put his finger-tips to my stinging cheek. 'It is forgotten,' he said. 'We must all learn to hold our tongues.'

I would have prostrated myself, but he raised me up. 'Go to bed, Bagoas. And don't lose sleep over your future, whatever may have been said. He will forget it, no doubt, tomorrow, or the day after.'

All night I scarcely closed my eyes; but not from fear for myself. He would not betray me. At Susa, I had grown used to the petty court intrigues; to office-seeking, backbiting of rivals, the endless play for favour. Now I knew that I had looked into far deeper places. He had not hidden his contempt; and it was not for me.

When my bruise was gone, the King sent for me to dance and gave me ten gold darics. But it was not the bruise that hung about my memory

7

With the turn of winter, we had good news from the north. The Scythians, those in alliance with Bessos, were to send us ten thousand bowmen, as soon as spring cleared the passes. The Kadousians, who live by the Hyrkanian sea, had answered the King's summons with a promise of five thousand foot.

The Governor of Persis, Ariobarzanes, also got a message through. He had walled, clean across, the great gorge of the Persian Gates, the pass into Persepolis. It could be held for ever; any army that went in would be destroyed from the heights above, with rocks and boulders. Alexander would, with any luck, be dead with his men before they reached the wall.

I overheard Bessos saying, as he passed me with a friend, 'Ah, it's there we should be, not here.' Happy for him, had some god fulfilled his wish.

It's a long hard ride from Persis to Ekbatana, with only one spare horse. Before that news even reached us, if we had known it, Alexander was in Persepolis.

He had tried the Persian Gates; soon found them deadly, and withdrew his men. They had thought him gone. But he'd heard from a shepherd, whom he later made rich for life, of some dizzy goat-track, by which if he did not break his neck he could outflank the pass. Over this he led his men through darkness and deep snow. He fell on the Persians from their rear, while the rest of his people forced the pass, now freed of its defenders. Our men were grain between the millstones. Meantime, we rejoiced at Ekbatana.

Days passed; the snow lay crisp, the sky was clear and windless. From the Palace windows I could see, between the orange battlements and the blue, the town lads throwing snowballs.

Long used to being with men, I had scarcely thought how it would be, to be a boy among others. I had just turned sixteen; now I would never know it. It came to me that I had no friends, as those boys down there would understand it. I had only patrons.

Well, I thought, no use lamenting; it won't put back what the slave-dealer cut away. There is the light and the dark, the Magus used to tell us, and all things that live have the power to choose.

So I rode out alone, to see the sevenfold walls with their colours and their metals, shining in the snow. On the hills a new air touched me, a scent of delight breaking through the whiteness. It was the first breath of spring.

The icicles melted from the water-spouts. Brown rusty grass showed through the snow; everyone went out riding. The King called a war-council, to plan for when the roads were open and the new troops came. I took out my bow, and shot a fox in a gully. It had a beautiful pelt, with a silver sheen. When I had taken it to a furrier in the town, to have a hat made out of it, I went back to tell Boubakes. Some servant said he was in his room, he had taken the news hard.

From the passage I heard him weeping. Once, I would not have dared go in, but those days were done. He lay prone on his bed, crying his heart out. I sat down by him and touched his shoulders. He lifted a face all blotched with tears.

'He has burned it. Burned it to the ground. Everything gone, ashes, cinders, dust.' 'Burned what?' I asked. He said, 'The Palace of Persepolis.'

He sat up and clutched a towel, fresh tears pouring down as soon as he had wiped his face. 'Has the King asked for me? I can't lie here like this.' I said, 'Never mind, someone will attend to him.' He went on, gasping and sobbing, about the lotus columns, the beautiful wall-carvings, the hangings, the gilded and coffered ceilings. It all sounded to me pretty much like Susa; but I grieved with him in his loss.

'What a barbarian!' I said. 'And a fool, to burn it when it belonged to him.' We had had that news some time.

'He was drunk, they say. You should not ride out so long, just because the King's in council. He would think it a liberty if he knew; it would do you harm.'

'I am sorry. Here, give me your towel, you need cold water.' I wrung it out for him, then ran down to the Guard Hall. I wanted to hear the messenger, before he was sick of telling his tale.

Those who had heard were still milling it over; but they had plied him with so much wine that he was now pretty near speechless, and was dozing on a pile of blankets. There was a crowd of Palace people, and some soldiers off duty.

A chamberlain told me, 'They were at a feast, all roaring drunk. Some whore from Athens asked him to set the place alight, because Xerxes had burned their temples. Alexander threw the first torch himself.'

'But he was living there!' I said.

'Where else? He sacked the city when first he took it.'

This too I had heard. 'But why? He never sacked Babylon. Or Susa.' I had thought, to tell the truth, of some houses there I would gladly have seen in flames.

A grizzled soldier, a captain of a hundred, said, 'Ah, there you have it. Babylon surrendered. So did Susa. Now in Persepolis, the garrison made a run for it, or started getting what they could out of the palace for themselves. So no one surrendered, not in form. Well, now; Alexander gave out prize-money to his men at Babylon, and again at Susa. But it's not the same. Two great cities fallen, and never a chance to loot. No troops will stand that for ever.'

His loud voice had roused the messenger. He had stolen two horses from the stables, while the Palace burned, and had enjoyed his importance here, till the wine had quenched him. 'No,' he said thickly, 'it was those Greeks. The King's slaves. They got free, they met him on the way, four thousand of them. Nobody knew there were so many, not till they came together.' His voice droned off. The soldier said, 'Never mind, I'll tell you later.'

'He cried over them.' The messenger gave a belch. 'One of them told me so; they're all free now, free and rich. He said he'd send them all home with enough to live on; but they didn't want to be seen there, not as they are now. They asked for some land they could farm together, being used to the sight of each other. Well, then he was angry like nobody ever saw him, and marched straight up to the city and let loose his men. Just kept the Palace for himself, till he burned that too.'

I remembered Susa, and the Greek slaves of the royal jeweller; their leg-stumps, their branded and noseless faces. Four thousand! Most must have been there since King Ochos' day. Four thousand! I recalled Boubakes, bewailing the ravaged beauty. I don't suppose such people had come much in his way; or not more than two or three of them.

'So,' said the soldier, 'there's an end to the New Year Festivals. I was posted there once; it was the sight of a life-time. Well, it's war. I was with Ochos' force in Egypt ...' He frowned to himself. Presently he looked up.

'I don't know how drunk he was. He saved his bonfire, till he was ready to be leaving.'

I understood him. Spring was breaking everywhere. But no soldier expects a eunuch to know anything.

'He's burned his quarters behind him. And you know where he'll be coming now? He'll be coming here.'

8

It was a day of late spring rain, with brown torrents in the gullies, when the King ordered the women to be sent north. They were to go through the pass of the Kaspian Gates, to safe keeping in Kadousia.

I helped load them into the wagons. You could see at a glance the favourites; they looked worn out, with blue streaks under their eyes. Even after these farewells, there were figures lingering on the palace roof, gazing after them.

To the common soldiers it meant nothing, unless it shortened their lords' tempers. Their own women would trudge behind them, with the sacks that were their households, as soldiers' women have done since wars began. Being more used than the ladies to shifting for themselves, not a few had scrambled off from Gaugamela.

Alexander had set out for Media. He seemed in no great haste, attending to this and that on his way. We would soon be on the north road, where the Kadousian and Scythian troops would march to meet us. With them, we would await him, and contest his passage to Hyrkania. So it was said. It was said also, though not so loudly, that if he were heard of within a hundred miles, we would be off through the passes ourselves, to Hyrkania and east to Baktria. 'When we serve the great, they are our destiny.' I tried to live each day as it came.

On a clear day in early summer we started out. Where the road turned into the hills, I turned as I rode, to see the light of sunrise gleam on the golden battlements. Beautiful city, I thought, I shall never see you again. Had I only known!

As we passed mountain hamlets, I noticed how lean the peasants were, and how sullenly they watched us. It was a poor countryside for an army to have lived off. Yet, when the King passed by, they all did reverence. He was a god to them, set above his servants' deeds. It has been in the blood of us Persians a thousand years. It was even still in mine, who knew what the god was made of.

We rode through bare open hills, under blue skies. The birds were singing. The cavalry sang as they rode; Baktrians mostly, on their stocky rough-coated mounts. Up here, it was hard to think one would not live for ever.

But as we advanced, the singing fell silent. We were nearing the meeting-place appointed with the Scythians. They had sent no fore-runners; nor had the Kadousians. Our own scouts had seen no signs of them.

The King retired early. Though the women were gone, he did not send for me. Perhaps what happened at Ekbatana had killed desire; or perhaps it had only happened because desire was waning. If so, I must prepare to be just a household eunuch, with my little daily duties. Had we been at court, I might already have been allotted them.

If that happens, I thought, I will take a lover. I remembered Oromedon; he had had the sheen on him that, when I looked back, told its tale. I myself had plenty of offers; discreet, of course, for fear of the King, but I had been let known where I was wanted.

With such follies the young, to whom each joy or trouble seems eternal, will concern themselves while the sky is about to fall.

Two days took us off the north road on to a country track. It led to the plain where the Scythians should be awaiting us.

We reached it about noon, a great space of upland grass and brush. Our camp had been pitched where a few starved trees leaned to the wind. There was a whining of curlews; coneys bobbed off among the stones. For the rest, in my life I had seen nothing look so empty.

The night came down. One grew used to the sounds of the camp; singing, the hum of talk, laughter or quarrelling, an order, the rattle of cookpots. Tonight there were just a low muttering, like the sound of a torrent grinding its stones. It went on late. I fell asleep at last to the sound.

At daybreak, I woke to bad-news voices. Five hundred cavalry had slipped off in the night; and nearly a thousand foot, taking all their gear but their shields.

There was a voice outside speaking Greek to the interpreter. It was Patron, the Greek commander. He had come to report his men all present.

Long since, they could have deserted to Alexander, and helped him sack Persepolis. Here they had just their wages, while the treasury held out. Patron was a thick-set grizzled man, with the square face not seen among Persians. He came from some part of Greece that had been beaten in war by Alexander's father, and had brought his men along with him; they had served in Asia since King Ochos' day. I was glad to see the King show him more warmth than usual. However, when at sun-up he called a war council, Patron was not invited. He was a hired soldier and an outlander. He did not count.

The throne was set on its dais; the royal tent was cleared and ready. The lords came straggling up, their coat-skirts flapping in the sharp wind, wearing the best clothes they had left; crowding outside, awaiting leave to enter. To one side, Bessos and Nabarzanes, were talking eagerly. Some shock, which felt long expected, came to me from their faces.

I went in, and said softly to Boubakes, 'Something dreadful is going to happen.'

'What do you mean?' He grasped my arm till it hurt.

'I don't know. Something against the King.'

'Why say such things, if you do not know?' He was cross because I had stirred his smothered fears.

The lords came in, did reverence, and took their stand in order of rank. We eunuchs, inside in the King's sleeping-place, listened through the leather curtains. This was mere custom; it was not a private audience. Though, if we could, we would listen to those as well.

The King spoke from the throne. It was soon too clear that he had composed the speech himself.

He praised his hearers' loyalty, reminding them – trusting man – how renegades like Mazaios of Babylon had been enriched by Alexander. He talked a good deal of past Persian glories, till I could feel the rising impatience with my skin. The pith came at last; he was for a last stand at the Kaspian Gates, victory or death.

There was a hush so thick, you could have stuck a knife in it upright. The Persian Gates, held by crack troops, had been forced in depth of winter. It was summer now; and as for our troops, could he not feel their temper?

But I, who had once been near him, thought I understood. He had not forgotten the song of my father's warriors. I felt his craving for lost honour. He had seen himself at the Kaspian Gates, gloriously redeeming Gaugamela. And not one man of all that were here had seen it with him. This was their answer, this dreadful silence.

On the toilet-table was the little knife we trimmed his nails with. I reached for it, jabbed it through the curtain, and put my eye to the slit. Boubakes looked shocked. I handed the knife to him. The King had his back to us; and for the rest of them, if we'd stuck our heads through the curtain, they'd not have noticed.

The King sat stiffly on his throne; I could see the peak of the Mitra, and a purple sleeve. And I saw what he saw – the faces. Though no one had dared a whisper in the Presence, they were all one glitter of moving eyes.

Someone stepped forward; old Artabazos, with his straight shrunk carriage and snow-white beard. When first I'd seen him, I had thought him in good shape for a man running up to eighty. In fact, he was ninety-five. As he approached, the King stepped down, and leaned him his cheek to kiss.

In his firm, high, ancient voice, Artabazos said that he and his sons would stand to the last man, with all their people in whatever field His Majesty should see fit to choose. The King embraced him. He withdrew to his place. For long moments, silence returned.

There was a movement, a low murmur. Nabarzanes came forward. I thought, It is now.

He was wearing the grey wool coat with embroidered sleeves, which he'd had on that night at Ekbatana. It was old and frayed. I daresay he had no better, so much had been lost. Power and danger hung about him, from his first words.

'My lord King. In this hour of so grave a choice, it seems to me we can look forward only by looking back. Firstly, our enemy. He has resource, great swiftness, and resolution. He has good troops, attached to his person. It is said, with what truth I cannot tell, that in hardships and in courage he is their example.' He made a tiny pause. 'At all events, he can now reward loyalty with Your Majesty's wealth. All this is said of him; but what else do we hear wherever his name is spoken? That he is fortunate; that he has all the luck.'

A longer pause. They hardly breathed, now. Something was coming; and some of them knew what.

'But is this so? I find a stray blood-horse on my land, you may call me fortunate. Or you may call its owner unlucky.'

People at the back, who knew nothing, shifted about. The stillness in front was louder. I could see the purple sleeve stir on the chair-arm.

'Let godless men,' said Nabarzanes smoothly, 'speak of chance. We, surely, reared in our fathers' faith, believe all things are disposed by heaven. Why should we think the Wise God favours Alexander, an out-land robber following other gods? Should we not rather, as I said, look back seeking some past impiety for which we suffer punishment?'

The silence was now entire. Even the most ignorant had caught, like dogs, the scent of thunder.

'Lord King, the world knows with what blameless honour Your Majesty assumed the throne, after horrors you had no share in.' His voice had sunk to a deep leopard purr of irony. 'Through your justice, a treacherous villain did not live to boast of them'. (He might just as well have added, 'or to accuse you'.) 'And yet, what has been our fortune since? We are the bowl

Alexander's luck has emptied. My lord, it is said that curses can outlive
the guilty dead. Is it not time to ask if Mithra, protector of honour, is yet
appeased?'

Stillness. They had begun to see, but did not yet believe.

Nabarzanes' voice altered. Towering Bessos moved up towards him.

'My lord King, our peasants, when they are lost in their own hills, turn
their coats, that the demon leading them astray may no longer know
them. There is old wisdom in simple folk. We too, I now believe, must turn
the unlucky garment, though it be of purple. Here is Bessos, who shares
with yourself the blood of Artaxerxes. Let him wear the Hood, and command till this war is over. When the Macedonians are driven out, Your
Majesty can return.'

At last, they believed. In the lifetimes of us all, two kings had died by
poison. But it was a thing unknown to man, that a Great King, robed and
enthroned, should be told to get up and go.

The silence broke; loud cries of assent, prompt and prepared; shouts of
dismay and outrage; mutterings of doubt. Suddenly a great shout of
'Traitor!' drowned all the rest. It was the King, striding down from the dais
in his purple robe, his scimitar drawn, making for Nabarzanes.

He was terrible in his size and fury. Even to me, in his royal state he
was clothed with godhead. I looked to see Nabarzanes blasted at his feet.

Instead, there was a crowd about him. Nabarzanes and Bessos and the
chief Baktrian lords, clinging in supplication. As they clung, begging
mercy, they pulled down his sword-arm. His sword hung, uncertainly.
They all prostrated themselves, bewailing their offence, saying they would
withdraw from his displeasure, till he gave them leave to see his face.

They backed out. And all the lords of Baktria followed them.

Someone was panting beside me. Boubakes had made a slit in the
curtain, about twice the size of mine. He was trembling from head to foot.

The tent now milled like a kicked ant-hill. Old Artabazos, his sons, and
loyal Persian lords crowded round the King, protesting their sacred faith.
He thanked them, and dismissed the Council. We had hardly time to put
ourselves in order, before he was inside.

In silence, he let Boubakes disrobe him and put on his leisure gown. He
lay down on the bed. His face looked sunken, as if from a month-long sick-
bed. I slipped outside, without obeisance, without leave. It was an
unheard-of thing to do. I simply knew that just now, there was no one
he would not sooner see about him. Boubakes never reproved me.

I went out into the camp. My clothes were well-worn, and smelled of
the stables now. I had no servant. No one noticed me.

The Baktrians were busy about their quarters. They were starting to
strike camp.

Quick work indeed! Had Bessos' fear of the King been real? Yet I could not see Nabarzanes giving up so easily. I pushed in among a crowd of Baktrians on their way; they were so full of their own concerns, I felt invisible. Mostly they were saying their lord ought to have his rights, it was time for a man to lead. But one said, 'Well, no one can say, now, that the King didn't have his chance.'

Separate and neat, as always, stood the Greek encampment. No one was striking tents there. They were just crowded together talking. Greeks are great talkers, but have often something to say. I walked over.

They were so engaged, I was in among them before anyone even spoke to me. Then one broke away and strode over. As he came, I'd taken him for forty, but now saw he was ten years younger; war and weather had done the rest.

'Beautiful stranger, do I see you here at last? Why do you never visit us?'

He still had real Greek clothes, though the stuff was threadbare. He was tanned as brown as cedar-wood, and the sun had faded his short beard much lighter than his hair. His smile looked honest.

'My friend,' I said, 'this is no day for beauty. Bessos wants to be King. He's just told the King so.' I did not see why I should keep from loyal men what every traitor knew.

'Yes,' he said. 'They wanted us to come over. They offered double pay.'

'Some of us Persians keep faith too, though by now you must be doubting it. Tell me, what are the Baktrians up to? Why are they striking camp?'

'They won't go far.' He was eating me with his eyes, quite frankly, yet without offence. 'I doubt they'll even go out of sight. From what they told Patron, on the face of it they're withdrawing from the King's presence on account of having offended him. Of course, it's really to show their strength. We'll be thin on the ground without them. That's what they want us to see. Well, I've not served as long in Asia as Patron and his Phokians; but I know what good Persians feel about the King. It's not our way in Athens; but our way's come to grief too, that's why I left. So I serve where I sign on, and where I serve I keep my bargain. A man must have something to put his pride in.'

'You may well do that. All of us know it.'

He looked at me wistfully with his bright-blue eyes, like a child asking for something it knows quite well it won't get. 'Well, *our* camp will still be here at nightfall. What do you say to slipping out for a drink with me? I could tell you about Greece, since you speak the language so well.'

I nearly laughed, and said I needed no telling. But I liked him; so I just said smiling, 'You know I serve the King. And just now he needs his friends.'

'Well, no harm in trying. My name's Doriskos. I found out yours.'

'Good-bye, Doriskos. I daresay we'll meet again.' I had no such expectation, but wanted to show goodwill. I gave him my hand, which I thought
he'd never let go of, and returned to the King's tent.

He was shut up alone. Boubakes said he would see no one, or even eat.
Nabarzanes had taken all his cavalry, and had made camp alongside
Bessos' men. Thus far he got, and broke down in tears. It was dreadful to
see him stuff his sash-end into his mouth, not to hide it from a young
nobody like me (that was all I was, now) but lest the King should hear.

'The Greeks are loyal,' I said. Once he would have scolded me for going
anywhere near them. Now he just asked what were two thousand men,
against more than thirty thousand Baktrians, and Nabarzanes' horsemen?

'There are the loyal Persians too. Who's commanding them now?'

He wiped his eyes on the other end of his sash and said, 'Artabazos.'

'*What?* I don't believe it.'

It was true. The ancient was doing a general's round of the Persian
camp, seeing the lords and captains, heartening them before their men.
Such fidelity must have moved a stone. It was strange to think that when
already old by most men's reckoning, he had been a rebel. But that was
against Ochos, who I daresay gave him little choice between that and
death.

Returning from his task, he came to the King, and got him to take food,
which they ate together. We were told to withdraw, but overheard their
talk. Since it was now unthinkable to lead the troops to battle, they would
be marched tomorrow through the Kaspian Gates, starting at dawn.

While we were eating supper in our tent, I said what I could no longer
contain in silence. 'Why didn't the King go round the camp himself? He
could be Artabazos' grandson; he's only fifty. He should make them *want*
to fight for him.'

They turned on me outraged, all together. Was I out of my mind? The
King to bare his countenance to common soldiers, like a mere captain?
Where would his royalty be, what reverence would they have for him? Far
better he should bear adversity, as now, with the dignity of his sacred rank.

'But,' I said, 'Kyros the Great was a general in the field. I know, I come
from his tribe. His men must have seen him every day.'

'Those were ruder times,' said Boubakes. 'They cannot return.'

'So we hope,' I said. I put on my coat again.

By now it was full dark, but for the watch-fires, the torches spiked here
and there into the ground, and the chinks of some lamplit tent. Passing
a dead torch, I smeared some of its soot across my face, made my way to
the nearest watch-fire, where I had heard a Baktrian accent, and squatted
down with the crowd.

You can tell God's curse is on him,' the Baktrian captain was saying. 'It's sent him mad. Marching us through the Gates, to be trapped like rats between the mountains and the Hyrkanian sea. When Baktria could hold out for ever.' He went on about its countless strongpoints, each one impregnable except to the birds of heaven. 'All we need, to finish the Macedonians there, is a King who knows the country. And how to fight.'

'Baktria,' said a Persian, 'I know nothing of. But don't talk of God's curses, if you turn against the King. That's god-cursed if anything ever was.'

There were murmurs of agreement. I wiped my nose on my fingers in a vulgar way, looked stupid, and slid off out of the firelight.

Hearing talk in a tent ahead of me, I was about to slip round it, away from the bright torch outside, when a man came out, so briskly that we collided. He took me by the shoulder, not roughly, and turned me round to the light.

'My poor Bagoas. We seem always to meet like this. Your face is quite black. Has he taken to beating you every night?'

His teeth grinned white in the torchlight. I knew he was as dangerous as a hunting leopard, yet could not fear him, nor even hate him as I knew I ought.

'No, my lord Nabarzanes.' By rights I should have bent my knee; I decided not to. 'But if he did, the King is the King.'

'Well, so. It would have disappointed me, if your loyalty had not matched your beauty. Do wipe that dirt off your face. I shan't harm you, my dear boy.'

I found myself rubbing it with my sleeve, as if I owed him obedience. He means, I thought, that it is too late.

'That is better.' He took off with one finger a smudge I had passed over. Then he laid his hands on my shoulders. His face was no longer mocking. 'Your father died for the King, I've heard. But Arses was the true-born heir, and fit to lead us. Yes, in Arses we would have had a warrior. Why do you think Alexander has not overtaken us? He could have done it long ago. I will tell you the reason; it is contempt. Your father died for our Persian honour. Remember that.'

'I don't forget it, my lord. And I know where my honour lies.'

'Yes, you are right.' He pressed my shoulders and let them go. 'Go back to him. You might lend him some of your manhood.'

It was like the pat of a leopard, claws pricking through the soft paw. As he left, I found that, without thinking, I had bent my knee.

At the royal tent, I met Artabazos leaving. I made reverence and would have passed, but he put out his blue-veined hand. 'You have come from the camp, my boy. What did you find?' I told him it was full of Baktrians, trying to subvert the loyal Persians. He clicked his tongue tetchily. 'I shall have to see these men.'

'Sir!' I said, careless of the impertinence. 'You must sleep. You have had no rest all day and half the night.'

'What I must do, my son, is see Bessos and Nabarzanes. At my age, we don't sleep as you young folk do.' He did not even take a staff to lean on.

He was right. As soon as I'd told Boubakes the news, I lay down, and fell asleep like the dead.

The horns aroused me, with the call 'Prepare to march'. I opened my eyes, and found all the others gone. Something was happening. I scrambled my clothes on, and went out. The King, dressed for the march, was standing before his tent, his chariot already waiting. At his feet knelt Bessos and Nabarzanes. Old Artabazos stood by.

The King was saying how their disloyalty had grieved him. Both hung their heads, and beat their breasts. Bessos' voice, one could have sworn had tears in it. His only wish, he cried, had been to ward off from the King a curse called down by others, as he would have lifted his shield in battle; he would have taken the curse on himself, and borne the wounds. Nabarzanes, touching the King's robe, said that they had withdrawn in awe of his displeasure; it would be their life's joy to be received in his grace again.

I looked with respect and wonder at Artabazos, whose work was thus rewarded; a soul beloved of Mithra, one to go straight to Paradise, whom the River of Ordeal would never scald. All was well again. Loyalty had returned. Light had conquered the dark Lie. I was still quite young.

The King, weeping, reached out his hands to them. They prostrated themselves and kissed the ground before him, declaring themselves the happiest of men and the most devoted. The King mounted his chariot. Artabazos' sons tried to get their father into a wagon, where he could rest. He scolded them soundly, and called for his horse. They withdrew abashed. The eldest was over seventy.

I went off towards the horse-lines. The soldiers, who had been milling and mixing and disputing through the night, were being shoved into marching order. The Persians were shaping best; but then, they were fewer. Fewer than last night, by far. So were the Baktrians; even with their numbers, it showed.

That came of the long night's trafficking. The Persians, knowing themselves outnumbered, had made off by hundreds; but they had put some Baktrians, too, in dread of vengeful Mithra. Between fear of him and Bessos, they had chosen the long walk home.

Riding back towards the Household wagons, I saw the Greeks lined up in column of march. They were all still there. Also, all armed.

On long marches, when no action threatened, they had always piled their armour, helmets and weapons in their carts, keeping only their swords; wearing their short tunics (made from all kinds of stuff, they had been so long from home) and the wide straw hats Greeks travel in, their skins being tender to sun. Now they had on corselets or cuirasses, helmets, even greaves if they owned them; and their round shields hung at their backs.

Just then one fell out, and waved to me. It was Doriskos. What does he take me for, I thought; I will show him if he can make a fool of me in public. I was just going to kick my horse to a canter, when I saw his face. It did not look like dalliance. I rode up.

He grabbed my boot, and motioned me to lean over. No dalliance in that either. 'Can you get word to the King?'

'I doubt it. He's on the road, I'm late. What is it?'

'Tell him not to be fooled. He's not seen the end of it.'

'Oh,' I said cheerfully, 'that's over, they've sued for pardon.'

'We know *that*. That's the thing; that's why Patron made us arm.'

My belly closed on itself. I said, 'What does it mean?'

'No one kept camp last night. It's common talk. They hoped to bring in the Persians; if they had, they'd have acted today. But the Persians said it was god-cursed; that's why so many made off. It'll be later now, when we're through the Gates; then they'll do it.'

I remembered my life, and despised my faith in men. 'Do what?'

'Take the King, and trade him to Alexander.'

I had thought that I knew treachery. I had been an unborn child.

'Steady-up, don't look so green.' He reached up to keep me in the saddle. 'Listen now; they're snakes, but they're not fools. The King's the King, but he's not the world's best general, let's admit. This one stroke would get him out of their way, and let them buy peace with Alexander. Then they'd go to Baktria, and make it ready for war.'

'Don't hold me on, people are looking.' I had quickly come to myself. 'Alexander would never trust them, men who had done that.'

'They say he's over-trusting, when faith's been pledged to him. On the other hand, God help you if you break it. I saw what he left of Thebes ... No matter; just tell the King.'

'But I haven't the rank to go up to him in public.' This would have been true even when I was in favour. 'It must be your general; no one less.'

'Patron? The King hardly knows his face.' He spoke not without bitterness.

'I know. But he must.' None too soon, I had started thinking. 'The King can speak Greek. Some of us do in the Household. But Bessos always asks for the interpreter; so does Nabarzanes. If they're listening, Patron can still warn the King.'

'That's worth knowing. I'll tell him that. We're a handful to the Baktrians, but if the King trusts us, we might still get him away.'

I soon overtook the Household; it had not gone a quarter-mile. The Sun Chariot had been lost at Gaugamela; but two Magi with the altar still walked in front. Behind that, all order was falling apart, all precedence shattered. Men of both kinds were edging each other to get near the King. Boubakes was riding just behind his chariot, a thing unheard-of. At his side, on a great Nisaian charger as heavy-boned as a bull, rode Bessos himself.

I fell in by Boubakes. He looked at me with dull sleepless eyes, as if to say, 'After all, what matter?' We were too near the King to talk.

The shaded litter was left behind at Arbela; those days were gone. He would be tired, after all day in a chariot. Something I felt for him still, beyond mere duty. I remembered him playful, kindly, amused, and in the follies of pleasure. He knew himself despised. Perhaps he had known it when he struck me.

The King was the King; he could not have believed this sacred state could be altered, except by death. Disaster after disaster, failure on failure, shame on shame; friend after friend turned traitor; his troops, to whom he should have been godlike, creeping off like thieves every night; Alexander approaching, the dreaded enemy; and, still unknown, the real peril at his elbow. And to trust in, whom? We few, who for the use of Kings had been made into less than men; and two thousand soldiers serving for hire, still faithful not for love of him, but to keep their pride.

As we marched, the road rising through bare uplands, I suppose there was no one in the Household who was not thinking, And what will become of *me*? We were only human. Boubakes thought, perhaps, of want, or a dreary life in some low-rank harem. But I had only one skill, I had only known one employment. I remembered slavery in Susa. I was no longer too young to find the means of dying. But I wished to live.

The road climbed higher. We were coming to the pass. Here was the barrier range of the Tapourians, great peaks, barren and harsh, so high that in summer they were still tipped with snow. Up the foothills wriggled our worm of road, and vanished in a cleft. In spite of all, my heart quickened. Beyond must be the sea, which I had never seen.

At each higher turn, rose a new wall of stark stone, weather-scoured, no living thing but a few cypresses bent like cripples. Here and there by a stream were poor fields and huts, whose wild people fled like rock-rabbits. But the air was like crystal. Ahead, plunging in shadow, was the steep gorge of the Gates.

Alexandria is a splendid city, with everything a sensible man can need. I daresay I shall end my life here, without ever again going far away. But when I remember the high hills, and a pass mounting to its unknown revelation, I will not think so. Even then, knowing the evil and the danger, knowing all I had known before, even then I felt it; ecstasy, prophecy, light.

A sheer cliff close above, a sheer drop below, far down the roar of water; we were in the Gates. Even so high, the rock-wall flung back the heat and the column laboured. Surely, this pass could have been held. Just ahead, Bessos on his great horse still rode beside the King. No sign of Patron. Why should he heed my message, second-hand, and from the King's minion at that?

The road flattened and opened. We were at the pass-head; Hyrkania lay below us. It was another country. The mountains were clothed with forests, green fold after green fold. Then a narrow plain; and beyond, the sea.

From this height, the horizon stretched immense round its sheet of silver. I caught my breath with delight. The black shores puzzled me; I did not know they were covered with flocks of cormorants, millions and millions, fed by its endless shoals of fish.

The Tapourian range is a great parting of the waters. Truly, it was to be so for me.

Soon we were winding down among the trees. Streams splashed and trickled over red-stained boulders; the water was delicious, very cold with a tang of iron. We made halt in a pine-grove, setting cushions for the King, and seeing to his retiring-tent.

When we set off again, the air grew closer and moister, tall trees held off the breezes that had tingled on the pass. We had halted late, because of its bleakness; now in the deep groves already the shadows darkened. Looking about, I was aware of someone new, riding just behind me. It was Patron.

He was a veteran. He had not laboured his horse uphill when the going would soon be easier. I caught his eye, and fell back to give him my place. He dismounted, and led his horse; in sign of respect, or to be noticed. His eyes never left the King.

It was Bessos who saw him first. His back stiffened; he came nearer the King, and started some kind of talk with him. Patron plodded along behind.

The road bent sharply. As the chariot turned, the King saw him, and showed surprise. No one should stare at the Great King's face, but Patron fixed his eyes on it. He made no gesture; just looked.

The King spoke to Boubakes, who fell back, and said to Patron, 'His Majesty asks if there is anything you want of him.'

'Yes. Tell His Majesty I would like a word, without interpreters. Say it is not for myself, but in his service. *Without interpreters.*'

Boubakes, his face changed, repeated the message. The chariot had its drags on for the slope, and was moving slowly. The King beckoned Patron up. I took his bridle, and led his horse for him.

He stepped up to the chariot, the other side from Bessos. His voice was low, I did not hear what he said; but Bessos could have heard it. Patron had taken the risk, on my bare word.

Soon he must have seen, from Bessos' look of baffled anger, that I'd not misled him. His voice grew louder. 'My lord King, pitch your tent in our camp tonight. We have served you a long time. If you ever trusted us, believe me, you need to now.'

The King was quite quiet. His countenance hardly altered. I was the better for his fortitude; one needs some pride in one's master. 'Why do you say this?' He spoke haltingly; his Greek was no better than mine. 'What do you fear for me?'

'Sire – it is your cavalry commander, and that one there beside you. You see why I can't speak names.'

'Yes,' said the King. 'Go on.'

'Sire, they lied this morning. It will be tonight.'

The King said, 'If it is ordained, so it will be.'

I understood his quiet. My heart sank like a stone. He had despaired.

Patron came nearer, leaning to the chariot. He was an old soldier, he knew what he had heard. He put out his strength, as if to hearten a flagging battle-line. 'You come over to us, sire. What men can do, every one of us will do it. Look at all this woodland. When night comes, we'll get you away.'

'To what, my friend?' With despair, he had recovered dignity. 'I live too long already, if my own people wish me dead.' I don't know what he read in Patron's face, which I could not see. 'Be assured, I trust you. But if what you say is true, you are outnumbered ten to one, you and the faithful Persians. I will not buy a few hours more of breath, at the cost of all your lives; that would be poor thanks to you. Go back to your men; and tell them that I value them.'

He saluted, and fell back behind the chariot. As he took back his horse, his eye said, 'Well done, boy. No fault of yours.' I turned to look at Bessos.

Dark blood engorged his dark face. He looked like a demon. He could not tell what Patron had revealed. For one moment I thought he would draw his sword upon the King, and butcher him out of hand. However, a dead King was spoiled merchandise. He took time to master himself; then he said to Darius, 'That man means treachery. No need to know his tongue, it was in his face.' He paused, hoping to draw some answer; but the King was silent. 'The scum of the earth. No stake in any country, on sale to the highest bidder. Alexander must have outbid you.'

Even from a kinsman, this was insolence. The King said only, 'I trust not. His suit was refused in any case.'

'Sire, I am happy for it. I hope you trust my good faith as you did this morning; may the gods witness it.'

The King said, 'May they be my witnesses also.'

'Then I am happier still.'

'But if Patron is the man you think, he will be foolish to count upon Alexander. He rewards surrender; but he is very harsh to treachery.'

Bessos looked sidelong under his black brows, and said no more. We wound downhill through the darkling forests. The high peaks, where we could glimpse them, still glittered golden. Here it would soon be night.

We made camp in a broad open glade. Long fading bars of red sunlight crossed it. It felt close and hot. I daresay at sunrise it would have looked delightful. None of us saw the sun rise on it, so I cannot say.

There was a village somewhere near. The Persian soldiers went off to forage in the usual way. When they were gone into the trees, the place was still full of men. The Baktrians had all remained, and were building watch-fires. They were still all under arms. We knew what it meant. It was like the last turn in a long fever.

Oxathres came to the King, and said that when the loyal Persians came back, they would make a fight of it. The King, embracing him, told him to do nothing without orders. He was a brave soldier, but none of that kin had the makings of a general. Patron could have done more with two thousand men than he with twenty thousand; I daresay the King knew it. When he had gone, he sent for Artabazos.

I found him, a little stiff from his ride but still alert. As I led him to the King, I saw the Greek camp by itself among the trees. They were still all armed, and had set outposts.

Round the royal tent stood the royal bodyguard; there were still some Immortals left, armed with their spears of honour. The gold pomegranates caught the firelight; and their eyes, staring sombrely before them.

From within, we heard the King give Artabazos Patron's news. He was some time silent, thinking no doubt of his long night's labours. Then he besought the King to make camp among the Greeks; the Persians, for whom he himself would answer, would rally in strength to the Greeks, if the King were with them. I was thinking, Poor good old man, you have lived too long for your peace, when he added briskly, 'These Greeks are soldiers by trade. The Baktrians are only called on levy. I saw discipline in Macedon. The difference between a blood-horse and an ox. Trust to the Greeks.'

How often we had listened like this from mere curiosity, or to be abreast of some small intrigue. We listened now for our lives.

'It is finished,' said the King. 'All my life I have hoped too willingly. Lately it has cost too much, to too many men. Now I have put hope away, do not wish it back to me.'

There was a smothered sound. It was Artabazos weeping.

'Dear friend,' said the King, 'you have lost many years with me. The rest are yours; go with the Wise God's blessing.'

The weeping went on. The King raised his voice and called to us. Artabazos was clinging to him, small against his height, the old face buried in his robe. He embraced him, saying, 'This faithful servant will not lay down his charge; but I have released him. Lead him away.'

He loosed the old man's hands, which clung like a child's; it took all of us to ease him out without roughness. The King hid his face from it. We saw Artabazos to his people; when we returned, and looked for the King, at first we did not see him. He lay prone on the ground, his head upon his arms.

One thought was in all our minds. But no weapon was near him, his shoulders moved with his breath. He lay like the run-down hare, coursed to its limit, awaiting the hounds or spear.

He had not dismissed us. We did not know what to do, but gazed at this painful sight in silence, feeling our own despair. After a while, a thought came to me; I fetched his sword from within, and laid it on the table where he could find it easily. Boubakes saw what I was about, but looked aside.

For my master, I had done this last thing. I could not feel, There lies the one who was my lover. I was in his service, and had served as I was called to do. He was the King.

After a while he moved his head, and gave us leave to go.

Our sleeping-tent had been half put up and left; one end sagging from a loose pole, the other end on the ground. No slaves were to be seen. From all around came a discord of quarrelling, arguing, orders shouted in vain. It was no longer an army, only a great confused crowd of tribes and factions. For a while we sat together on the slack tent-hides, whispering. Then I looked up and said, 'The bodyguard has gone.'

I went to make sure. Nothing, not so much as one gold-hafted spear. The Immortals had put off their immortality. We were alone.

After a time of silence, I said, 'I think he spoke. I'll see if he wants anything.'

He was lying as before. I stepped up softly, and knelt by him. I had heard nothing; but old days had come back to me. The very perfume I was wearing had been his gift. When all was said, I was not just like the others.

He lay, his head on one arm, the other flung forward. I dared not take his hand unbidden. He was the King.

He moved, aware of me, and said, 'Send me Boubakes.'

'Yes, sire.' I was someone to take a message. He had forgotten.

Boubakes went in. Suddenly he gave a great wail, such as is only heard at a death. All three of us ran inside. The sword still lay on the table, the King upon the ground. Boubakes knelt there, beating his breast, tearing his hair and clothes. We cried, 'What is it?' as if the King had not been there. All things we knew were breaking.

Boubakes sobbed, 'His Majesty bids us go.'

The King leaned up on one arm. 'You have all done your duty well. You can do no more for me. I acquit you of your service. Save yourselves while you can. This is my last command to you; you will all obey it.'

A vast horror overwhelmed us: the doomed King, the forsaken tent, the black strange forest full of wild beasts and enemies. I hope it was for him we wept; it is easy now to think so. We cried aloud in the night, drunk with fear, and grief; like mourners at a bier, each threw his voice into the outcry, no longer knowing which of its sounds was his.

As I flung my hair from my eyes, I saw someone at the entry. Even in my distraction, I remembered there was no guard. I went over just as I was. It was Bessos and Nabarzanes, with men behind them.

Bessos looked at the prone King, struck his fist into his palm, and said to Nabarzanes, 'Too late! I warned you.' He ground his teeth together.

Nabarzanes said, 'I never thought he could do it.' His face had no anger; only respect, and perhaps relief. He caught my eyes, and gravely nodded.

Bessos seized my shoulder in his huge paw and shook me. It lifted me off my feet. 'Did he finish it? Is he gone?'

Boubakes answered for me. 'I rejoice, my lord, His Majesty is in good health.'

Nabarzanes' face set hard as a wall-carving. He said to Bessos, 'So, then. Come.'

The King rose to his feet as they came inside. He said only, 'Why are you here?'

'I am here,' Bessos said, 'as King.'

The King was quite quiet. 'What kingdom has God given you?'

'I have obeyed the people's wishes. You should have done the same.'

The King said, 'As you see, I am no longer able to punish traitors. But I know who will.'

Bessos lifted his head. 'I am ready to abide the judgement of Mithra.'

'So I suppose, since you do these things. But I was speaking of Alexander.'

Nabarzanes, silent till now before him, said, 'Don't name the enemy to whom you have given our people. We do this to set them free.'

'Come with us,' said Bessos.

I thought, Shall I put his sword in his hand? But he was in reach of it. It was no right of mine, to tell my master when to die.

He stepped back; I think he meant to take it. But he was never swift in act, or certain in mind. As he moved they closed on him. He was a big man; but his muscles had grown slack. When their men came in, he ceased resistance. He stood with dignity; he could suffer like a king, at least. Perhaps Bessos felt it. He said, 'Well, if we must bind him, let his fetters match his rank.' He took off his massive gold neck-chain, and, while two Baktrians held the King's arms behind him, wound it round them like a rope.

They led him out between them, their hands on his shoulders as if he were a felon. From the Baktrians outside came low muttering, confused shouts, and laughter that was half fear.

Near by stood a common transport-cart, roofed with hides. The tents had been brought in it. Towards this they led him. We stared after him, unbelieving, helpless, dumb. Boubakes, rousing himself, cried out, 'At least let him have some cushions!' We ran back and fetched them. The King was already inside, two camp slaves with him; guards or attendants, I never knew. We threw in the cushions; then the soldiers shoved us away. The horses were hitched up, the driver mounted. We seemed to stand for an eternity while all this was done, and the cavalry mustered. The infantry was more a crowd than a column. Bessos gave an order; the cart began to jolt over the clearing towards the road.

A soldier ran past, carrying something I knew. It was the King's water-ewer. The tent was overrun with Baktrians, who had stayed to plunder it. Some were fighting outside over the best things. It was like a sack.

Boubakes looked at me with desperate eyes, cried, 'Let us go to Artabazos!' and ran off towards the Persian camp. The others followed. The soldiers let them go. They were just eunuchs, empty-handed, of no account.

I stood pressed to a tree. It looked a long way across the clearing. I remembered Susa. I was not like the others; I was loot.

The wagon had vanished. Close by was our sagging, half-set tent. I ran inside, pulled down the unsteady pole, and let the whole mass sink down on me.

The stiff folds let in some air. I should not smother. I lay there in pitch darkness, as if I were in my grave. Indeed, my life was buried here. When my sepulchre yielded me up, it would be to some fate unknown to me as to the child closed in the womb.

9

I lay in my lair. The cured leather was heavy, and stank, but I dared not stir. Sounds of commotion came through muffled, then lessened as the King's tent was picked clean. Once two men approached and I was in terror; but they thought, as I'd hoped, that if the tent had not been put up it must be empty. After that, there was nothing to do but wait.

I waited long, too muffled to trust my ears. At last, I squirmed till I could put my head out. The glade was empty but for smouldering camp-fires. After the darkness, even starlight seemed bright; but, beyond, the trees hid everything. There were sounds there of men, going away; loyal troops surely, Artabazos' men, who had left the rebels, being too few to fight them. I had better catch up.

Burrowing about in the tent, I gathered my belongings. Now for my horse. I had only to think it, to know the answer. All the same, I had to go stumbling over to the picket-lines. Of course nothing on four legs was left.

My poor beautiful little Tiger, the gift of a King; he was not bred to carry weight. I grieved for him, flogged along by some heavy oaf of a Baktrian in what time I had for it before I felt the truth of my own plight.

The enemy was gone. So were all those who would befriend me. Night must be far spent. I had no notion where they would be making for.

I would need food. In the King's tent, all that had been in his supper-dishes had been tossed out on the floor. Poor man, he had eaten nothing. I filled a napkin, and dipped my water-flask in the stream.

The sounds were now distant. I followed them, praying these were not Baktrians who had just deserted. They seemed to go along the mountain flank; they had left a well-beaten track. It crossed streams; I was wet to the knees, and my riding-boots oozed water. I had not gone cross-country since I was a child, with a scolding and dry clothes awaiting me.

There was no sign yet of dawn. I began to hear women's voices, and hastened on. They were camp-followers with their baggage, Persians. At this rate, I would soon be abreast of the column. A half-moon was giving a little light, I could go faster now.

Soon I saw a man ahead. He had stopped to make water; I turned away till he had done, and then approached him. He was a Greek; it was them I had overtaken. The women had misled me; of course, they would all be Persian. Hired men brought none from home.

He was a thick man, rather squat, black-bearded. It seemed I knew him, though of course this was impossible. He came and peered at me. His sweat stank. 'Why, by the dog!' he said. 'It's Darius' boy.'

'I am Bagoas, from the Household. I am trying to find Artabazos' Persians. Am I far out of my way?'

He paused, looking me over. Then he said, 'No, not too far. Just follow me, I'll put you on the path.' He led off into the wood. He was without his armour, as their custom was on the march.

No sign of a path appeared. The wood seemed to get thicker. We were not far in, when he faced about. One look was enough. There was no need of words, and he wasted none. He merely fell on me.

As he bore me to the ground, memory returned to me. He was indeed like someone I'd known: Obares, the jeweller at Susa. In an instant I lived it all again. But I was no longer twelve years old.

He was twice my weight; but I never felt a doubt that I would kill him. I struggled rather feebly, to hide what I was doing, till I had my dagger out; then I drove it between his ribs, up to the hilt. There was a dance I'd practised, a favourite of the King's at bedtime, which ends with a slow back-somersault off the hands. It is wonderful how strong it makes your arms.

He threshed about, choking blood. I dragged out the knife and thrust it into his heart. I knew where that was; I had heard it often enough, thudding away, along with heavy breathing in my ear. He yawned then, and died; but still I stabbed in the dagger, wherever I thought good. I was back at Susa, killing twenty men in one. It was not a pleasure I wish to know again; but I know it was one. I can feel it to this day.

Above me a voice said, 'Stop!' I had been aware of nothing but the body by which I knelt. Doriskos stood beside me. 'I heard your voice,' he said.

I stood up, my knife-hand bloody to the wrist. He did not ask why I had done it; my clothes had been pulled half off me. As if to himself, he said, 'I thought you were like a child.'

'Those days are long past,' I answered. We looked at each other in the dim light. He had his sword. If he wanted to avenge his comrade, he could kill me like a new-born pup. It was too dark to see his eyes.

Suddenly he said, 'Quick, get him out of sight. He has a kinsman here. Come on, take his feet. There in the thicket, down that gully.'

We parted the bushes. It was a winter watercourse, deep and steep. The body tumbled, the bushes closed again.

'He told me,' I said, 'that he would lead me towards the Persians.'

'He was lying, they're marching ahead of us. Clean your hand, and that dagger. There's water here.' He showed me a trickle down the rocks. 'There are leopards in this forest. We were warned not to straggle. He should have remembered.'

'You are giving me my life,' I said.

'I don't reckon you owe it. What do you mean to do with it, now?'

'I'll try Artabazos. For the King's sake, he might take me in.'

'We must move, we'll lose the column.' We scrambled through the rocky woods; when we came to anything steep, he helped me over it. I was wondering how Artabazos had really felt about the King's keeping a boy. And he was so old, a ride like this could kill him. About his sons, I knew next to nothing.

'I daresay,' said Doriskos, 'the old man will do what he can. But you know where he's going now? To surrender to Alexander.'

God knows why I had not thought of it. A friend of the young man's childhood could count on mercy. Oppression of spirit kept me silent.

'In the end,' said Doriskos, 'it will come to that with us. No way out of it. None of us will trust Bessos; at least Alexander has a name for keeping his word.'

'But where *is* Alexander?'

'He'll be through the pass by now. Two of the Persian lords went pelting off to meet him. They said the King would be better off with him than with the traitors. They won't lose by it, of course.'

'Pray God they won't be too late.'

'When Alexander hurries, he hurries. We'd no wish to be in his way. The Persians are well ahead of us; they want to make terms, not be ridden down. Ah, there's the column.' They were threading through the trees like shadows, keeping their voices low. He did not lead me across to them, but kept alongside. By now I was bruised and sore from the hard going, and glad of his helping hand. When I stumbled, he took my bag for me. A glimmer in open places proclaimed the first of dawn. He sat down on a fallen tree-bole. I was ready to rest.

'So the upshot is,' he said, 'we're skirting the hills, lying low, making for Hyrkania; and after that who knows? If you press on, I daresay you might overtake the Persians at the noon halt. It'll be a sweat for you, you're not used to going on foot.' He paused; the dim light now showed me his blue eyes. 'Or you could march with me, and let me give you a hand. However we get along, you won't need to use your knife on me.'

I remembered his smile from our first meeting. It was less wistful now, and more hopeful. With surprise I thought, I can say yes or no for myself. The first time in my life. I said, 'I'll come with you.'

So we joined the column. Even after daylight, I did not cause much stir. Several of the men had boys who marched beside them. There were many more with women; but they all had to keep behind.

When we halted to rest, I shared the last of my food with him; the only time, he said, he was likely to eat from a king's table.

He was the kindest of companions. When my feet grew sore, he searched all through the troop for some soldiers' salve, took off my boots, and dressed my feet himself, saying how slender and beautiful they were, though they were in such a state I was ashamed to have them seen. Once, when no one was looking, he even kissed them. It was lucky that when I fought in the thicket, my bow had fallen free, and the quiver had saved my arrows; so I was able to offer something – besides what would have contented him – by shooting for the pot.

From him I learned something of Athens, where, he said, his father had been well off, till some enemy brought a lawsuit against him unjustly; hiring a famous speech-maker to blacken his name with lies. The jury found against him; he was ruined, and Doriskos, the younger son, had to hire out his sword. He said this same speech-maker used to exhort the people how to vote, on the laws, and even on peace or war. This was called democracy, he told me, and had been a fine thing in the good old days, when speechmakers told the truth.

I said we were all brought up to speak the truth in Persia; it was our greatest proverb. No doubt Bessos and Nabarzanes had been taught it too.

It was sad that, with all this goodwill between us, I found his love-making quite without interest. I always pretended pleasure; he set store by this, and one could do no less for a friend. That was the only art I used with him. The Greeks, as it seems, are artless in these matters.

I remembered how, when I fell from the King's favour, I had said to myself that I would take a lover. I had pictured stolen meetings by moonlight in the park; the whisper of silk at a window; a jewel tied to a rose. Now here I was with a foreign foot-soldier, in a shelter made of brush.

One night he told me of a boy he'd loved in Athens, though his beauty was a pale star to the moon of mine. 'He hardly had the first down on his face, when I found he was spending my money on women. I thought it would break my heart.'

'But,' I said, 'that is nature, surely, if you take a boy up so young.'

'Beautiful stranger, it would never happen with you.'

I answered, 'No. That is why they do it.'

He was some time quiet, then asked if I was very angry. He had been good to me, so I said not. In Greece, he assured me, it was never done. But so long as they sold boys young into the brothels, I did not think the Greeks had so much to boast of.

Living among these was easier, from their having been in Persia so long, and knowing the customs. Though without modesty before each other, they understood it in me. They respected the sanctity of rivers, drawing off water for washing, not defiling the stream. Their own bodies they strangely cleaned by smearing them with oil, which they scraped off with blunt knives, exposing themselves so carelessly that from shame I used to go away. The smell of the oil was disagreeable close to; I never quite got used to it.

At night, the women would make a shelter for their men (some had children too) and cook them supper; they never saw them all day. As for the boys, pretty peasants bought from poor homes for a little silver, led leagues away, and losing all their Persian decencies, I did not like to think what their fate would be. The soldiers who bore the fewest burdens, and laid none on others, were those who had come already lovers from Greece.

In this manner, we journeyed, with adventures which then seemed great, for more than half a month, till we came to the eastern hills which end the snow-range, and look down on Hyrkania. Here the Greeks made camp, solid shelters in a wood; they would lie low till they knew where Alexander was. They planned to send him envoys under safe-conduct, not stumble into his hands.

Before long, some hunters told us he was moving along the mountain sides, beating the coverts, since these heights commanded his flank. They could not say if he knew that the Greeks were there.

It was only I who, when all these questions ceased, asked for news of the King. They said he was dead; they supposed Alexander killed him.

The time had come for me to be on my way. Somewhere, Artabazos must have left a camp, when he himself went to Alexander. I asked the hunters. They said a Persian lord was camped in the forest, a day's journey eastward; who, they did not know. He and his people were all strangers to those parts.

Doriskos and I said our farewells that night; I must start at dawn. No one else on earth cared if I lived or died, and now I felt it.

'I never had a boy like you,' he said, 'and I never shall have. You've spoiled me for all the rest. Henceforth I shall stick to women.'

All day I went through the forest by hunters' trails, fearful of snakes at my feet and leopards in the branches, wondering what I should do if the Persians had moved their camp. But before the sun was low I came to it, tucked away by a mountain stream; a thorn-hedge round it, and a guard at the gate who looked like a well-trained soldier. When he saw I was a eunuch, he lowered his spear and asked my business. I became aware I was almost in rags, my clothes worn out and filthy. I told him who I was, and begged for a night's shelter. After the forest, I did not care who they were, if they took me in.

He sent in the message. Presently a civil man, like a soldier servant, brought me inside. It was a camp for no more than a few hundred men; there had been thousands with Artabazos. Huts had been run up from timber and thatch; no tents. It seemed these people had come travelling light; but there was a corral of splendid Nisaian horses. I inquired the name of my host.

'Never mind. He offers you hospitality. These days, least said is best.'

His dwelling was built like the rest, but much bigger, with several rooms. To my astonishment, the servant led me to a well-furnished bathroom, which could only be the master's. 'You will like to bathe after your journey. The water will not be long.'

I was ashamed to soil the couch with my dirty clothes. Two Scythian slaves filled the bath with hot water and cold; there was scented oil in it. It was pleasure beyond words. I washed myself and my hair; scarcely noticing when the well-trained servant came in, his eyes politely downcast, and took away all my garments.

While, drowsy with contentment, I reclined in the warm water, the inner door-curtain moved a little. Well, I thought, what of it? That fight in the thicket has made me nervous as a girl. A man like that would have come in. Must I take everyone for an enemy? I got out and dried myself, and put on the fine wool robe that had been left ready.

Instead of my clothes, came a tray of excellent food; sucking kid with sauce, what bread, a fragrant wine. Wondering at all this in so rude a setting, I remembered glimpsing, below, the city of Zadrakarta. It seemed my host had arrived with nothing much, except a good deal of money.

I sat full of wellbeing, combing my hair, when the servant brought in a suit of clothes, saying, 'The master hopes you will find these fit.'

They were of fine cloth, a loose coat of dark red, blue trousers and embroidered slippers. They had been stitched here and there, to make them smaller; they must have been measured against mine. I felt like myself again. To honour the event, I touched up my eyes and put on my earrings.

The servant, returning, said, 'My master will see you now.'

It was only as I settled my sash that I remembered my dagger. It had been taken with my clothes, and not brought back.

In the master's room, a filigree lamp hung from the rafters; bright hangings of local work relieved the timbered walls. My host reclined on the divan, a wine-table before him. He smiled and raised a hand in greeting.

It was Nabarzanes.

I stood dumb as an ox, my mind in turmoil. Rather than come under this man's roof who had sold away my master's life, I ought to have slept out in the forest. Now, bathed, fed, clothed and sheltered, I could not help what I felt; it was gratitude that he had not told me.

'Come in, Bagoas.' He seemed not at all put out by my lack of manners. 'Come, sit down. I hope that they looked after you.'

I collected myself and bowed, the least I could do now, and said, speaking the bare truth, 'My lord, I am greatly in your debt.'

'By no means. Sit here and let us talk. It is rarely I have a guest here; I am grateful for your company.' I sat down on the divan, and took the wine he offered me. 'But,' he said, 'whom did you expect to find?'

I told him Artabazos, or his people.

'A fine old man, a pattern of antique virtue. Alexander will welcome him with open arms; it is the kind of thing that delights him.'

He must keep himself well informed here. But I was thinking how far he had gone beyond the duty of host to wayfarer, and how the curtain had moved. As far back as Babylon, I had sometimes wondered.

'You are anxious,' he said in the friendliest way. 'I understand it; you can have had no easy journey, your dagger has had use. Set your mind at rest; I do not take guests under my roof and then abuse them.'

My thoughts rebuked, I said that I was sure of it. His person had never been displeasing to me. I would have requited kindness gladly, but for what he had done. It was a matter of honour.

'I know your loyalty to the King.' He must have read my face. 'In one thing he was happy; he had devotion from his betters. There must have been something in him, though it was never my luck to find it.'

'He raised me from nothing, and gave me all I had. Not even a dog would have turned against him.'

'No. Even the beaten dog is true. Yet the master dies, and the faithful hound runs stray.'

'He is truly dead, then?' I thought of the cart and the golden bonds, and my heart was angry.

'Yes, truly dead.'

Of a sudden I wondered why, after making this good bargain, he was lurking here in the woods with so small a following. And where was Bessos?

I said, 'I hear Alexander killed him.'

'Peasant rumour, my dear boy.' He shook his head with a sad smile. 'Alexander would never have killed him. He would have entertained him graciously; set his son on his knee; given him some minor palace to retire to; married his daughter and courteously required to be named his lawful successor. If later he had rebelled, he would have been stamped on without pity; but of course he would never have done so. He could have lived quite peacefully into old age. All this he began to think of, while Alexander was overtaking us. He came like a Scythian wind; the pass must be strewn with foundered horses. The King's conveyance was too slow; we freed him and brought a horse. He refused to mount, saying he put more faith in Alexander than in us; he would remain, and make his own terms. By then

Alexander was cutting up our rearguard. Each moment was life or death. The King would not be moved. That was why we were forced to kill him with our own hands. Believe me, I regretted it.'

I was silent, gazing into the shadows beyond the lamplight.

'I know,' he said, 'what you would be saying, if the laws of hospitality did not restrain you. Take it as understood between us. He was the King, such as he was. But I am a Persian; for me, the second outweighed the first ... I did not seek, as the Vizier your namesake did, for a King who would be my creature; but for one who would lead us to honour, whom I could serve with pride. Well, Mithra has had the laugh of me. After all's done, I am a Persian without a King.'

Wine-softened I might be, but not yet stupid. Why was he telling me all this, why own he had killed the King? Why was he brushing off the difference of rank between us? I could make no sense of it. 'But my lord,' I said, 'you were all for proclaiming Bessos. Is he dead too?'

'Not yet. He has put on the Mitra and gone to Baktria. He will be dead whenever Alexander gets to him. I am punished, my dear boy, much more for my folly than my treason. I thought I had found a King for Persia. I had found a mountain bandit.'

He topped my wine-cup. 'I had supposed he could put on kingship, when it was laid in his lap. Not so. As soon as Darius was in bonds, the Baktrians became a rabble. He could not keep them from sacking the King's tent, which was now his own. They would even have had the treasure-chest, had I not arranged to secure it.'

He spoke with his leopard purr. Much was now made clear.

'That was a mere beginning. They rioted along as if in enemy country, plundering, raping, killing. Why not? They were not in Baktria. I reminded Bessos he was now Great King; they were violating his subjects. He thought it a fit reward for good service. I urged the need for haste; if Alexander overtook us, we would lose our whole enterprise. He made light of it. I saw the truth; he did not get them in hand because he could not. They had been good soldiers, serving in the old order they understood. Now they knew only that there was no King. And they were right. There was none indeed.'

His dark eyes stared beyond me. Since he holed-up here, maybe I was the first comer to whom he could tell the tale. 'So, when Alexander came storming down on us, with the handful who could keep up with him, he found our rearguard strolling like drunk peasants on market day. His hundreds rounded up thousands, like cattle. I had had enough. I had spent myself, my rank, my fortunes – my good faith too, you would tell me if you could – to change a useless coward for a useless bully. Even Issos was not so bitter. I took my own riders, who had still some discipline left, and led them cross-country to where you find us.'

There was nothing to say; but I remembered my debt to him. 'My lord, you are in danger here. Alexander is moving east.'

'Yes, I have heard so. I am planning as best I can. But, my dear boy, enough of my business. Let us think of yours. It distresses me, to think of you living hand to mouth like this. But what prospect can I offer you? Even should God permit me to see my home again, I should be at a loss. I must own to having wished often that you were a girl; or that I could find a girl with your face. But that is as far as my nature takes me. Indeed, you look far less girlish than you did in Babylon. It improves you, it has given you distinction. I would be out of my mind, to put you any-where in my harem.' He grinned at me; yet I felt something behind this play.

'And yet,' he said, 'you are without doubt the most lovely creature my eyes have rested on; woman, girl or boy. There can be only a few more years of it; it would be a crime to waste them. The truth is, you should serve only kings.'

Since he chose to amuse himself, I waited in patience.

'How I wish I could put some future in your way. But I have none myself. In fact, it is clear to me that I must go the way of Artabazos, with none of his fair prospects.'

'Do you mean,' I said startled, 'to Alexander?'

'Where else? He is the only Great King we have, or shall have now. Had he been a Persian, and what he is, we should all long since have followed him. All I hope for, at the best, is to be let live in quiet on my own estates. Kings are always affronted by king-killing, and yet ... He is a soldier. He has fought Darius twice. I think he may understand me.'

In honour I could not answer.

'He has given me, at least, a safe-conduct to know his terms. If he is set against me, I shall have safe-conduct back here. From then, I shall be driven game.'

'I hope not, my lord.' It was true. He smiled at me kindly.

'Did you see my gift-horses outside? They will be caparisoned, of course, with gold and silver. But he will have plenty just as good.'

In courtesy, I said he could have none finer.

'No, they are nothing much; not for Alexander. After all, he is now the richest man in the world. What can one give to such a man? If he wants it, he already has it. There is only one real gift for a man like that; something he has been wanting a long time, without being aware of it.'

'That would be hard to find, my lord, when you do not know him.'

'And yet, I believe I have seen the very thing.'
'I am glad, my lord. What is it?'
He answered, 'You.'

10

We Persians have a saying that one should deliberate serious matters first drunk, then sober.

I woke next morning on my pallet in Nabarzanes' room, where I had slept unmolested as with a kinsman. My head scarcely ached; it had been good wine. Dawn bird-song filled the forest. Trying to remember where I was, I saw across the room my host still sleeping. Memory stirred, together with the sense of some frightful thing impending.

We had talked and drunk, drunk and talked. I remembered saying, 'Is it true they paint themselves blue?' Yet at some much later time, it seemed to me he had taken me in a chaste but warm embrace, invoked the gods for me, and kissed me. I must have consented.

In the camp a hound bayed deeply. Men were stirring; I must think before he woke. Some of the talk was coming back to me. 'It is for you to choose. I have used no deceit with you. You would learn the truth when I had gone, and, if you prosper, might be a dangerous enemy. But you showed loyalty to Darius, in the presence of me who killed him. I trust you to keep as good faith with me. You will speak of me as you have found.'

He had said also, 'When I had my command, I made it my business to learn about Alexander. One should know one's enemy. Among matters of more use, I found that his pride extends into the bedchamber. He has never lain either with slave or captive. I daresay the first thing he will ask is whether you are free, and have come there willingly.'

'Well,' I had answered, 'then I shall know what to tell him.'

A little bird perched on the timbered window, singing so loudly its throat beat like a heart. Nabarzanes slept on, as peacefully as if his head had no price upon it. He had said, as I remembered, 'Twice to my knowledge, men seeking favour have offered to buy him Greek boys famed for beauty. He refused with indignation. But, my dear Bagoas, it appears that none of these eager sycophants took the trouble to offer him women.'

I seemed to recall his taking a lock of my hair still damp from the bath, and winding it round his fingers. We were fairly drunk by then. 'It takes no great fortitude,' he said, 'to resist a name in a letter, joined to the word beautiful. But the living presence, ah! that is another thing.'

What had my life been, I thought, since the King had died? There was no trade I knew to live by, but what I had. Only one thing had been wanted of me; even by Nabarzanes, though for another man. If I went tramping on with nothing, I should soon end where I began when I was twelve years old.

Yet it was terrible, to part from all I knew and make my life among barbarians. Who could say what this Macedonian was like in the inner room? I had learned at Susa that the outward man could be a mask for horrors. And then again, supposing I did not please him?

Well, I thought, better the unknown danger than creeping miseries, coming slow like leprosy, till one bears at last a life whose mere thought would once have made one end it. One throw, win or lose; so be it.

Nabarzanes stirred, yawned and smiled at me. It was not till we were at breakfast that he said, 'Does sober agree with drunk?'

'Yes, my lord, I'll go. On one condition, that you give me a horse. I've had enough of walking. And if you're presenting me to the richest man in the world, I should look as if I were worth something.'

He laughed aloud. 'Well begun! Never cheapen yourself with Alexander. You shall have clothes too, not those makeshifts; I am sending to Zadrakarta. In any case, we must give those scratches time to heal. Now I see you by daylight, you have certainly travelled rough.' He turned my face in his hand. 'Skin-deep. A few days merely.'

Four days later, our cavalcade rode down to Alexander's camp.

Nabarzanes had been generous. My horse, a chestnut with blond mane and tail, was even prettier than poor Tiger; I had two fine suits, the best one, which I was wearing, with real gold buttons and embroidered sleeves. 'I am sorry, my dear boy,' he'd said, 'that I can't give you your dagger back. Alexander would think I was sending him an assassin.'

Behind us came the string of Nisaian horses, with sparkling cheek-rosettes and bridles, and saddle-cloths fringed with bullion. Nabarzanes rode beside me, dressed as a noble suppliant; sombrely but becomingly, looking as well-bred as his horses. I hoped Mithra would forgive my kindly thoughts of him.

In front rode the guide, a Macedonian officer who spoke a few words of Persian. He pointed out the camp in the plain below, at the foot of the hills, beside a river. It was not very big; Alexander had divided his forces to search the mountains and man their strongpoints, and had only his own troops with him. We could see his tent. It was imposing, and had a Persian look.

Nabarzanes said, 'He took it at Issos. That was Darius' tent. I would know it anywhere.' He never spoke of Issos without bitterness. I remembered his men in Babylon, saying how well he'd fought till the King had fled.

We rode into camp through staring Macedonians, till we came to the open space before the tent. Grooms took our horses. Nabarzanes was announced to Alexander, who presently came out.

How clearly, even now, I remember him a stranger. He was not so small as I had expected. Of course, he would have measured like a boy against Darius; the young Macedonian who had come out behind him was taller, too. He was of middle height; but I suppose people had expected his stature to match his deeds.

Artabazos had said that even in Persia he would have been called beautiful. Just now, he had been riding about for days in an open helmet instead of a hat, and had been caught with sunburn. Being fair-skinned, he had gone rather red, a tint not much admired among us, recalling the northern savages. But he had not their rufous hair; his was bright gold. He wore it rough-cut, in a length between neck and shoulders; it was neither straight nor curling, but fell like a shining mane. When he turned to the interpreter, I perceived his features were very fine, though marred by a sword-cut on the cheekbone.

After a time, Nabarzanes bowed, and pointed to his train of gifts; then looked towards me. I was too far to hear his words; but Alexander looked, and for the first time I saw his eyes. Them I remember like yesterday; my own mind less clearly; a kind of shock, a sense that one should have been more prepared.

I came up with lowered gaze, and made the prostration. He said in Persian, 'You may rise.' At this time he scarcely knew any of our language, but had learned this off along with the words of greeting. He was unused to being bowed to down to the ground; you could tell it made him uneasy. One gets up in any case, without command; but no one had liked to tell him so.

I stood before him, my eyes cast down as is proper before a king. He said suddenly, 'Bagoas!' and I was startled into looking up, as he had intended.

As one might smile at the child of a stranger seeing it scared, so he did at me, and said to the interpreter, 'Ask the boy if he is here of his own free will.'

I said, 'My lord, I speak Greek a little.'

'You speak it quite well.' He looked surprised. 'Did Darius speak it, then?'

'Yes, my lord King.'

'Then you know what I just asked.'

I replied that I had come freely, hoping for the honour of serving him.

'But you come with the man who killed your master. How is this?' His eyes had changed. He was not trying to frighten me; but they had grown cold, and that was enough.

Nabarzanes had withdrawn to a decent distance. Alexander just glanced towards him. I felt myself being reminded that he knew no Greek.

'Lord King,' I said, 'Darius loaded me with kindness. I shall always grieve for him. But Lord Nabarzanes is a soldier. He thought that it was necessary.' I saw his eyes change as if at something he understood. I said, 'He repents it truly; that I know.'

He paused; then said abruptly, 'Has he been your lover?'

'No, my lord. Only my host.'

'Then that is not why you plead for him?'

'No, my lord.' I think it was his eyes, rather than Nabarzanes' counsel, which told me not to cheapen myself. I said, 'If he were my lover, I would not leave him.'

He raised his brows; then he turned with a smile to the young man behind him. 'You hear that, Hephaistion? An advocate worth having.'

The young man, without as much as a bow or a My Lord, said, 'All the same, they might at least have finished him off.'

To my surprise, Alexander did not notice the disrespect. 'We were treading on their tails,' he said. 'They were in a hurry. I'd no notion he spoke Greek. If only I'd been in time!'

He had a look at the horses, commended them through the interpreter, and invited Nabarzanes inside his tent.

I waited by the fidgeting horses, while the Macedonians looked at me. Among Persians, the eunuch knows himself marked out at sight by his lack of beard; it was most strange to be in a crowd where no young man had one. Alexander had shaved from his youth, and liked his fashion followed. Persian soldiers would have had any man's blood, who told them to make themselves like eunuchs; but I don't think this had even occurred to the Macedonians. They had no eunuchs. I was the only one.

No one molested me. There was discipline, but not the reverence one expects to surround a king. They stood about and stared, and discussed my looks as if I had been a horse, not knowing I could understand them. The lower ranks, I could not; but though they spoke Macedonian, which is barely Greek, I knew what they meant. I fought back the tears of wretchedness. What would become of me, among such people?

The tent-flaps opened. Alexander came out, with the interpreter and Nabarzanes. The King said something, and offered his right hand. I saw from Nabarzanes' face it was the sign of pardon.

He made a graceful speech of loyalty, and was given leave to depart. Turning to me, he said very solemnly (the interpreter was in hearing),

'Bagoas, serve your new master as well as you did your former one.' As he turned towards his horse, he winked at me.

He returned to his ancestral lands and his harem, and must have lived there, as he had said, in quiet. I never saw him again.

Alexander ordered the horses led away, then turned to me, as if he had only just remembered me. I have seen it better done. For an instant, I could have sworn I saw a look that one can't mistake. When it is hard and smug it is a bad lookout; but sometimes it is a softening. It vanished utterly, before I could be sure of it; there was only a soldier's briskness.

'Well, Bagoas, you are welcome to my service. See Chares, my chief steward, and he will find you quarters. I will see you again later.'

Well, I thought, that is plain enough.

The sun was sinking; my spirits also. I wondered what time he went to bed.

I ate with the clerks who kept his records. They looked surprised. There was no other place for people like me, except with soldiers or servants. The food was coarse and rough, but they seemed used to nothing better. After a while, one of them asked me how the archives were kept at Susa; as I knew this, they became more friendly; but they offered me no advice about my duties. I did not like to ask what sign the King gave, for one to stay when the rest retired. Eunuchs anywhere would have been more helpful.

The King was already at dinner with his chief officers. I returned to Chares, the chamberlain, a Macedonian of good rank. I did not think much of his service; even for a camp it was rough-and-ready to a Persian eye. When I appeared, he seemed not to know where to put me; but looking at my good clothes (I was deep in my host's debt, there) he gave me a damp towel and a dry, for the King to wipe his hands on. I stood by his chair, and he used the towels; yet I felt even he had not expected me.

I had heard already of their barbarous way with wine, bringing it in with the meat. But nobody had prepared me for the freedom of speech the King permitted. They called him Alexander, without title, like one of themselves; they laughed aloud in his presence, and far from rebuking them he joined in. The best you could say was that when he spoke, nobody interrupted him. They fought over their campaign like soldiers with their captain; once, one said, 'No, Alexander, that was the day before,' and even for this received no punishment, they just argued it out. How ever, I thought, does he get them to obey in battle?

When they had eaten (food like a peasants' feast-day, with no sweets at all) the servers left, but for the wine-pourers. So I went into the King's sleeping-place, to prepare his bed. It amazed me to find it not much better than a common soldier's, with scarcely room for two. There were a few fine gold vessels, I daresay from Persepolis; but the furniture was just the bed and clothes-stool, the washstand, a writing-table and chair, a rack of scrolls, and a fine bath of inlaid silver, which must have been Darius', taken with the tent.

I looked about for the perfume-sprinkler, but could not find it. Just then a Macedonian boy of about my age came in and said, 'What are *you* doing here?'

One would have supposed he had surprised a thief. I did not return his rudeness, but said I had been taken into service that day. 'It's the first I've heard of it,' he said. 'Who are you, to sneak in here without leave? I'm on guard here. For all I know you've come to poison him.'

He bawled out to another youth, who came in from outside, and they were about to lay hands on me, when a young man entered. The boys looked crestfallen before he had even spoken. 'In the name of Zeus!' he said. 'Can't you take guard, Antikles, without shouting and brawling like a market porter? I could hear you outside; you'll be lucky if the King didn't. What's this about?'

The youth stubbed his thumb at me. 'I found him in here, handling the King's things.'

The young man lifted his brows. 'You could have asked one of us, before you made this uproar. We're all sick of dry-nursing you. How the King manages with such raw oafs about him, I can't think.'

The boy, suddenly very angry, said, 'And how much longer did you want to do squire service, that you can't let go of it? I'm on duty. Am I meant to let in any spayed catamite some barbarian leaves behind?'

The young man stared at him till he flushed. 'For a start, don't be foul-mouthed, Alexander doesn't like it. For the rest, just take my word that the boy has leave to be here. I heard Alexander speak to him. I won't tax your understanding with more than that. By the dog of Egypt! If I were half such a fool as you, I'd hang myself.'

The boys muttered and went out. The young man gave me a long look over, smiled pleasantly, and departed also. I could make out none of it.

In fact, along with fresh troops from Macedon, the King had had fresh body-squires. By Macedonian custom, lords' sons did this duty, part of which was to guard his person at night. Two or three years was the usual time of service, but in four years of war, the squires he set out with had become grown men. He had chosen them himself in Macedon; they knew all his ways, and he was used to things running smoothly. Now, promoted to the cavalry, they were supposed to be training the new boys, whom they held in the greatest scorn. All this I found out later.

I was now alone in the tent. No one seemed to be waiting to help the King disrobe; but no doubt they would be there presently. I kindled the night-lamp from the hanging one, and set it by the bed; then went to an empty corner, and sat crosslegged in the shadow, thinking about my fate.

There were voices outside; the King came in with two officers. It was clear they had just walked over engaged in talk; they would not be putting him to bed. This was awkward; he might not wish them to know he'd sent for me; so I stayed quiet in my dark corner.

When they went, I was about to rise and disrobe him; but he began to pace about as if he were alone. It seemed he wished his thoughts to be undisturbed. One learns when to be quiet.

He walked to and fro, his head tilted sideways, his eyes looking, as it seemed, out through the tent. After a while he sat down at the table, opened a wax diptych, and began to write. It seemed a strange task for a king. He had clerks to write whatever he wanted. In all my time with Darius, I had never once seen him touch a writing-tool.

Suddenly, without a word with the guards outside, without a pause at the entry, without asking leave, a young man came in. I knew him; he had been with the King when Nabarzanes brought me. The King, his back to the entry, went on writing. This man came straight up behind him, and took him by the hair.

I was too terrified even to scream. In an instant I thought a thousand horrors. I must get to the forest before the body was found. The killer planned to accuse me, knowing the King had sent for me. I would be three days dying.

Then, just as I rose to run for it, I perceived no blow had been struck; the newcomer had no weapon; and the King, a quick-moving man, had made no resistance. His head had not been pulled back, nor his throat cut. Simply, the other was ruffling his hair with his fingers, as a man does with a boy.

Astonishment held me rooted. I had understood. The man – I remembered his name, Hephaistion – now leaned his head beside the King's, to read his writing. Coming a little to myself, I moved softly back to the concealing shadows. They both turned, and saw me.

My heart almost ceased to beat. I prostrated myself and kissed the floor. As I rose, Hephaistion was looking at the King with lifted brows, half laughing. The King, however, looked straight at me, and did not laugh at all.

He said, 'Why are you here?' but all Greek had failed me. He beckoned me up, felt me over with hard firm hands, and said, 'No weapon. How long have you been here?'

'My lord King, since after dinner.' I dared not remind him he had sent for me; no doubt he wished it forgotten. 'I am sorry, indeed, my lord. I – I thought I was to wait on you.'

'You heard me say I would tell you your duties later.'

At these words, I felt a blush of shame flood my whole body and scald my face. Gladly I would have been swallowed by the earth. I could say nothing.

He saw my confusion. His harshness gone, he said quite gently, 'Don't distress yourself. I see you misunderstood me. I am not angry with you, Bagoas. You have leave to go.'

I made reverence and went out. The night guard stood facing outwards. I paused on the dark side of the tent. I had no friend here, no one to advise me. I must learn whatever I could.

The King said, 'Since after dinner! And not a sound. He creeps about like a cat.'

'He was stiff with fright,' Hephaistion answered. 'What have you been doing with him, Alexander? Eh?' He was laughing.

'At a guess,' said the King, 'I should say he thought you meant to murder me. Remember he's used to Persian manners, and court manners at that. Poor little wretch! He was Darius' boy. I told him I'd see him later; of course he thought I wanted him for the night. I have put him to shame; all my fault; his Greek seemed good. I should have used the interpreter. One should have some Persian oneself for things like this.'

'That would be worse. It took you long enough to learn Greek. Well, there's your teacher. You might as well find some use for him; as it is, you've bought yourself talk enough.'

One of the guards moved; I had to slip away without hearing more.

My bed was in the clerks' tent. A torch outside lit it dimly through the entry. Two were sleeping; the third, who had seemed to be, peeped out as I took off my clothes. It was a fit end to a dreadful day. I pulled up my blanket, bit on the pillow, and soaked it with silent tears.

I remembered Nabarzanes' promises. What perfidy! How could he not have known this, knowing so much? The whole Macedonian army must know. How long must those two have been lovers, to behave like that, to talk like that? 'It took you long enough to learn Greek'! Ten years?

The Queen's Eunuch had told us how they had visited the royal tent together, and the Queen Mother had not known which to bow to. 'Never mind, Mother, you weren't far out; he too is Alexander.' Not even from her had he troubled to hide it.

Why, I thought, did he ever accept my service? What does he want with a boy? He is somebody's boy himself. And he must be twenty-five at least.

One of the clerks was snoring. For all my anger, I thought with longing of Nabarzanes' house. Tomorrow it would be forsaken; by next year, rotting back into the forest. So all that was Persian in me would rot away, as I trailed through strange lands, a servitor in this barbarian army.

I recalled Nabarzanes saying, in a haze of lamplight and wine, 'What can one give to a man like that? Something he has been wanting a long time, without being aware of it . . .' Well, he had fooled me as he did Darius; I should have expected it. And yet, he brought me here to win favour for himself; he never pretended otherwise. I am unjust, I thought. He must have acted in ignorance.

Soon after, worn out with trouble, I fell asleep.

11

When one is young, morning light does wonders. In the picket lines, my horse (I had called him Lion) had been well cared for. Though the faces of the Thracian grooms seemed at first hardly human – these were the men who really painted themselves blue – one of them told me with grins and gestures what a fine horse he was. As I cantered up river in first light, my heart revived; till I saw a sight so shocking, I hardly believed my eyes.

A dozen young men were in the river itself, their whole bodies in the sacred waters, washing themselves; and, as if delighting in this impious pollution, splashing about or swimming. Among them was a mane of golden hair, which, wet as it was, could be nobody's but the King's. I thought that he looked my way, and galloped off in horror.

Barbarians! I thought. What vengeance will Anahita of the Waters take on them? It was a beautiful morning, fresh but turning warm. Truly, I had left all civilized things behind me. All the same . . . if one knew no better, what pleasure to slide through the sparkling river, bare as a fish.

But where it flowed past the camp, I saw there was no insult these people would not offer the deity of the stream. They were not only washing themselves; they were scouring pots, watering horses. All my disgust returned. No wonder I had had trouble finding a vessel to draw water for my toilet!

Still worse a misery was the indecency of the privies. Just a trench, even for the Household, and people walking in, which was bad enough. But the squires, and other mannerless people, would try to take a look at me. Any Persian boy has satisfied his curiosity about eunuchs before he is six years old; but here, grown men supposed one had been cut down to the shape of a woman. The squires had had a bet on it. For some days, exposed to these immodesties, I had to get to the woods before nature would obey me.

I had heard no more about my duties, and dreaded presenting myself at the King's supper-table. However, instead of dismissing me, he gave me some promotion. During the day, a number of noble Persians had come in, to surrender and swear allegiance. Nabarzanes had been let go with a bare pardon, because he had killed his King; but these others had been received as guests of honour. More than once, when something choice had been put before Alexander, he would direct a server to take a portion, and say to me, 'Go to So-and-so, and tell him I hope he will enjoy this dish with me.' Though used to better food, the guests were pleased with this Persian compliment. I wondered he had learned so quickly; little knowing how.

Quite often, as he sent these delicacies away, I would warn him there would be nothing left for him; but he only smiled, and ate what everyone had. His sunburn had healed. One had to own that he was comely, even in Persia.

He never made me carry anything myself. He remembered last night, and was trying to heal my pride. It seemed that for someone reared in the wilds, he had much natural courtesy. One could not say as much for his Macedonians. His friends followed his lead; Hephaistion kept his eye on him all the time; but some (mostly those who had kept their beards) made it clear enough what they thought of eating with Persians. At any difference of manners, they would laugh or even point. There were lords here, whose forebears had been kings before Kyros' time; but I was sure these uncouth westerners would have wished to see them carrying in the dishes. More than once, Alexander turned a cold eye on these boors; a few took notice, others pretended not to see.

He has himself to blame, I thought. He lets them go on in his presence like untrained dogs who will not come to heel. He is feared in war, but not at his own table. What must my people think of him?

One or two of the Persians glanced at me. Not all knew who I was; Darius had never dreamed of showing me at his side in public. Yet Alexander, whom I was nothing to, seemed quite pleased to have me seen. Of course, I thought, I am spoils of war, like Darius' chariot. I am Darius' boy.

On the third day Chares the chamberlain gave me a written message, and sent me to find the King, saying, 'I daresay he is in the ball court.'

Inquiring for this place, I found a square of canvas walls, and heard shouting within, and the sound of thudding feet. The entry was a doorless overlap, without a guard. I went in; and paused frozen where I stood. Eight or ten young men were running about there, and every one stark naked.

It was beyond belief. The only grown men I had ever seen in such a state were the slaves who had been sold along with me, and criminals at the place of execution, whose offences had merited such disgrace. What sort of people had I come among? I was about to escape, when a big hairy young man came bounding up and asked me what I wanted. Averting my eyes, I said I had come here by mistake, having been sent by Chares to the King.

'Yes, he's here,' the young man said, and bounded a few steps off. 'Alexander! It's a message from Chares.' Next moment, there stood the King, as naked as all the rest.

From his lack of shame, you might have supposed he had never worn clothes nor felt the want of them. I cast down my eyes, too shocked even to speak, till he said, 'Well, what is this message from Chares?'

I begged his pardon, my confusion now complete. He took the note and read it. While the first young man's sweat had smelt as strong as a horse, the King seemed as fresh as if straight from the bath, though he was flushed with exercise. It was said of him that the ardour of his nature burned up the humours. Just then my only concern was to hide my own flush of shame.

'Tell Chares –' he said, and paused, I felt him look at me. 'No, tell him I'll send for him shortly.' Clearly he did not trust me with the simplest message; I could not wonder. 'That's all then,' he said; and then, 'Bagoas.' 'Yes, my lord?' I answered, looking at my feet. 'Cheer up, boy. You'll soon get used to it.'

I went off in a daze. Even though the Greeks were a byword for immodesty, I had never thought a king could sink so low. Why, I myself, trained in my calling to strip off in the inner room, would have been ashamed, outside of that, to be less decent than anyone else. It is something, I thought, when a king can put a courtesan to the blush. Has he no sense of his dignity at all?

We moved camp soon after. The speed of it amazed me. When the trumpet sounded, everyone seemed to know his task without orders. I was the last to get my horse, and the Horse-Master cursed me; when I rode back the tent was gone, and my things were sitting in the open. We were on the march, an hour before Darius would have been wakened.

I looked to see where Alexander would take his place; there was no sign of him, and I asked the clerk who rode beside me. He pointed outwards; some way off was a chariot, going at a fair pace; a man was jumping off it, running alongside without its slowing down for him, and jumping on again. I asked, 'Why does he make the man do that? Is it a punishment?' He threw back his head and laughed. 'But that's the King.' Seeing me bewildered, he added, 'He's taking exercise. He can't bear to dawdle at foot-pace. Often he hunts, when the game is good.'

I thought of the shaded litter, the Magi with their altar, the miles-long train of eunuchs and women and baggage. It seemed like another life.

We were moving north-east into Hyrkania. At the next camp, Artabazos came in to surrender.

He had been resting awhile after his long march, and getting his sons together. Beside the elder ones, he brought in nine handsome young men I had never seen before. He must have begotten them all between seventy and eighty.

Alexander met him outside the tent; came forward, took both his hands, and offered his cheek to kiss. These courtesies done, he embraced him as a son might do a father.

He of course spoke Greek, from his years of exile. Alexander put him at his right hand at supper. Standing by his chair, I heard him laughing with the old man over his childish scrapes, and recalling the tales of Persia he had heard upon his knee. 'Ah,' said Artabazos, 'but even then, my lord, you used to ask me what weapons King Ochos used.' Alexander smiled, and helped him to meat himself from his own dish. Even the rudest of the Macedonians held their peace.

Just after, an envoy came in from the Greek troops, asking for terms of surrender.

I was thankful for Artabazos, who I knew would speak for them, as indeed he did. But, taking it ill that Greek should fight against Greek, Alexander sent word they could come in to learn his terms, or stay away.

They came in two days later, the greater part of them. Some had gone off through the pass to try their fortunes; one Athenian had killed himself, being well-known in Greece as an enemy of Macedon. The rest were in good discipline, though rather lean. I could not get near, but thought I could glimpse Doriskos, and wondered how I could rescue him, if he was condemned to die.

But Alexander's only vengeance was the fright he gave them by refusing terms. Patron and his veterans, who had been serving before he declared war, he sent back to Greece with safe-conduct. Those like Doriskos, who had joined up after that, he reprimanded, said they did not deserve release, and simply hired them, at the wage they had had before (his own men were paid higher). They were marched straight off to their camp, and I had no chance to bid Doriskos farewell.

It was shortly after this that Alexander went off to fight the Mardians.

They lived in thick mountain forest, west in the range, and had sent no envoys. They were known for their fierceness; but as they had nothing worth taxing, Persian kings for generations had let them be. They were also famous robbers; Alexander did not mean to leave them in arms behind him, nor to have it said they were more than he could handle.

He went travelling light, for rough campaigning. Left in the base-camp, I tried to find my feet; helped in this by his having taken his squires along.

These boys, who seemed to think I had chosen my own condition, felt for me contempt, mingled with envy they did not own to. They could do their duties, in a rude and simple way, but knew nothing of such manners as I'd been trained in. It irked them that Alexander did not mock what they called my fawning barbarian ways, but chose me to compliment his guests of honour. They were forever plaguing me behind his back.

Chares, who had always treated me well, used to consult me about fine points of Persian etiquette, there being no one else from the court. I had time for riding, though the plain was humid and close. My having a good horse of my own was a great grievance with the squires, who thought it should have been taken from me. They themselves had army mounts, issued them by the Horse-Master.

The King was back in a half-month. He had chased the Mardians up the mountains, where they'd thought to sit him out; but finding him clamber after them, they gave up, and acknowledged him King.

That night at dinner, I heard him say to Ptolemy his bastard half-brother, 'He'll be back tomorrow!' So joyful did he sound, I thought he must mean Hephaistion; but the man was there at table.

Next morning there was a stir of expectation in the camp. I joined the crowd near the royal tent, though I had wakened with a headache. Seeing that the old Macedonian near me had a kindly face, I asked who was arriving. He said smiling, 'Boukephalas. The Mardians are bringing him back.'

'Boukephalas?' Surely this meant Oxhead; an odd name. 'Who is he, please?'

'You have never heard of Oxhead? Why, Alexander's horse.'

Remembering how satrap after satrap had brought him steeds matchless in their kinds, I asked why the Mardians were bringing this one. He answered, 'Because they stole him.'

'In that horse-thief country,' I said, 'the King was lucky to get him back so soon.'

'It had to be soon,' said the old man calmly. 'Alexander sent word that if he were not returned, he would fire the forests and put them all to the sword.'

'For a *horse*?' I cried, remembering his kindness to Artabazos, his mercy to the Greeks. 'But he would never really have done it?'

The old man considered. 'For Oxhead? Oh, yes, I think so. Not all at once. He would have begun, and gone on till they brought him back.'

The King had come out, and was standing before his tent, as he'd done to welcome Artabazos. Hephaistion and Ptolemy stood by him. Ptolemy was a bony-faced warrior with a broken nose, some ten years older than Alexander. Most Persian kings would have had such a person put out of the way when they assumed the throne; but these two seemed the best of friends. At the sound of approaching horns, all three were smiling.

A Mardian chief came first, in an ancient robe which looked as if it had been stolen in Artaxerxes' day. Behind was the string of horses. I saw at once there was not a Nisaian among them; but size is not everything.

I craned over all the shoulders, to glimpse this peerless pearl, this arrow of fire, that was worth a province and its people. He must be such, for the King even to have missed him, among so many. Darius had always been superbly mounted, and would soon have noticed a falling-off; but it was the Master of the Stables who knew which was which.

The cavalcade approached. The Mardians, in token of repentance, had adorned all the horses with their barbaric finery, plumes on their heads, on their foreheads nets of scarlet wool, glittering with beads and sequins. For some reason, they had made gaudiest of all an old black horse that was plodding along in front, looking dead-beat. The King took a few steps forward.

The old beast threw up its head and whinnied loudly; you could see, then, it had been a good horse once. Suddenly Ptolemy, running like a boy, took its bridle from the Mardian and loosed it. It broke into a stiff-legged canter, all its foolish fripperies jingling; made straight for the King, and nuzzled against his shoulder.

The King stroked its nose a time or two. He had been standing, it seemed, all this time grasping an apple, and with this he fed it. Then he turned round with his face pressed to its neck. I saw that he was crying.

There seemed nothing, now, with which he could still astonish me. I looked round at the soldiers, to see how they would take it. Beside me, two weathered Macedonians were blinking and wiping their noses.

The horse had been pushing at the King's ear, as if to confide in him. Now it sank creaking on its haunches. This done, it sat like one who has achieved something, and expects reward.

The King, his cheeks still wet, said, 'He's too stiff for this. He will keep it up. I'll never get him out of it.' He bestrode the saddle-cloth. The horse heaved itself up quite briskly. They trotted off towards the stables. The assembled army gave a cheer; the King turned and waved.

The old man by me turned to me with a smile. I said, 'I don't understand, sir. Why, that horse looks to be well past twenty.'

'Oh, yes, it is twenty-five; a year younger than Alexander. It was meant to be sold to his father, when he was thirteen. It had been mistreated on the way, and would let no one near it. King Philip would have none of it. It was Alexander who cried out that a great horse was being thrown away. His father thought him too forward, and gave him leave to try, thinking it would humble him. But it trusted him, as soon as it felt his hand. Yes, that was the first time he did what his father could not ... He had his first command at sixteen, and before that he was at war; all that time, he has ridden Oxhead. Even at Gaugamela, he saved him up for the charge, though he changed horses soon after. Well, Oxhead has fought his last battle. But as you see, he is still beloved.'

'That is rare,' I said, 'in kings.'

'In anyone. Well, I don't doubt he would do as much for me, seeing he has risked his life for me, though I am no more use to him now than that old horse. Once I told him tales of heroes, now he could better them himself. But though he was no more than a child when I stood between him and his tutor's harshness, he never forgets. In the hills behind Tyre, he got himself benighted with me, nearly alone, because I outwalked my strength and he would not leave me on anyone else's arm. My own fault too, I would go along. We were lying up in the rocks; winter, and a bitter wind, and the enemy watch-fires too near. He felt at me and said, "Phoinix, you're freezing. This won't do. Wait here." He was off like a flash; I heard shouts and cries from a watch-fire; back he came like a torch-racer, with a burning brand. Alone, with just his sword, and he put the fear of death in them. We kindled our blaze, and they all went running, they never looked to see what troops he had. So we sat warm for the night.'

I would have liked to hear more from this old man, who seemed fond of talking. But just then I felt sick, and had to run away and vomit. My head burned; I shivered. I told Chares I had fever, and he sent me to the hospital tents.

They were pretty well full of wounded from the Mardian war. The doctor put me in a corner, telling me not to walk among the others, in case my fever was catching. One thing it did for me, was break me in to Macedonian privies. My only thought was to get there fast enough.

I lay weak as a babe, keeping nothing down but water, hearing the men brag of the campaign, of women they had raped, or of Alexander. 'They were stoning us from up the cliff, rocks that could break your arm through your shield. Up he comes, strolling through it. "Well, men, what are we waiting for, enough stones to build a sheep-pen? This way up." And he's up the gully like a cat into a tree. We clawed up after him; they couldn't hit us there, we took them in flank. Some of them jumped off the cliff, but we got the rest.'

There were some whom pain kept quiet. One man near me had an arrow-head in his shoulder. They had cut down for it in the field, but could not draw it out; the wound was festering, and was to be searched that day. He had been dead silent a long while, before the surgeon came with his tools and servant. The others called awkward words of cheer, and fell silent too.

He bore it well at first, but soon began to groan, then to cry out; before long he struggled, and the servant had to hold him down. Just then a shadow crossed the doorway; someone came in and knelt beside the bed. At once the man was quiet, but for a hissing of his breath between his teeth. 'Hold on, Straton, it'll be quicker then. Hold on.' I knew the voice; it was the King's.

He stayed down there, taking the place of the doctor's servant. The man never cried again, though the probe was deep in the wound. The arrow-head came out; he gave a deep sigh, between relief and triumph. The King said, 'Look what you had in you. I never saw a man bear it better.' The wounded man said, 'We've seen one, Alexander'. There was a murmur of assent around the tent.

He laid a hand on the good shoulder, and stood up, his fresh white tunic all dirtied with blood and matter which the wound had spurted. I thought he would go to make himself presentable, but he just said to the surgeon, who was dressing the wound, 'Don't trouble with me'. A tall hunting-dog, which had sat quiet by the entry, got up and padded at his heel. He looked about him, and came towards my corner. I saw great red finger-weals on his upper arm. The wounded man must have been clutching at him – the sacred person of a king!

There was a common, wooden stool, used by the wound-dressers. He picked it up, himself, with his own hand, and came to sit beside me. The dog started to nose me over. 'Down Peritas. Sit,' he said. 'I hope dogs are not a pollution in your part of the world, as they are among the Jews?'

'No, my lord,' I said, trying to believe all this was happening. 'We honour them in Persia. They neither break faith, we say, nor do they lie.'

'A good saying. You hear that, Peritas? But how are you, boy? You looked clapped-out. Have you been drinking bad water?'

'I don't know, my lord.'

'Always ask about the water. Mostly, down in the plains, it's better in wine. Worse water, more wine. I've had your trouble. Sicker than a dog, and then a flux. You, too, I can see from the way your eyes are sunken. How many times today?'

I recovered my speech and told him; he was fast making me proof against any shock. 'That's no joke,' he said. 'Drink plenty, we've good water here. Nothing to eat but slops. I know a good infusion, but the herbs don't grow here; I must find out what the natives use. Look after yourself, boy, I'm missing you at dinner.' He stood up, the dog doing so too. 'I'll be here awhile; take no notice if you want to go outside. None of your Persian formality. I know what it is to be kept about, when you're doubled-up for a crap.'

He strolled on to another bed with his wooden stool. I was so stunned that I had to go out almost at once.

When he had left, I slid my hand-mirror from the purse under my pillow, and peered at it behind the blanket. I look dreadful, I thought, and he said so too. Did he truly mean he was missing me at dinner? No, he had a good word for everyone. 'You looked clapped-out,' he said.

I became aware of a youngish veteran, tough and big-boned, growling at me. Had he seen the mirror? 'Please speak Greek,' I said. 'I don't understand Macedonian.'

'Now, maybe, you know how he felt about the hospital at Issos.'

'Issos?' I must have been thirteen. 'I know nothing about a hospital.'

'Then I'll tell you now. Your people cut in at Issos when the King had marched beyond it; he turned back there to fight the battle. Meantime, he'd left the sick there, in a tent like this. And your royal whoremaster, who ran like a goat before Alexander's spear, was so brave with men too weak to stand on their feet, he had them cut up in bed alive. They . . . well, I suppose *you* know all about such things. I was there when we found them. If they'd been only barbarians it would still have made me sick. There were one or two left living; both hands off at the wrists and the stumps seared. I saw Alexander's face. We all thought he'd do the same the first chance he had, and we'd all have helped. But no, he had too much pride. Now my anger's cooled, I'm glad of it. So you can lie there safe, snugged-up with your bowl of gruel.'

I said, 'I did not know. I am sorry.' Then I lay down, and pulled up the blanket. Your royal whoremaster. Each time he had run away, I had thought. Who am I to judge? But now I judged him. Had it been coward's cruelty, or was he taking his ease, uncaring? Small odds. I was sad already with sickness; now this shame. I, who had given myself consequence because a king had chosen me. He had not done even that; some pandar had done it for him. I covered myself like a corpse, and gave myself up to grief.

Through the blanket and my sobs, I heard someone saying, 'See there what you've done. The boy's half dead; now you've put him in a convulsion. They're not made like us, you fool. You'll be sorry if he dies of it. The King fancies that boy, I could see it with half an eye.'

The next thing I knew, a heavy hand grasped my shoulder, and the first man (who should never have left his bed) told me not to take it so much to heart, it was no fault of mine. He pressed a fig into my hand, which I had sense enough not to eat; but I pretended to. The fever rose and burned in me. It scorched up even my tears.

It was sharp, but short. Even after we had been carted on wagons to the next camp, I mended, though most of the wounded had set-backs. The man with the arrow-wound died on the way. His shoulder mortified. In his delirium he called upon the King; the man beside me murmured that even Alexander had not yet conquered death.

The young heal quickly. Next time we moved camp, I was fit to ride.

There had been changes in my short absence. From a group of the Companion cavalry, the cream of the high-born Macedonians, a voice called to me in Persian, 'Here, Bagoas! Say something for me in Greek.' I could not credit my senses. It was Prince Oxathres, Darius' brother.

Being one of the fair Persians, he did not look strange among Macedonians, though taller and handsomer than any of them. He was not with the Companions by chance. Alexander had enrolled him.

At Issos, they had fought hand to hand before the royal chariot. They had met too over Darius' embassy, when Tyre had fallen. They had felt each other's quality. And now that Bessos had put on the Hood, rather than see his brother's murderer on his throne, Oxathres preferred Alexander, who would help him with his blood-feud.

Well might he be angry at that wretched death. It was only now that I learned all the story. Nabarzanes had told me only the truth he knew. They had stabbed Darius with their javelins, killed his two slaves, maimed the horses, left him for dead; but with Alexander hot on their heels they had struck clumsily. The cart dragged on, the wounded beasts sought water. The dying King heard them drink, while he lay covered with blood and flies, his mouth cracked dry. At last came a Macedonian soldier, puzzled that the horses should be slashed instead of stolen; pausing, he heard a groan. He was a decent man; so Darius got a drink before he died.

Alexander, coming too late, threw his own cloak over the body. He had sent it to Persepolis, to be buried with kingly honours; giving it to the Queen Mother first for tending.

I had now to think of my future. Since the King had no use for me in my calling, I must seek favour in other ways, if I was not to sink to a mere camp-follower. I could guess where that would end. So I looked for opportunity.

Since the capture of his old horse Oxhead, the King was displeased with his squires. His horses were their charge; they had been leading them through the forests, when the Mardians fell on them. They had reported themselves vastly outnumbered; but Alexander, who spoke Thracian, had had a word with the grooms. They, being unarmed, had had no face to save. He was still nursing Oxhead like a favourite child, taking him out each day in case he should be pining. He had pictured him, no doubt, ending his days as a half-starved beast of burden, beaten, and full of harness-sores.

These youths, though well-born, were new to courts, and were already tiresome to Alexander, coming after their well-trained elders. He had had patience with them at first, but now had less; and from ignorance, they did not know how to bear themselves under displeasure. Some were sullen, others nervous and clumsy.

Errands would often take me to his tent. I would take notice of any small service he was about to need – his wants were simple enough – and do it without fuss. Soon he would employ me for this or that; before long, he would keep me there to be at hand. I would hear him say to the squires, impatiently, 'Oh, leave it; Bagoas will see to it.'

Sometimes when I was there Persians came for audience. I would admit them with the right degree of respect for each man's rank; now and then I saw that he took a hint from me.

He was curt with the squires, as an officer to raw cadets. To me he was always civil, even when I showed ignorance. Indeed, I thought it his misfortune to have been born among barbarians. Such a man deserved to have been a Persian.

It seemed to me I might well be better where I was, than where Nabarzanes had meant for me. Who knows how long a king's fancy will endure? But a useful servant is not put away so lightly.

Yet he never called me to attend to his bath or bedtime. I didn't doubt it was because of that first night; and whenever Hephaistion came, I was gone beforehand. I had warning from Peritas, who knew his step, and would thump the floor with his tail.

My preferment so displeased the squires, that only in the King's presence was I safe from insults. I had been prepared for envy, but not for so much coarseness. I was not established enough to tell the King. Besides, he might have thought me soft.

Our next march was to the city of Zadrakarta, near the sea. It was a royal palace. I don't know when a king had last put up there. Darius had meant to make for it; it was swept and garnished, though rude and quaintly antique, its moth-holed rugs replaced with crude stuff from Scythia. A band of old eunuchs flocked about me, asking how the King liked things done. Though they had been mildewing here for forty years, it was something to hear my native speech from my own kind. They begged to know if they should stock up the harem. I said it would be better to await the King's commands. They looked at me slyly, and said no more.

He meant to rest his troops a half-month at Zadrakarta, give them games and shows, and sacrifice to his gods for victory. Meantime the men made holiday, and the streets were best left before dark.

The squires too had time on their hands, as I learned the very first day.

I was looking about the palace, doing no harm to anyone, and had come out among old courtyards, when I heard spears thudding on wood. They saw me, and ran out. 'Come along, lily-boy. We'll make a soldier of you.' There were eight or ten of them, and nobody else in sight. Their target was a great battered piece of planking, with a Scythian drawn life-size in the middle. They pulled out the javelins and made me throw. I had not handled a spear since my child's toy one, and could not even hit point-first. They roared with laughter; one, from bravado, stood up before the Scythian, while another lodged a spear each side of him. 'Your turn next!' someone shouted. 'Over there, No-balls, and don't wet your pretty trousers.'

I stood before the board; a spear struck on my left and on my right. I thought they had done; but they all yelled out that they had hardly started.

Just then a young cavalryman, one of the former squires, looked in and asked them what they were doing. They called out that they had no more need of nursemaids, and he went away.

This last hope gone, I gave myself up to death. I was sure they meant to kill me, and put it down to mischance. But first of all, they wanted to see the soft Persian eunuch crawling to their feet, entreating mercy. Oh, no, I thought. That's one thing they shall not have. I will die as I was born, Bagoas son of Artembares son of Araxis. No one shall say that I died Darius' boy.

So I held myself straight, while the best shot of them clowned about, pretending to be drunk, and threw his spear so close I could feel the whiffle. They had their backs to the courtyard gateway. Of a sudden I saw a movement there. A man had come in behind them; it was the King.

He opened his mouth; then saw one of them poised to throw, and waited, his breath drawn in, till the spear had landed safely. Then he shouted.

I had never before heard him use the uncouth tongue of Macedon. No one had yet told me it was a sign of danger. No one needed to tell me now.

Whatever he said caused them all to drop their javelins, and stand with crimsoning faces. Then he changed to Greek. 'You ran fast enough from the Mardians. But I see you can all be warriors, against one boy untrained to arms. And I tell you this – as I see him now, he looks more like a man to me than any of you do. Once and for all, I expect to be served by gentlemen. You will refrain from insulting the members of my household. Anyone disobeying this order will return his horse and join the column on foot. Second offence, twenty lashes. Have you heard me? Then get out.'

They saluted, stacked their arms, and left. The King walked towards me.

I would have prostrated myself. But the closest javelin had pierced my sleeve, pinning me to the target. He strode forward, looked to be sure it had not gone through flesh, wrenched it out and flung it away. I stepped from among the shafts, and again began the prostration.

'No, get up,' he said. 'You need not keep doing that, it is not our custom. A good coat spoiled. You shall have the price of a new one.' He touched the rent with his fingers. 'I am ashamed of what I have seen. They are raw; we have had no time to train them; but I am ashamed they are Macedonians. Nothing like that will ever happen again, that I can promise you.' He put his arm across my shoulders, patted me lightly, and, smiling into my eyes, said, 'You behaved yourself very well.'

I don't know what I had felt till then. Perhaps just awe of his splendid anger.

The living chick in the shell has known no other world. Through the wall comes a whiteness, but he does not know it is light. Yet he taps at the white wall, not knowing why. Lightning strikes his heart; the shell breaks open.

I thought, There goes my lord, whom I was born to follow. I have found a king.

And, I said to myself, looking after him as he walked away, I will have him, if I die for it.

12

The royal rooms were above the banquet hall, looking towards the sea. He was pleased with the sea, being used to it near in boyhood. Here I waited on him, as in his tent before; but, as before, never at night time.

In a half-month he would be at war again. It did not give me long.

I had thought myself skilled, at Susa, never having seen what my training lacked. I knew what to do when I was sent for. In all my life, I had never seduced anyone at all.

Not that he was indifferent. First love had not bereft me of all sense; something had been there when his eyes met mine. In his presence I felt more beautiful, a sign that one can't mistake. It was his pride I feared. I was his dependant; he thought I could not say no. How right he was! Yet if I offered myself, having been what I had been, what would he think? I might lose even what I had. He did not buy at market.

The squires were my unwilling friends. He kept me closer about him; to rebuke their spite, or so he let it seem. For my spoiled coat, he never even counted out the gold, just gave me a handful. I had something becoming made, and, you may be sure, put it on for his approval. He smiled; emboldened, I asked him to feel how fine the cloth was. For a moment, it seemed something might come of that. But no.

He was fond of reading, when he had the time. I knew when to be quiet; we all learned that at Susa. I would sit cross-legged by the wall, looking at the sky with its wheeling gulls that came for the palace offal, stealing a glance at him; one must not stare at a king. He did not read aloud to himself, like other people; one scarcely heard a murmur. But I knew when the murmur stopped.

He was aware of me. I felt it like a touch. I lifted my eyes, but he kept his on the book. I dared not come forward, or say, 'My lord, here am I.'

On the third day was the victory sacrifice and procession. He lived so simply, I had never guessed he had a love of spectacle. He rode in the cavalcade, in Darius' chariot (I found he had had the floor raised up a hand-span), his gold hair crowned with gold laurel, his purple cloak clasped with jewels. He loved every moment; but I was nowhere near, and at night there was a feast at which he stayed till dawn. I lost half next day, too, for he did not rise till noon.

Yet Eros, whom I had not yet learned to worship, did not forsake me. The next day he said, 'Bagoas, what did you think of the dancer last night at supper?'

'Excellent, my lord, for someone trained at Zadrakarta.'

He laughed. 'He claims it was Babylon. But Oxathres says he's nothing compared with you. Why have you never told me?'

I did not say I'd been racking my brains for a chance. 'My lord, I have had no practice since I left Ekbatana. I would be ashamed you should see me now.'

'Why, you could have used the ball-court any day. There must be somewhere here.' He strode out, attended only by me, through the ancient maze of rooms, till we found one with space and a good floor, which he had cleared and scoured before nightfall.

I could have exercised without music, but I hired a piper, in case it should be forgotten where I was. I got out my spangled loin-cloth, and let my hair hang free.

After a while the piper faltered, and glanced towards the door; but I, of course, was too intent on my dance to see. I finished with my slow back-somersault off the hands. By the time I came right side up, no one was there.

Later that day, I sat again in the King's room, while he read his book. His soft voice ceased. There was a silence like a note of music. I said, 'Your sandal-string is loose, my lord', and knelt beside him.

I felt him look down; I would have looked up, in another instant. But then the dog Peritas thumped the floor with his tail.

Having undone the string, I had to do it up again; so Hephaistion was in the room before I could get away. I bowed; he greeted me cheerfully, patting the dog which had come to fawn on him.

So ended the fifth day of fifteen.

Next morning, the King went out fowling, in the marshlands beside the sea. I thought he'd be gone all day; but he was back well before sundown. When he came from the bath (where still he had never sent for me) he said, 'Bagoas, I shan't sit late at dinner. I want you to teach me a little Persian. Will you wait up?'

I bathed, and put on my best suit, and tried to eat. He was dining with a few friends, and did not need me there. I went up and waited.

When he came, he paused at the door, making me fear he had forgotten to expect me. Then he smiled and came in. 'Good; you are here.' (Where else? As a rule he never said such things) 'Bring up that chair to the table, while I find the book.'

These words dismayed me. 'My lord King, could we do without a book?' He raised an eyebrow at me. 'I am very sorry, my lord, but I cannot read. Not even Persian.'

'Oh, that's no matter. I never thought you could. The book's for me.' He fetched it, and said, 'Come, sit here.' There was about a yard between us. The chairs quite put me out. There one is, trapped, and can get no nearer. I looked with regret at the divan.

'We'll work like this,' he said, setting out tablet and stylos. 'I shall read out a Greek word and write it down; you will tell me the Persian, and I shall write the sound as it seems to me. It's what Xenophon did, the man who wrote this book.'

It was an old book, much used, the split edges patched with glue. He opened it tenderly. 'I chose this for your sake; it's the life of Kyros. Is it true you come from his tribe?'

'Yes, my lord. My father was Artembarcs son of Araxis. He was killed when King Arses died.'

'I heard so,' he said, and looked at me with pity. Only Oxathres, I thought, could have told him that. He must have asked about me.

The big old lamp-cluster, a ring of lamplets, hung over the table, its many flames making double and treble shadows under his hands, the light touching his cheekbones but not his eyes. He was a little flushed, though I could tell he had drunk no more at dinner than they always did. I looked down at the book with its unknown markings, to let him look at me.

What can I do? I thought. Why ever did he get us into these stupid chairs, which is not at all what he wants, and how can I get us out of them? Things told me by Nabarzanes were coming back. I thought, Has *he* ever seduced anyone, either?

He said, 'Since I was a boy, Kyros has seemed to me the pattern for all kings, as Achilles – whom you won't know – is for all heroes. I have passed through your country, you know, and seen his tomb. When you were a child there, did you hear any tales of him?'

His arm rested quite near me. I wanted to grasp it and say, 'Won't Kyros keep?' He is in two minds, I thought, or we would not be sitting like this. If I lose him now, perhaps it will be forever.

'My father told me,' I said, 'that once upon a time there was a cruel king, called Astyages; and the Magi predicted that the son of his daughter would take his throne. So he gave the baby to a lord called Harpagos, to do away with. But the babe was beautiful and he could not kill it; so he gave it to a herdsman, to leave it on the mountain and be sure it died. The man went home first, and his wife's own baby was dead, and she was crying, "We are growing old, and who will feed us?" So the herdsman said, "Here is a son. But you must keep it secret for ever." He gave her the child, and put the dead one on the mountain in the royal clothes; and when jackals had gnawed it so that no one could know it again, he brought it to Harpagos. And Kyros grew up the herdsman's son; but he was brave as a lion and beautiful as morning, and the other boys made him their King. When he was about twelve, King Astyages came to hear of him, and sent to see him. By then he had the family looks; and Astyages made the herdsman tell. The King meant to kill the boy; but the Magi said that his being King in play had discharged the prophecy; so he was sent back to his parents. It was on Harpagos that the King took vengeance.' I dropped my voice to a whisper, just as my father had done. 'He took and killed his son, and roasted his flesh, and gave it Harpagos to eat at dinner. When he had eaten, he showed him the boy's head. It was in a basket.'

I had nothing near finished; but something made me stop. His eyes were on me, I almost swallowed my heart.

I said, I will love you forever, though what my tongue said was, 'Is that in your book, my lord?'

'No. But it's in Herodotos.' He pushed back his chair, and walked towards the window that faced the sea.

Thankfully I got up too. Would he make me sit down again? The clerks who wrote out his letters had to sit while he walked about. But he said nothing. He turned and came back to where I stood under the lamp, with my back against my chair.

Presently he said, 'You must tell me when I say the Persian wrongly.

Don't be afraid to correct me, or I shall never learn.' I took a step towards him. My hair had fallen forward over my shoulder. He put up his hand and touched it.

I said softly, 'My lord knows well that he only has to ask.'

Eros had gathered his net in the strong grip of a god, and pulled in his catch, no longer to be defied. The hand that had touched my hair slid under it; he said, 'You are here under my protection.' At this, without respect for the sacred person of a king, I put both arms round his neck.

That was the end of his pretences. Now here I stood, in the sole embrace which, out of so many, I had ever worked to get.

I did not speak. I had gone far enough above my place already. All I wished to tell him was, I have only one thing in the world to give you, but that is going to be the best you ever had. Just take it, that is all.

He still seemed hesitant; not from reluctance, that was sure; but from something; a kind of awkwardness. The thought broke in on me. Where has he lived, and he a soldier? He knows no more than a boy.

I thought of his famous continence, which I had supposed to mean only that he did not rape his captives. I thought of it when he went to the outer door, to tell the guard he was going to bed and needed no attendance (I expect they had had a bet on whether I would come out). As we went through to the bedchamber, I thought, Everyone else has always known what he wanted. Shall I have to find it out for him? I do not know his customs, I may offend against what is permitted. He must love me, or I shall die.

Peritas, who had heaved himself up from his corner and strolled in after us, curled up at the bed's foot where I had been taught to lay my clothes, lest the sight of them offend the King. But the King said, 'How does all this come off?' and in the end they were all in a heap with his own upon the clothes-stool.

The bed was ancient but grand, of painted and gilded cedar wood. And now it was time to serve him the royal Persian banquet he must be expecting from Darius' boy. I had it ready, with all the seasonings. But though in my calling I felt as old as time, my heart, which no one had trained, was young, and suddenly it mastered me. Instead of offering spices, I simply clutched him, like the soldier with the arrow-wound; uttering such follies as I blush even now to think of, and, when I remembered I was speaking Persian, repeating them in Greek. I said I had thought he would never love me. I did not beg him to take me with him wherever he was going, I did not think so far. I was like a traveller in the desert, who comes to water.

The last thing he could ever have looked for was to be eaten alive like this. I doubt he understood a word of it, smothered upon his shoulder.

'What is the trouble?' he asked. 'What is it, then, tell me, don't be afraid.'
I lifted my face and said, 'Oh, I am sorry, my lord. It is nothing. It is love.'
He said, 'Is that all?' and laid his hand on my head.

How foolish my plans had been! I should have learned better from seeing
him at table, giving away the best though he was left with none. He
distrusted taking pleasures for himself, from pride, and jealousy of his
freedom; and I, who had seen what I had seen, was not one to blame him.
Yet he did have something from those empty dishes. He was in love with
giving, almost to folly.

'Only love?' he said. 'Don't fret, then; we have enough to go round,
between us.'

I should have seen at table too that he never snatched. Except for
Oromedon, which did not count, he was the youngest man I had ever been
to bed with; yet his embrace had changed to comfort, as soon as he'd
thought I was in trouble; he would have heard out the whole tale, if there
had been one. Indeed, one learned soon enough, and some learned to his
cost, that he would do anything in return for love.

He really wanted love from me. I could not credit such fortune; nobody
ever had before. In the past, I had taken pride in giving pleasure, since it
was my skill; never had I known what it was to take delight in it. He was
not quite so ignorant as I had supposed; it was just that what he knew
had been very simple. He was a quick learner, though. All I taught him
that night, he thought that by some happy harmony of our souls, we were
discovering together. So, indeed, it seemed at last even to me.

Afterwards, he lay a long time stretched out as if he were dead. I knew
he was not asleep, and began to wonder if I was meant to go. But he drew
me back, though he did not speak. I lay quiet. My body echoed like a harp-
string after the note. The pleasure had been as piercing as the pain used
to be before.

At last he turned, and speaking gently, as if he had been a long time
alone, said, 'So they did not take that from you.' I murmured something,
I don't know what. 'And after,' he said, 'does it bring you grief?'

I whispered, 'No, my lord. It never happened to me till now.'

'Truly?' He took my face in his hand to look at by the night-lamp, then
kissed me, saying, 'May the omen be happy.'

'And my lord?' I said, gathering courage. 'Does my lord feel grief?'

'Always for a time. Take no account of it. All good things must be paid
for, either before or after.'

'You will see, my lord, I shall learn how to keep grief from you.'

He half laughed under his breath. 'Your wine is too strong, my dear,
to drink it often.'

I was amazed; all other men I'd known had pretended to more than they had. I said, 'My lord is as strong as a young lion. This is not the body's weariness.'

He raised his brows, and I feared he was displeased; but he only said, 'Well, learned physician, then tell me what it is.'

'It is like the bow, my lord; it is the strongest that wearies, if it is not unstrung. The bow must rest. So too the warrior's spirit.'

'Ah, so they say.' He ran a strand of my hair slowly between his fingers. 'How soft it is. I never felt hair so fine. Do you worship fire?'

'We did, my lord, at home.'

'You are right,' he said, 'for it is divine.'

He paused, seeking words; but there was no need, I had understood him. I laid down my head in submission, saying, 'For me let my lord never turn aside out of his way; let me be like a cup of water drunk down in haste at noon, and I am content.'

He reached out to my closed eyes, and touched my lashes. 'Ah, no. Is this how I repay you? No more, or we shall both be weeping. Who is talking about noon? The moon is only rising. There is no need of haste tonight.'

Later, when the moon stood high, and he lay sleeping, I leaned to look at him. Exaltation of spirit had kept me wakeful. His face was smoothed and beautiful; he was satisfied, and in sleep he was at peace with it. Though the wine is strong, I thought, you will come back for more.

What had Nabarzanes said? 'Something he has wanted a long time, without being aware of it.' That subtle serpent; how had he known?

His arm, darkened by sun, lay bare, and his shoulder, milk-white, but for the deep pitted wound from the catapult-bolt at Gaza. The stain was fading; it was the colour of watered wine. Softly I touched my lips to it. He slept soundly, and did not stir.

My art would not have been worth much, if I could not lead him, once I had understood. A light cloud crossed the moon. I remembered that first night in his tent; and how Hephaistion came and went just as he chose, pleasant with me as with the dog. Was he too secure to spare a thought for me? Too secure even to care? 'You can't guess what I did last night.' 'Of course I can. You slept with Darius' boy. I knew you would before long. And was he good?'

He was seemly in sleep, his mouth closed, his breathing silent, his body fresh and sweet. The room smelled of sex and cedarwood, with a tang of salt from the sea. Autumn drew on, the night wind blew from the north. I drew the blanket over him; without waking, he moved to me in the great bed, seeking warmth.

As I slid into his arm, I thought, We shall see who wins, tall Macedonian. All these years you have made a boy of him. But with me, he shall be a man.

13

At once the news was everywhere. Alexander took this with calm. He could be secret at need; he was never furtive. He did not conceal that my presence pleased him, but offered no foolishness to mockers. I was proud of his behaviour, coming so new to it, whereas I had been trained in the right deportment. It was I, now, who attended him at the bath; he used to send out the rest.

Once or twice, while I stood by his chair at table, I saw Hephaistion's eye on me; but he gave no other sign, coming and going as freely as before. I had no means of knowing what he said when I left the room. The walls are four feet thick, at Zadrakarta.

To me Alexander never spoke of him. I did not deceive myself with this. He was not forgotten; he was unassailable.

I thought of the King's old war-horse, for whose sake he would have sacked a province, though it would never carry him in the charge again. It is like that, I thought; he never turns love away, it is not in him. I thought Hephaistion had not done so badly. If the beautiful boy you caught in a haystack gets to be a general of cavalry at eighteen, and is still your boy, you have not much to complain of. And if he goes on to be Pharaoh and Great King, with the treasures of Babylon, Susa and Persepolis poured at his feet, and the world's fiercest troops adoring him, is it wonderful if he finds he is a boy no longer, and wants a boy of his own? How long, I wondered, since they'd done more than just think of themselves as lovers? Since last he rode the black horse to war? And yet . . .

But with the night my troubles left me. He knew what he wanted now, but I knew better. Sometimes in the dance one is lifted beyond oneself, and cannot fail; it was like that.

Once when through the deep window the moonlight glinted on gold, I was put in mind of my old room at Susa, and uttered the invocation of my dreams. 'Am I beautiful? It is for you alone. Say that you love me, for without you I cannot live.' Rightly I had believed it magical.

I doubt he'd ever in his life lain down with anyone for whom he had not felt some kind of fondness. He needed love as a palm-tree needs water, all his life long; from armies, from cities, from conquered enemies, nothing was enough. It laid him open to false friends, as anyone will tell you. Well, for all that, no man is made a god when he is dead and can do no harm, without love. He needed love and never forgave its betrayal, which he had no understanding of. For he himself, if it was not given him with a whole heart, never misused it, nor despised the giver. He took it gratefully, and felt bound by it. I should know.

It pleased him to think he'd given me what Darius could not; so I never told him Darius hadn't thought of such a thing. He always liked to surpass his rivals.

But still, when desire was spent, he fell back into heaviness of soul, so that I feared to break his solitude. Yet I wished to repay his gift of healing. I would draw a finger-tip from his eyebrow down to his throat, and he would smile to show me he was not sullen nor ungrateful. One night, remembering the book he had shown me, and that he had set store by it, I said softly in his ear, 'Did you know, my lord, that Kyros the Great once loved a Median boy?'

At the name his face lightened a little, and he opened his eyes. 'Truly? How did they meet?'

'He had won a great battle, my lord, against the Medes, and was going over the field to view the slain. He saw the boy, who was wounded almost to death, lying by his dead father. Seeing the King, he said, "Do what you choose with me, but do not deface my father's body; he kept his faith."

'Kyros said, "I do not do such things. Your father shall be buried with honour." For even as the boy lay in his blood, he loved him. And the boy looked up at Kyros, whom before he had seen only far off, flashing in arms, and thought, This is my King. Kyros had him taken up from the field and tended, and honoured him with love; and he was faithful for ever. And peace was made between the Medes and the Persians.'

I now had all his attention. His melancholy was gone. 'I never knew of this. Which was the battle? What was the boy's name?'

I told him; love gave my invention wings. 'Of course, my lord, in our part of the world people are full of these old stories. I can't say if they are all true.' I had made up every word of it, and could have done it better if I had had more Greek. For all I know, Kyros never loved a boy in all his life.

My spell had worked. I found a few more tales which, true or false, were really told in Anshan country. A little later, he said that not even Kyros' boy was more beautiful than Alexander's; and afterwards he did not grieve, but slept.

The very next day, he got out the book again, and started to read it me. I had him to myself for a full hour. He said he had read it at home while still a boy, and it had shown him the portrait of a true ruler's soul.

Well, so it might; but if it was meant to be a portrait of Kyros, Kyros would have been surprised. It had been written, not by some learned Persian who had read the records and talked to old men of the tribe, but by a hired Greek soldier of Artaxerxes' day, who had fought for Kyros the Younger against the King. After he had led his men safe out of that and back to Greece, I suppose it was no wonder they believed any tale he told there.

Of course, Alexander only read me his favourite pieces. As it was, with anyone else I don't know how I could have kept my eyes open. We were both rather short of sleep. Since I could have looked at his face forever, he never knew when I stopped listening. I could always tell when something he liked was coming.

'Not all of this,' he said, 'is history, as I've found since I was here. Your boys are not trained up in public barracks?'

'No, my lord. Our fathers train us for war.'

'And the young men too?'

'Yes, my lord. They fight with their fathers' tribesmen.'

'So I thought. He is far too fond of the Spartans. But it's true, I think, that Kyros liked to share his cooks' best dishes with his friends?'

'Oh, yes, my lord. It has been an honour ever since, from the King's table.' So *this* was where he had found it! The man Xenophon must have been in Persia just long enough for that. I was so touched, I nearly cried.

He read me a tale about how his lords chose for Kyros, from the spoils of battle, the loveliest of the noble ladies, who was weeping for her dead lord. But Kyros, who knew he was alive, would not even see her face, but kept her in honour among her own household, and sent the husband word of it. When he came in to surrender and swear loyalty, the King led her out and joined their hands. As Alexander read it me, I knew suddenly that this was what he had planned for Darius and his Queen. It was why he had mourned her fasting. I saw how he had pictured it, just like the book; and thought of the hide-roofed cart with its cushions dripping blood.

He had no harem with him any more. Before I came, he had settled the Queen Mother at Susa with the young princesses.

A king, the book said somewhere, *should not only prove himself better than those he rules; he should cast a kind of spell on them.* I said to him, 'Let me say that in Persian' and we smiled at one another.

'You must learn to read Greek,' he said. 'It's a great loss to you, not to read. I will find you a gentle teacher. Not Kallisthenes, he thinks himself too grand.'

For some days we read the book together, and he would ask me if this or that was true. He was so fond of it, I never liked to say that this Greek story-teller, coming from Athens where they had no kings, had dreamed of one and given him the name of Kyros. Where the book was wrong about Persian customs, I always told him, so that he should lose no face before my people. But when he read aloud some precept that had shaped his soul, I always said it had been handed down from Kyros' mouth in Anshan. There is nothing like giving joy to the one you love.

'I was mistaught as a boy,' he said. 'I won't insult you with what I was told to think about the Persians. The old man, I suppose, is saying the same things still in his school at Athens. It was Kyros who opened my eyes, in this book when I was fifteen. The truth is that all men are God's children. The excellent ones, he makes more his own than the rest; but one can find them anywhere.' He laid his hand on mine.

'Now tell me,' he said, 'is it really true that Kyros allied with the Medes to fight the Assyrians, as it says here? Herodotos says, and you were saying, that he beat the Medes in war.'

'He did, my lord. Any Persian will tell you so.'

He read from the book, *He ruled over these nations, even though they did not speak the same tongue as he, nor one nation the same as another's; yet he was able to spread the awe of him so far that all feared to withstand him; and he could rouse so eager a wish to please him, that they all desired to be guided by his will.*

'That is true,' I said. 'And will be again.'

'Yet he never made the Persians overlords of the Medes; he ruled over both as King?'

'Yes, my lord.' As I'd heard it, some of the chief Median lords had joined in revolt against Astyages, because of his cruelty. No doubt they made terms for this, and Kyros kept them like a man of honour. I said, 'It is true, Kyros made us all one kingdom.'

'So it should be. He did not make subject peoples; he made a greater empire. He chose men from what each man was in himself, not from hearsay and old wives' tales ... Well, I don't suppose he found it hard to persuade the conquered. To persuade the victors, that's the thing.'

I was seized with wonder. Why, I thought, he wants to follow Kyros even in this. No, to go before him; for Kyros was pledged, but he is free ... And I was the first Persian he had told.

It was long since I had remembered my father clearly. Now his face returned to me, blessing my sons to be. Maybe, after all, his words were not empty wind.

Alexander said, 'Yes, tell me your thought, what is it?'

I answered, 'That the sons of dreams outlive the sons of seed.'

'You are a seer. I have thought so often.'

I did not say, 'No, I am just a eunuch making the best of it,' but told him all about the New Year Festivals, which Kyros began as a feast of friendship; and how he led the peoples to conquer Babylon, the Medes and Persians vying to show valour before him. Sometimes from eagerness I stumbled in my Greek, and he would say, 'Never mind. I understand you.'

All day there was a shine on him; and at night, it was as if I'd come to him Kyros' boy, instead of Darius'. He fell without grief into smiling sleep; and I said to myself, That's one thing I've done for him that Hephaistion couldn't.

How perverse is the heart. Darius had neither offered love nor asked it; yet I had felt it right I should be grateful for all he gave me, a horse, a mirror, a bracelet. Now in my riches I scorched my soul because another came before me; I must have him all.

In all but words, he showed he had more pleasure with me than with anyone before me; he was too generous to belittle it. But the words were never spoken, and I well knew why. That would have violated loyalty.

'Never be importunate,' Oromedon had said to me long ago. 'Never, never, never, never. The quickest way to the dusty street outside. *Never.*' And he, who was always gentle as silk, had given my hair a twitch that made me yelp. 'I did that for your sake,' he said, 'to make you remember.'

Nobody owns the gods. But there are some they choose to make more their own than the rest. I remembered.

There were times when I could have grasped him in both hands, crying aloud, 'Love me best! Say that you love me best! Say that you love me best of all!' But I remembered.

Standing by the wall in the audience-room at Zadrakarta, I watched him giving audience to Macedonians. He had these people in without formality, walking about among them.

'You are a musician,' Oromedon had said. 'All you need is to know your instrument.' He had simpler ones in mind; this harp had many strings, some never for my sounding. And yet, we had made harmony.

So I was thinking, when a courier came in with a batch of letters from Macedon. The King took them from him, and sat down with them on the nearest divan he saw, like a common man. He would do these things. I longed to tell him they did him injury.

As he turned the letters over, Hephaistion strolled across, and sat down beside him. I gasped aloud; this passed all other effronteries. But Alexander just gave him some of the rolls to hold.

They were not very far away from me. I heard Alexander as he picked up the thickest letter, say, 'From Mother', and give a sigh.

'Read it first and get it over,' Hephaistion said.

Though I hated him, I could see how Darius' ladies had done him royal honours in their grief's confusion. By our Persian canons, I suppose he was the more beautiful; taller, with features regular to perfection. When his face was still, it was grave almost to sadness. His hair was a shining bronze though much coarser than mine.

Meantime, Alexander had opened Queen Olympias' letter. And Hephaistion, leaning easily on his shoulder, was reading it with him.

Through my own bitterness, I perceived this had shocked even the

Macedonians. Their murmurs reached me. 'Who does he think he is?' 'Well, we all know that. But he need not shout it.'

One of those veterans who stood out by their beards and their uncouth manners said, 'If he can read it, why can't all of us hear?' He spoke aloud.

Alexander looked up. He did not call his guards to arrest the man. He did not even rebuke him. He just drew off his signet-ring, turned to Hephaistion smiling, and laid on his lips the royal seal. They both returned to the letter.

I could always move smoothly, even if blind with tears. No one noticed me going. I ran to the stables, and rode off out of town, along by the sea-swamps, where clouds of black birds rose up wailing and screaming, like the thoughts of my heart. As I turned for home, my black thoughts settled, like crows upon a gibbet. I cannot bear my life while this man lives. He will have to die.

Walking my horse through sandy scrub, I thought it over. As boys they were vowed together, and while this man is faithful, Alexander feels himself bound. He will acknowledge him before all the world, though he loves me best in his heart, and my heart is scalding in fire. No! For Hephaistion, only one thing will do. I am going to kill him.

Tomorrow, then, I will go to the beggers' market and buy old clothes. Somewhere out here I will change, and hide my own clothes in the sand. I will wrap my head in a clout to hide my beardless face, and go to the little streets under the wall. I shall find a druggist there who will ask no questions. It cannot be long before I have the chance to get at his wine or food.

In the stables I called a groom to my lathered horse, and went back to the audience room, to look at him and think, You will soon be dead.

Quiet by the wall, I went over my plan. I would buy the poison; so far, good. Would it be in a phial, or a bag? I would keep it – where? In my clothes? Round my neck? How long would I have to hide it?

As my hot blood cooled, I began to think of a thousand mischances that could discover me, before I could use the drug; milling over these little things, till like a lightning-flash I saw the great one. If I were found with poison, who would ever doubt it was for the King? I had been brought to him by a man who had killed one king already.

So, then, Nabarzanes would be dragged from his home, and crucified beside me. I would be long remembered; the Persian boy, Darius' whore who fooled the great Alexander. So he too would remember me. Rather than that, I myself would take the poison, though it turned my entrails to shrivelling fire.

The Macedonians had had their audience. It was Persians now. Their presence reminded me whose son I was. What had been in my mind? To murder a faithful man, because he was in my way. So had King Arses' brothers been faithful, and in the way. So also had my father.

Next time I saw Hephaistion near the King, I said in myself, Well, I could kill you if I chose; you are lucky I will not stoop to it. I was young enough for this to make me feel better; too young, and too full of my own troubles, to think of his.

What he had had, would never again be anyone's. His claim was honoured; how could he ask for more? Well, he might have asked that his beloved should not become a lover, or have from a dark-eyed Persian boy what he'd never been thought to need. Maybe, since their youth, desire had faded (if so, I could guess whose had faded first); but the love was there, public as marriage. Lying alone in those nights at Zadrakarta, Hephaistion could not have slept at ease. I should have seen in his arrogance with the letter a plea for a proof of love. Alexander had seen; and given it in the face of everyone.

That night, between grief and guilt, I lost my sense of harmony, was strained and silly, and tried a trick I had learned at Susa, the kind of thing he had never guessed I knew. I felt my blunder. I feared disgust, not reckoning on his innocence. He exclaimed, 'Don't tell me you did that with Darius!' and laughed so much he nearly fell out of bed. I was so put out, I hid my face and would not look at him. 'What is it?' he asked. I said, 'I have displeased you. I will go.' He pulled me back. 'Don't sulk at me. What is it?' Then his voice altered, and he said, 'Do you miss Darius still?'

He was jealous; yes, even he! I flung myself on him, embracing him with a fury more like war than love. He was some time calming me down, before we could begin. Even then I was still strung-up, and at the end felt pain, almost like early days. Though I kept quiet, I suppose he felt some difference. I lay silent, doing nothing to divert his sadness. It was he who said, 'Come, tell.'

I answered, 'I love you too much, that's all.'

He drew me over, and ran my hair softly between his fingers. 'Never too much,' he said. 'Too much is not enough.' In sleep he did not toss himself free of me as he sometimes did; he let me stay in his side all night.

Next morning, as I got up, he said, 'How is your dancing?' I told him I was practising every day. 'Good. Today we are giving out the list of contests for the victory games. There will be one for dancers.'

I turned a cartwheel across the room, and a back-somersault after.

He laughed, then said seriously, 'One thing you must know; I never direct the judges. It's bound to make bad feeling. At the games at Tyre, I'd have given anything to see Thettalos crowned. For me, no tragedian touches him; he has been my envoy too, and done me very good service.

But they chose Athenodoros, and I had to put up with it. So I can only say, win for me.'

'If it kills me,' I said, doing a handstand.

'Oh, hush.' He made the Greek's sign against bad luck.

Later he gave me a fistful of gold for my costumes, and sent me the best flautist in Zadrakarta. If he had divined my trouble, and could not cure it, he knew how to make me forget.

I was tired of my old dances; for him I composed a new one. It began fast, Kaukasian style; then turned slow, with the bends that show one's balance and strength. The last part would have the sparks in it; not too many since I was a dancer and not an acrobat; but enough. For my costume, I ordered a Greek-style tunic, made all of scarlet ribbons, caught together just at the neck and waist. My sides were bare. I had anklets sewn with round tinkling rattles of beaten gold. For the first part, I would use the hand-clappers.

I practised for my life. The first day, when I'd done and sent off the flautist, Alexander came in and found me towelling-down, still out of breath. He took my shoulder between his hands. 'From now on till the games, you sleep in here. One thing at a time.'

He had a bed sent in for me. I knew he was right, but grieved he could do without me; still knowing less than the least of his soldiers what he could do without. I thought I could not bear a night away from him, but had worked so hard I slept as I lay down, and did not stir till morning.

On the day of the games, I went early to his room, where a squire was dressing him. As soon as he saw me he said, 'Oh, Bagoas will see to it; you can go.' Some of the squires had improved and the King had warmed to them, but this one was awkward. He went out sulkily; the King said, 'In all this time he can't hang a cloak.' I put in the brooches properly, saying, 'Next time, ask me.' He drew me by the hands and kissed me. 'We shall see each other when you dance.'

In the morning were the athletic events, running, jumping, throwing the disk and javelin, boxing, jumping, wrestling. This being the first time I had seen Greek games, I daresay I felt some interest, though they have bored me ever since. After the noon break came the dancing.

For this and for the music, the army carpenters had run up a theatre, with a stage and backdrop facing a gentle slope, benches for the important people, and a dais for the King's chair. The backdrops were painted with real-looking columns and curtains. We have no such art in Persia. I had never seen such a place before, but had been over it, and found that the floor was good.

The slopes were filling, the generals were taking their seats upon the benches. I went where I was shown, and joined the other dancers, on the grass near to the stage. We glanced sideways at each other; three Greeks. two Macedonians, and one other Persian. The King came in to the sound of trumpets. The other dancers all looked at me with hatred, knowing who I was.

But I don't think that, by the end, even they would have disputed my win. I knew it must be a good one, for his sake as well as mine. True enough, he never interfered with the judges; but judges are only human. Those at Tyre might have known he thought well of Thettalos; but this was not quite the same as being his lover. A near thing would not do.

At Susa, I had danced for favour, from the fear of being turned off, from conceit of myself. I danced now for the honour of our love.

Turns were settled by drawing lots; I came on fourth. And I was not halfway through my first quick dance with the handclappers, before the applause began. It was new to me. My biggest audience had been a handful of Darius' guests, who offered praise as courtesy. This roar was different; it carried me on wings. When I came to my somersaults at the end, I could hardly hear the music.

The judges made their choice in no time at all. I was sent to get my crown.

With the din following me all the way, I went up to the dais, and set my knee on its edge. Someone passed him the glittering wreath. I looked up, and met his smile.

He put the crown on my head, his touch caressing me. If happiness could overfill one like food or drink, I should have burst asunder. Hephaistion never did that for him, I thought.

The next contest was for kitharists. If the Wise God had sent his angels down to play, I would never have known the difference.

I remember nothing, between this paradise and standing by his chair at the evening feast. It was a grand banquet, quite well done for Macedonians, in the great hall of the palace, blazing with lamps; too many guests to use Greek couches. He had asked more Persian lords than ever before. All through the meal I was busy with gifts and messages. Everyone had something to say about my dance. I said to myself, He is honouring my people for what he finds in them; but a little, too, for me. And I thought with ecstasy of the coming night.

I went up before him. Instead of the bath-robe and towels, there were fresh clothes laid out. If I had not been living in a dream, I would have expected it; this I saw, in time not to make a fool of myself.

He came up, embraced me – the attendant squire had withdrawn when he saw me coming – and said, 'Today I was envied by all Zadrakarta, and not for being King.' I undid his cloak for him and helped him change. 'Don't wait up for me, my dear. It's all old friends, we shall be drinking until daylight. Go to bed and keep warm, or you'll be stiff tomorrow.'

A Macedonian night, I thought as I laid his purple cloak away. Well, he has given me warning. Never mind; however drunk he is, it shall be I who'll put him to bed, not that loutish squire. It's little enough to do for him.

I took a spare blanket from the chest, and rolled myself up in a corner. The hard floor did not keep me long awake.

I heard his voice. The birds were astir, but dawn had not yet broken.

'Every step on my feet. It took four of them to shift Philotas.'

'And they won't get far,' said Hephaistion. 'Now, can you get to bed?'

'Yes, but come in.' A pause. 'Oh, come in. No one is here.'

I felt very stiff. He'd been right about keeping warm. I drew up my blanket, lest my face should catch the light.

Hephaistion had Alexander's arm across his shoulders, not quite carrying him. He sat him down, took off his sandals and girdle, pulled his chiton over his head and eased him into bed. He placed the table, set there the water-pitcher and the cup, looked about for the chamber-pot and put it in easy reach. He wrung out a towel from the ewer, and wiped Alexander's forehead. Though unsteady on his feet, he did all this quite neatly. Alexander sighed, and said, 'That's good.'

'You'd better sleep it well off. Look, here's the water and there's the pot.'

'I'll sleep it off. Ah, that's good. You always think of everything.'

'I ought, by now.' He bent and kissed Alexander's forehead. 'Sleep well, my love.' He went, closing the door softly.

Alexander turned on his side. I waited a good while, to be sure he was fast asleep, then put back the blanket stealthily. I stole off to my cold bed, as dawn came with the squalling of the gulls.

14

At sixteen, in Zadrakarta, my youth began. Before, I had passed from childhood into some middle state, where youth was permitted only to my body. Now for seven years of my life it was given me back. All that long wandering has the taste of it.

There are places stamped on my memory; and long months when the face of the earth swims past me, as the shipping does when one sits beside the Nile. Mountain passes, wastes of snow, springtime forests, black lakes in upland moors, flatlands of pebbles or parched grass; rocks eaten into shapes of dragons; heavenly valleys full of fruit-blossom; mountains without end, spearing the sky, white and deadly; foothills with banks of unknown flowers; and rain – rain streaming down as if the heavens were dissolving, turning earth to mud, rivers to torrents, weapons to rust, men into helpless children. And the red-hot sandhills, day after day, by the glaring sea.

So we marched east from Zadrakarta, when I was sixteen and mad with love. We skirted the mountains that stretched on from Hyrkania, and entered wide empty land. Yet we lived in a moving city.

The King's train was now no less. He had crossed from Greece with a regent to rule his kingdom, free as a bird, just a general with the rank of King. Then the great cities fell, and Darius died. Now he was Great King in his own empire, and all its business travelled with him.

We were in a land without towns, like ancient Persis before Kyros' day. Hundreds of miles apart, were forts like my childhood home; bigger, because they had been seats of kings, but not really different; a strong house on a crag, a tribal village round it. They had passed from kings down to chiefs and satraps; but, ancient and rude as they were, were still called king-houses. For the rest, there were nomad herdsmen seeking pasture, or hamlets where there was water all year round. For league after league, our camp was the only town.

It held the army, and the second army that served it, of armourers, engineers, carpenters, tentmakers, sutlers, leather-workers, grooms; the womenfolk and children of all these; the slaves. There were a score of clerks by now. And these were only the army in Alexander's pay. A third army followed us for trade; horse-copers, cloth-sellers, jewellers, actors, musicians, jugglers, panders and bawds, whores of each sex or none. For even troopers were rich; as for the great generals, they lived like minor kings.

They had households of their own in wagon-trains, with chamberlains and stewards. Their courtesans lived as fine as Darius' women. They themselves after exercise were rubbed down by masseurs with oil of myrrh. Alexander only laughed at them, as the foibles of friends. I could not bear to see how he let them surpass him in state and pride. I knew what Persians would make of it.

He himself had no time for show; or, often, for me. At the end of every march there would be a day's business waiting; envoys and scouts and engineers and petitioners, and the common soldiers who brought him their troubles as of right. After all that, he wanted his bed only for sleep.

Darius, when he found desire to fail him, would feel wronged by nature, and send for someone, such as me, whose skill was to put things right. Alexander, his eyes upon tomorrow, thought nature meant him to get a good night's rest.

There are things one can't explain to a whole man. With people like me, sex is a pleasure but not a need. Much more I loved his body just to be near it, like a dog or a child. There was life in his warmth, and sweetness. But I never said to him, 'Let me in, I'll be no trouble.' Never be importunate, never, never. There were other things for which he needed me every day; and the nights of reward would come.

On one of these, he said to me, 'Were you angry that I burned Persepolis?'

'No, my lord; I was never there. But why did you burn it down?'

'Up. We burned it up. The god inspired us.' By the nightlamp, I saw his face like a rapt singer's. 'Curtains of fire, hangings of fire; tables, spread with great feasts of fire. And the ceilings were all of cedar-wood. When we had done throwing on the torches, and the heat drove us outside, it was going up like a torrent into the black sky, a great fire-fall pouring upward with sparks for spray; roaring and blazing right up to heaven. And I thought, No wonder they worship it. What is there on earth more godlike?'

He liked to be talked to after the act of love; there was still something in him that rebuked desire as weakness. At these times I would speak to him of serious things; laughter and play were for beforehand.

Once he said, 'Here we lie like this, and still you call me My Lord. Why do you do it?'

'It is what you are; in my heart, in everything.'

'Keep it in your heart, my dear, before the Macedonians. I have seen some looks.'

'You will always be my lord, whatever I call you. What must it be?'

'Alexander, of course. Any Macedonian trooper can call me that.'

'Iskander,' I said. My Greek accent was not very good yet.

He laughed and told me to try again. 'That's better. When they hear you lording me, they think, "So he's setting up as Great King".'

He had given me my chance at last. 'But my lord, my lord Iskander, you *are* the Great King of Persia. I know my people; they're not like the Macedonians. I know the Greeks say that the gods envy great men, that they punish hu –' I had been working hard at my books, but the word escaped me.

'Hubris,' he said. 'And they are watching me for that already.'

'Not the Persians, my lord. In a great man they look for grandeur. If he seems to hold himself cheap, they withhold respect.'

'Cheap?' he said from the bottom of his chest. It was too late to go back.

'My lord, courage and victory we honour. But the King ... he must be apart; great satraps must approach him like a god. For him they make the prostration, which only peasants would make for them.'

He was silent. I waited fearfully. At last he said, 'Darius' brother wanted to tell me that. But he did not dare.'

'Now my lord is angry?'

'Never, at counsel given in love.' He pulled me closer to prove it. 'But remember, Darius lost, and I'll tell you why. One can rule satraps that way; but never soldiers. They don't want to follow some royal image they have to approach on their bellies. They want to know you remember them in some action a year ago, and whether they've a brother serving; they like a word if he dies. If they're snowed on, they like to see the general snowed on too. And if rations are short, or water, and you keep ahead of the column, they want to know you're doing it on the army issue; *then* they'll follow you. And they like to laugh. I learned what they laugh at in my father's guard-house when I was six years old. They made me Great King of Persia, remember ... No, I'm not angry; you were right to speak. You know, I have the blood both of Greeks and Trojans in me.'

I knew nothing of it, but devoutly kissed his shoulder.

'Never mind. Say I like your people; or find something of myself in them. Why say yours or mine? They should all be ours. Kyros did not rest till he had achieved it. Now it's time to make a new thing again. The god does not lead us all this way for nothing.'

I said, 'I have talked too much. Now you are wide awake again.'

Last time I'd said this, he had replied, 'Why not?' Tonight he said, 'Yes', and went on thinking. I fell asleep beside his open eyes.

We were coming into Baktria, over huge rough uplands already touched with autumn, cut by harsh winds from the freezing mountains. I bought myself a coat of scarlet cloth lined with marten-skins, having lost my lynx-skin one at the Kaspian Gates. Camp-followers and soldiers bundled on extra warmth with sheep and goat-skins; the officers had cloaks of good woollen cloth; but it was only the sleeved and trousered Persians who looked really warm. Sometimes Macedonians gave me a glance of envy; but they would have died before they put on the garb of the defeated, the soft and rotten Mede. They'd as soon have eaten their mothers.

The first rains fell; the wet ground made heavy going, streams were in spate; we seemed now to move as cumbrously as Darius' train. I learned the difference, when news came in that Satibarzanes, Satrap of Areia, had rebelled behind us. He had given himself up freely at Zadrakarta; Alexander had offered him his right hand, asked him to dine, confirmed his satrapy, and given him a guard of forty Macedonians to help man his strongpoint. All these he'd murdered, once Alexander was gone; and was calling his tribesmen out to fight for Bessos.

Over our vast straggling horde, a trumpet sounded. The horse-train trampled and whinnied; orders barked in the snapping air; in less time than one could believe, the cavalry came out in column. Alexander mounted his war-horse; they plunged off into the weather, the ground shuddering under them. It was as if a slow giant had opened his cloak, and hurled a javelin.

We made camp and waited among all the winds of heaven; men and women were scratching the plain for firewood. I went to my Greek lessons with Philostratos, a grave young Ephesian, who did not despair of me. (To him I owe it that King Ptolemy let me use his library, and I have read most Greek authors worth mentioning, though I cannot to this day make out the simplest inscription in my native tongue.)

The clerks kept up the records, so I got the news. The tribesmen had fled at the mere rumour of Alexander; the satrap had escaped to Bessos. Alexander had marked him down for death; he could never abide treachery. None the less, the new satrap he had appointed for Areia was another Persian. He rode back in a snowstorm, and settled to his load of business.

The returning troops made a great rush for women, or whatever their fancy was. I knew better than to await any such summons. When he poured out his strength in war, he kept nothing back; and there was a half-month's work of government saved up for him. He got through it in five days. Then he asked in some friends, and they sat up all night drinking. He grew talkative, and fought over the whole war again. Then he slept all day, and on through the next night.

It was not the wine, though he had had a lot of it; he could have slept that off in half the time. Wine was what he used to bring his mind to a stop when it had forgotten rest. Drunk as he was, he managed to take a bath, which he liked at bedtime. He never laid a hand on me, except to steady his steps. Wine brings out hidden things, and it did with him; but coarseness in the bedchamber was never one of them.

The day after, he woke as fresh as a foal; got through another mountain of work; and said to me at bedtime. 'How can it have been so long?'

I made him welcome in every way I knew, and some I had only just thought of. It was a joke of his that I was making a Persian of him; the truth was that I was forgetting already how to please anyone else. A gentle subtlety was better for him than passion. Though I had the art to draw men into violent pleasures, and had done it also with him, it left a cloud on him; and for me it was only a taught skill. I should have obeyed my heart from the first; but no one before him had ever let me have one. Now

I had shown him his way about the garden of delight, or as much of it as ever would delight him, he wanted a companion there, not an entertainer. He was never clumsy; it was his nature to be a giver, here as elsewhere. And, here as elsewhere, if he was vain it was never about nothing.

Prince Oxathres had been promoted into the King's Bodyguard. Alexander liked handsome men there, and thought it due to his rank. He was within a thumb-breadth of Darius for height; Alexander said to me laughing that it was a change for Philotas, to have someone look down on him. I replied with constraint, which I hoped he noticed. This Philotas had been on my mind.

He was the grandest of the generals, Commander of the Companions, thought handsome, though too red for a Persian taste. Of all those who put on more state and luxury than the King, he was the chief. I swear he went hunting with more gear and attendance than Darius had, and the inside of his tent was like a palace. I had taken a message there, and he had looked at me with contempt. It did him no good with me, even that Hephaistion disliked him too.

When one knows the ways of court, one knows what to look for. Sometimes I would post myself outside the audience room, as I'd done at Babylon, to watch faces as men came out. There would be the usual run of relief, disappointment, pleasure, familiar ease; but Philotas' smile used to drop off his face too quickly, and once I could have sworn I saw a sneer.

I kept it in my heart. I dared say nothing. Alexander had known him all his life; with boyhood friends, he was loyal beyond sense. Not only that; the man's father, Parmenion, out-ranked every other general, even Krateros who outranked all others here. Parmenion had been King Philip's chief commander. I had never seen him, because his army was guarding the western roads behind us, a trust on which all our lives depended. So I held my peace; only praising Oxathres' Nisaian chargers and their splendid trappings, and adding, 'But of course, my lord, even at Darius' court he was never as rich as Philotas.'

'No?' he said, and I could see it had made him think; so I clasped him laughing, and went on, 'But now not you yourself are as rich as I.'

The only upshot of this, that I could see, was his looking at Oxathres' horse-trappings, and liking them so much that he had them copied for old Oxhead. No Greek horse looks wonderful to a Persian; but now he was fed, tended and fresh, you could believe he had carried Alexander in battle for ten years and never once shown fear. Most horses would have been bothered by the new finery, the headstall with the cockade, the silver cheek-pieces and the hanging plaques on the collar; but Oxhead thought very well of himself, and paced along making the most of them. There was a good deal in him of Alexander.

I was thinking this, as I sponged him down before dinner. He liked that as well as his bath at bed time; he was the cleanest man I ever knew, when his wars allowed it. I used to wonder at first what faint pleasant scent he used, and would look about for the phial; but there was none, it was the gift of nature.

I praised the horse-trappings, and Oxhead's looks in them, and he said he was having more made as gifts for his friends. I towelled him down; all muscle, not over-built as those clumsy Greek wrestlers are. I said, 'How well, my lord, you would wear the clothes that match the trappings.'

He looked round quickly. 'What put that in your head?'

'Only seeing you now.'

'Oh, no. You are a seer, I told you so. I have been thinking, in one's own kingdom one should look less like a stranger.'

His words delighted me. The wind was whistling around the tent. 'I can tell you, my lord, in this weather you'll be much warmer in trousers.'

'*Trousers?*' he asked, staring at me in horror, as if I had proposed he should paint himself blue all over. Then he laughed. 'My dear boy, on you they are enchanting; on Oxathres, they decorate the Guard. But to a Macedonian, there is something about trousers . . . Don't ask me why. I'm as bad as all the rest.'

'Well think of something, my lord. Something more like Persian court dress.' I longed to make him beautiful in the fashion of my people.

He sent for a bolt of fine wool, for me to drape on him. But I had hardly started, when it turned out that not only would he not wear trousers; he would not have long sleeves either. He said they would fidget him, but I could tell it was just a pretext. I told him it was Kyros himself who'd put the Persians into Median dress; what's more, it was true; but even this magic name had no power upon him. So I had to resort to the antique Persian robe, so terribly old-fashioned that no one had worn it in a hundred years, except the King at festivals. If I'd not seen Darius being put into it, I'd never have known how it was made. It has a long skirt, stitched in folds on a waistband; a kind of cape, with a hole for the head to go through, covers the upper part and hangs over the arms to the wrists. I cut it all out and tacked the skirt together, put it on him, and moved the mirror about for him to see.

'I remember this,' he said, 'in the wall-reliefs at Persepolis. What do you think?' He moved sideways to the mirror. He was like a woman for dressing-up, whenever he got a good excuse.

'It has great dignity,' I said. He could carry it off, though it really called for height. 'But do you like it to move in?'

He paced about. 'If one doesn't need to do anything. Yes, I'll have it made up. In white, with purple borders.'

So I found the best robe-maker (there were so many Persians in camp, that craftsmen followed them) and he made it with the real elaborate drapings. The King wore it, with a low open tiara, when entertaining Persians. I could see it increased respect. There are ways and ways of doing the prostration, which he did not see as I did. I had never told him, not wishing to betray my people; it hurt their pride, to see lower-born Macedonians make no reverence at all.

I told him now that they were well pleased with the robe. I did not say, though I longed to, that Philotas had looked down the length of the table and caught some crony's eye.

As I expected, Alexander soon found the robe tiresome; he said one could not stride out in it. I could have told him no one strode out at a Persian court. He had another made, pretty much like a long Greek chiton, except that the top overhung the arms. He wore a broad Median sash with it; purple on white. It suited him; but as far as the Macedonians were concerned, it might as well have had sleeves. He was so sure he had struck a happy mean, I hadn't the heart to tell him.

Hephaistion, as always, was on his side, and had taken to Persian horse-trappings. I heard murmurs about sycophancy as he passed; but I knew them mean. I had had time to consider Hephaistion. How easily he could have had me poisoned, or accused me through false witnesses, or had jewels hidden in my pack and charged me with their theft; something like that would have happened long ago at the Persian court, if I'd displeased a powerful favourite. He had a rough tongue among fellow-soldiers, yet had never used it on me. If we had to meet, he would just speak to me as if to some well-born page, civil and brisk. In return I offered respect without servility. Often I wished him dead, as, no doubt, so he did me; but we had reached an unspoken understanding. Neither of us would have robbed Alexander of anything he valued; so we had no choice.

Marching east over bare dun upland, and through rich valleys on which we fed, we halted at the king-house of the Zarangians. It was a rude old castle, rambling about over massive rocks with crazy rough-hewn steps, the windows mostly arrow-slits. The local chief moved out of the tower rooms; they smelled of his horses which had been stabled below. Alexander moved in, knowing he would lose face with the tribesmen if he did not. The squires had a guard-room half way up; above were the King's chamber and an anteroom; a sort of closet, used by the squire who had the care of his weapons; and another closet for me. Outside of that, the other rooms, where his friends were lodged, were reached by going outdoors.

I had a brazier brought up for him to take his bath by; the place had a whistling draught, and after the march he wanted a good clean-up before supper. The water was good and hot; I was rubbing down his back with ground pumice, when with a groaning creak the crude door flew open, and one of the squires burst in.

Alexander, sitting in the bath, said, 'Whatever is it, Metron?'

The youth stood breathless. This one had made efforts, and shaped quite well; if only from respect for Alexander, he was civil even to me. But he now stood white as a bed-sheet, trying to find his voice. Alexander told him to take a hold of himself, and speak up. He swallowed.

'Alexander. There's a man here says he knows of a plot to kill you.'

I rinsed the pumice off Alexander's back. He stood up. 'Where is he?'

'In the armoury, Alexander. There was nowhere else to put him.'

'His name?'

'Kebalinos, sir. Leonnatos' squadron. Sir, I brought your sword.'

'Good. You put a guard on him?'

'Yes, Alexander.'

'Good boy. Now tell me what he said.'

I was still drying and dressing him. Perceiving I was not to be sent out, Metron said, 'He's here for his brother, sir, young Nikomachos. He didn't dare come himself, they'd have guessed why. That's why he told Kebalinos.'

'Yes?' said Alexander very patiently. 'Told Kebalinos what?'

'About Dymnos, sir. He's the one.'

Alexander's brows went up a moment. Metron buckled his sword-belt on.

'He's – well, a friend of young Nikomachos, sir. He wanted him to join in, but Nikomachos said no. Dymnos had counted on him saying yes to anything; so he lost his head, and told Nikomachos they'd kill him if he didn't join. So then he pretended he would, and told his brother.'

'They? Who are the others?'

The youth strained his face. 'Alexander, I'm sorry. He told me, but I can't remember.'

'Honest at least. If you want to make a soldier, it's when taken by surprise you have to keep your wits. Never mind; go and fetch me the Captain of the Guard.'

He started pacing the room. He looked stern-faced, but hardly shocked at all. I'd learned already that more kings had been murdered in Macedon even than in Persia. There, they used the dagger. It was said his father had been struck down before his eyes.

When the Captain of the Guard came in, he said, 'Arrest Dymnos of Chalestra. He's quartered in the camp, not the Palace. Bring him here.' Then he went with Metron to the armoury.

From the anteroom, I heard the man inside cry, 'Oh, King! I thought I'd never get word to you in time.' Being scared he gabbled, so I missed some of his story. There was something about Dymnos feeling slighted by the King, then, 'But that's only what he told my brother. He couldn't account to me for the others being in it'; and he gave their names, which like Metron I have forgotten, even though I saw them die.

Alexander let him run on, never checking him when he rambled; then said, 'How long did your brother know this, before he told you?'

'Just till he could find me, Alexander. No time at all.'

'Today, then, while we were making camp, this happened.'

'Oh, no, Alexander. That's why I came like this. It was two days ago.'

'Two *days?*' His voice had altered. 'I've never been out of camp. How long were you in this, before you changed your mind? Arrest him.'

They pulled him out, a young soldier, gaping with fright. 'But Alexander,' he called, between a croak and a shout, 'I went the moment I heard. I swear it, I went straight to your tent. Didn't he tell you, then? He said he'd tell you as soon as you were free. And again next day. I swear it, King, by undying Zeus. Did he never tell you at all?'

There was a silence. Alexander searched the man with his deep eyes.

'Release him, but stand by. Now let me understand you. You are saying you told all this to someone at my headquarters, who undertook to report it?'

'Yes, Alexander!' He had nearly sunk down, when the soldiers let him go. 'I swear it, only ask him, King. He said I'd done right, and he'd report it as soon as he had the chance. Then yesterday he said you'd had too much business, but he'd do it before night. And then today, when we could see Dymnos and the rest still going free, my brother said I must see you somehow myself.'

'It seems your brother's no fool. To whom had you given this message?'

'To General Philotas, King. He –'

'*What?*'

The man repeated it, stammering in terror. But what I saw in Alexander's face was not disbelief. It was recollection.

Presently he said, 'Very well, Kebalinos. You and your brother will now be held as witnesses. You have nothing to fear if you speak the truth. So prepare your evidence, and be ready to give it clearly.'

The guards removed him. Alexander sent everyone else to summon men he needed. Meantime we were alone. I tidied the bath-things, stupidly concerned that all these people would be here before I could get hold of the slaves to carry the heavy bath away. I was not leaving him by himself till someone came.

Striding about the room, he came face to face with me. Words burst out of him. 'He was with me an hour that day. The last part of it, he was talking horses. Too much business! . . . We have been friends, Bagoas, we've been friends since I was a child.' He took another turn, and came back. 'He changed after I went to Siwah. He mocked it to my face, but he has always mocked the gods, and I forgave it him. I was warned of him in Egypt; but he was my friend; what was I, Ochos? Yet he has never been the same; he changed when I had the oracle.'

Before I could reply, the men he'd sent for began arriving, and I had to withdraw. The first was General Krateros, who had his lodging close by. As I went, I heard Alexander say, 'Krateros, I want a guard put on every road out of here; every track and riding-path. No one at all, for any reason, is to leave this place. Do that, it can't wait; then come back and I'll tell you why.'

The other friends he'd sent for, Hephaistion and Ptolemy and Perdikkas and the rest, were shut with him in his room, and I could hear nothing. Then came trudging feet upon the stairs. Young Metron, running ahead, now over his fright and full of self-importance, scraped at the door. 'Alexander, they're bringing Dymnos. Sir, he resisted arrest.'

Four soldiers brought on an army stretcher a youngish, fair-bearded Macedonian, with blood over his side and trickling from his mouth. His breath was rattled. Alexander said, 'Which of you did this?', and they all turned as white-faced as their burden. The leader, finding a voice of sorts, said, 'He did, King. I'd not even arrested him. He did it as soon as he saw us coming.'

Alexander stood by the stretcher. The man knew him, though his eyes were glazing. The King put a hand on his shoulder; meaning, I supposed, to shake out of him the names of his confederates while there was time. But he just said, 'How have I wronged you, Dymnos? What was it?'

The man's lips moved. I saw on his face a last shred of anger. His eyes rolled round and lighted on my Persian clothes; and his voice, half clotted, began to say 'Barbar –' Then the blood came up, and his eyes fixed in his head.

Alexander said, 'Cover him. Put him somewhere out of sight and set a guard.' The soldier of lowest rank spread, unwillingly, his cloak over the corpse.

Soon after, Krateros returned to say the guard-posts were being manned; then someone announced that the King's supper was ready.

As they all passed my closet, to which I had withdrawn, Alexander said, 'The outpost guards must still be on their way. He must know nothing, at all costs, till the roads are closed. We shall have to break bread with him, however little we like it.' Hephaistion answered, 'He has broken it with you, without any shame.'

It was a Macedonian supper; I was not needed. I should have liked to watch the faces. People like me are blamed for curiosity; having lost part of our lives, we are apt to fill the gap from the lives of others. In this I am like the rest, and make no pretences.

The royal hall was a stone barn, with a rock floor that stubbed one's toes. Not much of a place for his life's last feast; but I wished him nothing better.

I got rid of the bath, made the room fit for company, had supper, and came back to warm my hands at the brazier, and think about the closing of the roads. After a while it came to me. Philotas was son to Parmenion, the greatest man in Asia next the King. It was he who secured our rear. He was warden of the Ekbatana treasury; and had his own army, which from that hoard he could pay for ever. Many were hired men, who had only fought under him. Philotas was his one son left living; two others had died upon campaign. I understood.

The King's supper finished early. He came back with his friends, and sent for young Nikomachos, to hear his story. He was young, girlish and scared; the King treated him gently. After that, at about midnight, the conspirators he had named were all arrested. Philotas was taken last.

He was led in stumbling and blinking; he had drunk hard at supper, and been fast asleep. Now everyone was secured, they did not trouble closing doors for secrecy. I heard it all. Till now, the King had been like iron; now, for a moment, I seemed to hear the voice of a hurt angry boy, to an elder he once looked up to. Why had he hidden Kebalinos' warning? How could he do it? And, in the madness which, say the Greeks, the gods inspire in their chosen victims, Philotas answered the boy, and not the King.

With a blustering laugh, a little off the note, he said, 'Why, I thought nothing of it, who would? My dear Alexander, you don't want to hear of every spiteful little fancy-piece who has a tiff with his keeper.'

He was a great one for women, and boastful of it. The scorn in his voice was carelessness, and I daresay the drink. But it did his business. Fifteen years older in an instant, the King said, 'Dymnos has killed himself, rather than face his trial. But you will stand yours tomorrow. Guard! Confined to quarters under close arrest.'

The trials were held next day, on the heath outside the camp. It was cold, with grey scudding clouds threatening rain, but the whole army turned out, more than could get in hearing; the Macedonians in front, as was their right. Amazing to tell, the King could put no Macedonian to death without their vote. At home, any common peasant could have come and voted.

There being no place for me, I watched from the tower the small figures stand in the open square. Dymnos' accomplices were tried first. They had already confessed and accused each other. (Wolves howl every night in Baktria, so I can't be sure of the sounds I heard.) After each trial the Macedonians shouted, and the man was led away.

Last appeared Philotas, whom I knew by his height, and the King, whom I knew by everything. They seemed to stand a long time there; one could tell by their gestures which was speaking. Then witnesses testified, above a dozen. Then the King spoke again; the Macedonians shouted, louder than all the other times. Then it was over.

I was told the evidence later. Except for the brothers', it had all been about Philotas' pride and insolence, and his speaking against the King. He would call him The Boy, and credit all his victories to Parmenion and himself; used to say he'd been vain from a child, and would rather be King of fawning barbarians than a decent Macedonian. Now he had swallowed whole the politic flatteries of Egyptian priests, and would be content with no less than deity; God help the people ruled by a man who thought himself more than mortal.

The executions would be next day; stoning for the lesser men; for Philotas, a squad with javelins. In Persia, they would have bricked up such men in a cold furnace, and stoked it slowly. And the King would have asked no man's leave.

Had Philotas, when he hid the plot, just seized the chance to profit by others' risk; or was he himself behind it? This was still unproved.

The King being shut up in council, for pastime I went back to the tower-top. Already the stakes were being sunk for the executions. On the roads and passes, I could see the guard-posts. Something moved on the western road; three men in Arab dress, on racing dromedaries. They caught my eye by the beauty of their action, after the great shaggy Baktrian camels. No creature that carries man is swifter or more enduring. They went up with their smooth stride towards the pass, and I looked to see them turned back. But after a moment's pause at the guard-post, they were let through.

I went down, lest the King should need me. Soon after, his council left. As they turned to the stairs, Hephaistion was last. The King beckoned him back. He went in, and bolted the door.

At other times, I should have found some dark place to grieve in. But it was nothing like that, as their faces told me. So I left my slippers in my cell, and crept up barefoot. The door-bolt was a great wooden thing; Hephaistion had been some time coaxing it. While he was drawing it back, I could be well away. You cannot learn too much of the one you love.

Hephaistion was saying, 'I always thought he carried tales to your father. I told you so.'

'I know you did.' I heard again the voice of the distant boy. 'But you never liked him. Well, you were right.

'Yes, I was. He hung round you from ambition, he always envied you. You should have listened in Egypt. This time, we have to know.'

The King said, 'Yes. We must know now.'

'And don't take it to heart after. He's not worth it, never was.'

'No. I shan't do that.'

'He's been living soft, Alexander. It won't take long.'

His voice came close to the door, and I made ready to run; but the King said, 'Wait.' So I crept back again.

'If he denies his father knew, don't push him to extremity.'

'Why not?' Hephaistion asked. He sounded impatient.

'Because it makes no difference.'

'You mean,' said Hephaistion slowly, 'that you'll –?'

'It is done,' said the King. 'Nothing else was possible.'

There was a pause. Their eyes spoke, I suppose. Hephaistion said, 'Well, it's the law. A traitor's near kin. It's only the manner of it.'

'It's the only way.'

'Yes. But you'll feel better, if you know he's guilty.'

'Could I know from that? I won't lean on a lie, Hephaistion. It was necessary, and I know it. That is enough.'

'Very well. Let's have it over.' Hephaistion moved to the door again. I was in my cell long before he got it open.

After long enough, I asked the King if he needed anything. He was still standing where he must have been before. 'No,' he said. 'I have something to see to,' and went off by himself down the winding torchlit stair.

I waited, listening. At Susa, while still a slave, I had gone like other boys to the place of punishment, I had seen a man impaled, and flayings, and other things. Three times I had gone, drawn as boys are against their will to horrors. There were crowds that went every time; but I had had enough. I had now no wish to watch Hephaistion's work. It could be nothing much, to what I had seen already.

In time I heard the scream of a powerful voice. I felt no pity. What he had done to my lord, nothing undoes; the first betrayal by a friend. I, too, could remember losing childhood in a moment of time.

The scream sounded again, less like a man, more like a beast. Let him suffer, I thought. My lord has not only suffered a broken faith. He has taken a burden he will never again be free of.

I had understood his secret words to Hephaistion. Parmenion ruled like a king, in the lands behind us. Among his own troops, he could never be arrested, never be put on trial. Guilty or innocent, he would have his blood-feud the moment he got the news. I pictured our army and all its followers, in the freezing Baktrian winter, supplies cut off, no reinforcements; the conquered satraps, released by Parmenion's troops, taking us in rear; around us, Bessos and his Baktrians closing in.

I knew the errand of the dromedaries, swiftest of all beasts that carry man: to outrun the news, carrying death.

Such burdens fall only upon kings. He bore it all his life, and, as he foresaw, he bears it dead. Since I am one of many thousands who, because he took it on him, are still alive, it may be said I plead my own cause; but to the end of my days, I shall never see what else he could have done.

The screams did not last long. A man in Philotas' case has not much to lose by talking quickly.

The King came to bed late. He was stone-cold sober, as if at war. He scarcely spoke to me, except to thank me now and again, lest I should suppose him angry.

I lay in my little cell, wide awake, as I knew that he would be. The night wore on; the guard clanked and muttered below; the wolves of Baktria howled. Never be importunate, never, never, never. I dressed and gave on his door the tap he knew, and did not even wait for leave to enter.

He was lying half turned away; Peritas, who always slept down at his bed-foot, was standing by him, pawing the blanket as if concerned. Alexander was rubbing his ears.

I came and knelt on the other side, and said, 'My lord, may I say goodnight to you? Just goodnight?'

'Bed, Peritas,' he said. The dog went back to its blanket. He felt my face and hands. 'You're cold. Get in.'

I dropped off my things and came in beside him. He warmed my hands on his breast, as he had rubbed Peritas' ears, in silence. I reached up and stroked his hair back from his forehead. 'My father was betrayed by a false friend,' I said. 'He told me so before they killed him. It is terrible from a friend.'

'When we get back,' he said, 'you can tell me who it was.'

The dog, after turning round two or three times, got up to look, then went back to bed, as if satisfied he was now being well cared for.

I said, 'It is death to mock the gods. At Susa, I had a slave from Egypt; not a common man, he had served a temple. He said no oracle is as pure as the one at Siwah.'

He took a deep breath, and lay looking upward at the rafters, where the shadows of cobwebs moved with the flickering lamp. After a while, I put an arm across him, and he laid his hand on it to keep it there. He was silent a long time, holding my arm around him. Then he said, 'I have done a thing today that you don't know of, which I shall be blamed for by men to come. But it was necessary.'

'Whatever has to be done,' I answered him, 'you are the King.'

'It was necessary. There was no other way.'

I said, 'We lay our lives on the King, and he bears them all. He could never do it, without the hand of the god.'

He sighed, and drew my head upon his shoulder.

'You are my King,' I said softly. 'All you do is well done to me. If ever I am false, if ever my faith forsakes you, may I never enter Paradise, may the River of Ordeal scald me all away. You are the King, the son of the god.'

We lay quiet, just as we were, and at last he slept. I closed my eyes in contentment. Some Power must have directed me; I had come when I was truly needed.

15

Along with Philotas, there died by the javelins Alexandros of Lynkestis, next heir, by side-descent, to the throne of Macedon. His brothers had conspired in King Philip's murder; nothing being proved against the eldest, Alexander had taken him with the army. Now it seemed that Dymnos and the rest had meant to make him King; a decent Macedonian, who would keep barbarians in the place the Greek gods meant for them.

He had been warned of his trial, and prepared a speech of defence; but before the Assembly, could only utter a senseless stammer. He had looked, they said, like a croaking frog; and they condemned him out of contempt, saying they were well shot of such a king. One or two of the accused made good their case and were set free. We were on the march again, by the time the news came in of Parmenion's death.

The men took it quietly. They had themselves condemned Philotas; they were ready to suppose there was evidence against his father. It was the veteran officers, the old school of King Philip's training, who remembered Parmenion had won him a victory the day Alexander was born; it was these who brooded. Philip, it seemed, had been a proper Macedonian. Having freed the Greek cities of Asia, he would have been content to go home, and be master of Greece, which was what he had always wanted.

Our moving city dragged on over barren moors scorched brown with summer, now chilled with autumn winds that sang through the broken crags. It was harsh country; among the camp-followers the sickly died;

someone from their home place would scratch them a grave in the hard ground. Nobody starved; the wagon-trains came from the west, and droves of cattle lean with travelling. We laboured along, mostly without Alexander; he was scouring the wastes for Bessos, who was reported moving east.

After days or a half-month, they would come back, thin men upon thin horses, having outrun their supplies. Or now and again some stubborn hill-fort would hold out, and he would make a siege-train; catapults taken apart to load on mules, wood for the ladders if the land was treeless; if he could bring one up, a jolting siege-tower, drawn by ten yoke of oxen; litters for the wounded, if it was too rough for wagons. He would ride up and down the line, seeing everything for himself. It was almost beyond belief, out of so many thousand men, how many he knew. Often they laughed; the soldier with the King, or the King with the soldier.

The soldiers knew their part in him well enough. Most had not even seen him in Persian dress; they knew him in hard-worn Greek clothes, and armour of old leather with the bits of iron plating through at the edges. They wanted no properer Macedonian than their young unbeaten general, who sweated or froze or starved with them, never sitting down till he had seen them fed and their wounded cared for; never sleeping drier than they; snatching victory out of peril. What did they care if he appointed Persian satraps, when some Macedonian might have ruled and fleeced the province? They looked for their share of loot, and he shared it fairly. If he slept with Darius' boy when he had the time, what of it? He had a right to his share too. But they began to think about home.

They had had the cream of the spoils, the wealth of the great cities. They had swum in gold. Once, I was told, a transport mule in the treasure train had foundered; the trooper who led it, careful of the King's goods, had shouldered the heavy pack, staggering under it. Along came Alexander, and said, 'Bear up a little longer. Just get it to your tent. It's yours.' So they had lived. They had had their pickings from the Persians, and wanted no more part of us.

Not so with Alexander. His hunger grew by feeding. He loved victory; Bessos was still unconquered. He loved magnificence; our palaces, our manners, had shown him what that could be. As a boy he'd been taught to despise us; he had found beauty and valour among our lords, bred in for generations; also, he had found me. He loved kingcraft; here was a whole empire, weak with misrule, whose bridle had scarcely felt his hand. Above all, he had his Longing. That moment of eager joy I had felt at the Kaspian Gates with the pass ahead, with him reached far into the distance, craving for wonders rumoured in travellers' tales. Great anguish lies in wait for those who long too greatly.

Still he kept his soldiers faithful. Like Kyros, he cast his spell. He told them too that to retreat without settling Bessos would invite contempt, and a rising of all the tribes; they would lose their victories and their glory. They still cared for that. They had proved themselves masters of the barbarians, and valued it.

From them he would come back to me. As for sex, he was glad of it, having been a long time without; but he could have gone longer, there were things he needed more. He liked to return to his other kingdom, and find love there; to know there is one beauty of the sun, another of the moon. He liked, I found, to be sent to sleep with the long tales of the bazaar, about princes seeking the phoenix's egg, riding to towers of adamant ringed with flame, or coming in disguise to enchantress queens. He liked to hear about the court at Susa. At the rites of the getting-up, the bedtime and the bath, he could not keep from laughing; but to the etiquette of audience he listened carefully.

He trusted me. Without trust he could not live. He trusted Hephaistion, too; not all to my misfortune, as now it proved.

Philotas' power had proved too great for one man. The King now divided it between two commanders; Black Kleitos, a veteran officer he had known since childhood, and Hephaistion.

If trust were everything, Hephaistion would have had it all. But the army had its politics; already the parties were dividing. Hephaistion was known as the King's right hand in everything new he was doing. He had learned our forms of courtesy; was as tall and handsome as the Iranian lords, who admired and liked him; he was Persianized, said the men of the old school. Stocky bearded Kleitos, getting the same rank, was a surety they were not left out in the cold.

What all this meant to me, was that often Hephaistion would go out on his own campaigns.

He had proved himself well in war. He was a lord's son of Macedon, and required honour, even if it took him from Alexander's side. I wished him all of it he could go and find, I who required one thing alone.

About harvest time, we came to the Valley of the Benefactors. To find this place delighted Alexander. I had told him the story, left out like so much else from his book on Kyros, of how these people had brought his army food when they were starving in the wasteland; how he found them so virtuous, he freed them from tribute and let them rule themselves. It was he who named them. Their breed endured; slow, shy, quiet, broad-faced people, friendly even to soldiers, since none had troubled them since Kyros' day. Their valley was wide and fertile, sheltered from the lancing northern winds. Alexander rested his men here, bought their produce at the best rate they'd ever had, and promised a hanging out of hand to whoever harmed them.

He himself, who could never be idle anywhere, used to ride out hunting. Often he let me come along. Xenophon, he told me, said hunting was the image of war. It was for Alexander. Dangerous rocky ground, long runs, a fierce quarry, lion or boar for choice, were what he looked for. I remembered Darius in the royal park, shooting at driven game. After Alexander's hunts, I felt nearly dead. But I'd have died sooner than own it; before long I hardened and came back just hungry for my supper.

While we were camped there, a Persian lord gave a great birthday feast, and asked the King to honour it. He came to bed hardly drunk at all. Persians drink deep on their birthdays; but they hold it better than Macedonians. He was always careful among them, and watched his friends as well.

As I was settling him into bed, he said suddenly, 'Bagoas, I've never asked you, in all this time. When is *your* birthday?'

He could not make out why I was crying. I knelt by the bed with my head in my arms, and he patted me as if I had been Peritas. When at last I got it out, he leaned over me, and I heard him swallow a sob. It was absurd; I ought to have been ashamed.

He would not await the day, since, he said, I had missed so many, but next morning gave me a beautiful Arab horse and a Thracian groom; and two days later, when the jeweller had finished it, a ring with his portrait carved on chalcedony. I shall be buried with it. I have put that in my will; along with a curse, to keep the embalmers from stealing it.

Not only were the Benefactors a kindly people; they had worked out just laws among themselves. He greatly took to them. Before he went, he offered to double their lands; but they asked just for the tail-end of their valley, the one bit they did not own; it would round them off, which was all they wanted. He sacrificed to Apollo in their honour.

Bessos was lingering in the north, with no sign of raising a powerful army. Alexander, while his generals and satraps were subduing the country round about, moved eastward, towards the outer skirts of Great Kaukasos; taking his time, making his mark; here and there founding a city.

I remember the first I saw him make was upon this march; one of his Alexandrias. The site was a rocky hill, easy to defend; on a good trading route, as the Phoenician merchants told him; with a clean year-round spring for the public fountain, and good land next to it. It commanded a pass for caravans, which had harboured robbers. Every day he was scrambling over it, with his architect Aristoboulos; marking out the places for the garrison fort, the market, the gates and their defences; making sure the streets were well laid out, with channels to drain off the muck. He thought nothing like that beneath him. He had slaves to quarry and hew the stone, and free craftsmen to do the building. It amazed me, how quickly it all went up.

Then he had to people it. He would put in veteran soldiers, not all of them Macedonians; there were Greeks, and free Thracians, mostly with women and children they'd gathered on campaign; they were glad to be given a farm, though some grew homesick later. Some of the craftsmen settled there. They might not be very good, or they would have followed the lords and generals; but here they would not have rivals, and they brought something into the wilds, of Susa or of Greece. For all these people Alexander left law, never too foreign to their ways or the gods they followed. He had a feeling for what they would understand, and see the justice of.

He put his whole soul into this city, all day till supper-time. He did not get drunk – there was good water up there, so nobody sat down thirsty – but after the day's work, he liked to sit talking with the cup before him. Founding a city always stirred his mind. He knew it would make his name live among men to come; it made him think of his deeds. At these times he liked to go back over them, some said too much. Well, he did them. Does anyone deny it?

He would talk to me sometimes, after, the wine still in him, his spirit still burning it up. I asked him once if he had known, before he crossed to Asia, he would be Great King. He said, 'Not at first. It was my father's war; I wanted to win it faster than he'd have done. I was appointed general of the Greeks, to free the Greek Asian cities. When I'd done it, I disbanded their troops; and after that it was my own.' He paused; then, seeing that I understood, said, 'Yes, it was after Issos. When he ran away, leaving me his chariot and his royal mantle and all his arms; his friends' bodies who had died for him; his wife – even his mother! – then I said to myself. "If that's the Great King, I think I could do better."'

I answered, 'Kyros himself did less.'

I know the envious Greeks have written that I flattered him. They lie! Nothing was too good for him, or half good enough. I felt the impatience of his greatness, reined and curbed by the dullness of lesser men. They say I took his gifts. Of course I did. The best of them was to see his delight in giving. I took them in love; not, like some who claimed to be his friends, in covetousness soured with envy. If he had been a hunted man with a king's price on his head, I would have gone barefoot with him through Asia, starved with him, lain down in the market stews to buy him bread. All that is as true as the face of God. So had I no right to make him happy

in his victories? There was never a word that did not come from my
heart.

When the city was founded, he sacrificed, and dedicated it to Herakles
and Apollo. I did a dance for Apollo, who, Alexander thought, must be the
same as Mithra. I hope both gods were satisfied; I danced only for him.

I was someone now at court. I had my two horses, my baggage-mules,
my tent, and some pretty things in it. As for power, I wanted that over one
heart alone. Sometimes I remembered Susa, and all those who had tried
to buy my interest with the King. Only unwarned newcomers tried it now.
The Persians said, 'Bagoas the eunuch is Alexander's dog. He will feed
from no other hand; let him be.' Macedonians said, 'Watch out for the
Persian boy; he tells Alexander everything.'

Sometimes, when I waited on him in his bedchamber, he would say I
ought not to do servants' work; but that was just his courtesy. He knew
I lived for it. He would have been sorry, too, to do without me.

We marched eastward towards the heights, over high passes, with only
the tracks the herdsmen made, following the poor grass with the seasons.
In the rock-clefts grew little bright dry flowers like jewellers' work. Great
skies spread to dark horizons. I lived in the hour, I was young, the world
unrolled for me; as it did too for Alexander, riding always ahead, to see
the next turn of the road.

Of an evening he asked me to teach him Persian. (I had taught him
some, but not of a kind which would do at all for an audience.) The sounds
are hard for westerners; I never pretended he spoke it well. If he was cross
from disappointment, it was over in a moment. He knew I saved him from
making a fool of himself in public, which his pride could not endure.

'See what mistakes I still make in my Greek, Iskander.' I had put in a
slip or two, to cheer him up.

'How are the lessons? Has he tried you with reading yet?'

'He only has two books, and they're both too hard for me. He asked
Kallisthenes to lend us one; but he said the sacred treasures of Greek
thought were not to be smudged by barbarian fingers.'

'He said that to your face?'

I had not reckoned on his being quite so angry. This Kallisthenes was
so grand he must not be called a clerk, but a philosopher; and he was
writing Alexander's chronicle. I thought my lord deserved someone who
would better understand him; but one must go carefully with great men.

He said, 'I am tiring of this fellow. He's too full of himself by far. I only
took him on to please Aristotle, who's his uncle. But he has all the old
man's set notions, whose errors I had to find out for myself, and none of
his wisdom for which I honour him. He taught me what the soul should
reach after. He taught me the skill of healing, which I've saved some lives

with; and how to look at the natural world, which has enriched my life. I still send him specimens, wild beasts' skins, plants, anything that will travel . . . What's this blue flower?' He took it from behind my ear. 'I never saw that before.' It was nearly dead, but he pressed it carefully.

'Kallisthenes has none of that,' he said. 'Does he often insult you?'

'Oh, no, Sikander –'

'Al-ex-ander.'

'Al'skander, lord of my heart. No, mostly he doesn't see me.'

'Never mind if he thinks himself too good for you. I see signs that it will be my turn next.'

'Oh, no, my lord. He says it's he who will make your fame.' I had heard that myself, and thought he had better know.

His eyes turned pale. It was like watching a storm from shelter. 'Will he so? I have left a few marks about the world, to be remembered by.' He started pacing the tent; if he'd had a tail he would have lashed it. 'He wrote of me first with such fulsomeness that the truth stank like a lie. I was a boy, I didn't see the harm it did me. I rounded Cape Climax with god-sent luck and good guessing, but he had the waves bow before me. And heavenly ichor flowing in my veins! Men enough have seen the colour of my blood, and so I told him. And none of it from his heart.'

The sun was setting into a great horizon, the moorlands darkening in waves, the watch-fires budding flame. He stood to look, putting away his anger, till the slave kindled the lamps. 'So you've never read the *Iliad?*'

'What is that, Iskander?'

'Wait.' He went into his sleeping-place, and came back with something gleaming in his hands. 'If Kallisthenes is above bringing you Homer, I am not.'

He put on the table what he held; a casket of pure white silver, gold lions on its sides, the lid inlaid with malachite and lapis, carved into leaves and birds. There could not be two in the world. I gazed in silence.

He looked at my face. 'You have seen this before.'

'Yes, my lord.' It had stood by Darius' bed, under the golden vine.

'I might have thought. Does it hurt you? I'll put it away.'

'Truly no, my lord.'

He put it down again. 'Tell me, what did he keep in it?'

'Sweets, my lord.' Sometimes, when he was pleased with me, he used to put one in my mouth.

'See what I use it for.' He lifted the lid; I caught the scent of cloves and cinnamon. It choked me with the past; for a moment I closed my eyes.

He brought out a book, even more worn and mended than the Kyros one. 'I've had this since I was thirteen. It's old Greek, you know, but I'll make it a little easier. Too much would spoil the sound.'

He read a few lines, and asked if I had understood.

'He says he is going to sing about the anger of Achilles, which brought terrible trouble to the Greeks. Men died in great number and the dogs ate them. And the kites, also. But he says it fulfilled the will of Zeus. And it began when Achilles quarrelled with – with some lord who was powerful.'

'That's very good. It's a crying shame you've had no books yet. I'll see to that.' He put the book away, and said, 'Shall I tell you the story?'

I came and sat by his knees and laid my arm across them. If it kept me here, I did not care what kind of tale he told me. Or so I thought.

He told just the tale of Achilles; leaving out what I would not understand. So, after he had quarrelled with his Great King and refused allegiance, we came quite soon to Patroklos, who had been his friend from boyhood; who took his part and comforted his exile, and died of taking his place in battle; and how Achilles avenged him, though it had been foretold his own death must follow. And after the duel, while he slept in weariness, Patroklos' ghost came to him in his dream, to require his funeral rites and recall their love.

He did not tell it with art, like the tale-tellers in the market, but as if he had been there and remembered everything. At last I knew where my rival stood, grafted into his spirit, deeper than any memories of the flesh. There could be only one Patroklos. What was I, to that, but the flower one sticks behind one's ear and throws away dead at sunset? In silence I wept, and scarcely knew that my eyes were shedding tears, as well as my heart.

He lifted my face, and, smiling, wiped my eyes with his hand. 'Never mind. I cried too, the first time I read it. I remember it well.'

I said, 'I am sorry that they died.'

'They too. They loved their lives. But they died unfearing. It was living without fear, that made their lives worth loving. Or so I think.'

He rose and picked up the casket. 'Look, you have been nearer it than you knew.' He moved the pillow off his bed, and opened the bed-box. A dagger was there too, honed like a razor. Every second King of Macedon had been murdered, and sometimes two kings running.

Long after this, I caught my name as I approached his tent, and heard him say, 'I tell you, when he heard the story of Achilles, his eyes were full of tears. And that fool Kallisthenes talks of Persians as if they were Scythian savages. The boy has more poetry in one finger than that pedant has in his head.'

By summer's end we had reached the southern spurs of Parapamisos. They were already shawled with snow. Far to the east, they join Great Kaukasos, the wall of India, which goes on higher and higher, further than anyone knows.

On a spur of their foothills, sheltered from the north wind, he made the

year's third Alexandria. By the time of the first snowfall, it was ready for
us to winter in. After some of the king-houses, likes ogres' lairs in legends,
it was good to smell clean new wood and wall-paint. The governor's house
had a porch with columns, in the Greek style; and a plinth in front, for
a statue of Alexander.

It was the first he'd had done since I had been with him; but he, of
course, was as used to taking his clothes off for this as for his bath. The
sculptor made drawings from all around him, seven or eight studies, while
he gazed into the distance making himself look beautiful. Then he was
measured all over with the callipers. Then he could go off hunting, and
need not come back till the face was being finished. It was very fine, both
calm and eager; true to his soul, though of course it left out the swordcut.

One evening he said to me, 'The new thing has begun. Today I sent
orders back to the cities, to make me a new army. This one I'm growing
from seed. I'm having thirty thousand Persian boys taught Greek, and
trained to use Macedonian weapons. Does that please you?'

'Oh, yes, Al'skander. It would please Kyros too. When will they be
ready?'

'Not for five years. They must start young before their minds get fixed.
By then, I should hope, the Macedonians will be ready as well.'

I said I was sure of it. I was still of an age when five years seem half
a lifetime.

The air grew soft in the foothills, delicate flowers pierced the melting
snow. Alexander decided he could cross straight over the mountains after
Bessos.

I don't suppose even the local shepherds warned him. They only went
up with the summer snow-line. He guessed the high passes would be hard,
and went ahead with the soldiers; but I doubt he knew what they were
in for. It was terrible even for us, who had their beaten way to follow, with
more supplies. I, who love mountains, felt that these hated men. My breath
laboured, my feet and my fingers burned as I beat the blood back into
them. People huddled at night for warmth, and I had many offers, all with
fair promises to treat me like a brother; meaning that when it was too late
I would not dare to tell. I slept with Peritas, whom Alexander had left in
my care; he was a big dog, and there was a good deal of warmth in him.

Our hardships were nothing to the army's. With no fuel on the barren
rock to cook their meat, they had to thaw it on their bodies, or were lucky
to have it warm from some horse that had fallen dead. Their bread ran
out, and they fed on the herbs the cattle eat. Many would have slept in
the snow-death, but for Alexander struggling on foot along the column,
finding them where they lay, dragging them to their feet, and putting his
own life into them.

We overtook them at the border fort of Drapsaka, on the other side. There was food to be had; below, Bessos had wasted the land to starve us out.

I found him in a lodging of old rough-hewn stone. His face was all burned with cold, and it seemed that only his sinews held his frame together. I was still not used to a King who starved with his men. 'That's nothing,' he said. 'That soon comes back. But I can't yet believe I'll ever be warm again.'

He smiled at me, and I said, 'You will tonight.'

I did not have the chance to warm him long. Once his men were rested and fed, before a full month was up he was off down into Baktria.

I was now of fighting age. Eunuchs before, among them my wicked namesake, had borne arms. I kept thinking how Hephaistion had been with him on the mountains; keeping him warm, maybe. So the night before he went, I asked him to take me with him; saying my father had been a warrior, and if I could not fight at his side, I would be ashamed to live.

He answered gently, 'Dear Bagoas, I know you'd fight at my side. And you would die there, and quickly too. If your father had lived to train you, you would have made a soldier up to my best. But it takes time; and the gods willed otherwise. I need you now where you are.' He was proud, but not for himself alone; he had feeling for the pride in others.

Just then Peritas, who had been terribly spoiled from sleeping in my blankets, tried to creep by stealth on the bed, though he weighed it down and took up all the room. So it passed in laughter; but I was left behind again, for Alexander went ahead with the troops, expecting Bessos.

He was not there; nothing was there but snow, still thick on those high uplands. He had not found much to ravage; in winter the people there bury everything, their vines, their fruit-trees, even themselves, for they live in sunk beehive huts which the snows cover all over; they hole up with all their stores, and come out in spring. Soldiers clemmed with hunger would see a wisp of smoke rise through the snow, and dig down to the food. They said the stench was dreadful, and everything tasted of it; but they did not care.

With the spring, we followers caught up; the court and the royal city took form and travelled onward. Then news came that Bessos had crossed the Oxos, east. He was on the run, with a poor following. Nabarzanes had been the first, but not the last, to know he had looked for a King in vain.

Alexander marched slowly through Baktria. No one resisted him; so wherever he went, he had to take surrenders, and get his new lands administered. For Bessos, once again there was no hurry.

The next we heard of him, was from one of his own lords, a man well on in years, who came on a weary horse, his clothes and his beard full of dust, to give himself up to Alexander. This, he explained through me (I was interpreting, for the sake of secrecy), was what he had urged Bessos himself to do, when he held a war-council. Gobares, who now addressed us, had cited Nabarzanes as an example, which was surely rather simple of him. Bessos had taken drink, and at the mere sound of the name made for Gobares with drawn sword. He had scrambled off, faintly pursued since he was well respected; and here he was, ready in return for pardon to tell us all he knew.

Bessos' Baktrian levies had now deserted him. He had never led them, only fallen back before Alexander. They had gone home to their tribal villages; their surrenders could be trusted. All Bessos had left were those who had escorted Darius to his death; a remnant who shared his flight not from love, but fear.

He was making for Sogdiana, in which his last hopes lay. The Sogdians, Gobares said, do not like strangers, and would be loth ('at first' he said politely) to accept a foreign King. So Bessos would cross the Oxos, and burn his boats behind him.

'We will cross that river when we come to it.' Alexander said.

Meanwhile, he had to choose a satrap for Baktria. I awaited this with sadness; the second Persian Satrap of Areia had rebelled, and he had had to send them a Macedonian. None the less, he gave Baktria to a Persian. It was Artabazos. He had lately told Alexander he was getting too old to march about any longer; the mountain crossing had left him rather tired. I have heard he ruled his province with prudence, vigour and justice; retired from office at ninety-eight; and died at a hundred and two, from riding a horse that was too fresh for him.

So now it was time to go north and cross the Oxos. We'd been near it in the mountains; it takes its rise there; but for leagues it dashes through rocky gorges, where only a bird could go. The hills open out on the threshold of the desert; after that, it slows and widens on into the furthest wilderness, where at last, they say, it sinks into the sand. We were to cross at the first ferry, where the road goes on to Marakanda.

We went down pleasant warm slopes with vines and fruit-trees. The holy Zoroaster, who taught us to worship God through fire was born in those parts. Alexander heard this with reverence. He was sure the Wise God was the same as Zeus; and had seen him in fire, he said, since childhood.

We had enough of fire before long. When we came down into the Oxos valley, the desert wind from the north was blowing. It comes in mid-summer, and living things all dread it; it's as if the air had been passed through a furnace, and blown at you with bellows. We had to wrap our heads in cloth, to save them from the burning, pelting sand; four days of it, before we reached the river.

It's a great sight when you get to it; it was at least for me, and all who had not seen the Nile. The desert deer on the far side looked small as mice. The engineers stared at it in dismay. They had brought wagons full of timber with them; but what with its great width, its depth and its shifting sands, they could sink no piles. To bridge it was impossible.

Meantime the ferrymen met us with lifted hands, begging for bread. They had owned flat boats, with yoke-poles for a pair of horses, which were trained to swim them across. Bessos had burned the boats on the far side, gone off with the horses, and paid nothing. Alexander offered gold for anything they had left.

At this the poorest brought out their hidden wealth; rafts of hide blown up with air, to float with the current. That was all there was; and that, Alexander said, was what we would cross on, making the rest ourselves.

There were hides in plenty; the tents were made of them. The tent-makers studied the native craft, and oversaw the work. The insides were stuffed with straw and dry rushes, to keep them buoyant longer.

I've seldom been so scared as when the moment came to push off. My two servants shared the raft with me; we swam the horses and the mule. When the current tugged, the beasts began to flounder, the Thracian moaned out prayers to some Thracian god, and I saw further on a bigger raft overturning. I thought I was bound for another River. But this was the first time I had shared Alexander's danger, I who had talked of fighting at his side; and I could see my body-servant, a Persian from Hyrkania, watching me, in search of encouragement, or maybe to see how a eunuch would behave. I will see you dead, I said to myself, before you shall make a tale of me. So I said people crossed like this every day; and showed them that the men from the capsized raft were still holding on to it. The horses got the feel of the river and pulled us on; and we reached the shore hardly even wet.

Even the women and children crossed like this. They had to; it was leagues through the desert to the nearest ford. I saw one raft with a woman on it hiding her eyes, and five children screaming with pleasure.

All in all it took five days. The rafts had to be dried and made into tents again. Alexander gave timber to the ferrymen, to make good their boats.

Horses had died in the march through the burning wind. I thought I would lose Lion; his chestnut coat was staring and his head was down. Oryx, the one I'd had from Alexander, was a fine strong beast and bore up better; but Lion was dear to me. He just lived through it; so did old Oxhead, nursed all the way, often with the King's own hands. He was twenty-seven now, but built to last.

Soon we could take it easier. The last two Baktrian lords to follow Bessos sent word that Alexander could have him with their leave. The village where he was lodging would give him up.

We were now in Sogdiana. This was the first-fruit of it. They have no laws worth speaking of, but the law of blood-feud; even guest-friendship does not count for much there. If you are a little luckier than Bessos was, you may be safe under their roof; further along the road, if you have anything worth taking, they will ambush you and cut your throat. Their chief sports are robbery and tribal wars.

Alexander disdained to pick up Bessos himself. He sent Ptolemy, with a good-sized force since he had to deal with traitors. He did not need it; the Baktrian lords had made off; the mud-walled fort let him in for a small reward. Bessos was found in a peasant hut, with only a couple of slaves.

If Darius' spirit looked on, he must have felt well avenged. The lords who gave Bessos up had learned from his own example; they wanted him out of the way, to keep Alexander quiet while they prepared for war.

Ptolemy had had his orders. When Alexander came up with the army, Bessos was standing by the road, stripped naked, his hands tied up to a wooden yoke. At Susa I had seen this done to a famous bandit before they put him to death. I had never told the King of it; he must have asked Oxathres what was proper.

Nabarzanes had been right; there was nothing of a king in Bessos. I'm told that when Alexander asked him why he had dragged his lord and kinsman to so base a death, he pleaded he had been only one of many about Darius, who had agreed on it to win Alexander's favour. He did not say why in that case he had assumed the Mitra. The Susa bandit had put on a better face. Alexander ordered him flogged, and kept in chains for his trial.

The traitor lords, who had hoped to keep Alexander quiet, should have known better. He marched straight on into Sogdiana. It was part of the empire, and he meant to keep it so.

The Sogdians live in a land of great dun hills and fearsome gorges. Along every pass there are forts full of armed robbers; the caravans have to hire small armies of guards, to get safely through. Sogdians are handsome; hawk-faced, with the carriage of princes. Nearly all Sogdiana is made of rock; but they build on it in mud, like swallows, because the men think craftsmanship beneath them. They can ride horses where you'd not think a goat could go; but they don't regard their oaths if it does not suit them. Alexander was quite taken with them, till he found this out.

All seemed to go well at first. The city of Marakanda surrendered; so did the line of forts down by the Jaxartes river. Beyond that are the grasslands, and the Scythians against whom the forts had all been built.

Alexander now summoned the chiefs to his camp, to meet him in council. He wanted to tell them he would rule them justly, and ask what their laws were now. The chiefs, who knew just what they would do if they were Alexander, never doubted he wanted them there to take their heads. So of a sudden the river forts were stormed by yelling Sogdians, and their garrisons butchered; Marakanda was under siege; a forage-party from our own camp was cut to pieces.

He dealt first with that. The raiders had a roost on a mountain crag. The signal-smoke went up from the tall cresset by his tent; the troops fell in; he set out for the place, and took it.

They brought him back on a litter, and laid him on his bed. The surgeon was waiting in the tent, and so was I. An arrow had smashed into his shin, and split the bone. He had made them tug out the barb in the field and sat his horse till the fort was taken.

When we soaked the stuck bandages off, splinters of bone came with them. More chips were sticking through the skin; the doctor had to work them out.

He lay looking upward, still as his own statue; not even his mouth moved. Yet he had wept for the maimed slaves of Persepolis; for old Oxhead; for Achilles and Patroklos, dead a thousand years; for my forgotten birthdays.

The surgeon dressed the wound, told him to keep quiet, and left. I stood one side of the bed with a bowl of bloodstained water; on the other stood Hephaistion, waiting for me to go.

I turned with my dirty bowl. Alexander looked round, and said – the first sound he'd made – 'You were good with the bandages. Light-handed.'

He kept quiet for about seven days; that is, he went by litter, instead of riding, downhill towards the Jaxartes river forts. First he was carried by an infantry detail, till the cavalry complained of being denied the privilege. He then let them take turns. At night, when I changed the bandages, he confided to me that the cavalry, being unused to marching, were inclined to jolt.

I rode ahead with the army, this time; he was used to my doing the dressings. The doctor smelled at the wound each day; if the bone-marrow putrefies, it mostly kills a man. Bad as it looked, it scabbed-over clean at last; but it left a dent on his shin, which he had for life.

Before long he rid himself of the litter by getting on a horse. By the time we reached the river grasslands, he had started to walk.

Doriskos had once said to me, 'He's said to be over-trusting; but if you break your pledge, God help you.' I was now to see the truth of it.

He took five forts in two days; at three of the assaults he was there himself. All had sworn him loyalty, and all had helped murder their garrisons. If Sogdians thought that to honour his given word a man must be soft in the head, they were now shown reasons they would understand.

So now I saw what I'd not seen all through Baktria; the herd of wailing women and children, driven into camp like cattle, the spoils of war. All the men were dead.

It happens everywhere. Greeks do it to other Greeks. My own father must have done it, in Ochos' wars; though Ochos would never have given such people a first chance. However, this was the first time for me.

Alexander did not mean to drag along this horde of women; he was planning a new city here, and they would give the settlers wives. But meantime, soldiers short of a bedmate-slave were getting their pick. A woman would be led away; sometimes young children with wet dirty faces would stumble after, sobbing or screaming, to be cared for when her new master gave her time. Some of the young girls could scarcely walk; their bloodstained skirts showed why. I thought of my three sisters, whom I'd long managed to forget.

This was the slag of the fire, when the bright flame had passed. He knew what he was born to do; the god had told him. All those who helped, he would receive like kindred. If he was checked, he did whatever was necessary; then went on his way, his eyes on the fire he followed.

The sixth city was Kyropolis, the strongest; not built by the river, of mud-brick, but on a hill-flank, of stone. It had been founded by Kyros, no less; so Alexander had sent the siege-train on with Krateros, and ordered the assault saved up for him. He pitched his tent quite near the siege-lines, to save a walk, so I saw some of the battle. A great splinter of bone had just worked up through the scab on his shin. He made me tug it out, saying the doctor talked too much, and I was neater-handed. The blood was clean. 'I've good-healing flesh,' he said.

The engines were set up; two siege-towers, clad with hide; a row of catapults, like huge bows laid on their sides, shooting bolts of bronze; and the battering-rams under their housings. In honour of Kyros, he put on his best armour; his silver-burnished helmet with white wings, and his famous belt from Rhodes. Because of the heat, he refused his jewelled gorget. I heard the men cheering, as he rode up to the lines. The assault started soon after.

I felt the rams' thumping through the ground. Great clouds of dust flew up, but no breach appeared. For some time I saw the silver helmet, till it passed round a turn of the wall. Not so long after, yells and shouts rose up to heaven. The great gates of the fort were open; our men poured in. The walls were covered with soldiers fighting hand to hand; I could not think why, if the Sogdians had opened the gates. They had not; Alexander had done it.

The fort had its water from a river led under the walls. It was low in summer; its channel would let in a stooping man. He led his party in himself, wounded leg and all. The Sogdians, concerned about the rams, had not watched the gates well. He fought his way through, and pulled back the bolts.

Next day he came back to camp. A knot of officers was with him, asking how he felt. He shook his head fretfully, beckoned me up, and whispered, 'Bring me a tablet and stylus.'

That came of leaving off his gorget. In the street-fighting, a stone had hit his throat and bruised his voice-box. Only a little harder, it would have broken the bone and choked him. But he had stayed there in command, whispering his orders, till the citadel surrendered.

He could bear pain like no one I ever saw; but not being able to talk drove him nearly mad. He would not rest quiet alone with me, who at a finger-sign would have known just what he wanted; when his voice improved he strained it and it went again. He could not endure to hear the talk at supper and stay mute; he ate in his tent, with a clerk to read to him from one of the books he sent to Greece for. They had started building his new city, so he was soon riding out there, finding of course a hundred things to say. Even so, his voice was strengthening. He had a wonderful body for healing, in spite of all he did to it.

A new sight now appeared across the river; the house-wagons of Scythians, their horse-herds and black felt tents. They had heard of the Sogdian rising, and swept down like ravens to share the spoil. When they saw us, they withdrew and we thought them gone. Next day they were back; the men alone. They rode their small hairy mounts in whirling circles, waving their tufted spears and yelling. They tried to shoot across, but their arrows would not carry. Alexander, curious to know what they were saying with so much noise, sent for Pharneuches, the chief interpreter. The gist, it seemed, was, if Alexander wanted to know the difference between Baktrians and Scythians, let him cross the river.

We had this several days running, louder each time, and with gestures that needed no interpreter. Alexander was getting angry.

He had the generals in his tent, huddled around him so that he need not raise his voice. A whisper is catching; they all sounded like conspirators. I heard nothing till he said aloud, 'Of course I'm fit! I can do anything but shout.' 'Stop trying, then,' said Hephaistion, 'or you'll be dumb as a fish again.' As they argued their voices rose. Alexander said that if the Scythians got off now without a lesson, they would be sacking his new city the moment we had marched on. Since he meant to give the lesson himself, the others were much against it.

He supped in his tent, as sulky as Achilles. Hephaistion sat with him awhile, but left because he would keep talking. So I went back again; shook my head at all but sign-language, and in due course put him to bed. When he caught my hand to keep me, I must own it was not without my contrivance. The bow had been strung too long. We did very well without words; and, after, I told him old tales till he went to sleep.

I knew, however, he would not change his mind about the Scythians. He thought that if he did not go himself, they would suppose he was scared.

The Jaxartes is much smaller than the Oxos. He had the rafts started next day, and sent for the seer Aristander, who always took the omens for him. Aristander came back to say the entrails of the sacrifice were unlucky. (We Persians have cleanlier ways of consulting heaven.) I heard it said the generals had been at him; but I would not have cared for going to that old blue-eyed Magus, and asking him to bend a prophecy. Besides, he was right.

Next day more Scythians than ever came. They were now an army. Alexander had the sacrifice done again; got another No; and asked if the danger was to his men, or him. To him, Aristander said; which to my mind proves his honesty. Of course Alexander prepared at once to cross.

It was with anguish of heart that I watched him being armed. Before two squires, I could not shame him with unseemly grief. I returned his parting smile; smiles are well-omened.

The Scythians were waiting to cut up the troops as they struggled ashore. They had reckoned without the catapults. Their bolts did not fall short like Scythian arrows. After one rider was shot clean through his shield and armour, they kept their distance. Alexander sent the archers and slingers on ahead, to hold them while the phalanx and the cavalry got over. Not that he waited for that himself; he was on the first raft to cross.

From across the river, the battle looked neat as a dance: the Scythians wheeling around the Macedonian square; then the smashing charge of the cavalry, left and right, closing till they ran off inland. In a great cloud of dust (it was a very hot day) they went streaming over the plain. Alexander's horsemen after them. Then there was no more to be seen, but the rafts paddling over to bring in our dead and wounded, not many; and the kites screaming over Scythian corpses.

For three days we waited their returning dust. Then they came. Messengers paddled ahead. Once more the doctor was waiting, and so was I.

When the squires set down the litter, I took one look and thought, He is dead, he is dead. A great wail rose up in me, and I had almost uttered it, when I saw his eyelids move.

He was pale as a corpse; his fair skin had no colour when the bright blood had left it. His eyes were sunk as if into a skull. He stank, he who liked to be as clean as a bride's linen. I saw that though too weak to speak he had his senses, and that it shamed him. I took a step to his side.

'It's a flux, sir,' said a squire to the doctor. 'I was to tell you, he drank bad water. It was very hot, and he drank from a standing pool. He's been purging blood. He's very weak.'

'I can see that for myself,' the doctor said. Alexander's lips fluttered. They were speaking across him as if he were half-gone; which he was, but it made him angry. No one noticed but I.

The doctor gave him the draught he had prepared when the message reached him, and said to the squires, 'He must be put to bed.' They approached the litter. His eyes opened, and turned to me. I guessed what it was. He was lying in his dirt, he had been too weak to help himself. He did not want them uncovering him; it hurt his pride.

I said to the doctor. 'The King wants me to see to him. I can do everything.' Faint as a breath he said, 'Yes.' So they left him to me.

I sent the slaves for bowls and hot water and piles of linen. I got rid of the bloodstained muck, and washed him clean while he still lay on the litter, and had the mess carried away. His backside was raw; he had pressed on after the enemy long after he got sick, getting off his horse to purge, and back again, till he fainted. I rubbed him with oil, and lifted him into the clean bed – he'd lost so much weight, it was easy – and put a pad of clean linen under him, though he had emptied himself by now. As I laid my hand on his brow, feeling the fever, he whispered, 'Ah, that's good.'

Soon after, Hephaistion, having got his men across the river, came in to see him. I went, of course. It was like tearing my own flesh. I said to myself, If he dies, with that man and not with me, then truly I will kill him. Let him stay now, I will not grudge my lord his wish in his last hour. Yet he was glad of me.

However, he slept on right through the night on the doctor's opiate; wanted to get up next day, and did so the day after. Two days from that, he received an embassy from the Scythians.

Their King sent to say he was sorry Alexander had been vexed. The men who'd vexed him were lawless robbers, in whom the King had no part at all. Alexander sent back a civil answer. The Scythians, it seemed, had had their lesson, even though an unfinished one.

One evening, as I combed his hair, trying to ease out the tangles without hurting, I said. 'You were nearly dead. Did you know it?'

'Oh, yes. I thought the god had more left for me to do; but one must be ready.' He touched my hand; his thanks had been wordless, but none the worse for that. 'One must live as if it would be forever, and as if one might die each moment. Always both at once.'

I answered, 'That is the life of the gods, who only seem to die, like the sun at his setting. But do not ride too fast across the sky, and leave us all in darkness.'

'One thing,' he said, 'I've taken to heart from this. The water in the plains is poison. Do as I mean to do, and stick to wine.'

16

Spitamenes, one of Bessos' two traitor lords, was besieging Marakanda. When the first force Alexander sent had been cut up, he went himself. At the news of his approach, Spitamenes decamped, and escaped into the northern deserts. By the time the country was in order, winter was coming on. Alexander, to keep an eye upon the Scythians, wintered at Zariaspa-upon-Oxos.

It's a fair-sized town, north of the ferry; the river flows very wide there. They have channelled its waters round about, and made green things grow; beyond is the desert. In summer it must be a furnace. They've more cockroaches there than anywhere else I've known; most houses keep tame snakes to eat them.

Alexander had the governor's house, of real fired brick; a grandeur where mud-brick was the rule. He had good hangings and fine furniture to make it kingly. It pleased me to see him grow less careless in his state. He'd had a beautiful new robe made, purple bordered with white, the Great King's colours, for state occasions. For the first time, here, he put on the Mitra.

I took it on myself to say all Persians would expect it when he tried Bessos. To try pretenders, a king must look like a king.

'You are right,' he said. 'It's a Persian matter, and must be done the Persian way. I am taking advice upon the precedents.' He was pacing about the room, and frowning to himself. 'It will mean a Persian sentence. The nose and ears, beforehand. Oxathres will be content with nothing less.'

'Of course, my lord. He is Darius' brother.' I did not say, 'Why else should he accept a foreign King?' He could see that for himself.

'It is not our custom,' he said, still pacing. 'But I shall do it.'

He never said anything uncertain. Yet I feared he might change his mind, which would do him great harm among the Persians. My father had suffered only for keeping faith; why should this traitor escape? Besides, I owed another debt.

'Did I ever tell you, Al'skander, what Darius said before they dragged him away? "I no longer have power to punish traitors, but I know who will." Bessos thought he was speaking of our gods; but he said it was you he meant.'

He paused in his stride. 'Darius said that of me?'

'I myself heard it.' I thought of the horse and the silver mirror and the necklaces. Even I had my obligations.

He paced a while longer; then said, 'Yes, it must be by your custom.'

I said to myself, Be at peace, poor King, whatever the River of Ordeal has left of you to attain Paradise. Forgive me that I love your enemy. I have made what amends I can.

From the street I saw Bessos led to his trial. He had shrunk, since that night I had recalled; his face was heavy as clay. He knew his fate. When first they took him, he had seen Oxathres riding by Alexander.

If he had surrendered along with Nabarzanes, he would have been spared. Oxathres came in later, and would never have got Alexander to break his given word. He kept it to Nabarzanes, whatever Oxathres wished. I often wondered why Bessos ever put on the Mitra. For love of his people? If he had led them well, they would not have forsaken him. I suppose Nabarzanes first tempted him to kingship; but he had not Nabarzanes' suppleness. He could not wield it, yet could not let it go.

He was tried in Greek and Persian. The council agreed. He would lose his nose and ear-tips; then be sent to Ekbatana, where he had betrayed his lord; and be crucified, before an assembly of Medes and Persians. It was all in order, and according to custom.

I did not join the crowd that saw him go. His wounds would be fresh; I was afraid he'd look like my father.

In due time, word came from Ekbatana that he was dead. He had been nearly three days dying. Oxathres had ridden all the way there, to watch. When the body was taken down, he had it cut up small, and strewn on the mountain for the wolves.

The court stayed at Zariaspa most of that winter.

From all over the empire, people made the journey, and Alexander entertained them with splendour, as he had learned to do. One evening before supper, he had put on his Persian robe, and I was draping the folds for him.

'Bagoas,' he said, 'before now I've heard from you what the Persian lords daren't tell me. How much do they feel it, that they make the prostration, and the Macedonians not?'

I'd known he would ask me in the end.

'My lord, they do feel it. That I know.'

'How?' He turned round to look at me. 'Is it spoken of?'

'Not before me, Al-ex-ander.' I still had to go slowly, to get it right. 'No one would do that. But you in your courtesy keep your eyes on the man you are greeting, while I can look where I choose.'

'You mean they look angry, to see a Persian do it?'

This was less easy than I'd hoped. 'Not quite that, Al'skander. We're brought up to do it before the King.'

'You have said enough. It's when a Macedonian doesn't?'

I settled the pleats of his sash, and did not answer.

He moved restlessly, before I had finished. 'I know. Why put you to the pain of telling me? But from you I always get the truth.'

Well, sometimes he got what I knew would make him happy. But one thing he never got from me, was a lie that could do him harm.

That night at supper he kept his eyes well open. I think he saw a good deal, while they were fresh. This did not last all through supper, at Zariaspa.

He had said truly, that Oxos water is poison to those not bred to it. I suppose that among the natives, those whom it kills die young, before they have time to beget offspring.

No vines grow there; the wine comes in from Baktria. Baktrian wine is strong; but they reckon three parts of it to one of water, to kill the Oxos flux.

It was winter, and almost cool; no Persian host would have dreamed of offering wine before the sweets. But the Macedonians drank from the start, as always. Persian guests would sip for manners; the Macedonians drank deep as ever.

To be drunk now and then, what harm does it do a man? But give him strong wine night after night, and it takes a hold. If only my lord had wintered in the hills by a pure spring, he would have been spared much grief.

Not that he was really drunk every night. It would depend on how long he sat at table. He did not toss it down like the others, not at first. He would sit with the cup before him, and talk, and drink, and talk again. Cup for cup, he drank no more than before. But Baktrian wine should be mixed with two-thirds of water. Each cup he drank was twice the strength he was used to.

Sometimes after a late night he would sleep as late as noon; but for serious business he was always up, brisk and ready. He remembered even my birthday. At supper he called for a toast to me; commended my faithful service; gave me the gold cup he had drunk from, and then a kiss. The veteran Macedonians looked much scandalized; whether because I was a Persian, or a eunuch, or because he was not ashamed of me, I can't say. I suppose all three.

He did not forget the prostration. It was on his mind. 'It will have to be changed,' he said to me. 'And not with the Persians, it's far too old. If Kyros began it as they say, he must have had a good reason.'

'I think, Al'skander, to reconcile the peoples. It was the Median custom, before.'

'You see! Fealty from both, but neither people to lord it over the other. I tell you, Bagoas, when I see some Persian whose title goes back before Kyros' time, and who has it written all over him, bowing to the ground; and a Macedonian my father made out of nothing, whose own father wore sheep-skins, looking down as if at a dog, I could knock his head off his shoulders.'

'Don't do that, Al'skander,' I said, only half laughing.

The hall downstairs was quite big, but the upstairs rooms were cramped; he turned about like a leopard in a cage. 'In Macedon, the lords have learned so lately to obey the King at all, they think that's doing a favour. At home, in my father's day, he would put on fine manners for foreign guests; but when I was a boy, supper was like a feast of peasants. . . . I know how your people feel. I draw my blood from Achilles and from Hektor, and before that from Herakles; we won't speak of anything else.' He was on his way to bed; not very late, but still the wine had exalted him. I was afraid his bath would get cold.

'It's simple with the soldiers. They may think I have my fancies when off the field; but on it, we know each other. No, it's the men of rank, those I must entertain with Persians . . . You see, Bagoas, at home they think prostration is for gods.'

There was something in his voice, which told me he was not just instructing me. I knew him. I felt the current of his mind. Why not? I thought. Even the soldiers feel it, though they don't know what they feel.

'Al-ex-ander,' I said, letting him know I was weighing every word, 'everyone knows that the oracle at Siwah cannot lie.'

He looked at me with his deep grey eyes, saying nothing. Then he pulled his sash undone. I disrobed him. He gave me another look. I saw, as he meant, the catapult-wound on his shoulder; the sword-slash across his thigh; the purple dent on his shin. Truly, those wounds had run blood, not ichor. He was remembering, too, the time he had drunk bad water.

His eyes rested on mine, half smiling; yet with something in them that neither I nor anyone would reach. Perhaps the oracle had done, at Siwah.

I touched his shoulder, and kissed the catapult-wound. 'The god is present,' I said. 'The mortal flesh is his servant and his sacrifice. Remember us who love you, and do not let the god take it all away.'

He smiled and held out his arms. That night the mortal flesh received its due. Though gentle, it was as if he mocked himself. And yet the other presence stood waiting, ready to claim him back again.

Next day he was shut up with Hephaistion a long time alone, and the old sickness bit my heart. Then there was much coming and going among the King's best friends; then messengers went out, summoning guests to a great supper of fifty couches.

On the day, he said to me, 'Bagoas, you know what I've had in mind? Tonight we shall try for it. Put on your best clothes and look after my Persian guests. They know what to expect, Hephaistion has been seeing them. Just make them feel valued; you with your court manners can do that best.'

So, I thought, after all he needs me too. I put on my best suit, which by now was a very good one, crusted with gold embroidery on a dark-blue ground; and came to dress Alexander. He wore his grand Persian robe, but a low coronet, not the Mitra. He was dressed for Macedonians too.

If only, I thought, they would keep the wine till dessert-time. This will be delicate business.

The hall was splendidly garnished for the feast. I greeted the Persian lords, in the proper way, and led each to his supper couch, with compliments where they would be acceptable, on someone's famous ancestor, breed of horses, and so on; then I went to attend on Alexander. The meal went smoothly, in spite of all the wine; the dishes were carried out. Everyone made ready to toast the King. Someone got up; as people thought, to propose it.

This one was certainly sober. He was Anaxarchos, a tame philosopher who followed the court about; the kind Greeks call a sophist. As for wisdom, he and Kallisthenes had not half enough between them to make one good philosopher. When Anaxarchos rose, Kallisthenes looked as angry as an old wife with a young concubine, at not having been asked to speak first.

Certainly, he'd not have done it so well. Anaxarchos had a well-trained voice, and must have conned his speech by heart with every grace-note. He led off about some Greek gods who'd started life as mortals, and been deified for their glorious deeds. Herakles was one, the other Dionysos. Not a bad choice; though I doubt he had what I had in mind, which was that Alexander had some of both in him: the urge to great labours beyond reach of all other men; and the beauty, the dreams, the ecstasy ... did I think, then, the madness also? I expect not; I can't remember.

These divine beings, said Anaxarchos, while on earth, had shared the trials and sorrows of the human lot. If only men had seen their godhead earlier!

Then he rehearsed the deeds of Alexander. The plain truth, though known already, struck home even to me. Anaxarchos said that when it pleased the gods – let them keep the day long from us! – to call the King to themselves, no one would doubt that divine honours would at once be paid him. Why not offer them now, to comfort him through his labours; why wait till he was dead? We should all take pride in being the first to give them, and to symbolize it with the ritual of prostration.

All through the speech, I had been watching faces. Not the Persians'; they had been prepared, and were all grave attention. The King's friends, in the secret too, were doubly busy, applauding and watching others; all but Hephaistion, who for most of the time was watching Alexander, as grave as the Persians, and more attentive still.

I moved from behind his couch, to where I too could see him. I perceived that Anaxarchos' words, planned for use, had become a pleasure. Though nowhere near drunk, he had of course been drinking; the shine had come into his eyes. He fixed them on the distance, as he did for the sculptors' drawings. It would be beneath him, to look about and see how people took it.

Most of the Macedonians took it, at first, as a longwinded way of proposing a toast to the King. Cheerful with wine, even the veterans applauded. They were too slow to see where it was leading till the very end, when they looked as if hit suddenly on the head. Luckily I'd been trained against ill-timed laughter.

Others had seen it coming. The time-servers, each eager to be first in the race to please, could hardly wait for the speech to finish. Most of the younger men looked startled at first; but, for them, King Philip's day was when they were boys made to do as their fathers told them. Now was the time. Since Alexander led them, there had always been something new. He might be going rather far, but they would go along with him.

The older men were dead-set against it. Oh, yes! I thought. You are angry that he wants a god's salutation. If you guessed he was trying to level you with us, how much angrier you'd be! Sulk then; you're too few to matter.

Anaxarchos sat down. King's friends and Persians applauded; no one else. A kind of stir began. The Persians with gestures of respect stood by their couches, preparing to come forward. The King's friends got up too, saying, 'Come, let's begin.' The sycophants, twitching with eagerness, waited upon precedent. Slowly, the other Macedonians began to rise.

Suddenly Kallisthenes stood up, and in his harsh voice said loudly, 'Anaxarchos!' All movement ceased in the hall.

I'd been watching him. I knew the King had been cooler to him, since what I'd said. Resenting Anaxarchos' speech, he had hung on every word, and caught the drift quite early. I had guessed he would be up to something.

If both these were philosophers, they were pretty different. Anaxarchos' robe had embroidered borders; his silvery beard was combed like silk. Kallisthenes', which was black, was thin and straggly; his plainness of dress, since Alexander paid him well, was boorish for a state dinner. He stood well forward, to give us all a view of him. Alexander, who when his friends hailed him had returned from his distance to give them a welcoming smile, now turned, and fixed his eyes on him.

'Anaxarchos,' he led off, as if they were debating in some public street instead of in the Presence, 'I think Alexander not unworthy of any honour proper to mortal man. But bounds have been set between honours human and divine.' Of these latter, he gave a catalogue which I thought would go on for ever. But such honours, he said, when offered to a man, insult the gods, as royal honours offered a common man would insult the King. At this I heard, all about the hall, low murmurs of assent. Like the story-teller who has caught his audience, Kallisthenes started to bloom. He reminded Anaxarchos he was advising a leader of the Greeks, not some Kambyses or Xerxes. The contempt with which he named these Persian kings was much to the Macedonians' taste. I saw the Persians exchanging looks. Hiding my shame and anger, I went among those of the highest rank, and made a business of handing sweets. Since I started going to theatres, I've seen how an actor can spoil another's big scene. In my youth and ignorance, I had some such notion myself.

Not put out at all by me – what does a barbarian eunuch matter, serving a barbarian lord? – Kallisthenes went on to say that Kyros, who had founded the prostration, had been humbled by the Scythians who were poor but free. I would only have said myself that he failed to catch them; but more to the purpose, it was aimed at Alexander. Everyone must have known how he honoured Kyros; certainly Kallisthenes did, who had once had his trust. He gave it a clever turn by adding that Darius, who had received prostration, had been routed by Alexander who had done without. This licensed the Macedonians to applaud.

They did; and it was clear they were not applauding the hollow compliment. He had brought over all the doubtful ones, who would have complied if let alone. And what he'd caught them with was not respect for the gods, but contempt for Persians. When he named Darius, I didn't miss the spiteful glance that he aimed at me.

One must be just to the dead, who cannot answer. Maybe one should credit him with courage; maybe just with a blind complacency. The applause of the Macedonians was a brief delight; Alexander's anger would last.

Not that he made a show of it. After this slap in the face, he was concerned to keep his dignity. In his clear skin the flush showed like a flag; but his face was calm. He beckoned up Chares, spoke to him quietly, and sent him on a round of the Macedonian couches, to tell the guests that if the prostration was against their minds, they need think no more of it.

The Persians had not followed Kallisthenes' speech, since the interpreter had not thought fit to translate it. His voice when he named the kings must have told its tale. They saw Chares going round, and those who had risen settling back on their couches. There was a silence. The Persian lords looked at each other. Then, without a word exchanged among them, the lord of highest rank came forward, crossing the hall with the carriage such people have learned in childhood. He saluted the King, and went down in the prostration.

In order of precedence, all the others followed.

It was beautiful. No man of breeding could fail to see it was an act of pride. If these uncouth westerners thought themselves above the ancient courtesies, it was beneath a gentleman's notice. Most of all, though, it was done for Alexander, who had tried to offer them honour. As the foremost faced him, before making his bow, I saw their eyes meet in perfect understanding.

To each, as he made reverence, the King bent graciously; the Macedonians muttered on their couches; till near the end of the line came an oldish man, rather stout, and stiff in the knees, and got down as best he could. Everyone knows that one should not stick out one's backside; all the others had sunk with grace; but any fool could see the poor man's infirmities. I heard a snigger somewhere among the Macedonians; then one, a Companion called Leonnatos, gave a loud guffaw. The Persian, just then struggling to rise with a little dignity, was so shocked that he stumbled. I was behind him waiting my turn; I stepped forward, and helped him to his feet.

Concerned with this, I did not see Alexander till he was halfway there. His robe swinging about him, he came down the room as if his feet did not touch the ground, light as the lion running-up for its spring. I don't think Leonnatos saw him coming at all. Without a word, eyes fixed in a wide pale stare, he grasped Leonnatos' hair with one hand, his girdle with the other, and heaved him off his couch on to the floor.

They say that in battle Alexander seldom fought in anger; that mostly he was light of heart, and often smiling. Yet now I thought, How many men's last sight has that face been? Leonnatos, floundering upon the floor as angry as a bear, took one look and paled. Even I felt a little cold breath chill my neck. I looked at his sash, to see if he had a weapon.

But he just stood quietly, hands on hips, no more than a little short of breath, and said. 'Well, Leonnatos, now you're down there too. And if you think you look graceful, I wish you could see yourself.' Then he walked back to his supper-couch, and spoke coolly to those about him.

A boor has been punished, I thought. No one was hurt. It was foolish to be afraid.

The party broke up early. Alexander came to bed sober. The rage of the lion had gone; he was restless, pacing the room, spoke of the insult to my people, and then burst out, 'Why has Kallisthenes turned against me? How did I ever harm him? He's had gifts, consequence, anything he asked for. If he is a friend, give me an honest enemy. Some of those have done me good; he came to do me harm. He hates me, I saw it. Why?'

I thought, Perhaps he really believes divine honours should be kept for gods. But I remembered the Greeks had given them to men before. Besides, there had been something else. When you are used to courts, you get the feel of it. He was a Greek; I could not tell who might be behind him. I just said, therefore, that it seemed he wanted to form himself a faction.

'Yes; but why, that's the thing.' With some trouble, I got him to disrobe and take his bath. I had no comfort to offer which suited his mood just then, and I feared he would not sleep.

It was not only his being robbed of his rights, which he'd known for his due while they were being proclaimed. They had failed in love to him. He felt it too deeply to speak of it. Wounded in the moment of exaltation, he was bleeding still. Yet he had contained his anger; it was the insult to the Persian, had loosed it off. He had ended in thought for us, as he had begun.

I had put him to bed, and was seeking some word of comfort, when a voice at the door said, 'Alexander?' His face lightened as he said, 'Come in.' It was Hephaistion. I knew he'd have come in without knocking, but for knowing I would be there.

I left them together. On the day of the oracle, I thought, he was there waiting, he was told it all. Now he is here to do what I cannot. And once more I wished him dead.

As I tossed on my pillow, I said to myself at last, Do I grudge my lord the herb that will heal him, because another gathers it? No, let him be healed. Then I cried my eyes out, and fell asleep.

At the winter's end, Alexander moved his court to Marakanda. We were free of the poisonous Oxos and the hot plains. Now, I thought, all will be well.

It was like a paradise, after Zariaspa; a green river valley in mountain foothills; tall white peaks above; the water like liquid ice, and clean as crystal. Already in the many gardens almond trees were budding, and small delicate lilies sprang from the melting snows.

Though in Sogdiana, it is not wild like the backlands; it is a crossroads for caravans; you meet people from everywhere. The bazaars sell horse-collars set with turquoise, and daggers with wrought-gold sheaths. One can even buy Chin silk there. I got enough for a coat, sky-coloured, embroidered with flowers and flying serpents. The dealer said it had been a year upon the road. Alexander said Chin must be in India, there was nothing further than that but the Encircling Ocean. His eyes glowed, as always when he spoke of distant marvels.

The citadel perches westward above the city; a good-sized fort, with a real palace in it. Here Alexander did a great deal of business, which had not reached him in the north. He entertained many Persians of high rank; and, as I saw, felt no better about the prostration.

Leonnatos had been forgiven. He was a man, Alexander said to me, who was a good fellow in the main, and would have had more sense when sober. I answered that things would be better here, where we had mountain water.

I spoke only in hope for him. He had drunk strong wine too long beside the Oxos; he had the taste for it. Here he tempered it more, maybe half and half; but that's not enough for Baktrian wine.

If the talk was good, he would talk more than he drank, and even if he sat up late, all would be well. But at other times, he just set out to drink. All Macedonians do it; by the Oxos, they'd come to do it more than before.

Never in his life was he drunk upon campaign. His victories had been too brilliant; his enemies left him time for it. He never did it when he had to be up early, even if it was only to hunt. Sometimes he'd be two or three days at that, camping in the hills; it cleared his blood, and he'd come back fresh as a boy.

He was getting into our ways. At first, I think to show us we were not slighted; but then he took to them. Why not? He was far above the land he came from, as I'd seen from the very first. He was civilized in his soul; we showed him the outward forms of it. Often now, at audiences, he wore the Mitra. It suited him, being shaped so like a helmet. He had taken into his household several Palace chamberlains, who hired Persian cooks; Persian guests now got real Persian banquets, and though he always ate sparingly, he did not dislike the food. Feeling him move into harmony with our ways, many who had served him first from fear now did it willingly. His rule was both strong and just; it was a good while since Persia had had both together.

The Macedonians, though, were feeling wronged. They were the victors, and they thought it their due to have it shown. Alexander knew it. He was not a man to give up easily. He tried once more to bring them round to the prostration. This time, he started at the top.

No big feast this time, no Persian guests. Friends he could trust, and

Macedonians of importance, who he hoped could be persuaded. He told me the plan, which I thought would persuade anyone. He had the gift of grace.

I was not to be there. He did not tell me why; he knew well enough he need not. Still, resolved to witness it, I slipped into the service anteroom, and posted myself where I could see in through the door. Chares said nothing. Within reason, I could do pretty much what I chose.

All the King's close friends were there; Hephaistion, Ptolemy, Perdikkas, Peukestas; Leonnatos too, grateful for forgiveness and ready to make amends. As for the others, they knew what was to happen. When Alexander had told me one was Kallisthenes, I looked my doubts; but he said Hephaistion had talked to him and he'd agreed. 'And if he breaks his word, I don't intend to notice it. This won't be like the last time. It will do him no good with the others.'

It was quite a small party, fewer than twenty couches. I saw Alexander kept down the drinking. As long as he lived, there was no pleasure he was a slave to, when he put his will to it. He talked, and drank, and talked.

No one could talk like him, when he chose and had someone to talk to; with a Greek, plays and sculpture and poetry and painting, or the planning of cities; a Persian he would get to talk of his forebears, his horses, the customs of his province, or of our gods. Some of his Macedonian friends had gone to school with him, under Aristotle of whom he still thought so much. With most of the others, who had never read a book and could just about scrawl on wax, it had to be their concerns, their kills at the hunt, their love-affairs, or war; which, if the wine had gone briskly round, would soon lead to Alexander's victories. I suppose it's true that he sometimes talked too much of them. But any artist, even the greatest, likes to re-live the best of his art.

Tonight, with well-tempered wine, it all went smoothly. He had the right word for everyone. I heard him ask Kallisthenes if he'd lately heard from Aristotle, which for some reason he answered awkwardly, though he covered it just after. Alexander told the others that as well as his own rarities, he'd ordered the satraps of all the provinces to send anything strange their huntsmen found to the philosopher; and had given him a vast sum, eight hundred talents, to house his collection. 'Some day,' he said, 'I must go and look at it.'

The tables were cleared; no Persian sweets that night. There was an air of expectation. Chares himself, whose office was far above serving anything, bore in a beautiful gold loving cup. It was Persian work, I daresay from Persepolis. This he put in Alexander's hand.

Alexander drank; then held it towards Hephaistion, whose couch was on his right. Hephaistion drank, handed the cup to Chares, rose from his place; and, standing before Alexander, performed the prostration. He did it perfectly. He must have practised for days.

I drew well back out of sight. This I was not meant to witness, and I knew it was fair enough. I had been bowing to the ground most of my life; so had my forebears back to Kyros' day. It was just a ceremony, we did not feel it humbled us. For a Macedonian with his pride, it was something else. He had a right, this first time at least, not to have Persians there; and especially not me.

He got to his feet as gracefully as he'd gone down (I'd seen nothing better at Susa) and stepped towards Alexander, who took him by the shoulders and kissed him. Their eyes met smiling. Hephaistion got back on his couch; Chares took the cup to Ptolemy. So it went on; each saluted the King and was then embraced by the friend. This time, I thought, not even Kallisthenes can be sour.

His turn came near the end. As if by chance, Hephaistion spoke just then to Alexander, who turned his head to answer. Neither watched Kallisthenes.

I watched him. I wanted to decide how much respect he deserved. I soon knew. He did not refuse; he drank from the cup, then walked straight up to Alexander, who he thought had noticed nothing, and presented himself to be kissed. I could picture him later, boasting of having been the only one not to bow. One could scarcely believe a grown man could be such a fool.

Hephaistion's eyes signalled to Alexander. He said nothing. Kallisthenes had had the chance to keep his word. Having broken it, he would be despised by the most powerful men at court; also resented, for setting himself above them.

It was well reasoned; except that they resented him too much. As Alexander turned to him, one called out, 'Don't kiss him, Alexander! He never bowed.'

The King, having been told, now had to know. He raised his brows at Kallisthenes and turned his face away.

Enough, one would suppose. But Kallisthenes could never let either well or ill alone. He shrugged, and walked off saying, 'Oh, well! So I go short of a kiss.'

I suppose if you can keep cool in the front line of battle, to do it with a Kallisthenes is nothing much. Alexander just beckoned Chares, who overtook Kallisthenes as he reached his couch. Looking – if you can believe it! – quite surprised at his dismissal, he got up again and went out. I greatly approved the King's not deigning to address the man himself. Yes, I thought, he is learning.

The last few bowed, as if nothing had happened; the party went on like any friendly meeting. But it was spoiled. Kallisthenes had cut an ignoble figure; but he would make his own story out of it, and encourage others. I thought it over.

The King came to bed early. I listened to all he told me (remember, I'd not been there), then I said, 'I would do much more for a kiss than that. I will kill this man for you. It is time. Just give me the word.'

'Would you do that?' He sounded wondering, more than eager.

'Of course I would. Each time you go to war, your friends are killing your enemies. I've never killed anyone for your sake. Let me do it now.'

He said, 'Thank you, Bagoas. But it's not the same.'

'No one will know. The caravans bring subtle drugs from as far as India. I will disguise myself, when I buy. I know what to do.'

He took my face in his hand, and said, 'Have you done this for Darius?'

I did not reply: No, this is just the plan I made for killing your lover. 'No, Al'skander, I have only killed one man, and that was in a fight, to keep his hands off me. But I will do this for you; and I promise you, I won't botch it.'

He let my face go, quite gently. 'When I said it was not the same as war, I meant not for me.'

I should have known. He never killed by stealth in all his life. He had made no secret of Parmenion's death, once it was done. There must have been a score of men who could have rid him of Kallisthenes and made it look like nature; but what he would not own to, he would not do. And yet, if he had let me serve him as I wished, it would have saved much trouble, and some lives.

After this, he said no more about the prostration. With the Macedonians, he just went back to the old drinking-parties Yet there was a change. Those who had agreed to bow, from love, or loyalty, or understanding of his reasons, or simple flattery, resented those who'd refused as putting contempt upon them, and slighting the King. Men had now shown where they stood; where there had been uncertain talk, there was bitterness and faction.

Yet when we Persians bowed down, they thought nothing of it. Oh, no; we were just displaying our abject natures. It was only blasphemy when done by Macedonians.

There had been bad blood already between the parties. The force that had first failed to relieve Marakanda had been cut up with some disgrace. They had dislodged the besiegers; but had then gone on to attack a large force of Scythians, and were cornered in a river gorge. Pharneuches the interpreter had been attached to them as envoy; the Macedonian officers, of horse and foot, tried to get him to assume command. No one will know the whole truth; the few survivors put the blame here or there; but it seems the cavalry commander made off with his men across the river, leaving the foot in the lurch; they scrambled after as best they could; all were stranded on a river island, sitting targets for Scythian arrows; and not many swam away to tell the tale. Marakanda had been besieged again; Alexander himself relieved it, rode on to find what was left of the wretched corpses, and gave them burial.

He was furious at having good men butchered by such bungling, and said he could spare Pharneuches less than such commanders. His own friends said these were men who'd not thought Persians good enough to eat with; only to shoulder their commands when things looked bad. There was rancour about it; it made them more quarrelsome in their drink. Each night I was uneasy lest some brawl should start in the King's presence. That was the worst I feared. God spared me from foreknowledge.

It was about this time that Kleitos the Black (so called from his bushy beard) called at the Palace, asking for the King.

It was he who shared with Hephaistion command of the Companions. If you wanted a type of the old school, you found it here. Alexander always humoured him, because he had known him from the cradle; he was the younger brother of the royal nurse, a Macedonian lady of good blood. I suppose he was about a dozen years the King's elder. He had fought under King Philip; he liked the old ways, free-spoken among one's peers, despising foreigners. I suppose he could remember Alexander at a year old, tumbling about and puddling on the floor. It takes a small mind to remember such things against a great one; but I don't think, even by trying, Kleitos could have made his mind much larger. He was a very good soldier, and brave in battle. Every time he saw Persians, you could see him wishing he had killed more than he had.

It was a pity, therefore, that when he came for audience, Oxathres was the bodyguard on duty.

I was passing at the time; and hearing him addressed as if he were a servant, paused to look. Though he disdained to notice the rudeness, he did not mean to leave his post and run on errands; he beckoned me up, and said in Persian, 'Bagoas, tell the King that Kleitos the commander asks to see him.'

I replied in the same tongue, and made a little bow; it seemed proper not to forget what our stations had been at Susa. As I turned to go, I saw Kleitos' face. Two barbarians between him and the King, and one a eunuch! Till then it had all felt natural; now I saw what he thought of being announced by a Persian whore.

The King saw him quite soon. His business was nothing out of the way; I overheard it. It was only when he came out, and saw Oxathres at his post, that his brow grew black again.

Soon after this, the King gave a big supper, mostly for Macedonians; a few Greeks were there, envoys from western Asia; and some Persians of importance in the province, whose offices he had confirmed.

His household had grown to match his state; it was fit to look after guests of any rank. I could have gone shopping in the bazaar, or watched some dancing, or lit my lamp and read my Greek book, which had become a pleasure. Yet I went to the supper hall. No strange chance took me there. I was just anxious, and hung about. Such warnings may come from God; or from feeling the weather, as shepherds can. If God had sent me, he would have found me some good to do.

It was strange from the very outset. Alexander had done sacrifice that day to the Dioskouroi, the twin heroes of the Greeks. Kleitos had planned a sacrifice of his own; to Dionysos, for this was the god's day in Macedon, and he was always one for the old customs. He had poured libations on his two sheep, ready to slit their throats, when he heard the horn blow for supper; so he left everything, and went. But the silly sheep, taking their butcher for their shepherd, trotted along behind him, and followed him through the door. Everyone shouted with laughter; till it came out that these were beasts of sacrifice, dedicated already. The King was disturbed for Kleitos at this omen, and sent to the priests to sacrifice for his safety. Kleitos thanked him for the kind thought; and the wine came in.

I could see at once this was a night when Alexander felt like drinking. He set the pace; the wine-pourers went round so fast, everyone was tipsy by the time the meat was finished; when, at a decent Persian feast, the wine would first have come in. I am angry to this day, when ignorant Greeks say we taught the King deep drinking. Would to God he had learned from us.

There was a dessert that day; beautiful apples from Hyrkania. They had travelled well; Alexander had made me take one before supper, in case there should be none left. He was never too busy to think of things like that.

It seems the nature of man to turn God's good gifts to evil. At all events it was over these apples that the talk began to go wrong.

The fruits of all earth's four quarters, said Alexander's friends, now reached him from his own lands. The Dioskouroi had been deified for conquests far less than his.

Now I know, from my later reading, that this is true. The furthest the Twins ever got from their Spartan home was up to the Euxine in Jason's ship; about as far as from Macedon to western Asia, and just the coast at that. Their other wars had been these little Greek ones, cattle raids, or getting their sister back from some King of Athens; all quite near home. Good fighters, no doubt; but I never heard they could fight hand to hand while leading men in battle. One of them was just a boxer. So Alexander did not deny he had excelled them. Why should he? Yet I felt the breath of trouble.

Sure enough, the old school started to raise the cry of blasphemy. At this, the King's friends shouted out (by now everyone was shouting) that the Twins had been born as mortal as Alexander; and it was only spite and envy, putting on a false face of reverence, which had denied him the same honours, better earned.

As if touched by the ferment in the hall, I had helped myself well to wine out in the anteroom, and was in a haze; as one is in dreams where disasters loom, but one knows one can do nothing. Sober, though, I would have known the same.

'Alexander this, Alexander that, all Alexander!' Kleitos' thick raucous voice topped all the rest. It brought me from the anteroom to the entry. He was standing up in his place. 'Did he conquer Asia by himself? Did *we* do nothing?'

Hephaistion yelled back (he was as drunk as everyone else), 'He led us! You didn't get as far in Philip's day.'

This was just the thing to double Kleitos' anger. 'Philip!' he cried. 'Philip started with nothing! How did he find us? Tribes feuding, rival kings, enemies all round. He was struck down before he was fifty, and where was he then? Master of Greece; master of Thrace to the Hellespont; all ready to march to Asia. Without your father,' he shouted straight at Alexander, 'where would you be today? Without the army he left you ready? You'd be still beating off the Illyrians.'

I was shocked to the soul that such insolence was being heard by Persians. Whatever was done to the man later, he must be got out at once. I looked for the King to order it.

'What!' he shouted back. 'In seven years? Are you off your head?'

Never had I known him so to forget himself. It was like some trooper in a tavern. And the drunk fools of Macedonians did nothing but shout along with him.

'– still fighting the Illyrians!' bawled Kleitos over again.

Alexander, who was used to being heard above a battle when he raised his voice, lifted it now. 'My father was fighting the Illyrians half his life. And they never kept quiet till I was old enough to do it for him. I was sixteen. I drove them leagues beyond their borders, and there they've stayed. And where were you? Lying-up with him in Thrace, after the Triballians had thrashed you.'

I had long heard that Queen Olympias had been a turbulent jealous woman, who taught him to hate his father. This, I thought, is what comes of their having no one trained to manage their harems properly. I could have sunk with shame.

A roar of dispute broke out. The disaster by the river was fought over once again. During the hubbub Alexander came to himself a little. He called for silence, in a voice that at once procured it; I could see him fighting for calm. Presently he said to the Greek guests sitting near, 'You must feel like demigods among wild beasts, in all this uproar.'

Kleitos had heard. Purple with drink and fury, he yelled, 'Beasts now are we? And fools and bunglers. It'll be cowards next. That's what it will be! It's we, the men your father made us, *we* put you where you are. And now his blood's not good enough for you, you son of Ammon.'

Alexander was dead silent a moment; then he said, not loudly but in a voice so deadly it cut through everything, '*Get out*'.

'Yes, I'll go,' Kleitos said. 'Why not?' Suddenly his arm shot out and pointed straight at me. 'Yes, when we have to beg barbarians like that creature there for leave to see you, better stay away. It's the dead, it's Parmenion and his sons, it's the dead are lucky.'

Without a word, Alexander reached to his dish of apples, drew back his arm, and hurled one at Kleitos' head. It hit dead-on; I heard the clunk on his skull.

Hephaistion had jumped to his feet, and was standing by Alexander. I heard him say to Ptolemy, 'Get him outside. For the gods' love, get him *out*.'

Ptolemy went over to Kleitos, who was still rubbing his head, took his arm and eased him towards the outer doors. Kleitos turned and waved the other arm. 'And this right hand,' he said, 'saved you at Granikos, when you'd turned your back on Spithridates' spear.'

Alexander, who had on his half-Persian robe, grabbed at his sash, as if he hoped to find a sword there. Perhaps in Macedon they'd even worn them at supper. 'Turned my back?' he shouted. '*Liar*! Wait for me, don't run away.'

Now he had good cause for anger. Though Spithridates' kin had always claimed, at Susa, that he'd fallen hand to hand with Alexander, they had done him too much honour; he had tried to take him from behind when he was fighting someone else. Kleitos, coming up in turn behind Spithridates, had cut through his lifted arm. Any soldier in reach, I suppose, would have done the same; and Kleitos boasted of it so often that everyone was sick of it. To say Alexander had turned his back was truly infamous. He was already on his feet, when Hephaistion and Perdikkas gripped him round the middle. He struggled and cursed them, trying to break their hold, while Ptolemy shoved Kleitos towards the doors, still uttering some defiance swamped by the noise. Hephaistion said, 'We're all drunk. You'd be sorry after.'

Alexander, wrenching at their arms with both hands, said between his teeth, 'This is how Darius finished. Is it fetters next?'

He is possessed, I thought; it is more than the wine; he must be saved. I ran up to the struggling knot of men. 'Al'skander, it wasn't like this with Darius. These are your friends, they don't wish you harm.' He half-turned and said 'What?' Hephaistion said, 'Go away now, Bagoas'; speaking impatiently, as if to a child who comes up for notice when everyone is busy.

Ptolemy had walked Kleitos down the hall to the doors, and pulled them open. He nearly got away and back into the hall, but Ptolemy kept his hold. They vanished and the doors closed after them. Hephaistion said, 'He's gone. It's over. Don't make a show of yourself, come and sit down.' They let him go.

He threw back his head, and gave a great shout in Macedonian. A score of soldiers came running in from outside. He had called the guard.

'Trumpeter!' he said. The man stepped forward. It was his duty always to be in reach of the King. 'Sound the general alarm!'

The man lifted his trumpet, slowly, putting off the moment to blow. It would have turned the whole army out. From his post he must had heard nearly everything. Hephaistion, standing behind the King, signed to him 'No'.

'Sound the alarm,' said Alexander. 'Are you deaf? *Sound the alarm.*'

Again the man raised the trumpet. He saw the eyes of five or six generals fixed on him, saying no. He lowered it. Alexander hit him in the face.

Hephaistion said, 'Alexander.'

For a moment he paused, as it coming to himself. He said to the gaping guards. 'Go to your posts.' The trumpeter, after one anxious glance, went too.

Early in the uproar, the Persians had excused themselves to the chamberlains, and slipped away. The ever-curious Greeks had stayed much longer, then scrambled off without ceremony when the guard was called. It was now all Macedonians; their own quarrel forgotten, gaping like rustics beside whose village brawl a thunderbolt has fallen.

I thought, They should have let me near him. When I named Darius, he heard. Never mind what they do, I am going back to him.

But he was free now, striding down the hall, calling for Kleitos as if he were still in hearing. 'All this faction in the camp, it's all your doing!'

He passed by me unseeing; and I let him pass. How could I take hold of him before all these people? There had been enough unseemliness. That he should have wished to chastise this insolent boor with his own hands, instead of sending for the executioners! What King could think of such a thing, except one reared in Macedon? It was bad enough, without his Persian boy dragging at his arm in sight of everyone. I expect it made no difference, I daresay he would have shaken me off unheard. Yet even now, I wake in the night and think of it.

Just then, Ptolemy slipped in quietly through the service door, and said to the others, 'I walked him right outside the citadel. He'll cool off there.'

The King was still calling 'Kleitos!' but I felt better. He's just fighting drunk, I thought. It will soon go off. I'll get him into a good hot bath, and let him talk. Then he'll sleep till noon, and wake up himself again.

'Kleitos, where are you?' As he reached the outer doors, they burst wide open. There stood Kleitos, red-faced and panting. He must have started back as soon as Ptolemy left him.

'Here's Kleitos!' he shouted. 'Here I am!'

He had come back for the last word. He had thought of it too late, and would not forgo it. It was his fate to be given his wish.

From the doors behind him, a guard came in doubtfully, like a muddy dog. He'd had no orders to keep out the Commander; but he did not like it. He stood spear in hand, looking dutiful and ready. Alexander, checked in his stride, stared unbelievingly.

'Listen, Alexander. *Alas, ill rule in Hellas* . . .'

Even Macedonians knew their Euripides. I daresay everyone there but I could have completed these famous lines. The gist of them is that the soldiers do it all, the general gets it all. I don't know if he meant to go on.

A flash of white went to the door, and turned again. There was a bellow like a slaughtered bull's. Kleitos clutched with both hands at the spear stuck in his breast; fell and writhed grunting; jerked in the death-spasm. His mouth and eyes fixed, wide open.

It had been so quick, for a moment I thought the guard had done it. The spear was his.

It was the silence, all down the hall, that told me.

Alexander stood over the body, staring down. Presently he said, 'Kleitos.' The corpse glared back at him. He took the spear by the haft. When it would not come, I saw him begin the soldier's movement to brace his foot on the body; then flinch and pull again. It jerked out, a handspan deep in blood, splashing his clean white robe. Slowly he turned it round, the butt on the ground, the point towards him.

Ptolemy has always maintained that it meant nothing. I only knew I cried, 'No, my lord!' and got it away. I took him unready, as he had done the guard. Someone reached over and carried it out of sight. Alexander sank to his knees by the body, and felt over its breast; then covered his face with his bloody hands.

'Oh God,' he said slowly, 'God, God, God, God.'

'Come away, Alexander,' Hephaistion said. 'You can't stay here.'

Ptolemy and Perdikkas helped lift him to his feet. At first he resisted, still searching the corpse for life. Then he went with them, like a sleep-walker.

His face looked dreadful, all striped with blood. The Macedonians, in little knots, stared as he passed, I hurried after him.

At the door of his room, the squire on guard started forward, saying, 'Is the King wounded?' Ptolemy said. 'No. He doesn't need you.' Once inside, he flung himself on the bed, face downward, just as he was in his bloodstained robe.

I saw Hephaistion looking about, and guessed what for. I wetted a sponge and gave it him. He pulled at Alexander's hands and washed them, then turned his head this way and that, and cleaned his face.

Alexander pushed at him and said, 'What are you doing?'

'Getting the blood off you.'

'You will never do that.' He was sobered. He knew it all.

'Murder,' he said. He spoke the word over and over, like a foreign one he was trying to learn. He sat up. His face was nowhere near clean. I would have sent for warm water, gone quietly about it, and done it properly. 'Go, all of you,' he said. 'I want nothing. Leave me alone.'

They exchanged looks and moved towards the door. I waited, to care for him when his first grief was spent.

Hephaistion said, 'Come out, Bagoas, he wants no one here.'

'I am no one,' I answered. 'Just let me put him to bed.'

I took a step to him; but he said 'Everyone go'; so then I went. If Hephaistion had kept his mouth shut, I'd just have sat quietly in a corner till he forgot about me. Then, later in the night, when the life runs low, he would not have been sorry to have me tend him. They had not laid a blanket on him, and the nights were cold.

They went off talking together. In my room I kept my clothes on, in case he called for me. I could well understand, having brought on himself so dreadful an indignity, he could bear no one near him now. My heart shed blood for him. We had taught him enough in Persia, for him to feel his shame. When Nabarzanes had asked Darius to step down for Bessos, and the King had drawn his scimitar, it had been almost a courtly scene, compared with this.

I pictured such a person as Kleitos insulting the King at Susa, if such a thing could be conceived. The King would just have motioned with a finger, and the proper people would have appeared. The man would have been taken off with a hand over his mouth; the feast would have proceeded decently; and next day, when the King had rested, he would have decreed the mode of death. It would all have been quiet and seemly. The King would have done no more than move his hand.

I thought, He knows he forgot his dignity, before Greeks and even Persians. He feels he has lost esteem. He needs comfort, and to be reminded of his greatness. In all this trouble, he should not be alone.

In the dead hour after midnight, I went along to his room. The squire on duty looked at me, unmoving. From outside, I could hear the high whining of Peritas, and knew he must be weeping. 'Let me in,' I said. 'The King needs attendance.'

'Not your kind. Nor any other. Those are my orders.'

This youth, Hermolaos, had never left me in doubt of what he thought about eunuchs. He was glad to keep me out; he had no feeling for his master's grief. The sound tore at my heart; I could hear it now. 'You have no right,' I said. 'You know I have the entry.' He just held his spear across the doorway. Gladly I would have sunk a knife in him. I went back to bed, and did not close my eyes till morning.

When the night-guard had changed, between dawn and sunrise, I went again. It was Metron now. I said, 'The King will expect me. Nothing at all has been done for him since before supper.' He was sensible, and let me in.

He lay face upward, staring at the ceiling-beams. The blood on his robe had turned dark brown. He had done nothing for himself, not even pulled on the blanket. His eyes looked fixed like a dead man's.

'Al'skander,' I said. Dully his eyes moved, empty of welcome or displeasure. 'Al'skander, it's almost morning. You have grieved too long.'

I laid my hand on his brow. He let it lie just long enough not to slight me, and turned his head away. 'Bagoas. Will you take care of Peritas? He can't stay shut up here.'

'Yes, after I've seen to you. When you've taken these things off, and had a bath, you may still get a little sleep.'

'Let him run by your horse,' he said. 'It's good for him.'

The dog had jumped up, and was padding from one to the other of us, full of trouble. He sat down when I told him, but his head still turned about.

I said, 'The hot water's coming. Let us get these dirty clothes off.' I hoped this would work with him. He hated not to be clean.

'I have told you, I want nothing. Just take the dog and go.'

'Oh, my lord!' I cried. 'How can you punish yourself for such a fellow? Though the work was beneath you, it was still a good work done.'

'You don't know what I have done,' he said. 'How should you? Don't trouble me now, Bagoas. I want nothing. His leash is in the window.'

For a moment he growled at me; but Alexander spoke to him, and he went meekly. There were three jars of hot water standing by the door, and a slave was toiling up the stairs with another. I could only send them back.

Metron moved from the door, and said softly, 'Won't he have anything done?'

'No. Only the dog looked after.'

'He's taking it hard. It's because he killed a friend.'

'A *friend?*' I must have stared like an idiot. 'Do you know what Kleitos said to him?'

'Well, but he *was* a friend, since they were boys. He'd a name for being rough-spoken . . . You'd not understand, not having lived in Macedon. But haven't you found that friends' quarrels are the bitterest?'

'Are they?' I said, having no knowledge of it; and led the dog away.

After I'd given him his run, I hung about the door all day. I saw food brought in at noon, and sent out untasted. Later on, Hephaistion came. I could not hear what he said, because of the guard at the door; but I heard Alexander cry out, 'She loved me like a mother, and I give her this.' He must have meant his nurse, Kleitos' sister. Hephaistion left soon after. There was nowhere to withdraw to; but when he saw me he said nothing.

The King sent out, untouched, a good hot supper. Next morning, early, I brought an egg posset to put some strength in him. But a different guard was there, and turned me off. He lay fasting all that day.

After that, people of importance started coming, begging him to take some care of himself. Even the philosophers came, to preach to him. To me, it was beyond belief they should send Kallisthenes. I thought quickly and walked in after him. If *he* could enter, so could I. I wanted to see about the drinking-water; I remembered the pitcher had not had much in it.

It was just as it had been, quarter-full. In two days, and with the thirst a man has after wine, had not even drunk.

I sat down in a corner, too distressed to listen to Kallisthenes. I think he tried, in his way, to be of use, saying the virtue of repentance was next best to leaving the deed undone. To my mind, his mere presence, setting himself up, was an affront; but Alexander listened quietly, and at the end said without anger that he wanted nothing, but to be alone. I remained, as I'd hoped, unnoticed.

But then in came Anaxarchos, and asked why Alexander lay grieving there, when he was master of the world and had the right to do as he chose. Him too the King heard with patience, though in his state even the grasshopper might have been a burden. Then, just as the stupid man was going, he felt moved to add, 'Come, let Bagoas here bring you food and make you fit to be seen.' So I was noticed, and sent out with the sophist, my trouble all gone for nothing.

The third day came; nothing was changed. The news was all over the camp. The men were not strolling the town, but milling in their quarters, or sitting about before the palace; they kept sending to ask after the King. You could not be long with Macedonians, without guessing they killed each other in drinking-brawls pretty often; it had taken them some time to be anxious for him. But they knew that what he willed, he did; and they began to fear that he willed to die.

I had lain fearing it half the night.

I was glad to see Philippos the doctor go in. Though it was before my time, I knew the story of how the King, when very sick, had trusted him enough to take his draught, though Parmenion had just written that Darius had bribed the man to poison him. He'd handed him the letter to read, and meantime swallowed the medicine. But he came out, now, shaking his head.

I *must* get in, I thought; and I brought two gold staters, to bribe the guard. If he'd asked for a jar of my blood, I would have given that.

As I went to speak to him, the door opened, and Hephaistion came out. I stood aside. 'Bagoas,' he said, 'I want a word with you.'

He led me down into the open courtyard, away from eavesdroppers; then he said, 'I don't want you to see the King today.'

Because of his great power, I tried to hide my anger. What if he sent me from my lord? I said, 'Is that not for the King to order?'

'True.' I saw, surprised, that he too was holding back; what had he to fear from me? 'If he asks for you, no one will keep you out. But stay away till he does.'

It shocked me. I had thought better of him. I answered, 'He is killing himself like this. If he is saved, do you care who saves him? I do not care.'

'No,' he said slowly, looking down from his tall height. 'No, I daresay.' He still spoke as if to a tiresome child, but one he had half-forgiven. 'I doubt he will kill himself, He will remember his destiny. He has great endurance, as you'd know if you'd soldiered with him. He can stand a great deal of punishment.'

'Not without water,' I said.

'What?' he said sharply. 'He has water there, I saw it.'

'It is just as it was when you fetched me out the first night.' I added, 'I concern myself with these things, when I am allowed.'

Still he held back. 'Yes, he must take water. I will try to make him.'

'But not I?' I regretted, now, not having poisoned him at Zadrakarta.

'No. Because you will go in there and tell him the Great King can do anything.'

What I had meant to say was different, and no business of his. I answered, 'So he can. The King is the law.'

'Yes,' he said. 'I knew you would tell him that.'

'Why not? Who will give him respect, if traitors can spit in his face? At Susa, a man like Kleitos would have prayed for the death he got.'

'I don't doubt it,' he said. I thought of Philotas' screams, but did not remind him. I only said, 'Of course, if the King had been himself, he would not have soiled his hands with it. He knows that now.'

He took a deep breath, as if restraining himself from clouting my head.

'Bagoas,' he said slowly, 'I know the Great King can do anything. Alexander knows it too. But he also knows he is King of the Macedonians, who can't do everything. He cannot kill a Macedonian, with his own hand or anyone else's, unless Assembly has voted. This he forgot.'

I remembered him, then, saying, 'You don't know what I have done.'

'It is not our custom,' I said, 'to bring in the wine so early. Think how he was insulted and defied.'

'I know all about that. I knew his father ... But, that's no matter. He broke the first law of Macedon, And he was not master of himself. That's what he can't forget.'

'But,' I cried, 'he must forgive himself. He must, or he will die.'

'Of course he must. Do you know what the Macedonians are doing now? They are calling an Assembly, to try Kleitos for treason. They'll convict him, and then his death will be legal. It was the men who wanted it. They are doing it to make Alexander forgive himself.'

'But,' I said staring, 'don't you want that too?'

'Yes.' He spoke as if I might not understand Greek. 'Yes, but I am concerned with the terms on which he does it.'

I replied, 'I am concerned only for him.'

Suddenly he shouted at me, as if at some awkward soldier. 'You fool of a boy! Will you listen to sense?' It winded me like a blow, after his quiet.

'Have you noticed,' he said, standing over me with his fists upon his belt, 'that Alexander likes his men to love him? Yes or no? Well, his men are Macedonians. If you don't know what that means by now, you must be deaf and blind. In Macedon, any freeman can speak man to man with his chief; chief or freeman can speak to the King. And I tell you this; they can much better understand what Alexander did to Kleitos in the heat of anger, which might have happened to any one of them, than they'd understand an execution in cold blood next day. That would have threatened all their freemen's rights, and they'd have loved him less. If *you* love him, never tell him he is above the law.'

His earnestness transformed him. I said, 'Anaxarchos told him that.'

'Oh, Anaxarchos!' He shrugged. 'But he might listen to you.'

He had owned it. It could not have been easy. I owed him some return. 'I understand you. I see you must know best. I won't say those things to him; I promise. May I see him now?'

'Not now. It's not that I doubt your word; but at present, he's better among Macedonians.'

He went away. He had taken my promise, and given nothing back. I had never craved for power, as some eunuchs do; only for love. Now I understand what power is good for. He had it. If I had had it, someone would have let me in.

All that long day, I kept going to ask the guard if the King had eaten or drunk. The answer always was that he'd said he wanted nothing.

The soldiers had tried Kleitos, and pronounced him a traitor, justly put to death. Surely he would take heart from this proof of love? But not even this had moved him. Could it really be true he felt that he'd killed a friend? I remembered the bad omen of the sheep and his sacrifice for Kleitos' safety. He had asked him to come and share the good apples, too.

The sun rose to its zenith; the sun declined. How many suns more?

I kept to my room till the night was late, lest Hephaistion should see me. When all was quiet, I took a pitcher of fresh spring water, and a clean cup. All would depend on who was the night-guard squire before the door. God was kind to me. It was Ismenios. He had always treated me well; and he loved the King.

'Yes, go in,' he said. 'I don't care if he curses me after. I went in myself, when I came on guard. But he was asleep; I didn't dare wake him.'

My heart nearly ceased its motion. 'Asleep? Did you hear him breathing?'

'Oh, yes. But he looks half dead. Go in and try.'

The door made no noise. It was dark; he had put out the night-lamp. After the torch outside, at first I could only discern the glimmering windows. But there was a moon, and soon I saw him clearly. He was still asleep.

Someone had put a blanket on him, but it was tossed half off. He was still in his bloodstained robe. His hair was matted, his skin drawn. Fair though it was, his beard had begun to show. A filled pitcher stood untouched by him. His lips were cracked and dry; in his sleep he was trying to wet them with his tongue.

I filled my cup. Sitting by him, I dipped two fingers, and trickled the water on his mouth. He licked at it like a dog, still sleeping. I went on till I saw him start to wake; then I took his head on my arm, and tilted the cup gently. He drank, and gave a great sigh, and drank again. I refilled it, and he drank that too.

I stroked his hair and brow, and he did not draw away. I did not beg him to come back to us; he'd had enough of that. I said, 'Don't shut me out any longer. It is breaking my heart.'

'Poor Bagoas.' He laid a cold hand on mine. 'You can come in tomorrow.'

I kissed his hand. He had broken his fast before he knew it; he would end it now. Yes, now, I thought; not with officious fools around him, urging him on like a fractious child.

I slipped out of the door, and whispered to Ismenios, 'Send someone to wake a cook. Egg posset, with honey and wine, and soft cheese crumbled in. Hurry up, before he changes his mind.' His face lit up, and he gave me a great clap on the shoulder; which was more than Hermolaos would have done.

I went back to the bed. I didn't want him falling asleep before the posset came, then waking to say he would have nothing. But his eyes were open. He knew what I'd been about, and understood. He waited quietly, and I talked of little things, such as Peritas' doings, till Ismenios scratched at the door. The posset smelled good. I made no speeches, just lifted his head again. Soon he took the bowl from me, and finished it.

'Sleep now,' I said. 'But you must send for me in the morning, or they won't let me in. I shouldn't be here now.'

'Enough people have been let in,' he said, 'whom I didn't want. You I do.' He kissed me, and turned on his side. When I showed Ismenios the empty bowl, he was so pleased that he kissed me, too.

So next day I bathed and shaved and combed him, and he looked almost himself again, though very worn. He kept his rooms; it would take more courage to show himself again, than to lead the charge at Gaugamela; so he would do it soon. The soldiers, hearing he'd taken food, were giving themselves the credit, because they had condemned Kleitos. This was best; they were welcome to it, for me.

Later, the priest of Dionysos came for audience. He had taken omens, and the god had spoken. It was his anger had caused it all. On his Macedonian feast-day, Kleitos had left his sacrifice unfinished (had not his unoffered victims followed him in reproach?) and Alexander had worshipped the Heavenly Twins, instead. For this, the deity's sacred frenzy had been sent on both; and after that, neither was answerable for what he did.

I could see this gave Alexander comfort. I don't know why he had chosen the Twins that day. But I remembered the talk at supper, about his exploits surpassing theirs (which was true) and his deserving the same honours; and I guessed he had tried once more to have his people share the prostration with the Persians. Who could have guessed it would end so cruelly? But Dionysos is a cruel god. I had found a dreadful play about him, in one of the books Alexander had had sent from Greece.

He gave orders for a great propitiation sacrifice. Then he spent the day with his closest friends, and looked a little better. He retired early; it was suffering more than fasting that had worn him out. When he was settled, I put out the great lamp and set the night-lamp by him. He took my hand, saying, 'Before I woke last night, I dreamed of a good spirit.'

I thought of my life, and smiled. 'The god sent that, to tell you his wrath was over. He released you then; that was why you drank.'

'I dreamed of a good presence; and it was true.'

His hand felt warm. I remembered it before, stone cold. I said softly, 'The god's madness was truly there; I myself felt it. Do you know, my lord, I only went to have a look at the feast, and even so it seized me? I snatched at the wine as if compelled; and all that came after, I seemed to dream in madness. It was a visitation. I felt it everywhere.'

'Yes,' he said slowly. 'Yes, it was strange. I was driven out of myself. Kleitos, too. Look how he came back. The god led him, as he led Pentheus to his fate, and caused his own mother to perform it.' He knew I had read the play.

'No one can help himself when a god possesses him. Sleep in peace, my lord. He has forgiven you; he was only angry because you're dear to him. A slight from you hurt him more than from anyone else.'

I sat down by the wall, in case he should be wakeful and want to talk; but he slept soon, and lay quiet. I went away well content. What can compare with giving comfort to the one you love?

I had kept my promise to Hephaistion, too.

17

Most of that year, and the next, we were in Baktria and Sogdiana. It was a long, hard war. You never know where you are with Sogdians. They are mostly at blood-feud with the tribe in the next hill-fort, over the rights to water, or women carried off while gathering wood. They would swear loyalty to Alexander till he had reduced these people; then, if he took their surrender and did not cut all their throats, would turn on him themselves. Spitamenes, their best general, was killed by Sogdian enemies; they sent Alexander his head, for a reward, but were no more to be trusted after. Our men never left a dying man on the field, however hard-pressed they were, to be found by Sogdians. He would thank them for the death-stroke.

Alexander would be gone for weeks on these local wars. I missed him, and was forever anxious; but had my consolation. On campaign he was always sober. He had good mountain water. Soon he had sweated and rinsed the strong wine out of his blood, and was much as he used to be; enjoying sometimes a long night of spun-out talk and drinking, a long sleep after; moderate in between. The dreadful lesson of Marakanda lasted him all his days. He was never again seen disordered in his wine, let alone violent. Even his slanderers don't deny it.

A lesser man might have held it against me, that I'd seen him in despair and shame. But he only remembered I had brought him comfort. He never turned away love.

Once he had to re-cross the Oxos; it was easy this time, everything ready and better weather. I might hardly remember it, except that a miracle happened there. They had pitched the King's tent, and I was seeing his things set out, when I heard the squires exclaiming. Right by the tent, which was not far from the river, was a dark welling spring. They had skimmed the scum off, in case it might serve for horses; and found that it was oil!

Alexander was fetched to see the wonder. We all rubbed it upon our arms, and it spread smoothly. He sent for Aristander the seer, to read the omen. He sacrificed, and announced that as oil anoints the wrestler before the games, the portent stood for labours, but its generous flow for victory and wealth.

We tried some in the King's lamp at night. It burned quite well, but made a foul smoke; the lamp had to be taken outside. He wanted to taste it, but I said it might be as bad as Oxos water, which changed his mind. Leonnatos was for throwing a lighted torch into the pool, to see what happened; but Alexander thought it would be impious, towards a gift of the gods.

He had the labours it foretold. He was forever off in the mountains, often with small forces, for he had to divide his troops; he was resolved to bring Sogdiana under law. He learned wonderful skill and cunning in taking hill-forts. Many tales came back, of his endurance in cold or heat (you get extremes of both in Sogdiana); of a frightful storm, thunder and lightning-bolts followed by hailstones, and bitter cold, when men were perishing of despair and terror, freezing in their tracks, till, seeking the stragglers out in the maze of a black forest, he shook them alive and got them making fires. He was at last sitting down to get warm himself, when a soldier came staggering up, half-dead on his feet, hardly knowing where he was. Alexander took off with his own hands the icy armour whose straps made his fingers bleed, and sat the man in his own chair by the fire.

King Ptolemy, who was there, is putting such things in his book, to be known by men to come. Sometimes about other matters he sends for me, and I tell him whatever I think my lord would like to be remembered for. Seeing I followed his golden bier all the way here to Egypt, King Ptolemy in kindness found room for me in his household. He speaks louder than he knows, now he's a little hard of hearing (he is my elder by twenty years) and sometimes I hear him say, quietly as he supposes, to a foreign guest, 'Look there. Don't you see there has been great beauty? That is Bagoas, who was Alexander's boy.'

In camp I read Herodotos with Philostratos. He begged my pardon for the choice of book; he had not many; but as I told him, it was no news to me that Xerxes had been beaten in Greece; my great-great-grandfather had served with him.

Philostratos and I had grown fond of one another; only as teacher and pupil, though I saw Kallisthenes sniffing. When the King was at war, and the chronicle was up to date, he had not much to do till the King got back with his squires, whom Kallisthenes had the teaching of. They being of noble birth, and likely to command men later, Alexander did not want them ignorant. He had never taken this work from the philosopher, even after they were estranged. I thought it over-generous, myself; but then, he had Aristotle to consider.

Just now Kallisthenes was going over his library; we could see through his open tent-flap the racks of scrolls. Philostratos went in, and had another try at borrowing one, so that I could read Greek verse; he had only taught me what he knew by heart. I heard him get a dry no, and tell Kallisthenes he'd be lucky if one of his pupils showed half my promise. Kallisthenes said *his* pupils showed promise in the noble art of philosophy, not mere book-reading. Philostratos said, 'Can they read?' and walked out. They did not speak for a month.

Next time Alexander came back, I asked him to give Philostratos a present. He loved being asked for things. I don't think my story about Kallisthenes did the present any harm either. 'But what for yourself?' he said. 'Don't you think I love you enough?'

'I had presents at Susa without love,' I said. 'You give me all I need. And my best suit is still as good as new; or nearly.'

He laughed and said, 'Buy another. I like to see you come out in something new; like a pheasant in spring feathers.' He added gravely. 'My love you will always have. That is a sacred bond to me.'

Soon he was off again. I had my new suit made in deep red, embroidered with gold spangled flowers. The buttons were jewelled roses. I put it away to wear when he came back.

I should soon be twenty. Alone in my tent, I often looked in the mirror. For people like me, it is a dangerous age.

Though my looks had changed, it seemed I had beauty still. I was slim as ever; my face had not coarsened but fined. There is no salve like love.

It did not matter that I was a boy no longer. I had hardly been that when he saw me first. He was not a boy-lover; it was the comely young men around him that pleased his eye. One of them, a squire called Philippos, had lately died for it. I could see Alexander was fond of him; maybe there had been some nights upon campaign – I can think of it gently now. At all events, the youth felt a burning loyalty, which he longed to prove. They made a long pursuit after the Sogdians, in summer heat; his horse gave out, one of many; so he ran on foot by the King's horse, fully armed, and refused a mount he was offered, to show what he was made of. At the end of the chase, they found and fought the enemy. He stood by the King in the van; then, when it was over, suddenly the life went out in him, like the flame of an emptied lamp. He lasted just long enough to die in Alexander's arms. Even I could not grudge him that.

Yes, I thought at the mirror, he will always love me. He never takes love without return. But when desire begins to fail, it will be a day of grief. Holy Eros! (for I knew the god well by this time) let it not be yet.

As the country was subdued, he was founding cities. Hephaistion founded some of them. He had learned Alexander's eye for a good site, and though rough-tongued among Macedonians, had good manners and good sense with foreigners. Gladly I gave him credit for all his virtues, once he was out of sight.

What use to scourge oneself with jealousy of the past? He'd not had ten years of it before me, my first guess; he had had fifteen. They had been together since I was a baby learning to walk. The future no man knows; the past has been, now and forever.

We wintered in a rocky sheltered place called Nautika, with a waterfall and a cave. Alexander was up in the citadel tower again; reaching his bedchamber through a trapdoor in the floor. I was scared to death he would stumble on the ladder some night after supper, though he'd never been known to fall however drunk he was. The room had a big hearth under a hole in the roof; snow would come through it and hiss upon the fire. He and Hephaistion would sit by it talking, with Peritas stretched out like a great rug. But the nights were mine. Sometimes he'd say, 'You can't go out there, it's freezing', and take me in just to keep me warm. He was always a giver.

In the room below, heated by fire-baskets and full of draughts, he would do business most of the day. At one end was his chair of state and place of audience; at the other, behind a curtain, his working table, full of tablets and records, and letters from half the world. The more lands he conquered, the more work he had.

There were the soldiers to look after, and keep in shape through the idle time till the passes opened. He held games, for which everyone had to be ready on the first fine day. Once we even had a play, with a proper stage and good actors out from Greece. Actors would go through water, fire and ice, to go home and say they had played before Alexander. Philostratos sat by me, and explained in whispers the finer points. Kallisthenes, sitting among some of the squires he favoured, sniffed at us, and said something that made Hermolaos smirk.

Spring broke at last; huge snow-slides thundered down the mountains; streams turned to brown cataracts, hurling along the wreckage caught in their rush. The best passes opened. Sogdian robbers came out from their dens, awaiting the first caravans, but met with troops instead.

The land seemed quiet under Alexander's garrisons; till news came in that a powerful chief, who the year before had submitted and pledged fealty, was up in arms raising his tribesmen. An old story, except that he owned the Sogdian Rock.

It had the name of the strongest place in Asia; a huge sheer crag, its upper part full of caves. Generations of chiefs had burrowed there; it would hold a small army, with stores for years. They had tanks to catch the snow and rain, and store it against summer. It was reported snow still lay thick there; but the chief had already sent up his warriors, wealth and women, while he himself went rousing the countryside.

Alexander sent to him, offering a parley to his envoys. It was now known that envoys' heads returned from Alexander still on their shoulders; so two swaggering tribesmen came. When he offered free pardon for free surrender, the envoys laughed, and said he could go or stay; he would take the Sogdian Rock on the day his men grew wings.

Calmly he ordered them to be fed, and they took their heads safely home. A Sogdian chief, getting that message, would have left their heads till the last, when they'd have been glad to part with them. Alexander merely decided to have the Rock, if it took a year.

The whole camp marched there. One could see it for miles. Closer up, it really seemed a task for eagles. There was no easy side; it was precipice all round, plunging down to ragged rocks. One could just trace the goat-track the people had gone up by, because it had caught the snow; every yard was commanded by the mouths of the caves above.

The army made camp just out of bowshot. Behind them, the swarm of followers, sutlers and grooms and slaves, merchants and clerks and horse-traders, singers and painters and sculptors, carpenters and tanners, dancers and ironsmiths, jewellers and whores and bawds, spread about the Rock.

People have written of this enterprise, as if the King had been a boy taking up a dare. Of course that was always in him; he would have kept it into old age. But the Rock commanded leagues of country; he could not leave it unconquered in his rear. Also the Sogdians, who understand little except strength, would have despised his power, and cut his cities to bits as soon as he had moved on.

The chief, Oxyartes, did not live in this eyrie in peacetime. His house and his tribal village were at the foot of the trackway. Alexander would not let the soldiers burn them, least it be read as a sign that he meant to give no quarter. In the cave-mouth, little figures, as small as if carved on rings, stood looking down. On the steeps below, where in summer one would not have seen foothold for a rock-rabbit, winter had picked out in white the tiny ledges, or the cracks that gashed the cliffs. It was full moon. Even at night, one saw the gleam of the snow. Alexander rode all round it, looking.

Next morning, he called for a muster of mountaineers. A small crowd reported; mostly hillmen born, who had climbed for him in other sieges. From all who came forward he picked three hundred. To the first man on the summit, he would give twelve talents, riches for life; to the next eleven, and so on for the first twelve. They were to go up that night, by the steepest side, which could not be seen from the caves. Each would carry a wallet of iron tent-pegs, a mallet to drive them in, and a strong light rope, to hitch himself to one peg while he fixed the next.

It was a cold clear night. I had everything ready, but he would not come to bed. This was the first really dangerous action he had not led himself. There could be no leader; each took his own way to the top. He had not the skill. But he could scarcely bear it, not to be risking his neck with them. When they had climbed too high to be seen in the dim light, he came in, but still paced about. 'I saw three fall,' he said. 'We shall never find them for burial. They lodged up there in the snow.' He lay down at last in his clothes, with orders to be called at the first light.

He woke uncalled, while it was still too dark to see much. Some of the officers were waiting for him. The top of the Rock was a dark loom in the faint sky. As its edges sharpened, Alexander stared up devouringly. His eyes were good; but Leonnatos could see far things like a hawk, though when he wanted to read, he had to hold the writing out the length of his arm. He pointed up, and cried, 'They're there! They're signalling!'

The rising light showed them clustered on the blunt summit, as thick as cormorants. They had unrolled the long strips of linen they had carried bound around them; the signals streamed in the breeze.

Alexander stepped out, lifted his shield and flashed it at them. The trumpet squealed under the crags; the big voice of the herald bawled to the defenders to look above them; Alexander had found winged men.

The chief's son, who was in command, at once asked terms of surrender. He could not see how many were up there, or what arms they had, which were none; their pegs and mallets had been enough to carry. Thirty had died, one man in ten. Their graves were the maws of kites; but Alexander gave them a rite of honour, with an empty bier, after the custom of the Greeks.

It took two days for all the people to come down from the Rock with their goods and gear. I wondered how the women could manage the giddy path, in the wide skirts of Sogdiana; but I suppose they had done it often, in the endless tribal wars.

The chief's son, who never learned that the King's eagles had had no claws, came and pledged himself, promising to send a message to his father. To seal their compact, he begged the honour of entertaining the King to a royal feast.

It was agreed, for two days later. I was only afraid they meant to knife him as he sat at meat. It would be nothing much for Sogdians.

I dressed him for it, in the Mitra and his grandest robe. He was in good spirits. Though he grieved for his mountaineers, this stronghold might have cost many hundred lives. The enemy had shed no blood at all, and were grateful enough to promise anything.

'Take care, Al'skander,' I said as I combed his hair. 'He may offer you his daughter, like that Scythian king.'

He laughed. His friends had been very pleasant about the matter, picturing the bride being cut out of the clothes she'd been sewn up in some winters back, having the rancid mares' milk fat scraped from her hair, her vermin picked off, and so on, to make her lovely for the marriage bed.

'If that young man has a daughter, she's under five. You must come to the feast, it should be worth seeing. Put on that new suit of yours.'

The chief's son, Histanes, had certainly spared no pains. A lane of torches led from the camp to his hall. Music came out, quite good for Sogdiana. (I had once heard Alexander compare Persian singing to the yowl of mating cats; but he hadn't known I was listening.) The King was embraced by his host upon the threshold. It was a big hall. Oxyartes must be rich as well as powerful. Hangings of scarlet, stitched with ramping lions and leopards, smouldered in the light of torches enough to warm the air. The high table was set with gold and silver; gums I had not smelled since I left Susa burned in the fretted censers. If some of the Macedonians thought the place would have been worth sacking, they had to keep it to themselves.

The food was good and spicy; the caravans from India pass that way. Alexander and the host had an interpreter standing by them; the other Macedonian guests got along as best they could, letting their dishes be heaped up twice for good manners. Alexander, light eater as he was, performed this duty. He is wishing, I thought, they'd bring on the wine instead.

The sweets came in, and the wine. Histanes and Alexander pledged each other, exchanging compliments; then the interpreter stood forth and addressed us all in Greek. To honour the King, the ladies of the household would appear and dance. This was something indeed, in Sogdiana, where to look at their women is a matter for long knives.

I was at the foot of the table, near the royal squires. Ismenios had moved over to sit by me. His friendliness had increased; if he wished, as I thought, for more, he kept it to himself from loyalty to Alexander. I was his debtor for much kindness, and for smoothing my way with the others when he could.

The Sogdian youth on my other side now addressed me in their uncouth Persian, which I could barely understand. With both hands he drew female curves in the air, smiling and rolling his eyes. I said to Ismenios, 'It seems there's beauty in store.'

'They'll perform up at the top,' he said, 'for the King and generals. Only their backs for us. We must make do with one another.'

The musicians struck up a stately measure; the women entered stepping to the beat, not dancing yet. Their heavy clothes were crusted with embroidery; gold chains, hung with gold pendants, circled their brows; massive rings on their arms and ankles clashed as they moved, or tinkled with little bells. We had hardly glimpsed them before they turned away from us to bow, with arms crossed on their breasts, before the King.

Histanes pointed, no doubt at the chief's close kin, for some of them bowed again. Alexander inclined his head with a glance for each. I thought he paused, once, before his eye moved on. Ismenios said, 'Yes, one of them must be beautiful, to make the King look twice.'

The music quickened; they began to dance.

In Persia, only such women dance as are trained in it to rouse men. This dance was decent and seemly; they hardly showed more than their hennaed feet, as they twirled their heavy skirts and clashed their anklets. Their bending had grace, without invitation; their swaying arms were like rippling barley. But you would be foolish, to call this modest dancing. These ladies were above modesty. Its place was taken by pride.

Ismenios said, 'All very proper. One's own sister could do all that. Maybe we'll have real dancing later. Now *you* could have showed them something.'

I hardly heard him. The women wheeled in slow circles, or joined in a winding chain. Alexander's eyes, as they turned with the wheel or followed the chain along, were always fixed on one link.

He liked all things good of their kind. I had heard him praise a fine woman, often enough. Yet my belly shrank on itself, and my hands grew cold.

He spoke to the interpreter, who pointed questioning. Alexander nodded; he was asking who that one was. Histanes replied, with some increase of dignity. She must be someone of rank; no doubt his sister.

The music grew louder; the line of women turned, and came down the hall. All of us guests must have our share of honour.

I knew at once which she was. Yes, a sister; I saw the likeness, he was a handsome man. She was about sixteen, full womanhood in Sogdiana. Pure ivory, faintly tinted, and not by art; soft hair, blue-black, small fronds brushing her cheeks; a clear forehead under the gold pendants; brows with a perfect arch, over large brilliant eyes. She had the kind of beauty that is famed for leagues around, and made no pretence of not knowing it. Her one defect was that her fingers were not quite long enough, and the ends too pointed. I had learned to look for such things in Darius' harem.

Alexander's eyes were following her still, waiting for her to turn his way again. She passed by me, sitting there in the new suit he had liked so much; and he never saw me.

The Sogdian youth pulled at my sleeve, and said, 'Roxane'.

They danced back to the high table and made sweeping bows. Once more the interpreter hovered. As they turned to go, Histanes beckoned his sister. She came up; Alexander rose to his feet, and took her hands. He spoke and she replied. Her profile, now turned my way, was carved without flaw. When she went out, he stood till she had gone.

Ismenios said, 'Well, one knows one's in Sogdiana. No Persian girl would have done that, would she?'

I answered, 'No.'

'Still, Alexander asked to speak to her. I thought so, didn't you?'

'Yes. I thought so.'

'And sober as a judge. I expect he was just honouring the host. It's true, she's beautiful. Of course she's darker; but she had somehow a look of you.'

'You flatter me.' He had always been kind. He sat there smiling over his wine with his clear blue eyes, his flaxen hair a little damp from the heat, turning the knife in my heart.

Up at the high table, Histanes and the King were busy with the interpreter. Alexander had barely touched his wine. The room grew hot; I loosed the neck of my coat, with its ruby-clustered buttons. The last hand to open it had been his.

I had found him Hephaistion's boy, and with me he had wished for manhood. It had been my pride. So now I had given him to a woman. I sat in the hot torchlight, tasting death, and being pleasant to those around me, as I had been taught when I was twelve years old.

18

In his tent, I awaited his return, listening to my demons.

I answered them: So he has chosen a concubine. Darius had more than three hundred. How am I wronged? Any other king would have been married before he met me; from the first I would have shared him, with who knows how many, awaiting the night of favour.

Oh yes, they answered. But those were the days when you had a master. You have had a lover since then. Get ready, Bagoas, you have felt nothing yet. Wait till he comes to bed. Perhaps he will have her with him.

Perhaps so, I told the demons. But he is my lord whom I was born to follow. He never turns away love; nor can I take it back though it scalds my soul like the Fiery River. Thus it is. So go, and laugh somewhere else.

The feast had been over a long time. Was he still bargaining with her kin? At last I heard him; but he had with him most of his chief generals, the last thing I'd expected. Late as it was, they all came in, and talked in the outer chamber. It was well I listened; I had time to get over the shock of what I heard. At first, I could not believe it.

Hephaistion stayed on last. They talked too quietly for me to overhear. Then he went too, and Alexander came in.

'You shouldn't have waited up. I ought to have sent you word.'

I said it was nothing, and that his bathwater was on the way. He paced about; and no wonder. I knew he would speak before long; he could not keep it in.

'Bagoas.'

'Yes, Alexander.'

'Did you see Oxyartes' daughter, Roxane? She was presented, after the dance.'

'Yes, Alexander. We were all speaking of her beauty.'

'I shall marry her.'

Yes, it was well I was prepared. One more astounded silence would have been too much for his temper, I daresay.

'May you be happy, my lord. She is truly a pearl of light.' A Sogdian! A mere chief's daughter! Useless to hope he had not yet asked for her, and would wake in his right mind tomorrow. I could see it was too late.

He was pleased with my words. I'd had time to get them ready. 'They're all against me,' he said. 'Hephaistion will stand by me; but he's against it too.'

'My lord, they only think no one at all is worthy of you.'

He laughed. 'Oh, no! Some Macedonian girl I never set eyes on, carted out to me hit or miss; *she'd* have been worthy ... Roxane. What does it mean in Persian?'

I answered, 'Little Star.' He was pleased with that.

The bathwater came, and I had a chance to undress him. When the slaves had gone, he said, 'I've known a long time I ought to marry in Asia. It is necessary. The people *must* be reconciled. It can only begin with me. This is the one way left. This, they'll have to accept.'

I said, 'Yes, Alexander', thinking, Suppose they won't?

'But since I knew this, I've not seen a woman I could put up with, until tonight. Have you ever seen her equal?'

'Never, my lord, even among Darius' ladies.' I think this was really true, but for her hands. 'Of course, I never saw the Queen. That would not have been permitted.' I said this to make sure he never brought me into her presence.

'I only saw her once; and again when she was dead. Yes, she was beautiful; like a lily on a tomb. Her daughters were children then. They are older now, but ... Well, they are his too. I will not breed a son from the stock of cowards. This girl has spirit.'

'Without doubt, Alexander. One can see it in her eyes.' *That* was true enough. What sort, was another thing.

He was too restless to sleep, but paced about in his bath-robe, running on about the wedding, how he was sending word to Oxyartes her father, and so on. Strange to say, I found comfort in it. He would never had made me listen to all this if he meant to send me away; it was not in him. I could see such a thought had never entered his head.

Of course, he knew it was the girl he desired at present; but it was not from carelessness he did not know my pain. Affection ran deeper in him than passion, always. He had given it to Philotas, whose treachery had cut him like a lover's. He had given it to me, and still felt true to it. Suddenly I wondered if Hephaistion had felt as I did.

At last I got him to bed. It was not far short of morning. 'Bless you, in the name of both our gods. You are the only one who has understood.' He drew down my head and kissed me. The held-back tears flooded my eyes; but I got out before he knew it.

Oxyartes came in a few days later, to make peace. Of course Alexander did not give him back the Rock, which he meant to garrison; but the chief had made a pretty good bargain, if his grandson was to be Great King. When he got the news that Alexander meant to marry the girl, whom any other victor on earth would have taken as prize of war, I expect he could not believe his ears.

The wedding feast, now preparing, looked like making the last one seem a mere family supper. The kindred had been summoned, they were decking the bridal room. All I wished to know was what Alexander meant to do with her when he moved on. Sogdian women are not like ours. What if she expected to live with him in his tent, doing everything for him, only going inside when men appeared; seeing no reason for my presence but as her servant? If he lets that happen, I thought, it will be a good time to die.

Then appeared a fine new tent, and a splendid wagon, roofed and curtained with embroidered leather. My heart revived.

He called me to him and laid a hand on my shoulder. 'Will you do me a kindness?' 'How can you ask?' 'Come to Roxane's tent, and tell me what is wanting. I don't know much of these things. I have taken advice; but these people never lived at court.'

I smiled back at him and he led me in. I could have told him this Sogdian girl had never guessed such splendours existed, and would not know the use of half the toilet things. But I went gravely round, spoke well of orange-flower water if it could be obtained, and said nothing else was lacking. The bed was very grand, in the heavy style of the province. There came back to me the scent of cedar-wood, and the salt breeze of Zadrakarta.

As the day approached, it was clear the Sogdians were happy, but no one else was. Macedonians of rank took it very ill. If he had traded the girl for her brother's life, and had her dragged to his tent, it would have been a trifle; a scream or two would have been worth some bawdy jokes. But marriage, that affronted their victor's status. If he'd first taken a Macedonian Queen, and added this girl as a minor wife (his father, so they said, had had many such) they would not have grumbled. As it was, many had daughters at home, whom they thought should have been preferred. They were only kept quiet by his not conferring the rank of Queen on her. I was pleased to see he was not so far gone as that.

As for the men, all soldiers like oddities in a leader they admire; they like him to be a legend. They were used to the Persian dancing-boy; if he'd had no one for his bed, they'd have wondered what was wrong with him. But this was another thing. They had fought to subdue Sogdiana, because he said it was necessary; now it was rumoured he thought of India. They started wondering if he meant to go home at all. He had spread his wings; the whole earth was his home. But they thought of their villages, the hills where they'd herded goats in boyhood, and Macedonian children by Macedonian wives.

Whatever we all thought, the day arrived, true to its time as death. While I dressed him for the feast, he smiled to himself, as if now it was come he hardly believed it could be happening. A crowd of his friends came in, to wish him joy in the usual way. It pleased them when he did not put on the Mitra – he was taking a wife, not a Queen – and the jokes grew lively. Nobody noticed me; except that once Hephaistion glanced my way when he thought I did not see; in curiosity, or triumph, or pity, there was not time to guess.

The feast began; a blaze of light and heat and gold and colour, reeking with roast meats; the great barbaric heaps of the bride-goods on their stands; bridegroom and bride enthroned. It was a fine still night; all the flames burned upright. There was deafening music, everyone shouting over it. The bride looked about with her glowing eyes, as if no one had ever taught her to cast them down; till Alexander spoke to her through the interpreter, when she turned them upon him.

They brought in the ritual loaf, for him to divide with his sword. He broke off a piece from her half, gave it her to eat, and tasted his own. They were now man and wife. We all rose to our feet to cheer them. My throat closed; I could not utter a sound. The torches stifled me and burned my eyes. Yet I kept my place, ashamed to be seen going. If I stayed much longer, they would be bedding the bride.

In the shoving crowd, a hand slid under my arm. Without turning, I knew it was Ismenios.

'She is beautiful,' I said. 'Are you envying the bridegroom?'

'No,' he said in my ear. 'But I did before.'

I leaned a little nearer. It seemed to happen of itself, like blinking against dust. He eased me from the press. We found coat and cloak in the heap outside, and went out under the cold Sogdian stars.

It was nearly as bright outside as in; great cressets flaring everywhere, and a horde of tribesmen gorging on whole carcasses, spitting over the fires; singing, roaring, bragging, setting their dogs to fight each other, dancing in rings. However, they were all where the food and drink was; we soon got free of them.

No snow had fallen since before the siege; the ground had dried. We found a round hidden place among the boulders, and he spread his cloak. The grass had been well pressed down; I expect the whole village went there. I did not say so to Ismenios, who thought it a paradise created for us alone.

It surprised him how quickly I divined his wishes. I don't know why; they were nothing out of the way. I'd have thought myself lucky, any afternoon in Susa, to get such an easy client. He was eager to please, and I to be pleased by almost anything. Oromedon would have warned me what to expect; I had almost forgotten those early days. 'It comes of anger, and the soul's resistance.' When I caught my breath, Ismenios thought it was from rapture, and was happy. He had been a good friend, when other squires were plaguing me. I had learned young how to give thanks to those who did not ill-use me.

I don't know how long we were there; it felt like half the night. He had wanted me for a year, and seemed a stranger to fatigue. At last, after we had lain awhile under my coat, we agreed the night grew too cold to stay.

A late waning moon was up. Ismenios gazed at it floating beside the Rock; I leaned upon his shoulder. Making sure he got all he wanted had given me something to think about, which was worth as much to me as any of it to him. I said, 'We have dreamed, dear friend. Another time, we might awaken. Let it be a dream forgotten at morning.' That seemed a better way of saying it than, 'Never remind me of this, for fear I should stick a knife in you.'

He put an arm round my waist. A handsome youth; it had not always been my lot to pick and choose. Speaking quite sensibly – indeed he had never been stupid – he said, 'I promise. Never a word, not even if we're alone. I'm lucky having it to remember. Of course, he'll want you back. Anyone would.'

Up the Rock, a great fire leaped in the cave-mouth. Even on his wedding night, Alexander was not so besotted as to leave the place ungarrisoned; but had sent them plenty of good cheer to keep the feast.

In the hall there was lazy broken singing, from those guests who always linger till morning, to see the bride-sheet displayed. For the first time, I started wondering how he'd fared. He must be very much out of practice, if indeeed he'd ever been in it, and a virgin of sixteen would not be much help. For a moment my demons, returning, made me wish him to fail, and seek me for consolation. Then I thought what it would do to him, who had never known defeat; so I caught back my evil wish and killed it. When Ismenios had left me with speaking eyes, and gone to bed, I stayed, lost in the crowd, till daylight came with music, and some well-born old crone appeared to flap the sheet at us. It bore the red badge of victory. Alexander was still unconquered.

Next day, there was so much ceremony that I scarcely saw him, except when he came to his tent to change his clothes. He seemed pleased with himself (from bliss or from achievement who could say?) and looked brisk and fresh. Ismenios was on duty with blue lines under his eyes, and a soft secret smile he took care not to turn on me.

The bride was being visited by a hundred women; you could hear the chatter in the bride-room from out of doors. Not having travelled deaf in Darius' harem wagons, I knew the questions, and wondered how she replied.

I never went near the door, but would send a servant to leave his morning clothes with the eunuch there, or take away his supper-robe. One must start as one means to go on.

When he came for his bath at evening, I felt as I sluiced him down that I washed her off him; to such follies will jealousy bring the heart. Suddenly he said, 'I shall have to have her taught Greek.'

'Yes, Alexander.' How had he managed without speech? I had cured his old sadness – perhaps for good, perhaps not – by coaxing, gossiping, confiding, telling secrets or old tales. He loved a spell of this, before he was ready again. Sometimes he would just fall asleep to the sound of my voice; it was all one to me, so long as he kept me by him. Now there was this girl, without a word to say to him, just lying waiting for more.

'Your teacher, Philostratos, do you think he'd do?'

'None better,' I said, delighted to enrich him after all his kindness. 'And he has picked up a little Persian, from teaching me.'

'She doesn't understand mine.' Sogdian is to pure Persian as Macedonian is to Greek. He went on quickly, 'Yes, he seems just the man.'

'Not Kallisthenes?' I said, recalling an old joke; but he said unsmiling, 'When iron floats. He is taking more on himself than will do him good.'

I should have thought. Anyone could guess what Kallisthenes would say of barbarian weddings, and half-Sogdian heirs being bred to rule over Greeks.

'He must have written by now to Aristotle. Well, I have written too. The old man must try to understand what I am doing.'

'Yes, Alexander.' There was a purple bruise on his neck. She must have bitten him. How did that go, I wondered; it was not in his style at all.

However it went, a week had not gone by before, hearing of a tribe that had refused submission, he was off upon campaign. Since the rebels lived no great way off, he said it was not worthwhile to move the court, nor tire the Lady Roxane with rough travel over winter passes; he would soon be back.

At this news, I sat down to think.

If I just packed and assumed that I was going, he would quite likely take me along, I would be there, she not; what could be better? Well, perhaps one thing. What if we see who is missed the most? A big stake, upon one throw of the dice. All the same, I'll throw.

So I assumed I was to be left, as often before, and he marched away. As his long train vanished over the passes, I would have taken back my stake again. But it was down.

If I'd gone, he would not have had much time for me. The rebels lived in a rock-fort, with a great ravine before it, supposed to make it impregnable. Alexander spent about three parts of a month, in terrible weather, getting the ravine filled up, till he could bridge the gorge. Since no one inside had ever thought of such a thing being possible, they were much put out when arrows began to hit them, while their own, aimed at the working parties, fell on thick bull-hide screens. They sent down a herald, asking for Oxyartes to act as envoy.

Alexander sent for him; I think he was some kin to the chief. He went up, reported his daughter's marriage, declared Alexander both invincible

and merciful. The chief surrendered, invited Alexander into his stronghold, provisioned the army from his stores laid up for the siege; was
confirmed in his rank and given his fortress back. Thus the war ended.

Meantime, still at my Greek with Philostratos, I could not keep from
asking him how he got on in the harem. He said he had to teach in the
presence of two old women, the girl's three sisters, and a eunuch armed
to the teeth. 'You don't know when you're well off,' I said. 'Oxyartes
wanted to have you cut, before you were let inside.' I laughed aloud at
his courteous efforts to control his face. 'Don't worry, Alexander was very
firm. And how are the lessons going?'

He said the lady was eager to learn, even to impatience. On this he
looked uneasy, and quickly opened our book.

Soon after, the chief eunuch of Oxyartes' harem came seeking me. His
condescension surprised me; though unpolished, he was very pompous;
but his errand surprised me more. It was a summons to see the Lady
Roxane.

So, then, she knew. Never mind whether through spiteful tattle, or from
sending out spies herself; she knew.

Of course I was not going near her, now more than ever. I said I was
in despair that I could not rejoice my eyes with her gracious presence; but
I dared not attend the harem without the King's command. He nodded
gravely. It is not usual, anywhere, to bring people of my looks into a
harem, even when cut; Darius had never sent me once without him. I
could see the eunuch uneasy with his errand. Perhaps, I asked, he could
tell me why his lady had wished to see me?

'As I understand,' he said, looking me up and down, 'she wished to ask
why, since you are a dancer, you would not dance at her wedding, to bring
good fortune to her and to your master?'

'Dance at her wedding?' I must have stared like a fool. 'It is the custom
of our country,' he said, 'for a eunuch to do so, in woman's dress.'

'You may tell your lady that I did not refuse to dance; the King did not
command me. It is not a custom of his people.' Someone must have
performed after I left the hall. So he had crossed her will on his wedding
eve, rather than give me pain. Had she known then, already?

He came back soon after.

His fore-runners came at noon, he himself at sunset. No doubt he
excused himself to Oxyartes on account of his late return; he dined in
camp, with a few friends and the officers he'd had with him.

They did not sit long over the wine. They fought the campaign over,
debating how long it would have taken if the garrison had held out; then
he said he was going to bed. Nobody asked him where.

He came inside. I had everything ready as he liked it. He greeted me with a kiss, and it was a little more than a greeting; but I did not presume on that. What if he goes over there, I thought, as soon as he has bathed? I will not invite the cruelties of hope.

I bathed him; I rubbed him dry. Would he ask for fresh clothes? No. I turned back the bed for him.

Going about the sleeping-place, folding his things, kindling the night-lamp and putting out the great one, I felt his eyes. At last I ceased to rebuke my heart for singing. All the same, he would have to ask.

I stood the night-lamp by the bed, and said, 'Is there anything else, my lord?' He answered, 'You know well.'

As his arm received me, he gave a little sigh; just as when he came back from a fight and a long ride, dusty and bruised, and found his bath just right for him. A hundred verses of tenderest love, sung to the lute, could not have given me half the joy.

Next day, he set about the great pile of business that had come in while he was gone; envoys from cities of western Asia, men who'd ridden for leagues with grievances against satraps; letters from Greece, from Macedon, from his new cities. He was at it all day and on into the night. I don't know if he got in a courtesy call at the harem. At night he just dropped into bed and slept.

The day after, I heard that someone was asking for me at my tent. Here a young boy, whom I'd never seen, put in my hands an inlaid silver dish. Lifting the lid, he showed it was full of sweetmeats; with a slip of parchment in a fine Greek script. It read A GIFT FROM ALEXANDER.

I gazed in surprise. When I looked again for the boy, he'd gone.

I took the dish inside. Though I knew all his things, it was new to me. It was costly, but unrefined in style; it would have been thrown out of doors at Susa. It looked to me like Sogdian work.

The note was odd. He used no ceremony with me. Anything like this, he'd just send by a servant, whom I would know, with a message by mouth that he hoped I would enjoy it. The writing was delicate, nothing like his impatient hand. Recognition came to me. I thought that I understood.

I went out, and threw a sweet to the wretchedest of the pi-dogs that hung about the camp. He followed me in the hope of more. In my tent I gave him half the dishful. I had no need to tie him; the poor mangy creature sat down on my carpet, believing that at last he'd found a master to care for him. When he jerked about, and died with yellow foam upon his jaws, I felt like a host who has murdered a trusting guest.

I stared at the corpse, and thought of what I had planned once at Zadrakarta. Who was I to be angry? But at least I had not done it.

He will have to know, I thought; and not only because I want to go on living. Who can tell what next? By now, I doubt if the shock will kill him.

I went to his tent as his day's business was done, showed him the dish and told my story. He listened in silence, only his eyes looking deeper-set. 'This came in the dish, Alexander,' I said, and handed him the writing.

He took it between finger and thumb, as if it were poisoned too. 'Who wrote this? This is a scholar's hand.'

'My lord, it was Philostratos.' He stared at me. I said, 'I showed it him and he owned it freely. He could not understand how I came to have it. He wrote out a dozen, he said, for the Lady Roxane, to put in her chest with your wedding gifts to her. What must have happened,' I said, looking down, 'is that someone stole it.' I added, 'I told him nothing, my lord; I thought it best.'

He nodded, frowning. 'Yes, say nothing more to him. I shall not have him questioned.' He covered the dish and put it in a coffer. 'Eat only from the common table till I give you word. Drink nothing that has stood in your tent unwatched. Tell no one. I shall see to this myself.'

It was remarked that the King found leisure that afternoon to visit the harem. He was gone some time, which all thought proper in a bridegroom. At bedtime he said, 'You can feel safe now; I've dealt with it.'

I thought that would be all; but presently he said, 'We are bound in love; you have a right to know. Come and sit here.' I sat by him on the bed. He was tired, it would be a night for sleep. 'I took the sweets to her, and I could see she knew them. I offered her one, smiling at first. When she refused, I looked angry, and made as if to force her. She did not plead, she flung them down and trampled them. She has spirit, at least.' He spoke not without approval.

'But the time had come to tell her what she must not do. And here I met a difficulty. I could not bring in an interpreter to hear of such a business. The only one I could have trusted would have been yourself, and that would have been too much. She is, after all, my wife.'

I agreed that this was so. There was a lengthening silence. At last I dared to say, 'So, my lord, how did you manage?'

'I beat her. It was necessary. Nothing else was possible.'

Deprived of speech, I looked about the room. What had he used? He did not own a whip. Neither Oxhead nor Peritas had known the touch of one. But there it was on the table, with ten years' wear on it, borrowed, as I guessed, from a huntsman. She must have been awed by the use that it had seen.

Since there was nothing at all that could be said, I held my peace.

'She thought the more of me. I hadn't considered that.'

So that was why he'd been so long gone! I pulled my face straight in time. 'My lord, the Sogdian ladies have a great regard for strength.'

He eyed me sideways, considering whether he could permit himself to share the joke, and deciding it would be improper. I rose gravely and smoothed the bedclothes. 'Sleep well, Al'skander. You have laboured and earned your rest.'

Later I thought about it. He was warm, not hot; gentle, in giving and taking; his pace was slow, he liked the pauses of tenderness. I'm sure he had never asked himself whether we suited so well because I was what I was. I could imagine the care he would take with a young maiden. So now he knew that she'd simply thought him soft.

Soon after this, the camp was struck. The bride bade her kin farewell, and was received into her wagon-train. We were bound west for Baktria, to put the province in order. Some of its satraps and governors had failed their trust; and all must be left secure, before the march to India.

19

He visited his new cities, heard causes, removed a governor here and there who was extortionate, corrupt or weak. Except for a few short forays, against robber bands that were preying on the trade-roads, the court went with him. Now, beside the usual horde, there was the long wagon-train of Roxane, with her ladies and maids and eunuchs.

At first, he used to visit her pretty often, mostly in the afternoon. It soon appeared that he did not like sleeping the night there. He liked to have his own things around him, among them me; to retire late if he wished, and sleep on undisturbed next morning. In the afternoon, he could exchange civilities in such Greek as the lady had, perform his husband's duty, and go away.

She was not with child. Such things are not long a secret. Those who had known him from a boy in Macedon, said he had never yet had offspring; but then, they added, he had never cared for women, so that meant little.

No doubt her kin awaited the news with eagerness; but I saw none elsewhere. The Macedonians had not grown to love the Sogdians, having found them brave, but cruel, and not averse to treachery. True, the King was now kin to half the noble Sogdians, and the province was at peace. But the soldiers, who wanted no Sogdian heir to rule their sons, were hoping she would be barren.

Still they followed him. He drew them as a comet draws its tail, by his light and fire. Besides, he was head of their family. They could come to him as if to their tribal chief at home. Half his business was about their affairs. All who had campaigned with him, Macedonian, hired Greek, wild painted Thracian, knew some tale like that about the frozen soldier he'd set in his own chair by the fire. And he was undefeated. That above all.

As for me, my grief was healing. True, when he'd been with her he had nothing for me but his love; but I could live well on that, and I guessed my fasts would shorten. She tired him out. I could tell, though he never said so. He did two men's work, a king's and a general's; often enough a fighting soldier's as well. I had always been content with whatever the day's toil left him; he could come to me for a little drowsy pleasure, given with love, followed by rest; and I would slip away to let him sleep at ease. I don't think in the harem tent it was quite so simple. Perhaps the beating had raised false hopes.

Little by little, at any rate, his visits grew less frequent; or he was out again in barely the time it needed to ask after her health.

Philostratos had a box of new books, just come from Ephesus. He had been too poor to order from a good copying-house, and pay the costly cartage, till I'd asked Alexander to make him that first present. He unpacked them like an eager child; now, he said, we could read Greek verse.

It was strange, after the Persian; sparer in language, stricter in form; but in time yielding up its treasures. When I first read the entrance of Hippolytos, offering his mountain flowers to the pure goddess he alone can see, my eyes ran over. Philostratos, somewhat awkwardly, patted my hand, supposing I wept for my former life – who knows, perhaps even for my present one.

Not all my thoughts were on Euripides. In the next tent – the camp slaves always pitched them the same way – Kallisthenes taught the squires. I heard things as I passed; even where I sat, if he forgot to keep his voice down.

Ismenios, though he had kept his word with honour, would talk to me when he could. One day I asked him what he thought of the lessons. He laughed. 'I've not been for a three-month. I got sick and tired of them.'

'Truly? When I missed you, I thought you must be on duty. Do you mean he's never told on you? You could be punished, surely?'

'Oh, yes. I suppose he's glad to be rid of me; he thinks I'm too stupid for philosophy. It's all we get now; meaning his opinions, of which I've had enough. When first we joined, we used to learn something useful.'

Too stupid, or too loyal? Yes, maybe his absence was welcome. He was simple, compared with me who had served at Susa. Hearing what he disliked, he went away, when I would have stayed to listen.

My Greek was so fluent now, that Alexander was telling me not quite to lose my Persian accent, which he had grown fond of. But if Kallisthenes passed, I was always mute. It pleased him that a young barbarian could not master the tongue of Zeus' chosen race. I don't suppose it entered his head that Alexander ever *talked* to me.

I was indeed scarcely worth attention. The Persian boy was an old story; nothing in outrage, compared with the Sogdian wife.

Since the wedding, Kallisthenes had flaunted his austerity. He had been absent from the feast, pleading sickness, though he was about next day. Alexander, still willing to patch things up, even asked him to supper later, but got the same excuse. Few people were asking him anywhere; he was dour company and killed the mirth. Had I known it then, he was acting the new Athenian philosopher (old Sokrates, they say, was a good man at a party); and if I'd known more of Greece, perhaps I'd have guessed why. Even in my ignorance, I thought he called for watching, and would dawdle as I passed his class. For certain matters, he used a different voice.

Spring had broken. White flowers scented like jasmine opened on wayside thorns; lilies grew by the streams. Icy winds still whistled down the gorges. I remember a night when Alexander and I lay wound together; he disapproved of extra blankets, which he thought were softening, but did not object to me.

'Al'skander,' I said, 'who were Harmodios and Aristogeiton?'

'Lovers,' he said sleepily. 'Famous Athenian lovers. You must have seen their statues on the terrace at Susa. Xerxes took them from Athens.'

'The ones with the daggers? The man and boy?'

'Yes. It's in Thukydides ... What's the matter?'

'What were the daggers for?'

'Killing the tyrant Hippias. Though they never did it. They only got his brother, which made him more tyrannical.' He roused himself to tell the story. 'But they died with honour. The Athenians set great store by them. I'll send them back sometime. Very old statues. Stiff. The beautiful Harmodios, he's not fit to do up your shoes.'

He would be asleep in a few more moments. 'Al'skander, I heard Kallisthenes telling the squires they killed the tyrant, and it was a noble work.'

'Did he? Thukydides says it's a common error in Athens. There's an old song. I've heard it, about how they freed the city.'

I did not say, 'He spoke in a different voice.' I had seen conspiracy at Ekbatana; I had felt it first with my skin; I thought that I felt it now. But though I spoke the language, I had not yet learned its little mysteries, the changes of note, the pauses, where secrets show.

'Well, don't kill him.' He ran his hand over me laughing. 'Aristotle would never forgive me.' A draught came down the bed; we closed in a tighter knot. He had done three men's work that day, and was soon asleep.

A half-month later, while I combed his hair before supper, I told him that Kallisthenes had singled out Hermolaos and was forever in his company out of lesson-time. He replied that it was a pity, but love is blind.

'It's not love. Sostratos is his lover. I've watched him, he doesn't mind. Sometimes he's there too.'

'So? I've been wondering what has gone wrong with their manners. That must be Kallisthenes. He never did know the difference between civility and servility. How tedious the man is. But he's a southern Greek, you must remember. Six generations they've prided themselves on never owning a master; it's destroyed half their greatest men. Xerxes got down as far as Attica, only because they wouldn't follow one leader. That's why my father too could have sacked Athens if he'd wanted, and so could I. But between Xerxes and us, three generations, till envy wrecked them again, they were truly great, and Athens was the heart of it. I've only been there once. But one feels it still.'

'Al'skander, do you never comb it through when you're away? Underneath it's all in knots. If Kallisthenes hates a master, why did he come?'

'Because my father re-founded Aristotle's home town as a fee for tutoring me. It was burned out in the Thracian wars when I was a boy; so was Olynthos, where Kallisthenes comes from. He thinks he's worth as much, though he's never said so. But why Aristotle sent him, was to keep me Greek. That's the real reason.'

His hair was done, but I played with it to keep him talking.

'Ochos killed his best friend by torture, a man he'd studied with. He got the news in Macedon. "Never forget," he said to me, "to treat Greeks as men, and barbarians as cattle created for men's use." ' He laid my hand to his cheek.

'A great mind; but it's never followed me here. I write to him; I tell him each time I found a city, because he taught me civics and law. But I disappoint him. He can't see why, with a shake-up of Baktrians and Thracians and paid-off Macedonians and a few landless Greeks, I have to leave them a garrison and a code, not a constitution. The Greek cities of Asia, there I could make democracies; they understand it. But one must have justice, before all . . . I still send him gifts. I never forget my debt to him. I even put up with Kallisthenes, though he'll never know what it costs me.'

I said, 'I hope, my lord, he will never cost you more. It is time you had your hair cut.' He never had it curled, and left it to hang in careless locks like a lion's mane; but he had it cut with care, to keep its shape. In early days, I stole a piece from the barber's cloth. I have it now, in a little golden box. It is still as bright as the gold.

I said no more. If I made myself tiresome, he would listen less. His patience was shorter, on the days when he'd been to the harem.

With the spring, we moved our camp higher up the hills, to a slope by a tumbling river, clothed in a forest of ancient cedars. Even at noon the sun was sifted and mild. Anemones grew there. The stones in the clear brown stream were like polished bronze. The scent of the cedars bettered Arabian spices; their sheddings gave to the tread like harem carpets. It was a place for happiness.

Though the forest was a paradise to ride in, I still found time for my Greek, and for watching Kallisthenes and his favourite pupils.

He never, of course, had all the squires at once. Some were on duty, the night-guard would be sleeping. They were assigned to their watches, though Alexander was not strict if they asked to change. Hermolaos and Sostratos had been let serve together. It was their watch that Kallisthenes took trouble with.

I've thought of him often, since I lived in Egypt and read more books. He saw himself as a Greek philosopher; he knew, as I do now, that old Sokrates would never have made prostration; nor would Plato. But Alexander would no more have asked it of *them*, than he would of Aristotle if he'd made the journey. My lord recognized greatness of heart and honoured it, as later he showed in India. He did not honour Kallisthenes, who had first flattered, then insulted him. Why should he? There are always men who take their own measure against greatness and hate it, not for what it is, but for what they are. They can envy even the dead.

So much Alexander saw. He did not understand, since it was not in him, the power such men have to rouse in others the sleeping envy they once had a decent shame of; to turn respect for excellence into hate. Nor did Kallisthenes understand it in himself. Vanity begets it, vanity covers it up.

Did he see he was unlike his followers, almost their opposite? He looked back to a greater Greece long dead. To these Macedonian youths, Greece was just a name; he was something new, a fashion in defiance.

Certainly both Hermolaos and Sostratos showed it, and they were making their mark on others. Alexander was taking notice. The squires' privilege was that they served directly under the King; no one else could punish them. Sostratos was reprimanded and put on extra guard; Hermolaos was cautioned.

They were at the end of their term of service; as soon as a new batch arrived from Macedon, they would be relieved. They were not boys being watched for awkwardness, but men, for insubordination; this they knew. An uneasy time. Alexander, when he gave me one of his many presents, said, 'But for you, I'd be putting up with those louts in here.'

So things stood, when he went up the mountain hunting.

I loved the hunt, though I never killed much; the rough ride, the keen upland air, the tall hounds finding and baying; the waiting tiptoe at the covert, to see what would come out. From tusk-roughened bark and droppings, we knew this time; it would be boar.

One side of the range was bare, the other full of wooded folds and hollows. In a shade sweet with crushed flowers, the hounds bayed in the thick covert, rank for them with boar-scent. Alexander gave his horse to a squire; all the men dismounted. I too, though I was terribly scared of boar. They can knock you over, and tusk you open as you fall; if I got one on my spear I could never hold it. Well, I thought, if I die, he will remember me forever beautiful. And not a coward.

The men stood straddled firmly, spears levelled, knees bent a little to take the shock if the boar should break their way. The hounds were slipped into the covert. The squires stood near the King, a custom brought from Macedon.

Something black shot out; there were furious grunting squeals. Perdikkas had killed. He was briefly cheered; the hounds were still working within. The noise came the King's way; he smiled with eagerness, like a boy. Finding my own teeth clenched together, I made myself smile too.

A tusked snout pushed forth; a great boar stood at bay, a little sideways from Alexander, staring at the invaders of its home, choosing an enemy. Alexander, moving springily, stepped forward lest it should charge a squire. But at the moment the boar broke out, Hermolaos ran forward, and took it on his spear.

It was unheard-of insolence. Alexander would have yielded the game to any friend who had right of place when it broke; but the squires were only there to attend him, as they were in battle.

The boar had been badly struck, and fought fiercely. Alexander, himself not moving, signed to the other squires to help. When the bloody, untidy work was done, he beckoned Hermolaos. He came defiant, to meet eyes he'd seen in displeasure, but never before in anger. He paled. It was not a sight to forget.

'Go back to camp. Return your horse to the lines. Go to your quarters. Stay there till you are sent for.'

There was a hush among the rest. 'Return your horse' meant he was to be dismounted; a squire's greatest disgrace, save one.

We moved to another wood, and the hunt continued. I think we ran down a stag. Then we went back. Alexander never liked putting off.

That afternoon he had all the squires paraded; a good many, when one saw all the watches together. He told them he knew who was giving good service, and they had nothing to fear. Some had grown slack and impudent; they had been warned already, in vain. He gave out the offence of Hermolaos, who had been brought under guard, and asked him what he had to say.

I've been told that in Macedon, no youth comes of age till he has taken a boar alone. (It was a man as well, in King Philip's day.) I don't know if Hermolaos had this in mind; certainly Alexander imposed no such condition. At all events, Hermolaos said, 'I remembered I am a man.'

I too remembered something; Kallisthenes exhorting his class to remember they were men, and using his different voice. I don't know if Alexander guessed whence the words had come. He just said, 'Very good. Then you are fit to take a man's punishment. Twenty lashes, tomorrow at sunrise. The corps will attend to witness it. Dismiss.'

I thought, If Sostratos is anything of a lover, it will be worse for him. Well, he should not have encouraged his friend in insolence; he is the elder.

All the same, having myself seen wounds and pain in the body that I loved, I could not help but pity him.

It was the first time a squire had been flogged in Alexander's reign. He bore it quite well. The lash did not lay him open to the bone, as I'd seen it done at Susa; but it cut him, and I daresay he didn't know it could be worse. It would scar him, a disgrace whenever he stripped for exercise. A Persian could have kept it hidden.

I saw Kallisthenes put his hand on Sostratos' shoulder. A kindly gesture; but Sostratos, with eyes only for his beloved, could not see the face behind him. There was pleasure in it. Not a relishing of the pain, but the look of one who sees events fall out as he would wish.

Well, I thought, if he hopes this will turn the soldiers against the King, he's a fool; they understand discipline. I did not think it worth mentioning to Alexander; especially as things seemed to get better afterwards. The lessons I overheard were nothing out of the way; the different voice had gone. Perhaps he repented having harmed his pupil. Hermolaos, when after his cuts had scabbed he returned to duty, had become very correct; Sostratos also.

It was about this time, that the Syrian soothsayer began to hang about the King.

She had followed the camp for months, a little brown thing, young-old, in tattered clothes stitched with gold thread, and tawdry beads. She had a familiar spirit, and would wander about till he pointed out a man to her. Then she would tell him she'd luck to give him, for a loaf or a silver bit. They laughed at first, till they saw that those who gave, got the luck she promised. She would not divine for everyone; her Master must show the man. She came to be thought well-omened, and never starved. But once, some drunk bullies baited her; she was frightened at first, then looked at the leader suddenly, as if she'd only just seen him, and said. 'You will die about noon, the third day of this moon's waning.' He fell in a skirmish, on the day. After that she was left in peace.

Once or twice she had offered Alexander luck for nothing. He'd laughed, made her a gift, and not stopped to listen. You were pretty safe in prophesying him victory; but later, when he'd stayed for a word or two, he found small things she foretold fell pat, and would hear her out. With his gold, she bought herself a new gaudy dress; but as she slept in it, it soon looked much like the old one.

Of a morning, I used to enter the King's tent by the back way, that went straight into the sleeping-place. (It had been made for Darius, to bring in his women quietly.) One day I found her there, squatting cross-legged outside. The squires had not turned her off, because Alexander had told them not to. 'Why, Mother,' I said, 'have you been here all night? You look like it.'

She roused herself, and shook the coins in her ears, two that Alexander had given her. 'Yes, little son.' (I was a full head taller.) 'Master sent me. But now he says it's not yet.'

'Never mind, Mother. When the luck-day comes, you know the King will listen. Go along and sleep.'

About a month after the boar-hunt, Perdikkas gave a party for Alexander.

It was a big one; all his best friends; also their mistresses, if they were suitable; meaning as a rule Greek hetairas of good standing. There were of course no Persians. A Persian gentleman would rather die than show in public the very least of his concubines; even Macedonians who had ladies taken in conquered cities, did not put them to this disgrace. Alexander would not have allowed it.

Through the open tent-flap I saw Ptolemy's Thais, crowned with roses, sitting on his supper-couch near Alexander. She was an old friend, almost of his boyhood, having been Ptolemy's mistress before he crossed to Asia; being then quite young, she was in full beauty still. Ptolemy kept her almost like a wife, though not so strictly, which, after her fame in Corinth, she would not have endured. Alexander had always got on well with her. She was the girl who'd called to him, at Persepolis, to burn the palace.

He was dressed all Greek tonight, in a blue robe trimmed with gold, and a wreath of gold leaves, into which I had stuck fresh flowers for him. I thought, He has never been ashamed of me. I might be sharing his couch, if it weren't that he knows it would grieve Hephaistion. Already it was growing easier to forget Roxane. Hephaistion I never forgot.

Alexander had told me not to wait up. Yet in his tent I dragged out my little tasks. I felt an odd guilt at the thought of leaving, though, as I'd first watched the feast, it was already late.

Round the tent the night-guard was on duty, the usual watch of six; Hermolaos, Sostratos, Antikles, Epimenes, and a couple more. Antikles had changed over from another watch just lately. I stood in the back entry, smelling the night, hearing the hum of the camp, a dog baying – not Peritas, whom I'd left fast asleep inside – and the laughter from the feast. Light from the open tent slanted between the cedars.

The women were leaving. They squealed and giggled as the soft cedar-mast tripped their tipsy feet. Their torch-bearers led them off among the trees. In the tent, someone plucked a lyre, and they started singing.

Held by the beauty of the night, the flitting lights and the music, I lingered, I don't know how long. Suddenly Hermolaos was by me. I'd not heard him, on the soft ground. 'Are you waiting up, Bagoas? The King said he'd be very late.' In the past, he'd have put a sneer in it; now he spoke very pleasantly. I thought again how his manners had improved.

I was saying I was off to bed, when I saw a torch approaching. I must have dreamed a good while. It was lighting Alexander. Perdikkas and Ptolemy and Hephaistion were seeing him home. They looked steady enough on their feet, and were all laughing together.

Glad to have waited, I was about to go inside, when I saw in the jumping torchlight the Syrian woman. She came flitting along, like a night-owl, to Alexander; tugged at his robe, and reached up to straighten his chaplet. 'What now, Mother?' he said smiling. 'I've had my luck for tonight.'

'Oh, no, my King!' She grabbed him again with her little nut of a fist. 'No, child of fire! My Master sees you, he sees your best luck to come. Go back to the feast, rejoice till sun-up, your life's best luck is there for you. There's none for you here, my darling, none here at all.'

'You see?' said Perdikkas. 'Come back and bring luck to *us*.' Alexander looked at them laughing. 'The gods give good advice. Who's for a dip in the river, before we start again?'

'Not you,' Hephaistion said. 'It's snow-water, like the Kydnos, and you know that nearly killed you. Let's go and sing.'

They all went back, except Ptolemy and Leonnatos, who were on bodyguard duty next morning. Returning to the tent, I saw the squires had left their stations and were in a huddle, muttering. Slack discipline, I thought. Well, I'm for bed.

Yet still I did not go. After the soothsayer, the night now felt uncanny. I did not like her saying there was no luck for Alexander here. I went in. The squires still had their heads together; anyone could have entered, like me, unseen. I thought, They'll never make soldiers.

At the bed's foot, Peritas lay stretched out snoring. He was a dog who dreamed, jerking his paws, and with soft squeaks chasing his dream-quarry. But he was still, and never raised his head for me.

I will watch, I thought, for my lord's bad luck, since not even the dog is doing it. I rolled in my blanket, in a corner out of the way, in case the King's friends came in with him. The cedar-mast made the floor soft as a mattress. I closed my eyes.

I awoke to daylight. Alexander was there. The tent seemed full of people. They were the squires of the night-guard; why? Their watch ended at dawn. He was speaking to them with great kindness, saying he understood what they'd done, and here was something to mark it. He gave each a gold piece and a smile, and sent them off.

He did not seem much the worse for his long night; the talk must have been good. He never flung down the wine as he used by the Oxos, or at Marakanda.

The last squire out was Sostratos. By chance he looked my way, and gave a violent start. No wonder, I thought, when none of you had your eyes open.

Alexander said, as he dropped his clothes off, that I ought to be in bed. I asked if the promised luck had come to him.

'Yes. But I had it here, after all. You saw who the night-guards were; all the bad squad. They were relieved at dawn; but when I got back, they were all still at their stations, standing-by. They meant it for a sign to me. I've never yet been hard on a man who asked for pardon. If I'd turned in early, they'd have had no chance to do it. I must give the Syrian something. By Herakles, though, I'm tired! Let no one near me all day.'

I washed and changed, took a canter through the forest, and, the camp now growing busy, went back to make sure he was undisturbed. He slept like the dead; so, strangely, did Peritas still. I felt his nose, but it was cool.

There were voices in the outer tent, which I thought too loud. The bodyguards, Ptolemy and Leonnatos, had two men there, who seemed making a great to-do. In one, to my surprise, I recognized young Epimenes of the night-guard, sobbing, his face in his hands. The other said, 'Forgive him, sirs, he's been in such great distress.' At this I came forward, saying to Ptolemy that the King was sleeping, and had asked for quiet.

'I know that,' said Ptolemy shortly. 'But I shall have to wake him. He's lucky to be alive. Leonnatos, can I leave these two with you?'

Whatever was this? It was unheard-of, to wake him against orders in his first dead sleep. But Ptolemy was no fool. I went in behind him, without excuse, taking myself for granted.

Alexander had turned on his back and was snoring softly; he had to be very deep to do that. Ptolemy stood over him and called his name. His eyelids creased, but he did not stir. Ptolemy shook him.

He returned as if from death. His eyes looked blind. With a great sigh he forced back sight into them, and said, 'What is it?'

'Are you awake, Alexander? Listen. It's a matter of your life.'

'Yes. I'm awake. Go on.'

'There's a squire, Epimenes, was on guard last night. He says they'd all planned to kill you in your sleep. If you'd gone to bed, they'd have done it.'

Alexander's brow creased deeply. Slowly he sat up naked, and rubbed his eyes. I came with a towel wrung in cold water; he took it and wiped his face. Presently he said, 'Who's that weeping?'

'The boy. He says you were good to him this morning, and he was ashamed.'

He had smiled at them. I remembered the first time he'd smiled at me.

'He told his lover,' Ptolemy said, 'because he didn't know what to do; they'd all taken some oath together. The lover's in the Companions; he soon made up his mind for him, and told his elder brother to settle it.'

'I see. Get me the man's name, I owe him something. And the rest of them? What were they going to do?'

'Wait. Wait till their turn came round again. They've been a full month, the boy says, working themselves into the same watch together. That's why they hung about this morning after they were relieved. They couldn't make up their minds to having failed, after all their trouble.'

'Yes,' said Alexander slowly. 'Yes, I see. Are there any other names?'

'One or two. I've taken them down. Do you want them from him or me?'

He paused, wiping the towel across his eyes. 'No, arrest them all. I'll deal with it tomorrow. I can't come to a treason trial half asleep. But I'll see Epimenes.' He stood up. I put a fresh chiton on him.

In the outer tent, the brothers fell on their knees, the elder with outstretched hands. Alexander said, 'No, Eurylochos, don't ask your brother's life from me.' The man went ashen. 'No, you mistake me; I meant, don't deny me the pleasure of giving it you unasked.' He had not meant to torment him; he was still barely awake. 'I shall thank you later. You'll both be needed tomorrow, but set your minds at rest.' He gave his right hand to each, along with a smile. I could see that from now on, either would die for him at a word.

When they'd gone, he said to Ptolemy, 'Give out a free pardon for the next of kin, or they'll be running away all over Baktria. Why put them to that? We know where it all began. Arrest him. Keep him apart from the others.'

'You mean Hermolaos?'

'I mean Kallisthenes. It's time. Will you do all that for me? Then I'll get back to bed.'

He slept quite soon. He was used to living close to death.

At evening he woke, had a drink of water, ordered a night-guard from the Companions, and slept again till sunrise. Then he sent for me.

'You warned me,' he said. 'Again and again you warned me. I thought
...' He laid his hand on mine. He'd thought, of course, that I came from
a corrupt court, and it was not my fault if I brought its suspicions with
me. 'I thought you were over-anxious. You've heard Kallisthenes putting
this in their minds?'

'I think so. Among Persians I'd have known. But I think so, yes.'

'Tell it me all again. These people will be put to the question. I've no
wish to drag it on. With something to go on, I can make it shorter.'

I felt no such wish. My former pity had changed to sparks of fire.
Whatever had to be done, I would gladly have done myself, if I'd had the
skill. But I told all I remembered, starting with the Athenian lovers. 'Yes,'
he said. 'I read you a lesson and laughed at you. You asked me, what were
the daggers for?'

'He was forever on about some tyrants in Greece. I don't remember their
names. They lived in – in Si-Syracuse? And Tessaly.'

'Thessaly. He was killed in bed. Go on.'

'Then, after Hermolaos was beaten, it stopped. It was only the Good Life,
or figuring with numbers. I thought he knew he'd been wrong. Now, I
think he'd chosen his men, and wanted to keep it from the others. A few
days back, when I was riding in the woods, he was there with all of them,
and a couple more. I thought, then, he was teaching them about plants,
as Aristotle did you.'

'Why not, after I'd made light of you? Do you know who the others
were?'

I did, and told him. I felt no reproach to him for heeding me so late. I
loved him for finding it so hard to think the worst, even of a man he'd been
at odds with. I did not remind him that I'd wanted to rid him of the fellow
long ago. I remembered how he'd spoken gently to the waiting murderers,
and made them gifts. It would leave a mark on him, as deep as the
catapult-bolt at Gaza.

The squires were taken out of the camp for questioning. Ptolemy, who
I daresay was there, writes that they all confessed Kallisthenes had inspired them.

Later, Alexander found me in the tent giving milk to Peritas, who was
sick from the drug they'd dosed him with, and would not eat. He said, 'The
other two names were those you gave me. I'm grateful to you for that.'
He caressed the dog, who had staggered to his feet to greet him. 'I'm glad
you were not needed there; you are too gentle for such work.'

'Gentle?' I said. 'They would have killed you sleeping, when not all
together would have faced you waking, mother-naked with just your
sword. No, my lord, you would not have found me gentle.' He ran his hand
through my hair, and did not believe me.

They went to their trial able to walk, which I suppose was proper. Not being Macedonian, I was only there to see them stoned. The stones came from the river-bed; clean, round and good to grip. But it would have outraged everyone, for a Persian to stone a Macedonian. There were willing hands enough. The vote for death had been passed by acclamation: even the fathers, if they were there, agreeing. By the old law of Macedon, they should all have died as well; not so much for being suspect, as to protect the King from blood-feud. Alexander was the first to grant free pardon.

When the condemned were brought, Alexander asked if any wished to speak. I understood, after Hermolaos accepted.

I will say he kept a good countenance, though his voice grew shrill. But as he spoke, every word came like an echo. It was the voice of a disciple – a steadfast one, that I concede to the dead – paying his master homage. To most of the Macedonians it was mere insolence; Alexander had to restrain them till the youth had done; but to those who'd heard the speeches on the prostration, it was proof.

As they were led to the stakes, Sostratos passed me. It was he who had seen me in the tent that morning. He spat towards me. 'Yes, and we'd have had you too, filthy painted barbarian whore.'

It grieved me to stand still while others revenged my lord. Whenever I saw a strong man with a big stone, I prayed to Mithra, avenger of loyalty, 'Send that for me.' One such broke Hermolaos' head.

Kallisthenes I never saw again. Only Macedonians had right of trial before Assembly. Ptolemy thinks he was put to the question and then killed, but I doubt he was there, and I have heard a different story.

At the time, Alexander did not speak to me of it, so I did not ask. I felt things which went deep with him, and which he didn't think I would understand. But a long time after, when he was rather drunk and had forgotten he'd never told me, he said something from which I pieced it out. I think when they went over Kallisthenes' papers, they found letters from Aristotle. The philosopher had heard, it seemed, from his nephew how the King made barbarians his friends and officers; had required free Greeks to bow down to him along with this servile breed; had first taken to his bed a Persian eunuch, who'd even been in Darius' bed before; then stooped to marry a Sogdian savage, a mere dancer at a feast. And the philosopher had written (letters no doubt too precious to be destroyed) that such things would bring back the rule of tyranny and corrupt all good Greek ways. No means should be spared to make an end of it.

Old Sokrates and Plato, had both been soldiers; Aristotle never. Maybe he'd had no thought that his words would beget more than other words. If so, he did not know men. Alexander, who did, and now knew more, had seen the effect; small wonder if he doubted the intention.

At all events, I heard long after of Kallisthenes alive in bonds, and that Alexander meant to try him in Greece before Aristotle, to show where his words had led, but that in India Kallisthenes died of sickness. One thing is sure, that in Athens, which Alexander had spared only to hate and slander him, Kallisthenes would have been a great man indeed if the King had died. To me he did not speak of it.

To Hephaistion he did. They sat long of an evening, talking quietly with Peritas at their feet. They had studied together with the philosopher as boys in Macedon and shared their thoughts. Hephaistion knew it all; not like a boy from Susa whose only schooling had been in pleasing a king.

This I know; no more pressed flowers or strange beasts went from Alexander to the school at Athens. And this I understand; that as his power grew, he had often asked himself how his old teacher would advise him; but now it ended. Henceforward he would listen only to his own soul.

20

In the end we did not start that year for India. In Sogdiana, they sent the King a whole new army to train, from provinces all over Asia. Though they'd been drilled by Macedonian officers, it's one thing to school a colt, another to get him knowing the master's hand.

For me it was strange indeed, to see the very peoples who'd made up Darius' army (often the same men) once more in a great host, but one so changed; no longer a formless mass of peasants with home-forged arms, waiting for chiefs in chariots to call them on, with the whip-men behind to urge them; but phalanxes and squadrons, forming or wheeling at a word.

Alexander inspected them in all his parade armour; he knew they would want to see a King. He flamed in the sun like the image of a god. When he threw them into manoeuvre, they went at it as if for a prize. There he was on a little hill, with his generals and some Persian officers, directing this vast host from his conquered nations, which had only to charge as one to sweep him from the earth. It could not happen, simply because he knew it could not. He was Alexander.

He returned to the Rock, taking his wife to see her kindred; all very properly done. One could tell they were grieved she was not with child;

but he made them princely gifts, treated them courteously, and had taken no other wife. What could they say?

One was enough. He had far too much pride to bring the secrets of the marriage-chamber, even to me. He knew that I understood. I have heard it said that some men choose wives in whom they see their mothers. From all I could learn of Queen Olympias, her son was one of them. But that he learned too late.

Of Olympias, I've heard she was fierce and beautiful, and brawled with her lord till the day he died, which it was whispered she'd had a hand in. She ate Alexander up with love, and made sure he and his father were never friends for long. All of us knew she had never learned the conduct of a lady; for her letters followed him all over Asia, intriguing in the affairs of Macedon, and quarrelling with Antipatros, his regent there. Alexander had been heard to say, after reading one of them, that she charged high rent for the nine months' lodging she'd given him.

All of which goes to show, to my mind, that we Persians could teach the Greeks how to deal with women.

Maybe we'd taught Alexander. But also, gentle as he was with them, he had somewhere a deep core of iron, forged, I expect, when he freed himself from his mother. He had no brawls with Roxane. He never forgot he was Great King. She had her harem tent and her household; there she could rule. He would visit her now and again; if she was troublesome, he would leave, and be slower to return. I knew, as soon as he came back to me. There were certain signs, of relief from distaste elsewhere. I had been trained to understand such things.

The new squires had come out from Macedon. Even there, they'd learned of the traitors' fate. A scared huddle of boys, afraid to open their mouths, they were brought before the King. He was charming to them, and knew all their names in no time. In relief they fell over each other, trying to please him; spoke to me with respect, and gratefully took advice from me. They seemed very young. Since the last set came, I was four years older.

It was one of them who fetched me to Alexander, in the dark before dawn. He was sitting in his bath-robe on the side of his bed. Down the middle lay Peritas, taking up all the room. He had never been the same since the squires had drugged him.

Alexander said, 'He tried to climb up, and I told him to get down. After a while he tried again, and something warned me.'

'How old was he?'

'Eleven. He should have lived a few years more. He was quiet all yesterday. I had him in Illyria, from King Kotys' huntsman, when I'd fallen out with my father and gone away. He looked like a bear-cub. I had nothing much to do, and he was good company.'

'You must have his likeness put on his tomb,' I said, 'so that he will be remembered by men to come.'

'I'll do better for him that that. I'll name my next city after him.'

It has a fine site, approved by the soldiers and merchants, on a good pass to India. The tomb and the statue are by the gate as you go in. The city is called Perita.

When the passes froze, we wintered in eastern Baktria. Though urgent news came through, it was long before we learned how Kallisthenes was beginning already his long revenge, which he has not ceased from yet.

In Athens, the news of his arrest had been like kicking a wasp-nest. More than ten years had passed since King Philip had beaten them in a battle not of his seeking, which their speech-maker Demosthenes had talked them into, bringing ruin to Thebes as well. (It was Alexander, at eighteen, who first broke their line.) After, Philip had shown Athens a mercy that astonished Greece. In spite of this, or (for who knows man's heart?) because of it, they had loathed him, and were suspect of privity to his murder; they loathed his son, who had never set foot there but once on a peaceful mission. While my lord lived, they kept quiet from fear; after, like jackals when the lion dies, they began to tear him.

It did even the great Aristotle no good, that he'd warned his pupil against Persians; he had to run for his life, as a friend of Macedon, and never dared return. A smaller man took his school; then the philosophers joined the chorus.

So now, for mercy and honour shown to my people, my lord is barbarous; a tyrant, because he punished his would-be murderers, the right of their meanest citizen; a mere vaunting soldier, though wherever he went he brought Greece with him, the Greece he honoured, of which these liars are the unworthy heirs.

One good thing's come out of it; it determined King Ptolemy to write down the truth while he still has time. Now, he had rather work on his book than govern Egypt, which he mostly leaves to his son.

'Oh, my dear Bagoas!' my friends here say to me. 'A man like you, who reads the best of the Greeks, how can you be content to die without seeing Athens? The voyage is nothing, in the good season. I can recommend you a ship; I will write out all the things you ought to see; I will give you letters to men of learning. What holds you back, when you've travelled so much further? Do go, before age overtakes you and journeys become a burden.' So they say. But my lord in his house of gold here, my lord who is younger now than I – he understands why I shall never go to Athens.

Spring broke at last. It was time for India.

All winter the King had been seeing caravan-masters, and Greeks from beyond Kaukasos, who had gone trading with the caravans and stayed on. Craving for Greek speech again. or just for gold, they came to tell him about the country beyond the mountains, the Land of Five Rivers.

These rivers flowed down from Kaukasos, the greatest being the Indus which received the rest. The Indians who lived between them were mostly at feud, and would welcome anyone who fought their enemies. Alexander said that it had been the same in Greece, which was how his father had conquered it.

From the man who had journeyed furthest, he learned one day that a half-month's march from the Indus, was a river even greater. This stream, the Ganges, flowed not west but east, and ran into the ocean.

I have seldom seen him so exalted. He was still full of it at bedtime, though he'd been talking of it all day. 'The Encircling Ocean! We shall have crossed the world to its furthest end. We can sail home north to the Euxine, or round south to Babylon. We shall stand at the end of the world.'

'It will be remembered forever,' I said, 'by men to come.'

I had been wearing my coat of the silk from Marakanda, with its flying serpents and flowers. Its blue gleam caught my eye (I had taken it off to bath him); the buttons were of a pale green stone, heavy and cool to touch, carved with magic signs. According to the merchant, it had all been a year on the road. The liar, I thought; he was just putting up the price.

'What are you thinking of?' asked Alexander smiling. I was ashamed to have been so trivial, and said. 'Of the altar you'll build, Al'skander, at the world's end, carved with your name.'

'Ride with me tomorrow early. I must give Oxhead a canter, or he'll start grieving. His wind's still good. But I'm sorry he must cross the mountains.' He still missed Peritas. Friends had offered him good dogs, but he would not have one. 'You know,' he said, 'Oxhead is rising thirty.'

I bent, as I washed him, and kissed his head. I had seen, where the lamplight caught the gold, two threads of grey.

When spring opened the passes, we marked our leaving with a holocaust. The new troops had brought only their own necessaries; but the old army was lumbered up with wagons and wagons of heavy loot – furniture, beds and bedding, hangings, carpets, clothing; meant, I suppose, to be carted back to Macedon. They were no use meantime, unless to sell for a song by men in debt. The generals had whole trains of it. Alexander, though he always kept less than he gave, had some wagons of fine stuffs and carpets. He had everything carted out on a bit of heath, and the draught-beasts led away. Then he went up to his own wagons. A fire had been kindled near, with a pile of torches by it. Into each wagon, he threw a burning torch.

The officers, warned beforehand, followed suit. Even the men did not hang back too long. They had shed blood for all these goods, and carried them off in triumph; now they were tired of hauling them along. Besides, a love of fire is born in everyone; even a young child will try to grasp it; which proves that it is divine. As the splendid blaze went up, the men started flinging firebrands, at other men's things at first, then anywhere, laughing and shouting like boys, till the heat drove them back. But I watched the revel, I who had grown old without manhood when I was ten; remembered the burning rafters of my father's house, and thought of the waste of war.

This time we crossed Parapamisos without much hardship; Alexander had learned from the time before. He stayed a while in Alexandreia, putting it to rights, the governor having proved a fool and rogue; meantime, he sent heralds over to Omphis, the nearest of the Indian kings, asking for his allegiance. His land had been subject to the empire since the first Darius' day.

Omphis came himself; the first Indian, except a few common soldiers, the troops had seen. He came with twenty-five elephants, on the first of which he sat like a glittering image in his painted howdah; a handsome man of good stature, darker than a Mede, but not so dark as an Ethiop. He wore ivory earrings; his moustache and beard were dyed bright green. We Persians like rich colours; the Indians prefer brilliant ones. Besides the gold sequins stitched to his clothing everywhere, he was stuck all over with jewels so huge, I'd not have believed in them, if he had not been a king.

I don't know how much pomp he'd expected of Alexander. I could see him pause a moment, wondering where he was, till he saw the face and knew. He offered willing fealty, in exchange for help against his enemy, a king called Poros. This Alexander promised, if the man did not offer allegiance. He put on a great feast for Omphis, and gave him gold. None is mined in those parts, so the princes greatly prize it. Omphis promised, in return, all twenty-five of his elephants, as soon as he'd got home on them. Alexander in turn was pleased. He never used them for war, thinking them uncertain, as indeed they are; but he valued them for their strength and wisdom. They carried the parts from which he set up his catapults. Once or twice he rode one; but said he liked to feel the beast that bore him, not sit on it in a chair.

Soon he held his war-council, to plan the march on India. His sleeping-room at Alexandreia was just behind the room of audience, so I heard it all.

Hephaistion got command of his own army. He was to cross Great Kaukosos by the good pass, which Sogdians called Khyber; when he reached the Indus, he was to bridge it for Alexander. Khyber being the easiest way (but for the men who live there) he was to take in his charge the followers and all the women, not leaving out the harem. Alexander with his own army and the chief of the Companions, would take the hardest task; clearing the mountains which commanded the pass of anyone who threatened it.

As I listened, I thought, This is a crossroads in my life. Now or never.

I can't remember what he came in for after; to get a cloak or some such thing. 'Alexander,' I said, 'I happened to overhear your war-council.'

'You always do. I only put up with it because you keep your mouth shut. Why tell me now?' He looked stern. He knew well enough what I was after.

'Don't send me with the followers. Take me with you.'

'You should have listened better. Mine is a campaign, not a march. It may not be done by winter.'

'My lord, I know. It's too long to leave you.'

He frowned. He wanted to take me; but he believed in doing without comforts in the field. 'You've never been trained to hardship.'

'I come from the mountains that bred Kyros. Don't put me to shame.'

He stood, still frowning, and looking about for what he'd come in for. I knew what it was without telling, and gave it him with a smile. 'That's all very well,' he said. 'But war is war.'

'You take tanners and carpenters and cooks and bakers. You take slaves. Am I worth less?'

'Too much. I wish you knew what you're asking for. And there won't be much time for love.'

'For bed? I know. But for love, while I live, I shall always have time enough.'

He looked into my eyes, then said, 'I meant not to do this.' He went to his coffer and took out a fistful of gold. 'Get yourself more warm things, you'll need them. Pack away your dress-clothes and your tent-trimmings. Buy sheepskin horse-blankets. You may take one servant and one pack-mule.'

In the high passes it was already autumn. North of Khyber, the people were hunters and herders, whose second trade was robbery. They were reported fierce; Alexander wanted their submission.

Even up in the Parapamisos, I had not had mountain sickness. We were lower here than there; though Alexander climbed at first by slow stages, to temper our blood for the thin air. My childhood had not yet been lost in me; I went up without distress. Sometimes at evening I would count Alexander's breaths against mine, and they were faster; but he had more work to do. He never owned to fatigue.

Some say the Wise God's heaven is a rose-garden. For me, it is in the heights. After all, he lives there. Watching the dawn on snows no birds had touched, I shivered with joy. We were invading a land of gods, whose cold hands would soon fall on us; there were wars to come; but I could feel no dread.

In the end, Alexander had let me take my Thracian groom as well as my body-servant. I think he'd really feared I might die of hardship. At night in his campaign tent (made to his order; Darius had never owned anything so simple) he'd ask if I was well. At last, guessing what he'd never utter, I said, 'Al'skander, you think eunuchs are different in too many ways. If we're shut up with women and live soft with them, then we grow like them; but so would any man. Just because we have women's voices, it doesn't mean we have women's strength.'

He took my hand smiling. 'You've not a woman's voice; it is too pure. It's like the aulos, the deep-toned flute.' He was glad to be free of the harem.

In the night with its fierce white stars, before the snow-clouds had gathered, as I sat by my pine-wood fire the young squires would leave their own to squat beside me. 'Bagoas, tell us about Susa, tell us about Persepolis, tell us about the court in Darius' day.' Or I would watch the blaze where Alexander sat with Ptolemy and Leonnatos and his other officers. They would pass round the wine and talk and laugh; but there was no night when Alexander turned in with steps less steady than mine.

He never had me to bed. Always before hard tasks he would gather himself together, wasting nothing. Fire is divine He was glad of me; that was enough.

Then the wars began. The tribesmen's forts clung to the crags, like martins' nests. The first we came to looked impossible to storm. Alexander sent an interpreter, to offer terms, but they defied him. The Persian kings had never brought these lands under law.

The forts had done well against the assaults of other tribesmen, who had stones and arrows. Alexander had light catapults, whose bolts must have seemed to them like the darts of demons.

He had scaling-ladders too. When they saw his men coming over their walls, they left the fort and fled on the mountain-side. The Macedonians ran after them, and killed all they could overtake, while the fort was burned. I watched it from the camp. Though a long way off, I felt concern for these little figures caught in the rocks or on old snowfields. I had taken calmly the deaths of many, because I had not seen them as single men. It was folly, for they would have roused other tribes against us, if they'd got away.

When the fight was over, I learned what had made Alexander's troops so fierce. He had an arrow-wound in the shoulder. He'd made light of it; the corselet had stopped it from sinking in its barb. No one ever made less of his wounds than he did in battle; but it was always the same, if he got one his men went nearly mad. It was part love, part dread of being left without him.

When the doctor had gone, I took off his bandage and sucked the place clear; who could say what such people put on their arrows? It was to do such things that I'd come, though I'd had too much sense to tell him so; the way to persuade him was always to beg a gift.

The camp was noisy; the soldiers had come without women, all but the hardiest who never left their men; now they had all those from the fort, tall broad-faced hill women with strong black hair and jewels stuck through their noses.

Alexander took a fancy for me that night. The wound opened and I was covered in blood; he just laughed, and made me wash in case the guard thought I'd murdered him. The wound felt easier, he said; no physician like love. It is true that when dry they often fester.

The next fort surrendered, having heard about the first; so everyone was spared, as his custom was. As we marched onward, the mountain gods sent winter.

We pushed through thick driving snow like barley-grains; our clothes and our horses and the men's sheepskin cloaks were frosted white; the beasts slithered and stumbled on the drifted tracks, which we needed native guides to find. Then the sky would clear, and the white would dazzle till we rode with eyes almost closed; that light can blind a man.

We were amply fed, Alexander saw to that; and not climbing higher than timber grows, we had warm blazing fires at night. If the wind pushed cold fingers through my furs, I just wrapped my scarf to keep my face from burning, and thought of my luck to be here with no Roxane; above all with no Hephaistion.

Alexander took the hill-forts one by one, except those that surrendered. I hardly remember one from another now, though King Ptolemy remembers each one. He did some notable deeds of arms up there, among them a duel hand to hand with an important chief, whose shield he's kept to this day. He has put them all in his book, and who shall blame him?

After many battles and sieges, we sighted Massaga, stretched across a hill-spur; no mere tribal fort, but a strong walled town.

It gave Alexander four days' work. On the first, when they made a sortie from their gates, he fled to lure them out, then whipped round on them and caught a good many, though the rest got back inside. Then, lest they still thought he was scared, he marched up to the walls, for which he got an arrow in his ankle. By luck no sinew was cut; the doctor told him to rest it, as one might tell a river to run back up the hills.

Next day he brought up rams and breached the wall; but the breach was stoutly held. At night, he limped now and then when he forgot, but stopped himself next moment.

The day after, he ran a bridge across to the breach from a wooden siege-tower (he'd brought engineers to make such things on the spot) and led the assault himself. Before he'd crossed, so many had pressed up to be fighting next him, that the bridge broke in the middle.

I died many deaths, before they scrambled out from the rubble below, and I saw his white-winged helmet. He limped back all grazed and bruised, but only said he was lucky not to have broken a leg; he'd just come from seeing the wounded.

Next day, with a stronger bridge, he tried again and got over. While they fought on the walls, the tribal chief fell to a catapult bolt; and the town sued for a truce, which Alexander granted.

Seven thousand of their best fighting men turned out to have been hired, from somewhere beyond the rivers; they were shorter and darker than the rest. Alexander had them called out apart; he wanted to hire them himself. They had a different tongue from the hillmen's, but the interpreter said he knew it. In the King's presence he addressed them; the officers replied; after some parley, he said they agreed to the offered terms. So they camped by themselves on a hill near by, while the townspeople were treated with; and Alexander set scouts to watch them, they being strangers whose good faith he did not know, in a force that could be dangerous. He'd learned to take care, in Sogdiana.

'A good day's work,' he said to me after supper. He had bathed, and I was dressing his ankle, which seemed to be healing clean in spite of everything.

A night-guard squire came in. 'Sir. One of the outpost guards, asking to report.' Alexander said, 'I'll see him now.'

The man was young, but looked steady. 'Alexander. The Indians on the hill are getting ready to go.'

He stood up, stepping on my clean bandage. 'How do you know?'

'Well, King, the later it's grown, with everyone else asleep, the more they're stirring. It's not so dark you can't see them against the sky. Nobody's lying down; the whole camp's milling; the men are bearing arms, and I saw some leading pack-beasts. I've good eyes, Alexander, at night; I'm known for it. That's why the Commander sent me to report.'

Alexander's face set. He nodded slowly. Nothing was new, after two years in Sogdiana. 'Yes, you did well. Stand by outside. Bagoas, I'll dress again.' He called back the squire. 'Fetch the interpreter. And hurry.'

The man came, just out of bed. Alexander said, 'The hired soldiers you treated with today; are you really fluent in their language?'

The man, looking scared, assured him that he was; he had gone to their country with the caravans, and bargained for the merchants.

'You are sure they agreed, and understood what they agreed to?'

'Great King, without any doubt.'

'Very good. You can go. Menestas, have General Ptolemy waked, and ask him to see me now.'

He came, looking as always alert, steady and tough as well-cured leather. Alexander said, 'The Indian mercenaries are deserting. They must have sworn-in to put us off guard. We can't have them joining with the tribes and falling on the column. If they can't be trusted they're a standing danger, held or let go.'

'That's true. They're too many. And trained.' He paused, and looked at Alexander. 'Now? Tonight?'

'Yes. We'll take the whole force and do it quickly. Have the men turned out by word of mouth. No trumpets. While that's doing I'll make the dispositions. There's clear ground all round that hill. We've enough men to ring it.'

Ptolemy left. He called the squires to arm him. I heard the deep muttering stir as the camp was roused. The officers came for their orders. It seemed to take no time at all. His army was trained for swiftness, he only had to call for it. Soon the long files of men were stumbling and clanking off into the darkness.

After so much haste, the quiet seemed to last forever. Then the yells began. They seemed eternal too. They crossed the valley like the sound of the last battle which, we are told, will end the world. But that will be between Light and Dark. Here all was night.

I thought I heard, in the din, shrill screams like women's. I was right. They had been with the Indians; had picked up the arms of fallen men and were killed in the darkness, fighting.

At last the yells grew less, then were few and broken. Then there was only, here and there, a death-cry. After that, night's silence.

Two hours before the late winter dawn, the camp sounded with men again. Alexander came back.

The squires unbuckled his blood-slimed armour, and took it out to clean. He looked drawn and grey; lines that had hardly showed, were cut across his forehead. I took off his tunic; that was blood-soaked too, except where the armour had covered it. He seemed hardly aware of me, so that I looked at him as if myself unseen. Then his eyes turned to mine and knew them.

'It was necessary,' he said.

I had had the slaves get a bath ready. That too was necessary; even his face was splashed with blood, his arms and his knees were red with it. When he was in bed, I asked if he was hungry. He said, 'No. Just a little wine.' I brought him that, and the night-lamp, and was going away. 'Bagoas,' he said, looking up into my face. So I bent and kissed him. He received it like a gift, thanking me with his eyes.

I lay in my tent, in the cold before the dawn, with the fire dying outside, and thought, as I'd been thinking all night, that the interpreter was a Sogdian, and no Sogdian will own there is anything he cannot do. Still, if the Indians had believed they were free to go, they would have gone by day. Did they know they had broken faith, did they know they'd pledged it? Alexander had watched them. They must have looked as if they understood.

I thought of the heap of dead upon the hill, with the wolves and the jackals already tearing them; and I knew that other hands before his had sealed their death; the hand of Philotas; the hands of the dead squires; the hands of all those chiefs and satraps who had taken his right hand, sworn loyalty and been his welcome guests; then murdered his men whom he'd trusted to them, and fallen on his cities.

He had set out on his wars, as I knew while I still heard of him only from his enemies, looking for his own honour in all he met. Had he found it? Darius himself, if he'd lived to accept his mercy – would he have honoured his given word unless from fear? I remembered the soldier's tale of the hospital at Issos. Truly, my lord had not received as he had given. One by one I had seen the wounds fall on his trust. Tonight I had seen the scars.

And yet, I thought, this very grief I feel comes from him alone. Who else ever taught me mercy? While I served Darius, I would have said of this night's work, Such things are always done.

Yes; if tonight he had wanted all from me, instead of only a kiss to pardon him, I would not have withheld even my heart; no, not with all those dead men's souls drifting upon the air. It is better to believe in men too rashly, and regret, than believe too meanly. Men could be more than they are, if they would try for it. He has shown them that. How many have tried, because of him? Not only those I have seen; there will be men to come. Those who look in mankind only for their own littleness, and make them believe in that, kill more than he ever will in all his wars.

May he never cease believing, even though he grows angry at wasted faith. He is more weary than he knows, his breath comes fast in the thin air of the heights, and his sleep is broken. Yes, souls of the dead, I would go to him if he asked me.

But he did not ask. He lay alone with his thoughts, and when I came at morning I found him with open eyes.

21

We came down towards the river, after more victories, the greatest being the capture of the Aornos rock, said to have baffled even Herakles. Alexander added it to his chain of fortresses which secured the homeward road.

And there was the city of Nysa, pleasant in the spring air of the foothills, where the chief came out to meet him, asking mercy for the place, since, so said his interpreter, Dionysos himself had founded it; for proof, his sacred ivy grew there, alone in all the region. This interpreter was a Greek settler, who knew the right names of everything. I myself, going about the town, saw a shrine with the image of a beautiful youth playing a flute. I pointed him out to a passing Indian, saying 'Dionysos?' He answered, 'Krishna'; but doubtless it was the god.

Alexander and the chief got on well together, and agreed on terms. Then, being a lover of marvels all his life, Alexander had a longing to see the god's sacred hill behind the city. Not to have it over-trampled, he took only the Companions, the squires and me. Truly it was a paradise without art of man; green meadows and green shades, cedars and laurel-groves; dark-leaved bushes with clusters of bright flowers like lilies; and the god's ivy on all the rocks. Indeed the place was divine, for a pure happiness seized us all there. Someone wove Alexander a crown of ivy; soon we were all garlanded and singing, or hailing Dionysos by his sacred cry. A flute piped somewhere and I followed it, but never found the musician. As I walked by a brook that splashed down ferny rocks, I met Ismenios, whom I'd scarcely seen since he left the squires for the Companions. He had grown still handsomer with manhood. He came up smiling, embraced and kissed me; then he went singing on his way, and I on mine.

Rejoicing in spring after the harshness of winter war, we went down towards the rivers. The tall shade-trees and banks of flowers we left behind with the hills. Round the Indus is barren sand, scoured at its flood-times. A little above that, stretching a mile over dunes and scrub, Hephaistion had pitched the camp of the Macedonians. Across the river was his bridge.

He rode out to meet Alexander. He had worked well, he and his engineers. The bridge was of pointed boats linked side to side, with a firm road laid across them. It was longer than the river's width, for that spreads quickly when the snows melt at its source; he had great cables stretched far inland, ready for this. Alexander said he'd done better than Xerxes had with the Hellespont.

Near the place reserved for Alexander's tent was the camp of Roxane's household. But, so I heard, after the King had greeted Hephaistion and commended him, his next words were, 'How is Oxhead? Did the mountains tire him?'

He rode through the cheering soldiers, and then straight to the stables, hearing the old horse was short in the wind and had been missing him. Then he held a war-council. Some time that day, he paid his respects in the harem.

Soon we crossed the river and were in real India, whose marvels I have been asked to recount so often that I could do it in my sleep. The first of them was King Omphis, waiting to receive Alexander with all his kingdom's splendours; his whole army drawn up on the plain, flashing and bright, with its scarlet standards, its painted bedizened elephants, its clashing cymbals and booming gongs.

They were all armed to the teeth. Alexander had seen enough of treachery; he had the trumpets sounded, and came on in order of battle. Luckily, King Omphis had sense, and guessed something was wrong. He rode out in front with a couple of sons and princes; Alexander, always glad once more to believe in men, at once rode out to meet him.

We were all spendidly entertained and banqueted. King Omphis' chief wife went in her curtained carriage drawn by pure white oxen, to fetch Roxane to a ladies' feast. The soldiers, laden with pay they'd had no chance to spend for a year, filled the bazaars, bargaining by signs. They needed cloth, their tunics being in tatters. It dismayed them to find no good strong wool for any money. Even the linen was flimsy, made not from flax but from Indian tree-fluff; being either white or gaudy, it caused much discontent. However, they had no lack of women; they could be had there even in the temples.

I looked everywhere for more of the heavy silk I had bought from the caravan at Marakanda; I fancied another suit of it, now we were in India whence it came. But I could not find any at all.

On the city outskirts, I came on one of the Indian marvels; the offspring tree, which lets down from its branches roots that turn into new trees. It had spread so wide, a phalanx could have camped under its shade; this one tree spread like a wood. Walking up to look, I saw sitting under it groups of men, some quite venerable, naked as they were born.

Even after the Macedonians, this astonished me; even they did not sit about in such a state. Yet these old men seemed full of dignity, and did not vouchsafe me a glance. One, who seemed the chief of them, with an unkempt beard down to his middle, had a ring of pupils, old and young, who listened with admiration; another had for audience a young child and a white-haired ancient; yet another sat cross-legged, still as a block, his eyes cast down to his belly, hardly seeming to breathe. A passing woman laid before him a garland of yellow flowers, showing no shame for his nakedness; nor did he, he did not so much as move his eyes.

These, as I now remembered, must be the naked philosophers, whom Alexander had said he wanted to see. They were not much like Anaxarchos or Kallisthenes.

Sure enough, here was Alexander himself approaching with some friends, escorted by one of King Omphis' sons. Neither teachers nor pupils rose, nor indeed paid any attention. The prince showed no anger, but seemed even to expect it. He called his interpreter, who addressed them announcing Alexander; I heard his name.

At this, the chief man rose, followed by all the rest, except the cross-legged man still gazing at his belly. They stamped with their feet on the ground, two or three times, and then stood silent.

Alexander said, 'Ask them why they did that.'

At the sound of his voice, for the first time the cross-legged man looked up, and fixed his eyes on him.

The leader spoke to the interpreter, who said in Greek, 'He asks, lord King, why you have come so far with so much trouble, when wherever you go, nothing of earth is yours but what is under your feet, till you come to die, when you will have a little more, enough to lie in.'

Alexander looked at him earnestly for a while, then said, 'Tell him I do not only travel the earth to possess it. I seek to know what it is, and what men are, also.'

The philosopher bent down in silence, and held up a pinch of dust.

'But,' said Alexander, 'even the earth can be changed, and so can men.'

'Men indeed you have changed. Through you they have known fear and anger, pride and desire, chains which will bind their souls through many lives. And you, who think yourself free because you have mastered fear and the body's greeds; the desires of the mind consume you like raging fire. Soon they will burn you all away.'

Alexander thought a little. 'That may be. So is the sculptor's wax consumed within the clay, and is gone for ever. But in its room they cast the bronze.'

When this was interpreted, the philosopher shook his head. Alexander said, 'Tell him I should like to talk further with him. If he will come with me, I will see he is treated with honour.'

The old man's head lifted. Whatever he thought he was free of, I doubt he was free from pride. 'No, King. Nor would I permit the least of my children here. What can you give me, or what can you take away? All I have is this naked body, and even that I do not need; by taking it you would lift from me my last burden. Why should I go with you?'

'Why indeed?' said Alexander. 'We will trouble you no more.'

All this time, the man with the garland had sat still, gazing at Alexander. Now he stood up and spoke. I could see his words disturbed the others; the leader for the first time looked angry. The interpreter motioned for silence.

'He says this, lord King. "Even the gods grow weary of their godhead, and seek release at last. I will go with you till you are freed."'

Alexander smiled at him and said he would be welcome. He took from a crotch of the tree an old breech-cloth, which he wound on, and a wooden food-bowl, and followed barefoot after the King.

Later, I met a Greek who kept a shoe-shop in the city and knew the sages; I asked him why they had been so angry with the man. He said it was not because they thought he had gone from greed of wealth, but because he had been drawn in love to a mortal creature. They held that even though his love was of the soul, it would be a chain to him, and cause him to be reborn after his death, which they think a punishment. This was all I could understand.

Certainly, all he would take from the King was food for his wooden bowl, and not much of that. Since no one could pronounce his name, we called him Kalanos, from the sound of a word he used in greeting. Soon we all grew used to him, sitting under some tree near the King's pavilion. Alexander asked him inside, and talked to him alone but for the interpreter. He said to me once that though people thought Kalanos did nothing, he had fought and won great battles to be what he was, and was magnanimous in victory.

He had even a little Greek, picked up from the settlers there. It was said he had been a scholar, before he joined the naked men. But Alexander did not have long to study with him; he had to make war upon King Poros.

This was King Omphis' enemy, against whom he'd asked for help. His land was beyond the next river, the Hydaspes. This too had been taken into the empire, under Darius the Great; its kings were still satraps in name, but had been let alone for generations, and were kings again. So King Poros told Alexander's envoys, when they came asking for fealty; he added that he would pay no homage to any ally of Omphis, descended as he was from low-born slaves.

Alexander prepared for battle, but had first to rest his men, after the winter wars (Hephaistion's had had some hard fighting too, going through Khyber). He took his time, giving them games and festivals, though as it grew warm with spring, the rivers were rising. We were told that soon it would rain.

When we did march down to the Hydaspes along with King Omphis' troops, we were a vaster host than ever, in spite of the garrisons left in conquered strongholds. We made camp up above the river, while Alexander scouted for the best place to cross. It was brown and fierce already; one could tell it would never endure a bridge.

On one of these days, some person of consequence, whose name and race I forget, came to Alexander's tent for audience. He had been gone some time, so I said I would go and find him. I rode about the camp – no Persian will walk when he can ride – till I heard he had gone to the horse-lines. I went over to the endless rows of shelters, made from bamboo and grass and palm-leaves, which housed the cavalry mounts; a town in itself. At last a blue-tattooed Thracian slave, who was holding the King's charger, pointed me out a shelter standing alone, and handsomer than the rest. I dismounted and went inside.

After the Indian sun it seemed almost dark. Splinters of dazzle came through the chinks of the wall, making bars of light and shade. They fell on an old black horse, that lay in the straw with labouring sides; and on Alexander, sitting in the muck of the stable floor, with its head laid in his lap.

My shadow had darkened the doorway; he looked up.

I had no words, I just thought, I would do anything ... As if I had had the words all along, I said, 'Shall I fetch Hephaistion?'

He answered, 'Thank you, Bagoas.' I could just hear him. He'd not called the groom, because he could not command his voice. So I was not there for nothing.

I found Hephaistion by the river, among his engineers. They had brought his bridge-boats overland, in halves for cartage; he was seeing them put together. He stared at me in surprise; no doubt I looked out of place there. Besides, it was the first time I'd ever sought him out.

'Hephaistion,' I said, 'Oxhead is dying. Alexander wants you there.'

He looked at me in silence. Maybe he would have expected me to send someone else. Then he said, 'Thank you, Bagoas', in a voice he'd not used to me before, and called for his horse. I let him get well ahead, before I took the road.

Oxhead's funeral was held that evening; it has to be quick, in India. Alexander had him burned on a pyre, so as to have his ashes for a proper tomb. He only told his friends; but it was wonderful how many old soldiers came quietly up, who had fought at Issos, and Granikos, and Gaugamela. There were bowls of incense to throw upon the pyre; we must have given old Oxhead a full talent's worth. Some of Omphis' Indians, who stood further off, uttered loud cries to their gods, thinking Alexander had sacrificed the horse for victory.

When the fire had sunk, he went about his work again. But at night, I saw he looked older. When he first had Peritas he had been a man; Oxhead, he had had since boyhood. That little horse (all Greek horses look little to a Persian) had known things of him I'd never known. That day some of them died, and I shall never know them.

That night it thundered; and the rain came down.

In the morning the dust was laid, the sun was out, and all smelled of growing greenness. But clouds soon gathered; next time, it was as if the river had poured down from the sky. And I heard it said this was only the beginning.

In the downpour, plodding through mud, without a dry stitch on them, Alexander marched his men to the river banks.

He would not take me. He said he could not tell where he'd be from hour to hour, let alone day to day, or when he would cross the river. He found time to bid me good-bye, but, as always, did not make much of it. He saw no cause. He would win, and soon be back. Tender farewells were for the losers.

Yet this was the greatest and most perilous of all his battles; and I did not see it.

The rain drummed down, turning the camp to quagmire. The wretched followers huddled in leaky booths; a good tent was riches. In the drenching storms I would give some wayfarer shelter; a half-drowned Baktrian child, a Greek ballad-singer; and, once, Kalanos the philosopher, whom I saw standing in a waterfall, in his single breech-clout. When I beckoned him in, he signed a blessing; then crossed his feet upon his thighs, and sank into meditation. It was like being alone; but alone and happy.

At first, whenever the rain grew less, I would throw on a cloak and ride down to the river. There were troops along there for miles, but no one could tell me where the King was, nor what he meant to do. As it turned out, there was someone even more eager than I to know: King Poros, who had made his camp on the further shore, at the easiest point of crossing.

One night, in a lull of the roaring rain, we heard a great din of onset - trumpets, battle-yells, horses neighing. It had come at last. I lifted my hands to Mithra. The night was like pitch. All the camp was awake and listening. No word came back to us.

No wonder. No one had crossed the river. All that had happened was that Alexander had made a noise, and Poros had moved his whole army towards it, to stand-by all night in the pouring rain.

Next night, the same. Now the great battle had really started; we held our breath. No battle. The next night, and the next, when we heard clamours we took it easily. So did King Poros, too.

Alexander never minded looking a fool, or even a poltroon, in the first part of a battle. He could afford it. By now, he had to find distant places to be believed in; but here he was far enough. He had fought no war with Omphis, to warn King Poros of what he was. Poros was seven feet tall, his only mount an elephant. It can't have been hard for him, to think the little pup across the river was all bark, no bite.

Alexander kept barking, and running back to his kennel. He had great convoys of stores brought to his camp, giving out, to whoever would listen and spread the news, that he would wait if he must till the rains were over and winter shrank the stream. So Poros could camp all that time on a mud-bank in the wet while Alexander worked up his courage.

It must have gone on a full quarter-month. One night came the worst storm yet; torrents of rain, lightning so frightful one could see it through the tent; I put my pillow over my head. At least, I thought, tonight there'll be no battle.

At dawn, the thunder rumbled away; and then we heard. It was the din of onset, greater than on all those nights before, but further. Above it rose a new sound, furious and high; the trumpeting of elephants.

Alexander had crossed the river.

He had planned it for that night in any case. The storm, though a hardship, was a general's gift. He had crossed a little way up river of Poros, where there were thick woods to screen his march, and a wooded island to screen his crossing. He had to get over before Poros knew and brought up his elephants. If the cavalry mounts saw them as they came to land, they would plunge off the rafts and drown.

Ptolemy has the whole battle in his book, and has shown Alexander's skill and daring for men to come. His first peril was perhaps his worst. He made the crossing, first leaping ashore himself; then, while the cavalry were being landed, found that the bank had been cut off by a new flood-channel, and was an island.

At last they found a ford, though it was deep. Ptolemy writes that the water was breast-high on the men, and the horses could just keep their heads above. (You see what I mean, when I say Greek horses look little to a Persian.)

Already Poros' son had been sent with a chariot squadron, to push them back in the river. Alexander formed his men up just in time. The Prince fell; the chariots stuck in the mud; those who could, took flight. Poros had the news, chose a sandy stretch of firm land, and prepared for battle.

His front was unassailable; it had two hundred elephants spaced across. But he had an artist in war to deal with. To say much in little, Alexander lured out the cavalry by a show of weakness; attacked the front with mounted Scythian archers who shot and wheeled away; he himself charged the cavalry in front, Koines at rear; he maddened Poros' elephants with arrows or thrown javelins, or by shooting down their mahouts, till they did more damage on their own side than on his.

It's all in King Ptolemy's book; he read it me. He has it just as I heard it at the time, except that more Macedonians fell than he has written. When he read me that part, I daresay I looked up; for he smiled, saying those numbers were in the royal archives, and old soldiers understand each other.

We on the further shore came down to the bank at first light to see. The rains had laid the dust which hides most battles. We could see clearly the elephants with their swaying howdahs, the wheeling horse, the milling foot; but what this confusion signified, we could not tell. I could not even pick out Alexander by his flashing arms, for the river had muddied him all over. The sun grew high. The dreadful din seemed unending. Then at last, the flight and pursuit began.

It grieves me more than all else I missed, that I did not see Alexander meet with Poros. It was a thing after his own heart; also a true one, which neither time nor man's deceit ever took from him.

Long after the fight was lost, the tall King fought on in the van. His elephant, brave even among that race, had never flinched. At last while he cast a javelin he was hit under his lifted arm, through the gap in his coat of mail. At this he turned his steed, and rode slowly after the rout. Alexander had watched him eagerly and longed to meet him; he thought so noble a man should be summoned only by another king, and asked Omphis to be his envoy. This did not do; Poros detested Omphis, and at the sight of him reached left-handed for a javelin. Alexander found some-one more acceptable, and tried again. At this, Poros bade his elephant kneel; it put its trunk around him, and gently lifted him down. He asked for water – with the battle and his wound, he was parched with thirst – and went to meet Alexander.

'The finest-looking man I ever saw,' Alexander said to me later. He spoke without envy. I expect it grieved him in his youth that he was not tall; but if so it had ceased to trouble him, now that his shadow stretched from east to west. 'He is just like Homer's Ajax, but for his black skin and blue beard. He must have been in pain, but you'd never have known it. "Ask what you wish of me," I said. "How shall I deal with you?" "Like a king," he said. Do you know, I knew it before it was interpreted? I said, "That, I'd do for my own sake; ask something for yours." He answered, "There is no need, that is everything." What a man! I hope his wound heals quickly. I'm going to give him more land than he had before. He will balance Omphis' power; but above all, I trust him.'

He did not trust in vain. As long as he lived, no news of treachery came to him from there.

All that meant most to him, was fulfilled in that river battle. He fought mightily against man and nature; did not his hero Achilles fight a river? Happier than Achilles, he had Patroklos by him to share his glory;

Hephaistion was with him all that day. And he won with a welded army of all his peoples, just as Kyros fought with his welded Medes and Persians, though this was a greater thing. At the end, he found a brave enemy to make a friend of. Yes. that was my lord's last moment of perfect fortune.

Now it was done, his eyes were turned, as they always were, to the next horizon. What he lived for now was to make the march to Ganges, follow its shores, and reach the Encircling Ocean; his empire a finished work from sea to sea, crowned with a marvel. Thus his teacher Aristotle had told him the world was made, and I have not yet met a man who could deny it.

22

King Poros' flesh-wound soon healed, and Alexander feasted him. He was magnificent, still in his thirties though with sons of fighting age, for the Indians marry young. I danced for him, and he gave me some ruby earrings. To Alexander's pleasure, the faithful elephant, scar-seamed from earlier wars, recovered too.

There were victory games, and thank-offerings to the gods. Just when the victims had been consumed, the rain came down again and doused the fires. I have never grown used to watching the divine flame polluted with burning flesh; nor is any Persian easy when he sees it quenched from the sky. But I said nothing.

The King founded two cities, one each side the river. He named the right-bank one for Oxhead; his tomb was to be in the public square, with his statue cast in bronze.

After that, he and King Poros rode off to war together. Roxane he left in the palace, where she could have the company of King Poros' wives, and be in comfort out of the wet. Me he took with him.

They first had to fight Poros' cousin, a long-time enemy who'd declared war upon Alexander as soon as he learned that they were allies. His courage was not equal to his hate; he fled the test, and Alexander left Hephaistion's force to reduce the province, which he would give to Poros. He himself was for pushing on, drawn by the Encircling Ocean, making short work of anything in his way.

He offered peace to each town that surrendered; kept his word, and let them retain their laws. Those who fled their forts before him, he pursued without giving quarter, reckoning they would have made terms unless they meant to attack him in rear. It had often happened; yet, thinking how peasants will fly from the mere sight of soldiers, depending on what they've known of them before. I was sorry it had to be.

With Poros, he took the great fort of Sangala, despite its walls and its hill and its lake, and the triple wagon-wall drawn up all round them. Then he gave Poros leave to join Hephaistion in settling his new province. Himself, he pushed on towards the next river, the Beas; he would camp on its nearer shore, to rest his men. The rain came down.

We lumbered on, over ground trodden to mush by those before us. The elephants tugged their feet from the mud with sounds like great smacking kisses. The Scythians and Baktrians, to keep dry, wore in the wet swelter their hot felted clothes. The cavalry urged on footsore horses, each mile like three miles' work. The men of the phalanx trudged ankle-deep by the ox-carts which bore their gear; their boots warped with wetting and drying, now soaked again, the thin Indian stuff they'd had to buy for tunics plastered to their thighs; the edges of their cuirasses galled them through it as if they had been naked. The rain came down.

On rising ground above the river, they pitched the great tent of Darius; Alexander had brought it, to show himself as a king. It was green and fragrant here; we were coming towards hill-country; from the east I could swear I smelled the breath of the mountains, but the clouds hid every-thing. The rain came down, steady, unwearied, sighing through the trees and the tall green canes, as if it had fallen since the world began, and would not cease till the world was washed away.

The tent was leaking. I had that seen to, and looked out for him a dry robe and shoes. When he came, he felt my clothes, and would accept no service till I had changed them. I was so used to being wet, I had hardly noticed.

He had his generals to supper. Listening inside, I could tell he was in good spirits. He said he'd heard that beyond the Hyphasis the land was rich, the people were stout fighters, and the elephants bigger and stronger even than King Poros'. A last fine battle, before reaching the world's end.

But something odd had struck my ear. If he was a little drunk, his voice would always carry over the rest. But he was sober, and still it did. He was not loud; it was the others who were quiet.

He'd noticed, too. He bade them drink up, and chase the damp from their blood. They made a better show, till the meal was over and the servers gone. Then Ptolemy said, 'Alexander. I don't think the men are happy.'

He laughed. 'Happy! If they were they'd be insane. This rain, it's like wading through Styx and on through Lethe. They've shown a fine spirit, and they've seen I know it. The wet season's due to finish; Poros told me it's overlong this year. As soon as it clears, we'll hold games and give good prizes, and have them fresh to go on.'

They all said Yes, no doubt that would set them up.

At bedtime he said to me, 'This rain would dispirit lions. If only I could have settled Baktria a half-year sooner, we'd have been here in winter.' He did not say, 'If I'd waited there half a year.' He would have said it once. It was as if he felt, at last, the chariot of time pursuing him.

'After the rains,' I said, 'They say it's all fresh and beautiful.' I was glad he had made an early night of it. He'd been riding all day up and down the column, to see no one was bogged-down. He looked tired and the lines on his brow were back again.

Next day I came to his tent at dawn, to be first with good news. 'Al'skander! It has stopped raining.'

He jumped up, threw his blanket round him, and went to look. When first I'd known him he would have gone naked from his bed. He had grown more careful, from being often with Persians. A pale sun rose over the green leaves. Even its first rays had warmth; one could tell it was more than just a break in the rains.

'Thanks be to Zeus!' he said. 'Now I can get my poor men in heart again. They deserve a holiday.'

The river-banks smelled of sap and young flowers. He gave orders for the Games and invited entries. I took my horse Oryx (Lion was looking tired) and rode out to smell the breath of the mountains, before we turned for the plains.

I came back through the camp. Hundreds of times, all over Asia, I had ridden through it. Apart from land and weather, it was always much the same. But not today.

Even the camp-followers, whom I passed first, were restless. One noticed the carefree children, splashing in sunlit puddles, because the mothers had their backs to them chattering. In the quarter where the better-off, such as artists and merchants, lodged, one of the actors whom I knew came running; when I drew rein, he said, 'Bagoas. Is it true the King's turning back?' 'Back?' I said. 'Why, it's only a few days' march to the Stream of Ocean. Of course he's not turning back.' I rode on by the soldiers' camp. Then I knew something was wrong.

Soldiers in rest-camp have a thousand things to do; making good their kit and boots and weapons; buying things. There will be women, cock-fights and dice games; fortune-tellers, jugglers and men with dancing dogs. Such people were all about, dejected, getting no trade. The men did nothing. Nothing, that is, but talk.

A dozen with heads together; a score, hearing one man; two or three arguing; they talked. And I never heard a laugh.

When officers passed, one might be called to, as a friend for counsel; another would be scowled at silently. Some glanced even at me, as if I might carry tales of them. I only wished I knew what to tell. It was then a memory knocked at my mind – of a night on the high moors, above Ekbatana.

No! I thought. It's not as bad as that, and with him it never could be. But it's bad. His generals must tell him. It would be insolence from me.

They began about noon, by ones and twos. I'd been right, that it was not like Ekbatana. No one wished Alexander harm. No one dreamed of another King. The men wanted one thing only: to go no further.

I had thought he'd make light of it, at least at first. But he'd always had the feel of his troops, and he knew his officers; those who made much of little never reached these men's rank. He was calm, but serious. At the end he said to Ptolemy and Perdikkas, 'This must be taken in time. I shall speak myself. Give it out at once; every officer from brigade commander up, outside this tent an hour after sunrise tomorrow; allies and all. The rain's to blame for all this.'

No more rain fell. I rode through the camp again a few hours later. The feeling had changed. Instead of sullenness there was purpose. Each senior officer's tent had a crowd of men outside it, quite orderly, waiting to speak.

Next morning he was up early, pacing about. He hardly knew I was dressing him. I saw his lips move with the words his mind was forming.

From first light, they had been gathering outside; Macedonians, Persians, Baktrians, Indians, Thracians. Together, they made up a biggish crowd; about as many as his voice would reach.

A trestle had been brought out for him to stand on. He wore his best battle-armour, the winged silvery helmet, the jewelled belt from Rhodes. As he leaped on the rostrum, lithe as a boy, there was a breath like a sighing breeze. My actor friend had once said that he could have made his fortune in the theatre.

I listened behind the tent-flap. This play had no part for me.

He said he grieved to hear the men had lost so much spirit; he had called them in council, to decide along with him whether to go on. He meant, of course, that he would persuade and not compel them. I don't think the notion of really turning back had entered his head.

He had a splendid style, eloquent without rhetoric, though he'd not written down a word. He spoke of their unbroken victories; why need they fear the men beyond the river? The end of their task was near. They were coming to the Encircling Ocean; the very same that washed Hyrkania in the north, and Persia southward; earth's utmost boundary. He could not believe – I could hear it in his voice – that they felt no touch of his burning eagerness. Had he not shared their dangers, he said, and had they not

shared the spoils? Would they give up so near fulfilment? 'Keep steadfast-
ness!' he cried to them. 'It is a lovely thing, to live with courage, and die
leaving an everlasting fame.'

His clear voice ceased. He waited. It was so quiet, you could hear a shrill-
voiced bird, and the pi-dogs bickering.

After a while he said, 'Come! I've said my say; I sent for you to hear
yours.' At this, there was a shifting and shuffling about. Suddenly I
remembered the silence before Darius, at that last audience; and I felt the
difference. *He* had been despised. Alexander had awed and shamed them;
the words they'd come with had died before him. And yet, like Darius, he
had not moved their minds.

'Someone speak out,' he said. 'You've nothing to fear from me. Isn't my
word enough, do you want my oath on it?'

Someone muttered, 'Yes, Koinos, go on.'

A grizzled square man was shoved forward through the crowd. I'd
known him well by sight, even before his great part in the river battle. He'd
fought under Philip, but, a soldier first and last, never joined a faction.
Where good sense and stubborn fortitude were called for, the King chose
Koinos. They looked at each other. Koinos' face, the only one I could see,
said, You'll not like this; but I trust you.

'Sir,' he said, 'you've called us here in free council, we all know that.
But I'm not speaking for us commanders; I don't feel I've the right. With
all we've had from you, we'd be over-paid already for going on. If you want
to advance, it's for us to see it done; it's our duty, it's what we were
promoted for. So, with permission, I'd like to speak for the men. Not that
they come first with me, sir. You do. That's why I'm speaking.'

Alexander said nothing. I could see his back taut as a bowstring.

'I'm the eldest here, I think. If I can claim a good name, I have you to
thank, for giving me my chances. Well, sir. The men, as you said yourself,
have done more than any army did before them. Thanks to you, again.
But I put it to you, sir, that when they say it's enough, they deserve a
hearing. Think how many of us Macedonians came out with you. How
many of us are left?'

A good old man. A fine soldier. A Macedonian, speaking out to his King
in his forthright way. What were my people to him, the Persian horsemen
with their proud faces and slender strength? What were the strong
Baktrians, the hawk-nosed Sogdians, the red-haired Thracians, the tall
Indians in their jewelled turbans, the sharers in his victories? Chances
along the way which led to home.

'We've died in the field; we've died of fever and the flux. There are the
cripples who'll never fight again; and the men in your new cities; not all
of them happy there, but there they are. And look at the rest of us, fit to

scare the crows, dressed in Indian rags. When a soldier gets neither pride nor comfort from his turnout, it pulls down his spirits. The cavalry too, the horses' hooves are worn nearly down to the frogs. And, sir, we've wives and children at home. Already our children will be strangers; soon it will be our wives. Sir, the men want to get home with their loot, while they can still be somebody in their villages, looked up to. If they do that, you'll soon have a new army sprung up from the ground, asking to follow you. Go back, King. Your mother must be longing for a sight of you. Call up the young men who'll come out fresh. It's best, sir. Believe me, sir, it's best.'

His voice cracked, and he dragged his fingers across his eyes. A raucous sound came from him, as if he were going to spit; but it was a sob.

As if it had released the others, cries broke out everywhere; not of anger or defiance, but sheer pleading. They almost moaned. They stretched out their arms. If well-picked officers felt like this, what about the men?

Alexander stood unmoving. The sounds faded; they waited his reply.

'Council dismissed.' He turned his back, and went straight into his tent.

One or two senior generals, his friends, made a move to follow. He faced them in the entry and said again, 'Council dismissed.'

At Susa, I learned how to be invisible. One picked that up quickly. While he paced about, I vanished in a corner. When he tugged at his helmet-strap, I came silently and disarmed him, and once more made myself nothing. It gave me time to think.

Did the soldiers share his faith in the Stream of Ocean? I wondered. I thought of the teeming camp with its wandering traders; the interpreters, waiting to earn their small hire when the language of signs broke down. Interpreters called to a king will translate what they are told to. Market interpreters, once paid, will gossip. Their work being all with travellers, they will talk of far places and the road ahead. Did the soldiers know more than we?

The great Aristotle, wisest of all the Greeks, had told Alexander how the world was made. But one thing was sure; he had never been to look.

Alexander was pacing the great tent, back and forth, back and forth. He must have covered a mile. I remained a nothing; to his need, I was nothing more. He needed faith in his dream, and my faith was gone.

Suddenly he fetched up before me, and cried aloud, '*I will* go on!'

I rose, being now visible. 'My lord, you have surpassed Kyros. Herakles too, and Dionysos, and the Heavenly Twins. All the world knows it.'

He searched my face. I concealed my faithlessness from him.

'I must see World's End. It is not to possess it. It is not even for the fame. It is to see it, to be there . . . and it is so near!'

I said, 'They do not understand.'

Later he called back Ptolemy and Perdikkas and the other generals, and said he was sorry he'd been short with them. He would speak to the commanders again next day; meantime he could be planning the new campaign, for when he had talked them round. The generals sat down at the table, busily making notes on the river-crossing and the march beyond. They were no better than I.

He felt that with his skin. All evening he was brooding. I doubt he slept. Next morning when the commanders came, he made no speech to them, just asked if they'd changed their minds.

A confusion of voices followed. I think a few things came out, rumours of distances and so on. Someone had heard such and such, from the interpreter of a caravan. Someone spoke of a half-month march through desert. After a time of this, Alexander called for silence.

'I have heard you. I told you, you had nothing to fear from me. I will order no Macedonian to follow me unwillingly. There are others who will go forward with their King. I shall advance without you. Go, as soon as you wish. Go home. Nothing more is asked of you.'

He went in. I heard the voices outside, growing louder as they went off. Alexander said to the guard outside, 'Admit no one at all.'

But I was once more invisible. All day I came and went. Seeing me not dismissed at the outset, the guard let me back in. I would look through from the sleeping-place, lest he might have given way to distress, being alone. But he would be seated at the table, staring at his plans, or walking about. I saw he still clung to hope.

Whatever he had said, he would not go on without the Macedonians. This army, before which he had proved himself in boyhood, was part of his blood. It was like a lover. Why not? It had greatly loved him. He was shut up here, not in grief alone, but to bring the lover to his feet, asking for pardon.

No lover came. Over the great camp lay a heavy, brooding silence.

He did not send me away. I saw his solitude and did not trouble it. I brought him anything he seemed to need, went out if he looked restless, kindled the lamps at night. They brought him supper. He became aware of me, made me sit down and eat with him. Suddenly with the wine, though he did not take much, he began to talk. He said that all his life, now here or now there, some great longing had seized him, a certain deed to do, a certain wonder to reach and look at; longings so great, he knew that they came from a god. Always he had fulfilled them, always until now.

I hoped he would take me to bed. I could have done him good. But he was longing after another love than mine.

Next day, he stayed inside. The camp murmured sullenly. Everything was the same; except that this was the second day, and his hope was leaving him.

At evening I lit the lamp. Strange flying things threw themselves at the flame, shrivelled and fell dead. He sat at the table, his fists propping his chin. I had nothing to give him. This time, I could not even bring Hephaistion to him. I would have done it, if I could.

After a while, he took a book and opened it. He wants to compose his mind, I thought; and it put a thought in mine. I slipped away in the short Indian dusk, and went to the nearest shade-tree. There he was, his feet folded on his thighs and his hands laid in his lap. He knew enough Greek to converse in now, if one kept it simple.

'Kalanos,' I said, 'the King is in great grief.'

'God is good to him,' he answered; and, as I moved towards him, gently motioned me back. Right before me a great snake was coiled, in the dead leaves a yard away from him.

'Sit over there, and he will not be angry. He is the patient kind. He was angry when he was a man; now he is learning.'

I mastered my fear and sat. The snake's coils stirred gently, and were still.

'Don't sorrow for the King, my child. He is paying part of his debt; he will return with a lighter burden.'

I said, 'To what god can I sacrifice, so that when he is born again, I may be born with him?'

'That *is* your sacrifice; to that you are bound. You will return, to receive his service.'

'He is my lord and will always be. Can you lift his sorrow?'

'He is grasping his own wheel of fire. He has only to loose his hold. But it is hard for the gods to free themselves from god-head.' He unfolded himself, and in one movement was on his feet. The snake hardly shifted.

Alexander was still at his book. I said, 'Al'skander, Kalanos has been missing you. Will you see him, just for a little while?'

'Kalanos?' He gave me one of those looks that went right through one. 'Kalanos misses nobody. You brought him.' I cast down my eyes, 'Yes, bring him in. Now I think of it, he's the only one, but you, I could bear to see.'

When I had brought him past the guard, I went away. I did not try to listen. Healing magic is a sacred thing, and I feared to break it.

When at last I saw him leave, I entered. Alexander made me a sign of greeting, but was in thought, so I sat still. When supper came, he had me share it as before. Presently he said, 'Have you ever heard of Arjuna? No, nor I till tonight. He was an Indian king of times past and a great warrior. One day before a battle, he stood weeping in his chariot; not out of fear, but because honour bound him to fight his kindred. Then, just as you find in Homer, the shape of the charioteer was taken by a god, and the god addressed him.'

He fell quiet, and I asked what the god had said.

'A good deal. They'd both have missed the battle.' For a moment he grinned, then was grave again. 'He told Arjuna he was a warrior born and must fulfil his destiny; but he must do it without regret or desire; he must not want the fruits of it.'

'Could that be?' I asked. His seriousness surprised me.

'Almost, perhaps; by a man obeying orders. I've known men almost like that, and good men too, though they all valued a word of praise. But to lead men, to change their hearts, to make them brave – that, before anything can begin! – to see a new thing one must make, and not rest till one has made it – that needs a longing greater than for one's life.'

'There are so many things, Al'skander, you want more than your life. And your life is all I have.'

'Fire burns, dear Persian, and yet you worship it. I too. I have laid on it fear, and pain, and the body's needs, and the flames were beautiful.'

'Truly,' I said, 'I have worshipped before that fire.'

'But Kalanos, he wants me to lay on the fire all that the fire has given me – honour, fame among men now and men to come, the very breath of the god which says, Go further.'

'Yet he himself left his friends to follow you.'

'To free me, he says. But God gave us hands. If he'd meant them for folding in our laps, we should have no fingers.' I laughed. He said, 'Oh, he is a true philosopher. But ... I was with him once when we passed a dying dog, kicked almost to death, its ribs staved in, panting with thirst. He rebuked me because I drew my sword to end its pain. I should have let it complete its chosen path. Yet he himself would do no harm to any creature.'

'A strange man. Yet there is something one must love in him.'

'Yes. I enjoyed his company, I'm glad you brought him ... Tomorrow, I shall have the omens taken for the river crossing. If they're good, the men will think again.' Even yet, he was grasping his wheel of fire.

'Yes, Al'skander. You will know then for sure what the god means for you.' Something told me I was safe to say it.

It was done next morning. The Macedonians waited in muttering quiet. The victim struggled, itself an unlucky sign. When the liver was taken from the carcass, and laid in the hands of Aristander, the mutter died to a hush, as he turned the dark glossy flesh between his hands. Raising his voice for all to hear, he announced the signs were adverse in all their aspects.

Alexander inclined his head. He returned to his tent, asking the three generals with him. There he told them, quite calmly now, that he would not oppose the gods.

Soon after, he had in his friends and the eldest of the Companions, and told them they could give it out to the army. Nobody said much. They were thankful, but they knew what it was costing him. He sat down with the generals at his table, planning the march back; for a while, there was an everyday working calm. Then the sound began.

At that time, I had never heard a deep sea breaking; but it was like that. Then, as it came near, it was the noise of cheering. With grief I heard them rejoicing in his pain. Then there were voices close at hand, calling to the King. I asked if he would like the tent-flap opened.

'Yes,' he said. 'Yes, let's see how they're looking now.'

They were Macedonians; a full thousand. As he stepped out they cried to him. Their voices were rough and ragged with tears of joy. Many flung up their hands, as Greeks do to the gods. They shouldered each other for a sight of him. One seamed veteran, pushing in front, fell on his knees. 'Oh, King! Unconquered Alexander!' He was a man who had had some schooling. 'Only by yourself you have been conquered, and that for love of us. The gods reward you! Long life to you, and undying glory!' He clasped and kissed the hand of Alexander, who raised him and gave him a pat on the shoulder. He stood a while longer, acknowledging their praises, and then went in.

The lover had returned, still deep in love. But one thing the first lovers' quarrel always leaves behind – the knowledge that it could be. In times past, I thought, he would have kissed that veteran.

Night came. He had a few friends to supper. On his working table, the plans for the river crossing still lay, the wax not yet smoothed out, just scored with great strokes of the stylus. He was quiet at bedtime; I could picture him tossing all night. I set the night-lamp in its place, and knelt down by him. 'I would follow you to the last shores of the world, if it were a thousand miles.'

He said, 'Stay with me here instead.'

He was readier for love than he had known; but I had known it. I used up some of the fire within him, that would have stayed sealed in its furnace, scorching his heart. Yes, though I could not bring him Hephaistion, that night he was glad of me. I saw him fast asleep, before I went away.

23

He built twelve altars, so tall they were like broad towers, for the twelve gods of the Greeks, to mark the end of his journey. Wide stairs wound round them for the priests and victims; the celebrants did their rites against the sky. If he had to turn back, at least he would do it with grandeur.

He rested the men as he had planned, with games and shows; they were festive now, having what they wanted. After that, we marched back across the rivers, to Hephaistion's province that he had settled for Poros. He had built a new city there, and was in it, waiting for Alexander.

They were alone a long time together. Having nothing much else to do, I sought out Kalanos, and asked him about the gods of India. He told me a little, then smiled and said I was advancing on the Way. Yet I had told him nothing.

Hephaistion was a worker, no doubt of that. The province was in good order, appointments made; he was on the best of terms with Poros. He had a gift for such things. Once, before my time, Alexander having just conquered Sidon had even left him to choose its King. Asking here and there, he learned that the last of the old royal line, long since dispossessed by the Persians, still lived in the city, poor as a rat, a day-labourer in the gardens. But he had the name of a good honest man, so Hephaistion enthroned him. The rich nobles had nothing to fight each other for; and the King ruled very well. He is only quite lately dead, lamented by all. Oh, yes, Hephaistion had good sense.

Another boyhood friend of Alexander's had been busy too: Niarchos, a lean-waisted, small wiry man, of Kretan stock. He'd stuck firmly by Alexander in all his quarrels with his father, and shared his exile. He never forgot such things. Admiral of his fleet till he left the Middle Sea, Niarchos had come all the way east as a soldier, but now had again the water his race loves best. He had been making a fleet on the Hydaspes. Alexander meant to go down to the Indus, and on down the Indus to the sea. If he had been kept from going east to the Stream of Ocean, at least he would strike it westward.

The men, who'd hoped to go straight back through Khyber into Baktria, now learned they were to march beside the fleet along the rivers. Tribes there had not yet surrendered, and were reported fierce. The troops were not delighted; Alexander told them he hoped they would allow him to leave India, not run away from it. His temper had shortened, since they had turned him back. They looked at him and kept quiet. At least they were headed homeward.

Alexander had supposed, till lately, that the Indus, if followed far enough, would flow into the Nile. They both had lotuses, and crocodiles too. He had lately learned otherwise from some native river-men; but, as he said, there would still be things to see.

Old Koinos died here, of fever; he never saw Macedon after all. Alexander had kept his word, and never held his plain speech against him; now he gave him a fine funeral. Yet, within, something had altered. The many-headed lover had flawed its faith. They had patched things up, from need of one another; they still loved, but did not quite forget.

The fleet, beached on the sandy banks broadened with early summer, was a fine sight; long war-galleys, of thirty or twenty oars; light skiffs; round-sided tubs of all shapes and sizes; and the big flat horse-transports.

I kept my eyes on Alexander's galley, reckoning its space. Would he take me with him? It was a war-ship; would he think he should take only squires? On the land-march, there was no knowing when I'd get back to him. And I would be under Hephaistion's command. He was to lead on the left bank the greater part of the army, the followers, the elephants and the harem. Not that he would deign to show me spite; but I felt I could not bear it. There was another small matter, too; I had never travelled before where Roxane was and Alexander was not. From Hephaistion, I had nothing to fear but what was in myself. I felt no such assurance about *her*.

I had troubled myself for nothing. When I dared to ask him, Alexander said, 'What, would you like it? Well, why not? They've told me so often I'm Persianized, no one should be surprised. Can you swim?'

'Oh, yes, Al'skander, I'm sure I could.'

He laughed. 'Neither can I.'

We were seen off at dawn by King Poros and most of his subjects. The ships were strung out along the river as far as eye could see. Alexander's galley led; he stood in the prow, his hair wreathed from the embarkation sacrifice. He had invoked Ammon his father god, Poseidon of the waters, Herakles and Dionysos; also the rivers of our passage, for the Greeks do worship the holy waters, though they pollute them (I was growing careless myself). With each libation, he threw in the gold cup along with the wine. In the ships around, everyone raised the paean; the armies on both banks took it up; the horses neighed, the elephants trumpeted. Then to the time of the chanty-men, with the light still cool and grey on the broad waters, we went downstream.

Of all the gifts Alexander gave me, which were many and rich, one of the best was his taking me on the river. I say it still, who have seen the festivals of the Nile. First came the ornate war-galleys, their banks of oars beating like wings; then the motley fleet for miles; on either bank the long columns of the army, the heavy-armed phalanxes, the cavalry, the wagons, the painted elephants; and alongside, running to keep us in sight, thousands of Indians come for the marvel. Horses on ships were themselves a ten years' wonder. The Indians ran amazed, joining their chants to our chanties, till the river ran between cliffs and gorges; the land troops were lost to sight; for songs we had echoes from the cliffs, and the chatter of monkeys among their hanging green.

To me it was enchantment beyond all tales of the bazaar. In the galley's prow, Alexander grasped the figure-head's tall crest, gazing ahead. He gave off a flame of eagerness that caught us all. I ceased to care that all speech in a galley is public, that he had just a little shelter in the stern to sleep in, that we would barely touch hands till the voyage ended. Thrusting on into the unknown world, I entered a part of his soul that his men had known. Everything rang with him. One lost count of time, living in his wonder. Days of joy.

We were still some way from hostile country, and often put in on shore for the chiefs to do their homage. He would be set on a flower-decked throne; there would be horse-shows, dancing, often good; and singing, which seemed to me like the whine of market beggars. Then we would be off with the stream, waving to the troops on shore.

All good things must be paid for, Alexander always said. The river narrowed, the current tugged. Distant and faint at first, came a muffled roar, from the meeting of the waters, where the rapids are.

We had been warned that where the Hydaspes joined the Akisines between cliffs, the doubled waters boiled in whirlpools. Of the noise, no one had warned us. When we neared it, the rowers broke their beat from mere stunned fear; yet with the current we still plunged on. Onesikritos the chief pilot yelled out not to stop, but to row harder; they'd be dead men if the ships slewed round. They bent their backs into it. The pilot in the prows called back to the steersman, conning every yard. Near him stood Alexander, his eyes on the white water, his lips parted in half a smile.

In the giant hands of the river, I remember only wild motion, confusion, and deadly fear which luckily struck me dumb. Once thrown in that race, no one could save himself, nor Alexander. I found myself praying to an unknown god that when we'd been drowned we would be reborn together. Then we were through, still plunging and pitching, with the lower-bank oars all broken. In the tales, there is no enchantment without ordeal.

All the ships came through safe, but for two that collided, and some of their men were saved. Alexander made camp, as soon as we found good beaches.

That song was over.

We were nearing the Mallian country, whose cities had not submitted, and were preparing war. They were ruled by their priests; men quite unlike Kalanos, who indeed kept telling us he was just a god-seeker and not a priest at all. These priests were obeyed even by the warriors. They had proclaimed Alexander and all of us unclean barbarians. They abhor uncleanness, which is wherever they say it is. In Persia we own our slaves, but they are not unclean to us; here, the men of mean occupation, who come of a conquered race, though no one owns them, are so unclean that no priest or warrior will eat food their shadows have fallen on. But these men lived humbly. Not so Alexander. If his shadow could pollute them, what would his rule do?

These were the last people on his westward way, before he turned towards Persia; only these stood between him and the mastery of all India from the Beas to the Indus mouth. He had been robbed of his dream; now the matter of India was work to finish, once for all. The spell of the river was broken; the wondering boy at the prow, setting foot on land, changed to a daimon who burned the air before him.

He sent Hephaistion's troops on five days ahead, to meet any Mallians who fled before him. Ptolemy's men he left three days behind, to catch those who fled back. When the trap was set, he stalked his prey.

We marched through desert, a night and a day, because it was quick and no one went there. It was cruel going, but short. We had most of a night to sleep in. At dawn, Alexander led out the cavalry against the first Mallian town.

It was no great way from camp, so I rode to watch.

There were the mud-brick walls, the peasant fields teeming with men. They had set outposts on the road, to stop Alexander. No one had watched the desert, whence no one came.

The war-yell rose; the cavalry spurred into the fields. The men there were armed with farmers' tools, if they were armed at all. Sabres flashed in the dawn; the Mallians were reaped like barley.

I had thought he would call on them to surrender, as he'd always done. But they had refused already. He was giving no second chances.

He came back at evening, when they had stormed the citadel, covered with dust and blood. While the troops rested and ate, he was giving orders for a night-march, to surprise the next city before warning reached them. Himself he scarcely rested. The light that had shone on the river had turned to heat.

So it went on. Even when the Indians all knew where he was, they refused surrender. He took a good many slaves, those who gave themselves up at last; but many fought to the death, or burned themselves in their houses. The soldiers too had hardened. They, even more than he, wanted to be done for good with India; no revolts breaking out behind them, to make him march them back. They would not have taken prisoners, if he had not ordered it.

War is war. If this had been Darius, I would just have been glad for him, that he went bravely into battle. I had wondered at Alexander, not that he killed, but that so often he did not. Even now, he was letting the women and children get away. But I grieved that his dream had turned to bitterness.

This campaign the Macedonians had not bargained for; and it made them sullen. When I got him ready for his brief night's rest, he looked dried and drawn. 'The sappers brought down the wall,' he said. 'The men have always gone racing for a breach, before the dust could settle, to be in first. Today, I thought they'd never stop jostling about, waiting for each other. I went up and held the gap alone, till it put some shame in them.' Of course they had followed him then, and taken the town. But the lines on his brow had deepened.

'Al'skander, it is a weariness of the spirit. When we are back in Persia, your land and mine, it will all be well.'

'Yes, that will be good. But the frontiers must be secured, and well they know it. I've never asked them for blind obedience. We're Macedonians. I've always told them what we were about. They must sweat this through and make the best of it. As you do.' He kissed me, just in kindness. He never needed desire, to make him grateful for love.

On our next day's march we passed the fallen city, screaming with kites, stinking with rotten flesh in the hot sun, with a filthy smell from the charred houses where Indians had burned themselves. In my heart I prayed the Wise God to free him from all this, and quickly.

One should take care with one's prayers. One should not presume before the gods.

The next city, when he drew near, turned out to have been forsaken. He sent word back that he would go straight on in pursuit, and the camp must follow.

When you follow an army, you have no need of guides. We came to a river, and a ford all churned with horse-hooves. On the far side, there had been a battle. The dead lay everywhere, like some strange fruit of the land, darkened with ripeness against the pale withered grass and scrub. A faint sweet stench was starting; it was hot. I was taking a drink from my flask, when I heard a moan close by. It was an Indian, a little younger than I, stretching his hand to the water. He was done for; his entrails spilled from his wound. Yet I dismounted, and gave him a drink. Those who rode near me asked if I was mad. Why indeed does one do such things? I suppose he only lived longer in his pain.

Soon we overtook some ox-wagons, sent by Alexander for his dead and wounded. The wounded had awnings over them, and the water-bearer with his donkey went beside. Alexander always looked well after his people.

The wagoners told us there had been fifty thousand Mallians in the field. Alexander had held them somehow, just with his cavalry, till the archers and the infantry came up; then the enemy fled to the walled town, which we would see beyond the palm-grove. The King had it surrounded, and would rest his men for the night.

Before dusk we reached the round brown Mallian town, with its outer battlements, and the squat walls of its inner citadel. The tent-wagons trundled about with their slaves; the cooks unloaded their cauldrons and their sacks, set up their grids and earth-ovens, to give the men a good meal after the light mid-day ration. Alexander ate with his senior officers, Perdikkas, Peukestes and Leonnatos, planning the attack. 'I shan't get the men up before dawn. The infantry's had a long hot march, and the cavalry's had a battle. A good sleep and a good breakfast, then up and at it.'

At bedtime I looked at his splendid arms, which the squires had burnished, and his new corselet. He'd had it made in India, for the heat, lighter than his old one, with the plates quilted into Indian stuff. As if he had not shown up enough before, it was scarlet, with a gold lion worked on the breast.

'Al'skander,' I said, 'if you wore your old corselet tomorrow, I could get this cleaned. It's dirty from the battle.'

He turned round with raised brows, and grinned. 'You Persian fox! I know what you're up to. Oh, no. The men need to be shown, it's not enough to tell them.' He might have said that any time, but now it had a touch of sourness. Then he laid his hand on my shoulder. 'Don't try to keep me from it, even in love. I would rather end as I began ... Come, cheer up; won't you want to know tomorrow where to look for me?'

He slept well, as always before a battle. He used to say he left it then with the god.

Next day soon after sun-up they closed in round the town; the wagons moved up with the ladder and rams and catapults, and the sappers' tools. For some time we could see Alexander riding about, picked out, even when small with distance, by his scarlet and his silver helmet. Then he dismounted and was hidden in a mass of men before the wall. Soon they vanished into it; they must have forced a gate.

Troops poured in after them; ladder were carried through. The walls above, which had been packed with Indians, suddenly had emptied.

I rode forward to see better, on my own. There were few followers here but slaves; the crowd was with Hephaistion. No, there had been no surrender. The Mallians had run back to their inner citadel, and thronged its walls. Hidden by the town's low mud houses, the Macedonians must be below.

A ladder reared in sight against the wall, and settled. Then, mounting it, I saw a bright flash of scarlet. It went steadily up till it reached the battlements; hung there shoving and struggling; then stood upright on top, alone.

He was using the sword. One Indian fell; another he pushed off with his shield. Then three men swarmed up the ladder to fight beside him. The Indians fell back from them. The ladder was packed with clambering Macedonians. He had shown them once again. Suddenly like stones in a rock-fall, they tumbled down out of sight. The ladder had broken under them.

I rode nearer, scarcely knowing what I did. The four seemed to stand for ever, pelted with missiles from the wall and the fort within. Then Alexander was gone. He had leaped down – on the inner side.

After the shortest pause, I expect of unbelief, the others followed him.

I don't know how long it really was before the next Macedonians scaled the wall; about as long perhaps as it takes to peel and eat an apple, or die ten times. They went up on each other's shoulders, or with ladders, or by making footholds with spears. They poured over and were gone. I mustn't expect, I kept saying to myself, to get a sight of him yet.

A group of men mounted the wall from within. They were carrying something scarlet. Very slowly, they lowered it down a ladder out of my sight. I could not see it move.

I slashed at my horse's rump, and galloped towards the city.

The lower town was empty, even of the dead, quite peaceful; pumpkins and gourds ripened on the flat roofs. Ahead, from the citadel, came battle-yells and death-screams, which I scarcely heard.

At the door of a poor house, in a street just outside the wall, three of the squires were standing, looking in. I pushed between them.

The shield they'd carried him on lay with a pool of blood in it. He was on a peasant's dirty bed, with Peukestes and Leonnatos standing over him. More squires were huddled in a far corner. There were chickens running about.

His face was like chalk, but his eyes were open. In his left side, where all the bright scarlet cloth was darkened, stood a long thick arrow. It moved, and paused, and moved again with his shallow breath.

His lips were parted, drawing in, through the pain, just enough air for life. The breath hissed softly; not from his mouth, but from the wound. The arrow was in his lung.

I knelt by his head. He was too far gone to know. Peukestes and Leonnatos looked up briefly. Alexander's hand unclenched and felt at the arrow. He said, 'Pull it out.'

Leonnatos, almost as white as he, said, 'Yes, Alexander. We must just shift the corselet.' I had handled it often. I knew how strong that quilting was. It was pierced, not torn. The arrow-flights would not pass through it.

'Don't be a fool,' Alexander whispered. 'Cut the shaft.' He fumbled at his belt, got out his dagger, and sawed weakly. Then he coughed. Blood came from his mouth; the shaft jerked in his side. His face emptied of life. Faintly, still, the arrow moved in the wound.

'Quick,' said Peukestes, 'before he comes round again.' He took the dagger, and scraped at the hard cane. While he whittled it, and Leonnatos held it steady, I undid the corselet buckles. Alexander came round while Peukestes was still hard at it. He never stirred, as the barb ground in his side.

The shaft severed, leaving a handspan of pointed end. I slid the corselet from under him; we eased it off, hindered by the knots in the cane. Peukestes cut away the bloody chiton. The purple wound in the white flesh opened and closed, the air softly whistling through. Sometimes, it paused; he was trying not to cough.

'In God's name,' he whispered, 'pull and have done.'

'I'll have to cut for the barb,' Peukestes said.

'Get on, then,' said Alexander and closed his eyes.

Peukestes took a deep breath. 'Show me all your daggers.' Mine had the finest point; I had bought it in Marakanda. He thrust it in close by the shaft, and worked it outward. I took Alexander's head between my hands. I don't suppose he even knew of it, through all that pain.

Peukestes withdrew the blade, moved the arrow sideways, set his teeth and pulled. The thick iron barb came out; then a dark stream of blood.

Alexander said, 'Thank you, Peu-kes –' His head sagged; he lay like marble. Nothing moved but the blood; and even that soon ceased.

The doorway of the hut had been thronged with people. I heard the cry that the King was dead, spreading away.

In Persia, to bewail the dead comes without thought, like tears. But I offered him, as was his due, the gift of silence. Indeed, there was nothing else within me.

They were shouting up to the soldiers fighting in the citadel, that the King was dead. The clamour inside, which had gone on all this time, redoubled. You would have thought all the world's wicked had been flung at once into the Fiery River. It reached me without meaning.

'Wait,' Leonnatos said. He picked up from the dirty floor a chicken feather, and laid it on Alexander's mouth. For a moment it was still; then the down of the quill moved faintly.

I helped them bind up the wound with whatever we could find. Tears streamed from my eyes. That time, I was not the only one.

At last, when they dared to move him, he was put upon a litter. The squires carried it, walking softly. As I followed, something flew over the citadel wall, and thudded in the dust beside me. It was a three-month Indian child, with its throat cut from ear to ear.

Up there, the soldiers still thought him dead. They were taking his blood-price, and washing out their shame. They left no living thing there.

For two days he lay in the open hand of death. He was drained of blood. The arrow had chipped a rib. Though almost too weak to lift his hand, he did that rather than speak. He spoke when the doctor would not leave him; he ordered him to see the wounded. I had understood his sign; he never had to open his mouth with *me*.

The squires helped me with the nursing where they could; good lads, but nervous. I asked one, outside, 'Why did he do it? Did the men hang back?'

'I'm not sure. Perhaps a little. They were clumsy bringing the ladders. He snatched one and set it himself, and went straight up.'

The wound, though terribly torn and bruised, never went putrid. But as it healed, his sinews stuck to his ribs. Every breath caught him like a knife, then and long after. At first, a cough was such agony he had to press both hands to his side to hold it still. To the very end of his life, if his breath laboured hard he was in pain. He hid it, but I always knew.

On the third day he could speak a little; they gave him a taste of wine. So the generals came then, to scold him for his recklessness.

Of course they were right. It was a wonder he'd lived till the arrow hit him. He had fought on with it in, till he fell lifeless. In his tent was the old shield from Troy, with which Peukestes had covered him; often I saw him look at it. He took the rebukes with patience; he had to, because of the men whom the ladder's breaking had trapped along with him. One had died, he owed his life to the others. But he had done as he'd meant, and forced the men to follow him. The lover was still true to the beloved; it was their eager rush that broke the ladder. He couldn't have foreseen that.

Leonnatos told him all about the massacre, to show him their devotion. He said, 'The women and all the children?' and took a sharp breath and coughed up blood. Leonnatos was brave, but never quick in the head.

On the fourth day, when I was propping his pillows high to help him breathe, Perdikkas came in. He had been fighting on the far side of the town when Alexander was wounded. Having the highest rank, he was now in command; a tall man, dark-browed, both alert and steady. Alexander trusted him.

'Alexander, you're not fit to dictate a letter yet, so I've written one for you, with permission. It's for Hephaistion to give out to the army. Do you think you can just sign it?'

'Of course I can,' said Alexander. 'But I won't. Why disturb them? They'll start to say I'm dead. We've had enough of that.'

'It's unfortunate; but that's what they're saying now. It seems someone carried the rumour. They believe we're keeping it dark.'

Alexander pushed with his good arm (the left one dragged at his wound) and nearly sat up. I saw a stain of red on his clean bandage. 'Does Hephaistion himself think this?'

'It may well be. I've sent a dispatch; but something from you would clinch it.'

'Read me the letter.' He heard it through, then said, 'Add to that, before I sign, that I'll be coming in three day's time.'

Perdikkas brought down his brows. 'Better not. When you don't, it will make things worse.'

Alexander's hand gripped the blanket. The red on the bandage spread. 'Write down what I told you. If I say I'll go, I'll go.'

He went, seven days from when he took the wound.

Once more I was with him on the river. He had a little tent in the stern. Though it was not far to the water, the litter's jogging had worn him out. He lay like the dead. I remembered him standing in the prow, with the wreath on his hair.

It took two nights and three days. For all I could do, a galley is short of comforts; and he felt the pull of the oars. He never complained. I sat by him, fanning off the water-flies, changing the dressings on his great half-scabbed wound, and thinking, It's for Hephaistion you are doing this.

Now, I can see he would have gone for the men alone. He had never named any deputy, in case he should be past choosing one, nor any successor if he fell. It was not that he would not think of death; he lived with it; but that he would not give one man such a place of power, or expose him to so much envy. He knew well enough how it would be at the camp, while they thought him dead. Three great generals were based there, Krateros, Ptolemy and Hephaistion, each with equal claim to the high command; the troops well knowing it; knowing too that if he were dead, the Indians would rise up behind them and before. Had I asked him why he was going he would have answered, 'It is necessary.' But I remembered his voice saying, 'Does Hephaistion think that?' and I nursed my grief.

It was late afternoon when the camp was sighted. He had dozed off. As he had ordered beforehand, the awning was furled up, to let him be seen. He was already among the army; the whole river-bank was thick with men awaiting the ship. When they saw him lie unmoving, a great wail broke out, spreading all along to the camp. It could not have been more if a Great King had died at Susa. But it was not custom that drew it from the Macedonians. Sheer grief wrung it out.

He woke. I saw him open his eyes. He knew what it meant; they had felt what it was to be without him. I don't blame him, if he let them feel it a little longer. The galley was almost at the quay, before he lifted his arm and waved.

They roared and cheered and yelled. The noise was deafening. As for me, I was watching the three generals waiting at the landing-quay. I saw whose eyes he met first.

A shaded litter was waiting. They put down his stretcher by it. He said something I could not hear, being still on board. It seemed he disliked the litter. Something always goes wrong, I thought, when I have to leave him to other people; what is it now?

When I came down the gangplank, a horse was being led up. 'That's better,' he said. 'They can see now whether I'm dead.'

Someone gave him a leg-up. He sat as straight as if on parade. The soldiers yelled. The generals walked beside him; I hoped they were watching in case he fell. He'd not even been on his feet till the day before, and then for just long enough to make water.

Then the men came up.

They came in a great shouting wave, steaming with rank sweat in the Indian sun. The generals were shoved like nobodies. It was lucky they'd found him a quiet horse. The soldiers grasped at his feet, kissed the hem of his chiton, blessed him, or just got near and gazed. At last some of the squires fought through to him, knowing, as no one did on shore, the state he was really in. They led his horse towards the tent prepared for him.

I squeezed through the crush like a cat under a gate. They were so carried away, they never even noticed it was a Persian pushing them. I'd heard enough by now from those who'd seen chest wounds in the field, of how a man would live till he tried to rise, then spew up a pool of blood and die in moments. About twenty paces from the tent, when I'd almost caught up, he drew rein. He knows he's going to fall, I thought, and I struggled nearer.

'The rest I'll walk,' he said. 'Just to let them know I'm alive.'

He did it. They doubled the time for him, grasping his hands, wishing him health and joy. They tore flowers from the bushes, those waxen heavy-scented flowers of India, and flung them; some snatched wreaths from the shrines of Indian gods. He kept his feet, smiling. He never turned away love.

He went in. Kritodemos the doctor, who'd come by ship with him, hurried after. Coming out and seeing me outside – he knew me well by now – he said, 'He's bleeding, but not much. What kind of stuff is he made of?'

'I'll see to him, as soon as the generals go.' I'd brought along a bag with the things I needed. Ptolemy and Krateros came out fairly soon. So now, I thought, the real wait begins.

A crowd was milling before the tent. They seemed to think he would be giving audiences. The bodyguard turned them off. I waited.

The palm-trees were black against the sunset, when Hephaistion came out. 'Is Bagoas there?' he asked the guard. I came forward. 'The King's getting tired, he'd like to be settled down.'

Getting tired! I thought. He should have been settled an hour ago.

It was hot inside. He'd been propped up, after a fashion. I did it again properly. A wine-cup was standing by him. 'Oh, Al'skander!' I said. 'You know the doctor said not, if you were bleeding.'

'That's stopped, it was nothing.' It was rest he'd needed to pick him up, not wine.

I'd already sent for water, to sponge him down. 'Whatever have you been doing with this bandage?' I asked. 'The dressing's slipped half off.'

'It's nothing,' he said. 'Hephaistion wanted to see it.'

I just said, 'Lie over. It's stuck.' I soaked it off, bathed him, put on the salve, bandaged him, sent for his supper. He could barely eat. He was tired almost beyond rest. When I'd settled him, I sat quiet in a corner; he'd grown used to having me there when he went to sleep.

A little later, as he was dropping off, he gave a great sigh. I came up softly. His lips moved. I thought, He wants me to fetch Hephaistion back to sit with him. But what he said was, 'So much to do.'

24

Slowly he mended. The Mallians all sent envoys to surrender. He asked a thousand hostages, but, when they came, took that as proof of good faith and set them free.

Processions of honour came from his Indian lands, laden with gifts; gold bowls full of pearls, chests of rare wood filled with spices, embroidered awnings, gold necklaces thick with rubies, more elephants. Grandest of all were the tame tigers, hand-reared from cubs, pacing on silver chains. Alexander thought them more kingly even than lions, and said he'd have liked to hand-rear one himself, if he'd had time to care for it properly.

For each embassy he'd get out of bed, and be found enthroned as if he had nothing wrong with him. They always made long speeches, which had to be interpreted; he would reply, and be interpreted too. Then he would admire the gifts. I was afraid the tigers would smell his blood.

The wound dried up, though it still looked dreadful. One morning he said to me, pleased as a child who's pulled a loose milk-tooth, 'Look what I got out,' and showed a great splinter of rib. After that the pain was less sharp; but skin was still stuck to sinews, sinews to bone; and, so the doctor said, the lung inside to that. It hurt him to breathe deep, or use his arm; his strength was slow returning. This did not stop him from doing all the business which had heaped up while he was on campaign.

Soon after we arrived, Roxane came to his tent in her curtained litter, to greet her lord and ask how he did. She'd learned a little more Greek, as he told me after; it seemed she'd been gentle and meek and full of concern. I'd heard already that when the rumour came of his death, her screams had deafened the camp. Maybe it was true grief; on the other hand, she was still childless, and would have been no one at all, once he was gone.

After a month or so, he was on his feet; and we took to the river again, towards where it joins the Indus. It was a royal progress. The stream was broad and smooth; he took with him by water ten thousand foot alone, beside cavalry and their horses. The ships had coloured sails and painted eyes on their prows, and high stern-ornaments carved and gilded; half Greece, half India. It was good to see him stand again at his galley's prow, looking ahead.

Where the rivers join, he saw a fine site for a city, and set up camp. He still needed rest. We were there most of the winter; pleasant enough, though I missed the hills.

Now he was settled somewhere, people were coming from as far as Greece. But one guest was unexpected; Oxyartes, Roxane's father, arrived with his eldest son, in a good deal of state, Oxyartes claiming he was concerned about some revolt in Baktria. My own belief is, he'd come to see if his grandson, the next Great King, was on the way.

There'd been little of Alexander's Indian campaigning on which he could have taken Roxane if he'd wished; but I suppose Oxyartes had thought that where there's a will, there's a way. Alexander now claimed to be quite well, and was even riding ('It's only a stitch, it just needs to be loosened up') so could not blame his wound for slack attendance in the harem. For some weeks, in fact, he'd been well enough to make love – with someone who knew how to look after him. Therefore, I saw nothing of this state visit, having joined a pleasure-cruise up river, to view the crocodiles. One should always know when to vanish.

As a parting gift, Alexander gave his father-in-law a satrapy. It was under Parapamisos, about as far east as one could go and still be in Baktria; and a very long way from the royal cities of Persia. He was to have joint rule with a Macedonian general, who, I suspect, was asked to keep him busy there.

With spring, Alexander was ready to go west to Ocean. But between was all country of the ruler-priests, who gave him hard bloody wars. All peoples that acknowledged him, he welcomed in friendship; but if afterwards they rose up behind his back he did not pardon easily. He could never bear with treachery.

At first, he left to his generals the strenuous sieges. But it ate at him like a sickness; he was short even with me. It was not for long. He was off into battle, coming back ready to drop; whether he used his left arm for shield or bridle, it dragged at the stiffened wound. The doctor gave me some tinctured oil to soften it; the nearest to pleasure my hands could give him then, he was too tired for anything more.

He now disposed his forces. Krateros was to go back to Persia through Khyber, and settle Baktria on his way; taking along the old and crippled soldiers, the elephants and the harem. I don't know how Roxane took it; better, I should think, when she learned where Alexander was going next. Over winter, he had not quite neglected her; but there was no sign of the next Great King.

Once on a time, I too would have been packed off by the easy way. Now it was never thought of. And even if I had foreseen what lay ahead, I would not have chosen it.

It was summer before the frontier was settled, the new cities and ports were founded, and we were ready for the Ocean.

He did not embark an army; he went only to see the wonder; but we were still nearly a fleet. By now he'd rested from battle, to found a river-port, and was full of eagerness.

The Indus near its mouth makes even the Oxos look a rivulet. It seemed itself a sea, till we first felt the wind of Ocean. It nearly blew us under. The fleet just got to land with no one drowned. I thought that, all in all, Ocean might have treated Alexander more kindly.

The shipwrights made good; we set out with Indian pilots. Just as they said we'd almost reached Ocean, it blew again; we ran for shore and moored the ships. And then the water went away.

It went out and out. The ships were left high and dry, some in mud, some tilted on sandbanks. No one knew what to make of it; it seemed a most dreadful portent. Our seamen and rowers from the Middle Sea had none of them seen such a thing in all their days. The storm was just wind; but this . . . !

Some men from Egypt said that if this was like the Nile, we might be stranded here half a year. No one could get much sense out of the Indians, who spoke some local dialect; they made signs that the water would come back, but we could not make out when. We made camp to wait.

It returned with the fall of dark. Wave by wave it came lapping up, lifting the stranded ships, knocking their sides together. We prepared to remove the camp out of its path, not knowing how far to fly. But at the place where we found them first, the waters halted. Next morning they had sunk again. And this, as we learned when we'd found an interpreter for the Indians, Ocean does twice a day.

Whatever they say in Alexandria, I promise this is no market-tale. Only last year a Phoenician, who'd sailed past the Pillars to Iberia, told me that there it is just the same.

Once more the ships were mended; and there at last stretched Ocean. At the land's end, Alexander sacrificed to his special gods; then we put to sea.

The breeze was light, the sky blue; the sea much darker, almost the colour of slate. Small waves flung crystal spray. We passed two islands; then there was nothing between us and the very end of the world.

When Alexander had gazed his fill, he offered two bulls to Poseidon. Ocean had acted strangely on my belly; at the smell of the blood, I had to run to the side. And there I saw a silver fish, slender, about two spans long, rise from the water, fly skimming above, the full length of a spear-cast, and splash back again. No one saw it but I; and no one believed me after, except Alexander. Even he did not quite like to have it put in the Journal. But by Mithra, I swear it's true.

The bulls were flung overboard to the god. Alexander was not just thanking him for the sight of Ocean; he was asking favour for his old friend Niarchos, and all the fleet. They were to put out to sea, and go coastwise right from the Indus to the Tigris, looking for coastal towns or sites for ports. If a trade-route could be founded direct from Persia to India, saving the long perilous caravan-trail, Alexander thought it would be a great thing for mankind.

The coastal parts being reported harsh and barren, he would march the army alongside by land, to leave the fleet food-stores, and dig wells. Of course he chose the hardest part. We Persians all told him it was known for desert country, and Kyros himself had been in some trouble there. 'The Indians claim,' I said to him, 'that he only came through with seven men left. But that may be their vanity, because he'd meant to invade them.'

'Well,' he said smiling, 'he was a very great man. Still, we have gone a little further.'

About midsummer, we set out.

In spite of Krateros' convoy, we were still a big force of many peoples. There was a crowd of the soldiers' women and all their children; and the Phoenicians stuck to us. They will bear much hardship in the way of trade; and there was no knowing what we might come upon in unknown land. They found it well worth their trouble; that is, at first.

Eastern Gadrosia is a land of spices. Spikenard with its furry clusters grew under our feet like grass, its bruised perfume filled the air. The gum on the little myrrh-trunks caught the sun like amber. Groves of tall trees dropped pale sweet petals on us. When the hills and vales of this pleasant land started to fall behind us, so did the Phoenicians. They stayed among the spices. They'd heard what was coming next.

Spice-bushes turned to scrub, and trees to thorns. For green valleys, we had scoured water-courses carving dry earth, their stony beds bone-dry, or with a trickle you could barely fill a cup from. Mazes of soft rock were sculpted by weather into weird shapes of ruined forts, toothed battlements, or monsters rearing upright. Over plains of boulders and round stones we had to bruise our feet to save our horses'; then there would be cracked mud-flats, white with salt. Nothing grew, but what will grow without rain in stone or dust.

At first there would be water not far off; by scouting inland the foragers got supplies. Alexander sent a load to the shore for Niarchos, with orders to find him water. The men came back saying they'd set up a sea-mark, but there was no place for a port. No one lived there, but wretched creatures shy and mute as beasts, wizened and hairy, with nails like claws. Their only food was fish, for the land bore nothing. For water there were little brackish pools, not enough for a dog; it must be the wet in the raw fish that kept these people alive.

We marched on; and came to the sand.

Often in those two months I said to myself, If I live, I will wipe this time from my mind; I cannot even bear the memory. Yet now I turn to it. He is gone; and all times when he was there seem like lost riches. Yes, even that.

We marched by night. When the sun was high, no one could move and live for long. Scouts went ahead on camels, to find the next stream or water-hole, which we must reach wherever it was, or die. Sometimes we came to it before sun-up; more and more often not, as our strength lessened and our horses failed.

The grim fretted rock we'd left seemed kindly, compared with the scalding sand. Even at night it held the heat of the day. Its hills were too long to skirt; going up one slid back one pace in two, going down the men would glide. We horsemen must walk both ways – as long as we had horses. They gave out before the men; the wretched scrub and parched grass did not give them strength to reach the water-stages. It was not for long that the kites got them; after the foragers began to come back with nothing, a dead horse was a feast.

My Lion dropped halfway up a sandhill. I tried to get him up, but he just lay down. As if sprung from the ground, a horde with swords and cleavers appeared. 'Give him time to die!' I cried; I'd seen a mule carved up still breathing. They thought, when I showed my dagger, it was to keep the meat for myself. I made the sacrificer's cut into the neck-vein. I don't think it hurt him much. I took a share for myself and my servants; I gave them most of it. We in the King's household ate just like the King – the army ration, but at least nobody stole it.

Mules died whenever no officer was in sight; men would toss their own loot away, to get the beast of burden. The cavalry took to sleeping with their horses. I learned this trick too late; Oryx, who had held out well, vanished while I slept. I never asked Alexander for another; horses were for soldiers now.

Going on foot, I often came across Kalanos, making his way like some lean long-legged bird. He had refused to go with Krateros and leave Alexander, from whom he accepted a pair of sandals when we came to the stones. In the sunset hour, when everyone clung to the last bit of rest before the march, I would see him cross-legged, meditating with his gaze on the setting sun. Alexander mastered or hid his weariness; Kalanos seemed to feel none.

'Guess his age,' Alexander said to me one day. I guessed fifty-odd. 'You're twenty years short. He says he's never been ill all his life.'

'Wonderful,' I answered. He was happy in having only his god to think of, while Alexander was working like a wood-cutter's donkey, thinking about us all. I read his thoughts too well; that we were in this hell through his impatience, because he had not waited for winter to make the march.

About the third week out, when one no longer noticed whom one marched beside, but got along as one could, a soldier said to me, 'Well, the King led us into this, but at least he sweats it out with us. Leading the column on foot, now.'

'What?' I said. I wished I could not believe it. It was true.

We made camp two hours after sunrise, by a stream with real water running. I hurried with his drinking-jug before fools fouled it with their feet. I never trusted the slaves to bring it clean.

He came into the tent, bolt upright. I had his cup filled ready. He stood still in the entry, the first moment he'd not been on view, and pressed both hands to his side. His eyes were closed. I put down the cup and ran; I thought he'd fall. For a moment he leaned on me; then he straightened up and went to his chair, and I gave him water.

'Al'skander, how could you do it?'

'One can always do what one must.' He took three breaths to that.

'Well, you did it. Promise me never again.'

'Don't talk like a child. I must do it from now on. It is necessary.'

'Let's see what the doctor says.' I took the cup from him; it was spilling on his clothes.

'No.' When he'd fetched more breath, he said, 'It's good for me. It loosens the muscles up. That's enough, people are coming.'

They came with their troubles and questions; he dealt with everything. Then Hephaistion came, carrying his rations, to sup with him in the hot morning. I hated trusting anyone else to see he ate. Still, I found later he had, and had taken a drop of wine. He had even been put to bed; he only half woke when I smoothed the doctor's oil on the red burning scar. I had hidden the oil, in case the slaves should eat it.

From then on, he led each day's march on foot and set the pace; long or short, sand or stones. He was in pain every step, in torture before morning. He lived on will.

The men knew it; the marks were stamped on him. They knew his pride; but they knew too that he was punishing himself for what he had made them suffer. They forgave him; their spirits fed on his.

When in the rising heat I got him out of his clothes. I found myself thinking, Will he ever win back all the life this is bleeding out of him? I suppose that already I knew the answer.

He was distressed for the fleet off this cruel coast. Even now he sent another food-store. The officer in charge came back to say the men had unsealed it on the way, and eaten it. Sitting up straight in his folding chair, Alexander said, 'Tell them I reprimand their disobedience, and pardon their hunger. And if the mules have gone too, don't tell me. From now on' – he paused to get his breath – 'missing mules are presumed foundered. Men can take so much; one must know when to hold one's hand.'

Men had begun to die. A trifling sickness was mortal. They would fall out, in the dark of night, sometimes in silence, sometimes crying their own names, in hope that a friend would hear. There was much deafness in the night. What could anyone do, who was barely on his own feet? You would see a soldier with his child on his back, and knew his woman had died; but the children mostly died first. I remember I heard one crying in the dark – perhaps it had been left for dead – but I just trudged on. I had one thing to do, there was no room for any other.

One day we came to a broad water-course, with a fair stream in it, fresh and cold, good mountain water. It had been a shortish march; we were there before dawn, to make camp in the cool. Alexander had his tent pitched on the sands, where he could hear the stream. He had just come in, half-dead on his feet as usual, and I was sponging his face before people arrived, when a strange sound approached, between a rush and a roar. We listened, for an instant; Alexander leaped to his feet, cried 'Run!' and dragged me out by the wrist. Then we ran indeed. A great surge of brown water was bursting down the river-bed. The roar we had heard was the grinding of the boulders.

Alexander shouted a warning. People were scrambling everywhere. As we reached higher ground, I saw the tent tilt like a drunkard's hat, sink and go swirling off in the wrack of flood. I thought, 'The oil's still in my wallet,' and felt for it. Alexander caught his breath from the run. Then, the screaming.

Others too had camped upon the shore. The soldier's women had put up their little awnings, and started to make supper, while the children paddled. They were swept away in hundreds, only a few score left.

That was the most dreadful day of that dreadful march; men searching for the bodies, mostly in vain; everyone else, dead-tired already, making-good under the glaring sun. Alexander's tent was washed up somewhere, and spread to dry. All his things were lost. After hours on his feet, he slept in Hephaistion's tent. Meantime I'd gone begging among his friends; he'd not a change of clothes to his name. Some of the things I got were better than his own; he had travelled light. The squires, who had his arms in keeping, had saved them at least.

We made no march that night, from weariness, and to give rites to the dead. Though if one had to die in Gadrosia, it was something to die by water.

Young as I was, and lightly made, with a dancer's muscles, I felt my strength ebbing now from night to night. I lost count of time, just set foot before foot, my mouth full of dust from the feet around me; the nights began when I wanted only to lie down for ever. Then I would remember I had the oil, which helped him a little; and that if I dropped out, the terrible sun would rise and find me shelterless. So I flogged myself on, between love and fear.

All the marches were longer now; our pace was slower. Still he led, all night and in the heat of the morning. At bedtime we scarcely spoke; it was our understanding he need waste no breath on me. Sometimes I had to stop him from lying down just as he was; he'd curse me, I would snap like a cross nurse at a child; it meant nothing, it rested him from keeping up a face; when he was refreshed he'd thank me.

According to the survey men, we had long passed the half-way of the march. He sent out the camel-scouts, to seek the first fertile land and find supplies. We heard no more of them; each march stretched longer into the heat of day, before we came to water. Once it was so long, Alexander called a halt even in the sun, to let the stragglers catch up. It was by an old stony watercourse, dried up. In last night's well there had been so little, none was left to carry along. He was sitting on a boulder, in his sun-hat of plaited grass. Ptolemy was by him, I expect asking how he felt, for he looked dreadful, drained and drawn and dripping with sweat. I could see him panting, even from where I was.

Someone said, 'Where's the King?' I pointed; a Macedonian pushed past, followed by two Thracians, one of whom held a helmet upside down. It had water in it, not much, just enough to fill the crown. They must have scooped it from some crevice in the stream-bed, hidden by stones. God be thanked, I thought. I craved for it, but not so much as I craved to see him drink.

The tattooed Thracians shouldered along, guarding their treasure with drawn swords. Savage as they looked with their wild red hair, no troops had been more faithful. He'd had to wean them from bringing him severed heads and asking for a bounty; but they had not touched the water. They put up their weapons and ran to him; the first knelt down, with a grin all across his dusty blue-stained face, and held up the helmet.

Alexander took it. For a moment he looked inside. I don't think many felt envy, parched though we were. They could see his state for themselves.

He leaned forward, laid a hand on the Thracian's shoulder, said something in their language, and shook his head. Then he stood up, and lifting the helmet, poured out the water, as Greeks do when they make libation to a god.

There was a deep hum, all along the column, as word went from man to man. As for me, sitting on a boulder in the empty channel, I put my face in my hands and wept. I expect people thought it was at the waste of water. Presently, finding my tears on my hands, I put out my tongue and licked them.

We no longer camped close to water when we reached it. The rush was too great; men would jump in and muddy it, or bloat themselves and die. It was good that morning. I made him lie on his bed while I sponged him over. He looked like a cheerful corpse. 'Al'skander,' I said, 'there has never been anyone like you.'

'Oh, that was necessary.' He smiled at me. I saw it would still have been worth the price to him, if it had killed him.

'You needed it just as much,' he said. 'You look tired today.'

Perhaps he saw more than I knew myself. For a few nights later, in the hour before dawn, I thought, as if another were speaking for me, 'I can go no further.'

After the hours of night, the sand had a little coolness. I stumbled along to a bit of scrub, which would shelter my head when the sun came up. Don't ask why I wished to spin out my death; it seems the nature of man. To rest was wonderful. I watched the long column dragging past. I did not call, as I had heard those others calling. I could only have said, Forgive me.

I lay there taking my ease, till a glimmer showed in the east. By then I had felt some good from resting, and began to think, What am I doing here? Was I mad? I could have gone on.

I got to my feet, and found the track of the column. For a while I felt almost fresh, and was sure I could catch up. I tipped my water-flask, in case a drop was left, though I knew I'd finished it. The sand was heavy and deep; it stank from the ordure of men and horses, buzzing with flies, which flew from it to drink my sweat. From the crest of a dune I saw the dust far ahead. The sun rose higher. My strength was done.

There was a piece of rock, baked red mud, eaten with weather. While the sun still slanted, it gave a patch of shade. My whole body was dry heat, my feet failed. I crawled there and lay face downwards. This is my tomb, I thought. I have failed him. I have earned this death.

All was silent. The shadow began to shrink. I heard a horse's laboured breathing, and thought, Madness comes first. A voice said 'Bagoas.'

I turned over. Hephaistion stood looking down.

His face was white with dust, haggard with weariness. He looked like the dead. I said, 'Why have you come for my soul? I did not kill you.' But my throat was too dry to sound. He knelt and gave me water. 'Not too much yet. More later.'

'Your water,' I whispered, ashamed. 'No, I've come from camp,' he said, 'I've plenty. Get up, we haven't all day.'

He heaved me to my feet, and on to his horse. 'I'll walk him. He can't carry two, he'll die.' I could feel the beast's bones through the saddle-cloth; and it had had the day's march already. So had he. He dragged it along, hitting it when it stopped. My head was clearer. I said, 'You came yourself.'

'I couldn't have sent a man.' Of course not, at the end of such a march. No one went back for stragglers. If you fell out, you fell out.

From the next dune we plodded up, I saw the growing stuff that fringed a stream, and the dark scatter of the camp. He shared more water between us, then handed me back the flask. 'Finish it, it won't hurt you now.'

Once more I strove for speech. At Susa, I had learned to express thanks gracefully. But all I could bring out was, 'Now I understand.'

'Keep up with the column, then,' he said. 'And look after him. I can't, I've my work to do.'

Thanks to me, neither one of us had, that morning. The squires had done their best, but before them he always kept a face up. He was concerned for me, feeling my head to see if I had sunstroke. I said of my rescuer what was required by honour. He only answered, 'That is Hephaistion; it always has been'; and it was as if he closed again the curtain guarding a shrine. It was my punishment. He had meant none; but I knew its fitness.

It was at the next day's halt, that the wind came.

We'd had none before, and now it brought no coolness; only sand, and sand, and sand; blowing under the tents, piling against them till each had its sloping sandhill. Grooms with muffled faces ran to muffle the horses' eyes. It was in our mouths and ears and clothes and hair. It lulled; we slept; and at evening, all shapes were changed, all the landmarks gone, which the scouts had plotted to lead us to next day's water. The waves of sand had swallowed a dead tree whole.

Our water-hole was nearly silted up. I thought this must truly be the end. At least this time, I thought, I shall be somewhere near him, even though it's with Hephaistion he will want to die.

I should have known it was not in him to sit and wait for death. In the Mallian citadel, when he was lying with the arrow in him, he'd killed with his sword an Indian who came up to take his armour. So, now, he held a war-council in his tent. 'The guides have given up,' he said. 'We'll have to find our own landmark. There's only one we know which way to bear for, and that's the sea. We can steer for that by the sun. That's what we'll do.'

In the hour before dawn, he set off with thirty horsemen; they had found just so many horses fit for the work. To see their course, they had to go by day. They vanished beyond the dunes, carrying all our lives.

A score returned that night. Alexander had sent them back when he saw their horses failing. He himself had gone on with ten.

At next day's sunset, red in the sand-haze, we saw them black on the skyline. As they neared, Alexander looked leaner than ever, and the pain-lines were in his face; but he was smiling. We all drank his smile like life.

Five of the ten had fallen behind; with five he had pushed on. They crested a rise; there was the sea, and by the sea what no scouts had found before; green things growing which do not grow in brack. They jumped down and fell to digging, with daggers and bare hands, the thirsty horses nosing at their shoulders. Alexander was the first to strike water; and it was fresh.

The night after that we marched, Alexander leading to guide us. In sight of safety, he allowed himself to ride.

The sea was like polished iron; but it was wet, its mere sight refreshed us. Between it and the reeded dunes, was the strip of green where hidden streams seeped to the ocean.

For five days we followed it, cooled by sea breezes so that we marched by day; digging our wells, and drinking. At evening, we bathed in the sea. It was so delightful, that I forsook all my Persian modesty, and did not even care who saw what a eunuch looks like. We were all like children at play. The guides knew by the green that soon we should reach the road.

Then food began to arrive. The scouts had not died; they had reached the Gadrosian city to the north-west, and from there word had been sent round. The first camel-train came, well laden. It would have given us one spare meal all round, when the march began; now, fair shares made a feast. We were fewer now.

Going by easy stages, we felt strength return; and already faces looked less gaunt, when we came through the passes to the city of Gadrosia.

Here plenty welcomed us; corn and meat and fruit and wine, sent in from Karmania, the pleasant land ahead. We rested, ate and drank; our very skins seemed to drink in health from the green around us. Even Alexander began to gain some flesh, and have blood in his cheeks again. 'They look fit now to enjoy themselves a little,' he said, and led us on into Karmania, at strolling pace.

There was a feast at every halt, and plenty of wine; he had sent ahead to have it ready. Someone, Ptolemy or Hephaistion, devised a plan for getting him to take a rest himself. Craftily, they didn't tell him he looked to need it, but said that after his conquests and ordeals, he should make the same progress Dionysos had done before him. They had two chariots lashed together, with a platform across, and couches, green wreaths and a handsome awning. With good horses from the city, it looked very fine, and he did not disdain it. There was room for him and a friend or two; and the troops cheered him along. A great deal has been made of this, with much nonsense about Bacchic revels; but that is what it comes down to. A good device; it gave him a ride on cushions.

In fresh meadows, by sweet waters, under shady trees, we made our camp. He said to me, 'It's too long since I saw you dance.'

Shockingly out of training as I was, I was young; the sap flowed back into me as into a watered vine; each day my practice moved from labour towards pleasure. Also it kept me from over-eating; everyone's temptation then, and a dangerous one for eunuchs. Fat once put on is not shed so easily. Even since youth is past, I have managed to avoid it. I have him to think of. I've no wish to hear people saying, 'Is *that* what the great Alexander chose to love?'

A racecourse was levelled, a square for trick-riding and such shows; and the carpenters ran up a very good theatre. Singers and actors, dancers and acrobats were posting from everywhere in reach. All was gaiety, except for Alexander, who was getting news of what some of his satraps and governors had been up to, when they thought he was dying of his wound in India. In Gadrosia itself the satrap had been corrupt and slack. He was a Macedonian; Alexander put a Persian in his place. Meantime, the men must have rest and revelry; also he was awaiting Krateros and his army. Offenders elsewhere must wait.

His greatest trouble was getting no news of the fleet. Along that dreadful coast, he'd been able to leave them nothing. They were long overdue; if they perished, he would take it on himself for ever.

Krateros and his throng arrived; our camp was once more a city. Roxane was in good health. Alexander paid his respects without delay, though he left again without much delay either.

I fell in with Ismenios, asking about for news of me. We took wine under a tavern awning, and exchanged our tales. 'I always knew,' he said, 'that your bones were beautiful, but you must put a little more on them. But, Bagoas, the King! He looks – not older, I suppose – worn out.'

'Oh, he's building up,' I answered quickly. 'You should have seen him a month ago.' And I spoke of other things.

Just then, the governor of the district up the coast came posting by chariot, to say the fleet was safe, and Niarchos would be here directly.

Alexander lit up as if he'd slept for a week, and gave the governor presents. Nobody knew that this man, being as stupid as greedy, had offered them no help to lay up their ships, nor given them transport; just rushed off with his news lest anyone should get the reward before him. Days passed; Alexander sent out an escort but it found no seamen. The governor, still at court, was suspect and put under open arrest; Alexander looked more careworn than before, but sent out another escort. On the second day, it brought back two gnarled wizened men, their bodies like rawhide thongs, tanned almost black: Niarchos and his first officer. The escort had not known them, even when they asked for Alexander.

He came forward to embrace his boyhood friend, and wept. Seeing their state, he supposed them the sole survivors. When Niarchos told him the whole fleet was safe, he cried again for joy.

They'd had many hardships and adventures, which are all in Niarchos' book. Kretans are tough; he lived to campaign for years and write his memoirs. If you want to hear of huge whales who flee from the sound of trumpets, or the beastly lives of the Fish-Eaters, you can go to him.

He and his men were feted; Alexander began to look something like himself again. He entertained his friends and honoured the gods with festivals; and the revels followed. A whole crowd of entertainers had come in Krateros' convoy; things could be done in style.

There were games, of course. The riding events were mostly won by Persians; the foot-races by Greeks, who are fonder of using their legs.

(Alexander had given me two fine Karmanian horses.) Thracians won the archery. All the allies got a chance to shine. But we were almost in Persia now; when I saw him look with liking on my people's graces, I knew he was one of *us*.

The plays came next; all very Greek. Masks still came strange to me. When I confessed to Alexander that I'd sooner see the faces, he said he would agree if the face was mine. In this last month, I'd been teaching him once more to embrace delight, instead of pain. His very body felt different, strained into a habit of endurance. A little tending was what he needed; he looked years younger, when I'd loosened him up.

After the drama, the music contests. The day after that, the dancing.

There were nine or ten of us, from everywhere between Greece and India; some very good. This won't be my day, I thought; I'll just dance for him. If he likes it, that's prize enough.

I had just come from where water stood for joy. I wore white striped with green, and started with little tinkling finger-bells for the mountain stream. Then the river flashed and twisted, and took great leaps for the rapids; flowed in slow bends; and sank down, stretching out its arms for the sea's embrace.

Well, it was as he liked it. But it seemed all the army had liked it too. Considering how good some of the rest had been, I was amazed at the noise.

The Indian, who came last, I thought a serious rival; he did Krishna with a flute; and the boy from Susa was very polished indeed. To tell the truth, I have never been too sure about that contest. If I was no better than the runners-up, I daresay I was no worse; and, as always, Alexander did not direct the judges. But the army did.

It was for him, of course. I don't think I was badly liked; I did not flaunt myself, nor intrigue, nor sell my influence. I'd been with him a long time now; I expect it touched them to see how his love endured. He had suffered; they wanted to see him happy; they had watched his face as I danced. They did it for him.

The crown was of gold olive-sprays with sheet-gold ribbons. He put it on me, and stroked the ribbons to fall into my hair, and said softly, 'Beautiful. Don't go, sit here by me.' I sat on the edge of the dais by his chair; we smiled at one another. The army clapped and stamped; and someone with a voice of Stentor yelled, 'Go on! Give him a kiss!'

I looked down, confused. This was going too far, I wasn't sure how he'd take it. They were shouting it all round the theatre now. I felt him touch my shoulder. They had been with him a long time, too; he could tell affection from insolence. He drew me up into his arms, and gave me two firm kisses.

To judge from the applause, they liked it better than the dancing.

It is well that Persian ladies do not attend public spectacles, as Greek ones do. A most immodest custom.

That night he said to me, 'You've won back all your beauty from the desert, or even more.' Well, that's not so hard, at twenty-three, when you have never had a wound. He meant that it was good at last to feel a little life left to spare in him, at the end of the day.

I made him happy, without putting too much tax on it; how, was my secret, he never knew the difference. He was content, which was all that mattered to me just then, and fell asleep straight after.

When I rose, the cover slipped away, but he did not stir. I lifted the lamp and looked at him. He lay on his side. His back was smooth as a boy's, his wounds were all in front. There was no weapon devised to cut, or pierce, or fling, that had not left its mark on him. His body was white against his sun-scorched limbs; it was long since he'd run in the ball-court naked with his friends, which had once so shocked me. In his side, the knotted scar dragged on his ribs; even now in his first sleep, his brow was not quite smooth. His eyelids were wrinkled, old in the face of a boy at rest. His hair shone paler than it used when lamplight fell on it; the threads of silver had turned to streaks, since we marched into Gadrosia. He was thirty-one.

I reached to pull up the cover. But I had to draw back, lest my tears should fall and wake him.

25

To rest the desert troops, he sent them under Hephaistion by the coast roads to Persis; it would be mild there when winter came. He himself, as always, had work to do. With a small force, mostly cavalry, he went straight up country, to Pasargadai and Persepolis.

Had I been with Darius in time of peace, I should have known these places, the royal heartland of my country. It was Alexander who knew them. When we were up in the hills, he took me for an early ride, to taste, as he said, the clean air of Persis once again. I breathed it and said, 'Al'skander, we are home.'

'Truly. I too.' He looked towards the folded ranges, whose peaks had had the first snowfalls. 'I'd say this only to you; shut it in your heart. Macedon was my father's country. This is mine.'

I answered, 'You never gave me a greater gift than that.'

A fresh wind blew from the heights; the breath of our horses steamed in it. He said, 'In Pasargadai, we shall lie in Kyros' own house. Strange that you're of his tribe, yet it will be I who'll show you his tomb. I've trouble to deal with thereabouts; but that's one thing I look forward to. Lucky we're both slim; the doorway's so narrow, even you will have to go sideways. They must have walled it half-up against robbers, since they brought in that great gold coffin; it wouldn't go through now. His grave-offerings are still on the dais around it; you shall see his swords, the very clothes he wore, and his jewelled necklaces. They gifted him well, they must have loved him. I added something too; he taught me what it means to be a king.' His horse fidgeted, tired of walking. 'Behave,' he said, 'or Kyros shall have you . . . I left orders to sacrifice one horse a month to him; they said that was the ancient custom.'

Then we gave them their heads and galloped. His face was glowing, his hair flicked in the wind, his eyes lit up. When he told me, after, that he'd felt no more than a stitch in his ribs, I half believed him. Persis had done him good. I thought, Happiness begins again.

Kyros' palace was fine and spacious in its old simple way; solid, of black and white stone. The white columns stood out a landmark. Next morning early, Alexander set out to revisit the hero's tomb.

It was a short ride, through the royal park. A few friends came too (many had gone on with Hephaistion) but he kept me by him. The park had run wild, but was lovely in the gold of autumn; the game, so long unhunted, hardly heeded our passing. The tomb stood in a grove of shade-trees. Alexander had had water channelled there last time he came, and the grass was green.

Kyros' little house stood on a stepped plinth, a simple colonnade around it. Persian words were engraved over the door, which I could not read. Alexander said, 'I asked about that last time. It says, "MAN I AM KYROS SON OF KAMBYSES, WHO FOUNDED THE EMPIRE OF PERSIA AND RULED OVER ASIA. DO NOT GRUDGE ME MY MEMORIAL."' His voice shook a moment. 'Well, let's go in.'

He beckoned the guardian magi of the precinct. When first they came to prostrate themselves, I had thought they looked unhappy; the place was ill-kept and overgrown. He motioned them to unlock the door. It was narrow, very old, and made of some hard dark wood clasped with bronze. One magus brought on his shoulder the great wooden key. It moved the bolt quite easily. He opened the door, and withdrew into the distance.

'Come, Bagoas,' said Alexander smiling. 'You first; he was your King.' He took my hand; we edged into the shadows. The only light was from the door; I stood by him, my eyes dulled from the sun outside, smelling ancient spices and mould. Suddenly he snatched away his hand and strode forward. 'Who has done this?' Moving to follow him, I struck my foot on something. It was the thigh-bone of a man.

I could see now. There stood the dais, stripped bare. The gold coffin lay lidless on the floor, hacked with axes to break off pieces that would go through the doorway. Scattered beside it were the bones of Kyros the Great.

The entry darkened and lightened, as Peukestes, a biggish man, tried to get in and withdrew before he stuck. Alexander clambered fiercely into the sunshine. He was white with rage; the peak of his hair had risen. His eyes had looked less deadly when he struck down Kleitos. 'Call the wardens,' he said.

They were fetched from their house near by, while anyone who could squeeze inside the tomb described the desecration to those without. Alexander stood with clenched hands. The wardens were flung at his feet, and grovelled.

I interpreted, being the only other Persian there. Though of the priestly race, they seemed ignorant men, and terror made them foolish. They knew nothing, they had never entered the tomb, they had seen no one approach it, the thieves must have come by night (when their axes would have made a noise to wake the dead). They knew nothing, nothing at all.

'Take them to the prison,' Alexander said. 'I will have the truth.'

He took me, to interpret their confessions. But neither fire nor pincers could change their story; nor could the rack; Alexander had it stopped before they were disjointed. 'What do you think?' he said to me. 'Are they lying or not?'

'I think, Alexander, they had just been negligent, and are afraid to tell you. Perhaps they got drunk, or left the precinct. Maybe someone planned it.'

'Yes, perhaps. If so they have had their punishment. Let them go.'

They hobbled off, glad to get away so lightly. Any Persian King would have had them impaled.

Alexander sent for the architect, Aristoboulos, who'd been with him at his first visit and inventoried Kyros' grave-goods. He was to repair the coffin, and re-house the poor bones in proper state. So Kyros lies in gold again, and owns precious swords, though not those he fought with, and rich necklaces, though not the ones he wore. Alexander gave him a golden crown; then ordered the door walled up with a single slab, so that he should not be disturbed again. He was in there alone, before the masons started, saying farewell to his teacher.

A harsh welcome back to Persis. But harsher followed. Now he learned what had been done by men he'd left in trust, who had hoped he would never call them to account.

Some had been faithful; but some had set up like tyrants in the lands left to their charge; had plundered the rich, taxed the peasants to skin and bone, worked off old grudges on men who'd broken no law; enrolled themselves private armies. One Median lord had proclaimed himself Great King. One satrap had dragged from a lesser lord his maiden daughter, raped her, and passed her on to a slave.

I have heard it said that Alexander treated these people harshly. Tell that to someone who never saw what I did, when I was ten and the soldiers came to my home.

True, he grew hard, as proof after proof came in. True, after some time of this he punished beginnings. He said he'd learned the look of a budding tyrant, and what came after; and would depose them for showing the early signs. Whoever complained, it was not the peasants, nor the small lords of my father's kind. That he would not let even his own race oppress our people, was a wonder everywhere. He had been gone so long, they'd forgotten what he was like.

While he was away, one of the dearest friends of his childhood, a certain Harpalos, whom he'd left as treasurer at Babylon, had lived on the gold like a prince of India, set up his courtesans like queens, and fled with a load of money at the news of Alexander's return. This hurt him far more than the revolt of former enemies. 'We all trusted him; Hephaistion too, who never trusted Philotas. In exile he could always make us laugh. Of course, I had nothing then for him to steal. Perhaps he didn't know himself what he really was.'

All in all, he had enough to make him angry, before the new satrap of Persis obeyed his summons.

He was new because he had seized the satrapy. The Persian Alexander gave it to had died half a year before; of sickness it was said, though maybe of something he ate. Now envoys came with gifts, and a long letter, declaring the usurper had sent messages to Alexander, but getting no answer, had been looking after the province meanwhile, knowing of no one more fit to do it.

I was in his upper room with him when he read this letter, and threw it down. 'Fit to do murder, robbery and worse. He has ruled this province like a wolf in winter; I've heard it everywhere. Any man who crossed him, put to death without trial. He's looted even the royal sepulchres.' His brows came together; he was remembering Kyros. Perhaps indeed the magi had kept silent because of someone they feared more than the King.

'Well, I've witnesses enough already. Let him come; I shall like to see this Orxines ... Bagoas, what's the matter?'

'Nothing, Al'skander. I don't know. I don't know where I've heard that name.' It had been like some echo from a nightmare forgotten on waking.

'Was he cruel to you when you were with Darius? Let me know, if you remember anything.'

'No,' I said. 'No one was cruel there.' Of my life before, I'd only told him that I had been bought by a jeweller who ill-used me. The rest, he would only have pitied; but I'd wished to bury it, to forget for ever. Now I asked myself if this Orxines could have been some hated client; but his rank was too high; and the horror was even deeper. Perhaps I just dreamed it, I thought; I had bad dreams when I was a slave.

That night, Alexander said to me, 'Did they build this bed for elephants? Stay and keep me company.' It was years since he'd slept in a Persian royal bedchamber. We fell asleep quite soon. Dreams flung me into a terror long forgotten. My own scream woke me. It was the dead of night. Alexander was holding me to him. 'See you're with me, all's well. Whatever did you dream of?'

I clung to him wildly, like the child I had just been. 'My father. My father without his nose.' Suddenly I sat straight up in bed. 'The name! I remember the name!'

'What name?' He looked up; he was always very serious about dreams.

'The name he told me, when they dragged him away to kill him. "Orxines", that was what he said. "Remember the name. Orxines."'

'Lie down, and be quiet a little. You know, I told you today Orxines was a villain. I expect that gave you the dream.'

'No. I remember how he said it. His voice was different, because his nose was gone.' I shivered. He covered me up and warmed me.

Presently he said, 'It's not such a common name, but there may be others. Would you know this man again?'

'There was one lord from Persepolis. If that was he, I'll know him.'

'Listen. Be near when I give him audience. I'll say to you, "Bagoas, have you written that letter?" If it's not the man, say no, and go out. If it is, say yes, and stay; and I promise you, he shall know you before he dies. We owe it to your father's spirit.'

'That was his last wish, that I'd avenge him.'

'You loved him. In that, at least, you were fortunate ... Come, sleep. He knows you have heard him now, he will not trouble you.'

Next day the satrap came in state, as if confirmed in the rank already. He advanced to the throne, where Alexander sat in his Persian robes, and made the prostration gracefully. He had always had polished manners. His beard was grey now, and he'd grown a paunch. He made a tasteful speech about his seizure of the satrapy, all for the sake of good order and the King.

Alexander listened calmly, then beckoned me. 'Bagoas, did you write that letter I spoke of?'

I answered, 'Yes, lord King. You may be sure of it.'

So I was there to hear him charged with his many murders. Strange that I only remembered him as my father's friend whom everyone trusted. He seemed the same man still, so amazed to hear such things about himself that I almost doubted them, till Alexander took him by surprise with something proven. Then his face grew horrible; I would not have known him.

He was tried soon after. The kin of his victims testified; many in rags, their fathers having been killed for their estates. Then came the guardians of the royal tombs of Persepolis, those who had not resisted; the rest were dead. Darius the Great had given him the most loot, but he'd done well with Xerxes, and had robbed my own dead master of his modest grave-goods; I testified to things I remembered at Susa. Of stripping Kyros' bones he could not be convicted, since there were no witnesses; but it made no difference.

Alexander said at the end, 'You chose yourself to be shepherd of your people. If you had been a good one, you would have left here with honour. You have been a beast of prey, and you shall die like one. Take him away ... Bagoas, speak to him if you wish.'

As they were leading him off, I touched his arm. Even then, he had contempt to spare for a eunuch. I said, 'Do you remember Artembares son of Araxis, your friend and host, whom you betrayed when King Arses died? I am his son.'

I'd doubted it would mean much to him, after all the rest. But he had enough pride of birth to feel it. He flung off my hand; if he could, he would have stamped me underfoot. 'Do I owe all this to you, then? I should have thought to buy your favour. Well, old times come round again. A eunuch rules.'

Alexander said, 'A eunuch shall hang you, since he is the better man. Bagoas, I leave it in your charge. See it done tomorrow.'

I had nothing, really, to do; the captain whose usual work it was saw to it all, and only turned to me for the order to hoist him up. He kicked and writhed, on the high gallows against the wide sky of Pasargadai. I was ashamed to find it distasteful and take so little pleasure in it; it was disloyal to my father, and ungrateful to Alexander. I prayed in my heart, 'Dear father, forgive me that I am not a warrior, and have embraced my destiny. Accept this man through whom you died, and who robbed you of your son's sons. Give me your blessing.' He must have given it; for he never again returned to me in dreams.

Ptolemy has only put in his book that Orxines was hanged 'by certain persons, under Alexander's orders'. I expect he thinks it showed some loss of dignity, to have brought me forward. Never mind. He does not know of the night, while I was still a boy, when my lord drew the story out of me. He was very true to his promises, as Ptolemy himself has written.

He gave the satrapy to Peukestes, who had saved his life in the Mallian city. After Orxines, no one blamed him for not appointing a Persian; but he did the nearest thing. Peukestes had come to love the land; he understood us, and liked our way of living, even our clothes, which he was well made to wear; he had often practised his Persian on me. He ruled the province well, as much loved as Orxines had been hated.

We rode on to Persepolis. Alexander would have been there all this while, if there'd been a palace for him. Far off from the royal road we saw on the broad terrace the blackened ruins. He pitched his tent in open country outside; and I slipped away, to see what was left of the splendours Boubakes had wept for.

Already sand was drifted deep on the royal stairway, where the cavalcade of the lords had ridden. The sculpted warriors on the frieze marched up towards the roofless throne room, where only the sun held court between columns carved like flowers. Charred beams littered the harem; in its walled garden, a few tangled roses grew in a bed of cinders. I went back and said nothing of where I'd been. A long time had gone by, since that feast of young men with torches.

At night he said, 'Well, Bagoas, but for me we'd be better lodged tonight.'

'Don't mourn for it now, Al'skander. You will build something better, and hold the feast as Kyros did.'

He smiled, But he was brooding about Kyros' tomb; he was a great one for omens. Now these bones of grandeur, black and ragged against an angry sunset, revived his grief.

'Remember,' I said to him, 'how once you told me the blaze was godlike, an upward waterfall? How the tables were set with flame?' And I was going to add, 'No fire without ash, Al'skander.' But a shadow brushed me, and I closed my mouth on it.

We marched on towards Susa, where we were to meet Hephaistion's army. It gew cold in the passes, but the air was sweet and the great spaces stirred my heart. Alexander was happy too; he had some new plan, which he was not telling me yet. I felt him spark with it, and awaited his good time.

But one evening he came in looking troubled, and said, 'Kalanos is sick.'

'Kalanos? He's never ill. He was even well in the desert.'

'I sent for him this evening; I felt like a talk with him. He sent back asking me to go to him.'

'*He* sent for *you?*' I must admit, it shocked me.

'As a friend. I went, of course. He was sitting as he always does at his meditations, only propped against a tree. He usually gets up when I come, though he knows he needn't. But he asked me to sit down by him, because his legs had failed.'

'I've not seen him since Persepolis. How did he march today?'

'Someone lent him a donkey. Bagoas, he looks his age. When first he came to me, I'd no notion how old he was, or I'd never have taken him from his home. A man of seventy can't change all his bodily habits without harm. He'd lived for years in peace, every day the same.'

'He came for love of you. He says your fates were joined in some other life. He says . . .' I paused, having run on too fast. He looked up, saying, 'Come, Bagoas.' At last I answered, 'He says you're a fallen god.'

He was sitting naked for the bath, on the edge of his bed, with his hands on his sandal. Since first he was my lover, he'd never let me undo his shoes, unless he was wounded or dead tired, when any friend would do it. Now he sat still, his brows creased in thought. In the end he only said, as he took off his sandal, 'I tried to get him to bed, but he said he must finish his meditation. I should have ordered it. But I left him there.' I understood that; it was what he'd have wished himself. 'I don't like his look. He's too old to force his strength. Tomorrow I'll send a doctor.'

The doctor came back to report that Kalanos had a swelling in his entrails, and should travel in the sick-wagon. He refused, saying it would disturb his meditation, and that the foolish beast his body, if it would not obey, at least should not command him. Alexander gave him a soft-stepping horse to ride, and after each day's march went to see how he was; which was always thinner and weaker. Others went too; Lysimachos, for one, was very fond of him; but sometimes Alexander would stay alone. One evening he came back so distressed that all his friends remarked it. It was not till we were alone together that he said, 'He is resolved to die.'

'Al'skander, I think he is in pain, though he does not say so.'

'Pain! He wants to die by burning.'

I exclaimed in horror. It would have shocked me in the execution-place at Susa. Besides, it was a pollution of holy fire.

'I felt the same. He says in his own country women do it, rather than outlive their husbands.'

'So say the men! I saw it done to a child of ten, and she wished to live. They drowned her screams with music.'

'Some do consent. He says he will not outlive his life.'

'Could he get well?'

'The doctor won't answer for him. And he won't accept a regimen . . . I didn't refuse him flat; he might have done it himself at once, as best he could. With every day's delay, there's just a chance he might take a better turn. I don't think so now; I think I can see the death-marks. But one thing I'm resolved on; when he goes, he goes like a king. If it's true we live many lives, he was that before.' He paced about a little, then said, 'I will be there, as his friend. But I cannot watch it.'

So we reached Susa. Nothing was stranger to me than that. The Palace was just the same; even some old eunuchs, who had not marched with Darius, were still bustling about. When they learned who I was, they thought I must have been very clever.

Strangest of all was to stand again in the lamp-shadows of the golden vine, and see that head on the pillow. Even the inlaid casket was on the bed-table. I found him looking at me. He held my eyes, and stretched out his hand.

Afterwards he said, 'Was it better?' He couldn't even wait to be told, supposing he'd needed telling. In some things, he was like a child.

The fountain-court with its birds had been looked after. Alexander said it was just the place for Kalanos. He lay in the little room there; and each time I came to see him, he would ask me to open a cage. I hadn't the heart to tell him they were foreign birds, and might have trouble to make a living. It was his last pleasure, to watch them fly.

Hephaistion's army, with the elephants, had arrived before us. Alexander told his friends what Kalanos wanted, and ordered Ptolemy to prepare a royal pyre.

It was like a king's divan, decked with banners and garlands; underneath, it was filled with pitch and terebinth and tinder, and whatever would give the quickest and fiercest flame, mixed with Arabian incense.

In the square before the Palace, where all great ceremonies had been held since Darius the Great, the Companions stood drawn up, with the heralds and the trumpeters. On the fourth side were the elephants, newly painted, with sequinned draperies and gilded tusks. King Poros could have asked no more.

Alexander had chosen the cortege; the handsomest Persians and Macedonians on the tallest horses, in all their arms; then the offering-bearers, with grave-goods enough for a royal tomb, cloths sewn with gems and pearls, gold cups, vases of sweet oil and bowls of incense. They were to be laid on the pyre and burned with Kalanos. Alexander came in Darius' chariot, draped in white for mourning. His face looked drawn and set. I think he had devised all this magnificence, not just to honour Kalanos but to make it a little bearable.

Last of all came the living dead. Four big Macedonians carried his litter shoulder-high. The splendid Nisaian charger he had been meant to ride on, but was too weak to mount, was led beside him, to be sacrificed by the pyre.

He wore a thick wreath of flowers on his neck and breast, as the Indians do on their wedding day. As he came near, we heard that he was singing.

He still sang to his god, as they laid him on the bier. Then, at this funeral of the living, his friends came up to take their leave.

All kinds of people came; generals and troopers, Indians, musicians, servants. The offering-bearers began to pile their gifts on the pyre. He smiled, and said to Alexander, 'How like your kindness, to give me remembrances for my friends.'

He gave away everything; the horse to Lysimachos, the cloths and the rest to all who'd known him well. To me, when I took his hand, he gave a Persian goblet worked with a lion, saying, 'Do not fear, you shall drink to the very end, and no one shall take that from you.'

Last came Alexander; we moved aside from respect, as he leaned over to embrace him. But Kalanos said quietly – only those nearest heard – 'We need not say farewell. I will be with you in Babylon.'

All now withdrew. The torch-bearers came up, a troop of them to make the kindling quicker. As the flames leaped, Alexander shouted for the battle-paean. The trumpets sounded; the soldiers yelled; the mahouts cried to the elephants, who lifted their trunks and blared the salute they give to kings.

He was always tender to the pride of those he cared for. Feeling sure no old sick man could bear that searing pain without a cry, he'd ensured it should not be heard. He bowed his head as the fire rose roaring, and did not look. But I can witness that Kalanos lay with folded hands, while the flowers beneath them shrivelled; he neither changed countenance nor opened his mouth. I only watched till he began to be disfigured; but all who watched to the end agreed that he did not stir.

He'd made Alexander promise to feast for him, not mourn; good healing wisdom, except that, not touching wine himself, he'd never feasted with Macedonians. They were all rather mad that night, from horror or grief or both; someone proposed a drinking-contest by way of funeral games, and Alexander offered a prize. I think the winner downed two gallons. Many lay senseless until morning, on the couches or the floor; not the way to pass a cold winter night in Susa. The winner died of a chill, along with several more; so Kalanos got more than a horse for sacrifice.

Alexander had judged, not competed; he came to bed on his feet, already sobering and growing sad again.

'What did he mean,' he said to me, 'that he'd be with me in Babylon? Will he be reborn as a Babylonian? How shall I know the child?'

26

It was next day that he asked me, 'You have never seen Queen Sisygambis, have you?'

I heard the name as if in an ancient tale. She was the Queen Mother of Persia, whom Darius had left behind at Issos. 'No,' I said, 'she was with you already, before I joined the Household here.'

'Good. I want you to see her for me.' I had quite forgotten that it was here at Susa he'd installed her and the young princesses, soon after the Queen had died. 'If she would remember you at court, it might not quite do, you understand. But since she won't, I should like to send her someone charming, after so long with only letters and gifts. You remember, you chose me a chain of turquoises for her, at Marakanda? You'll find her well worth meeting. Give her my loving respects; say I've been impatient to see her, but business has held me back. Ask her if she'll do me the favour of receiving me in about an hour; and give her this.' He showed me in its casket a necklace of Indian rubies.

I made my way to the harem. When last I went, I had walked behind Darius, smelling the perfume from his robe.

At the Queen's entry, where I had never been, an old stately eunuch was fetched to sanction me. He was gracious, giving no sign of knowing what I had been, though of course such people know everything. I followed him down a corridor with sun-fretted lattices, and through an anteroom where matron ladies sat talking or playing chess. He scratched at a door beyond, announced me and who had sent me, then withdrew.

She sat straight in a tall straight chair, her arms along the chair-arms; over their ram-head ends, her fingers showed as fine as ivory spindles. She wore dark blue, with a dark blue veil over thin white hair. Her face was colourless, the face of an old white falcon brooding on its crag. Round her neck was the chain of turquoises from Marakanda.

I prostrated myself, with as much care as the first time before Darius. As I rose she spoke, in the high cracked voice of age.

'How is my son the King?'

It struck me dumb. How long had it been like this with her? She had had his body to deck for burial. Why had no one warned Alexander that her wits had gone? If I told the truth, she might fly into a frenzy, tear me with those long ivory nails, or dash her head on the wall.

Her old eyes stared at me fierce and bright, from their wrinkled lids. They blinked quickly once or twice, like an unhooded falcon's. They looked impatient. My tongue would not move. She struck one hand upon the chair-arm.

'I am asking you, boy, how is my son Alexander?' Her dark piercing gaze met mine, she had read my thought. She lifted her head against the chair-back. 'I have only one son a King. There has never been any other.'

Somehow I came to myself, remembered my training, gave her my message in proper form, and kneeling, offered Alexander's gift. She lifted out the rubies in both hands, and called to two old waiting-ladies by the window. 'See what my son has sent me.'

They admired, were allowed to touch, while I knelt with the casket till someone should think to take it, and remembered the son she had thrown away.

He must have guessed, after he fled at Issos; who could have known her and not guessed? It had only remained for him to know that his place was filled. In the fountain court I had played my harp, to soothe a grief I only now understood. It was this had turned his rage on poor Tyriotes. Did he know she'd refused his rescue at Gaugamela? Perhaps they had kept that from him. Well that they had not met again; poor man, he'd had sorrow enough.

She noticed me in time, and motioned one of her ladies to take the casket. 'Thank my lord the King for his gift, and say I shall receive him gladly.' When I went out, she was still stroking the jewels on her lap.

'Did she like it?' said Alexander, as eager as if he'd been her lover. I told him she had shown great pleasure in it. 'King Poros gave it me. I'm glad that she thought it worthy of her. *There* is the Great King who would have led your people, if God had made her a man. Both of us know it. We understand each other.'

'It's as well God made her a woman; or you'd have had to kill her.'

'Yes, there I was spared great grief. Did she look well? I've something important to say to her. I want to marry her granddaughter.'

Through my first amazement, he still read my face. 'That pleases you better than last time?'

'Alexander, it will please all the Persians.' He had not set eyes on Stateira since she was a child at Issos, with her face in her mother's lap. This was a real state marriage, to honour our people and breed a royal line; it would have Sisygambis' blood, he'd remembered, as well as Darius'. As for Roxane, as second wife she'd still be above her station; Darius would never have made her more than a concubine. Keeping all these thoughts to myself, I hastened to wish him joy.

'Ah, and that's not all.' We were in the fountain-court, a quiet retreat when the state rooms were full of envoys and officials. He cupped the fountain-fall in his palm and let it run out again. He was smiling.

'Now, Al'skander, tell me the secret. I've seen it in your face.'

'Oh, I knew that! I can tell you now. This won't be only my wedding; it will be a marriage of both our peoples.'

'Truly, Al'skander, yes.'

'No, wait. All my own friends, my generals, and the best of my Companions, will be marrying Persian ladies. I shall dower them all; and we shall all share the one wedding-feast. What do you think of that?'

'Al'skander, no one else could have conceived it.' Which was God's truth.

'I conceived it on the march, but it had to wait till I'd met the army. Most of them were serving there.'

Well, I could see why he hadn't told me. He could hardly announce to me Hephaistion's wedding, before the bridegroom knew.

'I've been thinking,' he said, 'how many couples would make a handsome feast, without crowding the pavilion. I decided eighty.' Getting back my breath, I said it sounded just right. 'All my soldiers who've married Persian women will get dowries too. About ten thousand, I think.'

He played smiling with the sunlit fountain-stream, which fell from his hands like gold.

'We'll make a new thing; two good wines blended to make a better, in a great loving-cup. Hephaistion will marry Stateira's sister. I should like his children to be my kin.'

I suppose he felt my silence.

He looked in my face, came over and embraced me. 'Dear one, forgive me. More than children are born of love. "The sons of dreams" – do you remember? All this you begot; from loving you, I first learned to love your people.'

After that, it was no pain to me to do my part; which was to call on the brides and their mothers, bring gifts, and tell them about procedure. I was well received in the harems; if they'd had plans of their own before Alexander had his, nobody said so. He had chosen, of course, for the greatest Macedonians the noblest brides; if these weren't always the best favoured, one can't have everything. The princesses, I did not see; but Drypetis would hardly disappoint Hephaistion; that was a handsome line. In all these years, I'd never heard he'd had a mistress; but if nephews and nieces were what Alexander asked him for, no doubt he would faithfully beget them.

Some silly man, whose name is not worth remembering, has written that Alexander slighted our people, because no Persian lord got a Macedonian wife. Where were these wives to come from? We were in Susa; there were only concubines or camp-followers. One can guess what the lady mothers of Macedon would have said, to despatching their maiden daughters to the beds of unknown 'barbarians'. But why waste words on such folly?

Alexander meant this to be the greatest festival since his reign began. Already, weeks ahead, every weaver and carver and goldsmith in Susa was working into the night. I did not go to see if my old master prospered. One does not return to the midden one was flung in.

Since the King's return, artists in everything had been streaming over from Greece; news of the festival made them race. One of these, a flute-player of some fame called Evios, caused a trifling quarrel; or what should have been trifling, had the men concerned not been at odds already. So wars begin, with peoples as with men. So with Eumenes and Hephaistion.

Eumenes I knew only at a distance; but he'd been Chief Secretary all through Alexander's reign, and to his father before him. He was a Greek, who had had time to do some soldiering in India, and with success. He was about forty-five, grizzled and shrewd. I don't know why he and Hephaistion had always brushed-up each other's fur. By my guess, it went back to Hephaistion's boyhood. Maybe Eumenes had envied him Alexander's love; maybe he just disapproved, as he did of me. I never took notice, knowing he could not harm me. It was different with Hephaistion. Since he led back the army, Alexander had made him Chiliarch, which is Greek for our Grand Vizier; he ranked next the King. He was incorruptible in office; but touchy about his dignity, among other things.

It had grown on him since India, where he'd had a jaundice fever. Doctors say you should not drink for a long time after; but try telling that to a Macedonian. Also he had a very constant nature; in love, and in resentment.

He was always polite to Persians; for Alexander's sake, and because our manners have civilized formality. It is impossible for Persians of decent breeding to brawl. We poison each other after consideration, or come to terms. Macedonians, who have no such restraints, are into it in a moment.

This flautist, Evios, was an old guest-friend of his from before my time; so he took charge of his entertainment. Susa was filling up; the lodging Hephaistion found for Evios had been taken by people of Eumenes' household; so Hephaistion turned them out.

Eumenes, a quiet man as a rule, went to him very angry. Whereas a Persian would have said it was all a dreadful mistake but too late for remedy, Hephaistion told Eumenes he must make room for guests of honour, like anyone else.

Eumenes, whose own rank was pretty high, went straight to Alexander, who had trouble to keep the peace. I know he had the flautist lodged elsewhere; I saw to that for him. What he said to Hephaistion, I could have overheard if I'd taken care; but I remembered that morning in the desert, and went away.

If, as I suspect, Hephaistion was asked to beg Eumenes' pardon, he thought it beneath him, and didn't do it. The enmity smouldered on. A petty squabble; why trouble to record it? Only because the end was to mix my lord's bitter grief with poison, and send him mad.

Meantime, being spared foreknowledge, I thought no more of it; nor I daresay did Alexander who was busier still. He saw a good deal of the Queen Mother, and was shown his bride. He told me she had her mother's looks, and was a gentle modest maid. There was none of that kindling with which he had seen Roxane. I dared not ask him how *she* had taken the news.

The feast-day came. Darius the Great may have seen such splendours; no one living had. The whole Palace square was turned into a vast pavilion; in the centre, the bridegroom's tent of fine cloth with bullion tassels, propped by gilt columns; all round it, awnings for the guests. The wedding would be by Persian rite; the bridal tent had gold chairs in couples. Our women being bred to modesty, the brides would only enter after the healths were drunk, when the grooms would take their hands, sit by them for the bridal song, and then retire.

Their fathers of course were present. Alexander asked me to help in their entertainment, because he wanted me to see the rite.

He wore the Mitra, and the royal robe of Persia, long sleeves and all. To tell the truth, his half-Greek dress suited him better; this called for Darius' height to set it off. But if there was one thing we'd learned in Persia, it was that a King is as tall as his soul.

For the crowd of lesser guests not to miss it all, he had heralds outside the tent, who would sound trumpets when the healths were drunk, give out the toasts, and announce the entry of the brides.

It all went perfectly. In the presence of the fathers-in-law, men of the noblest blood in Persia, the bridegrooms kept down their drinking, and did not even shout across the tent.

There were no prostrations. Alexander had given all the fathers the rank of Royal Kindred, which allowed them to kiss his cheek. There being no father-in-law for him, Oxathres took that place, and made a very fine figure, though he had to stoop for the kiss.

The King gave the bridal toast; the bridegrooms drank to the fathers, the fathers returned the honour, everyone drank to the King. The trumpets flourished for the entry of the brides. The fathers met them, took them by the hand and led them to the grooms.

Peasants apart, you seldom see the men and women of Persia walking together. Whatever Greeks may say, you won't find more beauty anywhere on earth than you do among our nobility, who have bred for it so choicely and so long. Handsomest of all was the foremost couple, Oxathres and his niece hand in hand. Alexander rose to meet them, and receive his bride. Yes, Darius had passed his good looks on to his children. Also his stature. She topped Alexander by a good half-foot.

He led her to her chair of honour by his throne; and the difference disappeared. He'd met her in the Queen Mother's rooms; and Alexander was nothing if not resourceful. He had had the legs of her chair cut down.

Of course they had to walk out together, when the bridal couples retired. I could almost hear his voice saying, 'It is necessary.' (Days later, I found pushed into some dark corner his wedding shoes. The soles had an inch of felt in them. He'd taken no such trouble when host to seven-foot Poros.)

Hephaistion and Drypetis matched up well. She was his height to an inch.

The feasting went on all night. I met old friends, and needed no pretence to share the merriment. Years had gone by, since he spared Susa and first rode in there. He had gone far away and become a legend, while wrong was done in his name. Now they knew him. In that city Kyros is remembered; how he did not profane the sanctuaries of the conquered Medes, nor dishonour their nobility, nor enslave their peasants, but was a just King to us all. That a westerner should prove to be such another, was a wonder everywhere. I saved up all I heard, to tell him later. He had done what he meant to do.

No doubt he did no less in the marriage-bed. Stateira was installed in her royal rooms; but his visits turned to mere calls of courtesy, much sooner than with Roxane. A few days later, indeed, he visited the Sogdian. It may have been just to heal her wounded feelings; but I'm not so sure. Stateira was, as he'd said, a gentle modest girl; and he was a lover of fire. Roxane had it, even if it smoked. He soon had enough of her; yet from time to time she always drew him back. Olympias his mother, that royal termagant, was still berating his regent by every post. He would throw down her letter in anger; yet with his answer would go a gift, lovingly chosen. Perhaps there is something in the proverb about how men choose their wives.

He had done what he meant to do. Yes – among *my* people.

I was too happy. Once or twice, going about, I got hard looks from Macedonians; but those whom kings love are always envied; so was Hephaistion, and in higher places than I. I never thought that all Persians were more hated, till I saw Peukestes ride by in our native dress. Our people, who'd already learned his worth, saluted him; then, when he'd passed I overheard some Macedonians. He had gone barbarian, it was disgusting, how could the King encourage it? For that matter, what was the King coming to himself?

I noted their faces and their regiment. I should not have been sorry to do them harm with Alexander. But it would only wound him, without doing him service. It was hearts, not words, he had hoped to change.

Soon after this, he got to know that Macedonian troops were waist-deep in debt, with creditors closing in. With the loot they'd had, they should have been as rich as princes; but they had no notion of bargaining, as we Persians understand it; they'd paid double the going price for all they bought, ate, drank or lay with. Hearing of their distress, as if he'd not spent enough upon their marriage dowers, Alexander gave out that he'd settle up for them. Few came forward; and at last the officers broke the truth to him; the men were saying he just wanted to know who was living beyond his pay.

It hurt him more than anything since that day in India, that they thought he'd lie to them. He could not understand it. I could have told him. He was growing foreign to them, as he came closer to us.

So he had banking-tables set up in the camp, and told his paymasters to sit there without writing things. Any soldier who showed up a debtor's bond had it paid off, and no record made. It cost close on ten thousand talents, that piece of magnanimity. I thought that should shut their mouths awhile.

Spring was just breaking; along by the river one smelled the rising sap. The lilies would not be long. As I rode there one morning with Alexander, he looked at the hills and said, 'Where was your home?'

'There, by that crag. The grey there, that looks like rock, that is the watch-tower.'

'A good place for a stronghold. Shall we ride up and see it?'

'Al'skander, I would see too much.'

'Don't see it now. Listen to some news I've kept for you. Do you remember, five years ago, I said I was starting an army of Persian boys?'

'Yes. We were in Baktria. Is it only five years since then?'

'It does seem longer. We've put a good deal into it.' Indeed, in thirty years he had filled three men's full lifetimes. 'Well, five years is up. They're ready, and on their way here.'

'That is wonderful, Al'skander.' Six years since I came to him; thirteen since I left those walls, riding with my father's head.

'Yes, their instructors are very pleased with them. Race me to the trees.' The gallop shook off my sadness, as he'd meant. As we breathed our horses, he said 'Thirty thousand, all eighteen years old. We'll see something, I think.'

They reached Susa seven days later. He had a dais set up on the Palace terrace, for him and his generals to see the new corps parade. Presently, from their camp beyond the walls, came the Macedonian bugle-call, 'Cavalry, march'.

They came in squadrons, Macedonian-armed, but on good Persian horses, not Greek scrubs. The Persians of Persis rode up first.

Macedonian dress or not, Persians are Persians. Their officers had not denied them those little touches that give an air; an embroidered saddle-cloth, a cuirass with a device, a pennant on the Macedonian lance, a glittering bridle, a flower stuck in the helmet. And they had the Persian face.

I don't suppose they had all been recruited willingly; but they had pride in their training now. Each squadron pranced up to the square with lances poised; slowed down, pacing to music; wheeled before the royal dais, saluting with their spears; then did their show-tricks, saluted again, and cantered off while the next rode in.

All Susa watched, from the walls and roof-tops. The sides of the square were crowded with Macedonians. No one denies they were the best-trained army the world has seen. All these young men did, they could have done as briskly. But we do have more sense of style. So had Alexander.

When the long review was over, he came glowing, and talking to the Persians of his bodyguard, Oxathres, and Roxane's brother, and one of Artabazos' sons. Right across the Great Hall, he caught my eye and smiled. He was late to bed, having sat up talking and drinking, as he did when he was pleased. 'I never saw so much beauty in one day; but still I have picked the best.' He pulled softly at my hair. 'You know what I call these boys? I call them my Successors.'

'Al'skander,' I said lifting off his chiton, 'did you call them that to the Macedonians?'

'Why not? They'll breed me successors too. What is it?'

'I don't know. You have taken nothing from them. But they don't like us to show excellence.'

He stood up, clothed only in his many wounds, tossing back his hair; not dulled but lit by the wine. 'To hate excellence is to hate the gods.' He spoke so loudly, the squire on guard looked in to see all was well. 'One must salute it everywhere, among unknown peoples, at the furthest ends of the earth; yet one must never cheapen it.' He began pacing about. 'I found it in Poros, though his black face was strange to me. And in Kalanos. I find it among your people. In respect for that, I hanged the Persian satraps along with the Macedonians. To excuse their crimes like something native to them, that would have been contempt.'

'Yes. We are an ancient race. We understand such things.'

'Those things and others,' he said, leaving off his oration, and stretching out his arms.

The Greeks have written that at this time he grew short-tempered. I
don't wonder. He wanted to be Great King in fact as well as name; and
all he did for it, his own people hated. A few friends understood – Hephaistion did, I allow – for the rest, they'd sooner have seen him master of a
race of slaves, with themselves as lesser masters. They didn't hide what
they felt about the new cadets. And then, though the wound in his side
had healed, he still tired more quickly than he used to do, though he'd
have died sooner than own it.

They said we'd spoiled him with servility; maybe to such uncouth folk
it seemed really so. *We* knew we'd made him used to decent manners and
a civilized court. *He* knew that it was necessary. Persians who were
allowed to upbraid a King would think him a low barbarian without
breeding or self-respect, whom it degraded them to serve. Any fool in
Persia knows that. I set it down for the ignorant.

What did they lose through us? He'd given all those marriage dowers;
he'd paid their debts; he'd held a parade of honour, with hosts of gifts and
prizes for bravery and good service. Yet afterwards, when he took into the
Companions some Persians of real distinction, it was resented. If his
temper was sometimes harsh, they asked for it. It never was with me.

Spring was well on; he decided to spend summer at Ekbatana, like the
Kings before him. Most of the troops, led by Hephaistion, were to march
up the Tigris valley to Opis, whence a good road leads through the passes;
Alexander, to see something new which might prove useful, went to Opis
by water. Down there the Tigris has lost its fierceness; it was a pleasant
voyage up the ever-winding stream, past the palm-groves and the margin
of fruitful fields, with the oxen turning the water-wheels. The river was
full of ancient useless weirs, which he caused to be cleared as he went;
we dawdled along, sleeping ashore or aboard as his fancy took him. It was
a rest from the court, from toil and anger. Green, peaceful days.

Near the end of the voyage, while they broke up one of these old weirs,
we were moored in a shady creek; he reclined in the stern under a striped
awning, with my head in his lap. Once he would have looked if there were
Macedonians watching; now he did as he liked and they could make the
best of it. In any case, there was no one about of much importance. He
looked up at the waving palm-fronds, and played lazily with my hair. 'At
Opis, we'll be on the Royal Road to the west, and I can send the old
veterans home. They've had work enough, since they told me in India how
tired they were. It's true as Xenophon says, the commander may bear the
same hardships, yet for him it's not the same. It was their tears that moved
me. Stubborn old fools ... still, stubborn in danger, too. When they go
home, it won't be my fault if they ever want again.'

The army arrived before us. It's a middle-sized city, with yellow mud-brick houses, and, like every town along the Royal Road, a stone lodging for the King. It was getting hot in the plain, but we were not staying. Nothing much had happened on the army's land-march, except that Hephaistion an Eumenes had been quarrelling all the way.

It had been building up before Susa. In Karmania, needing to repair the fleet, Alexander had asked a loan from his friends till he reached the capital. Their money, at least, had come through the desert safe, and he repaid with interest later. But Eumenes was close-fisted; when his offering came, Alexander said with irony that he would not rob the poor, and sent it back. 'I wonder,' he said to me that night, 'what he'd fetch out if his tent burned down.' 'Try it, Al'skander,' I said. He was rather drunk; we were laughing; I never thought he really would. The tent caught fire next day. The trouble was that it burned so fast, the royal journal and state letters went up along with it. The money came out as ingots; sure enough, about a thousand talents. Alexander asked for none; he'd had his joke, if it came expensive for him. Whether Eumenes thought it was Hephaistion who set him on to it, I don't know. After Susa, if Eumenes had only stepped in dogshit, he'd have suspected Hephaistion put it there.

On the march to Opis, being at open enmity, they had picked up factions. I doubt they'd aimed at this. Hephaistion had no need; Eumenes was a subtle Greek, who knew better than to put himself in the wrong. There had been no brawling; but those who hated the King's Persian ways, and knew his friend supported them, were drawn to Hephaistion's enemy without urging.

By the time we got there, it was making Eumenes anxious. He came to Alexander, said how much the estrangement grieved him, and declared himself eager to make it up. What he was chiefly eager for, was not to take the blame if it went on. Which it did; he had lost his temper over the flautist's lodging, and what he'd said, Hephaistion would not forget. It was seldom indeed he disobliged Alexander. But he was a great man now, and knew his dues. Alexander could not order him to swallow an insult. If he asked as a favour, it was one he didn't get. Hephaistion, who had not spoken to Eumenes for half a month, maintained his silence. Soon after, we had other things to think of.

Alexander had a platform put up on the parade-ground, to address the troops. He was to discharge the veterans, tell them their retirement-bounty, and give them their marching orders to the Middle Sea. A simple business. I only went up on the roof to watch because I was idle, and would always sooner look at him than not.

The troops filled the ground, right up to the rostrum with the bodyguard around it. The generals rode up the lane that had been left, and took their places; last came the King, gave a squire his horse, went up and began to speak.

Before long, they started to wave their arms. The discharge-bounty was wildly generous; I took it they were cheering.

Suddenly, he vaulted straight off the rostrum, and strode out through the Bodyguard among the soldiers. I saw him grab one with both hands, and shove him at the Guard, who took him in charge. The generals came scrambling after him. He moved about, pointing out some dozen men. They were marched away; he went round by the steps, came forward and spoke again.

There was no more arm-waving. He spoke for some time. Then he ran down the steps, jumped on his horse, and galloped towards his lodging. The generals followed as soon as they could get mounted.

I hurried down, to be in his room beforehand and hear what it was all about. The door opened; he said to the bodyguard outside, 'No one. On any business whatever. Do you understand?'

He flung in, slamming the door before the guard could close it. He didn't see me at first; I took one look and kept quiet. He was in a white-hot fury; his worn, brilliant face was blazing with outrage. His lips were moving, going over whatever he'd said out there. I just caught the end. 'Yes, tell them at home how you forsook me, and left me to the care of the foreigners you conquered. No doubt it will bring you glory among men, and heaven's blessing. Get out.'

He sent his helmet crashing into a corner, and started on his cuirass. I came forward to unbuckle it.

'I can do it.' He shoved away my fingers. 'I said nobody here.'

'I was inside. Alexander, whatever is it?'

'Go and find out. You'd better go, I don't trust myself with anyone. I'll send for you later. Go.'

I left him tugging at the straps, and cursing under his breath.

After a moment's thought, I went along to the squires' room. The one who had held the King's horse had just arrived. I joined the crowd around him.

'It was mutiny,' he said. 'They'd have killed any other man. Oh, Bagoas! Have you seen the King?'

'He won't talk. I only saw from the roof. What did he say to them?'

'Nothing! I mean, he gave the veterans their discharge, thanked them for their courage and their loyalty; all proper and nicely put. He was just getting on to their bounties, when some of the serving troops started shouting out, "Discharge us all!" When he asked them what they meant by it, they all took it up. "You don't want us now, it's all mother-fucking barbarians." ... Oh, I'm sorry, Bagoas.'

'Just get on,' I said. 'What then?'

'Somebody yelled, "Go marching with your father. The one with horns." He couldn't make himself heard. So he jumped straight down, right into the middle of them, and started arresting the ones who'd started it.'

'What?' someone said. 'Not on his own?'

'No one laid a finger on him. It was uncanny. As if he were really a god. He had on his sword, but he never touched it. The men just submitted like oxen; the first, he handled himself. You know why? I know. It's his eyes.'

'But then he spoke again,' I said.

'You saw that? He saw the prisoners taken off, then he went up and told them their fortune. He started by saying Philip brought them up from nothing, wearing sheepskins he said – is that really true?'

The squire from the noblest house said, 'My grandad told us only the lords wore cloaks. He said it showed who you were.'

'And the Illyrians came raiding right into Macedon?'

'He said all the peasants came up to the fort at night.'

'Well, the King said Philip had made them masters of all the people who used to kill them with fright, and when he died there were sixty talents in the treasury, a few gold and silver cups, and five hundred talents in debts. Alexander borrowed eight hundred more, and that's what he crossed to Asia with. Did you know that? Well, he reminded them of all the rest since then, and he said, I'll always remember this, "While I have led you, not one of you has ever been killed in flight." He said if they wanted to go home they could go today, and boast of it when they get there, and good luck to them. That's what he said.'

A young one called out, 'Let's go and see him, and tell him how *we* feel.' They often talked as if they owned him. I found it endearing.

'He won't have anyone in,' I said. 'He won't have me.'

'Is he weeping?' said the one with the softest heart.

'Weeping! He's as angry as a hit lion. Keep your heads out of his mouth.'

I kept mine out till evening. All his friends had been turned away, even Hephaistion. His quarrel with Eumenes was still on; I don't think Alexander had quite forgiven that. Servants with food were shut out like the rest. The wounded lion had no wish to see a doctor.

At night I went to see if he'd take a bath. The squires would have let me in, but I feared it might earn them a mauling from the cave, and made them announce me. The growl from within said, 'Thank him and tell him no.' I noted the thanks which I'd not had earlier; presented myself next morning, and was admitted.

He was still licking his wounds. Last night's anger had set into deep resentment. It was all he could talk about. I got him shaved and bathed and fed. Everyone else was still being kept out. He gave me most of his address to the army; fine fiery stuff, too good to keep to himself. He was like a women reliving her quarrel with her lover, word by word.

Just after, the guard scratched at the door. 'King, there are some Macedonians from the camp, asking leave to speak with you.'

His face altered. You could not quite say his eye lit up. He just tilted his head to one side a little. 'Ask them,' he said, 'what they are still doing here, when they discharged themselves yesterday. Tell them I am seeing no one; I am busy with their replacements. They can draw their pay and go. Bagoas, will you fetch me my writing things?'

He was at his table all day. At bedtime, he was deep in thought; there was a kind of sparkle in his eye, but he kept his counsel. Next morning he sent for the generals. From then on, the place teemed with officers, mostly Persian; and Opis seethed like an ant-hill with the top knocked off.

The Macedonian camp was still full of soldiers. Not wishing to be torn asunder, I sought in friendlier places the cause of all this stir. I soon found out. Alexander was forming an all-Persian army.

It was not just a new corps, like the young Successors. All the great Macedonian regiments, the Silver Shields, the Infantry Companions, were being made up from Persians. Only the chief Macedonian generals, and his most loyal friends, were left holding commands. The Companions themselves would be half Persian, at least.

The first day, orders went out. On the second, the commanders started work. On that day also, Alexander gave the rank of Royal Kin to the whole Persian nobility who'd had it under Darius; all could kiss his cheek instead of making the prostration. He added to these eighty Macedonians, those who had shared his wedding.

The dust outside was enough to choke you. Inside, Alexander in his Persian robe was being kissed in greeting by Persians assuming their new appointments. I watched in the shadows, thinking, He is all ours, now.

It was quiet; we know how to behave in the Presence. So the noise from the terrace sounded clearly; a heavy clatter, like ironwork being unloaded; and Macedonian voices, unhushed as they always are, but very sorrowful.

The sounds increased. The Macedonian generals looked at each other, and at Alexander. He tilted his head a little, and went on with what he was saying. I slipped off to a first-floor window.

The terrace was full of them, overflowing into the square. They were all unarmed; they had stacked their weapons. They stood before the Palace doors, with a lost murmuring; for all the world like dogs who've run truant to the woods, and come back to find the house locked for the night. Soon, I thought, they will put back their heads and howl.

Sure enough, with a noise to split your ears, they began to cry out like souls in ordeal, 'Alexander! Alexander! Alexander, let us come in!'

He came out. With one great cry, they fell upon their knees. The one nearest him clung weeping to the skirt of his Persian robe. He said nothing; just stood where he was and looked at them.

They implored his pardon. They would never do it again. They would condemn their ringleaders. They would stay on this spot night and day, just as they were, till he forgave and pitied them.

'So you say now.' He spoke sternly; but I thought his voice had a shake in it. 'Then what got into you all at the Assembly?'

There was another chorus. The one who had grasped his robe – I saw he was an officer – said, 'Alexander, you call Persians your kin. You let them kiss you; and which of us has done it?' Those were his words, I swear.

Alexander said, 'Get up.' He raised the man and embraced him. The poor fellow, knowing no etiquette, made a clumsy botch of the kiss; but you should have heard the cheering. 'You are all my kindred, every one of you from now on.' His voice, without disguise, had broken. He came forward with out-stretched hands.

I stopped counting how many pressed up to kiss him. His cheeks were glistening. They must have tasted his tears.

All the rest of the day, he spent re-arranging the new commands, under Persian names, alongside the Macedonian, without any Persian commander losing face. It did not seem to give him very much trouble. My belief is, he'd had it all in his head before.

He came to bed dead tired; but his smile was a smile of triumph. Well, he had earned it. 'They changed their minds,' he said. 'I thought they might. We have been a long time together.'

'Al'skander,' I said. He turned his smile on me. It was so close to the tip of my tongue, I almost said it: 'I have seen the great courtesans of Babylon and Susa. I have seen the cream from Corinth. I used to think I was not so mean in the art myself. But the crown is yours.'

However, one could not be quite sure he would understand; so I said instead, 'Kyros would have been proud to accomplish that.'

'Kyros ...? You've given me a thought. What would he do now? He would hold a Feast of Reconcilement.'

He held it before the veterans left for home. It was as grand as the wedding, except that we'd left the awnings at Susa. In the midst of the Palace square was an enormous dais, where all the nine thousand guests could see the royal table, at which sat around him the chief Macedonians and Persians, with the leaders of the allies. Greek seers and magi invoked the gods together. All those at the feast had equal honours; except that the Macedonians sat next him. He couldn't deny that to the old, forgiven lover, after all those kisses and tears.

To me, of course, it made a certain difference. At a real Persian court, a royal favourite, even though he takes no bribes, is treated with much respect. No one offends him. Still, it would have been a shadow of the substance I had already. I did not grieve that Hephaistion sat beside him; it was the Chiliarch's formal right. He had not used the great Reconcilement to make his peace with Eumenes. I thought to myself, Al'skander knows he'd not have asked *me* in vain.

So, when he lifted the great loving-cup to the sound of trumpets, and begged the gods to give us all kinds of blessings, but harmony between Macedonians and Persians above all, I drank with a whole heart, and drank again to the hope reborn in his face.

All is well, I thought. And soon we go to the hills. Once more, after so long, I shall see the sevenfold walls of beautiful Ekbatana.

27

The veterans were sent off with love and money. Krateros was leading them. In Macedon, he was to take the regency; Antipatros would come out in his place.

This was high politics. Alexander just said that Krateros needed sick-leave. Some said he wanted sick-leave himself from his mother's and regent's endless intrigues and bickerings, which might end in civil war; others, that he thought Antipatros had ruled like a king so long, he might start to think he was one. He had been faithful; but all this while he'd expected Alexander to be coming back. He was getting rather too purple, was what Alexander said.

In his parting speech to the veterans, he said, 'I honour you by trusting you to Krateros, my most loyal follower, whom I love as my own life.' *Most loyal* . . .? It passed well enough, in a speech of thanks and farewell.

To shake hands with Eumenes may well have been the first thing Hephaistion had refused to Alexander. Now every day made it harder. Eumenes had humbled himself to come forward first; no man of his standing, once rebuffed, was going to do it twice. Meeting, they exchanged cold stares; apart, each said what he thought of the other to whoever would pass it on.

You may say that here was my chance. Anyone used to courts will say so. I would have said it once; I knew better now. Alexander, of whom men tell many legends, lived by his own. Achilles must have Patroklos. He might love his Briseis; but Patroklos was the friend till death. At their tombs in Troy, Alexander and Hephaistion had sacrificed together. Wound Patroklos, and Achilles will have your blood. Eumenes knew; he'd known them since they were boys.

So, instead of telling tales and making mischief, I gave no sign that I even knew of trouble. That legend was a limb of Alexander. His very blood flowed into it. If anyone bruised it, let it be Hephaistion himself, not I. Besides, there was that morning in the desert.

The court set out for Ekbatana. Stateira was left with her grandmother at Susa. Roxane was brought along.

We had a diversion on the way. Atropates, satrap of Media, who'd heard of Alexander's dealings with other satraps, planned a little treat for him. The first time he'd passed that way, he'd asked whether the race of Amazons, mentioned by Herodotos, was still alive. Atropates had had none to offer, and must have been brooding on it ever since.

One morning, a silvery bugle-call echoed back and forth along the pass we'd camped in. Up pranced a troop of cavalry, daintily armed with round shields and little axes. The leader leaped from her horse, saluted Alexander, and told him they had been sent by Atropates. She had the right breast bare, as in all the legends, and small enough. As the left was covered, there was no knowing if that one was any bigger.

Having rejoined her troops, the lady put them through a very dashing display. The soldiers, eyeing all those bare breasts, nearly cheered their heads off. Alexander said to Ptolemy, 'Atropates must be out of his mind. Warriors? Those are just girls. Do they look to you like whores?'

'No,' Ptolemy said, 'they've been picked for their looks and riding.'

'What kind of fool does he take me for? Well, we must have them out of camp before the men get at them. Bagoas, do something for me. Tell them their show was so delightful, I'd like to see the musical ride again. Hydarnes, can you raise me an escort of sober, middle-aged Medes? And quickly?'

They looked prettier still, flushed from their riding; the men were licking their chops like dogs at a kitchen door. There were whistles and calls when the ride began again. In a great hurry, Alexander collected presents. He chose jewellery, not weaponry, but it was well received. The grizzled Medes led off their charges to a sound of groans.

We camped in the upland pastures of Nysa, the royal horselands. The brood-mares were still about fifty thousand, though so many had been lifted in the years of war. They were a delight to Alexander, who established a guard for them, and chose out some likely colts. He gave one to Eumenes. If it was by way of thanks for his thankless offer to Hephaistion, and a salve for pride, none of that was said; but Hephaistion, who had done the first wrong in the quarrel, may have read that into it. Certainly

Eumenes' faction did, and were saying that pride went before a fall.

I know, having seen the list, that Alexander had planned asking Hephaistion to dinner that night with some old friends. He'd have been charming to him before everyone, smoothed down his feathers, shown that Patroklos was Patroklos still.

That day, he came face to face with Eumenes in the camp.

I don't know if it was design or chance. I had ridden out to see the horse-herds, and was coming back; they were well away by the time I heard the shouting. Hephaistion was saying that Greeks had been played-out for a hundred years, that Philip had thrashed them everywhere, and Alexander had found them with only tongues for weapons; *those* they knew how to use. Eumenes said that swaggering braggarts needed no tale-bearers; their own noise told enough.

Each faction booed and cheered; the crowds were growing. It would be blood before long. I began to edge out. Already I heard the rasp of swords in scabbards; when there was a drumming of violent hooves, brought to a clattering halt. A high fierce voice shouted, once. All other sounds failed. Alexander, his bodyguard behind him, sat staring down, his mouth shut, his nostrils flaring. In the hush, one heard the shake of the horses' bridles.

The long pause ended. Hephaistion and Eumenes stepped towards him, each starting to blame the other.

'*Be silent!*'

I jumped down and held my horse, making myself small in the crowd. I did not want my face ever remembered, along with what was coming.

'Not a word. Either of you.' His speed had flicked back the hair from his brow; he had it rather short, for the summer heat. HIs eyes had paled, anger furrowed his brow like pain. 'I demand discipline from men I appoint to keep it. You are to lead my soldiers in battle, not in brawls. Both of you deserve to be put on a charge of mutiny. Hephaistion, I made you what you are. And not for this.'

Their eyes met. It was as if I saw them bleeding, letting the blood run down unheeding with faces of stone.

'I order you to renounce this quarrel. Under pain of death. If it breaks out again, you will both be on trial for treason. The proved aggressor will suffer the usual penalty. I shall not commute it.'

The crowd held its breath. It was not just the public reprimand of two such men, in itself a thing unheard-of. They were Macedonians. They knew the legend.

The factions were sheathing their swords in furtive quiet. 'At noon,' he said, 'you will both report to me. You will shake hands before me and swear a reconcilement, which you will keep to in look, and word, and deed. Is that understood?'

He wheeled his horse and rode off. I slipped away in the crowd. I dared not look at Hephaistion's face, in case he saw me there. I did not see it either when he took the oath before Alexander.

That night he had them both to supper. A gesture of forgiveness; but to both alike. That special kindness to Patroklos must be for another day.

I'd barely seen him, till it was time to dress. It was worse than I'd thought. He looked haggard, and hardly spoke. I dared say nothing. But when I was doing his hair, I took his head in my hands and laid my cheek on it. He gave a deep sigh and closed his eyes. 'I had to do it. Nothing else was possible.'

'There are wounds that only kings must suffer, for the sake of all.' I had been a long time thinking what to say, that he'd forgive me after.

'Yes. That is the thing.'

I longed to embrace him, and tell him I would never have made him suffer it. But, I thought, they will make it up; what then? Besides, there was always the desert. So I just kissed him once, and went on with what I was doing.

Supper broke up early. I thought he'd just been afraid of their getting drunk and starting again. But he loitered in his tent instead of coming to bed; then put a dark cloak on and went out. I saw him throw a fold about his head; he didn't want it seen where he was going, though he must have known I'd guess.

He was not very long away. They must have patched it up, after a fashion; one could tell that after. But if it had gone as he wished, he'd not have finished the night as he did with me. Nothing was said in words; much was said all the same, perhaps too much. I loved him, and could not help it.

Time passes, edges wear down. We camped three or four days more among the tall glossy horse-herds. Hephaistion and Eumenes addressed each other with quiet courtesy. Alexander went riding with Hephaistion, to choose him a horse. They came back laughing, much as they used, except that one knew it had been worked for. Time alone will not heal it, I thought; only the will to forget. 'I shall not commute it.' The one knows those words were forced upon him, the other that they were said. None of it can be undone, or talked away. But they have been bound so long, they will agree to forget; it is necessary, nothing else is possible.

We went up the passes, eastward to Ekbatana.

No snow, now, on the sevenfold ramparts; they glowed like jewelled necklaces on the mountain's breast. Not sleet, but cool delightful breezes blew through the high airy rooms. The makeshift shutters were cleared away; it was a summer palace, with the King expected. Beautiful carpets covered the royal floors. Lamps of fretted silver and gilded bronze hung from the gold-leafed rafters, in the bedchamber where Darius had struck my face, and I had stumbled out weeping into Nabarzanes' arms.

The hills were green and full of streams; one could smell the heights. I would ride in them at last; we were to stay all summer.

At night he walked out on his balcony, to cool his head from the wine. I stood beside him. The plant-tubs smelled of lemon flowers and roses; the breeze came pure from the mountains. He said, 'When first I came here, chasing Darius, though it was full winter, I said to myself, Some day I must come back.'

'I too. When I was with Darius, being chased by you, I said the same.'

'And here we are. Longing performs all things.' He gazed at the brilliant stars, conceiving new longings, as a poet conceives a song.

I knew the signs. He was absent and exalted, and would pace with brows creased in thought, which I always knew from trouble. One must never ask till he was ready. He would come out with it of a sudden, as if he'd given birth.

He was delivered one morning, so early that I was the first to hear. I found him up and walking about stark naked, as he must have been doing since before dawn. 'It's Arabia,' he said the moment he saw me. 'Not the inland parts, that's just a matter of seeing the tribesmen don't raid the ports. It's the coast we need; and no one knows how far it runs south or west. Just think. We can make harbours along Gadrosia, now we know where there's water. From Karmania up the Persian sea, that's easy sailing. But we need to round Arabia. Once up the Arabian Gulf – *that* end's well charted – you're in Egypt. And from there, do you know this, there's a channel right through to the Middle Sea? Their King Neko started it; and Darius the Great carried it through. It needs clearing and widening, that's all. Once we round Arabia, if we can, ships can go all the way from the Indus, not just to Susa – to Alexandria, Piraeus, Ephesos. Cities made from small towns, villages where there was nothing; poor savages like Niarchos' Fish-Eaters brought into the world of men; and all the great peoples sending their best to one another, sharing their thought. The sea's the great road. Man has hardly set his foot on it.'

I was nearly running, to keep up and listen. 'Italy, now. My sister's husband died making war there, he should have waited for me. They'll have to be brought into order before long, or that western tribe, the Romans, will have it all. Good fighters, I've heard. I should let them keep their own form of government; and I could use their troops to push the empire westward, along North Africa. I long to see the Pillars of Herakles; who knows what may lie beyond?'

There was much more. Sometimes snatches come back to me, and then I lose them; seeing only his face in the cool early light, worn and shining, worn fine like much-used gold; his deep eyes bright as a fire-altar; his tousled hair, faded yet still a boy's; and the strong obedient body forgetful of its wounds, ready to face the tasks of another life-span, pacing as if already on its way.

'So Babylon must be the capital at the centre. The harbour should have slips for a thousand galleys. I shall go straight from here, to get started, and prepare the fleet for Arabia ... Why are you looking sad?'

'Only at leaving Ekbatana. When do we go?'

'Oh, not till the cold begins. We will have our summer.' He turned his eyes to the mountains, and would have walked naked to the balcony, if I'd not put a robe on him. 'What a place for a festival! We'll have one before we go. It's time I offered something to the Immortals.'

We had our summer.

On the hills with the hounds crying, racing the clouds; in the rose-garden with its lotus pools; in the high hall whose columns were sheathed with gold and silver, as I did my Dance of the River to the sound of flutes; in the great bedchamber where I had been shamed and now was cherished, each day and night, I used to say to myself, I will miss nothing; I will never let my eye or my ear or my soul or my senses sleep, never forget to know that I am happy. For it will be a long campaign; who knows when we shall come back?

Thus the Wise God gives us prophecy enough, but not too much; as he does to the birds, who foresee the winter, but not the night of ice that will drop them from the bough.

Alexander started at once to put in train his plans for the fleet, and the great harbour at Babylon, sending orders ahead. He wanted the north of the Hyrkanian Sea explored, to see how the coast led round to India. He also did much state business Darius would have handed to someone else; it was the custom for the King to take a holiday at Ekbatana. When I told Alexander so, he looked surprised, and said he was taking one; he had never been so idle in his life.

The summer before, we had been in Gadrosia. I would dabble my hand in the lotus-pool, and think, I am happy. Let never a moment flow by me unthanked, unkissed.

One night I said, 'Are you happy, Al'skander?'

He said smiling, 'Couldn't you tell?'

'Oh, yes, that. I mean here, in Ekbatana.'

'Happy?' he said, turning it over. 'What is happiness?' He stroked me, so that I should know him grateful. 'To have achieved one's longing, yes. But also, when all one's mind and body are stretched to breaking, when one hasn't a thought beyond what to do next moment; one looks back after, and there it was.'

'You will never settle down, will you, Al'skander? Not even here.'

'Settle down? With all I have to do? I should hope not.'

He was already planning the autumn festival, and sent word of it to Greece. Hordes of actors and poets, singers and kitharists would be on the way. He was not inviting athletes. In the old days, he said, they had been all-round men, the heroes of their cities in war; now they had trained themselves into mere machines for winning one event. 'A catapult can throw further than any soldier, but it can't do anything else. It's not good for the men to have such people beat them. Nor for the boys to see it.'

'The boys' now meant one thing to him. When the veterans left, returning to their wives and leaving, as soldiers do, the women who'd followed them with so much hardship, he had made the children his wards. He would not have them suffer in Macedon as unwanted foreign bastards; they should be reared for what they were, half Persian half Macedonian, part of the harmony he'd prayed for at the Susa love-feast. Boys old enough to leave their mothers were at school already, and had come up here with the court. There were to be events for them at the games; he went sometimes to watch them training.

He went sometimes, too, along the latticed walk to the harem. Roxane was like a sharp sauce to him; nauseous if one fills one's plate with it, yet a little now and then will make one crave for the taste again. It did not trouble me.

Summer fled by in the cool sweet hills; the roses rested before their autumn flowering. There came a day of change. His face was smoothed with joy; he could talk about nothing long without 'Hephaistion thinks ...' or 'Hephaistion was saying ...' Somewhere, perhaps up in the mountains riding alone, they had broken the wall, cast themselves into each other's arms, were once again Achilles and Patroklos; they would begin forgetting.

In the wisdom of my hard schooling, I'd done nothing to delay it; no malice could be remembered against me now. I had shut in my silent heart, as always, 'Say that you love me best of all.' So I kept what I had. He'd no need to forget the nights when he'd turned to me, and known that I understood. I had not defaced the legend.

Now that it was restored, polishing and shining, I was aware of a relief. He'd not been himself without it. He had lived so long at stretch, in labours and wounds and sickness and endurance, it did not do for him to have the roots of his life disturbed.

Hephaistion must have known it; he was not a fool. I expect, indeed, in his heart he was still a lover. He'd felt he should be upheld against Eumenes, right or wrong. Just so the Macedonians felt about the Persians.

Just so I felt, but had the sense to keep it quiet. Alexander attracted jealousy. He was much beloved; and he never turned love away.

Even in the cool air of Ekbatana, and doing no more than two men's work, he still tired sooner than he'd done before his wound. I was glad this other wound was healing. He'd go more rested to Babylon, where the real work would begin.

Banners went up on gilded poles with sculptured finials. A city of tents arose, for the artists at the festival. The race-course and the stadium were cleared and levelled. The architects made a theatre, with a crane to fly on the gods, and a machine for wheeling in murdered corpses, which Greek poets set such store by. Thettalos, Alexander's favourite actor, a handsome Thessalian in his fifties, was welcomed with open arms and given the best tent. They came pouring in, flute-players, chorus boys, scene-painters, singers and dancers, rhapsodists, acrobats; high-class courtesans and low-class whores, among them some eunuchs so shameless and bedizened, I was ashamed to see them about. Traders swarmed everywhere, selling food and gewgaws and cloth and spices, and, of course, wine.

The Palace flowed with it. There was a party every night for the artists, or for Alexander's friends. Patroklos was back; he gave himself up to gaiety. For nights on end, I didn't get him sober to bed. He was never dead drunk, knowing he couldn't sleep it off next day; he had to be at the contests. His friends, not restrained by duty, often left the hall feet first. One gets used to this, when living among Macedonians.

While I was getting him into his state robe for the contest of choral odes, he said to me, 'Hephaistion's not well, he's running a fever.'

Once he used never to talk of him to me; now he often would, after all our unspoken secrets. I said I was sorry, and hoped it was nothing much.

'He must have had it on him last night, if he'd only known it. I wish I'd kept down the drinking.' He went off, and the trumpets sounded.

Hephaistion was worse next day, and had cramps in his belly. Busy as he was, Alexander spent all his spare time with him. Achilles had always bound Patroklos' wounds. He got him the most noted doctor in Ekbatana, a Greek called Glaukias; to whom he gave advice, as he told me after. But he really had some knowledge; Aristotle had taught it him, and he had kept it up. It was agreed the patient should take no solid food. The priests were told to sacrifice for his healing.

The third day he was lower; weak as a babe, rambling in his talk, and full of fever, so Alexander said. It was the day for the comedies and farces; he did not sit them out, just came from the sick-room in time to give the prizes. When I asked the news at evening, he said, 'He's better, I think. Restless and crotchety, a good sign. He's strong, he'll throw it off ... I was sorry to disappoint the artists, but that was necessary.'

There was a party that night, but he left it early to see how Hephaistion was; reporting him asleep, and looking easier. Next day, though still with some fever, he was much better. Alexander attended all the contests; his absence had much upset the comedians. In the evening he found Hephaistion sitting up, and asking for food.

'I wish,' he said to me later, 'I could have sent him something good from supper.' He was still fond of this pleasant custom. 'But the belly-cramps leave a weakness in the entrails; I saw that often in the Oxos country. I told the doctor to be sure and keep him on slops.'

He still kept his bed, much better, but with a little fever at night, when the artists' contests ended, and the games began.

Alexander loved the arts; but the games were his close concern. He presided over everything; always remembered the victor's record in battle and in earlier games, when he gave the crowns. For such things the army loved him. After two or three days of this, came the day for the boys.

I'd played truant from the men's events, finding better pastime in the artists' quarter; but I went to the stadium for the boys' race, to see the breed Alexander was rearing up. He was sure to want to talk about it after.

They looked healthy, having been well-fed since he took them over; with features from nearly everywhere, all crossed with Macedonian; no doubt there'd be half-Indians too, when they were old enough. The half-Persians were far the handsomest. I sat just across the track from Alexander. At the march-past, they went off with their faces lit from his smile.

They lined up; the trumpet sounded; they sped from the marks. They wore little breech-cloths from respect for Persian modesty, no more. A pretty sight, I was thinking; when I was aware of a stir about the throne. Some messenger was standing by Alexander. He had jumped to his feet. The steps behind had closed up with people; he shoved them aside before they could make way, he nearly stepped on them. He was gone, with those nearest him scrambling after.

I clambered from my place. I must know what it was; I might be needed. Being on the far side of the stadium delayed me. When I reached the palace, the royal rooms were deserted. It was then I guessed.

I went up the stairs, turned a crooked passage; I had no need to ask the way. I had heard from the stairway the dreadful sound of grief, which lifted the hair on my head.

No one was guarding the door. A knot of men stood outside. I slipped in among them, unnoticed as a household dog. I had never been before in Hephaistion's room. It was handsome, with red wall-hangings and a stand of silver vessels. A smell of sickness hung in the air. He lay on the bed, his face turned up, his mouth fallen open. Someone had closed his eyes. Grasping the body with both fists, lying across it, his mouth pressed to its face was Alexander. He lifted his head, and gave again that dreadful cry; then buried his head in the dead hair.

After a while Perdikkas, awkward with shame and pity (yes, and already fear) said, 'Alexander'.

He looked up. I stepped forward, caring for none of them. He had turned to me before, and knew that I understood. His gaze passed over me, empty. It seemed at that moment that for him I had never been. Lost, gone, possessed.

I looked at this strange room, never forgotten, where I stood like a dead thing unmourned, unburied, tossed naked into the night; at the bed with its burden, the wall-hangings of stags and archers, the silver ewers; the bed-table shoved askew, with something on it; an empty wine-jar tumbled on its side, and a platter with the picked carcass of a chicken.

Suddenly Alexander flung himself to his feet and stared at us, as if he might kill any one of us without caring which. 'Where is the doctor?'

Ptolemy looked round to ask the servants, but they had long since fled. He said, 'He must have gone to the games.'

I had withdrawn near the door, and was aware of something behind me. It was the man himself, slower than I had been to take alarm; just come, just aware of what he saw. Alexander sprang across like a beast of prey, fastened on him, and shook him to and fro, 'You murderer! Why did you leave him? Why did you let him eat?'

The man, almost past words, stammered that he had seemed to be out of danger, that he had ordered him chicken broth.

Alexander said, 'Hang him. Take him away and hang him. Do it now.'

Perdikkas looked at Ptolemy. His eyes were on Alexander; without moving them, he nodded. The man was dragged away, under Seleukos' escort. Alexander went back to the bed, stared down at it, and lay where he had been before. The corpse moved, shaken with his sobbing.

More people were at the door, men of rank who'd just had the news. Those within all looked at one another helplessly. Peukestes touched my shoulder, and said softly in Persian, 'You speak to him.'

I shook my head. Only one thing was wanting to my heart's death, that he should hate me for being the one who was left alive.

So I ran away; through the city, through the stink and litter of the fair, through the streets of the women, unseeing till I heard their laughter; into the country, I don't know where. A cold stream I stumbled in waked my mind. I looked back at the city; the sun was sinking, the coloured ramparts glowed. Did I run off, I thought, when his flesh was wounded? Now he is stricken in his mind and might hurt me in his madness, now I forsake him, a thing no dog would do.

Dusk was falling. My clothes were torn, my hands bleeding, from thorns

I could not recall. Without even thinking to make myself presentable, I went straight back. There was much the same knot about the door. Within, dead silence.

Two or three men came out to talk apart. Ptolemy said softly, 'We must get him out before it starts to stink, or he'll lose his reason. Maybe for good.'

'By force then?' said Perdikkas. 'He won't come else. It must be all of us; it's no time to be singled out.'

I slipped away. Nothing should get me in there, to see him look from that dead face to mine. I went to his room and waited.

He was quiet when they brought him in, no one was handling him. They all stood round him expressing grief and praising the dead, I daresay the first chance they'd had. His eyes moved from face to face, as if he were at bay among their spears. Suddenly he cried, 'Liars! You all hated and envied him, all of you. Go, leave me alone.'

They exchanged looks and went. He stood in the state robe he'd worn for the games, white upon purple, all creased from being lain on. A groan burst from him, as if all the wounds he had borne in silence found voice at once. Then he turned and saw me.

I could not read his face. He had no weapon; but his hands were very strong. I went and knelt, and reached for his hand and kissed it.

He stared down at me and said, 'You have mourned for him.'

It took me a moment to remember my briar-torn clothes, my scratched face and hands. I grasped a tear in my coat, and ripped it top to bottom.

He took me by the hair, and pulled back my face to look in it. I said to him with my eyes, When you come back I will be waiting, if I am alive. If not it was my destiny. It seemed he would search me forever with his mad eyes, grasping my hair. Then he said, 'You fetched him when Oxhead died. You honoured him when he saved you from the desert. *You* never desired his death.'

I praised the dead to him, kneeling, grasping his hand. It was my confession, though he did not know it. I had welcomed my rival's faults, hated his virtues. Now I drew them out with pain from where my wishes had buried them, and offered them, his trophies, wet with my blood. He was the victor for ever, now.

Alexander's eyes had wandered. He had not heard half I'd said. He let me go, returning to his solitude. Presently he lay down, and covered his face.

All next day he lay there, accepting no consolation. Though he let me take no care of him, he did not send me out; he seldom knew I was there. The generals acted on their own, cancelling the games, getting the banners changed to wreaths of mourning. Seleukos, who had kept the doctor unhanged lest the King should change his mind, dared not ask, and hanged him. The embalmers, summoned in time, did their work upon Hephaistion. There were many Egyptians with the camp.

At night, without really seeing me, he let me give him water. Without his leave, I brought in cushions and slept there. At morning I saw him wake from a brief sleep, and endure remembrance. That day he wept, as if he had only now learned how. It was as if he had been stunned, and began to stir. Once he even thanked me. But his face was strange, and I dared not embrace him.

Next morning he was awake before me. He was standing with a dagger in his hand, hacking off his hair.

For a moment I thought his senses were quite gone, that he might next cut his throat or mine. Greeks in our day only lay one lock on the funeral pyre. Then I remembered Achilles, shearing his hair for Patroklos. So I found the trimming-knife and said, 'Let me do it. I'll do it just as you want.'

'No,' he said, hacking away. 'No, I must do it myself.' But he grew impatient with the back, and let me finish it, so that he could be off. Roused from his living death, staring wide awake, he went like a trail of fire.

He asked where was Hephaistion; but the embalmers had him, steeped in nitre. He asked if the doctor had been hanged (Seleukos had been prudent there) and commanded the body to be nailed on a cross. He ordered the manes of all army horses to be cropped in mourning. He ordered the gold and the silver to be stripped from the battlements of Ekbatana, and the colours painted over black.

I followed where I could, in case he should lose his senses altogether, or become a child. I knew that he was mad. But he could tell where and with whom he was. He was obeyed in everything; Glaukios the doctor was black with crows.

I was trailing him, not too near in case he saw me, when he happened on Eumenes, who had seen his swift course too late. His face I couldn't see; but I saw the terror in Eumenes'. He knew he was suspect of wishing Hephaistion dead.

Soon after, a rich catafalque appeared in the square before the palace, hung with mourning wreaths. A message reached Alexander that friends of the dead had reared it, to dedicate their offerings. He came to see it. Eumenes was first; he dedicated his whole panoply of arms and armour, which were very costly. A whole procession followed him. Everyone came who'd had a cross word with Hephaistion any time in the last five years.

Alexander watched calmly, like a child who is lied to and not deceived. He spared them not for their pretences, but for their penitence and their fear.

When they had done, all who had really liked Hephaistion came and made offerings. I was surprised how many there were.

Next day Alexander planned the funeral. It was to be in Babylon, the new empire's centre, where his memorial would stand for ever. When Darius sued for peace after the fall of Tyre, he'd offered as ransom for his mother and wife and children ten thousand talents. On Hephaistion, Alexander was spending twelve.

It quietened his mind, making these dispositions, choosing an architect for a royal pyre two hundred feet high, planning the funeral games, which were to have three thousand competitors. He was clear and precise in everything.

At bedtime, he would talk to me of Hephaistion as if memory could give him life; what they did as boys, what he'd said of this or that, how he trained his dogs. Yet I felt something unsaid; I felt his eyes when I turned away. I knew; he was thinking that his taking me had grieved Hephaistion; that he should make amends. Quietly he would put me aside, punishing himself, not me, making his gift to the dead. He would do it, if once his resolve was set.

My mind ran like the hunted stag that scarcely knows it runs. I said, 'It's good that Eumenes and the rest made their dedications. He is at peace with them now. He has forgotten mortal anger. Of all men on earth he is only concerned with you, set as he is now among the immortals.'

He stepped away, leaving the towel in my hands, and pressed the heels of his hands against his eyes, till I feared he'd harm them. I don't know what he saw in that sparkling darkness. Coming out of it, he said, 'Yes. Yes. So it must be, nothing else is possible.'

I got him to bed and was going out, when he said, as briskly as he'd planned the games. 'I shall send to Ammon's oracle, tomorrow.'

I made some soft answer and crept off. What new turn had I given his madness? I had been thinking in Persian, when I spoke of the immortals; the souls of faithful men, safe through the River into Paradise. But Alexander, he had thought in Greek. He would ask the oracle for Hephaistion to be a god.

I tossed on my bed and wept. His resolve had set, he would do it. I thought of the Egyptians, the oldest people, scornful in their long history. They will mock him, I thought; they will mock him. Then I remembered; he is a deity himself already; Ammon acknowledged him. Without Hephaistion, he cannot bear even immortality.

So perfect was my grief, it made my mind white and empty, and I slept.

Next day he chose priests and envoys, and offerings for the god. The embassy left the day after.

After this he was much calmer; his madness healed a little from day to day, though all lived in fear of it. His friends made donations towards the funeral. Eumenes gave the most, no doubt remembering when his tent burned down; he would still walk a mile to avoid crossing Alexander's path.

To throw off sorrow, I rode out to the hills. From there I looked back, and saw the sevenfold walls stripped of their glories, seven rings of black; and I wept again.

28

Time passes, all things pass. He ate, and began to sleep, and to meet his friends. He even gave one or two audiences. His shorn hair began to grow. He would talk to me, sometimes, of daily things. But he did not recall the embassy on its way to Siwah.

Autumn drew to winter. It was past the time when the Kings had been used to leave for Babylon. There were embassies from half over the empire and beyond, on their way to meet him there.

The Egyptians had worked their skill upon Hephaistion. He lay in a gilded coffin, on a dais hung with precious cloths, in one of the state rooms. The trophies of arms, the dedications, were set up around him. They had not swaddled and cased and masked him, as they do it here in Egypt. A body they have treated, even unwrapped, will keep the features of life for many ages. Alexander often went to visit him. Once he took me, because I had worthily praised the dead, and lifted the lid for me to see him. He lay upon cloth of gold, in the pungent smell of spices and of nitre; he would blaze like a torch, when they came to burn him in Babylon. His face was handsome and stern, the colour of darkened ivory. His hands were crossed on his breast; they rested on the shorn locks of Alexander's hair.

Time passed; he could talk to his friends now; and then his generals in their soldiers' wisdom, doing what I could not, brought him the medicine that had power to do him good. Ptolemy came to him, to say that the Kossaians had sent to demand their tribute.

They were a tribe of famous brigands, who lived about the passes between Ekbatana and Babylon. Caravans which took that road would wait till they were big enough to hire a regiment of guards. Every year, it seems, even the Kings had been raided, till they'd agreed to pay a sackful of gold darics before the autumn progress, to buy the Kossaians off. This toll was overdue, and they had sent to ask for it.

Alexander's '*What?*' was almost like old times. 'Tribute?' he said. 'Let them wait. I'll give them tribute.'

'It's very difficult country,' said clever Ptolemy, rubbing his chin. 'Those forts are eagles' nests. Ochos could never reduce them.'

'You and I will, though,' said Alexander.

He set out within seven days. Any Kossaians he killed, he said, he would dedicate to Hephaistion, as Achilles had done the Trojans on Patroklos' pyre.

I packed my things without asking. He had given me no more of those hidden looks; he took me for granted, all that I asked just now. I had accepted in my heart that he might never take me to bed again, lest it grieve Hephaistion's spirit. That mourning had become an accustomed thing. I would live, if I could be near him.

In the passes, Alexander split his force between himself and Ptolemy. Up here it was already winter. We were an army camp as in Great Kaukasos, moving light as the forts fell one by one. Each night he turned in, no longer brooding, but full of the day's campaign. On the seventh day, for the first time he laughed.

Though the Kossaians were robbers and murderers, without whom mankind is better, I had dreaded for his sake some sick-brained, furious slaughter. But he'd been brought to himself. Certainly he killed when battle called for it; perhaps Hephaistion was pleased, if the dead like blood as much as Homer says. But he took prisoners as his custom was, and held the chiefs for bargaining. His mind was as clear as ever. He saw every goat-track to the eagles' nests; his ruses and surprises were an artist's work. Artists are healed by their art.

After one such triumph, he gave supper in his tent to his chief officers. I said beforehand, easily, 'Your hair wants trimming, Al'skander', and he let me take off the ragged ends. That night he got rather drunk. He had never done it since the death; it would have been base to drown that grief. Now he did it in victory, and as I helped him to bed my heart was lighter.

We moved on to the next stronghold. He set the siege-lines. The first snow whitened the tops, and the men drew close round the fires. He came in glowing from frost and flame, and greeted the guardian squires as he used to do. When I brought the night-lamp, he reached out and drew me by the hand.

I offered no art that night, or no more than had become my nature; only the tenderness from which pleasure springs of itself like flowers from rain. I had to rub my eyes on the pillow to hide my tears of joy. I saw on his sleeping face the marks of madness and pain and sleeplessness; but they were wounds turning to scars. He lay at peace.

I thought, He has rebuilt the legend in everlasting bronze. He will keep faith with it, if he lives to threescore and ten. Hephaistion's regiment is always to bear his name whoever may command it, just so he will be forever Alexander's lover; no one else will ever hear, 'I love you best'. But in that shrine will be only the legend dwelling; the man will be hissing blue flames, then dust. Let his place be in Olympos, with the immortals, so long as my place is here.

I stole off softly, before he woke. He was attacking the fort at daybreak; he would not have time to think of it overlong.

The Kossaians had never been hunted in midwinter, in all their wicked history. The last forts, starved out, surrendered in return for the captives' freedom. It had all taken forty days. Alexander garrisoned the strongpoints along the pass, pulled down the rest, and the war was over. The caravans poured through. The royal household was sent for, to come down to Babylon. Already hard red buds gemmed the bare bushes shedding their snow.

But for his madness, he could have wintered down there, in the mild season, planning the new harbour and the Arabian fleet. Now he'd be there when the Persian Kings would have been thinking of Persepolis. All through the Kossaian war, the troops of embassies had been kicking their heels, awaiting him.

They met him when he pitched camp beyond the Tigris. He had made ready for them in state; but no one had been prepared for what really came.

They were not just from the empire, but from most of the known world; from Libya, with a crown of African gold; from Ethiopia, with the teeth of hippocamps and the tusks of enormous elephants; from Carthage, with lapis and pearls and spices; from Scythia, with Hyperborean amber. Huge blond Kelts came from the north-west, russet Etruscans from Italy; even Iberians from beyond the Pillars. They hailed him as King of Asia; they brought disputes from far beyond his frontiers, begging his wise judgement. They came with dedications, asking oracles, as Greeks go to the greatest shrines of their gods.

Most of these distant folk must have looked for a man of towering stature; some of the Kelts were as tall as Poros; yet none left his presence wondering why he was what he was. He was equal even to having the earth laid in his hands.

Indeed, in our time his face has changed the very faces of the gods. Look where you like, at the statues and the paintings. All the world remembers his eyes.

It helped his sickness, to be seen for what he was. After all he'd suffered, the Greeks were muttering that he'd reached a fortune above the human lot, and the gods are envious. To one such I said, 'Speak for your own. Ours is Great King and envies no one; he rejoices in light and glory. That's why we offer him fire.' No wonder the Greeks have envious gods, being full of envy themselves.

For three days he had no time for grieving. He went on exalted in his mind, remembering Siwah, and thinking of the west, whose peoples he'd now first seen. But sometimes his face would change, as if sorrow touched his shoulder, saying, 'Had you forgotten me?'

In the river plains, already the corn pricked the rich earth with green. Babylon's black walls lay along the flat horizon, when to our last camp on the road a man came riding. It was Niarchos, from the city. Though his hardships had left their mark, you could now see he was only forty; yet he looked care-ridden, to me. Oh no, I thought; don't bring new troubles just when he is better. So I stayed to listen.

Alexander welcomed him, asked after his welfare and the fleet's; then said, 'And now tell me what's wrong.'

'Alexander, it's the Chaldean priests, the astrologers.'

'What's amiss with them? I gave them a fortune to rebuild the Zeus-Bel temple. What are they after now?'

'It's not that,' Niarchos said.

Though I could not see him from where I was, I felt a sinking. It was not his seaman's way, to beat about.

'Well, what, then?' said Alexander. 'What's the matter?'

'Alexander, they read me my stars before we marched to India. It all came true. So just now I went again. They told me something that . . . upset me. Alexander, I knew you when you were so-high. I know your birthday, the place, hour, everything they need. I asked them to read the stars for you. They say Babylon's in a bad aspect for you now. They were coming out on their own account, to warn you off. It's a lee shore for you, they say. Unlucky.'

There was a little pause. Alexander said, quietly, 'How unlucky?'

'Very. That's why I came.'

A shorter pause. 'Well, I'm glad to see you. Tell me, have they finished building the temple?'

'They're barely past the foundations. I don't know why.'

He laughed. 'I do. They've been drawing the sacred tax for the temple upkeep, ever since Xerxes pulled it down. For generations. They must be the richest priests on earth. They thought I'd never be back, and it could go on for ever. No wonder they don't want me through the gates.'

Niarchos cleared his throat. 'I didn't know that. But . . . they told me I'd be in ordeal by water, and live to be honoured by a king, and marry well with a foreign woman. I told you at the wedding-feast.'

'They knew you were an admiral and my friend. Wonderful! Come to supper.'

He arranged for Niarchos' lodging, and finished his day's work.

At bedtime, he looked up at me leaning over him, and said 'Eavesdropper! Don't look so woebegone. It serves you right.'

'Al'skander!' I fell on my knees beside him. 'Do as they say. Never mind if they keep the money. They're not seers, they don't need to be pure of heart; it's a learning they have. Everyone says so.'

He reached and ran a lock of my hair between his finger and thumb. 'So? Kallisthenes had learning, too.'

'They'd be afraid to lie. All their honour's in true predictions. I've lived in Babylon, I've talked to all sorts of people in the dancing-houses.'

'Have you indeed?' He tugged at the lock softly. 'Tell me more.'

'Al'skander, don't go into the city.'

'What's to be done with you? Get in, you're not fit to sleep alone.'

The Chaldeans met him next day.

They came in their sacred robes of a shape unchanged for centuries. Incense was burned before them; their wands bore the emblems of the stars. Alexander met them in his parade armour, all Macedonian. Somehow they persuaded him to come apart among them, with only the interpreter. Chaldeans have almost their own language, and Babylonians don't speak good Persian either; but I hoped enough would reach him to move his mind.

He came back looking serious. He was not one of those who think God has no name but the one they heard in childhood.

They had begged him to march east; which would have taken him to Susa. But all his dearest concerns were fixed in Babylon; the new harbour, the Arabian voyage, Hephaistion's funeral rites. He was still in doubt of their good faith. Old Aristander was dead, whom he could have asked to take the omens.

At all events, he said that since the west was unpropitious, he would go round the city on the eastward side, and reach the South Gate that way.

There is no Eastern Gate, and we soon knew why. That side, we came to a great stretch of marsh, treacherous and full of pools. The Euphrates seeped round into it. He could still have made a greater circuit, even if it crossed and re-crossed the Tigris, and come back to the Euphrates. But he said impatiently, 'That settles it. I'm not squatting like a frog in a swamp to please the Chaldeans.' Since the embassies, he knew the world's eyes were on him. Perhaps that really settled it. At all events he turned back by north and west.

Still he did not enter the gates, but camped up river. Then he heard more embassies were coming, this time from Greece.

Anaxarchos, ever officious, reminded him that Greek thinkers no longer believe in omens. It touched his pride.

The Palace had been long prepared for him. As he drove through the gates in Darius' chariot, ravens fought overhead, and one fell dead before his horses.

However, as if to confound the auguries, the first news that met him was of life and fortune. Roxane had travelled straight down from Ekbatana to the Palace harem. When he visited her there, it was to hear that she was with child.

She had known already, at Ekbatana; she told him she had waited to make quite sure. The truth, as I have no doubt, was that it was at the time of his madness, and she'd been afraid to give him news that would bring him near her.

He made her all the accustomed gifts of honour, and sent her father the news. He himself took it quietly. Perhaps he'd given up the thought that she would conceive by him, and had meant, in due time, to breed an heir from Stateira. Perhaps his mind was on other things.

When he gave me the news, I cried, 'Oh, Al'skander! May you live to see him victorious at your side!'

I grasped him in both hands, as if I had power to defy the heavens. We stood in silence, understanding each other. At last he said, 'If I'd married in Macedon, as my mother wanted, before I crossed to Asia, the boy would have been twelve by now. But there was never time. There is never time enough.' He kissed me and went away.

It was torment to me to have him out of my sight. I watched him move among the half-forgotten splendours known to my boyhood. Then, I had come here light of heart. Now fear and grief hung on me like a sickness. Why had he listened to the Chaldeans, obeyed their warning and then defied it? It is Hephaistion, I thought, reaching out to him from the dead.

One must live, he'd said to me long ago, as if it would be for ever, and as if each moment might be the last. He began at once to have the great harbour dug, and the fleet built for Arabia, which Niarchos would command. It was spring now, as warm as a Susa summer. He would ride back from the new harbour, and make for the royal bath. Nothing in the Palace gave him so much pleasure. He loved the cool walls, the fretted screens glimpsing the river, the great bath with its lapis-blue tiles and their golden fish. He would float there with the water lifting his hair.

But there was always Hephaistion. He was due now for his rite of burning.

The fleet and the new harbour were both in hand. Alexander had time; and soon he had time only for this. He returned a little into his madness. If one woke him, he was sensible; but he would drift back into dreams.

Alexander's dreams were daimons. He conjured them, and they obeyed him.

He had ten furlongs of the city wall knocked half down, and levelled out to a square. Within this he had a platform made of fine tiles, each side a furlong. That was the base of the pyre. From that it tapered up, storey upon storey; each tier with carved sculptures, as fine in wood as if they'd been meant to last for ever. At the bottom, ships' prows with archers and warriors, larger than life; then torches twenty feet long, adorned with eagles and serpents; then a scene of wild beasts and hunters, gilded. Next above, trophies of arms, both Macedonian and Persian, to show both races had held the dead in honour. Above that I don't know what elephants, lions, garlands. Near the top were figures of winged sirens, hollow behind, in which singers would lament before the pyre was kindled. Great crimson flags hung down between the stages. There was room inside for a stairway, to bring him up with dignity.

I thought, No king has gone like this since the world began. He has dreamed it as if it were for himself. I watched his face, his eyes lifted to the pyre in his quiet madness, and dared do nothing, not even touch him.

The funeral car had been escorted by Perdikkas from Ekbatana. Hephaistion lay in state in the palace, here as there. Alexander went oftener to see him now; he would soon be gone. Medios of Larissa, who had been his friend, had a little bronze likeness of him made by a sculptor who'd seen him often, to give Alexander. He received it so gladly, that one friend after another, vying in affection or for favour, had small statues made in gold or ivory or alabaster. Soon the room was full of them; he was there wheverever I looked. And I had thought that when the pyre was kindled, that would be the end of him.

One day, being alone, I took the best likeness into my hand, thinking, Who were you, what are you, that you can do this to my lord? He came in behind me, and said, 'Put that down!' with such anger that I nearly dropped it. I put it back somehow, shaking with fear of exile. He said more quietly, 'What were you doing?' I answered, 'He was dear to you. I wanted to understand him.'

He took a turn across the room, then said, 'He knew me.'

No more. I was pardoned, he meant no hurt. I had asked, he answered. They had been born in the same month, in the same hills, of the same race, with the same gods; had lived under one roof from their fourteenth year. Truly, when to me we had seemed like one, to how much I had been a stranger.

Time will pass, I thought. They could bear to be parted on campaign; it will come to seem only like that. If there is time.

The day came. In the dusk before dawn, they lined the square about the platform; generals, princes, satraps, priests; standard-bearers, heralds, musicians; the painted elephants. By the steps were the braziers and the torches.

The bearers took up the coffin by the hidden stairs. As they reached the topmost deck, looking small as toys, and laid it on its stand, the sirens sang, faint in the sky. They came down, still singing. The torches were kindled at the braziers.

The pyre stood on palm-wood columns; the space between was piled up with tinder and dry straw. Alexander came forward with his torch, alone.

He was exalted above his madness, into ecstasy. Peukestes, who'd seen him fight on with the Mallian arrow in him, said later that then he looked just the same. The elephants curled back their trunks and trumpeted.

He flung in his torch; flames leaped from it. The friends followed; the brands pelted in; the fire jumped through the gratings, into the tier of ships. It began to roar.

The pyre was tinder-filled up its centre, through all its two hundred feet. The blaze spired upward, past ships and archers and lions and eagles and shields and garlands. At the top it enwrapped the coffin, and burst in a great peak of flame, against the green sky of sunrise.

Once at Persepolis, that feast of fire, they had looked up side by side.

For a while the high tower stood in its fearful beauty; then tier after tier caved in. An eagle crashed to the platform with flaming wings; the sirens toppled inwards; the coffin vanished. The timbers, the heavy carvings, began to hurtle down, throwing up spark-clouds tall as trees. The pyre was a single torch burning to its socket, by whose light I saw his face alone.

The sun came up. The whole parade stood stupefied in the heat. When nothing was left but red embers and white ash, he gave the order to dismiss. He gave it himself. I had thought they would have to wake him.

As he was leaving, a crowd of priests approached him, robed from all kinds of temples. He answered briefly and passed on. They looked unhappy. I overtook one of the squires who had been near, and asked what it had been about.

He said, 'They asked if they could re-kindle the sacred fires now. He said not till sundown.'

I stared at him, unbelieving. 'The temple fires? He ordered them put out?'

'Yes, for the mourning. Bagoas, you look bad, it was all that heat. Come in the shade here. Does it mean something in Babylon?'

'They do it when the King is dead.'

Silence fell between us. At last, he said, 'But when he ordered it, they must have told him that.'

I hurried to the Palace, hoping to get him alone. Even to light them now might avert the omen. Had there not been enough, that he must make his own?

But already he had summoned a score of people, and was finishing off plans for the funeral contests. Grave Persian faces showed me that others had tried to warn him. Old Palace eunuchs who had lived to see the fires three times doused, were whispering, and rolled their eyes my way. I did not join them. The temples were dark till sunset. Alexander worked on the games all day. There had been nothing much left to do, but it seemed that he could not stop.

They lasted near half a month. All the best artists from all the Greek lands were there. I went to the plays, mostly to watch his face; only one of them stays with me, *The Myrmidons*, which Thettalos had done before for Alexander; it's about Achilles. and Patroklos' death. Thettalos himself had just lost a dear friend, a fellow-actor who had died on the journey down from Ekbatana. He carried it through; he was a professional. Alexander sat as if his mind were far away. I knew the look. He had had it when Peukestes cut out the arrow.

The music seemed to do him good; he looked released from himself when the kitharists were playing. Afterwards he entertained all the winners, saying just the right thing to each. Perhaps, I thought, the last of the madness had been seared out of him by so much burning.

He began to go down again to the river, to watch the seamen training; he held races for the rowers, and offered prizes. Then the embassies from Greece arrived.

They were envoys of compliment, to honour his safe return from the world's end. They brought gold crowns, exquisite wreaths of jewellers' work, and scrolls of honour. Even the envious Athenians came, full of lying compliments. He knew they lied. But he gave them in return the statues of the Liberators, fetched from Susa, to put back on their citadel. When he made the presentation, he pointed as if by chance to the daggers, and caught my eye.

The last embassy was from Macedon.

It was not like the rest. The regent, Antipatros, whom Krateros was to supersede, had sent his son to speak for him.

During all his years of regency, which went back to King Philip's day, Queen Olympias had hated him, my belief being that she wished to govern instead. Knowing of all her slanders it was perhaps no wonder if he thought they had made their mark, and he'd been sent for to go on trial; for ten years he'd not set eyes on Alexander, to know him better. Even so, one would have thought he'd have had more sense than to send his son Kassandros. That is, if his faith was good.

Whenever Alexander had told me about his boyhood, he'd mentioned this youth, as then he'd been, with detestation. They had disliked each other at sight, and on all through their school-days; once they had come to blows. The reason he had been left behind in Macedon was simply that Alexander would not have him in the army.

However, he had helped his father put down a rising in southern Greece, and done quite well there; no doubt both had hoped that this would recommend him now. He arrived, after so long, almost a stranger; only this stranger and Alexander hated each other on sight, as they'd done before.

He was an arrogant, freckled, red-haired man, with the old-time Macedonian beard. He was also, of course, a perfect stranger to court life in Persia. One had forgotten such people existed.

No doubt he was mad with envy. The throne-room had been re-furnished, to receive the embassies; about the throne was a great half-circle of couches with silver feet, where the King's chief friends, Persian and Macedonian, had a right to sit when he gave audience. All the Household would stand behind him. My own place, now we were back among real procedure, was near the throne. I was there to watch Kassandros when he came. While he awaited Alexander, I saw him look at us eunuchs as if we were noxious vermin.

The audience did not go well. There had been petitioners out from Macedon to plead causes against the regent. Kassandros was too hasty, in saying they had come to be well away from all the evidence; I think one, at least, had been sent by Queen Olympias. Only one man had ever been allowed to speak against her to Alexander, and he was dead. Alexander broke the audience off, and asked Kassandros to wait while he saw some Persians.

Barbarians before *him*! I could see his fury. He stepped back, and the Persians, who were below the rank of Royal Kin, made the prostration.

Kassandros sneered. It is not true, as some say, that he laughed aloud. He was an envoy with work to do. Nor is it true that Alexander knocked his head on the wall. He had no need.

It is true the sneer was open; I suppose anger made him reckless. He turned to some companion he'd brought with him, pointing a finger. Alexander let the Persians rise, spoke to them, dismissed them; then stepped down from the throne, grasped Kassandros in one hand by the hair, and stared into his face.

I thought, He is going to kill him. So did Kassandros I daresay. But it was more than that. It was more than the kingly power, more even than the word of Ammon's oracle. He had been through fire and darkness. All he needed was to lay it bare. Kassandros stared as the bird does at the serpent, white with pure naked terror of man for man.

'You have leave to go,' said Alexander.

It was a good way to the doors. He must have known his fear had marked him like a brand, and all we creatures of his scorn hàd seen it.

Later on, when I had Alexander alone, I said to him, 'Hate like that is dangerous. Why don't you pack him off home?' He answered, 'Oh, no. He'd go back and tell Antipatros I'm his enemy, urge him to revolt, kill Krateros when he gets there, and seize Macedon. He might do it, if he was put in fear of his life. Let alone he has more sense. If I meant him harm, I'd hardly have his other son as cupbearer. He's been where he is too long, that's all. No, till Krateros is in Macedon and Antipatros leaves it, Kassandros stays here under my eye ... Hephaistion could never stand him, either.'

In earlier days, I'd have begged him to have the man put quietly out of the way. I knew that what he would not own to, he would not do. It is my life's regret I did not take it on myself in secret. It torments me, to think that with one little phial I might have quenched that murderous hate that has pursued my lord even beyond the tomb; his mother, his wife, the son I never saw, who would have given us something more of him than memory.

Summer came on. All Persian Kings would have been at Ekbatana. I knew he would never ride through those gates again; I was only glad he had the fleet and harbour to keep him busy. It was four months since the Chaldeans' prophecy. Except when I saw the new Bel temple going up, I could almost forget them.

Soon we left the city for a while. Down the river, there were floods every year when the snows at its source were melting, and the people there, who were of old Assyrian stock, lived poor because of it. Alexander wanted to plan dams and canals against it, and make new farmlands. It was only a river cruise, but it cheered me to have him outside the walls.

He always loved rivers. The ships wound among man-tall reed-beds, the Assyrian pilots conning the channels. Sometimes great shade-trees met above, and we glided through green caves; sometimes we pushed through lily-pads in open pools; the river has many branches there. Alexander would stand in the prow, and sometimes take the helm. He had on the same old sun-hat he used to wear in Gadrosia.

The stream broadened between drooping willows which tossed in a flaw of wind. Among them stood blockish ancient stonework; with figures, worn by time and flooding, of winged lions and bulls, man-headed. When Alexander asked about them, the Babylonian shipmaster said, 'Great King, those are the tombs of the old-time kings, when the Assyrians ruled here. This was their burial-ground.'

On the words, a gust plucked off Alexander's sun-hat, and whirled it overboard. Its purple ribbon, the symbol of royalty, was loosened and carried away. It whipped itself round the rushes beside a tomb.

The ship glided on by its own way; the rowers had shipped their oars. All along the craft passed a murmur of awe and dread.

A rower, a young quick swarthy man, dived off, struck for the bank, and unwound the ribbon. He paused with it in his hand, thought of the muddy water, and wound it round his head to keep it dry. Alexander took it with a word of thanks. He was quiet. I had all I could do not to cry aloud. The diadem had gone to a tomb, and passed to another head.

When his work was done, he went back to Babylon. I could have beaten my breast, at the sight of those black walls.

When he told the seers about the omen, they all said that the head which had worn the diadem ought to be struck off. 'No,' he said. 'He meant well and did what anyone might. You can give him a beating, if the gods demand some expiation. Don't lay on too hard, and send him to me after.' When the man came he gave him a talent of silver.

We returned to nothing but prosperity. Peukestes proudly paraded a well-trained army of twenty thousand Persians. His province was in first-class order; he was better liked than ever. Alexander gave public commendations; and began a scheme for a new Persian–Macedonian force. No one mutinied; even Macedonians had started to think that Persians might be men. Some of our words were passing into their speech.

The day came, long waited for, when the embassy returned from Siwah.

Alexander received it in the Throne Room, his Companions round him on the silver couches. Ceremoniously, the chief envoy unrolled Ammon's papyrus. He had refused to share his god-head; but Hephaistion still had his place with the immortals. He had been proclaimed a divine hero.

Alexander was content. After his first madness, he must have guessed it was as far as the god would go. Hephaistion could still be worshipped.

Commands went out to all the cities, to build him a temple or a shrine. (Here in Alexandria, I often pass the empty site upon Pharos Isle. I expect Kleomenes, who was satrap then, took all the money.) Prayers and sacrifices were to be offered him, as an averter of evil. All solemn contracts must be sworn in his name, besides the names of the gods.

(The temple he should have had in Babylon was in the Greek style, with a frieze of lapiths and centaurs. That place is empty too. I don't suppose one stone of all those sacred places was ever set on another. Well, he should still be satisfied. He had his sacrifice.)

Alexander feasted the envoys, in honour of Hephaistion's immortality. The other guests were friends who would understand. He was light-hearted, almost radiant. One would have thought the omens all forgotten.

He was some days happy and busy, having drawings done for the shrines. He called on Roxane, whom he found healthy and strong; Sogdian women don't make much of pregnancy. Then he pressed on with plans for the new mixed army.

It meant changes in all the forces. When he was ready to re-assign commands, he sent for the officers, to appoint them. He was in the throne-room; he knew well by now what proper ceremony means to Persians. The Household was assembled behind the throne.

It was now full summer and very hot. He broke off halfway through, to take his friends to the inner room for a drink of cold citron-water mixed with wine. They would not be long; it was not worth going away; we waited behind the empty throne and the couches, and talked of trifles.

We never saw the man, till he was among us. A man in shabby clothes, a common man among thousands, but for his face. To his crazed intent-ness, all of us were invisible. Before we had time to move, he had sat down on the throne.

We stared, appalled, hardly believing. It is the most dreadful of all omens; that is why, through all our people's history, it has been a capital crime. Some of us leaped forward to drag him off, but the old ones cried out in warning. It would unman the kingdom, for eunuchs to free the throne. They began to wail and to beat their breasts, and we joined their lamentation. For a while it lulls the mind, and one need not think.

The officers down in the hall, aroused by the noise, ran up in horror, seized the man and had him down from the dais. He stared about, as if bewildered by this concern. Alexander came out from the inner room, his friends behind him, and asked what was going on.

One of the officers told him, and showed the man. He was a common soldier, unarmed, an Uxian if I remember. Of us the King asked nothing. I suppose our outcry had told enough.

He walked over and said, 'Why did you do this?' The man stood and blinked, without mark of respect, as if at any stranger. Alexander said, 'If he was sent for this, then I must know who sent him. Don't question him till I am there.'

To us he said, 'Quiet. That is enough. The audience is open.' He finished the assignments, without carelessness, without haste.

At sundown, he came up to change his clothes. Now we were at Babylon, we had the whole ceremonial. It was I who handled the Mitra. Reading my eyes, as soon as was proper he sent out the rest. Before I could ask, he said, 'Yes, we questioned him. I had it stopped. He knew nothing, not even what brought him there. He could only say he saw a fine chair and sat in it. He was due for courtmartial, for repeated disobedience; of course he had not understood his orders. I am satisfied he was out of his mind.'

He spoke coolly and firmly. All my blood stood still. I had longed to know that the man had confessed to deceit and a human plot, though one look at his face had told me. It is the true omens, that come without intent.

'Al'skander,' I said, 'this one you will have to kill.'

'That has been done. It is the law; and the seers said it was necessary.' He walked to the flagon-stand, filled a wine-cup and made me drink. 'Come, make a better face for me. The gods will do what they will. Meantime we live, and they will that too.'

I swallowed the wine like medicine, and tried to smile. He was wearing a thin white robe of Indian stuff, for the summer heat, which showed his body like the robes the sculptors carve. I set down the cup and threw my arms around him. He seemed to glow from within, as always. He felt unquenchable as the sun.

When he was gone, I looked about at the images of gold and bronze and ivory, watching gravely from their stands. 'Leave hold of him!' I said 'Are you not yet content? You died through your own fault, through disobedience, impatience, greed. Could you not love him enough to spare him that? Then leave him to me, who love him more.' They all looked back at me and answered, 'Ah, but I knew him.'

More embassies came from the Greeks, garlanded as they come before their gods. Once more they crowned him; with gold fruiting-olive, gold barley-ears, gold laurel, gold summer flowers. I can see him still, wearing each crown.

A few days later, his friends said that with all these triumphs, he himself had not yet celebrated his victory over the Kossaians. (They were now so much won over, he had taken some thousands into the army.) It was long, they said, since he'd held a komos; and the feast of Herakles was coming.

They meant no harm. Even the worst sought only favour; the best wanted in kindness to give him a carefree evening, make him remember his glory and forget his grief. The gods can do with anything what they will.

He proclaimed the feast, ordered sacrifices to Herakles, and gave the troops a free wine-issue all round. The komos began at sundown.

It as a sweltering Babylon night. They had soon done with the food. I had planned, with his friends, a small surprise for him; a dance of Macedonians and Persians, four a side, mock war first and then friendship. We were bare, but for helmets and kilts or trousers. Alexander was very pleased with it, called me to sit by him on his supper-couch, and shared his gold cup with me.

His face was flushed; no wonder, with the heat and wine, but there was a brightness about his eyes I didn't like. I had had a quick rub-down to take off the sweat, but was of course still warm. When he put his arm round me, I felt that he was hotter.

'Al'skander,' I said under the noise, 'you feel like fever.'

'No more than a touch. It's nothing. I'll turn in after the torch-song.'

Soon they took up the torches, and walked singing into the gardens, to get the night's first cool. I slipped off to the Bed-chamber, to see everything was ready. I was glad to hear the chant returning and tailing off. He came in. If we'd been alone, I'd have said, 'To bed with you now, and quick about it.' But before the Household I always observed the forms. I stepped forward to take the diadem. His robe came off damp with sweat, and I saw him shiver. He said, 'Just rub me down, and find me something a little warmer.'

'My lord,' I said, 'you are not going out again?'

'Yes, Medios has a little party, just old friends. I promised to look in.'

I gazed at him in entreaty. He smiled ahd shook his head. He was Great King, not to be disputed with before the Household. It is in our blood, that such things must not be done; therefore we cannot do them, without the air of insolence. As I rubbed him down, my eye caught the stands of images. Why are *you* not here, I thought, now when you could be useful, to say, 'Don't be a fool; you are going to bed if I have to push you in. Bagoas, go and tell Medios the King can't come'?

But the images held their hero poses; and Alexander in a Greek robe of fine wool went with his torchbearers down the great corridor with its lion frieze.

I said to the rest, 'You may all retire. I will wait up for the King. I will have you called, if he needs attendance.'

There was a divan I slept on, if he was going to be late; his coming always woke me. The moon climbed the sky before my open eyes. When he came, the cocks were crowing.

He looked flushed and tired, and walked unsteadily; he'd been drinking, on and off, from sunset till dawn; but he was very sweet-tempered, and praised my war-dance. 'Al'skander,' I said, 'I could be angry with you. You know wine's bad for a fever.'

'Oh, it's gone off. I told you it was nothing. I'll make up my sleep today. Come to the bath with me, you've been all night in your clothes.'

The first light shone through the screens, and the birds were singing. The bath left me refreshed and drowsy; when I'd put him to bed, I turned in myself and slept till nearly evening.

I went softly into the Bedchamber. He was just awake, turning restlessly. I went up and felt his brow. 'Al'skander, it has come back.'

'Nothing much,' he said. 'Cool hands. Don't take them away.'

'I'll have supper brought here. The river fish is good. And what about a doctor?'

His face hardened, and he moved his head from my hands. 'No doctors.

I've seen enough of *them*. No, I'll get up. I'm having supper with Medios.'

I argued, implored; but he had woken cross and impatient. 'I tell you it's nothing. The swamp-fever, I expect. It's over in three days.'

'Maybe for the Babylonians; they're seasoned. It can be bad. Why can't you take care of yourself? You're not at war.'

'With you I will be, if you go on like a wet-nurse. I've been sicker than this, riding all day over mountains. Give out that I want to dress.'

I wished he'd been going to anyone but Medios, who would take no care of him, or notice anything wrong. He'd been a great supporter of Hephaistion in his quarrel with Eumenes; making it worse, I'd heard, for he had a biting tongue, and some of his gibes had gone abroad in Hephaistion's name. No doubt his mourning had been sincere; but he'd not been slow to use the favour it brought him. He could speak honey as well as vinegar, knew how to amuse Alexander and make him laugh. Not a bad man; but not a good one either.

I was dozing, when Alexander returned. By the sky, it was not long past midnight. I was glad to get him back so early. 'I left them at it,' he said. 'The fever's up a little. I'll cool down in the bath, and get to bed.'

His breath shuddered as I disrobed him. He felt burning hot. 'Let me just sponge you,' I said. 'You ought not to bathe like this.'

'It will do me good.' He would hear no sense, but walked through in his bath-robe. He did not stay in the water long. I dried him, and had just put on his robe, when he said, 'I'll sleep here, I think,' and made for the couch by the pool. I went quickly over. He was shaking with ague in every limb; his teeth were chattering. He said, 'Get me a good warm blanket.'

In Babylon, in midsummer, at midnight! I ran off and fetched his winter cloak. 'This will do till the cold fit's over. I'll keep you warm.'

I covered him with it, and threw my own clothes on top, then got under and held him in my arms. He was shivering worse than ever, yet his skin was scorching. He said, 'Closer,' as if we were naked in a snowstorm. As I wrapped myself round him, the prophetic voice was silent, which had said at Ekbatana, 'Carve this upon your heart.' It spared me; it did not say, 'Never again.'

The shivering stopped, he began to feel hot and to sweat, and I let him be. He said he would sleep here where it was fresher. I dressed and waked the Keeper of the Bedchamber, to send what he would need, and a pallet for me. Before morning the fever lessened, he slept, and I closed my eyes.

I woke to his voice. The bath-house was full of people tip-toeing about. He had just waked and was ordering Niarchos to be summoned. Niarchos? I thought; whatever does he want *him* for? I had forgotten, in my concern, that it was getting near time for the Arabian voyage. Alexander was planning a morning's work.

He walked to the Bedchamber to be dressed; then, since he could hardly stand, lay on the divan. When Niarchos came, he asked if the propitiation sacrifice for the fleet was ready. Niarchos, who I could see was disturbed by his looks, said yes, and asked whom he would like to make the offering-prayer for him. 'What?' he said. 'I'll make it myself, of course. I'll go by litter. I'm a little shaky today; I expect this is the last of it.' He brushed off Niarchos' protests. 'It was the favour of the gods that brought you safe from Ocean. I sacrificed for you then, and they heard me. I shall do it now.'

They bore him off, under an awning against the crushing Babylonian sun, in which he stepped out and stood to pour the libations. When he came back he could scarcely touch the light meal I'd ordered; but he had in Niarchos and all his chief officers, with a clerk to take notes, and was four full hours talking of supply ships, water and stores.

Days passed. The fever did not leave him. He meant, when the fleet sailed, himself to lead a supporting coast-march, looking out for harbour sites; so he had to delay the sailing. Each morning he declared that he was better; each day he was carried to the household altar, to offer the morning prayer; each time he was weaker; each evening the fever began to mount.

The Bedchamber was full of people coming and going; the palace, of officers awaiting orders. Though its thick walls kept out the sun, he craved for green shade and the sight of water, and had himself ferried across the river to the royal gardens. There he would lie under the trees, his eyes half-closed, near a fountain that splashed into a basin of porphyry. Sometimes he sent for Niarchos and Perdikkas, to plan the voyage and the march, sometimes for Medios to gossip and play at knucklebones. Medios tired him, too proud of being chosen, staying too long.

Other times he chose the bath-house, and had his bed set by the edge where he could step down easily; he liked to cool himself in the tepid water, to be dried sitting on the blue-tiled verge, and get back into clean sheets. He slept there too, for the cool, and the sound of the river lapping outside.

I did not leave him, for Medios, or the generals, or anyone else. I had put off easily my palace dignities; the old man I had displaced gladly resumed them. I changed my court dress for serviceable linens. As Chief Eunuch of the Bedchamber, I would have had my daily offices, my occasions to withdraw. Now those who came saw only the Persian boy, holding a fan or drinking-cup, bringing blankets when an ague took him, sponging him and putting on dry sheets after a sweat, or sitting quiet on a cushion against the wall. I was safe, my place aroused no envy. Only one man would have taken it from me and he was white ash on the winds of heaven.

When my lord sent the great men away, it was to me that he turned his eyes. I had one or two quiet slaves to fetch and carry; all the needs of his person I saw to myself. Thus people ceased to see me, more than the pillows or the water-ewer. They still sent to the palace, by old custom, the pure spring water which had always been the drink of the Persian kings. It refreshed him; I kept it by him on the bed-table, in an earthen cooler.

At night I had my pallet set beside him. He could reach the water; if he wanted anything more, I always knew. Sometimes if the fever kept him restless he liked to talk to me, recalling old hardships and old wounds, to prove he would soon be victor of his sickness. He never spoke of the death-omens, any more than in the midst of battle he would have spoken of surrender. When he'd been ill a week, he still talked of marching in three days. 'I can begin by litter, as soon as the fever's down. This is nothing, to things I've thrown off before.'

They had given up asking him to have a doctor. 'I don't need the same lesson twice. Bagoas looks after me better than any doctor.'

'I would if you let me,' I said when they had gone. 'A doctor would make you rest. But you think it's only Bagoas, and do just what you like.' He had been carried out that day to sacrifice for the army. For the first time, he had poured the libation lying down.

'To honour the gods is necessary. You should be praising my obedience, gentle tyrant. I should like some wine, but I know better than to ask.'

'Not yet. You've the best water in Asia, here.' One reason I never went out when Medios came was for fear the fool would give him wine.

'Yes, it's good.' He emptied his cup; he'd only been teasing. When he grew lively, I knew the fever was coming up. But that evening it seemed less. I renewed my vows to the gods of what I'd give them for his recovery. When he rode out against the Scythians, the omens had been bad, but had been fulfilled by sickness only. I slept with my hopes reviving.

His voice woke me. It was still dark, the watch after midnight. 'Why have you not reported sooner? We have wasted half the night-march. It will be noon, before we come to water. Why have you let me sleep?'

'Al'skander,' I said, 'you were dreaming. This is not the desert.'

'Put a guard on the horses. Never mind the mules. Is Oxhead safe?'

His eyes wandered past me. I wrung out a sponge in mint-water and wiped his face. 'See, it's Bagoas. Is that better?' He pushed at my hand, saying, 'Water? Are you mad? There's not enough for the men to drink.'

His fever had mounted, at the time when it had always sunk. I tilted the cooler over the cup. It was half empty; and the stream was not clear but dark. It was wine. Someone had come while I slept.

Mastering my voice, I said softly. 'Al'skander. Who brought the wine?'

'Has Menedas had water? Give it him first, he has fever.'

'We all have water, truly.' I emptied the cooler and filled it from the great jar. He drank thirstily. 'Tell me, who gave you wine?'

'Iollas.' He had only named the King's cup-bearer. Disordered as he was, this may have been all he meant. Yet Iollas was Kassandros' brother.

I went over to ask the night-slave, and found him sleeping. I had asked none of them to serve night and day, as I was doing. I left him as he was, lest being forewarned he should escape his punishment.

Alexander dozed restlessly till morning. The fever had not remitted, as it had at this time before. When they carried him to the household altar and put the libation-cup in his hand, it shook so much that half the offering spilled before he could pour it. This change was from when he had the wine. Before, I could have sworn that he was mending.

The night-slave, when I questioned him, had known nothing; he must have slept for hours. I sent orders to the Household, that he should be flogged with the leaded whip. The night-guard squires knew nothing either, or so they said; it was not in my power to have them questioned. The bath-house was harder than the Bedchamber to guard; someone might have slipped in from the river.

It was a grilling hot day. Alexander asked to be carried over to the shady place by the porphyry fountain. If a breath of breeze was stirring, one caught it there. I had stocked the summerhouse with everything he might need. As I settled him on the bed, I heard his breathing. It had a harshness which was new.

'Bagoas, can you prop me up a little? It catches me here.' He put his hand to his side.

He was naked but for the sheet. He had his hand to the wound from the Mallian arrow. This, I think, was the moment when first I knew.

I fetched pillows and eased him up on them. Despair was treachery while he fought on. He must not feel it in my voice, in my hands' tenderness.

'I shouldn't have had the wine. My own fault, I asked you.' He panted even from so few words, and pressed his hand to his side again.

'Al'skander, I never gave it you. Can you remember who did?'

'No. No, it was there. I woke and drank it.'

'Did Iollas bring it?'

'I don't know.' He closed his eyes. I let him rest, and sat on the grass close by him. But he was resting to speak again. Presently he asked for the Captain of the Bodyguard. I went and beckoned him up.

Alexander said, 'General order. All officers from Commander up, assemble – in the inner courtyard – to await orders.'

I knew, then, that he began to guess.

There will be no farewell, I thought as I waved the palm-leaf fan to cool him and keep off the flies. He will not surrender. And nor must I.

A ferryload of his friends came over, to see how he was. I met them, to warn them he was short of breath. When they came up, he said, 'I had – better – go back.'

The bearers were called. People crowded with him on the ferry. He looked round and whispered, 'Bagoas'. So one got out, and made room for me.

They took him to the Bedchamber, where winged gilded daimons guarded the great bed. Long ago, in another life, I had prepared it for another King.

We propped him on high pillows, but still heard the rasp of his breath. If he wanted anything, he spoke to me without voice, as he used when his wound was fresh. He knew I would understand him.

After a while, Perdikkas came in, to tell him the officers were still in the courtyard awaiting orders. He signed to bring them in. They crowded into the Bedchamber. He made a gesture of greeting; I saw him draw breath to speak, but he coughed instead and brought up blood. He motioned them to dismiss, and they went away. Not till the last had gone, did he press his hand to his side.

After this, the generals brought the doctors without his leave. Three came. Weak as he was, they feared him because of Glaukios; but he suffered quietly their fingers on his wrist, their ears laid to his chest. He watched them, as they looked at one another. When they brought a draught he took it and slept awhile. One of them stayed with him, so I rested an hour or two. He would need me there at night, with my wits about me.

At night he was in high fever. They would no longer leave him to me alone; three of the Companions watched with him. One of the doctors would have sat by his pillow; but he put out his hand and held my arm, so the doctor went.

It was a long night. The Companions dozed in their chairs. He coughed blood and then slept a little. About midnight his lips moved. I bent to hear. He said, 'Don't drive it away.' I looked about but saw nothing. 'The snake,' he whispered, pointing to a shadowy corner. 'Nobody harm him. He is sent.'

'No one shall harm him,' I said, 'upon pain of death.'

He slept again. Then he said, 'Hephaistion.'

His eyes were closed. I kissed his forehead and did not speak. He smiled, and was quiet.

In the morning he knew me, and where he was. The generals came in and stood about his bed. All over the room one could hear his laboured breathing. He looked from one to the other. He knew well enough what it meant.

Perdikkas came forward and bent towards him. 'Alexander. We all pray the gods will spare you for many years. But if their will is otherwise, to whom do you leave your kingdom?'

He forced his voice, so as to speak aloud. He began, this I have always believed, to pronounce the name of Krateros. But his breath caught, and he finished with a gasp. Perdikkas murmured to the others, 'He says, To the strongest.'

Krateros, kratistos. The sounds so much alike, the meaning, even, of the name. Krateros, whom he had always trusted, was on his way to Macedon; I am persuaded he meant to leave him regent for the unborn child; King, even, if it should be a girl, or die. But Krateros was a long way off; his cause was no one's here.

Nor was it mine. What was Macedon to me, what did I care who ruled it? I looked only at my lord, to see if he was troubled; but he had not heard. While he was at peace, it was all one to me. If I gave offence to the others, they might take me from him. I held my tongue.

Presently he beckoned Perdikkas back; then drew from his finger the royal signet carved with Zeus enthroned, and gave it him. He had chosen a deputy, while he was too sick to rule. It need have meant no more than that.

Sitting quiet by the bed, only the Persian boy, I saw the faces begin to watch each other, reckoning policy and power, looking sideways at the ring.

He saw them. His eyes had been on the distance; but they moved, and I know he saw. I bent over him with a sponge; I thought he had seen enough. He looked at me as if we shared a secret. I laid my hand on his; there was a white band on his finger, where the ring had kept off the sun.

All was silent, but for his quick rough breath. In the quiet, I heard outside a deep stir, a many-voiced murmur. Ptolemy went out to see. When he did not return, Peukestes followed, then the others. Soon after, they all came in again.

Perdikkas said, 'Alexander. It's the Macedonians outside; all the men. They – they want to see you. I've told them it's impossible, that you're too ill. Do you think if I let in just a few, a score or so, to represent the others, do you think you could bear with that?'

His eyes opened wide. He began to cough. While I held the towel for the blood, he made a gesture of command, meaning, Wait till I am ready. Then he said, 'All. Every man.'

Wherever the ring might be, the King was here. Perdikkas went out.

Alexander pushed himself a little sideways, and looked at me, I moved the pillows, to prop him there. Someone opened the private postern, for the men to leave by when they had passed the bed. Their muttering voices approached. Peukestes looked at me with kindness, and made a little motion with his head. He had always shown me courtesy; so I understood him. I said to Alexander, 'I will come back after', and went out by the postern door.

As soldiers to their general, as Macedonians to their King, they had come to bid him farewell. Now at the last they must find him all their own, not with his Persian boy closer to him than they.

From the alcove where I stood unseen, I watched them leaving, a stream of men I thought would never end, one after one. They wept, or spoke in husky whispers; or just looked dazed, as if they had learned that the sun would not rise tomorrow.

They took hours to go by. The day wore towards noon. I heard one say. 'He greeted with his eyes. He knew me.' Another said, 'He recognized me right away. He tried to smile.' A young one said, 'He gave me a look, and I thought, The world is breaking.' A veteran answered, 'No, lad, the world goes on. But the gods alone know where.'

At last, no more came. I went in. He lay as I'd left him; all that time, he had held himself eyes-front to them, not letting one pass without a look of greeting. Now he lay like the dead, but for his panting breath. I thought, They have drained the last life from him, and left me nothing. May the dogs eat them.

I lifted him on one arm, and changed the pillows so that he lay easier. He opened his eyes, and smiled. I understood that this gift of theirs, whatever it had cost him, was what he would have asked of his guardian god. How could I grudge it him? I put away my anger.

The generals had stood aside while the men passed by. Ptolemy wiped his eyes. Perdikkas stepped over to the bed. 'Alexander. When you are received among the gods, at what times shall we offer you worship?'

I don't think he expected any answer; just wanted, if he could still be heard, to make a gift of honour, as he felt it due. He was heard. Alexander came back to us, as if out of deep water. The smile still hung about him. He whispered, 'When you are happy.' Then he closed his eyes, and returned where he had been.

All day he lay on the high pillows, between the gilded daimons with spread wings. All day the great men came and went. Towards evening, they brought Roxane. The child was big in her. She flung herself on him, beating her breast and tearing her hair, wailing as if he were already dead. I saw his eyelids creasing. Her I dared not speak to, for I had seen her look of hate; but I whispered to Peukestes, 'He can hear, it troubles him,' and they made her eunuchs lead her out.

Sometimes I could rouse him to take a drink of water; sometimes he seemed already in the death-sleep and would not stir for me; yet I felt his presence, and thought that he felt mine. I thought, I will not ask heaven for any sign from him; let him not be troubled by my love, only know of it if God pleases; for love is life to him, he has never turned it away.

Night fell and the lamps were kindled. Ptolemy stood by the bed, looking down, remembering him, I suppose, in Macedon as a child. Peukestes came up and said that he and a few friends were going to keep vigil for him at the shrine of Serapis. Alexander had brought the god's cult from Egypt; he is a form of the risen Osiris; they would ask his oracle whether he would heal Alexander, if he were carried to the shrine.

It is man's nature to hope even in extremity. As the flickering lamplight moved on his quiet face, mocking me with false shadows of life, I awaited some promise from the god. But my body knew. My body weighed with his death, as heavy as clay.

The night passed for me in starts and stretches. It was long since I had slept; sometimes I found myself with my head leaned on his pillow, and looked if he had stirred; but he slept on, with quick shallow breaths, broken with deep sighs. The lamps faded, the first pallor of dawn showed the shapes of the tall windows. His breathing had changed its sound, and something said to me, He is here.

I drew close and whispered, 'I love you, Alexander', and kissed him. Never mind, I thought, from whom his heart accepts it. Let it be according to his wish.

My hair had fallen on his breast. His eyes opened; his hand moved, and touched a strand, and ran it between his fingers.

He knew me. To that I will take my oath before the gods. It was to me that he bade farewell.

The others, who had seen him move, rose to their feet. But he had gone away. He was on the threshold of his journey.

Someone was at the door. Peukestes stood there. Ptolemy and Perdikkas went to meet him. He said, 'We watched all night, and at dawn we went to the oracle. The god said it would be better for him here.'

When his breath ceased, the eunuchs all bewailed him. I suppose that I did too. Outside the palace it was heard, and the sound spread through the city; there was no need to give out that the King was dead. As we took the high pillows from behind him, and laid him straight, the squires on guard came in and stood there bewildered, and walked out crying.

He had died with closed eyes and mouth, as seemly as in sleep. His hair was tousled from the tossing of the fever, and I combed it; I could not keep from doing it as if he could still feel. Then I looked for the great men who had half-filled the Bedchamber, for someone to order how he was to be cared for. But they had all gone. The world had broken; the pieces lay like shattered gold, spoil for the strongest. They had gone to gather them up.

After a while the palace eunuchs grew uneasy, not knowing who was King. One after another went off, to see how things stood; the lesser followed the greater. I did not notice at first that I was there alone.

I stayed, for I could not think of anywhere else to be. Someone will come, I thought; he is mine until they claim him. I uncovered his body, and looked at his wounds which I had known by touch in the dark, and covered him again. Then I sat down by the bed, and leaned my head on it, and I think that I fell asleep.

I woke to the slanting light of evening. No one had come. The air was heavy with heat. I thought, They must come soon, his body will not withstand it. But no breath of corruption came from him; he seemed no more than sleeping.

Always the life in him was stronger than in other men. I felt at his heart in vain; his breath did not mist the mirror; yet somewhere deep within him the soul might still remain, preparing to depart, but not yet gone. I spoke to that; not to his ears, I knew they would not hear me, but to whatever of him might hear.

'Go to the gods, unconquered Alexander. May the River of Ordeal be mild as milk to you, and bathe you in light, not fire. May your dead forgive you; you have given more life to men than you brought death. God made the bull to eat grass, but the lion not; and God alone will judge between them. You were never without love; where you go, may you find it waiting.'

At this, the memory came to me of Kelanos singing on his flower-wreathed bier. I thought, He has kept his word; he has put off for his sake being born again; himself having passed in peace through fire, he is here to lead him across the River. It eased my heart, to know he was not alone.

Suddenly, in this stillness, a great clamour approached the room. Ptolemy and Perdikkas rushed in with a band of soldiers, and the royal squires. Perdikkas shouted, 'Bolt the doors!' and they crashed them to. There were shouts and hammerings; those outside broke in the doors. Perdikkas and Ptolemy called to their men to defend the King's body from traitors and pretenders. I was almost crushed as they backed around the bed. The wars for the world had started; these people were fighting to possess him, as if he were a thing, a symbol, like the Mitra or the throne. I turned to him. When I saw him still lie calm, bearing all this without resentment, then I knew he was truly dead.

They had begun to fight, and were throwing javelins. I stood to shield him, and one of them grazed my arm. I have the scar to this day, the only wound I ever took for him.

Presently they parleyed, and went away to go on with their dispute outside. I bound up my arm with a bit of towel, and waited, for it was not proper he should be without attendance. I lit the night-lamp and set it by the bed, and watched with him, till at morning the embalmers came to take him from me, and fill him with everlasting myrrh.

Author's Note

All public acts of Alexander here recounted are based upon the sources, the most dramatic being the most authentic. It has been impossible to find room for all the major events, even, of his crowded life, or to demonstrate the full scope of his genius. This book attempts only an angle shot, with certain highlights.

Source histories all commend the 'moderation' of his sex life. None suggest that he was celibate; had he been, it would of course have been assumed that he was impotent; the Christian ideal of chastity was still unborn. A general pattern emerges of a fairly low physical drive – unsurprising, when such immense energies were spent elsewhere – coupled with a passionate capacity for affection. We know as little as we do of his love affairs, partly because they were few, partly because he was a good picker; none of his partners involved him in scandal.

That Hephaistion was his lover seems, on the evidence, probable to the verge of certainty, but is nowhere actually stated. Plutarch's account of a child by Memnon's widow after the fall of Damascus is, for sound reasons, doubted by modern historians, and there is no other record of his having had a mistress. Bagoas is the only person explicitly named in the sources as Alexander's *eromenos*.

He first appears in Curtius: *Nabarzanes, having received a safe conduct, met him* [Alexander] *bringing great gifts. Among these was Bagoas, a eunuch of remarkable beauty and in the very flower of boyhood, who had been loved by Darius, and was afterwards to be loved by Alexander; and it was especially because of the boy's pleading that he was led to pardon Nabarzanes.* This last is typical Curtius embroidery; the safe-conduct shows that Alexander was willing to hear Nabarzanes' account of himself, and no doubt this decided the issue. How Bagoas came into his hands, when none of Darius' suite were allowed with him after his arrest, and Nabarzanes himself escaped with only six hundred horsemen, is not explained.

There is a widespread modern delusion that all eunuchs became flabby and gross. To correct it one need go no further back than the eighteenth century and its famous operatic *castrati*, whose romantic looks caused them to be much pursued by women of fashion. A portrait of the greatest,

Farinelli, done in early middle age, shows a handsome sensitive face, and a figure many modern tenors might envy. The diarist Dr Burney, writing of him still later, said, 'He is tall and thin, but looks very well for his time of life, is lively and well bred.'

The story of Darius' last days occurs only in Curtius. It is vivid and detailed; is irrelevant to the bias for which Curtius is notorious, and is probably authentic. If so, the final scenes can only have been supplied to some early chronicler by one of Darius' eunuchs, who were the only witnesses; it is reasonable to suppose by Bagoas himself. With his favoured place at court he must have been known to all Alexander's contemporary historians.

History next knows Bagoas some six years later, when the anecdote of the kiss in the theatre is given both by Plutarch and Athenaeus. The location in Karmania is highly significant; there Alexander still had with him only those who had followed him through India and the desert march. After all these vicissitudes, Bagoas was not only still high in his affection, but evidently well-liked even by the xenophobe Macedonian troops, in itself surprising. Alexander always repaid with lifelong loyalty a personal devotion, and this seems the likeliest explanation of such a long attachment.

The young eunuch's origins are unknown; but the conjecture that he was of good birth is not fanciful. Such boys, whose looks had been taken care of and not spoiled by malnutrition or hardship, once enslaved were always at the highest risk of prostitution. Sokrates' disciple Phaidon (Phaedo) is the best-known case.

Bagoas' last appearance has been irretrievably garbled by Curtius; one can only do one's best with it. Luckily for Bagoas' reputation, we have the first-class evidence of Aristoboulos the architect, who actually restored Kyros' tomb for Alexander, that he went there when first at Persepolis, saw for himself the valuable grave-goods, and had them inventoried by Aristoboulos, whose description is preserved by Arrian, along with his account of the desecration. In Curtius, Alexander only goes to the tomb on his return from India, and finds it bare because Kyros has been buried only with his simple weapons; a notion which would no doubt delight Roman sentiment but surprise an archaeologist. Bagoas, who has a spite against Orxines for not having sent him a bribe, invents a non-existent treasure and accuses him of its theft. None of the crimes for which Orxines was in fact punished are mentioned; he is supposed an innocent victim. When the impossible is discarded from this tale not much is left. I have assumed that Bagoas did somehow enter the scene, having some grievance against the satrap with which Alexander sympathized. In view of Orxines' murderous record, I have supplied the commonest grudge of the ancient world, a family blood-feud.

Muddled sensationalism is typical of Curtius, an unbearably silly man with access to priceless sources now lost to us, which he frittered away in the cause of a tedious literary concept about the goddess Fortune, and many florid exercises in Roman rhetoric. (Alexander, exhorting his friends kindly to remove the arrow stuck in his lung, is impressively eloquent.) The favours of Fortune being conducive to hubris and nemesis, Alexander's story is bent that way by recourse to Athenian anti-Macedonian agitprop, written by men who never set eyes on him, and bearing about as much relation to objective truth as one would expect to find in a *History of the Jewish People* commissioned by Adolf Hitler. This had been revived in Augustus' time by Trogus and Diodorus, who found in a king three centuries dead a safe whipping-boy for the divine pretensions of the living ruler. No attempt is made at consistency with the undisputed facts. A corrupted tyrant would have been cut down by the Opis mutineers the moment he stepped down among them; they could have done it with perfect impunity (the fate of more than one Roman emperor) and elected a new king, as was their right. That instead they complained to Alexander of not being allowed to kiss him is not fiction but history.

As regards the ancient world, the political motives of these unconvincing attempts to show Alexander corrupted by success are clear enough. More puzzling is a present-day outbreak of what one may call blackwashing, since it goes far beyond a one-sided interpretation of facts to their actual misrepresentation. A recent popularization says only of Philotas' execution that it was 'on a trumped-up charge', though his concealment of the assassination plot is agreed on by all the sources (what would be the position of a modern security guard who, informed there was a bomb on the royal plane, decided not to mention it?). Hephaistion is 'fundamentally stupid' though in not one of his highly responsible independent missions, diplomatic as well as military, was he ever unsuccessful. Alexander is baldly accused of compassing his father's death, though not only is the evidence, literally, nil; Philip had not even a viable alternative heir to supply a motive. 'Severe alcoholism' is said to have hastened Alexander's end; any general practitioner could explain what a severe alcoholic's work-capacity is, and what his chance of surviving lung perforation, unanaesthetized field surgery, and a desert march. After the gesture of the troops at Alexander's deathbed, an event unique in history, it is somewhat surprising to be told that few people mourned him. That there are fashions in admiration and denigration is inevitable; they should not however be followed at the expense of truth.

In the same spirit, the most sinister motives have been sought for his policies of racial fusion. Yet no one took less trouble to conceal his aversions than he; it is staringly obvious that, once among Persians, he simply found he liked them. Surely in our day it takes a somewhat insular mind to find this either discreditable or strange.

Though accounts of Alexander's general deterioration do not hold water, there seems little doubt that he did suffer some severe mental disturbance just after Hephaistion's death. Whether such a breakdown could have recurred cannot be known. Alexander's nature was a kind of self-winding spring. The tensions of his childhood demanded compensation in achievement; achievement accumulated responsibilities, at the same time suggesting further achievements; the spiral was inexorably ascending, and one cannot be sure this process could have continued through a normal life-span without disaster. Perhaps Kalanos' parting words were more promise than warning.

Bury and other historians have pointed out the connection between a tainted water supply and heavier wine-drinking in the army. Aristoboulos, who was at court through Alexander's reign, says his usual habit was to sit over his wine talking into the night, but without getting drunk. According to Plutarch he got rather euphoric towards the end of the session; a phenomenon which can be observed today in persons not given to excess. Occasional drinking-bouts were however characteristically Macedonian, as we already find before Alexander's accession.

Rumours that he was poisoned, rife for centuries after his death, do not tally with the detailed case-history of his last illness. His loss of voice points to the most common fatal complication right up to the discovery of antibiotics – pneumonia. Pleurisy would be a certain sequel in view of his Mallian wound. Aristoboulos says that when in high fever he drank wine and became delirious; he is not said to have demanded it. If it was conveyed to him in malice then he was, morally speaking, poisoned, and the presence of a mortal enemy like Kassandros should not be overlooked.

Curtius has preserved a story that his body was found uncorrupted, in spite of the summer heat and of a long delay in fetching the embalmers, due to the chaos following his death. The period given, six days, is of course absurd; but it is quite possible that a deep coma deceived the watchers a good many hours before clinical death occurred. The embalmers did their work with skill. Augustus Caesar, visiting his tomb at Alexandria, admired the beauty of his features after three hundred years.

The account of Hephaistion's end suggests he had typhoid, where, though appetite often returns before the lesions in the gut have healed, solid food causes perforation and swift collapse. In our own century typhoid patients have been killed in hospital by misguided relatives smuggling them food. Hephaistion's boiled fowl, about the size of a modern bantam, would be enough. Poisoning is a possibility also.

Arrian has been followed for the squires' conspiracy, except for my own guess that letters from Aristotle were found among Kallisthenes' papers. Alexander's friendly correspondence with his tutor ceased from this time.

The romantic figure of Roxane has not been treated with a groundless scepticism. There is no need to dismiss the marriage as political; her rank was middling and her beauty famous. But about two months later, the squires could count upon finding Alexander in bed without her; and we know what she did when he died. She can have wasted no time in mourning. She sent, with such speed that it outstripped the news, a letter to his royal wife Stateira, written in his name, summoning her at once to Babylon; and had her murdered as soon as she arrived.

Sisygambis, the Queen Mother of Persia, when told of Alexander's death, bade her family farewell, shut herself up without food, and died five days later.

The royal Mitra of Persia, whose use by Alexander caused so much controversy, bore no resemblance to the modern church mitre, but fitted the head like a helmet, with deep flaps at the sides and back. It had a peak-shaped crown, which satraps wore flattened; to wear it upright was the sign of kingship. It was encircled by a diadem of purple ribbon.

Events this book has no room for, or which Bagoas would not have known of, have been taken into account in the portrayal of Alexander. It needs to be borne in mind today that not till more than a century later did a handful of philosophers even start to question the morality of war. In his time the issue was not whether, but how one made it. It is note-worthy that the historians most favourable to him, Ptolemy and Aristo-boulos, were those who knew him in life. They wrote when he was dead, with no incentive but to do him justice.

When his faults (those his own times did not account as virtues) have been considered, we are left with the fact that no other human being has attracted in his lifetime, from so many men, so fervent a devotion. Their reasons are worth examining.

Sources for the general reader

The best is Arrian, who drew mainly on the lost memoirs of Ptolemy and Aristoboulos, and wrote with a high sense of responsibility. His *Life of Alexander* is available in Penguin, or in the Loeb Classics with Greek and translation interleaved, and notes. Plutarch, whose *Lives* is published by Everyman, is colourful, but made little effort to evaluate his evidence, and should not be swallowed whole.

Proper names

It is of course implausible to have a Persian using Persian names in their Greek forms; but since in the Persian they would be unrecognizable and unpronounceable to almost all general readers (Darius for example is Darayavaush) I have retained the usual convention.

Roxane is pronounced with the accent on the first syllable.

FUNERAL
GAMES

I foresee great contests at my funeral games.

Reported deathbed words of Alexander the Great

Chief Events Preceding Alexander's Death

326 BC Alexander returns from India. During his march along the Indus he receives a dangerous chest wound.

325 BC Return march through the Gedrosian desert under extreme conditions.

324 BC Alexander at Susa. State wedding with Stateira, daughter of Darius III. She remains in the palace harem with her grandmother Sisygambis. Alexander goes to the summer palace of Ekbatana, accompanied by Roxane, his wife since 328, and by his friend Hephaistion. Roxane becomes pregnant. Hephaistion suddenly falls ill and dies.

323 BC Alexander goes to Babylon and conducts Hephaistion's funeral. He prepares for his next campaign, exploring the coast of Arabia. After boating on the lower Euphrates he contracts a fatal fever. When *in extremis* he hands the royal ring to Perdikkas, his second-in-command since Hephaistion's death.

323 BC

The ziggurat of Bel-Marduk had been half-ruinous for a century and a half, ever since Xerxes had humbled the gods of rebellious Babylon. The edges of its terraces had crumbled in landslides of bitumen and baked brick; storks nested on its ragged top, which had once held the god's golden bedchamber and his sacred concubine in his golden bed. But this was only defacement; the ziggurat's huge bulk had defied destruction. The walls of the inner city by the Marduk Gate were three hundred feet high, but the ziggurat still towered over them.

Near by was the god's temple; this Xerxes' men had succeeded in half demolishing. The rest of the roof was patched with thatch, and propped on shafts of rough-hewn timber. At the inner end, where the columns were faced with splendid but chipped enamels, there was still a venerable gloom, a smell of incense and burnt-offerings. On an altar of porphyry, under a smoke-duct open to the sky, burned in its bronze basket the sacred fire. It was low; the fuel-box was empty. Its shaven acolyte looked from it to the priest. Abstracted though he was, it caught his eye.

'Fetch fuel. What are you about? Must a king die when it serves your laziness? Move! You were got when your mother was asleep and snoring.'

The acolyte made a sketchy obeisance; the temple discipline was not strict.

The priest said, after him, "It will not be yet. Maybe not even today. He is tough as a mountain lion, he will die hard.'

Two tall shadows fell at the temple's open end. The priests who entered wore the high felt mitres of Chaldeans. They approached the altar with ritual gestures, bowing with hand on mouth.

The priest of Marduk said, 'Nothing yet?'

'No,' said the first Chaldean. 'But it will be soon. He cannot speak; indeed he can scarcely breathe. But when his homeland soldiers made a clamour at the doors, demanding to see him, he had them all admitted. Not the commanders; they were there already. The spearbearers, the common footmen. They were half the morning passing through his bedchamber, and he greeted them all by signs. That finished him, and now he is in the deathsleep.'

A door behind the altar opened to let in two Marduk priests. It gave a glimpse of a rich interior; embroidered hangings, a gleam of gold. There was a smell of spiced meats cooking. The door closed on it.

The Chaldeans, reminded of an old scandal, exchanged glances. One of them said, 'We did our best to turn him from the city. But he had heard that the temple had not been restored; and he thought we were afraid of him.'

A Marduk priest said stiffly, 'The year has not been auspicious for great works. Nebuchadrezzar built in an inauspicious year. His foreign slaves rioted race against race, and threw each other off the tower. As for Sikandar, he would still be fortunate, sitting safe in Susa, if he had not defied the god.'

One of the Chaldeans said, 'It seems to me he did well enough by the god, for all that he called him Herakles.' He looked round, pointedly, at the half-ruined building. He might as well have said aloud 'Where is the gold the King gave you to rebuild, have you eaten and drunk it all?'

There was a hostile silence. The chief of the Marduk priests said, with emollient dignity, 'Certainly you gave him a true prediction. And since then have you read the heavens?'

The tall mitres bent together in slow assent. The oldest Chaldean, whose beard was silver against his dark face and purple robes, signed to the Marduk priest, beckoning him to the broken end of the temple. 'This,' he said, 'is what is foretold for Babylon.' He swept round his gold-starred wand, taking in the crumbling walls, the threadbare roof, the leaning timber-props, the fire-stained paving. 'This is for a while, and then ... Babylon was.'

He walked towards the entry and stood to listen; but the night noises were unchanged. 'The heavens say it begins with the death of the King.'

The priest remembered the shining youth who, eight years before, had come offering treasure and Arabian incense; and the man who had returned this year, weathered and scarred, the red-gold hair sun-bleached and streaked with white; but with the deep eyes still burning, still ready with the careless, reflex charm of the youth beloved, still terrible in anger. The scent of the incense had lasted long on the air, the gold much longer in the treasury; even among men who liked good living, half was in the strongroom still. But for the priest of Bel-Marduk the pleasure had drained out of it. It spoke now of flames and blood. His spirit sank like the altar fire when the fuel was low.

'Shall we see it? Will a new Xerxes come?'

The Chaldean shook his head. 'A dying, not a killing. Another city will rise and ours will wane. It is under the sign of the King.'

'What? Will he live, then, after all?'

'He is dying, as I told you. But his sign is walking along the constellations, further than we can reckon in years. You will not see it setting in your day.'

'So? Well, in his life he did us no harm. Maybe he will spare us dead.'

The astrologer frowned to himself, like an adult seeking words to reach a child. 'Remember, last year, the fire that fell from heaven. We heard where it fell, and went there, a week's journey. It had lit the city brighter than full moon. But we found, where it had struck, it had broken into red-hot embers, which had charred the earth around them. One had been set up by a farmer in his house, because that day his wife bore twin sons. But a neighbour had stolen it for its power; they fought, and both men died. Another piece fell at a dumb child's feet, and speech came back to him. A third had kindled a fire that destroyed a forest. But the Magus of the place had taken the greatest piece, and built it into the fire-altar, because of its great light while it was in the sky. And all this from the one star. So it will be.'

The priest bowed his head. A fragrance drifted to him from the precinct's kitchen. Better to invite the Chaldeans than let the meal spoil with waiting. Whatever the stars said, good food was good food.

The old Chaldean said, looking into the shadows, 'Here where we stand, the leopard will rear her young.'

The priest made a decent pause. No sound from the royal palace. With luck, they might get something to eat before they heard the wailing.

The walls of Nebuchadrezzar's palace were four feet thick, and faced with blue-glazed tiles for coolness; but the midsummer heat seeped in through everything. The sweat running down Eumenes' wrist blotted the ink on his papyrus. The wax glistened moistly on the tablet he was fair-copying; he plunged it back into the cold water tub where his clerk had left it, with the other drafts, to keep the surface set. Local scribes used wet clay; but that would have set hard before one could revise on it. For the third time he went to the doorway, seeking a slave to pull the punkah cord. Once again the dim hushed noises – soft feet, soft voices furtive or awed or grieving – sent him back behind the drawn door-curtain to his listless task. To clap the hands, to call, to shout an order, were all unthinkable.

He had not sought his clerk, a garrulous man; but he could have done with the silent slave and the waft of the punkah. He scanned the unfinished scroll pinned to his writing-board. It was twenty years since he had written with his own hand any letter not of high secrecy; why now was he writing one that would never go, short of a miracle? There had been many miracles; but, surely, not now. It was something to do, it shut out the unknown future. Sitting down again he retrieved the tablet, propped it, dried his hand on the towel the clerk had left, and picked up his pen.

And the ships commanded by Niarchos will muster at the river mouth, where I shall review them while Perdikkas is bringing the army down from Babylon; and sacrifices will be made there to the appropriate gods. I shall then take command of the land force and begin the march to the west. The first stage ...

When he was five, before he'd been taught to write, he came to me in the King's business room. 'What's that, Eumenes?' 'A letter.' 'What's the first word that you've written big?' 'Your father's name. PHILIP, King of the Macedonians. Now I'm busy, run back to your play.' 'Make me my name. Do, dear Eumenes. Please.' I gave it him written, on the back of a spoiled dispatch. Next day he'd learned it, and carved it all over the wax for a royal letter to Kersobleptes of Thrace. He had my ruler across his palm ...

Because of the heat he had left open his massive door. A brisk stride, half hushed like all other sounds, approached it. Ptolemy pushed aside the curtain and drew it to behind him. His craggy war-weathered face was creased with fatigue; he had been up all night, without the stimulus of action. He was forty-three, and looked older. Eumenes waited, wordlessly.

'He has given his ring to Perdikkas,' Ptolemy said.

There was a pause. Eumenes' alert Greek face – not a bookish one, he had had his share of soldiering – searched the impassive Macedonian's. 'For what? As deputy? Or as Regent?'

'Since he could not speak,' said Ptolemy drily, 'we shall never know.'

'If he has accepted death,' Eumenes reasoned, 'we may presume the second. If not ...?'

'It's all one, now. He neither sees nor hears. He is in the death sleep.'

'Do not be sure. I have heard of men who were thought already dead, and who said later that they heard everything.'

Ptolemy suppressed an impatient gesture. These wordy Greeks. Or what is he afraid of? 'I came because you and I have known him since he was born. Don't you want to be there?'

'Do the Macedonians want me there?' An ancient bitterness pinched, for a moment, Eumenes' mouth.

'Oh, come. Everyone trusts you. We shall need you before long.'

Slowly the Secretary began to put his desk in order. He said, wiping his pen, 'And nothing, to the last, about an heir?'

'Perdikkas asked him, while he could still get a whisper out. He only said, "To the best man. *Hoti to kratisto.*"'

Eumenes thought, They say dying men can prophesy. He shivered.

'Or,' Ptolemy added, 'so Perdikkas told us. He was leaning over. Nobody else could hear.'

Eumenes put down the pen and looked up sharply. 'Or *Kratero?* You say he whispered, he was short of breath.' They looked at one another. Krateros, the highest-ranking of all Alexander's staff, was on the march to Macedon, to take over the Regency from Antipatros. 'If *he'd* been in the room ...'

Ptolemy shrugged. 'Who knows?' To himself he thought, If Hephaistion had been there ... But if *he'd* lived, none of this would have happened. He'd have done none of the crazy things he's dying of. Coming to Babylon in midsummer – boating about in the filthy swamps down river ... But one did not discuss Hephaistion with Eumenes. 'This door weighs like an elephant. Do you want it shut?'

Pausing on the threshold, Eumenes said, 'Nothing about Roxane and the child? Nothing?'

'Four months to go. And what if it's a girl?'

They moved into the shadowy corridor, tall big-boned Macedonian and slender Greek. A young Macedonian officer came blundering towards them, almost ran into Ptolemy, and stammered an apology. Ptolemy said, 'Is there any change?'

'No, sir, I don't think so.' He swallowed violently; they saw that he was crying.

When he had gone, Ptolemy said, 'That boy believes in it. I can't yet.'

'Well, let us go.'

'Wait.' Ptolemy took his arm, led him back into the room, and dragged-to the great ebony door on its groaning hinges. 'I'd best tell you this while we've time. You should have known before, but ...'

'Yes, yes?' said Eumenes impatiently. He had quarrelled with Hephaistion shortly before he died, and Alexander had never been easy with him since.

Ptolemy said, 'Stateira is pregnant, too.'

Eumenes, who had been fidgeting to be gone, was struck into stillness. 'You mean Darius' daughter?'

'Who else do you suppose? She *is* Alexander's wife.'

'But this changes everything. When did ... ?'

'Don't you remember? No, of course, you'd gone on to Babylon. When he came to himself after Hephaistion died' (one could not avoid the name forever) 'he went to war with the Kossaians. My doing; I told him they'd demanded road toll, and got him angry. He needed to be doing something. It did him good. When he'd dealt with them, and was heading here, he stopped a week at Susa, to call upon Sisygambis.'

'That old witch,' said Eumenes bitterly. But for her, he thought, the King's friends would never have been saddled with Persian wives. The mass wedding at Susa had gone by like some drama of superhuman magnificence, till suddenly he had found himself alone in a scented pavilion, in bed with a Persian noble-woman whose unguents repelled him, and whose only Greek consisted of 'Greeting, my lord.'

'A great lady,' said Ptolemy. 'A pity his mother was not like her. *She* would have had him married before he set out from Macedon, and seen that he got a son. He could have had an heir of fourteen by this time. *She'd* not have sickened him with marriage while he was a child. Whose fault was it that he wasn't ready for a woman till he met the Baktrian?' Thus, unofficially, did most Macedonians refer to Roxane.

'Done is done. But Stateira ... Does Perdikkas know?'

'That's why he asked him to name his heir.'

'And still he would not?'

'"To the best," he said. He left it to us, to the Macedonians, to choose when they came of age. Yes, he's a Macedonian at the last.'

'If they are boys,' Eumenes reminded him.

Ptolemy, who had been withdrawn into his thought, said, 'And if they come of age.'

Eumenes said nothing. They went down the dim corridor with its blue-tiled walls towards the death chamber.

Nebuchadrezzar's bedroom, once ponderously Assyrian, had been Persianized by successive kings from Kyros on. Kambyses had hung its walls with the trophies of conquered Egypt; Darius the Great had sheathed its columns with gold and malachite; Xerxes had pegged across one side the embroidered robe of Athene, looted from the Parthenon. The second Artaxerxes had sent for craftsmen of Persepolis to make the great bed in which Alexander now lay dying.

Its dais was covered with crimson tapestries worked in bullion. The bed was nine feet by six; Darius the Third, a man seven feet tall, had had ample room. The high canopy was upheld by four golden fire-daimons with silver wings and jewelled eyes. Propped on heaped pillows to help him breathe, and looking small among all these splendours, the dying man lay naked. A thin linen sheet had been spread half over him when he had ceased to toss about and throw it off. Damp with sweat, it clung to him as if sculpted.

In a monotonous cycle, his shallow rattling breath grew gradually louder, then ceased. After a pause during which no other breath was drawn in the crowded room, it started again, slowly, the same crescendo.

Until lately there had been scarcely another sound. Now that he had ceased responding to voice or touch, a soft muttering began to spread, too cautious and muted to be located; a ground-bass to the strong rhythm of death.

Perdikkas by the bed's head lifted at Ptolemy his dark heavy eyebrows;

a tall man, with the Macedonian build but not the colouring, and a face on which authority, long habitual, was growing. His silent gesture of the head signalled 'No change yet.'

The movement of a peacock fan drew Ptolemy's eye across the bed. There, as he had been for days, seemingly without sleep, seated on the dais was the Persian boy. So Ptolemy still thought of him though by now he must be three-and-twenty; with eunuchs it was hard to tell. At sixteen, he had been brought to Alexander by a Persian general involved in Darius' murder, to give exonerating evidence. This he was well placed to do, having been the King's minion, with inside knowledge of the court. He had stayed on to give his story to the chroniclers, and had never been far from Alexander since. Not much was on view today of the famous beauty which had dazzled two kings running. The great dark eyes were sunk in a face more drawn than the fever-wasted one on the pillows. He was dressed like a servant; did he think that if he was noticed he would be turned out? What *does* he think, Ptolemy wondered. He must have lain with Darius in this very bed.

A fly hovered over Alexander's sweat-glazed forehead. The Persian chased it off, then put down the fan to dip a towel in a basin of mint-scented water, and wipe the unmoving face.

At first Ptolemy had disliked this exotic presence haunting Alexander's living quarters, encouraging him to assume the trappings of Persian royalty and the manners of a Persian court, having his ear day and night. But he was a fixture one had grown used to. Through Ptolemy's own grief and sense of looming crisis, he felt a stir of pity. Walking over he touched him on the shoulder.

'Get some rest, Bagoas. Let one of the other chamberlains do all this.' A knot of court eunuchs, ageing relics of Darius and even of Ochos, advanced officiously. Ptolemy said, 'He won't know now, you know.'

Bagoas looked round. It was as if he had been told he was condemned to immediate execution, a sentence long expected. 'Never mind,' said Ptolemy gently. 'It's your right; stay if you wish.'

Bagoas touched his fingers to his forehead. The interruption was over. With his eyes fixed once more on the closed eyes of Alexander, he waved the fan, shifting the hot Babylonian air. He had staying power, Ptolemy reflected. He had weathered even the brainstorm after Hephaistion's death.

Against the wall nearest the bed, on a massive table like an altar, Hephaistion was still enshrined. Enshrined and multiplied; here were the votive statuettes and busts presented by condolent friends, assiduous place-seekers, scared men who had once had words with the dead; commissioned by the best artists found at short notice, to comfort Alexander's grief. Hephaistion stood in bronze, a nude Ares with shield and spear; precious in gold armour with ivory face and limbs; in tinted marble with a gilded laurel crown; as a silver battle-standard for the squadron which was to bear his name; and as a demigod, the first maquette for the cult-statue of his temple in Alexandria. Someone had cleared a space to put down some sick-room object, and a small Hephaistion in gilded bronze had fallen over. With a quick glance at the blind face on the pillows, Ptolemy set it up again. Let them wait till he's gone.

The small sound drew Eumenes' eye, which quickly looked away again.

Ptolemy thought, You've nothing to fear now, have you? Oh yes, he could be arrogant now and then. Towards the end, he thought he was the only one who understood – and how far was he wrong? Accept it, Eumenes, he was good for Alexander. *I* knew when they were boys at school. He was somebody in himself and both of them knew it. That pride you didn't like was Alexander's salvation; never fawning, never pushing, never envious, never false. He loved Alexander and never used him, kept pace with him at Aristotle's lessons, never on purpose lost a match to him. To the end of his days he could talk to Alexander man to man, could tell him he was wrong, and never for a moment feared him. He saved him from solitude, and who knows what else? Now he's gone, and this is what we have. If he were alive, we'd all be feasting today in Susa, whatever the Chaldeans say.

A frightened physician, pushed from behind by Perdikkas, laid a hand on Alexander's brow, fingered his wrist, muttered gravely and backed away. As long as he could speak, Alexander had refused to have a doctor near him; and even when he was light-headed, none could be found to physic him, lest they should later be accused of having given him poison. It was all one now; he was no longer swallowing. Curse that fool quack, Ptolemy thought, who let Hephaistion die while he went off to the games. I'd hang him again if I could.

It had long seemed that when the harsh breathing changed, it could only be for the death-rattle. But as if the doctor's touch had stirred a flicker of life, the stridor took a more even rhythm, and the eyelids were seen to move. Ptolemy and Perdikkas each took a step forward. But the self-effacing Persian by the bed, whom everyone had forgotten, put down the fan and, as if no one else were in sight, leaned intimately over the pillowed head, his long light-brown hair falling around it. He whispered softly. Alexander's grey eyes opened. Something disturbed the silky cloak of hair.

Perdikkas said, 'He moved his hand.'

It was still now, the eyes shut again, though Bagoas, as if transfixed, was still gazing down at them. Perdikkas' mouth tightened; all kinds of people were here. But before he could walk up with a reprimand, the

Persian had resumed his station and picked up his fan. But for its movement, he could have been a statue carved from ivory.

Ptolemy became aware of Eumenes speaking to him. 'What?' he said
harshly. He was near to tears.

'Peukestes is coming.'

The huddled functionaries parted to admit a tall well-built Macedonian
dressed as a Persian, even – to most of his countrymen's shocked disapproval – down to the trousers. When given the satrapy of Persis he had
adopted the native dress to please Alexander, not unaware that it suited him.
He strode forward, his eyes on the bed. Perdikkas advanced to meet him.

There was a low buzz of talk. The eyes of the two men exchanged their
message. Perdikkas said formally, for the benefit of the company, 'Did you
receive an oracle from Sarapis?'

Peukestes bowed his head. 'We kept the night-watch. The god said at
dawn, "Do not bring the King to the temple. It will be better for him where
he is."'

No, thought Eumenes, there will be no more miracles. For a moment,
when the hand had moved, he had almost believed in another.

He turned round looking for Ptolemy; but he had gone off somewhere
to put his face in order. It was Peukestes who, coming away from the
bedside, said to him, 'Does Roxane know?'

The palace harem was a spacious cloister built around a lily-pond. Here
too were hushed voices, but differently pitched; the few men in this female
world were eunuchs.

None of the women whose home the harem was had set eyes on the
dying King. They had heard well of him; they had been kept by him in
comfort and unmolested; they had awaited a visit that never came. And
that was all, except that they knew of no male heir who would inherit
them; in a little while there would even, it seemed, be no Great King. The
voices were muted with secretive fear.

Here were all the women Darius had left behind him when he marched
to his fate at Gaugamela. His favourites, of course, he had taken with him;
these who remained were something of a mixture. His older concubines,
from his days as a nobleman unplaced in line for the throne, had long been
installed at Susa; here were girls found for him after his accession, who
had failed to retain his interest, or had come too late to be noticed by him
at all. As well as all these, there were the survivors of King Ochos' harem,
who could not in decency be put out of doors when he died. An unwelcome
legacy, they formed with one or two old eunuchs a little clique of their
own, hating the women of Darius, that usurper they suspected of complicity in their master's death.

For Darius' concubines it was another matter. When brought here they had been fourteen, fifteen, eighteen at most. They had known the real drama of the harem; the rumours and intrigues; the bribery to get first news of a royal visit; the long intricacies of the toilet, the inspired placing of a jewel; the envious despair when the menstrual days enforced retirement; the triumph when a summons was received in a rival's presence; the gift of honour after a successful night.

From a few such nights had come one or two little girls of eight or so, who were dabbling in the pool and telling each other solemnly that the King was dying. There had been boys too. When Darius fell, they had been spirited away with every kind of stratagem, their mothers taking it for granted that the new, barbarian King would have them strangled. Nobody, however, had come looking for them; they had returned in time and now, being of an age to be brought out from among women, were being reared as men by distant kindred.

With the long absence of any king from Babylon, the harem had grown slack. At Susa, where Sisygambis the Queen Mother lived, everything was impeccable. But here they had seen little even of Darius, nothing of Alexander. One or two of the women had managed to intrigue with men from outside and run away with them; the eunuchs, whom Ochos would have impaled for negligence, had kept it quiet. Some girls in the long idle days had had affairs with one another; the resulting jealousies and scenes had enlivened many hot Assyrian nights. One girl had been poisoned by a rival; but that too had been hushed up. The Chief Warden had taken to smoking hemp, and disliked being disturbed.

Then, after years in the unknown east, after legendary victories, wounds, perils in deserts, the King sent word of his return. The harem had aroused itself as if from sleep. The eunuchs had fussed. All through the winter, the Babylonian season of gentle warmth, when feasts were held, he was expected but did not come. Rumour reached the palace that a boyhood friend had died – some said a lover – and it had sent him mad. Then he had come to himself, but was at war with the mountain Kossaians. The harem slipped back into its lethargy. At last he was on his way, but had broken his march at Susa. Setting out again, he had been met by embassies from all the peoples of the earth, bringing him golden crowns and asking him for counsel. Then, when late spring was heating up for summer, the earth had shaken under the horses and the chariots, the elephants and the marching men; and the palace had seethed with the long-forgotten bustle of a king's arrival.

Next day, it was announced that the King's Chief Eunuch of the Bedchamber would inspect the harem. This formidable person was awaited with dread; but turned out, shockingly, to be little more than a youth, none other than the notorious Bagoas, minion of two kings. Not that he failed to impress. He was wearing silk, stuff never seen within those walls, and shimmered like a peacock's breast. He was Persian to his fingertips, which always made Babylonians feel provincial; and ten years at courts had polished his manners like old silver. He greeted without embarrassment any eunuchs he had met in Darius' day, and bowed respectfully to some of the older ladies. Then he came to business.

He could not say when the King's urgent concerns would give him leisure to visit the harem; no doubt he would find in any case the perfect order which declares respect. One or two shortcomings were obliquely hinted at ('I believe the custom is so-and-so at Susa') but the past was left unprobed. The wardens were concealing sighs of relief, when he asked to see the rooms of the royal ladies.

They led him through. These rooms of state were secluded from the rest, and had their own courtyard, exquisitely tiled. There had been some dismay at their abandoned state, the dry plants and withered creepers, the clogged fountain with green scum and dead fish. All this had been seen to, but the rooms still had the dank smell of long disuse. Silently, just opening his delicate nostrils, Bagoas indicated this.

The rooms of the Royal Wife, despite neglect, were still luxurious; Darius though self-indulgent had been generous too. They led him on to the smaller, but still handsome rooms for the Queen Mother. Sisygambis had stayed here in an early year of her son's short reign. Bagoas looked them over, his head tilted slightly sideways. Unconsciously, over the years, he had picked up this tic from Alexander.

'Very pleasant,' he said. 'At any rate it can be made so. As you know, the lady Roxane is on her way from Ekbatana. The King is anxious that she should have an easy journey.' The eunuchs pricked up their ears; Roxane's pregnancy was not yet public news. 'She will be here in about seven days. I will order some things, and send in good craftsmen. Please see they do all they should.'

In a speaking pause, the eunuchs' eyes turned towards the rooms of the Royal Wife. Those of Bagoas followed them, inexpressively.

'Those rooms will be closed at present. Just see they are well aired and kept sweet. You have a key for the outer door? Good.' No one said anything. He added, blandly, 'There is no need to show these rooms to the lady Roxane. If she should ask, say they are in disrepair.' He left politely, as he had come.

At the time, they had decided that Bagoas must have some old score to pay. Favourites and wives were traditional antagonists. The rumour ran that early in her marriage Roxane had tried to poison him, but had never again tried anything, so dreadful had been the anger of the King.

The furniture and hangings now sent in were costly, and the finished rooms lacked nothing of royal splendour. 'Don't be afraid of extravagance,' Bagoas had said. 'That is to her taste.'

Her caravan duly arrived from Ekbatana. Handed down the steps of her travelling wagon she had proved to be a young woman of striking, high-nosed beauty, with blue-black hair and dark brilliant eyes. Her pregnancy hardly showed except in opulent softness. She spoke fluent Persian, though with a Bactrian accent which her Bactrian suite did nothing to correct; and had gained a fair command of Greek, a tongue unknown to her before her marriage. Babylon was as foreign to her as India; she had settled without demur in the rooms prepared for her, remarking that they were smaller than those at Ekbatana, but much prettier. They had their own courtyard, elegant and shady. Darius, who had held his mother in awe as well as in esteem, had always been attentive to her comfort.

Next day a chamberlain, this time of venerable age, announced the King.

The eunuchs waited anxiously. What if Bagoas had acted without authority? The King's anger was said to be rare, but terrible. However, he greeted them courteously in his scanty, formal Persian, and made no comment when shown to Roxane's rooms.

Through chinks and crannies known in the harem since the days of Nebuchadrezzar, the younger concubines glimpsed him on his way. They reported him handsome in countenance, for a westerner at least (fair colouring was not admired in Babylon); and he was not tall, a grave defect, but this they had known already. Surely he must be older than thirty-two, for his hair had grey in it; but they owned that he had presence, and awaited his return to see him again. They expected a lengthy vigil; but he was back in barely the time it would take a careful woman to bathe and dress.

This made the younger ladies hopeful. They cleaned their jewels and reviewed their cosmetics. One or two, who from boredom had let themselves get grossly fat, were derided and cried all day. For a week, each morning dawned full of promise. But the King did not come. Instead, Bagoas reappeared, and conferred in private with the Chief Warden. The heavy door of the Royal Wife's room was opened, and they went inside.

'Yes,' said Bagoas. 'Not much is needed here. Just there, and there, fresh hangings. The toilet vessels will be in the treasury?'

Thankfully (they had tempted him more than once) the Warden sent for them; they were exquisite, silver inlaid with gold. A great clothes-chest of cypress wood stood against the wall. Bagoas raised the lid; there was a drift of faded fragrance. He lifted out a scarf stitched with seed-pearls and small gold beads.

'These, I suppose, were Queen Stateira's?'

'Those she did not take with her. Darius thought nothing too good for her.'

Except his life, each thought in the awkward pause. His flight at Issos had left her to end her days under the protection of his enemy. Under the scarf was a veil edged with green scarab-wings from Egypt. Bagoas fingered it gently. 'I never saw her. "The loveliest woman of mortal birth in Asia" – was that true?'

'Who has seen every woman in Asia? Yes, it well may be.'

'At least I have seen her daughter.' He put back the scarf and closed the chest. 'Leave all these things. The lady Stateira will like to have them.'

'Has she set out from Susa yet?' A different question trembled on the Warden's lips.

Bagoas, well aware of it, said deliberately, 'She will be coming when the worst of the heat is over. The King is anxious she should have an easy journey.'

The Warden caught a sharp breath. Fat old chamberlain and slender glittering favourite, their eyes exchanged the immemorial communication of their kind. It was the Warden who spoke first.

'So far, everything has gone smoothly *there*.' He glanced towards the other set of rooms. 'But as soon as these apartments are opened, there will be talk. There is no preventing it. You know that as well as I do. Does the King intend to tell the lady Roxane?'

For a moment, Bagoas' urbane polish cracked, revealing a deep settled grief. He sealed it off again. 'I will remind him if I can. It is not easy just now. He is planning the funeral of his friend Hephaistion, who died at Ekbatana.'

The Warden would have liked to ask if it was true that this death had sent the King out of his mind for a month or more. But Bagoas' polish had hardened, warningly. Quickly the Warden smoothed away curiosity. They said of Bagoas that, if he chose, he could be the most dangerous man at court.

'In that case,' said the Warden carefully, 'we might delay the work for a while? If I am asked questions, without any sanction from the King . . .?'

Bagoas paused, looking for a moment uncertain and still quite young. But he answered crisply, 'No, we have had our orders. He will expect to find them obeyed.'

He left, and did not return. It was reported in the harem that the funeral of the King's friend surpassed that of Queen Semiramis, renowned in story; that the pyre had been a burning ziggurat two hundred feet high. But, said the Warden to anyone who would listen, that was a little fire to the one he had had to face when the Royal Wife's rooms were opened, and news reached the lady Roxane.

At her mountain home in Baktria, the harem eunuchs had been family servants and slaves, who knew their place. The ancient dignities of the palace chamberlains seemed to her mere insolence. When she ordered the Warden a flogging, she was enraged to find no one empowered to inflict it. The old Baktrian eunuch she had brought from home, dispatched to tell the King, reported that he had taken a flotilla down the Euphrates to explore the swamps. When he got back she tried again; first he was busy, and then he was indisposed.

Her father, she was sure, would have seen to it that the Warden was put to death. But the satrapy conferred on him by the King was on the Indian frontier; by the time she could hear back from him, her son would have been born. The thought appeased her. She said to her Baktrian ladies, 'Let her come, this great tall flagpole from Susa. The King cannot abide her. If he must do this to please the Persians, what is that to me? Everyone knows that I am his real wife, the mother of his son.'

The ladies said in secret, 'I would not be that child, if it is a girl.'

The King did not come, and Roxane's days hung heavy. Here, at what was to be the centre of her husband's empire, she might as well be encamped in Drangiana. She could, if she wished, have entertained the concubines. But these women had been living for years in royal palaces, some of them since she had been a child on her father's mountain crag. She thought with dread of assured Persian elegance, sophisticated talk tossed spitefully over her head. Not one had crossed her threshold; she had rather be thought haughty than afraid. One day however she found one of the ancient crannies; it passed the time to lay an ear to it and hear them talking.

So it was that, when Alexander had been nine days down with marsh-fever, she heard a palace chamberlain gossiping with a harem eunuch. From this she learned two things; that the sickness had flown to the King's chest, and he was like to die; and that the daughter of Darius was with child.

She did not pause, even to hear them out. She called her Baktrian eunuch and her ladies, threw on a veil, brushed past the stunned Nubian giant who guarded the harem, and only answered his shrill cries with, 'I must see the King.'

The palace eunuchs came running. They could do nothing but run after her. She was the King's wife, not a captive; she stayed in the harem only because to leave it was unthinkable. On the long marches, out to India and back to Persia and down to Babylon, wherever the King pitched camp her baggage-wagons had unpacked the wicker screens which had made her a travelling courtyard, so that she could leave her covered wagon and take the air. In the cities she had her curtained litter, her latticed balconies. All this was not her sentence but her right; it was only whores whom men displayed. Now, when the unprecedented happened, to lay hands on her was inconceivable. Guided by her trembling eunuch, her progress followed by astonished eyes, she swept through corridors, courtyards, anterooms, till she reached the Bedchamber. It was the first time she had entered it; or, for that matter, his own sleeping-place anywhere else. He had never summoned her to his bed, only gone to hers. It was the custom of the Greeks, so he had told her.

She paused in the tall doorway, seeing the high cedar ceiling, the daimon-guarded bed. It was like a hall of audience. Generals, physicians, chamberlains, stupid with surprise, stood back as she made her way to him.

The heaped pillows that propped him upright gave him still the illusion of authority. His closed eyes, his parted and gasping mouth, seemed like a willed withdrawal. She could not be in his presence without believing that everything was still under his control.

'Sikandar!' she cried, slipping back into her native dialect. 'Sikandar!'

His eyelids, creased and bloodless in sunken sockets, moved faintly but did not open. The thin skin tightened, as if to shut out a harsh glare of sun. She saw that his lips were cracked and dry; the deep scar in his side, from the wound he had got in India, stretched and shrank with his labouring breath.

'Sikandar, Sikandar!' she cried aloud. She grasped him by the arm.

He took a deeper breath, and choked on it. Someone leaned over with a towel, and wiped bloody froth from his lips. He did not open his eyes.

As if she had known nothing till now, a cold dagger of realization stabbed her. He was gone out of reach; he would no longer direct her journeys. He would decide nothing, ever again; would never tell her what she had come to ask. For her, for the child within her, he was already dead.

She began to wail, like a mourner over a bier, clawing her face, beating her breast, tearing at her clothes, shaking her dishevelled hair. She flung herself forward, her arms across the bed, burying her face in the sheet, hardly aware of the hot, still living flesh beneath it. Someone was speaking; a light, young voice, the voice of a eunuch.

'He can hear all this; it troubles him.'

There was a strong grasp on her shoulders, pulling her back. She might have recognized Ptolemy, from the triumphs and processions seen from her lattices; but she was looking across the bed, perceiving who had spoken. She would have guessed, even if she had not seen him once in India, gliding down the Indus on Alexander's flagship, dressed in the brilliant stuffs of Taxila, scarlet and gold. It was the hated Persian boy, familiar of this room she had never entered; he, too, a custom of the Greeks, though her husband had never told her so.

His menial clothes, his haggard exhausted face, conceded nothing. No longer desirable, he had become commanding. Generals and satraps and captains, whose obedience should be to her, who should be rousing the King to answer her, to name his heir – they listened, submissive, to this dancing-boy. As for her, she was an intrusion.

She cursed him with her eyes, but already his attention was withdrawn from her, as he beckoned a slave to take the blood-stained towel, and checked the clean pile beside him. Ptolemy's hard hands released her; the hands of her attendants, gentle, supplicating, insistent, guided her towards the door. Someone picked up her veil from the bed and threw it over her.

Back in her own room, she flung herself down in a furious storm of weeping, pummelling and biting the cushions of her divan. Her ladies, when they dared speak to her, implored her to spare herself, lest the child miscarry. This brought her to herself; she called for mare's milk and figs, which she chiefly craved for lately. Dark fell; she tossed on her bed. At length, dry-eyed, she got up, and paced to and fro in the moon-dappled courtyard, where the fountain murmured like a conspirator in the hot Babylonian night. Once she felt the child move strongly. Laying her hands over the place, she whispered, 'Quiet, my little king. I promise you ... I promise ...'

She went back to bed, and fell into a heavy sleep. She dreamed she was in her father's fort on the Sogdian Rock, a rampart-guarded cavern under the mountain's crest, with a thousand-foot drop below, the Macedonians were besieging it. She looked down at the swarming men, scattered like dark grains up the snow; at the red starry camp-fires plumed with faint smoke; at the coloured dots of the tents. The wind was rising, moaning over the crag. Her brother called to her to fit arrow-heads with the other women; he rebuked her idleness, and shook her. She woke. Her woman let go her shoulder, but did not speak. She had slept late, the sun was hot in the courtyard. Yet the wind soughed on; the world was full of its noise, rising and falling, like its winter voice when it blew from the immeasurable ranges of the east ... But this was Babylon.

Here it died down and there it rose, and now it came close at hand, the high wailing of the harem; she could hear now its formal rhythm. The women beside her, seeing her awake, at once began lamenting, crying out the ancient phrases offered to the widows of Baktrian chieftains time out of mind. They were looking at her. It was for her to lead the dirge.

Obediently she sat up, dragged her hair, drummed with her fists on her breast. She had known the words since her childhood: 'Alas, alas! The light is fallen from the sky, the lion of men is fallen. When he lifted his sword, a thousand warriors trembled; when he opened his hand, it shed gold like the sands of the sea. When he rejoiced, it gladdened us like the sun. As the storm-wind rides the mountains, so he rode to war; like the tempest that fells great forest trees, he rode into the battle. His shield was a strong roof over his people. Darkness is his portion, his house is desolate. Alas! Alas! Alas!'

She laid her hands in her lap. Her wailing ceased. The women, startled, stared at her. She said, 'I have lamented; I have finished now.' She beckoned her chief waiting-woman and waved the rest away.

'Bring my old travelling gown, the dark blue one.' It was found, and dust shaken out of it from the Ekbatana road. The stuff was strong; she had to nick it with her paring-knife before it would tear. When she had rent it here and there, she put it on. Leaving her hair uncombed, she ran her hand over a dusty cornice and smeared her face. Then she sent for her Baktrian eunuch.

'Go to the harem, and ask the lady Badia to visit me.'

'Hearing is obedience, madam.' How did she know the name of Ochos' first-ranking concubine? But it was clearly no time for questions.

From her listening-place, Roxane could hear the fluster in the harem. Some were still wailing for the King, but most were chattering. After a short delay for preparation, Badia appeared, dressed in the mourning she had put on for King Ochos, fifteen years before, smelling of herbs and cedar-wood. For Darius she had not worn it.

Ochos had reigned for twenty years, and she had been a concubine of his youth. She was in her fifties, graceful once, now gaunt. Long before his death she had been left behind in Babylon while younger girls were taken along to Susa. But she had ruled the harem in her time, and did not forget.

Some minutes were passed in orthodox condolences. Badia lauded the valour of the King, his justice, his bounty. Roxane responded as was proper, swaying and keening softly. Presently she wiped her eyes, and made a few broken answers. Badia offered the immemorial consolation.

'The child will be his remembrance. You will see him grow to rival his father's honour.'

All this was formula. Roxane abandoned it. 'If he lives,' she sobbed, 'If Darius' accursed kindred let him live. But they will kill him. I know, I know it.' She grasped her hair in both hands and moaned.

Badia caught her breath, her lean face shocked with memory. 'Oh, the good God! Will those days come again?'

Ochos had achieved the throne by wholesale fratricide, and died by poison. Roxane had no wish to hear reminiscences. She flung back her hair. 'How can they not? Who murdered King Ochos when he lay sick?

And the young king Arses and his loyal brothers? And Arses' little son, still at the breast? And when it was done, who killed the Vizier his creature, to stop his mouth? Darius! Alexander told me so.'

('I used to think so,' Alexander had told her not long before, 'but that was before I'd fought him. He'd not spirit enough to be more than the Vizier's tool. He killed him after because he was afraid of him. That was just like the man.')

'Did the King say so? Ah, the lion of justice, the redresser of wrongs!' Her voice rose, ready to wail again; Roxane lifted a quick repressive hand.

'Yes, he avenged your lord. But my son, who will avenge him? Ah, if you knew!'

Badia raised sharp black eyes, avid with curiosity. 'What is it, lady?'

Roxane told her. Alexander, still sick with grief for his boyhood friend, had gone before, leaving her in safety at Ekbatana, to purge of bandits the road to Babylon. Then, weary from the winter war, he had stayed to rest at Susa, and been beguiled by Queen Sisygambis; that old sorceress who, if truth were known, had set on her son, the usurper, to all his crimes. She had brought to the King the daughter of Darius, that clumsy, long-legged girl he had married to please the Persians. Very likely she had drugged him, she was skilled in potions. She had got her grandchild into the King's bed, and told him she was with child by him, though who was to know the truth? And, since he had married her in state in the presence of the Persian and Macedonian lords, what could they do but accept her infant? 'But he married her only for show, for policy. He told me so.'

(Indeed it was true that before the wedding, appalled by Roxane's frenzy, deafened by her cries, and feeling remorseful, Alexander had said something to this effect. He had made no promises for the future, it being a principle of his to keep the future open; but he had dried her tears, and brought her some handsome earrings.)

'And so,' she cried, 'under this roof she will bear a grandchild to Ochos' murderer. And who will protect us, now that the King is gone?'

Badia began to cry. She thought of the long dull peaceful years in the quiet ageing harem, where the dangerous outside world was only rumour. She had outgrown the need of men and even of variety, living contentedly with her talking bird and her little red-coated monkey and her old gossiping eunuchs, maintained in comfort by the wandering, distant King. Now there opened before her dreadful ancient memories of betrayal, accusations, humiliation, the waking dread of the new day. It had been a cruel rival who had displaced her with King Ochos. The peaceful years fell from her. She sobbed and wailed; this time for herself.

'What can we do?' she cried. 'What can we do?'

Roxane's white, plump, short-fingered hand grasped Badia's wrist. Her great dark eyes, which had cast their spell upon Alexander, were fixed on hers. 'The King is dead. We must save ourselves as best we can.'

'Yes, Lady.' The old days were back; once more it was a matter of survival. 'Lady, what shall we do?'

Roxane drew her near and they talked softly, remembering the crannies in the wall.

Some time later, quietly by the servants' door came an old eunuch from Badia's household. He carried a box of polished wood. Roxane said, 'It is true that you can write Greek?'

'Certainly, madam. King Ochos often called on me.'

'Have you good parchment? It is for a royal letter.'

'Yes, madam.' He opened the box. 'When the usurper Darius gave my place to one of his people, I took a little with me.'

'Good. Sit down and write.'

When she gave him the superscription, he almost spoiled the scroll. But he had not come quite ignorant of his errand; and Badia had told him that if Darius' daughter ruled the harem, she would turn all Ochos' people out in the street to beg. He wrote on. She saw that the script was even and flowing, with the proper formal flourishes. When he had done, she gave him a silver daric and let him go. She did not swear him to silence; it was beneath her dignity, and Badia would have seen to it.

He had brought wax, but she had not sealed it in his presence. Now she drew off a ring Alexander had given her on their wedding night. It was set with a flawless amethyst the colour of dark violets, on which Pyrgoletes, his favourite engraver, had carved his portrait. It was nothing like the royal ring of Macedon, with its Zeus enthroned. But Alexander had never been conventional, and she thought that it would serve.

She turned the stone in the light. The work was superb, and though somewhat idealized had caught a vivid look of him. He had given it her when they were at last alone in the bridal chamber; something to serve them in place of words, since neither could speak the other's tongue. He had put it on her, finding a finger it would fit at the second try. She had kissed it respectfully, and then he had embraced her. She remembered how unexpectedly pleasing his body was, with a warm freshness like a young boy's; but she had expected a harder grasp. He should have gone out to be undressed and have a wedding shift put on him; but, instead, he had just tossed off his clothes and stood there stark naked, in which state he had got into bed. She had been too shocked at first to think of anything else, and he had thought she was afraid of him. He had taken a good deal of trouble with her, some of it quite sophisticated; he had had expert tuition, though she did not yet know whose. But what she really wanted was to be taken by storm. She had adopted postures of submission, proper in a virgin; for anything livelier on the first night, a Baktrian bridegroom would have strangled her. But she could feel he was at a loss, and had a dreadful fear that there would be an unstained bridal sheet for the guests to view next morning. She had nerved herself to embrace him; and afterwards all was well.

She dropped the hot wax on the scroll and pressed in the gem. Suddenly a piercing memory came to her of a day a few months ago in Ekbatana, one summer afternoon by the fish pool. He had been feeding the carp, coaxing the old sullen king of the pool to come to his hand from its lair under the lily-pads. He would not come in to make love till he had won. After, he had fallen asleep; she remembered the fair boyish skin with the deep dimpled scars, the soft margins of his strong hair. She had wanted to feel and smell him as if he were good to eat, like fresh-baked bread. When she buried her face in him, he half-woke and held her comfortably, and slept again. The sense of his physical presence came back to her like life. At last, alone, in silence, she shed real tears.

She wiped them soon. She had business that would not wait.

In the Bedchamber, the long days of dying were over. Alexander had ceased to breathe. The lamenting eunuchs had drawn out the heaped-up pillows; he lay straight and flat in the great bed, restored by stillness to a monumental dignity, but, to the watchers, shocking in his passiveness. A dead man, a corpse.

The generals, hastily called when the end was plainly coming, stood staring blankly. For two days they had been thinking what to do now. Yet, now, it was as if the awaited certainty had been some mere contingency with which their imaginations had been playing. They gazed stupefied at the familiar face, so finally untenanted; feeling almost resentment, so impossible did it seem that anything could happen to Alexander without consent of his. How could he die and leave them in this confusion? How could he throw off responsibility? It was quite unlike him.

A cracked young voice at the outer door suddenly cried out, 'He's gone, he's gone!' It was a youth of eighteen, one of the royal body squires, who had been taking his turn on guard duty. He broke into hysterical weeping, which rose above the keening of the eunuchs around the bed. Someone must have led him away, for his voice could be heard receding, raw with uncontainable grief.

It was as if he had invoked an ocean. He had blundered, sobbing, into half the Macedonian army, gathered around the palace to await the news.

Most of them had passed through the Bedchamber the day before; but he had known them still, he had remembered them; they, most of all, had good cause to expect a miracle. Now a huge clamour rose; of grief, of ritual mourning; of protest, as if some authority could be found to blame: of dismay at the uncertainties of the shattered future.

The sound aroused the generals. Their reflexes, trained to a hair by the dead man on the bed, snapped into action. Panic must be dealt with instantly. They ran out to the great platform above the forecourt. A herald, wavering at his post, was barked at by Perdikkas, lifted his long-stemmed trumpet, and blew the assembly call.

The response was ragged. Only yesterday, believing the call to be from Alexander, they would in silent minutes have sorted themselves into their files and phalanxes, each troop competing to get into formation first. Now, nature's laws were suspended. Those in front had to shout back to the rear that it was Perdikkas. Since Hephaistion's death he had been Alexander's second-in-command. When he roared at them, it gave them some sense of security; they shuffled and shoved themselves into a semblance of order.

The Persian soldiers fell in with the rest. Their mourning outcries had counterpointed the Macedonians' clamour. Now they grew quiet. They were – they had been – soldiers of Alexander, who had made them forget they were a conquered people, given them pride in themselves, made the Macedonians accept them. The early frictions had been almost over, Greek soldier slang was full of Persian words, a comradeship had begun. Now, suddenly, feeling themselves once more defeated natives on sufferance in an alien army, they looked at each other sidelong, planning desertion.

At Perdikkas' signal, Peukestes strode forward, a reassuring figure; a man renowned for valour, who had saved Alexander's life in India when he took his near-mortal wound. Now, tall, handsome, commanding, bearded in the fashion of his satrapy, he addressed them in Persian as correct and aristocratic as his dress. Formally he announced to them the death of the Great King. In due course, his successor would be proclaimed to them. They might now dismiss.

The Persians were calmed. But a deep muttering growl arose from the Macedonians. By their ancestral law, the right to choose a king belonged to them; to the Assembly of all male Macedonians able to bear arms. What was this talk of a proclamation?

Peukestes stood back for Perdikkas. There was a pause. For twelve years, both of them had watched Alexander dealing with Macedonians. They were not men who could be told to hold their peace and await authority's pleasure. They had to be talked to, and he had done it; only once, in all the twelve years, without success. Even then, once they had made him turn back from India, they were all his own. Now, faced with this disorder, for a moment Perdikkas expected to hear approaching the brisk impatient footsteps; the crisp low-spoken reprimand, the high ringing voice creating instant stillness.

He did not come; and Perdikkas, though he lacked magic, understood authority. He fell, as Alexander had done at need, into the Doric patois of the homeland, their own boyhood tongue before they were schooled into polite Greek. They had all lost, he said, the greatest of kings, the bravest and best of warriors, that the world had seen since the sons of the gods forsook the earth.

Here he was stopped by a huge swelling groan; no voluntary tribute, but an outburst of naked misery and bereavement. When he could be heard again, he said, 'And the grandsons of your grandsons will say so still. Remember, then, that your loss is measured by your former fortune. You out of all men, past or to come, have had your share in the glory of Alexander. And now it is for you, his Macedonians, to whom he has bequeathed the mastery of half the world, to keep your courage, and show you are the men he made you. All will be done according to the law.'

The hushed crowd gazed up in expectation. When Alexander had talked them quiet, he had always had something to tell them. Perdikkas knew it; but all he had to tell was that he himself was now, effectively, the King in Asia. It was too soon; they knew only one King, alive or dead. He told them to go back to camp and wait for further orders.

Under his eye they began to leave the forecourt; but when he had gone in, many came back by ones and twos, and settled down with their arms beside them, ready for night, to keep the deathwatch.

Down in the city the sound of lamentation, like a brush-fire with a high wind behind it, spread from the crowded streets nearest the palace, on through the suburbs to the houses built along the walls. Above the temples the tall thin smoke-plumes, which had been rising upright in the still air from the sacred fires, one after another dipped and died. By the heat of damp ashes in Bel-Marduk's brazier, the priests reminded each other that this was the second time in little more than a month. The King had ordered it on the day of his friend's funeral. 'We warned him of the omen, but he would hear nothing. He was a foreigner, when all is said.'

Theirs was the first fire quenched. In the temple of Mithra, guardian of the warrior's honour, lord of loyalty and the given word, a young priest stood in the sanctuary with a water-ewer in his hand. Above the altar was carved the symbol of the winged sun, at war with the dark, age after age till the last victory. The fire still burned high, for the young man had been feeding it extravagantly, as if it had power to rekindle the sinking life of the King. Even now, when he had been ordered to extinguish it, he put down his ewer, ran to a coffer of Arabian incense, and flung a handful to sparkle into fragrance. Last of the officiants, it was not till his offering had lifted into the summer sky that he poured the water hissing upon the embers.

On the Royal Road to Susa, a courier travelled, his racing dromedary eating the miles with its smooth loping stride. Before it needed rest he would have reached the next relay-post, whence a fresh man and beast would carry his charge on through the night.

His stage was half-way of the journey. The parchment in his saddle-bag had been passed to him by the man before, without pause for questions. Only the first stage out from Babylon had been run by a rider unknown to his relief. This stranger, when asked if it was true that the King was sick, had replied that it might be so for all he knew, but he had no time for gossiping. Silent haste was the first rule of the corps; the relief had saluted and sped away, showing, wordlessly, to the next man in the chain, that his letter was sealed with the image of the King.

It was said that a dispatch by Royal Messenger would outstrip even the birds. Winged rumour itself could not overtake it; for at night rumour stops to sleep.

Two travellers, who had reined in to let the courier past, were nearly thrown as their horses squealed and reared at the detested smell of camel. The elder man, who was about thirty-five, stocky, freckled and red-haired, mastered his mount first, wresting back its head till the rough bit dripped blood. His brother, some ten years younger, auburn and conventionally good-looking, took longer because he had tried to reassure the horse. Kassandros watched his efforts with contempt. He was the eldest son of the Regent of Macedon, Antipatros, and was a stranger in Babylonia. He had reached it lately, sent by his father to find out why Alexander had summoned him to Macedon and sent Krateros to assume the Regency in his stead.

Iollas, the younger, had marched with Alexander, and till lately been his cupbearer. His appointment had been by way of an appeasing gesture to their father; Kassandros had been left behind on garrison duty in Macedon, because he and Alexander had disliked each other since they were boys.

When the horse was quiet, Iollas said, 'That was a Royal Messenger.'

'May he and his brute drop dead.'

'Why is he riding? Perhaps – it's all over now.'

Kassandros, looking back towards Babylon, said, 'May the dog of Hades eat his soul.'

For some time they rode in silence, Iollas looking at the road before him.

At last he said, 'Well, no one can turn Father out now. Now he can be King.'

'King?' growled Kassandros. 'Not he. He took his oath and he'll keep it. Even to the barbarian's brat, if it's a boy.'

Iollas' horse started, feeling its rider's shock. 'Then why? Why did you make me do it? . . . Not for Father? . . . Only for hate! Almighty God, I should have known!'

Kassandros leaned over and slashed his riding-quirt down on the young man's knee. He gave a startled cry of pain and anger.

'Don't dare do that again! We're not at home now, and I'm not a boy.'

Kassandros pointed to the red weal. 'Pain's a reminder. You did nothing. Remember, nothing. Keep it in your head.' A little way further on, seeing tears in Iollas' eyes, he said with grudging forbearance, 'Like as not he took fever from the marsh air. By now he must have drunk dirty water often enough. The peasants down river drink swamp-water, and *they* don't die of it. Keep your mouth shut. Or *you* might die of it.'

Iollas swallowed and gulped. Dragging his hand across his eyes, and streaking his face with the black dust of the Babylonian plain, he said huskily, 'He never got back his strength after that arrow wound in India. He couldn't afford a fever . . . He was good to me. I only did it for Father. Now you say he won't be King.'

'*He* won't be King. But whatever name they call it by, he'll die the ruler of Macedon and all Greece. And he's an old man now.'

Iollas gazed at him in silence; then spurred his horse and galloped ahead through the yellow wheatfields, his sobs catching their rhythm from the pounding of the hooves.

Next day in Babylon the leading generals prepared for the Assembly that was to choose a ruler of the Macedonians. Their law did not demand primogeniture as inalienable. It was the right of the men in arms to choose among the royal family.

When Philip had died, it had been simple. Almost all the fighting men were still at home. Alexander at twenty had already made a name for himself, and no other claimant had been so much as named. Even when Philip, a younger brother, had been chosen before the child of King Perdikkas, lately fallen in battle, that had been simple too; Philip had been a tried commander, the child an infant in arms, and they were at war.

Now, Macedonian troops were scattered in strongpoints all over central Asia. Ten thousand veterans were marching home for discharge under the command of Krateros, a youngish man, whom Alexander had ranked next after Hephaistion, and who was one of the royal kindred. There were the garrison troops in Macedon, and in the great stone forts which commanded the passes into southern Greece. All this the men at Babylon knew. But no one of them questioned that theirs was the right to choose a king. They were the army of Alexander, and that was everything.

Outside on the hot parade ground they waited, disputing, conjecturing, passing rumours on. Sometimes, as their impatience and disquiet mounted, the noise would surge like a breaker on a pebble beach.

The generals inside, the high command known as the Royal Bodyguard, had been trying to get hold of the chief officers of the aristocratic Companions, with whom they wished to confer in their dilemma. Failing in this, they ordered the herald to blow a call for quiet, and summon them by name. The herald, knowing no army call for quiet alone, blew 'Assemble for orders'. It was received by the impatient men as 'Come to Assembly'.

Clamorously they poured through the great doors into the audience hall, while the herald shouted against the din the names he had been given, and the officers he named, those who could hear him, tried to shove themselves through the crowd. The crush inside grew dangerous; the doors were shut, in desperation, on everyone who had entered, authorized or not. The herald, gazing helplessly at the milling, cursing mob left in the courtyard, said to himself that if Alexander had seen it, someone would soon be wishing he'd never been born.

First to get in, because others had made way for them, were the men of the Companions, the horse-owning lords of Macedon, and any officers who had been near the doors. The rest of the crowd was a mixture of high and low, thrown anyhow together. The one thing they had in common was a deep unease, and the aggressiveness of worried men. It had come home to them that they were isolated troops in conquered country, half their world away from home. They had come here through faith in Alexander, in him alone. What they craved now was not a king but a leader.

The doors once closed, all eyes sought the royal dais. There, as often before, were the great men, Alexander's nearest friends, standing around the throne, the ancient throne of Babylon; its arms carved into crouching Assyrian bulls, its back re-carved for Xerxes into the winged image of the unconquered sun. Here they had seen the small, compact, bright figure, needing a footstool, glowing like a jewel in too large a box, the spread wings of Ahura-Mazda above his head. Now the throne was empty. Across its back was the royal robe, and on its seat the diadem.

A low, sighing groan ran through the pillared hall. Ptolemy, who read the poets, thought it was like the climax of a tragedy, when the upstage doors are flung open, disclosing to the chorus that their fears are true and the King is dead.

Perdikkas stepped forward. All Alexander's friends here present, he said, would witness that the King had given him the royal ring. But, being speechless, he could not say what powers he was conferring. 'He looked at me fixedly, and it was clear he wished to speak, but his breath failed him. So, men of Macedon, here is the ring.' He drew it off, and laid it beside the crown. 'Bestow it as you choose, according to ancestral law.'

There were murmurs of admiration and suspense, as at a play. He waited, still downstage, like a good actor who could time his lines. So Ptolemy thought, glancing at the alert arrogant face, now set in impassive dignity; a well-carved mask; a mask for a king?

Perdikkas said, 'Our loss is beyond all measure, that we know. We know it is not to be thought of that the throne should pass to anyone not of his blood. Roxane his wife is five months with child; let us pray it will be a boy. He must first be born, and then he must come of age. Meantime, whom do you wish to rule you? It is for you to say.'

The voices murmured; the generals on the dais looked restively at each other; Perdikkas had not presented another speaker. Suddenly, unannounced, Niarchos, the admiral, stepped forward; a spare, lean-waisted Cretan, with a brown weathered face. The hardships of the dreadful voyage down the Gedrosian coast had put ten years on him; he looked fifty, but still wiry and fit. The men quietened to hear him; he had seen monsters of the deep, and put them to flight with trumpets. Unused to public speaking upon the land, he used the voice with which he hailed ships at sea, startling them with its loudness.

'Macedonians, I put before you as Alexander's heir the son of Darius' daughter Stateira. The King left her pregnant when last he passed through Susa.' There were surprised, disconcerted murmurs; he raised his voice over them, as he would have done in a noisy storm. 'You saw their wedding. You saw it was a royal one. He meant to send for her here. He told me so.'

This wholly unexpected news of a woman who, barely glimpsed on her bridal day, had vanished at once into the recesses of the Susa harem, caused a surge of confusion and dismay. Presently a broad-spoken peasant voice called out, 'Ah, but did he say aught about the bairn?'

'No,' said Niarchos. 'In my belief he meant to bring up both sons under his eye, if both were sons, and choose the better one. But he's not lived to do it; and Stateira's child has right of rank.'

He stepped back; he had nothing more to say. He had done what seemed his duty, and that was all. Looking out over the sea of heads, he remembered how Alexander, lean as a bone and hollow-eyed from the desert march, had greeted him when he brought the fleet safe back, embracing him with tears of relief and joy. Since they were boys, Niarchos had been in love with him in an unsexual, undemanding way; that moment had been the climax of his life. What he would do with the rest of it, he could not begin to think.

Perdikkas' teeth were set with anger. He had urged the men to appoint a regent – who but himself? Now, they had been side-tracked into debating the succession. Two unborn children, who might both be girls. It was in the family; Philip had sired a horde of daughters, and only one son unless you counted the fool. The regency was the thing. Philip himself had started out as regent for an infant heir, but the Macedonians had not wasted much time in electing him King. Perdikkas himself had a good strain of the royal blood ... What had possessed Niarchos? There was no heading the men off now.

Their debate grew noisy and acrimonious. If, in their view, Alexander had had a fault, it was letting himself get Persianized. The Susa weddings, a serious manifesto, had caused much more unease than the campaign marriage with Roxane, the sort of thing his father used to do time and again. They had been indulgent towards the dancing boy, as towards a pet monkey or dog; but why could he not have married a girl from a decent old Macedonian family, instead of two barbarians? Now this was what had come of it.

Some argued that any offspring of his must be accepted, half-breed or not. Others said there was no knowing if he would have acknowledged either; and you could be sure, if either of those women had a stillbirth or a girl, they would smuggle something in. They were crawling on their bellies to no Persian changeling.

Ptolemy watched the scene with grief and anger, longing to be gone. From the time when Alexander's death had become a certainty, he had known where he wished to go. Ever since Egypt had opened its arms to Alexander as its liberator from the Persian yoke, Ptolemy had been entranced by it, its immemorial mellow civilization, its stupendous monuments and temples, the rich life of its sustaining river. It was defensible as an island, protected by sea and desert and wilderness; one had only to win the people's trust to hold it secure for ever. Perdikkas and the rest would gladly give him the satrapy; they wanted him out of the way.

He was dangerous, a man who could claim to be Alexander's brother, even though from adultery when Philip was in his teens. His paternity was unproved and unacknowledged; but Alexander had always had a special place for him, and everyone knew it. Yes, Perdikkas would be glad to see him off to Africa. But did the man think he could make himself Alexander's heir? That was what he was after; it was written all over him. Something must be done; and now.

The soldiers, when Ptolemy stepped forward, broke off their disputes to give him a hearing. He had been a boyhood friend of Alexander; he had presence without Perdikkas' arrogance; men who had served under him liked him. A group of them gave him a cheer.

'Macedonians, I see you do not wish to choose a king from the offspring of the conquered.'

There was loud applause. The men, who had all come armed – it was the proof of their voting right – beat their spears on their shields till the high hall echoed. Ptolemy raised a hand for quiet.

'We do not know if either wife of Alexander will bear a boy. If one or both should, when they come of age they must be brought before you and your sons, for Assembly to decide whom the Macedonians will accept. In the meantime, you await Alexander's heir. But who will act for him? Here before you are those whom Alexander honoured with trust. Lest too much power go to one man, I propose a Council of Regency.'

The voices were tempered. Reminded that in fifteen years or so they could still reject both claimants, they saw where the day's serious business lay. Ptolemy said into the new quiet, 'Remember Krateros. Alexander trusted him like himself. He sent him to govern Macedon. That is why he is not present now.'

That got home to them. They honoured Krateros next to Alexander; he was of royal stock, capable, brave, handsome and careful of their needs. Ptolemy could feel the eyes of Perdikkas, red-hot in his back. Let him make the best of it; I did as I had to do.

As they buzzed and muttered below, Ptolemy thought suddenly, Only a few days back we were all alike the Friends of Alexander, just waiting for him to get up again and lead us. What are we now, and what am I?

He had never set great store on being Philip's son; it had cost him too much in childhood. Philip had been a nobody, a younger son held hostage by the Thebans, when he was born. 'Can't you make your bastard behave?' his father would say to his mother when he was in trouble. Philip had won him more than one boy's share of beatings. Later, when Philip was King and he himself a Royal Squire his luck had turned; but what he had learned to care for was not being Philip's son, if indeed he was. He had cared, with affection and with growing pride, to be Alexander's brother. Never mind, he thought, whether it is the truth of my blood, or not. It is the truth of my heart.

A new voice broke his brief reverie. Aristonous, one of the Bodyguard, came forward to point out that whatever Alexander might have meant, he had given his ring to Perdikkas. He had looked around first, and knew what he was doing. This was fact, not guesswork; and Aristonous was for abiding by it.

He spoke simply and frankly, and carried the Assembly. They shouted

Perdikkas' name, and many called to him to take back the ring. Slowly, scanning them, he took a few steps forward towards it. For a moment his eye met Ptolemy's, noting him in the way a man notes a new-found enemy.

It would not yet do, Perdikkas thought, to look over-eager. He needed another voice in Aristonous' support.

The hall, crowded with sweating men, was stiflingly close and hot. To the stink of humanity was added that of urine, where a few men had surreptitiously relieved themselves in corners. The generals on the dais were growing stupefied by their varied feelings of grief, anxiety, resentment, impatience and frustration. Suddenly, shouting something indistinct, an officer elbowed his way forward through the crowd. What, they all thought, can Meleager have to say?

He had been a phalanx commander since Alexander's first campaigns, but had risen no higher. Alexander had confided to Perdikkas, one night at supper, that he was a good soldier if one did not stretch his mind.

He arrived below the dais, red-faced with the heat, with anger, and, by his looks, with wine; then lifted a harsh furious voice which stunned the crowd almost silent. 'That's the royal ring! Are you letting that fellow take it? Give it him now, he'll keep it till he dies! No wonder he wants a king who's not yet born!'

The generals, calling for order, were barely heard above the sudden roar. Meleager had aroused, from a kind of restless torpor, a mass of men who had not been heard before, the mental lees of the crowd. They took notice now, as they would of a knife-duel in the street, a man beating his wife, or a vicious dog-fight; and shouted for Meleager, as if for the winning dog.

In the camp, Perdikkas could have restored order in minutes. But this was Assembly; he was not so much Commander-in-Chief as candidate. Repression might seem to forecast tyranny. He made a gesture of tolerant contempt, meaning 'Even such a man must be heard.'

He had seen the naked hatred in Meleager's face. The rank of their fathers had been much the same; they had both been Royal Squires to Philip; both had looked with secret envy at the tight-knit circle round the young Alexander. Then, when Philip was assassinated, Perdikkas had been the first to run down the fleeing assassin. Alexander had praised him, noticed and promoted him. With promotion came opportunity; he had never looked back. When Hephaistion died, he had been given his command. Meleager had remained an infantry phalanx leader, useful if not too much was put on him. And, as Perdikkas saw, the knowledge that burned him was that they had started equal.

'How do we know,' Meleager shouted, 'that Alexander gave him anything? Whose word do we have for it? His and his friends! And what are they after? Alexander's treasure here, which all of us helped to win! Will you stand for that?'

The noise turned to turmoil. The generals, who had thought that they knew men, saw incredulously that Meleager was beginning to lead a mob; men ready to sack the palace like a conquered town. Chaos broke out around it.

Perdikkas summoned, desperately, all his expert powers of dominance. '*Halt!*' he thundered. There was a reflex response. He barked his orders; sufficient men obeyed them. Solid ranks with locked shields formed before the inner doors. The yelling sank to growls. 'I am glad to see,' said Perdikkas in his deep voice, 'that we still have here some soldiers of Alexander.'

There was a hush, as if he had invoked the name of an offended god. The mob began to lose itself in the crowd. The shields were lowered.

In the uncertain pause, a rustic voice, from somewhere deep in the press, made itself heard. 'Shame on you all, I say! Like the Commander says, we're soldiers of Alexander. It's *his* blood we want to rule us, not regents for foreign children. When we've Alexander's true-born brother, here in this very house.'

There was an astonished silence. Ptolemy, stunned, felt all his well-considered decisions shaken by a surge of primitive instinct. The ancient throne of Macedon, with its savage history of tribal rivalries and fratricidal wars, reached out its beckoning spell. Philip – Alexander – Ptolemy . . .

The peasant spearman below, having gained a hearing, went on with gathering confidence. 'His own brother, which King Philip himself acknowledged, as every one of you knows. Alexander always cared for him like his own. I do hear say he was backward as a boy, but it's not a month since the both of them were sacrificing for their father's soul at the household altar. I was on escort, and so were my mates here. He done everything right.'

There were sounds of assent. Ptolemy could barely repress the stare and dropped jaw of utter stupefaction. *Arridaios!* They must be mad.

'King Philip,' persisted the soldier, 'married Philinna lawful, which was his right to have more wives than one. So I say, pass by the foreign babes, and let's have his son, which is his rightful heir.'

There was applause from law-abiding men, who had been shocked by Meleager. On the dais, the silence was general and appalled. Simple or devious, not one of them had thought of this.

'Is it true?' said Perdikkas quickly to Ptolemy through the noise. '*Did* Alexander take him to the shrine?' Urgency overcame enmity; Ptolemy would surely know.

'Yes.' Ptolemy remembered the two heads side by side, dark and fair, the apprentice piece and the sculptor's. 'He's been better lately. He's not had a fit in a year. Alexander said he must be kept in mind of who his father was.'

'Arridaios!' came a growing shout. 'Give us Alexander's brother! Long live Macedon! Arridaios!'

'How many saw him?' said Perdikkas.

'The Companion escort and the foot guard, and anyone looking on. He behaved quite properly. He always does . . . did, with Alexander.'

'We can't have this. They don't know what they're doing. This must be stopped.'

The speaker, Peithon, was a short wiry man with a foxily pointed, rufous face and a sharp foxy bark. He was one of the Bodyguard, a good commander, but not known for the spirit of persuasion. He stepped out, forestalling Perdikkas, and snapped, 'Alexander's brother! You'd do better to choose his horse!'

The bite in his voice produced a brief, but not friendly silence; he was not on the parade ground now. He went on, 'The fellow's a halfwit. Dropped on his head as a baby, and falls down in fits. Alexander's kept him like a child, with a nurse to tend him. Do you want an idiot for a King?'

Perdikkas swallowed a curse. Why had this man ever been promoted? Competent in the field, but no grip on morale in quarters. He himself, if this fool had not stepped in, would have recalled to the men the romantic winning of Roxane, the storming of the Sogdian rock, the victor's chivalry; winning back their minds to Alexander's son. Now their feelings had been offended. They saw Arridaios as a victim of obscure intrigues. They had *seen* the man, and he had behaved like anyone else.

Alexander was always fortunate, thought Ptolemy. Already people wore his image cut on rings, for luck charms. What spiteful fate inspired him, so near his end, with this kindly impulse towards a harmless fool? But, of course, there was a ceremony to come, at which he *must* appear. Perhaps Alexander had thought of that . . .

'Shame!' the men were shouting up to Peithon. 'Arridaios, Arridaios, we want Arridaios!' He yapped at them; but they drowned his voice with boos.

Nobody noticed, till too late, that Meleager was missing.

It had been a long, dull day for Arridaios. No one had come to see him except the slave with his meals, which had been overcooked and half cold. He would have liked to hit the slave, but Alexander did not allow him. Someone from Alexander came nearly every day to see how he was, but today there had been no one to tell about the food. Even old Konon, who looked after him, had gone off just after getting-up time, saying he had to attend a meeting or some such thing, and hardly listening to a word he said.

He needed Konon for several things; to see he had something nice for supper, to find him a favourite striped stone he had mislaid, and to say why there had been such a terrible noise that morning, wailing and howling which seemed to come from everywhere, as if thousands of people were being beaten at once. From his window on the park, he had seen a crowd of men all running towards the palace. Perhaps, soon, Alexander would come to see him, and tell him what it was all about.

Sometimes he did not come for a very long time, and they said he was away on a campaign. Arridaios would stay in camp, or sometimes, as now, in a palace, till he came back again. Often he brought presents, coloured sweets, carved painted horses and lions, a piece of crystal for his collection, and once a beautiful scarlet cloak. Then the slaves would fold the tents and they would all move on. Perhaps this was going to happen now.

Meantime, he wanted the scarlet cloak to play with. Konon had said it was far too hot for cloaks, he would only make it dirty and spoil it. It was locked in the chest, and Konon had the key.

He got out all his stones, except the striped one, and laid them out in pictures; but not having the best one spoiled it. A flush of anger came over him; he picked up the biggest stone and beat it on the table top again and again. A stick would have been better, but he was not allowed one, Alexander himself had taken it away.

A long time ago, when he lived at home, he had been left mostly with the slaves. No one else wanted to see him. Some were kind when they had time, but some had mocked him and knocked him about. As soon as he began to travel with Alexander, the slaves were different and more polite, and one was even afraid of him. It seemed a good time to get his own back, so he had beaten the man till his head bled and he fell down on the floor. Arridaios had never known till then how strong he was. He had gone on hitting till they carried the man away. Then, suddenly, Alexander had appeared; not dressed for dinner, but with armour on, all dirty and splashed with mud, and out of breath. He had looked quite frightening, like a different person, his eyes pale grey and large in his dirty face; and he had made Arridaios swear on their father's head never to do such a thing again. He had remembered it today when his food was late. He did not want his father's ghost to come after him. He had been terrified of him, and had sung with joy on hearing he was dead.

It was time for his ride in the park, but he was not allowed to go without Konon, who kept him on a leading-rein. He wished Alexander would come, and take him again to the shrine. He had held everything nicely, and poured on the wine and oil and incense after Alexander did, and had let them take the gold cups away though he would have liked to keep them; and afterwards, Alexander had said he had done splendidly.

Someone was coming! Heavy feet, and a clank of armour. Alexander was quicker and lighter than that. A soldier came in whom he had never seen before; a tallish man with a red face and straw-coloured hair, holding his helmet under his arm. They looked at one another.

Arridaios, who knew nothing of his own appearance, knew still less that Meleager was thinking, Great Zeus! Philip's face. What is inside it? The young man had, in fact, much of his father's structure, square face, dark brows and beard, broad shoulders and short neck. Since eating was his chief pleasure he was overweight, though Konon had never allowed him to get gross. Delighted to see a visitor at last, he said eagerly, 'Are you going to take me to the park?'

'No, sir.' He stared avidly at Arridaios, who, disconcerted, tried to think if he had done anything wrong. Alexander had never sent this man before. 'Sir, I have come to escort you to Assembly. The Macedonians have elected you their King.'

Arridaios stared at him with alarm, followed by a certain shrewdness. 'You're telling lies. *I'm* not the King, my brother is. He said to me, Alexander said, "If I didn't look after you, someone would try to make you King, and you'd end up being killed." ' He backed away, eyeing Meleager with growing agitation. 'I won't go to the park with you. I'll go with Konon. You fetch him here. If you don't, I'll tell Alexander of you.'

His retreat was blocked by the heavy table. The soldier walked right up to him, so that he flinched instinctively, remembering boyhood beatings. But the man just stared into his eyes, and, very slowly, spoke.

'Sir. Your brother is dead. *King Alexander is dead.* The Macedonians are calling for you. Come with me.'

Since Arridaios did not move, he grasped his arm and guided him to the door. He came unresisting, not heeding where he was led, striving to come to terms with a world which Alexander did not rule.

So expeditious had Meleager been that the crowd in the hall was still shouting 'Arridaios!' when he himself appeared upon the dais. Confronted by this sounding sea of men, he gazed in a numb astonishment, giving a brief illusion of dignified reserve.

Most of the dumbfounded generals had never seen him before; only a few of the men had glimpsed him. But every Macedonian over thirty had seen King Philip. There was a pause of perfect silence; then the cheers began.

'Philip! Philip! Philip!'

Arridaios sent a terrified look over his shoulder. Was his father coming, had he never been really dead? Meleager beside him caught the revealing change of countenance and whispered swiftly, 'They are cheering *you*.' Arridaios gazed about, slightly reassured, but still bewildered. Why did they call for his father? His father was dead. *Alexander* was dead ...

Meleager stepped forward. So much, he thought triumphantly, for that upstart Perdikkas and his unborn ward. 'Here, Macedonians, is the son of Philip, the brother of Alexander. Here is your rightful King.'

Spoken loudly and almost in his ear, it reached Arridaios with awful comprehension. He knew why all these men were here and what was happening. 'No!' he cried, his high plaintive voice issuing incongruously from his large hirsute face. 'I'm not the King! I told you, I can't be King. Alexander told me not to.'

But he had addressed himself to Meleager, and was inaudible beyond the dais, drowned by the cheering. The generals, appalled, all turned upon Meleager, talking across him. He listened with mounting fear to the loud angry voices. Clearly he recalled Alexander's large deep-set eyes, fixed upon his, warning him of what would happen if they tried to make him King. While Meleager was quarrelling with the tall dark man in the middle of the dais, he bolted for the now unguarded door. Outside, in the warren-like passages of the ancient palace, he wandered sobbing to himself, seeking the way back to his familiar room.

In the hall, new uproar began. None of this had precedent. Both the last two kings had been elected by acclamation, and led with traditional paeans to the royal palace at Aigai, whence each had confirmed his accession by directing his predecessor's funeral.

Meleager, wrangling with Perdikkas, had not missed his fugitive candidate till he was warned by sounds of derision from the floor. Feeling was swinging against him; the powerful presence of Perdikkas had appeal for men seeking some source of confidence and strength. Meleager saw that only instant resource would avail. He turned and ran, followed by boos, through the door Arridaios had used. The most vocal of his supporters – not the loot-hungry mob, but kinsmen and fellow-clansmen and men with grudges against Perdikkas – took alarm and hurried after.

Before long they ran down their quarry, standing where two passages met, debating with himself which way to turn. At sight of them he cried out, 'No! Go away!' and started to run. Meleager grasped his shoulder. He submitted, looking terror-stricken. Clearly in this state he could not appear. Gently, calmingly, Meleager changed his grip to a protective caress.

'Sir, you must listen. Sir, you've nothing to fear. You were a good brother to Alexander. He was the rightful King; it would have been wrong, just as he said, for you to take his throne. But now he is dead, and *you* are the rightful King. The throne is yours.' A flash of inspiration came to him. 'There is a present for you on it. A beautiful purple cloak.'

Arridaios, already soothed by the kindly voice, now brightened visibly. No one had laughed; things were too urgent and too dangerous.

'Can I keep it all the time?' he asked cannily. 'You won't lock it up?'

'No, indeed. The moment you have it, you can put it on.'

'And have it all day?'

'All night too, if you wish.' As he began to guide his prize along the passage, a new thought struck him. 'When the men called "Philip!" it was you they meant. They are honouring you with your father's name. You will be King Philip of Macedon.'

King Philip, thought Arridaios. It gave him confidence. His father must be really dead, if his name could be given away, like a purple cloak. It would be well to take them both. He was still buoyed by this decision when Meleager steered him on to the dais.

Smiling around at the exclamations, he saw at once the great swathe of colour draped upon the throne, and walked briskly towards it. Sounds which he had mistaken for friendly greetings died; the Assembly, arrested by his changed demeanour, watched the drama almost in silence.

'There, sir, is our present to you,' said Meleager in his ear.

To a ground-bass of restless murmurs, Philip Arridaios lifted the robe from the throne, and held it up before him.

It was the robe of state, made at Susa for the marriage of Alexander to Stateira daughter of Darius, and of his eighty honoured friends to their Persian brides, with the whole of his army as his wedding guests. In this robe he had given audience to envoys from half the known world, during his last progress down to Babylon. It was of wool as dense as velvet and soft as silk, dyed with Tyrian murex to a soft glowing crimson just tinged with purple, pure as the red of a dark rose. The breast and back were worked with the sunburst, the Macedonian royal blazon, in balas rubies and gold. A sleeveless dalmatic, it was clasped on the shoulders with two gold lion-masks, worn at their weddings by three kings of Macedon. The hot afternoon sun slanted down from a high window on the lions' emerald eyes. The new Philip gazed at it in rapture.

Meleager said, 'Let me help you put it on.'

He raised it, and slipped it over Philip's head. Radiant with pleasure, he looked out at the cheering men. 'Thank you,' he said, as he had been taught when he was a child.

The cheers redoubled. The son of Philip had come in with dignity, looking like a king. At first he must simply have been abashed and modest. Now they were for the royal blood against the world.

'Philip! Philip! Long live Philip!'

Ptolemy felt almost choked with grief and anger. He remembered the wedding morning, when he and Hephaistion had gone to Alexander's room in the Susa palace to dress the bridegroom. They had exchanged the jokes which were traditional, along with private ones of their own. Alexander, who had been planning for weeks this great ceremony of racial concord, had been almost incandescent; one could have taken him for a man in love. It was Hephaistion who had remembered the lion brooches and pinned them on the robe. To see it now on a grinning idiot made Ptolemy long to split Meleager on his sword. Towards the poor fool himself he felt horror rather than anger. He knew him well; he had often gone, when Alexander was busy, to make sure he was not neglected or ill-used; such things, it was tacitly agreed, were better kept in the family. Philip ...! Yes, it would stick.

He said to Perdikkas, who was beside him, 'Alexander should have had him smothered.'

Perdikkas, unheeding, strode forward, blazing with rage, trying vainly to be heard above the din. Pointing at Philip, he made a sweeping gesture of rejection and scorn.

Shouts of support came from just below him. The Companions, foremost by right of rank, had had the clearest view. They had heard of the fool; they had watched, in silent grief or sheer incredulity, the assumption of the robe. Now their outrage found vent. Their strong voices, trained in the piercing war-paean of the charging cavalry, overpowered all other sound.

It was as if the robe of Alexander had been a battle standard, suddenly unfurled. Men started to put their helmets on. The hammering of spears on shields grew to a volume like the sound of onset. Nearer, more deadly, came the hiss and whisper of the Companions' unsheathed swords.

In alarm Meleager saw the powerful aristocracy of Macedon rallying in force against him. Even his own faction might fall off from him, unless forced to commit themselves beyond retreat. Each common soldier now shouting 'Philip!' was, after all, the tribesman of some lord. He must divide them from tribal allegiances, create new action. With the thought, the answer came to him. His own genius amazed him. How could Alexander have passed such a leader by?

Firmly, but imperceptibly, he guided the smiling Philip to the edge of the dais. The impression that he meant to speak procured a moment's quiet, if only from curiosity. Meleager spoke into it.

'Macedonians! You have chosen your King! Do you mean to stand by him?' The spearmen replied with defiant cheers. 'Then come with him now, and help him confirm his right. A king of Macedon must entomb his predecessor.'

He paused. He had real silence now. A ripple of shock could almost be felt, passing through the packed, sweat-stinking hall.

Meleager lifted his voice. 'Come! The body of Alexander awaits its rites. Here is the heir to perform them. Don't let them cheat him of his heritage. To the death-chamber! Come!'

There was confused, seething movement. The sounds had changed. The most determined of the infantry surged forward; but they did not cheer. Many held back; there was a deep mutter of opposing voices. Companions began to clamber on the dais, to guard the inner doors. The generals, all trying to protest at once, only added to the confusion. Suddenly, rising above everything, came the cracked new-broken voice of a youth, hoarse with passionate fury.

'Bastards! You bastards! You filthy, slave-born bastards!'

From a corner of the hall alongside the Companions, shoving through everyone regardless of age or rank, yelling as if in battle, came the Royal Squires.

The watch on duty had been with Alexander till he died, standing on after sunrise. They had been several years in attendance on him. Some of them had turned eighteen and had a vote, the rest had crowded into Assembly with them. They leaped and scrambled up on the dais, waving their drawn swords, wild-eyed, crop-headed, their fair Macedonian hair shorn raggedly almost to their scalps in mourning. There were nearly fifty of them. Perdikkas, seeing their fanatic rage, knew them at sight for the readiest killers in the hall. Unless stopped they would have Philip dead, and then there would be a massacre. 'To me!' he shouted to them. 'Follow me! Protect the body of Alexander!'

He ran to the inner door, Ptolemy neck and neck with him, the other generals close behind, and then the Squires, so fierce in their rush that they outdistanced the Companions. Pursued by the angry cries of the opposition, they ran through the King's reception room, through his private sanctum, and on into the Bed-chamber. The doors were closed, not locked. The foremost men burst through them.

Ptolemy thought, with a shuddering realization, He has lain here since yesterday! In Babylon, in midsummer. Unconsciously, as the doors burst open, he held his breath.

There was a faint scent of almost burned-out incense; of the dried flowers and herbs which scented the royal robes and bed, mixed with the scent of the living presence which Ptolemy had known since boyhood. In the vast forsaken room he lay on the great bed between its watchful daimons, a clean fresh sheet drawn over him. Some aromatic sprinkled on it had cheated even the flies. On the dais, half-propped against the bed with an arm thrown over it, the Persian boy lay in an exhausted sleep.

Roused by the clamour, he staggered dazedly to his feet, unaware of Ptolemy's touch upon his shoulder. Ptolemy walked to the bed's head and folded back the sheet.

Alexander lay in an inscrutable composure. Even his colour seemed hardly changed. His golden hair with its bright silver streaks felt, to the touch, still charged with life. Niarchos and Seleukos, who had followed Ptolemy, exclaimed that it was a miracle, that it proved Alexander's divinity. Ptolemy, who had been his fellow-student with Aristotle, looked down in silence, wondering how long a secret spark of that strong life had burned in the still body. He laid a hand on the heart; but it was over now, the corpse was stiffening. He drew the sheet over the marmoreal face, and turned to the ranks that were forming to hold the bolted doors.

The Squires, who knew the room in detail, dragged up the heavy clothes-chests to form a barricade. But it could not last for long. The men outside were well used to pushing. Six or seven deep, they leaned upon the doors as, ten years back, they had leaned with their fifteen-foot sarissas on Darius' levies; and, like the Persians at the Granikos, at Issos, at Gaugamela, the doors gave way. Grinding along the floor, the bronze-bound chests were heaved aside.

As the foremost thrust in, Perdikkas knew himself unable to cut them down, and be first with the shame of bloodshed in this room. He called back his men to bar the way to the royal bed. In a brief pause, the attackers looked about them. The ranks of the defenders screened the body, they saw only the spread wings of the gold daimons and their fierce alien eyes. They shouted defiance, but came no nearer.

There was movement behind them. Philip came in.

Though Meleager was with him, he was here of his own accord. When a person died, his family must see to him. All motives of policy had passed over Philip like unmeaning noise; but he knew his duty.

'Where's Alexander?' he called to the bristling barrier before the bed. 'I'm his brother. I want to bury him.'

The generals gritted their teeth in silence. It was the Squires whose yells of wrath and spat-out insults broke the loaded pause. They had no reverence for the dead, because in their central consciousness Alexander was still alive. They shouted for him as if he were lying on a battlefield senseless with wounds, beset by cowards who would not have faced him on his feet. Their whoops and war-cries set off all the young men in the Companions, who remembered their own days as Squires. 'Alexander! Alexander!'

From somewhere in the press, making a little whiffling sound as the spinstrap launched it, a javelin hurtled across and rang on Perdikkas' helmet.

In moments more were flying. A Companion knelt pouring blood from a severed leg-vein; a squire who had come helmetless had a slashed scalp and was masked in scarlet, his blue eyes staring through. Till it came to close quarters, the defenders were sitting game. They had brought only their short curved cavalry sabres, symbol of their rank, to what should have been a purely civil occasion.

Perdikkas picked up the javelin that had struck him and hurled it back. Others, plucking them from the bodies of the wounded, held them to serve as spears. Ptolemy, taking a step back to avoid a missile, collided with someone, cursed, and turned to look. It was the Persian boy, blood staining his linen sleeve from a gashed arm. He had thrown it up to ward a javelin from Alexander's body.

'Stop!' shouted Ptolemy across the room. 'Are we wild beasts or men?'

From beyond the doors, the hubbub still continued; but it trailed off, damped by the hush of those in front to a kind of shamefaced muttering. It was Niarchos the Cretan who said, 'Let them look.'

Grasping their weapons, the defenders made a gap. Niarchos uncovered Alexander's face and stood back, silent.

The opposing line fell still. The crowd behind, jostling to see, felt the change and paused. Presently in the front a grizzled phalanx captain stepped a pace forward and took his helmet off. Two or three veterans followed. The first faced around to the men behind him, lifted his arm and shouted, 'Halt!' Sombrely, in a kind of sullen grief, the parties looked at one another.

By ones and twos the senior officers unhelmed themselves and stood forth to be known. The defenders lowered their weapons. The old captain began to speak.

'There's my brother!' Philip, who had been elbowed aside, pushed forward. He still had on the robe of Alexander, pushed askew and crumpled. 'He has to have a funeral.'

'Be quiet!' hissed Meleager. Obediently – moments like this were familiar in his life – Philip let himself be hustled out of sight. The old captain, red-faced, recovered his presence of mind.

'Gentlemen,' he said, 'you are outnumbered, as you see. We have all acted in haste, and I daresay we all regret it. I propose a parley.'

Perdikkas said, 'On one condition. The body of the King shall be left inviolate, and every man here shall swear it by the Gods Below. I will take my oath that when a fitting bier is ready, I will have it taken to the royal burial ground in Macedon. Unless these vows are solemnized, none of us will leave this place while we can stand and fight.'

They agreed. They were all ashamed. Perdikkas' words about the royal burial ground had brought them sharply down to earth. What would they have done with the body if they had taken it? Buried it in the park? One look at that remote proud face had sobered them. A miracle he was not stinking; yet you would have thought he was still alive. A superstitious shiver had run down many backs; Alexander would make a powerful ghost.

On the terrace a goat was slaughtered; men touched the carcass or the blood, invoking the curse of Hades if they were forsworn. Owing to their numbers it took some time; as twilight fell they were still swearing by torchlight.

Meleager, the first to swear under Perdikkas' eye, watched, brooding. He had lost support and knew it. Only some thirty, the hard core of his partisans, still rallied round him; and even those because they were now marked men, frightened of reprisals. He must keep them, at least. While the sunset dusk hummed with the noises of an anxious fermenting city, he had been giving the matter thought. If he could separate the Bodyguard ... thirty to only eight ...

The last men had scrambled through their oaths. He approached Perdikkas with a sober placating face. 'I acted rashly. The King's death has overset us all. Tomorrow we can meet and take better counsel.'

'So I hope.' Perdikkas frowned under his dark brows.

'All of us would be ashamed,' went on Meleager smoothly, 'if the near friends of Alexander were kept from watching beside him. I beg you' – his gesture embraced the Bodyguard – 'return and keep your vigil.'

'Thank you,' said Niarchos, quite sincerely. He had hoped to do it. Perdikkas paused, his soldier's instinct indefinably wary. It was Ptolemy who said, 'Meleager has taken his oath to respect Alexander's body. Has he taken one for ours?'

Perdikkas' eyes sought Meleager's, which shifted in spite of him. All together, with looks of profound contempt, the Bodyguard walked off to join the Companions encamped in the royal park.

Presently they sent messengers to the Egyptian quarter, summoning the embalmers to begin their work at dawn.

'Where were you all day, Konon?' said Philip, as his hot clothes were lifted off him. 'Why didn't they fetch you when I said?'

Konon, an elderly veteran who had served him for ten years, said, 'I was at Assembly, sir. Never mind, you shall have your nice bath now, with the scented oil.'

'I'm King now, Konon. Did they tell you I'm the King?'

'Yes, sir. Long life to you, sir.'

'Konon, now I'm King, you won't go away?'

'No, sir, old Konon will look after you. Now let me have this beautiful new robe to brush it and keep it safe. It's too good for every day ... Why, come, come, sir, you've no call to cry.'

In the royal bedchamber, as the evening cooled, the body of Alexander stiffened like stone. With a bloodstained towel round his arm, the Persian boy put by the bed the night-table of malachite and ivory, and kindled the night-lamp on it. The floor was strewn with the debris of the fighting. Someone had lurched against the console with the images of Hephaistion; they lay sprawled like the fallen after a battle. In the faint light, Bagoas took a long look at them, and turned away. But in a few minutes he went back and stood them up neatly, each in its place. Then, fetching a stool lest sitting on the dais he might sleep again, he folded his hands and composed himself to watch, his dark eyes staring into the dark shadows.

The harem at Susa was Persian, not Assyrian. Its proportions were elegantly balanced; its fluted columns had capitals sculpted with lotus buds by craftsmen from Greece; its walls were faced with delicately enamelled tiles, and the sunlight dappled them through lattices of milky alabaster.

Queen Sisygambis, the mother of Darius, sat in her high-backed chair, a granddaughter on either side. At eighty she kept the hawk-nosed, ivorine face of the old Elamite nobility; the pure Persian strain, unmixed with Median. She was brittle now; in her youth she had been tall. She was robed and scarved in deep indigo, but for her breast, on which glowed a great necklace of polished pigeon-blood rubies, the gift of King Poros to Alexander, and of Alexander to her.

Stateira, the elder girl, was reading a letter aloud, slowly, translating it from Greek to Persian. Alexander had had both girls taught to read Greek as well as speak it. From affection for him, Sisygambis had allowed him to indulge this whim, though in her view clerking was somewhat menial, and more properly left to the palace eunuchs. However, he must be allowed the customs of his people. He could not help his upbringing, and was never purposely discourteous. He should have been a Persian.

Stateira read, stumbling a little, not from ignorance but from agitation.

ALEXANDER, KING OF THE MACEDONIANS AND LORD OF ASIA, to his honoured wife Stateira.

Wishing to look upon your face again, I desire you to set out for Babylon without delay, so that your child may be born here. If you bear a boy, I intend to proclaim him my heir. Hasten your journey. I have been sick, and my people tell me there is ignorant talk that I am dead. Do you pay no heed to it. My chamberlains are commanded to receive you with honour, as the mother of a Great King to be. Bring Drypetis your sister, who is my sister also for the sake of one who was dear to me as myself. May all be well with you.

Stateira lowered the letter, and looked down at her grandmother. The child of two tall parents, she stood nearly six feet without her slippers. Much of her mother's famous beauty had passed to her. She was queenly in everything but pride. 'What shall we do?' she said.

Sisybambis looked up impatiently under her white brows. 'First finish the King's letter.'

'Madam grandmother, that is all.'

'No,' said Sisygambis with irritation. 'Look again, child. What does he say to *me*?'

'Madam grandmother, that is the end.'

'You must be mistaken. Women should not meddle with writing; I told him so, but he would have his way. You had better call a clerk, to read it properly.'

'Truly, there is no more writing paper. *May all be well with you*. See, it stops here.'

The strong lines of Sisygambis' face slackened a little; her years showed like sickness. 'Is the messenger still here? Fetch him, see if he has another letter. These men tire on the road and it makes them stupid.'

The rider was brought, gulping from his meal. He pledged his head he had received one letter only, one from the King. He shook out his wallet before them.

When he had gone, Sisygambis said, 'Never has he sent to Susa without a word to me. Show me the seal.' But her sight had lengthened with age, and even at arms' length she could not make out the figure.

'It is his likeness, madam grandmother. It is like the one on my emerald, that he gave me on my wedding day; only here he has a wreath, and on mine he wears a diadem.'

Sisygambis nodded, and sat awhile in silence. There were earlier royal letters in the care of the head chamberlain; but she did not like to let such people know that her eyes were failing.

Presently she said, 'He writes that he has been sick. He will be behind-hand with all his business. Now he is overtaxing himself, as his nature is. When he was here, I saw he was short of breath ... Go child, fetch me your women; you too, Drypetis. I must tell them what to pack for you.'

Young Drypetis, the widow of Hephaistion (she was seventeen) moved to obey, then ran back to kneel beside the chair. 'Baba, please come with us to Babylon.'

Sisygambis rested her fine-boned old ivory hand on the young girl's head. 'The King has told you to hurry on the road. I am too old. And besides, he has not summoned me.'

When the women had been instructed, and all the flurry had moved to the girls' bedchamber, she sat on in her straight-backed chair, tears trickling down her cheeks and falling upon King Poros' rubies.

In the royal bedchamber of Babylon, now redolent of spices and of nitre, the Egyptians who were the heirs of their fathers' art pursued the elaborate task of embalming the latest Pharaoh. Shocked at the delay which would surely undo their skill, they had tiptoed in by dawnlight, and beheld the corpse with awed amazement. As their slaves brought in the instruments, the vessels and fluids and aromatics of their art, the single watcher, a white-faced Persian youth, extinguished his lamp and vanished like a ghost in silence.

Before slitting the torso to remove the entrails, they remembered, far though they were from the Valley of the Kings, to lift their hands in the traditional prayer, that it might be lawful for mortals to handle the body of a god.

The narrow streets of ancient Babylon hummed with rumour and counter-rumour. There were lamps burning all night. Days passed; the armies of Perdikkas and Meleager waited in armed truce; the infantry around the palace, the cavalry in the royal park, beside the horse-lines where Nebuchadrezzar had kept his chariots for the lion-hunt.

Outnumbered four to one, they had discussed moving to the plains outside, where there was room for horse to deploy. 'No,' said Perdikkas. 'That would concede defeat. Give them time to take a look at their booby King. They'll come round. Alexander's army has never been divided.'

On the parade ground and in the palace gardens, the men of the phalanx bivouacked as best they could. Stubbornly they clung to their victors' pride and their rooted xenophobia. No barbarian should rule their sons, they told each other across the camp fires, where their Persian women, whom Alexander had induced them to marry lawfully, were stirring their supper pots. They had long ago spent Alexander's dowries; not one man in a hundred meant to take home his woman when he was paid-off.

They thought with confused resentment of the young bloods in the Companions, drinking and hunting beside the sons of Persian lords with their curled beards and inlaid weapons and bedizened horses. It was well enough for the cavalry; *they* could afford to Persianize without losing face. But the foot-men, sons of Macedonian farmers, herdsmen and hunters, masons and carpenters, owned only what the wars had won them, their little hoards of loot, and, above all, the just reward for all their toils and dangers, the knowledge that whoever their fathers might have been, they were Alexander's Macedonians, masters of the world. Clinging to this treasure of self-esteem, they spoke well of Philip, his modesty, his likeness to his great father, his pure Macedonian blood.

Their officers, whose affairs took them into the royal presence, came back increasingly taciturn. The enormous business of Alexander's empire could not come to a standstill. Envoys, tax-collectors, shipbuilders, officers of the commissariat, architects, disputing satraps seeking arbitration, still appeared in the anterooms; indeed, in augmented numbers, many having waited for audience through Alexander's illness. Not only had they to be dealt with; they had to find a visible, believable King.

Before each appearance, Meleager briefed Philip carefully. He had learned to go, unled, straight to his throne, without wandering off to speak to some chance person who had caught his eye; to keep his voice down so that he was seen, but not heard to speak, enabling Meleager beside him to proclaim suitable replies. He had learned not to call while enthroned for lemonade or sweets, or to ask permission from his guard of honour when he wanted to go outside. His scratching himself, picking his nose and fidgeting could never be quite controlled; but if his appearances were kept short, he presented as a rule a quiet and sober figure.

Meleager had appointed himself to the post of Chiliarch, or Grand Vizier, created for Hephaistion and inherited by Perdikkas. Standing at the King's right hand, flamboyantly panoplied, he knew that he looked impressive; but he knew too, all too well, what a soldier thinks when the chief to whom he has come for orders speak through an intermediary and never looks him in the face. His officers, all of whom had had free access to Alexander, could not be kept out; nor could the royal guard. And all of them, he felt it through his skin, were looking at the stout stocky figure on the throne, the slack mouth and wandering stare, and seeing in mind's eye the dynamic vanished presence, the alert responsive face, the serene authority, that now lay stilled for ever in the locked bedchamber, submerged in the embalmers' bath of nitre, preparing to abide the centuries.

Beyond all this, Persian officers appointed by Alexander could not be refused audience, and were not fools. The thought of a concerted rising, against a mutinous divided army, gave him waking nightmares.

Like other men who have indulged a long rancorous hate, he blamed all adversity upon its object, never considering that his hatred, not his enemy, had created his predicament. Like other such men before and after him, he saw only one remedy, and resolved to seek it.

Philip was still in his old apartments, which, having been chosen for him by Alexander, were pleasant and cool, at least for Babylon in midsummer. When Meleager had tried to move him into more regal quarters, he had refused with shouts so loud that the palace guard had come running, thinking murder was being done. Here Meleager sought him, taking with him a kinsman, a certain Duris, who carried writing things.

The King was occupied happily with his stones. He had a chest full, collected over thousands of miles of Asia as he trailed along after the army; pebbles he had picked up for himself, mixed with bits of amber, quartz, agate, old seals, and coloured glass jewels from Egypt, which Alexander or Ptolemy or Hephaistion had brought him when they happened to remember. He had arranged them in a long winding path across the room, and was on his knees and hands improving it.

At Meleager's entrance he scrambled guiltily to his feet, clutching a favourite lump of Scythian turquoise, which he hid behind his back lest it be taken away.

'Sire!' said Meleager harshly.

Philip, recognizing this as a severe rebuke, hastened over to the most important chair, carefully stuffing the turquoise under the cushion.

'Sir,' said Meleager standing over him, 'I have come to tell you that you are in grave danger. No, don't be afraid, I will defend you. But the traitor Perdikkas, who tried to steal Alexander's body and rob you of the throne, is plotting to take your life, and make himself King.'

Philip jumped to his feet, stammering incoherently. Presently Meleager made out, 'He said ... Alexander *said* ... He can be King if he wants to. I don't mind. Alexander told me they mustn't make me King.'

With some trouble, Meleager freed his arm from a grip he had feared would break it. 'Sir, if he is King his first act will be to kill you. Your only safety is in killing *him*. See, here is the paper ordering his death.' Duris set it, with pen and ink, upon the table. 'Just write PHILIP here, as I taught you. I will help you, if you like.'

'And then you'll kill him before he kills me?'

'Yes, and all our troubles will be over. Write it here.'

The blot with which he began did not efface the writing; and he produced, after that, a quite tolerable signature.

Perdikkas' lodging was one of the grace-and-favour houses built in the royal park by the Persian kings, and bestowed on his friends by Alexander. Around it were encamped the Royal Squires. They had attached themselves to Perdikkas as Alexander's chosen Regent. Though they had not offered to wait upon his person, and he had known better than to ask it, they rode with his messages, and guarded him in their accustomed rota by day and night.

He was consulting with Ptolemy when one of them came in. 'Sir. An old man is asking for you.'

'Thirty at least,' said Ptolemy flippantly. Perdikkas said crisply, 'Well?' 'He says, sir, he's the servant of Arridaios.' The honorific Philip was not used on the Companions' side of the river. 'He says it's urgent.'

'Is his name Konon?' said Ptolemy sharply. 'Perdikkas, I know this man. You had better see him.'

'So I intended.' Perdikkas spoke rather stiffly. He found Ptolemy too easygoing and informal, traits which Alexander had regrettably not discouraged. 'Bring him in, but search him for weapons first.'

Old Konon, profoundly ill at ease, gave an old soldier's salute, stood to attention, and said nothing till given leave.

'Sir, with permission. They've made my poor master sign a paper against you. I was in his bedroom, seeing to his things, they never thought to look. Sir, don't hold him to blame. They took advantage of him. He never meant harm to you, not of his own accord.'

'I believe you,' said Perdikkas frowning. 'But it seems that harm is done.'

'Sir. If he falls into your hands, don't kill him, sir. He was never any trouble, not in King Alexander's day.'

'Rest assured we have no such wish.' This man could be useful, his charge more useful still. 'When the army returns to duty, I will have your master well cared for. Do you want to stay with him?'

'Sir, yes sir. I've been with him nearly from a boy. I don't know how he'd go on without me.'

'Very good. Permission granted. Tell him, if he will understand you, that he has nothing to fear from me.'

'I will, sir, and God bless you.' He left, saluting smartly.

'An easy favour,' said Perdikkas to Ptolemy. 'Did he think we could afford to kill Alexander's brother? Meleager, now . . .'

Later, his day's business done, Perdikkas was sitting down to supper when raised voices sounded outside. From the window he saw a company of a hundred foot-soldiers. The squires on duty numbered sixteen.

He was too old a campaigner to have changed into a supper-robe. In moments, with the speed of two decades' practice, he had whipped his corselet from the stand and clasped it on. A panting squire dashed in, saluting with one hand while the other waved a paper.

'Sir! It's a summons from the rebels. A royal warrant they call it.'

'Royal, eh?' said Perdikkas calmly. The missive was brief; he read it aloud.

PHILIP SON OF PHILIP KING OF THE MACEDONIANS AND LORD OF ASIA. To the former Chiliarch Perdikkas. You are hereby summoned to appear before me, to answer a charge of treason. If you resist, the escort has orders to use force.

'Sir, we can hold them. Do you want a message sent?'

Not for nothing had Perdikkas served directly under Alexander. He laid his hand on the boy's shoulder, shaping his austere face into the needed smile. 'Good lad. No, no message. Guard, stand to arms. I will talk to this

squad of Meleager's.' The squire's salute had the faint reflection of a
remembered ardour. Perhaps, thought Perdikkas, I can show Acting
Chiliarch Meleager why I, and not he, got promoted to the Bodyguard.

He had had twelve years to absorb a basic Alexander precept: Do it with
style. Unlike Alexander, he had had to work for it, but he knew what it was
worth. On his own account, needing instruction from no one, he could
deliver a memorable dressing-down.

Striding bareheaded on to the porch, the summons in his hand, he
paused formidably for effect, and began to speak.

He had recognized the officer – he had a good general's memory – and
reviewed in detail the last campaign in which they had all served under
his own command. Alexander had once spoken highly of them. What did
they suppose themselves to be doing, disgracing themselves like this; they
who had once been men, and even, God help them, soldiers? Could they
face Alexander now? Even before he was King, the wittol bastard had been
used in intrigue against him; anyone else would have had him put out of
the way; but he in the greatness of his heart had cared for him as a
harmless innocent. If King Philip had wished a fool to bear his name, he
would have said so. King Philip! King Ass. Who would believe that men
of Alexander's could come here as servants of Meleager, a man he had
known too well to trust with a division, to sell the life of the man he himself
had chosen to command them? Let them go back to their comrades, and
remind them who they had been, and what they had sunk to now. Let
them ask themselves how they liked it. They could now dismiss.

After an uneasy, shuffling, silence the troop captain rapped out gruffly,
'About turn! March.'

Meantime, the squires on watch had been joined by every squire in
hearing. When the troop departed, they gathered round Perdikkas and
cheered. Without effort this time, he returned their triumphant grins.
Almost, for a moment, he felt like Alexander.

No, he thought as he went in. People used to eat *him* alive. They had
to touch him, his hands, his clothes. I've seen them fighting to reach him.
Those fools at Opis, when he'd forgiven them for rioting, demanded the
right to kiss him ... Well, that was his mystery, which I shall never have.
But then, nor will anyone else.

Slowly, against the stream, the rowers' labour lightened sometimes by
a flaw of wind from the south, the canopied barge meandered along the
Tigris. On linen cushions stuffed with wool and down, waving their fans,
the two princesses stretched like young cats, luxuriating in smooth movement and the cool air off the water, after the jolting heat of their covered
wagon. Within the awning, their duenna was fast asleep. Along the

towpath trundled the wagon and the baggage-cart. the escort of armed mounted eunuchs, the muleteers and the household slaves. When the caravan passed a village, all the peasants would gather on the bank to stare.

'If only,' sighed Stateira, 'he had not told us to hurry. One could go nearly all the way by water, down river instead to the Gulf, and up the Euphrates to Babylon.' She settled the cushions in her back, which had the ache of pregnancy.

Drypetis, fingering her dark-blue widow's veil, looked over her shoulder to be sure the duenna was sleeping. 'Will he give me another husband?'

'I don't know.' Stateira looked away at the river bank. 'Don't ask him yet. He won't like it. He thinks you still belong to Hephaistion. He won't let Hephaistion's regiment ever have another name.' Feeling a desolate silence behind her, she said, 'If I have a boy, I'll ask him.' She lay back in the cushions and closed her eyes.

The sun, splintering through tall clumps of papyrus, made shifting patterns in the rose-red light that filtered through her eyelids. It was like the sun-glowing crimson curtains of the wedding pavilion at Susa. Her face burned, as always when the memory came back to her.

She had been, of course, presented to the King before. Grandmother had ensured that she made the deepest curtsey, before he took his tall chair and she her low one. But the wedding ritual could not be evaded; it had followed the Persian rite. She had been led in by her dead mother's brother, a fine tall man. Then the King had risen from his chair of state, as the bridegroom must, to greet her with a kiss and lead her to the chair beside him. She had performed, for the kiss, the little genuflexion Grandmamma had taught her; but then she had had to stand up, there was no way out of it. She was half a head taller, and ready to die of shame.

When the trumpets had sounded, and the herald announced that they were man and wife, it was Drypetis' turn. The King's friend, Hephaistion, had stood up and come forward, the most beautiful man she had ever seen, stately and tall – with his dark-gold hair, he could have been one of the fair Persians – and taken her sister's hand, matching her height to a hair. All the King's friends, the other bridegrooms, had given a kind of sigh; she knew that when the King had stepped out to meet her they had been holding their breath. At the end, he and she had had to lead out the procession to the bridal chambers. She had wished that the earth might swallow her.

In the crimson pavilion with its golden bed, he had likened her to a daughter of the gods (her Greek was quite good by then), and she had seen that he meant well; but since nothing could do away those dreadful moments, she would have preferred him to keep silence. His was a powerful presence, and she was shy; though the defect was his, it was she who had felt like an ungainly tentpole. All she had been able to think about in the marriage bed was that her father had run away in battle, and Grandmother would never speak his name. She must redeem the honour of her house by courage. He had been kind, and hardly hurt her; but it had all been so strange, so overpowering, she could hardly utter a word. No wonder she had not conceived, and that though he had paid her visits of compliment while still at Susa, and brought her gifts, he had never once had her to bed again.

To crown these miseries, she had known that somewhere in the palace was the King's Baktrian wife, whom he had taken along to India. A stranger to sexual pleasure, Stateira knew no sexual jealousy; but its fiercest torments could hardly have been more wounding than her thoughts of Roxane, Little Star, favourite and confidante. She pictured them lying side by side in tender love-making, intimate talk, amusing gossip, laughter – perhaps at her. As for Bagoas the Persian, she had heard nothing of him at her father's court, and nothing since. She had been carefully brought up.

The King's sojourn at Susa had gone by, its great political events dimly heard of and little understood. Then he had gone on his summer progress to Ekbatana. He had called to take leave of her (would he have done even that, except to see Grandmother?) without a word of when he would send for her or where. He had gone, taking the Baktrian woman; and she had cried all night from shame and anger.

But last spring, when he had come to Susa after the mountain war, it had all been different; no ceremony, no crowds. He had been shut up alone with Grandmother, and it almost seemed that she had heard him weeping. In the evening they had all dined together; they were his family, he said. He looked lean, weather-beaten and weary; but he talked, as she had never heard him do before.

At the first sight of Drypetis in her widow's veil, his face had frozen in a dreadful grief; but he had covered it quickly, and enthralled them with tales of India, its marvels and its customs. Then he spoke of his plans to explore the coast of Arabia, to make a road along north Africa and extend his empire westward. And he had said, 'So much to do, so little time. My mother was right; long before now, I should have begotten an heir.'

He had looked at her; and she had known it was she, not the Baktrian, who was the chosen one. She had come to him in a passion of gratitude, which had proved as efficacious as any other ardour.

Soon after he had gone, she knew that she had conceived, and Grandmother had sent him word. It was good that he had summoned her to Babylon. If he was still sick, she would tend him with her own hands. She would make no jealous scenes about the Baktrian. A King was entitled to his concubines; and, as Grandmother had warned her, much trouble could spring from quarrels in the harem.

The soldiers sent to arrest Perdikkas had taken his advice. They had considered what had become of them; and they did not like it. They went among their comrades, reporting his courage and their discomfiture; and relating, what he himself had first revealed to them, that Meleager had meant to have his head. They had been anxious, restless, volatile. While Meleager was still digesting failure, suddenly they were roaring at his doors like a human sea. The guards on duty abandoned their posts and joined them.

In a cold sweat, he saw himself dying, like a boar at bay, in a ring of spears. With the speed of desperation, he made for the royal rooms.

In a cheerful lamplight, Philip was seated at his evening meal, a favourite dish, spiced venison with pumpkin fritters. A jug of lemonade stood by him; he was not reliable if given wine. When Meleager burst in, he expressed annoyance with his eyes, since his mouth was full. Konon, who was waiting at table, looked up sharply. He was wearing his old sword; he had heard the noise.

'Sir,' panted Meleager, 'the traitor Perdikkas has repented, and the soldiers want him spared. Please go and tell them you have pardoned him.'

Philip bolted his mouthful to reply indignantly, 'I can't come now, I'm having my dinner.'

Konon took a step forward. Looking Meleager in the eye, he said, 'He was taken advantage of.' His hand rested, as if by chance, on his well-polished sword belt.

Keeping his head, Meleager said, 'My good man, the King will be safer on his throne than anywhere else in Babylon. You know that; you were at Assembly. Sir, come at once.' A persuasive argument occurred to him. 'Your brother would have done so.'

Philip put down his knife and wiped his mouth. 'Is that right, Konon? Would Alexander go?'

Konon's hand fell to his side. 'Yes, sir. Yes, he would go.'

As he was steered to the door, Philip looked back regretfully at his dinner-plate, and wondered why Konon was wiping his eyes.

The army was placated for the time, but far from satisfied. Audiences in the throne-room were going badly. The envoys' regrets for the late King's untimely death grew less formal and more pointed. Meleager felt his power increasingly unstable, and discipline crumbling by the day.

Meantime, the cavalry had taken counsel. Suddenly one morning they were found to have disappeared. The park was empty of everything but horse-droppings. They had made their way through the crumbling outer walls, and deployed to invest the city. Babylon was under siege.

Much of the terrain outside was swampy; it needed no great force to close the solid causeways and the firm open ground. As planned, the refugees were unmolested. At all the gates, with a hubbub of shouting men, wailing children, burbling camels, bleating goats and cackling poultry, the country people who feared war were pouring into the city, and the city people who feared famine were pouring out.

Meleager could have dealt with a foreign enemy. But he knew too well that he could no longer trust his troops for even the briefest contact with their former comrades. They were forgetting the threat of unborn barbarian heirs, and homesick for the familiar discipline of the old triumphant days, the officers who had linked them to Alexander. Less than a month ago, they had been limbs of a well-knit body directed by a fiery spirit. Now each man felt his isolation in a foreign world. Soon they would take revenge for it.

In this extremity, he went to consult Eumenes.

Throughout the turmoil since Alexander's death, the Secretary had gone quietly about his business. A man of humble origins, discovered and trained by Philip, advanced by Alexander, he had been, and remained, uncommitted in the present strife. He had neither joined the Companions nor denounced them. His work, he said, was to carry on the kingdom's business. He had helped with replies to the envoys and embassies, drawing on his records, and had drafted letters in the name of Philip, but without the title of King (it had been added by Meleager). When pressed to take sides, he would only say that he was a Greek, and politics were the concern of the Macedonians.

Meleager found him at his writing table, dictating to his clerk, who was taking it down on wax.

Next day he bathed agin, and sacrificed the appointed offerings, and after the sacrifice remained in constant fever. Yet even so, he sent for the officers, and ordered them to see that everything was ready for the expedition. He bathed again in the evening, and after that became gravely ill ...

'Eumenes,' said Meleager, who had been standing ignored in the doorway, 'let the dead rest awhile. You are needed by the living.'

'The living need the truth, before rumour pollutes it.' He motioned to his clerk, who folded his tablet and went out. Meleager outlined his dilemma, aware as he went on that the Secretary had long since assessed it all, and was waiting impatiently for him to finish. He trailed to a lame conclusion.

Eumenes said without emotion, 'My opinion, since you ask it, is that it is not too late to seek a compromise. And it is too late for anything else.'

Meleager had already been driven to this view, but wanted to have it confirmed by someone else, whom he could blame if things went wrong. 'I accept your advice. That is, if the men agree.'

Eumenes said drily, 'Perhaps the King can persuade them.'

Meleager ignored the double edge. 'One man could do it; yourself. Your honour is unquestioned, your experience known. Will you address the Macedonians?'

Eumenes had long since taken his measure. His own sole loyalty was to the house of Philip and Alexander, who had lifted him from obscurity to prestige and power. Had Philip Arridaios been competent, he would have felt divided loyalties; but he knew what the elder Philip had thought about that, and was for the son of Alexander, unborn, unseen. Yet Philip was the son of Philip his benefactor, who had seen fit to acknowledge him; and Eumenes would protect him if he could. He was a dry, cool man, whose inward feelings few suspected; he had no taste for protestations. He said, 'Very well.'

He was well received. A man in his fifties, spare and erect, with the subtler features of the south yet a soldier's bearing, he said what was needed and no more. He made no attempt to emulate Alexander, whose sense of his audience had been an artist's gift. Eumenes' talent was for sounding reasonable, and keeping to the point. Reassured by hearing their confused misgivings reduced to logic, the Assembly accepted his conclusions with relief. Envoys were sent to the camp of Perdikkas, to treat for terms. As they rode out at sunrise from the Ishtar gate, crowds of anxious Babylonians watched them off.

They were back before noon. Perdikkas would raise the siege and reconcile the armies, as soon as Meleager and his accomplices gave themselves up to justice.

By now, any discipline still left among the troops in Babylon was self-imposed from dim feelings of dignity, depending chiefly on the popularity of any officer concerned. The returning envoys shouted back their message to anyone who stopped them in the street to ask. While Meleager was still reading Perdikkas' letter, the troops were pouring into the Hall of Audience, having called their own Assembly.

Eumenes in his business room listened to the rumble of conflicting voices, and the scrape of boot-nails continuing the ruin of the marble floor. A stair in the thickness of the wall had a window which overlooked the Hall. He saw that the soldiers had not come armed only with token weapons; despite the heat, they had on their corselets; helmets were worn, not held. A visible division was starting; on one side the men who were for accepting the conditions; on the other, alarmed and angry, those who had committed themselves irretrievably to Meleager. The rest were waiting to have their minds made up for them. This, Eumenes thought, is how civil wars begin. He made his way to the royal rooms.

Meleager was there, standing over Philip and coaching him in a speech. Philip, more aware of his sweating desperation than of anything he said, was fidgeting, not taking in a word. 'What,' asked Eumenes bluntly, 'are you telling him to say?'

Meleager's light-blue eyes, always prominent, were now bloodshot too. 'To say no, of course.'

In the level voice to which even Alexander in anger had paid attention, Eumenes said, 'If he says that, swords will be out before you can take breath. Have you looked in the Hall? Look now.'

A big, heavy hand clutched Eumenes' shoulder. He turned, startled. It had never occurred to him that Philip would be strong.

'I don't want to say it. I can't remember it. Tell him I've forgotten.'

'Never mind,' said Eumenes quietly. 'We will think of something else.'

The royal fanfare made a brief silence in the hall. Philip came forward, Eumenes just behind him.

'Macedonians!' He paused, reminding himself of the words the kind, calm man had taught him. 'There is no need for strife. The peacemakers will be the victors here.' He almost turned round for approval; but the kind man had told him not to.

A pleased murmur went round the hall. The King had sounded just like anyone else.

'Do not condemn free citizens ...' prompted Eumenes softly.

'Do not condemn free citizens, unless you wish for civil war.' He paused again; Eumenes, screening his lips with his hand, gave him his lines. 'Let us try again for reconcilement. Let us send another embassy.' He drew a breath of triumph. Eumenes whispered, 'Don't look round.'

There was no serious opposition. All welcomed a breathing-space, and argued only the ways and means; but as the voices grew louder, they brought back to Philip that dreadful day when he had run away from the hall, and they had given him a robe to make him come back again, and then ... Alexander had been lying dead, as if he were carved in marble. Alexander had told him ...

He felt at his head, at the gold diadem they always made him wear when he came out here. He took it off, and, holding it out, walked forward.

Behind him, Meleager and Eumenes gave a united gasp of dismay. He extended, confidently, the crown to the staring soldiers. 'Is it because I'm

King? It doesn't matter. I'd sooner not be King. Here, look; you can give it to someone else.'

It was a curious moment. Everyone had been at stretch, till the half-relief of borrowed time. Now this.

Always prone to emotion – a trait which Alexander had used with unfailing skill – the Macedonians were borne on a flood of sentiment. What a decent, good fellow; what a law-abiding King. Living under his brother's shadow had made him over-modest. No one laughed as he looked about for someone to take the crown. There were reassuring cries of 'Long live Philip, Philip for King!'

With happy surprise, Philip resumed his crown. He had got everything right, and the kind man would be pleased with him. He was still beaming when they shepherded him inside.

Perdikkas' tent was pitched in the shade of a tall palm grove. He was settled back into surroundings so familiar that he seemed never to have left them; the light bed and folding chair, the armour stand, the chest (there had been a pile of chests in the days of victorious loot, but that was over), the trestle table.

His brother Alketas and his cousin Leonnatos were with him when the new envoys came. Leonnatos was a long-boned auburn-haired man, who reminded the world of his connections with the royal house by copying Alexander's leonine hair-cut, even, said his enemies, reproducing its wave with the tongs. His ambitions, though high, were as yet inchoate; meantime he supported Perdikkas.

The envoys had been sent out while their message was considered. Peace was offered in King Philip's name, if his claim was recognized, and his deputy, Meleager, was appointed to share the supreme command with Perdikkas.

Leonnatos tossed back his hair; a gesture rarely used by Alexander, which in his pupil had become a mannerism. 'Insolence! Do we need to disturb the others?'

Perdikkas glanced up from the letter. 'Here,' he said easily, 'I see the hand of Eumenes.'

'No doubt,' said Alketas, surprised. 'Who else would write it?'

'We will accept. Nothing could be better.'

'*What?*' said Leonnatos, staring. 'You can't take that brigand into the command!'

'I told you, I see the hand of Eumenes.' Perdikkas stroked the dark stubble on his chin. 'He knew what bait would draw the beast from his lair. Yes, let us have him out. Then we shall see.'

*

The barge on the Tigris was nearing the bend where the ladies must disembark, to join their caravan and proceed by land.

Dusk was falling. Their tent had been pitched on grass, away from the river damp and the mosquitoes. They stepped ashore as the first torches were kindled about the camp; there was a smell of burnt fat as the lamb for supper sizzled over the fire.

The chief eunuch of the escort, as he handed Stateira off the gang-plank, said softly, 'Madam. The villagers who came selling fruit are saying that the Great King is dead.'

'He warned me of it,' she answered calmly. 'He said there was this rumour among the peasants. It is in his letter; he said we should not heed it.'

Holding up her gown from the rushes heavy with dew, she swept on towards the lamplit tent.

To a spirited music of trumpets and double flutes, the foot-soldiers marched out under the towers of the Ishtar Gate, watched by the relieved Babylonians, to seal their peace with the Companions.

At their head rode Meleager, the King beside him. Philip made a cheerful and seemly figure, wearing the scarlet shoulder-cloak that Alexander had once given him, sitting a well-trained, solid horse that would walk half a length ahead of Konon with the leading-rein. He hummed to himself the tune that the pipes were playing. The air was still fresh with morning. All would be well, everyone was to be friends again. It would be no trouble, now, to go on being King.

The Companions waited on their glossy horses, restive from leisure; their bridles sparkled with gold pendants and silver cheek-rosettes, a fashion set by Alexander for Boukephalas. Dressed in the workmanlike panoply of campaign, plain Thracian helmet and stamped leather cuirass, Perdikkas watched with grim satisfaction the marching phalanx, the gaudy rider leading it. Meleager had had his parade armour adorned with a large gold lion-mask, and his cloak was edged with bullion. So! The beast was drawn.

They accorded Philip the royal salute. Well, coached, he acknowledged it and reached out his arm; Perdikkas bore, with resolute affability, the crushing of his huge paw. But Meleager, with a look offensively familiar, had pushed up after, his own hand ready for the clasp of reconciliation. It was with far greater reluctance that Perdikkas returned that grip. He told himself that Alexander had once had to break bread with the traitor Philotas, biding his time; and if he had balked at it, few of his advance force, including Perdikkas probably, would be alive today. 'It was necessary' was what Alexander had said.

*

It was settled that the absent Krateros, considering his high rank and royal lineage, should be appointed Philip's guardian. Antipatros should keep the regency of Macedon. Perdikkas should be Chiliarch of all the Asian conquests, and, if Roxane bore a boy, should be joint guardian with Leonnatos. They were Alexander's kinsmen, which Meleager could not claim; but since he was to share the high command, the distinction did not trouble him. He had begun already to give them his views on the management of the empire.

When all this business was done, Perdikkas made a last proposal. It was the ancient custom of Macedon, after civil war (another ancient custom) to exorcize discord with a sacrifice to Hekate. He proposed that all the troops in Babylon, horse and foot, should assemble on the plain for the Purification.

Meleager willingly agreed. He planned an impressive appearance, proper to his new rank. He would have his helmet topped with a double crest, like Alexander's at Gaugamela. Conspicuous; and a lucky omen.

Shortly before the rite, Perdikkas asked the Bodyguard to a private supper. He was back, now, at his house in the royal park. The generals rode or strolled over in the falling twilight, under the ornamental trees brought from far and wide by the Persian kings to adorn the paradise. A simple occasion, a meeting of old friends.

When the servants had left them with the wine, Perdikkas said, 'I have chosen the men and briefed them. I think that Philip – I suppose we must get used to calling him that – will have learned his part.'

Till Krateros, his new guardian, could take charge of him, Perdikkas was doing so. Since he lived in his accustomed rooms, with his accustomed comforts, he had scarcely noticed the change, except for the welcome absence of Meleager. He was getting new lessons; but that was to be expected.

'He has taken to Eumenes,' Ptolemy said. 'Eumenes doesn't bully him.'

'Good. He can help to coach him. Let us hope the noise and spectacle won't confuse him ... There will be the elephants.'

'Surely,' said Leonnatos, 'he has seen elephants by now?'

'Of course he has,' Ptolemy said impatiently. 'He travelled from India with them, in Krateros' convoy.'

'Yes, true.' Perdikkas paused. There was a silence, a sense of more to come. Seleukos, to whose command the elephant corps belonged, said 'Well?'

'King Omphis,' said Perdikkas slowly, 'had a certain use for them in India.'

There were sharply-drawn breaths all round the supper-couches. It was Niarchos who said distastefully, 'Omphis maybe. Never Alexander.'

'Alexander was never in our dilemma,' said Leonnatos unwisely. 'No,' returned Ptolemy. 'Nor like to be.'

Perdikkas cut in, with brusque authority. 'No matter. Alexander knew very well the power of fear.'

The men were astir at cockcrow, to march to the Field of Purgation at break of day, and get the rite finished before the crushing heat of noon.

The rich wheatfields, which bore three crops a year, had been lately harvested. The sun, floating up from the flat horizon, slanted its first beams over miles of stubble, gleaming like golden fur. Here and there, scarlet pennants marked the limits of the parade ground, which were significant to the rite.

Thick and squat, their ancient Assyrian brick mortared with black bitumen, jagged and crumbling with the centuries and with the lassitude of a long-conquered race, the walls of Babylon, impassive, overlooked the plain. They had seen many deeds of men, and looked incapable of amazement. A wide stretch of their battlements had been flattened down into a new, smooth platform. Its smoke-blackened bricks still smelled of burning; streams of molten pitch had hardened down its sides. In the ditch below was a great pile of debris; half-charred timber with broken carvings of lions and ships and wings and trophies, still dimly picked out with gilding. It was the remains of the two-hundred-foot pyre on which, not long before his death, Alexander had burned the body of Hephaistion.

Long before dawn, the crowds had started to gather along the walls. They had not forgotten the splendours of Alexander's entry into Babylon; a free show, for it had surrendered peacefully, and he had forbidden his men to plunder it. They remembered the streets flower-strewn and wafted with frankincense; the procession of exotic gifts, gold-bedizened horses, lions and leopards in gilded cages; the Persian cavalry, the Macedonian cavalry; and the gold-plated state chariot with the slight, glittering figure of the victor like a transfigured boy. He had been twenty-five, then. They had hoped for more splendours when he came back from India; but he had given them only that stupendous funeral.

Now they waited, to see the Macedonian men of war march out in their pride, and offer their gods appeasement; the citizens, the soldiers' women and children, the smiths and tent-makers and sutlers and wagoners and whores, the shipwrights and seamen from the galley-slips. They loved a show; but under expectation was a deep unease. A time had gone, a time was coming; and they did not like the auspices of its birth.

Most of the army had crossed the river overnight, by Queen Nitokris' bridge, or by the innumerable ferry-boats of reed and pitch. They slept in the open, and polished their gear for the morrow. The watchers on the walls saw them getting up by torchlight, the sound of their stirring like a murmuring sea. Further away, the Companions' horses whinnied.

Hooves drummed on the timbers of Nitokris' Bridge. The leaders arrived, to direct the sacrifice which would cleanse men's hearts from evil.

The rite was very old. The victim must be dedicated, killed and disembowelled, its four quarters and its entrails carried to the boundaries of the field. The army would march into the space thus purified, would parade, and sing a paean.

The sacrifice was, as it had always been, a dog. The finest and tallest wolfhound had been chosen from the royal kennels; pure white, handsomely feathered. Its docility, as the huntsman led it forward to the altar, promised the good omen of a consenting sacrifice; but when its leash was handed to the sacrificer, it growled and flew at him. Even for its size, it was immensely strong. It took four men to overpower it and get the knife to its throat; they finished with more of their own blood on them than the victim's. To make things worse, in the midst of the struggle the King had rushed up shouting, and only with trouble had been coaxed away.

Hastily, before there could be brooding on the augury, the four horsemen, appointed to asperse the plain, galloped to its four corners with their bloody offerings. The lumps of white and scarlet were flung outward with averting invocations to triple Hekate and the infernal gods; and the exorcized field was ready to receive the army of Alexander.

The squadrons and the phalanxes were ready. The burnished helmets of the horsemen gleamed; their crests of red or white horsehair, the pennants of their lances, stirred in the morning breeze. Their short sturdy Greek ponies whinnied at the tall horses of the Persian cavalry. Most of the Persian foot had melted away, trudging dusty caravan trails to their distant villages. The Macedonian foot was present to a man. They stood in close order, their whetted spear-tips making a glitter above them.

A square had formed on the wide stubbled plain. Its base was the wall of Babylon; its left side was the infantry; its right, the cavalry. Between them, making the fourth side, were the royal elephants.

Their mahouts, who had come with them from India, and knew them as a mother knows her child, had worked on them all yesterday in the high thatched elephant-sheds among the palm trees; crooning and clucking and slapping, washing them in the canal; painting on their foreheads, in ochre or scarlet or green, sacred symbols enlaced with elaborate scrollwork; draping their wrinkled flanks with tasselled nets brilliantly dyed and threaded with gold bullion; fastening jewelled rosettes through slits in their leather ears; grooming their tails and toes.

It was a year since the mahouts had had a chance to make their children fine. They had had their schooling on the royal maidan at Taxila; their children also. They had talked to them softly, reminding them of old days beside the Indus, while they reddened their feet with henna, as the custom had always been for such occasions. Now in the pink early light they sat proudly on their necks, wearing their ceremonial silks and turbans with peacock feathers, their beards freshly dyed blue or green or crimson; each holding the gold-bound ivory goad, studded with gems, which King Omphis in his magnificence had presented with each elephant to King Iskandar. They had served two famous kings; the world should see that they and their children knew how things were done.

The generals, who had been pouring their libations at the bloody altar, went off to join their detachments. As Ptolemy and Niarchos rode side by side towards the ranks of the Companions, Niarchos rubbed a splash of blood from his bridle arm, saying, 'The gods below don't seem disposed to cleanse us.'

'Are you surprised?' said Ptolemy. His craggy face was set in creases of disgust. 'Well, God willing, I shall be far away before long.'

'And I God willing ... Do the dead watch us, as poets say?'

'Homer says the unburied dead do ... He never did let go easily.' He added, not altogether to Niarchos, 'I shall make him what amends I can.'

It was time for the King to take his time-honoured place at the right of the Companions. His horse was ready. He had been well rehearsed. Eager to produce him and get to business, Perdikkas was grinding his teeth in the effort to keep his temper.

'Sir, the army awaits you. The men are watching. You cannot let them see you cry. You are the King! Sir, compose yourself. What is a dog?'

'He was Eos!' Philip was scarlet-faced, tears running into his beard. 'He knew me! We used to play tug-of-war. Alexander said he was strong enough to look after himself. He knew me!'

'Yes, yes,' said Perdikkas. Ptolemy was right, Alexander should have had him smothered. Most of the crowd had thought he was assisting in the sacrifice; but all the omens had been disquieting. 'The gods required him. It is done now. Come.'

Obedient to authority and to a voice far more impressive than Meleager's, Philip wiped his eyes and nose with the corner of his scarlet cloak, and let a groom hoist him up on his embroidered saddle-cloth. His horse, a seasoned veteran of parades, followed each manoeuvre of the one beside it. Philip felt the leading-rein must still be there.

The troops awaited the final ceremony; the sound of the trumpet, giving the note of the paean for them to sing.

Perdikkas, the King beside him, turned to the officers strung out behind him, leading their squadron. 'Forward!' he barked. 'Slow – march!'

The pipers struck up, instead of the paean, the cavalry walk familiar at parades. The sleek and glittering lines paced smoothly forward, rank upon rank, stepping delicately as they had done on triumphant days in the years of miracle at Memphis, at Tyre, at Taxila, at Persepolis, and here on this very field. At their head rode Perdikkas, and, carried by his wise charger, the King.

The infantry, taken unawares by this manoeuvre, stood in their ranks and muttered. The decay of discipline showed; spears dipped or leaned askew. They were light parade spears, not the tall sarissas; suddenly their bearers felt half-armed. The advancing cavalry looked formal and ceremonious; had there been some muddle in the briefing? Such doubts, once unthinkable, were common nowadays. Under Meleager their morale was low, their bonding shaky.

Perdikkas gave an order. The left and centre wings reined to a halt; the right, the royal squadron, still advanced. He said to Philip, 'When we stop, sir, make your speech. You remember?'

'Yes!' said Philip eagerly. 'I'm to say –'

'Hush, sir, not now. When I have said "Halt!" '

Neatly, stylishly, the royal squadron advanced till it was fifty feet from the phalanx. Perdikkas halted it.

Philip lifted his arm. He was used by now to his comfortable horse. Set firmly on the embroidered saddle-cloth, in a loud and unexpectedly deep voice, surprising even to himself, he shouted, 'Surrender the mutineers!'

There was a moment of absolute, stunned silence. This was their own, their chosen Macedonian King. The front ranks, staring across incredulous, saw his face strained in the simple effort of a child getting his lesson right; and knew at last what they had done.

Voices broke out among the lines, suddenly raised, appealing for support. They came from Meleager's ringleaders. Among uncertain undertones, their own noise isolated them; it could be heard how few they were.

Slightly at first, looking almost accidental, spaces began to open around them. It was coming home to their former comrades that they themselves were not precisely threatened. And who, after all, had been to blame? Who had foisted on them this hollow King, the tool of anyone who, for the moment, owned him? They forgot the peasant spearman who had first called for Philip's son; remembering only how Meleager had dressed the fool in Alexander's robe, and tried to profane Alexander's body. What did anyone owe his creatures?

Perdikkas beckoned the herald, who rode up with a paper in his hand. In his trained, carrying voice, he read out the names of Meleager's thirty. Meleager's own name was not called.

In his station of honour before the right-wing phalanx, he felt, around him, the last lees of loyalty ebb away, leaving him high and dry. If he stepped forward, challenged Perdikkas' perfidy – that was the signal they were waiting for over there. He froze, the statue of a soldier, sweating cold under the brazen Babylonian sun.

Sixty men dismounted from Perdikkas' squadron. On foot they formed pairs; one holding a set of fetters, the other a coil of rope.

There was a crucial pause. The thirty turned here and there, protesting. Some spears were waved, some voices urged resistance. In the confusion, the trumpet spoke again. Quietly, seeming only to confer with him, Perdikkas had been rehearsing Philip in his next speech.

'Deliver them up!' he shouted. 'Or we will ride against you!' He began, unprompted, to gather up his reins.

'Not now!' hissed Perdikkas, to his relief. He had no wish to go any nearer the spears. They used to point all one way, when Alexander was there.

The spaces widened about the thirty as the fetter-men approached them. Some gave up and submitted; some struggled, but their captors had been picked for strength. All were soon standing, with fettered feet, in the space between the lines. They awaited they knew not what. There had been something odd in the faces of their captors, who had not met their eyes.

'Bind them,' said Perdikkas.

Their arms were trussed to their sides. The cavalry fell back to its first line, leaving once more a hollow square. The fetter-bearers pushed the bound men over; they fell forward helplessly, twisting in their bonds, alone under the sky in the field hallowed to Hekate.

From the far side came the shrilling of an eastern pipe and a roll of drums.

The hot sun flashed on the goads of gold and ivory, King Omphis' gifts. Gently the mahouts pricked the necks of their good children, shouting the old command.

Rising like one, fifty trunks curled backward. The troops heard with awe the high blare of their war cry. Slowly, then at a steady thudding roll, their tread felt through the ground, the huge bedizened beasts moved forward.

The mahouts in their gleaming silks flung off their well-trained silence. They drummed with their heels, hallooing, slapping the necks of their mounts with their jewelled hands or the butts of the goads. They sounded like boys let out of school. The elephants fanned out their great ears, and, squealing with excitement, began to run.

A kind of groan, of horror and a dreadful fascination, ran through the watching lines. Hearing it, the men on the ground writhed to their knees staring about them. At first they looked at the goads; then one man, still struggling, saw the hennaed feet as they drummed closer, and understood. He screamed. Others tried to roll away in the thick grey dust. They had only time to move a yard or two.

With drawn hissing breath, the army of Alexander saw the treading of the human vintage; the bursting of the rind, the scarlet juices running from the pounded flattened flesh. The elephants moved with well-trained intelligence, catching the rolling bodies with their trunks, and steadying them while the feet came down, trumpeting as the war-smell steamed up from the ground.

From his station beside Perdikkas, Philip uttered little breathless cheers. This was not like the killing of Eos. He was fond of elephants – Alexander had let him ride one – but nobody was hurting them. His eye was filled with their splendid trappings, his ear with their proud brayings. He hardly noticed the bloody mash below them. In any case, Perdikkas had told him that those were all wicked men.

The mahouts, seeing the work well done, calmed and praised their children, who willingly came away. They had done such things in battle, and several still bore the scars. This had been painless and quick. Following their leader, an elephant of great age and wisdom, they formed in line, red to the knees; paraded past Perdikkas and the King, touching brow with trunk in a grave salute; then went their way to the shady elephant-houses, the reward of palm-kernels and melons, the cool pleasant bathe which would sluice off the scent of war.

As indrawn breaths escaped, and the silence in the ranks was breaking, Perdikkas signed to the herald to blow again, and rode forward, a length ahead of the King.

'Macedonians!' he said, 'with the death of these traitors the army is truly cleansed, and fit again to defend the empire. If there is anyone among you who, deserving these men's fate, has today escaped it, let him thank his fortune and learn loyalty. Trumpeter! The paean.'

The stirring air sang out; the cavalry took it up. After a dragging moment, the infantry came in. Its ancient fierceness was reassuring as a lullaby. It took them back to days when they knew who and what they were.

It was over. Meleager left the ground, alone. His confederates were dead; out of all his hangers-on, not one came near him. He might have had the plague.

The servant who had held his horse seemed to look at him not with meant insolence, but with an inquisitiveness which was worse. Behind, in the vacant square, two covered wagons had appeared, and men with pitchforks were heaving the corpses into them. Two cousins and a nephew of his were there; he ought to arrange their funerals, there was no one else. The thought of searching that trampled meat for shreds of identity revived his nausea; dismounting, he vomited till he was cold with emptiness. As he rode on, he was aware of two men behind him. When he stopped they had drawn rein while one adjusted his saddle-cloth. Now they moved on.

He had fought in many battles. Ambition, comradeship, the bright fierce certainty radiated by Alexander, enemies on whom one could revenge and redeem one's fear, all these had carried him along and made him brave. Never before had he faced a lonely end. His mind began to run, like a hunted fox's, upon likely refuge. Above him, thick and ragged and pitch black, sullen with the blood of worked-out slaves, loomed the walls of Babylon and the crumbling ziggurat of Bel.

He rode through the tunnelled gateway. The men were following. He turned off into narrow streets where women crushed themselves into doorways to give him room; filthy deep courts between eyeless houses, where huddles of thievish men stared at him dangerously. The pursuit was no longer in sight. Suddenly he came out into the wide Marduk Way, the temple just before him. A hallowed place, to Greeks as well as to bar-barians. Everyone knew that Alexander had sacrificed there to Zeus and Herakles. Sanctuary!

He hitched his horse to a fig-tree in the weed-grown outer precinct. Through rank greenery a trodden path led to the ruined entry; from the gloom beyond came the universal temple smell of incense, burned meat and wood-ash, the Babylonian smell of foreign unguents and foreign flesh. As he walked towards it in the dazzling heat, someone stood in the sunlight facing him. It was Alexander.

His heart stopped. Next moment he knew what he was looking at, but still he could not move. The statue was marble, tinted like life; a dedication eight years old from the first Babylonian triumph. It stood at ground level, the plinth as yet unbuilt. Nude but for a red chlamys across one shoulder, grasping a spear of gilded bronze, Alexander calmly awaited the new temple he had endowed. His deepset eyes, with their smoke-grey enamel irises, gazed out at Meleager, saying 'Well?'

He stared back, attempting defiance, at the searching face, the smooth young body. You were lean and sinewy and hacked about with scars. Your forehead was creased, you were drawn about the eyes, your hair was fading. What is that idol? An idea . . . But memory, once invoked, conjured all too potently the real presence. He had seen the living anger . . . He strode on into the temple.

At first the gloom almost blinded him after the harsh sun. Presently, by the light of a smoke-shaft high above, he saw looming in shadow the colossal image of Bel, Great King of Gods, enthroned with fists on knees.

His towering mitre almost touched the roof; he was flanked by winged lions with the heads of bearded men. His sceptre was tall as a man; his robe, from which the gold leaf was peeling, glimmered dimly. His face was blackened with age and smoke, but his ivory-inlaid eyes glared fiercely yellow. Before him was the fire-altar, covered with dead ash. No one, it seemed, had told him there was a new King of Babylon.

No matter, an altar was an altar. Here he was safe. Content at first to get back his breath and enjoy the cool from the thick high walls, soon he started to peer about for signs of life. The place seemed deserted; yet he felt a sense of being observed, assessed, considered.

In the wall behind Bel, there was a door set in the dark-glazed tiles. He felt, rather than heard, stirrings of life behind it; but he dared not knock. Authority had drained from him. Time dragged by. He was a temple suppliant, someone should attend to him. He had not eaten since day-break; behind the ebony door were men, food, wine. But he did not go to tell them he was there. He knew they knew it.

A rusty sunset light lowered in the courtyard. The shadows deepened round frowning Bel, drowning all but his yellow eye-whites. With the dark, he came into possession. The temple seemed peopled with the ghosts of men like stone, treading with stony feet the necks of their conquered enemies, offering their blood to this stone demon. More than for food, Meleager craved for the open skies of a mountain shrine in Macedon, the colour and light of a Greek temple, the gracious and human countenance of its god.

The last light-ray left the courtyard; there was only a square of dusk, and, within, thick dark. Behind the door, low voices sounded and went away.

His horse stamped and whinnied outside. He could not stay here and rot; under cover of dark he could be gone. Someone would take him in ... but those who were safe were dead. Better to leave the city now, go west, hire out his sword to some satrap in nearer Asia. But he must get first to his rooms; he would need gold, he had taken bribes from scores of petitioners to the King ... The dusk in the courtyard moved.

Two shadows showed in the glimmering square. They came on, into the broken entry. They were not the shadows of Babylonians. He heard the rasp of drawn swords. 'Sanctuary!' he shouted. 'Sanctuary!'

The door beyond Bel's image opened a crack, lamplight bright in the darkness. He shouted again. The crack closed. The shadows approached, vanishing into blackness. He set his back to the unlit altar and drew his sword. As they came close, it seemed to him he knew them; but it was only the familiar smell and outline of men from home. He called their names aloud, recalling old friendships in the army of Alexander. But the names were wrong; and when they dragged back his head across the altar, it was remembering Alexander that they cut his throat.

Stripped of its banners and plumes, wreathed with cypress and weeping willow, the lamenting caravan paced slowly under the Ishtar Gate. Perdikkas and Leonnatos, warned by the fore-runners of its coming, had ridden to meet the wife of Alexander and tell her that she was widowed. Bareheaded, their hair still cropped in mourning, they rode beside the wagon train, which had now the air of a cortège. The princesses sobbed, their women keened and chanted ritual threnodies. The keepers of the gate heard wondering these new tears, so long after the days prescribed.

In the harem, the rooms of the chief wife waited, perfumed and immaculate, as ordained by Bagoas two months before. The Warden had feared that after Alexander's death Roxane would demand them; but to his deep relief she seemed settled where she was. No doubt her pregnancy had quietened her. So far, thought the Warden, so good.

Perdikkas escorted Stateira there, concealing his surprise at her arrival; he had supposed her established in Susa to bear her child in quiet. Alexander, she said, had summoned her. He must have done so without informing anyone. He had done some very odd things, after Hephaistion's death.

Handing her down the wagon steps to the Warden, he thought her more beautiful than at the Susa wedding. Her features had purity of line, the Persian delicacy, fined-down by pregnancy and fatigue, which had put smudges of faint cobalt under her large dark eyes; their lids with their long silky lashes looked almost transparent. The Persian kings had always bred for looks. Her hand on the curtain was long-fingered and smooth as cream. She had been wasted on Alexander; he himself, a good inch taller, could have stepped out with her very well. (His own Susa bride, a swarthy Median chosen for exalted birth, had greatly disappointed him.) At least, Alexander had finally had the sense to get a child on her. It should be certain of beauty, if nothing else.

Leonnatos, assisting Drypetis, noted that her face, though still immature, held distinguished promise. He too had a Persian wife; but this need not keep him from looking higher. He rode off in thought.

An obsequious train of eunuchs and waiting-women led the princesses through Nebuchadrezzar's devious corridors to the once-familiar rooms. As in childhood, they felt after the space and light of the Susa palace the frowning Babylonian strength. But then they came through to the sunny courtyard, the fishpool where they had floated their boats of split bamboo in lily-leaf archipelagos, or reached shoulder-deep after the carp. In the room that had been their mother's they were bathed and scented and fed.

Nothing seemed changed since that summer eight years before, that watershed of time, when their father had brought them here before marching to meet the King of Macedon. Even the Warden had remembered them.

Their meal done, their attendants dismissed to be settled in their own quarters, they explored their mother's clothes-chest. The scarves and veils still released their memory-stirring scent. Sharing a divan, looking out on the sunlit pool, they recollected that other life; Stateira, who had been twelve when it ended, reminding Drypetis who had only been nine. They talked of their father whom Grandmother would never name, remembering him in their mountain home before he had been King, laughing as he tossed them eight feet in the air. They thought of their mother's perfect face, framed in the scarf with the seed-pearls and gold beads. Everyone gone – even Alexander – except for Grandmother.

They were growing sleepy when a shadow crossed the doorway. A child came in, with two silver cups on a silver tray. She was about seven years old, enchantingly pretty, with a blend of Persian and Indian looks, cream-skinned, dark-eyed. She dipped a knee without spilling a drop. 'Honoured ladies,' she said carefully. This, clearly, was all her Persian, learned by heart. They kissed and thanked her; she dimpled at them, said something in Babylonian, and trotted away.

The silver cups were misted with coolness, pleasant to touch. Drypetis said, 'She had beautiful clothes, and gold earrings. She wasn't a servant's child.'

'No,' said Stateira, worldly-wise. 'And if not, you know, she must be our half-sister. I remember, Father brought most of the harem here.'

'I'd forgotten,' Drypetis, a little shocked, looked round her mother's room. Stateira had gone out into the courtyard, to call back the child again. But she had gone, and no one was in sight; they had told their women they wished to rest undisturbed.

Even the palms seemed bleached in the dazzling heat. They lifted the cups, admiring their chased birds and flowers. The drink tasted of wine and citron, with a delicate bitter-sweet tang.

'Delicious,' said Stateira. 'One of the concubines must have sent it to make us welcome; she was too shy to come herself. Tomorrow we might invite her.'

The heavy air was still perfumed with their mother's clothes. It felt homely, secure. Her grief for her parents, for Alexander, grew dim and drowsy. This would be a comforting place to bear his child in. Her eyelids closed.

The shadow of the palms had barely slanted when pain awoke her. She thought at first that her child must be miscarrying, till Drypetis clasped her belly and screamed aloud.

Perdikkas, as Regent of Asia, had moved into the palace. He was seeing petitioners in the small audience room when the Warden of the Harem appeared, unheralded, his clay-grey face and evident terror having passed him through the guards. Perdikkas, after one look, had the room cleared and heard him.

When the princesses began to cry for help no one had dared go near them; everyone in hearing had guessed the cause. The Warden, desperate to exculpate himself (he had in fact had no hand in it), had not waited for them to breathe their last. Perdikkas ran with him to the harem.

Stateira lay sprawled on the divan. Drypetis on the floor where she had rolled in her death-throes. Stateira drew her last gasp as Perdikkas entered. At first, transfixed with horror, he was aware of no one else in the room. Then he perceived that in the ivory chair before the toilet table a woman was sitting.

He strode across and stared down at her, silent, hardly able to keep his hands from her throat. She smiled at him.

'You did this!' he said.

Roxane raised her brows. 'I? It was the new King. Both of them said so.' She did not add that, before the end, she had taken pleasure in undeceiving them.

'The King?' said Perdikkas furiously. 'Who will believe that, you accursed barbarian bitch?'

'All your enemies. They will believe it because they wish. I shall say that he sent the draught to me too; but when these fell sick I had not yet drunk it.'

'You ...' For a while he vented his rage in curses. She listened calmly. When he paused, for sufficient answer she laid her hand over her womb.

He looked away at the dead girl. 'The child of Alexander.'

'*Here*,' she said, 'is the child of Alexander. His only child ... Say nothing, and so will I. She came here without ceremony. Very few will know.'

'It was *you* who sent for her!'

'Oh, yes. Alexander did not care for her. I did as he would have wished.'

For a moment she felt real fear; his hand had dropped to his sword-hilt. Still gripping it, he said, 'Alexander is dead. But if ever again you say that of him, when your brat is born I will kill you with these hands. And if I knew it would take after you, I would kill you now.'

Growing cool again, she said, 'There is an old well in the back court. No one draws from it, they say the water is foul. Let us take them there. No one will come.'

He followed her. The well-cover had lately been loosened from its seal of grime. As he lifted it a smell of ancient mould came out.

He had no choice and knew it. Proud as he was, ambitious and fond of power, he was loyal to Alexander, dead as alive. His son should not, if Perdikkas could prevent it, enter the world branded as a poisoner's child.

He returned in silence, going first to Drypetis. Her face was soiled with vomit; he wiped it with a towel before he carried her to the dark hole of the well. When she had slipped from his hands, he heard her clothes brushing the brick till, about twenty feet down, she reached the bottom. He could tell, then, that the well was dry.

Stateira's eyes were staring open, her fingers clutched the stuff of the divan. The eyes would not close: while Roxane waited impatiently, he went to the chest for something to cover her face, a veil stitched with scarab wings. When he began to move her, he felt wet blood.

'What have you done to her?' He drew back in revulsion, wiping his hands on the coverlet.

Roxane shrugged. Stooping, she lifted the robe of embroidered linen. It could be seen that Alexander's wife in her death-pangs had brought forth his heir.

He stared down at it, the four-month manikin, already human, the sex defined, even the nails beginning. One of the fists was clenched as if in anger, the face with its sealed eyes seemed to frown. It was still tied to its mother; she had died before she could pass the afterbirth. He drew his dagger and cut it free.

'Come, hurry,' said Roxane. 'You can see that the thing is dead.'

'Yes,' said Perdikkas. It hardly filled his hands, the son of Alexander, the grandson of Philip and Darius, carrying in its threadlike veins the blood of Achilles and of Kyros the Great.

He went again to the chest. A scarf trailed out, stitched with seed pearls and gold beads. Carefully, like a woman, he wrapped the creature in its royal shroud, and gave it its own journey to the burial-place, before returning to send its mother after it.

Queen Sisygambis sat playing chess with the Head Chamberlain. He was an elderly eunuch with a distinguished past going back to King Ochos' reign. An expert survivor of countless court intrigues, he played a canny game, and offered more challenge than the waiting-ladies. She had invited him to relieve her boredom, and mere courtesy demanded that she should attend to him. She brooded over the ivory armies on the board. Now that the girls were gone with their young attendants, the harem seemed to have been left behind by time. Everyone here was old.

The Chamberlain saw her lethargy and guessed the cause. He fell into one or two of her traps and rescued himself, to enliven the game. In a pause, he said, 'Did you find, when the King was here, that he had remembered your instruction? You said, before he marched east, that he had promise if he would apply his mind.'

She said smiling, 'I did not test him. I knew he would have forgotten.' For a moment, reflected from the distance, rays of vitality seemed to surge through the muted room. 'I used to tell him it was called the royal war-game, and for my sake he pretended to care who won. But when I scolded him and told him he could do better, he said, "But, Mother, these are *things*."'

'He is not a man for sitting still, indeed.'

'He needed more rest. It was not the time to go down to Babylon. Babylon has always been to winter in.'

'It seems he means to winter in Arabia. We shall scarcely see him this year. But when he marches, for sure he will send Their Highnesses back to you, as soon as the child is born and the lady Stateira can travel.'

'Yes,' she said a little wistfully. 'He will want me to see the child.' She returned to the board, and moved an elephant to threaten his vizier. A pity, he thought, that the boy had not sent for her; she doted on him still. But, as she had said, it was no time to go down to Babylon, and she was turned eighty.

They had finished the game, and were drinking citron, when the Chamberlain was summoned, urgently, by the commander of the garrison. When he came back, she looked at his face, and grasped the arms of her chair.

'Madam . . .'

'It is the King,' she said. 'He is dead.'

He bowed his head. It was as if her body had known already; at his first word the chill had reached her heart. He came up quickly, in case she was going to fall; but after a moment she motioned him to his chair, and waited for him to speak.

He told her as much as he had learned, still watching her; her face was the colour of old parchment. But she was not grieving only; she was thinking. Presently she turned to a table near her chair, opened an ivory casket, and took out a letter.

'Please read me this. Not the substance only. Word for word.'

His sight was not what it had been; but by bringing it close he could see quite clearly. He translated scrupulously. At *I have been sick, and there is ignorant talk that I am dead*, he looked up and met her eyes.

'Tell me,' she said, 'is that his seal?'

He peered at it; at a few inches, the detail was sharp enough. 'It is his likeness, and a good one. But it is not the royal seal. Has he used this before?'

Without speaking, she put the casket into his hands. He looked at the letters, written in elegant Persian by a scribe; his eyes caught one ending: *I commend you, dear Mother, both to your gods and mine, if indeed they are not the same, as I think they are.* There were five or six letters. All had the royal seal, Olympian Zeus enthroned, his eagle perched on his hand. She read the answer in his face.

'When he did not write to me ...' She took the casket and set it down beside her. Her face was pinched as if with cold, but without astonishment. All her middle years had been passed in the dangerous reign of Ochos. Her husband had had royal blood enough to be in danger whenever the King felt insecure. Trusting almost no one, he had trusted her and told her everything. Intrigue, revenge and treachery had been daily weather. In the end, Ochos had killed him. She had believed that he lived again in her tall son; his flight from Issos had almost killed her with shame. In the desolate tent, the young conquerer was announced, to visit the family his enemy had abandoned. For the children's sake, performing dignity like a well-trained animal its trick, she had knelt to the tall handsome man before her. He stepped back; everyone's dismay made her aware of a frightful error; she began to bow to the smaller man she had overlooked. He had taken her hands and raised her, and for the first time she saw his eyes. 'Never mind, Mother ...' She had had Greek enough for that.

The Chamberlain, the old survivor, almost as pale as she, was trying not to look at her. Just so someone had looked away when her husband had had his last summons to the court.

'They have murdered him.' She said it as something evident.

'This man says the marsh-fever. It is common at Babylon in summer.'

'No, they have poisoned him. And there is no word of my grand-daughters?'

He shook his head. There was a pause while they sat silent, feeling disaster strike on their old age, a mortal illness, not to be shaken off.

She said, 'He married Stateira for policy. It was my doing he got her with child.'

'They may still be safe. Perhaps in hiding.'

She shook her head. Suddenly she sat up in her chair, like a woman thinking, Why am I idling like this, when I have work to do?

'My friend, a time is over. I shall go to my room now. Farewell. Thank you for your good service in all these years.'

She read new fear in his face. She understood it; they had both known Ochos' reign. 'No one will suffer. No one will be charged with anything. At my age, to die is easy. When you go, will you send my women?'

The women found her composed and busy, laying out her jewels. She talked to them of their families, advised them, embraced them and divided her jewels among them, all but King Poros' rubies, which she kept on.

When she had bidden them all farewell, she lay down on her bed in the inner room and closed her eyes. They did not try, after her first refusals, to get her to eat or drink. It was no kindness to trouble her, still less to save her alive for the coming vengeance. For the first few days, they left her alone as she had ordered. On the fourth, seeing her begin to sink, one or other kept watch beside her; if she knew of them, she did not turn them away. On the fifth day at nightfall, they became aware that she was dead; her breathing had been so quiet, no one could be sure when it had ended.

Galloping day and night, by dromedary, by horse, by mountain mule as the terrain needed, man throwing to man the brief startling news, the King's Messengers had carried their tidings of death from Babylon to Susa, Susa to Sardis, Sardis to Smyrna, along the Royal Road which Alexander had extended to reach the Middle Sea. At Smyrna, all through the sailing season, a dispatch-boat was ready to carry his letters to Macedon.

The last courier of the long relay had arrived at Pella, and given Perdikkas' letter to Antipatros.

The tall old man read in silence. Whenever Philip had gone to war he had ruled Macedon; since Alexander crossed to Asia he had ruled all Greece. The honour which had kept him loyal had also stiffened his pride; he looked far more regal than had Alexander, who had looked only like himself. It had been a joke of his among close friends that Antipatros was all white outside, with a purple lining.

Now, reading the letter, knowing he would not after all be replaced by Krateros (Perdikkas had made that clear), his first thought was that all south Greece would rise as soon as the news had broken. The news itself, though shocking, was a shock long half-expected. He had known Alexander from his cradle; it had always been inconceivable that he would make old bones. Antipatros had almost told him so outright, while he was preparing to march to Asia without begetting an heir.

It had been a false move to hint at his own daughter; the boy could hardly have done better, but it had made him feel trapped, or used. 'Do you think I've time now to hold wedding-feasts and wait about for children?' he had said. He could have had a half-grown son, thought Antipatros, with our good blood in him. And now? Two unborn half-breeds; and meantime, a pride of young lions, slipped off the leash. He remembered, not without misgivings, his own eldest son.

He remembered, too, a scrap of gossip from the first year of the young

King's reign. He had told someone, 'I don't want a son of mine reared here while I'm away.'

And that was behind it all. That accursed woman! All through his boyhood she had made him hate his father, whom he might have admired if let alone; she'd shown him marriage as the poisoned shirt of Herakles (that, too, a woman's doing!), then, when he'd reached the age for girls and could have had his pick, she was outraged that he'd taken refuge with another boy. He could have done far worse than Hephaistion – his father had, and got his death by it – but she could not live with what she'd brought about, had made an enemy where she could have had an ally; and all she'd achieved was to come second instead of first. No doubt she'd rejoiced to hear of Hephaistion's death. Well, she had another to hear of now, and let her make the best of it.

He checked himself. It was unseemly to mock a mother's grief for her only son. He would have to send her the news. He sat down at his writing-table with the wax before him, seeking some decent and kindly word for his old enemy, some fitting eulogy of the dead. A man, he reflected, whom he had not seen for more than a decade, whom he thought of still as a brilliantly precocious boy. What had he looked like, after those prodigious years? Perhaps one might still see, or guess. It would be something suitable with which to end his letter, that the body of the King had been embalmed to the likeness of life, and only awaited a worthy bier to begin its journey to the royal burial-ground at Aigai.

TO QUEEN OLYMPIAS, *health and prosperity . . .*

It was full summer in Epiros. The high valley on its mountain shoulder was green and gold, watered from the deep winter snows which Homer had remembered. The calves were fattening, the sheep had yielded their fine soft wool, the trees bent, heavy with fruit. Though it was against all custom, the Molossians had prospered under a woman's rule.

The widowed Queen Kleopatra, daughter of Philip and sister of Alexander, stood with the letter of Antipatros in her hand, looking out from the upper room of the royal house to the further mountains. The world had changed, it was too soon to know how. For Alexander's death she felt awe without grief, as for his life she had felt awe without love. He had entered the world before her, to steal her mother's care, her father's notice. Their fights had stopped early, in the nursery; after that they had not been close enough. Her wedding day, the day of their father's murder, had made her a pawn of state; him it had made a king. Soon he had become a phenomenon, growing with distance more dazzling and more strange.

Now for a while, the paper in her hand, she remembered the days when, boy and girl with only two years between them, their parents' ceaseless strife had brought them together in defensive collusion; remembered, too, how if their mother had to be braved in one of her dreadful weeping rages, it had been he who would always go and face the storm.

She laid Antipatros' letter down. The one for Olympias was on the table beside it. He would not face her now; she herself must do it.

She knew where she would find her; in the ground-floor state guest room where she had been first received to attend the funeral of Kleopatra's husband, and where she had since remained. The dead King had been her brother; more and more she had encroached on the kingdom's business, while she pursued through a horde of agents the feud with Antipatros which had made her position in Macedon impossible.

Kleopatra set resolutely the square chin she had inherited from Philip, and, taking the letter, went down to her mother's room.

The door was ajar. Olympias was dictating to her secretary. Kleopatra, pausing, could hear that she was drawing up a long indictment against Antipatros, going back ten years, a summary of old scores. *Question him on this, when he appears before you, and do not be deceived if he claims that* . . . She paced about impatiently while the scribe caught up.

Kleopatra had meant to behave, on so traditional an occasion, as a daughter should; to show the warning of a grave sad face, to utter the usual preparations. Just then her eleven-year-old son came in from a game of ball with his companion pages; a big-boned auburn boy with his father's face. Seeing her hesitating at the door, he looked at her with an air of anxious complicity, as if sharing her caution before the seat of power.

She dismissed him gently, wanting to hug him to her and cry, 'You are the King!' Through the door she saw the secretary busily scratching the wax. He was a man she hated, a creature of her mother's from long ago in Macedon. There was no knowing what he had known. '

Olympias was a few years over fifty. Straight as a spear, and slender still, she had begun to use cosmetics as a woman does who means only to be seen, not touched. Her greying hair had been washed with camomile and henna; her lashes and brows were lined-in with antimony. Her face was whitened, her lips, not her cheeks, were faintly reddened. She had painted her own image of herself, not enticing Aphrodite but commanding Hera. When, catching sight of her daughter in the doorway, she swept round to rebuke the interruption, she was majestic, even formidable.

Suddenly, Kleopatra was swept by a red surge of anger. Stepping forward into the room, her face like stone, making no gesture to dismiss the scribe, she said harshly, 'You need not write to him. He is dead.'

The perfect silence seemed deepened by each slight intrusive sound; the click of the man's dropped stylus, a dove in a nearby tree, the voices of children playing a long way off. The white cream on Olympias' face stood out like chalk. She looked straight before her. Kleopatra, nerved for she could not tell what elemental furies, waited till she could no longer bear it. Quiet with remorse, she said, 'It was not in war. He died of fever.'

Olympias motioned to the scribe. He made off, leaving his papers in disorder. She turned towards Kleopatra.

'Is that the letter? Give it to me.'

Kleopatra put it into her hand. She held it, unopened, waiting, dismissive. Kleopatra shut the thick door behind her. No sound came from the room. His death was something between the two of them, as his life had been. She herself was excluded. That, too, was an old story.

Olympias grasped the stone mullion of the window, its carvings biting, unfelt, into her palms. A passing servant saw the staring face and thought, for a moment, that a tragic theatre mask had been propped there. He hurried on lest her sightless gaze should light on him. She stared at the eastern sky.

It had been foretold her before his birth. Perhaps as she slept he had stirred within her – he had been restless, impatient for life and it had made her dream. Billowing wings of fire had sprung from her body, beating and spreading till they were great enough to waft her into the sky. Still the fire had streamed from her, an ecstasy, flowing over mountains and seas till it filled the earth. Like a god she had surveyed it, floating on the flames. Then, in a moment, they were gone. From some desolate crag where they had abandoned her, she had seen the land black and smoking, sparked with hot embers like a burned-out hillside. She had started wide awake, and put out her hand for her husband. But she was eight months gone, he had long since found other bedfellows. She had lain till morning, remembering the dream.

When, later, the fire was running over the wondering world, she had said to herself that all life must die, the time was far off and she would not live to see it. Now all was fulfilled; she could only clench her hands upon the stone and affirm that it must not be. It had never been in her to accept necessity.

Down on the coast, where the waters of Acheron and Kokytos met, was the Nekromanteion, the Oracle of the Dead. She had gone there long ago, when for her sake Alexander had defied his father, and they had both come here in exile for a time. She remembered the dark and winding labyrinth, the sacred drink, the blood libation which gave the shades strength to speak. Her father's spirit had stirred in the gloom and spoken faintly, saying her troubles would soon end and fortune shine on her.

It would be a long day's ride, she must set out at dawn. She would make the offering and take the draught and go into the dark, and her son would

come to her. Even from Babylon, from the world's end, he would come ...
Her mind paused. What if the first comers were those who had died at
home? Philip, with Pausanias' dagger in his ribs? His new young wife, to
whom she had offered poison or the rope? Even for a spirit, even for
Alexander, it was two thousand miles from Babylon.

No; she would wait till his body came; that, surely, would bring his
spirit nearer. When she had seen his body, his spirit would seem less
strange. For she knew that she feared its strangeness. When he left,
he had been still a boy to her; she would receive the body of a man
nearing middle age. Would his shade obey her? He had loved her but
seldom obeyed.

The man, the ghost, slipped from her grasp. She stood there empty.
Then, uninvoked, vivid to sight and touch, came the child. The scent of
his hair, nuzzled into her neck; the light scratches on his fine skin, his
grazed dirty knees; his laughter, his anger, his wide listening eyes. Her dry
eyes filled; tears streaked her cheeks with eye-paint; she bit on her arm
to muffle her crying.

By the evening fire, she had told him the old family tales of Achilles
handed down by word of mouth, always reminding him that it was from
her side that the hero's blood came down to him. When school days began
he had come eagerly to the Iliad, colouring it with the Achilles of the tales.
Reaching the Odyssey, he came upon Ulysses' visit to the land of shades.
('It was in my country, in Epiros, that he spoke with them.') Slowly and
solemnly, looking out past her at a reddening sunset sky, he had spoken
the words.

> 'Achilleus,
> no man before has been more blessed than you, nor ever will be.
> Before, when you were alive, we Argives honoured you
> as we did the gods, and now in this place you have great
> authority over the dead. Do not grieve, even in death, Achilleus.'
>   So I spoke, and he in turn said to me in answer,
> 'O shining Odysseus, never try to console me for dying.
> I would rather follow the plough as thrall to another
> man, one with no land allotted him and not much to live on,
> than be a king over all the perished dead.'

Because he did not cry when he was hurt, he was never ashamed of
tears. She saw his eyes glitter, fixed on the glowing clouds, and knew that
his grief was innocent; only for Achilles, parted from hope and expectation, the mere shadow of his glorious past, ruling over the shadows of past
men. He had not yet believed in his own mortality.

He said, as if it were her he was reassuring, 'But Odysseus did console
him for dying, after all, it says so.

So I spoke, and the soul of the swift-footed scion of Aiakos
stalked away in long strides across the meadow of asphodel,
happy for what I had said of his son, and how he was famous.'

'Yes,' she had said. 'And after the war his son came to Epiros, and we are both descended from him.'

He had considered it. Then: 'Would Achilles be happy if I were famous too?'

She had bent and ruffled his hair. 'Of course he would. He would stride through the asphodel and sing.'

She let go of the window-column. She felt faint and ill; going to her inner room she lay down and wept fiercely. It left her almost too weak to stand, and at last she slept. At dawn, she woke to the recollection of great grief, but her strength was almost recovered. She bathed and dressed and painted her face, and went to her writing table. TO PERDIKKAS REGENT OF THE ASIAN KINGDOMS, PROSPERITY...

On the roof of their house, a few miles inland from Pella, Kynna and Eurydike were practising with the javelin.

Kynna, like Kleopatra, was one of Philip's daughters, but by a minor marriage. Her mother had been an Illyrian princess, and a noted warrior, as the customs of her race allowed. After a war against her formidable old father Bardelys, Philip had sealed the peace treaty with a wedding, as he had done several times before. The lady Audata would not have been his choice for her own sake; she was comely, but he had trouble remembering which sex he was in bed with. He had paid attention enough to get one daughter on her, given them a house, maintained them, but seldom called on them till Kynna was of marriageable age. Then he had given her in wedlock to his nephew Amyntas, his elder brother's child, the same whom the Macedonians had passed over in his infancy, to make Philip king.

Amyntas, obedient to the people's will expressed in the Assembly, had lived peaceably through Philip's reign. Only when conspirators were planning the King's murder had he fallen to temptation, and agreed when the deed was done to accept the throne. For this, when it came to light, Alexander had put him on trial for treason, and the Assembly had condemned him.

Kynna, his wife, had withdrawn from the capital to his country estate. She had lived there ever since, rearing her daughter in the martial skills her Illyrian mother had taught her. It was her natural bent; it was an occupation; and she felt, instinctively, that one day it would be of use. She had never forgiven Amyntas' death. Her daughter Eurydike, only child of an only child, had known as long as she could remember that she should have been a boy.

The core of the house was a rugged old fort going back to the civil wars; later the thatched house had been built beside it. It was on the flat roof of the fort that the woman and the girl were standing, throwing at a straw man propped on a pole.

A stranger could have taken them for sisters; Kynna was only just thirty, Eurydike was fifteen. They both took after the Illyrian side, tall, fresh-faced, athletic. In the short men's tunics they wore for exercise, their brown hair plaited back out of their way, they looked like girls of Sparta, a land of which they knew almost nothing.

Eurydike's javelin had left a splinter in her palm. She pulled it out, and called in slave-Thracian to the tattooed boy who was bringing back the spears from the target, and who should have seen they were rubbed smooth. As he worked they sat to rest on a block of stone set for an archer, stretched, and took deep breaths of the mountain air.

'I hate the plains,' said Eurydike. 'I shall mind that more than anything.'

Her mother did not hear; she had been looking out at the hill-road that led between the village huts to their gate. 'A courier is coming. Come down and change your clothes.'

They climbed down the wooden steps to the floor below, and put on their second-best dresses. A courier was a rare event, and such people reported what they saw.

His gravity and sense of drama almost made Kynna ask his errand before she broke the seal. But it would be undignified; she sent him off to be fed before she read Antipatros' letter.

'Who is dead?' asked Eurydike. 'Is it Arridaios?' Her voice was eager.

Her mother looked up. 'No. It is Alexander.'

'*Alexander!*' She spoke with disappointment more than grief. Then her face lightened. 'If the King is dead, I needn't marry Arridaios.'

'Be quiet!' said her mother. 'Let me read.' Her face had changed; it held defiance, resolution, triumph. The girl said anxiously, 'I needn't marry him, mother? Need I? Need I?'

Kynna turned to her with glowing eyes. 'Yes! Now indeed you must. The Macedonians have made him King.'

'*King?* How can they? Is he better, have his wits come back?'

'He is Alexander's brother, that is all. He is to keep the throne warm for Alexander's son by the barbarian. If she has a son.'

'And Antipatros says I am to marry him?'

'No, he does not. He says that Alexander had changed his mind. He may be lying, or not. It's no matter which.'

Eurydike's thick brows drew together. 'But if it's true, it might mean Arridaios is worse.'

'No, Alexander would have sent word; the man is lying, I know it. We must wait to hear from Perdikkas in Babylon.'

'Oh, mother, let us not go. I don't want to marry the fool.'

'Don't call him the fool, he is King Philip, they have named him after your grandfather ... Don't you see? The gods have sent you this. They mean you to right the wrong that was done your father.'

Eurydike looked away. She had been barely two when Amyntas was executed, and did not remember him. He had been a burden on her all her life.

'Eurydike!' The voice of authority brought her to attention. Kynna had set herself to be father as well as mother, and done it well. 'Listen to me. You were meant for great things, not to grow old in a village like a peasant. When Alexander offered you his brother's hand to make peace between our houses, I knew that it was destiny. You are a true-born Macedonian and royal on both sides. Your father should have been King. If you were a man, they would have chosen you in Assembly.'

The girl listened in a growing quiet. Her face lost its sullenness; aspiration began to kindle in her eyes.

'If I die for it,' said Kynna, 'you shall be reigning Queen.'

Peukestes, Satrap of Persia, had withdrawn from his audience-chamber to his private room. It was furnished in the manner of the province, except for the Macedonian panoply on the armour-stand. He had changed from his formal robe to loose trousers and embroidered slippers. A tall fair man, with features of lean refinement, he had curled his hair Persian style; but at Alexander's death, conforming to Persian custom, had shaved it to the scalp, instead of cropping it as he would in Macedon. When exposed it still felt chilly; to warm his head he had put on his cap of office, the helmet-shaped kyrbasia. This gave him an unintended look of state; the man he had summoned approached him with downcast eyes, and prepared to go down in the prostration.

Peukestes looked at him startled, at first not knowing him; then he put out his hand. 'No, Bagoas. Get up, be seated.'

Bagoas rose and obeyed, acknowledging, with some gesture of the face, Peukestes' smile. His dark-circled eyes looked enormous; there was just enough flesh on him to display the elegance of his skull. His scalp was naked of hair; when it began to grow he must have shaved again. He looked like an ivory mask. Yes, something must be done for him, Peukestes thought.

'You know,' he said, 'that Alexander died leaving no will?'

The young eunuch made an assenting gesture. After a pause he said, 'Yes. He would not surrender.'

'True. And when he understood that the common fate of man had overtaken him, his voice had gone. Or he would not have forgotten his faithful servants ... You know, I kept vigil for him at the shrine of Sarapis. It was a long night, and a man had time to think.'

'Yes,' said Bagoas. 'That was a long night.'

'He told me once that your father had an estate near Susa, but was unjustly dispossessed and killed while you were young.' No need to add that the boy had been castrated and enslaved, and sold to pleasure Darius. 'If Alexander could have spoken, I think he would have bequeathed you your father's land. So I shall buy out the man who has it, and give it you.'

'The bounty of my lord is like rain on a dry river bed.' A beautiful movement of the hand went with it, like an absentminded reflex; he had been a courtier since he was thirteen. 'But my parents are both dead; so are my sisters, at least if they were fortunate. I had no brother; and I shall have no son. Our house was burned to the ground; and for whom should I rebuild it?'

He has made a grave-offering of his beauty, Peukestes thought; now he is waiting to die. 'And yet, it might please your father's shade to see his son restore his name with honour in the ancestral place.'

Bagoas' hollow eyes seemed to consider it, like something infinitely distant. 'If my lord, in his magnanimity, would give me a little time ...?'

He wants only to be rid of me, Peukestes thought. Well, I can do no more.

That evening Ptolemy, on the eve of departing to the satrapy of Egypt, was his guest at supper. Since it seemed they might never meet again, their talk grew reminiscent. Presently it turned upon Bagoas.

'He could make Alexander laugh,' Ptolemy said. 'I have heard them often.'

'You would not think so now.' Peukestes related the morning's interview. The talk passed to other things; but Ptolemy, who had a mind that wasted nothing, pleaded tomorrow's press of business and left the party early.

Bagoas' house stood in the paradise a little way from the palace. It was small but elegant; often Alexander had spent an evening there. Ptolemy remembered the torches in their sconces by the door, the sound of harps and flutes and laughter, and, sometimes, the eunuch's sweet alto singing.

At first sight all was dark. Nearer, he saw a dim single lamp yellowing a window. A small dog barked; after a while, a sleepy servant peered through the grille, and said the master had retired. These courtesies over, Ptolemy went round towards the window.

'Bagoas,' he said softly, 'it's Ptolemy. I am going away for ever Won't you bid me good-bye?'

There was only a short silence. The light voice said, 'Let the lord Ptolemy in. Light the lamps. Bring wine.'

Ptolemy entered, politely disclaiming ceremony, Bagoas politely insisting. A taper was brought, light shone on his ivory head. He was dressed, in the formal clothes he must have worn to call on Peukestes. They looked now as if he had slept in them; he was buttoning the jacket up. On the table was a tablet covered with score-marks; what was erased looked like an attempt to draw a face. He pushed it aside to make room for the wine-tray, and thanked Ptolemy for the honour of his visit with impeccable civility; peering at him blankly from deep hollow eyes, as the slave kindled the lamps, like an owl revealed in daylight. He looked a little mad. Ptolemy thought, Am I too late already?

He said, 'You have truly mourned for him. I too. He was a good brother.'

Bagoas' face remained inexpressive; but tears ran from his eyes in silence, like blood from an open wound. He brushed them absently away, as one might a lock of hair which has a habit of straying, and turned to pour the wine.

'We owed him tears,' Ptolemy said. 'He would have wept for us.' He paused. 'But, if the dead care for what concerned them in life, he may be needing more from his friends than that.'

The ivory mask under the lamp turned to a face; the eyes, in which desperation was tempered by older habits of gentle irony, riveted themselves on Ptolemy's. 'Yes?' he said.

'We both know what he valued most. While he lived, honour and love; and, after, undying fame.'

'Yes,' said Bagoas. 'So . . .?'

With his new attention had come a profound and weary scepticism. Why not, thought Ptolemy; three years among the labyrinthine intrigues of Darius' court before he was sixteen – and, lately, why not indeed?

'What have you seen since he died? How long have you been shut up here?'

Raising his large dark disillusioned eyes, Bagoas said with a vicious quiet, 'Since the day of the elephants.'

For a moment Ptolemy was silenced; the wraith had hardened, dauntingly. Presently he said, 'Yes, that would have sickened him. Niarchos said so, and so did I. But we were overborne.'

Bagoas said, answering the unspoken words, 'The ring would have gone to Krateros, if he had been there.'

There was a pause. Ptolemy considered his next move; Bagoas looked like a man just waked from sleep, considering his thoughts. Suddenly he looked up sharply. 'Has anyone gone to Susa?'

'Bad news travels fast.'

'News?' said Bagoas with unconcealed impatience. 'It is protection they will need.'

Suddenly, Ptolemy remembered something said by his Persian wife, Artakama, a lady of royal blood bestowed by Alexander. He was leaving her with his family till, as he had said, the affairs of Egypt were settled. He had been uneasy with a harem, its claustral and stifling femininity, after the free-and-easy Greek hetairas. He meant his heir to be a pure-bred Macedonian, and had, in fact, offered for one of Antipatros' many daughters. But there had been some piece of gossip . . . Bagoas' eyes were boring into his.

'I have heard a rumour – worth nothing I daresay – that a Persian lady came from Susa to the harem here, and was taken sick and died. But –'

Bagoas' breath hissed through his teeth. 'If Stateira has come to Babylon,' he said in a soft deadly voice, 'of course she has been taken sick and died. When first the Baktrian knew of me, I would have died of the same sickness, if I had not given some sweetmeats to a dog.'

Ptolemy felt a sickening conviction. He had been with Alexander on that last visit to Susa, been brought once to dine with Sisygambis and the family. Pity and disgust contended with the thought that if this had happened, and Perdikkas had condoned it, his own design was justified.

'Alexander's fame,' he said, 'has not been very well served since the gods received him. Men who cannot match his greatness of soul should try at least to honour it.'

Bagoas brooded on him, thoughtfully, in a grey calm; as if he stood on the threshold of a door he had been going out of, and could not be sure it was worth while to turn back. 'Why have you come?' he said.

The dead are not respectful, Ptolemy reflected. Good, it saves time.

'I will tell you why. I am concerned for the fate of Alexander's body.'

Bagoas hardly stirred, but his whole frame seemed to change, losing its lethargy, becoming wiry and tense. 'They took their oath!' he said. 'They took it on the Styx.'

'Oath . . .? Oh, all that is over. I'm not talking of Babylon.'

He looked up. His hearer had come in from the threshold; the door of life had swung-to behind him. He listened, rigidly.

'They are making him a golden bier; nothing less is due to him. It will take the craftsmen a year to finish. Then, Perdikkas will have it sent to Macedon.'

'To *Macedon*!' The look of stunned shock quite startled Ptolemy, his homeland customs taken for granted. Well, so much the better.

'That is the custom. Did he not tell you how he buried his father?'

'Yes. But it was *here* they . . .'

'Meleager? A rogue and a halfwit, and the rogue is dead. But in

Macedon, that is different. The Regent is nearly eighty; he may be gone before the bier arrives. And his heir is Kassandros, whom you know.'

Bagoas' slender hand closed in a sinewy fist. 'Why did Alexander let him live? If he had only given me leave. No one would have been the wiser.'

I don't doubt it, thought Ptolemy, glancing at his face. 'Well, in Macedon the King is entombed by his rightful heir; it confirms his succession. So, Kassandros will be waiting. So will Perdikkas; he will claim it in the name of Roxane's son – and, if there is no son, maybe for himself. There is also Olympias, who is no mean fighter either. It will be a bitter war. Sooner or later, whoever holds the coffin and the bier will need the gold.'

Ptolemy looked for a moment, and looked away. He had come remembering the elegant, epicene favourite; devoted certainly, he had not doubted that, but still, a frivolity, the plaything of two kings' leisure. He had not foreseen this profound and private grief in its priestlike austerity. What memories moved behind those guarded eyes?

'This, then,' Bagoas said inexpressively, 'is why you came?'

'Yes. I can prevent it, if I have help that I can trust.'

Bagoas said, half to himself, 'I never thought they would be taking him away.' His face changed and grew wary. 'What do you mean to do?'

'If I have word of when the bier sets out, I will march from Egypt to meet it. Then, if I can treat with the escort – and I think I can – I will take him to his own city, and entomb him in Alexandria.'

Ptolemy waited. He saw himself being weighed. At least there were no old scores between them. Less than delighted when Alexander took a Persian to his heart and bed, he had been distant to the boy, but never insolent. Later, when it was clear the youth was neither venal nor ambitious, simply a tactful and well-mannered concubine, their chance meetings had been unstrained and easy. However, one did not sleep with two kings and remain naive. One could see the assessment he was making now.

'You are thinking of what I stand to gain; and why not? A great deal, of course. It may even make me a king. But – and this I swear before the gods – never a king of Macedon and Asia. No man alive can wear the mantle of Alexander, and those who grasp at it will destroy themselves. Egypt I can hold, and rule it as he wanted. You were not there, it was before your time; but he was proud of Alexandria.'

'Yes,' said Bagoas. 'I know.'

'I was with him,' said Ptolemy, 'when he went to Ammon's oracle at Siwah in the desert, to learn his destiny.'

He began to tell of it. Almost at once the worldly alertness in his hearer's face had faded; he saw the single-minded absorption of a listening child. How often, he thought, must that look have drawn the tale from Alexander! The boy's memory must read like a written scroll. But to hear it from someone else would give some new and precious detail, some new sight-line.

He took trouble, therefore, describing the desert march, the rescuing rain, the guiding ravens, the serpents pointing as they lay, the sand's mysterious voices; the great oasis with its pools and palm-glades and wondering white-robed people; the rocky acropolis where the temple was, with its famous courtyard where the sign of the god was given.

'There is a spring in a basin of red rock; we had to wash our gold and silver offerings in it, to cleanse them for the god, and ourselves as well. It was icy cold in the hot dry air. Alexander of course they did not purify. He was Pharaoh. He carried his own divinity. They led him into the sanctuary. Outside, the light was all shimmering white, and everything seemed to ripple in it. The entrance looked black as night, you'd have thought it would have blinded him. But he went in as though his eyes were on distant mountains.'

Bagoas nodded, as if to say, 'Of course; go on.'

'Presently we heard singing, and harps and cymbals and sistra, and the oracle came out. There is not room for it inside the sanctuary. He stood there to watch it, somewhere in the dark.

'The priests came out, forty pairs of them, twenty before and twenty behind the god. They carried the oracle like a litter, with long shoulder-poles. The oracle is a boat. I don't know why the god should speak through a boat on land. Ammon has a very old shrine at Thebes. Alexander used to say it must have come first from the river.'

'Tell me about the boat.' He spoke like a child who prompts an old bedtime story.

'It was long and light, like the bird-hunters' punts on the Nile. But sheathed all over with gold, and hung with gold and silver votives, all kinds of little precious things swinging and glittering and tinkling. In the middle was the presence of the god. Just a simple sphere.

'The priest came out into the court with Alexander's question. He had written it on a strip of gold and folded the gold together. He laid it on the pavement before the god, and prayed in his own tongue. Then the boat began to live. It stayed where it was, but you could see it quicken.'

'You saw it,' said Bagoas suddenly. 'Alexander said he was too far.'

'Yes, I saw. The carriers stood with empty faces, waiting; but they were like flotsam on a still river-pool, before the flow of the river lifts it. It does not stir yet; but you know the river is under all.

'The question lay shining in the sun. The cymbals sounded a slow beat and the flutes played louder. Then the carriers began to sway a little where they stood, just as flotsam sways. You know how the god answers; back for no, forward for yes. They moved forward like all one thing, a skein of water-weed, a drift of leaves, till before the question they stopped, and the prow dipped. Then the trumpets sounded, and we waved our hands and cheered.

'We waited, then, for Alexander to come out from the sanctuary. It was hot; or we thought so, not having yet been in Gedrosia.' A shadowy smile replied to him. They were both survivors of that dreadful march.

'At last he came out with the high priest. I think more had happened than he had come to ask. He came out with the awe still in him. Then, I remember, he blinked in the sudden brightness, and shaded his eyes with his hand. He saw us all, and looked across and smiled.'

He had looked across at Hephaistion and smiled; but there was no need to say so.

'Egypt loved him. They welcomed him with hymns as their saviour from the Persians. He honoured all their temples that Ochos had profaned. I wish you had seen him laying out Alexandria. I don't know how far it has gone up now, I don't trust the governor; but I know what he wanted, and when I am there I shall see it done. There is only one thing he left no mark for; the tomb where we shall honour him. But I know the place, by the sea. I remember him standing there.'

Bagoas' eyes had been fixed upon a light-point on his silver cup. He raised them. 'What is it you want done?'

Silently, Ptolemy caught his breath. He had been in time.

'Stay here in Babylon. You refused Peukestes' offer; no one else will make you his concern. Bear with it if they take your house for some creature of Perdikkas'. Stay till the bier is ready and you know when it will set out. Then come to me. You shall have a house in Alexandria near where he lies. You know that in Macedon that could not be.'

In Macedon, he thought, the children would stone you in the street. But you have guessed that; there is no need to be cruel.

'Will you take my hand on it?' he said.

He held out his big-boned right hand, calloused from the spearshaft and the sword, its seams picked out by the lamp as he held it open. Pale, slender and icy cold, Bagoas' hand took it in a precise and steady grip. Ptolemy remembered that he had been a dancer.

In a last fierce spasm, Roxane felt her infant's head thrust out of her. More gently, with swift relief, turned by a skilful midwife, the moist body slid after. She stretched her legs out, dripping with sweat and panting; then heard the child's thin angry cry.

Shrill with exhaustion, she cried out, 'A boy, is it a boy?'

Acclamation and praise and good-luck invocations rose in chorus. She gave a great groan of triumph. The midwife lifted the child to view, still on its blue-white cord. From the half-screened corner where he had vigilantly watched the birth, Perdikkas came forward, confirmed the sex, uttered a conventional phrase of good omen, and left the room.

The cord was tied, the afterbirth delivered; mother and child were washed with warm rose-water, dried, anointed. Alexander the Fourth, joint King of Macedon and Asia, was laid in his mother's arms.

He nuzzled for warmth, but she held him at arms' length to look at him. He was dark-haired.

The midwife, touching the fine fluff, said it was birth-hair that would fall away. He was still red and crumpled, his face closed up in the indignation of the newly-born; but she could see through the flush an olive, not a rosy colouring. He would be dark, a Baktrian. And why not? Alone in a harsh alien element, missing the womb's blind comfort, he began to cry.

She lowered him to her body, to take the weight from her arms. He hushed; the slave-girl with the feather fan had come back to the bedside; after the bustle, the women with silence and soft feet were setting to rights the rooms of the Royal Wife. Beyond the door, the courtyard with its fishpool lay under the mild winter sun. Reflected light fell on the dressing table, and on the gold and silver toilet set that had been Queen Stateira's; her jewel-box stood beside it. All was triumph and tranquillity.

The nurse came fussing up with the antique royal cradle, plated with gold and time-yellowed ivory. Roxane drew the coverlet over the sleeping child. Under her fingers, almost disguised by the elaborate embroidery, was a smear of blood.

Her stomach heaved. When she had moved into this room it had all been refurbished and re-draped. But the bed was a fine one and they had not changed it.

She had stood by while Stateira writhed and tried to clutch at her and moaned 'Help me! Help me!', and fumbled blindly with her clothes. Roxane had flung them back to see her beaten enemy, her son's rival, come naked into the world he would never rule. Could it be true that the thing had opened its mouth and cried? Disturbed by her tightened fingers, the infant wailed.

'Shall I take him, madam?' said the nurse timidly by her side. 'Would madam like to sleep?'

'Later.' She softened her grip; the child quietened and curled itself against her. He was a king and she was a king's mother; no one could take it from her. 'Where is Amestrin? Amestrin, who put this filthy cover on my bed? It stinks, it is disgusting, give me something clean. If I see it again, your back will know it.'

After panic scurryings, another cover was found; the state one, a year's work in Artaxerxes' day, was whisked out of sight. The baby slept. Roxane, her body loosening into comfort from its labour, sank into drowsiness. In a dream she saw a half-made child with the face of Alexander, lying in blood, its grey eyes staring with anger. Fear woke her. But all was well; he was dead and could do nothing, it was her son who would rule the world. She slept again.

322 BC

The army of King Philip was encamped in the Pisidian hills. Perdikkas, blood-spattered and smeared with ash, was picking his way down a stony path strewn with dead men and abandoned weapons. Above him, circling a cloud of stinking smoke, vultures and kites made exploring swoops, their numbers thickening as news of the banquet spread. The Macedonians, prompter than the birds, scavenged the charred ruins of Isaura.

Spared by Alexander because they had surrendered without a fight, the Isaurians had been left with orders to pull down the robber fort from which they had plagued their neighbours, and to live peaceably. In his long absence they had murdered his satrap and fallen back into old ways. This time, from bad consciences or from having less trust in Perdikkas than in Alexander, they had defended their craggy nest to the bitter end. When their outworks fell, they had locked into their houses their goods, their wives and children, set timber and thatch alight, and to the hellish music of the fires had hurled themselves on the Macedonian spears.

Some fifteen years of war had made Perdikkas almost nightmare-proof; in a few days he would be dining out on the story; but with the stench of burned flesh still hanging in the air he had had enough for today, and had welcomed the news that a courier awaited him in his camp below. His brother Alketas, a hard man and his second-in-command, would oversee the raking of the cinders for half-melted silver and gold. His helmet was scorching hot; he took it off and wiped his sweating forehead.

From the royal tent of dyed and emblazoned leather, Philip came out and ran towards him. 'Did we win?' he asked.

He was armed in cuirass and greaves, a thing he had insisted on. In Alexander's day, when he had followed the army much as now, he had worn civil dress; but now that he was King, he knew what was due to him. He had in fact been eager to fight; but, used to obedience, had not insisted, since Alexander had never let him do it. 'You're all bleeding,' he said. 'You ought to see a doctor.'

'It's a bath I need.' When alone with his sovereign, Perdikkas dispensed with formality. He told him as much as it was good for him to know, went to his own tent, cleaned himself, put on a robe, and ordered the courier brought.

This person was a surprise. The letter he brought was reticent and formal; he himself had much to say. A hardy grizzled man in his early sixties, with a missing thumb lost at Gaugamela, he was a minor Macedonian nobleman, and not so much a messenger as an envoy.

With elation, tinged by well-founded misgivings, Perdikkas re-read the letter to gain time for thought. TO PERDIKKAS, REGENT OF THE ASIAN KINGDOMS, FROM KLEOPATRA, DAUGHTER OF PHILIP AND SISTER OF ALEXANDER, GREETING. After the usual well-wishings, the letter glanced at their cousinship, recalled his distinguished services to Alexander, and proposed a conference, to discuss *matters concerning the wellbeing of all the Macedonians*. These matters were not specified. The last sentence disclosed that the Queen had set out already from Dodona.

The envoy, affecting negligence, was toying with his wine-cup. Perdikkas coughed. 'Am I to hope that if I should beg the honour of the lady Kleopatra's hand, my suit would be graciously received?'

The envoy gave a reassuring smile. 'So far, the Kings have been elected only by the Macedonians in Asia. Those in the homeland might like their own chance to choose.'

Perdikkas had had a gruelling and hideous, even though successful, day. He had come back for a bath, a rest and a drink, not to be offered at short notice the throne of Macedon. Presently he said, with a certain dryness, 'Such happiness was beyond my hopes. I feared she might still be mourning Leonnatos.'

The veteran, whom Perdikkas' steward had refreshed while he was waiting, settled into his chair. The wine was strong, with no more than a splash of water, Perdikkas having felt he needed it. The diplomat gave way visibly to the soldier.

'I can tell you, sir, why he was her first choice, for what it's worth. She remembered him from her childhood at home. He climbed a tree once, to get down her cat for her, when he was a boy. You know what women are.'

'And in the end I believe they did not meet?'

'No. When he crossed from Asia to fight the southern Greeks, he'd only time to raise his troops in Macedon and ride on down. Bad luck that he fell before our victory.'

'A pity that his troops were so cut up. I hear he fought while he could stand. A brave man; but hardly the stuff of kings?'

'She was well out of it,' said the soldier bluntly. 'All her friends tell her so. It was a fancy; she soon got over her grieving. Lucky for her she has the chance to think better now.' He tipped back his cup; Perdikkas refilled it. 'If she had seen *you*, sir, at Gaugamela . . .'

This word of power diverted them into reminiscence. When they came back to business, Perdikkas said, 'I suppose the truth is, she wants to get away from Olympias.'

The envoy, flushed and relaxed, planked down his cup and leaned his arm on the table. 'Sir. Let me tell you, between ourselves, that woman is a gorgon. She's eaten that poor girl piece by piece, till she's hardly mistress of her house, let alone the kingdom. Not that she lacks spirit; but left as she is, without a man to stand by her, there's no fighting Olympias. She has the Molossians treating her like a queen. She *is* a queen. She looks like a queen; she has the will of a king. And she's Alexander's mother.'

'Ah. Yes . . . So Kleopatra has a mind to leave her Dodona, and make a bid for Macedon?'

'She's Philip's daughter.'

Perdikkas, who had been thinking quickly, said, 'She has a son by the late King.' He had no wish to be caretaker for a stepson.

'*He'll* inherit at home, his granddam will see to that. Now Macedon . . . No woman has ever reigned in Macedon. But Philip's daughter, married to a royal kinsman who's ruled like a king already . . .' Abruptly, remembering something, he hitched at his belt-purse, and brought out a flat package wrapped in embroidered wool. 'She sent you this, seeing it's a long time since you had a sight of her.'

The portrait was painted with skill, in encaustic wax on wood. Even allowing for convention, which smoothed away personality like a blemish, it could be seen that she was Philip's daughter. The strong hair, the thick upswept eyebrows, the resolute square face, had defeated the artist's well-meant insipidity. Perdikkas thought, Two years younger than Alexander – about thirty-one, now. 'A queenly and gracious lady,' he said aloud. 'A dowry in herself, kingdom or no.' He found more of this kind to say, while he played for time. Danger was great; ambition also. Alexander had taught him long ago to assess, decide, and act.

'Well,' he said, 'this is serious business. She needs something more than a yes. Let me sleep on this. When you dine with us tonight, I'll tell them all you brought a letter from Olympias. She's forever writing.'

'I have brought one. She approves, as you may well suppose.'

Perdikkas set the thick roll aside, summoned the steward to find his guest a lodging, and, left alone, sat with his elbows on the rough camp table and his head between his hands.

Here he was found by his brother Alketas, whose servants carried two rattling sacks filled with stained, smoked gold, cups and armrings and necklaces and coin; the Isaurians had been successful robbers. The slaves gone, he showed Perdikkas the loot, and was annoyed by his abstraction. 'Not squeamish?' he said. 'You were there in India, when the men thought the Mallians had killed Alexander. You should have a strong stomach after that.'

Perdikkas looked at him in irritation. 'We'll talk later. Is Eumenes back in camp? Find him, he can bath and eat later, I have to see him now.'

Eumenes appeared quite shortly, washed, combed and changed. He had been in his tent, dictating his memoir of the day's events to Hieronymos, a young scholar who, under his patronage, was writing a chronicle of the times. His light compact body was toughened and tanned from the campaign; soon he would be riding north to get his satrapy of Kappadokia in order. He greeted Perdikkas with a calm alert expectancy, sat down, and read the letter Perdikkas handed him. At the end, he allowed himself a slight lift of the brows.

Looking up from the scroll, he said, 'What is she offering? The regency or the throne?' Perdikkas understood him perfectly. He meant, Which do you plan to take?

'The regency. Or would I be talking to you now?'

'Leonnatos did,' Eumenes reminded him. 'And then decided that I knew too much.' He had, in fact, barely escaped with his life, having affirmed his loyalty to Alexander's son.

'Leonnatos was a fool. The Macedonians would have cut his throat; and they'd cut mine if I disinherited Alexander's boy. If they elect him when he comes of age, so be it. But he's the Baktrian's son; by that time, they may not be so fond of him. Then we'll see. Meantime, I'll have been King in all but name for fifteen years or so, and I shan't complain.'

'No,' said Eumenes grimly. 'But Antipatros will.'

Perdikkas sat back in his leather-slung camp chair, and stretched out his long legs. 'That's the crux. Advise me. What shall I do with Nikaia?'

'A pity indeed,' said the Greek, 'that Kleopatra didn't write a few months sooner.' He sat reflecting, like a mathematician before a theorem. 'You won't need her now. But you've sent her the betrothal gifts. She's the Regent's daughter. And she's on her way.'

'I offered for her too soon. Everything seemed in chaos; I thought I should make sure of an ally while I could ... Alexander would never have tied his hands like that. *He* always made alliances when he could dictate the terms.' It was rarely, now, that he was self-critical; he must be disturbed, Eumenes thought. He tapped absently at the letter. Perdikkas noted that even his nails were clean.

'Antipatros puts out his daughters as a fisherman puts out lines.'

'Well, I took the bait. What now?'

'You've bitten at the bait. The hook's not yet in your belly. Let us think.' His neat thin lips came together. Even on campaign, he shaved every day. Presently, looking up, he said crisply, 'Take Kleopatra. Take her now. Send an escort to meet Nikaia; tell her you're sick, wounded; be civil, but have her taken home. Act at once, before Antipatros is ready. Or he'll hear of it, you won't know how or when; and he'll act before *you're* ready.'

Perdikkas bit his lip. It sounded prompt and decisive; probably it was what Alexander would have done. Except that he would never have put himself in need of it. Among these doubts, a disturbing thought intruded: Eumenes hated Antipatros. The Regent had been snubbing him ever since he had been a junior secretary, advanced by Philip because of his quick mind. The old man had all the prejudices of his race against the effete, fickle, subtle men of the south. Eumenes' loyalty, his distinguished war record, had never made any difference. Even when he was in Asia as Chief Secretary to Alexander, Antipatros had tried often to go over his head. Alexander, whom it irritated, had made a point of replying through Eumenes.

Now that Perdikkas had been counselled to burn his boats, he felt a certain flinching. He said to himself that here was an old enmity, of the kind that warps a man's better judgement.

'Yes,' he said, affecting gratitude. 'You are right. I'll write by her envoy tomorrow.'

'Better use word of mouth. Letters can go astray.'

'.. But I'll tell her, I think, that I've already married Nikaia. It will be true by the time it reaches her. I'll ask her to wait till I can decently get free. I'll put the palace of Sardis at her disposal, and ask her to consider us betrothed in secret. That will give me room to manoeuvre.'

Seeing Eumenes looking at him in silence, he felt the need to justify himself. 'If there were only Antipatros to consider ... But I don't like what I hear of Ptolemy. He's raising too big an army down in Egypt. It only needs one satrap to make a kingdom of his province, and the empire will fall apart. We must wait a little and see what he means to do.'

A bland winter sun shone down through the columned window into Ptolemy's small audience-room. It was a handsome house, almost a small palace, built for himself by the previous administrator, whom Ptolemy had executed for oppression. The slight rise commanded a view of new straight streets and handsome public buildings, their pale unweathered stone touched up with paint and gilding. New wharves and quays fringed the harbour; hoists and scaffolding surrounded a couple of nearly finished temples ordered by Alexander. Another temple, less advanced, but promising to be the most imposing, stood near the waterfront, where it would dominate the prospect for incoming ships.

Ptolemy had had a busy but congenial morning. He had seen the chief architect, Deinokrates, about the sculpture on the temples; some engineers, who were replacing insanitary canals with covered drains; and the heads of several nomes, to whom he had restored the right to collect taxes. This, to the Egyptians who had suffered under his predecessor, meant something like a fifty per cent tax reduction. A rapacious man, resolved to execute his commission and enrich himself as well, he had imposed forced levies and forced labour, extorted fortunes by threats to kill the sacred crocodiles, or to pull down villages for building sites (which he would do in the end, when he had squeezed them dry). Moreover, he had done all this in the name of Alexander, which had so enraged Ptolemy that he had gone through the administration like a consuming fire. It had made him extremely popular, and he had remained so.

He was now busy recruiting. Perdikkas had only allowed him two thousand men when he took over the satrapy. He had found, when he got there, its garrison almost mutinous, the men's pay in arrears while the interest was being skimmed off it. Things were different now. Ptolemy had not been the most brilliant of Alexander's commanders; but he was reliable, resourceful, brave and loyal, all things Alexander valued; and, above all, he was good at looking after his men. He had fought under Philip before Alexander had his first command; the pupil of two great masters, he had learned from both. Trusted, sufficiently feared, and liked, he was apt with small touches of personal concern. Before his first year was out, thousands of active veterans settled in Alexandria were begging to re-enlist; by now, volunteers were arriving by land and sea.

He had not allowed this to inflate ambition. He knew his limits, and had no wish for the stresses of boundless power. He had what he had wanted, was content with it and meant to keep it; with luck, to add a little more. His men were well paid and fed; they were also well trained.

'Why, Menandros!' he said warmly as the last applicant came in. 'I thought you were in Syria. Well, this is an easier climb than the Birdless Rock. You got here without a rope.'

The veteran, recognized at sight as a hero of that renowned assault, grinned with delight, feeling that after an uncertain year he had arrived where he belonged. The interview was happy. Ptolemy decided to take a break in his inner sanctum. His chamberlain, an Egyptian of great discretion, scratched at the door.

'My lord,' he murmured, 'the eunuch of whom you spoke has come from Babylon.'

The broken nose in Ptolemy's craggy face pointed like a hound's at a breast-high scent. 'I'll see him here,' he said.

He waited in the pleasant, cool, Greek-furnished room. Bagoas was shown in.

Ptolemy saw a Persian gentleman, soberly suited in grey, equipped for travel with a businesslike sword belt, its slots well stretched by the weapons left outside. He had grown his hair; a modest length of it fringed his round felt hat. He looked handsome, lean, distinguished and of no particular age. Ptolemy supposed he must be twenty-four.

He made the graceful genuflexion due to a satrap, was invited to sit, and offered the wine which had awaited the morning's leisure. Ptolemy made the proper enquiries about his health and journey; he knew better than to be precipitate with a Persian. It was clear that the midnight encounter in the paradise was to be remembered in substance only; etiquette was to be preserved. He remembered from old days Bagoas' infinite resources of tact.

The courtesies fully observed, he asked, 'What news?'

Bagoas set aside his wine-cup. 'They will be bringing him out from Babylon two months from now.'

'And the convoy? Who's in command?'

'Arybbas. No one has questioned it.'

Ptolemy sighed audibly with relief. Before marching south, he had proposed this officer to design and supervise the bier, citing his expertise; he had devised several important shrines for Alexander, and could handle craftsmen. Not cited was that he had served in India under Ptolemy's command, and been on excellent terms with his commander.

'I waited,' said Bagoas, 'till I was sure of it. They would need him, in case of mishap, to see the bier repaired.'

'You have made good time, then.'

'I came up the Euphrates, and then by camel to Tyre. The rest by sea. Forty days in all.'

'You will be able to rest awhile, and still be in Babylon before they start.'

'If God permits. As for the bier, in a hundred days it could hardly reach the coast. The roadmakers are out already, smoothing the way. Arybbas reckons it will travel ten miles a day on level ground, or five over hills, if sixty-four mules pull it. To bring it from Asia into Thrace, they plan to bridge the Hellespont.'

The quiet madness of the house in the park was gone. He spoke with the concentration of a man going about his chosen calling. He looked lean and fit after his long journey.

'You have seen it then?' Ptolemy asked. 'Is it worthy of Alexander?'

Bagoas considered. 'Yes, they have done all that men can.'

Arybbas must have excelled himself, Ptolemy thought. 'Come to the window. There is something you must see.'

He pointed to the temple rising on the waterfront, the sea, pale blue under the mild sky, shining between the unfinished columns.

'There is his shrine.'

For a moment, the reticent face beside him lit and glowed. Just so, Ptolemy remembered from another life, the boy had looked when Alexander rode past in a victory parade.

'It should be ready in another year. The priests of Ammon would like him to go to Siwah; they say it would have been his wish. I have considered it, but I think this is his place.'

'When you have seen the bier, sir, you will know it could never go to Siwah. If once its wheels sank into sand, a team of elephants could not drag it free ... That is a fine temple. They have worked quickly to get so far.'

Ptolemy had known that this must some time be met. He said gently, 'It was begun before I came. Alexander approved the plan himself. It is the temple he ordered for Hephaistion ... He did not know how soon he himself would need it.'

Bagoas' face turned to agelessness. He gazed in silence at the sunlit shafts of stone. Presently he said calmly, 'Hephaistion would give it him. He would have given him anything.'

Except his pride, thought Ptolemy; that was his secret, it was why Alexander felt him as a second self. But it was only possible because they were boys together. Aloud he said, 'Most men would welcome Alexander as a guest, even in death. Well, let us come to ways and means.'

At the table he unlocked a silver-clasped document box. 'This letter I shall give you when you leave, along with funds for your journey. Do not deliver it in Babylon. When the bier sets out, no one will wonder that you wish to follow it. Do nothing till it reaches Thapsakos – the Syrian border will be soon enough – and give it to Arybbas then. It commits him to nothing. It says I shall meet him at Issos, to do honour to Alexander. He will hardly suppose, I think, that I shall come alone.'

'I will see, said Bagoas coolly, 'that he is prepared.'

'Don't lose the letter in Babylon. Perdikkas would send an army corps for escort.' Wasting no words, Bagoas smiled.

'You have done well. Tell me, have you heard anything of Roxane's child? He must be walking now. Does he favour Alexander?'

One of Bagoas' fine brows moved upward a very little. 'I myself have not seen him. But the harem people say he takes after his mother.'

'I see. And King Philip, how is he?'

'Very well in health. He has been allowed to ride on an elephant, which made him happy.'

'So. Well, Bagoas, you have earned my gratitude; trust in it from now on. When you are rested, see the city; it will be your home.'

Bagoas made the elegant half-prostration of the gentleman to the satrap, learned at Darius' court, and took his leave.

Later, as the sun declined towards the western desert, he walked down to the temple. This was the evening promenade of the Alexandrians, who would pause to notice the progress of the work; off-duty soldiers of Macedon and Egypt, merchants and craftsmen from Greece and Lydia and Tyre and Cyprus and Judaea; wives and children, and hetairas looking for trade. The crowd was not yet oppressive; the city was still young.

The workmen on the site were packing their tools in their straw bags; the nightwatchmen were coming with their cloaks and food-baskets. From the ships tied to the waterfront men were going ashore; the ship-guards on board kindled torches whose tarry smell hung over the water. As dusk fell, on the temple terrace a burning cresset was hoisted on a tall pole. It was not unlike the one Alexander used to have by his tent in central Asia, to show where his headquarters was.

The strollers drifted towards home; soon no one was about but the watchmen and the silent traveller from Babylon. Bagoas looked at Hephaistion's house, where Alexander would be his guest for ever. It was fitting, it was what he would have wished, and after all it made no difference. What was, was, as it had always been. When Alexander breathed his last, Bagoas had known who would be awaiting him beyond the River. That was why he had not killed himself; the thought was not to be borne of intruding on that reunion. But Alexander had never been ungrateful, he had never turned love away. One day, after faithful service done, there would be, as there had always been, a welcome.

He turned back towards the palace guest house, where they were lighting the lamps. Alexander would be served worthily here. Nothing else had ever mattered.

In the manor house of the late prince Amyntas, Kynna and Eurydike were trimming each other's hair. They were preparing for their journey. Till they were out of Macedon, they planned to travel as men.

The Regent, Antipatros, was besieging stubborn forts in the mountains of Aitolia, where the last of the Greek revolt still smouldered on. He had taken most of his troops. This was their chance.

'There,' said Kynna, standing back with the shears. 'Many young men wear it as long as that, since Alexander set the fashion.'

Neither of them had had to sacrifice much hair; it was strong and wavy, not long. A maid was called to sweep up the clippings. Eurydike, who had already prepared her mule-packs, went to the stack of spears in the corner, and chose out her favourite javelins.

'We shan't have much chance to practise on the road.'

'Let us hope,' said Kynna, 'that we may not need them in earnest.'

'Oh, robbers won't attack ten men.' They were taking an escort of eight retainers. She glanced at her mother's face, and added, 'You're not afraid of Olympias?'

'No, she is too far away, we shall be in Asia before she hears.'

Eurydike looked again. 'Mother, what is it?'

Kynna was pacing the room. On stands and tables and shelves were the family treasures, her dead husband's heritage from his royal father, and pieces from her dowry; her own father, King Philip, had given her a handsome wedding. She was wondering how much she dared entrust to such a journey. Her daughter could not go empty-handed, but ...

'Mother, there is something ... Is it because we've heard nothing from Perdikkas?'

'Yes. I don't like it.'

'How long since you wrote to him?'

'I did not. It was proper for him to write.' She turned to a shelf and picked up a silver cup.

'There is something else you've not told me. I know there is. Why is Antipatros against our going? Have they betrothed the King to someone else? ... Mother, don't pretend you don't hear me. I'm not a child. If you don't tell me, I won't go.'

Kynna turned round, with the face that would have meant a whipping a few years back. The tall girl, implacable, stood her ground.

Kynna put down the cup with its boar-hunt chasing. She bit her lip.

'Very well, since you will have it; I daresay it's better. Alexander said frankly it was an empty marriage. He offered you wealth and rank; I daresay you could have gone home after, for all he cared.'

'You never told me so!'

'No, because you were not meant to grow old in a village. Be quiet and listen. He never looked further than the reconcilement of our houses. That was because he believed what his mother told him. He believed that his brother was born a fool.'

'So are all fools. I don't understand.'

'Don't you remember Straton the mason?'

'But that was because a stone fell on his head.'

'Yes. He was not born stumbling in his speech, or asking for a tree when he wanted bread. That was done by the stone.'

'But all my life, I've heard Arridaios was a fool.'

'All your life he has been one. You are fifteen, and he is thirty. When your father was hoping to be King, he told me a good deal about Philip's house. He said that when Arridaios was born, he was a fine strong child, and forward. It is true your father was still a child himself, and it was servants' talk; but he listened, because it concerned another child. They said that Philip was pleased with the boy, and Olympias knew it. She swore Philinna's bastard should not disinherit her son. The child was born in the palace. Maybe she gave him something, maybe she saw to it that something should hit his head. So your father heard them say.'

'What a wicked woman! Poor baby, I would not do it to a dog. But it's done; where is the difference now?'

'Only born fools beget fools. Straton's children are all sound.'

Eurydike drew a sharp, shocked breath. Her hands gripped defensively the javelin she was holding. 'No! They said I need not. Even Alexander said so. You promised me!'

'Hush, hush. No one is asking it. That is what I'm telling you. That is why Antipatros is against it and Perdikkas doesn't write. It is not what they want. It is what they fear.'

Eurydike stood still, absently passing her hand up and down the shaft of the javelin; it was a good one, of smooth hard cornel wood. 'You mean, they are afraid I could found a royal line, to displace Alexander's?'

'So I think.'

The girl's hand tightened on the shaft so that the knuckles paled. 'If that is what I must do to avenge my father, then I will. Because he left no son.'

Kynna was appalled. She had only wanted to explain their dangers. Quickly she said that it had been only slaves' talk; there had always been gossip about Olympias, that she coupled with serpents, and had conceived Alexander by the fire from heaven. It might well be true that Philinna had borne a fool, and it had not shown till the child was growing.

Eurydike looked carefully at the javelin, and put it aside with the few she meant to take. 'Don't be afraid, mother. Let's wait till we are there, and I can see what I ought to do. Then I will do it.'

What have I made, thought Kynna; what have I done? Next moment she reminded herself that she had made what she had planned, and done what she had long resolved. She sent word to the herdsman to bring an unblemished kid, for a sacrifice to dedicate their enterprise.

Arybbas, the creator of Alexander's bier, made his way to the workshop for his daily visit. He was a dandified but not effeminate man, soldier and aesthete, a remote kinsman of the royal house, and of course too aristocratic ever to have worked for hire. Alexander had made him lavish presents whenever he had created a shrine, a royal barge, or a public

spectacle, but that had been just between friends. Alexander, who loved
to give money away, took offence when it was stolen, and valued his
probity as well as his gifts. Ptolemy, when recommending him to
Perdikkas, had stressed this virtue, so necessary in a man handling a great
deal of gold.

He had in fact watched it jealously; not a grain had stuck to his fingers,
nor anyone else's. Weighing was a daily rite. A sumptuous designer, used
by Alexander when notable splendour was required, he had used with
gusto the whole treasure entrusted to him, for Alexander's honour and
his own. As the magnificent structure he had inspired took shape under
the hammers and gouges and graving-tools of his hand-picked craftsmen,
exultation mingled with solemnity; he pictured Alexander surveying it
with approval. *He* had appreciated such things. Arybbas had never cared
much for Perdikkas.

Outside the workshop he noticed that Bagoas the eunuch was loitering
about again, and, smiling graciously, beckoned him up. Though hardly
a person whose company one would seek in public, he had shown impeccable taste, and an eye for the finer points. His devotion to the dead was
touching; it was a pleasure to let him view the work.

'You will find a change,' he said. 'Yesterday they mounted it on the
wheel-base. So now you can see it whole.'

He rapped with his staff. Bolts grated; the little postern opened in the
great door. They stepped into shadow surrounding a blaze of glory.

The broad matting on the roof, which kept out bad weather and thieves
at night, had been rolled back to open the great working skylight. The
spring sun shafted down dazzlingly on a miniature temple, sheathed all
over with gold.

It was some eighteen feet long; its vaulted roof was of gold scales set with
gems, glowing balas rubies, emerald and crystal, sapphire and amethyst.
On its ridge like a banner stood a laurel wreath with leaves of shimmering
sheet-gold; on its corners victories leaned out, holding triumphant
crowns. It was upheld by eight golden columns; around the cornice was
festooned a flower-garland in fine enamels. On the frieze were pictured the
exploits of Alexander. The floor was of beaten gold; the wheels were
sheathed with it, their axles capped with lion-heads. A net of gold wire
half-hid the inner sanctuary on three sides; on the fourth, two couchant
gold lions guarded the entry.

'See, they have hung the bells.'

Those too were of gold; they hung from the tassels of the garland. He
lifted his staff and struck one; a clear musical sound, of surprising
resonance, throbbed through the shed. 'They will know of his coming.'

Bagoas swept his hand across his eyes. Now he had entered the world again he was ashamed of tears; but he could hardly bear that Alexander would not see it.

Arybbas did not notice; he was talking to the overseer about making good the dents and scratches caused by the hoisting. Perfection must be restored.

In a far corner of the shed gleamed, dimly, the sarcophagus, blazoned with the royal sunburst of Macedon. Six men could scarcely lift it; it was solid gold. Only at last, at the outset of his journey, would Alexander be brought out in his cedar coffin where, hollow and light, he lay in a bed of spices and sweet herbs, to be laid among more spices in his final resting place. Satisfied that it was undamaged, Arybbas left.

Outside, Bagoas offered unstinted praise, the price of admission, willingly paid. 'It will be counted among the wonders of the world.' He added deliberately, 'The Egyptians are proud of their funeral arts; but even there I saw nothing to compare with it.'

'You have been to Egypt?' Arybbas asked, surprised.

'Since my service with Alexander ended, I have travelled a little to pass my time. He spoke so much of Alexandria, I wished to see it for myself . . . You, sir, of course, were there at its foundation.'

He said no more, leaving Arybbas to ask questions. To these he replied obligingly, leaving loose ends which prompted further questions. These led to a modest confession that he had been granted an audience with the Satrap.

'As it happened, though officers and friends of Alexander had come from most of nearer Asia to join his army, I was the only one from Babylon, so he asked for news. He had heard, he said, that Alexander's bier was to be a marvel, and asked who had been charged with it. When he knew, he exclaimed that Alexander himself could wish for no one better. "If only", he said, "Arybbas could be here to adorn the Founder's temple." . . . Perhaps, sir, that is indiscreet of me.' Fleetingly, like a reflection upon water, appeared the smile which had entranced two kings. 'But I don't think that he would mind.'

They talked for some time, Arybbas having found his curiosity about Alexandria sharpened. Riding back to his house, he was aware he had been delicately probed; but he did not pursue this thought. If he knew what Ptolemy wanted, it might be his duty to divulge it; and this, he suspected, might be to his disadvantage.

In the thick-walled palace of red stone on the red rock citadel of Sardis, Kleopatra and her women were settled in modest comfort by the standards of nearer Asia; in luxury by those of Epiros. Perdikkas had had the royal apartments refurnished and redraped, and staffed with well-trained slaves.

To Nikaia his bride, during their brief honeymoon, he had explained the arrival of the Molossian queen by saying she was in flight from her mother, who had usurped her power and threatened her life; a daughter of Antipatros would believe anything of Olympias. After some ceremonious festivities suited to her rank, he had dispatched the lady to an estate of his near by, on the grounds that war continued and he would soon be taking the field. Returning to Sardis, he resumed his courtship of Kleopatra. His visits and costly gifts had all the conventions of betrothal.

Kleopatra had enjoyed her journey; the family restlessness had not passed her by. The sight of new horizons had consoled her even for leaving her son behind. His grandmother would treat him like a son of her own whom she could train for kingship. When she herself was married and living in Macedon, she could see him often.

She had assessed Perdikkas more as a colleague than a husband. He was a dominating man, and she had sounded him for signs that he would overrule and bully her. It seemed, however, he had the sense to know that without her support he could neither get nor keep the regency. Later, depending on how he behaved, she might help him to the throne. He would be a hard king; but after Antipatros a soft one would be despised.

With a certain detachment, she imagined him in bed with her, but doubted it would be of much importance to either of them once she had produced an heir. Clearly, it would be more valuable and more lasting to make a friend of him than a lover; this she was already doing with some success.

On this day of early spring he was to take the midday meal with her. Both preferred the informality of noon and the chance of undisturbed talk. The single dish would be good; he had found her a Karian cook. She studied his tastes against the time when they would be married. She did not mean to deal hardly with Antipatros' poor plain little girl, as her mother had done with rivals; Nikaia could go back safe to her family. The Persian wife from Susa had done so long ago.

He arrived on foot from his quarters at the other end of the rambling palace, whose buildings clambered about the rock. He had dressed for her with a jewelled shoulder-brooch and a splendid arm-ring clasped with gold gryphon heads. His sword-belt was set with plaques of Persian cloisonné. Yes, she thought, he would make a convincing king.

He liked to talk of his wars under Alexander, and she to listen; only fragmented news had reached Epiros, and he had seen the whole. But before they had reached the wine, her eunuch chamberlain coughed at the door. A dispatch had arrived for His Excellency's urgent attention.

'From Eumenes,' he said as he broke the seal. He spoke rather too easily, aware that Eumenes called nothing urgent without good cause.

As he read, she saw his weathered tan go sallow, and sent out the slave who was serving them. Like most men of his time, he sounded the words he read (it was thought remarkable in Alexander to have suppressed this reflex); but his jaw had set, she heard only an angry mutter. Seeing his face at the end, she guessed that he would look like this in war. 'What is it?' she said.

'Antigonos has fled to Greece.'

'Antigonos . . .?' while he stared before him, she remembered that this was the Satrap of Phrygia, nicknamed One-Eye. 'Was he not under arrest for treason? I suppose he was afraid.'

He gave a snort like a horse's. 'He, afraid? He has gone to betray me to Antipatros.'

She saw that he wanted only to be thinking ahead; but there was more here than she had been told, and she had a right to know. 'What was the treason? Why was he being held?'

He answered savagely, 'To stop his mouth. I found out that he knew.'

She took this in without trouble; she was not a daughter of Macedon for nothing. My father, she thought, would not have done it; nor Alexander. In the old days . . . must we go back to that? She only said, 'How did he come to know?'

'Ask the rats in the wall. He was the last man I'd have confided in. He was always close with Antipatros. He must have smelled something and sent a spy. It's all one now, the harm's done.'

She nodded; there was no need to spell it out. They must be married with royal ceremony before attempting Macedon. There was no time now; Antipatros would be marching north from Aitolia the moment he got the news. A scrambled wedding would bring them nothing but scandal. She thought, This will mean war.

He swung himself down from his dining-couch and began to stride the room; she had a stray thought that they might as well be married already. Wheeling round, he said, 'And I still have to deal with those accursed women.'

'What women?' She let her voice sharpen; he was keeping too much, lately, to himself. 'You've said nothing of women; who are they?'

He made a sound, compounded of impatience and embarrassment. 'No. It was hardly fitting; but I should have told you. Philip, your brother . . .'

'Pray, don't call that wittol my brother!' She had never shared Alexander's tolerance of Philinna's son. Her only passage of arms with Perdikkas had taken place when he had wanted to instal the King in the palace, as became his rank. 'If he comes, I go.' He had seen in her face a flash of Alexander's will. Philip had stayed in the royal tent; he was used to it, and had no thought of any other arrangement. 'What has *he* to do with women, in god's name?'

'Alexander betrothed him to Adeia, your cousin Amyntas' daughter. He even granted her the royal name of Eurydike, which she's made a point of using. I don't know what he meant by it. Shortly before he died, Philip took a turn for the better. Alexander seemed pleased. You'd not know, it's too long since you saw either of them. Alexander took him along in the first place to keep him safe out of the way, in case someone should use him in Macedon. Also, as he told me one night when he was drunk, because Olympias might have killed him if he was left behind. But he got a kind of fondness for him, after taking care of him all those years. He was glad to see him looking more like a man, and let him be seen with him, helping at the sacrifices and so on. Half the army saw it, that's why we've the trouble we have today. But there were no plans for any wedding. If he'd not fallen ill, he'd have marched to Arabia within the month. In the end, I expect, the marriage would have been by proxy.'

'He never told me!' For a moment her face was an injured child's; a long story was there, if Perdikkas had cared to read it.

'That was on account of your mother. He was afraid, if she knew, she'd do the girl an injury.'

'I see,' said Olympias' daughter, without surprise. 'But he should never have done it. Of course we must free her now, poor child.' He did not answer. In a new voice of authority, she said, 'Perdikkas, these are my kin. It is for me to say.'

'Madam, I know.' He spoke with studied respect; he could well afford it. 'But you have misunderstood. Antipatros cancelled the contract with my agreement, some months ago. In his absence, without his leave, her mother Kynna has brought the girl to Asia. They are demanding that the marriage shall proceed.'

His exasperation spoke for his truth. 'Shameless!' she cried. 'There you see the barbarian blood!' It might almost have been Olympias speaking.

'Indeed. They are true Illyrians. I hear that they travelled as far as Abdera dressed as men, and carrying arms.'

'What will you do with them? *I* can have no dealings with such creatures.'

'They will be dealt with. I have no time; I must meet with Eumenes, before Antipatros crosses to Asia. Krateros will be sure to join him, which is much worse. The men love Krateros ... My brother will have to meet them, and keep them from making mischief.'

Presently he left to make his dispositions. One of these was to send to Ephesos, summoning Roxane and her child. He had known better than to quarter the Baktrian on the daughter of Philip and Olympias; besides, if she knew of their plans she would probably have him poisoned. But now it was time to move, and she must follow the army. At least, he thought, she was used to that.

On the high road to the Syrian coast, flashing in the sun and ringing all its bells, the bier of Alexander trundled towards Issos. The sixty-four mules drew it, four yoke-poles hitching each four teams of four. The mules wore gold wreaths, and little gold bells on their cheeks. Their tinkling, and the deep clear chime of the bells upon the bier, mingled with the shouts of the muleteers.

In the shrine, between the gold columns and the shimmering golden nets, the sarcophagus lay draped with its purple pall. On it was displayed Alexander's panoply of arms, his helmet of white iron, his jewelled sword-belt, his sword and shield and greaves. The cuirass was the parade one; the one he had used in battle was too worn and hacked to match the splendours around.

When the iron-bound felloes of the gold-sheathed wheels jolted on rough ground, the bier only swayed gently; there were hidden springs above the axles. Alexander would come whole to his tomb. Veterans in the escort said to each other that if he had been anywhere near as careful of his body while he was alive, he would be with them yet.

All along the road sightseers stood in expectant clusters, awaiting the sound of the distant bells. The fame of the bier had far outstripped its progress. Peasants had walked a day from mountain hamlets, and slept in the open to await it; riders on horses or mules or asses kept along by it for miles, unwilling to relinquish it. Boys ran themselves to a standstill, dropping like spent dogs, when the escort struck camp at night, creeping to the cook-fires to beg a crust, and listening half in dreams to the soldiers' tales.

At each town on the way, sacrifices were offered to the deified Alexander; the local bard would extol his deeds, inventing marvels where his store of history failed. Arybbas presided calmly over these solemnities. He had had Ptolemy's letter, and knew what he would do.

Save for his one visit to Arybbas' tent, Bagoas made himself imperceptible. By day he rode among the changing sightseers; at night he slept among the Persian soldiers who formed the rearguard. They all knew who he was, and no one troubled him. He was keeping faith with his lord, as a true follower of Mithra ought. They respected his pious pilgrimage, and thought no more of it.

Kynna and her daughter had travelled as armed men, sleeping in their baggage-cart with their retainers in the open round them, till they could take ship from Abdera. There the people were Greek, there was plenty of merchant shipping, and the only question asked was whether they could pay. Kynna, who could deceive no one at close quarters, resumed female dress; Eurydike travelled as her son.

The ship carried hides on deck; the retainers found them a grateful bed at night, but their smell made Eurydike sick at the first flurry of wind. At last, they sailed into the green sheltering arms of the long gulf of Smyrna. From now on, their progress must be very different.

Smyrna consisted of ancient ruins, an old village, and a brand-new town re-founded by Alexander, whom the harbour had impressed. The traffic had grown with his conquests, and it was now a busy port. Here they would be seen and spoken of; though Babylon was still far off, they must think about appearances. The old man who acted as their major-domo – he remembered Amyntas' father – went before them to seek good lodgings, and hire transport for the long journey overland.

He returned with startling news. The journey to the east was not required of them. Perdikkas, and King Philip with him, were no further off than Sardis, some fifty miles.

They felt a shock, as people do when a distant crisis leaps up close; then told each other that luck was speeding them. Eurydike went ashore with a long cloak over her tunic, and, in the lodging, assumed himation and robe.

They must travel at once with public consequence, a king's betrothed travelling to her bridal. They should of course have been met at the port by a kinsman or friend of the groom; but the greater their state, the less they would be questioned. They could afford lavishness for so short a journey; Amyntas' estates had never been confiscated, their quiet life had not been due to poverty.

When, two days later, they set out, their train was an imposing one. Thoas the major-domo, who had purchased them maids and porters, reported that according to people here they should have a eunuch chamberlain. Kynna, much outraged, replied that they were Greek, as was her daughter's bridegroom, and they had not crossed to Asia to adopt the disgusting customs of the barbarians. Alexander, she had heard, had been given too much that way.

The faithful Thoas, transacting all this business, made no secret of his ladies' rank, or of their purpose. It was no spy, but the eternal gossip of travellers on the road, that ran ahead of them with the news to Sardis.

The field of Issos still yielded up old weapons and old bones. Here, where Darius had first fled from Alexander's spear leaving mother and wife and children to await the victor, two armies sacrificed a milk-white bull before the golden bier. Ptolemy and Arybbas poured incense side by side. The escort had been much moved by Ptolemy's address, affirming the divine hero's wish that his body return to his father Ammon.

Each of Arybbas' men had been given a hundred drachmas, a bounty worthy even of Alexander. Arybbas himself had received, in private, a talent of silver, and in public the rank of general in the Satrap's army, whither all his Macedonian troops had agreed to follow him. There was a feast at night in Alexander's honour; a whole spit-roast sheep and an amphora of wine to each camp fire. Next morning, satrap and general riding either side the bier, the funeral cortège turned south towards the Nile.

Bagoas, whose name had been proclaimed in no citation, followed behind the rearguard. The other Persians had gone home; but the troops from Egypt made the column a very long one, and he was far, now, from the bier. When he topped a rise, he could just see its glittering crest. But he rode contented. His task was done, his god was served; and there would still be his fame to tend in his chosen city. A Greek might have seen in him the serenity of the initiate, fresh from a celebration of his mystery.

Kynna's caravan was within a day's journey from Sardis. They were not hurrying; they meant to arrive there next morning before the heat began. Its fame had reached even Macedon for wealth and luxury; the bride of a king must not be outshone by his subjects. Overnight they would prepare their entry.

Along the road, the stony heights were topped with old forts, newly repaired by Alexander to command the passes. They passed rock-slabs carved with symbols, and inscriptions in unknown writing. The travellers who passed them making for the port were all barbarians, strange to sight and smell; Phoenicians with blue-dyed beards, Karians with heavy earrings dragging down their lobes; a train of negro carriers bare to the waist, their blackness strange and terrible to a northern eye used only to the red-haired slaves from Thrace; sometimes a trousered Persian, the legendary ogre of Greek children, with embroidered hat and curved sword.

To Eurydike all was adventure and delight. She thought with envy of world-wandering Alexander and his men. Kynna, beside her under the striped awning, kept a cheerful countenance, but felt her spirits flag. The alien speech of the passers-by, the inscrutable monuments, the unknown landscape, the vanishing of all she had pictured in advance, were draining her of certainty. Those black-veiled women, carrying burdens beside the donkeys their menfolk rode, if they knew her purpose would think her mad. The two-wheeled cart jolted over stones, her head was aching. She had known that the world was vast, that Alexander in ten years had never reached the end of it; but at home in her native hills it had had no meaning.

Now, on the mere threshold of the illimitable east, she felt like a desolation its indifferent strangeness.

Eurydike, who had been admiring the defences of the forts and pointing out their chain of beacons, said, 'Is it true, do you think, that Sardis is three times as big as Pella?'

'I daresay. Pella is only two generations old; Sardis is ten maybe, or even more.' The thought oppressed her. She looked at the girl in her careless confidence, and thought, I brought her here from home, where she could have lived out her life in quiet. She has no one but me to turn to. Well, I am healthy and still young.

Night would soon fall. An outrider brought news that they were within ten miles of Sardis. Soon they must find a camping-place. A rocky turn shut off the westering sun, and the road grew dusky. The slope above them, dark against a reddening sky, was scattered with great boulders. Somewhere among them a man's voice called, 'Now!'

Stones and shale fell rattling on the road, dislodged by scrambling men. Thoas at the escort's head shouted out, 'Ware thieves!'

The men reached the road, thirty or forty of them, on foot, with spears. Among them the escort looked what it was, a troop of willing, confused old men. Those who had ever fought had done it in Philip's wars. But they were true Macedonians, with the archaic virtues of the liegeman. They shouted defiance, and thrust at the bandits with their spears.

The squeal of a wounded horse echoed against the rocks. Old Thoas fell with his mount; a huddle of men closed stabbing over him.

There was a high shout, a wordless 'Hi-yi!' of challenge. Kynna leaped down from the cart, Eurydike beside her. Their spears had been at hand; with practised speed they had kilted their skirts into their girdles. With their backs to the cart, which rocked with the shifting of the frightened mules, they stood to face the enemy.

Eurydike felt a shiver of exultation. Here at last was war, real war. Though she could guess the consequence of defeat if they were taken alive, it was mainly a good reason for fighting well. A man reached out at her, fair-skinned, with a week's red stubble on his chin. He had on a hide cuirass, so she went for his arm. The spear sunk in; he leaped back crying out 'You hellcat!' grasping the wound. She laughed at him; then realized with a sudden shock that here, in Lydia, a bandit had spoken Macedonian.

One of the lead mules, hurt by a spear, suddenly squealed and leaped forward. The whole team bolted, the cart bucking and bouncing behind it. It struck her, but she just kept her feet. There was a cry beside her. Kynna had fallen; she had been braced against the cart when it moved off. A soldier was leaning over her with a spear.

A man came forward with upheld hand. The men around her withdrew.

It grew quiet, except for the struggling mules which had been pulled up
by the soldiers, and the groans of three of the escort on the ground. The
rest had been overpowered, save for old Thoas, who was dead.

Kynna moaned; the almost animal sound of a warm-blooded creature
struggling in pain to breathe. Her breast was stained with red.

Eurydike's first impulse was to run to her, take her in her arms, entreat
the bandits for mercy. But Kynna had trained her well. This too was war;
there would be no mercy for asking, only for winning. She looked at the
chief who had been at once obeyed, a tall dark man with a lean cold face.
Knowledge was instant; not bandits, soldiers.

Kynna groaned again; the sound was fainter now. Pity and rage and
grief lit like one flame in Eurydike, as they did in Achilles, shouting for dead
Patroklos on the wall. She leaped to her mother's body and stood across
it.

'You traitors! Are you men of Macedon? This is Kynna, King Philip's
daughter, the sister of Alexander.'

There was a startled pause. The men all turned towards the officer. He
looked angry and disconcerted. He had not told them.

A thought came to her. She spoke this time in the language of the
soldiers, the peasant dialect of the countryside she had known before she
was taught Greek. 'I am Philip's grandchild, look at me! I am Amyntas'
daughter, the grandchild of King Philip and King Perdikkas.' She pointed
at the glowering officer. 'Ask him. *He* knows!'

The oldest soldier, a man in his fifties, walked across to him. 'Alketas.'
He used the name without honorific, as a freeman of Macedon could do
to kings. 'Is what she says true?'

'No! Obey your orders.'

The soldier looked from him to the girl, and from her to the other men.
'I reckon it's true,' he said.

The men drew together; one of them said, 'They're no Sarmatians, like
he said. They're as Macedonian as I am.'

'My mother ...' Eurydike looked down. Kynna stirred, but blood was
running from her mouth. 'She brought me here from Macedon. I am
betrothed to Philip, your king, the brother of Alexander.'

Kynna stirred. She rose a little on one arm. Chokingly she said, 'It is true.
I swear by ...' She coughed. A rush of blood came out, and she fell back.
Eurydike dropped her spear and knelt beside her. Her eyes fixed, showing
the whites.

The old soldier who had faced Alketas came over and stood before her,
confronting the rest. 'Let them alone!' he said. Another and another joined
him; the rest leaned on their spears in a confused and sullen shame.
Eurydike flung herself on her mother's body and wept aloud.

Presently, through the sound of her own crying, she heard voices raised. It was the sound of mutiny. Had she known, it was one with which Macedonian generals were growing over familiar. Ptolemy had confided to close friends in Egypt that he was glad to hand-pick his men, and be rid of the standing army. It put one in mind of Alexander's old horse Boukephalas, liable to kick anyone else who tried to mount him. Like the horse, it had been too long used to a rider with clever hands.

More urgently now, Eurydike thought of throwing herself upon their mercy, begging them to burn her mother's body decently, give her the ashes to bury in the homeland, and take her back to the sea. But, as she wiped the blood from Kynna's face, she knew it for the face of a warrior steadfast to the death. Her shade must not find that she had borne a coward.

Under her hand was the gold pendant her mother always wore. It was bloodstained, but she slipped it over the lifeless head, and stood erect.

'See. Here is my grandfather King Philip's likeness. He gave it to my grandmother Audata on her wedding day, and she to my mother when she married Amyntas, King Perdikkas' son. Look for yourself.'

She put it in the veteran's cracked horny hand; they crowded round him, poring over the gold roundel with the square-boned, bearded profile. 'Aye, Philip it is,' the veteran said. 'I saw him many a time.' He rubbed it clean on a fold of his homespun kilt and gave it back to her. 'You should take care of that,' he said.

He spoke as if to a young niece; and it struck a chord in all of them. She was their foundling, the orphan of their rescue and adoption. They would take her to Sardis, they told Alketas; she had Philip's blood in her as any fool could see; and if Alexander had promised her his brother, wed they should be, or the army would know why.

'Very well,' said Alketas. He knew by now that discipline hung by a thread, and maybe his life. 'Then get the road cleared, and look alive.'

With rough competence the soldiers laid Kynna out in the cart, and covered her with a blanket; brought their own transport-cart for the dead and wounded guards, picked up the baggage which the porters had dropped when with the maids they fled into the hills. They settled the cushions for Eurydike, to ride beside her dead.

One of them rode off willingly with Alketas' dispatch to his brother Perdikkas. On his way would be the main camp of Perdikkas' and Eumenes' armies, where he could spread the news.

So, when the last turn of the road showed her the red-rock citadel with the city around its feet, it showed her also a great throng of soldiers, crowding the road, and parting to make an avenue of honour, as if for a king.

As she came they cheered her. Close to her by the road she heard gruff murmurs; 'Poor maid.' 'Forgive them, lady, he told them wrong.' The strangeness, the dreamlike consummation of their long intent, made her mother's death dreamlike too, though she could have reached out and touched the body.

From the high window, Kleopatra looked down with Perdikkas, fuming, beside her. She saw his impotence, and struck her hand in anger on the sill. 'You are permitting this?'

'No choice. If I arrest her, we shall have a mutiny. Now of all times ... They know that she's Philip's grandchild.'

'And a traitor's daughter! Her father plotted my father's murder. Will you let her marry his son?'

'Not if I can help it.' The cart was coming nearer. He tried to descry the face of Amyntas' daughter, but it was too far. He must go down and make some gesture which would preserve his dignity and, with luck, gain time. Just then new movement below, from a new direction, caught his eye. He leaned out, stared, and, cursing, swung back into the room.

'What is it?' His rage and dismay had startled her.

'Hades take them! They are bringing Philip out to her.'

'What? How can –'

'They know where his tent is. You wouldn't have him here. I must go.' He flung out, without even the curtest apology. For a very little, she thought, he would have cursed her, too.

Down below in the thick outer walls the huge gates stood wide. The cart halted. A group of soldiers, pulling something, came running out of the gateway.

'Lady, if you'll please to step down, we've something here more fit for you.'

It was an old and splendid chariot, its front and sides plated with silver gryphons and gold lions. Lined with tooled red leather, it had been built for Kroisos, that legend for uncounted riches, the last Lydian king. Alexander had made a progress in it, to impress the people.

This moving throne made her sense of dream grow deeper. She came to herself to say that she could not leave her mother's body untended.

'She'll be watched with, lady, like she ought, we've seen to that.' Worn black-clad women came forward with eager pride; veterans' wives, looking from work and weather old enough to be their mothers. A soldier approached to hand Eurydike down. At the last moment Alketas, making a virtue of necessity, came up to do the office. For a moment she flinched; but that was not the way to take an enemy's surrender. She inclined her head graciously and took his offered arm. A team of soldiers grasped the chariot-pole, and pulled it forward. She sat like a king on Kroisos' chair.

Suddenly, the sound of the cheering altered. She heard the ancient Macedonian cries: 'Io Hymen! Euoi! Joy to the bride! Hail to the groom!'

The groom was coming towards her.

Her heart gave a lurch. This part of the dream had been blurred.

The man came riding, on a beautiful, slow-pacing dapple grey. A grizzled old soldier led it by the rein. The face of the bearded rider was not unlike the one on the gold medallion. He was looking about him, blinking a little. The old soldier pointed towards her. When he looked straight at her, she saw that he was frightened, scared to death. Among all she had thought of, so far as she had allowed herself to think at all, she had not thought of this.

Urged by the soldiers, he dismounted and walked up to the chariot, his blue eyes, filled with the liveliest apprehension, fixed on her face. She smiled at him.

'How are you, Arridaios? I am your cousin Eurydike, your uncle Amyntas' daughter. I have just come from home. Alexander sent for me.'

The soldiers all around murmured approval, admiring her quick address, and cried, 'Long live the King!'

Philip's face had brightened at the sound of his old name. When he was Arridaios he had had no duties, no bullying rehearsals with impatient men. Alexander had never bullied, only made one pleased to get things right. This girl reminded him, somehow, of Alexander. Cautiously, less frightened now, he said, 'Are you going to marry me?'

A soldier burst into a guffaw, but was manhandled by indignant comrades. The rest listened eagerly to the scene.

'If you would like it, Arridaios. Alexander wanted us to marry.'

He bit his lip in a crisis of irresolution. Suddenly he turned to the old soldier who led his horse. 'Shall I marry her, Konon? Did Alexander tell me to?'

One or two soldiers clapped hands over their mouths. In the muttering pause, she was aware of the old servant subjecting her to a search of scrutiny. She recognized a resolute protector. Ignoring the voices, some of them growing ribald, which were urging the King to speak up for the girl before she changed her mind, she looked straight at Konon, and said, 'I will be kind to him.'

The wariness in his faded eyes relaxed. He gave her a little nod, and turned to Philip, still eyeing him anxiously. 'Yes, sir. This is the lady you're betrothed to, the maid Alexander chose for you. She's a fine, brave lady. Reach out your hand to her, and ask her nicely to be your wife.'

Eurydike took the obedient hand. Large, warm and soft, it clung to hers appealingly. She gave it a reassuring pressure.

'Please, cousin Eurydike, will you marry me? The soldiers want you to.'

Keeping his hand, she said, 'Yes, Arridaios. Yes, King Philip, I will.'

The cheers began in earnest. Soldiers who were wearing their broad-brimmed hats flung them into the air. The cries of 'Hymen!' redoubled. They were trying to coax Philip into the chariot beside her, when Perdikkas, red and panting from his race down the steep and winding steps of the ancient city, arrived upon the scene.

Alketas met him, speaking with his eyes. Both knew too well the mood in which Macedonians grew dangerous. They had seen it in the time of Alexander, who had dealt with it at Opis by leaping from his dais and arresting the ringleaders with his bare hands. But such things had been Alexander's mystery; anyone else would have been lynched. Alketas met with a shrug of the shoulders his brother's furious stare.

Eurydike in the chariot guessed at once who Perdikkas was. For a moment she felt like a child before a formidable adult. But she stood her ground, sustained by strength she was largely unaware of. She knew she was the grandchild of Philip and King Perdikkas, great-grandchild of Illyrian Bardelys, the old terror of the border; but she did not know they had bequeathed her more than pride in them; she had some of their nature, too. Her sequestered youth, fed upon legends, let her see in her situation nothing absurd or obscene. All she knew was that these men who had cheered her should not see her afraid.

Philip had been standing with one hand upon the chariot, arguing with the men who had been trying to hoist him into it. Now he grabbed her arm.

'Look out!' he said. 'Here comes Perdikkas.'

She put her hand over his. 'Yes, I see him. Come up here, and stand by me.'

He scrambled up, encouraging soldiers steadied the chariot as his weight rocked it. Grasping the rail, he stood rigid with scared defiance; she rose to her feet beside him, summoning her nerve. Briefly, they presented an uncanny semblance of a triumphant pair, remote in pride and power. Tauntingly, the soldiers flung at Perdikkas the marriage cry.

He reached the chariot; there was a moment of held breath. Then he raised his hand in salute.

'Greeting, King. Greeting, daughter of Amyntas. I am glad that the King has been prompt to welcome you.'

'The soldiers made me,' mumbled Philip warily. Eurydike's clear voice cut in, 'The King has been very gracious.'

Philip gazed anxiously at these two protagonists. No vengeance from Perdikkas happened. The soldiers were pleased, too. He gave a conniving grin. Hiding with care her almost incredulous amazement, Eurydike knew that, for the present, she had won.

'Perdikkas,' she said, 'the King has asked for my hand with the goodwill of the Macedonians. But my mother, the sister of Alexander, is lying here murdered, as you know. First of all I must have leave to direct her funeral.'

Loud, respectful sounds of approval greeted this. Perdikkas agreed with as good a grace as he could. Scanning the sullen faces, thinking of Antipatros' forces making for the Hellespont, he added that the death of her noble mother had been a shocking error, due to ignorance and to the valour of her defence. The matter would of course be searched to the bottom shortly.

Eurydike bowed her head, aware that she would never know what Alketas' orders had really been. Kynna would at least meet the flame with all the honours of war; one day her ashes must return to Aigai. Meantime, her funeral offerings must be courage and resolve. As for her blood-price, that would be with the gods.

The funeral was barely over, when news reached Perdikkas that Alexander's bier was proceeding in state to Egypt.

It struck him like a thunderbolt. All his plans had been directed against the threat from the north, the outraged father-in-law to whom he had already dispatched Nikaia. Now, from the south, came a clear declaration of war.

Eumenes was still in Sardis, summoned when danger came from the north alone. It had come, as they both knew, from neglect of his advice to marry Kleopatra openly, to send Nikaia still virgin home, and advance at once on Macedon. This was not spoken of. Like Kassandra, Eumenes was fated never to reap much good from being right. A Greek among Macedonians had no business to know best. He refrained, therefore, from pointing out that Perdikkas could now have been Regent of Macedon with a royal bride, a power against which Ptolemy could have attempted nothing; and merely voiced a doubt that he was planning war.

'All he has done so far in Egypt has been to dig in and make himself snug. He's ambitious, yes; but what are his ambitions? It was a fine piece of insolence to steal the body; but even that may be only to glorify Alexandria. Will he trouble us if he's let alone?'

'He's already annexed Kyrene. And he's raising a bigger army than he needs.'

'How does he know? If you march against him he'll need it.'

Perdikkas said with sudden venom, 'I hate the man.'

Eumenes offered no comment. He remembered Ptolemy as a gangling youth, hoisting the child Alexander up on his horse for a ride. Perdikkas had been a friend of the King's manhood, but it had never been quite the same. Alexander promoted on merit – even Hephaistion had started at the bottom – and Perdikkas had outstripped Ptolemy in the end. But it was Ptolemy who had suited Alexander like a well-worn, comfortable shoe; the trusted Perdikkas had never quite matched that ease. Ptolemy, by instinct and from watching Alexander, had a way with men; he knew when to relax discipline as well as when to tighten it; when to give, when to listen, when to laugh. Perdikkas felt the absence of that sixth sense as a man might feel short sight; and envy ate at him.

'He's like a vicious dog, that eats the flock it should be guarding. If he's not whipped back, the rest will be at it too.'

'Maybe; but not yet. Antipatros and Krateros will be marching *now*.'

Perdikkas' dark jaw set stubbornly. He has changed, thought Eumenes, since Alexander died. His desires have changed. They grow hubristic, and he knows it. Alexander contained us all.

Perdikkas said, 'No, Ptolemy can't wait. That asp of Egypt must be stepped upon in the egg.'

'Then we divide the army?' His voice was neutral; a Greek among Macedonians had said enough.

'Needs must. You shall go north, and refuse Antipatros the Hellespont. I will settle with Ptolemy, and settle for good . . . But before we march, we must have this accursed wedding. The men won't move else. I know them too well.'

Later that day, Perdikkas spent an hour reasoning with Kleopatra. In the end, with flattery, cold logic, appeal, and as much charm as he could conjure, he persuaded her to act as Eurydike's matron of honour. The troops were set on the marriage; it must be done with a good grace. Any grudging would be remembered against them both, which they could not afford.

'The girl was a child at nurse,' he said, 'when they murdered Philip. I doubt even Amyntas was more than on the fringe of it. I was there when he was tried.'

'Yes, I daresay. But it is all disgusting. Has she no shame at all? Well, you have dangers enough without my making more for you. If Alexander was willing to give it countenance, I suppose I can do the same.'

Eumenes did not await the feast. He marched at once to meet the forces of Antipatros and Krateros (another of his sons-in-law); leading his Macedonians with their loose and dubious loyalty to the alien Greek. For Eumenes, that was an old story. Perdikkas, whose business was less urgent, stayed on another week to give his troops their show.

Two days before the wedding, a flustered maid announced to Eurydike in her inner room – built for the chief wife of old Kroisos – that the Queen of the Epirotes had come to visit her.

Kleopatra arrived in state. Olympias had not stinted her since she left home; meanness had never been one of her sins. Her daughter came dressed like a queen, and with queenly gifts; a broad gold necklace, a roll of Karian embroidery stitched with lapis and gold. For a moment, Eurydike was overwhelmed. But Kynna had trained her in manners as well as war; she achieved a kind of naive dignity which moved Kleopatra against her will. She remembered her own wedding, to an uncle old enough to be her father, at seventeen.

The compliments paid, the formal sweet cakes tasted, she went dutifully over the wedding ritual. It was a dry business, since there could be no question of the sly feminine jokes traditional at such a conference. Careful correctness resulted. Kleopatra's sense of duty nagged at her. This grave guarded girl, left alone in the world at fifteen; what did she know? Kleopatra smoothed her gown over her knees, and looked up from her ringed fingers.

'When you met the King' – how allude to so disgraceful an occasion? – 'did you have time to talk with him? Perhaps you saw he is a little young for his years?'

Eurydike's straight eyes met hers, deciding that she meant well and must be answered civilly. 'Yes. Alexander told my mother so; and I see it is so.'

This was promising. 'Then, when you are married, what do you mean to do? Perdikkas would give you an escort to your kin in Macedon.'

Eurydike thought, It is not quite a command, because it cannot be one. She answered quietly, 'The King has a right that I should be his friend, if he needs a friend. I will stay for a while and see.'

Next day, such ladies of standing as Sardis could supply – wives of senior officers and administrators, with a few timid ornate Lydians – paid their respects. Later, in the quiet afternoon, sacred since Kroisos' day to the siesta, came a different caller. A twittering maid announced a messenger from the household of the bridegroom.

Old Konon, when shown in, eyed the attendants meaningly. She sent them out, and asked what message he brought.

'Well, madam ... to wish you health and joy, and God speed the happy day.' Delivered of this set speech, he swallowed audibly. What could be coming? Eurydike, dreading the unknown, looked withdrawn and sullen. Konon, his nervousness increased, marshalled his words. 'Madam, he's taken a real liking to you, that's sure. He's forever talking of cousin Eurydike, and setting out his pretty things to show you ... But, madam, I've cared for him man and boy, and I know his ways, which he sets store by, seeing he was ill-used before I came. If you please, madam, don't turn me off. You'll not find me taking liberties or putting myself forward. If you'll just keep me on trial, to see if I suit; I won't ask more.'

So that was all! In her relief she could have embraced him; but of course one must not show it. 'Did I not see you with the King? Your name is Konon, is it not? Yes, you will be welcome to stay on. Please tell the King so, if he should ask.'

'He's never thought to ask, madam. It would have put him in a terrible taking.' They eyed each other, a little relaxed, still cautious. Konon was reaching for words, even for the little that could be said at all. 'Madam, he's not used to big feasts, not without Alexander giving him the lead and seeing him through it. I daresay they told you, he has a bad turn sometimes. Don't be afraid, if you just leave him to me, he'll soon be right again.'

Eurydike said she would. Echoing silence engulfed them. Konon swallowed again. The poor girl would give anything to know what he didn't know how to tell her – her groom had no notion that the act of sex could be performed with a second party. At length, turning crimson, he managed, 'Madam, he thinks the world of you. But he'll not trouble you. It wouldn't be his way.'

She was not too naive to understand him. With as much dignity as she could summon, she said, 'Thank you, Konon, I am sure the King and I will agree together. You have leave to go.'

Philip woke early on his wedding morning. Konon had promised that he could wear the purple robe with the great red star. Besides, he was going to be married to cousin Eurydike. She would be allowed to stay with him, and he could see her whenever he liked, Perdikkas himself had said so.

That morning, the bath-water came in a big silver ewer, carried by two well-dressed young men who stayed to pour it over him, wishing him good luck. This, Konon explained, was because he was a bridegroom. He saw the young men exchange a grin across him; but such things often happened.

A good many people were singing and laughing outside the door. He was no longer in his familiar tent, but had a room in the palace; he did not mind, he had been allowed to bring all his stones. Konon had explained that there was no room in the tent for a lady, while here she could stay next door.

The young men helped him put on the beautiful robe; then he was taken by Perdikkas to sacrifice at the little temple of Zeus at the top of the hill. Alexander had built it there, where fire had fallen from heaven. Perdikkas told him when to throw incense on the burning meat, and what to say to the god. He got everything right, and the people sang for him; but nobody praised him afterwards, as Alexander used to do.

Perdikkas, indeed, had had trouble enough to plan a convincing ceremony. Thanks to Alketas, the bride had no family to give the marriage feast. He was grateful to Kleopatra for consenting to hold the torch of welcome in the bridal chamber. But what mattered most, because the troops would see it, was the wedding procession.

Then, to compound his troubles, at midday two fore-runners announced the approach of the lady Roxane. Since this affair, he had entirely forgotten having sent for her, and had not even asked her to the wedding.

Lodgings were hastily prepared; her closed litter was carried up through the city. The Sardians crowded to see; the soldiers gave a few restrained greetings. They had never approved of Alexander's foreign marriages; but now he was dead, a kind of aura clung to her. Besides, she was the mother of his son. The child was with her. A Macedonian queen would have held him up for them to see; but Baktrian ladies did not show themselves in public. The child was teething and fretful, and could be heard whimpering as the litter passed.

Dressed in his wedding robe, and putting a good face on it, Perdikkas greeted her and invited her to the feast; prepared, he said, at short notice owing to the imminence of war.

'You told me nothing of it!' she said angrily. 'Who is this peasant girl you have found for him? If the King is to marry, he should have married me.'

'Among Macedonians,' said Perdikkas frostily, 'a dead king's heir does not inherit his harem. And the lady is granddaughter to two kings.'

A crisis of precedence now arose. Alexander and his officers had married their foreign wives by the local rites; Roxane, ignorant of Macedonian custom, could not be brought to see that Kleopatra was taking a mother's place and could not be removed from it. 'But I,' she cried, 'am the mother of Alexander's son!'

'So,' said Perdikkas, very nearly shouting, 'you are the kinswoman of the *bridegroom*. I will send someone to explain the rite to you. See to it that your part is properly done, if you want your son accepted by the soldiers. Don't forget they have the right to disinherit him.'

This sobered her. He had changed, she thought; grown colder, harsher, more overbearing. He had not forgiven Stateira's death, it seemed. She was unaware that others had noticed a change as well.

Philip had looked forward all day to the wedding ride. It did not disappoint him. Not since the time he rode an elephant had he enjoyed himself so much.

He wore the purple robe, and a gold diadem. Eurydike beside him had a yellow dress, and a yellow veil flung back from a wreath of gold flowers. He had thought they would have the car all to themselves, and had been displeased when Perdikkas got up on the other side. Eurydike was married to *him*, and Perdikkas could not marry her as well. Hastily people had explained that Perdikkas was best man; but it was cousin Eurydike he listened to. Now he was married, he felt much less frightened of Perdikkas; he had been on the point of pushing him out of the car.

Drawn by white mules, they drove along the processional Sacred Way, which bent and turned to bring it downhill without stairs. It was adorned with old statues and shrines, Lydian, Persian, Greek. Flags and garlands were everywhere, as the sun sank they were starting to light the torches. People were standing and cheering all the way, climbing up on the house-roofs.

The tasselled, sequin-netted mules were led by soldiers wearing scarlet cloaks and wreaths. Behind and in front, musicians played Lydian airs on flutes and pipes, shook sistra with their little tinkling bells, and clanged great cymbals. Auspicious cries in mingled tongues rose like waves. The sunset glow faded, the torches came out like stars.

Full of it all, Philip turned and said, 'Are you happy, cousin Eurydike?'

'Very happy.' Indeed, she had imagined nothing to compare with it. Unlike her groom, she had never before tasted the pomps of Asia. The music, the shouts of acclamation, elated her like wine. This was her element, and till now she had never known it. Not for nothing was she the daughter of Amyntas, a king's son who, when a crown was offered him, could not forbear to reach for it. 'And now,' she said, 'you must not call me cousin any more. A wife is more important than a cousin.'

The wedding feast was set out in the great hall, with a dais for the women in their chairs of honour, a flower-decked throne for the bride. Her gifts and her dowry were displayed on stands around her. With wondering and distanced eyes, she saw again the jewels and cups and vases, the bolts of fine dyed wool, which Kynna had brought with cherishing care from Macedon. Only one piece was missing, the silver casket which now held her calcined bones.

Kleopatra led her to the King's high table to take her piece of the bride-loaf, sliced with his sword. It was clear that he had never handled a sword before; but he hacked a piece off bravely, broke it in two when told, and, as she tasted hers – the central rite of the wedding – asked her if it was nice, because his own piece was not sweet enough.

Back at her dais, she listened to a hymn by a choir of maidens; Lydians mostly, mangling the words, a few Greek daughters trying hard to be heard. Then she became aware that the women round her were murmuring together, stirring with little fidgets of preparation. With a sudden clutch in her midriff, she knew that when the song ended, they would lead her to the nuptial chamber.

All through the ride, nearly all through the feast, she had overleaped this moment, throwing her mind ahead to next month, next year, or living in the present only.

'Have you had instruction?'

She looked round with a start. The voice, with a strong foreign accent, came from just beside her. Not till this morning had she met the widow of Alexander. She had bowed to the small jewelled woman, stiff with embroideries of gold and pearl, rubies like pigeon's eggs hanging from her ears. Her surface had been so stunning that she had seemed hardly human, a kind of splendid adornment for the feast. Now, Eurydike met the gaze of two large black eyes, their whites brilliantly clear between eyelids dark with kohl, fixed on her in concentrated malice.

'Yes,' she said quietly.

'So, truly? I had heard your mother was a man, as well as your father. To look at you, one might think so.'

Eurydike gazed back, fascinated as the prey by the predator. Roxane, bright as a little shrike, leaned out from her chair of honour. 'If you know all you should, you will be able to teach your husband.' Her rubies flashed; the song, rising to its climax, did not cover her rising voice. 'To Alexander he was like a dog under his table. He trained him to heel, then sent him back to the kennel. It is *my* son who is King.'

The song was over. Along the dais there were agitated rustlings.

Kleopatra rose to her feet, as she had seen Olympias do it. The others stood up with her. After a moment Roxane followed, staring defiantly. In the formal, studied Greek of her father's court, looking down from her Macedonian height at the little Baktrian, she said, 'Let us remember where we are. And who we are, if we can. Ladies, come. The torches. Io, Hymen! Joy to the bride!'

'Look!' said Philip to Perdikkas, who had the place of honour beside him. 'Cousin Eurydike is going away!' He scrambled anxiously to his feet.

'*Not now!*' Grabbing him by his purple robe, Perdikkas thumped him back on his supper-couch. With savage geniality he added, 'She is changing her dress. We will take you to see her presently.'

The guests in hearing, even the elegant young Lydian servers who had picked up a bit of Greek, made stifled noises. Perdikkas, lowering his voice, said, 'Now listen to the speeches, and when they look at you, smile. We are going to drink your health.'

Philip pushed forward his wine-cup, an engraved gold Achaemenid treasure from the Persian occupation. Konon, standing behind his chair, got it quickly back from a too zealous server. and filled it from a jug of watered wine, in the strength given to Greek children. He looked incongruous among the graceful Lydians and well-born Macedonian pages waiting at table.

Perdikkas rose to make the best man's speech, recalling the groom's heroic ancestry, the exploits of his grandfather whose name he had auspiciously assumed; the lineage of his mother, the noble lady of horse-loving Larissa. His compliments to the bride were adequate, though rather vague. Philip, who had been occupied in feeding someone's curly white poodle which had been sitting under the table, looked up in time to acknowledge the cheers with an obedient grin.

A harmless person, a distant royal connection, responded for the bride, uttering bland platitudes about her beauty, virtue and high descent. Once more the health was given, and honoured with ritual shouts. It was the time for serious drinking.

Goblets were emptied and briskly filled, faces reddened under tilting wreaths, voices grew louder. Captains still in their thirties argued and bragged about past wars and women; Alexander had died young with young men all about him. For the older men, a real Macedonian wedding brought back the feasts of their youth. Nostalgically, they roared out the time-honoured phallic jokes remembered from their family bridals.

The noble pages had slipped out to get their share. Presently one said, 'Poor fellow. Old Konon might let him have a mouthful he can taste, at his own wedding. It might put heart in him.' He and a friend came up behind Philip's couch. 'Konon, Ariston over there told me to say he pledges you.' Konon beamed, and looked about for his wellwisher; Perdikkas was talking to the guest on his other side. The second page filled up the royal cup with neat wine. Philip tasted his new drink, liked it, and tilted back his cup. By the time Konon noticed and angrily diluted it, he had had more than half.

Some of the men started to sing a skolion. It was not yet lewder than a wedding feast allowed, but Perdikkas pulled himself together. He had known all along that this could not be a long drinking-bout. A little time yet could be allowed for hospitality, but soon he must break it up. He stopped drinking, to keep alert.

Philip felt a surge of wellbeing, strength and gaiety. He banged the table in time with the skolion, singing loudly, 'I'm married, married, married to Eurydike!' The white poodle pawed at his leg; he picked it up and put it on the table, where it ran about, scattering cups, fruit and flowers, till someone hurled it off, when it fled yelping. Everyone laughed; some men far gone in drink bawled ancient encouragements to first-night prowess.

Philip gazed at them with blurred eyes, in which lurked a dim anxiety and suspicion. His purple robe felt too hot, in the stew of torch-warmed humanity. He heaved at it, trying to take it off.

Perdikkas saw that it was high time. He called for a torch, and gave the signal to conduct the bridegroom.

Eurydike lay in the great perfumed bed, in her night-robe of fine mussel-silk, the brideswomen gathered round her. They talked among themselves; at first they had dutifully included her, but none of them knew her, and the wait for the men was always tedious; the more since coy jokes were barred. Mostly the floor was held by Roxane, who described the far more splendid ceremonies of Alexander's day, and patronized Kleopatra.

Solitary in the little crowd, with its warm smell of female flesh, of the herbs and cedar-wood of clothes chests, essence of orange and of rose, Eurydike heard the rising sounds of the men's revelry. It was warm, but her feet felt icy cold in the linen sheets. They had slept in wool at home. The room was huge, it had been King Kroisos' bedchamber; the walls were patterned in coloured marbles, and the floor was porphyry. A Persian lamp-cluster of gilt lotuses hung over the bed, bathing her in light; would anyone put it out? She had an overpowering memory of Philip's physical presence, his strong stocky limbs, his rather sweetish smell. The little she had eaten lay in her like lead. Supposing she was sick on the bed. If her mother were only here! The full sense of her loss came home to her; she felt, terrified, a surge of approaching tears. But if Kynna were here, she would be ashamed to see her cry in the presence of an enemy. She pulled in her stomach muscles, and forced back the first sob in silence.

Behind the matrons the bridesmaids clustered whispering. Their song sung, their small rite done of turning back the bride-bed and sprinkling it with perfume, they had nothing to do. Among a little set of sisters and cousins and friends, the tittering began; dying away if one of the great ladies looked round, rustling like a faint breeze in leaves. Eurydike heard it; she too had nothing to do. Then suddenly she knew that the sounds from the hall had altered. Supper-couches scraped along the floor, the slurred singing stopped. They were getting up.

Like a tense soldier released by the call to onset, she summoned up her courage. Soon all these people must go, and leave her alone to deal with him. She would talk to him, tell him stories. Old Konon had said he would not trouble her.

Roxane too had heard the sounds. She turned, clashing her intricate ruby earrings. 'Joy to the bride!' she said.

Surrounded and pushed on by laughing, drunken, torch-bearing men, stumbling over his robe on the shallow stately stairs with their painted murals, Philip made his way towards the royal bedchamber.

His head swam, he sweated in his purple robe; he was angry about the dog being chased away. He was angry with Perdikkas for fetching him from the table, and with all the men for mocking him, as he knew they were; they had stopped even pretending. They were laughing at him because they knew he was scared. He had heard the jokes in the hall; there was something he was expected to do with Eurydike; so bad that one must not do it even by oneself, if anyone could see. He had been beaten long ago for being seen. Now, he believed – no one had thought to tell him otherwise – they would all stand and watch him. He didn't know how, and was sure cousin Eurydike would not like it. Perdikkas was holding him by the arm, or he would have run away.

He said despairingly, 'It's my bedtime. I want to go to bed.'

'*We'll* put you to bed,' they chorused. 'That's why we're here.' They roared with laughter. It was like the bad old days at home, before Alexander had taken him away.

'Be quiet.' Perdikkas' voice, suddenly unfestal, an angry martinet's, sobered everyone down. They led Philip to an anteroom, and started to undress him.

He let them take off the hot purple robe; but when they undid the girdle of his sweat-soaked tunic, he fought them, and knocked two flying. The rest all laughed; but Perdikkas, looming and awful, commanded him to remember he was King. So he let them strip him, and put him into a long white robe with a gold-embroidered hem. They let him use the chamber-pot (where was Konon?); then there was no more to stay for. They led him to the door. He could hear inside a murmur of women's voices. *They* would be watching, too!

The wide doors opened. There was Eurydike, sitting up in the great bed. A little brown slave-girl, laughing, ran before him with a long snuffer, ready to quench the hanging lamps. A great wave of anger and misery and fear built up in him. It hummed and boomed in his head, booom, booom, booom. He remembered, he knew that soon the white flash would come. Oh, where was Konon? He shouted, 'The light! The light!' and it flashed, a lightning that struck all through him.

Konon, who had been standing in shadow along the passage, ran in. Without apology he shoved aside the horrified group, shocked sober, which bent over the rigid figure on the floor; pulled from his belt-pouch a wooden wedge; prised Philip's jaws apart, so that his tongue should not fall back and choke him. For a moment, he looked up at the men with bitter reproach and anger; then his face settled back into the blank mask of the soldier confronted with stupid officers. He said to Perdikkas, 'Sir, I can see to him. I know what to do. If the ladies could leave, sir.'

Disgusted and ashamed, the men stood aside to let the women go first.

In panic disregard for precedence, the bridesmaids ran at once, their slippers pattering on the stairs. The matrons of middle rank, obsessed all day with etiquette and protocol, clustered helplessly, waiting for the queens.

Eurydike sat in the bed, grasping around her the crimson gold-fringed coverlet, looking for help. She had on only her thin wedding shift; how could she get up in the presence of the men; of Konon, who was staying? Her clothes were on an ivory stool, at the far end of this great room. Would none of them remember her, stand to shield her, put something round her?

She heard a sound from the floor. Philip, stiff as a board till now, had begun to twitch. In a moment he was in the throes of the clonic spasm, his whole frame jerking and thrashing, his robe flung up by his kicking legs.

'Joy to the bride!' It was Roxane, looking down over her shoulder as she swept towards the door.

'Come, ladies.' Kleopatra gathered in a glance the huddled matrons, averting her face from scandal. Making for the door she paused, and turned back to the bed. Eurydike saw the long look of contempt, the unwilling pity. 'Will you come? We will find you something to wear.' Her eye moved to the clothes-stool; an officious matron bustled over.

Eurydike looked after the widow of Alexander, whose gold embroideries gleamed beyond the door; she looked up at Alexander's sister, to whom she was like a beaten whore, whose shame must be covered for the house's honour. She thought, What do I know even of *him*, except that he killed my father? May the gods curse them all. If I die for it, I will make them kneel at my feet.

The matron brought her himation of dyed saffron, the lucky colour of fertility and joy. She took it in silence, and wrapped it round her as she rose. Philip's tremor was growing weaker; Konon was holding his head, to keep it from striking the floor. Standing between him and the watching faces, she said, 'No, lady, I will not come. The King is sick, and my place is with my husband. Please leave us and go away.'

She fetched a pillow from the bed, and laid Philip's head on it. He was hers now, they were both victims together. He had made her a queen, and she would be a king for both of them. Meantime, he must be put into bed and covered warmly. Konon would find her a place to sleep.

321 BC

South down the ancient coast road that followed the eastern shore of the Middle Sea, the army of Perdikkas marched with its long following train; grooms and chandlers, smiths and carpenters and harness-makers, the elephants, the endless wagons, the soldiers' women, the slaves. At Sidon, at Tyre, at Gaza, the people looked down from the mended walls. It was eleven years since Alexander had passed that way alive, whom they had just seen on his last progress, going to Egypt with a chime of bells. This army was no business of theirs; but it meant a war, and war has a way of spreading.

Flanked by its guard of armed Baktrian and Persian eunuchs, Roxane's wagon followed the march, as it had followed from Baktria to India, to Drangiana, to Susa, to Persepolis, to Babylon. Each part had been many times renewed as its journeys lengthened, but it seemed the same, smelling as before of the stamped dyed leather that roofed it, of the essences which at each new city her eunuchs had brought for her approval; even now, a drift of scent on a cushion could bring back the heat of Taxila. Here were the heavy turquoise-studded bowls and trinkets of her dowry, the vessels of chased gold from Susa, a censer from Babylon. It might all have been the same, except for the child.

He was nearly two, and seen to be small for his age; but, as she said, his father must have been so. Otherwise, it was clearly her looks he favoured; the soft dark hair, the bright dark eyes. He was lively, and seldom ill; curious and exploring; a terror to his nurses who must watch his safety at peril of their lives. Though he must be protected, she did not like him thwarted; he must learn from the beginning that he was a king.

Perdikkas called on her every few days; he was the King's guardian, as he reminded her whenever they fell out, which happened often. He was offended that the child shrank from him; it came, he said, of never seeing any other man. 'His father, you should remember, was not reared among eunuchs.'

'Among *my* people they leave the harem at five, and still make warriors.'

'However, he beat them. That is why you are here.'

'How dare you,' she said, 'call me a captive of the spear! You who were our wedding guest! Oh, if he were here!'

'You may well wish that,' Perdikkas said, and left to visit his other ward.

When the army made camp, Philip had his tent just as before. Eurydike, as became a lady of rank, had her wagon; and in this she slept. It lacked Roxane's splendours; but, as she had not seen them, she found it comfortable, and even handsome when her dowry things were set out. It had a roomy locker; and in this, disguised in a roll of blankets, at the hour of departure she had concealed her arms.

Philip was quite happy with these arrangements. He would have been gravely disconcerted by her presence in his tent at night; she might even have wanted Konon to go. In the daytime he was delighted to have her company; would often ride beside her wagon, and point out the sights as they passed. He had traversed this whole route in the train of Alexander, and from time to time something would jog an inconsequent flash of memory. He had been encamped for months before the huge walls of Tyre.

In the evening, she dined with him in his tent. She hated at first to watch him eat, but with instruction he improved a little. Sometimes at sunset, if the camp was near the shore, she would walk with him, guarded by Konon, helping him to look for stones and shells; and then she talked to him, telling the legends of the royal house of Macedon she had heard from Kynna, right back to the boy who took the sunbeam for his wages. 'You and I,' she said, 'will be King and Queen there soon.'

A dim anxiety stirred in his eyes. 'But Alexander told me ...'

'That was because he was King himself. All that is over. You *are* the King. You must listen to me, now that we are married. I will tell you what we can do.'

They had passed the Sinai, and in the lands of Egypt made camp by the flat green coast. A few miles ahead was the ancient port of Pelusion; beyond that, the spread-fingered delta of the Nile, webbed with its intricate veins of canal and stream. Beyond the Nile was Alexandria.

Among the date-palms and little black irrigation canals and clumps of tall papyrus, the army spread itself restlessly. The warm dry wind from the southern sands was just beginning; the Nile was low, the crops stood deep in the rich silt, the patient oxen toiled at the wooden water-wheels. By the elephant lines, the mahouts stripped off their dhotis to wash their children in the canal, gaily splashing them as they showered themselves with their trunks after the hot trudge across Sinai. The camels, drinking prodigiously, refilled their secret storage tanks; the soldiers' women washed their clothes and their children. The sutlers went out to find supplies. The soldiers prepared for war.

Perdikkas and his staff scanned the terrain. He had been here with Alexander; but that was eleven years back, and for the last two, Ptolemy had been making himself at home. The land's long vistas showed where, at vital points of access, where a mound or a rocky outcrop offered foundation, stout forts of brick or timber had appeared. They could get no further coastwise; Pelusion was well defended by the salt marsh between. He must strike south, below the marshes of the delta.

The main camp must stay here. He would take a mobile force, light and unencumbered. Alexander had taught him that. He rode back to his tent in the quick-falling dusk which the breath of the desert reddened, to make his plans.

Through the wide straggling camp, the cook-fires budded and bloomed; little fires of the women, big ones – for the nights were cold still – where twenty or thirty men would share their bean soup and porridge, their bread and olives, with a relish of dates and cheese, washed down with rough wine.

It was in the hour between food and sleep, when men talked idly, told tales or sang, that the voices began to sound around the camp, just beyond the reach of the firelight. They called softly, speaking good Macedonian; uttering familiar names, recalling old battles under Alexander, old fallen friends, old jokes. First unrebuffed, then hesitantly welcomed, the speaker would come up to the fire. Just a jar together for old times' sake, seeing he'd brought one. Tomorrow, who could say, they might have to kill each other, but meantime, good health and no hard feelings. As for himself, he could only speak as he'd found; now Alexander was gone, Ptolemy was next best. He was a soldier and no one's fool; but he looked after you, he had time for your troubles, and where else would you find that today? What wage, by the way, was Perdikkas paying veterans? *What?* (A shake of the head, a long contemptuous whistle.)

'He promised you loot, I suppose? Oh, yes, it's *there*; but not so you'll ever get to it. The country's murder to those who don't know the waterways. Look out for the crocodiles; they're bigger than in India, *and* cunning.'

To a growing audience, he would go on to the comforts and pleasures of Alexandria, the shipping from everywhere, the good fresh food, the wineshops and the girls, the good air all the year round; and Alexander to bring the city luck.

The wine-jar emptied, his mission done, the visitor would slip away, his footfalls merging into the uncanny noises of the Egyptian night. As he threaded his way back to his fort, he would reflect comfortably that he'd not given them a word of a lie, and doing old friends a kindness was a very good way of earning a hundred drachmas.

Perdikkas made his last camp a little above the wrist of the Nile, from which the fingers of the Delta spread northwards. The non-combatants he had brought thus far would await him; among them the Kings, whom he wanted under his eye. From here he would make his march towards the river.

They watched him and his soldiers go into the shimmer of morning mist, horse and foot, the pack-mules with the rations, the camel-train with the parts for the catapults, the elephants plodding after. For a long time they grew smaller in the flat distance, vanishing at last into a low horizon of tamarisk and palm.

Pacing the royal tent, Eurydike waited restlessly for news. Konon had found an escort, and taken Philip riding. She too had liked to ride, free on the hills of Macedon, sitting astride; but she had to remember, now, what would be acceptable in a queen. Perdikkas had told her so.

Now that for the first time she was with an army in the field, all her training and her nature rebelled at being laid aside with slaves and women. Her marriage she had felt as a grotesque necessity, something to be managed, altering nothing of herself; even more, now, she felt women an alien species, imposing no laws upon her.

Over by her wagon, her two maids sat in its shade, chattering softly in Lydian. Both were slaves. She had been offered ladies-in-waiting, but had refused, telling Perdikkas she would not ask softly-nurtured women to endure the hardships of the march. The truth was that she would not endure the tedium of female talk. To sex she was indifferent; in this respect she needed women even less than men. Her wedding night had killed the last of that. In adolescent dreams she had fought, like Hippolyta, at a hero's side. Since then she had become ambitious, and her dreams were otherwise.

By the third morning she was impatient even of ambition, which had no outlet. The day stretched before her, empty and flat as the land. Why should she endure it? She remembered the locker in the wagon which contained her arms. Her man's tunic was there as well.

She was Queen; Perdikkas should have sent reports to her. If no one would bring her news, she would go and see.

All she knew of the expedition she had heard from Konon, who had many friends in the camp. Perdikkas, he had said, had started out without telling anyone his objective, neither the camp commandant nor the senior officers who were going with him. He had heard there had been spies about the camp. The officers had not liked it; Seleukos, who commanded the elephants, liked to know how they would be used. Konon kept to himself much more than he had told; they were saying in camp that Perdikkas was far higher-handed these days than Alexander ever was; Alexander had known how to talk you round.

He had confided, however, to Eurydike that with the stores and remounts they'd taken, he reckoned they would not be marching above thirty miles. And that was the distance to the Nile.

Eurydike changed into her tunic, clasped on her tooled-hide corselet, laced down the shoulder pieces, put on riding-boots and greaves. Her breasts were small and the corselet hid their curve. Her helmet was a simple, unplumed Illyrian war cap; her grandmother, Audata, had worn it on the border. The drowsy servants never saw her go. Down at the horse-lines the grooms took her for one of the royal squires, and at her imperious order led a sound horse out.

Even after three days, the spoor of the troops was plain: the ploughed-up grass, the bared dust, the horse and camel droppings, the trampled banks of the irrigation canals, the leaked water caking in the little fields. The peasants labouring to mend the dykes looked up with sullen hatred of all destructive soldiers.

She was only a few miles out when she met the messenger.

He was riding a camel; a dusty, drawn-faced man, who stared at her angrily for not making way for him. But he was a soldier; so she wheeled round and overtook him. Her horse shied from the camel: she called, 'What news? Has there been a battle?'

He leaned over to spit; but his mouth was dry, and only the sound came out. 'Get out of my way, boy. I've no time for you. I've dispatches for the camp. They must get ready to take the wounded . . . what are left of them.' He switched his mount; it bobbed its scornful head and left her in its dust.

An hour or two later, she met the wagons. As they came nearer, she guessed their freight from the groaning, from the water-carriers on their donkeys, and the doctor leaning under one of the awnings. She rode down the line, hearing the humming flies, a curse or a cry when a wagon jolted.

The fourth of them had men talking and looking out; men with disabled limbs, not too weak to be alert. She saw inside a familiar face; it was the veteran who had first taken her part on the Sardis road, when her mother died.

'Thaulos!' she called, riding up to the tail-board. 'I am sorry to see you hurt.'

She was hailed with amazement and delight. Queen Eurydike! And they had taken her for some young blood in cavalry! What was she doing here? Had she meant to lead them into battle? A daughter of the house – her granddad would have been proud of her. Ah well, lucky she had been too late for yesterday's work. It did one good to see her.

She did not understand that it was her youth they found endearing; that had she been thirty instead of fifteen they would have made a barrack-room joke of her for a mannish termagant. She looked like a charming boy without having lost her girlishness; she was their friend and ally. As she walked her horse beside the cart, they poured out their discontents to her.

Perdikkas had marched them to a place on the Nile called Camelford. But of course the ford was guarded by a fort across the stream, with a palisade, a scarp, and the wall of the fort on top. Perdikkas' scouts had reported it lightly manned.

A younger veteran said resentfully, 'But what he forgot was that Ptolemy learned his trade from Alexander.'

'Perdikkas hates him,' said another, 'so he underrates him. You can't afford that in war. Alexander knew better.'

'That's it; of course the fort was undermanned. Ptolemy was keeping mobile, till he knew where the stroke would be. Once he did know, he came like the wind; I doubt Alexander would have been much quicker. By the time we were half across, he was in the fort with a regiment.'

'And another thing I'll tell you,' Thaulos said. 'He didn't want to shed Macedonian blood. He could have lain low, and fallen on us as we crossed; for he'd come up out of sight. But up he stood on the walls, with a herald, and his men all shouting, trying to scare us back. He's a gentleman, Ptolemy. Alexander thought the world of him.'

With a grunt of pain, he eased himself over on the straw to favour his wounded leg. She asked if he needed water; but they were all in need of talk. The desperately wounded were in other carts.

Perdikkas, they said, had made a speech calling upon their loyalty. It was he who was guardian of the Kings, who had his appointment direct from Alexander. This they could not deny; moreover he was paying them, and their pay was not in arrears.

Scaling ladders had been carried by the elephants; and it was they, too, who had torn down the palisades on the river bank, as their mahouts directed them, plucking out the stakes like the saplings whose leaves they fed on, their thick hides making little of javelins from above. But the defenders had been well trained; the glacis was steep; the men dislodged from the ladders had rolled down the broken palisade into the river, where the weight of their armour drowned them. It was then that Perdikkas had ordered the elephants to assault the walls.

'Seleukos didn't like it. He said they'd done their stint. He said there was no sense in a beast carrying two men up where they'd be level with a dozen, and exposing its head as well. But he was told pretty sharply who was in command. And he didn't like that either.'

The elephants were ordered to give their war-cry. 'But it didn't scare Ptolemy. We could see him up on the wall with a long sarissa, poking back our men as they came up. An elephant can scare any man down on the ground; but not when he's on a wall above it.'

The elephants had laboured up the scarp, digging their heavy feet into the earth, till Old Pluto, the one the others followed started to pull at the wall-timbers. Old Pluto could shift a battering-ram. But Ptolemy stood his ground, threw off the missiles with his shield, reached out his long spear and got Old Pluto's eyes. The next elephant up, someone picked off the mahout. So there were these two great beasts, one blind and the other unguided, pounding and blundering down the scarp, trampling anyone in their way.

'And that,' said one man, 'is how I got a broken foot. Not from the enemy. And if I never walk straight again, it's not Ptolemy I'll blame for it.'

There was a growl of anger from every man in the cart. They had seen little more of the action, having been wounded about this time; they thought it had gone on all day. She rode by them a little longer, offering sympathy, then asked them the way to Camelford. They urged her to take care, to do nothing rash, they could not spare their Queen.

As she rode on, a dark moving bulk appeared in the middle distance, coming slowly from a palm-grove that fringed a pool. As it drew near, she saw two elephants in single file, the smaller going first, the bigger one holding it by the tail. Old Pluto was going home, led as he had been by his mother forty years ago in his native jungle, to keep him safe from tigers. His mahout sat weeping on his neck; his wounded eyes, dropping bloody serum, seemed to be weeping too.

Eurydike noted him, as proof of Ptolemy's prowess. At home her chief diversion had been the hunt; she took for granted that animals were put into the world for men to use. Questioning the other mahout, who seemed to have his wits about him, she learned that Perdikkas had abandoned the assault at evening, and marched after dark, the man did not know where. Clearly, if she rode on she risked falling among the enemy; so she turned back to the camp.

No one had missed her but old Konon, who recognized her as she came back; but, as she warned him with her eyes, it was not his place to rebuke her. He would not dare give her away. For the rest, Philip's wedding had been a nine days' wonder, and just now they had other concerns. It was she herself who began, dimly and gropingly, to see her way ahead.

The army of Perdikkas, what was left of it, came back next day.

Stragglers came first, unofficered, undisciplined, unkempt. Clothes, armour and skin were plastered with dried Nile mud; they were black men, but for their light angry eyes. They went about the camp, seeking water to drink and clean themselves, spreading each his tale of confusion and disaster. The main force followed, a sullen, scowling mass, led by Perdikkas with a face of stone, its tight-lipped officers keeping their thoughts to themselves. Her female dress and seclusion resumed, she sent out Konon to learn the news.

While he was gone, she became aware that round the small circle of the royal quarters a ring of men was gathering. They settled down in groups, not talking much, but with the air of men agreed upon their business. Puzzled and disturbed, she looked for the sentries who should have been somewhere near; but they had joined the silent watchers.

Some instinct dispelled her fear. She went to the entry of the royal tent, and let herself be seen. Arms went up in salute; it was all quiet, it had an air of reassurance, almost of complicity.

'Philip,' she said, 'stand in the opening there, and let those men see you. Smile at them and greet them as Perdikkas taught you. Show me – yes, like that. Say nothing, just salute them.'

He came in, pleased, to say, 'They waved to me.'

'They said, "Long live Philip." Remember, when people say that, you must always smile.'

'Yes, Eurydike.' He went to lay out with his shells some beads of red glass she had bought him from a pedlar.

A shadow darkened the tent-mouth. Konon paused for leave to enter. When she saw his face, her eyes moved to the corner, where they kept Philip's ceremonial spear. She said, 'Is the enemy coming?'

'Enemy?' He made it sound like an irrelevance. 'No, madam ... Don't be in a worry about the lads out there. They've taken it on themselves, just in case of trouble. I know them all.'

'Trouble? What trouble?'

She saw his old soldier's stone-wall face. 'I can't say, madam. They say one thing and another in the camp. They were cut up badly, trying to cross the Nile.'

'I've seen the Nile.' Philip looked up. 'When Alexander ...'

'Be quiet and listen. Yes, Konon. Go on.'

Perdikkas, it seemed, had given his men a few hours' rest after the assault upon the fort. Then he had ordered them to strike camp and be ready for a night march.

'Konon,' said Philip suddenly, 'why are all those men shouting?'

Konon too had heard; his narrative had been flagging. 'They're angry, sir. But not with you or the Queen. Don't fret about it, they won't come here.' He took up his tale again.

Perdikkas' men had fought through the heat of the day and on till evening. They were discouraged and dog-tired; but he had promised them an easy crossing, further south at Memphis, down the east bank of the river.

'Memphis,' said Philip brightening. Long ago, from a window, he had watched the tremendous pageant of Alexander's enthronement as Pharaoh, Son of Ra. He had seemed to be made all of gold.

Konon was saying, 'Alexander, now; *he* knew how to make a man throw his heart into it.'

Outside, the voices of the encircling soldiers rose a tone or two, as if receiving news. The sound sank again.

In the dark before dawn, Konon went on, they had come to the crossing-place. Here the river was split by a mile-long island, breaking its force, and the forks were shallower. They were to cross in two stages, assembling on the island in between.

'But it was deeper than he'd thought. Half over from this side, they were chest deep. With the current pulling at their shields, some of them keeled over; the rest had all they could do to keep their feet. So then Perdikkas remembered how Alexander crossed the Tigris.'

He paused, to see if she knew about this famous exploit. But she had encouraged no one to talk about Alexander.

'It's a fast stream, the Tigris. Before he sent the infantry across, he stood two columns of cavalry in the river, upstream and down of them. Upstream to break the current, downstream to catch any man carried away. He was the first man in on foot, feeling out the shoals with his spear.'

'Yes,' said Eurydike cooling. 'But what did Perdikkas do?'

'What *he* did was to use the elephants.'

'They didn't get drowned?' said Philip anxiously.

'No, sir. It was the men that drowned ... Where's that idle loafing Sinis? Trust a Karian to go off at a time like this. A moment, madam.' He took a taper to the little clay day-lamp which kept a source of fire, and kindled the cluster on the big branched lamp-stand. Outside, a red glow showed that the soldiers were making a cook-fire. Konon's shadow, made huge by the light behind him, loomed dark and manifold on the worn linen hangings of the tent.

'He put the elephants upstream, in line across, and the cavalry downstream; then he told the phalanx to advance. They went in, the phalanx leaders each with his men. And when they got to the middle, it was as if the Nile had come up in flood. It was over their heads; the horses downstream had to swim for it. It was the weight of the elephants did it; it stirred up the muddy bottom, which the Tigris didn't have. But the worst of all, they all say, was to see their mates being taken by the crocodiles.'

'I've seen a crocodile,' said Philip eagerly.

'Yes, sir, I know ... Well, before it deepened too much, a good few men had scrambled up on the island. Perdikkas saw there was no going ahead; so he hailed them, and ordered them to come back.'

'Come *back*?' said Eurydike. She listened with new ears to the sounds outside; the muttering that rose and fell, a long keening from the bivouacs of the soldiers' women. 'He ordered them back?'

'It was that or leave them there. It meant throwing away their arms, which no Macedonian did as long as Alexander led them, and they don't forget it. Some of them shouted out they'd as soon take their chance in the west channel, and give themselves up to Ptolemy. No one knows what became of them. The rest went back in the water, which was deeper than ever, full of blood and crocodiles. A few got out. I've talked with them. One of them left his hand in a crocodile's mouth. The rest of his arm's in ribbons, he'll never live ... They lost two thousand men.'

She thought of the groaning hospital carts, a mere drop now in the ocean of disaster. A sweeping impulse, compounded of anger, pity, contempt, and ambition grasping at opportunity, lifted her out of herself. She turned to Philip.

'Listen to me.' He waited, attentive; recognizing as a dog would do the note of imperative command. 'We are going out to see the soldiers. They have been treated badly, but they know we are their friends. This time, *you* must speak to them. First return their salute; then say – now, listen very carefully – "Men of Macedon. My brother's spirit would grieve to see this day." Don't say anything more, even if they answer you. I will talk to them then.'

He repeated it after her; they went out into the falling dark, lit from behind by the lamps inside the tent, and from before by the soldiers' fire.

An instant cheer greeted them; the word ran round, men ran up crowding to hear. Philip did not falter; she had not charged him with more than he could retain. She saw him pleased with himself, and, lest he should be tempted to improvise, turned to him quickly with a show of wifely assent. Then she spoke.

They were all ears. The King's sense of their wrongs had amazed and pleased them; he could not be as slow as people said. A man of few words. No matter, the Queen would be worth hearing.

Roxane, near by in her wagon, had supposed the troop to have been posted for her own protection. Her eunuchs had told her there was trouble in the camp; but their Greek was poor, and no soldier had had time for them. Now with bewildered anger she heard the young ringing voice crying out against the waste of the gallant dead; promising that when the time came for the King himself to rule them, he would see to it that good men's lives were not thrown away.

Roxane heard the cheers. All her five years of marriage had been told with cheers; shouts of acclamation, the rhythmic roar as the victory parade went by. This sound was different; starting with indulgent affection, but ending with a chorus of revolt.

There, thought Roxane, was an unsexed virago! That bastard and fool the husband should never share *her* child's throne. Just then the child, who had been on edge all day, bumped into something and began to cry.

Eurydike, the cheering over, heard the sound, and said to herself that the barbarian's brat should never reign in Macedon.

Perdikkas sat in his tent at his trestle table, stylus in hand, a wax diptych blank before him. He was alone. Before this he should have called his staff to a war council, to decide on his next move; but, he thought, he must give them time to cool. Seleukos had answered him in monosyllables; Peithon had looked foxily under his reddish brows and down his pointed nose, saying this or that, but none of what he thought; Archias, though known to be in camp, had not reported at all. Once more he regretted having sent Alketas north with Eumenes; there was nothing like a kinsman in treacherous times.

Round the double bowl of his tall-stemmed table lamp, brittle bronze beetles and papery moths fluttered and fell in a ring of ephemeral death. Outside the tent, the squires on duty were talking softly together. It was a breach of discipline, but he was strangely reluctant to go out and deal with it. All he could hear was, now and then, a name. Through the slit of his tent-flap, like a fiery crack, shone the flame of the fire at which the rest were sitting. He had not – yet – the royal right to choose fresh boys from the noble houses of Macedon. One or two had died of fever, or fallen in war; the rest were all here still, his inheritance from the death-chamber in Babylon. He had not had much time for them lately, just taken for granted that they would be there at call. They had been with him at the Nile, ready with spare horses, waiting till he was ready to cross.

The soft voices buzzed, a little nearer now, or a little less careful. 'Alexander always used to ...' 'Alexander would no more have ...' 'Never! Remember how he ...' The voices sank; voices not of protest but of intimate, private judgement. He got to his feet, then sat down again, staring at the tiny holocaust around the lamp. Well, he trusted me with his ring; do they forget that? But as if he had spoken aloud, he seemed to hear a murmur: 'But Krateros was in Syria. And Hephaistion was dead.'

Seeking warmth and comfort, his memory groped back to the days of youth and glory; further yet, to the moment of exultation when, the blood of Philip's assassin red on his sword, he had first looked into those searching intent grey eyes. 'Well done, Perdikkas.' (He knew my name!) 'When my father has had his rites, you will hear from me.' The long pageant of the short years unrolled. He rode in triumph through Persepolis.

There was a break in the sound outside. The squires had fallen silent. New voices now; older, terser, more purposeful. 'You may dismiss.' A single, uncertain, 'Sir?' Then, a little louder – Peithon surely – 'I said, dismiss. Go to your quarters.'

He heard the click of weapons and armour, the fall of departing feet. Not one had come in, to ask for orders, to give a warning. Two years ago, they had cheered him for defying Meleager. But then, they had only just come from the room in Babylon.

His tent-flap opened. For a moment he saw the bright leap of the fire, before the press of men blotted it out. Peithon; Seleukos; Peukestes with his Persian scimitar. And more behind them.

Nobody spoke; there was no need. He fought while he could, grimly, in silence. He had his pride; he had been, even though not for long, second to Alexander. His pride chose for him, when it was too late to think, not to die calling for help that would not come.

From the royal tent, Eurydike heard the rising confusion of rumour and counter-rumour, contention and savage cheers. Their protectors grew restless, seeking news. There was a sudden stir; a young man ran up, helmetless, red and sweating with excitement and the heat of the fire.

'King, lady. Perdikkas is dead.'

She was silent, more shocked than she would have supposed. Before she could speak, Philip said with simple satisfaction, 'Good. That's good. Did you kill him?'

'No, sir.' (Just as if, she thought subconsciously, a real man had asked.) 'It was the generals, as I understand. They . . .'

He paused. A new sound had pierced the vague fluctuant din; the roar of a lynch-mob making for its prey. Soon it was mingled with the shrieks of women. For the first time she was afraid. A mindless thing was abroad, a thing that could not be spoken with. She said, 'What is it?'

He frowned and bit his lip. 'There's always some will go too far once they begin. They'll be after Perdikkas' people. Don't be afraid, lady; they won't harm the Kings.'

She was startled by a strong voice just beside her. 'If they come here, I'll kill them.'

Philip had found his ceremonial spear, and was fiercely grasping it. The ornate blade was pointed. It took her a little time to coax it from his hands.

Ptolemy arrived in the camp next day.

He had been informed of Perdikkas' death as soon as it took place – some said before – and arrived with a cavalcade which, though impressive, had no appearance of threat. Relying on his informants, he chose to present himself as a man of honour trusting in his peers.

He was warmly welcomed, even cheered. The soldiers saw in this intrepid confidence a touch of Alexander. Peithon, Seleukos and Peukestes met and escorted him.

He had brought Arybbas, riding at his right hand. The bier of Alexander had been installed at Memphis, to await the completion of his tomb; Perdikkas from across the fatal river might almost have caught the gleam of its gold crest. Its architect now gave the generals a friendly salute. After the briefest pause they returned it; things had to be lived with as they were.

Ptolemy's terms had been agreed beforehand. The first of them was that he should address the army, to answer Perdikkas' accusation of treason. The generals had little choice. He had offered a gentleman's undertaking not to incite their own troops against them. The need for this reassurance spoke, after all, for itself.

The engineers, working at speed, had run up a rostrum. As Alexander had accustomed them to do, they put it near the royal quarters. Eurydike took it at first for a scaffold, and asked who was being put to death. They told her that Ptolemy was to make a speech.

Philip, who had been arranging his stones in an elaborate spiral, looked up alertly. 'Is Ptolemy coming? Has he brought me a present?'

'No, he is only coming to talk to the soldiers.'

'He always brings me a present.' He fondled a memorable lump of yellow crystal from central Asia.

Eurydike was staring at the tall dais, deep in thought. Now Perdikkas was dead, the only appointed guardian of the Kings was the distant Krateros, campaigning somewhere in Syria against Eumenes. There was no regent of Asia, either. Was this the moment destiny had appointed? 'Men of Macedon, I claim the right to govern in my own name.' She could teach him that, and afterwards speak herself, as she had done last night. Why not?

'Philip. Put that away now.' Carefully she gave him his words. He was not to interrupt Ptolemy's speech; she would tell him when to begin.

A ring of soldiers cordoned the royal quarters. It was only to protect them from the crush of the Assembly; but it gave space, one could step out and be heard. She rehearsed her speech in her head.

Ptolemy, flanked by Peithon and Arybbas, mounted the steps to the rostrum, welcomed with cheers.

Eurydike was astounded. She had heard cheers already that day, but it had never occurred to her that they could be in honour of the recent enemy. She had heard of Ptolemy – he was, after all, a kind of left-handed kinsman – but had never seen him. She was young, still, in the history of Alexander's army.

However often told by Perdikkas that he was a traitor, the troops knew Ptolemy as a well-liked man, and one who led from the front. From the start, none of them had really wanted to go to war with him; when they met disasters, there had been no bracing hatred of the enemy to stiffen their morale. Now they hailed him as a revenant from better days, and heard him eagerly.

He began with an epitaphion for the dead. He mourned as they did the loss of brave former comrades, against whom it would have grieved him to lift his spear. Many had been cast up on his side of the river, whom, had they lived, he would have been proud to enrol under his command. They had had their due rites and he had brought their ashes. Not a few, he was glad to say, had reached shore alive. He had brought them back; they were here now at Assembly.

The rescued men led the cheering. All had been freed without ransom; all had enlisted with Ptolemy.

And now, he said, he would speak of him who, while he lived, had united all Macedonians in pride, victory and glory. Moving many to tears, he told them of Alexander's wish to return to the land of Ammon. (Surely, thought Ptolemy, he would have said so if he could have spoken at the last.) For doing Alexander right, he had been accused of treason, though he had never lifted sword against the Kings; and this by a man who had himself been reaching for the throne. He had come here to submit himself to the judgement of the Macedonians. Here he stood. What was their verdict to be?

The verdict was unanimous; it verged on the ecstatic. He waited, without anxiety or unbecoming confidence, till it had spent itself.

He was glad, he said, that the soldiers of Alexander held him in remembrance. He would subvert no man's loyalty; the army of the Kings could march north with his goodwill. Meantime, he had heard that through the late misadventures the camp was short of supplies. Egypt had had a good harvest; it would be his pleasure to send some victuals in.

Rations were indeed disorganized, stale and scanty; some men had not eaten since yesterday. There was a furore of acclamation. Seleukos mounted the dais. He proposed to the Assembly that Ptolemy, whose magnanimity in victory had equalled even Alexander's, should be appointed regent in Asia, and guardian of the Kings.

Cries of assent were hearty and unanimous. Hands and hats waved. No Assembly had ever spoken with a clearer voice.

For a moment – all the time he had – he stood like Homer's Achilles, this way and that dividing the swift mind. But he had made his choice, and nothing had really happened to change it. As regent, he would have had to leave prospering friendly Egypt, where he was as good as king already; to lead his troops, who liked and trusted him, into a cut-throat scrimmage where one could trust no one – look at Perdikkas, his body hardly cold! No. He would keep his own good land, husband it, and leave it to his sons.

Gracefully but firmly, he made his speech of refusal; the satrapy of Egypt, and the building of Alexandria, were a great enough charge for such a man as himself. But since he had been honoured with their vote, he would take it on himself to name two former friends of Alexander to share the office of guardian. He gestured to Peithon and Arybbas.

In the royal tent, Eurydike heard it all. Macedonian generals learned how to make their voices carry, and Ptolemy's soundbox was resonant. She heard him end his speech with some homespun army anecdote, mysterious to her, delightful to the soldiers. With a sense of hopeless defeat she observed his height, his presence, his air of relaxed authority; an ugly, impressive man, talking to men. Philip said, 'Does your face hurt you?' and she found she had covered it with her hands. 'Shall I make my speech now?' he said. He began to step forward.

'No,' she said. 'Another day you shall make it. There are too many strangers here.'

He went back happily to play with his toys. She turned to find Konon just behind her. He must have been standing there quietly for some time. 'Thank you, madam,' he said. 'I think it's better.'

Later that day, an aide announced that Ptolemy would shortly pay his respects to the King.

He arrived soon after, saluted Eurydike briskly, and clapped Philip's shoulders in a fraternal embrace, to his beaming pleasure. It was almost as good as Alexander coming. 'Have you brought me a present?' he asked.

His face scarcely flickering, Ptolemy said heartily, 'Of course I have. Not here; I had to talk to all these soldiers. You'll get it tomorrow ... Why Konon! It's a long time, eh? But I see you take good care of him; he looks as fit as a warhorse. Alexander used to say, "That was a good posting."'

Konon saluted with glistening eyes; no one since Alexander had commended him. Ptolemy turned to go, before remembering his manners. 'Cousin Eurydike, I hope that all goes well with you. Philip's been fortunate, I see.' He paused, and took a long second look at her. In a pleasant, but different voice, he added, 'A sensible wife like you will keep him out of mischief. He's had enough in his life of people trying to use him. Even his father, if Alexander hadn't ... well, never mind. Now Alexander's gone, he needs someone to watch out for him. Well – health and prosperity, cousin. Farewell.'

He was gone, leaving her to ask herself what had possessed her, a queen, to bow to a mere governor. He had meant to warn, not praise her. Another of Alexander's arrogant kindred. At least she would never see *him* again.

Roxane received him with more formality. She still took him for her son's new guardian, and offered the sweetmeats kept for important guests, warning him against the intrigues of the Macedonian vixen. He disillusioned her, praising Peithon and Arybbas. Where, he wondered as he nibbled his candied apricot, would she be today if Alexander were alive? Once Stateira had borne a boy, would he have put up with the Baktrian's tantrums?

The child was clambering over him, clutching his clean robe with sticky hands. He had grabbed at the sweets, thrown his first choice on the rug, and helped himself to more, with only the fondest of maternal chiding. None the less, Ptolemy took him on his knee, to see Alexander's son who bore his name. His dark eyes were bright and quick; he knew better than his mother did that he was being appraised, and put on a little performance, bouncing and singing. His father was always a showman, thought Ptolemy; but he had a good deal to show. What will this one have?

He said, 'I saw his father when he was as young as this.'

'He takes after both our houses,' said Roxane proudly. 'No, Alexander, don't offer a guest a sweet after you have bitten it ... He means it for a compliment, you know.' He tried another, this time throwing it down.

Ptolemy lifted him firmly down and set him on his feet. He resented it (That's his father, Ptolemy thought) and started to howl (And that's his mother). It dismayed rather than surprised him to see Roxane picking him out his favourites from the dish, and feeding him in her lap. 'Ah, he will have his way. Such a little king as he is already.'

Ptolemy got to his feet and looked down at the child; who looked up, from the cosseting lap, with a strange uneasy gravity, pushing his mother's hands away.

'Yes,' he said. 'He is the son of Alexander. Do not forget that his father could rule men because he had first learned to rule himself.'

Roxane caught the child to her breast and stared at him resentfully. He bowed and saw himself out. At the entrance of the tent with its precious rugs and gem-studded hanging lamps, he turned to see the boy gazing after him with wide dark eyes.

In the palace of Sardis, seated in the same room where she had entertained Perdikkas, Kleopatra confronted Antipatros, the Regent of Macedon.

Perdikkas' death had shocked her to her roots. She had not loved him; but she had committed her life to him, and founded on him her future. Now she looked into a void. She was still trying to come to terms with her desolation when Antipatros arrived from his campaign in Kilikia.

She had known him all her life. He had been fifty when she was born. Except that his hair and beard and brows had turned from grizzle to white, he seemed unchanged, and as formidable as ever. He sat in the chair Perdikkas had often used, spear-straight, fixing her with a faded but fierce blue eye of inflexible authority.

It was his fault, she said to herself, that Olympias had come from Macedon to Dodona to make her life intolerable. It was his fault she was here. But the habit of youth still held; he was the Regent. It was she who felt in his presence like a child who has wickedly broken something old and precious, and awaits a well-earned chastisement.

He had not rebuked her; simply addressed her as someone whose deep disgrace could be taken for granted. What was there to say? It was she who had set the landslide moving. Through her, Perdikkas had rejected the Regent's daughter, after marrying her for policy; had planned to usurp his power, loyally wielded through two kings' reigns. She sat silent, twisting a ring on her finger, Perdikkas' betrothal gift.

After all, she thought, trying to summon up defiance, he is not the rightful Regent. Alexander said he was too oppressive, Perdikkas told me so. By rights, Krateros should be Regent now.

Antipatros said in his slow harsh voice, 'Did they tell you that Krateros is dead?'

'Krateros?' She stared, almost too dulled to feel it. 'No, I had not heard.' Handsome commanding Krateros, the soldiers' idol next to Alexander; never Persianized, Macedonian dyed in grain. She had adored him at twelve years old when he was one of her father's squires; she had treasured a strand of horsehair left in a tree by his helmet crest. 'Who killed him?'

'It would be hard to say.' He stared back under his white thatched brows. 'Perhaps he might think that you did. As you know, Perdikkas sent Eumenes north to hold the straits against us. He was too late for that; we crossed, and divided our forces, and it was he who met with Eumenes. The Greek is clever. He guessed that if his own Macedonians knew whom they were to fight, they would mutiny and go over; so he kept it from them. When the cavalry met, Krateros' horse went down. His helmet was closed, he was not recognized; the horses trampled him. When it was over they found him dying. I am told that even Eumenes wept.'

She was past tears. Hopelessness and humiliation and grief lay on her like black stones. It was grey winter with her; in silence she bore the cold.

He said drily, 'Perdikkas was unfortunate.' Was it possible, she thought, that there was more to come? He sat there like a judge counting the hangman's lashes. 'Eumenes' victory was complete. He sent a courier south to Egypt, to tell Perdikkas. If he had heard in time, he might have persuaded his men that his cause was still worth following. When it reached the camp he was dead.'

What did we do, she thought, to make the gods so angry? But she knew the annals of the throne of Macedon. She had the answer: we failed.

'And so,' Antipatros was saying, 'all Eumenes got for his trouble – and he is wounded too, I hear – was to be condemned in his absence, for treason and for the death of Krateros. Perdikkas' army condemned him in Assembly ... also, when they mutinied, a mob of them murdered Atalante, Perdikkas' sister. Perhaps you knew her.'

She had sat in this room, tall and dark like her brother; rather grave, because of his other marriage, but civilly planning for the wedding; a woman with dignity. For a moment Kleopatra shut her eyes. Then she straightened. She was Philip's daughter. 'I am sorry for it. But they say, Fate rules all.'

He said only, 'And now? Will you go back to Epiros?'

It was the final stroke, and he must know it. He knew why she had left her dead husband's land, which she had governed well. He knew that she had offered herself to Leonnatos and then Perdikkas, not in ambition but in flight. No one knew more than he about Olympias. His wronged daughter was in his house in Macedon; and Olympias' daughter was wholly in his power. If he chose, he could pack her off like a runaway child, in custody to her mother. Rather than that she would die; or even beg.

'My mother is governing in Epiros till my son succeeds. It is her country; she is Molossian. There is no place for me in Epiros any more. If you will grant it me' – the words almost scorched her throat – 'I will stay here in Sardis and live privately. You have my word I shall do nothing more to trouble you.'

He kept her waiting, not to punish her but to think. She was still worth, to any well-born adventurer, what she had been to two dead pretenders. In Epiros she would be restless and resentful. It would be wisest to have her killed. He looked, and saw her father in her face. For two reigns he had kept his oath of loyalty to absent kings; now his pride was invested in his honour. He could not do it.

'These are uncertain times. Sardis has been fought for time out of mind, and we are still at war. If I do as you ask, I cannot ensure your safety.'

'Who is safe in this world?' she said, and smiled. It was her smile that for the first time made him pity her.

The army of the Kings had struck camp in Egypt. Generously victualled and politely seen off by Ptolemy, it was marching north to its rendezvous with Antipatros.

The guardians of the Kings, appointed after Alexander's death, were now both dead within two years of it. Their office was held, at present, by Peithon and Arybbas.

In the two royal households, only Roxane had known the fallen
Krateros. He had convoyed her back from India with the non-combatants,
while Alexander was shortening his life in the Gedrosian desert. She had
greatly preferred him to Perdikkas, and looked forward to being in his
charge again. She had had a new gown made to receive him in; her
mourning for Krateros had been sincere. The new guardians were both
unpromising. Peithon, fiercely devoted to Alexander, had always regarded
her as a campaign wife who ought to know her place. Arybbas she
suspected of preferring boys. Besides, they had only visited her both
together; a precaution privately agreed between them.

To Eurydike, Krateros had been only a name. She had heard of his death
with relief; his fame had threatened a powerful force; more powerful, she
had been quick to sense, than the present guardians could command.

Soon after the mutiny she had felt the change of air. Morale had altered.
These were now men who had successfully defied their leaders; some were
men who had shed blood. They had won; but their inward certainty was
wounded, not strengthened by their victory. They had been led dis-
astrously and did not repent rebellion; but a navel-cord that had nourished
them had been broken, a common trust. Without it they felt restless and
bereaved.

Peithon and Arybbas had not filled up their emptiness. Peithon they
knew by repute, as all the eight Bodyguards were known; but few, as it
happened, had ever served with him. His quality was untested, and in the
meantime they found him uninspiring. As for Arybbas, his record under
Alexander had been undistinguished except in the field of art, which did
not interest them.

If either one had given signs of hidden fire, the army would have been
his own; it was like a pack of powerful dogs missing a master's voice. But
on both alike their office sat uneasily; both alike were anxious to avoid all
occasion for disorder, all look of rivalry or of forming factions. Both went
about their duties with sober competence.

Thus the drama dragged, the action sagged; the audience fidgeted,
coughed and yawned, began fingering its apple-cores and half-bitten
onions and crusts, but was not quite ready yet to throw them at the actors.
The play was a gift to any talented supporting actor who had the wit to
steal it. Eurydike, waiting in the wings, felt the theatre pausing and knew
that her cue had come.

Had Peithon had about him the wily veterans of his old command, some
gnarled and canny phalanx-leader would have come to his tent and said,
'Sir, with respect. That young wife of King Philip's is going about among
the men and making trouble ... Oh, not that kind of trouble, she's a lady
and knows it too; but ...' But Peithon's crafty old veterans had marched

with Krateros, carrying the gold with which Alexander had paid them off. It was Eurydike who had her allies and her faithful spies.

Her chief problem was Philip. On the one hand he was indispensable; on the other, he could not safely be produced for more than minutes. To receive men without him would invite scandal; with him, disaster.

And yet, she thought, my blood is as good and better. What is he but the bastard of a younger son, even if his father did seize the throne? *My* father was the rightful king; what's more, I was born in wedlock. Why should I hold back?

She picked up her faction first from soldiers who already knew her; her saviours on the Sardis road, the men who had guarded the tent in Egypt; some of the walking wounded who had survived the battle on the Nile. Soon many found pretexts to approach her wagon on the march, give a respectful greeting, and ask if she or the King had need of anything. She had taught Philip, if he was riding beside her, to smile and salute and go a short way ahead. Thus sanctioned by her husband, the ensuing talk was relieved of any awkwardness.

Soon, by devious ways known to soldiers not keenly scrutinized, the King had his own unofficial guard, and his wife commanded it. It was proud of itself, and its unrostered numbers grew.

The march dragged on, at foot pace with all its followers. A young officer of her troop, remembering Alexander (they were all prone to this, and she had learned better than to check them) told how he used to leave the sluggish column and go hunting with his friends. The idea delighted her. One or other of them would ask leave to ride out for the day and join the column at sunset, taking a few comrades, a common indulgence in a peaceful area. She would get into her men's clothes and, asking no one's leave, go with them.

Of course the news got round; but it did her no harm. She was played into her role by now, fed by her audience. A confiding gallant boy, a girl receiving gratefully their protection and support, a Queen who was wholly Macedonian; in all these parts they loved her.

In upland pastures, sharing a breakfast of barley-cake and thin wine, she would tell them stories of the royal house, from her great-grandfather Amyntas down; of his gallant sons, Perdikkas and Philip, both kings and both her grandfathers, fighting the Illyrians on the border when Perdikkas fell. 'And because of Philip's valour they made him king. My father was a child and could not help them; so they passed him by. He never questioned the people's will, he was always loyal; but when Philip was murdered, false friends accused him falsely, and the Assembly put him to death.'

They hung on her words. All of them in their youth had heard old garbled tales around the family fire; but now they were getting the real truth, straight from a queen of the royal line; they were proud, impressed and deeply grateful. Her chastity, so evident to them, so natural to her as to be unconsidered, awed them. Each one of them would boast of her notice to a dozen envious comrades when the wineskin went round at night.

She talked, too, of Philip. He had been delicate, she said, in youth; when he grew strong, Alexander was in the full tide of his victories, and his brother felt abashed beside him. Now, he would be glad no longer to be ruled by guardians, but himself to be the guardian of the Macedonians, whose good he had at heart. But because of his modesty, Perdikkas had usurped his rights; and the new guardians did not know him, or care to know.

Philip was pleased, when he rode through the camp, to be so often and so warmly greeted. He would salute and smile; soon she advanced his instruction. He learned to say, 'Thank you for your loyalty,' and was happy to see how much the soldiers liked it.

Arybbas, going about, once or twice noticed these greetings, but saw no harm in them and did not report them to Peithon. Peithon for his part was paying the price for his own resentment of Perdikkas' overbearing ways. On the march to Egypt he had shrugged his shoulders and lost interest in administration. By the time catastrophe had prompted them to kill Perdikkas, Peithon was out of touch with the men. Mutiny had made them truculent; all he wanted was to get the army in one piece to the rendezvous with Antipatros. Once an Assembly could be mustered there, a permanent guardian could be elected. He would stand down with relief.

Discipline, meantime, he left to the junior officers, who in turn thought it wiser to take things easy. Eurydike's faction grew and fermented. When the army made camp at Triparadisos, the brew was ready.

Triparadisos – Three Parks – was in north Syria, the creation of some past Persian satrap who must have wished to emulate the Great King himself. Its small river had been channelled into pools and cascades and fountains, with marble bridges and whimsical stepping-stones of obsidian and porphyry. Rhododendron and azalea jewelled the gentle hills; specimen trees of great rarity and beauty, brought here by ox-train in a solid bed of their native earth, made laced or spreading patterns against a springlike sky. There were glades starred with lilies, whose green perspectives were overlooked by summerhouses with fretted screens, designed for harem ladies; and hunting-lodges of cedar-wood for the satrap and his guests.

During the years of war, the deer had been mostly poached, the peacocks eaten, and a good deal of timber felled; but to restless weary soldiers it was Elysium. Here was the ideal rest-camp in which to await Antipatros, reported a few days' march away.

The generals ensconced themselves in the chief hunting-lodge, built on a central eminence and commanding long man-made vistas. In the glades and clearings the army camped, bathing in the sparkling streams, cutting the trees for cook-fires, snaring conies and liming birds for the pot.

Arybbas found it delightful, and went off on long rambling rides with a dear friend. Peithon so much outranked him that it seemed more graceful, as well as much more pleasant, to leave discipline to him.

Peithon, who thought him a lightweight, scarcely missed him, but thought uneasily that Alexander would have found the men something to do. Games very likely, with prizes big enough to keep them on their toes for a few days' practice . . . He considered talking to Seleukos; but Seleukos, who thought he had a better claim to the guardianship than Arybbas, had been sulking lately. Well, thought Peithon, better leave it alone.

Philip and Eurydike were lodged in the summerhouse of the old satrap's chief wife. By now she had the remount officer among her partisans; a good horse was always hers for the asking. She rode about her business, wearing her man's tunic now all day. Peithon and Arybbas saw from their knoll, if they happened to look out, only a distant horseman like any other.

By now, most of the camp knew what was going on. Not everyone approved; but Philip was King, there was no getting past that; and no one loved either guardian well enough to risk the dangerous task of talebearing. No matter, the doubtful thought; any day now Antipatros would arrive.

As it happened, however, an inland cloudburst had brought the river Orontes down in flood, across Antipatros' line of march. Seeing no pressing need for haste in peaceful country, and preferring to keep his eighty-year-old bones dry, he made camp on rising ground and awaited the sinking of the waters.

In Triparadisos the weather was fresh and fine. Bright and early one day, when the dew lay on the spring lilies in crystal globes, and the birds were singing high in the fifty-year-old trees, Peithon was wakened by an aide who rushed into his room half dressed, still tying his girdle. 'Sir, the men . . .'

His voice was drowned by a trumpet-call which brought Peithon to his feet, naked and staring. It was the royal fanfare which announced a king.

Arybbas came running in, a robe thrown round him. 'It must be Antipatros. Some fool of a herald . . .'

'No,' said Peithon. 'Listen.' He peered through the little window. 'What in the Furies' name . . .? Get dressed! Get armed!'

It was quick work for Alexander's veterans. They came out on the verandah from which the satrap had aimed his arrows at driven game. The broad glade before them was filled with soldiers. At their head, mounted, were Philip and Eurydike. The trumpeter stood by them, looking defiant, and full of the importance of a man who is making history.

Eurydike spoke. She was wearing her man's tunic, and all her armour except her helmet. She was uplifted, glowing; her skin was clear and transparent; her hair shone; the vitality of great daring flowed through her and rayed out of her. She did not know, nor would have wished to know, that Alexander had glowed like this on his great days; but her followers knew it.

Young, clear and hard, her voice carried as far as Ptolemy's bass had done in Egypt. 'In the name of King Philip son of Philip! Perdikkas his guardian is dead. He has no need of new guardians. He is of age, thirty years old, and able to reign for himself. He claims his throne!'

Beside her, Philip threw up his hand. His shout, startlingly loud, unfamiliar to all his hearers, boomed out. 'Macedonians! Do you take me for your King?'

The cheers came crashing back, making the birds beat up from the treetops. 'Long live King Philip! Long live Queen Eurydike!'

A galloping horse thudded over to the lodge. The rider threw his bridle to a scared slave and strode up to the verandah. Seleukos, whose courage was legendary and who knew it, was having no one say he had skulked in his quarters during a mutiny. He was a well-liked general. In his presence, incipient shouts of 'Death to the guardians!' sank away. The cheers for Philip went on.

Through the din, Seleukos bawled in Peithon's ear, 'They're not all here. Play for time. Call for a full Assembly.'

It was true that about a third of the men looked to have stayed away. Peithon stepped forward; shouts sank to muttering. 'Very well. You're free Macedonians, you have your rights. But remember, Antipatros' men are only a few miles off, and they have *their* rights. This touches all the citizens.'

There was a surge of discontent. They were keyed-up, impatient. It needed only Eurydike's 'No! Now!' to set them off again.

Something made her look round. Philip was drawing his sword.

She had had to let him wear it if he was to look like a man, let alone a king. In another moment, by the look of his eyes, he would be charging at the lodge. For an instant she hesitated. Would they follow him . . . ? But he would be helpless in combat, all would be lost. 'Let's kill them!' he said eagerly. 'We can kill them, look.'

'No. Put it back.' He did so, obedient though regretful. 'Now call out to the men, "Let Peithon speak".'

He was at once obeyed. Never before had he so impressed the soldiers. Peithon knew he could do no more. 'I hear you,' he said. 'Yes, you can call Assembly. Don't blame me when the Regent comes and it's all to be done again. Herald, you down there. Come up here and sound.'

The Assembly was held in the glade before the hunting lodge. The men who had stayed aloof answered the summons; there were rather more than Eurydike had thought. But the glow of success was on her when, with Philip, she mounted the verandah which was to serve as rostrum. Smiling she looked around the cheering faces. The silent ones she could do without well enough.

At the far end of the platform, Peithon was talking quietly to Seleukos. She ran over in her mind what she meant to say.

Peithon came up to her. 'You shall have the last word. A woman's privilege.' He was sure of himself, she thought. Well, let him learn.

He stepped forward briskly to the front of the platform. He got a few boos, but soon the sound died down. This was Assembly, and ancient custom held.

'Macedonians!' His crisp bark cut through the last murmurs. 'In Egypt, in full Assembly, you appointed me and Arybbas as guardians of the Kings. It seems that you've changed your minds, never mind why. So be it. We accept. No need to put it to the vote; we are both agreed. We resign the guardianship.'

There was complete, stunned silence. They were like men in a tug-of-war when the other team lets go. Peithon made the most of it.

'Yes, we resign. *But*, the office of guardian stands. The office was decreed in full Assembly when Alexander died. Remember, you have two kings, one of them too young to speak for himself. If you vote Philip to rule in his own right, you appoint him guardian of Alexander's son, till he comes of age. Before you vote, consider all these things.'

'Yes! Yes!' They were like the audience at a play when the actors are slow to enter. Eurydike saw it. It was for her that they were waiting; and she was ready.

'Here, then,' said Peithon, 'is Philip son of Philip, who claims his right to rule. King Philip, come here.' Meekly, with a look of faint surprise, Philip joined him at the head of the central steps. 'The King,' said Peithon, falling back a pace, 'will now address you and state his case.'

Eurydike stood frozen. The sky had fallen on her, and she had not seen that it was inevitable from the first.

She was crushed by the shock of her own folly. She sought no excuse, did not remind herself that she was only just turned sixteen. In her own mind she was a king, a warrior. She had blundered, and that was all.

Philip gazed around him, smiling vaguely. He was greeted with friendly, encouraging cheers. They all knew he was a man of few words, and over modest. 'Long live Philip!' they called. 'Philip for King!'

Philip's head went up. He knew quite well what the meeting was about, Eurydike had told him. But she had told him, too, never to say a word she had not taught him first. He shot an anxious look at her, to see if she would talk instead; but she was looking straight before her. Instead, the voice of Arybbas just behind him, smooth and insistent, said, 'Sir, speak to the soldiers. They are all waiting.'

'Come on, Philip!' they shouted. 'Silence for the King!' He waved his hand at them; they hushed each other to hear.

'Thank you for your loyalty.' That was safe, he knew; yes, they all liked it. Good. 'I want to be King. I'm old enough to be King. Alexander told me not to, but he's dead.' He paused, collecting his thoughts. 'Alexander let me hold the incense. He told Hephaistion, I heard him, he said I'm not as slow as I'm made out to be.' There were indeterminate noises. He added, reassuringly, 'If I don't know what to do, Eurydike will tell me.'

There was a moment's stupefied pause, then confused uproar. They turned on one another, abusive, expostulating, wrangling. 'I told you, now you see.' 'He spoke to me like any man, only yesterday.' 'He has the falling sickness, it takes men so.' 'Well, he told us the truth, you can give him that.'

Eurydike stood as if bound to the execution post. Gladly she would have been dispersed in air. Everywhere, repeated as the joke was relished, she heard, 'Eurydike will tell me what to do.' Encouraged by his reception, Philip was still speaking. 'When I'm King, I shall always ride an elephant.'

Behind him, Peithon and Arybbas looked complacently at each other.

Something in the laughter began to give Philip doubts. It reminded him of the dreadful wedding night. He remembered the magic phrase, 'Thank you for your loyalty'; but they did not cheer, only laughed louder. Should he run away, would he be caught? He turned on Eurydike a face of panic appeal.

At first she moved like an automaton, carried by her pride. She gave the smug guardians a look of scorn. Without a glance at the buzzing crowd below, she went on to Philip and took him by the hand. With ineffable relief and trust he turned to her. 'Was the speech right?' he said.

Holding up her head, for a moment she faced the crowd before she answered him. 'Yes, Philip. But it is finished now. Come, we can sit down.'

She led him to the benches by the wall, where once the satrap and his guest had sat with their wine to await the huntsman's call.

The Assembly continued without them.

It was involved and fretful. The factions had collapsed into absurdity. A few hundred voices urged Peithon and Arybbas to resume their charge, meeting a vigorous refusal. Seleukos in turn declined. While lesser names were being tossed about, a courier rode in. He announced that Antipatros with his army was crossing the Orontes, and would arrive within two days.

Peithon, giving out this news, reminded the men that ever since Perdikkas' death both the Kings had been on their way to Macedon, where they belonged. Who, then, was more fitted than the Regent to be their guardian, now Krateros was dead? Sullenly they settled for this solution, since no one had a better one.

Quietly, during the debate, Eurydike had led her husband away. Over their midday meal he repeated his speech to Konon, who praised it and avoided meeting her eyes.

She hardly heard them. Beaten to her knees, faced with surrender, she felt her blood remembering its sources. The shade of Alexander taunted her; he, at sixteen, had held Macedon as Regent, and fought a victorious war. The fire of her ambition smouldered still under its embers. Why had she been humbled? Not for reaching too high, but too low. I was mocked, she thought, because I did not dare enough. From now on, I will claim my rights for myself.

At evening, when the sun sank over Asia and the first smoke rose, she put on her man's tunic, called for her horse, and rode out among the watch-fires.

Two days later, riding ahead of the Regent and his army, Antigonos One-Eye reached the camp at Triparadisos.

He was the man who had escaped to Macedon to reveal Perdikkas' plot. Alexander had made him satrap of Phrygia; the grateful Regent had appointed him commander-in-chief of all the troops in Asia. He was now on the way to take up his command.

He rode a Persian 'great horse', being so tall that no Greek horse could carry him far. But for his eye-patch – he had lost the eye winning Phrygia for Alexander – he was still a handsome man. His even handsomer young son Demetrios, who went with him everywhere, worshipped him. Riding side by side, they made an impressive pair.

With the small column of his entourage, he entered the woodland fringes of the park. Soon, cocking his ear, he motioned his train to halt.

'What is it, father? Is it a battle?' The boy's eyes kindled. He was fifteen, and had never yet fought in war.

'No,' said his father, listening. 'It's a brawl. Or mutiny. High time I came, by the sound. Forward.' To his son he said, 'What's Peithon about? He did well enough under Alexander. Never think you know a man whom you've only seen acting under orders. Well, he's a stopgap here. We'll see.'

The prospect did not displease him. His own ambitions were great.

Eurydike had rallied to her cause about four-fifths of the army. At the head of her troops, she had appeared before the generals' lodge, announced with the royal fanfare, demanding, this time, joint rule for Philip and herself.

The three generals gazed down with revulsion, not unmixed with fear, at the mob below. It looked worse than mutinous; it looked anarchic. Eurydike herself was half aware of this. Her training in weaponry had not included military drill, and she had not considered in advance that her following would be more manageable, as well as more impressive, if she drew it up in some kind of formation. A year ago, the junior officers (the senior had held aloof) would have managed for her; but much had happened in a year, and most of it bad for discipline. So now an armed rabble followed her; men shouldered each other to get in front, and hurled insults at the generals.

It was as boos and jeers were drowning Peithon's voice that Antigonos and his suite had come into earshot.

After his first distant glimpse, he sent Demetrios to scout ahead; it was good training for the boy. He cantered gaily into the trees, coming back to report that there was a horde of men gathered in front of what looked like headquarters, but no one to speak of at the back.

Meantime, Eurydike felt, behind her, the mass begin to seethe. She must lead them on, now, or somehow hold them back. Inherited instinct told her she would not lead them long. They would surge past her and lynch the generals. After that, her frail authority would be swept away.

'Herald, blow halt!' She faced them with lifted arms; they swayed restlessly, but came no further. She turned again to confront the generals.

The verandah was empty.

During the uproar of the last few minutes, the generals had learned that their new commander-in-chief had arrived in camp. He was in the lodge behind them.

The room inside, with its dark wood and little windows, had an air of dangerous gloom, in which, peering, they made out the towering form of Antigonos, seated in the satrap's chair; glaring at them, like a cyclops, with his single eye. The young Demetrios, a splinter of light picking out his dazzling profile, stood like a fierce attendant spirit behind him.

Antigonos said nothing. He pierced them with his eye, and waited.

As he heard out their lamentable tale, his face changed slowly from grimness to sheer incredulity. After a disturbing pause, he said, 'How old *is* this girl?'

Shouting against the impatient roar from outside, Seleukos told him.

Antigonos swivelled his head to sweep them with his eye, ending at Peithon. 'Thundering Zeus!' he said. 'Are you soldiers or pedagogues? Not even pedagogues, by God! Stay here.' He strode out on the verandah.

The apparition from nowhere of this huge, formidable and famous man, instead of the expected victims, startled the crowd into almost total silence. Eurydike, who had no idea who he was, stared at him blankly. Philip, whom she had forgotten, began, 'That's Antigonos. He ...'

He was drowned by a boom from Antigonos' great chest. Soldiers in the front, despite themselves, straightened up and made vain shuffling efforts to dress their line.

'*Stand* back there, you sons of fifty fathers!' Antigonos roared. '*Get* back, Hades and the Furies take you! What do you think you are, a horde of naked savages? Stand up and let me look at you. Soldiers, are you? I've seen better soldiers robbing caravans. Macedonians are you? Alexander wouldn't know you. Your own mothers wouldn't know you, not if they could help. If you want to hold Assembly, you'd better look like Macedonians, before some real ones come here and see you. That will be this afternoon. Then you can hold Assembly, if the rest agree. Clean yourselves up, curse you, you stink like goats.'

Eurydike heard, dismayed, defiant shouts change to an indeterminate grumbling. Antigonos, who had ignored her, seemed to see her for the first time.

'Young lady,' he said, 'take your husband back to his quarters, and look after him. It's a wife he needs, not a female general. Go about your work, and leave me to mine. I learned it from your grandfather before ever you were born.'

There was a wavering pause; the edges of the press began to fall away, the centre to loosen. Eurydike cried out, 'We will have our rights!', and some voices took it up; but not enough. The hateful giant had beaten her, and she did not know even his name.

Back in the tent, Konon told her. While she considered her next move, the smell of food reminded her that her young stomach was hungry. She waited till Philip had done – she hated to see him eating – and sat down to her meal.

Somewhere outside, a high imperious voice was arguing with the guard. Konon, who was pouring her wine, looked up. A youth came in; stunningly handsome, and hardly as old as herself. With his perfect features and clustering short gold curls, he could have posed for a Hermes to any sculptor. Like Hermes he entered lightly, and stood poised before her, fixing her with the gaze of a scornful god.

'I am Demetrios, son of Antigonos.' He sounded, too, like a deity announcing himself at the opening of a play. 'I am here to warn you, Eurydike. It is not my custom to make war on women. But if you harm a hair of my father's head, your life shall pay for it. That is all. Farewell.'

He was gone, as he had come, through the disorganized army; his speed, his youth and arrogance cleaving his way.

She stared after this first antagonist of her own age. Konon snorted. 'The insolent young dog! Who let him in? "Not my custom to make war on women"! Who is *he* used to make war on, I'd like to know? His father should take a strap to him.'

Eurydike ate quickly and went out. The visitation had spurred her flagging purpose. Antigonos was a force of nature with which she could not contend; but he was one man alone. The troops were still mutinous and ripe for revolt. She dared not assemble them, which would bring him down on her again; but she went among them, reminding them that Antipatros, who was coming, was not the rightful Regent, that he feared being displaced by a rightful King. If he was allowed, he would seek out Philip and herself and all the best of their followers, to be put to death.

Antigonos, meanwhile, had sent one of his suite to meet the Regent and warn him to prepare for trouble. But the Regent and his escort had come by short cuts over the hills; the messenger missed his way, arriving late at the tail-end of the column. There he was told that the old man had gone ahead with his bodyguard, long before noon.

Sitting straight on his easy-pacing charger, his stiff legs aching on the saddle-cloth, his face set in the harsh stare which was his mask for the pains and infirmities of age, the Regent rode to Triparadisos. His doctor had urged him to go by litter. But so had his son Kassandros, back in Macedon; who was only waiting to insist that his failing strength called for a deputy – naturally, himself. Antipatros neither trusted nor much liked his eldest son. Here in Syria, since Perdikkas' death, anything might have happened; and he meant to arrive, the gods and physic helping him, looking like a man to be obeyed.

The main gate into the park was dignified with great columns topped with stone lotuses. Antipatros took the good road which duly led him there.

Noises came from beyond; but to his annoyed surprise no escort was there to meet him. He told his herald to announce him with a trumpet blast.

In the lodge, the generals knew with dismay that his main force could not have come so quickly. Their envoy had missed him. Almost at once a rising commotion was heard; and a squadron leader, who had not joined the revolt, came galloping up. 'Sir! The Regent's here with no more than fifty horse, and the rebels are mobbing him.'

They ran for their helmets – the rest of their armour was on – and shouted for their horses. Neither Peithon nor Arybbas had ever lacked personal courage; they reached for their javelins briskly. Antigonos said, 'No, not you two. If you come they'll fall on all of us. Stay here, get anyone you can find and hold the lodge. Come, Seleukos. We'll go and talk to them.'

As Seleukos mounted, vaulting upon his spear, Antigonos on his tall horse beside him, he felt for a moment the old elation of the golden years. It was welcome after the squalid affair in Egypt, from which he did not yet feel clean. When, though, in those years had he ever felt in danger from his own men?

The Regent had reached an age when discomfort and fatigue bothered him more than danger. Expecting nothing worse than disaffection, he had come in a light riding tunic and straw sun-hat, armed only with his sword. Seleukos and Antigonos, galloping down between huge cedars and deodars and spreading planes, saw the tight knot of the bodyguard sway in the press around it, the broad-brimmed hat fly off among the helmets, the vulnerable gleam of silver hair.

'Try not to draw blood,' called Antigonos to Seleukos. 'They'll kill us then.' With a bellow of 'Halt, there!' he shoved down into the press.

Their firmness, their fame, Antigonos' great height and overwhelming presence, got them through to the Regent, glaring under his white brows like an ancient eagle beset by crows, and grasping his old sword. 'What's this, what's this?' he said. Antigonos gave him a brief salute (did he think there was time to chat? the old man must be failing at last) and addressed the soldiers.

Had they no shame? They claimed to respect the King; had they no respect for Philip his great father, the maker of their nation, who had appointed this man and trusted him? He had never been deposed by Alexander, only summoned for a conference while a deputy relieved him ... Antigonos when he chose could persuade as well as dominate. The crowd sullenly parted; the Regent and his rescuers rode up to the Lodge.

Eurydike had been preparing her speech for the coming Assembly, and knew nothing of the fracas till it was over. It shocked her that followers of hers might have butchered this ancient man. It offended her poetic image of war. Besides, they should be under her control and seen to be so. Only Athenian demagogues made speeches while others fought.

An hour before sunset, Antipatros' main force arrived. She heard, rumbling on into the dusk, the horse and foot filing into the parks, the shouting and creaking of the supply-trains, the bustle of camp slaves pitching tents, the rattle of stacked arms, the whinnying of horses scenting their kind; and, lasting long after, the hubbub of men in animated talk, exchanging news and rumours and opinions. It was the sound of the agora, the wine-shop, the gymnasium, the forum; age-long leitmotiv of the lands by the Middle Sea.

After sundown, a few of her following came, to say they had been arguing her cause with Antipatros' men; one or two had cuts and bruises. But these had been little fights, stopped quickly by authority. She read the omens of discipline restored, and not wholly unwelcome. When a senior officer of the Regent's staff came to the tent, they all, to a man, saluted.

He announced that a full Assembly would be held next day, to decide the kingdom's affairs. King Philip would no doubt wish to attend it.

Philip had been building himself a little fort on the floor, and trying to man it with some ants who persisted in deserting. Hearing the message, he said anxiously, 'Must I make a speech?'

'That, sir, is as you wish,' the envoy said impassively. He turned to Eurydike. 'Daughter of Amyntas, Antipatros sends you greeting. He says that though it is not the custom of the Macedonians for women to address Assembly, you have his leave to do so. When he himself has spoken, they will decide if they wish to hear you.'

'Tell him I shall be there.'

When he had gone, Philip said eagerly, 'He promised I needn't make a speech if I didn't want to. Please don't make me.'

She felt she could have struck him; but she held back, fearing to lose her hold on him. Indeed, she had some fear of his strength.

The Assembly was held next day with ancient procedure. Foreign soldiers, the legacies of Alexander's catholic racial mix, were barred. An impressive rostrum was raised in the biggest clearing, with seats of honour below it. As Eurydike took her place, whispering to Philip a last order to keep still, she felt in the huge throng a new, impalpable change. Something was different, and yet somehow familiar. It was the feel of the homeland, the native hills.

Antigonos spoke first. Here, at Assembly, the angry general was gone. A statesman spoke, not without the skills of oratory. With dignity he reminded them of their heroic past under Alexander, urged them not to disgrace it, and introduced the Regent.

The old man stepped briskly up to the rostrum. His own army cheered him; no hostile sound was heard. As he looked about him; as with perfect timing he signed for silence, an unwanted voice said within Eurydike, This man is a king.

He had reigned over Macedon and Greece throughout Alexander's wars. He had crushed the sporadic risings of the south, imposed on its cities the rulers of his choice, exiled his opponents. He had defeated even Olympias. Now he was old and brittle, his height had begun to shrink, his deep voice to crack; but still, given off from his inner core, the aura of power and command surrounded him.

He told them of their forefathers, he told them of Philip who had rescued their fathers from invasion and civil war, and begotten Alexander who had made them masters of the world. They had become a tree with wide and spreading branches – he gestured to the noble timber standing round – but the greatest tree will die if its roots are sundered from its native earth. Could they bear to sink down among the barbarians they had conquered?

He told them of the birth of Arridaios, the lackwit they had honoured with Philip's name; he told them what Philip had thought of him, ignoring his presence in the seats below. He reminded them that in all their history, they had never had a woman ruler. Would they now choose a woman and a fool?

Philip, who had followed his peroration, nodded sagely. He found it somehow reassuring. Alexander had told him he ought not to be King, and now this forceful old man agreed. Perhaps they would tell him, now, that he could be Arridaios again.

Antipatros' own men had been for him from the start. For the rebels, it was like a slow awakening from restless dreams. All round her, like the sough of shingle on an ebbtide beach, Eurydike felt the lapse of the withdrawing sea.

She would not, could not admit defeat. She would speak, it was her right; she had won them once and would again. Soon this old man would finish talking, and she must be ready.

Her hands had clenched, her back and her shoulders tightened; her stomach contracted, achingly. The aching turned to a cramp, a low heavy drag which, with dismay, she tried at first not to recognize. In vain; it was true. Her menses, not due for four days, had started.

She had always counted carefully, always been regular. How could it happen now? It would come on quickly, once begun, and she had not put on a towel.

She had been strung-up this morning; what had she failed to notice in all the stress? Already she felt a warning moisture. If she stood on the rostrum, everyone would see.

The Regent's speech approached its climax. He was talking of Alexander; she hardly heard. She looked at the thousands of faces round her, on the slopes, in the trees. Why, among all these humans made by the gods, was she alone subject to this betrayal, she only who could be cheated by her body at a great turn of fate?

Beside her sat Philip, with his useless gift of a strong man's frame. If she had owned it, it would have carried her up to the rostrum and given her a voice of bronze. Now she must creep from the field without a battle; and even her wellwishers would think, Poor girl!

Antipatros had finished. When the applause subsided, he said, 'Will the Assembly now hear Eurydike, daughter of Amyntas, the wife of Arridaios?'

No one dissented. Antipatros' men were curious; her partisans were ashamed to vote against her. Their minds were made up, but they were prepared at least to listen. Now was the moment for a true leader to compel their hearts ... She had come, the morning being fresh, with a himation round her shoulders. Now, carefully, she slipped it down to her elbows, to drape in a curve over her buttocks, as elegant ladies wore it in fresco paintings. Getting to her feet, taking care over her draperies, she said, 'I do not wish to address the Macedonians.'

Roxane had kept her tent in a good deal of alarm, among scared eunuchs and terrified women; sure that if the mutiny succeeded, Eurydike's first action would be to kill her and her child; it was, as Roxane saw it, the natural thing to do.

It took her some time to learn the Assembly's decision, since only Macedonians had attended. At length her wagoner, a Greek-speaking Sidonian, came back to report that the wife of Philip had been quite put down without a word to say; that Antipatros the Regent had been made guardian of both the Kings; and that, as soon as the great lords had agreed to divide the satrapies, he would take both royal households back to Macedon.

'Ah!' she cried, and threw off fear like a cloak. 'All will be well, then. It is my husband's kingdom. They know the fool Philip from his childhood days; of course they will have none of him. It is my child they will wish to see. Alexander's mother will be waiting.'

Alexander had never read her the letter Olympias had sent him when he had informed her of his marriage. She had advised him, if the barbarian girl should bear a boy, to have it smothered lest it should some day pretend to the throne. It was high time for him to visit the homeland and beget a Macedonian, as she had begged him to do before he crossed to Asia. This letter had not been placed in the royal archives. He had shown it to Hephaistion, and then burned it.

319 BC

Beside the great palace of Archelaos at Pella stood Antipatros' house. It was solid but unpretentious; scrupulously correct, he had always avoided a regal style. Its only adornments were a columned portico and a terrace.

The house was hushed and closed. Straw and rushes were laid on the terrace paving. Small groups of people stood at decent distances, to watch the comings and goings of the doctors and the kin: townspeople drawn by curiosity and the sense of drama; guest-friends awaiting the signal for condolence and funeral plans; dealers in mourning wreaths and grave-goods. Hovering more discreetly, or represented by spies, were the consuls of client cities, who had the most at stake.

Nobody knew who would inherit power when the old man unclenched at last his grasp of life, or whether his policies would be continued. His last action, before he took to his bed, had been to hang two envoys bringing a petition from Athens, a father and son who he found had corresponded with Perdikkas. Neither age nor his wasting sickness had softened Antipatros. Now the watchers scanned, whenever it appeared, the set frowning face of his son Kassandros, trying to read the omens.

Near by in the palace, that famous wonder of the north, where both the Kings maintained their separate households, the tension was like the string of a drawn bow.

Roxane stood in her window, looking from behind a curtain at the silent crowd. She had never felt at home in Macedon. The mother of Alexander had not been there to receive her or admire her son, having vowed, it seemed, never to set foot in Macedon while Antipatros lived; she was still in Dodona. To Roxane the Regent had behaved with formal courtesy; but before they had crossed the Hellespont he had sent her eunuchs home. They would cause her, he told her, to be taken for a barbarian, and people would ill-use them. She was now fluent in Greek, and could be attended by Macedonian ladies. The ladies had instructed her, politely, in the local customs. Politely, they had dressed her suitably; and, very politely, made it clear that she spoiled her son. In Macedon, boys were made ready to be men.

He was now four, and in this foreign place inclined to cling to her; she in her loneliness could hardly bear him out of her sight. Soon Antipatros had reappeared – no doubt the women were his spies – and declared himself amazed that Alexander's son should have only a few words of Greek. It was time that he had a pedagogue. This person arrived next day.

The customary sober slave, Antipatros had decided, was not enough. He had chosen a vigorous young patrician, already at twenty-five a veteran of the Greek rebellion. Antipatros had noticed the strictness of his army discipline. He had had no occasion to notice that he was fond of children.

It had been the dream of Kebes' life to fight under Alexander; he had been drafted to go with the contingent Antipatros would have brought to Babylon. He had borne in silence his shattered hopes, and performed his distasteful duty of fighting fellow-Greeks instead, though his men thought him rather dour. From habit rather than intent he had accepted his appointment dourly, betraying nothing to the Regent of the elation within.

The first sight of the dark-haired, soft-skinned, plump child had disappointed him; but he had not expected an Alexander in little. For the mother he had been prepared. She clearly supposed that once out of her care her son would be bullied and beaten; the child, seeing he was expected to be frightened, struggled and whined. Taken out firmly without fuss, he displayed a lively curiosity and swiftly forgot his tears.

Kebes knew the maxim of the famous Spartan nurses; never expose a small child to fear, let him enter confidently on boyhood. By small safe stages, he introduced his charge to horses, to large dogs, to the noise of soldiers drilling. Roxane, waiting at home to comfort her ill-used child, found him full of himself, trying to describe the delights of his morning, for which he knew only Greek.

He picked up the language quickly. Soon he was talking incessantly of his father. Roxane had told him he was the son of the world's most powerful king; Kebes related the legendary exploits. He himself had been a boy of ten when Alexander crossed to Asia; he had seen him in the height of his glowing youth, and imagined the rest. If the child was still too small to emulate, he could already learn to aspire.

Kebes had been happy in his work. Now, waiting with the rest before the straw-strewn terrace, he felt the uncertain future shadowing his achievement. Had the child, after all, any more in him than boys at home whom he had known at the same age? Had the great days gone forever? What world would he and his like inherit?

He was brooding on this when the ritual wails began.

Roxane heard them from her window, saw the waiting people turning to one another, and went in to pace her room, pausing sometimes to clutch the child to her breast. Alarmed, he asked what was the matter, getting no answer but, 'What will become of us now?'

Five years before, in the summer palace of Ekbatana, Alexander had told her of Kassandros, the Regent's heir, whom he had left behind in Macedon from fear of treachery. When Alexander died he had been in Babylon; very likely he had had him poisoned. In Pella he had come to pay his respects to her, professedly on behalf of his sick father; really, no doubt, to look at Alexander's son. He had been civil, but unmeaningly, merely accounting for his presence; she had hated and feared his reddish freckled face, his harsh pale eyes, his look of undisclosed purpose. Today she was more frightened than during the mutiny in Syria. If only she could have stayed in Babylon, in a world she knew, among people she could understand! As it was, she must plan as best she could.

Kassandros in the death chamber stared with embittered anger at his father's shrunken corpse. He could not bring himself to lean and close his eyes; an old aunt, looking reproach, pressed down the withered lids and pulled up the blanket.

Across the bed from him stood stolid, fifty-year-old Polyperchon, his grey stubbled chin unshaven from the night watch; making a matter-of-fact gesture of respectful grief, his mind already on his new responsibilities. To him, not to Kassandros, Antipatros had bequeathed the guardianship of the Kings. Thorough to the last, before he drifted into coma he had sent for all the chief noblemen to witness his intent, and elicited their oath to vote for it at Assembly.

He had been senseless since yesterday; the ceasing of the breath was a mere formality. Polyperchon, who had respected him, was glad to end the tiring vigil and get to business, which was in arrears. He had not sought his new charge; Antipatros had had to plead with him. It had been shocking and terrible, like seeing his own stern father grovelling at his feet.

'Do this for me,' he had wheezed. 'Old friend, I beg you.' Polyperchon was not even an old friend; he had been in Asia with Alexander until he rode back with Krateros. He had been in Macedon when Alexander died, and made himself useful in the southern rebellion. While the Regent had been away in nearer Asia fetching home the Kings, Polyperchon had been left as deputy. That had been the start of it.

'I took my oath to Philip.' The dying man had cleared his throat, even that an effort. His voice rustled like dry reeds. 'And to his heirs. I will *not*' – he choked, and paused – 'be forsworn by my son. I know him. I know what . . . Promise me, friend. Swear by the Styx. I beg you, Polyperchon.' In the end he had sworn, only to stop it and escape. Now he was bound.

As Antipatros' last gasps tainted the air, he could feel Kassandros' hatred flowing out at him across the body. Well, he had faced hard men under Philip at Chaironeia, under Alexander at Issos and Gaugamela. He had not risen above brigade commander, yet Alexander had picked him for the Bodyguard, and trust went no higher than that. Polyperchon, he had said, holds on.

Soon he must make himself known to the royal households, taking his eldest son; an Alexandros, he liked to think, who would bring no discredit on the name. Kassandros, who cared greatly what people thought of him, could at least be trusted to put on a handsome funeral.

Eurydike had been out riding when the Regent died. She had known the news was near; when she had had it, she would be pent in the dreary, stifling rites of mourning, which it would be indecent to neglect.

For company on her ride she had a couple of grooms, and a strapping young lady of her household, chosen only because she was a hill-woman and rode well. The days of her cavalry escorts were over; Antipatros had had her vigilantly watched for conspiracy with soldiers. Only Philip himself, by bursting into tears, had persuaded him to leave old Konon. Even so, she sometimes got salutes, and still acknowledged them.

Turning back towards Pella with the westering sun behind her, the hill shadows creeping out over the lagoon, she felt a stirring of destiny, a change of pace in the wheel of fortune. It was not without hope that she had awaited the cries of mourning.

To her, as well as to Roxane, Kassandros had paid his respects during his father's illness. Formally speaking, he had paid them to the King her husband; but with some finesse had conversed respectfully with Philip, while making it clear that his words were meant for her. The looks which, to Roxane, had seemed fierce and savage, were to Eurydike those of a fellow-countryman; not notable for beauty, but engraved with resolution and strength. He would have, no doubt, his father's hardness; but also his father's competence.

She had assumed, since he clearly did so, that he would succeed his father. She had known what he meant when he said that the Macedonians were fortunate in having *one* King of the true blood, and a Queen who was no less so. He had hated Alexander, he would never allow the barbarian's child to rule. It had seemed to her that they understood each other.

The news of Polyperchon's election had disconcerted her. She had never met him, barely knew him by sight. Now, when she came back from her ride, she found him in the royal rooms, talking with Philip.

He must have been there some time. Philip seemed quite at ease with him, and was telling him a rambling story about snakes in India. 'Konon found it under my bath. He killed it with a stick. He said the little ones were the worst.'

'Quite right, sir. They could get into a boot, a man of mine died of it.' He turned to Eurydike, complimented her on her husband's health, begged her to call on him if he could be of service, and took his leave. Clearly it was too soon, with the Regent still unburied, to ask him about his plans;

but she was angry that he had told her nothing, and presented himself to Philip without regard for her absence.

All through the long pompous funeral rites, walking in the procession with shorn hair and ash on her black dress, adding her wail to the chant of lamentation, she scanned Kassandros' face, whenever he came in sight, for some hint of purpose. It was only solid, correct, shaped for the occasion.

Later, when the men went to the pyre to burn the body, and she stood apart with the women, she heard a loud cry, and saw some kind of stir beside the fire. Then Konon was running through all the men of rank towards it. Soon he came out, with a couple of the guard of honour, carrying Philip, with flaccid limbs and open mouth. Lagging, ashamed, she went over and walked with them towards the palace.

'Madam,' Konon muttered, 'if you could speak to the General. He's not used to the King, he doesn't know what upsets him. I had a word with him, but he told me to remember my place.'

'I will tell him.' With the back of her head, she could feel scornful Roxane looking after her. One day, she thought, you will not make light of me.

In the palace, Konon undressed Philip, washed him – in the fit he had wetted his robe – and put him to bed. Eurydike in her room took off her mourning dress and combed the soft wood-ash from her ritually dishevelled hair. She thought, He is my husband. I knew what he was before I took him. I did it from free choice; so I am bound to him in honour. My mother would tell me so.

She called for a warm egg posset with a splash of wine, and took it in to him. Konon had gone off with the dirty clothes. He looked up at her pleading, like a sick dog at a hard master. 'See,' she said, 'I have brought you something nice. Never mind that you were taken ill, you couldn't help it. Many people don't like to watch a funeral pyre.'

He looked at her thankfully and put his face to the bowl. He was glad that she asked no questions. The last thing he remembered, before the drumbeat in his head and the terrible white light, was the beard of the corpse blackening and stinking in the fire. It had brought back to him a day a long time ago, before he went journeying with Alexander. That had been the funeral of the King, so they had told him, but he had not known whom they meant. They had cut short his hair and put a black robe on him and dirtied his face, and made him walk with a lot of people crying. And there was his frightening father, whom he had not seen for years, lying on a bed of logs and brushwood, with a grand bedspread, grimfaced and dead. He had never seen a dead man before. Alexander was there. He too had had a haircut, the fair crop shone in the sun. He had made a speech, quite a long one, about what the King had done for the Mace-

donians; then, suddenly, he had taken a torch from someone who had
been holding it, and stuck it in among the brushwood. Horrified, Philip
had watched as the flames rushed in, roaring and crackling, running
along the edges of the embroidered pall, then bursting through it; then the
hair and the beard ... For a long time afterwards, he would wake with
a scream in the night, and could tell no one that he had dreamed of his
burning father.

The polished marble doors closed on Antipatros' tomb, and an uneasy
calm fell upon Macedon.

Polyperchon gave out that he had no wish for arbitrary powers. Antipatros had governed for an absent ruler. It was now proper that the chief
men should share his counsels. Many Macedonians approved this sign of
antique virtue. Some others said that Polyperchon was incapable of
decision and wished to avoid too much responsibility.

The calm became no easier. Every eye was upon Kassandros.

His father had not wholly passed him over. He had been appointed
Chiliarch, Polyperchon's second-in-command, a rank to which Alexander
had given high prestige. Would he be content with it? Men watched his
rufous impassive face as he came and went in Pella, and said to each other
that he had never been a man to swallow slights.

However, having buried his father he went quietly about his business
through the mourning month. When it was up, he paid his respects to
Philip and Eurydike.

'Greet him,' she said to her husband when he was announced, 'and then
don't talk. It may be important.'

Kassandros' greetings to the King were brief. He addressed himself to
the Queen. 'I shall be gone for a time; I am going to our country place.
I have had a good deal to try me; now I mean to make up a hunting party
of old friends, and forget public affairs.'

She wished him well with it. He did not miss the questioning in her
eyes.

'Your goodwill,' he said, 'has been a solace and support to me. You and
the King may count on me in these troubled times. You, sir' – he turned
to Philip – 'are your father's undoubted son. *Your* mother's life was never
a public scandal.' To Eurydike he said, 'As no doubt you know, there have
always been doubts about the birth of Alexander.'

When he had gone, Philip said, 'What did he mean about Alexander?'

'Never mind. I am not sure what he meant. We shall find out later.'

Antipatros' country place was an old run-down hill fort, overlooking
a well-managed rich estate. He had lived at Pella, and run the land with

a bailiff. His sons had used the place for hunting parties, such as this one had, till now, appeared to be.

In the upper room of the rude keep a fire was burning on the round hearth under the smoke-hole; autumn nights were sharp in the hills. Around it, on old benches or sheepskin-covered stools, sat a dozen or so of youngish men, dressed in the day's leather and tough-woven wool, smelling of the horses which could be heard stirring and champing on the floor below, where grooms speaking Thracian were mending and waxing tack.

Kassandros, a red man in the red firelight, sat by his brother Nikanor. Iollas had died soon after he got home from Asia, of a quartan fever picked up in the Babylonian swamps; he had gone down quickly, showing little fight. The fourth brother, Alexarchos, had not been invited. He was learned, slightly mad, and mainly employed in inventing a new language for a utopian state he had seen in visions. Besides his uselessness, he could not be trusted to hold his tongue.

Kassandros said, 'We've been here three days and no one's come spying. We can begin to move. Derdas, Atheas, can you start early tomorrow?'

'Yes,' said the two men across the hearth.

'Get fresh horses at Abdera, Ainos; Amphipolis if you must. Take care at Amphipolis, keep away from the garrison, someone might know you. Simas and Antiphon can start next day. Keep a day between you on the road. Two men aren't noticed, four make people look.'

Derdas said, 'And the message for Antigonos?'

'I'll give you a letter. You'll be safe enough if you don't draw notice. Polyperchon's a blockhead. I'm hunting, good, he can go to sleep again. When Antigonos reads the letter, tell him anything he wants to know.'

They had been hunting boar in the woods all day, to keep up appearances; soon afterwards the party went off to bed, at the far end of the big room behind a dressed hide curtain. Kassandros and Nikanor lingered by the hearth, their soft voices muted by the stable sounds below.

Nikanor was a tall, lean, sandy-coloured man; a capable soldier, who stood by the family loyalties and feuds and looked no further. He said, 'Are you sure you can trust Antigonos? He wants more than he has, that's plain.'

'That's why I can trust him. While he's stretching out in Asia, he'll be glad to have Polyperchon kept busy in Greece. He'll leave me Macedon; he knows Asia will take him all his time.'

Nikanor scratched at his head; one seemed always to pick up lice on a hunting party. He caught one and dropped it in the fire. 'Are you sure of the girl? She'd be as dangerous as Antigonos, if she knew how. She made trouble enough for Father, and for Perdikkas before that. But for her, Philip would be a nothing.'

'M-m,' said Kassandros reflectively. 'That's why I asked you to watch her while I'm gone. I told her nothing, of course. She'll take our side, to keep out the barbarian's child. She showed me that.'

'Good so far. But she's the King's wife and she means to be reigning Queen.'

'Yes. With her descent, I daresay I shall need to marry her.'

Nikanor's pale eyebrows rose. 'And Philip?'

Kassandros made a simple gesture.

'I wonder,' said Nikanor thoughtfully, 'if she'd consent to that.'

'Oh, I daresay not. But when it's done, she won't settle down with the loom and the needle, it's not in her. She'll marry me sure enough. Then she can behave herself. Or . . .' He made the gesture again.

Nikanor shrugged. 'Then what about Thessalonike? I thought you'd settled for her. *She's* Philip's daughter, not his granddaughter.'

'Yes, but the blood's only on the father's side. Eurydike first. When I'm King I can marry both. Old Philip would have made nothing of that.'

'You're sure of your luck,' Nikanor said uneasily.

'Yes. Ever since Babylon, I've known that my time has come.'

A half-month later, towards evening on a day of mist and rain, Polyperchon came to the palace, urgently demanding to see the King.

He barely waited to be announced. Philip, with Konon's help, was still gathering up an arrangement of his stones which he had been elaborating all day. Eurydike, who had been waxing the leather of her cuirass, had not time to hide that either. She looked resentfully at Polyperchon, who bowed formally, having first saluted the King.

'I've nearly put it away,' said Philip apologetically. 'It was a Persian paradise.'

'Sir. I must ask your presence at a council of state tomorrow.'

Philip looked at him in horror. 'I won't make a speech. I don't want to make a speech.'

'You need not, sir; only assent when the rest have voted.'

'On what?' asked Eurydike sharply.

Polyperchon, a Macedonian in the old tradition, thought, A pity Amyntas lived long enough to beget this meddlesome bitch. 'Madam. We have news that Kassandros has crossed to Asia, and that Antigonos has welcomed him.'

'What?' she said, startled. 'I understood he was hunting on his estate.'

'That,' said Polyperchon grimly, 'is what he wished us to understand.

We may now understand that we are at war. Sir, please be ready at sun-up; I will come and escort you. Madam.' He bowed, about to depart.

'Wait!' she said angrily. 'With whom is Kassandros at war?'

He turned on the threshold. 'With the Macedonians. They voted to obey his father, who had thought him unfit to govern them.'

'I wish to attend the council.' ·

Polyperchon jutted at her his grizzled beard. 'I regret, madam. That is not the custom of the Macedonians. I wish you good night.' He strode out. He was furious with himself for not having had Kassandros watched; but at least he need not put up with insolence from a woman.

The council of state considered the country's dangers and found them grave. Kassandros, it was clear, would only stay in Asia to get the forces he needed. Then he would make for Greece.

Since the last years of Philip's reign, and all through Alexander's, the Greek states had been governed as Macedon ordained. Democrat leaders had been exiled, the franchise confined to men of property, whose oligarch leaders had to be pro-Macedonian. Alexander had been a long way off, and Antipatros had had a free hand. Since his supporters had enriched themselves at the expense of the many exiles, there had been violent consternation when Alexander, returning from the wilderness, had ordered them brought home and their lands restored. He had summoned the Regent to report to him in Babylon; Kassandros had gone instead. When Alexander died, the Greeks had risen, but Antipatros had crushed them. The cities, therefore, were still governed by his satellites, whose support for his son would be a matter of course.

All this time, the Greek envoys were hanging about in Pella, waiting, as they had done since the funeral, to learn the policy of the new regime towards their various states. They were now hastily summoned, and handed a royal proclamation. Much had been done in Greece, it said, which Alexander had never sanctioned. They could now with the goodwill of the Kings, his heirs, restore their democratic constitutions, expel their oligarchs, or execute them if desired. All their citizen rights would be defended, in return for loyalty to the Kings.

Polyperchon, escorting Philip from the council chamber, explained these decisions to Eurydike with punctilious care. Like Nikanor, he had reflected that she had a great capacity for mischief. She should not be idly provoked.

She listened without much comment. While the council deliberated, she too had had time for thought.

'A dog came in,' said Philip as soon as his mentor had gone. 'He had a great bone, a raw one. I said to them, he must have stolen it from the kitchen.'

'Yes, Philip. Quiet now, I must think.'

She had guessed right, then; when Kassandros came to see her, he had been offering her alliance. If he won this war, he would depose the child of the barbarian, assume the guardianship, enthrone Philip and herself. *He* had spoken to her as an equal. He would make her a queen.

'Why,' asked Philip plaintively, 'do you keep walking about?'

'You must change your good robe, you will get it dirty. Konon, are you there? Please help the King.'

She paced the room with its carved windows and great painted inner wall, covered with a life-sized mural of the sack of Troy. Agamemnon was carrying off Kassandra, shrieking, from the sanctuary; the wooden horse loomed between the gate towers; in the foreground, at the household altar, Priam was lying in his blood; Andromache clasped to her bosom her dead child. All the background was fighting, flames and blood. It was an antique piece, the work of Zeuxis, commissioned by Archelaos when he built the palace.

About the hearth with its worn old stones clung faded aromatic odours, a fume of ancient burnings, and curious stains. It had been, for many years, the room of Queen Olympias. Much magic, people used to say, had been worked in it. Her sacred snakes had had their basket by this hearth, her spells their hiding-places. One or two were indeed still where she had left them, for she meant to return. Eurydike only knew that the room had a presence of its own.

Striding about it, she pondered her unspoken bargain with Kassandros, and for the first time thought, What then?

Only the child of the barbarian could beget a new generation. When he had been driven out, she and Philip would reign alone. Who would succeed them?

Who fitter than the grandchild of Philip and Perdikkas to carry on their line? To do that, she could put up with childbirth. For a moment she thought shrinkingly of teaching Philip; after all, there were women in every city who for a drachma put up with worse. But no, she could not. Besides, what if he should sire a fool?

If I were a man! she thought. On the hearth a bright fire of dry lichened apple-wood was burning, for winter was drawing on. The blackened stones under the fire-basket released drifts of old tainted incense in the heat. If I were a king, I could marry twice if I chose, our kings have often done so. A vivid recollection came to her of Kassandros' powerful presence. He had offered to be her friend ... But then, there was Philip.

For a moment, recalling that moment of silent speech, she was on the edge of comprehension. To the last tenant of this room it would have been a simple thing, a matter of ways and means. Eurydike felt it loom, and flinched away from it. To see it must be to choose, yes or no, and she would not. She only said to herself that she must be able to depend upon Kassandros, and it was useless to think too far ahead. But the smell of the old myrrh in the stones was like the smoke of the hidden thought, buried under the smouldering embers, waiting its time.

318 BC

Eumenes sat in his tent on the kindly coastland of Kilikia, looking across the sea towards Cyprus' distant hills. The warm fruitful plain was a paradise after the cramped fort, perched on the high Tauros, where Antigonos had kept him invested all through last winter in the bitter mountain wind. A spring of good water, plenty of grain, and precious little else. The men's gums had started to rot from lack of greenstuff; he had had hard work to stop them from eating the horses, on which their lives might yet depend; he had kept the beasts exercised by having their forequarters hoisted up once a day in slings, and making the grooms shout and hit at them, so that they thrashed about and got into a sweat. He had almost made up his mind to slaughter them when, of a sudden, Antigonos sent an envoy to offer terms. The Regent was dead, it was every man for himself, and Antigonos wanted an ally.

He had demanded an oath of loyalty before he lifted the siege. To Antigonos and the Kings, the envoy said. Eumenes had changed it, in the act of swearing, to Olympias and the Kings. The envoy had let it pass. Antigonos had not liked it; but by the time he heard, they had all got out. This was as well, for soon Eumenes had heard from Polyperchon, appointing him in the Kings' name to Antigonos' command; which, since Antigonos would certainly not resign it, he would have to get by force. Meantime, he was to take over the provincial treasury of Kilikia, and the command of its garrison regiment, the Silver Shields.

He was now in camp with them, while they made themselves snug with stolen comforts, won by every devious ruse known to campaigners who had been, many of them, fifty years under arms. None of them had been serving for less than forty; tough, wicked old sweats whom Alexander had

thought himself well shot of, and whom even he had not rid himself of
without a mutiny. They had been his legacy from his father Philip, men
of the phalanx, wielders of the long sarissa, all of them hand-picked
fighters. They had been young men along with Philip; many were older
than he would have been if he were still alive. Now, when they should be
living with their loot and Alexander's bounty on their homeland farms,
here they still were, hard as their boot-nails, their discharge held up by
the death of Krateros and their own obdurate resistance; never yet beaten,
and ready to march again.

Not a man was under sixty; most of them were past seventy; their
arrogance was a proverb; and Eumenes, a generation younger, and an
alien Greek, had to take them over.

He had almost refused; but while, after the siege, he was salvaging his
scattered forces, he had a letter brought by land and sea from Epiros. It
was from Olympias.

I beg you to help us. Only you, Eumenes, are left, most loyal of all my friends,
and best able to rescue our forsaken house. I entreat you, do not fail me. Let me
hear from you; shall I entrust myself and my grandson to men who claim, one after
another, to be his guardians, and then are found planning to steal his heritage?
Roxane his mother sends me word that she fears for his life, once Polyperchon
leaves Macedon to fight the traitor Kassandros. Is it best she flies to me here,
bringing the boy; or shall I raise troops and go to Macedon?

The letter had deeply moved him. He had been still young when first
he had met Olympias, and so had she. Often in Philip's absences the
Regent, who loathed her, had sent Eumenes with messages to her, partly
to slight her with his lower rank, partly to keep out of her way. During
many domestic quarrels Philip had done the same. To the young Greek,
she had a quality of archaic myth; a bacchic Ariadne, waiting the embrace
of a Dionysos who never came. He had seen her in tears, in savage mirth,
in blazing anger and sometimes in regal grace. He had no more desired
her than one desires a splendid play of lightning over the sea; but he had
adored her. Even when he had known well that she was in the wrong,
and that he had to tell her so, he had never gone to face her without a
thrill at the heart. In fact, she had often unbent to him. He had been a
handsome young man; though she had never been able to make him her
partisan or subvert his faith to Philip, she had enjoyed his admiration.

He knew she had harassed Alexander all through Asia, pursuing her
feud with the Regent; he remembered how, handing him one such letter,
her son had said, 'By God, she charges high rent for the nine-months'
lodging she gave me!' But he had said it half laughing; he, too, had loved
her through everything. He had left her still beautiful; and, like Eumenes,
was never to see her old.

One thing he now knew at once; on no account must she go to Macedon, with or without an army. She knew moderation no more than a hunting leopardess; she would not be there a month before she destroyed her cause. He had written to her exhorting her to stay in Epiros till the present war was settled; meantime, she could count on his fidelity, to her and to Alexander's son.

He did not refer to Roxane and her fears. Who could say what fancies might scare the Baktrian? During his long campaign, followed by the winter siege, he had had little news from Europe. Since the wedding at Sardis, he had barely heard of Eurydike.

Soon Antigonos would be after him – clearly the man meant to make a kingdom for himself in Asia – and he must be moving, with his native levies and their stiffening, the battle-hardened Silver Shields. From his tent opening, he could see them now, sitting in their groupings established over half a century, while their women made their breakfasts; Lydian women, Tyrian women, Baktrians and Parthians and Medes and Indians, the spoils of their long wanderings, with a few old hardy Macedonians who had come with them from home and somehow survived. The resultant children – a third, perhaps, of those begotten along the way – chattered softly round the cook-fires, wary of a clout from their father; brown and honey-coloured and fair, speaking their lingua franca. When camp broke, the women would pack the wagon-train with all its worldwide pickings, and march once more.

On the next knoll, Eumenes could see the tents of the two commanders, Antigenes and Teutamos; crafty and stubborn old wardogs, each old enough to be his father. Today he must call them to a war council; and would they defer to him without resentment? From wounded pride, he knew too well, comes treachery. He sighed wearily, his mind going back to the days when he and they had not been flotsam on the stream of history, but had proudly shaped its course. Those old sinners over there, he thought, even they must remember.

His mind had been suppled by years of precarious survival; now it took one of those leaps which had saved him in places tighter than this. The day was still young, the sunlight upon Cyprus fresh and tender. He shaved, dressed himself neatly without ostentation and called the herald.

'Sound,' he said, 'for the officers to assemble.'

He had his slaves set out the stools and camp chairs casually, without precedence, on the grass. As the leathery ancients, taking their time, approached, he waved them affably to be seated. From the chair they left for him, he rose and addressed them standing.

'Gentlemen, I have called you together to give you serious news. I have received an omen.'

As he had foreseen, dead silence fell. Old soldiers were as superstitious as sailors. They all knew what chance can do to a man in war.

'If ever the gods gave a man a powerful dream, they gave one to me at cockcrow. A dream more real than waking. My name was called. I knew the voice, it was Alexander's. He was in my tent, in that very chair that you, Teutamos, are sitting on. "Eumenes!" he said.'

They sat forward in their chairs. Teutamos' gnarled hands stroked the pinewood arms as if he touched a talisman.

'I begged his pardon for sleeping in his presence as if he had been alive. He had on his white robe edged with purple, and a gold diadem. "I am holding a council of state," he said. "Are you all here?" And he looked about him. Then it seemed the tent was not mine but his, the tent he took from Darius. He was there on his throne, with the Bodyguard around him; and you too were there, with the other generals, waiting for his words. He leaned forward to address us; but as he began, I woke.'

Skilled in the arts of rhetoric, he had tried none here. He had looked and spoken like a man remembering something momentous. It had worked. They were looking at one another, but not in distrust, only wondering what it meant.

'I believe,' he said, 'that I divined Alexander's wish. He is concerned for us. He wants to be present at our councils. If we appeal to him, he will guide us in our decisions.' He paused for questions; but they hardly murmured.

'So, let us not receive him meanly. Here we have the gold of Koyinda which you, gentlemen, have guarded for him faithfully. Let us send for craftsmen to make him a golden throne, a sceptre and a diadem. Let us dedicate a tent to him, and lay the insignia on the throne and offer incense to his spirit. Then we will confer before him, making him our supreme commander.'

Their shrewd, scarred faces considered him. He was not, it seemed, setting himself above them; he was not planning to steal the treasure; if Alexander had appeared only to him, after all he had known him well. And Alexander liked his orders obeyed.

The tent, the throne and the insignia were ready within a week. Even some purple was found, to dye a canopy. When it was time to march towards Phoenicia, they met in the tent to discuss the coming campaign. Before they sat down, each offered his pinch of incense at the little portable altar, saying, 'Divine Alexander, favour us.' All of them deferred to Eumenes, whose divination was manifest around them.

It did not matter that scarcely any of them had seen Alexander enthroned. They remembered him in old leather cuirass and burnished greaves, his helmet off for them to see him, riding along the line before an action, reminding them of their past victories and telling them how to win another. They did not care that the local goldsmith was not of the highest skill. The shining of the gold, the smoke of frankincense, wakened a memory long silted over by the weather and war and weariness of thirteen years; of a golden chariot driving in triumph through the flower-strewn streets of Babylon; the trumpets, the paean, the censers and the cheers. For a little while, standing before the empty throne, it seemed to them that they might become what they once had been.

317 BC

The spring sun warmed the hills, melting the snows; first filling, then tempering the streams. Roads deep in mud and silted with scree grew firm again. The land opened to war.

Kassandros, with the fleet and army Antigonos had lent him, crossed the Aegean and landed at Piraeus, the port of Athens. Before his father was dead, he had sent a man of his own to take command of the Macedonian garrison in the harbour fort. While the Athenians were still discussing the royal decree and the offer of their ancient liberties, they found that the garrison had come down and occupied the harbour. Kassandros had sailed in unopposed.

Polyperchon, getting this news, dispatched advance troops under his son Alexandros. The campaign hung fire; he prepared to set out himself. When he began to mobilize, he came to the palace to see King Philip.

Eurydike received him with the offerings of formal hospitality; she was resolved to have her presence recognized. Polyperchon, as formally, asked after both their health, listened to Philip's account of a cock-fight to which Konon had lately taken him, and then said, 'Sir. I have come to tell you that we shall soon be marching south together. The traitor Kassandros must be dealt with. We shall start in seven days. Please tell your people to have your baggage ready. I will see your man about your horses.'

Philip nodded cheerfully. He had been on the march for nearly half his life, and took it as a matter of course. He did not understand what the war was about; but Alexander had seldom told him. 'I shall ride Whitefoot,' he said. 'Eurydike, which horse will you ride?'

Polyperchon cleared his throat. 'Sir, this is a campaign. The lady Eurydike will of course remain at Pella.'

'But I *can* take Konon?' said Philip anxiously.

'By all means, sir.' Polyperchon did not look her way.

There was a pause. He awaited the storm. But in fact Eurydike said nothing.

It had never occurred to her that she could be left behind. She had looked forward to the escape from the tedium of the palace to the freedom of the camp. In the first moment of learning that she had been relegated to the women's rooms she had been as angry as Polyperchon had expected, and had been on the point of protest, when there came into her mind Kassandros' unspoken message. How could she influence affairs, trailing along with the army, watched at every turn? But here at home, with the guardian away at war ...

She swallowed her anger at being so belittled, and held her peace. Afterwards, she found a lingering hurt that Philip had found Konon more necessary than her. After all I have done for him, she thought.

Polyperchon meantime was at the other end of the palace. Here were the quarters where the elder Philip had moved, when he ceased to share the great bedchamber with Olympias. They were handsome enough to satisfy Roxane, and her son did not complain of them. They opened on to an old orchard where he liked to play now that the days grew warmer. The plum-trees were already budding, and the grass smelled of hidden violets.

'Considering his tender years and need of his mother,' Polyperchon said, 'I shall not expose the King to the hardships of the march. In any treaties I may sign or edicts I may issue, his name will of course appear with King Philip's, as if he were present too.'

'So,' said Roxane, 'Philip will go with you?'

'Yes; he is a grown man, it will be expected.'

'Then his wife will go to care for him?' Her voice had sharpened.

'No, madam. War is not women's business.'

She opened her black eyes till the clear white showed all round. 'Then,' she cried, 'who will protect my son and me?'

What could the foolish woman mean? He brought down his brows in irritation, and answered that Macedon would be left well garrisoned.

'Macedon? Here, in this house, who will protect us from that she-wolf? She will only wait to see you gone before she murders us.'

'Madam,' he said testily, 'we are not now in the wilds of Asia. The Queen Eurydike is a Macedonian and will obey the law. Even if she wished otherwise, she would not dare touch the son of Alexander. The people would have her blood.'

He left, thinking, Women! They make war seem a holiday. The thought consoled him among his cares. Since the new decree, nearly all the Greek cities were in a state of civil war, or on the verge of it; the coming campaign promised every kind of confusion and uncertainty. Roxane's notion that he would add to his troubles by taking that termagant girl along was enough to make a man laugh.

A week later the army marched. From the balcony of the great bed-chamber, Eurydike had watched the troops assemble on the great drill field where Philip and Alexander had trained their men; had seen the long column wind slowly down alongside the lagoon, making for the coast road to the south.

As the lumbering baggage train began to follow the soldiers, she looked about her at the horizons of the land she still meant to rule. Over the near hills was her father's house where Kynna had taught her war. She would keep it for her hunting lodge, her private place, when she was Queen.

She looked down idly at the grandiose front of the palace with its painted pediment and columns of coloured marble. On the broad steps the tutor Kebes came down, the child Alexander beside him, trailing a wooden hobby-horse by its scarlet bridle. The child of the barbarian, who must not reign. How would Kassandros deal with that? She frowned.

Roxane behind her curtains grew weary of watching wagons, a sight too long familiar. Her eyes wandered. There on a balcony, brazenly showing herself to the world like a harlot looking for trade, stood Philip's mannish wife. What was she staring at so fiercely? Roxane's ear caught the sound of her own child's piping chatter. Yes, it was at him that she was looking! Swiftly, Roxane made the sign against the evil eye, and ran to her casket. Where was the silver charm her mother had given her against the malice of harem rivals? He must put it on. A letter was beside it, with the royal seal of Epiros. She re-read it, and knew what she must do.

Kebes proved easy to persuade. The times were doubtful; so was his own future. He could well believe that the son of Alexander was in danger, and not only from his mother's spoiling. He had softened to Roxane; she might need protection too. It was eleven years since her beauty had hit Alexander like a fiery arrow across a torchlit hall; but her looks had been tended, her legend lived in them still. It seemed to the young man that he too could enter the legend, rescuing the woman Alexander had loved, and his only child.

It was he who chose the litter-bearers and the armed escort of four; who swore them to secrecy, who bought the mules, who found a messenger

to ride ahead with news of their coming. Two days later, just before dawn,
they were on the mountain road making for Dodona.

The royal house had a steep-pitched roof to throw off the winter snows.
Roofs in Molossia gave no platform for watchers. Olympias stood in the
window of the King's bedchamber, which she had taken when her
daughter left it. Her eyes were fixed on a curl of smoke from the nearest
hill-top. On three heights in an eastward line she had had beacons laid,
to signal the approach of her daughter-in-law and grandson. Now she sent
for the captain of the palace guard, and ordered him to meet them with
an escort.

Olympias had assented to her age. In the month of mourning for
Alexander she had washed the paint from her face and covered her hair
with a dark veil. When the month was over, and she put the veil away,
her hair was silky white. She was sixty, and lean where she had been slim.
Her fine red-head's skin was brittle like pressed petals; but lacking colour
the proud bones showed more. Under their white brows, the smoky grey
eyes could still pale dangerously.

She had waited long for this day. As the emptiness of loss came home
to her, she had craved to touch this last living vestige of him; but the child
was unborn, there was no remedy for waiting. With the wars' delays, her
longing dulled and earlier doubts returned. The mother was a barbarian,
a campaign wife, whose son he had meant to pass over – in a secret letter
he had told her so – if the Great King's daughter had borne a boy. Would
anything remain of him in this stranger?

When the child reached Macedon, her feud with Antipatros had left her
only two ways to go back there, submission or war. The first was unthinkable; against the second Eumenes, on whom she must depend, had warned
her. Then Roxane had written begging for a refuge, and she had answered,
'Come.'

Next day the cavalcade arrived; the tough Molossian troopers on their
shaggy ponies, two dishevelled waiting women on stumbling donkeys, a
covered litter with its mules. Her eyes on the litter, she did not see at first
the young man who carried across his horse's withers a six-year-old boy.
He lifted him down and spoke to him, quietly, pointing. Resolutely, on legs
more a boy's than a child's, he walked up the steps, gave her a soldier's
salute, and said, 'May you live, Grandmother. I am Alexander.'

She took him between her hands while the company made respectful
gestures, and kissed his brow, dirty with travel, and looked again. Kebes
had fulfilled his trust. Alexander's son was no longer the podgy nurseling
of the harem tent. Olympias saw a beautiful young Persian, fine-boned and
dark-eyed. The hair was cut sloping to the nape, as Alexander used to wear

it, but it was straight, heavy and raven-black. He looked up at her from under his fine dark brows and his blue-brown, thick-lashed eyelids; and though there was nothing of him anywhere that was Macedonian, she saw Alexander in his upward, deep-set gaze. It was too much, it took her a few moments to gather herself together. Then she took his pale slender hand. 'Welcome, my child. Come, bring me to your mother.'

The roads from Pella down into Greece had been smoothed since old Philip's reign for the swift march of armies. The roads to the west were rough. Despite the difference in distance, therefore, it was at about the same time that Polyperchon in the Peloponnese, and Olympias in Dodona, got news from Macedon that Eurydike had assumed the regency.

Polyperchon got, in addition, an order signed by her, directing him to hand over to Kassandros the Macedonian forces in the south.

Speechless for a while, the old soldier kept his head, offered the courier wine without disclosing the message, and asked for news. It seemed that the Queen had called Assembly, and addressed it with great spirit. The barbarian woman, she told them, had fled the land with her child, fearing the anger of the Macedonians; she would do well not to return. All who had known Alexander would testify that the child looked nothing like him. He had died before the birth, had never acknowledged the infant; there was no proof that he was the father. Whereas she herself had on both sides the Macedonian royal blood.

For a time, Assembly had been in doubt. But Nikanor, Kassandros' brother, had given her his voice and the whole clan had come in with him. That had carried the vote. She was now giving audiences, receiving envoys and petitioners, and in all ways acting as reigning Queen.

Polyperchon thanked the man, rewarded and dismissed him, cursed to relieve his feelings, and sat down to think. He quickly decided what he himself would do; and, soon afterwards, what to do with Philip.

He had had hopes of him, if he could be removed from his wife's control; but he had soon learned better. At first, he had been so docile that it had seemed safe to produce him, set up impressively on a gold-canopied throne, for a delegation from Athens. In the midst of a speech he had guffawed at a rhetorical trope which, like a child, he had taken literally. Later, when Polyperchon had rebuked a speaker, the King had grabbed at his ceremonial spear; if Polyperchon had not grappled with him in front of everyone, the man would have been run through. 'You said,' he had protested, 'that he told lies.' The delegation had been dismissed too hastily, costing a political disaster and some lives.

It was now clear to Polyperchon that all Philip was good for was to hold the throne for Alexander's son, who had better come of age quickly. As for Eurydike, her claim was plain usurpation.

Konon came when sent for, saluting woodenly. His silent 'I told you so' had irked Polyperchon after the incident of the spear and several others. Good riddance to both of them. 'I have decided,' he said, 'to send back the King to Macedon.'

'Sir.' The general felt, reverberating from this blank surface, knowledge that the campaign had gone badly, that he had had to raise the important siege of Megalopolis, that Kassandros still held the Piraeus and might well get Athens, in which event the Greek cities would join him. But that was irrelevant now.

'I will give you an escort. Tell the Queen that I am sending back the King in obedience to her wishes. That is all.'

'Sir.' Konon left, relieved. He could have told them all beforehand, if he had been asked. Now, he thought, they would all have a chance to live in peace.

At a massive table of inlaid hardstones with lion-feet of gilded bronze, Eurydike sat in the royal study. King Archelaos, nearly a century ago, had designed this splendid sanctum when he built the palace to stun foreigners with its magnificence. From it, whenever they were at home, Philip the Second had ruled Macedon and his spreading conquests, and Alexander had ruled all Greece. Since Alexander had gone to rule the world from a moving tent, no king had sat at the table under Zeuxis' mural of Apollo and the Muses. Antipatros, rigidly correct, had governed from his own house. She had found everything swept, polished, scrupulously neat, and empty.

It had awaited a tenant for seventeen years, as long as she had lived. Now it was hers.

When she called Assembly to claim the regency, she had not told Nikanor of what she meant to do. She had guessed he would think it rash, but that confronted with the fact he would support her, sooner than hurt his brother's cause. She had thanked him afterwards, but had fended off his efforts to advise her. She meant to rule for herself.

Awaiting news from the south, she had spent most of her time on what she most enjoyed, exercising the army. She felt, at last, that she was fulfilling her true destiny when she rode along a line of cavalry, or took the salute of the phalanx presenting their great sarissas. She had seen a good deal of army drill and talked to many soldiers; she knew all the procedure. They were amused and delighted with her. After all, they thought, they were just a garrison army; if there was action the generals would of course resume command. Taking this for granted, they performed for her indulgently.

Her fame was spreading, Eurydike, the warrior Queen of Macedon. One day she would strike her own coinage. She was tired of seeing the eager long-nosed face of Alexander hooded in his lion-skin. Let Herakles give place to Athene, lady of citadels.

Each day she waited to hear whether Polyperchon had surrendered his command to Kassandros as she had ordered. So far she had heard from neither. Instead, unheralded, Philip returned to Pella. He carried no dispatches and did not know where his guardian was going next.

He was delighted to be home, and ran on at length about his adventures on campaign, though all he knew of the débâcle at Megalopolis was that the wicked people in the fort had put down spikes to hurt the elephants' feet. Even so, had she had patience to listen to his ramblings she might have learned something of value. He had been present, as a matter of form, at several councils from which Konon was excluded. But she was busy, and answered him with half her mind. She seldom asked where he was; Konon took him about and amused him. She had ceased to issue orders in his name, and used only her own.

Until just lately, everything had gone smoothly. She understood the disputes of Macedon, nearly all brought by petitioners in person. But suddenly, all at once, a flood of business was coming in from the south, even from Asia. It had not yet occurred to her that all these matters had been going to Polyperchon, who had dealt with them in Philip's name. Now, Philip was here; and Polyperchon, for good reasons, was no longer accessible.

She looked with dismay at petitions from towns and provinces she had never heard of, seeking judgements on land claims; reports on delinquent, distant officials; long obscure letters from priests of temples founded by Alexander, seeking guidance about rituals; reports from Asian satraps on the encroachments of Antigonos; passionate protests from pro-Macedonians of Greek cities, exiled or dispossessed under the new decree. Often she had trouble even in reading the script with its many contractions. Turning over in helpless bewilderment this heap of documents, she reflected unwillingly that it must be a fraction of what Alexander had dealt with in an army camp, in the rest-breaks of conquering an empire.

The chief secretary, who knew all this business, had gone south with Polyperchon, leaving only a subordinate at Pella. She would have to send for this underling and try to hide her ignorance. She rang the silver bell with which, long ago, her grandfather had summoned Eumenes.

She waited. Where was the man? She rang again. Urgent muttering voices sounded outside the door. The secretary came in, shaken, without apology for delay, without asking her what she wanted. She saw fear in his face, and the resentment of a frightened man towards someone who cannot help.

'Madam. There is an army on the western border.'

She sat up with brightening eyes. The border wars were the ancient proving-ground of the Macedonian kings. Already she saw herself in arms, leading the cavalry. 'The Illyrians? Where have they crossed?'

'Madam, no. From the south-west. From Epiros. Won't you see the messenger? He says Polyperchon is leading them.'

She straightened in her chair, her pride answering his fear. 'Yes, I will see him. Bring him in.'

It was a soldier, anxious and dusty, from a garrison fort on the Orestid hills. He begged pardon, his horse had gone lame, he had had to come on by mule, a poor beast, all he could get. It had lost him a day. He gave her the dispatch from his commander, shocked to discover how young she was.

Polyperchon was on the border, announcing by heralds that he had come to restore Alexander's son. He was in the country of his clan and kindred, and many of them had joined him. From the fort itself there had, unhappily, been some desertions, and the post was gravely undermanned. Between the lines, she read the intention to surrender.

She sent the man out, and sat looking before her. On the far side of the room stood a bronze youth looking back, a Hermes, holding a lyre. He stood on a plinth of green marble, Attic, poised; his gravity seeming stern to an eye used to modern prettiness. A subtle melancholy in his face had once made her ask an old palace steward who he was. Some athlete, said the man, done by Polykleitos the Athenian; he had heard it was during the great siege when the Spartans won the war, and Athens was broken. No doubt King Archelaos' agents had picked it up cheaply afterwards; there was a great deal, then, to be had for very little.

The bronze face gazed at her with eyes of dark-blue lapis laid into white glass, between lashes of fine bronze wire. They seemed to say, 'Listen. I hear the footsteps of fate.'

She got to her feet, confronting him. 'You lost. But I am going to win.' Presently she would give orders to raise the army and prepare to march. But first she must write to Kassandros and call him to her aid.

Travel to the south was quick. Her letter reached him in three days.

He was camped before a stubborn fort in Arkadia. That dealt with, he planned to reduce the Spartans, those relics of an outworn past. They had come down to walling their city, that proud open town whose only bulwark had been its warriors' shields. Their soul was cowed, they would soon be under his hand.

Athens had made terms and had let him appoint its governor. The officer who had taken the Piraeus for him had expected the post; but he had been looking too ambitious, and Kassandros had had him disposed of in a dark alley. The new governor was a harmless, obedient client. Soon, thought Kassandros, he must visit the Lyceum. There was a great deal to be done there.

Eurydike's appointment of him as supreme commander, though too precipitate, had helped to sway many wavering Greek allegiances. Even some who had killed their oligarchs and restored democracy were now thinking again. He would be glad to finish with the south; he was interested in war only as an instrument of policy. He was not a coward, he could get his orders obeyed, he was a competent strategist, and that was all. Deep in his being, burned there since his youth, was a bitter envy of Alexander's magic. No one would cheer himself hoarse for Kassandros, no one be proud to die for him; his men would do what they were paid to do. That vain tragedian, he thought; let us see how he looks to the new age.

The news that Polyperchon was withdrawing his forces and heading north had been no great surprise. He was old and tired and a loser; let him go home with his tail between his legs, and bed down in his kennel.

Eurydike's dispatch, therefore, had been a rude shock to him. The stupid reckless girl, he thought. Had this been the time to denounce Alexander's brat? He fully intended, once Philip was out of the way, to govern at first as the boy's regent. There would be plenty of time before he came of age. Now, instead of biding the hour, as anyone would who had the beginning of statecraft, she had flung the country into a succession war. Did she know no history? One of her family should have remembered better than that.

Kassandros reached a decision. He had made a bad bargain and must get it off his hands, quickly, like an unsound horse. Afterwards, everything would be simpler.

He sat down to write a letter to his brother Nikanor.

With banners and standards streaming, with shrill flutes and the deep-toned aulos giving the time, the royal army of Macedon marched through the high western hills towards Epiros.

Summer had come. The thyme and sage bruised by the trampling feet censed them with aromatics; the uncurled bracken stood waist-high; heather and sorrel purpled the moors. The burnished helmets, the dyed horsehair plumes, the little bright pennants on the tall sarissas, glittered and glowed in long streams of moving colour, winding down through the passes. Herd-boys on the crags cried the warning that soldiers were coming, and called their little brothers to help drive in the sheep.

Eurydike in burnished armour rode at the head of the cavalry. The heady air of the hills exalted her; the wide prospects from the heights stretched before her like worlds to conquer. She had always known that this was her nature and her fate, to ride to victory like a king, her land behind her and her horsemen at her side. She had her Companions as a ruler of Macedon should. Before she marched she had made it known that when the war was won the lands of the western traitors would reward her loyal followers. Not far off, led by Nikanor, rode the clan of the Antipatrids, a hearteningly solid force.

Kassandros had not appeared, nor sent her word. Clearly, as Nikanor said, some misadventure had overtaken her messenger. It would be better to send again, and she had done so. Then, too, the troops in the Peloponnese were often on the move, and that might have caused delay. At all events, said Nikanor, he himself was doing as he knew Kassandros would wish.

Philip on his big steady horse was riding near by; he, also, panoplied for war. He was still the King, and the troops would expect to see him. Soon, when they came near the enemy, he must be settled in a base-camp out of the way.

He was placid and cheerful, travelling with an army; he could hardly remember when this had not been his life. Konon was with him, riding as usual half a length behind. Philip had wanted him alongside, the better to talk about the sights upon the way; but Konon, as usual, had said it would not be proper before the men. Dimly, after the years, Philip still missed the days of strangeness and changing marvels, when his life had moved with the journeys of Alexander.

Konon had withdrawn into his thoughts. He, too, could have wished for Alexander, and for more urgent reasons. Ever since his young master Arridaios had become King Philip, he had known that the time would come which was coming now, had felt it in his bones. Well, he thought, it was an old proverb, not to look back at the end. He was nearly sixty, and few men lived longer.

A rider showed briefly on the crest of the ridge ahead. A scout, he thought; had the girl seen? He looked at Philip ambling along, a half-smile on his broad face, enjoying some pleasant fantasy. She ought to take more thought for him. Supposing . . .

Eurydike had seen. She too, long before this, had sent out scouts. They were overdue; she sent off two more. The army moved on, bright, burnished, the flutes giving the time.

Presently, when they reached the next ridge, she herself would ride up and survey the terrain. That, she knew, was the duty of a general. If the enemy was in sight she would study his dispositions, then hold a war council and dispose her troops.

Derdas, her second-in-command – a new promotion, so many of the higher ranks had marched with Polyperchon – rode up to her, young, lank-limbed, frowning with responsibility. 'Eurydike, the scouts ought to be back, they may have been taken. Shouldn't we make sure of the high ground? We may be needing it.'

'Yes.' It had seemed that the gallant march in the fresh morning would go on till she herself chose to end it. 'We will lead with the cavalry, and hold it till the infantry comes up. Form them up, Derdas; you take the left wing, and of course I shall take the right.'

She was issuing further orders, when a harsh, peremptory cough sounded at her elbow. She turned, startled and put out. 'Madam,' said Konon. 'What about the King?'

She clicked her tongue impatiently; far better to have left him behind at Pella. 'Oh, take him back to the wagon train. Have a tent set up there.'

'Will there be a battle?' Philip had come up, looking interested and eager.

'Yes,' she said quietly, mastering her irritation before the onlookers. 'Go to the camp now, and wait till we come back.'

'Must I, Eurydike?' A sudden urgency disturbed Philip's placid face. 'I've never been in a battle. Alexander never let me. None of them let me. Please let me fight in this one. Look, here's my sword.'

'No, Philip, not today.' She motioned to Konon; but he did not move. He had been watching his master's face; now he looked into hers. There was a short silence. He said, 'Madam. If the King wishes. Maybe it would be best.'

She stared at him, at his sorrowful and sober eyes. Understanding, she caught her breath. 'How dare you? If there were time I would have you flogged for insolence. I will see you later. Now obey your orders.'

Philip hung his head. He saw that he had misbehaved, and everyone was angry. They would not beat him; but the memory of ancient beatings moved in his mind. 'I'm sorry,' he said. 'I hope you win the battle. Alexander always did. Good-bye.' She did not look after him as he went.

Her favourite horse was led up, snorting and tossing its head, full of high spirits. She patted the strong neck, grasped the tough mane on the withers, and vaulted with her spear on to the scarlet saddle-cloth. The herald stood near, his trumpet at the ready, waiting to sound the advance.

'Wait!' she said. 'First I will address the men.'

He gave the brief flourish for attention. One of the officers, who had been watching the ridge ahead, began to speak; but the trumpet drowned it.

'Men of Macedon!' Her clear voice carried as it had on the march from Egypt, at Triparadisos, at the Assembly where they had voted her the regency. Battle was near; let them only be worthy of their fame. 'If you

were brave fighting against foreign enemies, how much more gloriously
you will fight now, defending your land, your wives, your ...'

Something was wrong. They were not hostile; they were simply not
attending, staring past her, speaking to one another. Suddenly, young
Derdas, gravity changed to urgency, grasped her horse's headstall,
wheeled it round to face forward and shouted, 'Look!'

All along the crest of the ridge ahead, a dark dense bristle had sprouted.
It was thick with spears.

The armies faced each other across the valley. Down at the bottom was
a stream, low now in summer, but with a wide bed of stones and boulders
bared by winter scour. The horsemen on both sides looked at it with
distaste.

The western rise which the Epirote army commanded was higher than
the Macedonian position. If their full strength was on view, however, they
were outnumbered three to two on foot, though somewhat stronger in
cavalry.

Eurydike standing on an outcrop to survey the field, pointed this out to
Derdas. The enemy flanks were on broken, brushy ground which would
favour infantry. 'Yes,' he said, 'if they let our infantry get there. Polyperchon may be no' – he just stopped himself from saying Alexander – 'but
he knows better than that.'

The old man could be clearly seen on the opposite slope, in a clump of
horsemen, conferring. Eurydike's men pointed him out to one another, not
feeling him a great menace in himself, but bringing the comfortless
thought that they were about to fight old comrades.

'Nikanor.' (He had left his contingent to join the council of war.) 'There
is still no signal from the beacon?'

He shook his head. The beacon had been laid on a peak behind them,
commanding a view of the southern pass. 'Without a doubt Kassandros
would be here, if something had not prevented him. Perhaps he has been
attacked upon the march. You know the confusion in the Greek states,
thanks to Polyperchon.'

Derdas made no comment. He did not like Nikanor's disposition of his
men, but this was no time to say so.

Eurydike stood on the tall flat rock, shading her eyes to look across at
the enemy. In her bright helmet and gold-studded cuirass, her knee-high
kilt of scarlet wool above her shining greaves, she looked a gallant figure.
Derdas thought to himself that she looked like a boy actor in a play,
masked to enact the young Achilles at Aulis. It was she, however, who
first saw the herald.

He emerged from the knot around Polyperchon, and rode down towards them; unarmed, bareheaded, with a white wool fillet round his grey hair, carrying a white rod bound with olive; a man with presence.

At the stream-bed he dismounted, to let his horse pick its way over the stones. Having crossed, he walked a few paces forward and waited. Eurydike and Derdas came down to meet him. She turned to Nikanor to join them, but he had disappeared into the mass.

The herald had voice as well as presence, and the curve of the slope threw up his words like the hollow bowl of a theatre.

'To Philip son of Philip, to Eurydike his wife, and to all the Macedonians!' He sat at ease on his strong stocky horse, a ward of the gods, protected by immemorial custom. 'In the name of Polyperchon, guardian of both the Kings.' He paused, just long enough for suspense. 'Also,' he added slowly, 'in the name of Queen Olympias, daughter of King Neoptolemos of Molossia; wife of Philip, King of the Macedonians; and mother of Alexander.'

In the silence, a dog could be heard to bark in a village half a mile away.

'I am charged to say this to the Macedonians. Philip found you pressed by enemies and torn with civil wars. He gave you peace, reconciled your factions, and made you masters of all Greece. And by Queen Olympias herself he was the father of Alexander, who made the Macedonians masters of the world. She asks you, have you forgotten all these benefits, that you will drive out Alexander's only son? Will you take up arms against Alexander's mother?'

He had thrown his voice past Eurydike and her staff, to the silent ranks of men. When he ceased, he wheeled round his mount, and pointed.

Another rider was coming from the group above. On a black horse, in a black robe and veil, Olympias paced slowly down towards the stream.

She rode astride in a wide skirt that fell to the tops of her crimson riding-boots. The headstall of her horse glittered with gold rosettes and silver plaques, the spoils of Susa and Persepolis. She herself wore no ornaments. A little way above the stream, where she could be seen by everyone, and where Eurydike had to look up to her, she drew rein and threw back the dark veil from her white hair. She said nothing. Her deep-set grey eyes swept the hushed murmuring ranks.

Eurydike was aware of the distant gaze pausing upon her. A light breeze floated back the black veil, stirred the horse's long mane and ruffled the snowy hair. The face was still. Eurydike felt a shiver go through her. It was like being glanced at by Atropos, the third Fate, who cuts the thread.

The herald, who had been forgotten, now suddenly raised his loud voice again. 'Macedonians! There before you is the mother of Alexander. Will you fight against her?'

There was a pause, like the pause of a rearing wave before it topples to break. Then a new sound began. It was a slight rapping, at first, of wood on metal. Then it was a spreading rattle, a mounting beat; then, echoing back from along the hillside, a thunderous drumming, the banging of thousands of spear-shafts upon shields. With a united roar the royal army cried, 'No!'

Eurydike had heard it before, though never so loudly. It had greeted her when she was voted regent. For many long seconds, she thought they were defying the enemy, that the shouting was for her.

Across the stream, Olympias raised her arm in a regal gesture of acknowledgement. Then, with a beckoning movement, she turned her horse. She moved up the hill like a leader of warriors, who need not look back to be sure that they will follow.

As she went up in triumph, the whole prospect on the opposite slope fragmented. The royal army drawn up in its formation, the phalanx, the cavalry, the light-armed skirmishers, ceased to be an army, as a village struck by an earthquake ceases to be a street. There was just a mass of men, with horses heaving about among them; shouting to each other, gravitating to groups of friends or clansmen; the whole united only in a single disordered movement, going like landslide pebbles down towards the stream.

Eurydike was overwhelmed by it. When she began to shout orders, to exhort them, she was scarcely heard. Men jostled her unnoticing; those who saw her did not meet her eyes. Her horse grew restive in the crush and reared, she was afraid of being thrown and trampled.

An officer thrust through to her, held the horse and quieted it. She knew him, he was one of her partisans from the very first days in Egypt, a man about thirty, light-haired, with a skin still yellowed from some Indian fever. He looked at her with concern. Here at last, she thought, was a man in his right mind. 'How can we rally them?' she cried. 'Can you find me a trumpeter? We must call them back!'

He ran his hand over her horse's sweating neck. Slowly, like a man explaining something simple to a child, which even a child must see, he said, 'But madam. That is Alexander's mother.'

'Traitor!' She knew it was unjust, her anger belonged elsewhere. She had seen, at last, her real enemy. Not the terrible old woman on the black horse; she could be terrible only because of him, the glowing ghost, the lion-maned head on the silver drachmas, directing her fate from his golden bier.

'There's no help for it,' said the man, forbearingly, but with little time to spare for her. 'You don't understand. You see, you never knew him.'

For a moment she grasped her sword; but one cannot kill a ghost. The jostling press below was beginning to cross the stream. Names were shouted, as the soldiers of Polyperchon welcomed back old friends.

He sighted a brother in the crush, and gave an urgent wave, before turning back to her. 'Madam, you were too young, that's all. You made a good try of it, but . . . There's not a man wishes you harm. You've a fresh horse there. Make for the hills before her people cross over.'

'No!' she said. 'Nikanor and the Antipatrids are over there on the left. Come, we'll join them and fall back and hold Black Pass. *They'll* never make peace with Olympias.'

He followed her eyes. 'They won't do that. But they're off, you see.'

She saw then that the force on the heathery rise was moving. Its shining shields were facing the other way. Its head was dipping already over the skyline.

She looked round. The man had sought his brother, and vanished down the hill.

Dismounting, she held her horse, the only living thing that would still obey her. As the man had said, she was young. The despair she felt was not the grim resignation of Perdikkas, paying the price of failure. Both had played for power and lost; but Perdikkas had never put his stake upon love. She stood by the fretting horse, her throat choking, her eyes blinded with tears.

'Eurydike, come, hurry.' A little group, some of her court, had found its way to her. Wiping her eyes, she saw they were not defiant but afraid; marked men all of them, old allies of Antipatros, who had thwarted Olympias' intrigues, had intrigued against her, had crossed her will and wounded her pride and helped drive her out of Macedon. 'Quickly,' they said. 'Look, that cavalry there, those are Molossians, they're heading this way, it is you they will be looking for. Quickly, come.'

She galloped with them cross-country, cutting the corners of the rutted road, letting her horse pick its line over the heath; thinking how Nikanor had said that he was doing as he knew his brother would wish; remembering Kassandros' red hair and inflexible pale eyes. No messenger from her had fallen among thieves; he had had her cry for help, and decided she was expendable.

On the shoulder of the next hill they stopped to breathe their horses, and looked back. 'Ah!' said one of them. 'That was what they were after, to loot the baggage train. There they are at it; so much the better for us.' They looked again; and there was a silence which no one liked to break. In the distance they saw, among the wagons, a single tent with men surrounding it. A small far-off figure was being led outside. Eurydike realized that from the moment when Olympias had appeared and her army melted, she had forgotten Philip entirely.

They made their way east towards Pella, avoiding the look of fugitives as best they could, using for hospitality the mesh of guest-friendship that webbed every Greek land, excusing by their haste their lack of servants. They kept ahead of the news, pretending that a treaty had been signed upon the border, that they were hurrying to Pella to call Assembly and confirm the terms which the army in the west had agreed to. In this way they lodged for several nights, and left each morning aware of a cloud of doubt.

Nearing Pella, she glimpsed the tall keep of her father's house. With unbearable longing she remembered the quiet years with Kynna, the small boyish adventures and heroic dreams, before she entered the great theatre of history, to enact a tragedy in which no god came down at last from the machine to vindicate Zeus' justice. From her childhood on she had been given her role and taught her lines and shown the mask she must wear. But the poet was dead, and the audience had booed the play.

At Mieza, they passed an old manor whose overgrown gardens scented the warm air with roses. Someone said that this was the schoolhouse where Aristotle had taught many years ago. Yes, she thought bitterly; and now his boys were ranging the earth to pick up the leavings of their schoolfellow, who, grasping at power to serve a use beyond it, had put his stake upon love and swept the board.

They dared not enter Pella. They had only travelled at their own horses' pace; a courier with remounts on the way could have been there long before them, and they could not be sure of the garrison after the news from the western army. One of her suite, a certain Polykles, was brother to the commandant of Amphipolis, an old stronghold near the Thracian border. He would help them to get away by sea.

Henceforward they must try not to be seen. Their arms discarded, wearing homespun bartered for with peasants, they nursed their weary horses, skirting the great timeworn road that had carried Darius the Great towards Marathon, Xerxes to Salamis, Philip to the Hellespont and Alexander to Babylon. One by one, pleading sickness, or just disappearing in the night, her small company fell away. On the third day, there was only Polykles.

From a long way off they saw the great keep of Amphipolis, commanding the mouth of the Strymon river. There was a ferry there; troops were there also. They turned inland to seek the nearest ford. But at the ford, too, they were awaited.

When they brought her into Pella, she asked them to untie her feet, which were bound under the mule she rode, to let her wash and comb her hair. They replied that Queen Olympias had ordered her brought just as she was.

On the low hill above the town stood what looked at first like a thicket of stunted trees, laden with birds. When they came near, ravens and crows and kites rose, angrily cawing, from the branches. It was Gallows Hill, where the corpses of criminals were nailed up after execution, like vermin in a gamekeeper's larder. Philip's murderer had hung there once. The present corpses were no longer to be recognized – the scavengers had fed well – but their names had been painted on boards nailed at their feet. NIKANOR, SON OF ANTIPATROS one board said. There were more than a hundred crosses; the reek almost reached the town.

In the audience hall, on the throne where Eurydike had heard petitioners and envoys, Olympias was seated. She had changed her black robes and was dressed in crimson, with a gold diadem on her head. Beside her on a chair of state sat Roxane, the young Alexander on a stool at her knee. He stared with round dark eyes at Eurydike when she was led in, unkempt and dirty, with fetters on legs and wrists.

The irons had been forged to restrain strong men. Her wrists with their dead weight hung down before her. She could only walk by sliding each foot in turn along the floor, and every step chafed her ankles. To keep the fetters from tripping her, she had to walk with an ungainly straddle. But she held her head high as she shuffled towards the throne.

Olympias nodded to one of the guards. He gave Eurydike a hard shove in the back; she toppled forward, bruising her chained hands. Struggling to her knees she looked up at their faces. Some had laughed; the child had laughed with them, but was suddenly grave. Roxane was still smiling. Olympias watched under dropped lids, intently, like the cat that waits for the caught mouse to move.

She said to the guard, 'Is this slut the woman who claims to be Queen of Macedon?' He assented, woodenly. 'I do not believe you. You must have found her in the harbour stews. You, woman. What is your name?'

Eurydike thought, I am alone. No one wishes me courage or will praise it. Any courage I have is for me, alone. She said, 'I am Eurydike, the daughter of Amyntas son of Perdikkas.'

Olympias turned to Roxane, and said conversationally, 'The father a traitor, the mother a barbarian's bastard.'

She stayed on her knees; if she tried to rise, her weighted wrists would pull her over. 'And yet, your son the King chose me to marry his brother.'

Olympias' face tautened with an old anger; the flesh seemed to grow dense. 'I see he did well. The trull is well matched with the fool. We will keep you apart no longer.' She turned to the guards and for the first time smiled. Eurydike could see why she did it seldom; one of her front teeth was black. The guards seemed to blink before they saluted. 'Go,' she said. 'Take her to the marriage chamber.'

When she had toppled twice trying to rise, the guards set her on her feet. She was led to the rear courts of the palace. Dragging her fetters, she passed the stables, and heard her horses whinny; the kennels, where the deep-voiced hounds she had hunted with barked at the foreign sound of her weighted footsteps. The guards did not hustle or harry her. They walked awkwardly at her dragging pace; once, when she tripped over a rut, one of them caught her to keep her from falling; but they did not look at her or speak to one another.

Today or tomorrow, or soon, she thought; what matter? She felt death present in her flesh, its certainty like a sickness.

Ahead was a low-walled stone hut with a pointed roof of thatch. A stink came from it; a privy, she thought, or perhaps a sty. They steered her towards it. A muffled sobbing sounded from within.

They lifted the crossbar from the rough timber door. One of them peered into the fetid gloom. 'Here's your wife, then.' The sobbing ceased. They waited to see if she would go in without being forced. She stooped under the low lintel; the roof inside was hardly higher, the thatch pricked her head. The door closed behind her, the crossbar clattered back.

'Oh, Eurydike! I will be good! I promise I'll be good. Please make them let me out now.'

By the light of a foot-square window under the eaves she saw Philip, in fetters, hunched sideways against the wall. The whites of his eyes glittered in the tear-stained dirt of his face. He gazed at her pleadingly and held out his hands. The wrists were rubbed raw.

The room was furnished with a wooden stool, and a litter of straw like a horse's. At the further end was a shallow pit, reeking with excrement and buzzing with great blue flies.

She moved to the space under the high roof-peak, and he saw her fetters. He wept again, wiping his running nose. The smell of his unwashed flesh repelled her as much as the privy. Involuntarily she drew back against the far wall; her head met the roof again and she had to crouch on the filthy floor.

'Please, please, Eurydike, don't let them beat me again.'

She saw then why he did not sit with his back to the wall. His tunic was stuck to his skin with dark stripes of clotted blood; when she came near he cried, 'Don't touch it, it hurts.' Flies were clustering on the yellow serum.

Fighting back her nausea she said, 'Why did they do it?'

He gulped a sob. 'I hit them when they killed Konon.'

A great shame filled her. She covered her eyes with her chained hands.

He eased his shoulder against the wall, and scratched his side. She had felt already the trickle of insects around her legs. 'I shouldn't have been

King,' he said. 'Alexander told me I shouldn't be. He said if they made me King someone would kill me. Will they kill me?'

'I don't know.' Having brought him here, she could not refuse him hope. 'We may be rescued. You remember Kassandros? He didn't help us in the war; but now Olympias has killed his brother and all his kin. Now he must come. If he wins, he will let us out.' She sat down on the stool, holding her wrist-chains in her lap to ease the weight, and looking at the window-square, whose patch of sky was edged by a distant tree. A gull, seeking the pickings of the kitchen midden, floated across from the wide free waters of the lagoon.

He asked her unhappily for permission to use the pit. When necessity drove her there, the flies flew up and she saw their crawling maggots.

Time passed. At length he sat up eagerly. 'Supper-time,' he said, and licked his lips. It was not only squalor that had changed him; he had lost several stone. A tuneless whistling was coming towards the hut.

A grimy, broken-nailed hand appeared in the window-hole, grasping a hunk of black bread smeared with greasy dripping. Another followed, then a crock of water. She could see nothing of the face but the end of a coarse black beard. The whistling receded.

Philip seized his bread and tore at it like a starving dog. It seemed to her she would never eat again; but her captors had fed her that morning. She had no need to ask if he had eaten that day. She said, 'You can have my piece today; I will eat tomorrow.'

He looked at her, his face illuminated, radiant. 'Oh, Eurydike, I'm so glad you've come.'

Afterwards he told her, ramblingly, the tale of his captivity. His sufferings had confused his mind, he was often hardly coherent. She listened dully. Far off and muted, as they might reach a sick-room, came the sounds of early evening, the lowing of cattle, horses returning from the stables, dogs barking, peasants hailing each other after work, the stamp and rattle of the changing guard. A cart lumbered near with a heavy load; she could hear the oxen straining, the driver cursing and beating them. It did not pass by, but creaked to a halt, and, rumbling and rattling, tipped its load. She listened dully, aware that she was exhausted, thinking of the crawling straw. She propped her back to the wall and fell into an un-sleeping doze.

Footsteps approached. Is it now? she thought. Philip was stretched out and snoring. She waited to hear the bar withdrawn. But there came only the indistinct sounds of peasants at heavy work. She called, 'What is it? What do you want?'

The mutterings died into silence. Then, as if a stealthy sign had been made, the stirrings began again. There was a kind of patting and scraping against the door, then a thud, and another.

She went to the little window, but it did not overlook the door. All she could see was part of a heap of rough-dressed stone. She was tired, and slow to understand, but suddenly the sound came clearly; the slap of wet mortar, and the scraping of a trowel.

Kassandros was walking his siege-lines on the damp Arkadian plateau under the walls of Tegea; thick, dark, mossy, impacted brick, stuff that would only dent under a ram that could have loosened ashlar. The town had a perpetual spring inside it; it was a slow business to starve them out. They had told his heralds that they were under the special patronage of Athene, who had promised in some oracle of remote antiquity that their city would never be taken by force of arms. He was resolved to make Athene eat her words.

He did not hurry to meet the courier from Macedon; it was sure to be another appeal from Eurydike. Then as he came near he saw the face of disaster, and took the man to his tent.

He was a servant who had escaped the massacre of the Antipatrids. To the tale of death he added that Olympias had had the tomb of his brother Iollas battered down and his bones scattered for beasts to eat, claiming that he had poisoned her son in Babylon.

Kassandros, who had listened in rigid silence, leaped from his chair. There would be a time for grief; all he could feel was a blazing hate and rage. 'That wolf-bitch! That gorgon! How did they let her set foot in Macedon? My father warned them against her with his dying breath. Why did they not kill her on the border?'

The messenger said, without expression, 'They would not fight the mother of Alexander.'

For a moment, Kassandros felt that his head would burst. The man looked with alarm at his staring eyes. Aware of it, he fought for composure. 'Go, rest, eat. We will speak again later.' The rider went off, not wondering that a man should be moved by such a slaughter of his kin.

When he had come to himself, he sent an envoy to make terms with the Tegeans. He excused them from allegiance to himself, if they would merely agree not to help his enemies. Face-saving formulae were exchanged; the siege was lifted; the Tegeans went in procession to the old wooden temple of Athene, to bring her thank-offerings for keeping her ancient promise.

Behind the walled-up door, time passed like the days of a slow fatal illness, bringing misery by small additions; more stink, more flies and lice and fleas, more festering of their sores, weakness and hunger. But still the bread and water came every day to the window hole.

At first Eurydike had counted the days, scratching with a pebble on the wall. After seven or eight she missed one and lost count, and ceased to make the effort. She would have sunk into blank apathy, broken only by fighting with the insects, but for Philip.

His mind could not hold the sum of disaster long enough to be capable of despair. He lived from day to day. Often he would complain to the man who brought the food, and he would sometimes answer, not cruelly but like a sulky servant unjustly blamed, saying he had his orders and that was the end of it. She scorned to utter a word to him; but as time passed he grew a little more forthcoming, bringing out old saws about the ways of fortune. One day he even asked Philip how his wife was. He looked at her and answered, 'She says I'm not to tell.'

She drowsed away half the day but could not sleep at night. Philip's snores were noisy, the vermin as tormenting as her thoughts. One morning early, when they were awake and already hungry, she said to him, 'Philip. I made you claim the throne. It was for myself I wanted it. It is my fault you are shut up here, my fault that you were beaten. Do you want to kill me? I do not mind. If you like I will show you how.' But he only said with a whine like a sick child's, 'The soldiers made me. Alexander told me not to.'

She thought, I need only give up my bread to him. He would take it gladly if I gave it, though he will not rob me. I would surely die quickly, now. But when the time came she could not bear the hunger, and ate her share. To her surprise, she was aware that the portion had grown larger. Next day there was still more, enough to save for a frugal breakfast.

At the same time, they began to hear the voices of the guard outside. They must have been told to keep their distance – her record of subversion was well known – their comings and goings had been only measures of time. But discipline was relaxing, they talked and gossiped carelessly, weary perhaps of guarding a place without an exit. Then one night, as she lay watching through the window hole a single star, there was a soft approach, the click of leather and metal; the opening was darkened for a moment, and when it lightened, there were two apples on the sill. The mere smell was ambrosia.

After that something came every night, and with less stealth, as if the officer of the watch was himself conniving. No one stayed to talk at the window, no doubt a hanging matter; but they talked to their relief, as if they meant to be heard. 'Well, we've our orders, like it or not.' 'Rebels or no, enough's enough.' 'And too much is hubris, which the gods don't like.' 'Aye, and by the look of it they won't wait long.'

Well versed in the tones of mutiny, she sensed here something else. These men were not plotting; they were talking openly the common talk of the streets. She thought, we are not that woman's only victims; the people have sickened of her. What did they mean by the gods not waiting long? Can it be that Kassandros is marching north?

There had been cheese and figs in the night, and the jug had had watered wine in it. With better food her listlessness had left her. She dreamed of rescue, of the Macedonians staring with pity at their filth and wretchedness, clamouring for retribution; of her hour of triumph when, washed and robed and crowned, she resumed her throne in the audience chamber.

Kassandros' sudden departure for the north had left confusion behind him; his forsaken allies in the Peloponnese had to face alone the Macedonians led by Polyperchon's son. When their desperate envoys overtook his column, he only said he had business that would not wait.

Democrat Aitolians had manned Thermopylai against his passage. Such challenges had no romance for him. More practical than Xerxes, he commandeered everything that would float in the busy strait between Euboia and the mainland, and bypassed the Hot Gates by sea.

In Thessaly, Polyperchon himself awaited him, still faithful, despite Olympias, to Alexander's son. He too was side-stepped; some troops were detached to tie him up, while the main force pressed on north-east. Skirting Olympos, they were soon on the borders of Macedon.

The coastal fortress of Dion lay ahead. Kassandros' envoys promised an end to the unlawful tyranny of women and a return to the ancient customs. After a short conclave within, the gates were opened. Here he held court, receiving all who offered support or brought him intelligence. Many kinsmen of Olympias' victims, or men whom she had proscribed, came to join him, full of their wrongs and clamouring for vengeance. But others came by stealth who till lately would not have come; men who had refused to fight the mother of Alexander, and who said now that no one but Alexander could have held such a woman in check. These would go back, spreading news of Kassandros' pledges, and his claim to the regency on behalf of Roxane's son.

One day, he remembered to ask of such a visitor, 'And when they took Amyntas' daughter, how did she die?'

The man's face lightened. 'There at least I have good news for you. She was alive when I left and Philip too. They are treated shockingly, walled-up in a wretched sty; there is a great deal of anger among the people. I'm told they were in a very poor way, till even the guards took pity on them and gave them a little comfort. If you hurry, you can save them still.'

Kassandros' face had set in a moment's stillness. 'Shameful!' he said. 'Olympias should have borne her good fortune more becomingly. Can they have lived so long?'

'You can count on that, Kassandros. I had it from one of the guard.'

'Thank you for the news.' He leaned forward in his chair, and spoke with sudden animation. 'Let it be known I mean to right their wrongs. They shall be restored to all their dignities. As for Olympias, I shall hand over her person to Queen Eurydike, to punish as she sees fit. Tell the people.'

'Indeed I will; they will be glad to hear. I'll get word, if I can, to the prison. It will cheer them to have hope at last.'

He left, big with his mission. Kassandros sent for his officers, and told them he would delay his march for a few days more. It would give his friends time, he said, to gather more support.

Three mornings later, Eurydike said, 'How quiet it is. I don't even hear the guard.'

The first dawn was glimmering in the window hole. The night had been cool, the flies were not yet awake. They had eaten well on what the night guard had brought. The watch had changed just before dawn as usual; but the relief had been quiet, and now there was no sound of their movements. Had they deserted, mutinied? Or been called to help defend the city, which would mean Kassandros had come?

She said to Philip, 'Soon we shall be free, I feel it.'

Scratching at his groin, he said, 'Can I have a bath?'

'Yes, we shall have baths and good clean clothes, and beds to sleep in.'

'And I can have my stones back?'

'Yes, and some new ones too.' Often in their close quarters his nearness, his smell, the way he ate and belched and relieved himself, had been barely endurable; she would gladly have exchanged him for a dog; but she knew that she owed him justice. She must care for her mind, if she was to be fit again for ruling. So she seldom scolded him, and, if she did, gave him a kind word after. He never sulked, always forgave, or perhaps simply forgot.

'When will they let us out?' he said.

'As soon as Kassandros wins.'

'Listen. People are coming now.'

It was true, there were footsteps; three or four men by the sound. They were on the door side, where the window did not look. Their voices muttered but she could not make out their words. Then, suddenly, came a sound there was no mistaking – the blow of a pick on the wall that closed the door.

'Philip!' she cried. 'They have come to rescue us!'

He whooped like a child. and peered vainly through the window. She stood up in the space under the roof-point, listening to the fall of rubble and thud of stones. The work went quickly; the wall had been a shoddy job by men without their hearts in it. She called out, 'Are you Kassandros' men?'

There was a pause in the pick-strokes; then a thick foreign voice said, 'Yes, Kassans men,' but she could tell he had not understood her. His next words, to his workmates. were not in Greek, and now she recognized the sound.

'They are Thracians,' she said to Philip. 'They are slaves sent to knock down the wall. When that's done, someone will come to unbar the door.'

Philip's face had altered. He withdrew as far from the door as he could without falling into the privy. Old days, before the benevolent reign of Konon, were coming back to him. 'Don't let them come in,' he said.

She had begun to reassure him, when there was a laugh outside.

She stiffened. It was not the laughter of slaves, complaisant or discreet. She knew. with a crawling of the flesh, the nature of this archetypal mirth.

The last stones fell. The crossbar clattered from the door. It creaked open; the sunrise burst dazzling in.

Four Thracians stood on the threshold, staring across the rubble.

They choked, clapping hands to their mouths and noses; men bred in the clean hill air, with hundred-foot cliffs to receive the ordure of their villages. In this pause. she saw on their cheeks and foreheads their warrior tattoos, saw their pectorals of engraved bronze etched with silver, their cloaks with bands of tribal colours, the daggers in their hands.

Sickly she thought, the Macedonians would not do it. She stood straight, in the centre where the roof was high.

The leading Thracian confronted her. He wore an arm-bracelet of a triple-coiled snake, and greaves with women's faces embossed upon the kneecaps. Spiral blue tattoos on his brow, and on his cheeks to his dark-red beard, made his expression impenetrable. 'Kill me then!' she cried, lifting her head. 'You can boast that you killed a queen.'

He put out his arm – not the right, with the dagger, but the left with the coiled bronze snake – and swept her out of his way. She lost her footing and fell.

'You slave, don't you dare hit my wife!' In a moment, the cowering form by the privy had hurled itself straight forward from a bent-kneed crouch. The Thracian, taken unawares with a butted midriff, had the breath knocked out of him. Philip, fighting like an ape enraged, using feet and knees and nails, struggled to get the dagger. He had sunk his teeth in the Thracian's wrist when the others fell on him.

Between his roars of pain as the knives went in, she thought that he called for Konon; then he gave a guttural choke, his head arched back gaping, he clawed at the dirt floor and lay still. One of the men shoved at him with a foot, but he did not move.

They turned to each other, like men whose task is done.

She rose on her hands and knees. A booted foot had trodden on her leg; she wondered that she could still move it. They were staring down at the body, comparing the bites and scratches Philip had given them. She caught in their unknown jargon a note of admiration; they had found, after all, a king.

They saw her movement and turned to look at her. One of them laughed. A new horror gripped her; till now she had thought only of the knives.

The man who had laughed had a round, smooth-skinned face and a pale scanty beard. He came towards her smiling. The leader who wore the greaves called something out, and the man turned away with a gesture which said he could do better for himself than this stinking drab. They looked at their red blades and wiped them on Philip's tunic. One of them threw it back to show the groin; the leader, rebukingly, pulled it down again. They went out, picking their way over the scattered stones.

She tottered to her feet, shaking and dazed and cold with shock. It had all taken, perhaps, two minutes from the time when the door gave way.

Clear early sun streaming through the doorway picked out the stale filth, the fresh scarlet blood of the body. She blinked in the unaccustomed light. Two shadows fell across it.

They were Macedonians, and unarmed, the second attendant on the first, for he stood half a pace behind and carried a bundle. The first came forward, a thickset middle-aged man in a decent drab tunic and shoulder cloak. He gazed for a few moments in silence at the scene, clicking his tongue in disapproval. Turning to the other he said, 'Mere butchery. A disgrace.'

He stepped into the entry, confronting the haggard, mat-haired woman with her grimy feet and black nails, and spoke in the flat, rather pompous voice of a minor functionary doing his office with regard to his own importance.

'Eurydike, daughter of Amyntas. I act under command, do you therefore hold me guiltless before the gods. Olympias, Queen of the Macedonians, says this by me. Because your father was born lawfully of royal blood, she does not condemn you to execution like the bastard your husband. She gives you leave to end your own life, and offers you a choice of means.'

The second man came forward, and looked for somewhere to put his bundle down. Seeming disconcerted to find no table, he opened it on the ground, and, like a pedlar, set out the contents on the cloth; a short fine dagger, a stoppered flask, and a cord of plaited flax with a running noose.

Silently she considered them, then looked away from them to the sprawling corpse beside her. If she had joined him as he fought, perhaps it would all be over. Kneeling she picked up the phial; she had heard that the Athenian hemlock killed with a creeping cold, giving no pain. But this came from Olympias, and if she asked what it was they might lie. The dagger was sharp; but she knew she was too weak to strike it home; half-dead, what would they do to her? She fingered the rope. It was smooth, well-made and clean. She looked up at the peak of the hut where the roof stood eight feet high, and said, 'This will do.'

The man gave a business-like nod. 'A good choice, lady, and quickly over. We'll soon have it fixed, you've a stool there I see.' When the servant mounted it, she saw there was even an iron hook, fixed to a little cross-beam, such as is found in places where tools or tackle are kept. No, they would not be long.

So, she thought, nothing at all remained. Not even style; she had seen hanged men. She looked down at Philip, left tumbled like a slaughtered beast. Yes, after all, something was still left. Piety remained to her. This was the King her husband, who had made her a queen, who had fought and died for her. As the executioner, his task done, stepped down from the stool, she said, 'You must wait awhile.'

The jug of watered wine, left by the night-guard for their comfort, stood untouched in the window. She knelt beside him, and wetting a corner of her tunic hem, washed his wounds as well as she could, and cleaned his face. She straightened his legs, laid his left arm on his breast and his right beside him, closed his eyes and mouth and smoothed his hair. Set in the gravity of death he looked a comely man. She saw the executioners looking at him with a new respect; she had done that at least for him. Scraping her hand along the earth floor, she strewed on him the ritual pinch of dust which would free him to cross the river.

There was one thing still, she thought; something for herself. It was not for nothing that her blood came down from the warring Macedonian kings and the chieftains of Illyria. She had her blood feud; and if she could not pursue it, the powers whose work it was must do it for her. She stood up from the body, stretching her hands palm downwards over the trampled and blood-stained earth.

'Witness, you gods below,' she cried aloud, 'that I received these gifts from Olympias. I call upon you, by the waters of Styx, and by the power of Hades, and by this blood, to give her in turn such gifts as these.' She turned to the men, saying, 'I am ready.'

She kicked the stool away for herself, not flinching or leaving them to take it, as they had seen strong men do many a time. All in all they thought she had shown a good deal of spirit, not unworthy of her ancestry; and when it seemed that her struggle might last longer than was needful, they dragged her down by the knees, to pull the noose tight and help her die.

Olympias, these needful things attended to, summoned her council.

Few of the men about her were bound, now, by loyalty to her person. Some had blood-feuds with the Antipatrids; many knew they had given Kassandros cause for vengeance; others, she guessed, were loyal only to the son of Alexander. She sat at the great table of gilt and hardstone where her husband Philip had sat, a young king, in the old days of the civil wars which men of no more than sixty could still remember, and men of seventy had fought in. She did not ask them for advice. Her own will sufficed for her. The old men and soldiers sitting before her saw her impenetrable solitude, her enclosure in her will.

She did not mean, she told them, to sit at ease in Pella while rebels and traitors overran her frontiers. She would go south to Pydna; it was only some fifteen miles north of Dion where Kassandros had insolently set up his standard. Pydna had a harbour; it was well fortified; from there she would direct the war.

The soldiers approved. They thought of the bloodless victory in the west.

'Good,' she said. 'In two days I shall move the court to Pydna.'

The soldiers stared. This was another thing entirely. It meant a horde of women, servants and non-combatants taking up room, getting under the feet of the garrison, having to be fed. After a pause in which everyone waited for someone else to speak first, they told her so.

She said, unmoved, 'Our allies can join us by sea, without losses from fighting on the march. When we are in full strength, when Polyperchon has joined us, we will meet Kassandros.'

Agenor, a veteran of the east who had been given the chief command, cleared his throat and said, 'No one questions the honour of Polyperchon. But it is said he has had desertions.' He paused; everyone wondered if he would dare go on. 'And, as you know, we can expect nothing now from Epiros.'

She stiffened in her ivory-inlaid chair. The Epirotes who had followed her to the border had mutinied when ordered to fight in Macedon, and gone home. Only a handful of Molossians was left. She had shut herself up for two days to nurse her pride, and Kassandros' secret partisans had made the most of them. The councillors looked angrily at Agenor; they had seen her face harden. She fixed on them her inflexible dangerous eyes, looking out from her mask of will. She said, 'The court will move to Pydna. This session is closed.'

The men left, looking at one another. not speaking till they were in the open. Agenor said, 'Let her have her way. But she must be out before the winter.'

Kassandros had had good news from the officer he had sent to deal with Polyperchon. Avoiding battle, he had infiltrated the straggling camp with men who had a clansman or kinsman there. They spread the news that Olympias had shed the royal blood of Macedon, herself a foreigner and a usurper; and offered a bounty of fifty drachmas to any good Macedonian who would join Kassandros' force. Every morning the numbers in Polyperchon's camp were fewer; soon he and his faithful remnant were too few to consider more than their own defence. They dug themselves into the best of the local hillforts, mended its walls, provisioned it, and waited upon events.

The corn and the olives ripened, the grapes were trodden, the women took to the mountains to honour Dionysos; in the dark before dawn the shrill Bacchic cry answered the first cock-crow. In Pydna, the watchers on the harbour walls scanned the sea, which the first autumn winds were ruffling. No sails appeared but those of the fisher-boats, already running for home.

Before the first gales began, Kassandros appeared from the passes he now commanded, and surrounded Pydna with a palisade.

316 BC

It was spring in the valleys. The peaks of Olympos still dazzled with winter snow under a clear pale sky. A single wreath of cloud hid the Throne of Zeus. His eagles had forsaken its lifeless purity to fend for themselves on the lower crags. Around the summits, only sheer cliffs that would not hold a snowflake slashed the white cloak with black.

In the foothills, the waters of the thaw scoured ravines and gullies in torrents that ground the boulders like thunder. Below, under the walls of Pydna, a mild sun warmed the corpses which the cold had stiffened, releasing their carrion reek, and the kites returned to them.

Olympias, pacing the walls, looked out beyond the siege-lines to the wild mountain ranges where the lynxes and wolves ran free, where the pines were shrugging the snow from their furry shoulders like awakening bears.

Her gaunt face looked out from a shapeless mass of clothing, layer upon layer. She had come in mild autumn weather, resolved that the war would be over in a month and Kassandros dead. Alexander had always done what he resolved, that she knew. He had seldom discussed with her the complex calculations which had preceded action. There was a sharp wind today; she was wearing even her state robe heaped over her shoulders like a wrap. With hunger one felt the cold.

The other women were huddled indoors over their tiny fire. The men upon the ramparts, skull-faced, glanced dully at her as she passed, their vitality too low to nourish a hot hate. All through the winter there had been no assault upon the walls; the corpses in the ditch were all dead of starvation. They had been flung there not from callousness but necessity; there was no room left in the fort to dig more graves.

Scattered among them were the huge bones of the elephants. The horses and mules had soon been eaten; but elephants were instruments of war, and, besides, no one had dared to slaughter them. They had tried to keep them alive on sawdust; for a time their complaining moans and forlorn trumpetings had disturbed the night, then one by one they had sunk down in their stalls, and what meat was left on them, all sinew, had been something to chew on for a while. The mahouts, who were useless now, had been taken off the ration list; they too were below the walls.

Somewhere in the fort a camp woman's child was crying; new born, soon gone. The young Alexander was too old to cry. She had seen to it that he still had enough; he was a king and must not have the strength of his manhood crippled in his youth. Though the food was wretched he had been unexpectedly good, telling her that his father had gone hungry with his men. But often she would find herself looking through him, seeing the tall grandson she could have had if her son had obeyed her, and married before he rode to war. Why, she asked herself; why?

On the rampart that faced the sea the air was cleaner, with a sharp scent of spring. The Olympian massif with its snowy crests called to her like the trees to a captive bird. Last autumn's Dionysia was the first for forty years that she had not spent with her maenads in the mountains. Never again, said the caw from the kite-haunted bones. She refused it angrily. Soon, when it was sailing weather, Eumenes, whose loyalty had never failed, would cross with his troops from Asia.

There was a stirring along the ramparts. A little crowd was gathering and growing, coming towards her. She drew back from the brink and waited.

The band of emaciated men approached without sign of violence. Few looked to have strength for it. Their clothes hung on them like half-empty sacks; several leaned on a comrade's shoulder to keep their feet. Men of thirty could have been sixty. Their skin was blotched with scurvy and many had toothless gums. Their hair was falling. One, to whom still clung vestiges of command, came forward and spoke, lisping a little because his front teeth had gone.

'Madam. We request permission to leave.'

She looked at them, speechless. Anger surfaced in her eyes and fell away into their depths. The old, thin voice seemed not a man's but a fate's.

Answering her silence, he said, 'If the enemy attacked he could lay us out bare-handed. All we can do here now is share the last of the stores, and then go *there*.' He made a tired uneconomical gesture towards the ditch. 'Without us, what's left will last a little longer. Permission, madam?'

'But,' she said at last, 'Kassandros' men will butcher you.'

'As God wills, lady. Today or tomorrow, what's the odds?'

'You may go,' she said. He stood a few moments looking at her mutely as the rest began shambling away. She added, 'Thank you for your good service.'

She went in then, because of the cold; but a little later she went up again to watch them depart.

They had broken off branches from some scrawny pines that grew in the cracks of the stone, and as the gates creaked open they waved them in sign of peace. Slowly they eased themselves down the scarp, and plodded across no-man's-land towards the siege works. The rough timber gate in the stockade was lifted open; they trickled through and stood in a clump inside. A single, helmeted figure came out to them, seemed to address them, and went away. Presently soldiers came among them with baskets and tall jars. She watched the bread and wine distributed, the sticklike arms reached out in eager gratitude.

She returned to her room in the gate-tower, to crouch over her little fire. A ribbon of ants was streaming along the hearth to a basket that stood beside it. She lifted the lid; inside, they were swarming over a dead snake. It was the last one left from the Thracian sanctuary of Dionysos, her oracle. What had killed it? The rats and mice had been trapped and eaten, but it could have lived on the creeping things. It was only a few years old. She gazed at the moving mass and shivered, then put the basket with its seething heap on to the fire.

The air grew mild, the breezes gentle. It was sailing weather; but the only sails were those of Kassandros' warships. The ration was down to a handful of meal a day, when Olympias sent envoys to ask for terms.

From the ramparts she saw them go into his tent. Beside her stood her stepdaughter Thessalonike, a legacy from one of Philip's campaign weddings. Her mother had died when she was born, and Olympias had tolerated her in the palace because she gave herself no airs, and was quiet and civil. She was thirty-five, tall and plain, but carried herself well. She had not dared confess that in Pella she had had an offer from Kassandros; she had come to Pydna letting it be thought it was her life she had feared for. Now, pale and lank-haired, she waited for the envoys, keeping her thoughts to herself.

The envoys came back, their lassitude a little lifted by the hospitality in the tent. Kassandros' envoy was with them.

He was a man called Deinias, who had done many secret errands for Olympias in the past and been well rewarded. How much had he told Kassandros? He behaved as if those days had never been, insolently bland. Florid, well-fleshed, his very body was an arrogance in that company. He refused a private parley, demanding to speak before the garrison. Having no choice, she met him in the central court where, while they were able, the soldiers used to exercise.

'Kassandros son of Antipatros sends you greetings. If your people give themselves up to him, they will be spared like those who have now surrendered. As for yourself, his terms are that you put yourself in his hands, without any conditions.'

She pulled herself upright, though a twinge reminded her that her back was stiffening. 'Tell Kassandros to come with better terms.' A whispering sigh ran through the ranks below her. 'When Eumenes comes, your master will run like a hunted wolf. We will hold out till then.'

He raised his brows in overplayed surprise. 'Madam, forgive me. I had forgotten news does not reach you here. Do not set your hopes on a dead man.'

Her vitality seemed to drain, like wine from a cracked jar. She kept her feet but did not answer.

'Eumenes was given up lately to Antigonos. He was sold by the Silver Shields whom he commanded. By the chance of battle, Antigonos seized their baggage-train. Their loot of three reigns was in it; also their women and children – one cannot tell how much that weighed with such men. At all events, Antigonos offered it back in exchange for their commander, and they struck the bargain.'

A rustling shudder passed through the brittle ranks. Horror perhaps, the knowledge that nothing was now unthinkable; or, perhaps, temptation.

Her face was parchment-coloured. She would have been glad of the stick she used sometimes to get about the rough places of the fort. 'You may tell Kassandros we will open the gates without condition, in return for our lives alone.'

Though her head felt icy cold, and a dazzle of darkness was spinning in her eyes, she got to her room and shut the door before she fainted.

'Excellent,' said Kassandros when Deinias returned to him. 'When the men come out, feed them and recruit any who are worth it. Get a trench dug for the carrion. The old bitch and her household will stay here for the time.'

'And after?' said Deinias with feigned carelessness.

'Then ... well. She is still the mother of Alexander, which awes the ignorant. The Macedonians won't bear her rule again; but, even now ... I shall frighten her, and then offer her a ship to escape to Athens. Ships are wrecked every year.'

The dead were shovelled into their trench; the thin, pasty-faced women moved from the fortress into the town house reserved for royal visits. It was roomy and clean; they got out their mirrors, and put them quickly away; girdled their loose clothes round them, and ate cravingly of fruit and curds. The boy picked up quickly. He knew he had survived a memorable siege, and that the Thracian archers, in the secrecy of their guard-room, had made stew from the flesh of corpses. The inner defences of childhood were making it like a tale to him. Kebes, whose fine physique had lasted him well, did not check this talk; the haunted ones were those who kept silent. All kings of Macedon were heirs to the sword; it was well to know that war was not all flags and trumpets. As man and boy gained strength, they began to exercise again.

It was Roxane who had changed most to the outward eye. She was twenty-six; but in her homeland this was matronhood. Her glass had showed it her, and she had accepted it. Her consequence was now a dowager's; she saw herself not as the last King's widow, but as the mother of the next.

Pella had surrendered, on Olympias' orders, dictated by Kassandros. This done, she sent to ask him if she might return to her palace rooms. He replied that at present it was not convenient. At Pella he had things to do.

She would sit in a window that looked on the eastward sea, considering the future. She was exiled now from Epiros; but there was still the boy. She was sixty; she might have ten years or more to rear him and see him on his father's throne.

Kassandros held audience at Pella. The Epirotes made alliance with him; he sent an adviser to direct their King, the young son of Kleopatra. He buried his brother Nikanor, and restored his brother Iollas' desecrated tomb. Then he asked where were the bodies of the royal pair, so foully murdered. They led him to a corner of the royal burial-ground, where in a little brick-lined grave Philip and Eurydike had been laid like peasants. They were hardly to be recognized, by now, as man and woman; but he burned them on a ceremonial pyre, denouncing the outrage of their deaths, and had their bones laid up in precious coffers while a handsome tomb was built for them. He had not forgotten that kings of Macedon were entombed by their successors.

There were many graves around Pella after Olympias' purge. The withered wreaths still hung upon the stones, tasselled with the mourners' hair. The kindred still came with tears and offering-baskets. Kassandros made it his business to go among them, commiserating their losses, and asking if time was not ripe for justice on the guilty.

Soon it was announced that the bereaved wished an Assembly called, to accuse Olympias of shedding without trial the blood of Macedonians.

She was sitting with the other women at the evening meal when a messenger was announced. She finished, drank a cup of wine, and then went down to him.

He was a well-spoken man with the accent of the north; a stranger, but there were many after her long absence in the west. He warned her that her trial was to be demanded; then he said, 'I am here, you understand, at the instance of Kassandros. He pledged your safety when the siege was raised. Tomorrow at dawn, there will be a ship for you in the harbour.'

'A ship?' It was dusk, the lamps in the hall had not been lit yet. Her cheeks were hollowed with shadow, her eyes dark wells with a faint gleam in the depths. 'A ship? What do you mean?'

'Madam, you have good guest-friends in Athens. You have supported their democrats.' (It had been part of her feud with Antipatros.) 'You will be well received. Let Assembly try you in absence. No one yet died of that.'

Till now she had spoken quietly; she had not yet lost the lassitude of the siege. But her raised voice was full and rounded. 'Does Kassandros think I shall run away from the Macedonians? Would my son have done so?'

'No, madam. But Alexander had no cause?'

'Let them see me!' she cried. 'let them try me if they wish. Say to Kassandros only to tell me the day, and I shall be there.'

Disconcerted, he said, 'Is that well-advised? I was to warn you that some of the people wish you harm.'

'When they have heard me, we will see what their wish is then.'

'Tell her the day?' said Kassandros when this news was brought him. 'She is asking too much. I know the fitful hearts of the Macedonians. Call Assembly for tomorrow, and give out that she refused to come.'

*

The bereaved appeared before Assembly in torn mourning clothes, their hair newly shorn and strewn with ashes. Widows led orphaned children, old men bewailed the sons who had propped their age. When it was made known that Olympias would not appear, no one stood up to speak for her. By acclamation, Assembly voted for death.

'So far so good,' said Kassandros afterwards. 'We have authority. But for a woman of her rank, a public execution is unseemly. She would be able to address the people, a chance that she would not waste. I think we will make a different plan.'

The household at Pydna was busy with small mid-morning tasks. Roxane was embroidering a girdle; Thessalonike was washing her hair. (She had been told, on Kassandros' authority, that she was free to return to the palace; a distinction received with dread, and not responded to.) Olympias, sitting in her window, was reading Kallisthenes' account of the deeds of Alexander. He had had it copied for her by a Greek scribe somewhere in Baktria, and sent it her by the royal road. She had read it often; but today it had come into her mind that she would like to read it again.

There was an urgent tap on her door. Kebes came in. 'Madam. There are soldiers asking for you outside. They're here for no good; I have barred the doors.'

As he spoke, battering and clanging began, with shouted oaths. Roxane ran in with her sewing still in her hand. Thessalonike, a towel wound round her hair, said only, 'Is *he* with them?' The boy came in, saying sharply, 'What do they want?'

She had been putting her book aside; now she picked it up again. She gave it to him, saying, 'Alexander, keep this for me.' He took it with grave quiet eyes. The battering on the door grew louder. She turned to the women. 'Go in. Go to your rooms. And you too, Kebes. It is for me they are here. Leave them to me.'

The women withdrew. Kebes paused; but the boy had taken his hand. If he had to die, it would be for the King. He bowed and led him away.

The door was splintering. Olympias went to her clothes-chest, dropped to her feet the house-gown she was wearing, and put on the crimson robe in which she had given audiences. Its girdle was Indian cloth of gold, embroidered with bullion and rubies. She took from her casket a necklace of great pearls which Alexander had sent her from Taxila, clasped it on, and walking without haste to the stairhead, stood there waiting.

The doors gave way. A press of men stumbled in and stood staring about them. They began pulling out their swords, ready to ransack the house and seek such hiding-places as the sacking of towns had made them cunning in. Then, as they moved towards the stairs, they saw the silent figure looking down on them, like an image on a plinth.

The leaders stopped. Those behind them, even those still at the gaping doors, saw what they saw. The clamour died into an eerie silence.

'You wished to see me,' said Olympias. 'I am here.'

'Did you run mad?' said Kassandros when the leader reported back to him. 'Do you tell me she was standing there before you, and you did nothing? Slunk off like dogs chased out of a kitchen? The old hag must have put a spell on you. What did she say?'

He had struck the wrong note. The man felt resentful. 'She said nothing, Kassandros. What the men said was, she looked like Alexander's mother. And nobody would strike first.'

'*You* were paid to do that,' said Kassandros tartly.

'Not yet, sir. So I've saved you money. Permission to withdraw.'

Kassandros let him go. Affairs were at a crux, commotion must be avoided. He would see the man got some dangerous mission later. At present, he must think of another plan. When it came to him, it was so simple that he wondered he could have been so slow to see it.

It was drawing towards evening. At Pydna they were looking forward to supper, not so much from hunger – their stomachs were still somewhat shrunken – as because it broke the tedium of the day. Alexander was being read to by his tutor from the Odyssey, the book where Circe changes the hero's men to swine. The women were making small changes in their toilet, to keep good manners alive. The sun hung over the high peaks of Olympos, ready to sink behind them and plunge the coast in dusk.

The little crowd came quietly along the road, not with the tramp of army boots, but with the soft shuffling tread that becomes a mourner. Their hair was cropped, dishevelled and dusted with wood-ash, their clothing ritually torn.

In the last sunlight they came to the broken door, shored-up by a local carpenter. It was ramshackle work. While passers-by stared, wondering what burial these people came from at such an hour, they ran up to the door and tore the planks apart.

Olympias heard. When the frightened servants ran up to her, she had already understood, as though she had known already. She did not change the homely gown she had on. She looked in the box where she kept the *Deeds of Alexander.* Good, the boy had it still. Walking to the stairs she saw the ash-streaked faces below, like masks of tragedy. She did not go through the farce of standing there, appealing to those unrelenting eyes. She went down to them.

They did not seize her at once. Each wanted his say. 'You killed my son, who never injured anyone.' 'Your people cut my brother's throat, a good man who had fought for your son in Asia.' 'You hung my husband on a cross and his children saw it.' 'Your men killed my father, and raped my sisters too.'

The voices rose, lost words, became a gabble of rage. It seemed they might tear her to pieces where she stood. She turned to the older men, steadier in their sternness. 'Will you not see that this is decently done?'

Though they felt no pity she had touched their pride. One of them lifted his staff for quiet, and cleared a place around her.

Above in the house the women servants were keening. Thessalonike moaning softly, Roxane wildly sobbing. She heard it like the noises of some foreign town which did not concern her. She cared only that the boy should not see.

The old man pointed his staff. They led her to a piece of waste land near the sea, too poor for farming, where glaucous shore-plants grew in the stony ground, and a mat of flotsam edged the water. The stones that strewed it were smoothed by the sea's grinding, cast up in the winter storms. The people drew away from her, and stood round her in a ring, as children do in games. They looked at the old man who had appointed himself to speak.

'Olympias, daughter of Neoptolemos. For killing Macedonians without trial, contrary to justice and the law, we pronounce you worthy of death.'

Alone in the circle, she stood with her head up while the first stones struck her. Their force made her stagger, and she sank to her knees to prevent an unseemly fall. This offered her head, and soon a big stone struck it. She found herself lying, gazing upwards at the sky. A cloud of great beauty had caught the light from the sinking sun, itself hidden behind the mountain. Her eyes began to swim, their images doubled; she felt her body breaking under the stones, but it was more shock than pain; she would be gone before the real pain had time to start. She looked up at the whirling effulgent cloud, and thought, I brought down the fire from heaven; I have lived with glory. A thunderbolt struck from the sky and all was gone.

315 BC

The Lyceum stood in a pleasant suburb of Athens, near the plane-shaded Ilissos stream beloved by Sokrates. It was a new and handsome building. The humbler one, where Aristotle had set up his strolling university, was a mere annexe now. A long elegant stoa with painted Corinthian columns now sheltered the Principal and his students when they paced discoursing. Within, it smelled benignly of old vellum, ink and writing-wax.

It was all the gift of Kassandros, presented through his cultured Athenian governor. The Principal, Theophrastos, had long been eager to entertain their benefactor, and the auspicious day had arrived.

The distinguished guest had been shown the new library, many of its shelves consecrated to Theophrastos' works; he was a derivative but prolific author. Now they had returned to the Principal's rooms to take refreshment.

'I am glad,' said Kassandros, 'that you study history, and delighted that you compile it. It is for the scholars of each generation to purge it of its errors, before they infect the next.'

'Aristotle's philosophy of history ...' began Theophrastos eagerly. Kassandros, who had had an hour of learned garrulity, lifted a courteous hand.

'I myself sat at his feet, in my youth when he was in Macedon.' Hateful days, tasting of gall, seeing the charmed circle always from outside, exiled from the bright warmth by the centrifuge of his own envy. He said meaningly, 'If only the *chief* of his students had put his privilege to better use.'

Cautiously, the Principal murmured something about the corruption of barbarian ways and the temptations of power.

'You suffered a grievous loss when Kallisthenes met his end. A brilliant scholar, I believe.'

'Ah yes. Aristotle feared, indeed predicted it. Some unwise letters ...'

'I am persuaded that he was falsely accused of inspiring his students to plot the death of the King. The voice of philosophy had become unwelcome.'

'I fear so ... We have no one here who accompanied Alexander, and our records suffer.'

'You have at least,' said Kassandros smiling, 'a guest who visited the court at Babylon in its last weeks. If you would like to call a scribe, I can give you some account of what I found.'

The scribe came, well furnished with tablets. Kassandros dictated at a smooth, measured pace. '... But long before this he had given way to arrogance and wantonness, preferring the godlike hauteur of a Persian Great King to the wholesome restraints of the homeland.' The scribe would have no polishing to do; he had prepared it all in advance. Theophrastos, whose own career had been wholly scholastic, hung fascinated on this voice from the theatre of great events.

'He made his victorious generals fall down to the ground before his throne. Three hundred and sixty-five concubines, the same in number as Darius had, filled his palace. Not to speak of a troop of effeminate eunuchs, used to prostitution. As for his nightly carouses . . .' He continued for some time, noting with satisfaction that every word was going down on the wax. At length the scribe was thanked, and dismissed to begin the work of copying.

'Naturally,' Kassandros said, 'his former companions will give such accounts of him as they hope will tend to their own glory.' The Principal nodded sagely, the careful scholar warned of a dubious source.

Kassandros, whose throat was dry, sipped gratefully at his wine. He, like the Principal, had looked forward to this meeting. He had never managed to humble his living enemy; but at least, now, he had begun to damp-down the fame he had set such store by, for which he had burned out his life.

'I trust,' said Theophrastos civilly at parting, 'that your wife enjoys good health.'

'Thessalonike is as well as her condition allows at present. She has her father King Philip's good constitution.'

'And the young King? He must be eight years old, and beginning his education.'

'Yes. To keep him from inclining to his father's faults, I am giving him a more modest upbringing. Granted that the custom was an old one, still it did Alexander no good that all through his boyhood he had his Companions to dominate – a troops of lords' sons who competed to flatter him. The young King and his mother are installed in the castle at Amphipolis, where they are protected from treachery and intrigue; he is being reared like any private citizen of good birth.'

'Most salutary,' the Principal agreed. 'I shall venture, sir, to present you with a little treatise of my own, *On the Education of Kings*. When he is older, should you think of appointing him a tutor . . .'

'That time,' said the Regent of Macedon, 'will certainly be in my thoughts.'

315 BC

The castle of Amphipolis crowned a high bluff above a sweeping curve of the Strymon, just before it reached the sea. In old days it had been fortified by Athens and by Sparta, strengthened and enlarged by Macedon, each of its conquerors adding a bastion or a tower. The watchmen on its ashlar walls could see wide prospects on every side. They would point out to Alexander, when the air was clear, distant landmarks in Thrace, or the crest of Athos; and he would try to tell them of places he himself had seen before he came here, when he was a little boy; but the years are long between seven and thirteen, and it was growing dim for him.

He remembered confusedly his mother's wagon, the women and eunuchs in her tent, the palace at Pella, his grandmother's house in Dodona; he remembered Pydna too well; he remembered how his mother would not tell him what had happened to grandmother, though of course the servants had said; he remembered his aunt Thessalonike crying terribly although she was going to be married; and his mother crying too on the journey here, though she was settled now. Only one thing had been constant all his life, the presence of soldiers round him. Since Kebes had been sent away, they were his only friends.

He seemed never to meet other boys; but he was allowed out riding so long as soldiers went with him. It always seemed that as soon as he got to know them, to joke and race with them and get their stories out of them, they would be assigned somewhere else and he had a different pair. But in five years a good many turns had come round again, and one could pick up the threads.

Some of them were dour and no fun to ride with; but in five years he had learned policy. When Glaukias, the Commandant, came to see him, which happened every few days, he would say that these soldiers were most interesting people, who were telling him all about the wars in Asia; and soon after they would be transferred. When his friends were mentioned he looked glum, and they stayed on for some time.

Thus he had learned that Antigonos, the Commander-in-Chief in Asia, was making war on his account, wishing to get him out of Amphipolis and be his guardian. He had been two years old when Antigonos had come his way, and remembered only a huge one-eyed monster whose approach had made him scream with fright. He knew better now, but had still no wish to be his ward. His present guardian was no trouble because he never came.

He wished his guardian had been Ptolemy; not that he remembered him, but the soldiers said he was the best-liked of all Alexander's friends, and behaved in war almost as handsomely, which was rare these days. But Ptolemy was far off in Egypt, and there was no way of getting word to him.

Lately, however, it seemed the war was over. Kassandros and Antigonos and the other generals had made a peace, and agreed that Kassandros should be his guardian till he came of age.

'When *shall* I come of age?' he had asked his friends. For some reason this question had alarmed them both; they had enjoined him, with more than their usual emphasis, not to go chattering about what they'd said, or that would be the last he'd ever see of them.

There had always been two of them, until yesterday, when Peiros' horse had gone lame in the first mile, and he had begged Xanthos for one canter before they had to go home. So they had one while Peiros waited; and when they paused to breathe the horses, Xanthos had said, 'Never a word. But there's a lot of talk about you, outside of here.'

'Is there?' he said, instantly alert. 'No one outside of here knows anything about me.'

'So you'd think. But people talk, like we're talking now. Men go on leave. The word goes round that at your age your father had killed his man, and that you're a likely lad who should be getting to know your people. They want to see you.'

'Tell them I want to see them, too.'

'I'll tell them that I want my back tanned. Remember; never a word.'

'Silence or death!' This was their usual catchword. They trotted back to the waiting Peiros.

Roxane's rooms were furnished from her long travels. The splendours of the Queen's rooms in Babylon, the fretted lattices and lilied fishpond, were twelve years away; all she had of them were Stateira's casket and jewels. Lately, she hardly knew why, she had put them away out of sight. But she had plenty of ornaments and comforts; Kassandros had allowed her a wagon train to carry her things to Amphipolis. He was sending them both there, he had said, only for their protection after all the perils they had undergone; by all means, let her make her stay agreeable.

She had however been very lonely. In the beginning the Commandant's wife, and some of the officers' ladies, had made overtures; but she was the Queen Mother, she had not expected a long stay, and she had exacted her proper dignities. As months became years she had regretted this, and put out small signals of condescension; but it was too late, formality was coldly kept.

It distressed her that the King her son should have no company but women and common soldiers. Little as she knew of Greek education she knew that he should be getting it; or how, when he came to reign, would he hold his own at court? He was losing his tutored Greek, and falling into the uncouth Doric patois of his escorts. What would his guardian think of him when he came?

And he would come today. She had just had word that he had arrived without warning at the castle, and was closeted with the Commandant. At least, the boy's ignorance should convince the Regent of his need for schooling and civil company. Besides, she herself should long since have been installed in a proper court with her ladies and attendants, not penned up among provincial nobodies. This time she must insist.

When Alexander came in, dusty and flushed from his ride, she sent him to bathe and change. In her long leisure she had worked beautiful clothes for both of them. Washed, combed, dressed in his blue tunic bordered with gold thread and his embroidered girdle, she thought that he had added to the grace of Persia the classic beauty of Greece. Suddenly the sight of him moved her almost to tears. He had been growing fast, and was already taller than she. His soft dark hair and his fine delicate brows were hers; but his eyes, though they were brown, had something in their deep-set intensity that stirred her memories.

She put on her best gown, and a splendid gold necklace set with sapphires which her husband had given her in India. Then she remembered that among Stateira's jewels were sapphire earrings. She found the casket in the chest, and put them on.

'Mother,' said Alexander as they waited, 'don't forget, not a word about what Xanthos told me yesterday. I promised. You've not told anyone?'

'Of course not, darling. Whom should I find to tell among these people?'

'Silence or death!'

'Hush. He is coming.'

Escorted by the Commandant, whom he dismissed with a nod, Kassandros entered.

He noticed that she had grown stout in the idle years, though she had kept her clear ivory skin and splendid eyes; she, that he looked older and thin to gauntness, and that his cheekbones had a flush of broken veins. He greeted her with formal civility, asked after her health and, without awaiting an answer, turned to her son.

Alexander, who had been sitting when he came in, got up, but only on reflection. He had long ago been told that kings should not rise for anyone. On the other hand, this place was his home, and he had a duty as host.

Kassandros, noting this, did not remark on it. He said without expression, 'I see your father in you.'

'Yes,' said Alexander, nodding. 'My mother sees it, too.'

'Well, you would have outgrown him. Your father was not tall.'

'He was strong, though. I exercise every day.'

'And how else do you spend your time?'

'He needs a tutor,' Roxane cut in. 'He would forget how to write, if I did not make him. His father was taught by a philosopher.'

'These things can be attended to. Well, Alexander?'

The boy considered. He felt he was being tested, to see how soon he could come of age. 'I go to the ramparts and look at the ships and ask where they all come from, and what the places and the people are like, if anyone can tell me. I go riding every day, under guard, for exercise. The rest of the time,' he added carefully, 'I think about being King.'

'Indeed?' said Kassandros sharply. 'And how do you plan to rule?'

Alexander had given this thought. He said at once, 'I shall find all the men I can whom my father trusted. I'll ask them all about him. And before I decide anything, I shall ask them what he'd do.'

For a moment, to his surprise, he saw his guardian turn quite white, so that the red patches on his cheeks looked almost blue; he wondered if he was ill. But his face grew red again, and he only said, 'What if they do not agree?'

'Well, I'm the King. So I must do what I think myself. He had to.'

'Your father was a –' Kassandros checked himself, greatly though he had been tempted. The boy was naive, but the mother had shown cunning in the past. He finished '. . . man of many aspects. So you would find . . . Well, we will consider these matters, and do what is expedient. Farewell, Alexander. Roxane, farewell.'

'Did I do well?' Alexander asked when he had gone.

'Very well. You looked truly your father's son. I saw him in you more than ever before.'

'And we kept the secret. Silence or death!'

Next day brought the first frost of autumn. He rode out with Xanthos and Peiros along the shore, their hair blowing, tasting the sea wind. 'When I come of age,' he shouted over his shoulder, 'I shall sail to Egypt.'

He came back full of this thought. 'I must see Ptolemy. He's my uncle, or partly. He knew my father from when he was born to when he died. Kebes told me so. And my father's tomb is there, and I ought to offer at it. I've never offered him anything. You must come too, mother.'

Someone tapped at the door. A young girl slave of the Commandant's wife came in, with a jug that steamed spicily and two deep goblets. She set it down, curtseyed, and said, 'Madam brewed it for you, and hoped you will honour her by taking it, to keep out the cold.' She sighed with relief at having remembered it. She was a Thracian and found Greek hard.

'Please thank your mistress,' Roxane said graciously, 'and tell her that we shall enjoy it.' When the girl had gone, she said, 'She is still hoping to be noticed. After all, we shall not be much longer here. Perhaps tomorrow we will invite her.'

Alexander was thirsty from the salt air, and tossed down his cupful quickly. Roxane, who was at a tricky stage of her embroidery, finished the flower that she was stitching, and drank hers then.

She was telling him a story about her own father's wars – he must remember, after all, that there were warriors on her side too – when she saw his face tauten and his eyes stare past her. He looked urgently at the door, then rushed to a corner and bent over, reaching and straining. She ran to him and took his head in her hands, but he fought her off like a hurt dog, and strained again. A little came up, smelling of vomit and spices; and of something else, that the spices had masked before.

It was from her eyes that he understood.

He staggered to the table, emptied the jug out on the floor, and saw the grounds at the bottom. Another spasm cramped him. Suddenly his eyes burned with pure rage; not like the tantrums of his childhood, but like a man's; like the blazing anger of his father which she had, once only, seen.

'You told!' he shouted. 'You told!'

'No, no, I swear!' He hardly heard her, clenched in his agony. He was going to die, not when he was old but now; he was in pain and afraid; but overwhelming even pain and fear was the knowledge that he had been robbed of his life, his reign, his glory; of the voyage to Egypt, of proving himself Alexander's son. Though he clung to his mother, he knew that he craved for Kebes, who had told him his father's deeds, and how he had died game to the last, greeting his men with his eyes when his voice was gone. If only Xanthos and Peiros had been here, to be his witnesses, to tell his story ... there was no one, no one ... The poison had entered his veins, his thoughts, dissolved in pain and sickness; he lay rigid, staring at the roof-beams.

Roxane, the first qualms working in her, crouched over him, moaning and weeping. Instead of the stiffened face with the blue mouth, the white forehead sweating under the damp hair, she saw with dreadful clarity the half-made child of Stateira, frowning in Perdikkas' hands.

Alexander's body contracted violently. His eyes set. In her own belly the gripe became a stabbing, convulsive pain. She crept on her knees to the door and cried, 'Help me! Help me!' But no one came.

286 BC

King Ptolemy's book-room was on the upper floor of the palace, looking out over Alexandria harbour; it was cool and airy, its windows catching the sea breeze. The King sat at his writing-table, a large surface of polished ebony which had once been crowded with the papers of his administration, for he had been a great planner and legislator. Now the space was clear but for some books, some writing things, and a sleeping cat. The business of Egypt went to his son, who was discharging it very capably. He had relinquished it by degrees, and with increasing satisfaction. He was eighty years old.

He looked over the writing on his tablet. It was a little shaky, but the wax was readably engraved. In any case, he hoped to live long enough to oversee the scribe.

Despite stiffness, fatigue and the other discomforts of old age, he was enjoying his retirement. He had never before had time to read enough; now he was making up for it. Besides, he had had a task saved up, to whose completion he had long looked forward. Many things had hampered it in earlier years. He had had to exile his eldest son, who had proved incurably vicious (the mother, married too soon, for policy, had been Kassandros' sister) and it had taken time to train this much younger son for kingship. The crimes of the elder were the one sorrow of his age; often he reproached himself for not having killed him. But his thoughts today were serene.

They were interrupted by the entrance of his heir. Ptolemy the Younger was twenty-six, pure Macedonian; Ptolemy's third wife had been his stepsister. Big-boned like his father, he entered softly, seeing the old man so quiet in his chair that he might be dozing. But his mere weight on a floorboard was enough to dislodge two scrolls from one of the crowded shelves that lined the walls. Ptolemy looked round smiling.

'Father, another chest of books has come from Athens. Where can they go?'

'Athens? Ah, good. Have them sent up here.'

'Where will you put them? You've books on the floor already. The rats will have them.'

Ptolemy reached out his wrinkled freckled hand and scratched the cat's neck above its jewelled collar. Svelte and muscular, it flexed its smooth bronze-furred back and stretched luxuriously, uttering a resonant, growling purr.

'Still,' said the son, 'you do need a bigger book-room. In fact, you need a house for them.'

'You can build one when I'm dead. I will give you another book for it.'

The young man noticed that his father was looking as complacent as the cat. Almost he had purred too.

'What? Father! Do you mean that *your* book is finished?'

'In this very hour.' He showed the tablet, on which was written above a flourish of the stylus, HERE ENDS THE HISTORY OF ALEXANDER. His son, who had an affectionate nature, leaned down and embraced him.

'We must have the readings,' he said. 'In the Odeion of course. It's nearly all copied already. I'll arrange it for next month, then there will be time to give out word.' To this late-born child, his father had been always old, but never unimpressive. This work, he knew, had begun before he himself was born. He was in haste to see his father enjoy the fruits of it; old age was fragile. He ran over in his mind the names of actors and orators noted for beauty of voice. Ptolemy pursued his thoughts.

'This,' he said suddenly, 'must kill Kassandros' poison. I was there, as everyone knows, from the beginning to the end ... I should have done it sooner. Too many wars.'

'Kassandros?' Dimly the young man recalled that King of Macedon, who had died during his boyhood and been succeeded by disastrous sons who were both dead too. He belonged to the distant past; whereas Alexander, who had died long before his birth, was as real to him as someone who might now walk in at the door. He had no need to read his father's book, he had been hearing the tales since childhood. 'Kassandros ... ?'

'In the pit of Tartaros, where he is if the gods are just, I hope he learns of it.' The slack folds of the old face had tightened; it looked, for a moment, formidable. 'He killed Alexander's son – I know it, though it was never proved – he hid him through all his growing years, so that his people never knew him, nor will he be known by men to come. The mother of Alexander, his wife, his son. And not content with that, he bought the Lyceum, which will never be the same again, and made a tool of it to blacken Alexander's name. Well, he rotted alive before he died, and between them his sons murdered their mother ... Yes, arrange the readings. And then the book can go to the copy-house. I want it sent to the Lyceum – the Academy – the school at Kos. And one to Rhodes, of course.'

'Of course,' said his son. 'It's not often the Rhodians get a book written by a god.' They grinned at each other. Ptolemy had been awarded divine honours there for his help in their famous siege. He gently stirred the cat, which presented its cream belly to be tickled.

The younger Ptolemy looked out of the window. A blinding flash made him close his eyes. The gold laurel-wreath above the tomb of Alexander had caught the sun. He turned back into the room.

'All those great men. When Alexander was alive, they pulled together like one chariot-team. And when he died, they bolted like chariot-horses when the driver falls. And broke their backs like horses, too.'

Ptolemy nodded slowly, stroking the cat. 'Ah. That was Alexander.'

'But,' said the young man, startled, 'you always said –'

'Yes, yes. And all of it true. That was Alexander. That was the cause.' He picked up the tablet, looked at it jealously, and put it down.

'We were right,' he said, 'to offer him divinity. He had a mystery. He could make anything seem possible in which he himself believed. And we did it, too. His praise was precious, for his trust we would have died; we did impossible things. He was a man touched by a god; we were only men who had been touched by him; but we did not know it. We too had performed miracles, you see.'

'Yes,' said his son, 'but they came to grief and you have prospered. Is it because you gave him burial here?'

'Perhaps. He liked things handsomely done. I kept him from Kassandros, and he never forgot a kindness. Yes, perhaps ... But also, when he died I knew he had taken his mystery with him. Henceforward we were men like other men, with the limits that nature set us. Know yourself, says the god at Delphi. Nothing too much.'

The cat, resenting his inattention, jumped into his lap and began kneading itself a bed. He unhooked its claws from his robe and set it back on the table. 'Not now, Perseus, I have work to do. My boy, get me Philistos, he knows my writing. I want to see this book set down on paper. It is only in Rhodes that I am immortal.'

When his son had gone, he gathered the new tablets together with shaky but determined hands, and set them neatly in order. Then he waited at the window, looking out at the gold laurel wreath that stirred as if alive in the breeze of the Middle Sea.

Author's Note

Among the many riddles of Alexander's life, one of the strangest surrounds his attitude to his own death. His courage was legendary; he consistently exposed himself in the most dangerous part of any action; if he believed himself to be god-begotten, this did not in Greek belief make men immortal. He had had several dangerous wounds and nearly fatal illnesses. One might have supposed that a man so alert to the contingencies of war would have provided for this obvious one. Yet he ignored it totally, not even begetting an heir till the last year of his life, when after his severe wound in India he must have felt his dynamic vitality begin to flag. This psychological block, in a man with immense plans meant to outlast his life, will always be an enigma.

Had Hephaistion survived, he would presumably have been left the regency as a matter of course. His record reveals, besides a devoted friend and, probably, lover, an able intelligent man, sympathetic to all Alexander's ideas of statecraft. His sudden death seems to have shattered all Alexander's certainties, and it is clear that he had not yet recovered from the shock when, partly as a result of it, his own life ended. Even so, during his last illness he continued to plan for his next campaign till he could no longer speak. Perhaps he held the view Shakespeare gives to Julius Caesar: 'Cowards die many times before their deaths; The valiant never taste of death but once.'

His responsibility for the murderous power struggle which followed does not lie in his personality as a leader. On the contrary, his standards were high in terms of his own day, and he demonstrably checked in his chief officers the unscrupulousness and treachery which surfaced when his influence was gone. In so far as he was to blame, it was in not making a good dynastic marriage, and begetting an heir, before he crossed to Asia. Had he left a son of thirteen or fourteen, the Macedonians would never have considered any other claimant.

As it was, the earlier history of Macedon makes it plain that his successors simply reverted to the ancestral pattern of tribal and familial struggles for the throne; except that Alexander had given them a world stage on which to do it.

The deeds of violence which this book describes are all historical. It has indeed been necessary, for the sake of continuity, to omit several murders of prominent persons; the most notable being that of Kleopatra. After Perdikkas' death, she lived quietly at Sardis till she was forty-six, refusing an offer of marriage from Kassandros. In 308, probably from sheer ennui, she made overtures to Ptolemy. It seems unlikely that this prudent ruler meant to repeat Perdikkas' rash adventure; but he agreed to marry her, and she prepared to set out for Egypt. Her plans became known to Antigonos, who, fearing an obstacle to his own dynastic aims, had her murdered by her women, afterwards executing them for the crime.

Peithon allied himself with Antigonos, but became powerful in Media and seemed to be planning revolt. Antigonos killed him too.

Seleukos outlived even Ptolemy (he was a younger man) but when nearly eighty invaded Greece to attempt the throne of Macedon, and was killed by a rival claimant.

Aristonous, at the time of Olympias' surrender to Kassandros, was garrison commander of Amphipolis. Kassandros lured him out under a pledge of safety and had him murdered.

Pausanias says of Kassandros, 'But he himself had no happy end. He was filled with dropsy, and from it came worms while he was still alive. Philip, his eldest son, soon after coming to the throne took a wasting disease and died. Antipatros, the next son, murdered his mother Thessalonike, Philip's and Nikasepolis' daughter, accusing her of being too fond of Alexandros, the youngest son.' He goes on to relate that Alexandros killed Antipatros his brother, but was killed in turn by Demetrios. This extirpation of the entire line reads like the vengeance of the Furies in some Greek tragedy.

Antigonos strove for years to conquer Alexander's empire for himself, till Ptolemy, Seleukos and Kassandros made a defensive alliance and killed him at the battle of Ipsos in Phrygia, before his son Demetrios, who was always loyal to him, could come to his help.

The remarkable career of Demetrios cannot be summarized in a note. A brilliant, charming, volatile and dissipated man, after notable achievements, which included the Macedonian throne, he was captured by Seleukos in whose humane custody he drank himself to death.

The strange phenomenon of Alexander's uncorrupted body is historical. In Christian times this was considered the attribute of a saint; but there was no such tradition in Alexander's day to attract hagiographers, and allowing for exaggeration it does seem that something abnormal occurred, which the great heat of Babylon made more remarkable. The likeliest explanation is of course that clinical death took place much later than the watchers supposed. But it is evident that someone must have taken care of the body, protecting it from flies; the probability being that this was done by one of the palace eunuchs, who had no part in the dynastic brawls going on outside.

Alexander's eight chief officers were known as the Bodyguard; this is a literal translation of the Greek, but it would be wrong to suppose that they were in constant attendance on his person. Many held important military commands. They have therefore been described as staff officers in the List of Characters. The title of Somatophylax, or Bodyguard, is probably rooted deeply in Macedonian history.

PRINCIPAL SOURCES: Quintus Curtius, Book X, for events immediately after Alexander's death: thereafter, Diodorus Siculus, Books XVIII and XIX. Diodorus' source for this period is a good one: Hieronymos of Kardia, who followed the fortunes first of Eumenes, afterwards of Antigonos, and was close to many of the events he describes. For the quotation from *The Odyssey* on page 101 I am grateful for Richmond Lattimore's translation.

Principal Characters

Invented characters are italicized; all those in Roman type are historical. Persons marked * are dead before the story opens. Minor characters making a brief appearance are omitted.

ALEXANDER III — The Great. All further references to Alexander refer to him unless his son, Alexander IV, is specified.

ALEXANDER IV — His posthumous son by Roxane

ALKETAS — Brother of Perdikkas, the general.

*AMYNTAS — Son of Philip II's elder brother, King Perdikkas. An infant when Perdikkas died, he was passed over in favour of Philip, after whose murder he was executed for treason. Husband of Kynna, father of Eurydike.

ANTIGONOS — General of Alexander; Satrap of Phrygia. Later a king, and founder of the Antigonid dynasty.

ANTIPATROS — Regent of Macedon during Alexander's years in Asia, and at the time of his death.

ARISTONOUS — A staff officer of Alexander; later loyal to Alexander IV.

ARRIDAIOS — See Philip III.

ARYBBAS — A Macedonian nobleman, designer of Alexander's funeral car. His real name was Arridaios; he is here given a rather similar Epirote name to distinguish him from Philip Arridaios.

BADIA — *A former concubine of *King Artaxerxes Ochos of Persia.*

BAGOAS   A young Persian eunuch, favourite successively of
                      Darius III and Alexander. Though a real person, he
                      vanishes from history after Alexander's death, and
                      his appearance in this story is fictional.

*DARIUS III   The last Persian Great King; murdered by his
                      generals after his defeat by Alexander at Gaugamela.

DEMETRIOS   Son of Antigonos. (Later known as the Besieger, he
                      became King of Macedon after Kassandros' death.)

DRYPETIS   Younger daughter of Darius III and widow of
                      Hephaistion.

EUMENES   Chief Secretary and general of Alexander; loyal to
                      the royal house.

EURYDIKE   Daughter of Amyntas and Kynna. Her given name
                      was Adeia; Eurydike was the dynastic name con-
                      ferred on her at her marriage (or betrothal) to Philip
                      III. She was the granddaughter of Philip II and of
                      Perdikkas III his elder brother.

*HEPHAISTION   Alexander's lifelong friend, who died a few months
                      before him.

IOLLAS   Son of Antipatros the Regent of Macedon, younger
                      brother of Kassandros; formerly Alexander's cup-
                      bearer.

KASSANDROS   Eldest son of Antipatros; lifelong enemy of Alexander
                      (became King of Macedon after the murder of Alex-
                      ander IV).

KEBES   *Tutor to the boy Alexander IV.*

KLEOPATRA   Daughter of Philip II and Olympias, sister of Alex-
                      ander. Married to King Alexandros of Molossia,
                      which she ruled after his death in Italy. Her father,
                      Philip, was assassinated in her wedding procession.

KONON   *A Macedonian veteran, attendant on Philip Arridaios.*

KRATEROS   Alexander's highest-ranking officer, absent on a
                      mission to Macedon when Alexander died.

KYNNA   Daughter of Philip II by an Illyrian princess, from
                      whom she learned the skills of war. Widow of Amyn-
                      tas, mother of Eurydike.

LEONNATOS — Staff officer and kinsman of Alexander; betrothed to Kleopatra before his death in battle.

MELEAGER — (Greek spelling Meleagros.) A Macedonian officer, enemy of Perdikkas, supporter of Philip III.

NIARCHOS — Boyhood friend and admiral of Alexander.

NIKAIA — Daughter of the Regent Antipatros, married and divorced by Perdikkas.

NIKANOR — Brother of Kassandros; general in Eurydike's army.

*OCHOS — (King Artaxerxes Ochos.) Great King of Persia before the short reign of *Darius III.

OLYMPIAS — Daughter of King Neoptolemos of Molossia; widow of Philip II; mother of Alexander.

PEITHON — Staff officer of Alexander, later of Perdikkas.

PERDIKKAS — Second-in-command to Alexander after Hephaistion's death. Betrothed to Kleopatra after death of Leonnatos.

*PERDIKKAS III — Elder brother of *Philip II, who succeeded him after his death in battle. (See *Amyntas.)

PEUKESTES — Staff officer of Alexander; Satrap of Persia.

*PHILIP II — The founder of Macedonian supremacy in Greece; father of Alexander.

PHILIP III — (Philip Arridaios.) His son by Philinna, a minor wife. The royal name of Philip was conferred at his accession.

POLYPERCHON — Staff officer of Alexander; Regent of Macedon after Antipatros' death.

PTOLEMY — (Greek spelling Ptolemaios.) Staff officer, kinsman and reputed half-brother of Alexander. Later King of Egypt, founder of the Ptolemaic dynasty, and author of a History of Alexander extensively used by Arrian.

ROXANE — Wife of Alexander, married on campaign in Baktria. Mother of Alexander IV.

SELEUKOS — Staff officer of Alexander. (Later King of the Seleucid Empire in Nearer Asia.)

SISYGAMBIS   Mother of Darius III, befriended by Alexander.

STATEIRA   Daughter of Darius III, married in state by Alexander
                  at Susa.

THEOPHRASTOS   Aristotle's successor as head of the Lyceum Univer-
                  sity at Athens, patronized by Kassandros.

THESSALONIKE   Daughter of Philip II by a minor wife; later wife of
                  Kassandros.